EVERYMAN,
I WILL GO WITH THEE,
AND BE THY GUIDE,
IN THY MOST NEED
TO GO BY THY SIDE

JAMES ELLROY

THE
L.A. QUARTET

THE BLACK DAHLIA
THE BIG NOWHERE
L.A. CONFIDENTIAL
WHITE JAZZ

WITH AN INTRODUCTION
BY TOM NOLAN

EVERYMAN'S LIBRARY

Alfred A. Knopf NewYork London Toronto

388

F
E11

C O N T E N T S

――――

Introduction	..	..	..	..	..	vii
Select Bibliography	..	..	..	..	..	xv
Chronology	..	..	..	..	..	xvi
THE BLACK DAHLIA	..	..	..	..	1
THE BIG NOWHERE	..	..	..	..	305
L. A. CONFIDENTIAL	..	..	..	..	697
WHITE JAZZ ..	..	..	..	..	..	1069

INTRODUCTION

James Ellroy's breakthrough into crime-fiction success in the late 1980s was comparable in its impact and controversy to—what? Perhaps the 1913 Paris debut of Igor Stravinsky's notorious, upsetting, violent ballet-score *The Rite of Spring*. Splice that with anyone's first glimpse of the eyeball scene in Bunuel and Dali's 1929 *épater-les-bourgeois* film *Un Chien Andalou*. A more American parallel might be the furor created in swing-jazz circles in the 1940s when a cadre of New York musicians gave birth to the raucous, frenzied sounds of bebop—or when, in the '50s, rhythm and blues and rockabilly spawned the decadent, repetitive, aggressive sounds of rock'n'roll: a musical-verbal-sensual poke in the ear to white-bread sensibilities.

This author's in-your-face novels gave you verbatim police reports, period radio-chatter, self-righteous scandal-sheet tease, sober newspaper prose, thought-patterns, brainstorms, stream of subconsciousness dreads: all transcribed or tele-pathed with kaleidoscope clarity. Place-names and call-letters and street-numbers and local celebs put you right back in the 1950s: KGFJ, KMPC, Hody's on Vine Street, the Pacific Dining Car; Scrivner's Drive-in, Tiny Naylor's, Sy Devore, Spade Cooley, Jerry Geisler.

Ellroy's books, especially the four gathered in this volume, seemed unlike any detective- or crime-fiction written yet: a scary mélange of grisly murders, perverse obsessions, civic corruption, corrosive cynicism and contagious evil. And butch-erous violence. These books had protagonists, not heroes. Ostensibly police-procedurals, their cops were often as thug-gish, larcenous, and murderous as the gangsters with whom they oft collaborated. Expediency was the best policy for them, and their first commandment was survival.

Ellroy's semi-antiheroes reminded some older readers and critics of Mickey Spillane's Mike Hammer, that post-World War II private-eye who inflicted mayhem on foes both male and female with a glee that could seem fascistic. The English novelist and detective-fiction scholar Julian Symons, for one, was repelled by the matter-of-fact manner in which Ellroy depicted (hence, it might seem, condoned) violence: "I banged his head against the wall, threw him out the window screaming" (chapter 2, *White Jazz*). But other knowledgeable commentators saw Ellroy as being squarely (if jarringly) in the all-American hard-boiled tradition: Richard Layman, the premier chronicler of Dashiell Hammett (whose *Red Harvest* was, it could be said, the *White Jazz* of 1929) judged of *The Black Dahlia* and its author: "Ellroy is here to stay. Our great-grandchildren will be reading this book."

It was in *The Black Dahlia* (1987)—a fiction work based on the nightmarish real-life murder of Elizabeth Short, the most notorious unsolved crime in Los Angeles history—that James Ellroy displayed his mature vision and was rewarded with best-selling success.

The hallmarks of Ellroy's soon-familiar style are on full display here. The intersection of historical figures with fictional characters is presented in audacious, take-it-or-leave-it fashion. The scenes of slaughter and depravity are worthy of a Tijuana-bible drawn by H. Bosch (the painter, not Michael Connelly's cop). Racial epithets—the n-word, the j-word, the other j-word, and on and beyond—are ubiquitous, seeming much more shocking on the page of a 1980s depiction of 1950s L.A. than they were in Raymond Chandler's 1930s/'40s books; our awareness of those ugly words coming out of Philip Marlowe's mouth somehow gets lost in Chandler's romantic fog.

Framing the novel's search for the Black Dahlia killer is the friendship and sometimes partnership of two cops, Bucky Bleichert (the novel's narrator) and Lee Blanchard: both ex-boxers, both in love with the smart and passionate Kay, an experienced woman who bears a checkered and traumatic past with dignity. The cop duo negotiate a milieu in which they interact with such real-life figures as mobsters Bugsy Siegel and Mickey Cohen, and where police higher-ups and civic officials take advantage of high-profile crimes to advance their own careers and inflate their budgets. Inexorably but in unpredictable ways, Lee and Bucky each become possessed by the memory of Elizabeth Short ("Betty") whose brief, sordid life and cruel death stir up and supplement their own worst memories of physical and moral pain suffered and inflicted.

Of *The Black Dahlia*, Ellroy would later write: "The novel is phrased as a young man coming of age in a hell of his own making. Bucky Bleichert is solely responsible for his own descent. He made specious moral choices early in life and brought a grievously flawed soul to the Dahlia." But in moving forward, he is able in part to mend: "Love requires self-sacrifice and deference. Bucky Bleichert learns that and achieves a tenuous peace."

There seems no peace in store at first in *The Big Nowhere*, Ellroy's unrelenting follow-up to the best-selling *Dahlia*. Set in 1950, three years after the (still unsolved of course) killing of Elizabeth Short, it too begins with a horrific murder involving a mutilated corpse: "Eyes poked out. Sex organs mauled. Bare flesh gored down to the quick." But this victim is male, the killing has apparent homosexual aspects, and the powers that be want to clamp a lid on press coverage, hoping to avoid "another Black Dahlia mess."

Catching the unwanted case is L.A. Sheriff's deputy Danny Upshaw: a studious, ascetic rookie whose career choice was prompted by the haunting memory of glimpsing two men in a farmhouse at night attacking a blonde woman with axes, this surreal vision ("a half-second flash of an arm severed off") viewed as Upshaw raced a stolen car to Bakersfield during an adolescent criminal stint. Thus the would-be crook became a cop instead, with an abiding need to comprehend the roots of evil: "to know WHY."

It never rains but it pours: soon Upshaw encounters two more related murders, even more brutal (you may not want the details, but you'll get them). To win the chance to be in charge of investigating these linked slaughters, Upshaw agrees to join a covert grand-jury investigation documenting Communist infiltration of the movie business. Among the other Red-hunters is Turner "Buzz" Meeks, native of Lizard Ridge, Oklahoma: "heroin skimmer, shakedown artist, bagman and now a glorified pimp for Howard Hughes" and "the man who held the possible distinction of being the single most crooked cop in the history of the Los Angeles Police Department." Meeks is comfortable in the niche he's found between law and ordure, but he develops a fatal flaw (or, in Ellroy's theology, a chance for redemption): his lust-driven love for Audrey "the Va-Va-Voom Girl" Anders, mobster Mickey Cohen's stripper girlfriend. "I'm glad bein' with you is dangerous," Buzz tells Audrey, once their crush is physically consummated. "It feels good."

Also among the elite Red-hunters is Lt. Mal Considine, District Attorney's investigator, a man trapped in a wretched marriage entered into to protect a stepson he dotes upon; Mal develops an unexpected romantic interest in Claire De Haven, glamorous Hollywood activist and fiancée of a fading movie star. Rounding out the conspiracy committee (under the leadership of hyper-ambitious Ellis Loew, head of the DA's Criminal Division) is LAPD Homicide Detective Dudley Smith: Dublin-born, Jesuit-trained, glib, blarney-spouting oozer of insidious charm, wily as the snake in Genesis: "Knock knock, who's there? Dudley Smith, so Reds beware."

Ellroy's conflicted characters have fault-lines as deep as the San Andreas. They battle and indulge their obsessions, compulsions and repulsions in the context of their work, which plays into and out against a broader historical context. The gruesome murders Upshaw probes have evidentiary links to the Zoot Suit riots and Sleepy Lagoon killings of a few years back—which also have relevance for the DA commission's charting of left-wing Hollywood activism. The liberals' current cause, in support of a Hollywood trade-union picketing Howard Hughes' studio for better pay, puts the left-wingers in opposition to Mickey Cohen's mob, which supports the rival Teamsters union. The crime mobs themselves are in long-standing opposition, with Cohen's outfit pitted against Jack Dragna's crew—which is protected by a squad of the LAPD, while the West Hollywood Sheriff's Department gives Mickey Cohen cover.

Agendas clash. Egomaniacs rage. Yet the bizarre cases (which may or may not have much to do with the "larger issues" at hand) still must in some fashion or other be solved. Cops as different from one another as Upshaw and Meeks, driven by the best and worst of motives, comb through old booking slips and arrest reports, coerce witnesses, call in favors, break as many rules as they hope to enforce in search of THE fiendish soul whose repulsive acts go beyond baroque into the obscenely rococo.

Guilt proves especially difficult to fix in *L.A. Confidential*, third and longest of the L.A. Quartet books. Trying as hard as anyone to prove who's responsible for the after-hours deaths of six customers at Hollywood's Nite Owl Café in 1953 is the cold and manipulative Ed Exley, son of a former policeman turned construction magnate. Though decorated for his World War II service (thanks to a somewhat padded official record), Ed is despised by his LAPD colleagues as a cowardly martinet. Though a desk-officer, not a field cop, he takes a hands-on approach to the Nite Owl case when the obvious (convenient) suspects—three young black men the police claim have confessed—escape from jail but are soon run to ground. Exley beards them in their lair and single-handedly assassinates them (what, self-defense?)—then lives to confront the unexpected consequences, when in '58 new evidence proves the shot-gunned suspects couldn't have been the Nite Owl killers after all.

No worries. "That's blood under the bridge," says Dudley Smith, one of several recidivist characters making recurring appearances throughout the Quartet. Exley, Smith and the other men serving with and under Ed simply "solve" the case again—this time, they insist, for real. Among Exley's minions: Wendell "Bud" White: "frustrated because he wasn't that smart, he wasn't really a Homicide detective—he was the guy they brought in to scare other guys shitless." Then there's Jack "the Big V" Vincennes, official police adviser to the TV show *Badge of Honor* (a lot like *Dragnet*, aka *Badge 714*), engineer of juicy cop stories for *Hush-Hush* magazine (remember *Confidential?*), whose sex life has been turned rancid by twisted fantasies and who lives in despair of being exposed as a cop fraud and political fixer.

Multiple homicides, a botched pornography racket, strange interlocking criminal conspiracies and personality-disorder flameouts complicate matters. For plot twists and switchbacks and Mobius-strip encounters, post-modern authors such as John Barth or Thomas Pynchon have nothing on Ellroy, whose moments of surprising subtlety and out-of-the-blue sentiment nonetheless ground his fiction in the real world in which we live.

That world is no less astounding and perilous in the Quartet's final novel, *White Jazz*, set in 1958. After decades of having things their own ways, L.A.'s cops and mobsters are to come under the scrutiny of federal investigators hoping to indict those enmeshed in the crooked local prize-fight racket and maybe sundry other illicit endeavors to boot. Down-on-his-luck Mickey Cohen has meanwhile branched into low-budget film-making on location in Griffith Park. And in the nearby Hollywood Hills, a creepy killer has been victimizing alcoholic hobos; the gutter-press dubs the fiend the "Wino Will-o-the-Wisp."

Ed Exley, now LAPD Chief of Detectives, gives Lt. Dave Klein (a cop with a law degree, and the novel's narrator) the task of rousting a few bookie joints, thus earning the Department some favorable press to counter the Feds' bad-mouthng. Klein, who hates the condescending Exley (but who knows? that may change) is another deeply compromised officer—not averse to accepting money to kill people whose continued existence proves troublesome to Mickey Cohen or his even scarier friends. (As noted earlier: "I banged his head against the wall, threw him out the window screaming.") Also, up pops Dudley Smith again, at last to get a fair-sized comeuppance. (Apologies if that spoils things for anyone. Think of it as something to look forward to.)

Thumbnail summaries do not suffice. These books spiel out with a mind-boggling, memory-taunting complexity of plot, thought and conjecture that rivals or surpasses the crazy cat's-cradles of Ross Macdonald (*aka* Kenneth Millar), a writer Ellroy dedicated a book to and invoked in the epigraph to *White Jazz*. As with Macdonald, even the minor characters in Ellroy's books are fleshed out with quick strokes that would do Goya or Daumier proud. But then that sudden violence: blood-soaked action fit to make Spillane chuckle—or gasp, depending.

For some, Ellroy's most notable achievement will be the inducement in readers of sympathy (or at least empathy) (or at the very least, some understanding) for initially unforgivableseeming characters such as Dave Klein. How understand his villainous deeds in any context other than greed and evil? But as Klein shares his backstory in first-person voice, we comprehend: passionate (okay, incestuous) family loyalty made him vulnerable to gangsters who twisted his chivalric impulses to homicidal ends, then insisted he keep "paying them back" with more killings until he felt hooked for life.

This is the sort of thing that happens in Ellroy's world, a universe of raunchy sex with movie stars, bordellos with fake-believe actresses, and once-real people—L.A. police chief Bill Parker, police chemist Ray Pinker—saying and doing made-up things. (Justified by poetic license and the powers of invention? As fair as Gore Vidal portraying Thomas Jefferson in *Burr* as a dullard and nerd?)

Here are professional and personal blood rivalries that prevail for years and years. Here be high-end homosexual escort services and penny-ante prostitution rings. Here crime solutions and nested conspiracies disprove the thesis of Occam's Razor—for the simplest answers are not the best, they're mere starting-points.

Here live the jaded children and seedy grandkids of the blood-simple extras and crazed "atmosphere people" of Nat "Pep" West's *The Day of the Locust*, and also the descendants of James M. Cain's low-end losers. Still here are the nasty thrills of Kenneth Anger's *Hollywood Babylon*, the bug-eyed kicks of Todd Browning's *Freaks*. See too the lit-by-lightning movie-house gropes and sidewalk bleed-outs of press photographer Weegee the Famous. Stag films. Heroin shoot-ups. Strip clubs. Eight-by-ten glossies of bestiality. Body parts tossed in the trash.

As Bob Dylan once asked in a liner note: "And just how far would you like to go in?"

James Ellroy's popularity soon became widespread among young readers and writers. His influence was noticeable in others' books and movies and TV series, and he himself was seen and heard—looming frame, shaven head, stern gaze, unsmiling lips—over NPR, on PBS, at book events that combined the fervor of an Aimee Semple McPherson revival with the jocular abuse of *The Jerry Springer Show*. He was a raucous performer, a crowd natural; yet, encountered one-on-one, courteous: near-courtly, good with children: "Naw, you can't hurt me, you know why? 'Cause I'm a *tough* guy."

The art stands on its own of course. But—be we biographers, psych students, curious book-club members or just plain nosy parkers—it's human nature to wonder, who would or could cook up this psychic grue? And why? Who "is" the author behind these grotesque, convoluted, oft-unpleasant stories?

Everything begins in childhood, experts insist. Nothing in this novelist's history belies that claim. He's been kind enough to provide us himself with the necessary proof—for instance, in a 2006 afterword to *The Black Dahlia* in which he wrote of his family and upbringing with candor and heroic respect. Of the mother who was murdered in 1958 when he was ten (another unsolved L.A. homicide): "I hated her and lusted for her and got my wish of her dead," he described his first reactions. When he later learned (through a book by Jack Webb, star of TV's *Dragnet*) the story of Elizabeth Short, he conflated the Black Dahlia's fate with his mother's. His obsession with crime and punishment was sealed.

As a youth, he's written, he broke into houses, committed petty crimes, felt he was "born to think single-mindedly and live obsessively." When his father died in 1965: "I spent the next twelve years in a near-insane spiral. I cleaned up at twenty-nine. I wrote six good novels"—then came the psychic and artistic breakthrough of *The Black Dahlia*.

After that, his growing knowledge of and appreciation and love for the woman who bore him inspired a well-received nonfiction work and no doubt influenced his fiction in crucial ways. Like the worthiest of his novels' problematic personae, the author "made specious moral choices early in life" but learned "love requires self-sacrifice and deference"—and hence, like Bucky Bleichert, he's achieved "a tenuous peace."

Ellroy, son of a Calvinist-raised mother, writes: "I tell redemptive tales aimed at women." He urges: "Love God. Fear God. Seek goodness as dark forces assail you." Words to live by—and to write by.

Or, as one of his own blunt characters once put it: "No shit, Sherlock."

Tom Nolan

SELECT BIBLIOGRAPHY

GRAY, PAUL, "James Ellroy: The Real Pulp Fiction" in *Time Magazine*, 4/10/1995. Review of *American Tabloid*.

MANCALL, JIM, *James Ellroy: A Companion to the Mystery Fiction*, McFarland Companions to Mystery Fiction (series editor Elizabeth Foxwell), McFarland & Company, Inc., Jefferson NC, 2014.

POWELL, STEVEN (ed.), *Conversations with James Ellroy* (Literary Conversations Series), University Press of Mississippi, Jackson MS, revised edition 2012.

POWELL, STEVEN, *James Ellroy: Demon Dog of Crime Fiction*, Palgrave Macmillan UK, Basingstoke, 2016.

VOLLMAN, WILLIAM T., "En Route to the Grassy Knoll" in *The New York Times*, 2/26/1995. Review of *American Tabloid*.

WOLFE, PETER, *Like Hot Knives to the Brain: James Ellroy's Search for Himself*, Lexington Books, Lanham MD, 2006.

TOM NOLAN is the author of biographies of Ross Macdonald and Artie Shaw. He edited the Macdonald short story collection *The Archer Files* and Macdonald's wife Margaret Millar's volume *The Couple Next Door*. With Suzanne Marrs, Nolan coedited *Meanwhile There Are Letters: The Correspondence of Eudora Welty and Ross Macdonald*.

CHRONOLOGY

DATE	AUTHOR'S LIFE	LITERARY CONTEXT
1948	Born March 4, in Los Angeles, California.	Capote: *Other Voices, Other Rooms.* Carr: *The Skeleton in the Clock.* Faulkner: *Intruder in the Dust.* Mailer: *The Naked and the Dead.*
1949		Algren: *The Man with the Golden Arm.* Miller: *Death of a Salesman.* Orwell: *Nineteen Eighty-Four.* Stout: *The Second Confession.*
1950		Hemingway: *Across the River and Into the Trees.* Highsmith: *Strangers on a Train.* Welch: *A Voice Through a Cloud.*
1951		Jones: *From Here to Eternity.* Salinger: *The Catcher in the Rye.* Williams: *The Rose Tattoo.* Wouk: *The Caine Mutiny.*
1952		Ellison: *Invisible Man.* Hemingway: *The Old Man and the Sea.* O'Connor: *Wise Blood.* Steinbeck: *East of Eden.*
1953		Baldwin: *Go Tell It on the Mountain.* Bellow: *The Adventures of Augie March.* Burroughs: *Junkie.* Chandler: *The Long Goodbye.* Grubb: *The Night of the Hunter.* Levin: *A Kiss Before Dying.* Thompson: *Savage Night.*
1954		Huxley: *The Doors of Perception.* Réage: *Story of O.* Thompson: *Not as a Stranger.*
1955	Late November: parents separate and acrimoniously divorce.	Highsmith: *The Talented Mr. Ripley.* Mailer: *The Deer Park.* Miller: *A View from the Bridge.* Nabokov: *Lolita.*

President Harry Truman signs the Marshall Plan, authorizing $13 billion in aid to Western Europe in the aftermath of World War II. State of Israel established. Soviet blockade of Berlin and Allied airlift. Communist coup in Czechoslovakia. *Apartheid* becomes official policy in South Africa. Assassination of Gandhi.

North Atlantic Treaty signed, creating NATO, involving United States, Canada, and several Western European nations in collective security pact against the Soviet Union. Communists seize power in China after Civil War.

U.S. Senator McCarthy begins investigating alleged Communist infiltration of federal government. Korean War breaks out.

Great flood in U.S. Midwest. First oral contraceptive invented by Luis E. Miramontes.

Eisenhower elected U.S. President. U.S. explodes first thermonuclear bomb at Enewetak Atoll. Richard Nixon's "Checkers speech" on TV attracts audience of 56 million.

Stalin dies. Korean War ends.

Vietnam War begins. Nasser comes to power in Egypt.

Soviet Union and Eastern Bloc allies sign Warsaw Pact as response to NATO. U.S. begins involvement in Vietnam War. Rosa Parks arrested in bus protest in Montgomery, Alabama.

DATE	AUTHOR'S LIFE	LITERARY CONTEXT
1955 *cont.*		O'Connor: *A Good Man Is Hard to Find.* Stout: *Before Midnight.*
1956		Algren: *A Walk on the Wild Side.* Bellow: *Seize the Day.* Ginsberg: *Howl.* McBain: *Cop Hater.* O'Neill: *Long Day's Journey Into Night.*
1957		Cheever: *The Wapshot Chronicle.* Kerouac: *On the Road.* Rand: *Atlas Shrugged.* Williams: *Baby Doll.*
1958	June 22: mother, Jean Hilliker, murdered in Los Angeles County suburb. The crime remains unsolved.	Carr: *The Dead Man's Knock.* MacDonald: *The Executioners.* Williams: *Suddenly, Last Summer.*
1959		Bloch: *Psycho.* Burroughs: *Naked Lunch.* Jackson: *The Haunting of Hill House.* Roth: *Goodbye, Columbus.*
1960		Lee: *To Kill a Mockingbird.* O'Connor: *The Violent Bear It Away.* Updike: *Rabbit* tetralogy (to 1981).
1961		Fanon: *The Wretched of the Earth.* Heller: *Catch-22.* Highsmith: *This Sweet Sickness.* Yates: *Revolutionary Road.*
1962		Albee: *Who's Afraid of Virginia Woolf?* Baldwin: *Another Country.* Carson: *Silent Spring.* Jackson: *We Have Always Lived in the Castle.* Kesey: *One Flew Over the Cuckoo's Nest.* Nabokov: *Pale Fire.*
1963		Baldwin: *The Fire Next Time.* McCarthy: *The Group.* Pynchon: *V.* Thompson: *The Grifters.*

CHRONOLOGY

Soviet invasion of Hungary. Suez Crisis. Elvis Presley performs "Hound Dog" on U.S. television, scandalizing the nation.

Civil Rights Commission established in U.S. to safeguard voting rights. The U.S. military sustains its first combat fatality in Vietnam.

U.S. launches first satellite, Explorer 1. Integrated circuit created by Jack Kilby. Khrushchev becomes Premier of Soviet Union.

Fidel Castro seizes power in Cuba, forms Socialist government.

Kennedy elected U.S. President.

Attempted U.S. invasion of Cuba, Bay of Pigs. Berlin Wall erected. Yuri Gagarin first man in space.

Cuban Missile Crisis. Telstar, world's first commercial communications satellite, launched and activated.

Kennedy assassinated in Dallas, Lyndon Johnson becomes President. Civil rights leader Martin Luther King Jr. arrested.

DATE	AUTHOR'S LIFE	LITERARY CONTEXT
1964		Bellow: *Herzog*.
		Berne: *Games People Play*.
		Cheever: *The Wapshot Scandal*.
		Selby: *Last Exit to Brooklyn*.
1965	Expelled from high school for truancy and disruptive behavior. Numerous arrests and short county-jail terms for misdemeanor offenses (until 1975).	Herlihy: *Midnight Cowboy*. Mailer: *An American Dream*. Wolfe: *The Kandy-Kolored Tangerine-Flake Streamline Baby*.
1966		Capote: *In Cold Blood*.
		Pynchon: *The Crying of Lot 49*.
		Stout: *Death of a Doxy*.
		Styron: *The Confessions of Nat Turner*.
		Susann: *Valley of the Dolls*.
		Thompson: *Hell's Angels*.
1967		Levin: *Rosemary's Baby*.
		Manchester: *The Death of a President*.
		Thomas: *Down These Mean Streets*.
1968		Cleaver: *Soul on Ice*.
		Derleth: *Wisconsin Murders*.
		Mailer: *Armies of the Night*.
		Updike: *Couples*.
		Vidal: *Myra Breckinridge*.
1969		Greenlee: *The Spook Who Sat by the Door*.
		Leonard: *The Big Bounce*.
		Oates: *Them*.
		Puzo: *The Godfather*.
		Roth: *Portnoy's Complaint*.
1970		Dickey: *Deliverance*.
		Fo: *Accidental Death of an Anarchist*.
		Morrison: *The Bluest Eye*.
1971		Blatty: *The Exorcist*.
		McCarthy: *Birds of America*.
		O'Connor: *The Complete Stories*.
		Selby: *The Room*.
		Stegner: *Angle of Repose*.
		Wolfe: *The Electric Kool-Aid Acid Test*.

CHRONOLOGY

Warren Report into Kennedy assassination published. Civil Rights Act outlaws racial discrimination. Martin Luther King receives Nobel Peace Prize.

U.S. bombs North Vietnam. Malcolm X assassinated.

Black Panthers founded, Oakland, California. Vietnam War: U.S. planes bomb Hanoi and Haiphong. China: Mao launches Cultural Revolution.

Racial violence in many U.S. cities, Johnson appoints commission to investigate causes. "Summer of Love," Haight-Ashbury, California. Six-Day War between Israel and Arab states. Che Guevara shot dead, Bolivia.

Students protest in U.S. and throughout Europe. Martin Luther King and Robert Kennedy assassinated. Nixon elected U.S. President. Soviet invasion of Czechoslovakia.

Neil Armstrong first man on moon. U.S. troops begin withdrawal from Vietnam. Woodstock rock festival attended by 400,000 in New York State.

Nixon orders invasion of Cambodia. Jordan: Black September conflict. Chile: Allende becomes world's first democratically elected Marxist head of state. France: De Gaulle dies.

U.S. voting age lowered to eighteen. India and Pakistan border disputes erupt into full-scale war.

DATE	AUTHOR'S LIFE	LITERARY CONTEXT
1972		Higgins: *The Friends of Eddie Coyle.* Levin: *The Stepford Wives.* Thompson: *Fear and Loathing in Las Vegas.*
1973		Algren: *The Last Carousel.* Pynchon: *Gravity's Rainbow.* Schumacher: *Small Is Beautiful.* Thompson: *Fear and Loathing on the Campaign Trail '72.*
1974		Benchley: *Jaws.* Heller: *Something Happened.* Jong: *Fear of Flying.* King: *Carrie.* Roth: *My Life as a Man.*
1975		Agee: *Inside the Company.* Bellow: *Humboldt's Gift.* Doctorow: *Ragtime.* Stout: *A Family Affair.*
1976		Selby: *The Demon.* Woodward & Bernstein: *The Final Days.*
1977		Cheever: *Falconer.* Coover: *The Public Burning.* King: *The Shining.* Morrison: *Song of Solomon.*
1978		Levin: *Deathtrap.* Said: *Orientalism.* Selby: *Requiem for a Dream.* Yates: *A Good School.*
1979		Mailer: *The Executioner's Song.* Roth: *The Ghost Writer.* Straub: *Ghost Story.* Styron: *Sophie's Choice.* Wolfe: *The Right Stuff.*
1980		King: *Firestarter.* Ludlum: *The Bourne Identity.* Toole: *A Confederacy of Dunces.*
1981	First novel, *Brown's Requiem,* published.	Carver: *What We Talk About When We Talk About Love.* Irving: *The Hotel New Hampshire.*
1982	Second novel, *Clandestine,* published.	Galeano: *Memory of Fire.* McCullough: *An Indecent Obsession.* Walker: *The Color Purple.*

CHRONOLOGY

HISTORICAL EVENTS

U.S. and U.S.S.R. sign Strategic Arms Limitation Treaty (SALT I). Eleven Israeli athletes killed by Arab guerrillas at Olympic Village, Munich.

U.S. Supreme Court suspends capital punishment (until 1976).
Chile: Allende and over 2,500 others killed in coup led by Pinochet.

Nixon resigns after Watergate scandal, Ford becomes U.S. President.

Vietnam War ends. Oil price tops $13.00 a barrel.

Carter becomes U.S. President. China: Chairman Mao dies.

Elvis Presley dies. Egyptian President Sadat recognizes Israel.

Camp David Agreement signed by Carter, Sadat and Israeli prime minister Begin.

Iran: Shah forced into exile, Ayatollah Khomeini establishes Islamic state. U.K.: Thatcher becomes country's first female prime minister. Carter and Brezhnev sign SALT II. Soviet troops occupy Afghanistan.

Reagan elected U.S. President. Iran–Iraq War begins (to 1988). Lech Walesa, shipyard worker, leads strikes in Poland.

Assassination attempt on Reagan, Washington. Egypt: Sadat killed by Islamic fundamentalists.

Beginning of 1980s stock market boom in U.S. Lebanese Civil War: multinational force lands in Beirut to oversee the P.L.O. withdrawal from Lebanon.

DATE	AUTHOR'S LIFE	LITERARY CONTEXT
1983		Mailer: *Ancient Evenings.*
		Vidal: *Duluth.*
1984	Third novel, *Blood on the Moon,* published.	Amis: *Money.*
		King & Straub: *The Talisman.*
		Updike: *The Witches of Eastwick.*
1985	Fourth novel, *Because the Night,* published.	DeLillo: *White Noise.*
		Ellis: *Less than Zero.*
		McCarthy: *Blood Meridian.*
1986	Fifth and sixth novels, *Suicide Hill* and *Silent Terror,* published.	Amis: *The Moronic Inferno.*
		Ford: *The Sportswriter.*
		Hiaasen: *Tourist Season.*
1987	First novel of *The L.A. Quartet, The Black Dahlia,* published.	Auster: *The New York Trilogy.*
		Morrison: *Beloved.*
		Turow: *Presumed Innocent.*
		Wolfe: *The Bonfire of the Vanities.*
1988	Second novel of *The L.A. Quartet, The Big Nowhere,* published.	Chabon: *The Mysteries of Pittsburgh.*
		DeLillo: *Libra.*
		Harris: *The Silence of the Lambs.*
		Rushdie: *The Satanic Verses.*
		Tyler: *Breathing Lessons.*
1989		Irving: *A Prayer for Owen Meany.*
		King: *The Dark Half.*
1990	Third novel of *The L.A. Quartet, L.A. Confidential,* published.	Crichton: *Jurassic Park.*
		Leonard: *Get Shorty.*
		Pynchon: *Vineland.*
1991		Ellis: *American Psycho.*
		Grisham: *The Firm.*
		Madonna: *Sex.*
		Smiley: *A Thousand Acres.*
1992	Concluding novel of *The L.A. Quartet, White Jazz,* published.	Algren: *America Eats.*
		Grisham: *The Pelican Brief.*
		Morrison: *Jazz.*
		Tartt: *The Secret History.*
1993		Proulx: *The Shipping News.*
		Welsh: *Trainspotting.*
1994	Unsuccessfully investigates unsolved murder of Jean Hilliker (until 1995).	Grisham: *The Chamber.*
		King: *Insomniac.*
1995	First novel of *The Underworld U.S.A. Trilogy, American Tabloid,* published, named *Time Magazine*'s Novel of the Year.	Baudrillard: *The Gulf War Did Not Take Place.*
		Ford: *Independence Day.*
		Kane: *Blasted.*
		Roth: *Sabbath's Theater.*

CHRONOLOGY

HISTORICAL EVENTS

U.S. troops invade Granada after government overthrown.

Reagan re-elected in landslide. India: Indira Gandhi assassinated. Famine in Ethiopia.

U.S.S.R.: reform begun under new General Secretary of the Communist Party, Gorbachev.

U.S. bombs Libya. Gorbachev–Reagan summit. Nuclear explosion in Chernobyl, U.S.S.R.

Reagan makes Berlin Wall speech. World population reaches 5 billion.

George Bush elected U.S. President. Soviet troops withdrawn in large numbers from Afghanistan.

Berlin Wall dismantled, Communism collapses in Eastern Europe. U.S.S.R. holds first democratic elections. China: Tiananmen Square masssacre.

Hubble Space Telescope launched during Space Shuttle Discovery mission. South Africa: Nelson Mandela released. Yeltsin elected first leader of Russian Federation after end of Communist rule.
Gulf War begins. War breaks out in former Yugoslavia. South Africa: *Apartheid* ends. Bush and Gorbachev sign START arms reduction treaty.

Clinton elected U.S. President. Riots in Los Angeles.

World Trade Center bombed. Palestinian leader Arafat signs peace agreement with Israeli prime minister Rabin.
South Africa: Mandela's A.N.C. takes power after elections. Rwanda: civil war. Russia takes military action in Chechen Republic.

Oklahoma City bombing: 168 people, including eight Federal Marshals and nineteen children, killed. Israel: Rabin assassinated.

DATE	AUTHOR'S LIFE	LITERARY CONTEXT
1996	*My Dark Places*, memoir of the Jean Hilliker murder investigation, published.	Atwood: *Alias Grace.* Huntington: *The Clash of Civilizations and the Remaking of World Order.* Palahniuk: *Fight Club.* Wallace: *Infinite Jest.*
1997	Much-heralded film version of *L.A. Confidential* released.	Bellow: *The Actual.* DeLillo: *Underworld.* Pynchon: *Mason & Dixon.* Roth: *American Pastoral.*
1998		Bolaño: *The Savage Detectives.* Roth: *I Married a Communist.*
1999		Coatzee: *Disgrace.* Hiaasen: *Sick Puppy.* Southwell: *Conspiracy Theories.* Stephenson: *Cryptonomicon.*
2000		Brown: *Angels & Demons.* Kingsolver: *Prodigal Summer.* Roth: *The Human Stain.*
2001	*The Cold Six Thousand*, second novel of *The Underworld U.S.A. Trilogy*, published.	Frantzen: *The Corrections.* Moore: *Stupid White Men.*
2002		Auster: *The Book of Illusions.* Patchett: *Bel Canto.* Tartt: *The Little Friend.*
2003		Brown: *The Da Vinci Code.* DeLillo: *Cosmopolis.* Gibson: *Pattern Recognition.* Moore: *Dude, Where's My Country?*
2004		Robinson: *Gilead.* Roth: *The Plot Against America.* Stephenson: *Baroque Trilogy* (concludes).
2005		Didion: *The Year of Magical Thinking.* Ellis: *Lunar Park.* Koontz: *Velocity.* Larsson: *The Girl with the Dragon Tattoo.*
2006	Much-scorned film version of *The Black Dahlia* released.	Dawkins: *The God Delusion.* Ford: *Lay of the Land.* McCarthy: *The Road.* Pynchon: *Against the Day.* Updike: *Terrorist.*

CHRONOLOGY

HISTORICAL EVENTS

Clinton re-elected U.S. President. Dolly the sheep successfully cloned in Scotland.

Economic crisis: stock markets around the world crash, Dow Jones Industrial Average plummets. New York Stock Exchange inaugurates "circuit breaker" rule to block trading.

Clinton impeached over sex scandal (acquitted 1999).

Ethnic Albanians attacked by Serbs in Kosovo; U.S. leads NATO in bombing of Belgrade.

George W. Bush elected U.S. President. Putin succeeds Yeltsin as Russian President. More conflict in Chechen Republic. Milosevic's regime collapses in former Yugoslavia.
Al-Qaeda attacks New York's World Trade Center and the Pentagon (known thereafter as "9/11"); 2,977 killed. U.S. and allies take action against Taliban in Afghanistan.
Bush declares "War on Terror." Moscow theater hostage crisis.

U.S. and British troops invade Iraq; Saddam Hussein captured.

Bush re-elected U.S. President. Spain: terrorist bombings, Madrid. Tsunami in Indian Ocean.

U.S.: Hurricane Katrina floods New Orleans. Terrorist bombings in London.

Iran joins "nuclear club"; North Korea tests nuclear weapon.

THE L.A. QUARTET

DATE	AUTHOR'S LIFE	LITERARY CONTEXT
2007		Klein: *The Shock Doctrine*.
2008		Bolaño: *2666*.
		Robinson: *Home*.
		Roth: *Indignation*.
2009	*Blood's a Rover*, concluding volume of *The Underworld U.S.A. Trilogy*, published.	Foer: *Eating Animals*.
		Larsson: *The Girl Who Played with Fire*.
		Moore: *The Gate at the Stairs*.
		Prebble: *ENRON*.
		Roth: *The Humbling*.
2010	*The Hilliker Curse*, companion volume to *My Dark Places*, published.	Coover: *Noir*.
		Egan: *A Visit from the Goon Squad*.
		Ferris: *The Unnamed*.
		Larsson: *The Girl Who Kicked the Hornets' Nest*.
		Roth: *Nemesis*.
2011		Child: *The Affair*.
		Patchett: *State of Wonder*.
		Wallace: *The Pale King*.
2012		Ford: *Canada*.
		Leonard: *Raylan*.
		Robinson: *2312*.
2013		Kimmel: *Angry White Men*.
		Tartt: *The Goldfinch*.
2014	*Perfidia*, first novel of *The Second L.A. Quartet*, published.	Grossman: *A Horse Walks into a Bar*.
		Klein: *This Changes Everything*.
2015		Beatty: *The Sellout*.
		Franzen: *Purity*.
		Lee: *Go Set a Watchman*.
		Stephenson: *Seveneves*.
2016		Alderman: *The Power*.
		Smith: *Swing Time*.
2017		Auster: *4 3 2 1*.
		Saunders: *Lincoln in the Bardo*.
		Strout: *Anything Is Possible*.
2018	*This Storm*, second novel of *The Second L.A. Quartet*, in preparation for publication 2019.	Burns: *Milkman*.
		Wolff: *Fire and Fury*.

CHRONOLOGY

HISTORICAL EVENTS

Bush reduces U.S. forces in Iraq; 853 military deaths. Al Gore and U.N. climate scientists win Nobel Peace Prize. Russia: Yeltsin dies.
Barack Obama, Democratic Senator from Illinois, becomes first black presidential nominee.

Ongoing world financial crisis. H1N1 ("swine flu") global pandemic.

Healthcare Reform Bill passed by President Obama. Deepwater Horizon (B.P. rig) oilspill in Gulf of Mexico.

"Arab Spring": uprisings against repressive regimes across Middle East; civil war in Syria. Osama Bin Laden killed by U.S. Navy Seals.

Obama re-elected U.S. President. Mars Science Laboratory ("Curiosity Rover") lands on Mars.

Nelson Mandela and Margaret Thatcher die. Pope Benedict XVI resigns.

Russia annexes Crimea. ISIS declares Islamic Caliphate.

Black Lives Matter protests begin in U.S. Greek debt crisis. France: Islamic terrorists attack offices of satirical magazine *Charlie Hebdo*.

Donald Trump elected U.S. President.

Trump takes up office of President, promising to "make America great again" and fueling rise of populism worldwide.

Trump announces his intention to withdraw the United States from the Iranian nuclear agreement, but negotiates with North Korea's Kim Jong-un over denuclearization. Populism continues to proliferate worldwide.

THE BLACK DAHLIA

To Geneva Hilliker Ellroy
1915–1958

Mother:
Twenty-nine Years Later,
This Valediction in Blood

Now I fold you down, my drunkard, my navigator,
My first lost keeper, to love and look at later.

ANNE SEXTON

PROLOGUE

I NEVER knew her in life. She exists for me through others, in evidence of the ways her death drove them. Working backward, seeking only facts, I reconstructed her as a sad little girl and a whore, at best a could-have-been—a tag that might equally apply to me. I wish I could have granted her an anonymous end, relegated her to a few terse words on a homicide dick's summary report, carbon to the coroner's office, more paperwork to take her to potter's field. The only thing wrong with the wish is that she wouldn't have wanted it that way. As brutal as the facts were, she would have wanted all of them known. And since I owe her a great deal and am the only one who does know the entire story, I have undertaken the writing of this memoir.

But before the Dahlia there was the partnership, and before that there was the war and military regulations and manuevers at Central Division, reminding us that cops were also soldiers, even though we were a whole lot less popular than the ones battling the Germans and Japs. After duty every day, patrolmen were subjected to participation in air raid drills, blackout drills and fire evacuation drills that had us standing at attention on Los Angeles Street, hoping for a Messerschmitt attack to make us feel less like fools. Daywatch roll call featured alphabetical formations, and shortly after graduating the Academy in August of '42, that was where I met Lee.

I already knew him by reputation, and had our respective records down pat: Lee Blanchard, 43-4-2 as a heavyweight, formerly a regular attraction at the Hollywood Legion Stadium; and me: Bucky Bleichert, light-heavy, 36-0-0, once ranked tenth by *Ring* magazine, probably because Nat Fleisher was amused by the way I taunted opponents with my big buck teeth. The statistics didn't tell the whole story, though. Blanchard hit hard, taking six to give one, a classic headhunter; I danced and counterpunched and hooked to the liver, always keeping my guard up, afraid that catching too many head shots would ruin my looks worse than my teeth already had. Style-wise, Lee and I were like oil and water, and every time our shoulders brushed at roll call, I would wonder: who would win?

For close to a year we measured each other. We never talked boxing or police work, limiting our conversation to a few words about the weather. Physically, we looked as antithetical as two big men could: Blanchard was blond and ruddy, six feet tall and huge in the chest and shoulders, with stunted bowlegs and the beginning of a hard, distended gut; I was pale and dark-haired, all lanky muscularity at six foot three. Who would win?

I finally quit trying to predict a winner. But other cops had taken up the question, and during that first year at Central I heard dozens of opinions: Blanchard by early KO; Bleichert by decision; Blanchard stopped/stopping on cuts—everything but Bleichert by knockout.

When I was out of eye shot, I heard whispers of our non-ring stories: Lee coming on the LAPD, assured of rapid promotion for fighting private smokers attended by the high brass and their political buddies, cracking the Boulevard-Citizens bank heist back in '39 and falling in love with one of the heisters' girlfriends, blowing a certain transfer to the Detective Bureau when the skirt moved in with him—in violation of departmental regs on shack jobs—and begged him to quit boxing. The Blanchard rumors hit me like little feint-jabs, and I wondered how true they were. The bits of my own story felt like body blows, because they were 100 percent straight dope: Dwight Bleichert joining the Department in flight from tougher main events, threatened with expulsion from the Academy when his father's German-American Bund membership came to light, pressured into snitching the Japanese guys he grew up with to the Alien Squad in order to secure his LAPD appointment. Not asked to fight smokers, because he wasn't a knockout puncher.

Blanchard and Bleichert: a hero and a snitch.

Remembering Sam Murakami and Hideo Ashida manacled en route to Manzanar made it easy to simplify the two of us—at first. Then we went into action side by side, and my early notions about Lee—and myself—went blooey.

It was early June of '43. The week before, sailors had brawled with zoot suit wearing Mexicans at the Lick Pier in Venice. Rumor had it that one of the gobs lost an eye. Skirmishing broke out inland: navy personnel from the Chavez Ravine naval base versus pachucos in Alpine and Palo Verde. Word hit the papers that the zooters were packing Nazi regalia along with their switch-blades, and hundreds of in-uniform soldiers, sailors and marines descended on downtown L.A., armed with two-by-fours and baseball bats. An equal number of pachucos were supposed to be forming by the Brew 102 Brewery in Boyle Heights, supplied with similar weaponry. Every Central Division patrolman was called in to duty, then issued a World War I tin hat and an oversize billy club known as a nigger knocker.

At dusk, we were driven to the battleground in personnel car-riers borrowed from the army, and given one order: restore order. Our service revolvers had been taken from us at the station; the brass did not want .38's falling into the hands of reet pleat, stuff cuff, drape shape, Argentine ducktail Mexican gangsters. When I jumped out of the carrier at Evergreen and Wabash holding only a three-pound stick with a friction-taped handle, I got ten times as frightened as I had ever been in the ring, and not because chaos was coming down from all sides.

I was terrified because the good guys were really the bad guys.

Sailors were kicking in windows all along Evergreen; marines in dress blues were systematically smashing streetlights, giving them-selves more and more darkness to work in. Eschewing inter-service rivalry, soldiers and jarheads overturned cars parked in front of a bodega while navy youths in skivvies and white bell-bottoms truncheoned the shit out of an outnumbered bunch of zooters on the sidewalk next door. At the periphery of the action I could see knots of my fellow officers hobnobbing with Shore Patrol goons and MPs.

I don't know how long I stood there, numbed, wondering what to do. Finally I looked down Wabash toward 1st Street, saw small houses, trees and no pachucos, cops or blood-hungry GIs. Before I knew what I was doing, I ran there full speed. I would have kept running until I dropped, but a high-pitched laugh issuing from a front porch stopped me dead.

I walked toward the sound. A high-pitched voice called out, "You're the second young copper to take a powder from the com-motion. I don't blame you. Kinda hard to tell who to put the cuffs on, ain't it?"

I stood on the porch and looked at the old man. He said, "Radio says cabdrivers been makin' runs to the USO up in Hollywood, then bringin' the sailor boys down here. KFI called it a naval assault, been playin' 'Anchors Aweigh' every hour on the half hour. I saw some gyrenes down the street. You think this is what you call an amphibious attack?"

"I don't know what it is, but I'm going back."

"You ain't the only one turned tail, you know. 'Nuther big fella came runnin' this way pronto."

Pops was starting to look like a wily version of my father.

"There's some pachucos who need their order restored."

"Think it's that simple, laddy?"

"I'll make it that simple."

The old man cackled with delight. I stepped off the porch and headed back to duty, tapping the knocker against my leg. The streetlights were now all dead; it was almost impossible to distinguish zooters from GIs. Knowing that gave me an easy way out of my dilemma, and I got ready to charge. Then I heard "*Bleichert!*" behind me, and knew who the other runner had been.

I ran back. There was Lee Blanchard, "The Southland's good but not great white hope," facing down three marines in dress blues and a pachuco in a full-drape zoot suit. He had them cornered in the center walkway of a ratty bungalow court and was holding them off with parries from his nigger knocker. The jarheads were taking roundhouse swipes at him with their two-by-fours, missing as Blanchard moved sideways and back and forth on the balls of his feet. The pachuco fondled the religious medals around his neck, looking bewildered.

"Bleichert code three!"

I waded in, jabbing with my stick, the weapon hitting shiny brass buttons and campaign ribbons. I caught clumsy truncheon blows on my arms and shoulders and pressed forward so the marines would be denied swinging room. It was like being in a clinch with an octopus, and no referee or three-minute bell, and on instinct I dropped my baton, lowered my head and started winging body punches, making contact with soft gabardine midsections. Then I heard, "Bleichert step back!"

I did, and there was Lee Blanchard, the nigger knocker held high above his head. The marines, dazed, froze; the club descended: once, twice, three times, clean shots to the shoulders. When the trio was reduced to a dress blue rubble heap, Blanchard said, "To the halls of Tripoli, shitbirds," and turned to the pachuco. "Hola, Tomas."

I shook my head and stretched. My arms and back ached; my right knuckles throbbed. Blanchard was cuffing the zooter, and all I could think to say was, "What was that all about?"

Blanchard smiled. "Forgive my bad manners. Officer Bucky Bleichert, may I present Señor Tomas Dos Santos, the subject of an all-points fugitive warrant for manslaughter committed during the commission of a Class B Felony. Tomas snatched a purse off a hairbag on 6th and Alvarado, she keeled of a heart attack and croaked, Tomas dropped the purse, ran like hell. Left a big fat juicy set of prints on the purse, eyeball witnesses to boot." Blanchard nudged the man. "Habla Ingles, Tomas?"

Dos Santos shook his head no; Blanchard shook his head sadly. "He's dead meat. Manslaughter Two's a gas chamber jolt for spics. Hepcat here's about six weeks away from the Big Adios."

I heard shots coming from the direction of Evergreen and Wabash. Standing on my toes, I saw flames shooting out of a row of broken windows, crackling into blue and white flak when they hit streetcar wires and phone lines. I looked down at the marines, and one of them gave me the finger. I said, "I hope those guys didn't get your badge number."

"Fuck them sideways if they did."

I pointed to a clump of palm trees igniting into fireballs. "We'll never be able to get him booked tonight. You ran down here to roust them? You thought—"

Blanchard silenced me with a playful jab that stopped just short of my badge. "I ran down here because I knew there wasn't a goddamn thing I could do about restoring order, and if I just stood around I might have gotten killed. Sound familiar?"

I laughed. "Yeah. Then you—"

"Then I saw the shitbirds chasing hepcat, who looked suspiciously like the subject of felony warrant number four eleven dash forty-three. They cornered me here, and I saw you walking back looking to get hurt, so I thought I'd let you get hurt for a reason. Sound reasonable?"

"It worked."

Two of the marines had managed to get to their feet, and were helping the other one up. When they started for the sidewalk three abreast, Tomas Dos Santos sent a hard right foot at the biggest of the three asses. The fat PFC it belonged to turned to face his attacker; I stepped forward. Surrendering their East L.A. campaign, the three hobbled out to the street, gunshots and flaming palm trees. Blanchard ruffled Dos Santos' hair. "You cute little shit, you're a dead man. Come on, Bleichert, let's find a place to sit this thing out."

* * *

We found a house with a stack of daily papers on the porch a few blocks away and broke in. There were two fifths of Cutty Sark in the kitchen cupboard, and Blanchard switched the cuffs from Dos Santos' wrists to his ankles so he could have his hands free to booze. By the time I made ham sandwiches and highballs, the pachuco had killed half the jug and was belting "Cielito Lindo" and a Mex rendition of "Chattanooga Choo Choo." An hour later the bottle was dead and Tomas was passed out. I lifted him onto the couch and threw a quilt over him, and Blanchard said, "He's my ninth hard felon for 1943. He'll be sucking gas inside of six weeks, and I'll be working Northeast or Central Warrants inside of three years."

His certainty rankled me. "Ixnay. You're too young, you haven't made sergeant, you're shacking with a woman, you lost your high brass buddies when you quit fighting smokers and you haven't done a plainsclothes tour. You—"

I stopped when Blanchard grinned, then walked to the living room window and looked out. "Fires over on Michigan and Soto. Pretty."

"Pretty?"

"Yeah, pretty. You know a lot about me, Bleichert."

"People talk about you."

"They talk about you, too."

"What do they say?"

"That your old man's some sort of Nazi drool case. That you ratted off your best friend to the feds to get on the Department. That you padded your record fighting built-up middle-weights."

The words hung in the air like a three-count indictment. "Is that it?"

Blanchard turned to face me. "No. They say you never chase cooze and they say you think you can take me."

I took the challenge. "All those things are true."

"Yeah? So was what you heard about me. Except I'm on the Sergeants List, I'm transferring to Highland Park Vice in August and there's a Jewboy deputy DA who wets his pants for boxers. He's promised me the next Warrants spot he can wangle."

"I'm impressed."

"Yeah? You want to hear something even more impressive?"

"Hit me."

"My first twenty knockouts were stumblebums handpicked by my manager. My girlfriend saw you fight at the Olympic and said you'd be handsome if you got your teeth fixed, and maybe you *could* take me."

I couldn't tell if the man was looking for a brawl then and there or a friend; if he was testing me or taunting me or pumping me for information. I pointed to Tomas Dos Santos, twitching in his booze sleep. "What about the Mex?"

"We'll take him in tomorrow morning."

"You'll take him in."

"The collar's half yours."

"Thanks, but no thanks."

"Okay, partner."

"I'm not your partner."

"Maybe someday."

"Maybe never, Blanchard. Maybe you work Warrants and pull in repos and serve papers for the shysters downtown, maybe I put in my twenty, take my pension and get a soft job somewhere."

"You could go on the feds. I know you've got pals on the Alien Squad."

"Don't push me on that."

Blanchard looked out the window again. "Pretty. Make a good picture postcard. 'Dear Mom, wish you were here at the colorful East L.A. race riot.'"

Tomas Dos Santos stirred, mumbling, "Inez? Inez? Qué? Inez?" Blanchard walked to a hall closet and found an old wool overcoat and tossed it on top of him. The added warmth seemed to calm him down; the mumbles died off. Blanchard said, "Cherchez la femme. Huh, Bucky?"

"What?"

"Look for the woman. Even with a snootful of juice, old Tomas can't let Inez go. I'll lay you ten to one that when he hits the gas chamber she'll be right there with him."

"Maybe he'll cop a plea. Fifteen to life, out in twenty."

"No. He's a dead man. Cherchez la femme, Bucky. Remember that."

I walked through the house looking for a place to sleep, finally settling on a downstairs bedroom with a lumpy bed way too short for my legs. Lying down, I listened to sirens and gunshots in the distance. Gradually I dozed off, and dreamed of my own few and far between women.

* * *

By the morning the riot had cooled off, leaving the sky hung with soot and the streets littered with broken liquor bottles and discarded two-by-fours and baseball bats. Blanchard called Hollenbeck Station for a black-and-white to transport his ninth hard felon of 1943 to the Hall of Justice jail, and Tomas Dos Santos wept when the patrolmen took him away from us. Blanchard and I shook hands on the sidewalk and walked separate routes downtown, him to the DA's office to write up his report on the capture of the purse snatcher, me to Central Station and another tour of duty.

The L.A. City Council outlawed the wearing of the zoot suit, and Blanchard and I went back to polite conversation at roll call. And everything he stated with such rankling certainty that night in the empty house came true.

Blanchard was promoted to Sergeant and transferred to Highland Park Vice early in August, and Tomas Dos Santos went to the gas chamber a week later. Three years passed, and I continued to work a radio car beat in Central Division. Then one morning I looked at the transfer and promotion board and saw at the top of the list: Blanchard, Leland C., Sergeant; Highland Park Vice to Central Warrants, effective 9/15/46.

And, of course, we became partners. Looking back, I know that the man possessed no gift of prophecy; he simply worked to assure his own future, while I skated uncertainly toward mine. It was his flat-voiced "Cherchez la femme" that still haunts me. Because our partnership was nothing but a bungling road to the Dahlia. And in the end, she was to own the two of us completely.

PART ONE

FIRE AND ICE

1

THE ROAD to the partnership began without my knowing it, and it was a revival of the Blanchard-Bleichert fight brouhaha that brought me the word.

I was coming off a long tour of duty spent in a speed trap on Bunker Hill, preying on traffic violators. My ticket book was full and my brain was numb from eight hours of following my eyes across the intersection of 2nd and Beaudry. Walking through the Central muster room and a crowd of blues waiting to hear the P.M. crime sheet, I almost missed Johnny Vogel's, "They ain't fought in years, and Horrall outlawed smokers, so I don't think that's it. My dad's thick with the Jewboy, and he says he'd try for Joe Louis if he was white."

Then Tom Joslin elbowed me. "They're talking about you, Bleichert."

I looked over at Vogel, standing a few yards away, talking to another cop. "Hit me, Tommy."

Joslin smiled. "You know Lee Blanchard?"

"The Pope know Jesus?"

"Ha! He's working Central Warrants."

"Tell me something I don't know."

"How's this? Blanchard's partner's topping out his twenty. Nobody thought he'd pull the pin, but he's gonna. The Warrants boss is this felony court DA, Ellis Loew. He got Blanchard his appointment, now he's looking for a bright boy to take over the partner's spot. Word is he creams for fighters and wants you. Vogel's old man's in the Detective Bureau. He's simpatico with Loew and pushing for his kid to get the job. Frankly, I don't think either of you got the qualifications. Me, on the other hand ..."

I tingled, but still managed to come up with a crack to show Joslin I didn't care. "Your teeth are too small. No good for biting in the clinches. Lots of clinches working Warrants."

* * *

But I did care.

That night I sat on the steps outside my apartment and looked at the garage that held my heavy bag and speed bag, my scrapbook of press clippings, fight programs and publicity stills. I thought about being good but not really good, about keeping my weight down when I could have put on an extra ten pounds and fought heavyweight, about fighting tortilla-stuffed Mexican middle-weights at the Eagle Rock Legion Hall where my old man went to his Bund meetings. Light heavyweight was a no-man's-land division, and early on I pegged it as being tailor-made for me. I could dance on my toes all night at 175 pounds, I could hook accurately to the body from way outside and only a bulldozer could work in off my left jab.

But there were no light heavyweight bulldozers, because any hungry fighter pushing 175 slopped up spuds until he made heavyweight, even if he sacrificed half his speed and most of his punch. Light heavyweight was safe. Light heavyweight was guaranteed fifty-dollar purses without getting hurt. Light heavy-weight was plugs in the *Times* from Braven Dyer, adulation from the old man and his Jew-baiting cronies and being a big cheese as long as I didn't leave Glassell Park and Lincoln Heights. It was going as far as I could as a natural—without having to test my guts.

Then Ronnie Cordero came along.

He was a Mex middleweight out of El Monte, fast, with knockout power in both hands and a crablike defense, guard high, elbows pressed to his sides to deflect body blows. Only nineteen, he had huge bones for his weight, with the growth potential to jump him up two divisions to heavyweight and the big money. He racked up a string of fourteen straight early-round KOs at the Olympic, blitzing all the top L.A. middles. Still growing and anx-ious to jack up the quality of his opponents, Cordero issued me a challenge through the *Herald* sports page.

I knew that he would eat me alive. I knew that losing to a taco bender would ruin my local celebrity. I knew that running from the fight would hurt me, but fighting it would kill me. I started looking for a place to run to. The army, navy and marines looked good, then Pearl Harbor got bombed and made them look great. Then the old man had a stroke, lost his job and pension and started sucking baby food through a straw. I got a hardship deferment and joined the Los Angeles Police Department.

I saw where my thoughts were going. FBI goons were asking me if I considered myself a German or an American, and would I be willing to prove my patriotism by helping them out. I fought what was next by concentrating on my landlady's cat stalking a bluejay across the garage roof. When he pounced, I admitted to myself how bad I wanted Johnny Vogel's rumor to be true.

Warrants was local celebrity as a cop. Warrants was plainclothes without a coat and tie, romance and a mileage per diem on your civilian car. Warrants was going after the real bad guys and not rousting winos and wienie waggers in front of the Midnight Mission. Warrants was working in the DA's office with one foot in the Detective Bureau, and late dinners with Mayor Bowron when he was waxing effusive and wanted to hear war stories.

Thinking about it started to hurt. I went down to the garage and hit the speed bag until my arms cramped.

*   *   *

Over the next few weeks I worked a radio car beat near the northern border of the division. I was breaking in a fatmouthed rookie named Sidwell, a kid just off a three-year MP stint in the Canal Zone. He hung on my every word with the slavish tenacity of a lapdog, and was so enamored of civilian police work that he took to sticking around the station after our end of tour, bullshitting with the jailers, snapping towels at the wanted posters in the locker room, generally creating a nuisance until someone told him to go home.

He had no sense of decorum, and would talk to anybody about anything. I was one of his favorite subjects, and he passed station house scuttlebutt straight back to me.

I discounted most of the rumors: Chief Horrall was going to start up an interdivisional boxing team, and was shooting me Warrants to assure that I signed on along with Blanchard; Ellis Loew, the felony court comer, was supposed to have won a bundle betting on me before the war and was now handing me a belated reward; Horrall had rescinded his order banning smokers, and some high brass string puller wanted me happy so he could line his pockets betting on me. Those tales sounded too farfetched, although I knew boxing was somehow behind my front-runner status. What I credited was that the Warrants opening was narrowing down to either Johnny Vogel or me.

Vogel had a father working Central dicks; I was a padded 36-0-0 in the no-man's-land division five years before. Knowing the only way to compete with nepotism was to make the weight, I punched bags, skipped meals and skipped rope until I was a nice, safe light heavyweight again. Then I waited.

2

I WAS a week at the 175-pound limit, tired of training and dreaming every night of steaks, chili burgers and coconut cream pies. My hopes for the Warrants job had waned to the point where I would have sold them down the river for pork chops at the Pacific Dining Car, and the neighbor who looked after the old man for a double sawbuck a month had called me to say that he was acting up again, taking BB potshots at the neighborhood dogs and blowing his Social Security check on girlie magazines and model airplanes. It was reaching the point where I would have to *do* something about him, and every toothless geezer I saw on the beat hit my eyes as a gargoyle version of Crazy Dolph Bleichert. I was watching one stagger across 3rd and Hill when I got the radio call that changed my life forever.

"11-A-23, call the station. Repeat: 11-A-23, call the station."

Sidwell nudged me. "We got a call, Bucky."

"Roger it."

"The dispatcher said to call the station."

I hung a left and parked, then pointed to the call box on the corner. "Use the gamewell. The little key next to your handcuffs."

Sidwell obeyed, trotting back to the cruiser moments later, looking grave. "You're supposed to report to the Chief of Detectives immediately," he said.

My first thoughts were of the old man. I leadfooted the six blocks to City Hall and turned the black-and-white over to Sidwell, then took the elevator up to Chief Thad Green's fourth-floor offices. A secretary admitted me to the Chief's inner sanctum, and sitting in matched leather chairs were Lee Blanchard, more high brass than I had ever seen in one place and a spider-thin man in a three-piece tweed suit.

The secretary said, "Officer Bleichert," and left me standing there, aware that my uniform hung on my depleted body like a

tent. Then Blanchard, wearing cord slacks and a maroon letterman's jacket, got to his feet and played MC.

"Gentlemen, Bucky Bleichert. Bucky, left to right in uniform,
we have Inspector Malloy, Inspector Stensland and Chief Green.
The gentleman in mufti is Deputy DA Ellis Loew."

I nodded, and Thad Green pointed me to an empty chair facing
the assembly. I settled into it; Stensland handed me a sheaf of
papers. "Read this, Officer. It's Braven Dyer's editorial for this
coming Saturday's *Times*."

The top page was dated 10/14/46, with a block printed
title—"Fire and Ice Among L.A.'s Finest"—directly below it.
Below that, the typed text began:

> Before the war, the City of the Angels was graced
> with two local fighters, born and raised a scant five
> miles apart, pugilists with styles as different as fire
> and ice. Lee Blanchard was a bowlegged windmill of
> a leather slinger, and sparks covered the ringside seats
> when he threw punches. Bucky Bleichert entered
> the ring so cool and collected that it was easy to
> believe he was immune to sweat. He could dance
> on his toes better than Bojangles Robinson, and his
> rapier jabs peppered his opponents' faces until they
> looked like the steak tartare at Mike Lyman's Grill.
> Both men were poets: Blanchard the poet of brute
> strength, Bleichert the counter poet of speed and
> guile. Collectively they won 79 bouts and lost only
> four. In the ring as in the table of elements, fire and
> ice are tough to beat.
>
> Mr. Fire and Mr. Ice never fought each other.
> Divisional boundaries kept them apart. But a sense
> of duty brought them together in spirit, and both
> men joined the Los Angeles Police Department and
> continued fighting out of the ring—this time in the
> war against crime. Blanchard cracked the baffling
> Boulevard-Citizens bank robbery case in 1939, and
> captured thrill-killer Tomas Dos Santos; Bleichert
> served with distinction during the '43 Zoot Suit
> Wars. And now they are both officers in Central
> Division: Mr. Fire, 32, a sergeant in the prestigious
> Warrants Squad; Mr. Ice, 29, a patrolman working a

dangerous beat in downtown L.A. I recently asked both Fire and Ice why they gave up their best ring years to become cops. Their responses are indicative of the fine men they are:

Sergeant Blanchard: "A fighter's career doesn't last forever, but the satisfaction of serving your community does."

Officer Bleichert: "I wanted to fight more dangerous opponents, namely criminals and Communists."

Lee Blanchard and Bucky Bleichert made great sacrifices to serve their city, and on Election Day, November 5, Los Angeles voters are going to be asked to do the same thing—vote in a five-million-dollar bond proposal to upgrade the LAPD's equipment and provide for an 8 percent pay raise for all personnel. Keep in mind the examples of Mr. Fire and Mr. Ice. Vote "Yes" on Proposition B on Election Day.

Finishing, I handed the pages back to Inspector Stensland. He started to speak, but Thad Green shushed him with a hand on his shoulder. "Tell us what you thought of it, Officer. Be candid."

I swallowed to keep my voice steady. "It's subtle."

Stensland flushed, Green and Malloy grinned, Blanchard hooted outright. Ellis Loew said, "Proposition B is going to lose hands down, but there's a chance to reintroduce it in the off-year election next spring. What we had in—"

Green said, "Ellis, please," and turned his attention to me. "One of the reasons the bond is going to fail is that the public is less than pleased with the service we've been giving them. We were shorthanded during the war, and some of the men we hired to remedy that turned out to be rotten apples and made us look bad. Also, we're top-heavy with rookies since the war ended, and a lot of good men have retired. Two station houses need to be rebuilt and we need to offer higher starting salaries to attract better men. All this takes money, and the voters aren't going to give it to us in November."

I was beginning to get the picture. Malloy said, "It was your idea, counselor. You tell him."

Loew said, "I'm laying dollars to doughnuts we can pass the proposal in the '47 Special. But we need to drum up enthusiasm for the Department to do it. We need to build up morale within the Department, and we need to impress the voters with the quality of our men. Wholesome white boxers are a big draw, Bleichert. You know that."

I looked at Blanchard. "You and me, huh?"

Blanchard winked. "Fire and Ice. Tell him the rest of it, Ellis."

Loew winced at his first name, then continued. "A ten-round bout three weeks from now at the Academy gym. Braven Dyer is a close personal friend of mine, and he'll be building it up in his column. Tickets will go for two dollars apiece, with half allotted for policemen and their families, half for civilians. The gate goes to the police charity program. From there we build up an interdivisional boxing team. All good wholesome white boys. The team members get one duty day off a week to teach underprivileged kids the art of self-defense. Publicity all the way, straight to the '47 Special Election."

All eyes were on me now. I held my breath, waiting for the offer of the Warrants spot. When no one said a word, I glanced sidelong at Blanchard. His upper body looked brutally powerful, but his stomach had gone to flab and I was younger, taller and probably a whole lot faster. Before I could give myself reasons to back down, I said, "I'm in."

The brass gave my decision a round of applause; Ellis Loew smiled, exposing teeth that looked like they belonged on a baby shark. "The date is October 29, a week before the election," he said. "And both of you will have unlimited use of the Academy gym for training. Ten rounds is a lot to ask of men as inactive as you two have been, but anything else would look sissy. Don't you agree?"

Blanchard snorted, "Or communistic"; Loew shot him a shark-tooth grimace. I said, "Yes, sir," and Inspector Malloy raised a camera, chirping, "Watch the birdy, son."

I stood up and smiled without parting my lips; a flashbulb popped. I saw stars and got a back pounding, and when the camaraderie stopped and my vision cleared, Ellis Loew was standing in front of me, saying, "I'm betting on great things from you. And if I don't miss my bet, I expect we'll be colleagues soon."

I thought, You're a subtle bastard, but said, "Yes, sir." Loew gave me a limp handshake and walked away. I rubbed the last of the stars out of my eyes and saw that the room was empty.

I took the elevator down to street level, thinking of tasty ways to regain the weight I had lost. Blanchard probably weighed 200, and if I came in at my safe old 175 against him he would wear me down every time he managed to get inside. I was trying to decide between the Pantry and Little Joe's when I hit the parking lot and saw my adversary in the flesh—talking to a woman blowing smoke rings up at a picture postcard sky.

I went over. Blanchard was leaning against an unmarked cruiser, gesturing at the woman, still intent on her rings, putting them out three and four at a time. She was in profile as I approached, head tilted up, back arched, one hand on the cruiser's door for support. Auburn hair in a pageboy cut brushed her shoulders and long, thin neck; the fit of her Eisenhower jacket and wool skirt told me she was thin all over.

Blanchard caught sight of me and nudged her. Letting out a lungful of smoke, she turned. Up close, I saw a strong-pretty face, all mismatched parts: high forehead that made her hairdo look incongruous, crooked nose, full lips and big black-brown eyes.

Blanchard made the introductions. "Kay, this is Bucky Bleichert. Bucky, Kay Lake."

The woman ground out her cigarette. I said, "Hello," wondering if this was the girlfriend that Blanchard met at the Boulevard-Citizens robbery trial. She didn't play as a heister's quail, even if she had been shacking with a cop for years.

Her voice had a slight prairie twang. "I saw you box several times. You won."

"I always won. Are you a fight fan?"

Kay Lake shook her head. "Lee used to drag me. I was taking art classes back before the war, so I brought my sketch pad and drew the boxers."

Blanchard put an arm around her shoulders. "Made me quit fighting smokers. Said she didn't want me doing the vegetable shuffle." He went into an imitation of a punch-drunk fighter sparring, and Kay Lake flinched away from him. Blanchard shot a quick look at her, then fired off some left jabs and right crosses at the air. The punches were telegraphed, and in my mind I countered a one-two at his jaw and midsection.

I said, "I'll try not to hurt you."

Kay smoldered at the remark; Blanchard grinned. "It took weeks to talk her into letting me do it. I promised her a new car if she didn't pout too much."

"Don't make any bets you can't cover."

Blanchard laughed, then moved into a side-by-side drape with Kay. I said, "Who thought this thing up?"

"Ellis Loew. He got me Warrants, then my partner put in his papers and Loew started thinking about you to replace him. He got Braven Dyer to write that Fire and Ice horseshit, then he took the whole pie to Horrall. He never would have gone for it, but all the polls said the bond issue was heading for the deep six, so he said okay."

"And he's got money on me? And if I win I get Warrants?"

"Something like that. The DA himself don't like the idea, thinks the two of us wouldn't work as partners. But he's going along—Horrall and Thad Green convinced him. Personally, I almost hope you do win. If you don't, I get Johnny Vogel. He's fat, he farts, his breath stinks and his daddy's the biggest nose-bleed in Central dicks, always running errands for the Jewboy. Besides—"

I tapped Blanchard's chest with a soft forefinger. "What's in it for you?"

"Betting works both ways. My girl's got a taste for nice things, and I can't afford to let her down. Right, babe?"

Kay said, "Keep talking about me in the third person. It sends me."

Blanchard put up his hands in mock surrender; Kay's dark eyes burned. Curious about the woman, I said, "What do you think about the whole thing, Miss Lake?"

Now her eyes danced. "For aesthetic reasons, I hope you both look good with your shirts off. For moral reasons, I hope the Los Angeles Police Department gets ridiculed for perpetrating this farce. For financial reasons, I hope Lee wins."

Blanchard laughed and slapped the hood of the cruiser; I forgot vanity and smiled with my mouth open. Kay Lake stared me straight in the eye, and for the first time—strangely but surely—I sensed that Mr. Fire and I were becoming friends. Sticking out my hand, I said, "Luck short of winning"; Lee grabbed it and said, "The same."

Kay took in the two of us with a look that said we were idiot children. I tipped my hat to her, then started to walk away. Kay called out "Dwight," and I wondered how she knew my real name. When I turned around, she said, "You'd be very handsome if you got your teeth fixed."

3

THE FIGHT became the rage of the Department, then L.A., and the Academy gym was sold out within twenty-four hours of Braven Dyer's announcement of it in the *Times* sports page. The 77th Street lieutenant tapped as official LAPD oddsmaker installed Blanchard as an early 3 to 1 favorite, while the real bookie line had Mr. Fire favored by knockout at 2½ to 1 and decision by 5 to 3. Interdepartmental betting was rampant, and wager pools were set up at all station houses. Dyer and Morrie Ryskind of the *Mirror* fed the craze in their columns, and a KMPC disc jockey composed a ditty called the "Fire and Ice Tango." Backed by a jazz combo, a sultry soprano warbled, "Fire and Ice ain't sugar and spice; four hundred pounds tradin' leather, that sure ain't nice. But Mr. Fire light my torch and Mr. Ice cool my brow, to me that's all-night service with a capital wow!"

I was a local celebrity again.

At roll call I watched betting markers change hands and got attaboys from cops I had never met before; Fat Johnny Vogel gave me the evil eye every time he passed me in the locker room. Sidwell, ever the rumor monger, said that two nightwatch blues had bet their cars, and the station commander, Captain Harwell, was holding the pink slips until after the fight. The dicks in Administrative Vice had suspended their bookie shakedowns because Mickey Cohen was taking in ten grand a day in markers and was kicking back 5 percent to the advertising agency employed by the city in its effort to pass the bond issue. Harry Cohn, Mr. Big at Columbia Pictures, had put down a bundle on me to win by decision, and if I delivered I got a hot weekend with Rita Hayworth.

None of it made sense, but all of it felt good, and I kept myself from going crazy by training harder than I ever had before.

At end of watch each day I headed straight for the gym and *worked*. Ignoring Blanchard and his brownnosing entourage and the off-duty cops who hovered around me, I hit the heavy bag, left jab—right cross—left hook, five minutes at a crack, on my toes the whole time; I sparred with my old pal Pete Lukins and rolled sets at the speed bag until sweat blinded me and my arms turned to rubber. I skipped rope and ran through the Elysian Park hills with two-pound weights strapped to my ankles, jabbing at tree limbs and bushes, outracing the trash can dogs who prowled there. At home, I gorged myself on liver, porterhouse steak and spinach and fell asleep before I could get out of my clothes.

Then, with the fight nine days away, I saw the old man and decided to take a dive for the money.

The occasion was my once-a-month visit, and I drove out to Lincoln Heights feeling guilty that I hadn't shown up since I got the word that he was acting crazy again. I brought gifts to assuage that guilt: canned goodies scrounged from the markets on my beat and confiscated girlie mags. Pulling up in front of the house, I saw that they wouldn't be enough.

The old man was sitting on the porch, swigging from a bottle of cough syrup. He had his BB pistol in one hand, absently taking shots at a formation of balsa wood airplanes lined up on the lawn. I parked, then walked over to him. His clothes were flecked with vomit and his bones protruded underneath them, poking out like they were joined to him at all the wrong angles. His breath stank, his eyes were yellow and filmy and the skin I could see underneath his crusty white beard was flush with broken veins. I reached down to help him to his feet; he swatted my hands, jabbering, "Scheisskopf! Kleine Scheisskopf!"

I pulled the old man up into a standing position. He dropped the BB pistol and Expectolar pint and said, "Guten Tag, Dwight," like he had just seen me the day before.

I brushed tears from my eyes. "Speak English, Papa."

The old man grabbed the crook of his right elbow and shook his fist at me in a slapdash fungoo. "Englisch Scheisser! Churchill Scheisser! Amerikanisch Juden Scheisser!"

I left him on the porch and checked out the house. The living room was littered with model airplane parts and open cans of beans with flies buzzing around them; the bedroom was wallpapered with cheesecake pics, most of them upside down. The bathroom stank of stale urine and the kitchen featured three cats snouting around in half-empty tunafish cans. They hissed at me as I approached; I threw a chair at them and went back to my father.

He was leaning on the porch rail, fingering his beard. Afraid he would topple over, I held his arm; afraid I would start to cry for real, I said, "Say something, Papa. Make me mad. Tell me how you managed to fuck up the house so bad in a month."

My father tried to pull free. I held on tighter, then loosened my grip, afraid of snapping the bone like a twig. He said, "Du, Dwight? Du?" and I knew he'd had another stroke and lost his memory of English again. I searched my own memory for phrases in German and came up empty. As a boy I'd hated the man so much that I made myself forget the language he'd taught me.

"Wo ist Greta? Wo, mutti?"

I put my arms around the old man. "Mama's dead. You were too cheap to buy her bootleg, so she got some raisinjack from the niggers in the Flats. It was rubbing alcohol, Papa. She went blind. You put her in the hospital, and she jumped off the roof."

"Greta!"

I held him harder. "Ssssh. It was fourteen years ago, Papa. A long time."

The old man tried to push me away; I shoved him into the porch stanchion and pinned him there. His lips curled to shout invective, then his face went blank, and I knew he couldn't come up with the words. I shut my eyes and found words for him: "Do you know what you cost me, you fuck? I could have gone to the cops clean, but they found out my father was a fucking subversive. They made me snitch off Sammy and Ashidas, and Sammy died at Manzanar. I know you only joined the Bund to bullshit and chase snatch, but you should have known better, because I didn't."

I opened my eyes and found them dry; my father's eyes were expressionless. I eased off his shoulders and said, "You couldn't have known better, and the snitch jacket's all on me. But you were a cheap stingy fuck. You killed Mama, and that's yours."

I got an idea how to end the whole mess. "You go rest now, Papa. I'll take care of you."

* * *

That afternoon I watched Lee Blanchard train. His regimen was four-minute rounds with lanky light heavys borrowed from the Main Street Gym, and his style was total assault. He crouched when he moved forward, always feinting with his upper body; his jab was surprisingly good. He wasn't the headhunter or sitting duck I expected, and when he hooked to the breadbasket I could feel the punches twenty yards away. For the money he was no sure thing, and money was the fight now.

So money made it a tank job.

I drove home and called up the retired postman who kept an eye on my father, offering him a C-note if he cleaned up the house and stuck to the old man like glue until after the fight. He agreed, and I called an old Academy classmate working Hollywood Vice and asked him for the names of some bookies. Thinking I wanted to bet on myself, he gave me the numbers of two independents, one with Mickey Cohen and one with the Jack Dragna mob. The indies and the Cohen book had Blanchard a straight two to one favorite, but the Dragna line was even money, Bleichert or Blanchard, the new odds coming from scouting reports that said I looked fast and strong. I could double every dollar I put in.

In the morning I called in sick, and the daywatch boss bought it because I was a local celebrity and Captain Harwell wouldn't want him rattling my cage. With work out of the way, I liquidated my savings account, cashed in my Treasury bonds and took out a bank loan for two grand, using my almost new '46 Chevy ragtop as collateral. From the bank, it was just a short ride out to Lincoln Heights and a talk with Pete Lukins. He agreed to do what I wanted, and two hours later he called me with the results.

The Dragna bookie I had sent him to had taken his money on Blanchard by late-round knockout, offering him two to one odds against. If I took my dive in rounds eight through ten, my net would be $8,640—enough to maintain the old man in a class rest home for at least two or three years. I had traded Warrants for a close-out on bad old debts, with the late-round stipulation just enough of a risk to keep me from feeling too much like a coward. It was a tradeoff that someone was going to help me pay for, and that someone was Lee Blanchard.

With seven days left before the fight, I ate myself up to 192, increased the distance on my roadwork and upped my heavy bag stints to six minutes. Duane Fisk, the officer assigned as my trainer and second, warned me about overtraining, but I ignored him and kept pushing up until forty-eight hours before the bout. Then I decelerated to light calisthenics and studied my opponent.

From the back of the gym I watched Blanchard spar in the center ring. I looked for flaws in his basic attack and gauged his reactions when his sparring partners got cute. I saw that in clinches his elbows were tucked in to deflect body shots, leaving him open for jarring little uppercuts that would bring up his guard and set him up for counter hooks to the ribs. I saw that his best punch, the right cross, was always telegraphed with two half steps to the left and a head feint. I saw that on the ropes he was deadly, that he could keep lighter opponents pinned there with elbow steers alternated with short body blows. Moving closer, I saw eyebrow scar tissue that I would have to avoid in order to prevent a stoppage on cuts. That rankled, but a long scar running down the left side of his ribcage looked like a juicy place to throw him a lot of hurt.

"At least he looks good with his shirt off."

I turned to face the words. Kay Lake was staring at me; out of the corner of my eye I saw Blanchard, resting on his stool, staring at us. "Where's your sketch pad?" I asked.

Kay waved at Blanchard; he blew her a kiss with two gloved hands. The bell rang, and he and his partner moved toward each other popping jabs. "I gave that up," Kay said. "I wasn't very good, so I changed my major."

"To what?"

"To pre-med, then psychology, then English lit, then history."

"I like a woman who knows what she wants."

Kay smiled. "So do I, but I don't know any. What do *you* want?"

I eyeballed the gym. Thirty or forty spectators were seated in folding chairs around the center ring, most of them off-duty cops and reporters, most of them smoking. A dissipating haze hung over the ring, and the spotlight shining down from the ceiling gave it a sulfurous glow. All were on Blanchard and his punchy, and all the shouts and catcalls were for him—but without me getting ready to avenge old business none of it meant a thing. "I'm part of this. That's what I want."

Kay shook her head. "You quit boxing five years ago. It's not your life anymore."

The woman's aggressiveness was making me itchy. I blurted, "And your boyfriend's a never-was just like me, and you were some sort of gang skirt before he picked you up. You—"

Kay Lake stopped me by laughing. "Have you been reading my press clippings?"

"No. You been reading mine?"

"Yes."

I didn't have a retort for *that*. "Why'd Lee quit fighting? Why'd he join the Department?"

"Catching criminals gives him a sense of order. Do you have a girlfriend?"

"I'm saving myself for Rita Hayworth. Do you flirt with a lot of cops, or am I a special case?"

Shouts rose from the crowd. I glanced over and saw Blanchard's sparring partner hit the canvas. Johnny Vogel climbed into the ring and popped out his mouthpiece; the punchy expelled a long jet of blood. When I turned to Kay she was pale, hunching into her Ike jacket. I said, "Tomorrow night'll be worse. You should stay home."

Kay shuddered. "No. It's a big moment for Lee."

"He told you to come?"

"No. He would never do that."

"The sensitive type, huh?"

Kay dug in her pockets for cigarettes and matches, then lit up. "Yes. Like you, but without the chip on the shoulder."

I felt myself go red. "You're always there for each other? thick and thin and all that?"

"We try."

"Then why aren't you married? Shacking's against the regs, and if the brass decided to get snotty they could nail Lee for it."

Kay blew rings at the floor, then looked up at me. "We can't."

"Why not? You've been shacked for years. He quit fighting smokers for you. He lets you flirt with other men. Sounds like an ace deal to me."

More shouts echoed. Glancing sidelong, I saw Blanchard pounding a new punchy. I countered the shots, duking the stale gym air. After a few seconds I saw what I was doing and stopped. Kay flipped her cigarette in the direction of the ring and said, "I have to go now. Good luck, Dwight."

Only the old man called me that. "You didn't answer my question."

Kay said, "Lee and I don't sleep together," then walked away before I could do anything but stare.

* * *

I hung around the gym for another hour or so. Toward dusk, reporters and cameramen started arriving, making straight for center ring, Blanchard and his boring knockdowns of glass-chinned pugs. Kay Lake's exit line stayed with me, along with flashes of her laughing and smiling and turning sad at the drop of a hat. When I heard a newshound yell, "Hey! There's Bleichert!" I exited, running out to the parking lot and my twice-mortgaged Chevy. Pulling away, I realized I had no place to go and nothing I wanted to do except satisfy my curiosity about a woman who was coming on like gangbusters and a big load of grief.

So I drove downtown to read her press clippings.

The clerk at the *Herald* morgue, impressed with my badge, led me to a reading table. I told him I was interested in the Boulevard-Citizens bank robbery and the trial of the captured robber, and that I thought the date was sometime early in '39 for the heist, maybe fall of the same year for the legal proceedings. He left me sitting there and returned ten minutes later with two large, leather-bound scrapbooks. Newspaper pages were glued to heavy black cardboard sheets, arranged chronologically, and I flipped from February 1 to February 12 before I found what I wanted.

On February 11, 1939, a four-man gang hijacked an armored car on a quiet Hollywood side street. Using a downed motorcycle as a diversion, the robbers overpowered the guard who left the car to investigate the accident. Putting a knife to his throat, they forced the other two guards still inside the car to let them in. Once inside, they chloroformed and trussed all three men and substituted six bags filled with phone book scraps and slugs for six bags filled with cash.

One robber drove the armored car to downtown Hollywood; the other three changed into uniforms identical to the ones the guards wore. The three in uniform walked in the door of Boulevard-Citizens Savings & Loan on Yucca and Ivar, carrying the sacks of paper and slugs, and the manager opened the vault for them. One of the robbers sapped the manager; the other two grabbed sacks of real money and headed for the door. By this time, the driver had entered the bank, and had rounded up the tellers. He herded them into the vault and sapped them, then shut the door and locked it. All four robbers were back on the sidewalk when a Hollywood Division patrol car, alerted by a bank-to-station alarm, arrived. The officers ordered the heisters to halt; they opened fire; the cops fired back. Two robbers were killed and two escaped—with four bags filled with unmarked fifties and C-notes.

When I saw no mention of Blanchard or Kay Lake, I skimmed a week of page one and two accounts of the LAPD investigation.

The dead heisters were identified as Chick Geyer and Max Ottens, San Francisco muscle with no known L.A. associates. Eyeball witnesses at the bank could not identify the two escapers from mug shots or provide adequate descriptions of them—their guard hats were pulled low and both wore lacquered sunglasses. There were no witnesses at the hijack scene, and the chloroformed guards had been overpowered before they got good looks at their attackers.

The heist went from page two and three to the scandal columns. Bevo Means featured it for three days running, milking the angle that the Bugsy Siegel mob was chasing the escaped heisters because one of the armored car's stops was the Bug Man's haberdashery front. Siegel had sworn to find them, even though it was the bank's money that the two got away with—not his.

Means' columns got further and further afield, and I turned pages until I hit the February 28 headline: "Tip From Ex-Boxer Cop Cracks Bloody Bank Robbery."

The account was loaded with praise for Mr. Fire, but was short on facts. Officer Leland C. Blanchard, 25, a Los Angeles policeman attached to Central Division and a former "popular fixture" at the Hollywood Legion Stadium, questioned his "fight game acquaintances" and "informants" and got tips that Robert "Bobby" De Witt was the brains behind the Boulevard-Citizens job. Blanchard relayed the tip to Hollywood Division detectives, and they raided De Witt's Venice Beach house. They found stashes of marijuana, guard uniforms and money bags from Boulevard-Citizens Savings & Loan. De Witt protested his innocence, and was arrested and charged with two counts of Armed Robbery One, five counts of Aggravated Assault, one count of Grand Theft Auto, and one count of Harboring Felonious Drugs. He was held without bail—and there was still no mention of Kay Lake.

Tiring of cops and robbers, I kept flipping pages. De Witt, a San Berdoo native with three pimping priors, kept yelping that the Siegel mob or the police had framed him: the mob because he sometimes ran cooze in Siegel territory, the cops because they needed a patsy for the Boulevard-Citizens job. He had no alibi for the day of the heist, and said he didn't know Chick Geyer, Max Ottens or the still-at-large fourth man. He went to trial, and the jury didn't believe him. He was convicted on all counts, and drew a ten-to-life jolt at San Quentin.

Kay finally appeared in a June 21 human interest piece titled "Gang Girl Falls In Love—With Cop! Going Straight? To Altar?" Beside the story there were photographs of her and Lee Blanchard, along with a mug shot of Bobby De Witt, a hatchet-faced guy sporting a greasy pompadour. The piece started with a recounting of the Boulevard-Citizens job and Blanchard's part in solving it, then segued to sugar:

> … and at the time of the robbery, De Witt was providing shelter for an impressionable young girl. Katherine Lake, 19, came west from Sioux Falls,

South Dakota, in 1936, not seeking Hollywood stardom, but seeking a college education. What she got was a degree in the college of criminal hard knocks.

"I fell in with Bobby because I had no place to go," "Kay" Lake told *Herald Express* reporter Aggie Underwood. "It was still the Depression, and jobs were scarce. I used to take walks near this awful boardinghouse where I had a cot, and that was how I met Bobby. He gave me my own room at his house, and he said he'd enroll me at Valley J.C. if I kept the house clean. He didn't do that, and I got more than I bargained for."

Kay thought Bobby De Witt was a musician, but he was really a dope peddler and procuror. "At first he was nice to me," Kay said. "Then he made me drink laudanum and stay home all day to answer the telephone. After that it got worse."

Kay Lake declined to state how it "got worse," and she was not surprised when police arrested De Witt for his part in the bloody February 11 robbery. She found lodging at a career girls' residence in Culver City, and when called by the prosecution to testify at De Witt's trial, she did—even though she was terrified of her former "benefactor."

"It was my duty," she said. "And of course at the trial I met Lee."

Lee Blanchard and Kay Lake fell in love. "As soon as I saw her I knew she was the girl for me," Officer Blanchard told crime scribe Bevo Means. "She has that waiflike beauty I'm a sucker for. She's had a rough life, but now I'm going to set it straight."

Lee Blanchard is no stranger to tragedy himself. When he was 14, his 9-year-old sister disappeared, never to be seen again. "I think that's why I quit fighting and became a policeman," he said. "Catching criminals gives me a sense of order."

So out of tragedy, a love story has begun. But where will it end? Kay Lake says: "The important things now are my education and Lee. Happy days are here again."

And with Big Lee Blanchard on Kay's case, it looks like they're here to stay.

I closed the scrapbook. Except for the kid sister, none of it surprised me. But all of it made me think of big wrong moves: Blanchard blowing the juice from his glory case by refusing to fight smokers; a little girl obviously snuffed and dumped somewhere like garbage; Kay Lake shacking on both sides of the law. Opening the book again, I stared at the Kay of seven years before. Even at nineteen she looked way too smart to speak the words Bevo Means put in her mouth. And seeing her portrayed as naive made me angry.

I gave the scrapbooks back to the clerk and walked out of the Hearst building wondering what I'd been looking for, knowing it was more than just evidence to prove Kay's come-on was legit. Driving around aimlessly, killing time so I'd be exhausted and able to sleep through to the afternoon, it hit me: with the old man taken care of and Warrants dead, Kay Lake and Lee Blanchard were the only interesting prospects in my future, and I needed to know them past wisecracks, insinuations and the fight.

I stopped at a steak joint on Los Feliz and wolfed a king-size porterhouse, spinach and hash browns, then cruised Hollywood Boulevard and the Strip. None of the movie marquees looked inviting, and the clubs on Sunset looked too rich for a flash-in-the-pan celebrity. At Doheny the long stretch of neon ended, and I headed up into the hills. Mulholland was rife with motorcycle bulls in speed traps, and I resisted the urge to leadfoot to the beach.

Finally I got tired of driving like a law-abiding citizen and pulled over to the embankment. Movie searchlights out of Westwood Village strafed the sky just above me; I watched them swivel and pick out low cloud formations. Following the lights was hypnotic, and I let the act numb me. Cars racing by on Mulholland hardly dented my numbness, and when the lights went off I checked my watch and saw that it was past midnight.

Stretching, I looked down at the few house lights still glowing and thought of Kay Lake. Reading between the lines of the newspaper piece, I saw her servicing Bobby De Witt and his friends, maybe selling it for him, a heister's hausfrau jacked on laudanum. It read true, but ugly, like I was betraying the sparks between us. Kay's exit line started coming on as true, and I wondered how Blanchard could live with her without possessing her completely.

The house lights went off one by one, and I was alone. A cold wind blew down from the hills; I shivered and got the answer.

You come off a winning fight. Sweat-drenched, tasting blood, high as the stars, still wanting to *go*. The handbooks who made money on you bring you a girl. A pro, a semipro, an amateur tasting her own blood. You do it in the dressing room, or in a backseat too cramped for your legs, and sometimes you kick the side windows out. When you walk outside after it, people mob you and swarm to touch you, and you go high as the stars again. It becomes another part of the game, the eleventh round of a ten-round fight. And when you go back to an ordinary life, it's just a weakness, a loss. As long as he'd been away from the game, Blanchard had to know it, had to want to keep his love for Kay separate from that.

I got in the car and headed home, wondering if I would ever tell Kay that I didn't have a woman because sex tasted like blood and resin and suture scrub to me.

4

WE LEFT our dressing rooms simultaneously, at the sound of a warning bell. Pushing out the door, I was an adrenaline live wire. I had chewed a big steak two hours before, swallowing the juice and spitting out the meat, and I could smell animal blood in my sweat. Dancing on my toes, I moved toward my corner through the most incredible fight mob I had ever seen.

The gym was packed to more than capacity, the spectators crammed together in narrow wooden chairs and bleachers. Every human being seemed to be shouting, and people in aisle seats plucked at my robe and urged me to kill. The side rings had been removed; the center ring was bathed in a perfect square of hot yellow light. Grabbing the bottom rope, I hoisted myself into it.

The referee, an old foot beat hack from Central nightwatch, was talking to Jimmy Lennon, on one-night leave from his announcer's gig at the Olympic; at ringside I saw Stan Kenton huddled with Misty June Christy, Mickey Cohen, Mayor Bowron, Ray Milland and a shitload of high brass in civvies. Kenton waved at me; I yelled "Artistry in rhythm!" at him. He laughed, and I bared my buck choppers at the crowd, who roared their approval. The roars grew to a crescendo; I turned around and saw that Blanchard had entered the ring.

Mr. Fire bowed in my direction; I saluted him with a barrage of short punches. Duane Fisk steered me to my stool; I took off my robe and leaned against the turnbuckle with my arms draped over the top rope. Blanchard moved into a similar position; we locked eyes. Jimmy Lennon waved the ref to a neutral corner, and the ring mike slinked down from a pole attached to the ceiling lights. Lennon grabbed it and shouted above the roar: "Ladies and gentlemen, policemen and supporters of L.A.'s finest, it is time for the Fire and Ice tango!"

The crowd went batshit, howling and stomping. Lennon waited until they quieted down to a buzz, then crooned: "Tonight we have ten rounds of boxing in the heavyweight division. In the white corner, wearing white trunks, a Los Angeles policeman with a professional record of forty-three wins, four losses and two draws. Weighing two hundred and three and one half pounds, ladies and gentlemen, Big Lee Blanchard!"

Blanchard slipped off his robe, kissed his gloves and bowed in all four directions. Lennon let the spectators go nuts for a few moments, then made his amplified voice rise above it all: "And in the black corner, weighing one ninety-one, a Los Angeles police-man, undefeated with thirty-six straight pro wins—Tricky Bucky Bleichert!"

I soaked up my last hurrah, memorizing the faces at ringside, pretending I wasn't going to dive. The noise in the gym leveled off; I walked to the center of the ring. Blanchard approached; the ref mumbled words that I didn't hear; Mr. Fire and I touched gloves. I got scared shitless and moved back to my corner; Fisk slipped my mouthpiece in. Then the bell rang, and it was all over and just starting.

Blanchard charged. I met him in the middle of the ring, pop-ping double jabs as he went into a crouch and stood in front of me weaving his head. The jabs missed, and I kept moving left, making no move to counter, hoping to sucker him into a right hand lead.

His first punch was a looping left hook to the body. I saw it coming and stepped inside, connecting with a short left cross to the head. Blanchard's hook grazed my back; it was one of the most powerful missed punches I'd ever taken. His right hand was low, and I brought in a short uppercut. It landed cleanly, and while Blanchard covered up I banged a one-two to his rib cage. Backpedaling before he could clinch or go to the body himself, I caught a left hand on the neck. It shook me, and I got up on my toes and started circling.

Blanchard stalked me. I stayed out of reach, peppering his always moving head with jabs, connecting more than half the time, reminding myself to hit low, so I wouldn't open up his scarred eyebrows. Moving from a crouch, Blanchard winged body hooks; I stepped back and countered them with on-target combinations. After a minute or so I had his feints and my jabs synchronized, and when his head snapped I dug in short right hooks to the ribs.

I danced, circled and threw punches in flurries. Blanchard stalked and looked for openings to land the big one. The round was winding down, and I realized that ceiling light glare and crowd smoke had distorted my ring bearings—I couldn't see the ropes. On reflex, I looked over my shoulder. Turning back, I caught the big one flush on the side of the head.

I staggered into the white corner turnbuckle; Blanchard was all over me. My head rang and my ears buzzed like Jap Zeros were dive-bombing inside them. I put up my hands to protect my face; Blanchard slammed pulverizing left-right hooks at my arms to bring them down. My head started clearing, and I leaped out and grabbed Mr. Fire in a bear hug clinch, holding him with all my juice, getting stronger each second as I stagger-pushed the two of us across the ring. Finally the ref intervened and yelled "Break!" I still held on, and he had to pry us apart.

I backpedaled, the dizziness and ear buzzing gone. Blanchard came at me flat-footed, wide open. I feinted with my left, and Big Lee stepped straight into a perfect overhand right. He hit the canvas flat on his ass.

I don't know who was more shocked. Blanchard sat there slack-jawed, taking the ref's count; I moved to a neutral corner. Blanchard was on his feet at seven, and this time I charged. Mr. Fire was dug in, feet planted wide apart, ready to kill or die. We were almost within swinging distance when the ref stepped between us and shouted, "The bell! The bell!"

I walked back to my corner. Duane Fisk removed my mouth-piece and doused me with a wet towel; I looked out at the fans, on their feet applauding. Every face I saw told me what *I* now knew: that I could cancel Blanchard's ticket plain and simple. And for a split second I thought that every voice was screaming for me not to throw the fight.

Fisk turned me around and popped in my mouthpiece, hissing, "Don't mix it up with him! Stay outside! Work off the jab!"

The bell rang. Fisk stepped out of the ring; Blanchard made a beeline for me. His stance was straight up now, and he threw a series of jabs that stopped just short of the money, moving in a step at a time, measuring me for a big right cross. I stayed on my toes and flicked doubled-up jabs from too far out to hurt, trying to set up a rhythm that would lull Blanchard into leaving his body open.

Most of my shots hit; Blanchard kept pressing. I banged a right to his ribs; he leaped in with a counter-right to mine. At close range, we threw body shots two handed; with no swinging room, the blows were nothing more than arm action, and Blanchard kept his chin dug into his collarbone, obviously wise to my inside uppercuts.

We stayed in close, landing only glancing blows to the arms and shoulders. I felt Blanchard's superior strength through all of it, but made no move to get out, wanting to put some hurt on him before I got back on my bicycle. I was settling into serious trench warfare when Mr. Fire got as cute as Mr. Ice at his cutest.

In the middle of a body exchange, Blanchard took one simple step backward and shot a hard left to my lower gut. The blow stung, and I backed up, getting ready to dance. I felt the ropes and brought up my guard, but before I could move sideways and away, a left-right caught me in the kidneys. My guard came down, and a Blanchard left hook connected with my chin.

I bounced off the ropes and hit the canvas on my knees. Shock waves pulsed from my jaw to my brain; I caught a jiggly picture of the referee restraining Blanchard, pointing to a neutral corner. I got up on one knee and grabbed the bottom rope, then lost my balance and flopped on my stomach. Blanchard had reached a neutral turnbuckle, and being prone took the jiggle out of my vision. I sucked in deep breaths; the new air eased the crackling feeling in my head. The ref came back and started counting, and at six I tried my legs. My knees buckled a little, but I was able to stand steady. Blanchard was blowing glove kisses to the fans, and I began hyperventilating so hard that my mouthpiece almost popped out. At eight the referee wiped my gloves on his shirt and gave Blanchard the signal to fight.

I felt out of control with anger, like a humiliated child. Blanchard came at me loose-limbed, his gloves open, like I wasn't worth a closed fist. I met him head-on, throwing a mock-woozy jab as he got into firing range. Blanchard slipped the punch easily—just like he was supposed to. He loaded up a huge right cross to finish me, and while he was rearing back I pounded a full-force counter-right at his nose. His head snapped; I followed through with a left hook to the body. Mr. Fire's guard fell; I stepped inside with a short uppercut. The bell rang just as he staggered into the ropes.

The crowd was chanting, "Buck-kee! Buck-kee! Buck-kee!" as I weaved to my corner. I spat out my mouthpiece and gasped for air; I looked out at the fans and knew that all bets were off, that I was going to pound Blanchard into dog meat and milk Warrants for every process and repo dollar I could get my hands on, put the old man in a home with *that* money and have the whole enchilada.

Duane Fisk shouted: "Box him! Box him!" The high brass judges at ringside grinned at me; I flashed them the bucktoothed Bucky Bleichert salute in return. Fisk shoved a bottle of water at my mouth, I guzzled and spat in the pail. He popped an ammonia cap under my nose and replaced my mouthpiece—then the bell rang.

Now it was straight cautious business—my specialty.

For the next four rounds I danced, feinted and jabbed from the outside, utilizing my reach advantage, never letting Blanchard tie me up or get me on the ropes. I concentrated on one target—his scarred eyebrows—and flicked, flicked, flicked my left glove at them. If the jab landed solidly and Blanchard's arms raised in reflex, I stepped inside and right-hooked to the breadbasket. Half the time Blanchard was able to counter to *my* body, and each shot that landed took a little bounce off my legs, a little *oomph* off my wind. By the end of the sixth round Blanchard's eyebrows were a gashed ridge of blood and my sides were welted from trunk line to rib cage. And we were both running out of steam.

Round seven was trench warfare fought by two exhausted warriors. I tried to stay outside and work the jab; Blanchard kept his gloves high to wipe blood out of his eyes and protect his cuts from further ripping. Every time I stepped in, firing a one-two at his gloves and gut, he nailed me to the solar plexus.

The fight had turned into a second-to-second war. Waiting for the eighth stanza, I saw that my welts were dotted with pinpoints of blood; the shouts of "Buck-kee! Buck-kee!" hurt my ears. Across the ring, Blanchard's trainer was swabbing his eyebrows with a styptic pencil and applying tiny adhesive bandages to the flaps of skin hanging loose. I slumped on my stool and let Duane Fisk feed me water and knead my shoulders, staring at Mr. Fire the whole sixty seconds, making him look like the old man so I'd have the hate juice to top out the next nine minutes.

The bell sounded. I moved toward the center of the ring on wobbly legs. Blanchard, back in a crouch, came at me. His legs were trembling just like mine, and I saw that his cuts were closed.

I fired off a weak jab. Blanchard caught it coming in and still kept coming, muzzling my glove out of the way as my dead legs refused to backpedal. I felt the laces rip open his eyebrows; my gut caved in just as I saw Blanchard's face streaming with blood. My knees buckled; I spat my mouthpiece, toppled backward and hit the ropes. A right hand bomb was arching toward me. It looked like it was launched from miles and miles away, and I knew I'd have time to counter. I put all my hate into my own right and shot it straight at the bloody target in front of me. I felt the unmistakable crunch of nose cartilage, then everything went black and hot yellow. I looked up at blinding light and felt myself being lifted; Duane Fisk and Jimmy Lennon materialized beside me, holding my arms. I spat blood and the words "I won"; Lennon said, "Not tonight, laddie. You lost—eighth-round KO."

When it all sank in, I laughed and pulled my arms free. The last thing I thought of before passing out was that I had cut the old man loose—and *clean*.

* * *

I got ten days off from duty—at the insistence of the doctor who examined me after the fight. My ribs were bruised, my jaw was swollen to twice its normal size and the punch that did me in loosened six of my teeth. The croaker told me later that Blanchard's nose was broken, and that his cuts required twenty-six stitches. On the basis of damage inflicted, the fight was a draw.

Pete Lukins collected my winnings, and together we scouted rest homes until we found one that looked fit for human habitation— the King David Villa, a block off the Miracle Mile. For two grand a year and fifty a month deducted from his Social Security check, the old man would have his own room, three squares and plenty of "group activities." Most of the oldsters at the home were Jewish, and it pleased me that the crazy Kraut was going to be spending the rest of his life in an enemy camp. Pete and I installed him there, and when we left he was fungooing the head nurse and ogling a colored girl making up beds.

After that I stuck to my apartment, reading and listening to jazz on the radio, slopping up ice cream and soup, the only food I could handle. I felt content in knowing I had played as hard as I could—winning half the apples in the process.

The phone rang constantly; since I knew it had to be reporters or cops offering condolences, I never answered. I didn't listen to sports broadcasts and I didn't read the newspapers. I wanted a clean break with local celebrity, and holing up was the only way to accomplish it.

My wounds were healing, and after a week I was itchy to go back on duty. I took to spending afternoons on the back steps, watching my landlady's cat stalk birds. Chico was eyeing a perched bluejay when I heard a reedy voice call out, "Ain't you bored yet?"

I looked down. Lee Blanchard was standing at the foot of the steps. His eyebrows were laced with stitches and his nose was flattened and purple. I laughed and said, "Getting there."

Blanchard hooked his thumbs in his belt. "Wanta work Warrants with me?"

"*What?*"

"You heard me. Captain Harwell's been calling to tell you, only you were fucking hibernating."

I was tingling. "But I lost. Ellis Loew said—"

"Fuck what Ellis Loew said. Don't you read the papers? The bond issue passed yesterday, probably because we gave the voters such a good show. Horrall told Loew that Johnny Vogel was out, that you were his man. You want the job?"

I walked down the steps and stuck out my hand. Blanchard shook it and winked.

So the partnership began.

5

CENTRAL DIVISION Warrants was on the sixth floor of City Hall, situated between the LAPD's Homicide Bureau and the Criminal Division of the DA's Office—a partitioned-off space with two desks facing each other, two file cabinets spilling folders and a map of the County of Los Angeles covering the window. There was a pebbled glass door lettered with DEPUTY DISTRICT

ATTORNEY ELLIS LOEW separating the cubicle from the Warrants boss and DA Buron Fitts—his boss—and nothing separating it from the Homicide dicks' bullpen, a huge room with rows of desks and corkboard walls hung with crime reports, wanted posters and miscellaneous memoranda. The more battered of the two desks in Warrants had a plate reading SERGEANT L.C. BLANCHARD. The desk facing it had to be mine, and I slumped into the chair picturing OFFICER D.W. BLEICHERT etched on wood next to the phone.

I was alone, the only one on the sixth floor. It was just after 7:00 A.M., and I had driven to my first day's duty early, in order to savor my plainclothes debut. Captain Harwell had called to say that I was to report to my new assignment on Monday morning, November 17, at 8:00, and that the day would begin with attending the reading of the felony summary for the previous week, which was mandatory for all LAPD personnel and Criminal Division DA's. Lee Blanchard and Ellis Loew would be briefing me on the job itself later, and after that it would be the pursuit of fugitive warrantees.

The sixth floor housed the Department's elite divisions: Homicide, Administrative Vice, Robbery and Bunco, along with Central Warrants and the Central Detective Squad. It was the domain of specialist cops, cops with political juice and up-and-comers, and it was my home now. I was wearing my best sports jacket and slacks combo, my service revolver hung from a brand-new shoulder rig. Every man on the Force owed me for the 8 percent pay raise that came with the passage of Proposition 5. My departmental juice was just starting. I felt ready for anything.

Except rehashing the fight. At 7:40 the bullpen started filling up with officers grumbling about hangovers, Monday mornings in general and Bucky Bleichert, dancemaster turned puncher, the new kid on the block. I stayed out of sight in the cubicle until I heard them filing into the hall. When the pen fell silent, I walked down to a door marked DETECTIVES' MUSTER ROOM. Opening it, I got a standing ovation.

It was applause military style, the forty or so plainclothesmen standing by their chairs, clapping in unison. Looking toward the front of the room, I saw a blackboard with "8%!!!" chalked on it. Lee Blanchard was next to the board, standing beside a pale fat man with the air of high brass. I sighted in on Mr. Fire. He grinned, the fat man moved to a lectern and banged on it with his knuckles.

The claps trailed off; the men sat down. I found a chair at the back of the room and settled into it; the fat man rapped the lectern a last time.

"Officer Bleichert, the men of Central Dicks, Homicide, Ad Vice, Bunco, et cetera," he said. "You already know Sergeant Blanchard and Mr. Loew, and I'm Captain Jack Tierney. You and Lee are the white men of the hour, so I hope you enjoyed your ovation, because you won't get another one until you retire."

Everyone laughed. Tierney rapped the podium and spoke into an attached mike. "Enough horseshit. This is the felony summary for the week ending November 14, 1946. Pay close attention, it's a doozy.

"First off, three liquor store stickups, on the nights of 11/10, 11/12 and 11/13, all within ten blocks on Jefferson in University Division. Two teenaged Caucasians with sawed-offs and the heebie-jeebies, obviously hopheads. The University dicks have got no leads, and the squad boss there wants a Robbery team on it full-time. Lieutenant Ruley, see me at 0900 on this, and all you men put out the word to your snitches—hophead-heister is a bad MO.

"Moving east, we've got freelance prosties working the restaurant bars in Chinatown. They're servicing their johns in parked cars, lowballing the girls Mickey Cohen's been running there. Misdemeanor stuff so far, but Mickey C. doesn't like it and the Chinks don't like it because Mickey's girls use the hot sheet flops on Alameda—all Chink owned. Sooner or later we're looking at grief, so I want the restaurant owners pacified and forty-eight-hour detentions on every Chinatown whore we can grab. Captain Harwell's detaching a dozen nightwatch blues for a sweep later in the week, and I want the Ad Vice whore files gone through and mug shots and rap sheets pulled for every independent hooker known to work Central. I want two men from Central dicks in on this, with Ad Vice supervising. Lieutenant Pringle, see me at 0915."

Tierney paused and stretched; I looked around the room and saw that most of the officers were writing in notebooks. I was cursing myself for not bringing one when the captain slammed the lectern with two flattened palms. "Here's a collar that would please old Captain Jack no end. I'm talking about the Bunker Hill house burglaries Sergeants Vogel and Koenig have been working on. Fritzie, Bill, have you read the SID memo on it?"

Two men sitting side by side a few rows up from me called out, "No, Cap" and "Nossir." I got a good profile look at the older of them—the spitting image of Fat Johnny Vogel, only fatter.

Tierney said, "I suggest you read it immediately after this briefing. For the benefit of you men not directly involved in the investigation, the print boys found a set of latents at the last break-in, right near the silverware cupboard. They belonged to a white male named Coleman Walter Maynard, age 31, two sodomy priors. A surefire degenerate baby raper.

"County Parole's got no line on him. He was living at a transient hotel on 14th and Bonnie Brae, but he hotfooted around the time the burglaries started. Highland Park's got four sodomy unsolveds, all little boys around eight years old. Maybe it's Maynard and maybe it isn't, but between them and the B&Es we could fix him up with a nice one-way to Q. Fritzie, Bill, what else are you working on?"

Bill Koenig hunched over his notebook; Fritz Vogel cleared his throat and said, "We've been working the downtown hotels. We collared a couple of key thieves and rousted some pickpockets."

Tierney tapped the podium with one heavy knuckle. "Fritzie, were the key thieves Jerry Katzenbach and Mike Purdy?"

Vogel squirmed in his chair. "Yessir."

"Fritzie, did they snitch each other off?"

"Ah . . . yessir."

Tierney rolled his eyes up to heaven. "Let me enlighten those of you not familiar with Jerry and Mike. They're homos, and they live with Jerry's mother in a cozy little love nest in Eagle Rock. They've been bedmates since God was a pup, but every once in a while they have spats and get the urge to chase jailhouse chicken, and one rats the other off. Then the other reciprocates and they both draw a county jolt. They stool on the gangs while they're in stir, pork nancy boys and get sentence reductions for their snitch duty. This has been going on since Mae West was a virgin. Fritzie, what *else* have you been working on?"

There was a rumble of laughter throughout the room. Bill Koenig started to get up, twisting his head to see who the laughers were. Fritz Vogel pulled him back down by his coat sleeve, then said, "Sir, we've also been doing some work for Mr. Loew. Bringing in witnesses for him."

Tierney's pale face was working toward beet red. "Fritzie, I am the commander of Central Detectives, not Mr. Loew. Sergeant

Blanchard and Officer Bleichert work for Mr. Loew, you and Sergeant Koenig do not. So drop what you're doing for Mr. Loew, leave the pickpockets alone and bring in Coleman Walter Maynard before he rapes any more little boys, would you please? There's a memo on his known associates on the squadroom bulletin board, and I suggest all officers acquaint themselves with it. Maynard's a lamster now, and he might be holing up with one of them."

I saw Lee Blanchard leave the muster room by a side exit. Tierney leafed through some papers on the lectern and said, "Here's one that Chief Green thinks you should know about. Over the past three weeks someone's been tossing chopped-up dead cats into the cemeteries off Santa Monica and Gower. Hollywood Division's taken a half dozen reports on it. According to Lieutenant Davis at 77th Street, that's a calling card of nigger youth gangs. Most of the cats have been dumped on Thursday nights, and the Hollywood roller rink's open to shines on Thursdays, so maybe there's something to that. Ask around, talk to your informants and relay anything pertinent to Sergeant Hollander at Hollywood dicks. Now the homicides. Russ?"

A tall, gray-haired man in an immaculate double-breasted suit took the podium; Captain Jack plopped into the nearest available chair. The tall man carried himself with an authority that was more like a judge or hotshot lawyer than a cop; he reminded me of the smooth Lutheran preacher who palled around with the old man until the Bund went on the subversive list. The officer sitting next to me whispered, "Lieutenant Millard. Number two in Homicide, but the real boss. A real piece of velvet." I nodded and listened to the lieutenant speak in a velvet-smooth voice:

". . . and the coroner ruled the Russo-Nickerson job murder-suicide. The Bureau is handling the hit-and-run on Pico and Figueroa on 11/10, and we located the vehicle, a '39 La Salle sedan, abandoned. It's registered to a male Mexican named Luis Cruz, age 42, of 1349 Alta Loma Vista in South Pasadena. Cruz is a two-time loser with a Folsom jacket—both falls Robbery One. He's long gone, and his wife claims the La Salle was stolen in September. She says it was snatched by Cruz's cousin Armando Villareal, age 39, who's also missing. Harry Sears and I took the initial squeal on this one, and eyeball witnesses said there were two male Mexicans in the car. Have you got anything else, Harry?"

A squat, disheveled man stood up, turned around and faced the room. He swallowed a few times, then stammered, "C-C-C-Cruz's wife is sc-screwing the c-c-c-cousin. The c-c-c-car was never reported st-stolen, and the neighbors s-say the wife wants the c-cousin's parole violated so C-C-Cruz won't find out about them."

Harry Sears sat down abruptly. Millard smiled at him and said, "Thanks, partner. Gentlemen, Cruz and Villareal are now state parole absconders and priority fugitives. APBs and absconder warrants have been issued. And here's the punch line: both of these guys are boozehounds, with over a hundred plain drunks between them. Hit-and-run drunks are a damn menace, so let's get them. Captain?"

Tierney stood up and shouted, "Dismissed!" Cops swarmed me, offering hands and back slaps and chucks under the chin. I soaked it in until the muster room cleared and Ellis Loew approached, fiddling with the Phi Beta Kappa key dangling from his vest.

"You shouldn't have slugged with him," he said, twirling the key. "You were ahead on all three cards."

I held the DA's stare. "Proposition 5 passed, Mr. Loew."

"Yes, it did. But some patrons of yours lost money. Play it smarter here, Officer. Don't blow this opportunity like you did the fight."

"You ready, canvasback?"

Blanchard's voice saved me. I went with him before I did something to blow it then and there.

* * *

We headed south in Blanchard's civilian car, a '40 Ford coupe with a contraband two-way under the dashboard. Lee rambled on about the job while I looked out at the downtown L.A. street scene.

"... mostly we go after priority warrantees, but sometimes we chase down material witnesses for Loew. Not too often—he's usually got Fritzie Vogel running his errands, with Bill Koenig along for muscle. Shitbirds, both of them. Anyway, we get slack periods sometimes, and we're supposed to go by the other station houses and check the squadrooms for their priority stuff— warrants filed in the regional courts. Every LAPD station has two men working Warrants, but they spend most of their time catching squeals, so we're supposed to help out. Sometimes, like today, you hear something at the felony summary or get something hot off the bulletin board. If it's *really* slow, you can serve papers for the Department 92 shysters. Three bucks a throw, chump change. The real moolah's in repos. I've got delinquent lists from H.J. Caruso Dodge and Yeakel Brothers Olds, all the nigger stiffs the credit agents are too pansy to move on. Any questions, partner?"

I resisted the urge to ask, "Why aren't you screwing Kay Lake?" and "While we're on the subject, what's the story on her?"

"Yeah. Why'd you quit fighting and join the Department? And don't tell me it was because your kid sister disappeared and catching criminals gives you a sense of order. I've heard that one twice, and I don't buy it."

Lee kept his eyes on traffic. "You got any sisters? Kid relatives you really care about?"

I shook my head. "My family's dead."

"So's Laurie. I figured it out when I was fifteen. Mom and Dad kept spending money on handbills and detectives, but I knew she was a snuff job. I kept picturing her growing up. Prom queen, straight A's, her own family. It used to hurt like a bastard, so I pictured her growing up wrong. You know, like a floozy. It was actually comforting, but it felt like I was shitting on her."

I said, "Look, I'm sorry."

Lee gave me a gentle elbow. "Don't be, because you're right. I quit fighting and joined the cops because Benny Siegel was putting the heat on me. He bought out my contract and scared off my manager, and he promised me a shot at Joe Louis if I took two dives for him. I said no and joined the Department because the Jew syndicate boys have got a rule against killing cops. I was scared shitless that he'd kill me anyway, so when I heard that the Boulevard-Citizens heisters took some of Benny's money along with the bank's, I shook down stoolies until I got Bobby De Witt on a platter. I gave Benny first crack at him. His number two man talked him out of a snuff, so I took the dope to Hollywood dicks. Benny's my pal now. Gives me tips on the ponies all the time. Next question?"

I decided not to push for information on Kay. Checking out the street, I saw that downtown had given way to blocks of small, unkempt houses. The Bugsy Siegel story stayed with me; I was running with it when Lee slowed the car and pulled to the curb.

I blurted, "What the hell"; Lee said, "This one's for my own personal satisfaction. You remember the baby raper on the felony sheet?"

"Sure."

"Tierney said there's four sodomy unsolveds in Highland Park, right?"

"Right."

"And he mentioned that there was a memo on the rape-o's KAs?"

"Sure. What—"

"Bucky, I read that memo and recognized the name of a fence—Bruno Albanese. He works out of a Mex restaurant in Highland Park. I called Highland Park dicks and got the addresses on the assaults, and two of them were within a half mile of the joint where the fence hangs out. This is his house, and R&I says he's got a shitload of unpaid traffic tickets, bench warrants issued. You want a diagram of the rest of it?"

I got out of the car and walked across a weedy front yard strewn with dog turds. Lee caught up with me at the porch and rang the bell; furious barks issued from inside the house.

The door opened, held to the frame by a chain. The barks grew to a crescendo; through the crack I glimpsed a slatternly woman. I shouted, "Police officers!" Lee wedged his foot into the space between the doorjamb and runner; I reached inside and twisted the chain off. Lee pushed the door open, and the woman ran out onto the porch. I stepped inside the house, wondering about the dog. I was eyeballing a seedy living room when a big brown mastiff leaped at me, his jaws wide open. I fumbled for my piece—and the beast started licking my face.

We stood there, the dog's front paws resting on my shoulders like we were doing the Lindy Hop. A big tongue lapped at me, and the woman yelped, "Be nice, Hacksaw! Be nice!"

I grabbed the dog's legs and lowered him to the floor; he promptly turned his attention to my crotch. Lee was talking to the slattern, showing her a mug shot strip. She was shaking her head no, hands on hips, the picture of an irate citizen. With Hacksaw at my heels, I joined them.

Lee said, "Mrs. Albanese, this man's the senior officer. Would you tell him what you just told me?"

The slattern shook her fists; Hacksaw explored Lee's crotch. I said, "Where's your husband, lady? We don't have all day."

"I told him and I'll tell you! Bruno's paid his debt to society! He doesn't fraternize with criminals and I don't know any Coleman what's his name! He's a businessman! His parole officer made him quit hanging out at that Mexican place two weeks ago, and I don't know where he is! Hacksaw, be nice!"

I looked at the real senior officer, now stagger-dancing with a two-hundred-pound dog. "Lady, your husband's a known fence with outstanding traffic warrants. I've got a hot merchandise list in the car, and if you don't tell me where he is, I'll turn your house upside down until I find something dirty. Then I'll arrest *you* for receiving stolen goods. What's it gonna be?"

The slattern beat her fists into her legs; Lee wrestled Hacksaw down to all fours and said, "Some people don't respond to civility. Mrs. Albanese, do you know what Russian roulette is?"

The woman pouted, "I'm not dumb and Bruno's paid his debt to society!" Lee pulled a .38 snubnose out of his back waistband, checked the cylinder and snapped it shut. "There's one bullet in this gun. You feeling lucky, Hacksaw?"

Hacksaw said, "Woof"; the woman said, "You wouldn't dare." Lee put the .38 to the dog's temple and pulled the trigger. The hammer clicked on an empty chamber; the woman gasped and started turning pale; Lee said, "Five to go. Prepare for doggie heaven, Hacksaw."

Lee squeezed the trigger a second time; I held in belly laughs when the hammer clicked again and Hacksaw licked his balls, bored over the whole thing. Mrs. Albanese was praying fervently with her eyes shut. Lee said, "Time to meet your maker, doggy"; the woman blurted, "No no no no no! Bruno's tending bar in Silverlake! The Buena Vista on Vendome! Please leave my baby alone!"

Lee showed me the .38's empty cylinder, and we walked back to the car with Hacksaw's happy barks echoing behind us. I laughed all the way to Silverlake.

* * *

The Buena Vista was a bar and grill shaped like a Spanish rancho—whitewashed adobe walls and turrets festooned with Christmas lights six weeks before the holiday. The interior was cool, all dark wood. There was a long oak bar just off the entrance foyer, with a man behind it polishing glasses. Lee flashed his shield at him and said, "Bruno Albanese?" The man pointed to the back of the restaurant, lowering his eyes.

The rear of the grill was narrow, with Leatherette booths and dim lighting. Wolfish eating noises led us to the last booth—the only one occupied. A thin, swarthy man was hunched over a plate piled high with beans, chili and huevos rancheros, shoveling the slop in like it was his last meal on earth.

Lee rapped on the table. "Police officers. Are you Bruno Albanese?"

The man looked up and said, "Who, me?"

Lee slid into the booth and pointed to the religious tapestry on the wall. "No, the kid in the manger. Let's make this fast, so I don't have to watch you eat. You've got outstanding warrants, but me and my partner like your dog, so we're not taking you in. Ain't that nice of us?"

Bruno Albanese belched, then said, "You mean you want some skinny?"

Lee said, "Whiz kid," and smoothed the Maynard mug shot strip on the table. "He cornholes little boys. We know he sells to you, and we don't care. Where is he?"

Albanese looked at the strip and burped. "I never seen this guy before. Somebody steered you wrong."

Lee looked at me and sighed. He said, "Some people don't respond to civility," then grabbed Bruno Albanese by the scruff of the neck and smashed his head face first into the plate of goo. Bruno sucked in grease through his mouth, nose and eyeballs, flapping his arms and banging his legs under the table. Lee held him there, intoning, "Bruno Albanese was a good man. He was a good husband and a good father to his son Hacksaw. He wasn't very cooperative with the police, but who expects perfection? Partner, can you give me a reason to spare this shitbird's life?"

Albanese was making gurgling sounds; blood was leaking into his huevos rancheros. "Have mercy," I said. "Even fences derserve a better last supper."

Lee said, "Well put," and let go of Albanese's head. He came up for air bleeding and gasping, wiping a whole Mexican cookbook off his face. When he got breath he wheezed out, "The Versailles Apartments on 6th and Saint Andrews room 803 and please don't give me a rat jacket!"

Lee said, "Bon appetit, Bruno"; I said, "You're good." We ran out of the restaurant and highballed it code three to 6th and Saint Andrews.

* * *

The mail slots in the Versailles lobby listed a Maynard Coleman in Apartment 803. We rode the elevator up to the eighth floor and rang the buzzer; I put my ear to the door and heard nothing. Lee took a ring of skeleton keys from his pocket and worked them into the lock until one hit and the mechanism gave with a sharp click.

We entered a hot, dark little room. Lee flicked on the overhead light, illuminating a Murphy bed covered with stuffed animals—teddy bears, pandas and tigers. The crib stank of sweat and some medicinal odor I couldn't place. I wrinkled my nose, and Lee placed it for me. "Vaseline with cortisone. The homos use it for ass lube. I was gonna turn Maynard over to Captain Jack personally, but now I'm gonna let Vogel and Koenig have him first."

I moved to the bed and examined the animals; they all had ringlets of soft children's hair taped between their legs. Shivering, I looked at Lee. He was pale, his features contorted by facial tics. Our eyes met, and we silently left the room and took the elevator downstairs. On the sidewalk, I said, "What now?"

Lee's voice was shaky. "Find a phone booth and call the DMV. Give them Maynard's alias and this address and ask if they've processed any pink slips on it the past month or so. If they have, get a vehicle description and a license number. I'll meet you at the car."

I ran to the corner, found a pay phone and dialed the DMV police information line. A clerk answered, "Who's requesting?"

"Officer Bleichert, LAPD badge 1611. Auto purchase information, Maynard Coleman or Coleman Maynard, 643 South Saint Andrews, L.A. Probably recent."

"Gotcha—one minute."

I waited, notebook and pen in hand, thinking of the stuffed animals. A good five minutes later, "Officer, it's a positive," jarred me.

"Shoot."

"De Soto sedan, 1938, dark green, license B as in boy, V as in Victor, 1-4-3-2 Repeat, B as in boy—"

I wrote it down, hung up and ran back to the car. Lee was scrutinizing an L.A. street atlas, jotting notes. I said, "Got him."

Lee closed the atlas. "He's probably a school prowler. There were elementary schools near the Highland Park jobs, and there's a half dozen of them around here. I radioed the Hollywood and Wilshire desks and told them what we've got. Patrol cars are gonna stop by the schools and put out the skinny on Maynard. What's the DMV got?"

I pointed to my notesheet; Lee grabbed the radio mike and switched on the outgoing dial. Static fired up, then the two-way went dead. Lee said, "Fuck it, let's roll."

* * *

We cruised elementary schools in Hollywood and the Wilshire District. Lee drove, I scanned curbs and school yards for green De Sotos and loiterers. We stopped once at a gamewell phone, and Lee called Wilshire and Hollywood stations with the DMV dope, getting assurances that it would be relayed to every radio car, every watch.

During those hours we hardly spoke a word. Lee gripped the wheel with white-knuckled fingers, slow lane crawling. The only time his expression changed was when we pulled over to check out kids at play. Then his eyes clouded and his hands shook, and I thought he would either weep or explode.

But he just kept staring, and the simple act of moving back into traffic seemed to calm him. It was as if he knew exactly how far to let himself go as a man before getting back to strict cop business.

Shortly after 3:00 we headed south on Van Ness, a run by Van Ness Avenue Elementary. We were a block away, going by the Polar Palace, when green De Soto BV 1432 passed us in the opposite direction and pulled into the parking lot in front of the rink.

I said, "We've got him. Polar Palace."

Lee hung a U-turn and drew to the curb directly across the street from the lot. Maynard was locking the De Soto, eyeing a group of kids skipping toward the entrance with skates slung over their shoulders. "Come on," I said.

Lee said, "You take him, I might lose my temper. Make sure the kids are out of the way, and if he pulls any hinky moves, kill him."

Solo plainclothes rousts were strictly against the book. "You're crazy. This is a—"

Lee shoved me out the door. "Go get him, goddamnit! This is Warrants, not a fucking classroom! Go get him!"

I dodged traffic across Van Ness to the parking lot, catching sight of Maynard entering the Polar Palace in the middle of a big throng of children. I sprinted to the front door and opened it, telling myself to go smooth and slow.

Cold air stunned me; harsh light reflecting off the ice rink stung my eyes. Shielding them, I looked around and saw papier mâché fjords and a snack stand shaped like an igloo. There were a few kids twirling on the ice, and a group of them oohing and aahing at a giant taxidermied polar bear standing on its hind legs by a side exit. There was not an adult in the joint. Then it hit me: check the men's room.

A sign pointed me to the basement. I was halfway down the stairs when Maynard started up them, a little stuffed rabbit in his hands. The stench of room 803 came back; just as he was about to pass me, I said, "Police officer, you're under arrest," and drew my .38.

The rape-o threw up his hands; the rabbit went flying. I shoved him into the wall, frisked him and cuffed his hands behind his back. Blood pounded in my head as I pushed him up the stairs; I felt something pummeling my legs. "You leave my daddy alone! Leave my daddy alone!"

The assailant was a little boy in short pants and a sailor's jumper. It took me half a second to make him as the rape-o's kid—their resemblance was bone deep. The boy attached himself to my belt and kept bawling, "Leave my daddy alone"; the father kept bawling for time to say good-bye and get a babysitter; I kept moving, up the stairs and through the Polar Palace, my gun at the rape-o's head, my other hand pushing him forward, the kid dragging behind me, yowling and punching with all his might. A crowd had formed; I shouted, "Police officer!" until they separated and gave me a shot at the door. An old geezer opened it for me, blurting, "Hey! ain't you Bucky Bleichert?"

I gasped, "Grab the kid and call for a matron"; the junior tornado was yanked off my back. I saw Lee's Ford in the parking lot, shoved Maynard all the way to it and into the backseat. Lee hit the horn and peeled; the rape-o mumbled Jesus mumbo jumbo. I kept wondering why the horn blare couldn't drown out the little boy's shrieks for his daddy.

* * *

We dropped Maynard off at the Hall of Justice jail, and Lee phoned Fritz Vogel at Central squadroom, telling him the rape-o was in custody and ready to be interrogated on the Bunker Hill burglaries. Then it was back to City Hall, a call to notify Highland Park dicks of Maynard's arrest and a call to Hollywood Juvie to ease my conscience on the kid. The matron I talked to told me that Billy Maynard was there, waiting for his mother, Coleman Maynard's ex-wife, a car hop with six hooking convictions. He was still bawling for his daddy, and I hung up wishing I hadn't called.

Three hours of report writing followed. I wrote the arresting officer's summary longhand; Lee typed it up, omitting mention of our break-in at Coleman Maynard's apartment. Ellis Loew hovered around the cubicle as we worked, muttering, "Great collar" and "I'll kill them in court with the kid angle."

We finished our paperwork at 7:00. Lee made a check mark in the air and said, "Chalk another one up for Laurie Blanchard. You hungry, partner?"

I stood up and stretched, food suddenly a great idea. Then I saw Fritz Vogel and Bill Koenig approaching the cubicle. Lee whispered, "Make nice, they've got juice with Loew."

Up close, the two resembled gone-to-seed refugees from the L.A. Rams' middle line. Vogel was tall and fat, with a huge flat head that grew straight out of his shirt collar and the palest blue eyes I'd ever seen; Koenig was plain huge, topping my six foot three by a couple of inches, his linebacker's body just starting to go soft. He had a broad, flattened nose, jug ears, a crooked jaw and tiny chipped teeth. He looked stupid, Vogel looked shrewd, they both looked mean.

Koenig giggled. "He confessed. The kiddie porks and the burglaries. Fritzie says we're all gonna get commendations." He stuck out his hand. "Good fight you gave blondie."

I shook the big fist, noticing fresh blood on Koenig's right shirt cuff. I said, "Thanks, Sarge," then extended my hand to Fritz Vogel. He took it for a split second, bored into me with coldly furious eyes and dropped it like it was a hot turd.

Lee slapped my back. "Bucky's aces. Smarts *and* cojoñes. You talked to Ellis about the confession?"

Vogel said, "He's Ellis to lieutenants and up."

Lee laughed. "I'm a privileged character. Besides, you call him kike and Jewboy behind his back, so what do you care?"

Vogel flushed; Koenig looked around with his mouth open. When he turned, I saw blood spatters on his shirtfront. Vogel said, "Come on Billy"; Koenig dutifully followed him back to the squadroom.

"Make nice, huh?"

Lee shrugged. "Shitbirds. If they weren't cops they'd be in Atascadero. Do as I say, not as I do, partner. They're afraid of me, and you're just a rookie here."

I racked my brain for a snappy reply. Then Harry Sears, looking twice as sloppy as he did in the morning, poked his head in the doorway. "I heard something I thought you should know, Lee." The words were spoken without a trace of a stutter; I smelled liquor on the man's breath.

Lee said, "Shoot"; Sears said, "I was over at County Parole, and the supervisor told me Bobby De Witt just got an 'A' number. He'll be paroled to L.A. around the middle of January. Just thought you should know."

Sears nodded at me and took off. I looked at Lee, who was twitching like he did up in room 803 of the Versailles. I said, "Partner—"

Lee managed a smile. "Let's get ourselves some chow. Kay's making pot roast, and she said I should bring you home."

* * *

I tagged along for the woman and was astounded by the pad: a beige Deco-streamline house a quarter mile north of the Sunset Strip. Going in the door, Lee said, "Don't mention De Witt; it'll upset Kay." I nodded and took in a living room straight out of a movie set.

The wainscoting was polished mahogany, the furniture was Danish Modern—gleaming blond wood in a half dozen shades. There were wall prints representing hotshot twentieth-century artists, and carpets embroidered with modernistic designs, mist-hung skyscrapers or tall trees in a forest or the spires of some German Expressionist factory. A dining area adjoined the living room, and the table held fresh flowers and chafing dishes leaking the aroma of good eats. I said, "Not bad on a cop's pay. You taking a few bribes, partner?"

Lee laughed. "My fight stash. Hey babe, you here?"

Kay Lake walked in from the kitchen, wearing a floral dress that matched the tulips on the table. She took my hand and said, "Hello, Dwight." I felt like a punk kid crashing the junior prom.

"Hello, Kay."

With a squeeze she dropped my hand, ending the longest shake in history. "You and Leland partners. It makes you want to believe in fairy tales, doesn't it?"

I looked around for Lee, and saw that he'd disappeared. "No. I'm the realistic type."

"I'm not."

"I can tell."

"I've had enough reality to last me a lifetime."

"I know."

"Who told you?"

"The L.A. *Herald Express.*"

Kay laughed. "Then you did read my press clippings. Come to any conclusions?"

"Yeah. Fairy tales don't work out."

Kay winked like Lee; I got the feeling that she was the one who taught him. "That's why you have to turn them into reality. Leland! Dinnertime!"

Lee reappeared, and we sat down to eat; Kay cracked a bottle of champagne and poured. When our glasses were full, she said, "To fairy tales." We drank, Kay refilled, Lee said, "To Bond Issue B." The second dose of bubbly tickled my nose and made me laugh; I proposed, "To the Bleichert-Blanchard rematch at the Polo Grounds, a bigger gate than Louis and Schmeling."

Lee said, "To the second Blanchard victory"; Kay said, "To a draw and no gore." We drank, and killed the bottle, and Kay retrieved another from the kitchen, popping the cork and hitting Lee in the chest. When our goblets were full, I caught my first blast of the juice and blurted, "To us." Lee and Kay looked at me in something like slow motion, and I saw that our free hands were all resting a few inches apart on the tabletop. Kay noticed me notice and winked; Lee said, "That's where I learned how." Our hands moved together into a sort of triad, and we toasted "To us" in unison.

* * *

Opponents, then partners, then friends. And with the friendship came Kay, never getting between us, but always filling in our lives outside the job with style and grace.

That fall of '46, we went everywhere together. When we went to the movies, Kay took the middle seat and grabbed both our hands during the scary parts; when we spent big band Friday evenings at the Malibu Rendezvous, she alternated dances with the two of us and always tossed a coin to see who got the last slow number. Lee never expressed an ounce of jealousy, and Kay's

come-on subsided into a low simmer. It was there every time our
shoulders brushed, every time a radio jingle or a funny billboard or
a word from Lee hit us the same way and our eyes met instant-
aneously. The quieter it got, the more available I knew Kay was—
and the more I wanted her. But I let it all ride, not because
it would have destroyed my partnership with Lee, but because it
would have upset the perfection of the three of us.

After tours of duty, Lee and I would go to the house and find
Kay reading, underlining passages in books with a yellow crayon.
She'd cook dinner for the three of us, and sometimes Lee would
take off to run Mulholland on his motorcycle. Then we talked.

We always spoke around Lee, as if discussing the brute center
of the three of us without him present was a cheat. Kay talked
about the six years of college and two master's degrees that Lee
had bankrolled with his fight stash and how her work as a substi-
tute teacher was perfect for the "overeducated dilettante" she'd
become; I talked about growing up Kraut in Lincoln Heights. We
never spoke of my snitching for the Alien Squad or her life with
Bobby De Witt. We both sensed the other's general story, but neither of us wanted details. I had the upper hand there: the Ashida
brothers and Sam Murakami were long gone and dead, but Bobby
De Witt was a month away from L.A. parole—and I could tell Kay
was afraid of his return.

If Lee was frightened, he never showed it past that moment
when Harry Sears gave him the word, and it never hindered him
during our best hours together—the ones spent working Warrants.
That fall I learned what police work really was, and Lee was my
teacher.

From mid-November through the New Year we captured a
total of eleven hard felons, eighteen traffic warrantees and three
parole and probation absconders. Our rousts of suspicious loiterers
got us an additional half dozen arrests, all of them for narcotics
violations. We worked from Ellis Loew's direct orders, the felony
sheet and squadroom scuttlebutt, filtered through Lee's instincts.
His techniques were sometimes cautious and roundabout and
sometimes brutal, but he was always gentle with children, and
when he went strong-arm to get information, it was because it
was the only way to grab results.

So we became a "good guy–bad guy" interrogation team;
Mr. Fire the black hat, Mr. Ice the white. Our boxing reputations
gave us an added edge of respect on the street, and when Lee

rabbit-punched for information and I interceded on the pun-chee's behalf, it got us what we wanted.

The partnership wasn't perfect. When we worked twenty-four-hour tours, Lee would shake down hopheads for Benzedrine tablets and swallow handfuls to stay alert; then every Negro roustee became "Sambo," every white man "Shitbird," every Mexican "Pancho." All his rawness came out, destroying his considerable finesse, and twice I had to hold him back for real when he got carried away with his black-hat role.

But it was a small price to pay for what I was learning. Under Lee's tutelage I got good fast, and I wasn't the only one who knew it. Even though he'd dropped half a grand on the fight, Ellis Loew warmed to me when Lee and I brought in a string of felons he was drooling to prosecute, and Fritz Vogel, who hated me for snatching Warrants from his son, reluctantly admitted to him that I was an ace cop.

And, surprisingly, my local celebrity lingered long enough to do me some extra good. Lee was a favored repo man with H.J. Caruso, the auto dealer with the famous radio ads, and when the job was slow we prowled for delinquent cars in Watts and Compton. When we found one, Lee would kick in the driver's side window and hot-wire the sled, and I would stand guard. Then we'd run a two-car convoy to Caruso's lot on Figueroa, and H.J. would slip us a double sawbuck apiece. We gabbed cops and robbers and fight stuff with him, and afterward he kicked back a good bottle of bourbon, that Lee always kicked back to Harry Sears to keep us greased up with good tips from Homicide.

Sometimes we joined H.J. for the Wednesday night fights at the Olympic. He had a specially constructed ringside booth that kept us protected when the Mexicans in the top tier tossed coins and beer cups full of piss down at the ring, and Jimmy Lennon introduced us during the prefight ceremonies. Benny Siegel stopped by the booth occasionally, and he and Lee would go off to talk. Lee always came back looking slightly scared. The man he'd once defied was the most powerful gangster on the West Coast, known to be vindictive, with a hair-trigger temper. But Lee usually got track tips—and the horses Siegel gave him usually won.

So that fall went. The old man got a pass from the rest home at Christmas, and I brought him to dinner at the house. He had recovered pretty well from his stroke, but he still had no memory of English, and rambled on in German. Kay fed him turkey and

goose and Lee listened to his Kraut monologues all night, interjecting, "You tell 'em, pop" and "Crazy, man" whenever he paused
for breath. When I dropped him back at the home, he gave me
the fungoo sign and managed to walk in under his own steam.

On New Year's Eve, we drove down to Balboa Island to catch
Stan Kenton's band. We danced in 1947, high on champagne, and
Kay flipped coins to see who got last dance and first kiss when
midnight hit. Lee won the dance, and I watched them swirl across
the floor to "Perfidia," feeling awe for the way they had changed
my life. Then it was midnight, the band fired up, and I didn't know
how to play it.

Kay took the problem away, kissing me softly on the lips,
whispering, "I love you, Dwight." A fat woman grabbed me and
blew a noisemaker in my face before I could return the words.

We drove home on Pacific Coast Highway, part of a long
stream of horn-honking revelers. When we got to the house, my
car wouldn't start, so I made myself a bed on the couch and
promptly passed out from too much booze. Sometime toward
dawn, I woke up to strange sounds muffling through the walls.
I perked my ears to identify them, picking out sobs followed by
Kay's voice, softer and lower than I had ever heard it. The sobbing
got worse—trailing into whimpers. I pulled the pillow over my
head and forced myself back to sleep.

6

I DOZED through most of the lackluster January 10 felony summary, coming awake when Captain Jack barked, "That's it. Lieutenant Millard, Sergeant Sears, Sergeant Blanchard and Officer
Bleichert, go to Mr. Loew's office immediately. Dismissed!"

I walked down the corridor to Ellis Loew's inner sanctum.
Lee, Russ Millard and Harry Sears were already there, milling
around Loew's desk, examining a stack of morning *Herald*s.

Lee winked and handed me a copy, folded over to the local section. I saw a piece titled, "Criminal Division DA to Try for Boss's
Job in '48 Republican Primary?" read three paragraphs lauding
Ellis Loew and his concern for the citizens of Los Angeles and
tossed the paper on the desk before I threw up. Lee said, "Here
comes the man now. Hey Ellis, you going into politics? Say 'The
only thing we have to fear is fear itself.' Let's see how you sound."

Lee's FDR imitation got a laugh all around; even Loew chuckled as he handed out rap sheet carbons with mug shot strips attached. "Here's the gentleman we all have to fear. Read those and find out why."

I read the sheet. It detailed the criminal career of Raymond Douglas "Junior" Nash, white male, born in Tulsa, Oklahoma, in 1908. Nash's convictions went back to 1926, and included Texas State Prison jolts for statutory rape, armed robbery, first degree mayhem and felonious assault. There were five California charges filed against him: three armed robbery warrants from up north in Oakland County and two 1944 L.A. papers—first degree statch rape and felony contributing to the delinquency of a minor. The rap sheet ended with notations from the San Francisco PD Intelligence Squad, stating that Nash was suspected of a dozen Bay Area stickups and was rumored to be one of the outside men behind the May '46 Alcatraz crash-out attempt. Finishing, I checked out the mug shots. Junior Nash looked like a typical inbred Okie shitkicker: long bony head, thin lips, beady eyes and ears that could have belonged to Dumbo.

I glanced at the other men. Loew was reading about himself in the *Herald*; Millard and Sears were still on the sheets, pokerfaced. Lee said, "Give us the good news, Ellis. He's in L.A. and acting uppity, right?"

Loew fiddled with his Phi Beta Kappa key. "Eyewitnesses have made him for two market stickups in Leimert Park over the weekend, which is why he wasn't in the felony summary. He pistol-whipped an old lady during the second robbery, and she died an hour ago at Good Samaritan."

Harry Sears stammered, "Kn-kn-known as-s-sociates?"

Loew shook his head. "Captain Tierney talked to the SFPD this morning. They said Nash is a lone wolf type. Apparently he was recruited for his part in the Alcatraz thing, but that's an exception. What I—"

Russ Millard raised his hand. "Is there a common denominator in Nash's sex beefs?"

"I was getting to that," Loew said. "Nash apparently likes Negro girls. Young ones, still in their teens. All of his sex offense complainants have been colored."

Lee motioned me toward the door. "We'll hit University Station, read the dick's report and take it from there. My bet is that Nash is holing up somewhere in Leimert Park. It's white, but there's shines from Manchester on south. Lots of places to prowl for poontang."

Millard and Sears got up to leave. Loew walked up to Lee and said, "Try to avoid killing him, Sergeant. He richly deserves it, but try anyway."

Lee flashed his patented demon grin. "I'll try, sir. But you be sure to kill him in court. The voters want boys like Junior fried, makes them feel safe at night."

* * *

Our first stop was University Station. The squadroom boss showed us the Robbery reports and told us not to waste our time canvassing the area near the two markets, that Millard and Sears were doing it, concentrating on getting a better description of Nash's car, believed to be a postwar white sedan. Captain Jack had called University with word on Nash's poontang penchant, and three plainclothes Vice officers had been dispatched to check out southside whorehouses specializing in young colored girls. Newton Street and 77th Street divisions, almost entirely colored, would be sending night-watch radio cars by juke joints and playgrounds where Negro youths congregated, eyeballing for Nash and telling the kids to watch out.

There was nothing *we* could do but cruise the area on the chance that Nash was still around and put out the word to Lee's stoolies. We decided on a long Leimert Park tour and took off.

The district's main drag was Crenshaw Boulevard. Broad, running north all the way to Wilshire and south to Baldwin Hills, it spelled "postwar boom" like a neon sign. Every block from Jefferson to Leimert was lined with dilapidated, once grand houses being torn down, their facades replaced by giant billboards advertising department stores, jumbo shopping centers, kiddie parks and movie theaters. Completion dates ranging from Christmas '47 to early '49 were promised, and it hit me that by 1950 this part of L.A. would be unrecognizable. Driving east, we passed vacant lot after vacant lot that would probably soon spawn houses, then block after block of prewar adobe bungalows distinguished only by their color and the condition of their front lawns. Southbound, old wood frame houses took over, getting more and more unkempt.

And no one resembling Junior Nash was on the street; and every late model white sedan we saw was either driven by a woman or squarejohn type.

Nearing Santa Barbara and Vermont, Lee broke our long silence. "This grand tour stuff is the shits. I'm calling in some favors."

He pulled into a filling station, got out and hit the pay phone; I listened to calls on the two-way. I was at it for ten minutes or so when Lee came back, pale and sweating. "I got a tip. A snitch of mine says Nash is shacking with some poon in a crib near Slauson and Hoover."

I shut the radio off. "It's all colored down there. You think—"

"I think we fucking roll."

We took Vermont to Slauson, then headed east, passing storefront churches and hair-straightening parlors, vacant lots and liquor stores with no names—only neon signs blinking L-I-Q-U-O-R at one in the afternoon. Hanging a right turn on Hoover, Lee slowed the car and started scanning tenement stoops. We passed a group of three Negro men and an older white guy lounging on the steps of a particularly seedy dump; I saw the four make us as cops. Lee said, "Hopheads. Nash is supposed to run with jigs, so let's shake them. If they're dirty we'll squeeze for an address on him."

I nodded; Lee ground the car to a halt in the middle of the street. We got out and walked over; the four stuck their hands in their pockets and shuffled their feet, the dance routine of rousted hoodlums everywhere. I said, "Police. Kiss the wall nice and slow." They moved into a search position, hands above their heads, palms on the building wall, feet back, legs spread.

Lee took the two on the right; the white guy muttered, "What the—Blanchard?"

Lee said, "Shut it, shitbird," and started frisking him. I patted down the Negro in the middle first, running my hands along the arms of his suit coat, then dipping into his pockets. My left hand pulled out a pack of Luckys and a Zippo lighter; my right a bunch of marijuana cigarettes. I said, "Reefers" and dropped them to the pavement, then gave Lee a quick sidelong glance. The zoot suit Negro beside him reached toward his waistband; light gleamed on metal as his hand came away. I shouted, "Partner!" and pulled my .38.

The white man swung around; Lee shot him twice in the face point blank. The zooter got a shiv free just as I extended my gun. I fired, he dropped the knife, grabbed his neck and slammed into the wall. Wheeling, I saw the jig at the end fumbling at the front of his trousers and shot him three times. He flew backward; I heard *"Bucky duck!"* Hitting the cement, I got a topsy-turvy view of Lee and the last Negro drawing on each other from a couple of feet apart. Lee's three shots cut him down just as he managed to aim a tiny derringer. He fell dead, half his skull blown off.

I stood up, looked at the four bodies and blood-covered sidewalk, stumbled to the curb and vomited into the gutter until my chest ached. I heard sirens approaching, pinned my badge to my jacket front, then turned around. Lee was pulling out the stiffs' pockets, tossing shivs and reefers onto the sidewalk, away from the pools of blood. He walked over, and I was hoping he'd have a wisecrack to calm me down. He didn't; he was bawling like a baby.

* * *

It took the rest of the afternoon to put ten seconds down on paper.

We wrote out our reports at 77th Street Station, and were questioned by the team of Homicide dicks who investigated all officer-involved shootings. They told us that the three Negroes—Willie Walker Brown, Caswell Pritchford and Cato Early—were known grasshoppers, and that the white man—Baxter Fitch—took two strong-arm falls back in the late '20s. Since all four men were armed and harboring marijuana, they assured us that there would be no Grand Jury hearing.

I took the questioning calmly; Lee took it rough, shivering and muttering that he'd rousted Baxter Fitch for loitering a bunch of times when he worked Highland Park, and he sort of liked the guy. I stuck close to him at the station, then steered him out to his car through a throng of reporters hurling questions.

When we got to the house, Kay was standing on the front porch; one look at her gaunt face told me she already knew. She ran to Lee and embraced him, whispering, "Oh baby, oh babe." I watched them, then noticed a newspaper on the railing.

I picked it up. It was the bulldog edition of the *Mirror*, featuring a banner headline: "Boxer Cops in Gun Battle! Four Crooks Dead!!" Below were publicity stills of Fire and Ice crouched in gloves and trunks, along with mug shots of the dead men. I read a jazzed-up account of the shoot-out and a replay of October's fight, then heard Lee shout: "You'll never understand, so just leave me fucking alone!"

Lee took off running, around the driveway to the garage, Kay right behind him. I stood on the porch, amazed at the soft center in the toughest son of a bitch I'd ever known. I heard Lee's motorcycle starting up; seconds later he peeled out on it, screeching into a hard right turn, undoubtedly heading for a brutal run at Mulholland.

Kay came back just as the cycle noise died in the distance. Taking her hands, I said, "He'll get over it. He knew one of the guys, so that made it worse. But he'll get over it."

Kay looked at me strangely. "You're very calm."

"It was them or us. You look after Lee tomorrow. We're off-duty, but when we go back we're going after a real beast."

"And you look after him, too. Bobby De Witt gets out in a week or so, and he swore at his trial to kill Lee and the other men who arrested him. Lee's scared, and I know Bobby. He's as bad as they come."

I put my arms around Kay and held her. "Ssssh. Fire and Ice are on the job, so rest easy."

Kay shook herself free. "You don't know Bobby. You don't know the things he made me do."

I brushed a lock of hair away from her eyes. "Yes, I do, and I don't care. I mean I do care, but—"

Kay said, "I know what you mean," and pushed me away. I let her go, knowing if I pursued it she'd tell me a shitload of things I didn't want to hear. The front door slammed, and I sat down on the steps, glad to be alone to sort things out.

Four months ago, I was a radio car hack going nowhere. Now I was a Warrants detective instrumental in passing a million-dollar bond issue, with a double shine killing on my record. Next month I would be thirty years old with five years on the job, eligible to take the Sergeant's Exam. If I passed it, then played my cards right, I could be detective lieutenant before I was thirty-five, and that was just the beginning.

I started to get itchy, so I went inside and puttered around the living room, thumbing through magazines, checking out the book-shelves for something to read. Then I heard the sound of water drumming hard, coming from the rear of the house. I walked back, seeing the wide-open bathroom door, feeling the steam, knowing it was all for me.

Kay was standing nude under the shower. Her expression stayed fixed in no expression at all, even when our eyes met. I took in her body, from freckled breasts with dark nipples to wide hips and flat stomach, then she pirouetted for me. I saw old knife scars criss-crossing her backside from thighs to spine, choked back tremors and walked away wishing she hadn't showed me on the day I killed two men.

PART TWO

39th AND NORTON

7

THE PHONE woke me up early Wednesday morning, cutting off a dream featuring Tuesday's *Daily News* headline—"Fire and Ice Cops KO Negro Thugs"—and a beautiful blonde with Kay's body. Figuring it was the newshounds who'd been pestering me since the shoot-out, I fumbled the receiver onto the nightstand and dived back to slumberland. Then I heard, "Rise and shine, partner!" and picked it up.

"Yeah, Lee."

"You know what day this is?"

"The fifteenth. Payday. You called me up at six A.M. to—" I stopped when I caught an edge of nervous glee in Lee's voice. "Are you okay?"

"I'm swell. I ran Mulholland at a hundred ten, played house with Kay all day yesterday. Now I'm bored. Feel like doing some police work?"

"Keep going."

"I just talked to a snitch who owes me big. He says Junior Nash has got a fuck pad—a garage on Coliseum and Norton, in back of a green apartment building. Race you there? Loser buys the beer at the fights tonight?"

New headlines danced in front of my eyes. I said, "You're on," hung up and dressed in record time, then ran out to my car and gunned it the eight or nine miles to Leimert Park. And Lee was already there, leaning against his Ford, parked at the curb in front of the only structure on a huge block of vacant lots—a puke-green bungalow court with a two-story shack at the rear.

I pulled up behind him and got out. Lee winked and said, "You lost."

I said, "You cheated."

He laughed. "You're right, I called from a pay phone. Reporters been bothering you?"

I gave my partner a slow eyeballing. He seemed relaxed but itchy underneath, with his old jocular front back in place. "I holed up. You?"

"Bevo Means came by, asked me how it felt. I told him I wouldn't want it for a steady diet."

I pointed to the courtyard. "You talk to any of the tenants? Check for Nash's car?"

Lee said, "No vehicle, but I talked to the manager. He's been renting Nash that shack in the back. He's used it a couple of times to entertain poon, but the manager hasn't seen him in a week or so."

"You shake it?"

"No, waiting for you."

I drew my .38 and pressed it to my leg; Lee winked and aped me, and we walked through the courtyard to the shack. Both floors had flimsy-looking wooden doors, with rickety steps leading to the second story. Lee tried the bottom door; it creaked open. We pressed ourselves to the wall on opposite sides of it, then I wheeled and entered, my gun arm extended.

No sound, no movement, only cobwebs and a wood floor strewn with yellowed newspapers and bald tires. I backed out; Lee took the lead up the steps, walking on his toes. At the landing, he gave the doorknob a jiggle, shook his head no and kicked the door in, clean off its hinges.

I ran up the stairs; Lee moved inside gun first. At the top, I saw him reholstering his piece. He said, "Okie trash," and made a gesture that took in the whole room. I stepped over the door and nodded my head in agreement.

The crib reeked of rotgut wine. A bed fashioned from two folded-out car seats took up most of the floor space; it was covered with upholstery stuffing and used rubbers. Empty muscatel short dogs were piled in corners, and the one window was streaked with cobwebs and dirt. The stench got to me, so I walked over and opened the window. Looking out, I saw a group of uniformed cops and men in civilian clothes standing on the sidewalk on Norton, about halfway down the block to 39th Street. All of them were staring at something in the weeds of a vacant lot; two black-and-whites and an unmarked cruiser were parked at the curb. I said, "Lee, come here."

Lee stuck his head out the window and squinted. "I think I see Millard and Sears. They were supposed to be catching squeals today, so maybe—"

I ran out of the pad, down the steps and around the corner to Norton, Lee at my heels. Seeing a coroner's wagon and a photo car screech to a halt, I sprinted. Harry Sears was knocking back a drink in full view of a half dozen officers; I glimpsed horror in his eyes. The photo men had moved into the lot and were fanning out, pointing their cameras at the ground. I elbowed my way past a pair of patrolmen and saw what it was all about.

It was the nude, mutilated body of a young woman, cut in half at the waist. The bottom half lay in the weeds a few feet away from the top, legs wide open. A large triangle had been gouged out of the left thigh, and there was a long, wide cut running from the bisection point down to the top of the pubic hair. The flaps of skin beside the gash were pulled back; there were no organs inside. The top half was worse: the breasts were dotted with cigarette burns, the right one hanging loose, attached to the torso only by shreds of skin; the left one slashed around the nipple. The cuts went all the way down to the bone, but the worst of the worst was the girl's face. It was one huge purpled bruise, the nose crushed deep into the facial cavity, the mouth cut ear to ear into a smile that leered up at you, somehow mocking the rest of the brutality inflicted. I knew I would carry that smile with me to my grave.

Looking up, I felt cold all over; my breath came in spurts. Shoulders and arms brushed me and I heard a jumble of voices: "There's not a goddamned drop of blood—" "This is *the* worst crime on a woman I've seen in my sixteen years—" "He tied her down. Look, you can see the rope burns on her ankles—" Then a long, shrill whistle sounded.

The dozen or so men quit jabbering and looked at Russ Millard. He said calmly, "Before it gets out of hand, let's put the kibosh on something. If this homicide gets a lot of publicity, we're going to get a lot of confessions. That girl was disemboweled. We need information to eliminate the loonies with, and that's it. Don't tell *anyone*. Don't tell your wives, don't tell your girlfriends, don't tell any other officers. Harry?"

Harry Sears said, "Yeah, Russ," palming his flask so the boss wouldn't see it. Millard caught the act and rolled his eyes in disgust. "No reporters are to view the body. You photo men, take your pictures *now*. You coroner's men, put a sheet over the body when they finish. You patrolmen, stake up a crime scene perimeter from the street all the way to six feet in back of the body. Any reporter who tries to cross it, you arrest immediately. When the lab men get here to examine the body, you move the reporters over to the opposite side of the street. Harry, you call Lieutenant

Haskins at University Station and tell him to send over every man he can spare for canvassing."

Millard glanced around and noticed me. "Bleichert, what are you doing here? Is Blanchard here, too?"

Lee was squatting beside the stiff, writing in a pocket notebook. Pointing north, I said, "Junior Nash is renting a garage in back of that building over there. We were shaking it down when we saw the hubbub."

"Was there blood on the premises?"

"No. This isn't Nash, Lieutenant."

"We'll let the lab men be the judge of that. Harry!"

Sears was sitting in a black-and-white, talking into a radio mike. Hearing his name, he yelled, "Yeah, Russ!"

"Harry, when the lab men get here have them go up to that green building on the corner and test the garage for blood and latent prints. Then I want the street sealed—"

Millard stopped when he saw cars swinging onto Norton, beelining for the commotion; I glanced down at the corpse. The photo techs were still snapping pictures from all angles; Lee was still jotting in his notebook. The men milling around on the sidewalk kept looking at the stiff, then averting their eyes. On the street, reporters and camera jockeys were pouring out of cars, Harry Sears and a cordon of blues standing at the ready to hold them back. I got itchy to stare, and gave the girl a detailed eyeing.

Her legs were spread for sex, and from the way the knees buckled I could tell that they were broken; her jet-black hair was free of matted blood, like the killer had given her a shampoo before he dumped her. That awful death leer came on like the final brutality—it was cracked teeth poking out of ulcerated flesh that forced me to look away.

I found Lee on the sidewalk, helping string up crime scene ropes. He stared through me, like all he could see was the ghosts in the air. I said, "Junior Nash, remember?"

Lee's gaze zeroed in on me. "He didn't do this. He's trash, but he didn't do this."

Noise rose from the street as more reporters arrived and a line of blues linked arms to restrain them. I shouted to make myself heard: "He beat an old woman to death! He's our priority warrantee!"

Lee grabbed my arms and squeezed them numb. "This is our priority, and we're staying! I'm senior, and I say so!" The words

rumbled over the scene, causing heads to turn in our direction.
I pulled my arms free and snapped to who Lee's ghost was.

"Okay, partner."

* * *

Over the next hour, 39th and Norton filled up with police
vehicles, reporters and a big crowd of rubberneckers. The body
was removed on two sheet-covered stretchers; in the back of the
meat wagon a lab team rolled the dead girl's prints before hauling
her downtown to the morgue. Harry Sears gave the press a handout that Russ Millard composed, the straight dope of everything
except the gutting of the stiff. Sears drove to City Hall to check
the records of the Missing Persons Bureau, and Millard stayed
behind to direct the investigation.

Lab technicians were dispatched to prowl the lot for possible
murder weapons and women's clothing; another forensic team
was sent to check for latents and bloodstains at Junior Nash's fuck
pad. Then Millard counted cop heads. There were four men directing traffic and keeping civilian ghouls in line, twelve bluesuits
and five plainclothesmen, Lee and me. Millard dug a street atlas
out of his cruiser and divided the entire Leimert Park area into
foot beats, then assigned each man his territory and mandatory
questions to be asked of every person in every house, apartment
and store: Have you heard female screams at any time over the past
forty-eight hours? Have you seen anyone discarding or inciner-
ating women's clothing? Have you noticed any suspicious cars or
people loitering in the area? Have *you* passed by Norton Avenue
between 39th and Coliseum Streets during the past twenty-four
hours, and if so, did you notice anyone in the vacant lots?

I was assigned Olmsted Avenue, three blocks east of Norton,
from Coliseum south to Leimert Boulevard; Lee was given the
stores and building sites on Crenshaw, from 39th north to Jefferson.
We made plans to meet at the Olympic at 8:00 and split up;
I started pounding pavement.

I walked, rang doorbells and asked questions, getting negative
answers, writing down the addresses where no one was at home,
so that the second wave of canvassing cops would have the numbers to work from. I talked to sherry-sneaking housewives and
bratty little kids; to pensioners and on-leave servicemen, even an
off-duty cop who worked West L.A. Division. I threw in questions
on Junior Nash and the late model white sedan and showed

around his mug shots. All I got was a big fat zero; at 7:00 I walked back to my car disgusted by what I'd blundered into.

Lee's car was gone, and forensic arclights were being set up at 39th and Norton. I drove to the Olympic hoping for a good series of bouts to take the bad taste of the day out of my mouth.

H.J. Caruso had left tickets for us at the front turnstile, along with a note saying he had a hot date and wouldn't be showing up. Lee's ticket was still in the envelope; I grabbed mine and headed for H.J.'s box. The first prelim of an all-bantamweight card had already started, and I settled in to watch and wait for Lee.

The two tiny Mex warriors put on a good fight, and the crowd ate it up. Coins rained down from the top tier; shouts in Spanish and English filled the arena. After four rounds I knew that Lee wasn't going to show; the bantys, both cut bad, made me think of the butchered girl. I got up and left, knowing exactly where Lee was.

I drove back to 39th and Norton. The entire lot was lit up by arclights—as bright as day. Lee was standing just inside the crime scene rope. The night had turned cold; he was hunched into his letterman's jacket as he watched the lab techs poke around in the weeds.

I walked over. Lee saw me coming and did a quick draw, shooting me with finger pistols, his thumbs the hammers. It was a routine he pulled when he was jacked up on Benzedrine.

"You were supposed to meet me. Remember?"

Arclight glow gave Lee's raw nerved face a blue-white cast. "I said this was priority. Remember that?"

Looking off in the distance, I saw other vacant lots illuminated. "It's priority for the Bureau, maybe. Just like Junior Nash is priority for us."

Lee shook his head. "Partner, this is *big*. Horrall and Thad Green were down here a couple of hours ago. Jack Tierney's been detached to Homicide to run the investigation, with Russ Millard backstopping. You want my opinion?"

"Shoot."

"It's a showcase. A nice white girl gets snuffed, the Department goes all out to get the killer to show the voters that passing the bond issue got them a bulldog police force."

"Maybe she wasn't such a nice girl. Maybe that old lady that Nash killed was somebody's loving granny. Maybe you're taking this thing too personal, and maybe we let the Bureau handle it and get back to our job before Junior kills somebody else."

Lee balled his fists. "You got any other maybes?"

I stepped forward. "Maybe you're afraid of Bobby DeWitt getting out. Maybe you're too proud to ask me for help to scare him away from the woman we both care for. Maybe we let the Bureau chalk up that dead girl for Laurie Blanchard."

Lee uncoiled his fists and turned away; I watched him rock on his heels, hoping he'd be fighting mad or wisecracking or anything but hurt when I finally saw his face. I made fists, then shouted: "Talk to me, goddamnit! We're partners! We killed four fucking men together, now you pull this shit on me!"

Lee turned around. He flashed his patented demon grin, but it came off nervous and sad, used up. His voice was raspy, stretched thin.

"I used to watchdog Laurie when she played. I was a scrapper, and all the other kids were afraid of me. I had a lot of girlfriends—you know, kiddie romance stuff. The girls used to tease me about Laurie, go on about how much time I spent with her, like she was my real sweetheart.

"See, I doted on her. She was pretty and she was a trouper.

"Dad used to talk about getting Laurie ballet lessons and piano lessons and singing lessons. I was gonna work goon squad at Firestone Tire like him, and Laurie was gonna be an artiste. It was just talk, but I was a kid, and it was real to me.

"Anyway, right around the time she disappeared, Dad was talking up this lesson stuff a lot, and it made me mad at Laurie. I started ditching her when she went to play after school. There was this wild girl who'd moved into the neighborhood. She was a roundheels, and she used to get tanked on bathtub and put out for all the boys. I was dicking her when Laurie got snatched, when I should have been protecting my sister."

I reached for my partner's arm to tell him I understood; Lee pushed my hand away. "Don't tell me you understand, because I'll tell you what makes it bad. Laurie got snuffed. Some degenerate strangled her or chopped her up. And when she died, I was thinking ugly things about her. About how I hated her because Dad thought she was a princess and I was a thug. I pictured my own sister cut up like that stiff this morning, and I laughed about it while I was with that floozy, screwing her and drinking her father's booze."

Lee took a deep breath and pointed to the ground a few yards away. A separate, inside perimeter had been staked, the two halves of the body marked in quicklime. I stared at the outline of the spread legs; Lee said, "I'm gonna get him. With you or without you, I'm gonna get him."

I dredged up a ghost of a smile. "See you at the Hall tomorrow."

"With you or without you."

I said, "I heard you," and walked back to my car. Hitting the ignition, I saw another empty lot a block to the north light up.

8

THE FIRST thing I saw when I walked into the squadroom the next morning was Harry Sears reading the *Herald* headline: "Hunt Werewolf's Den in Torture Slaying!!!"; the second thing I saw was a chain of five men—two derelicts, two squarejohn types and one in county jail denims, manacled to a bench. Harry put his paper down, stammering, "C-c-con-fessors. S-s-said they s-sliced the girl." I nodded, hearing screams coming from the interrogation room.

A moment later, Bill Koenig led a doubled-over fat man out the door, announcing to the bullpen at large, "He didn't do it." A couple of officers clapped satirically at their desks; a half dozen looked away, disgusted.

Koenig shoved the fat man out to the corridor. I asked Harry, "Where's Lee?"

Harry pointed to Ellis Loew's office. "W-with Loew. R-r-reporters, too."

I walked over and peered through the crack in the doorway. Ellis Loew was standing in back of his desk, playing to a score of newshounds. Lee was seated at the DA's side, dressed in his only suit. He looked tired—but nowhere near as edgy as he did last night.

Loew was sternly enunciating, "... and the heinous nature of the killing deems it imperative that we make every effort to catch this fiend as soon as possible. A number of specially trained officers, including Mr. Fire and his partner Mr. Ice, have been detached from their regular duties to aid in the investigation, and with men like them on the job, I think we can expect positive results soon. Moreover ..."

I couldn't hear for the pounding of blood in my head. I started to nudge the door open; Lee saw me, bowed to Loew and exited the office. He dogged me back to the Warrants cubicle; I wheeled around. "You got us detached, right?"

Lee put restraining hands on my chest. "Let's take this slow and easy, okay? First off, I gave Ellis a memo. It said we got verified dope Nash blew our jurisdiction."

"Are you fucking crazy!"

"Sssh. Listen, it was just to grease the skids. The APB on Nash still stands, the fuck pad is being staked out, every southside cop is out to cancel the bastard's ticket. I'm gonna stay at the pad tonight myself. I've got binoculars, and I figure between them and the arclights I'll be able to catch the plates on the cars that cruise down Norton. Maybe the killer's gonna drive by to gloat. I'll get all the license numbers, and check them against the DMV and R&I."

I sighed. "Jesus, Lee."

"Partner, all I want is a week on the girl. Nash is covered, and if he doesn't get collared by then, we go back to him as our priority warrantee."

"He's too dangerous to let go. You know that."

"Partner, *he's covered*. Now don't tell me you don't want to build on your shine killings. Don't tell me you don't know that the dead girl is a better piece of pie than Junior Nash."

I saw more Fire and Ice headlines. "One week, Lee. No more."

Lee winked. "Copacetic."

Captain Jack's voice came over the intercom: "Gentlemen, everybody to the muster room. Now."

I grabbed my notebook and walked through the bullpen. The ranks of the confessors had swollen, the new ones cuffed to radiators and heating pipes. Bill Koenig was slapping an old guy demanding to talk to Mayor Bowron; Fritzie Vogel was taking down names on a clipboard. The muster room was SRO, packed with Central and Bureau men and a shitload of plainclothes cops I'd never seen before. Captain Jack and Russ Millard were at the front, standing beside a floor microphone. Tierney tapped the mike, cleared his throat and spoke:

"Gentlemen, this is a general briefing on the 187 in Leimert Park. I'm sure you've all read the papers and you all know it's a damn rough piece of work. It's also a damn big piece of work. The mayor's office has gotten a lot of calls, we've gotten a lot of calls, the City Council has gotten a lot of calls and Chief Horrall has gotten personal calls from a lot of people we want to keep happy. This werewolf stuff in the papers is going to get us a lot more calls, so let's get going on it.

"We'll start with the chain of command. I'm supervising, Lieutenant Millard is exec, Sergeant Sears is the runner between divisions. Deputy DA Loew is liaison to the press and civilian authorities, and the following officers are detached to Central Homicide, effective 1/16/47: Sergeant Anders, Detective Areola, Sergeant Blanchard, Officer Bleichert, Sergeant Cavanaugh, Detective Ellison, Detective Grimes, Sergeant Koenig, Detective Liggett, Detective Navarette, Sergeant Pratt, Detective J. Smith, Detective W. Smith, Sergeant Vogel. You men see Lieutenant Millard after this briefing. Russ, they're all yours."

I got out my pen, giving the man next to me a gentle elbow to get more writing room. Every cop around me was doing the same thing; you could feel their attention rivet to the front of the room.

Millard spoke in his courtroom lawyer's voice: "Yesterday, seven A.M., Norton Avenue between 39th and Coliseum. A dead girl, naked, cut in half, right off the sidewalk in a vacant lot. Obviously tortured, but I'll hold off on that until I talk to the autopsy surgeon—Doc Newbarr's doing the job this afternoon at Queen of Angels. No reporters—there's some details we don't want them to know.

"The area has been thoroughly canvassed once—no leads so far. There was no blood where we found the body; the girl was obviously killed somewhere else and dumped in the lot. There's a number of vacant lots in the area, and they're being searched for weapons and bloodstains. An armed robbery–homicide suspect named Raymond Douglas Nash was renting a garage down the street—the place was checked for prints and bloodstains. The lab boys got zero, and Nash is not a suspect on the girl.

"There's no ID on her yet, no matchup to anyone in the Missing Persons files. Her prints have been teletyped, so we should get some kind of report soon. An anonymous call to University Station started it all, by the way. The officer who caught the squeal said it was a hysterical woman walking her little girl to school. The woman didn't give her name and hung up, and I think we can eliminate her as a suspect."

Millard switched to a patient, professorial tone. "Until the body is ID'd, the investigation has to be centered on 39th and Norton, and the next step is recanvassing the area."

A big collective groan rose. Millard scowled and said, "University Station will be the command post, and there'll be clerks there to type up and collate the field officers' reports. Clerical officers will be working up summary reports and evidence indexes. They'll be posted on the squadroom board at University, with carbons distributed to all LAPD and Sheriff's divisions. You men here from other squads are to take what you hear at this briefing back to your station houses, put it on every crime sheet, every watch. Any information you get from patrolmen, you phone in to Central Homicide, extension 411. Now, I've got lists of recanvassing addresses for everyone but Bleichert and Blanchard. Bucky, Lee, take the same areas as yesterday. You men from other divisions, stand by; the rest of you men that Captain Tierney detached, see me now. That's it!"

I jockeyed out the door and took service stairs down to the parking lot, wanting to avoid Lee and put some distance between him and my okay on the Nash memo. The sky had turned dark gray, and all the way to Leimert Park I thought of thunderstorms obliterating leads in the vacant lots, washing the sliced girl investigation and Lee's grief over his little sister into the sewer until the gutters overflowed and Junior Nash popped his head out, begging to be arrested. As I parked my car, the clouds started to break up; soon I was canvassing with the sun beating down—and a new string of negative answers kiboshed my fantasies.

I asked the same questions I asked the day before, stressing Nash even harder. But this time it was different. Cops were combing the area, writing down the license numbers of parked cars and dragging sewers for women's clothing—and the locals had listened to the radio and read the papers.

One sherry-breathing hairbag held out a plastic crucifix and asked me if it would keep the werewolf away; an old geezer wearing skivvies and a clerical collar told me the dead girl was God's sacrifice because Leimert Park voted Democrat in the '46 Congressional. A little boy showed me a movie pinup of Lon Chaney, Jr. as the Wolfman and said that the vacant lot at 39th and Norton was the launching pad for his rocket ship, and a boxing fan who recognized me from the Blanchard fight asked me for my autograph, then told me straight-faced that his neighbor's bassett hound was the killer, and would I please shoot the cocksucker? The sane nos I got were as boring as the nut answers were fanciful, and I started to feel like the straight man in a monstrous comedy routine.

At 1:30, I finished and walked back to my car, thinking about lunch and checking in at University Station. There was a piece of paper stuck under the wiper blades—a sheet of Thad Green's personal stationery, with "Official Police Witness—admit this officer to autopsy of Jane Doe #31, 2:00 P.M., 1/16/47" typed in the middle of the page. Green's signature was scrawled at the bottom—and it looked suspiciously like the writing of Sergeant Leland C. Blanchard. Laughing against my will, I drove to Queen of Angels Hospital.

The corridors were crowded with nun-nurses and oldsters on gurneys. I showed an elderly sister my badge and inquired after the autopsy; she crossed herself and led me down the hall, pointing to a double-doored entranceway marked PATHOLOGY. I walked up to the patrolman standing guard and flashed my invitation; he snapped to attention and swung the doors open, and I entered a small cold room, all antiseptic white, a long metal table in the middle. Two sheet-covered objects lay on top of it. I sat down on a bench facing the slab, shivering at the thought of seeing the girl's death smile again.

The double doors opened a few seconds later. A tall old man smoking a cigar came in, along with a nun carrying a steno pad. Russ Millard, Harry Sears and Lee followed them, the Homicide exec shaking his head. "You and Blanchard keep turning up like bad pennies. Doc, can *we* smoke?"

The old man took a scalpel from his back pocket and wiped it on his trouser leg. "Sure. Won't bother the girl any, she's in dreamland for keeps. Sister Margaret, help me get that sheet off, will you?"

Lee sat down on the bench beside me; Millard and Sears lit cigarettes, then dug out pens and notebooks. Lee yawned, and asked me, "Get anything this morning?"

I saw that his Benzedrine juice was all but dead. "Yeah. A wolf-man killer from Mars did the snuff. Buck Rogers is chasing him in his spaceship, and you should go home and sleep."

Lee yawned again. "Later. My best tip was the Nazis. A guy told me he saw Hitler in a bar on 39th and Crenshaw. Oh Jesus, Bucky."

Lee lowered his eyes; I looked at the autopsy slab. The dead girl was uncovered, her head lolling in our direction. I stared at my shoes while the doctor rambled on in medicalese:

"On gross pathology, we have a female Caucasian. Muscle tone indicates her age is between sixteen and thirty. The cadaver is presented in two halves, with bisection at the level of the umbilicus.

On the upper half: the head is intact, with massive depressed skull fractures, facial features significantly obscured by massive ecchymoses, hematomas and edema. Downward displacement of nasal cartilage. Through-and-through laceration from both mouth corners across masseter muscles, extending through temporal mandibula joints upward to both earlobes. No visible signs of neck bruises. Multiple lacerations on anterior thorax, concentrated on both breasts. Cigarette burns on both breasts. Right breast almost completely severed from thorax. Inspection of upper half abdominal cavity reveals no free-flowing blood. Intestines, stomach, liver and spleen removed."

The doctor took an audible breath; I looked up and watched him puff on his cigar. The steno nun caught up with her note taking and Millard and Sears eyeballed the stiff deadpan while Lee stared at the floor, wiping sweat from his brow. The doc felt both breasts, then said, "Lack of hypertrophy indicates no pregnancy at time of death." He grabbed his scalpel and started poking around inside the bottom half of the corpse. I shut my eyes and listened.

"Inspection of the lower half of the cadaver reveals a midline longitudinal incision extending from the umbilicus to the symphysis pubis. Mesentery, uterus, ovaries and rectum removed, multiple lacerations on both posterior and anterior cavity walls. Large triangular gouge on left thigh. Sister, help me turn her over."

I heard the doors open; a voice called out, "Lieutenant!" I opened my eyes to see Millard getting up and the doctor and nun wrestling the stiff onto its stomach. When it was backside up, the doctor lifted the ankles and flexed the legs. "Both legs broken at the knee, and healing, light lash marks on the upper back and shoulders. Ligature marks on both ankles. Sister, hand me a speculum and swab."

Millard came back and handed Sears a piece of paper. He read it and nudged Lee. The doctor and nun turned the bottom half of the body over, spreading the legs wide. My stomach flip-flopped; Lee said, "Bingo." He stared at a teletype sheet while the doc droned on about lack of vaginal abrasions and the presence of old semen. The coldness in his voice made me angry; I grabbed the sheet and read: "Russ—she's Elizabeth Ann Short, DOB 7/29/24, Medford, Mass. Feds ID'd the prints—she was arrested in Santa Barbara 9/43. Background check in progress. Report back to Hall following autopsy. Call in all available field officers. —J.T."

The doctor said, "That's it on preliminary postmortem. Later on I'll have some more specifics, and I'll run some toxicological tests." He draped both halves of Elizabeth Ann Short and added, "Questions?" The nun headed for the door clutching her steno pad.

Millard said, "Can you give us a reconstruction?"

"Pending the test results, sure. Here's what she wasn't: she wasn't pregnant, she wasn't raped, but she had had voluntary intercourse sometime during the past week or so. She took what you might call a gentle whipping within the past week; the last marks on her back are older than the cuts on her front side. Here's what I think happened. I think she was tied down and tortured with a knife for a minimum of thirty-six to forty-eight hours. I think her legs were broken with a smooth, rounded instrument like a baseball bat while she was still alive. I think she either got beaten to death with something like a baseball bat, or she choked to death on her blood from the mouth wound. After she was dead, she was cut in half with a butcher knife or something resembling it, and the killer went in after her internal organs with something like a penknife. After *that*, he drained the blood from the body and washed it clean, my guess is in a bathtub. We took some blood samples from the kidneys, and in a few days we'll be able to tell you if she had any dope or liquor in her system."

Lee said, "Doc, did this guy know anything about medicine or anatomy? Why'd he go after that inside stuff?"

The doctor examined his cigar butt. "You tell me. The top-half organs he could have pulled out easily. The bottom organs he hacked with a knife to get at, like that was what interested him. He could have had medical training, but then again he could have had veterinary training, or taxidermist's training, or biological training, or he could have taken Physiology 104 in the L.A. city school system or my Pathology for Beginners class at UCLA. You tell me. I'll tell you what you've got for sure: she was dead six to eight hours before you found her, and she was killed someplace secluded that had running water. Harry, has this girl got a name yet?"

Sears tried to answer, but his mouth just fluttered. Millard put a hand on his shoulder and said, "Elizabeth Short."

The doctor saluted heaven with his cigar. "God love you, Elizabeth. Russell, when you get the son of a bitch who did this to her, give him a kick in the balls and tell him it's from Frederick D. Newbarr, M.D. Now all of you get out of here. I've got a date with a jumper suicide in ten minutes."

*   *   *

Walking out of the elevator, I heard Ellis Loew's voice, an octave louder and deeper than normal, echoing down the corridor. I caught "Vivisection of a lovely young woman," "Werewolf psychopath" and "My political aspirations are subservient to my desire to see justice done." Opening a connecting door into the Homicide pen, I saw the Republican bright boy emoting into radio mikes while a recording crew stood by. He was wearing an American Legion poppy on his lapel—probably purchased from the wino legionnaire who slept in the Hall of Records parking lot—a man he had once vigorously prosecuted for vagrancy.

The bullpen was taken over by ham antics, so I walked across the hall to Tierney's office. Lee, Russ Millard, Harry Sears and two old-timer cops I hardly knew—Dick Cavanaugh and Vern Smith— were huddled around Captain Jack's desk, examining a piece of paper the boss was holding up.

I looked over Harry's shoulder. Three mug shots of a show-stopper brunette were taped to the page, with three close-up face photos of the corpse at 39th and Norton affixed next to them. The slashed-mouth smile jumped out at me; Captain Jack said, "The mugs are from the Santa Barbara PD. They popped the Short girl in September '43 for underaged drinking, sent her home to her mother in Massachusetts. Boston PD contacted her an hour ago. She's flying out to ID the stiff tomorrow. The Boston cops are doing a background check back east, and all Bureau days off are cancelled. Anybody complains, I point to those pictures. What did Doc Newbarr say, Russ?"

Millard said, "Tortured for two days. Cause of death the mouth wound or the head bashing. No rape. Internal organs removed. Dead six to eight hours before the body was dumped in the lot. What else have we got on her?"

Tierney checked some papers on his desk. "Except for the juvie roust, no other record. Four sisters, parents divorced, worked in the Camp Cooke PX during the war. The father's here in L.A. What's next?"

I was the only one who blinked when the big boss asked number two for advice. Millard said, "I want to recanvass Leimert Park with the mugs. Me, Harry and two other men. Then I want to go to University Station, read reports and answer calls. Has Loew given the press a look at the mugs?"

Tierney nodded. "Yeah, and Bevo Means told me the father sold the *Times and* the *Herald* some old portrait pictures of the girl. She'll be front page on the evening editions."

Millard barked, "Damn," the only word of profanity anyone ever heard him use. Seething, he said, "They'll be coming out of the woodwork to greet her. Has the father been questioned?" Tierney shook his head and consulted some memo slips. "Cleo Short, 1020½ South Kingsley, Wilshire District. I had an officer call him and tell him to stay put, that we'd be sending some men by to talk to him. Russ, you think the strange-o's will fall in love with this one?"

"How many confessions so far?"

"Eighteen."

"Double that by morning, more if Loew got the press excited with his purple prose."

"I would say I got them motivated, Lieutenant. And I would say my prose fit the crime."

Ellis Loew was standing in the doorway, Fritz Vogel and Bill Koenig behind him. Millard locked eyes with the radio ham.

"Too much publicity is a hindrance, Ellis. If you were a police-man you'd know that."

Loew flushed and reached for his Phi Beta Kappa key. "I'm a ranking civilian-police liaison officer, specially deputized by the City of Los Angeles."

Millard smiled. "You're a civilian, counselor."

Loew bristled, then turned to Tierney. "Captain, have you sent men to talk to the victim's father?"

Captain Jack said, "Not yet, Ellis. Soon."

"How about Vogel and Koenig? They'll get us what we need to know."

Tierney looked up at Millard. The lieutenant gave an almost imperceptible head shake; Captain Jack said, "Aah, Ellis, in big homicide jobs the whip assigns the men. Aah, Russ, who do you think should go?"

Millard scrutinized Cavanaugh and Smith, me trying to look inconspicuous and Lee yawning, slouched against the wall. He said, "Bleichert, Blanchard, you bad pennies question Miss Short's father. Bring your report to University Station tomorrow morning."

Loew's hands jerked his Phi Beta key clean off its chain; it fell to the floor. Bill Koenig squeezed in the doorway and picked it up; Loew about-faced into the hall. Vogel glared at Millard, then followed him. Harry Sears, breathing Old Grand Dad, said, "He sends a few niggers to the gas chamber and it goes to his head."

Vern Smith said, "The niggers must have confessed."

Dick Cavanaugh said, "With Fritzie and Bill they all confess."

Russ Millard said, "Shit-brained, grandstanding son of a bitch."

* * *

We took separate cars to the Wilshire District, rendezvousing in front of 1020½ South Kingsley at dusk. It was a garage apartment, shack sized, at the rear of a big Victorian house. Lights were burning inside; Lee, yawning, said, "Good guy–bad guy," and rang the buzzer.

A skinny man in his fifties opened the door and said, "Cops, huh?" He had dark hair and pale eyes similar to the girl in the mug shots, but that was it for familial resemblance. Elizabeth Short was a knockout; he looked like a knockout victim: bony frame in baggy brown trousers and a soiled undershirt, moles all over his shoulders, seamed face pitted with acne scars. Pointing us inside, he said, "I got an alibi, just in case you think I did it. Tighter than a crab's ass, and that is *air* tight."

Mr. White Hat to the hilt, I said, "I'm Detective Bleichert, Mr. Short. This is my partner Sergeant Blanchard. We'd like to express our condolences for the loss of your daughter."

Cleo Short slammed the door. "I read the papers, I know who you are. Neither one of you would have lasted one round with Gentleman Jim Jeffries. And as far as your condolences go, I say *c'est la vie.* Betty called the tune, so she had to pay the piper. Nothing's free in this life. You want to hear my alibi?"

I sat down on a threadbare sofa and eyeballed the room. The walls were lined floor to ceiling with shelves spilling dime novels; there was the couch, one wooden chair and nothing else. Lee got out his notebook. "Since you're so anxious to tell us, shoot."

Short slumped into the chair and ground the legs into the floor, like an animal pawing the dirt. "I was Johnny on the spot at my job from Tuesday the fourteenth at two P.M. to five P.M. Wednesday the fifteenth. Twenty-seven straight hours, time and a half for the last seventeen. I'm a refrigerator repairman, the best in the west. I work at Frost King Appliances, 4831 South Berendo. My boss's name is Mike Mazmanian. You call him. He'll alibi me up tighter than a popcorn fart, and that is *air* tight."

Lee yawned and wrote it down; Cleo Short crossed his arms over his bony chest, daring us to make something of it. I said, "When was the last time you saw your daughter, Mr. Short?"

"Betty came west in the spring of '43. Stars in her eyes and hanky-panky on her mind. I hadn't seen her since I left that dried-up old ginch of a wife of mine in Charlestown, Mass., on March 1, 1930 A.D. and never looked back. But Betty wrote me and said she needed a flop, so I—"

Lee interrupted: "Cut the travelogue, pop. When was the last time you saw Elizabeth?"

I said, "Back off, partner. The man is cooperating. Go on, Mr. Short."

Cleo Short dug in with his chair, glaring at Lee. "Before punchy here got wise, I was gonna tell you that I reached into my own savings and sent Betty a C-note to come west on, then I promised her three squares and a five-spot a week mad money if she kept the house tidy. A generous offer, if you want my opinion. But Betty had other things on her mind. She was a lousy housekeeper, so I gave her the boot on June 2, 1943 A.D., and I ain't seen her since."

I wrote the information down, then asked, "Did you know she was in L.A. recently?"

Cleo Short quit glaring at Lee and glared at me. "No."

"Did she have any enemies that you knew of?"

"Just herself."

Lee said, "No cute answers, Pops."

I whispered, "Let him talk," then said out loud, "Where did Elizabeth go when she left here in June of '43?"

Short jabbed a finger at Lee. "You tell your pal he calls me Pops I call him stumblebum! Tell him disrespect's a two-way street! Tell him I repaired Chief CB Horrall's Maytag 821 model myself, and I mean *air* tight!"

Lee walked into the bathroom; I saw him chasing a handful of pills with sink water. I put on my calmest white hat voice: "Mr. Short, where did Elizabeth go in June of '43?"

Short said, "That palooka lays a hand on me, I'll fix his wagon *air* tight."

"I'm sure you will. Would you ans—"

"Betty moved up to Santa Barbara, got a job at the Camp Cooke PX. She sent me a postcard in July. It said some soldier beat her up bad. That was the last I ever heard from her."

"Did the card mention the soldier's name?"

"No."

"Did it mention the names of any of her friends up at Camp Cooke?"

"No."

"Any boyfriends?"

"Hah!"

I put my pen down. "Why 'hah'?"

The old man laughed so hard that I thought his chicken chest would explode. Lee walked out of the bathroom; I gave him a sign to ease off. He nodded and sat down next to me; we waited for Short to laugh himself out. When he was down to a dry chortle, I said, "Tell me about Betty and men."

Short giggled. "She liked them and they liked her. Betty believed in quantity before quality, and I don't think she was too good at saying no, unlike her mother."

"Be specific," I said. "Names, dates, descriptions."

"You musta caught too many in the ring, Sonny, 'cause your seabag's leaky. Einstein couldn't remember the names of all Betty's boyfriends, and my name ain't Albert."

"Give us the names you do remember."

Short hooked his thumbs in his belt and rocked in the chair like a cut-rate cock of the walk. "Betty was man crazy, soldier crazy. She went for lounge lizards and anything white in a uniform. When she was supposed to be keeping house for me she was out prowling Hollywood Boulevard, cadging drinks off servicemen. When she was staying here this place was like a branch of the USO."

Lee said, "Are you calling your own daughter a tramp?"

Short shrugged. "I've got five daughters. One bad apple ain't so bad."

Lee's anger was oozing out of him; I put a restraining hand on his arm and could almost feel his blood buzzing. "What about names, Mr. Short?"

"Tom, Dick, Harry. Those punks took one look at Cleo Short and amscrayed with Betty pronto. That's as specific as I can get. You look for anything not too ugly in a uniform, you won't go wrong."

I flipped to a fresh notebook page. "What about employment? Was Betty holding down a job when she stayed here?"

The old man shouted: "Betty's job was working for me! She said she was looking for movie work, but that was a lie! All she wanted to do was parade the Boulevard in those black getups of hers and chase men! She ruined my bathtub dying her stuff black, then she took off before I could dock the damage out of her wages! Prowling the streets like a black widow spider, no wonder she got hurt! It's her mother's fault, not mine! No-count shanty Irish bitch! Not my fault!"

Lee drew a hard finger across his throat; we walked out to the street, leaving Cleo Short screaming at his four walls. Lee said, "Jesus fuck"; I sighed, "Yeah," thinking of the fact that we'd just been handed the entire U.S. armed forces as suspects.

I dug in my pockets for a coin. "Toss you for who writes it up?"

Lee said, "You do it, okay? I want to stick at Junior Nash's pad and get some license numbers."

"Try and get some sleep, too."

"I will."

"No, you won't."

"I can't shit a shitter. Look, will you go over to the house and keep Kay company? She's been worried about me, and I don't want her to be alone."

I thought of what I'd said at 39th and Norton last night— that statement of what all three of us knew but never talked about, that move forward that only Kay had the guts to take. "Sure, Lee."

*   *   *

I found Kay in her usual weeknight posture—reading on the living room couch. She didn't look up when I walked in, she just blew a lazy smoke ring and said, "Hi, Dwight."

I took a chair across the coffee table from her. "How'd you know it was me?"

Kay circled a passage in the book. "Lee stomps, you tread cautiously."

I laughed. "It's symbolic, but don't tell anybody."

Kay stubbed out her cigarette and put the book down. "You sound worried."

I said, "Lee's all bent out of shape on the dead girl. He got us detached to work the investigation when we should be going after a priority warrantee, and he's taking Benzedrine and starting to go a little squirrely. Has he told you about her?"

Kay nodded. "A little."

"Have you read the papers?"

"I've avoided them."

"Well, the girl is being played up as the hottest number since the atom bomb. There's a hundred men working a single homicide, Ellis Loew's looking to get fat off of it, Lee's cuckoo on the subject—"

Kay disarmed my tirade with a smile. "And *you* were front page news on Monday, but you're stale bread today. And you want to go after your big bad robber man and get yourself another headline."

"Touché, but that's only part of it."

"I know. Once you got the headline, you'd hide out and not read the papers."

I sighed. "Jesus, I wish you weren't so much smarter than me."

"And I wish you weren't so cautious and complicated. Dwight, what is going to happen with us?"

"The three of us?"

"No, *us*."

I looked around the living room, all wood and leather and Deco chromium. There was a glass-fronted mahogany cabinet; it was filled with Kay's cashmere sweaters, all the shades of the rainbow at forty dollars a pop. The woman herself, South Dakota white trash molded by a cop's love, sat across from me, and for once I said exactly what was on my mind. "You'd never leave him. You'd never leave this. Maybe if you did, maybe if Lee and I were quits as partners, maybe then we'd have a chance together. But you'd never give it all up."

Kay took her time lighting a cigarette. Exhaling a breath of smoke, she said, "You know what he's done for me?"

I said, "And for me."

Kay tilted her head back and eyed the ceiling, brushed stucco with mahogany wainscoting. Blowing smoke rings, she said, "I had such a schoolgirl crush on you. Bobby De Witt and Lee used to drag me to the fights. I brought my sketch pad so I wouldn't feel like one of those awful women buttering up their men by pretending they liked it. What I liked was you. The way you made fun of yourself with your teeth, the way you covered up so you wouldn't get hit. Then you joined the Department, and Lee told me how he heard you informed on those Japanese friends of yours. I didn't hate you for it, it just made you seem more real to me. The zoot suit thing, too. You were my storybook hero, only the stories were real, little bits and pieces here and there. Then the fight came along, and even though I hated the idea of it I told Lee to go ahead, because it seemed to mean the three of us were meant to be."

I thought of a dozen things to say, all of them true, and just about the two of us. But I couldn't, and ran to Lee for cover.

"I don't want you to worry about Bobby De Witt. When he gets out, I'll lean on him. Hard. He'll never come near you or Lee."

Kay took her eyes off the ceiling and fixed me with a strange look, hard but sad underneath. "I've given up worrying about Bobby. Lee can handle him."

"I think Lee's afraid of him."

"He is. But I think it's because he knows so much about me, and Lee's afraid he'll let everyone know. Not that anyone cares."

"I care. And if I lean on De Witt, he'll be lucky to talk at all."

Kay stood up. "For a man with an up-for-grabs heart, you are such a hardcase. I'm going to bed. Good night, Dwight."

When I heard a Schubert quartet coming from Kay's bedroom, I took pen and paper from the stationery cupboard and wrote out my report on the questioning of Elizabeth Short's father. I included mention of his "air tight" alibi, his account of the girl's behavior when she lived with him in '43, the beating she got from a Camp Cooke soldier and her parade of nameless boyfriends. Padding the report with unnecessary details kept my mind most of the way off Kay, and when I finished I made myself two ham sandwiches, chased them with a glass of milk and fell asleep on the couch.

My dreams were mug shot flashes of recent bad guys, Ellis Loew representing the right side of the law with felony numbers stenciled across his chest. Betty Short joined him in black and white, full face and left profile views. Then all the faces dissolved into LAPD report forms rolling out endlessly as I tried to jot down information on Junior Nash's whereabouts in the blank spaces. I woke up with a headache, knowing I was in for a very long day.

It was dawn. I walked out to the porch and picked up the morning *Herald*. The headline was "Hunt Boyfriends in Torture Killing," a portrait photo of Elizabeth Short centered directly below it. It was captioned, "The Black Dahlia," followed by, "Authorities today were searching into the love life of 22-year-old Elizabeth Short, victim of the 'Werewolf Murder,' whose romances had changed her, according to friends, from an innocent girl to a black-clad, man-crazy delinquent known as the Black Dahlia."

I felt Kay beside me. She grabbed the paper, skimming the front page, giving a slight shudder. Handing it back, she asked, "Will all this be over soon?"

I flipped through the front section. Elizabeth Short took up six whole pages, most of the ink portraying her as a slinky femme fatale in a tight black dress. "No," I said.

9

REPORTERS WERE surrounding University Station. The parking lot was packed and the curb was lined with radio trucks, so I double-parked, stuck "Official Police Vehicle" signs under my wiper blades and pushed through the cordon of newshounds, ducking my head to avoid being recognized. It didn't work; I heard "Buck-kee!" and "Blei-chert," then hands grabbed at me. My jacket pocket was ripped loose, and I shoved myself the rest of the way inside.

The entrance hall was filled with daywatch blues going on duty; a connecting door opened up into a bustling squadroom. Cots lined the walls; I saw Lee passed out on one of them, sheets of newspaper covering his legs. Phones were ringing at desks all around me, and my headache came back, the pounding twice as bad. Ellis Loew was tacking slips of paper to a bulletin board; I tapped him hard on the shoulder.

He turned around. I said, "I want out of this circus. I'm a War-rants officer, not a Homicide dick, and I've got priority fugitives. I want to get un-detached. *Now*."

Loew hissed, "No. You work for me, and I want you on the Short case. That's final, absolute and irrevocable. And I'll brook no prima donna demands from you, Officer. Do you understand?"

"Ellis, goddamnit!"

"You get stripes on your sleeve before you call me that, Bleichert. Until then it's Mr. Loew. Now go read Millard's summary report."

I stormed over to the rear of the squadroom. Russ Millard was asleep in a chair, his legs propped up on the desk in front of him. Four typed sheets of paper were tacked to the corkboard wall a few feet away. I read:

First Summary Report
187 P.C., Vict: Short, Elizabeth Ann, W.F.
D.O.B. 7/29/24. Filed 1/17/47 0600 Hrs.

Gentlemen—
Here's the 1st summary on E. Short, D.O.D. 1/15/47, 39th and Norton, Leimert Park.

1. 33 phony or probable phony confessions so far. Obviously innocent confessors have been released, incoherent and seriously imbalanced being held at City Jail awaiting alibi checks and sanity hearings. Known deviates being questioned by Dr. De River, consulting psychiatrist, with Det. Div. backup. Nothing solid yet.

2. *Results of prlim. post mort. and follow-up: vict. choked to death on ear to ear knife slash thru mouth. No alcohol or narcotics in blood at time of death. (For det. see case file 14-187-47)*

3. *Boston P.D. doing background check on E. Short, family and old boyfriends and their whereabouts at time of murder. Father (C. Short) has valid alibi—he is eliminated as suspect.*

4. *Camp Cooke CID is checking out reports of beating E. Short received from soldier when she worked at PX in 9/43. E. Short arrested for underaged drinking in 9/43, CID says soldiers she was arrested with are all overseas, thus eliminated as suspects.*

5. *Sewers being dragged citywide for E. Short's clothing. All women's clothing found will be analyzed at Central Crime Lab. (See crime lab sum. rpts. for det.)*

6. *Citywide field interrogation rpts. 1/12/47— 1/15/47 collated and read. One follow-up: Hollywood woman called in complaint about shouts of "weird sounding gibberish" in H.W. Hills nights of 1/13 and 1/14. Result of follow-up: put off as party revelers making noise. Field officers: disregard this occurrence.*

7. *From verified phone tips: E. Short lived most of 12/46 in San Diego, at home of Mrs. Elvera French. Vict. met Mrs. French's daughter, Dorothy, at movie theater where Dorothy worked, told (unverified) story about being abandoned by husband. Frenches took her in, and E. Short told them conflicting stories: she was widow of air corps major; pregnant by navy pilot; engaged to army flyer. Vict. had many dates with different men during her stay at French house. (See 14-187-47 interviews for det.)*

8. *E. Short left French house on 1/9/47 in company of man she called "Red." (Desc. as: W.M., 25-30, tall, "handsome", 170-180, red hair, blue eyes.) "Red" allegedly salesman. Drives a pre-war Dodge sedan with Huntington Park tags. Vehicle cross-check initiated. APB issued on "Red".*

9. Verified info: Val Gordon (W.F.) Riverside, Calif. called in, said she is sister of deceased air corps major Matt Gordon. Said: E. Short wrote to her and her parents in Fall of '46, shortly after Maj. Gordon died in plane crash. Lied about being Gordon's fiancee, requested $ from them. Parents, Miss Gordon, denied request.

10. Trunk belonging to E. Short located at Railway Express office, downtown L.A. (R.E. clerk saw vict.'s name and picture in papers, recalled her storing trunk in late 11/46.) Trunk being gone over. Carbons of 100's of love letters to various men (mostly servicemen) found, and (many fewer) mash notes written to her. Also, many photos of E. Short with servicemen in trunk. Letters being read, names and descriptions of men being collated.

11. Verified phone info: former Air Corps Lt. J.G. Fickling called from Mobile, Ala. when he saw E. Short's name and picture in Mobile papers. Said he and vict. had "brief affair" in Boston in late '43, and "she had about 10 other boyfriends on line at all times." Fickling has verified alibi for time of murder. Eliminated as suspect, also denies ever having been engaged to E. Short.

12. Numerous tips being phoned in to all LAPD and Sheriff's divisions. Crank-sounding dismissed, others routed to applicable area squadrooms thru Cent. Homicide. All tips being cross-filed.

13. Address verified info: E. Short lived at these addresses in 1946. (Names following addresses are of caller or verified residents of same address. All but Linda Martin verified by D.M.V. records.)

13-A-1611 N. Orange Dr., Hollywood. (Harold Costa, Donald Leyes, Marjorie Graham) 6024 Carlos Ave., Hollywood. 1842 N. Cherokee, Hollywood (Linda Martin, Sheryl Saddon) 53 Linden, Long Beach.

14. Results of SID findings in Leimert Park vact lots: no woman's clothing found, numerous knives and knife blades found, all too rusted to be murder weapon. No blood found.

15. Results of Leimert Park canvasing (with mugs of E. Short): zero (all sightings obvious crank stuff.)

In conclusion: I believe all investigatory efforts should be centered around questionings of E. Short's known associates, particularly her numerous boyfriends. Sergeant Sears and I will be going to San Diego to question her K.A.'s there. Between the APB on "Red" and the L.A. K.A. questionings we should get salient information.

Russell A. Millard, Lt.,
Badge 493, Central Homicide

I turned around to find Millard watching me. He said, "Off the top of your head, what do you think?"

I fingered my ripped pocket. "Is she worth it, Lieutenant?"

Millard smiled; I noticed that rumpled clothes and a razor stubble didn't dent his aura of class. "I think so. Your partner thinks so."

"Lee's chasing bogeymen, Lieutenant."

"You can call me Russ, you know."

"Okay, Russ."

"What did you and Blanchard get from the father?"

I handed Millard my report. "Nothing specific, just more dope on the girl as a tramp. What's with this Black Dahlia stuff?"

Millard slapped the arms of his chair. "We can thank Bevo Means for that. He went down to Long Beach and talked to the desk clerk at the hotel where the girl stayed last summer. The clerk told him Betty Short always wore tight black dresses. Bevo thought of that movie with Alan Ladd, *The Blue Dahlia*, and took it from there. I figure the image is good for at least another dozen confessions a day. As Harry says when he's had a few, 'Hollywood will fuck you when no one else will.' You're a smart bad penny, Bucky. What do you think?"

"I think I want to go back to Warrants. Will you grease it with Loew?"

Millard shook his head. "No. Will you answer my question?"

I choked down the urge to smash or beg. "She said yes or no to the wrong guy, at the wrong time, at the wrong place. And since she's had more rubber burned on her than the San Berdoo Highway, and doesn't know how to tell the truth, I'd say that finding that wrong guy is going to be a hell of a job."

Millard stood up and stretched. "Bright penny, you go up to Hollywood Station and meet Bill Koenig, then you two go question the tenants at the Hollywood addresses on my summary. Stress the boyfriend angle. Keep Koenig on a tight leash if you can, and you write the report, because Billy's practically illiterate. Report back here when you're finished."

My headache going migraine, I obeyed. The last thing I heard before hitting the street was a group of cops chortling over Betty Short's love letters.

* * *

I picked up Koenig at Hollywood Station and drove with him to the Carlos Avenue address. Parking in front of 6024, I said, "You're ranking, Sarge. How do you want to play this?"

Koenig cleared his throat loudly, then swallowed the wad of phlegm he brought up. "Fritzie does the talking, but he's home sick. How about you talk, I stand backup?" He opened his jacket to show me a leather sap stuck into the waistband. "You think it's a muscle job?"

I said, "Talk job," and got out of the car. There was an old lady sitting on the porch of 6024, a three-story brown clapboard house with a ROOMS FOR RENT sign staked on the lawn. She saw me walking over, closed her Bible and said, "I'm sorry, young man, but I only rent to career girls with references."

I flashed my shield. "We're police officers, ma'am. We came to talk to you about Betty Short."

The old woman said, "I knew her as Beth," then shot a look at Koenig, standing on the lawn surreptitiously picking his nose.

I said, "He's looking for clues."

The woman snorted, "He won't find them inside that big beak of his. Who killed Beth Short, Officer?"

I got out pen and notepad. "That's what we're here to find out. Could I have your name, please?"

"I'm Miss Loretta Janeway. I called the police when I heard Beth's name on the radio."

"Miss Janeway, when did Elizabeth Short live at this address?"

"I checked my records right after I heard that news broadcast. Beth stayed in my third-floor right-rear room from last September fourteenth to October nineteenth."

"Was she referred to you?"

"No. I remember it very well, because Beth was such a pretty girl. She knocked on the door and said she was walking up Gower when she saw my sign. She said she was an aspiring actress and needed an inexpensive room until she got her big break. I said I'd heard that one before, and told her she'd do well to lose that awful

Boston accent of hers. Well, Beth just smiled and said, 'Now is the time for all good men to come to the aid of their party' with no accent at all. Then she said, 'See! See how I take direction!' She was so eager to please that I rented her the room, even though my policy is not to rent to movie types."

I wrote the pertinent info down, then asked, "Was Beth a good tenant?"

Miss Janeway shook her head. "God rest her soul, but she was an awful tenant, and she made me regret bending my policy on movie picture types. She was always late on her rent, always hocking her jewelry for food money and trying to get me to let her pay by the day instead of the week. A dollar a day she wanted to pay! Can you imagine how much space my ledgers would take up if I let all my tenants do that?"

"Did Beth socialize with the other tenants?"

"Good lord, no. The third-floor right-rear room has got private steps, so Beth didn't have to come in through the front door like the other girls, and she never attended any of the coffee klatches I put on for the girls after church on Sunday. Beth *never* went to church herself, and she told me, 'Girls are good for chitchat once in a blue moon, but give me boys any day.'"

"Here's my most important question, Miss Janeway. Did Beth have any boyfriends while she was living here?"

The old woman picked up the Bible and hugged it to herself. "Officer, if they'd come in the front door like the other girls' beaus, I would have seen them. I don't want to blaspheme the dead, so let's just say I heard lots of footsteps on Beth's stairs at the most ungodly hours."

"Did Beth ever mention any enemies? Anybody she was afraid of?"

"No."

"When was the last time you saw her?"

"Late October, the day she moved out. She said, 'I've found more simpatico digs' in her best California girl voice."

"Did she say where she was moving to?"

Miss Janeway said "No," then leaned toward me confidingly and pointed to Koenig, loping back to the car tugging at his crotch. "You should talk to that man about his hygiene. Frankly, it's disgusting."

I said, "Thank you, Miss Janeway," walked to the car and got in behind the wheel.

Koenig grunted, "What did the cooze say about me?"

"She said you're cute."

"Yeah?"

"Yeah."

"What else did she say?"

"That a man like you could make her feel young again."

"Yeah?"

"Yeah. I told her to forget it, that you're married."

"I ain't married."

"I know."

"Then why'd you tell her that?"

I pulled out into traffic. "You want her sending you mash notes at the Bureau?"

"Oh, I get it. What did she say about Fritzie?"

"Does she know Fritzie?"

Koenig looked at me like *I* was mentally defective. "Lots of people talk about Fritzie behind his back."

"What do they say?"

"Lies."

"What kind of lies?"

"Bad lies."

"For instance?"

"Lies like he got the syph fucking hooers when he worked Ad Vice. Like he got docked off a month from duty to take the mercury cure. Like he got bounced to Central dicks for it. Bad lies, even worse stuff than that."

Chills were tickling my spine. I turned onto Cherokee and said, "Such as?"

Koenig slid closer to me. "You pumping me, Bleichert? You looking for bad things to say about Fritzie?"

"No. Just curious."

"Curiosity killed the kitty cat. You remember that."

"I will. What did you get on the Sergeant's Exam, Bill?"

"I don't know."

"What?"

"Fritzie took it for me. Remember the kitty cat, Bleichert. I don't want nobody saying nothing bad about my partner."

1842, a big stucco apartment house, came into view. I pulled over and parked, muttered, "Talk job," then headed straight for the lobby.

A wall directory listed S. Saddon and nine other names—but no Linda Martin—in apartment 604. I took the elevator up to the sixth floor, walked down a hallway smelling faintly of marijuana and rapped on the door. Big band music died out, the door opened and a youngish woman in a sparkly Egyptian outfit was standing there, holding a papier mâché headdress. She said, "Are you the driver from RKO?"

I said, "Police." The door shut in my face. I heard a toilet flushing; the girl returned a moment later, and I walked into the apartment uninvited. The living room was high-ceilinged and arched; sloppily made-up bunk beds lined the walls. Suitcases, valises and steamer trunks were spilling out of an open closet door, and a linoleum table was wedged diagonally against a set of bunks without mattresses. The table was covered with cosmetics and vanity mirrors; the cracked wood floor beside it was dusted with spilled rouge and face powder.

The girl said, "Is this about those jaywalking tickets I forgot to pay? Listen, I've got three days on *Curse of the Mummy's Tomb* at RKO, and when I get paid I'll send you a check. Is that all right?"

I said, "This is about Elizabeth Short, Miss—"

The girl put out a big stage groan. "Saddon. Sheryl with a Y-L Saddon. Listen, I talked to a policeman on the phone this morning. Sergeant something or other with a bad stutter. He asked me nine thousand questions about Betty and her nine thousand boyfriends, and I told him nine thousand times that lots of girls bunk here and date lots of guys, and most of them are fly-by-nights. I told him that Betty lived here from early November to early December, that she paid a dollar a day just like the rest of us, and I didn't remember the names of any of her dates. So can I go now? The extra truck's due any minute, and I need this job."

Sheryl Saddon was out of breath and sweating from her metallic costume. I pointed to a bunk bed. "Sit down and answer my questions, or I'll roust you for the reefers you flushed down the toilet."

The three-day Cleopatra obeyed, giving me a look that would have withered Julius Caesar. I said, "First question. Does a Linda Martin live here?"

Sheryl Saddon grabbed a pack of Old Golds off the bunk and lit up. "I told Sergeant Stutter already. Betty mentioned Linda Martin a couple of times. She roomed at Betty's other place, the one over on De Longpre and Orange. And you need evidence to arrest someone, you know."

I took out my pen and notebook. "What about Betty's enemies? Threats of violence against her?"

"Betty's trouble wasn't enemies, it was too many friends, if you follow my drift. Get it? Friends like in *boy*friends?"

"Smart girl. Any of them ever threaten her?"

"Not that I know of. Listen, can we hurry this up?"

"Simmer down. What did Betty do for work while she was staying here?"

Sheryl Saddon snorted, "Comedian. Betty didn't work. She bummed change from the other girls here, and she cadged drinks and dinner off grandfather types down on the Boulevard. A couple of times she took off for two or three days and came back with money, then she told these fish stories about where it came from. She was such a little liar that nobody ever believed a word she said."

"Tell me about the fish stories. And about Betty's lies in general."

Sheryl stubbed out her cigarette and lit another one immediately. She smoked silently for a few moments, and I could tell that the actress part of her was warming to the idea of caricaturing Betty Short. Finally she said, "You know all this Black Dahlia stuff in the papers?"

"Yes."

"Well, Betty always dressed in black as a gimmick to impress casting directors when she made rounds with the other girls, which wasn't often, because she liked to sleep till noon every day. But sometimes she'd tell you she was wearing black because her father died or because she was mourning the boys who died in the war. Then the next day she'd tell you her father was alive. When she was out for a couple of days and came back flush, she'd tell one girl a rich uncle died and left her a bundle and another that she won the money playing poker in Gardena. She told everybody nine thousand lies about being married to nine thousand different war heroes. You get the picture?"

I said. "Vividly. Let's change the subject."

"Goody. How about international finance?"

"How about the movies? You girls are all trying to break in, right?"

Sheryl gave me a vamp look. "I have broken in. I was in *The Cougar Woman*, *Attack of the Phantom Gargoyle* and *Sweet Will Be the Honeysuckle*."

"Congratulations. Did Betty ever get any movie work?"

"Maybe. Maybe once, but then again maybe not, because Betty was such a liar."

"Go on."

"Well, on Thanksgiving all the kids on the sixth floor chipped in for a potluck supper, and Betty was flush and bought two whole cases of beer. She was bragging about being in a movie, and she was showing around this viewfinder that she said the director gave her. Now lots of girls have got chintzy little viewfinders that movie guys give them, but this was an expensive one, on a chain, with a little velvet case. I remember that Betty was on cloud nine that night, talking up a blue streak."

"Did she tell you the name of the movie?"

Sheryl shook her head. "No."

"Did she mention any names associated with the movie?"

"If she did, I don't remember."

I looked around the room, counted twelve bunk beds at a dollar a night apiece and thought of a landlord getting fat. I said, "Do you know what a casting couch is?"

The mock Cleopatra's eyes burned. "Not me, buster. Not this girl *ever.*"

"Betty Short?"

"Probably."

I heard a horn honking, walked to the window and looked out. A flatbed truck with a dozen Cleopatras and pharaohs in the back was at the curb directly behind my car. I turned around to tell Sheryl, but she was already out the door.

*　*　*

The last address on Millard's list was 1611 North Orange Drive, a pink stucco tourist flop in the shadow of Hollywood High School. Koenig snapped out of his nose-picking reverie as I double-parked in front of it, pointing to two men perusing a stack of newspapers on the steps. "I'll take them, you take the skirts. You got names for them?"

I said, "Maybe Harold Costa and Donald Leyes. You look tired, Sarge. Don't you want to sit this one out?"

"I'm bored. What should I ask them guys?"

"I'll handle them, Sarge."

"You remember the kitty cat, Bleichert. Same thing happened to him happens to guys who try to jerk my chain when Fritzie ain't around. Now what do I roust them guys for?"

"Sarge—"

Koenig sprayed me with spittle. "I'm ranking, hotshot! You do what Big Bill says!"

Seeing red, I said, "Get alibis and ask them if Betty Short ever engaged in prostitution"; Koenig snickered in reply. I took the lawn and steps at a run, the two men moving aside to let me through. The front door opened into a shabby sitting room; a group of young people were sitting around, smoking and reading movie mags. I said, "Police. I'm looking for Linda Martin, Marjorie Graham, Harold Costa and Donald Leyes."

A honey blonde in a slacks suit dog-eared her *Photoplay*. "I'm Marjorie Graham, and Hal and Don are outside."

The rest of the people got up and fanned out into the hallway, like I was a big dose of bad news. I said, "This is about Elizabeth Short. Did any of you know her?"

I got a half dozen negative head shakes, shocked and sad looks; outside I heard Koenig shouting, "You tell me true! Was the Short bimbo peddling it?"

Marjorie Graham said, "I was the one who called the police, Officer. I gave them Linda's name because I knew she knew Betty, too."

I pointed to the door. "What about those guys outside?"

"Don and Harold? They both dated Betty. Harold called you because they knew you'd be looking for clues. Who's that man yelling at them?"

I ignored the question, sat down beside Marjorie Graham and got out my notebook. "What can you tell me about Betty that I don't know already? Can you give me *facts*? Names of other boy-friends, descriptions, specific dates? Enemies? Possible motives for somebody wanting to kill her?"

The woman flinched; I realized I was raising my voice. Keeping it low, I said, "Let's start with dates. When did Betty live here?"

"Early December," Marjorie Graham said. "I remember because there was a bunch of us sitting here listening to a radio program on the fifth anniversary of Pearl Harbor when she checked in."

"So that was December seventh?"

"Yes."

"And how long was she here?"

"No more than a week or so."

"How did she know about this place?"

"I think Linda Martin told her about it."

Millard's memo stated that Betty Short spent most of December in San Diego. I said, "But she moved out shortly afterward, right?"

"Yes."

"Why, Miss Graham? Betty lived in three places that we know of last fall—all in Hollywood. Why did she move around so much?"

Marjorie Graham took a tissue from her purse and fretted it. "Well, I don't really know for sure."

"Was some jealous boyfriend after her?"

"I don't think so."

"Miss Graham, what *do* you think?"

Marjorie sighed. "Officer, Betty used up people. She borrowed money from them and told them stories, and … well, a lot of pretty hard-nosed kids live here, and I think they saw through Betty pretty quick."

I said, "Tell me about Betty. You liked her, didn't you?"

"Yes. She was sweet and trusting and sort of dumb, but … inspired. She had this strange gift, if you want to call it that. She'd do anything to be liked, and she sort of took on the mannerisms of whoever she was with. Everybody here smokes, and Betty started smoking to be one of the kids, even though it was bad for her asthma and she hated cigarettes. And the funny thing is that she'd try to walk and talk like you, but she was always herself when she was doing it. She was always Betty or Beth or whatever nickname for Elizabeth she was going by at that moment."

I kicked the sad dope around in my head. "What did you and Betty talk about?"

Marjorie said, "Mostly I just listened to Betty talk. We used to sit here and listen to the radio, and Betty told stories. Love stories about all these war heroes—Lieutenant Joe and Major Matt and on and on. I knew they were just fantasies. Sometimes she talked about becoming a movie star, like all she had to do was walk around in her black dresses and sooner or later she'd get discovered. That sort of made me mad, because I've been taking classes at the Pasadena Playhouse, and I know that acting is hard work."

I flipped to my notes from the Sheryl Saddon questioning. "Miss Graham, did Betty talk about being in a movie sometime in late November?"

"Yes. The first night she was here she was bragging about it. She said she had a co-starring role, and she showed around a viewfinder. A couple of boys pressed her for details, and she told one of them it was at Paramount, another that it was at Fox. I thought she was just fibbing to get attention."

I wrote "Names" on a clean page and underlined it three times. "Marjorie, what about names? Betty's boyfriends, people you saw her with?"

"Well, I know she went out with Don Leyes and Harold Costa, and I saw her once with a sailor, and I ..."

Marjorie faltered; I caught a troubled look in her eyes. "What is it? You can tell me."

Marjorie's voice was stretched thin. "Right before she moved out I saw Betty and Linda Martin talking to this big older woman up on the Boulevard. She was wearing a man's suit, and she had short hair like a man. I only saw them with her that one time, so maybe it doesn't mean—"

"Are you saying the woman was a lesbian?"

Marjorie bobbed her head up and down and reached for a Kleenex; Bill Koenig stepped inside and hooked a finger at me. I walked over to him. He whispered, "Them guys talked, said the stiff peddled her twat when she got strapped bad. I called Mr. Loew. He said to keep that zipped, 'cause it's a better caper if she's a nice young cooze."

I bit off an urge to spill the dyke lead; the DA and his flunky would probably quash it, too. I said, "I've got another quick one here. Get statements from those guys, okay?"

Koenig giggled and walked outside; I told Marjorie to sit still and moved to the rear of the lobby. There was a registration desk, an open ledger on top of it. I stood at the counter and leafed through the pages until I saw a childishly scrawled "Linda Martin," with "Room 14" printed across from it.

I took the first-floor corridor back to the room, knocked on the door and waited for an answer. When none came after five seconds, I tried the knob. It gave, and I pushed the door open.

It was a cramped little room containing nothing but an unmade bed. I checked the closet; it was dead empty. The nightstand held a stack of yesterday's papers folded open to "Werewolf Murder" brouhaha; suddenly I *knew* the Martin girl was a lamster. I got down on the floor and ran a hand under the bed, brushed a flat object and pulled it out.

It was a red plastic change purse. I opened it and found two pennies, a dime and an identification card for Cornhusker High School, Cedar Rapids, Iowa. The card was made out to Lorna Martilkova, DOB 12/19/31. There was a photo of a beautiful young girl below the school's crest; in my mind I was already typing out an all-points juvie runaway warrant.

Marjorie Graham appeared in the doorway. I held out the ID card; she said, "That's Linda. God, she's only fifteen."

"Middle-aged for Hollywood. When did you see her last?"

"This morning. I told her I called the police, that they'd be coming by to talk to us about Betty. Was that the wrong thing to do?"

"You couldn't have known. And thanks."

Marjorie smiled, and I found myself wishing her a speedy one-way trip out of movieland. I kept the wish silent as I smiled back and walked outside. On the porch, Bill Koenig was standing at parade rest and Donald Leyes and Harold Costa were sprawled in lounge chairs with that green-at-the-gills look that comes with taking a few rabbit punches.

Koenig said, "They didn't do it."

I said, "No shit, Sherlock."

Koenig said, "My name ain't Sherlock."

I said, "No shit."

Koenig said, "What?"

* * *

At Hollywood Station I exercised the Warrants cops' special prerogative, issuing an all-points juvenile runaway warrant and a priority material witness warrant on Lorna Martilkova/Linda Martin, leaving the report forms with the daywatch boss, who told me the APBs would hit the air within the hour, and that he would send officers over to 1611 North Orange Drive to question the tenants on Linda/Lorna's possible whereabouts. With that taken care of, I wrote my report on the series of questionings, stressing Betty Short as a habitual liar and the possibility that she acted in a movie sometime in November of '46. Before finishing it up, I wavered on whether to mention Marjorie Graham's lead on the old dyke. If Ellis Loew got ahold of the dope he would probably quash it along with the skinny on Betty as a part-time prostie, so I decided to omit it from the report and give the information verbally to Russ Millard.

From a squadroom phone I called the Screen Actor's Guild and Central Casting and inquired about Elizabeth Short. A clerk told me that no one by that name or any diminutive of the name Elizabeth was ever listed with them, making it unlikely that she had appeared in a legit Hollywood production. I hung up thinking of the movie as another Betty fairy tale, the viewfinder a fairy-tale prop.

It was late afternoon. Being free of Koenig felt like surviving cancer and the three interviews felt like an overdose of Betty/Beth Short and her low-rent last months on earth. I was tired and hungry, so I drove to the house for a sandwich and a nap—and walked straight into another installment of the Black Dahlia Show.

Kay and Lee were standing around the dining room table, examining crime scene photos shot at 39th and Norton. There was Betty Short's bashed head; Betty Short's slashed breasts; Betty Short's empty bottom half and Betty Short's wide-open legs—all in glossy black and white. Kay was nervously smoking and shooting little glances at the pictures; Lee was eyeballing them, his face twitching in a half dozen directions, the Benzedrine man from outer space. Neither said a word to me; I just stood there playing straight man to the most celebrated stiff in L.A. history.

Finally Kay said, "Hi, Dwight," and Lee stabbed a shaky finger at a close-up of the torso mutilations. "It's not a random job, I know it. Vern Smith says some guy just picked her up on the street, took her someplace and tortured her, then dumped her in the lot. Horseshit. The guy who did this hated her for a reason and wanted the whole goddamn world to know. Jesus, two fucking days he cut her. Babe, you took pre-med classes, you think this guy had medical training? You know, like some kind of mad doctor type?"

Kay put out her cigarette and said, "Lee, Dwight's here"; Lee wheeled around.

I said, "Partner—" and Lee tried to wink, smile and speak at the same time.

It came off as one awful grimace; when he got out, "Bucky, listen to Kay, I knew all the college I bought her would do me some good," I had to look away.

Kay's voice was soft, patient. "This kind of theorizing is just nonsense, but I'll give you a theory if you'll eat something to calm yourself down."

"Theory on, teach."

"Well, it's just a guess, but maybe there were two killers, because the torture cuts are crude, while the bisection and the cut on the abdomen, which are obviously both postmortem, are neat and clean. Maybe there's just one killer though, and after he killed the girl he calmed down, then bisected her and made the abdominal cut. And anybody could have removed the internal organs with the body in two parts. I think mad doctors are only in the movies. Sweetie, *you* have to calm down. You have to quit taking those pills and you have to eat. Listen to Dwight, he'll tell you that."

I looked at Lee. He said, "I'm too hopped-up to eat," then stuck out his hand like I'd just walked in. "Hey, partner. You learn anything good about our girl today?"

I thought of telling him I learned she wasn't worth a hundred full-time cops; I thought of spilling the dyke lead and Betty Short as a sad little floozy-liar to back the claim up. But Lee's dope-juiced face made me say, "Nothing that's worth you doing this to yourself. Nothing that's worth seeing you useless when a bimbo you sent to Quentin is three days away from L.A. Think of your little sister seeing you this way. Think of her—"

I stopped when tears started streaming from Lee's outer-space eyes. Now *he* just stood there like the straight man to his own blood kin. Kay moved between us, a hand on each of our shoulders. I walked out before Lee began weeping for real.

*   *   *

University Station was another outpost of Black Dahlia mania.

A wager pool sign-up list was posted in the locker room. It was in the form of a crudely drawn crap table felt, featuring betting spaces labeled "Solved—pay 2 to 1," "Random sex job—pay 4 to 1," "Unsolved—even money," "Boyfriend(s) pay 1 to 4," and "'Red'—no odds unless suspect captured." The "House $ man" was listed as Sergeant Shiner, and so far the big action was on "boyfriend(s)," with a dozen officers signed up, all plopping down a sawbuck to win two-fifty.

The squadroom was more comic relief. Someone had hung the two halves of a cheap black dress from the doorway. Harry Sears, half gassed, was waltzing around the Negro cleaning woman, introducing her as the real Black Dahlia, the best colored songbird since Billie Holiday. They were taking nips from Harry's flask, the cleaning lady belting gospel numbers while officers trying to talk on the phone clamped hands to their free ears.

The straight business was frenzied, too. Men were working with DMV registrations and Huntington Park street directories, trying to put together a lead on the "Red" Betty Short left San Dago with; others were reading her love letters, and two officers were on the DMV police line getting info on the license numbers Lee had gotten last night while camped out at Junior Nash's fuck pad. Millard and Loew were gone, so I dropped my questioning report and a note on the warrants I'd issued into a large tray marked FIELD DETECTIVE'S SUMMARIES. Then I took off before some ranking clown forced me to join the circus.

Being at loose ends made me think of Lee; thinking of Lee made me wish I was back at the squadroom, where at least there was a sense of humor about the dead girl. Then thinking of Lee made me mad, and I started thinking about Junior Nash, professional gunman more dangerous than fifty jealous boyfriend killers. Itchy, I went back to being a Warrants cop and prowled Leimert Park for him.

But there was no escape from the Black Dahlia.

Passing 39th and Norton, I saw rubberneckers gawking around the vacant lot while ice cream and hotdog vendors dispensed chow; an old woman was peddling Betty Short portrait glossies in front of the bar at 39th and Crenshaw, and I wondered if the charming Cleo Short had supplied the negatives for a substantial percentage cut. Pissed off, I pushed the buffoonery out of my mind and *worked*.

I spent five straight hours walking South Crenshaw and South Western, showing Nash's mug shots and talking up his MO of statch rape on young Negro tail. All I got was "No" and the question "Why ain't you after the guy who chopped up that nice Dahlia girl?" Toward mid-evening I surrendered myself to the notion that maybe Junior Nash really had blown L.A. And still itchy, I rejoined the circus.

After a wolfed burger dinner, I called the night number at Administrative Vice and inquired about known lesbian gathering places. The clerk checked the Ad Vice intelligence files and came back with the names of three cocktail lounges, all on the same block of Ventura Boulevard out in the Valley: the Dutchess, the Swank Spot and La Verne's Hideaway. I was about to hang up when he added that they were out of the LAPD's jurisdiction in the unincorporated county territory patrolled by the Sheriff's

Department, and were probably operating under their sanction—for a price.

I didn't think about jurisdictions on the ride out to the Valley. I thought about women with women. Not lez types, but soft girls with hard edges, like my string of fight giveaways. Going over the Cahuenga Pass, I tried to put pairs of them together. All I could come up with was their bodies and the smell of liniment and car upholstery—no faces. I used Betty/Beth and Linda/Lorna then, mug shots and high school ID combined with the bodies of the girls I remembered from my last pro fights. It got more and more graphic; then the 11000 block of Ventura Boulevard came into view and I got women-and-women for real.

The Swank Spot had a log cabin facade and double swinging doors like the saloons in western movies. The interior was narrow and poorly lit; it took long moments for my eyes to adjust to the darkness. When they did I saw a score of women trying to stare me down.

Some of them were bull dykes in khaki shirts and GI issue trousers; some were soft girls in skirts and sweaters. One hefty dagger eyed me head to toe; the girl standing next to her, a svelte redhead, put her head on her shoulder and slinked an arm around her thick waist. Feeling myself start to sweat, I looked for the bar and someone with the air of top dog. I spotted a lounge area at the back of the room, bamboo chairs and a table covered with liquor bottles, all of it encircled by wall neon blinking purple, then yellow, then orange. I walked over; arm-draped couples separated to let me through, giving me just enough room to maneuver.

The lezzie behind the serving bar poured a shot glass full of whiskey and placed it in front of me, saying, "You from the Beverage Control?" She had piercing light eyes; neon reflections turned them almost translucent. I got a weird feeling that she knew what I was thinking about on the way over.

Downing the booze, I said, "LAPD Homicide"; the dyke said, "Not your bailiwick, but who got snuffed?" I fumbled for my snapshot of Betty Short and the Lorna/Linda ID card, then placed them on the bar. The whiskey lubed my hoarse voice: "Have you seen either of them?"

The woman gave the two pieces of paper, then me, a long once-over. "You tellin' me the Dahlia's a sister?"

"You tell me."

"I'll tell you I've never seen her except in the papers, and the little schoolgirl twist I've never seen, because me and my girls don't truck with underaged stuff. Capice?"

I pointed to the shot glass; the dyke refilled it. I drank; my sweat warmed, then cooled off. "Capice when your girls tell me that and I believe them."

The woman whistled, and the lounge area filled up. I grabbed the pictures and handed them to a femme draped around a lumberjack lady. They checked the photos out and shook their heads, then passed them to a woman in a Hughes Aircraft jumpsuit. She said, "No, but USDA choice tail," and gave them to a couple next to her. They muttered "Black Dahlia," real shock in their voices. Both said, "No"; the last lezzie said, "Nyet, nein, no, and not my type besides." She shoved the pictures at me, then spat on the floor. I said, "Good night, ladies," and made for the door, the word "Dahlia" whispered over and over behind me.

The Dutchess was two more free shots, a dozen more hostile looks and "No" answers, all in an old English motif. Walking into La Verne's Hideaway, I was half juiced and itchy for something I couldn't put my finger on.

La Verne's was dark inside, baby spots affixed to ceiling beams casting shadowy light on walls covered with cheap palm tree paper. Lezbo couples were cooing at each other in wraparound booths; the sight of two femmes kissing forced me to stare, then look away and seek out the bar.

It was recessed into the left wall, a long counter with colored lights reflecting off a Waikiki Beach scene. There was nobody tending it, no customers sitting on any of the stools. I walked to the back of the room, clearing my throat so the lovebirds in the booths could jump off cloud nine and return to earth. The strategy worked; clinches and kisses ended, angry and startled eyes looked up at the coming of bad news.

I said, "LAPD Homicide," and handed the pics to the nearest lezzie. "The dark-haired one is Elizabeth Short. The Black Dahlia if you've been reading the papers. The other one's her pal. I want to know if any of you have seen them, and if so who with."

The pictures made the rounds of the booths; I studied reactions when I saw that I'd have to use a bludgeon to get simple yes or no answers. Nobody said a word; all I got from reading faces was curiosity tinged with a couple of cases of lust. The photos came back to me, handed over by a diesel dagger sporting a flat top. I grabbed them and headed for the street and fresh air, stopping when I saw a woman behind the bar polishing glasses.

I moved to the bar and placed my wares on the counter, hooking a finger at her. She picked up the mug shot strip and said, "I seen her picture in the paper and that's it."

"What about this girl? She goes by the name Linda Martin."

The barmaid held up the Lorna/Linda ID card and squinted at it; I saw a flicker of recognition pass over her face. "No, sorry."

I leaned over the counter. "Don't fucking lie to me. She's fifteen fucking years old, so you come clean now, or I slap a contributing beef on you, and you spend the next five years eating pussy in Tehachapi."

The lezbo recoiled; I half expected her to go for a bottle and brain me with it. Eyes on the bar, she said, "The kid used to come in. Maybe two, three months ago. But I've never seen the Dahlia, and I think the kid liked boys. I mean, she just cadged drinks off the sisters, that was it."

Sidelong, I saw a woman just starting to sit down at the bar change her mind, grab her purse and make for the door, as if spooked by my words with the barmaid. The baby spotlight caught her face; I caught a fleeting resemblance to Elizabeth Short.

I gathered up my pictures, counted to ten and pursued the woman, getting to my car just as I saw her unlock the door of a snow-white Packard coupe parked a couple of spaces up from me. When she pulled out, I counted to five, then followed.

The rolling surveillance led me over Ventura Boulevard to the Cahuenga Pass, then down into Hollywood. Late-night traffic was scarce, so I let the Packard stay several car lengths in front of me as it headed south on Highland, out of Hollywood, into the Hancock Park District. At 4th Street, the woman turned left; within seconds we were in the heart of Hancock Park—an area Wilshire Division cops called "Pheasant Under Glass Acres."

The Packard turned the corner at Muirfield Road and stopped in front of a huge Tudor mansion fronted by a lawn the size of a football field. I continued on, my headlights picking up the car's rear plate: CAL RQ 765. Checking my rearview mirror, I saw the woman locking the driver's side door; even from a distance her trim sharkskin figure stood out.

I took 3rd Street out of Hancock Park. At Western I saw a pay phone, got out and called the DMV night line, requesting a vehicle make and criminal record check on white Packard coupe CAL RQ 765. The operator kept me waiting for close to five minutes, then returned with his read-out:

Madeleine Cathcart Sprague, white female, DOB 11/14/25, L.A., 482 South Muirfield Road; no wants, no warrants, no criminal record.

Driving home, the shots of booze wore off. I started wondering if Madeleine Cathcart Sprague had anything at all to do with Betty/Beth and Lorna/Linda, or whether she was just a rich lezzie with a taste for low life. Steering with one hand, I took out my Betty Short mugs, superimposed the Sprague girl's face over them and came away with a common, everyday resemblance. Then I saw myself peeling off her sharkskin suit and knew I didn't care one way or the other.

10

I PLAYED the radio on the ride to University Station the next morning. The Dexter Gordon quartet was bebopping me into good spirits when "Billie's Bounce" quit bouncing, replaced by a feverish voice: "We interrupt our regular broadcast to bring you a bulletin. A major suspect in the investigation into the slaying of Elizabeth Short, the raven-haired party girl known as the Black Dahlia, has been captured! Previously known to the authorities only as 'Red,' the man has now been identified as Robert 'Red' Manley, age twenty-five, a Huntington Park hardware salesman. Manley was captured this morning at the South Gate home of a friend and is now being held and questioned at the Hollenbeck police station in East Los Angeles. In an exclusive handout to KGFJ, Deputy DA Ellis Loew, ace legal beagle working on the case as civilian-police liaison, said: 'Red Manley is a hot suspect. We've got him pegged as the man who drove Betty Short up from San Diego on January ninth, six days before her torture-ravaged body was found in a vacant lot in Leimert Park. This looks like the big break we've all been hoping and praying for. God has answered our prayers!'"

Ellis Loew's sentiments were replaced by a commercial for Preparation H, guaranteed to reduce the painful swelling of hemorrhoids or double your money back. I flipped the radio off and changed direction, heading for Hollenbeck Station.

The street in front of it was blocked off with sawhorse detour signs; patrolmen were holding reporters at bay. I parked in the alley behind the station and entered through the back door to the holding tank. Drunks jabbered in cells on the misdemeanor side of the catwalk; hardcase types glowered from the felony row. It was a jailhouse full house, but there were no jailers anywhere. Opening a connecting door into the station proper, I saw why.

What looked like the entire in-station contingent was crammed into a short corridor inset with interrogation cubicles, every man straining for a look through the one-way glass of the middle room on the left side. Russ Millard's voice was coming out of a wall-mounted speaker: smooth, coaxing.

I nudged the officer nearest to me. "Has he confessed?"

The man shook his head. "No. Millard and his partner are giving him the Mutt and Jeff."

"Did he admit knowing the girl?"

"Yeah. We got him from the DMV cross-checks, and he came along peacefully. Wanna make a little bet? Innocent or guilty, take your pick. I'm feelin' lucky today."

I ignored the offer, gently elbowed my way up to the glass and peered in. Millard was seated at a battered wooden table, a handsome young guy with a carrot-hued pompadour across from him fingering a pack of cigarettes. He looked scared shitless; Millard looked like the nice-guy priest in the movies—the one who's seen it all and granted absolution for the whole enchilada.

Carrot top's voice came over the speaker. "Please, I've told it three times now."

Millard said, "Robert, we're doing this because you didn't come forward. Betty Short has been on the front page of every L.A. newspaper for three days now, and you knew we wanted to talk to you. But you hid out. How do you think that looks?"

Robert "Red" Manley lit a cigarette, inhaled and coughed. "I didn't want my wife to know I was chipping on her."

"But you didn't chip on her. Betty wouldn't put out. She cock-teased you and didn't come across. That's no reason to hide from the police."

"I dated her down in Dago. I danced slow dances with her. It's the same thing as chipping."

Millard put a hand on Manley's arm. "Let's go back to the beginning. Tell me how you met Betty, what you did, what you talked about. Take your time, nobody's rushing you."

Manley stubbed out his cigarette into an overflowing ashtray, lit another one and wiped sweat from his brow. I looked around the corridor and saw Ellis Loew leaning against the opposite wall, Vogel and Koenig flanking him like twin dogs awaiting the command to attack. A static-filtered sigh came over the loudspeaker; I turned back and watched the suspect squirm in his chair. "And this is the last time I'll have to tell it?"

Millard smiled. "That's right. Go ahead, son."

Manley got up and stretched, then paced as he talked. "I met Betty the week before Christmas, at this bar in downtown Dago. We just started gabbing, and Betty let it slip that she was sort of on her uppers, staying with this woman Mrs. French and her daughter, sort of temporarily. I bought her dinner at an Italian joint in Old Town, then we went dancing at the Sky Room at the El Cortez Hotel. We—"

Millard interrupted. "Do you always chase tail when you're out of town on business?"

Manley shouted, "I wasn't chasing tail!"

"What were you doing, then?"

"I was infatuated, that's all. I couldn't tell if Betty was a gold digger or a nice girl, and I wanted to find out. I wanted to test my loyalty to my wife and I just …"

Manley's voice died down; Millard said, "Son, for God's sake tell the truth. You were looking for some pussy, right?"

Manley slumped into his chair. "Right."

"Just like you always do on business trips, right?"

"No! Betty was different!"

"How was she different? Out-of-town stuff is out-of-town stuff, right?"

"No! I don't chip on my wife when I'm on the road! Betty was just …"

Millard's voice was so low that the loudspeaker barely picked it up. "Betty just set you off. Right?"

"Right."

"Made you want to do things you'd never done before, made you mad, made you—"

"No! No! I wanted to fuck her, I didn't want to hurt her!"

"Sssh. Sssh. Let's go back to Christmastime. You had that first date with Betty. Did you kiss her good night?"

Manley gripped the ashtray with both hands; they shook, butts spilled onto the table. "On the cheek."

"Come on, Red. No heavy pass?"

"No."

"You had a second date with Betty two days before Christmas, right?"

"Right."

"More dancing at the El Cortez, right?"

"Right."

"Soft lights, drinks, soft music, then you made your move, right?"

"Goddamn you, quit saying 'Right'! I tried to kiss Betty and she gave me this song and dance about how she couldn't sleep with me because the father of her child had to be a war hero and I was only in the army band. She was goddamn nuts on the subject! All she did was talk about these horseshit war heroes!"

Millard stood up. "Why do you say 'horseshit,' Red?"

"Because I knew they were lies. Betty said she was married to this guy and engaged to that guy, and I knew she was trying to make me look small because I never saw combat."

"Did she mention any names?"

"No, just ranks. Major this and Captain that, like I should be ashamed of being a corporal."

"Did you hate her for it?"

"No! Don't put words in my mouth!"

Millard stretched and sat down. "After that second date, when was the next time you saw Betty?"

Manley sighed and rested his forehead on the table. "I've told you the whole story three times."

"Son, the sooner you tell it again, the sooner you'll be able to go home."

Manley shivered and wrapped his arms around himself. "After the second date I didn't hear from Betty until January eighth, when I got this telegram at my office. The telegram said she'd like to see me when I made my next sales run down to Dago. I wired back, saying I had to be in Dago tomorrow afternoon, and I'd pick her up. Then I picked her up, and she begged me to drive her up to L.A. I said—"

Millard held up a hand. "Did Betty say why she had to get to L.A.?"

"No."

"Did she say she was meeting somebody?"

"No."

"You agreed to do it because you thought she'd put out for you?"

Manley sighed. "Yes."

"Go ahead, son."

"I took Betty with me on my rounds that day. She stayed in the car while I called on customers. I had some calls in Oceanside the next morning, so we spent the night in a motel there, and—"

"Let's have the name of the place again, son."

"It was called the Cornucopia Motor Lodge."

"And Betty CT'd you again that night?"

"She ... she said she had her period."

"And you fell for that old chestnut?"

"Yes."

"Did it make you mad?"

"Goddamn it, I didn't kill her!"

"Sssh. You slept in the chair and Betty slept on the bed, right?"

"Right."

"And in the morning?"

"In the morning we drove up to L.A. Betty went with me on my rounds and tried to float me for a five-spot, but I turned her down. Then she handed me a cock-and-bull story about meeting her sister in front of the Biltmore Hotel. I wanted to get rid of her, so I dropped her in front of the Biltmore that night, right around five o'clock. And I never saw her again, except for all that Dahlia stuff in the papers."

Millard said, "That was five o'clock, Friday, January tenth when you last saw her?"

Manley nodded. Millard looked straight at the glass, adjusted the knot of his necktie, then stepped outside. In the corridor, officers swarmed him, hurling questions. Harry Sears slipped into the room; next to me a familiar voice rose above the commotion. "Now you'll see why Russ keeps Harry around."

It was Lee, grinning a shit-eating grin, looking like a million tax-free dollars. I cuffed him around the neck. "Welcome back to earth."

Lee cuffed me back. "It's your fault I look this good. Right after you left, Kay slipped me a Mickey Finn, some stuff she got at the drugstore. I slept seventeen hours, got up and ate like a horse."

"Your own goddamn fault for bankrolling her chemistry classes. What do you think of Red?"

"A pussy hound at worst, a divorced pussy hound by the end of the week. You agree?"

"In spades."

"You get anything yesterday?"

Seeing my best friend looking like a new man made it easy to twist the truth. "You read my FI report?"

"Yeah, at University. Good work on the juvie warrant. You get anything else?"

I lied flat-out, a trim sharkskin figure dancing in the back of my head. "No. You?"

Staring through the one-way, Lee said, "No, but what I said about getting the bastard still goes. Jesus, look at Harry."

I did. The mild-mannered stutterer was circling the interrogation room table, twirling a metal-studded sap, whacking it hard into the tabletop each time he circuited. "Ka-thack's" filled the speaker; Red Manley, arms wrapped around his chest, quivered as each blow reverberated.

Lee nudged me. "Russ has got one rule—no actual hitting. But watch how—"

I shrugged off Lee's hand and stared through the one-way. Sears was tapping the sap on the table a few inches in front of Manley, his stutterless voice dripping cold rage. "You wanted some fresh gash, and you thought Betty was easy. You came on strong, and that didn't work, so you begged. That didn't work, so you offered her money. She told you she was on the rag, and that was the final straw. You wanted to make her bleed for real. Tell me how you sliced her titties. Tell me—"

Manley screamed, "No!" Sears smashed the sap into the ashtray, the glass cracked, butts flew off the table. Red bit his lip; blood spurted out, then dribbled down his chin. Sears sapped the pile of broken glass; shards exploded all over the room. Manley whimpered, "No no no no no"; Sears hissed, "You knew what you wanted to do. You're an old cunt chaser, and you knew lots of places to take girls. You plied Betty with a few drinks, got her to talk about her old boyfriends and came on like a pal, like the nice little corporal willing to leave Betty to the *real men*, the men who saw combat, who deserved to get laid with a fine cooze like her—"

"No!"

Sears hit the table, ka-thack! "*Yes*, Reddy-poo, *yes*. I think you took her to a toolshed, maybe one of those abandoned warehouses out by the old Ford plant in Pico-Rivera. There was some twine and lots of cutting tools lying around, and you got a hard-on. Then you shot your load in your pants before you could stick it in Betty. You were mad before, but now you were *really* mad. You started thinking about all the girls who laughed at that tiny little dick of yours and all the times your wife said, 'Not tonight, Reddy-poo, I've got a headache.' So you hit her and tied her down and beat her and cut her! Admit it, you fucking degenerate!"

"No!"

Ka-thack!

The table jumped off the floor from the force of the blow. Manley almost jumped out of his chair; only Sears' hand on the back slats kept him from toppling over.

"Yes, Reddy-poo. *Yes.* You thought of every girl who said 'I don't suck,' every time your mommy spanked you, every evil eye you got from real soldiers when you played your trombone in the army band. Goldbrick, needle-dick, pussy-whipped, that's what you were thinking. That's what Betty had to pay for. Right?"

Manley dribbled blood and spittle into his lap and gurgled. "No. Please, as God is my witness, no"; Sears said, "God hates liars," and sapped the table three times—*Ka-thack! Ka-thack! Ka-thack!* Manley lowered his head and began to dry sob; Sears knelt by his chair. "Tell me how Betty screamed and begged, Red. Tell me, then tell God."

"No. No. I didn't hurt Betty."

"Did you get another hard-on? Did you come and come and come the more you cut her?"

"No. Oh God, oh God."

"That's right, Red. Talk to God. Tell God all about it. He'll forgive you."

"No, please God."

"Say it, Red. Tell God how you beat and tortured and ripped up Betty Short for three fucking days, then cut her in two."

Sears smashed the table once, twice, three times, then hurled it over onto its side. Red fumbled himself out of his chair and onto his knees. He clasped his hands and mumbled, "The Lord is my shepherd, I shall not want," then started weeping. Sears looked straight at the one-way, self-loathing etched into every plane of his flabby juicehound face. He gave the thumbs-down sign, then walked out of the room.

Russ Millard met him just outside the door and led him away from the general crowd of officers, in my direction. Eavesdropping on their whispered conversation, I picked up the gist of it: they both thought Manley was clean, but wanted to shoot him with Pentothal and give him a polygraph test to make sure. Looking back through the one-way, I saw Lee and another plainsclothesman handcuffing Red, easing him out of the interrogation room. Lee was giving the man the kid gloves treatment he usually reserved for children, talking softly to him, one hand on his shoulder. The crowd broke up when the three of them disappeared into the holding tank. Harry Sears went back into the cubicle and began cleaning up his mess; Millard turned to me. "Good report yesterday, Bleichert."

I said, "Thanks," knowing I was being sized up. We locked eyes. I asked, "What's next?"

"You tell me."

"First you send me back to Warrants, right?"

"Wrong, but keep going."

"Okay, then we canvass around the Biltmore and try to reconstruct Betty Short's movements from the tenth, when Red dropped her off, to the twelfth or thirteenth, when she got snatched. We blanket the area and collate the FIs and hope to hell the legit leads don't get lost with all the phonies this publicity is getting us."

"Keep going."

"We know Betty was movie-struck and promiscuous, and that she bragged about being in a movie last November, so my bet is that she wouldn't turn down a roll on the casting couch. I think we should query producers and casting directors, see what we get."

Millard smiled. "I called Buzz Meeks this morning. He's an ex-cop, works as head of security at Hughes Aircraft. He's the Department's unofficial liaison to the studios, and he'll be asking around. You're doing well, Bucky. Run with the ball."

I wavered—wanting to impress a senior officer; wanting to roust the rich lezzie myself. Millard's pump job came on as condescending, bones of praise to keep a young cop from balking at his unwanted assignment. Madeleine Cathcart Sprague framed in my mind, I said, "All I know is that you should keep an eye on Loew and his boys. I didn't put it in my report, but Betty Short sold it outright when she needed money bad enough, and Loew's been trying to keep it kiboshed. I think he'll sit on anything that makes her look like an outright tramp. The more sympathy the

public has for the girl, the more juice he gets as prosecuting attorney if this mess ever gets to court."

Millard laughed. "Bright penny, are you calling your own boss
an evidence suppressor?"

I thought of myself as the same thing. "Yeah, and a shit-brained,
grandstanding son of a bitch."

Millard said, "Touché," and handed me a piece of paper. "Betty
sightings—restaurants and bars in Wilshire Division. You can
work it single or with Blanchard, I don't care."

"I'd rather canvass around the Biltmore."

"I know you would, but I want foot beat men who know the
area to work there, and I need smart pennies to eliminate the
phonies from the tip list."

"What are you going to be doing?"

Millard smiled sadly. "Keeping an eye on the evidence suppressor shit-brained son of a bitch and his minions to make sure
they don't try to coerce a confession out of that innocent man in
the holding tank."

* * *

I couldn't find Lee anywhere around the station, so I checked
out the tip list as a single-o. The canvassing territory was centered in the Wilshire District, restaurant bars and juke joints on
Western, Normandie and 3rd Street. The people I talked to were
mostly barflies, daytime juicers eager to suck up to authority or
gab with someone other than the usual boon acquaintances they
found in gin mills. Pressing for facts, I got sincere fantasy—
virtually every person had Betty Short giving them a long spiel
taken from the papers and radio when she was really down in
Dago with Red Manley or somewhere getting tortured to death.
The longer I listened the more they talked about themselves,
interweaving their sad tales with the story of the Black Dahlia,
who they actually believed to be a glamorous siren headed for
Hollywood stardom. It was as if they would have traded their
own lives for a juicy front-page death. I included questions on
Linda Martin/Lorna Martilkova, Junior Nash and Madeleine
Cathcart Sprague and her snow-white Packard, but all it got
me was stuporous deadpans. I decided that my FI report would
consist of two words: "All bullshit."

I finished shortly after dark, and drove to the house to grab
dinner.

Pulling up, I saw Kay storming out the door and down the steps, hurling an armful of paper onto the lawn, then storming back while Lee stormed beside her, shouting and waving his arms. I walked over and knelt beside the discarded pile; the papers were carbons of LAPD report forms. Sifting through them, I saw FIs, evidence indexes, questioning reports, tip lists and a complete autopsy protocol—all with "E. Short, W.F. D.O.D. 1/15/47" typed at the top. They were obviously bootlegged from University Station—and the very possession of them was enough to guarantee Lee a suspension from duty.

Kay came back with another load, shouting, "After all that's happened, all that might happen, how can you do this? It's sick and it's insane!" She dumped the papers beside the other pile; 39th and Norton glossies glinted up at me. Lee grabbed her by the arms and held her while she squirmed. "Goddamnit, you know what this is to me. You *know*. Now I'll rent a room to keep the stuff in, but babe, you stick by me on this. It's *mine*, and I need you ... and you *know*."

They noticed me then. Lee said, "Bucky, you tell her. You reason with her."

It was the funniest Dahlia circus line I'd heard so far. "Kay's right. You've pulled at least three misdemeanors on this thing, and it's getting out—" I stopped, thinking of what *I'd* pulled, and where I was going at midnight. Looking at Kay, I shifted gears. "I promised him a week on it. That means four more days. On Wednesday it's over."

Kay sighed, "Dwight, you can be so gutless sometimes," then walked into the house. Lee opened his mouth to say something funny. I kicked a path through official LAPD paper to my car.

* * *

The snow-white Packard was in the same spot as last night. I staked it out from my car, parked directly in back of it. Huddled low in the front seat, I spent angry hours watching foot traffic enter and leave the three bars on the block—daggers, femmes and obvious sheriff's dicks with that edgy look indigenous to bagmen. Midnight came and went; the foot traffic picked up— mostly lezzies headed for the hot sheet motels across the street. Then she walked out the door of La Verne's Hideaway alone, a showstopper in a green silk dress.

I slid out the passenger side door just as she stepped off the curb, giving me a sidelong glance. "Slumming, Miss Sprague?"

Madeleine Sprague stopped; I closed the distance between us. She dug in her purse, pulling out car keys and a fat wad of cash. "So Daddy's spying again. He's on one of his little Calvinist crusades, and he said you shouldn't be subtle." She switched to a deft imitation of a Scotchman's burr: "Maddy girl, ye should not be congregating in such unsuitable places. It would not do to have ye seen by the wrong people there, lassie."

My legs were trembling, like they did while I waited for the first-round bell. I said, "I'm a police officer."

Madeleine Sprague went back to her normal voice. "Oh? Daddy's buying policemen now?"

"He didn't buy me."

She held out the cash and looked me over. "No, probably not. You'd be dressing better if you worked for him. So let's try the West Valley Sheriffs. You're already extorting La Verne, so you thought you'd try extorting her patrons."

I took the money, counted over a hundred dollars, then handed it back. "Let's try LAPD Homicide. Let's try Elizabeth Short and Linda Martin."

Madeleine Sprague's brassy act died fast. Her face scrunched up with worry, and I saw that her resemblance to Betty/Beth was more hairdo and makeup than anything else; on the whole her features were less refined than the Dahlia's, and only superficially similar. I studied that face: panicky hazel eyes caught by streetlight glow; forehead creased, like her brain was working overtime. Her hands were shaking, so I grabbed the car keys and money, stuffed them into her purse and tossed it on the hood of the Packard. Knowing I might have a major lead by the short hairs, I said, "You can talk to me here or downtown, Miss Sprague. Just don't lie. I know you knew her, so if you jerk me off on that it's the station and a lot of publicity you don't want."

The brass girl finally composed herself. I repeated, "Here or downtown?" She opened the Packard's passenger door and got in, sliding over behind the wheel. I joined her, flicking on a dashboard light so I could read her face. The smell of leather upholstery and stale perfume hit me; I said, "Tell me how long you knew Betty Short."

Madeleine Sprague fidgeted under the light. "How did you know I knew her?"

"You rabbited last night when I was questioning the barmaid. What about Linda Martin? Do you know her?"

Madeleine ran long red fingertips over the wheel. "This is all a fluke. I met Betty and Linda at La Verne's last fall. Betty said it was her first time there. I think I talked to her one time after that. Linda I talked to several times, just cocktail lounge chitchat."

"When last fall?"

"November, I think."

"Did you sleep with either of them?"

Madeleine flinched. "No."

"Why not? That's what that dive is all about, right?"

"Not entirely."

I tapped her green silk shoulder, hard. "Are you lez?"

Madeleine went back to her father's burr. "Ye might say I take it where I can find it, laddie."

I smiled, then patted the spot I'd jabbed a moment before. "You're telling me that your sole contact with Linda Martin and Betty Short was a couple of cocktail bar conversations two months ago, right?"

"Yes. That's exactly what I'm telling you."

"Then why did you take off so fast last night?"

Madeleine rolled her eyes and rolled "Laddie," Scotch-voiced; I said, "Cut the shit and tell it straight." The brass girl spat out: "Mister, my father is Emmett Sprague. *The* Emmett Sprague. He built half of Hollywood and Long Beach, and what he didn't build he bought. He does not like publicity, and he would not like to see 'Tycoon's Daughter Questioned in Black Dahlia Case—Played Footsie with Dead Girl at Lesbian Nightclub' in the papers. Now do you get the picture?"

I said, "In Technicolor," and patted Madeleine's shoulder. She pulled away from me and sighed, "Is my name going into all kinds of police files where all kinds of slimy little policemen and slimy little yellow journalists will see it?"

"Maybe, maybe not."

"What do I have to do to keep it out?"

"Convince me of a few things."

"Such as?"

"Such as first you give me your impression of Betty and Linda. You're a bright kid—give me your play on them."

Madeleine stroked the wheel, then the gleaming oak dashboard. "Well, they weren't sisters, they were just using the Hideaway to cadge drinks and dinner."

"How could you tell?"

"I saw them brush off passes."

I thought of Marjorie Graham's mannish older woman. "Any passes stand out? You know, rough stuff? Bull daggers getting persistent?"

Madeleine laughed. "No, the passes I saw were very ladylike."

"Who made them?"

"Street trade I never saw before."

"Or since?"

"Yes, or since."

"What did you talk about with them?"

Madeleine laughed again, harder. "Linda talked about the boy she left behind in Hicktown, Nebraska, or wherever it was she came from and Betty talked about the latest issue of *Screenworld*. On a conversational level, they were right down there with you, only they were better looking."

I smiled and said, "You're cute."

Madeleine smiled and said, "You're not. Look, I'm tired. Aren't you going to ask me to prove I didn't kill Betty? Since I can prove it, won't that put an end to this farce?"

"I'll get to that in a minute. Did Betty ever talk about being in a movie?"

"No, but she was movie-struck in general."

"Did she ever show you a movie viewfinder? A lens gadget on a chain?"

"No."

"What about Linda? Did she talk about being in a movie?"

"No, just her hicktown sweetheart."

"Do you have any idea where she'd go if she was on the lam?"

"Yes. Hicktown, Nebraska."

"Besides there."

"No. Can I—"

I touched Madeleine's shoulder, more of a caress than a pat. "Yeah, tell me your alibi. Where were you and what were you doing from last Monday, January thirteenth, through to Wednesday the fifteenth."

Madeleine cupped her hands to her mouth and blew a horn fanfare, then rested them on the seat by my knee. "I was at our house in Laguna from Sunday night through Thursday morning. Daddy and Mommy and sister Martha were there with me, and so were our live-in servants. If you want verification, call

Daddy. Our number is Webster 4391. But be discreet. Don't tell him where you met me. Now, do you have any other questions?"

My private Dahlia lead was blown, but it gave me the green light in another direction. "Yeah. You ever do it with men?"

Madeleine touched my knee. "I haven't met any lately, but I'll do it with you to keep my name out of the papers."

My legs were Jell-O. "Tomorrow night?"

"All right. Pick me up at eight, like a gentleman. The address is 482 South Muirfield."

"I know the address."

"I'm not surprised. What's your name?"

"Bucky Bleichert."

Madeleine said, "It goes with your teeth."

I said, "Eight o'clock," and got out of the Packard while my legs could still function.

11

LEE SAID, "You want to catch the fight films at the Wiltern tonight? They're showing oldies—Dempsey, Ketchel, Greb. What do you say?"

We were sitting at desks across from each other in the University squadroom, manning telephones. The clerical flunkies assigned to the Short case had been given Sunday off, so regular field dicks were doing the drudge work, taking down tips, then writing out slips assessing the tipsters and routing possible follow-ups to the nearest detective division. We'd been at it for an hour without interruption, Kay's "gutless" remark hanging between us. Looking at Lee, I saw that his eyes were just starting to pin, a sign that he was coming on to a fresh Benzie jolt. I said, "I can't."

"Why not?"

"I've got a date."

Lee grinned-twitched. "Yeah? Who with?"

I changed the subject. "Did you smooth it out with Kay?"

"Yeah, I rented a room for my stuff. The El Nido Hotel, Santa Monica and Wilcox. Nine scoots a week, chump change if it makes her feel good."

"De Witt gets out tomorrow, Lee. I think I should lean on him, maybe get Vogel and Koenig to do it."

Lee kicked at a wastebasket. Paper wads and empty coffee cups flew out; heads darted up from other desks. Then his phone rang. Lee picked it up. "Homicide, Sergeant Blanchard speaking."

I stared at my routing slips; Lee listened to his caller. Wednesday, Dahlia kiss-off time, came into focus as an eternity away, and I wondered if he'd need weaning off the Benzedrine. Madeleine Sprague jumped into my mind—her nine millionth jump since she said, "I'll do it with you to keep my name out of the papers." Lee had been on his call for a long time without interjecting comments or questions; I started wishing that my phone would ring and make Madeleine jump away.

Lee put down the receiver. I said, "Anything interesting?"

"Another loony. Who's your date tonight?"

"A neighbor girl."

"Nice girl?"

"A honey. Partner, if I find you hopped-up after Tuesday, it's the Bleichert-Blanchard rematch."

Lee gave me an outer space grin. "It's Blanchard-Bleichert, and you'd lose again. I'm getting coffee. You want some?"

"Black, no sugar."

"Coming up."

* * *

I logged in a total of forty-six phone tips, about half of them reasonably coherent. Lee took off in the early afternoon, and Ellis Loew stuck me with the job of typing up Russ Millard's new summary report. It stated that Red Manley had been released to his wife after conclusively passing lie detector and Pentothal tests, and that Betty Short's love letters had been thoroughly gone through. A number of her swains had been ID'd and cleared as suspects, as had most of the guys who appeared in her photographs. Efforts to identify the remaining men were continuing, and the Camp Cooke MPs had called in with the word that the soldier who beat up Betty in '43 was killed in the Normandy Invasion. As for Betty's many marriages and engagements, a forty-eight-state capital record check revealed that no marriage licenses had ever been issued to her.

The report went downhill from there. The license numbers that Lee had glommed from the window of Junior Nash's fuck pad had yielded zero; over three hundred Dahlia sightings a day were flooding LAPD and Sheriff's Department switchboards.

There had been ninety-three phony confessions so far, with four seriously cracked loonies without alibis held at the Hall of Justice Jail, awaiting sanity hearings and probable shipment to Camarillo. Field interrogations were still going full speed—190 full-time men now on the case. The only ray of hope was the result of my 1/17 FI questionings: Linda Martin/Lorna Martilkova was spotted in a couple of Encino cocktail lounges, and a big push to grab her was being centered in that area. I finished up the typing job gut certain that Elizabeth Short's killer was never going to be found, and put money on it—a double sawbuck on "Unsolved-pay 2 to 1" in the squadroom pool.

* * *

I rang the doorbell of the Sprague mansion at exactly 8:00. I was dressed in my best outfit—blue blazer, white shirt and gray flannels—and put money on myself as a fool for kowtowing to the surroundings—I'd be taking the clothes off as soon as Madeleine and I got to my place. The ten hours of phone work stuck with me despite the shower I'd taken at the station, I felt even more out of place than I should have and my left ear still ached from the barrage of Dahlia talk.

Madeleine opened the door, a knockout in a skirt and a tight cashmere sweater. She once-overed me, took my hand and said, "Look, I hate to pull this, but Daddy has heard about you. He insisted you stay for dinner. I told him we met at that art exhibit at Stanley Rose's Bookshop, so if you have to pump everybody for my alibi, try to be subtle about it. All right?"

I said, "Sure," let Madeleine link her arm through mine and lead me inside. The entrance foyer was as Spanish as the outside of the mansion was Tudor: tapestries and crossed wrought-iron swords on the whitewashed walls, thick Persian carpets over a polished wood floor. The foyer opened into a giant living room with a men's club atmosphere—green leather chairs arranged around low tables and settees; huge stone fireplace; small Oriental throw rugs, multicolored, placed together at different angles, so that just the right amount of oak floor bordered them. The walls were cherry wood, and featured framed sepias of the family and their ancestors.

I noticed a stuffed spaniel poised by the fireplace with a yellowed newspaper rolled into its mouth. Madeleine said, "That's Balto. The paper is the L.A. *Times* for August 1, 1926. That's the day

Daddy learned he'd made his first million. Balto was our pet then. Daddy's accountant called up and said, 'Emmett, you're a millionaire!' Daddy was cleaning his pistols, and Balto came in with the paper. Daddy wanted to consecrate the moment, so he shot him. If you look closely, you can see the bullet hole in his chest. Hold your breath, lovey. Here's the family."

Slack-jawed, I let Madeleine point me into a small sitting room. The walls were covered with framed photographs; the floor space was taken up by the three other Spragues in matching easy chairs. They all looked up; nobody stood up. Smiling without exposing my teeth, I said, "Hello." Madeleine made the introductions while I gawked down at the still-life ensemble.

"Bucky Bleichert, may I present my family. My mother, Ramona Cathcart Sprague. My father, Emmett Sprague. My sister, Martha McConville Sprague."

The ensemble came to life with little nods and smiles. Then Emmett Sprague beamed, got to his feet and stuck out his hand. I said, "A pleasure, Mr. Sprague," and shook it, eyeing him while he eyed me. The patriarch was short and barrel-chested, with a cracked, sun-weathered face and a full head of white hair that had probably once been sandy colored. I placed his age as somewhere in his fifties, his handshake as the grip of someone who'd done a good deal of physical labor. His voice was cut-glass Scottish, not the broad burr of Madeleine's imitation: "I saw you fight Mondo Sanchez. You boxed the pants off him. Another Billy Conn you were."

I thought of Sanchez, a built-up middleweight stiff I'd fought because my manager wanted me to get a rep for creaming Mexicans. "Thanks, Mr. Sprague."

"Thank you for giving such a dandy performance. Mondo was a good boy, too. What happened to him?"

"He died from a heroin overdose."

"God bless him. Too bad he didn't die in the ring, it would have spared his family a lot of grief. Speaking of families, please shake hands with the rest of mine."

Martha Sprague stood up on command. She was short, plump and blonde, with a tenacious resemblance to her father, blue eyes so light that it looked like she sent them out to be bleached and a neck that was acned and raw from scratching. She looked like a teenaged girl who'd never outgrow her baby fat and mature into beauty. I shook her firm hand feeling sorry for her; she caught what I was thinking immediately. Her pale eyes fired up as she yanked her paw away.

Ramona Sprague was the only one of the three who looked like Madeleine; if not for her I would have thought the brass girl was adopted. She possessed a pushing-fifty version of Madeleine's lustrous dark hair and pale skin, but there was nothing else attractive about her. She was fat, her face was flaccid, her rouge and lipstick were applied slightly off center, so that her face was weirdly askew. Taking her hand, she said, "Madeleine has said so many nice things about you," with a trace of a slur. There was no liquor on her breath; I wondered if she was jacked on drugstore stuff.

Madeleine sighed, "Daddy, can we eat? Bucky and I want to catch a nine-thirty show."

Emmett Sprague slapped me on the back. "I always obey my eldest. Bucky, will you entertain us with boxing and police anecdotes?"

"Between mouthfuls," I said.

Sprague slapped my back again, harder. "I can tell you didn't catch too many in the cabeza. Like Fred Allen you are. Come on, family. Dinner is served."

We filed into a large, wood-paneled dining room. The table in the middle of it was small, with five place settings already laid down. A serving cart was stationed by the door, leaking the unmistakable aroma of corned beef and cabbage. Old Man Sprague said, "Hearty fare breeds hearty people, haute cuisine breeds degenerates. Dig in, lad. The maid goes to her voodoo revival meetings on Sunday nights, so there's no one here but us white folks."

I grabbed a plate and piled it with food. Martha Sprague poured the wine and Madeleine dished herself out a small portion of each item and sat down at the table, motioning for me to sit beside her. I did, and Martha announced to the room: "I want to sit opposite Mr. Bleichert so I can draw him."

Emmett caught my eye and winked. "Bucky, you are in for a cruel caricaturing. Martha's pencil never flinches. Nineteen years old she is, and a high-paid commercial artist already. Maddy's my pretty one, but Martha's my certified genius."

Martha winced. She placed her plate directly across from me and sat down, arraying a pencil and a small sketch pad beside her napkin. Ramona Sprague took the adjoining seat and patted her arm; Emmett, standing by his chair at the head of the table, proposed a toast: "To new friends, prosperity and the great sport of boxing."

I said, "Amen," forked a slice of corned beef into my mouth and chewed it. It was fatty and dry, but I put on a yum-yum face and said, "This is delicious."

Ramona Sprague gave me a blank look; Emmett said, "Lacey, our maid, believes in voodoo. Some sort of Christian variation on it. She probably put a spell on the cow, made a pact with her nigger Jesus so the beast would be nice and juicy. Speaking of our colored brethren, how did it feel to shoot those two jigaboos, Bucky?"

Madeleine whispered, "Humor him."

Emmett caught the aside and chuckled. "Yes, lad, humor me. In fact, you should humor all rich men pushing sixty. They might go senile and confuse you with their heirs."

I laughed, exposing my choppers; Martha reached for her pencil to capture them. "I didn't feel much of anything. It was them or us."

"And your partner? That blond lad you fought last year?"

"Lee took it a bit harder than I did."

Emmett said, "Blonds are overly sensitive. Being one, I know. Thank God I've two brownies in the family to keep us pragmatic. Maddy and Ramona have that bulldog tenacity that Martha and I lack."

Only the food I was chewing kept me from braying outright. I thought of the spoiled sewer crawler I was going to screw later that night and her mother smiling numbly across the table from me. The impulse to laugh came on stronger and stronger; I finally got my mouthful swallowed, belched instead of howled and raised my glass. "To you, Mr. Sprague. For making me laugh for the first time in a week."

Ramona gave me a disgusted look; Martha concentrated on her artwork. Madeleine played footsie with me under the table and Emmett toasted me back. "Rough week you had, lad?"

I laughed. "In spades. I've been detached to Homicide to work on the Black Dahlia thing. My days off have been cancelled, my partner's obsessed with it, and the crazies have been coming out of the woodwork. There's two hundred cops working a single case. It's absurd."

Emmett said, "It's tragic, is what it is. What's your theory, lad? Who on God's earth could have done a thing like that to another human being?"

I knew then that the family didn't know about Madeleine's tenuous connection to Betty Short, and decided not to press for her alibi. "I think it's a random job. The Short girl was what you might call easy. She was a compulsive liar with a hundred boyfriends. If we get the killer, it'll be a fluke."

Emmett said, "God bless her, I hope you get him and I hope he gets a hot date with that little green room up at San Quentin."

Running her toes up my leg, Madeleine pouted, "Daddy, you're monopolizing the conversation and you're making Bucky sing for his supper."

"Shall I sing for mine, lassie? Even though I'm the breadwinner?"

Old Man Sprague was angry—I could see it in his rising color and the way he hacked at his corned beef. Curious about the man, I said, "When did you come to the United States?"

Emmett beamed. "I'll sing for anyone who wants to hear my immigrant success story. What kind of name is Bleichert? Dutch?"

"German," I said.

Emmett raised his glass. "A great people, the Germans. Hitler was a bit excessive, but mark my words that someday we'll regret not joining forces with him to fight the Reds. Where in Germany are your people from, lad?"

"Munich."

"Ah, München! I'm surprised they left. If I'd grown up in Edinburgh or some other civilized place I'd still be wearing kilts. But I came from godawful Aberdeen, so I came to America right after the first war. I killed a lot of your fine German countrymen during that war, lad. But they were trying to kill me, so I felt justified. Did you meet Balto out in the parlor?"

I nodded; Madeleine groaned, Ramona Sprague winced and speared a potato. Emmett said, "My old dreamer friend Georgie Tilden taxidermied him. Scads of odd talents dreamer Georgie had. We were in a Scots regiment together during the war, and I saved Georgie's life when a bunch of your fine German countrymen got obstreperous and charged us with bayonets. Georgie was enamored of the flickers; he loved a good nickelodeon show. We went back to Aberdeen after the armistice, saw what a dead dog town it was, and Georgie persuaded me to come to California with him—he wanted to work in the silent flicker business. He was never worth a damn unless I was there to lead him around by the snout, so I looked around Aberdeen, saw that it was a third-class destiny and said, 'Aye, Georgie,

California it is. Maybe we'll strike rich. And if we don't, we'll fail where the sun always shines.'"

I thought of my old man, who came to America in 1908 with big dreams—but married the first German emigrant woman he met and settled for wage slavery with Pacific Gas and Electric. "What happened then?"

Emmett Sprague rapped the table with his fork. "Knock wood, it was the right time to arrive. Hollywood was a cow pasture, but the silents were moving into their heyday. Georgie got work as a lighting man, and I found work building damn good houses— damn good and cheap. I lived outdoors and put every damn good dime back into my business, then took out loans from every bank and shylock willing to lend money and bought damn good property—damn good and cheap. Georgie introduced me to Mack Sennett, and I helped him build sets out at his studio in Edendale, then touched him for a loan to buy more property. Old Mack knew a lad on the make when he saw one, being one him- self. He gave me the loan on the proviso that I help him with that housing project he was putting up—Hollywoodland—underneath that godawful hundred-foot sign he erected on Mount Lee to ballyhoo it. Old Mack knew how to squeeze a dollar dry, he did. He had extras moonlighting as laborers and vice versa. I'd drive them over to Hollywoodland after ten or twelve hours on a Key- stone Kops flicker, and we'd put in another six hours by torchlight. I even got an assistant director's credit on a couple of movies, old Mack was so grateful for the way I squeezed his slaves."

Madeleine and Ramona were picking at their food with sullen faces, like they'd been captive audiences to the story before; Martha was still drawing, staring intently at me, *her* captive. "What happened to your friend?" I asked.

"God bless him, but for every story of success there's a corres- ponding one of failure. Georgie didn't butter up the right people. He didn't have the drive to complement his God-given talent, and he just fell by the wayside. He was disfigured in a car crash back in '36, and now he's what you might call a never was. I give him odd jobs tending some of my rental property and he does some rubbish hauling for the city—"

I heard a sharp screechy sound, and looked across the table. Ramona had missed stabbing a potato, and her fork had slid off the plate. Emmett said, "Mother, are you feeling well? Is the food to your liking?"

Ramona stared in her lap and said, "Yes, Father"; it looked like Martha was bracing her elbow. Madeleine went back to playing footsie with me; Emmett said, "Mother, you and our certified genius have not been doing a very good job of entertaining our guest. Would you care to participate in the conversation?"

Madeleine dug her toes into my ankle—just as I was about to try to lighten things up with a joke. Ramona Sprague forked herself a small mouthful of food, chewed it daintily and said, "Did you know that Ramona Boulevard was named after me, Mr. Bleichert?"

The woman's out-of-kilter face congealed around the words; she spoke them with a strange dignity. "No, Mrs. Sprague, I didn't know that. I thought it was named after the Ramona Pageant."

"I was named after the pageant," she said. "When Emmett married me for my father's money he promised my family that he would use his influence with the City Zoning Board to have a street named after me, since all his money was tied up in real estate and he couldn't afford to buy me a wedding ring. Father assumed it would be a nice residential street, but all Emmett could manage was a dead-end block in a red light district in Lincoln Heights. Are you familiar with the neighborhood, Mr. Bleichert?" Now the doormat's voice held an edge of fury.

"I grew up there," I said.

"Then you know that Mexican prostitutes expose themselves out of windows to attract customers. Well, after Emmett succeeded in getting Rosalinda Street changed to Ramona Boulevard he took me for a little tour there. The prostitutes greeted him by name. Some even had anatomical nicknames for him. It made me very sad and very hurt, but I bided my time and got even. When the girls were small I directed my own little pageants, right outside on our front lawn. I used the neighbor's children as extras and reenacted episodes out of Mr. Sprague's past that he would rather forget. That he would—"

The head of the table was slammed; glasses toppled and plates rattled. I stared at my lap to give the family infighters back some of their dignity and saw that Madeleine was gripping her father's knee so hard that her fingers were blue-white. She grabbed my knee with her free hand—with ten times the strength I thought she'd be capable of. An awful silence stretched, then Ramona Cathcart Sprague said, "Father, I'll sing for my supper when Mayor Bowron or Councilman Tucker comes to dinner, but not for Madeleine's male whores. A common policeman. My God, Emmett, how little you think of me."

I heard chairs scraping the floor, knees bumping the table, then footsteps moving out of the dining room; I saw that my hand was gripping Madeleine's the same way I curled it into an eight-ounce glove. The brass girl was whispering, "I'm sorry, Bucky. I'm sorry." Then a cheery voice said, "Mr. Bleichert?" and I looked up because it sounded so happy and sane.

It was Martha McConville Sprague, holding out a piece of paper. I took it with my free hand; Martha smiled and walked away. Madeleine was still muttering apologies when I looked at the picture. It was the two of us, both naked. Madeleine had her legs spread. I was between them, gnawing at her with giant Bucky Bleichert teeth.

* * *

We took the Packard down to hot sheet row on South La Brea. I drove, and Madeleine had the smarts not to talk until we passed a cinderblock auto court called the Red Arrow Inn. Then she said, "Here. It's clean."

I parked beside a line of pre-war jalopies; Madeleine went to the office and returned with the key to room eleven. She opened the door; I flicked on the wall light.

The flop was done up in dreary shades of brown and reeked of its previous inhabitants. I heard a dope sale being transacted in number twelve; Madeleine started to look like the caricature in her sister's drawing. I reached for the light switch to blot it all out. She said, "No. Please, I want to see you."

The narco sale burst into an argument. I saw a radio on the dresser and turned it on; an ad for Gorton's Slenderline Shop ate up the angry words. Madeleine pulled off her sweater and removed her nylons standing up; she was down to her undergarments before I began fumbling at my clothes. I snagged the zipper stepping out of my trousers; I ripped a shirt seam unhitching my shoulder holster. Then Madeleine was naked on the bed—and the kid sister's picture was obliterated.

I was nude inside of a second and joined with the brass girl inside of two. She muttered something like, "Don't hate my family, they're not bad," and I silenced her with a hard kiss. She returned it; our lips and tongues played until we had to break for breath. I ran my hands down to her breasts, cupping and kneading; Madeleine gasped little words about making up for the other Spragues. The more I kissed and felt and tasted her and the more she loved it, the more she murmured about *them*—so I grabbed her hair and hissed, "Not them, *me*. Do *me*, be with *me*."

Madeleine obeyed, going between my legs like a reverse of Martha's drawing. Captured that way, I felt myself getting ready to burst. I pushed Madeleine away so as not to explode, whispering, "Me, not them," stroking her hair, trying to concentrate on an inane radio jingle. Madeleine held me harder than any fight give-away girl ever did; when I was cooled down and ready, I eased her onto her back and pushed myself inside her.

Now it was no common policeman and rich girl slut. It was us together, arching, shifting and moving, hard, but with all the time in the world. We moved together until the dance music and jingles ended and the radio dial tone came and went, the cinderblock rutting room silent except for us. Then we ended it—perfectly, together.

We held each other afterward, pockets of sweat binding us head to toe. I thought of going on duty in less than four hours and groaned; Madeleine broke our embrace and aped my trademark, flashing her perfect teeth. Laughing, I said, "Well, you kept your name out of the papers."

"Until we announce the Bleichert-Sprague nuptials?"

I laughed harder. "Your mother would love that."

"Mother's a hypocrite. She takes pills that the doctor gives her, so she's not a hophead. I fool around, so I'm a whore. She's sanctioned, I'm not."

"Yes, you are. You're my—" I couldn't quite say, "whore."

Madeleine tickled my ribs. "Say it. Don't be a cop from squaresville. *Say it*."

I grabbed her hand before the tickling made me helpless. "You're my paramour, you're my inamorata, you're my sweetheart, you're the woman I suppressed evidence for—"

Madeleine bit my shoulder and said, "I'm your whore."

I laughed. "Okay, you're my violator of 234-A PC."

"What's that?"

"The California penal code designation for prostitution."

Madeleine waggled her eyebrows. "*Penal* code?"

I put up my hands. "You got me there."

The brass girl nuzzled me. "I like you, Bucky."

"I like you, too."

"You didn't start out liking me. Tell true—at first you just wanted to screw me."

"That's true."

"Then when did you start liking me?"

"The moment you took off your clothes."

"Bastard! You want to know when I started liking you?"

"Tell true."

"When I told Daddy I met this nice policeman Bucky Bleichert. Daddy's jaw dropped. He was impressed, and Emmett McConville Sprague is a very hard man to impress."

I thought of the man's cruelty to his wife and made a neutral comment: "He's an impressive man."

Madeleine said, "Diplomat. He's a hardcase, tightwad Scotchman son of a bitch, but he's a man. You know how he really made his money?"

"How?"

"Gangster kickbacks and worse. Daddy bought rotten lumber and abandoned movie facades from Mack Sennett and built houses out of them. He's got firetraps and dives all over L.A., registered to phony corporations. He's friends with Mickey Cohen. His people collect the rents."

I shrugged. "The Mick's thick with Bowron and half the Board of Supervisors. You see my gun and handcuffs?"

"Yes."

"Cohen paid for them. He put up the dough for a fund to help junior officers pay for their equipment. It's good public relations. The city tax assessor never checks his books, because the Mick pays for the gas and oil on all his field agents' cars. So you're not exactly shocking me."

Madeleine said, "Do you want to hear a secret?"

"Sure."

"Half a block of Daddy's Long Beach houses collapsed during the '33 earthquake. Twelve people were killed. Daddy paid money to have his name expunged from the contractor's records."

I held Madeleine out at arm's length. "Why are you telling me these things?"

Caressing my hands, she said, "Because Daddy's impressed with you. Because you're the only boy I've ever brought home that he thought was worth spit. Because Daddy worships toughness and he thinks you're tough, and if we get serious he'd probably tell you himself. Those people weigh on him, and he takes it out on Mother because it was her money he built that block with. I don't want you to judge Daddy by tonight. First impressions last, and I like you and I don't want—"

I pulled Madeleine to me. "Be still, babe. You're with me now, not your family."

Madeleine held me tightly. I wanted to let her know things were copacetic, so I tilted her chin up. Tears were in her eyes; she said, "Bucky, I didn't tell you all of it about Betty Short."

I gripped her shoulders. "What?"

"Don't be mad at me. It's nothing, I just don't want to keep it a secret. I didn't like you at first, so I didn't—"

"Tell me *now.*"

Madeleine looked at me, a stretch of sweat-stained bedsheet separating us. "Last summer I was bar hopping a lot. Straight bars in Hollywood. I heard about a girl who was supposed to look a lot like me. I got curious about her and left notes at a couple of places—'Your lookalike would like to meet you' and my private number at the house. Betty called me, and we got together. We talked, and that was it. I ran into her again with Linda Martin at La Verne's last November. It was just a coincidence."

"And that's all of it?"

"Yes."

"Then babe, you'd better prepare yourself. There's fifty-odd cops canvassing bars, and if even one of them gets hold of your little lookalike number, you're headed for a trip across page one. There's not a goddamned thing I could do about it, and if it happens, don't ask me—because I've done all I'm going to."

Drawing away from me, Madeleine said, "I'll take care of it."

"You mean your Daddy will?"

"Bucky lad, are ye telling me you're jealous of a man twice your age and half your size?"

I thought of the Black Dahlia then, her death eclipsing my shoot-out headlines. "Why did you want to meet Betty Short?"

Madeleine shivered; the red neon arrow that gave the flop its name blinked through the window and across her face. "I've worked hard at being loose and free," she said. "But the way people described Betty it sounded like she was a natural. A real wild girl from the gate."

I kissed my wild girl. We made love again, and I pictured her coupled with Betty Short the whole time—both of them naturals.

12

RUSS MILLARD took in my rumpled clothes and said, "A ten-ton truck or a woman?"

I looked around at University squadroom starting to fill up with daywatch dicks. "Betty Short. No phone work today, okay, boss?"

"In the mood for some fresh air?"

"Keep talking."

"Linda Martin was spotted last night out in Encino, trying to get served at a couple of bars. You and Blanchard go out to the Valley and look for her. Start at the twenty-thousand block of Victory Boulevard and work west. I'll be sending some other men as soon as they report in."

"When?"

Millard checked his watch. "Immediately, if not sooner."

I eyeballed for Lee and didn't see him, nodded assent and reached for the phone on my desk. I called the house, the City Hall Warrants office and Information for the number of the El Nido Hotel. I got a no answer for the first call and two no Blanchards for the others. Then Millard came back, with Fritz Vogel and—amazingly—Johnny Vogel in plainclothes.

I stood up. "I can't find Lee, Skipper."

Millard said, "Go with Fritzie and John. Take an unmarked radio car so you can keep in touch with the other men out there."

The fat Vogel boys stared at me, then at each other. The look they exchanged said my unkempt state was a Class B Felony. "Thanks, Russ," I said.

*   *   *

We drove to the Valley, the Vogels in the front seat, me in the back. I tried to doze, but Fritzie's monologue on hooers and woman killers made it impossible. Johnny nodded along; every time his father paused for breath, he said, "Right, Dad." Going over the Cahuenga Pass, Fritzie ran out of verbal steam; Johnny's yes-man act fell silent. I closed my eyes and leaned against the window. Madeleine was doing a slow striptease in concert with motor hum when I heard the Vogels whispering.

"... he's alseep, Daddy."

"Don't call me 'Daddy' on the job, I've told you a million goddamn times. It makes you sound like a nancy boy."

"I proved I'm not no nancy boy. Homos couldn't do what I did. I'm not cherry no more, so don't say nancy boy."

"Be still, damn you."

"Daddy, I mean Dad—"

"I said be still, Johnny."

The fat braggart cop reduced to a child grabbed my interest; I faked a snore-wheeze so the two would keep it up. Johnny whispered, "See, Dad, he's asleep. And he's the nance, not me. I proved it. Buck-tooth bastard. I could take him, Dad. You know I could. Job-stealing bastard, I had Warrants in the bag until—"

"John Charles Vogel, you hush this instant or I'll take a strap to you, twenty-four-year-old policeman or not."

The radio started barking then; I faked a big yawn. Johnny turned around and smiled. He said, "Catch up on your beauty sleep?" wafting his legendary halitosis.

My first instinct was to call him on his crack about taking me—then my sense of squadroom politics took over. "Yeah, I had a late night."

Johnny winked ineffectually. "I'm a quiff hound myself. I go a week without it, I'm climbing the walls."

The dispatcher droned, "... repeat, 10-A-94, roger your location."

Fritzie grabbed the mike. "10-A-94, rogering at Victory and Saticoy."

The dispatcher replied, "See the barman at the Caledonia Lounge, Victory and Valley View. Warrantee Linda Martin reported there now. Code three."

Fritzie hit the siren and punched the gas. Cars pulled to the curb; we shot forward in the middle lane. I sent one up to the Calvinist God I believed in as a kid: don't let the Martin girl mention Madeleine Sprague. Valley View Avenue appeared in the windshield; Fritzie hung a hard right turn, killing the siren in front of a mock-bamboo hut.

The bar's mock-bamboo door burst open; Linda Martin/ Lorna Martilkova, looking as fresh-scrubbed as her picture, burst out. I tumbled from the car and hit the sidewalk running, Vogel and Vogel huffing and puffing behind me. Linda/Lorna ran like an antelope, clutching an oversized purse to her chest; I closed the distance between us by sprinting flat-out. The girl reached a busy side street and darted into traffic; cars swerved to avoid hitting her.

She looked over her shoulder then; I dodged a beer truck and motorcycle on a collision course, sucked wind and *hauled*. The girl stumbled over the opposite curb, her purse went flying, I made a final leap and grabbed her.

She came up off the pavement spitting and beating at my chest; I grabbed her tiny fists, twisted them behind her back and cuffed her wrists. Lorna tried kicking then, well-aimed little shots at my legs. One kick connected with my shinbone; the girl, off balance from the cuffs, hit the ground ass-first. I helped her up, catching a wad of spittle on my shirtfront. Lorna yelped, "I'm an emancipated minor and if you touch me without a matron present I can sue you!" Catching my breath, I push-pulled her over to where her purse was lying.

I picked it up, surprised by the bulk and weight. Looking inside, I saw a small metal film can. I said, "What's the movie about?" The girl stammered, "P-P-Please, mister, my p-p-parents."

A horn tooted; I saw Johnny Vogel leaning out the window of the cruiser. "Millard said to bring the girl to Georgia Street juvie."

I hauled Lorna over and shoved her into the backseat. Fritzie hit the siren, and we leadfooted.

*   *   *

The run to downtown L.A. took thirty-five minutes.

Millard and Sears were waiting for us on the steps of Georgia Street Juvenile Hall. I led the girl in while Vogel and Vogel strode ahead. Court matrons and juvie dicks cleared a path for us inside; Millard opened a door marked DETENTION INTERVIEWS. I removed Lorna's cuffs, Sears walked into the room, pulled out seats and arranged ashtrays and notepads. Millard said, "Johnny, you go back to University and work the phones."

Fat Boy started to protest, then looked at his father. Fritzie nodded yes; Johnny exited, looking wounded. Fritzie announced, "I'm gonna call Mr. Loew. He should be in on this."

Millard said, "No. Not until we have a statement."

"Give her to me, I'll get you a statement."

"A voluntary statement, Sergeant."

Fritzie flushed. "I consider that a goddamn insult, Millard."

"You consider it what you damn well like, but you do what I damn well say, Mr. Loew or no Mr. Loew."

Fritz Vogel stood perfectly still. He looked like a human A-bomb about to explode, his voice the fuse: "You whored with the Dahlia, didn't you, girlie? You peddled your little twat with her. Tell me where you were during her lost days."

Lorna said, "Screw you, Charlie."

Fritzie stepped toward her; Millard moved between them. "I'll ask the questions, Sergeant."

You could have heard a pin drop. Vogel stood toe to toe with Millard. Seconds stretched, and then Fritzie squeaked, "You're a goddamned bleeding heart Bolshevik."

Millard took one step forward; Vogel took one step back. "Get out, Fritzie."

Vogel took three steps backward. His heels hit the wall, and he pivoted out the door, slamming it. The echo reverberated; Harry disarmed the remnants of the bomb: "How does it feel to be the object of such a fuss, Miss Martilkova?"

The girl said, "I'm Linda Martin," and tugged at the pleats of her skirt.

I took a seat, caught Millard's eye and pointed to the purse resting on the table, the film can poking out. The lieutenant nodded and sat down next to Lorna. "You know this is about Betty Short, don't you, sweetheart?"

The girl lowered her head and began sniffling; Harry handed her a Kleenex. She tore it into strips and smoothed them out on the table. "Does this mean I'll have to go back to my folks?"

Millard nodded. "Yes."

"My dad hits me. He's a dumb Slovak, and he gets drunk and hits me."

"Sweetheart, when you get back to Iowa you'll be on non-court probation. You tell your probation officer your father hits you and he'll put a stop to it damn quick."

"If my dad finds out what I did in L.A., he'll hit me bad."

"He won't find out, Linda. I told those other two officers to leave to make sure what you say stays confidential."

"If you send me back to Cedar Rapids, I'll just run away again."

"I'm sure you will. Now the sooner you tell us what we want to know about Betty and the sooner we believe you, the sooner you'll be on the train and able to escape. So that gives you a good reason to be truthful with us, doesn't it, Linda?"

The girl went back to playing with her Kleenex. I sensed a jaded little brain considering all the angles, all the possible outs. Finally she sighed, "Call me Lorna. If I'm going back to Iowa I should get used to it."

Millard smiled; Harry Sears lit a cigarette and poised his pen over his steno pad. My blood pressure zoomed to the tune of "No Madeleine, no Madeleine, no Madeleine."

Russ said, "Lorna, are you ready to talk to us?"

The former Linda Martin said, "Shoot."

Millard asked, "When and where did you meet Betty Short?"

Lorna mussed up her Kleenex strips. "Last fall, at this career girls' place on Cherokee."

"1842 North Cherokee?"

"Uh-huh."

"And you became friends?"

"Uh-huh."

"Say yes or no please, Lorna."

"Yes, we became friends."

"What did you do together?"

Lorna bit at her cuticles. "We talked girl talk, we made casting rounds, we bummed drinks and dinner at bars—"

I interrupted: "What kind of bars?"

"What do you mean?"

"I mean nice places? Dives? Servicemen's hangouts?"

"Oh. Just places in Hollywood. Places where we figured they wouldn't ask me for ID."

My blood pressure decelerated. Millard said, "You told Betty about the rooming house on Orange Drive, the place where you were staying, right?"

"Uh-huh. I mean yes."

"Why did Betty move out of the place on Cherokee?"

"It was too crowded, and she'd tapped all the girls for a dollar here, a dollar there, and they were mad at her."

"Were any of them particularly mad?"

"I don't know."

"Are you sure Betty didn't move out because of boyfriend trouble?"

"I'm sure."

"Do you recall the names of any of the men Betty went out with last fall?"

Lorna shrugged. "They were just pickups."

"What about names, Lorna?"

The girl counted on her fingers, stopping when she got to three. "Well, there were these two guys at Orange Drive, Don Leyes and Hal Costa, and a sailor named Chuck."

"No last name on Chuck?"

"No, but I know he was a gunnery mate second class."

Millard started to ask another question, but I held up my hand to cut him off. "Lorna, I talked to Marjorie Graham the other day, and she said she told you the police were coming by Orange Drive to talk to the tenants about Betty. You ran then. Why?"

Lorna bit a hangnail off and sucked at the wound. "Because I knew that if my picture got in the papers as Betty's friend my parents would see it and make the police send me home."

"Where did you go when you rabbited?"

"I met a man in a bar and got him to rent me a room at an auto court in the Valley."

"Did you—"

Millard silenced me with a chopped hand gesture. "You said you and Betty made casting rounds together. Did you ever get any movie work?"

Lorna twisted her fingers together in her lap. "No."

"Then could you tell me what's in that film can in your purse?"

Eyes on to the floor and dripping tears, Lorna Martilkova whispered, "It's a movie."

"A dirty movie?"

Lorna nodded mutely. The girl's tears were rivers of mascara now; Millard handed her a handkerchief. "Sweetheart, you have to tell us all of it, from the beginning. So think it all out, and take your time. Bucky, get her some water."

I left the room, found a drinking fountain and cup dispenser in the hall, filled a large paper container and returned with it. Lorna was speaking softly when I placed the cup on the table in front of her.

"... and I was cadging at this bar in Gardena. This Mexican man—Raoul or Jorge or something—started talking to me. I thought I was pregnant, and I was desperate wicked bad for money. He said he'd give me two hundred dollars to act in a nudie film."

Lorna stopped, slugged down the water, took a deep breath and kept going. "The man said he needed another girl, so I called Betty at the Cherokee place. She said yes, and the Mexican man and me picked her up. He got us hopped on reefers, I think 'cause he was afraid we'd get scared and back out. We drove down to Tijuana, and we made the movie at this big house outside town.

The Mex man worked the lights and ran the camera and told us what to do and drove us back to L.A., and that's *all of it, from the beginning*, so will you call my folks now?"

I looked at Russ, then Harry; they were staring at the girl impassively. Wanting to fill in the blank spaces of my own private lead, I asked, "When did you make the film, Lorna?"

"Around Thanksgiving."

"Can you give us a description of the Mexican man?"

Lorna stared at the floor. "Just a greasy Mex. Maybe thirty, maybe forty, I don't know. I was on hop, and I don't remember too good."

"Did he seem particularly interested in Betty?"

"No."

"Did he touch either of you? Get rough with you? Make passes?"

"No. He just moved us around."

"Together?"

Lorna whimpered, "Yes"; my blood buzzed. My voice sounded weird to my own ears, like I was some ventriloquist's puppet. "Then this wasn't just nudie stuff? This was you and Betty playing lez?"

Lorna gave a little dry sob and nodded; I thought of Madeleine and pushed ahead, oblivious to where the girl might take it: "You lez? Was Betty lez? You do any *lez* pub crawling?"

Millard barked, "Bleichert, can it!" Lorna leaned forward in her chair, grabbed the soft daddy cop and hugged him fiercely. Russ looked at me and brought a flat palm slowly down, like a conductor asking the orchestra for a hush. He stroked the girl's head with his free hand, then cocked a finger at Sears.

The girl moaned, "I'm not lez, I'm not lez, it was just that one time"; Millard cradled her like a baby.

Sears asked, "Was Betty a lesbian, Lorna?"

I held my breath. Lorna wiped her eyes on Millard's coat front and looked at me. She said, "I'm not lezzie, and Betty wasn't, and we only bummed at normal-type bars, and it was just that one time in the movie because we were broke and on hop, and if this gets in the papers my daddy'll kill me."

I glanced at Millard, sensed that he bought it, and got a strong instinct that the whole dyke offshoot of the case was a fluke. Harry asked, "Did the Mexican man give Betty a viewfinder?"

Lorna muttered "Yes," her head on Millard's shoulder.

"Do you remember his car? The make, the color?"

"I ... I think it was black and old."

"Do you remember the bar where you met him?"

Lorna lifted her head; I saw that her tears had dried. "I think it was on Aviation Boulevard, near all those aircraft plants."

I groaned; that part of Gardena was a solid mile of juke joints, poker parlors and cop-sanctioned whorehouses. Harry said, "When did you see Betty last?"

Lorna moved back to her own chair, clenching herself against another display of emotion—a hardcase reaction for a fifteen-year-old kid. "The last time I saw Betty was a couple of weeks later. Right before she moved out of the Orange Drive place."

"Do you know if Betty ever saw the Mexican man again?"

Lorna picked at the chipped polish on her nails. "The Mex was a fly-by-nighter. He paid us, drove us back to L.A. and left."

I butted in: "But you saw him again, right? There's no way he could have made a copy of the movie before you all drove back from TJ."

Lorna studied her nails. "I went looking for him in Gardena, when I read in the papers about Betty. He was about to go back to Mexico, and I conned him out of a print of the movie. See ... he didn't read the papers, so he didn't know that all of a sudden Betty was famous. See ... I figured that a Black Dahlia stag film was a collector's item, and if the police tried to ship me back to my folks I could sell it and hire a lawyer to fight my extradition. You'll give it back to me, won't you? You won't let people look at it?"

Out of the mouths of babes. Millard said, "You went back to Gardena and found the man again?"

"Uh-huh. I mean yes."

"Where?"

"At one of those bars on Aviation."

"Can you describe the place?"

"It was dark, with flashing lights out front."

"And he willingly gave you a copy of the film? For nothing?"

Lorna eyed the floor. "I did him and his friends."

"Can you improve on your description of him, then?"

"He was fat and he had a tiny little pecker! He was ugly and so were his friends!"

Millard pointed Sears to the door; Harry tiptoed quietly out. Russ said, "We'll try to keep this out of the papers, and we'll destroy the film. One question before the matron takes you up to your room. If we take you down to Tijuana, do you think you could find the house where the movie was shot?"

Shaking her head, Lorna said, "No. I don't want to go down to that awful place. I want to go home."

"So your father can hit you?"

"No. So I can get out again."

Sears returned with a matron; the woman led hard/soft/pathetic/feisty Linda/Lorna away. Harry, Russ and I looked at one another; I felt the girl's sadness smothering me. Finally the senior man said, "Comments?"

Harry kicked in first. "She's hedging on the Mex and the pad in TJ. He probably beat her up and screwed her, and she's afraid of reprisals. Aside from that, I buy her story."

Russ smiled. "What about you, bright penny?"

"She's covering on the Mex angle. I think she might have been screwing him regularly, and now she's protecting him from a smut rap. I'd also lay odds the guy is white, that the Mex routine is a cover-up to go along with the TJ stuff—which I do buy—because that place is a cesspool, and most of the smuthounds I rousted working Patrol got their stuff there."

Millard winked à la Lee Blanchard. "Bucky, you are a very bright penny today. Harry, I want you to talk to Lieutenant Waters here. Tell him to hold the girl incommunicado for seventy-two hours. I want a private cell for her, and I want Meg Caulfield detached from Wilshire Clerical to play cellmate. Tell Meg to give her a good pumping and report in every twenty-four hours.

"When you finish that, call R&I and Ad Vice for the rap sheets on white and Mexican males with pornography convictions, then call Vogel and Koenig and send them down to Gardena to check the bars for Lorna's movie man. Call the Bureau too, and tell Captain Jack we've got a little Dahlia film to look at. Then call the *Times* and give them the smut lead before Ellis Loew sits on it. Give them a Jane Doe for Lorna, have them add an appeal for pornography tips and pack a bag, because we're going down to Dago and TJ later tonight."

I said, "Russ, you know this is a long shot."

"The biggest one since you and Blanchard beat the crap out of each other and became partners. Come on, bright penny. It's blue movie night at City Hall."

* * *

A projector and screen had already been set up in the muster room; an all-star cast was awaiting the all-star smut movie. Lee, Ellis Loew, Jack Tierney, Thad Green and Chief of Police C.B. Horrall himself were seated in front of the screen; Millard handed the film can to the clerical stooge manning the projector, muttering, "Where's the popcorn?"

The big chief walked over and gave me a gladhander's shake. "A pleasure, sir," I said.

"A mutual pleasure, Mr. Ice, and my wife sends her belated regards for the pay raise you and Mr. Fire got us." He pointed to a seat next to Lee. "Lights! Camera! Action!"

I sat down beside my partner. Lee looked drawn, but not dope-juiced. A *Daily News* was unfolded on his lap; I saw "Boulevard-Citizens Mastermind to be Released Tomorrow— L.A. Bound After 8 Years in Custody." Lee checked out my raggedy state and said, "Getting any?"

I was about to respond when the lights went off. A blurred image hit the screen; cigarette smoke wafted into it. A title flashed—*Slave Girls From Hell*—then a big, high-ceilinged room with Egyptian hieroglyphics on the walls came into view in grainy black and white. Pillars shaped like coiled serpents were stationed throughout the room; the camera zoomed in for a close-up of two inset plaster snakes swallowing each other's tails. Then the snakes dissolved into Betty Short, wearing only stockings, doing an inept hoochie-koochie dance.

My groin clenched; I heard Lee draw a sharp breath. An arm entered the screen, passing a cylindrical object to Betty. She took it; the camera moved in. It was a dildo, scales covering the shaft, fangs extending from the large circumcised head. Betty put it in her mouth and sucked it, eyes wide open and glassy.

There was an abrupt cut, then Lorna, naked, was lying on a divan, her legs spread. Betty entered the picture. She knelt between Lorna's legs, stuck the dildo inside her and simulated sex with it. Lorna buckled and rotated her hips, the screen went out of focus, then blipped to a close-up—Lorna writhing in phony ecstasy. Even a two-year-old could tell she was contorting her face to hold back screams. Betty re-entered the frame, poised between Lorna's thighs.

She looked up at the camera, mouthing, "No, please." Then her head was shoved down, and she worked her tongue next to the dildo in a shot so close in that every ugly detail seemed to be magnified ten million times.

I wanted to shut my eyes, but couldn't. Next to me, Chief Horrall said calmly, "Russ, what do you think? You think this has got anything to do with the girl's murder?"

Millard answered with a hoarse voice. "It's a long shot, Chief. The movie was made in November and from what the Martilkova girl said, the Mexican doesn't play as a killer. It's got to be checked out, though. Maybe the Mex showed the movie to somebody, and *he* got a case on Betty. What I—"

Lee kicked his chair over and shouted: "Who gives a fuck if he didn't kill her! I've sent Boy Scouts to the green room for less than that! So if you won't do something about it, I will!"

Everyone sat there, shock-stilled. Lee stood in front of the screen, blinking from the hot white light in his eyes. He wheeled and ripped the obscenity down; the screen and tripod hit the floor with a crash. Betty and Lorna continued their sex on a chalked-up blackboard; Lee took off running. I heard the projector knocked over in back of me; Millard yelled, "Bleichert, get him!"

I got up, tripped, got up again and tore out of the muster room, catching sight of Lee stepping into the elevator at the end of the hall. When the doors shut and the elevator descended, I ran for the stairs, hurtled down six flights and out into the parking lot just in time to see Lee peeling rubber northbound on Broadway. There was a string of unmarked cruisers lined up on the Department's side of the lot; I jogged over and checked under the driver's seat of the nearest one. The keys were right there. I hit the ignition, then the gas, and took off.

I gained ground quickly, coming up behind Lee's Ford as he swerved into the middle lane on Sunset, heading west. I gave him three short horn blasts; he responded by tapping his horn in the LAPD semaphore that meant "Officer in Pursuit." Cars pulled over to let him through—there was nothing I could do but hit my own horn and stay glued to his tail.

We hauled ass out of downtown, through Hollywood and over the Cahuenga Pass to the Valley. Turning onto Ventura Boulevard, I got spooked by the proximity of the lez bar block; when Lee ground his Ford to a halt smack in the middle of it, I choked on a wave of panic and thought: *He can't know about my brass girl, there's no way; the lezzie film must have flipped his switch.* Then Lee got out and pushed through the door of La Verne's Hideaway. Worse panic made me stomp the brakes and fishtail the cruiser into the sidewalk; thoughts of Madeleine and evidence suppression raps propelled me into the dive after my partner.

Lee was facing off booths full of daggers and femmes, shouting curses. I flailed with my eyes for Madeleine and the barmaid I'd rousted; not seeing them, I got ready to cold cock my best friend.

"You fucking quiff divers seen a little movie called *Slave Girls From Hell*? You buy your stag shit from a fat Mex about forty? You—"

I grabbed Lee from behind in a full nelson and spun him around toward the door. His arms were clenched and his back was arched, but I was able to use his weight against him. We stumbled outside, then tripped together in a jumble of arms and legs and hit the pavement. I kept the hold clamped on with all my strength, then heard a siren approaching and snapped that Lee wasn't resisting— he was just lying there, muttering "Partner" over and over.

The siren wailed louder, then died; I heard car doors slamming. I extricated myself from Lee and helped him, rag doll limp, to his feet. And Ellis Loew was right there.

Loew had murder in his eyes. It hit me that Lee's explosion came from his weird chastity, a week of death and dope and its pornographic capper. Safe myself, I put an arm around my partner's shoulders. "Mr. Loew, it was just that goddamn movie. Lee thought the dykes here could give us a lead on the Mex."

Loew hissed, "Bleichert, shut up," then turned his velvet rage on Lee: "Blanchard, I got you Warrants. You're *my* man, and you made *me* look like a fool in front of the two most powerful men in the Department. This is no lesbian killing, those girls were on drugs and hated it. Now I covered for you with Horrall and Green, but I don't know how much good that will do you in the long run. If you weren't *Mr. Fire, Big Lee Blanchard*, you'd be suspended from duty already. You've gotten personally involved in the Short case, and that's an unprofessionalism I will not tolerate. You're back on Warrants duty as of tomorrow morning. Report to me at 0800, and bring in formal letters of apology to Chief Horrall and Chief Green. For the sake of your pension, I advise you to grovel."

Lee, his body limp, said, "I want to go to TJ to look for the smut man."

Loew shook his head. "Under the circumstances, I would call that request ridiculous. Vogel and Koenig are going to Tijuana, you're back on Warrants, and Bleichert, you're to remain on the Short case. Good day, Officers."

Loew stormed over to his black-and-white; the patrolman driver hung a U-turn out into traffic. Lee said, "I have to talk to Kay." I nodded, and a sheriff's patrol car cruised by, the passenger cop blowing kisses to the lezzies in the doorway. Lee walked to his car murmuring, "Laurie. Laurie, oh babe."

13

I SHOWED up at the Bureau at 8:00 the next morning, wanting to ease Lee through the ignominy of his return to Warrants and share the diet of crow Ellis Loew would undoubtedly be feeding him. Identical memo slips from Chief Green were on both of our desks: "Report to my office tomorrow, 1/22/47, 6:00 P.M." The handwritten words looked ominous.

Lee did not report in at 8:00; I sat at my desk for the next hour, picturing him fretting over Bobby De Witt's release, a captive of his ghosts, his ghost chaser redemption gone now that he was off the Dahlia case. Across the partition in the DA's office, I heard Loew barking and pleading on the phone to the city editors of the *Mirror* and *Daily News*—Republican rags rumored to be sympathetic to his political aspirations. The gist of his talk was that he would help them cutthroat the *Times* and *Herald* with inside Dahlia info on the proviso that they softpedal their coverage of Betty Short's roundheeled ways and portray her as a sweet but misguided young girl. From the hotshot's self-satisfied farewells, I could tell that the newsmen went for it, buying Loew's line that "The more sympathy we attract for the girl, the more juice we get when I prosecute the killer."

When Lee didn't show up by 10:00, I went into the muster room and read through the bulging E. Short case file, wanting to satisfy myself that Madeleine's name wasn't in it. Two hours and two hundred form pages later I was satisfied—her name was not listed among the hundreds of people questioned, nor was she fingered by tipsters. The only mention of lesbians was obvious nut case stuff—religious crackpots calling in poison phone clues, informing on rival sect members as "Nun dykes sacrificing the girl to Pope Pius XII" and "Lezbos performing communistic anti-Christ rituals."

By noon, Lee still hadn't put in an appearance. I called the house, University squadroom and the El Nido Hotel, with no success. Wanting to look busy so that no one would put me to work, I prowled the bulletin boards reading summary reports.

Russ Millard had compiled a new update before leaving for San Diego and Tijuana last night. It stated that he and Harry Sears would be checking the R&I and Ad Vice files for convicted and suspected pornographers, and would be searching for the smut movie filming site down in TJ. Vogel and Koenig had been unable to locate Lorna Martilkova's "Mexican man" in Gardena, and were also going to Tijuana to work on the stag film angle. The coroner's inquest had been held yesterday; Elizabeth Short's mother was present, and identified her remains. Marjorie Graham and Sheryl Saddon testified about Betty's life in Hollywood, Red Manley as to how he drove Betty up from Dago and dropped her off in front of the Biltmore Hotel on January tenth. Intensive canvassing of the area around the Biltmore had thus far yielded no verified sightings, the records of convicted sex loonies and regis- tered sex offenders were still being combed, the four drool case confessors were still being held at City Jail awaiting alibi checks, sanity hearings and further questioning. The circus was continuing, phone tips flooding in, resulting in third-, fourth- and fifth-hand questionings—officers talking to people who knew people who knew people who knew the exalted Dahlia. Needle in a haystack stuff straight down the line.

I was getting goldbrick looks from the men working at their desks, so I went back to my cubicle. Madeleine jumped into my head; I picked up the phone and called her.

She answered on the third ring: "Sprague residence."

"It's me. You want to get together?"

"When?"

"Now. I'll pick you up in forty-five minutes."

"Don't come here, Daddy's having a business soiree. Meet you at the Red Arrow?"

I sighed. "I've got an apartment, you know."

"I only rut in motels. One of my rich girl idiosyncrasies. Room eleven at the Arrow in forty-five?"

I said, "I'll be there," and hung up. Ellis Loew tapped the par- tition. "Go to work, Bleichert. You've been skating all morning, and it's getting on my nerves. And when you see your phantom partner, tell him his little no-show has cost him three days' pay. Now check out a radio car and roll."

* * *

I rolled straight to the Red Arrow Motel. Madeleine's Packard was parked in the alley behind the bungalows; the door to room eleven was unlocked. I walked in, smelled her perfume and squinted into the darkness until I was rewarded with a giggle. Undressing, my eyes got accustomed to the lack of light; I saw Madeleine—a nude beacon on a tattered bedspread.

We joined so strongly that the bedsprings banged the floor. Madeleine kissed her way down to between my legs, made me hard, then did a quick turn onto her back. I went in her thinking of Betty and the snake shaft thing, then blotted it out by concentrating on the ripped wallpaper in front of my eyes. I wanted to go slow, but Madeleine gasped, "Don't hold back, I'm ready." I pushed hard, slamming the two of us together, my hands braced on the bed rail. Madeleine locked her legs around my back, grabbed the rail over her head and pushed, pulled and gyrated against me. We came seconds apart, moving in a stretching, slamming counterpoint; when my head hit the pillow, I bit at it to stanch my tremors.

Madeleine slid out from under me. "Sugar, are you all right?"

I was seeing the snake thing. Madeleine tickled me; I twisted around and looked at her to make it go away. "Smile at me. Look soft and sweet."

Madeleine gave me a Pollyanna grin. Her smeared red lipstick reminded me of the Dahlia's death smile; I shut my eyes and grabbed her hard. She stroked my back softly, murmuring, "Bucky, what is it?"

I stared at the curtains on the far wall. "We picked up Linda Martin yesterday. She had a print of a stag movie in her purse, her and Betty Short playing lez. They filmed it down in TJ, and there was all this spooky stuff in it. It spooked me, and it spooked my partner bad."

Madeleine stopped her caresses. "Did Linda mention me?"

"No, and I checked through the case file. There's no mention of that note-leaving number you pulled. But we've got a police-woman planted in the girl's cell to pump her, and if she blabs, you're sunk."

"I'm not worried, sugar. Linda probably doesn't even remember me."

I slid over to where I could eyeball Madeleine up close. Her lipstick was a bloody disarray, and I daubed at it with the pillow. "Babe, I'm withholding evidence for you. It's a fair trade for what I'm getting, but it still spooks me. So you be damn sure you come clean. I'll ask you one time. Is there anything you haven't told me about you and Betty and Linda?"

Madeleine ran her fingers down my rib cage, exploring the welt scars I'd gotten in the Blanchard fight. "Sugar, Betty and I made love once, that one time we met last summer, I just did it to see what it would be like to be with a girl who looked so much like me."

I felt like I was sinking; like the bed was dropping out from under me. Madeleine looked like she was at the end of a long tunnel, captured by some kind of weird camera trick. She said, "Bucky, that's all of it, I swear that's all of it," her voice wobbling from deep nowhere. I got up and dressed, and it was only when I strapped on my .38 and cuffs that I felt like I'd quit treading quicksand.

Madeleine pleaded, "Stay, sugar, stay"; I went out the door before I could succumb. In my cruiser, I flipped on the two-way, looking for good sane cop noise to distract me. The dispatcher barked, "Code four all units at Crenshaw and Stocker. Clear robbery scene, two dead, suspect dead, unit 4-A-82 reports suspect is Raymond Douglas Nash, white male, object fugitive warrant number—"

I yanked the radio cord and hit the ignition, gas and siren in what felt like a single swipe. Pulling out, I heard Lee pacifying me with "Don't tell me you don't know the dead girl is a better piece of pie than Junior Nash"; speedballing downtown, I saw myself kowtowing to my partner's ghosts even though I knew the Okie killer was a real live killer bogeyman. Jamming into the Hall parking lot, I saw Lee cajoling, wheedling, pushing, pulling and twisting at me to get his way; running up to the Bureau, I saw red.

I came out of the stairway yelling, "Blanchard!" Dick Cavanaugh, walking out of the bullpen, pointed to the bathroom. I kicked in the door; Lee was washing his hands in the sink.

He held them up to show me, blood oozing from cuts on the knuckles. "I beat up a wall. Penance for Nash."

It wasn't enough. I let the crimson loose all the way, smashing my best friend until my own hands were ruined and he was senseless at my feet.

14

LOSING THE first Bleichert-Blanchard fight got me local celebrity, Warrants and close to nine grand in cash; winning the rematch got me a sprained left wrist, two dislocated knuckles and a day in bed, woozy from an allergic reaction to the codeine pills Captain Jack gave me when he got word of the punch-out and saw me in my cubicle trying to tape up my fist. The only thing good that came of my "victory" was a twenty-four-hour respite from Elizabeth Short; the worst was yet to come—bracing Lee and Kay to see if I could salvage the three of us, without giving up my balls.

I drove to the house Wednesday afternoon, Dahlia kiss-off day and the one-week anniversary of the celebrity stiff's first appearance. The confab with Thad Green was scheduled for 6:00 that evening, and if there was any way to work a patch job with Lee before then, it had to be tried.

The front door was standing open; the coffee table held a copy of the *Herald*, folded open to pages two and three. The detritus of my messy life was smeared all over it—the Dahlia, hatchet-faced Bobby De Witt homeward bound, Junior Nash shot by an off-duty sheriff's dick after he knocked off a Jap greengrocer, killing the proprietor and his fourteen-year-old son.

"We're famous, Dwight."

Kay was standing in the hallway. I laughed; my bad knuckles throbbed. "Notorious, maybe. Where's Lee?"

"I don't know. He left yesterday afternoon."

"You know he's in trouble, don't you?"

"I know you beat him up."

I walked over. Kay's breath reeked of cigarettes, her face was mottled from crying. I held her; she held me back and said, "I don't blame you for it."

I nuzzled her hair. "De Witt's probably in L.A. by now. If Lee isn't back by tonight, I'll come and stay with you."

Kay pulled away. "Don't come unless you want to sleep with me."

I said, "Kay, I can't."

"Why? Because of that neighbor girl you're seeing?"

I remembered my lie to Lee. "Yes ... no, not that. It's just that ..."

"It's just *what*, Dwight?"

I grabbed Kay so she wouldn't be able to look in my eyes and know that half of what I was saying made me a child, half made me a liar. "It's just that you and Lee are my family, and Lee's my partner, and until we get this trouble he's in settled and see if we're still partners then you and me together is just no damn good. The girl I've been seeing is nothing. She doesn't really mean a thing to me."

Kay said, "You're just frightened of anything that doesn't involve fighting and cops and guns and all that," and tightened her grip. I let myself be held, knowing she'd nailed me clean. Then I broke it off and drove downtown to "All That."

* * *

The clock in Thad Green's waiting room hit 6:00, and there was no Lee; at 6:01 Green's secretary opened his door and ushered me in. The Chief of Detectives looked up from his desk. "Where's Blanchard? He's the one I really wanted to see."

I said, "I don't know, sir," and stood at parade rest; Green pointed me to a chair. I sat down, and the COD fixed me with a hard stare. "You've got fifty words or less to explain your partner's behavior Monday night. Go."

I said, "Sir, Lee's little sister was murdered when he was a kid, and the Dahlia case is what you might call an obsession with him. Bobby De Witt, the man he sent up on the Boulevard-Citizens job, got out yesterday, and a week ago we killed those four hoods. The stag film was the capper. It set Lee off, and he pulled that stunt at the dyke bar because he thought he could get a lead on the guy who made the film."

Green quit nodding along. "You sound like a shyster trying to justify his client's actions. In my police department, a man checks his emotional baggage when he pins on his badge, or he checks out. But just to let you know that I'm not entirely unsympathetic, I'll tell you this, I'm suspending Blanchard for a trial board, but not for his Monday night tantrums. I'm suspending him for a memo he submitted stating that Junior Nash blew our jurisdiction. I think it was a phony. What do you think, Officer?"

I felt my legs fluttering. "I believed it, sir."

"Then you're not as intelligent as your Academy scores led me to believe. When you see Blanchard, tell him to turn in his gun and badge. You stay on the Short investigation, and kindly refrain from fisticuffs on city property. Good night, Officer."

I stood up, saluted and about-faced out of the office, maintaining my military gait until I was down the hall in the muster room. Grabbing a desk phone, I called the house, University squadroom and the El Nido Hotel—all with zero results. Then a dark thought crossed my mind, and I dialed the number of the County Parole office.

A man answered: "Los Angeles County Parole, may I help you?"

"This is Officer Bleichert, LAPD. I need the disposition on a recent parolee."

"Shoot, Officer."

"Robert 'Bobby' De Witt. Came out of Quentin yesterday."

"That's easy. He hasn't reported to his PO yet. We called the bus depot at Santa Rosa, and found out that De Witt didn't buy a ticket for L.A., he bought one for San Diego, with a transfer to Tijuana. We haven't issued an absconder warrant yet. De Witt's PO figured he might have gone down to TJ to get laid. He's giving him until tomorrow morning to show up."

I hung up, relieved that De Witt didn't head straight for L.A. Thinking of prowling for Lee, I took the elevator down to the parking lot and saw Russ Millard and Harry Sears walking toward the back stairs. Russ noticed me and hooked a finger; I trotted over.

I said, "What happened in TJ?"

Harry, breathing Sen-Sen, answered: "Goose egg on the stag movie. We checked for the pad and couldn't find it, rousted some smut peddlers. Double goose egg. We checked some of the Short girl's acquaintances in Dago—triple gooser. I—"

Millard put a hand on his partner's shoulder. "Bucky, Blanchard's down in Tijuana. A border patrolman we talked to saw him, recognized him from all the fight publicity. He was hobnobbing with a bad-looking bunch of Rurales."

I thought of De Witt TJ bound and wondered why Lee would be talking to the Mex state police. "When?"

Sears said, "Last night. Loew and Vogel and Koenig are down there too, at the Divisidero Hotel. They've been talking to the TJ cops. Russ thinks they're measuring spics for a frame on the Dahlia."

Lee chased smut demons through my mind; I saw him bloody at my feet and shivered. Millard said, "Which is crap, because Meg Caulfield got the straight dope on the smut man out of the Martilkova girl. He's a white guy named Walter 'Duke' Wellington. We checked his Ad Vice jacket, and he's got a half dozen pandering and pornography beefs. All well and good, except Captain Jack got a letter from Wellington, postmarked three days ago. He's hiding out, gun-shy from all the Dahlia publicity, and he copped to making the film with Betty Short and Lorna. He was afraid of getting tagged for the snuff, so he sent in a detailed alibi for

Betty's missing days. Jack checked it out personally, and it's iron-clad. Wellington sent a copy of the letter to the *Herald*, and they're publishing it tomorrow."

I said, "So Lorna was lying to protect him?"

Sears nodded. "That looks like the picture. Wellington's still on the lam from old pimping warrants, though, and Lorna clammed up when she got wise to Meg. And here's the kicker: we called Loew to tell him the Mex man was horseshit, but a Rurale buddy of ours says that Vogel and Koenig are still rousting spics."

The circus was turning into a farce. I said, "If the newspaper letter kiboshes their Mex job, they'll be looking for patsies up here. We should hold our info back from them. Lee's on suspension, but he made carbons from the case file, and he's got them stored in a hotel room in Hollywood. We should hold on to it, use it to store our stuff."

Millard and Sears nodded slowly; the real kicker kicked me. "County Parole said Bobby De Witt bought a ticket for TJ. If Lee's down there too, it could be trouble."

Millard shivered. "I don't like the feel of it. De Witt's a bad piece of work, and maybe he found out that Lee was headed down there. I'll call the Border Patrol and have them put out a detain order on him."

Suddenly I knew it all came down to me. "I'm going."

15

I CROSSED the border at dawn. Tijuana was just coming awake as I turned onto Revolución, its main drag. Child beggars were digging for breakfast in trash cans, taco venders were stirring pots of dog-meat stew, sailors and marines were being escorted out of whorehouses at the end of their five-spot all-nighters. The smarter ones stumbled over to Calle Colon and the penicillin pushers; the stupidos hotfooted toward East TJ, the Blue Fox and Chicago Club—no doubt eager to catch the early morning donkey show. Tourist cars were already lined up outside the cut-rate upholstery joints; Rurales driving prewar Chevys cruised like vultures, wearing black uniforms that looked almost like Nazi issue.

I cruised myself, looking for Lee and his '40 Ford. I thought about stopping at the Border Patrol hut or Rurale substation to seek help, then remembered my partner was suspended from duty, illegally armed and probably stretched so thin that words from the wrong greaser would provoke him to God knows what. Recalling the Divisidero Hotel from my high school excursions south, I drove to the edge of town to seek American aid.

The pink Art Deco monstrosity stood on a bluff overlooking a tin roof shantytown. I intimidated the desk clerk; he told me the "Loew party" was in suite 462. I found it on the ground floor rear, angry voices booming on the other side of the door.

Fritzie Vogel was yelling, "I still say we get ourselves a spic! The letter to the *Herald* didn't say stag movie, it just said Wellington saw the Dahlia and the other girlie in November! We can still—"

Ellis Loew shouted back: "We *can't* do that! Wellington admitted making the movie to Tierney! He's the supervising officer, and we can't go over his head!"

I opened the door and saw Loew, Vogel and Koenig huddled in chairs, all of them holding eight-star *Herald*s obviously hot off the presses. The framing session fell silent; Koenig gawked; Loew and Vogel muttered, "Bleichert," simultaneously.

I said, "Fuck the fucking Dahlia. Lee's down here, Bobby De Witt's here and it's got to go bad. You—"

Loew said, "Fuck Blanchard, he's suspended"; I beelined for him. Koenig and Vogel formed a wedge between us; trying to move through them was like bucking a brick wall. The DA backed off to the other side of the room, Koenig grabbed my arms, Vogel put his hands on my chest and pushed me outside. Loew evil-eyed me from the doorway, then Fritzie chucked my chin. "I've got a soft spot for light heavyweights. If you promise not to hit Billy, I'll help you find your partner."

I nodded, and Koenig let me go. Fritzie said, "We'll take my car. You don't look fit to drive."

* * *

Fritzie drove; I eyeballed. He kept up a stream of chatter on the Short case and the lieutenancy it was going to get him; I watched beggars swarm turistas, hookers dispense front seat blow jobs and zoot suit youths prowl for drunks to roll. After four fruitless hours the streets became too car-choked to maneuver in, and we got out and walked.

On foot, the squalor was worse. The kiddie beggars got right up in your face, jabbering, shoving crucifixes at you. Fritzie swatted and kicked them away, but their hunger-ridden faces got to me, so I changed a fiver into pesos and tossed handfuls of coins into the gutter whenever they converged. It spawned scratching, biting and gouging free-for-alls, but it was better than looking into sunken eyes and seeing nada.

An hour of prowling two abreast got us no Lee, no Lee's '40 Ford and no gringos resembling Bobby De Witt. Then a Rurale in black shirt and jackboots, lounging in a doorway, caught my eye. He said, "Policia?" and I stopped and flashed my badge in answer.

The cop dug in his pockets and pulled out a teletype photo strip. The picture was too blurred to identify, but the "Robert Richard De Witt" was plain as day. Fritzie patted the cop's epaulets. "Where, Admiral?"

The Mex clicked his heels and barked, "Estación, vamanos!" He marched ahead of us, turning into an alley lined with VD clinics, pointing to a cinderblock hut fenced in with barbed wire. Fritzie handed him a dollar; the Mex saluted like Mussolini and about-faced away. I strode for the station, forcing myself not to run.

Rurales holding tommy guns flanked the doorway. I showed my badge; they heel clicked and let me in. Fritzie caught up with me inside; dollar bill in hand, he went straight for the front desk. The desk cop grabbed the buck and Fritzie said, "Fugitivo? Americano? De Witt?"

The deskman smiled and hit a switch beside his chair, barred doors in the side wall clicked open. Fritzie said, "Precisely what is it we want this scum to tell us?"

I said, "Lee's down here, probably chasing smut leads on his own. De Witt came here directly from Quentin."

"Without checking in with his PO?"

"Right."

"And De Witt has a hard-on for Blanchard from the Boulevard-Citizens job?"

"Right."

"Enough said."

We walked down a corridor lined with cells. De Witt was alone in the last lock-up, sitting on the floor. The door buzzed open; Kay Lake's defiler stood up. The years in stir had not been kind to him: the hatchet-faced tough of the '39 newspaper pictures was now a well-used piece of work, bloated in the body, grizzled in the face, his pachuco haircut as outdated as his Salvation Army suit.

Fritzie and I walked in. De Witt's greeting was con bravado tinged with just the right amount of subservience. "Cops, huh? Well, at least you're Americans. Never thought I'd be glad to see you guys."

Fritzie said, "Why start now?" and kicked De Witt in the balls. He doubled over; Fritzie grabbed his duck's ass scruff and gave him a hard backhand. De Witt started to foam at the mouth; Fritzie let go of his neck and wiped pomade on his sleeve. De Witt hit the floor, then crawled over to the commode and vomited into it. When he tried to get himself upright, Fritzie pushed his head back into the bowl and held it there with a big spit-shined wing-tip brogue. The ex-bank-robber-pimp drank piss water and puke.

Vogel said, "Lee Blanchard's here in TJ, and you came here flush out of Big Q. That's a goddamned strange coincidence, and I don't like it. I don't like you, I don't like the syphilitic whore you were born out of, I don't like being down here in a rat-infested foreign country when I could be at home with my family. I *do* like inflicting pain on criminals, so you had better answer my questions truthfully, or I'll hurt you bad."

Fritzie released his foot; De Witt came up gasping for air. I picked a soiled skivvy shirt up off the floor, and was about to hand it to him when I remembered the lash scars on Kay's legs. The image made me throw the shirt at De Witt, then grab a chair from the catwalk and reach for my handcuffs. Fritzie swabbed the ex-con's face, I shoved him into the seat and cuffed his wrists to the back slats.

De Witt looked up at us; his trouser legs darkened as his bladder went. Fritzie said, "Did you know that Sergeant Blanchard is here in Tijuana?"

De Witt shook his head back and forth, spraying off the remnants of his toilet dip. "I ain't seen Blanchard since my fucking trial!"

Fritzie shot him a little backhand, his Masonic ring severing a cheek vein. "Don't use profanity with me, and address me as sir. Now, did you know that Sergeant Blanchard is here in Tijuana?"

De Witt blubbered, "No"; Fritzie said, "No, *sir*," and slapped him. De Witt hung his head, lolling his chin on his chest. Fritzie prodded it up with one finger. "No, what?"

De Witt screeched, "No, sir!"

Even through my hate haze I could tell he was coming clean. I said, "Blanchard's afraid of you. Why?"

Twisting in the chair, greasy pompadour wilted over his fore-head, De Witt laughed. Wild laughter, the kind that cuts through pain, then makes it worse. Livid, Fritzie balled a fist to punish him; I said, "Let him be." Vogel relented; De Witt's loony chuckles trailed off.

Sucking in breath, De Witt said, "Man o Manieschewitz, what a laugh. Lee beauty gotta be scared of me 'cause of how I flapped my trap at the trial, but all I know is what I read in the papers, and I gotta tell you that little reefer roust put the fear of God into me, if I'm lyin', I'm flyin'. Maybe I was thinkin' revenge up to then, maybe I was talkin' trash to my cellies, but when Lee beauty killed them niggers and—"

Vogel right hooked De Witt, toppling him, chair and all, to the floor. Spitting blood and teeth, the aging lounge lizard moaned and laughed at the same time; Fritzie knelt beside him and pinched his carotid artery, shutting off the blood to his brain. "Bobby boy, I do not like Sergeant Blanchard, but he is a fellow officer, and I will not have syphilitic scum like you defaming him. Now you risked a parole violation and a trip back to Q for a trip down here. When I let go of your neck you will tell me why, or I will pinch your neck again until your gray cells go snap, crackle and pop like Kellogg's Rice Krispies."

Fritzie released the hold; De Witt's face went from blue to dark red. With one hand, Vogel grabbed suspect and chair and placed them upright. Lounge lizard Bobby started to laugh again, then sputtered blood and stopped. Looking up at Fritzie, he reminded me of a dog who loves his cruel master because it's the only one he's got. His voice was a beaten dog whimper: "I came down to cop some horse and bring it back to L.A. before I reported in to my PO. The guy I got is supposed to be a softie, you tell him 'Gee, sir, I been in stir eight years and I hadda get my ashes hauled,' and he don't violate you for bein' late."

De Witt took a deep breath; Fritzie said, "Snap, crackle, pop." Bobby boy dog whimpered the rest of his confession rapidamente: "The man down here is this cholo named Felix Chasco. He's sup-posed to meet me at the Calexico Gardens Motel tonight. The L.A. man's the brother of this guy I knew at Quentin. I ain't met him and please don't hurt me no more."

Fritzie let out a huge whoop and ran out of the cell to report his booty; De Witt licked blood off his lips and looked at me, his dog master now that Vogel was gone. I said, "Finish up on you and Lee Blanchard. And don't get hysterical this time."

De Witt said, "Sir, all that's between me and Blanchard is that I fucked this cunt Kay Lake."

I remember moving toward him and I remember picking him up two-handed by the neck, wondering how hard you had to squeeze a dog's throat to make its eyeballs pop out. I remember him changing color and voices in Spanish, and Fritzie shouting, "His story checks." Then I remember being hurled backward, thinking, so that's what bars feel like. Then I remember nothing.

* * *

I came to thinking I'd been knocked down in a third Bleichert-Blanchard fight, wondering how much hurt I'd put on my partner. I babbled, "Lee? Lee? Are you all right?" then sighted in on two greaser cops with ridiculous dime store regalia on their blackshirts. Fritzie Vogel towered over them, saying, "I let Bobby boy go so we could tail him to his pal. But he blew the tail while you were catching up on your beauty sleep, which was too bad for him."

Someone hugely strong lifted me up off the cell floor; coming out of my haze I knew it had to be Big Bill Koenig. Woozy and rubberlegged, I let Fritzie and the Mex cops lead me through the station and outside. It was dusk, and the TJ sky was already lit with neon. A Studebaker patrol car pulled up; Fritzie and Bill ushered me into the backseat. The driver hit the loudest siren the world had ever heard, then gunned it.

We drove west out of town, stopping in the gravel center of a horseshoe-shaped auto court. TJ cops in khakis and jodhpurs were standing guard in front of a back unit, holding pump shotguns. Fritzie winked and offered me his arm to lean on; I spurned it and got out of the car under my own steam. Fritzie led the way over; the cops saluted us with their gun barrels, then opened the door.

The room was a cordite-reeking slaughterhouse. Bobby De Witt and a Mexican man lay dead on the floor, bullet holes oozing blood all over them. Brain spatters leaking fluid covered one entire wall; De Witt's neck was bruised from where I'd been throttling him. My first coherent thought was that I'd done it during my blackout, vigilante vengeance to protect the only two people I loved. Fritzie must have been a mind reader, because he laughed and said, "Not you, boyo. The spic is Felix Casco, a known dope trafficker. Maybe it was other dope scum, maybe it was Lee, maybe it was God. I say let our Mexican colleagues handle their own dirty laundry and let's us go back to L.A. and get the son of a bitch who sliced the Dahlia."

16

BOBBY DE Witt's murder got a half column in the L.A. *Mirror,* I got a day off from a surprisingly solicitious Ellis Loew, Lee's disappearance got a squad of Metropolitan Division cops full-time.

I spent most of the day off in Captain Jack's office, being interrogated by them. They asked me hundreds of questions about Lee—from the reasons for his outbursts at the stag film and La Verne's Hideaway, to his obsession with the Short case, to the Nash memo and his shack job with Kay. I played fast and loose with facts, and lied by omission—keeping it zipped about Lee's Benzedrine use, his file room at the El Nido Hotel and the fact that his cohabitation was chaste. The Metro bulls repeatedly asked me if I thought Lee killed Bobby De Witt and Felix Chasco; I repeatedly told them he wasn't capable of murder. Asked for an interpretation of my partner's flight, I told them about beating Lee up over the Nash job, adding that he was an ex-boxer, maybe soon to be an ex-cop, too old to go back to fighting, too volatile to live a squarejohn life—and the Mexican interior was probably as good a place as any for a man like that. As the interrogation wound down, I sensed that the officers weren't interested in securing Lee's safety—they were building a case for his LAPD expulsion. I was repeatedly told not to stick my nose in their investigation and each time I agreed I dug my fingers into my palms to keep from hurling insults and worse.

From City Hall I went to see Kay. Two Metro goons had already paid her a visit, putting her through the wringer about her life with Lee, rehashing her old life with Bobby De Witt. The iceberg look she gave me said I was slime for belonging to the same police department; when I tried to comfort her and offer words of encouragement about Lee's return, she said, "And all that," and pushed me away.

I checked out room 204 of the El Nido Hotel then, hoping for some kind of message, some kind of clue that said, "I'll be back, and the three of us will keep going." What I found was a shrine to Elizabeth Short.

The room was a typical Hollywood bachelor flop: Murphy bed, sink, tiny closet. But the walls were adorned with Betty Short portrait pictures, newspaper and magazine photos, horror glossies from 39th and Norton, dozens of them enlarged to magnify every gruesome detail. The bed was covered with cardboard boxes—an entire detective's case file, with carbons of miscellaneous memos, tip lists, evidence indexes, FIs and questioning reports all cross-filed alphabetically.

Having nothing to do and no one to do it with, I leafed through the folders. The bulk of the information was staggering, the manpower behind it more staggering, the fact that it was all over one silly girl the most staggering of all. I didn't know whether to toast Betty Short or rip her off the walls, so I badged the desk clerk on my way out, paid him a month's rent in advance and kept the room like I promised Millard and Sears—even though I was really holding it for Sergeant Leland C. Blanchard.

Who was somewhere out there in the Big Nowhere.

I called up the classified desks of the *Times*, *Mirror*, *Herald* and *Daily News*, placing a personals ad to run indefinitely: "Fire—Nightflower room will remain intact. Send me a message—Ice." With that behind me, I drove to the only place I could think of to send him one.

39th and Norton was just a block of empty lots now. No arclights, no police cars, no nighttime gawkers. A Santa Ana wind blew in while I stood there, and the more I pulled for Lee to come back to me the more I knew my hotshot cop life was as gone as everybody's favorite dead girl.

17

IN THE morning I sent the big boys a message. Hiding out in a storage room down the hall from my cubicle, I typed copies of a transfer request letter, one each for Loew, Russ Millard and Captain Jack. The letter read:

> I request to be detached from the Elizabeth Short investigation immediately, and returned to my duties at Central Division Warrants. I feel that the Short case is more than adequately staffed, by far more experienced officers than myself, and that I could more

effectively serve the Department working Warrants. Moreover, with my partner, Sergeant L.C. Blanchard, missing, I will be in the position of Senior Officer, and I will need to break in a replacement at a time when there is most likely a large backlog of priority papers. In preparation for my duties as Senior Warrants officer, I have been studying for the Sergeant's Examination, and expect to take it at the next promotion board this spring. This, I feel, will give me leadership training, and will make up for my relative lack of experience as a plainclothes field officer.

Respectfully,
Dwight W. Bleichert, Badge 1611,
Central Detectives

Finishing, I read the letter over, deciding that it worked in just the right blend of respect and exasperation, with the half-truth about the Sergeant's Exam a good closing line. I was signing the copies when I heard a tremendous ruckus coming from the bullpen.

I folded the pages into my jacket pocket and went to investigate. A group of detectives and crime lab techs in white smocks were surrounding a table, looking down at it, jabbering and gesturing away. I joined the throng, muttering "Holy fuck," when I saw what was jazzing them.

An envelope was lying on a metal evidence tray. It was stamped and postmarked and smelled faintly of gasoline. The front of it was covered with letters clipped from newspapers and magazines, glued to the plain white surface. The words spelled out:

TO THE HERALD AND OTHER L.A. PAPERS.
HERE IS DAHLIA'S BELONGINGS.
LETTER TO FOLLOW.

A lab man wearing rubber gloves slit the envelope and pulled out the contents—a little black address book, a plastic-sheathed Social Security card and a thin stack of photographs. Squinting, I read the name on the card—Elizabeth Ann Short—and knew the Dahlia case had blown wide open. The man next to me was talking the delivery up—a postal carrier found the envelope in a mailbox near the downtown library, almost keeled from a heart attack, then grabbed a pair of radio car bulls, who code three'd the booty over.

Ellis Loew pushed his way up against the lab techs, Fritzie Vogel at his heels. The head tech flailed his hands in anger; a cacophony of speculation hit the pen. Then there was a loud whistle, and Russ Millard yelled, "Damnit, back off and let them work. And give them some quiet."

We did.

The techs descended on the envelope, dusting it with print powder, leafing through the address book, examining the snapshots and calling out their findings like surgeons at an operating table:

"Two partial latents on the back flap, smudged, no more than one or two comparison points, not enough to run a make on, maybe enough to compare to incoming suspects—"

"No prints on Social Security card—"

"Pages of address book readable, but gasoline saturated, no chance of sustaining latents. Names and phone numbers mostly men, not listed alphabetically, some pages ripped out—"

"Photographs are of Short girl with servicemen in uniform, the men's faces crossed out—"

Stunned, I wondered: *Would* a letter follow? Was my random snuff theory blown? Since the stuff was obviously sent in by the killer, was *he* one of the servicemen in the pictures? Was the mailing cat and mouse, or the precursor to surrender and confession? All around me, other officers were running with the same dope, the same questions, talking in knots of two and three, or looking rapt, like they were talking with themselves. The lab techs took off with the plethora of new leads, cradling them in rubber-gloved hands. Then the only calm man in the room whistled again.

And again the commotion froze. Russ Millard, poker-faced, counted the heads and pointed us over to the rear bulletin board. We lined up there; he said, "I don't know what it means, except I'm pretty sure the killer sent the stuff. The lab boys are going to need more time on the envelope, then they'll photograph the pages and give us a list of names to do interviews from."

Dick Cavanaugh said, "Russ, he's playing with us. Some of the pages were ripped out, and I'll lay you ten to one his name was on one of them."

Millard smiled. "Maybe, maybe not. Maybe he's crazy and wants to get caught, maybe some of the people in the book know him. Maybe the techs will get latents off the photos or be able to identify some of the men from the insignia of their uniforms. Maybe the bastard *will* send a letter. That's a lot of maybes, so I'll tell you what we've got for sure: all eleven of you are going to drop what you're doing and canvass the area around the mailbox where that envelope was found. Harry and I will be going over the case file to see if any of our previous suspects live or work around there. *Then*, when we've got the list of names from the book, we'll go at it *discreetly*. Betty spread herself pretty thin with men, and homewrecking isn't my style. Harry?"

Sears was standing by the wall map of downtown L.A., holding a pen and clipboard. He stuttered, "W-w-we'll do f-f-foot beats." I saw my transfer request stamped "Rejected." Then I heard an argument on the opposite side of the squadroom.

The arguers were Ellis Loew and Jack Tierney, both of them trying to score points and keep it sotto voce. They ducked behind a wall post for privacy, I ducked over to an adjacent phone cubicle to eavesdrop—hoping for skinny on Lee.

It wasn't about Lee—it was about *Her*.

"...Jack, Horrall wants to take three quarters of the men off the investigation. Bond issue or no bond issue, he thinks he's given the voters enough of a show. We can get around him by going at the names in the book a hundred percent. The more publicity the case gets, the more truck we've got with Horrall—"

"Goddamn it, Ellis—"

"No. Just listen to me. Before, I wanted to downplay the girl as a floozy. The way I see it now is that it's too far out in the open already to sit on. We know what she was, and we'll get it confirmed a couple of hundred times by the men in that little black book. We keep our men questioning them, I'll keep feeding the names to my newspaper contacts, we'll keep a head of steam on this thing until we get the killer."

"It's a sucker play, Ellis. The killer's name probably isn't in the book. He's a psycho, and he's showing us his backside and saying, 'Make something out of it.' The girl's a gravy train, Ellis. I've known it from the beginning, just like you. But this has got to backfire on us. I'm working a half dozen other homicides with skeleton crews, and if the married men in that book get their names in the paper, then their lives will be shot to shit because they copped Betty Short for a quick piece of tail."

There was a long stretch of silence. Then Loew said, "Jack, you know I'll be DA sooner or later. If not next year, in '52. And you know that Green will be retiring in a few years, and you know who I want to replace him. Jack, I'm thirty-six and you're forty-nine. I may get another shot at something this big. You won't. For God's sake take the farsighted view on it."

More silence. I pictured Captain Jack Tierney weighing the pros and cons of selling his soul to Satan with a Phi Beta Kappa key and a hard-on for the City of Los Angeles. When he said, "Okay, Ellis," I tore up my transfer request and walked back to rejoin the circus.

18

OVER THE next ten days the circus turned into wholesale farce, with an occasional tragedy thrown in.

No other leads were gleaned from the "Death Letter," and the 243 names in the book were divvied up between four detective teams, the low number of cops Jack Tierney's ploy aimed at padding that part of the investigation into extended newspaper and radio juice. Russ Millard argued for twenty teams and a fast, clean sweep; Captain Jack, backstopped by the DA Satan, refused. When Big Bill Koenig was deemed too combustible to work the questionings and was given clerical duties, I was paired with Fritz Vogel. Together, we questioned fifty-odd people, mostly men, about their association with Elizabeth Short. We heard predictable stories of them meeting Betty in bars and buying her drinks and dinner, listening to her fantasies of being the bride or widow of war heroes, bedding or not bedding her. A number of the men did not even know the notorious Dahlia—they were "friends of friends," their names passed on out of pussy hound camaraderie.

Of our parcel of names, sixteen of the guys were what Fritzie labeled "Certified Dahlia Fuckers." They were mostly lower-echelon movie minions: agents, talent scouts and casting directors who hung out at Schwab's Drugstore chasing gullible would-be starlets, empty promises on their lips, Trojan "value packs" in their pockets. They told proud or shamefaced casting couch stories every bit as sad as Betty's tales of bliss with studs in uniform. Finally, the men in Elizabeth Short's little black book had two things in common—they got their names in the L.A. dailies and they coughed up alibis that eliminated them as suspects. And word filtered back to the squadroom that the publicity eliminated more than a few of them as husbands.

The women were a mixed bag. Most were just pals—girl talk acquaintances, fellow cocktail lounge cadgers and aspiring actresses heading nowhere. A dozen or so were hookers and semi-pro B girls, instant soulmates that Betty met in bars. They gave us leads that petered out on follow-up investigation—basically, the word that Betty sold herself freelance to conventioneers at several lower-class downtown hotels. They hedged that Betty rarely peddled it, and could not identify any of her tricks by name; Fritzie's canvassing of the hotels got him an angry zero, and the fact that several other women—R&I confirmed as prostitutes—couldn't be located, pissed him off even more.

Madeleine Sprague's name did not appear in the book, nor did it turn up in any of my subsequent questionings. No dyke or dyke bar leads came out of the 243 names, and every night I checked the University squadroom bulletin boards to see if any of the other teams had latched on to her monicker. None of them did, and I started to feel very safe regarding my evidence suppression tango.

While the book queries got most of the headlines, the rest of the circus continued on: tips, tips and more tips wasted thousands of police man-hours; poison phone and poison pen communiques had local squadroom dicks bracing spiteful loonies implicating their enemies for hundreds of major and minor grievances. Discarded women's garments were sifted through at the Central crime lab, and every piece of size eight black female apparel that was found launched another extensive neighborhood run-through.

The biggest surprise of my little black book tour was Fritz Vogel. Free of Bill Koenig, he possessed a surprising wit, and in his muscle fashion he was as adept an interrogator as Russ Millard. He knew when to punch for information, hitting fast and hard, fueled by personal rancor but capable of putting it out of his mind when the interrogee coughed up what we wanted. Sometimes I sensed that he was holding back out of respect for my nice guy questioning style, that the pragmatist in him knew it was the best way to get results. We became an effective Mutt and Jeff duo fast, and I could tell that I was a restraining influence on Fritzie, a check and balance on his admitted fondness for hurting criminals. He gave me a wary respect for the hurt I'd put on Bobby De Witt, and a few days into the temporary partnership we were bullshitting in broken German, a way to kill time driving to and from question-ings. With me, Fritzie spoke less in tirades and came across as one of the guys—with a mean streak. He talked up the Dahlia and his coveted lieutenancy, but didn't talk frames, and since he never tried to pull any railroad jobs around me and was straight in his FI reports, I got the notion that Loew had either given up the idea or was biding his time. I could also tell that Fritzie was constantly sizing me up, that he knew Koenig wouldn't cut it as partner to Detective Division brass, but with Lee gone, I would. The appraisal process flattered me, and I kept myself razor sharp during interro-gations. I had played second banana to Lee working Warrants, and if Fritzie and I partnered up I wanted him to know that I wouldn't play stooge—or lacky—like Harry Sears to Russ Millard.

Millard, Fritzie's cop antithesis, exerted his own pull on me. He took to using Room 204 at the El Nido as his field office, going there at end of watch to read Lee's superbly cross-filed col-lection of paper. With Lee gone, time weighed heavy on me, so I joined him most evenings. When he looked at the Dahlia horror pictures, he always made the sign of the cross and murmured "Elizabeth" with reverence; walking out, he said, "I'll get him, dear." He always left at 8:00 on the dot, to go home to his wife and sons. That a man could care so deeply yet put it aside so casually amazed me. I asked him about it; he said, "I will not let brutality rule my life."

From 8:00 on, my own life was ruled by two women, a crossfire of their strange, strong wills.

From the El Nido, I'd go to see Kay. With Lee gone and no longer footing the bills, she had to find full-time work, and she did—getting a job teaching sixth grade at an elementary school a few blocks off the Strip. I'd find her grading book reports and perusing kiddie artwork stoically, glad to see me, but caustic underneath, like maintaining a business-as-usual front would keep her grief over Lee's absence and her contempt for my reluc-tance at bay. I tried denting the front by telling her I wanted her, but would only move on it when Lee's vanishing act was resolved; she answered with overeducated psychological claptrap about our missing third, turning the education he bought her around, using it as a weapon against him. I exploded at phrases like "paranoid tendencies" and "pathological selfishness," coming back with "He *saved* you, he *made* you." Kay's comeback for that was, *"He only helped me."* I had no comeback for the truth behind the jargon and the fact that without Lee as a centerpiece, the two of us were loose ends, a family sans patriarch. It was that stasis that drove me out the door ten nights running—straight to the Red Arrow Motel.

So I brought Kay with me to Madeleine.

We'd rut first thing, talk later. The talk was always of Madeleine's family, followed by fantasies that I concocted so as not to feel impoverished in the wake of her tales. The brass girl had robber baron Daddy, *the* Emmett Sprague, confrere of Mack Sennett in the Hollywood salad days; art poseur and elixir-guzzling Mommy, a direct descendant of *the* California land grant Cathcarts; genius sister Martha, hotshot commercial artist, rising star on Ad Agency Row downtown. For a supporting cast there was Mayor Fletcher Bowron, public relations–minded thug Mickey Cohen, "Dreamer" Georgie Tilden, Emmett's former stooge, the son of a famous Scottish anatomist and wastrel nickolodeon artiste. The Dohenys and Sepulvedas and Mulhollands were also close friends, as were Governor Earl Warren and DA Buron Fitts. Having only senile Dolph Bleichert, the late Greta Heilbrunner Bleichert, the Japs I snitched off and fight acquaintances, I spun yarns out of thin air: scholastic medals won and proms attended; bodyguarding FDR in '43. I dissembled away until it was time to rut again, grateful that we always kept the lights off between bouts, so Madeleine couldn't read my face and know I was coming from hunger.

Or from the Dahlia.

The first time it happened accidentally. We were making love, both of us close to peaking. My hand slipped off the bed rail and hit the light switch on the wall, illuminating Betty Short below me. For just a few seconds I believed it was her, and I called out for Lee and Kay to help me. When my lover was Madeleine again, I reached for the switch, only to have her grab my wrist. Moving hard, springs creaking, light glaring, I made Madeleine Betty— made her eyes blue instead of hazel, made her body Betty's body from the stag film, made her silently mouth, "No, please." Coming, I knew it could never be that good with just plain Madeleine; when the brass girl whispered, "I knew she'd get to you sooner or later," I dry sobbed that all my pillow stories were lies and poured out the nonstop true story of Lee and Kay and Bucky, straight

through to Mr. Fire's fix on the dead girl and his jump off the
face of the earth. When I finished, Madeleine said, "I'll never be
a schoolteacher from Sioux Falls, South Dakota, but I'll be Betty
or anyone else you want me to be." I let her stroke my head,
grateful not to have to lie anymore, but sad that she—and not
Kay—was my confessor.

So Elizabeth Short and I were formally joined.

19

LEE STAYED gone and Madeleine stayed Betty, and there was
nothing I could do about either transformation. Heeding the
Metro goons' warning, I kept my nose out of their investigation,
constantly wondering if Mr. Fire took his powder preplanned or
accidentally. I did check his bank records, finding an $800 balance
with no recent withdrawals, and when I heard that a nationwide
and Mexico APB had been issued on Lee and his '40 Ford, yielding goose egg, my instincts told me he had fled way south of the
border, where the Rurales used gringo police bulletins as toilet
paper. Russ Millard told me that two Mexican men, both well-
known dope traffickers, had been arrested in Juarez for the murder of Bobby De Witt and Felix Chasco, which eased my mind
on Metro making Lee for the job—but then scuttlebutt filtered
down from high, high brass circles. Chief Horrall had rescinded
the APB and decreed, "Let sleeping dogs lie." Thad Green's secretary told Harry Sears that she had heard Lee was going to be
dismissed from the LAPD if he did not show up within thirty
days of the time he vanished.

January dwindled out, rainy days with only one spark of
excitement. An envelope arrived by mail at the Bureau. It had a
clipped word address, with a clipped word letter on plain bond
paper inside:

HAVE CHANGED MY MIND.
YOU WOULD NOT GIVE ME A SQUARE DEAL.
DAHLIA KILLING JUSTIFIED.
—BLACK DAHLIA AVENGER.

Taped to the page was a photograph of a short, heavyset man
wearing a business suit, his face scratched out. No prints or other
forensic leads were gleaned from the snapshot or envelope, and

since the servicemen pics from the first letter had been withheld from the press as a suspect elimination device, we knew letter number two was legit. The Bureau consensus was that the photo was of the killer, symbolically eliminating himself from the overall "picture."

With the death letter and stag film leads ground to dust, a second consensus took over: we were never going to get the bastard. The odds on "Unsolved" dropped to even money in the squadroom pool; Thad Green told Russ and Captain Jack that Horrall was going to pull the chain on the Dahlia mess on February 5, returning a large number of officers to their normal duties. Rumor had it that I would be one of the returnees, breaking in Johnny Vogel as my partner. Bad Breath Johnny rankled, but going back to Warrants came on as Paradise regained. Betty Short would then exist the only place I wanted her to—as the spark point of my imagination.

20

"THE FOLLOWING Central Division and Detective Bureau officers temporarily assigned to the E. Short investigation are to return to their normal assignments, effective tomorrow, 2/6/47:

Sgt. T. Anders - ret. to Central Bunco.

Det. J. Arcola - ret. to Central Burglary.

Sgt. R. Cavanaugh - ret. to Central Robbery.

Det. G. Ellison - ret. to Central Detectives.

Det. A. Grimes - ret. to Central Detectives.

Det. C. Ligget - ret. to Central Juvenile.

Det. R. Navarette - ret. to Central Bunco.

Sgt. J. Pratt - ret. to Central Homicide. (See Lt. Ruley for assignment.)

Det. J. Smith - ret. to Central Homicide. (See Lt. Ruley.)

Det. W. Smith - ret. to Central Detectives.

Chief Horrall and Deputy Chief Green wish me to thank you for your help on this investigation, most especially the many overtime hours logged in. Commendation letters will be sent to all of you.

My thanks also—

Capt. J.V. Tierney, Commander, Central Detectives.

*   *   *

The distance between the bulletin board and Millard's office was about ten yards; I covered it in about a tenth of a second. Russ looked up from his desk. "Hi, Bucky. How's tricks?"

"Why wasn't I on that transfer list?"

"I asked Jack to keep you on the Short case."

"Why?"

"Because you're getting to be a damn good detective, and Harry's retiring in '50. Want more?"

I was wondering what to say when the phone rang. Russ picked it up and said, "Central Homicide, Millard," then listened for a few moments and pointed to the extension on the desk across from him. I grabbed the receiver, catching a deep male voice in mid-sentence:

"... attached to the CID unit here at Fort Dix. I know you've had a lot of confessions peter out on you, but this one sounds good to me."

Russ said, "Go on, Major."

"The soldier's name is Joseph Dulange. He's an MP, attached to the headquarters company at Dix. He made the confession to his CO, coming off a bender. His buddies say he carries a knife, and he flew to Los Angeles on furlough on January eighth. On top of that, we found bloodstains on a pair of his trousers—too small an amount to type. Personally, I think he's a bad apple. He got in a lot of brawls overseas, and his CO says he's a wife beater."

"Major, is Dulange near you right now?"

"Yes. He's in a cell across the hall."

"Do this for me, please. Ask him to describe Elizabeth Short's birthmarks to you. If he does it accurately, my partner and I will be on the next transport flight out of Camp MacArthur."

The major said, "Yes, sir"; the Fort Dix half of the conversation broke off. Russ said, "Harry's got the flu. Feel like a trip to New Jersey, bright penny?"

"Are you serious?"

"If that soldier comes up with the moles on Elizabeth's rear end, I am."

"Ask him about the slash marks, the stuff that didn't make the papers."

Russ shook his head. "No. It might excite him too much. If this is legit, we're flying out on the QT and reporting in from Jersey. If Jack or Ellis get hold of this they'll send Fritzie, and he'll have that soldier in the electric chair by morning, guilty or otherwise."

The Fritzie crack irked me. "He's not that bad. And I think Loew's given up on the frame idea."

"You're an impressionable penny, then. Fritzie's as bad as they get, and Ellis—"

The major came back on the line: "Sir, Dulange said the girl had three little dark moles on the left cheek of her, uh … derriere."

"You could have said ass, Major. And we're on our way."

* * *

Corporal Joseph Dulange was a tall, hard-muscled man of twenty-nine, dark-haired, horse-faced, with a pencil-thin mustache. Dressed in olive drab fatigues, he sat across a table from us in the Fort Dix provost marshal's office, looking incorrigibly mean. A judge advocate captain sat beside him, probably to make sure Russ and I didn't try the civilian third degree. The eight-hour plane ride had been bumpy; at 4:00 A.M. I was still on L.A. time, exhausted but keyed-up. On the ride over from the airstrip, the CID major we'd talked to on the phone had briefed us on Dulange. He was a twice-married combat vet, a boozehound, a feared brawler. His statement was incomplete, but buttressed by two hard facts: he flew to L.A. on January eighth, and was arrested for Plain Drunk in New York City's Pennsylvania Station on January seventeenth.

Russ kicked it off. "Corporal, my name is Millard, and this is Detective Bleichert. We're from the Los Angeles Police Department, and if you convince us you killed Elizabeth Short, we'll arrest you and take you back with us."

Dulange shifted in his chair and said, "I sliced her," his voice high and nasal.

Russ sighed. "A lot of other people have told us that."

"I fucked her, too."

"Really? You cheat on your wife?"

"I'm a Frenchman."

I moved into my bad guy role. "I'm a German, so who gives a shit? What's that have to do with you cheating on your wife?"

Dulange flicked his tongue like a reptile. "I give it the French way. My wife don't like it like that."

Russ elbowed me. "Corporal, why did you take your furlough in Los Angeles? What were you interested in?"

"Cunt. Johnnie Red Label. Excitement."

"You could have found that across the river in Manhattan."

"Sunshine. Movie stars. Palm trees."

Russ laughed. "L.A.'s got all of that. It sounds like your wife gives you a long leash, Joe. You know, furlough all by yourself."

"She knows I'm a Frenchman. I give it to her good when I'm home. Missionary style, ten inches. She got no complaints."

"What if she did complain, Joe? What would you do to her?"

Deadpan, Dulange said, "One complaint, I use my fists. Two complaints, I slice her in half."

I broke in: "Are you telling me you flew three thousand miles to eat some pussy?"

"I'm a Frenchman."

"You look like a homo to me. Gash divers are all repressed fruits, it's been proven. You got an answer for that, shitbird?"

The soldier-lawyer got up and whispered in Russ's ear; Russ nudged me under the table. Dulange cracked his deadpan into a big grin. "I got my answer hangin' ten hard, flatfoot."

Russ said, "You'll have to excuse Detective Bleichert, Joe. He's got a short fuse."

"He's got a short pecker. All Krauts do. I'm a Frenchman, I know."

Russ laughed uproariously, like he'd just heard a real knee-slapper at the Elks Club. "Joe, you're a pisser."

Dulange waggled his tongue. "I'm a Frenchman."

"Joe, you're a hot sketch, and Major Carroll told me you're a wife beater. Is that true?"

"Can niggers dance?"

"They certainly can. Do you enjoy hitting women, Joe?"

"When they ask for it."

"How often does your wife ask for it?"

"She asks for the big tensky every night."

"No. Asks to get hit, I mean."

"Every time I'm pallin' with Johnnie Red and she cracks wise, then she's askin' for it."

"You and Johnnie go back a ways?"

"Johnnie Red's my best friend."

"Did Johnnie go with you to L.A.?"

"In my pocket."

Sparring with a psycho drunk was wearing me down; I thought of Fritzie and the direct approach. "Are you having the DTs, shitbird? You want a little rap in the cabeza to clear things up for you?"

"Bleichert, enough!"

I shut up. The JA man glared at me; Russ straightened the knot in his necktie—the signal for me to keep it zipped. Dulange cracked the knuckles on his left hand one by one. Russ tossed a pack of cigarettes on the table, the oldest "I'm your pal" ploy in the book.

The Frenchman said, "Johnnie Red don't like me to smoke 'cept in his company. You bring Johnnie in, I'll smoke. I confess better in Johnnie's company, too. Ask the Catholic chaplain at North Post. He told me he always smells Johnnie when I go to confession."

I started smelling Corporal Joseph Dulange as an attention-seeking drool case. Russ said, "Booze confessions aren't valid in court, Joe. But I'll tell you what. You convince me you killed Betty Short, and I'll make sure Johnnie comes back to L.A. with us. A nice eight-hour flight would give you plenty of time to renew your acquaintance with him. What do you say?"

"I say I chopped the Dahlia."

"I say you didn't. I say you and Johnnie are going to stay parted for a while."

"I chopped her."

"How?"

"On her titties, ear to ear and in half. Chop. Chop. Chop."

Russ sighed. "Let's backtrack, Joe. You flew out of Dix on Wednesday, January eighth, you landed at Camp MacArthur that night. You and Johnnie are in L.A., anxious to sow some wild oats. Where did you go first? Hollywood Boulevard? Sunset Strip? The beach? Where?"

Dulange cracked his knuckles. "Nathan's Tattoo Parlor, 463 North Alvarado."

"What did you do there?"

Crazy Joe rolled up his right sleeve, revealing a forked snake's tongue with "Frenchy" emblazoned below it. Flexing his bicep, the tattoo stretched. Dulange said, "I'm a Frenchman."

Millard pulled his patented reversal. "I'm a cop, and I'm getting bored. When I get bored, Detective Bleichert takes over. Detective Bleichert was once the tenth-ranked light heavyweight in the world, and he is not a nice man. Right, partner?"

I balled my fists. "I'm a German."

Dulange laughed. "No tickee, no washee. No Johnnie, no story."

I almost leaped across the table at him. Russ grabbed my elbow and held it, viselike, while he bargained. "Joe, I'll make you a deal. First you convince us you *knew* Betty Short. Give us some facts. Names, dates, descriptions. You do that, and when we take our first break, you and Johnnie can go back to your cell and get reacquainted. What do you say?"

"Johnnie pint?"

"No, his big brother Johnnie fifth."

The Frenchman grabbed the pack of butts and shook one loose; Russ had his lighter out and extended. Dulange took a monumental drag, exhaling a rush of words along with the smoke:

"After the tattoo joint, me and Johnnie got a cab downtown and got a room. Havana Hotel, Ninth and Olive, deucesky a night, big cockroaches. They started makin' a ruckus, so I put out mousetraps. That killed 'em. Me and Johnnie slept it off, then the next day we went cunt chasin'. No luck. Next day I get me this Filipino cunt at the bus depot. She says she needs bus fare to Frisco, so I offer her a fivesky to take on me and Johnnie. She says tensky minumum for two guys. I say Johnnie's hung like Jesus, she should pay me. We go back to the hotel, all the cockroaches got loose from the traps. I introduce her to Johnnie, tell her he goes first. She gets scared, says, 'You think you're Fatty Arbuckle?' I tell her I'm a Frenchman, who does she think she is, thinks she can high-hat Johnnie Red?

"Cockroaches start howlin' like niggers. The Filipino says Johnnie's got sharp teeth, no sir. She runs like sixty, me and Johnnie hole up till late Saturday. We want cunt bad. We go by this army-navy on Broadway, and I get me some ribbons for my Ike jacket. DSC with oak leaf, silver star, bronze star, ribbons for all the Jap campaigns. I look like George S. Patton, only hung bigger. Me and Johnnie go to this bar called the Night Owl. Dahlia sashays in, Johnnie says, 'Yes sir, that's my baby, no sir, don't mean maybe, yes sir, that's my baby now.'"

Dulange stubbed out his cigarette and reached for the pack. Russ jotted notes; I figured time and location, remembering the Night Owl from my days working Central Patrol. It was on 6th and Hill— two blocks from the Biltmore Hotel, where Red Manley dropped Betty Short on Friday, January tenth. The Frenchman, DT recollections notwithstanding, had gained another notch of credibility.

Russ said, "Joe, this was Saturday the eleventh into Sunday the twelfth you're talking about?"

Dulange fired up another cigarette. "I'm a Frenchman, not a calendar. Sunday follows Saturday, you figure it out."

"Go on."

"Anyhow, Dahlia, me and Johnnie have a little chat, and I invite her over to the hotel. We get there and the cockroaches are loose, singin' and bitin' at the woodwork. Dahlia says she won't spreadsky 'less I kill 'em. I grab Johnnie and start boppin' 'em with him, Johnnie told me it don't hurt. But the Dahlia cunt won't spreadsky till the roaches are disposed of scientific style. I go down the street and get this doctor. He gives the roaches poison injections for a fivesky. Me and Dahlia fuck like bunnies, Johnnie Red watches. He's mad, 'cause Dahlia's so good I don't want to give him none."

I threw in a cut-the-shit question: "Describe her body. Do a good job, or you won't see Johnnie Red until you get out of the stockade."

Dulange's face went soft; he looked like a little kid threatened with the loss of his teddy bear. Russ said, "Answer the man's question, Joe."

Dulange grinned. "Till I cut 'em off, she had perky little titties with pink nipples. Kinda thick legs, nice bush. She had them moles I told Major Carroll about, and she had these scratches on her back, real fresh, like she'd just took a whippin'."

I tingled, remembering the "soft lash marks" the coroner mentioned at the autopsy. Russ said, "Go on, Joe."

Dulange ghoul grinned. "Then Dahlia starts actin' nutso, sayin', 'How come you're only a corporal if you won all them medals?' She starts callin' me Matt and Gordon and keeps talkin' about our baby, even though we just did it once, and I wore a safe. Johnnie gets spooked, and him and the cockroaches start singin', 'No sir, that *ain't* my baby.' I want more cuntsky, so I take Dahlia down the street to see the roach doctor. I slip him a tensky, and he gives her a fake examination and tells her, 'The baby will be healthy and arrive in six months.'"

More confirmation, smack in the middle of a DT haze—the Matt and Gordon were obviously Matt Gordon and Joseph Gordon Fickling, two of Betty Short's fantasy husbands. I thought 50-50, let's close it out for Big Lee Blanchard; Russ said, "Then what, Joe?"

Dulange looked genuinely puzzled—past bravado, booze-brain memories and a desire to be reunited with Johnnie Red. "Then I sliced her."

"Where?"

"In half."

"No, Joe. Where did you perform the murder?"

"Oh. At the hotel."

"What room number?"

"116."

"How'd you get the body to 39th and Norton?"

"I stole a car."

"What kind of car?"

"A Chevy."

"Make and model?"

"'43 sedan."

"American cars weren't manufactured during the war, Joe. Try again."

"'47 sedan."

"Somebody left the keys in a nice new car like that? In downtown L.A.?"

"I hot-wired it."

"How do you hot-wire a car, Joe?"

"What?"

"Explain the procedure to me."

"I forget how I did it. I was drunk."

I cut in: "Where's 39th and Norton?"

Dulange toyed with the cigarette pack. "It's near Crenshaw Boulevard and Coliseum Street."

"Tell me something that wasn't in the papers."

"I cut her to ear to ear."

"Everybody knows that."

"Me and Johnnie raped her."

"She wasn't raped, and Johnnie would have left marks. There weren't any. Why'd you kill her?"

"She was a bad fuck."

"Bullshit. You said Betty fucked like a rabbit."

"A bad rabbit."

"All cats are gray in the dark, shitbird. Why'd you kill her?"

"She wouldn't go French."

"That's no reason. You can get French at any five-dollar whorehouse. A Frenchman like you should know that."

"She gave bad French."

"There's no such thing, shitbird."

"I chopped her!"

I slammed the tabletop à la Harry Sears. "You're a lying frog son of a bitch!"

The JA man got to his feet; Dulange bawled, "I want my Johnnie."

Russ told the captain, "Have him back here in six hours," and smiled at me—the softest smile I'd ever seen him give.

*   *   *

So we left it at 50–50 moving toward 75–25 against. Russ left to call in his report and dispatch an SID team over to Room 116 of the Havana Hotel to check for bloodstains; I went to sleep in the BOQ room Major Carroll assigned us. I dreamed of Betty Short and Fatty Arbuckle in black and white; when the alarm went off I reached for Madeleine.

Opening my eyes, I saw Russ, dressed in a clean suit. He handed me a newspaper and said, "Never underestimate Ellis Loew."

It was a Newark tabloid job bearing the headline: "Fort Dix Soldier Culprit in Sinsational Los Angeles Murder!" Below the banner print were side-by-side photos of Frenchman Joe Dulange and Loew, posed theatrically behind his desk. The text read:

> In a scoop to our sister publication the Los An-
> geles *Mirror*, Los Angeles Deputy District Attorney
> Ellis Loew, Chief Legal Officer on the mystifying
> "Black Dahlia" murder case, announced a major
> breakthrough last night. "I have just been informed
> by two of my closest colleagues, Lieutenant Russell
> Millard and Officer Dwight Bleichert, that Fort Dix,
> New Jersey Corporal Joseph Dulange has confessed
> to the murder of Elizabeth Short, and that the con-
> fession has been validated by facts that only the killer
> would know. Corporal Dulange is a known degen-
> erate, and I will be supplying the press with more
> facts on the confession as soon as my men return
> Dulange to Los Angeles for arraignment."
>
> The Elizabeth Short case has baffled authorities
> since the morning of January 15, when Miss Short's
> nude, mutilated body, cut in half at the waist, was found
> in a vacant lot in Los Angeles. Deputy DA Loew would
> not reveal the details of Corporal Dulange's confession,
> but he did say that Dulange was a known intimate of

Miss Short. "Details will be forthcoming," he said. "The important thing is that this fiend is in custody, where he will not kill again."

I laughed. "What did you really tell Loew?"

"Nothing. When I talked to Captain Jack the first time, I told him Dulange was a strong possible. He bawled me out for not reporting before we left, and that was it. The second time I called I told him Dulange was starting to look like another crazy. He got very upset, and now I know why."

I stood up and stretched. "Let's just hope he really killed her."

Russ shook his head. "SID said there's no bloodstains in the hotel room, and no running water to drain the body. And Carroll had a tri-state bulletin out on Dulange's whereabouts January tenth through the seventeenth—drunk tanks, hospitals, the works. We just got a kickback: Frenchy was in the jail ward of St. Patrick's Hospital in Brooklyn January fourteenth to the seventeenth. Severe DTs. He was released that morning and picked up in Penn Station two hours later. *The man is clean.*"

I didn't know who to be mad at. Loew and company wanted to clear the slate any way possible, Millard wanted justice, I was going home to headlines that made me look like a fool.

"What about Dulange? You want to brace him again?"

"And hear about more singing cockroaches? No. Carroll confronted him with the kickback. He said he made up the killing story to get publicity. He wants to reconcile with his first wife, and he thought the attention would get him some sympathy. I talked to him again, and it was nothing but DT stuff. There's nothing more he can tell us."

"Jesus Christ."

"The savior indeed. Joe's getting a quickie discharge and we're getting a flight back to L.A. in forty-five minutes. So get dressed, partner."

I put on my stale clothes, then Russ and I walked out to the sallyport to wait for the jeep that would take us to the airstrip. In the distance, I could see a tall uniformed figure approaching. I shivered against the cold; the tall man got closer. I saw that it was none other than Corporal Joseph Dulange.

Reaching the sallyport, he held out a morning tabloid and poked at his picture on the front page. "I got the whole hog, you're small print where Krauts belong."

I smelled Johnnie Red on his breath and sucker-punched him square in the chops. Dulange went down like a ton of bricks; my right hand throbbed. Russ Millard's look reminded me of Jesus getting ready to rebuke the heathens. I said, "Don't be so goddamn proper. Don't be such a fucking saint."

21

ELLIS LOEW said, "I called this little meeting for several reasons, Bucky. One is to apologize for jumping the gun on Dulange. I was precipitious in talking to my newspaper people, and you got hurt. I apologize for that."

I looked at Loew, and at Fritz Vogel sitting beside him. The "little meeting" was in the living room of Fritzie's house; the two days of Dulange headlines portrayed me as no worse than an overeager cop on a wild goose chase. "What do you want, Mr. Loew?"

Fritzie laughed; Loew said, "Call me Ellis."

The setup hit a new bottom in the subtlety department—way below the highballs and bowl of pretzels Fritzie's hausfrau had served as amenities. I was supposed to meet Madeleine in an hour—and off-duty fraternizing with my boss was the last thing in the world I wanted. "Okay, Ellis."

Loew bristled at my tone. "Bucky, we've clashed a number of times in the past. Maybe we're even clashing now. But I think we agree on a few things. We'd both like to see the Short case closed out and get back to normal business. You want to go back to Warrants, and as much as I would like to prosecute the killer, my part in the investigation has gotten out of hand, and it's time that I returned to the old cases on my docket."

I felt like a bush league cardsharp holding a royal flush. "What do you want, Ellis?"

"I want to return you to Warrants tomorrow, and I want to give the Short case a last go before I return to my old caseload. We're both comers, Bucky. Fritzie wants you for his partner when he gets his lieutenancy, and—"

"Russ Millard wants me when Harry Sears retires."

Fritzie took a belt of his highball. "You're too raw for him, boyo. He's told people you can't control your temper. Old Russ is a sob sister, and I'm much more your type."

It was a good wild card; I thought of the disgusted look Russ gave me after I coldcocked Joe Dulange. "What do you want, *Ellis*?"

"Very well, *Dwight*, I'll tell you. There are four confessors still being held at City Jail. They've got no alibis for Betty Short's missing days, they weren't coherent when they were first questioned, and they are all violent, frothing-at-the-mouth lunatics. I want them reinterrogated, with what you might call 'appropriate props.' It's a muscle job, and Fritzie wanted Bill Koenig for it, but he's a bit too enamored of violence, so I picked you. So, *Dwight*, yes or no. Back to Warrants or Homicide shitwork until Russ Millard gets tired of you? Millard is a patient, forbearing man, *Dwight*. That might be a long time."

My royal flush collapsed. "Yes."

Loew beamed. "Go to the city jail now. The night jailer has released waivers for the four men. There's a drunk wagon in the nightwatch lot, keys under the mat. Drive the suspects to 1701 South Alameda, meet Fritzie. Welcome back to Warrants, *Dwight*."

I stood up. Loew took a pretzel from the bowl and nibbled it daintily; Fritzie drained his glass, his hands shaking.

* * *

The loonies were waiting for me in a holding tank, wearing jail denims, chained together and manacled at the ankles. The waivers the jailer had given me came with mug shots and rap sheet carbons attached; when the cell door was racked electronically, I matched pictures to faces.

Paul David Orchard was short and burly, with a flat nose spread across half his face and long, pomade-lacquered blond hair; Cecil Thomas Durkin was a fiftyish mulatto, bald, freckled, close to six and a half feet tall. Charles Michael Issler had enormous sunken brown eyes, and Loren (NMI) Bidwell was a frail old man, shaking from palsy, liver spots covering his skin. He looked so pathetic that I double-checked his sheet to make sure I had the right man; child molesting beefs running back to 1911 told me I did. "Out in the catwalk," I said. "Roll it up now."

The four shuffled out, scissor-walking sideways, their chains dragging the floor. I pointed them to a side exit adjoining the catwalk; the jailer opened the door from outside. The loony conga line scissored into the parking lot; the jailer held a bead on them while I found the drunk wagon and backed it up.

The jailer opened the wagon's back door; I checked the rearview mirror and watched my cargo climb aboard. They were whispering among themselves, taking gulps of the crisp night air as they stumbled up and in. The jailer locked the door behind them and signaled me with his gun barrel; I took off.

1701 South Alameda was in the East L.A. Industrial District, about a mile and a half from the city jail. Five minutes later, I found it—a giant warehouse smack in the middle of a block of giant warehouses, the only one with its street facade illuminated: KOUNTY KING LUNCH MEAT—SERVING LOS ANGELES COUNTY WITH INSTITUTIONAL FOOD SINCE 1923. I tapped the horn as I parked; a door beneath the sign opened up, the light went off, Fritzie Vogel was standing there with his thumbs hooked in his belt.

I got out and unlocked the back door. The loonies stumbled into the street; Fritzie called, "This way, gentlemen." The four scissor-walked in the direction of the voice; a light went on in back of Fritzie. I secured the van and walked over.

Fritzie ushered the last loony in and greeted me in the doorway. "County kickbacks, boyo. The man who owns this place owes Sheriff Biscailuz, and he's got a plainclothes lieutenant who's got a doctor brother who owes me. You'll see what I'm talking about in a while."

I shut the door and bolted it; Fritzie led me past the scissorwalkers and down a hall reeking of meat. At the end, it opened into a huge room—sawdust-covered cement floors, row after row of rusted meathooks hanging from the ceiling. Sides of beef dangled from over half of them, in the open at room temperature while horseflies feasted. My stomach looped; then, at the rear, I saw four chairs stationed directly beneath four unused hooks and got the picture for real.

Fritzie was unlocking the loonies' manacles and cuffing their hands in front of them. I stood by and gauged reactions. Old Man Bidwell's palsy was going into overdrive, Durkin was humming to himself, Orchard sneered, his head cocked to one side, like his butch-waxed pompadour was weighing it down. Only Charles Issler looked lucid enough to be concerned—he was fretting his hands and looking from Fritzie to me, his eyes constantly darting.

Fritzie took a roll of tape from his pocket and tossed it to me. "Tape the rap sheets to the wall next to the hooks. Alphabetically, straight across."

I did it, noticing a sheet-draped table wedged diagonally into a connecting doorway a few feet away. Fritzie led the prisoners over and made them stand on the chairs, then dangle their hand-cuff chains loosely over the meathooks. I skimmed the rap sheets, hoping for facts that would make me hate the four enough to get me through the night and back to Warrants.

Loren Bidwell was a three-time Atascadero loser, the falls for aggravated sexual assault on minors. Between prison jolts, he confessed to all the big sex crimes, and was even a major suspect in the Hickman child snuff case back in the '20s. Cecil Durkin was a hophead, a knife fighter and a jailhouse rape-o who played jazz drums with some good combos; he took two Quentin jolts for Arson and was caught masturbating at the scene of his last torch—the home of a bandleader who had allegedly stiffed him on payment for a nightclub gig. That fall cost him twelve years in stir; since his release he'd been working as a dishwasher, living at a Salvation Army domicile.

Charles Issler was a pimp and career confessor specializing in copping to hooker homicides. His three procuring beefs had netted him a year county jail time; his phony confessions two ninety-day observation stints at the Camarillo nut farm. Paul Orchard was a jack roller, a male prostitute, and a former San Bernardino County deputy sheriff. On top of his vice beefs, he had two convictions for grievous aggravated assault.

A little surge of hate juice entered me. It felt tenuous, like I was about to go into the ring against a guy I wasn't sure I could take. Fritzie said, "A charming quartet, huh, boyo?"

"Real choirboys."

Fritzie curled a come-hither finger at me; I walked over and faced the four suspects. My hate juice was holding as he said, "You all confessed to killing the Dahlia. We can't prove you did, so it's up to you to convince us. Bucky, you ask questions about the girlie's missing days. I'll listen in until I hear syphilitic lies."

I braced Bidwell first. His palsy spasms had the chair rocking underneath him; I reached up and grabbed the meathook to hold him steady. "Tell me about Betty Short, pops. Why'd you kill her?"

The old man beseeched me with his eyes; I looked away. Fritz-ie, perusing the rap sheets on the wall, picked up on the silence. "Don't be timid, boyo. That bird made little boys suck his hog."

My hand twitched and jerked the hook. "Come clean, pop. Why'd you snuff her?"

Bidwell answered in a breathless geezer's voice: "I didn't kill her, mister. I just wanted a ticket to the honor farm. Three hots and a cot's all I wanted. Please, mister."

The geez didn't look strong enough to *lift* a knife, let alone tie a woman down and carry the two halves of her stiff out to a car. I moved to Cecil Durkin.

"Tell me about it, Cecil."

The hepcat mocked me. "Tell you about it? You get that line from *Dick Tracy* or *Gang Busters?*"

Out of the corner of my eye I saw Fritzie watching, measuring me. "One more time, shitbird. Tell me about you and Betty Short."

Durkin giggled. "I fucked Betty Short and I fucked your mama! I'm your daddy!"

I one-two'd him in the solar plexus, hard little shots. Durkin's legs buckled, but he kept his feet on the chair. He gasped for breath, got a lungful and went back to bravado: "You think you clever, don't you? You the bad guy, your buddy the nice guy. You gonna hit me, he gonna rescue me. Don't you clowns know that bit went out with vaudeville?"

I massaged my right hand, still bone bruised from Lee Blanchard and Joe Dulange. "I'm the nice guy, Cecil. Keep that in mind."

It was a good line. Durkin fumbled for a comeback; I turned my attention to Charles Michael Issler.

He looked down and said, "I didn't kill Liz. I don't know why I do these things, and I apologize. So please don't let that man hurt me."

His manner was quietly sincere, but something about him put me off. I said, "Convince me."

"I ... I can't. I just didn't."

I thought of Issler as a pimp, Betty as a part-time prostie, and wondered if there was a possible connection between them— then remembered that the hookers in the little black book questionings said she always worked freelance. I said, "Did you know Betty Short?"

"No."

"Did you know of her?"

"No."

"Why'd you confess to her murder?"

"She ... she looked so sweet and pretty and I felt so bad when I saw her picture in the paper. I ... I always confess to the pretty ones."

"Your rap sheet says you only cop to hooker snuffs. Why?"

"Well, I ..."

"You hit your girls, Charlie? You get them gone on hop? You make them service your pals—"

I stopped, thinking of Kay and Bobby De Witt. Issler bobbed his head up and down, slowly at first, then harder and harder. Soon he was sobbing, "I do such bad things, nasty, nasty things. Nasty, nasty, nasty."

Fritzie walked over and stood beside me, brass knuckles coiled in both fists. He said, "This kid gloves routine is getting us nowhere," and kicked Issler's chair out from under him. The confessor-pimp screamed and flopped like an impaled fish; bones snapped as the cuffs caught the brunt of his weight. Fritzie said, "Watch, boyo."

Shouting, "Jack Roller!" "Nigger!" "Baby fucker!" he kicked the other three chairs to the floor. Now there were confessors dangling four abreast, shrieking, grabbing at one another with their legs, an octopus in county jail denim. The screams sounded like one voice—until Fritzie zeroed in on Charles Michael Issler.

He roundhoused the knuckle dusters into his midsection, left-right, left-right, left-right. Issler screamed and gurgled; Fritzie yelled, "Tell me about the Dahlia's missing days you syphilitic whoremonger!"

My legs felt like they were about to go. Issler screeched, "I ... don't ... know ... anything." Fritzie shot him an uppercut to the crotch.

"Tell me what you know!"

"I knew you at Ad Vice!"

Fritzie winged rabbit punches. "Tell me what you know! Tell me what your girls told you, you syphilitic whoremonger!"

Issler retched; Fritzie moved in close and worked his body. I heard ribs cracking, then stared off to my left, to a burglar alarm lever on the wall by the connecting doorway. I stared and stared and stared; Fritzie ran into my field of vision and wheeled over the sheet-covered table I'd noticed before.

The loonies flopped on their hooks, moaning low. Fritzie got right up next to me, cackled in my face, then whipped off the sheet.

The table held a naked female corpse, cut in half at the waist—a pudgy girl coiffed and made up to look like Elizabeth Short. Fritzie grabbed Charlie Issler by the scruff of the neck, hissing, "For your cutting pleasure, may I present Jane Doe number forty-three. You're all going to slice her, and the best slicer buys the ticket!"

Issler shut his eyes and bit through his lower lip. Old Man Bidwell went purple, starting to foam at the mouth. I smelled loosed feces on Durkin and saw Orchard's wrists broken, twisted to right angles, bones and tendons exposed. Fritzie pulled out a pachuco toad stabber and popped the blade. "Show me how you did it, you filths. Show me what didn't get in the papers. Show me and I'll be nice to you and make all your hurt go away. Bucky, take off their cuffs."

My legs went. I stumbled into Fritzie, hurled him to the floor, ran for the alarm and pulled the lever. A code three response siren went off so good, so loud, so hard that it felt like its sound waves were what propelled me out of the warehouse and into the drunk wagon and all the way to Kay's door with no excuses and words of loyalty for Lee.

So were Kay Lake and I formally joined.

22

TRIPPING THAT alarm was the costliest act of my life.

Loew and Vogel succeeded in putting the hush on it. I was booted off Warrants and back into uniform—swingwatch foot patrol out of Central Station, my old home. Lieutenant Jastrow, the watch boss, was thick with the demon DA. I could tell he was checking out my every act—waiting for me to snitch or rabbit or somehow follow up on the big wrong move I had to make.

I did nothing about it. It was the word of a five-year officer versus a twenty-two-year man and the city's future District Attorney, backed by their hole card: the radio car officers who responded to the alarm were made the new Central Division Warrants team, a piece of serendipity guaranteed to keep them quiet and happy. Two consolations kept me from going crazy: Fritzie didn't kill anybody, and when I checked the city jail release records I learned that the four confessors had been treated for "car crash injuries" at Queen of Angels and shipped to different state ding farms for "observation." And my horror pushed me where I'd been too scared and stupid to go for a long, long time.

Kay.

That first night she was as much my grief catcher as my lover. I was afraid of noise and abrupt movement, so she undressed me and made me be still, murmuring, "And all that," every time I tried to talk about Fritzie or the Dahlia. She touched me so softly that it was hardly touching at all; I touched every whole and healthy part of her until I felt my own body cease to be fists and cop muscle. Then we roused each other slowly and made love, with Betty Short far away.

A week later I broke it off with Madeleine, the "neighbor girl" whose identity I had kept secret from Lee and Kay. I didn't offer a reason, and the rich gutter crawler aced me as I was about to hang up the phone. "Find somebody *safe*? You'll be back, you know. I look like her."

Her.

A month passed. Lee didn't return, the two dope traffickers were convicted and hanged for the De Witt-Chasco killings, my Fire and Ice ad continued to run in all four L.A. dailies. The Short case moved from headlines to back pages, tips fell off to almost zero, everyone but Russ Millard and Harry Sears went back to their regular assignments. Still assigned to *Her*, Russ and Harry kept putting in straight eights at the Bureau and in the field, spending evenings at the El Nido, going over the master file. When I got off duty at 9:00, I'd visit for a while on my way to see Kay, quietly amazed at how obsessed Mr. Homicide was becoming, his family neglected as he prowled paper until midnight. The man inspired confession; when I told him the story of Fritzie and the warehouse, his absolution was a fatherly embrace and the admonishing, "Take the Sergeant's Exam. In a year or so I'll go to Thad Green. He owes me one, and when Harry retires you'll be my partner."

It was a promise to build on, and it kept bringing me back to the file. With my days free and Kay at work, I had nothing to do, so I read it over and over. The "R," "S," and "T" folders were missing, which was an annoyance, but other than that it was perfection. My real woman had Betty Short pushed back across a Maginot Line into professional curiosity, and I kept reading, thinking and hypothesizing from the standpoint of becoming a good detective—the road I was on until I tripped that alarm. Sometimes I felt connections begging to be made, sometimes I cursed myself for not having ten percent more gray matter, sometimes the report carbons just made me think of Lee.

I continued with the woman he saved from a nightmare. Kay and I played house three and four times a week, the hours late now that I was working swingwatch. We made our tender kind of love and talked around the bad events of the past months, and as gentle and good as I was, I kept churning inside for an outside conclusion—Lee back, the Dahlia killer on a platter, one more Red Arrow shack with Madeleine or Ellis Loew and Fritzie Vogel nailed to a cross. What always came with it was a big, ugly replay of me hitting Cecil Durkin, followed by the question: how far would you have gone that night?

The beat was where it ate at me the most. I worked East 5th Street from Main to Stanford, skid row. Blood banks, liquor stores selling half pints and short dogs exclusively, fifty-cent-a-night flophouses and derelict missions. The unspoken rule down there was that foot beat hacks worked strong-arm. You broke up bottle gangs by whacking winos with your billy club; you hauled jigs out of the day labor joints when they insisted on getting hired. You rounded up drunks and ragpickers indiscriminately to meet the city quota, beating them down if they tried to run from the drunk wagon. It was attrition duty, and the only officers good at it were the transplanted Okie shitkickers hired in the manpower shortage during the war. I patrolled half-heartedly: little jabs with my stick, handing winos dimes and quarters to get them off the street and into the wine bars where I wouldn't have to roust them, low quotas on my drunk sweeps. I got a rep as the Central swingwatch "sob sister"; twice Johnny Vogel saw me passing out chump change and hooted uproariously. Lieutenant Jastrow gave me a Class D fitness report my first month back in uniform—a clerical aide told me he cited my "Reluctance to employ sufficient force with recalcitrant misdemeanants." Kay got a kick out of the line, but I saw a stack of bum paper building up so high that all Russ Millard's juice wouldn't be able to return me to the Bureau.

So I was back where I was before the fight and the bond issue, only further east and on foot. Rumors raged on my way up to Warrants; now speculation centered on my fall. One story had me shitcanned for beating up Lee, others had me infringing on East Valley Division's process-serving territory, punking out on a bout with the 77th Street rookie who won the '46 Golden Gloves, incurring Ellis Loew's wrath by leaking Dahlia info to a radio station opposed to his upcoming DA candidacy. Every

rumor portrayed me as a backstabber, a Bolshevik, a coward and
a fool; when my second month's fitness report ended with the
line, "This officer's passive patrol behavior has earned him the
enmity of every enforcement-minded policeman on his watch,"
I started thinking of handing out five-spots to the winos and
beatings to every bluesuit who looked at me even slightly hinky.

Then *she* came back.

I never thought about her on the beat; when I studied the file,
it was just detective drudge work, facts and theorizing on a common DOA. When my lovemaking with Kay got too involved in
affection, she came to help, served her purpose and was banished
as soon as we finished. It was when I was asleep and helpless that
she lived.

It was always the same dream. I was at the warehouse with
Fritz Vogel, beating Cecil Durkin to death. She watched, screaming that none of the drool cases killed her, promising to love me
if I made Fritzie quit hitting Charlie Issler. I stopped, wanting the
sex. Fritzie continued his carnage, and Betty wept for Charlie
while I had her.

I always woke up grateful for daylight, especially when Kay
was beside me.

On April 4, almost two and a half months after Lee's disappearance, Kay got a letter on official LAPD stationery:

4/3/47

Dear Miss Lake-

This is to inform you that Leland C. Blanchard
has been formally dismissed from the Los Angeles
Police Department on grounds of moral turpitude,
effective 3/15/47. You were the beneficiary of his
Los Angeles City Credit Union account, and since
Mr. Blanchard remains out of touch, we feel it is only
fair to send you the existing balance.

> Best wishes,
> Leonard V. Strock,
> Sergeant,
> Personnel Division

A check for $14.11 was included. It made me killing mad, and
I attacked the master file so I wouldn't attack my new enemy—
the bureaucracy that owned me.

23

TWO DAYS later the connection jumped up off the carbon and grabbed me by the balls.

It was my own FI report, filed on 1/17/47. Under "Marjorie Graham," I had written: "M.G. stated E. Short used nickname variations of 'Elizabeth' according to the company she was with."

Bingo.

I had heard Elizabeth Short called "Betty," "Beth," and once or twice "Betsy," but *only* Charles Michael Issler, a *pimp*, referred to her as "Liz." At the warehouse he had denied knowing her. I recalled that he didn't impress me as a killer, but that I still found him hinky. When I'd thought about the warehouse before, it was Durkin and the stiff that came on strong; now I replayed it strictly for facts:

Fritzie had beat Issler half to death, ignoring the other three loonies.

He had stressed side issues, shouting: "Tell me what you know about the Dahlia's missing days," "Tell me what *you* know," "Tell me what your girls told you."

Issler had answered back, "I knew you at Ad Vice."

I thought of Fritzie's hands shaking earlier that night; I remembered him shouting at Lorna Martilkova: "You whored with the Dahlia, didn't you, girlie? *Tell me where you were during her lost days.*" Then the finale hit: Fritzie and Johnny Vogel whispering on the ride out to the Valley.

"I proved I'm not no nancy boy. Homos couldn't do what I did."

"Be still, damn you!"

I ran out to the hall, fed the pay phone a nickel and dialed Russ Millard's number at the Bureau.

"Central Homicide, Lieutenant Millard."

"Russ, it's Bucky."

"Something wrong, bright penny? You sound shaky."

"Russ, I think I've got something. I can't tell you now, but I need two favors."

"This is about Elizabeth?"

"Yes. Goddamnit, Russ—"

"Hush, and tell me."

"I need you to get me the Ad Vice file for Charles Michael Issler. He's got three pimping priors, so I know he'll have one."

"And?"

I dry swallowed. "I want you to check on Fritz Vogel's and John Vogel's whereabouts January tenth through fifteenth."

"Are you telling me—"

"I'm telling you maybe. I'm telling you maybe real strong."

There was a long silence, then: "Where are you?"

"The El Nido."

"Stay there. I'll call you back inside of half an hour."

I hung up and waited, thinking of a sweet package of glory and revenge. Seventeen minutes later the phone rang; I pounced on it. "Russ, what—"

"The file's missing. I checked the 'I's' myself. They were all put back unevenly, so my guess is that it was snatched recently. On the other, Fritzie was on duty at the Bureau straight through those days, racking up overtime on old cases, and Johnny was on vacation leave, where I don't know. Now, will you explain all this?"

I got an idea. "Not now. Meet me here tonight. *Late.* If I'm not here, wait for me."

"Bucky—"

"Later, padre."

* * *

I called in sick that afternoon; that night I committed two felony B & E's.

My first victim was working swingwatch; I called Personnel Division and impersonated a city payroll clerk to get his home address and phone number. The catching officer kicked loose; at dusk I parked across the street and eyeballed the apartment house that John Vogel called home.

It was a stucco four flat on Mentone near the L.A.–Culver City border, a salmon-pink structure flanked by identical buildings painted light green and tan. There was a pay phone at the corner; I used it to dial Bad Breath Johnny's number, an extra precaution to make sure the bastard wasn't in. Twenty rings went unanswered. I walked calmly over, found a bottom floor door with "Vogel" on the mail slot, worked a doubled-over hairpin into the keyhole and let myself in.

Inside, I held my breath, half expecting a killer dog to leap at me. I checked the luminous dial on my watch, decided ten minutes was tops and squinted for a light to turn on.

My eyes caught a floor lamp. I moved to it and pulled the cord, lighting up a tidy living room. There was a tidy bargain basement sofa with matching chairs, an imitation fireplace, cheese-cake glossies of Rita Hayworth, Betty Grable and Ann Sheridan Scotch taped to the walls, what looked like a genuine captured Jap flag draped over the coffee table. The phone was on the floor by the sofa, with an address book next to it; I allotted half my time right there.

I checked every page. There was no Betty Short or Charles Issler, and none of the names listed were repeats from the master file or the names in Betty's "little black book." Five minutes down, five to go.

A kitchen, dinette and bedroom adjoined the living room. I turned off the lamp, moved in darkness to the half-open bedroom doorway and patted the inside wall for a light switch. Finding one, I flipped it on.

An unmade bed, four walls festooned with Jap flags and a big, scuffed chest of drawers were revealed. I opened the top drawer, saw three German Lugers, spare clips and a scattering of loose shells—and laughed at the taste of Axis Johnny. Then I opened the middle one, and a tingling was all over me.

Black leather harnesses, chains, whips, studded dog collars, Tijuana condoms that gave you a bludgeon-headed extra six inches. Smut books with pictures of naked women getting whipped by other women while they sucked harness-clad guys with big dicks. Close-up photos that captured fat, needle marks, chipped nail polish and dope-glazed eyes. No Betty Short, no Lorna Mar-tilkova, no *Slave Girls from Hell* Egyptian backdrop or tie-in to Duke Wellington, but a parlay—whips to the coroner's "light lash marks"—that was enough to nail Johnny Vogel as Dahlia suspect number one.

I shut the drawers, flicked off the light, tingle walked into the living room and turned on the lamp, then reached for the address book. "Daddy & Mom's" number was GRanite-9401; if I got a no answer, B & E number two was a ten-minute drive away.

I dialed; Fritz Vogel's phone rang twenty-five times. I turned off the light and hauled ass.

Vogel Senior's small wood frame house was totally dark when I pulled up across from it. I sat behind the wheel remembering the layout from my previous visit, recalling two bedrooms off a long hallway, the kitchen, a rear service porch and a closed door across the hall from the bathroom. If Fritzie had a private den, that had to be it.

I took the driveway to the back of the house. The screen door to the service porch was open; I tiptoed past a washing machine to the barrier to the house proper. That door was solid wood, but feeling at the jamb I found it connected to the wall with a simple hook and eyelet. I shook the knob and felt plenty of give; if I could pop the little piece of metal, I was in.

I got down on my knees and patted the floor, stopping when my hand hit a skinny piece of metal. Pawing at it like a blind man, I realized I'd found an oil gauge dipstick. I smiled at my luck, stood up and popped the door open.

Thinking fifteen minutes tops, I moved through the kitchen, over to the hallway and down it, my hands in front of me to deflect unseen obstacles. A nightlight glowed inside the bathroom doorway—pointing me straight across to what I hoped was Fritzie's hideaway. I tried the knob—and the door opened.

The little room was pitch dark. I banged along the walls, hitting picture frames, feeling iceberg spooky until my leg grazed a tall wobbly object. It was about to topple when I snapped that it was a gooseneck lamp, reached for the top part and flipped the switch.

Light.

The pictures were photographs of Fritzie in uniform, in plainclothes, standing at attention with the rest of his 1925 Academy class. There was a desk positioned against the back wall, facing a window covered with a velvet curtain, a swivel chair and a filing cabinet.

I slid the top compartment open and fingered through manila folders stamped "Intelligence Rpt—Bunco Division," "Intelligence Rpt—Burglary Division," "Intelligence Rpt—Robbery Division"—all with the names of individuals typed on side tabs. Wanting some kind of common denominator, I checked the first sheets of the next three folders I came to—finding only one carbon page in each of them.

But those single pieces of paper were enough.

They were financial accountings, lists of bank balances and other assets, tallies made on known criminals that the Department couldn't legally touch. The routing designations at the top of each sheet spelled it out plain—it was the LAPD shooting the feds hot dope so that they could initiate tax evasion investigations. Handwritten notes—phone numbers, names and addresses—filled the margins, and I recognized Fritzie's Parker penmanship hand.

My breath came in short cold bursts as I thought: shakedown. He's either putting the screws to the hoods based on info in the rest of the files or selling them tip-offs on impending fed rousts.

Extortion, first degree.

Theft and harboring of official LAPD documents.

Impeding the progress of federal investigations.

But no Johnny Vogel, Charlie Issler or Betty Short.

I tore through another fourteen folders, finding the same scrawled-over financial reports in all of them. I memorized the side tab names, then moved to the bottom compartment. I saw "Known Offender Rpt—Administrative Vice Division" on the first file inside it—and knew I'd gotten the whole ball of wax.

Page one detailed the arrests, MO and confessing career of Charles Michael Issler, white male, born in Joplin, Missouri, in 1911; page two listed his "Known Associates." A June 1946 "whore book" check by his probation officer yielded six girls' names, followed by phone numbers and the arrest dates and dispositions of their hooking convictions. There were an additional four female names below the heading "?—No Prostitution Record." The third name was "Liz Short—Transient?"

I turned to page three and read down the column headed "KAs, cont"; one name harpooned me. "Sally Stinson" was in Betty Short's little black book, and none of the four questioning teams had been able to locate her. In brackets beside her name, some Ad Vice dick had penciled in, "Works out of Biltmore bar—conventioneer Johns." Doodles in Fritzie's ink color surrounded the entry.

I forced myself to think like a detective, not a revenge-happy kid. The extortion stuff aside, it was certain that Charlie Issler knew Betty Short. Betty knew Sally Stinson, who hooked out of the Biltmore. Fritz Vogel didn't want anybody to know it. He probably arranged the warehouse stunt to find out how much Sally and/or his other girls had told Issler about Betty and the men she was recently with.

"I proved I'm not no nancy boy. Homos couldn't do what I did. *I'm not cherry no more*, so don't say nancy boy."

I put the folders back in order, closed the cabinet, hit the light and relatched the backdoor before walking out the front like I owned the place, wondering briefly if there was any connection between Sally Stinson and the missing "S's" in the master file. Treading air to my car, I knew it couldn't be—Fritzie didn't know that the El Nido work room existed. Then another thought took over: if Issler had blabbed about "Liz" and her tricks I would have overheard. Fritzie was confident he could keep me quiet. It was an underestimation that I was going to bleed him for.

* * *

Russ Millard was waiting for me with two words: "Report, Officer."

I told him the whole story in detail. When I finished, he saluted Elizabeth Short on the wall, said, "We're making progress, dear," and formally stuck out his hand.

We shook, sort of like father and son after the big game. "What next, padre?"

"Next you go back to duty like none of this happened. Harry and I will brace Issler at the nut farm, and I'll assign some men to look for Sally Stinson on the QT."

I swallowed. "And Fritzie?"

"I'll have to think about it."

"I want him nailed."

"I know you do. But you keep one thing in mind. The men that he extorted are criminals who would never testify against him in court, and if he gets wind of this and destroys the carbons, we wouldn't even be able to get him for an interdepartmental offense. *All* of this is going to require corroboration, so for now it's just us. And *you* had better settle down and control your temper until it's over."

I said, "I want in on the collar."

Russ nodded. "I wouldn't have it any other way." He tipped his hat to Elizabeth on the way out the door.

* * *

I went back to swingwatch and played sob sister; Russ put men out to look for Sally Stinson. A day later, he called me at home with one dose of bad news, one of good:

Charles Issler had found a lawyer to file him a writ of habeas corpus; he had been released from the Mira Loma ding farm three weeks before. His L.A. apartment had been cleaned out; he couldn't be found. That was a kick in the balls, but the confirmation on the Vogel extortion front made up for it.

Harry Sears checked Fritzie's felony arrest records—from Bunco in 1934 up through his current position in Central Detectives.

At one time or another Vogel had arrested every single man on the LAPD-FBI financial carbons. And the feds did not indict a single one of them.

I rotated off-duty the next day, and spent it with the master file, thinking *corroboration*. Russ called to say that he hadn't got any leads on Issler, that it looked like he'd blown town. Harry was keeping Johnny Vogel under a loose surveillance on and off duty; a buddy working West Hollywood Sheriff's Vice had kicked loose with some KA addresses—friends of Sally Stinson. Russ told me a half dozen times to take it easy and not jump the gun. He knew damn well I already had Fritzie in Folsom and Johnny in the Little Green Room.

I was scheduled to go back on duty Thursday, and got up early in order to spend a long morning with the master file. I was making coffee when the phone rang.

I picked it up. "Yes?"

"It's Russ. We've got Sally Stinson. Meet me at 1546 North Havenhurst in half an hour."

"Rolling."

* * *

The address was a Spanish castle apartment house: white-washed cement shaped into ornamental turrets, balconies topped by sun-weathered awnings. Walkways led up to the individual doors; Russ was standing by the one on the far right.

I left the car in a red zone and trotted over. A man in a disheveled suit and paper party hat strutted down the walkway, a slap-happy grin on his face. He slurred, "Next shift, huh? Twosies on onesies, ooh la la!"

Russ led me up the steps. I rapped on the door; a not-young blonde with mussed hair and smeared makeup threw it open, spat, "What did you forget this time?" then, "Oh, shit."

Russ held out his badge. "LAPD. Are you Sally Stinson?"

"No, I'm Eleanor Roosevelt. Listen, I put out for the Sheriff's more ways than one lately, so I'm tapped in the cash department. You want the other?"

I started to elbow my way inside; Russ grabbed my arm. "Miss Stinson, it's about Liz Short and Charlie Issler, and it's here or the women's jail."

Sally Stinson clutched the front of her robe and pressed it to her bodice. She said, "Listen, I told the other guy," then stopped and hugged herself. She looked like the floozy victim confronting the monster in old horror movies; I knew exactly who *her* monster was. "We're not with him. We just want to talk to you about Betty Short."

Sally appraised us. "And he ain't gonna know?"

Russ flashed his father-confessor smile and lied. "No, this is strictly confidential."

Sally stood aside. Russ and I entered an archetypal trick pad front room—cheap furniture, bare walls, suitcases lined up in one corner for a quick getaway. Sally bolted the door. I said, "Who's this guy we're talking about, Miss Stinson?"

Russ straightened the knot in his necktie; I clammed up. Sally jabbed a finger at the couch. "Let's do this quicksville. Rehashing old grief is against my religion."

I sat down; stuffing and the point of a spring popped out a few inches from my knee. Russ settled into a chair and got out his notebook; Sally took a perch on top of the suitcases, back to the wall and eyes on the door like a seasoned getaway artist. She started with the most often heard Short case intro line: "I don't know who killed her."

Russ said, "Fair enough, but let's take it from the beginning. When did you meet Liz Short?"

Sally scratched a hickey on her cleavage. "Last summer. June, maybe."

"Where?"

"At the bar at the Yorkshire House Grill downtown. I was half in the bag, waiting for my … waiting for Charlie I. Liz was putting the moves on this rich-looking old hairbag, coming on too strong. She scared him off. Then we started talking and Charlie showed up."

I said, "Then what?"

"Then we all discovered we had a lot in common. Liz said she was broke, Charlie says 'you wanta make a quick double-saw,' Liz says 'yeah,' Charlie sends us over for a twosie at the textile sales-man's convention at the Mayflower."

"And?"

"And Liz was gooood. You want details, wait till I publish my memoirs. But I'll tell you this. I'm pretty good at faking like I'm loving it, but Liz was great. She had this bee in her bonnet about keeping her stockings on, but she was like a virtuoso. Academy Award stuff."

I thought of the stag film—and the strange gash on Betty's left thigh. "Do you know if Liz ever appeared in any pornographic movies?"

Sally shook her head. "No, but if she did she'd be gooood."

"You know a man named Walter 'Duke' Wellington?"

"No."

"Linda Martin?"

"Ixnay."

Russ took over. "Did you turn any other tricks with Liz?"

Sally said, "Four or five, last summer. Hotel jobs. All conventioneers."

"Remember any names? Organizations? Descriptions?"

Sally laughed and scratched her cleavage. "Mr. Policeman, my first commandment is keep your eyes shut and try to forget. I'm good at it."

"Were any of the hotel jobs at the Biltmore?"

"No. The Mayflower, the Hacienda House. Maybe the Rexford."

"Did any of the men react strangely to Liz? Get rough with her?"

Sally hooted. "Mostly they were just happy 'cause she faked it so good."

Itchy to get at Vogel, I changed the subject. "Tell me about you and Charlie Issler. Did you know he confessed to the Dahlia killing?"

Sally said, "Not at first I didn't. Then ... well, anyway, I wasn't surprised when I did hear. Charlie's got this what you might wanta call compulsion to confess. Like if a prostie gets killed and it makes the papers, bye-bye Charlie and get out the iodine when he comes back, 'cause he always makes sure the rubber hose boys work him over."

Russ said, "Why do you think he does it?"

"How's a guilty conscience sound?"

I said, "How's this sound? You tell us where you were January tenth through fifteenth, and you tell us about this guy we all don't like."

"Sounds like I've really got a choice."

"You do. Talk to us here or to a butch matron downtown."

Russ tugged at his tie—hard. "Do you remember where you were on those dates, Miss Stinson?"

Sally fished cigarettes and matches from her pockets and lit up. "Everybody who knew Liz remembers where they were then. You know, like when FDR died. You keep wishing you could go back, you know, and change it."

I started to apologize for my tactics; Russ beat me to it. "My partner didn't mean to get nasty, Miss Stinson. This is a grudge thing for him."

It was the perfect come-on. Sally Stinson tossed her cigarette on the floor, ground it out with her bare feet, then patted the suitcases. "I'm adios as soon as you walk out the door. I'll tell you, but I won't tell no DAs, no Grand Juries, no other cops. I mean it. You walk out that door and it's bye-bye Sally."

Russ said, "It's a deal." Sally's color rose; that and the anger in her eyes knocked a good ten years off her. "On Friday the tenth I got a call at this hotel where I was staying. A guy said he's a friend of Charlie and he wants to buy me for this young guy he knows who's cherry. Two-day session at the Biltmore, a C-note and a half. I say I ain't seen Charlie in a while, how'd you get my number? The guy says 'Never mind, meet me and the kid outside the Biltmore tomorrow at noon.'

"I'm broke, so I say okay, and I meet the two guys. Big fat peas in a pod packing hardware, I know it's a father and son cop act. Money changes hands, sonny's got halitosis but I've seen worse. He tells me daddy's name and I get a little scared, but daddy amscrays and the kid's so lame I know I can take care of him."

Sally lit another cigarette. Russ passed me Personnel photos of the Vogel boys; I handed them to her. She said, "On the button," burned their faces off with the tip of her Chesterfield, then got on with it.

"Vogel had a suite set up. Sonny and I tricked, and he tried to get me to play with these creepy sex gadgets he brought. I said, 'Ixnay, ixnay, ixnay.' He said he'll give me an extra twenty if he can whip me soft for fun. I said, 'When hell freezes.' Then he—"

I broke off the story. "Did he talk about stag films? Lezzie stuff?"

Sally snorted. "He talked about baseball and his peter. He called it the Big Schnitzel, and you know what? It wasn't."

Russ said, "Go on, Miss Stinson."

"Well, we screw all afternoon, and I listen to the kid prattle about the Brooklyn Dodgers and the Big Schnitzel until I am blue in the face. Then I say, 'Let's get dinner and some fresh air,' and we go down to the lobby.

"And there's Liz, sitting all by herself. She tells me she needs money, and since I can tell sonny likes her, I set up a trick within a trick. We go back up to the suite, and I take a breather while they go at it in the bedroom. Liz skips out about twelve-thirty, whispers 'Little Schnitzel' to me, and I never saw her again until I saw her picture all over the papers."

I looked at Russ. He mouthed the word, "Dulange"; I nodded, picturing Betty Short on the loose until she met Frenchman Joe on the morning of the twelfth. The missing Dahlia days were coming together.

Russ said, "And you and John Vogel went back to your assignation then?"

Sally tossed the Personnel photos on the floor. "Yes."

"Did he talk to you about Liz Short?"

"He said she loved the Big Schnitzel."

"Did he say that they'd made plans to meet again?"

"No."

"Did he mention his father and Liz in any context at all?"

"No."

"What did he say about Liz?"

Sally hugged herself. "He said she liked to play his kind of games. I said, 'What kind of games?' Sonny said, 'Master and Slave' and 'Cop and Whore.'"

I said, "Finish it up. Please."

Sally eyed the door. "Two days after Liz got in all the papers, Fritz Vogel came by my hotel and told me Sonny said he'd tricked with her. He told me he'd got my name from some police file, and he questioned me about my ... procurers. I mentioned Charlie I., and Vogel remembered him from when he worked this hotshot Vice detail. Then he got spooked, 'cause he remembered Charlie had this confessing problem. He called some partner of his on my phone and told him to yank some Vice file of Charlie's, then he made another call and went crazy, 'cause whoever he talked to told him Charlie was already in custody, that he'd already confessed to Liz.

"He beat me up then. He asked me all these questions, like whether Liz would mention tricking with a cop's son to Charlie. I told him Charlie and Liz were just acquaintances, that he'd just sent her out a few times, months and months ago, but he kept hitting me anyway, and he told me he'd kill me if I told the police about his son and the Dahlia."

I got up to go; Russ sat still. "Miss Stinson, you said that when John Vogel told you his father's name you got scared. Why?"

Sally whispered, "A story I heard." Suddenly she looked beyond used-up—ancient.

"What sort of story?"

Sally's whisper cracked. "How he got kicked off that hotshot Vice job."

I remembered Bill Koenig's rendition—that Fritzie caught syphilis from hookers when he worked Ad Vice, and was canned to take the mercury cure. "He caught a bad dose. Right?"

Sally dredged up a clear voice: "I heard he got the syph and went crazy. He thought a colored girl gave it to him, so he shook down this house in Watts and made all the girls do him before he took the cure. He made them rub his thing in their eyes, and two of the girls went blind."

My legs were weaker than they were the night at the warehouse. Russ said, "Thank you, Sally."

I said, "Let's go get Johnny."

* * *

We took my car downtown. Johnny had been working a day-watch foot beat with overtime on swing, so at 11:00 A.M. I knew there was a good chance of snagging him alone.

I drove slowly, looking for his familiar blue serge figure. Russ had a syringe and Pentothal ampule he'd kept from the Red Manley interrogations out on the dashboard; even he knew this was a muscle job. We were cruising the alley in back of the Jesus Saves Mission when I spotted him—solo rousting a pair of piss bums scrounging in a trash can.

I got out of the car and yelled, "Hey, Johnny!" Vogel Junior shook a finger at the winos and sidled over, thumbs in his Sam Browne belt.

He said, "What you doin' in civvies, Bleichert?" and I hooked him to the gut. He bent over double, and I grabbed his head and banged it into the roof of the car. Johnny slumped, his lights dimming. I held him; Russ rolled up his left sleeve and jacked the silly syrup into the vein at the crook of his elbow.

Now he was out cold. I took the .38 from his holster, tossed it on the front seat and stuffed Johnny into the back. I got in with him; Russ took the wheel. We peeled rubber down the alley, the piss bums waving their short dogs at us.

The ride to the El Nido took half an hour. Johnny giggled in his dope slumber, almost coming awake a couple of times; Russ drove silently. When we got to the hotel, Russ checked the lobby, found it empty and gave me the high sign from the door. I slung

Johnny over my shoulder and hauled him up to room 204—the hardest minute's work of my life.

The trip upstairs half roused him; his eyes fluttered as I dumped him into a chair and cuffed his left wrist to a heating pipe. Russ said, "The Pentothal's good for another few hours. No way he can lie." I soaked a bath towel in the sink and swathed Johnny's face with it. He coughed, and I pulled the towel away.

Johnny giggled. I said, "Elizabeth Short," and pointed to the glossies on the wall. Johnny, rubber-faced, slurred, "What about her?" I gave him another dose of the towel, a cobweb-clearing bracer. Johnny sputtered; I let the wad of cold terrycloth drop into his lap. "How about *Liz* Short? You remember her?"

Johnny laughed; Russ motioned for me to sit beside him on the bed rail. "There's a method to this. Let me ask the questions. You just hold on to your temper."

I nodded. Johnny had the two of us in focus now, but his eyes were pinned and his features were slack and goofy. Russ said, "What's your name, son?"

Johnny said, "You know me, loot," the slur on its way out.

"Tell me anyway."

"Vogel, John Charles."

"When were you born?"

"May 6, 1922."

"What's sixteen plus fifty-six?"

Johnny thought for a moment, said, "Seventy-two," then fixed on me. "Why'd you hit me, Bleichert? I never did you no dirt."

Fat Boy seemed genuinely befuddled. I kept it zipped; Russ said, "What's your father's name, son?"

"You know him, loot. Oh ... Friedrich Vogel. Fritzie for short."

"Short like in Liz Short?"

"Uh sure ... like Liz, Betty, Beth, Dahlia ... lots of monickers."

"Think about this January, Johnny. Your dad wanted you to lose your cherry, right?"

"Uh ... yeah."

"He bought you a woman for two days, right?"

"Not a woman. Not a *real* one. A hooer. A hoooooer." The long syllable turned into a laugh; Johnny tried to clap his hands. One hand hit his chest; the other jerked at the end of its cuffed tether. He said, "This ain't right. I'll tell Daddy."

Russ answered him calmly: "It's only for a little while. You had the prostitute at the Biltmore, right?"

"Right. Daddy got a rate because he knew the house dick."

"And you met Liz Short at the Biltmore, too. Right?"

Spastic movements hit Johnny's face—eye tics, lip twitches, veins popping on his forehead. He reminded me of a knocked-down fighter trying to haul himself up off the canvas. "Uh … that's right."

"Who introduced you?"

"What's her name … The hooer."

"And what did you and Liz do then, Johnny? Tell me about it."

"We … divvied on ten scoots for three hours and played games. I gave her the Big Schnitz. We played 'Horse and Rider,' and I liked Liz, so I just whipped her soft. She was nicer than the blondie hooer. She kept her stockings on, 'cause she said she had this birthmark nobody could look at. She liked the Schnitz, and she let me kiss her without the Listerine like the blondie made me gargle."

I thought about Betty's thigh gouge and held my breath. Russ said, "Johnny, did you kill Liz?"

Fat Boy jerked in his chair. "No! No no no no no no! No!"

"Ssssh. Easy, son, easy. When did Liz leave you?"

"I didn't slice her!"

"We believe you, son. Now when did Liz leave you?"

"Late. Late Saturday. Maybe twelve, maybe one."

"You mean early Sunday morning?"

"Yeah."

"Did she say where she was going?"

"No."

"Did she mention any men's names? Boyfriends? Men she was going to see?"

"Uh … some flyboy she was married to."

"That's all?"

"Yeah."

"Did you see her again?"

"No."

"Did your father know Liz at all?"

"No."

"Did he force the house detective to change the name on the registration book after Liz's body was found?"

"Uh … yes."

"Do you know who killed Liz Short?"

"No! No!"

Johnny was starting to sweat. I was too—anxious for facts to nail him with now that it looked like he and the Dahlia were just a one-night stand. I said, "You told your father about Liz when she made the papers, is that right?"

"Uh ... yes."

"And *he* told *you* about a guy named Charlie Issler? A guy who used to pimp Liz Short?"

"Yes."

"And he told you Issler was in custody as a confessor?"

"Uh ... yes."

"Now you tell me what he said he was going to do about that, shitbird. You tell me damn good and slow."

Fat Boy's cut-rate heart rose to the challenge. "Daddy tried to get Ellis Jewboy to cut Issler loose, but he wouldn't. Daddy knew this morgue attendant who owed him, and he got this DOA cooze and talked Jewboy into this idea. Daddy wanted Uncle Bill for it, but Jewboy said no, take you. Daddy said you'd do it 'cause without Blanchard to tell you what to do you were jelly. Daddy said you were a sob sister, weak sister, buck tooth ..."

Johnny started laughing hysterically, shaking his head, spraying sweat, rattling his cuffed wrist like a zoo animal with a new plaything. Russ stepped in front of me. "I'll make him sign a statement. You take a half hour or so to calm down. I'll feed him coffee, then when you get back we'll figure out what's next."

I walked out to the fire escape, sat down and dangled my legs over the edge. I watched cars head up Wilcox to Hollywood and got it all down, the cost to myself, the whole enchilada. Then I played license plate blackjack, southbound versus northbound, out-of-state cars as wild cards. Southbound was me, the house; northbound was Lee and Kay. Southbound stood on a chicken-shit seventeen; northbound got an ace and a queen for pure blackjack. Dedicating the enchilada to the three of us, I went back to the room.

Johnny Vogel was signing Russ's statement, flushed and sweaty, with a bad case of the shakes. I read the confession over his shoulder: it laid out the Biltmore, Betty, and Fritzie's beating of Sally Stinson succinctly, to the tune of four misdemeanors and two felonies.

Russ said, "I want to sit on this for now, and I want to talk to a legal officer."

I said, "No, padre," and turned to Johnny.

"You're under arrest for suborning prostitution, withholding evidence, obstruction of justice and accesory to first-degree assault and battery."

Johnny blurted, "Daddy" and looked at Russ. Russ looked at me—and held out the statement. I put it in my pocket and cuffed Junior's wrists behind his back while he sobbed quietly.

The padre sighed. "It's the shithouse until you retire."

"I know."

"You'll never get back to the Bureau."

"I've already got a taste for shit, padre. I don't think it'll be so bad."

*   *   *

I led Johnny down to my car and drove him the four blocks to Hollywood Station. Reporters and camera jockeys were lounging on the front steps; they went nuts when they saw the plainclothesman with the uniformed cop in bracelets. Flashbulbs popped, newshounds recognized me and shouted my name, I yelled back, "No comment." Inside, bluesuits goggle-eyed the sight. I shoved Johnny to the front desk and whispered in his ear: "Tell your daddy I know about his extortion deal with the fed reports, and about the syph and the whorehouse in Watts. Tell him I'm going to the papers with it tomorrow."

Johnny went back to his quiet sobbing. A uniformed lieutenant came over and blurted, "What on God's earth is this here?"

A flashbulb went off in my eyes; there was Bevo Means with his notepad at the ready. I said, "I'm Officer Dwight Bleichert and this is Officer John Charles Vogel." Handing the statement to the lieutenant, I winked. "Book him."

*   *   *

I dawdled over a big steak lunch, then drove downtown to Central Station and my regular tour of duty. Heading into the locker room, I heard the intercom bark: "Officer Bleichert, go to the watch commander's office immediately."

I reversed directions and knocked on Lieutenant Jastrow's door. He called out, "It's open." I walked in and saluted like an idealistic rookie. Jastrow stood up, ignored the salute and adjusted his horn-rims like he was seeing me for the first time.

"You're on two weeks vacation leave as of now, Bleichert. When you return to duty, report to Chief Green. He'll assign you to another division."

Wanting to milk the moment, I asked, "Why?"

"Fritz Vogel just blew his brains out. That's why."

My farewell salute was twice as crisp as my first one; Jastrow ignored it again. I walked across the hall thinking of the two blind whores, wondering if they'd find out or care. The muster room was crammed with blues waiting for roll call—a last obstacle before the parking lot and home. I took it slow, standing GI straight, meeting the eyes that sought mine, making them look down. The hisses of "Traitor" and "Bolshevik" all came when my back was turned. I was almost out the door when I heard applause and turned to see Russ Millard and Thad Green clapping good-bye.

24

EXILED TO the shithouse and proud of it; two weeks to kill before I began serving my sentence at some putrid LAPD outpost. The Vogel arrest-suicide whitewashed as interdepartmental offenses and a father's shame over the ignominy. I closed out my glory days the only way that seemed decent—I chased the gone man.

I started at the L.A. end of his vanishing act.

I got nothing from repeated readings of Lee's arrest scrapbook; I questioned the lezzies at La Verne's Hideaway, asking whether Mr. Fire showed up to abuse them a second time—and got no's and jeers. The padre sneaked me a carbon of the complete Blanchard felony arrest file—it told me nothing. Kay, content in our monogamy, told me I was worse than a fool for what I was doing—and I knew it scared her.

Dredging up the Issler/Stinson/Vogel connection had convinced me of one thing—that I was a detective. Thinking like one as far as Lee was concerned was another matter, but I forced myself to do it. The ruthlessness I had always seen—and secretly admired—in him came across even deeper, making me care for him even more unequivocally. As did the facts I always came back to:

Lee disappeared when the Dahlia, Benzedrine and Bobby De Witt's imminent parole converged on him;

He was last seen in Tijuana at a time when De Witt was heading there and the Short case was centered on the U.S.–Mexico border;

De Witt and his dope partner Felix Chasco were murdered then, and even though two Mexican nationals were nailed for the job, it could have been a railroad—the Rurales wiping an unwanted homicide off their books;

Conclusion: Lee Blanchard could have murdered De Witt and Chasco, his motive a desire to protect himself from revenge attempts and Kay from lounge lizard Bobby's possible abuse. Conclusion within that conclusion: I didn't care.

My next step was to study the transcript of De Witt's trial. At the Hall of Records, more facts sunk in:

Lee named the informants who gave him the dope on De Witt as the Boulevard-Citizens "brains," then said that they left town to avoid reprisals from Lizard's friends. My follow-up call to R&I was unsettling—the snitches had no records at all. De Witt asserted a police frame because of his prior dope arrests, and the prosecution based its case on the marked money from the robbery found at De Witt's house and the fact that he had no alibi for the time of the heist. Of the four-man gang, two were killed at the scene of the crime, De Witt was captured and the fourth man remained at large. De Witt claimed not to know who he was—even though stooling might have gotten him a sentence reduction.

Conclusion: maybe it *was* an LAPD frame, maybe Lee *was* in on it, maybe he initiated it to curry favor with Benny Siegel, whose money was clouted by the real heisters, and who Lee was terrified of for good reason—he had stiffed the Bug Man on his fight contract. Lee then met Kay at De Witt's trial, fell in love with her in his chaste-guilty way and learned to hate Bobby for real. Conclusion within that conclusion: Kay couldn't have known. De Witt was scum who got what he deserved.

And the final conclusion: I had to hear the man confirm or deny himself.

Four days into my "vacation," I took off for Mexico. In Tijuana, I passed out pesos and American dimes and showed snapshots of Lee, holding quarters back to barter for "información importante." I acquired an entourage, no leads and the certainty that I would be trampled if I kept showing coin. From then on, I stuck to the traditional gringo cop–Mex cop one-dollar handout confidential exchange.

The TJ cops were black-shirted vultures who spoke only broken English—but they understood the international language very well. I stopped a score of individual "patrolmen" on the street, flashed my shield and pictures, pressed dollar bills into their hands and asked questions in the best English-Spanish I could muster. The singles quickly snapped up, I got headshakes, bilingual bullshit broadsides and a strange series of tales that rang true.

One had "el bianco explosivo" weeping at a stag film smoker held at the Chicago Club in late January; another featured a big blond guy beating the shit out of three jack rollers, then buying off the cops with double-saws peeled from a large roll. The capper was Lee donating 200 scoots to a leper ministry priest he met in a bar, buying drinks for the house, then driving to Ensenada. That bit of dope earned a five spot and a demand for an explanation. The cop said, "The priest my brother. He ordain himself. Vaya con Dios. Keep your money in your pocket."

I took the coast road eighty miles south to Ensenada, wondering where Lee got that kind of money to throw around. The drive was pleasant—scrub-lined bluffs giving way to the ocean on my right, hills and valleys covered with dense foliage to the left of me. Car traffic was scarce, with a steady trickle of pedestrians walking north: whole families lugging suitcases, looking scared and happy at the same time, like they didn't know what their dash across the border would bring them, but it had to be better than sucking Mexican dirt and tourist chump change.

Approaching Ensenada at twilight, the trickle became a migration march. A single line of people hugged the northbound roadside, belongings wrapped in blankets and slung over their shoulders. Every fifth or sixth marcher carried a torch or a lantern, and all the small children were strapped papoose-style onto their mothers' backs. Coming over the last hill outside the city limits, I saw Ensenada, a smear of neon below me, torchlights punctuating the darkness until the overall fluorescence swallowed them.

I drove down into it, quickly sizing up the burg as a sea breeze version of TJ catering to a higher class of turista. The gringos were well behaved, there were no child beggars on the streets and no barkers in front of the profusion of juice joints. The wetback line originated out in the scrubland, and only cut through Ensenada to reach the coast road—and to pay tribute to the Rurales for letting them through.

It was the most blatant shakedown I had ever seen. Rurales in brownshirts, jodhpurs and jackboots were walking from peasant to peasant, taking money and attaching tags to their shoulders with staple guns; plainsclothes cops sold parcels of beef jerky and dried fruit, putting the coins they received into changemakers strapped next to their sidearms. Other Rurales were stationed one man to a block to check the tags; when I turned off the main drag onto an obvious red light street, I glimpsed two brownshirts rendering a man senseless with the butts of their weapons: sawed-off pump shotguns.

I decided that it would be wise to check in with the law before going out to question the Ensenada citizenry. Also, Lee had been spotted talking to a group of Rurales up near the border shortly after leaving L.A., and it might be possible to shake the locals for a line on him.

I followed a caravan of '30s-vintage prowl cars down the red light block and across to the street paralleling the beach—and there was the station. It was a converted church: barred windows, the word POLICÍA painted in black over religious scenes carved into the white adobe facade. A searchlight was stationed on the lawn; when I got out of the car, badge out, American grin on, it was shined right at me.

I walked into it, eyes shielded, face smarting from the heat blast. A man cackled, "Yanqui copper, J. Edgar, Texas Rangers." His hand was out as I passed him. I pressed a dollar bill into it and entered the station.

The interior was even more churchlike: velvet wall hangings depicting Jesus and his adventures decorated the entrance hall; the benches filled with lounging brownshirts looked like pews. The front desk was a big block of dark wood, Jesus on the cross carved into it—most likely a retired altar. The fat Rurale standing sentry there licked his lips when he saw me coming—he reminded me of a child molester who would never retire.

I had my obligatory onesky out, but held back. "Los Angeles Police to see the chief."

The brownshirt rubbed his thumbs and forefingers together, then pointed to my badge holder. I handed it over along with the dollar; he led me down a Jesus-frescoed hallway to a door marked CAPITÁN. I stood there while he went in and talked in rapid-fire Spanish; when he exited, I got a heel click and a belated salute.

"Officer Bleichert, come in please."

The non-accented words surprised me; I walked in to answer them. A tall Mexican man in a gray suit was standing there with his hand out—for a shake, not a dollar bill.

We shook. The man sat down behind a big desk and tapped a plate reading CAPITÁN VASQUEZ. "How can I help you, Officer?"

I grabbed my badge holder off the desk and put a picture of Lee down in its place. "That man is a Los Angeles police officer.

He's been missing since late January, and when he was last seen he was heading here."

Vasquez examined the snapshot. The corners of his mouth twitched; he immediately tried to cover up the response by turning it into a negative head shake. "No, I haven't seen this man. I will put out a bulletin to my officers and have them inquire in the American community here."

I answered the lie. "He's a hard man to miss, Captain. Blond, six feet, built like a brick shithouse."

"Ensenada attracts rough trade, Officer. That is why the police contingent here is so well armed and vigilant. Will you be staying awhile?"

"At least overnight. Maybe your men missed him, and I can get some leads."

Vasquez smiled. "I doubt that. Are you alone?"

"I have two partners waiting for me in Tijuana."

"And what division are you assigned to?"

I lied big. "Metropolitan."

"You are very young for such prestigious duty."

I picked up the photo. "Nepotism, Captain. My dad's a deputy chief and my brother's with the consulate in Mexico City. Good night."

"And good luck, Bleichert."

* * *

I rented a room at a hotel within walking distance of the nightclub/red light strip. For two dollars I got a ground-floor flop with an ocean view, a bed with a pancake-thin mattress, a sink and a key to the community john outside. I dumped my grip on the dresser, and as a precaution on the way out, yanked two hairs from my head and spit-glued them across the door-doorjamb juncture. If the fascisti prowled the pad, I would know.

I walked to the heart of the neon smear.

The streets were filled with men in uniform: brownshirts, U.S. marines and sailors. There were no Mex nationals to be seen, and everyone was quite orderly—even the knots of jarheads weaving drunk. I decided that it was the walking Rurale arsenal that kept things pacified. Most of the brownshirts were scrawny bantam-weights, but they were packing firepower grande: sawed-offs, tommys, .45 automatics, brass knucks dangling from their cart-ridge belts.

Fluorescent beacons pulsated at me: Flame Klub, Arturo's Oven, Club Boxeo, Falcon's Lair, Chico's Klub Imperial. "Boxeo" meant "boxing" in Spanish—so I made that dump my first stop.

Expecting darkness, I walked into a garishly lit room crowded with sailors. Mexican girls danced half naked on top of a long bar, dollar bills tucked into their G-strings. Canned marimba music and catcalls made the joint a deafening pocket of noise; I stood on my tiptoes looking for someone with the air of proprietor. At the back I saw an alcove papered with fight publicity stills. It drew me like a magnet, and I threaded my way past a new shift of nudies slinking to the bar to get to it.

And there *I* was, in great light heavyweight company, sandwiched between Gus Lesnevich and Billy Conn;

And there was Lee, right next to Joe Louis, who he could have fought if he'd dived for Benny Siegel.

Bleichert and Blanchard. Two white hopes gone wrong.

I stared at the pictures for a long time, until the raucousness around me dissipated and I wasn't in some upholstered sewer, I was back in '40 and '41, winning fights and rutting with giveaway girls who looked like Betty Short. And Lee was scoring knockouts and living with Kay—and, strangely, we were a family again.

"First Blanchard, now you. Who's next? Willie Pep?"

I was back in the sewer immediately, blurting, "When? When did you see him?"

Whirling around, I saw a hulking old man. His face was cracked leather and broken bones—a punching bag—but his voice was nothing like a stumblebum's: "A couple of months ago. The heavy rains in February. We musta talked fights for ten hours straight."

"Where is he now?"

"I ain't seen him since that one time, and maybe he don't want to see you. I tried to talk about that fight you guys had, but Big Lee won't have any. Says 'We ain't partners no more' and starts tellin' me the featherweights are the best division pound for pound. I tell him, nix—it's the middles. Zale, Graziano, La Motta, Cerdan, who you kiddin'?"

"Is he still in town?"

"I don't think so. I own this place, and he ain't been back here. You lookin' to settle a grudge? A rematch maybe?"

"I'm looking to get him out of a shitload of trouble he's in."

The old pug measured my words, then said, "I'm a sucker for dancemasters like you, so I'll give you the only piece of skinny I've

got. I heard Blanchard caused a ruckus over at the Club Satan, had
to bribe his way out big with Captain Vasquez. You walk over five
blocks to the beach, there's the Satan. You talk to Ernie the cook.
He saw it. You tell him I said to be kosher with you, and take a
deep breath when you walk in, 'cause there ain't nothin' like that
place where you're comin' from."

* * *

The Club Satan was a slate-roofed adobe hut sporting an
ingenious neon sign: a little red devil poking the air with a
trident-headed hard-on. It had its very own brownshirt doorman,
a little Mex who scrutinized incoming patrons while fondling
the trigger housing of a tripod BAR. His epaulet flaps were
stuffed with yankee singles; I added one to the collection as
I walked in, bracing myself.

From the sewer to the shitstorm.

The bar was a urinal trough. Marines and sailors masturbated
into it while they gash dived the nudie girls squatting on top.
Blow jobs were being dispensed underneath tables facing the
front of the room and a large bandstand. A guy in a Satan costume
was dicking a fat woman on a mattress. A burro with red velvet
devil horns pinned to his ears stood by, eating hay out of a bowl
on the floor. To the right of the stage, a tuxedo-clad gringo was
crooning into a microphone: "I've got a rich girl, her name's
Roseanne, she uses a tortilla for a diaphragm! Hey! Hey! I've got
a girl, her name is Sue, she's a one-way ticket to the big fungoo!
Hey! Hey! I've got a girl her name's Corrine, she knows how to
make my banana cream! Hey! Hey! ..."

The "music" was drowned out by chants from the tables—"Donkey! Donkey!" I stood there getting sideswiped by revelers, then
garlicky breath smothered me. "Joo want the bar, handsome?
Breakfast of champions, one dollar. Joo want *me*? Roun' the world,
two dollar."

I got up the guts to look at her. She was old, fat, her lips crusted
with chancre sores. I pulled bills from my pocket and shoved them
at her, not caring what denomination they were. The whore genuflected before her nightclub Jesus; I shouted, "Ernie. I have to see
him now. The guy at Club Boxeo sent me over."

Mamacita exclaimed, "Vamanos!" and ran interference for me,
pushing through a line of jarheads waiting for dinner seats at the
bar. She led me to a curtained passageway beside the stage and

down it to the kitchen. A spicy aroma perked my tastebuds—until I saw the rear end of a dog carcass hanging out of a stewpot. The woman spoke in Spanish to the chef—a strange-looking guy who came off as a Mex-Chink halfbreed. He nodded along, then walked over.

I had the snapshot of Lee out. "I heard this man gave you some trouble a while back."

The guy gave the photo a cursory eyeball. "Who wants to know?"

I flashed my badge, giving the breed a glimpse of hardware. He said, "He your friend?"

"My best friend."

The breed tucked his hands under his apron; I knew one of them was holding a knife. "Your friend drink fourteen shots of my best Mescal, house record. That I like. He make lots of toasts to dead women. That I don't mind. But he try to fuck with my donkey show, and that I don't take."

"What happened?"

"Four of my guys he take, fifth he don't. Rurales take him home to sleep it off."

"That's it?"

The breed pulled out a stiletto, popped the button and scratched his neck with the dull side of the blade. "Finito."

I walked out the backdoor into an alley, scared for Lee. Two men in shiny suits were lounging by a streetlight; when they saw me they picked up the tempo of their foot shuffling and studied the ground like dirt was suddenly fascinating. I took off running; gravel scraping behind me said the two were in hot pursuit.

The alley ended at a connecting road to the red light block, with another, barely navigable dirt fork angling off in the direction of the beach. I took it at a full sprint, my shoulders brushing chicken wire fencing, penned-up dogs trying to get at me from the opposite sides. Their barks destroyed the rest of the street noise; I had no idea if the two were still on my tail. I saw the ocean-front boulevard looming in front of me, got my bearings, figured the hotel to be a block to the right and slowed to a walk.

I was half a block off—in my favor.

The dump was about a hundred yards away. Catching my breath, I strolled there, Mr. Square American slumming. The courtyard was empty; I reached for my room key. Then light from the second floor fluttered across the door—now minus my spit hair warning trap.

I drew my .38 and kicked the door in. A white man sitting in the chair by the bed already had his hands up and a peace offering on his lips: "Whoa, boy. I'm a friend. I'm not heeled, and if you don't believe me then I'll stand a frisk right now."

I pointed my gun at the wall. The man got up and placed his palms on it, hands over head, legs spread. I patted him down, .38 at his spine, finding a billfold, keys and a greasy comb. Digging the muzzle in, I examined the billfold. It was stuffed with American cash; there was a California private investigator's license in a laminated holder. It gave the man's name as Milton Dolphine, his business address as 986 Copa De Oro in San Diego.

I tossed the billfold on the bed and eased the pressure on my gun; Dolphine squirmed. "That money's jackshit compared to what Blanchard was holding. You go partners with me and it's easy street."

I kicked his legs out from under him. Dolphine hit the floor and sucked dust off the carpet. "You tell me all of it, and you watch what you say about my partner, or it's a B&E roust and the Ensenada jail."

Dolphine pushed himself up onto his knees. He gasped, "Bleichert, how the fuck did you figure I knew to come here? It occur to you that maybe I was nearby when you did your gringo cop routine with Vasquez?"

I sized the man up. He was past forty, fat and balding, but probably tough—like an ex-athlete whose hardness reverted to smarts when his body went. I said, "Somebody else is tailing me. Who is it?"

Dolphine spat cobwebs. "The Rurales. Vasquez has got a vested interest in you not finding out about Blanchard."

"Do they know I'm staying here?"

"No. I told Cap I'd start the tail. His other boys must have picked you up. You lose them?"

I nodded and flicked Dolphine's necktie with my gun. "How come you're so cooperative?"

Dolphine put a light hand on the muzzle and eased it away from him. "I got my own vested interest, and I am damn good at playing both ends against the middle. I also talk a sight better sitting down. You think that's possible?"

I grabbed the chair and placed it in front of him. Dolphine got to his feet, brushed off his suit and plopped himself into it. I reholstered my piece. "Slow and from the beginning."

Dolphine breathed on his nails and buffed them on his shirt. I took the only other chair in the flop and sat down facing the slats so that I'd have something to grab. "Talk, goddamnit."

Dolphine obliged. "About a month ago, this Mexican woman walked into my office in Dago. Chubby, wearing ten tons of makeup, but dressed to the nines. She offered me five hundred to locate Blanchard, and she told me she thought he was somewhere down around TJ or Ensenada. She said he was an L.A. cop, some kind of lamster. Knowing the L.A. cops love that green stuff, I started thinking money pronto.

"I asked my TJ snitches about him, showed around this newspaper picture the woman gave me. I heard that Blanchard was in TJ around late January, getting in fights, boozing, spending lots of dough. Then a pal on the Border Patrol tells me he's hiding out in Ensenada, paying protection to the Rurales—who are actually letting him booze and brawl in their town—something Vasquez just about never tolerates.

"Okay, so I came down here and started tailing Blanchard, who's playing the rich gringo to the hilt. I see him beat up these two spics who insult this señorita, with Rurale troopers standing by doing nothing. That means the protection tip is straight dope, and I start thinking money, money, money."

Dolphine traced a dollar sign in the air; I grabbed the chair slats so hard that I could feel the wood start to give. "Here's where it gets interesting. This one pissed-off Rurale who's not on the Blanchard payroll tells me that he heard Blanchard hired a couple of Rurale plainclothesmen to kill two enemies of his in Tijuana in late January. I drive back to TJ, pay out some bribe money to the TJ cops and learn that two guys named Robert De Witt and Felix Chasco were bumped off in TJ on January twenty-third. De Witt's name sounded familiar, so I called a friend working San Diego PD. He checked around and called me back. Now get this, if you didn't already know. Blanchard sent De Witt up to Big Q in '39, and De Witt vowed to get even. I figure that De Witt got early parole, and Blanchard had him snuffed to protect his own ass. I called my partner in Dago, and left a message with him for the Mexican woman. Blanchard is in Ensenada, protected by the Rurales, who probably snuffed De Witt and Chasco for him."

I let go of the slats, my hands numb. "What was the woman's name?"

Dolphine shrugged. "She called herself Delores Garcia, but it was obviously a phony. After I heard about the De Witt-Chasco angle, I pegged her as one of Chasco's bimbos. He was supposed to be a gigolo with plenty of rich Mex gash on the line, and I figured the dame wanted revenge for the snuff. I figured she already knew somehow that Blanchard was responsible for the killings, and she just needed me to finger him."

I said, "You know the Black Dahlia thing up in L.A.?"

"The Pope a guinea?"

"Lee was working on the case right before he came down here, and in late January there was a Tijuana angle on it. Did you hear of him asking questions about the Dahlia?"

Dolphine said, "Nada. You want the rest of it?"

"Rapidamente."

"Okay. I went back to Dago, and my partner told me that the Mex dame got the message I left. I took off for Reno and a little vacation, and I blew the money she paid me at the crap table. I started thinking of Blanchard and all that money he had, wondering what the Mex dame had in mind for him. It really got to be a bug up my ass, and I went back to Dago, worked some missing persons jobs and came back to Ensenada about two weeks later. And you know what? There was no fucking Blanchard.

"Only a fool would've asked Vasquez or the troopers about him, so I hung around town picking up skinny. I saw this punk wearing Blanchard's old letterman's jacket, and this other punk with that Legion Stadium sweatshirt of his. I get word that two guys got hanged in Juarez for the De Witt-Chasco job, and I think, Rurale railroad all the way. I stay in town sucking up to Vasquez, snitching hopheads to him to stay on his good side. Finally I piece the Blanchard thing together. So if he was your buddy, get ready."

At "was," my hands broke off the chair slat I was grabbing. Dolphine said, "Whoa, boy."

I gasped, "Finish it."

The PI spoke slowly and calmly, like he was addressing a hand grenade. "He's dead. Chopped up with an axe. Some punks found him. They broke into the house he was staying in, and one of them blabbed to the troopers, so they wouldn't get tagged for it. Vasquez bought them off with pesos and some of Blanchard's belongings, and the Rurales buried the body outside town. I heard rumors that none of the money was found, and I stuck around because I figured Blanchard was rogue and sooner or later some

American cop would come looking for him. When you showed up at the station with that horseshit about working Metropolitan, I knew it was you."

I tried to say no, but my lips wouldn't move; Dolphine speed-balled the rest of his pitch: "Maybe the Rurales did it, maybe it was the woman or friends of hers. Maybe one of them got the money and maybe they didn't, and *we* can. You *knew* Blanchard, you could get a grip on who—"

I leaped up and roundhoused Dolphine with the chair slat; he caught the blow on the neck, hit the floor and sucked carpet again. I aimed my gun at the back of his head; the shitbird private eye whimpered, then double-speeded a mercy plea: "Look, I didn't know it was so personal with you. I didn't kill him, and I'll back off if you want to get whoever did it. Please, Bleichert, goddamn it."

I whimpered myself. "How do I know it's true?"

"There's a sand pit by the beach. The Rurales dump stiffs there. A kid told me he saw a bunch of troopers burying a big white man right around the time that Blanchard got it. Goddamn you, it's true!"

I eased down the .38's hammer. "Then show me."

*   *   *

The burial ground was ten miles south of Ensenada, just off the coast road on a bluff overlooking the ocean. A big, burning cross marked the spot. Dolphine pulled up next to it and killed the engine. "It's not what you think. The locals keep the damn thing lit up because they don't know who's buried there, and lots of them have got missing loved ones. It's a ritual with them. They burn the crosses, and the Rurales tolerate it, like it's some kind of panacea to keep the great unwashed gun-shy. Speaking of which, you want to put that thing away?"

My service revolver was pointed at Dolphine's midsection; I wondered how long I'd been holding the bead. "No. Have you got tools?"

Dolphine swallowed. "Gardening stuff. Listen—"

"No. You take me to the spot the kid told you about, and we dig."

Dolphine got out of the car, walked around and popped open the trunk. I followed, watching him remove a large earth spade. Flame glow illuminated the PI's old Dodge coupe; I noticed a pile of fence pickets and rags next to the spare tire. Tucking the .38 into my waistband, I fashioned two torches out of them, wrapping the rags around the ends of the posts, then igniting them in the cross. Handing one to Dolphine, I said, "Walk ahead of me."

We strode into the sand pit, outlaws holding fireballs on a stick. The softness made the going slow; torchlight let me pick out grave offerings—little bouquets and religious statues placed atop dunes here and there. Dolphine kept muttering how gringos got dumped on the far side; I felt bones cracking beneath my feet. We reached an especially high drift, and Dolphine waved his torch at a tattered American flag spread out on the sand. "Here. The punk said by el bannero."

I kicked the flag away; a swarm of insects buzzed up. Dolphine screeched, "Cocksuckers," and swatted them with his torch.

A putrid smell rose from a big crater at our feet. "Dig," I said.

Dolphine went at it; I thought of ghosts—Betty Short and Laurie Blanchard—waiting for the shovel to hit bones. The first time it did I recited a psalm the old man had force-fed me; the second time, it was the "Our Father" that Danny Boylan used to chant before our sparring sessions. When Dolphine said, "Sailor. I can see his jumper," I didn't know if I wanted Lee alive and in grief or dead and nowhere—so I pushed Dolphine aside and shoveled myself.

My first blow sheared off the sailor's skull, my second tore into the front of his tunic, pulling the torso free from the rest of the skeleton. The legs were in crumbled pieces; I shoveled past them into plain sand glinting with mica. Then it was maggot nests and entrails and a blood-mattted crinoline dress and sand and odd bones and nothing—and then it was sunburned pink skin and blond eyebrows covered with stitch scars that looked familiar. Then Lee was smiling like the Dahlia, with worms creeping out of his mouth and the holes where his eyes used to be.

I dropped the shovel and ran. Dolphine shouted, "The money!" behind me; I tore for the burning cross thinking that I put those scars on Lee, I did it to him. Reaching the car, I got in, gunned it in reverse, plowed the crucifix into the sand, then gnashed through the gears one-two-three going forward. I heard, "My car! The money!" as I fishtailed onto the coast road northbound, reaching for the siren switch, slamming the dashboard when it hit me that civilian vehicles didn't have them.

I made it to Ensenada, highballing at double the speed limit. I ditched the Dodge on the street by the hotel, then ran for *my*

car—slowing when I saw three men approaching me in a flanking movement, their hands inside their jackets.

My Chevy ten yards away; the middle man coming into focus
as Captain Vasquez, the other two fanning out to close me in
from the sides. The only shelter a phone booth near the first door
on the left U of the courtyard. Bucky Bleichert about to be DOA
in a Mexican sand pit, his best friend along for the ride. I decided
to let Vasquez get right up next to me and blow his brains out
point-blank. Then a white woman walked out the left-hand door,
and I saw my ticket home.

I ran over and grabbed her by the throat. She started to scream.
I stifled the sound by moving my left hand to her mouth. The
woman flailed with her arms, then clenched herself rigid. I pulled
my .38 and pointed it at her head.

The Rurales advanced cautiously, hand cannons pressed to
their sides. I shoved the woman into the phone booth, whispering,
"Scream and you're dead. Scream and you're dead." Inside, I pinned her
to the wall with my knees and removed my hand; the screams she
put out were silent. I aimed my gun at her mouth to keep them
that way, grabbed the receiver, fed the slot a nickel and dialed "O."
Vasquez was standing in front of the booth now, livid, reeking
of cheap American cologne. The operator came on the line with
"Que?" I blurted, "Habla inglés?"

"Yes, sir."

I held the receiver chin to shoulder and fumbled all the
coins in my pocket into the slot; I kept my .38 glued to the
woman's face. When a shitload of pesos were swallowed up,
I said, "Ferderal Bureau of Investigation, San Diego field office.
It's an emergency."

The operator muttered, "Yes, sir." I heard the call going
through. The woman's teeth chattered against my gun barrel.
Vasquez tried bribery: "Blanchard was very rich, my friend. We
could find his money. You could live very well here. You—"

"FBI, Special Agent Rice."

I stared daggers at Vasquez. "This is Officer Dwight Bleichert,
Los Angeles Police Department. I'm in Ensenada, and I screwed
up with some Rurales. They're getting ready to kill me for nothing, and I thought you could talk Captain Vasquez here out of it."

"What the—"

"Sir, I'm a legit L.A. policeman and you had better do this fast."

"You jerking my chain, son?"

"Goddamn it, you want proof? I worked Central Homicide with Russ Millard and Harry Sears. I worked DA's Warrants, I worked—"

"Put the spic fellow on, son."

I handed the receiver to Vasquez. He took it and leveled his automatic at me; I kept my .38 on the woman. Seconds ticked; the standoff held as the Rurale boss listened to the fed, getting paler and paler. Finally he dropped the phone and lowered his piece. "Go home, puta. Get out of my city and get out of my country."

I holstered my gun and squeezed out of the booth; the woman shrieked. Vasquez stood back and waved his men away. I got in my car and peeled out of Ensenada on fear overdrive. It was only when I was back in America that I started obeying speed laws— and that was when it got bad with Lee.

* * *

Dawn was pushing up over the Hollywood Hills when I knocked on Kay's door. I stood on the porch shivering, storm clouds and streaks of sunlight looming as strange things I didn't want to see. I heard "Dwight?" inside, followed by the sound of bolts being unlatched. Then the other remaining partner in the Blanchard/Bleichert/Lake triad was there, saying, "And all that."

It was an epitaph I didn't want to hear.

I walked inside, stunned at how strange and pretty the living room was. Kay said, "Lee's dead?"

I sat down in his favorite chair for the first time. "The Rurales or some Mexican woman or her friends killed him. Oh, babe, I—"

Using Lee's endearment jarred me. I looked at Kay, standing by the door, backlighted by the weird sunstreaks. "He hired the Rurales to kill De Witt, but that doesn't mean shit. We've got to get Russ Millard and some decent Mexican cops on it ..."

I stopped, noticing the phone on the coffee table. I started dialing the padre's home number. Kay's hand halted me. "No. I want to talk to you first."

I moved from the chair to the couch; Kay sat beside me. She said, "You'll hurt Lee if you go crazy with this."

That was when I knew she'd been expecting it; that was when I knew she knew more than I did. "You can't hurt something dead."

"Oh, yes you can, babe."

"Don't call me that! That's his!"

Kay moved closer and touched my cheek. "You can hurt him and you can hurt us."

I pulled away from the caress. "You tell me why, *babe.*"

Kay cinched the belt on her robe and fixed me with a cold look. "I didn't meet Lee at Bobby's trial," she said. "I met him before. We became friends, and I lied about where I was staying so Lee wouldn't know about Bobby. Then he found out on his own, and I told him how bad it was, and he told me about a business opportunity he had coming up. He wouldn't tell me the details, and then Bobby was arrested for bank robbery and everything was chaos.

"Lee planned the robbery and got three men to help him. He'd bought his way out of his contract with Ben Siegel, and it cost him every cent he'd made as a boxer. Two of the men were killed during the robbery, one escaped to Canada, and Lee was the fourth. Lee framed Bobby because he hated him for what he did to me. Bobby didn't know we were seeing each other, and we made it look like we met at the trial. Bobby knew it was a frame, but he didn't suspect Lee, just the LAPD in general.

"Lee wanted to give me a home, and he did. He was very cautious with his part of the robbery money, and he always talked up his boxing savings and his gambling so the brass wouldn't think he was living above his means. He hurt his career by living with a woman, even though we weren't together that way. It was like a happy fairy tale until last fall, right after you and Lee became partners."

I moved toward Kay, awed by Lee as the most audacious rogue cop in history. "I knew he had it in him."

Kay drew away from me. "Let me finish before you get sentimental. When Lee heard about Bobby getting an early parole date, he went to Ben Siegel to try to get him killed. He was afraid of Bobby talking about *me*, upsetting our fairy tale with all the ugly things he knew about yours truly. Siegel wouldn't do it, and I told Lee it didn't matter, that there were three of us now and the truth couldn't hurt us. Then, right before New Year's, the third man from the robbery showed up. He knew that Bobby De Witt was getting out on parole, and he made a blackmail demand: Lee was to pay him ten thousand dollars, or he would tell Bobby that Lee masterminded the robbery and framed him.

"The man said Lee's deadline was Bobby's release date. Lee put him off, then went to Ben Siegel to try to borrow the money.

Siegel wouldn't do it, and Lee begged him to have the man killed. He wouldn't do that either. Lee learned that the man hung out with some Negroes who sold marijuana, and he—"

I saw it coming, huge and black like the headlines it got me, Kay's words the new fine print: "That man's name was Baxter Fitch. Siegel wouldn't help Lee, so he got you. The men were armed, so I guess you were legally justified, and I guess you were damn lucky that no one looked into it. It's the one thing I can't forgive him for, the one thing I hate myself for tolerating. Still feeling sentimental, triggerman?"

I couldn't answer; Kay did it for me. "I didn't think so. I'll finish up, and you tell me if you still want revenge.

"The Short thing happened then, and Lee latched on to it for his little sister and who knows what else. He was terrified that Fitch had already talked to Bobby, that Bobby knew about the frame. He wanted to kill him or have him killed, and I begged and pleaded with him to just let it be, no one would believe Bobby, so just don't hurt anybody else. If it wasn't for that fucking dead girl I might have convinced him. But the case went down to Mexico, and so did Bobby and Lee and you. I knew that the fairy tale was over. And it is."

FIRE AND ICE COPS KO NEGRO THUGS
SOUTHSIDE SHOOTOUT—COPS: 4, HOODLUMS: 0

FOUR HOPHEADS SLAIN BY BOXER—POLICEMEN IN
BLOODY L.A. GUN BATTLE

Limp all over, I started to stand up; Kay grabbed my belt with both hands and brought me back down. "No! You don't pull the patented Bucky Bleichert retreat this time! Bobby took pictures of me with animals, and Lee stopped it. He pimped me to his friends and hit me with a razor strap, and Lee stopped it. He wanted to love me, not fuck me, and he wanted us to be together, and if you weren't so intimidated by him you would have known it. We can't drag his name down. We have to give it all up and forgive him and get on with just us and—"

I retreated then, before Kay destroyed the rest of the triad.

* * *

Triggerman.

Stooge.

Bumfuck detective too blind to clear the case he was a homicide accessory to.

The weak point in a fairy tale triangle.

Best friend to a cop–bank robber, now the keeper of his secrets.

"Give it all up."

I stuck to my apartment for the next week, killing off the remainder of my "vacation." I hit the heavy bag and skipped rope and listened to music; I sat on the back steps and took finger sights at blue jays perching on my landlady's clothesline. I convicted Lee of four homicides connected to the Boulevard-Citizens bank job and granted him a pardon based on homicide number five—himself. I thought of Betty Short and Kay until they blurred together; I reconstructed the partnership as a mutual seduction and figured out that I lusted for the Dahlia because I had her number, that I loved Kay because she had mine.

And I examined the past six months. It was all there:

The money Lee had been spending in Mexico was probably a separate stash of robbery swag.

On New Year's Eve I heard him weeping; Baxter Fitch had made his blackmail demand a few days before.

That fall, Lee had sought out Benny Siegel—in private—every time we went to the fights at the Olympic; he was trying to talk him into killing Bobby De Witt.

Right before the shoot-out, Lee had spoken on the phone to a snitch—allegedly about Junior Nash. The "snitch" had fingered Fitch and the Negroes, and Lee came back to the car looking spooked. Ten minutes later four men were dead.

On the night I met Madeleine Sprague, Kay shouted at Lee: *"After all that might happen"*—a portentous line, probably her predicting disaster with Bobby De Witt. During our time working the Dahlia case, she had been jittery, morose, concerned for Lee's well-being, yet weirdly accepting of his lunatic behavior. I thought she was upset over Lee's obsession with Betty Short's murder; she was really running toward and from the fairy tale's finale.

It was all there.

"Give it all up."

When my refrigerator was empty, I took the patented Bucky Bleichert retreat down to the market to stock up. Walking in, I saw a box boy reading the local section of the morning *Herald*.

Johnny Vogel's picture was at the bottom of the page; I looked over the kid's shoulder and saw that he'd been dismissed from the LAPD on a graft whitewash. A column over, Ellis Loew's name caught my eye—Bevo Means was quoting him that "The Elizabeth Short investigation is no longer my raison d'etre—I have more pertinent fish to fry." I forgot all about food, and drove to West Hollywood.

It was recess. Kay was in the middle of the schoolyard, supervising kids flopping around in a sandbox. I watched her awhile from the car, then walked over.

The kids noticed me first. I flashed my teeth at them until they started laughing. Kay turned around then. I said, "It's the patented Bucky Bleichert advance."

Kay said, "Dwight"; the kids looked at us like they knew it was a big moment. Kay caught on a second later. "Did you come here to tell me something?"

I laughed; the kids chortled at another shot of my choppers. "Yeah. I decided to give it all up. Will you marry me?"

Kay, expressionless, said, "And we'll bury the rest of it? The f-ing dead girl too?"

"Yes. Her too."

Kay stepped into my arms. "Then yes."

We embraced. The children called out, "Miss Lake's got a boyfriend, Miss Lake's got a boyfriend!"

* * *

We were married three days later, May 2, 1947. It was a rush job, the vows given by the LAPD Protestant chaplain, the service held in the backyard of Lee Blanchard's house. Kay wore a pink dress to satirize her lack of virginity; I wore my blue dress uniform. Russ Millard was best man, and Harry Sears came along as a guest. He started out with a stutter, and for the first time I saw that it was precisely his fourth drink that quashed it. I got the old man out of the rest home on a pass, and he didn't know who the hell I was, but seemed to have a good time anyway—swigging from Harry's flask, goosing Kay, hopping around to the music from the radio. There was a table laid out with sandwiches and punch, hard and soft. The six of us ate and drank, and total strangers walking down to the Strip heard the music and laughter and crashed the party. By dusk the yard was filled with people I didn't know, and Harry made a run to the Hollywood Ranch Market for more food and booze. I unloaded my service revolver and let the unknown civilians play with it, and Kay danced polkas with the chaplain. When darkness hit, I didn't want it to end, so I borrowed strings of Christmas lights from the neighbors and strung them over the backdoor and the clothesline and Lee's favorite Yucca tree. We danced and drank and ate under a fake constellation, the stars red and blue and yellow. Around 2:00 A.M., the clubs on the Strip let out, revelers from the Trocadero and Mocambo made the scene, and Errol Flynn hung around for a while, his tux coat doffed for my jacket, replete with badge and pistol medals. If it weren't for the thunderstorm that struck, it might have gone on forever—and I wanted it to. But the crowd broke up amidst frantic kisses and hugs, and Russ drove the old man back to the rest bin. Kay Lake Bleichert and I retired to the bedroom to make love, and I left the radio on to help distract me from Betty Short. It wasn't necessary—she never crossed my mind.

PART THREE

KAY AND MADELEINE

25

TIME PASSED. Kay and I worked and played at being a young married couple.

After our quickie San Francisco honeymoon, I returned to what remained of my police career. Thad Green talked turkey to me: he admired what I did with the Vogels, but considered me useless as a patrol cop—I had earned the enmity of rank and file blues, and my presence in a uniformed division would only create grief. Since my year of junior college showed straight A's in chemistry and math, he assigned me to the Scientific Investigation Detail as an evidence technician.

The job was quasi-plainclothes—smocks in the lab and gray suits in the field. I typed blood, dusted for latent prints and wrote ballistics reports; scraped ooze off the walls at crime scenes and examined it under a microscope, letting the Homicide dicks take it from there. It was test tubes and beakers and clinical gore—an intimacy with death that I never became inured to; a constant reminder that I wasn't a detective, that I couldn't be trusted to follow up on my own findings.

From various distances I followed the friends and enemies the Dahlia case had given me.

Russ and Harry kept the El Nido file room intact, continuing to work overtime hours on the Short investigation. I had a key to the door, but didn't use it—per my promise to Kay to bury "that———dead girl." Sometimes I met the padre for lunch and asked him how it was going; he always said, "Slowly," and I knew that he would never find the killer and never quit trying.

In June of '47, Ben Siegel was shot to death in his girlfriend's Beverly Hills living room. Bill Koenig, assigned to 77th Street dicks after Fritz Vogel's suicide, caught a shotgun blast in the face on a Watts street corner early in '48. Both killings went unsolved. Ellis Loew was soundly trounced in the June '48 Republican primary, and I celebrated by cooking up beakers of moonshine on my Bunsen burner, getting everyone in the crime lab fried.

The '48 general election brought me news of the Spragues. A slate of reform Democrats were running for seats on the L.A. City Council and Board of Supervisors, "City Planning" their basic campaign theme. They asserted that there were faultily designed, unsafe dwellings all over Los Angeles, and were calling for a grand jury probe on the contractors who built the structures back during the '20s real estate boom. The scandal tabloids took up the hue and cry, running articles on the "boom barons"—Mack Sennett and Emmett Sprague among them—and their "gangster ties." *Confidential* magazine ran a series on Sennett's Hollywoodland tract and how the Hollywood Chamber of Commerce wanted to lop the L-A-N-D off the giant Hollywoodland sign on Mount Lee, and there were photographs of the Keystone Kops director standing beside a stocky man with a cute little girl in tow. I couldn't quite tell if it was Emmett and Madeleine, but I clipped the pictures anyway.

My enemies;

My friends;

My wife.

I processed evidence and Kay taught school, and for a while we reveled in the novelty of living a squarejohn life. With the house paid off in full and two salaries, there was plenty of money to spend, and we used it to pamper ourselves away from Lee Blanchard and the winter of '47. We took weekend trips to the desert and the mountains; we ate in restaurants three and four nights a week. We checked into hotels pretending to be illicit lovers, and it took me well over a year to realize that we did those things because it got us out of the pad the Boulevard-Citizens bank job paid for. And I was so heedless in my pursuit of pampering that it required a live-wire shock to spell it out.

A floorboard in the hallway came loose, and I pulled it all the way off so I could reglue it. Looking in the hole, I found a cash roll, two thousand dollars in C-notes secured by a rubber band. I didn't feel joyous or shocked; my brain went tick, tick, tick, and came up with the questions my rush into normal life had quashed:

If Lee had this money, plus the dough he was spending in Mexico, why didn't he pay off Baxter Fitch?

If he had the money, why did he go to Ben Siegel to try to borrow ten grand to meet Fitch's blackmail demand?

How could Lee have bought and furnished this house, put Kay through college and still have had a substantial sum left when his cut from the aborted heist couldn't have amounted to more than fifty grand or so?

Of course I told Kay; of course she couldn't answer the questions; of course she loathed me for dredging up the past. I told her we could sell the house and get an apartment like other normal squarejohns—and of course she wouldn't have it. It was comfort, style—a link to her old life that she would not give up.

I burned the money in Lee Blanchard's Deco-streamline fireplace. Kay never asked me what I did with it. The simple act gave me back some smothered part of myself, cost me most of what I had with my wife—and returned me to my ghosts.

Kay and I made love less and less. When we did it was perfunctory reassurance for her and a dull explosion for me. I came to see Kay Lake Bleichert as wasted by the obscenity in her old life, just short of thirty and already going chaste. I brought the gutter to our bed then, the faces of hookers I saw downtown attached to Kay's body in the darkness. It worked the first few times, until I saw where I really wanted to go. When I finally made the move and came gasping, Kay stroked me with mothering hands, and I sensed that she knew I'd broken my marriage vow—with her right there.

1948 became 1949. I turned the garage into a boxing gym, complete with speed bag and heavy bag, jump ropes and barbells. I got back into fighting trim, and decorated the garage walls with fight stills of young Bucky Bleichert, circa '40–'41. My own image glimpsed through sweat-streaked eyes brought me closer to her, and I scoured used book stores for Sunday supplements and news magazines. I found sepia candids in *Colliers*; some family snapshots reproduced in old issues of the *Boston Globe*. I kept them out of sight in the garage, and the stack grew, then vanished one afternoon. I heard Kay sobbing inside the house that evening, and when I went to talk to her the bedroom door was locked.

26

THE PHONE rang. I reached for the bedside extension, then snapped that I'd been a couch sleeper for the past month and flailed at the coffee table. "Yeah?"

"You still sleeping?"

It was the voice of Ray Pinker, my supervisor at SID. "I was sleeping."

"Past tense is right. Are you listening?"

"Keep going."

"We've got a gunshot suicide from yesterday. 514 South June Street, Hancock Park. Body removed, looks open and shut. Do a complete work-up and drop the report off with Lieutenant Reddin at Wilshire dicks. Got it?"

I yawned. "Yeah. Premises sealed?"

"The stiff's wife will show you around. Be courteous, this is filthy rich we're dealing with."

I hung up and groaned. Then it hit me that the Sprague mansion was a block from the June Street address. Suddenly the assignment was fascinating.

*   *   *

I rang the bell of the pillared colonial manse an hour later. A handsome gray-haired woman of about fifty opened the door, dressed in dusty work togs. I said, "I'm Officer Bleichert, LAPD. May I express my condolences, Mrs.—"

Ray Pinker hadn't given me a name. The woman said, "Condolences accepted, and I'm Jane Chambers. Are you the lab man?"

The woman was trembling underneath her brusqueness; I liked her immediately. "Yes. If you'll point me to the place I'll take care of it and leave you alone."

Jane Chambers ushered me into a sedate, all-wood foyer. "The study in back of the dining room. You'll see the rope. Now, if you'll excuse me I want to do some gardening."

She took off dabbing at her eyes. I found the room, stepped over the crime scene rope and wondered why the bastard did himself in where his loved ones would see the gore.

It looked like a classic self-inflicted shotgun job: overturned leather chair, the outline of the stiff chalked on the floor beside it. The weapon, a double-barreled .12 gauge, was right where it should have been—three feet in front of the body, the muzzle coated with blood and shredded tissue. The light plaster walls and ceiling showed off blood and caked-on brains to full advantage, the teeth fragments and buckshot a dead giveaway that the victim had stuck both barrels in his mouth.

I spent an hour measuring trajectories and spatter marks, scraping matter into test tubes and dusting the suicide weapon for latents. When I finished, I took a bag from my evidence kit and wrapped up the shotgun, knowing full well it would end up the property of some LAPD sportsman. Then I walked out to the entrance hall, stopping when I saw a framed painting hung at eye level.

It was a portrait of a clown, a young boy done up in court jester's garb from long, long ago. His body was gnarled and hunched; he wore a stuporous ear-to-ear smile that looked like one continuous deep scar.

I stared, transfixed, thinking of Elizabeth Short, DOA at 39th and Norton. The more I stared the more the two blended; finally I pulled my eyes away and settled them on a photo of two arm-linked young women who looked just like Jane Chambers.

"The other survivors. Pretty, aren't they?"

I turned around. The widow was twice as dusty as before, smelling of insect spray and soil. "Like their mother. How old are they?"

"Linda's twenty-three and Carol's twenty. Are you finished in the study?"

I thought of the daughters as contemporaries of the Sprague girls. "Yes. Tell whoever cleans it up to use pure ammonia. Mrs. Chambers—"

"Jane."

"Jane, do you know Madeleine and Martha Sprague?"

Jane Chambers snorted, "Those girls and that family. How do you know them?"

"I did some work for them once."

"Count yourself lucky it was a brief encounter."

"What do you mean?"

The hallway phone rang. Jane Chambers said, "Back to con-dolences. Thank you for being so nice, Mr.—"

"It's Bucky. Good-bye, Jane."

"Good-bye."

*　*　*

I wrote out my report at Wilshire Station, then checked the routine suicide file on Chambers, Eldridge Thomas, DOD 4/2/49. It didn't tell me much: Jane Chambers heard the shotgun explosion, found the body and called the police immediately. When detectives arrived, she told them her husband was de-pressed over his failing health and their eldest daughter's failing marriage. Suicide: case closed pending forensic crime scene work-up.

My work-up confirmed the verdict, plain and simple. But it didn't feel like enough. I liked the widow, the Spragues lived a block away, I was still curious. I got on a squadroom phone and put in calls to Russ Millard's newspaper contacts, giving them two names: Eldridge Chambers and Emmett Sprague. They did their own digging and calling, and got back to me on the station extension I was hogging. Four hours later I knew the following:

That Eldridge Chambers died enormously wealthy;

That from 1930 to 1934 he was president of the Southern California Real Estate Board;

That he nominated Sprague for membership in Wilshire Country Club in 1929, but the Scotsman was rejected because of his "Jewish business associates"—i.e. East Coast hoodlums;

And the kicker: Chambers, through intermediaries, got Sprague kicked off the real estate board when several of his houses collapsed during the '33 earthquake.

It was enough for a juicy newspaper obit, but not enough for a test-tube cop with a foundering marriage and time on his hands. I waited four days; then, when the papers told me Eldridge Chambers was in the ground, I went back to talk to his widow.

She answered the door in gardening clothes, holding a pair of shears. "Did you forget something or are you as curious as I thought you were?"

"The latter."

Jane laughed and wiped dirt from her face. "After you left I put your name together. Weren't you some sort of athlete?"

I laughed. "I was a boxer. Are your daughters around? Have you got someone staying with you?"

Jane shook her head. "No, and I prefer it that way. Will you join me for tea in the backyard?"

I nodded. Jane led me through the house and out to a shaded veranda overlooking a large bent grass yard more than half dug up into furrows. I sat down in a lounge chair; she poured iced tea. "I've done all that garden work since Sunday. I think it's helped more than all the sympathy calls I've gotten."

"You're taking it well."

Jane sat down beside me. "Eldridge had cancer, so I half expected it. I didn't expect a shotgun in our own home, though."

"Were you close?"

"No, not anymore. With the girls grown up, we would have divorced sooner or later. Are you married?"

"Yes. Almost two years."

Jane sipped tea. "God, a newlywed. There's nothing better, is there?"

My face must have betrayed me. Jane said, "Sorry," then changed the subject. "How do you know the Spragues?"

"I was involved with Madeleine before I met my wife. How well do you know them?"

Jane considered my question, staring out at the uprooted yard. "Eldridge and Emmett went way back," she said finally. "They both made a lot of money in real estate and served on the Southern California board together. Maybe I shouldn't be saying this, since you're a policeman, but Emmett was a bit of a crook. A lot of his houses went down during the big quake in '33, and Eldridge said that he has lots of other property that has to go bad sooner or later—houses made out of *the* worst possible material. Eldridge got Emmett booted off the board when he found out that phony corporations controlled the rentals and sales—he was enraged that Emmett would never be held responsible if more lives were lost."

I remembered talking with Madeleine about the same thing. "Your husband sounds like a good man."

Jane's lips curled into a smile—it looked like against her will. "He had his moments."

"He never went to the police about Emmett?"

"No. He was afraid of his gangster friends. He just did what he could, a little nuisance to Emmett. Being removed from the board probably cost him some business."

"'He did what he could' isn't a bad epitaph."

Now Jane's lips curled into a sneer. "It was out of guilt. Eldridge owned slum blocks in San Pedro. When he learned he had cancer, he really started feeling guilty. He voted Democratic last year, and when they got in he had meetings with some of the new City Council members. I'm sure he gave them his dirt on Emmett."

I thought of the Grand Jury probe the scandal sheets were predicting. "Maybe Emmett's heading for a fall. Your husband could have been—"

Jane rapped her ring finger on the tabletop. "My husband was rich and handsome and did a mean Charleston. I loved him until I found out he was cheating on me, and now I'm starting to love him again. It is so strange."

"It's not so strange," I said.

Jane smiled very softly. "How old are you, Bucky?"

"Thirty-two."

"Well, I'm fifty-one, and I think it's strange, so it is strange. You shouldn't be so all-accepting of the human heart at your age. You should have illusions."

"You're teasing me, Jane. I'm a cop. Cops don't have illusions."

Jane laughed—heartily. "Touché. Now *I'm* curious. How did an ex-boxer cop get involved with Madeleine Sprague?"

Now I lied. "I stopped her for a red light and one thing led to another." My gut clenching, I asked casually, "What do you know about her?"

Jane stomped her foot at a crow eyeing the rose bushes just off the veranda. "What I know about the distaff Spragues is at least ten years old and quite strange. Baroque, almost."

"I'm all ears."

Jane said, "Some might say all teeth." When I didn't laugh, she looked across the dug-up yard to Muirfield Road and the boom baron's estate. "When my girls and Maddy and Martha were little, Ramona directed pageants and ceremonies on that huge front lawn of theirs. Little enactments with the girls dressed up in pinafores and animal costumes. I let Linda and Carol participate, even though I knew Ramona was a disturbed woman. When the girls all got a bit older—in their teens—the pageants got stranger. Ramona and Maddy were very good at makeup, and Ramona staged these … epics, reenacting the things that happened to Emmett and his friend Georgie Tilden during World War I.

"So, she had children wearing soldier kilts and pancake faces, carrying toy muskets. Sometimes she smeared fake blood on them, and sometimes Georgie actually filmed it. It got so bizarre, so out of proportion, that I made Linda and Carol quit playing with the Sprague girls. Then one day Carol came home with some pictures Georgie took of her. She was playing dead, all smeared with red dye. That was the last straw. I stormed over to the Sprague house and berated Georgie, knowing Ramona wasn't really responsible for her actions. The poor man just took my abuse, and I felt terrible about it later—he was disfigured in a car wreck, and it turned him into a bum. He used to manage property for Emmett, now he just does yard work and weeds lots for the city."

"And what happened to Madeleine and Martha then?"

Jane shrugged. "Martha turned into some sort of art prodigy and Madeleine turned into a roundheels, which I guess you already know."

I said, "Don't be catty, Jane."

Tapping the table with her ring, Jane said, "I apologize. Maybe I'm wishing *I* could pull it off. I certainly can't spend the rest of my life gardening, and I'm too proud for gigolos. What do you think?"

"You'll find yourself another millionaire."

"Unlikely, and one was enough to last me a lifetime. You know what I keep thinking? That it's almost 1950 and I was born in 1898. That floors me."

I said what I'd been thinking for the past half hour. "You make me wish things were different. That time was different."

Jane smiled and sighed. "Bucky, is that the best I can expect from you?"

I sighed back. "I think it's the best anyone can."

"You're a bit of a voyeur, you know."

"And you're a bit of a gossip."

"Touché. Come on, I'll walk you out."

We held hands on the way to the door. In the entrance hall, the scar mouth clown painting grabbed me again. Pointing to it, I said, "God, that is spooky."

"Valuable, too. Eldridge bought it for my forty-ninth birthday, but I hate it. Would you like to take it with you?"

"Thanks, but no thanks."

"Thank you, then. You were my best condoler."

"And you were mine."

We embraced for a moment, then I took off.

27

BUNSEN BURNER jockey.

Couch sleeper.

Detective without a case.

I worked at all three throughout the spring of '49. Kay left for school early each morning; I pretended to sleep until she was gone. Alone in the fairy tale house, I touched my wife's things—the cashmere sweaters Lee bought her, her essays to be graded, the books she had stacked up waiting to be read. I kept looking for a diary, but never found one. At the lab I pictured Kay prowling *my* belongings. I toyed with the idea of writing a journal and leaving it out for her to find—detailed accounts of my coupling with Madeleine Sprague—rubbing her nose in it to either gain forgiveness for my fix on the Dahlia or blow our marriage out of its stasis. I got as far as five pages scrawled in my cubicle—stopping when I smelled Madeleine's perfume melding with the Lysol stench of the Red Arrow Motel. And wadding the pages up and throwing them away only fanned the brush fire into a blaze.

I kept the Muirfield Road mansion under surveillance for four nights running. Parked across the street, I watched lights go on and off, saw shadows flicker across leaded glass windows. I played with notions of crashing the Spragues' family life, cashing in on being a hard boy to Emmett, coupling with Madeleine all over hot sheet row. None of the family left the manse during those nights—all four of their cars remained on the circular driveway. I kept wondering what they were doing, what shared history they were rehashing, what the odds were on someone mentioning the cop who came to dinner two years before.

On the fifth night, Madeleine, dressed in slacks and a pink sweater, walked to the corner to mail a letter. When she returned, I saw her notice my car, passing headlights illuminating the surprise on her face. I waited until she hurried back inside the Tudor fortress, then drove home, Jane Chambers' voice taunting, "Voyeur, voyeur."

Walking in, I heard the shower running; the bedroom door was open. Kay's favorite Brahms quintet was on the phonograph. Remembering the first time I saw my wife naked, I undressed and lay down on the bed.

The shower went off; Brahms came on that much stronger. Kay appeared in the doorway wrapped in a towel. I said, "Babe," she said, "Oh, Dwight," and let the towel drop. We both began talking at once, apologies from both sides. I couldn't quite make out her words, and I knew that she couldn't unscramble mine. I started to get up to turn off the phonograph, but Kay moved to the bed first.

We fumbled at kisses. I went open-mouthed too fast, forgetting how Kay liked to be coaxed. Feeling her tongue, I pulled away, knowing she hated it. Closing my eyes, I trailed my lips down her neck; she moaned, and I knew it was a fake. The love sounds got worse—like something you'd expect from a stag film actress. Kay's breasts were flaccid in my hands, her legs closed, but braced up against me. A knee nudge parted them—the response was jerky, spasmodic. Hard now, I made Kay wet with my mouth and went inside her.

I kept my eyes open and on hers so she would know it was just us; Kay turned away, and I knew she saw through it. I wanted to ease off and go slowly, softly, but the sight of a vein throbbing in Kay's neck made me go as hard as I could. I came grunting, "I'm sorry goddamn you I'm sorry," and whatever Kay said back was muffled by the pillow she was burying her head in.

28

THE FOLLOWING night I was parked across the street from the Sprague mansion, this time in the unmarked Ford I drove to SID field jobs. Time was lost on me, but I knew that every second was bringing me closer to knocking on the door or bolting outright.

My mind played with Madeleine nude; I wowed the other Spragues with killer repartee. Then light cut across the driveway, the door slammed and the Packard's headbeams went on. It pulled out onto Muirfield, hung a quick left turn on Sixth Street and headed east. I waited a discreet three seconds and followed.

The Packard stayed in the middle lane; I dogged it from the right one, a good four car lengths behind. We traveled out of Hancock Park into the Wilshire District, south on Normandie and east on 8th Street. I saw glittery bar beacons stretching for a solid mile—and knew Madeleine was close to something.

The Packard stopped in front of the Zimba Room, a dive with crossed neon spears above the entrance. The only other parking space was right behind it, so I glided up, my headlights catching the driver locking the door, my brain wires unraveling when I saw who it wasn't and *was*.

Elizabeth Short.

Betty Short.

Liz Short.

The Black Dahlia.

My knees jerked into the steering wheel; my trembling hands hit the horn. The apparition shielded her eyes and squinted into my beams, then shrugged. I saw familiar dimples twitch, and returned from wherever it was I was going.

It was Madeleine Sprague, completely made over as the Dahlia. She was dressed in an all-black clinging gown, with makeup and hairdo identical to Betty Short at her portrait photo best. I watched her sashay into the bar, saw a dot of yellow in her upswept black curls and knew that she'd taken her transformation all the way to the barrette Betty wore. The detail hit me like a Lee Blanchard one-two. On punch-drunk legs, I pursued the ghost.

The Zimba Room interior was wall-to-wall smoke, GI's and juke box jazz; Madeleine was at the bar sipping a drink. Looking around, I saw that she was the only woman in the place and already creating a hubbub—soldiers and sailors were elbowing the good news to one another, pointing to the black-clad figure and exchanging whispers.

I found a zebra-striped booth at the back; it was filled with sailors sharing a bottle. One glance at their peach fuzz faces told me they were underage. I held out my badge and said, "Scram or I'll have the SP's here inside of a minute." The three youths took off in a blue swirl, leaving their jug behind. I sat down to watch Madeleine portray Betty.

Guzzling half a tumbler of bourbon calmed my nerves. I had a diagonal view of Madeleine at the bar, surrounded by would-be lovers hanging on her every word. I was too far away to hear anything—but every gesture I saw her make was *not* hers, but that of some other woman. And every time she touched a member of her entourage my hand twitched toward my .38.

Time stretched, in a haze of navy blue and khaki with a jet black center.

Madeleine drank, chatted and brushed off passes, her attention narrowing down to a stocky sailor. Her coterie dwindled out as the man shot them mean looks; I killed off the bottle. Staring at the bar kept me from thinking, the loud jazz kept my ears perked for the sound of voices above it, the booze kept me from rousting the stocky man on a half dozen trumped-up charges. Then the woman in black and the sailor in blue were out the door, arms linked, Madeleine inches taller in her high heels.

I gave them a bourbon-calmed five seconds, then hauled. The Packard was turning right at the corner when I got behind the wheel; gunning it and hanging a hard right myself, I saw taillights at the end of the block. I zoomed up behind them, almost tapping the rear bumper; Madeleine's signal arm shot out the window, and she veered into the parking lot of a brightly lit auto court.

I skidded to a stop, then backed up and killed my headlights. From the street I could see sailor boy standing by the Packard smoking a cigarette, while Madeleine hit the motel office for the room key. She came outside with it a moment later, just like our old routine; she made the sailor walk ahead of her, just like she did with me. The lights went on and off inside the room, and when I listened outside it the blinds were drawn and our old station was on the radio.

*   *   *

Rolling stakeouts.

Field interrogations.

The Bunsen burner jockey now a detective *with* a case.

I kept Madeleine's Dahlia act under surveillance for four more nights; she pulled the same MO every time: 8th Street gin mill, hard boy with lots of confetti on his chest, the fuck pad at 9th and Irolo. When the two were ensconced, I went back and questioned bartenders and GIs she gave the ixnay to.

What name did the black-clad woman give?

None.

What did she talk about?

The war and breaking into the movies.

Did you notice her resemblance to the Black Dahlia, that murdered girl from a couple of years ago, and if so, what do you think she was trying to prove?

Negative answers and theories: She's a loony who thinks she's the Black Dahlia; she's a hooker cashing in on the Dahlia's look; she's a policewoman decoy out to get the Dahlia killer; she's a crazy woman dying of cancer, trying to attract the Dahlia slasher and cheat the Big C.

I knew the next step was to roust Madeleine's lovers—but I didn't trust myself to do it rationally. If they said the wrong thing or the right thing, or pointed me in the wrong/right direction, I knew I couldn't be held accountable for what I would do.

The four nights of booze, catnaps in the car and couch naps at home with Kay sequestered in the bedroom took their toll on me. At work I dropped slides and mislabeled blood samples, wrote evidence reports in my own exhaustion shorthand and twice fell asleep hunched over a ballistics miscroscope, awakening to jagged shots of Madeleine in black. Knowing I couldn't hack night five by myself or give it a pass, I stole some Benzedrine tablets awaiting processing for Narcotics Division. They juiced me out of my fatigue and into a clammy feeling of disgust for what I'd been doing to myself—and they gave me a brainstorm to save me from Madeleine/Dahlia and make me a real cop again.

Thad Green nodded along as I plea-bargained him: I had seven years on the Department, my run-in with the Vogels was over two years before and mostly forgotten, I hated working SID and wanted to return to a uniformed division—preferably nightwatch. I was studying for the Sergeant's Exam, SID had served me well as a training ground for my ultimate goal—the Detective Bureau. I started to launch a tirade on my shitty marriage and how nightwatch would keep me away from my wife, faltering when images of the lady in black hit me and I realized I was close to begging. The Chief of Detectives finally silenced me with a long stare, and I wondered if the dope was betraying me. Then he said, "Okay, Bucky," and pointed to the door. I waited in the outer office for a Benzedrine eternity; when Green walked out smiling, I almost jumped loose of my skin. "Newton Street nightwatch as of tomorrow," he said. "And try to be civil with our colored brethren down there. You've got a bad case of the yips, and I wouldn't want you passing it on to them."

* * *

Newton Street Division was southeast of downtown L.A., 95 percent slums, 95 percent Negroes, all trouble. There were bottle gangs and crap games on every corner; liquor stores, hair-straightening parlors and poolrooms on every block, code three calls to the station twenty-four hours a day. Footbeat hacks carried metal-studded saps; squadroom dicks packed .45 automatics loaded with un-regulation dum-dums. The local winos drank "Green Lizard"—cologne cut with Old Monterey white port, and the standard pop for a whore was one dollar, a buck and a quarter if you used "her place"—the abandoned cars in the auto graveyard at 56th and Central. The kids on the street were scrawny and bloated, stray dogs sported mange and perpetual snarls, merchants kept shotguns under the counter. Newton Street Division was a war zone.

I reported for duty after twenty-two hours of sack time, booze-weaned off the Benzies. The station commander, an ancient lieutenant named Getchell, supplied a warm welcome, telling me that Thad Green said I was kosher, and he'd accept me as such until I fucked up and proved otherwise. Personally, he hated boxers and stoolies, but he was willing to let bygones be bygones. My fellow officers would probably take some persuading, however; they *really* hated glory cops, boxers and Bolsheviks, and Fritzie Vogel was warmly remembered from his Newton Street tour years before. The cordial CO assigned me to a single-o foot beat, and I left that initial briefing determined to out-kosher God himself.

My first roll call was worse.

Introduced to the watch by the muster sergeant, I got no applause and a wide assortment of fisheyes, evil eyes and averted eyes. After the reading of the crime sheet, seven men out of the fifty-five or so stopped to shake my hand and wish me good luck. The sergeant gave me a silent tour of the division and dropped me off with a street map at the east edge of my beat; his farewell was, "Don't let the niggers give you no shit." When I thanked him, he said, "Fritz Vogel was a good pal of mine," and sped off.

I decided to kosherize myself fast.

My first week at Newton was muscle rousts and gathering information on who the *real* bad guys were. I broke up Green Lizard parties with my billy club, promising not to roust the winos if they fed me names. If they didn't kick loose, I arrested them; if they did, I arrested them anyway. I smelled reefer smoke on the sidewalk outside the gassed hair joint on 68th and Beach, kicked the door in and drew down on three grasshoppers holding felony quantities of maryjane. They snitched off their supplier and fingered an upcoming rumble between The Slausons and Choppers in return for my promise of leniency; I called in the info to the squadroom and flagged down a black-and-white to haul the hopheads to the station. Prowling the hooker auto dump got me prostitution collars, and threatening the girls' johns with calls to their wives got me more names. At week's end I had twenty-two arrests to my credit—nine of them felonies. And I had names. Names to test my courage on. Names to make up for the main events I'd dodged. Names to make the cops who hated me afraid of me.

I caught Downtown Willy Brown coming out of the Lucky Time Wine Bar. I said, "Your mother sucks a mean dick, Sambo"; Willy charged me. I took three to give six; when it was over

Brown was blowing teeth out his nose. And two cops shooting the breeze across the street saw the whole thing.

Roosevelt Williams, paroled rape-o, pimp and policy runner, was tougher. His response to "Hello, shitbird" was "You a whitey motherfuck"—and he hit first. We traded shots for close to a minute, in full view of a cadre of Choppers lounging on front stoops. He was getting the better of me, and I almost went for my baton—not the stuff of which legends are made. Finally I pulled a Lee Blanchard move, rolling upstairs-downstairs sets, wham-wham-wham-wham, the last blow sending Williams to dreamland and me to the station nurse for two finger splints.

Bare knuckles were now out of the question. My last two names, Crawford Johnson and his brother Willis, operated a rigged card game out of the rec room of the Mighty Reedeemer Baptist Church on 61st and Enterprise, catty corner from the greasy spoon where Newton cops ate for half price. When I came in the window, Willis was dealing. He looked up and said, "Huh?"; my billy club took out his hands and the card table. Crawford went for his waistband; my second baton blow knocked a silencer-fitted .45 from his grip. The brothers crashed out the door howling in pain; I picked up my new off-duty piece and told the other gamblers to grab their money and go home. When I walked outside, I had an audience: bluesuits chomping sandwiches on the sidewalk, watching the Johnson brothers hotfoot it, holding their broken paws. "Some people don't respond to civility!" I yelled. An old sergeant rumored to hate my guts yelled back, "Bleichert, you're an honorary white man!" and I knew I was kosherized.

* * *

The Johnson Brothers roust made me a minor legend. My fellow cops gradually warmed to me—the way you do to guys too crazy-bold for their own good, guys that you're grateful not to be yourself. It was like being a local celebrity again.

I got straight 100's on my first month's fitness report, and Lieutenant Getchell rewarded me with a radio car beat. It was a promotion of sorts, as was the territory that came with it.

Rumor had it that both the Slausons and the Choppers were out to do me in, and if they failed, Crawford and Willis Johnson were next in line to try. Getchell wanted me out of harm's way until they cooled off, so he assigned me to a sector on the western border of the division.

The new beat was an invitation to boredom. Mixed white and Negro, small factories and tidy houses, the best action you could hope for was drunk drivers and hitchhiking hookers soliciting motorists, trying to pick up a few bucks on their way down to the niggertown dope pads. I busted DDs and thwarted assignations by flashing my cherry lights, wrote traffic tickets by the shitload and generally prowled for anything out of the ordinary. Drive-in restaurants were popping up on Hoover and Vermont, spangly modern jobs where you could eat in your car and listen to music on speakers attached to the window posts. I spent hours parked in them, KGFJ blasting bebop, my two-way on low in case anything hot came over the air. I eyeballed the street while I sat and listened, trawling for white hookers, telling myself that if I saw any who looked like Betty Short, I'd warn them that 39th and Norton was only a few miles away and urge them to be careful.

But most of the whores were jigs and bleached blondes, not worth warning and only worth busting when my arrest quota was running low. They were women, though, safe places to let my mind dawdle, safe substitutes for my wife at home alone and Madeleine crawling 8th Street gutters. I toyed with the idea of picking up a Dahlia/Madeleine lookalike for sex, but always quashed it—it was too much like Johnny Vogel and Betty at the Biltmore.

Going off-duty at midnight, I was always itchy, restless, in no mood to go home and sleep. Sometimes I hit the all-night movies downtown, sometimes the jazz clubs on South Central. Bop was moving into its heyday, and all-night sessions with a pint of bonded were generally enough to ease me home and into a dreamless sleep shortly after Kay left for work in the morning.

But when it didn't work, it was sweats and Jane Chambers' smiling clown and Frenchman Joe Dulange smashing cockroaches and Johnny Vogel and his whip and Betty begging me to fuck her or kill her killer, she didn't care which. And the worst of it was waking up alone in the fairy tale house.

Summer came on. Hot days sleeping it off on the couch; hot nights patrolling west niggertown, bonded sourmash, the Royal Flush and Bido Lito's, Hampton Hawes, Dizzy Gillespie, Wardell Gray and Dexter Gordon. Restless attempts to study for the Sergeant's Exam and the urge to blow off Kay and the fairy tale house and get a cheap pad somewhere on my beat. If it weren't for the spectral wino it might have gone on forever.

I was parked in Duke's Drive-in, eyeing a gaggle of trampy-looking girls standing by the bus stop about ten yards in front of me. My two-way was off, wild Kenton riffs were coming out of the speaker hook-up. The breezeless humidity had my uniform plastered to my body; I hadn't made an arrest in a week. The girls were waving at passing cars, one peroxide blonde gyrating her hips at them. I started synchronizing the bumps and grinds to the music, playing with the idea of pulling a shakedown, running them through R&I for outstanding warrants. Then a scraggy old wino entered the scene, one hand holding a short dog, the other out begging for chump change.

The bottle blonde quit dancing to talk to him; the music went haywire—all screeches—without her accompaniment. I flashed my headlights; the wino shielded his eyes, then shot me the finger. I was out of the black-and-white and on top of him, Stan Kenton's band my backup.

Roundhouse lefts and rights, rabbit punches. The girl's shrieks out-decibeling Big Stan. The wino cursing me, my mother, my father. Sirens in my head, the smell of rotting meat at the warehouse, even though I knew it couldn't be. The old geez blubbering, "Pleeese."

I staggered to the corner pay phone, gave it a nickel and dialed my own number. Ten rings, no Kay, WE-4391 without thinking. Her voice: "Hello, Sprague residence." My stammers; then, "Bucky? Bucky, is that you?" The wino weaving toward me, sucking his bottle with bloody lips. Hands inside my pockets, pulling out bills to throw him, cash on the pavement. "Come over, sweet. The others are down at Laguna. It could be like old—"

I left the receiver dangling and the wino scooping up the better part of my last paycheck. Driving to Hancock Park, I ran, just this one time, just to be inside the house again. Knocking on the door, I had myself convinced. Then Madeleine was there, black silk, upswept coiffure, yellow barrette. I reached for her; she stepped back, pulled her hair loose and let it fall to her shoulders. "No. Not yet. It's all I have to keep you with."

PART FOUR

ELIZABETH

29

FOR A month she held me in a tight velvet fist.

Emmett, Ramona and Martha were spending June at the family's beach house in Orange County, leaving Madeleine to look after the Muirfield Road estate. We had twenty-two rooms to play in, a dream house built from immigrant ambition. It was a big improvement over the Red Arrow Motel and Lee Blanchard's monument to bank robbery and murder.

Madeleine and I made love in every bedroom, tearing loose every silk sheet and brocade coverlet, surrounded by Picassos and Dutch masters and Ming Dynasty vases worth hundreds of grand. We slept in the late mornings and early afternoons before I headed for niggertown; the looks I got from her neighbors when I walked to my car in full uniform were priceless.

It was a reunion of avowed tramps, rutters who knew that they'd never have it as good with anyone else. Madeleine explained her Dahlia act as a strategy to get me back; she had seen me parked in my car that night, and knew that a Betty Short seduction would keep me returning. The desire behind it moved me even as the elaborateness of the ruse elicited revulsion.

She dropped the look the second the door shut that first time. A quick rinse brought her hair back to its normal dark brown, the pageboy cut returned, the tight black dress came off. I tried everything but threats of leaving and begging; Madeleine kept me mollified with "Maybe some day." Our implicit compromise was Betty talk.

I asked questions, she digressed. We exhausted actual facts quickly; from then on it was pure interpretation.

Madeleine spoke of her utter malleability, Betty the chameleon who would be anyone to please anybody. I had her down as the center of the most baffling piece of detective work the Department had ever seen, the disrupter of most of the lives close to me, the human riddle I had to know *everything* about. That was my final perspective, and it felt bone shallow.

After Betty, I turned the conversation to the Spragues themselves. I never told Madeleine that I knew Jane Chambers,
broaching Jane's inside stuff in roundabout ways. Madeleine said
that Emmett was mildly worried about the forthcoming demolitions up by the Hollywoodland sign; that her mother's pageantry
and love of strange books and medieval lore were nothing but
"Hophead stuff—Mama with time on her hands and a snootful
of patent medicine." After a while, she came to resent my probes
and demanded turnabout. I told lies and wondered where I would
go if my own past was all I had left.

30

PULLING UP in front of the house, I saw a moving van in the
driveway and Kay's Plymouth, top down, packed with boxes. The
run for clean uniforms was turning into something else.

I double-parked and bolted up the steps, smelling Madeleine's
perfume on myself. The van started backing out; I yelled, "Hey!
Goddamn it, come back here!"

The driver ignored me; words from the porch kept me from
going after him. "I didn't touch your things. And you can have
the furniture."

Kay was wearing her Eisenhower jacket and tweed skirt, just
like when I'd first met her. I said, "Babe," and started to ask
"Why?" My wife counterpunched: "Did you think I'd let my
husband vanish for three weeks and do nothing about it? I've had
detectives following you, Dwight. She looks like that fucking
dead girl, so you can have *her*—not me."

Kay's dry eyes and calm voice were worse than what she was saying.
I felt shakes coming on, bad heebie-jeebies. "Babe, goddamn it—"

Kay backed out of grabbing range. "Whoremonger. Coward.
Necrophile."

The shakes got worse; Kay turned and made for her car, a deft
little pirouette out of my life. I caught another scent of Madeleine
and walked into the house.

The bentwood furniture looked the same, but there were no
literary quarterlies on the coffee table and no cashmere sweaters
folded in the dining room cabinet. The cushions on my couch-
bed were neatly arrayed, like I'd never slept there. My phonograph was still by the fireplace, but all Kay's records were gone.

I picked up Lee's favorite chair and threw it at the wall; I hurled Kay's rocker at the cabinet, reducing it to glass rubble. I upended the coffee table and rammed it into the front window, then tossed it out on the porch. I kicked the rugs into sloppy piles, pulled out drawers, tipped over the refrigerator and took a hammer to the bathroom sink, smashing it loose from the pipes. It felt like going ten rounds full blast; when my arms were too limp to inflict more damage I grabbed my uniforms and my silencer .45 and got out, leaving the door open so scavengers could pick the place clean.

With the other Spragues due back in L.A. any day, there was only one place to go. I drove to the El Nido, badged the desk clerk and told him he had a new tenant. He forked over an extra room key; seconds later I was smelling Russ Millard's stale cigarette smoke and Harry Sears' spilled rye. And I was eyeball to eyeball with Elizabeth Short on all four walls: alive and smiling, dumbstruck with cheap dreams, vivisected in a weedy vacant lot.

And without even saying it to myself, I knew what I was going to do.

I removed the file cases from the bed, stacked them in the closet and ripped off the sheets and blankets. The Dahlia photos were nailed to the wall; it was easy to drape the bedding over them so that they were completely covered. The pad perfect, I went prowling for props.

I found a jet-black upswept wig at Western Costume, a yellow barrette at a dime store on the Boulevard. The heebie-jeebies came back—worse than bad. I drove to the Firefly Lounge, hoping it still had Hollywood Vice's sanction.

One eyeball circuit inside told me it did. I sat down at the bar, ordered a double Old Forester and stared at the girls congregating on a matchbook-size bandstand. Footlights set in the floor shined up at them; they were the only thing in the dump illuminated.

I downed my drink. They all looked typical—hophead whores in cheap slit kimonos. Counting five heads, I watched the girls smoke cigarettes and adjust their slits to show more leg. None was anywhere near close.

Then a skinny brunette in a flouncy cocktail dress stepped onto the bandstand. She blinked at the glare, scratched her pert button nose and toed figure eights on the floor.

I hooked a finger at the bartender. He came over with the bottle; I held a palm over my glass. "The girl in the pink. How much to take her to my place for an hour or so?"

The barman sighed. "Mister, we've got three rooms here. The girls don't like—"

I shut him up with a crisp new fifty. "You're making an exception for me. Be generous with yourself."

The fifty disappeared, then the man himself. I filled my glass and downed it, eyes on the bartop until I felt a hand on my shoulder.

"Hi, I'm Lorraine."

I turned around. Close up she could have been any pretty brunette—perfect molding clay. "Hi, Lorraine. I'm ... B-B-Bill."

The girl snickered, "Hi, *Bill*. You wanna go now?"

I nodded; Lorraine walked outside ahead of me. Straight daylight showed off the runs in her nylons and old needle scars on her arms. When she got in the car I saw that her eyes were dull brown; when she drummed her fingers on the dashboard I saw that her closest link to Betty was chipped nail polish.

It was enough.

We drove to the El Nido and walked up to the room without saying a word. I opened the door and stood aside to let Lorraine enter; she rolled her eyes at the gesture, then gave a low whistle to let me know the place was a dive. I locked the door behind us, unwrapped the wig and handed it to her. "Here. Take off your clothes and put this on."

Lorraine did an inept strip. Her shoes clunked on the floor, she snagged her nylons pulling them off. I made a move to unzip her dress, but she saw it coming, turned away and did it herself. With her back to me, she unhooked her bra, stepped out of her panties and fumbled with the wig. Facing me, she said, "This your idea of a big thrill?"

The coiffure was askew, like a gag rug on a vaudeville comic; only her breasts were a good match. I took off my jacket and started to work at my belt. Something in Lorraine's eyes stopped me; I snapped that she was afraid of my gun and handcuffs. I got the urge to calm her down by telling her I was a cop—then the look made her seem more like Betty, and I stopped.

The girl said, "You won't hurt—"; I said, "Don't talk," and straightened the wig, bunching her lank brown hair up inside it. The fit was still all wrong, whorish and out of kilter. Lorraine was shaking now; head-to-toe shivers as I stuck the yellow barrette into the coif to make things right. All it did was rip loose strands of black as dry as straw and tilt everything off to one side, like the girl was the slash mouth clown, not my Betty.

I said, "Lie down on the bed." The girl complied, legs rigid and pressed together, hands underneath her, a skinny length of tics and twitches. Prone, the wig was half on her head, half on the pillow. Knowing the pictures on the wall would spark perfection, I pulled off the sheets covering them.

I stared at portrait-perfect Betty/Beth/Liz; the girl screamed, *"No! Killer! Police!"*

Wheeling around, I saw a naked fraud transfixed by 39th and Norton. I hurled myself onto the bed, pressed my hands over her mouth and held her down, talking it right and perfect: "It's just that she has all these different names to be, and this woman won't be her for me, and I can't be just anybody like her, and every time I try I fuck it up, and my friend went crazy because his little sister might have been her if somebody didn't kill her—"

"KILL—"

The wig in disarray on the bedspread.

My hands on the girl's neck.

I let go and stood up slowly, palms out, no harm meant. The girl's vocal cords stretched, but she couldn't come up with a sound. She rubbed her throat where my hands had been, the imprint still bright red. I backed off to the far wall, unable to talk.

Mexican standoff.

The girl massaged her throat; something like ice came into her eyes. She got off the bed and put on her clothes facing me, the ice getting colder and deeper. It was a look I knew I couldn't match, so I got out my ID buzzer and held up LAPD badge 1611 for her to see. She smiled; I tried to imitate her; she walked up to me and spat on the piece of tin. The door slammed, the pictures on the wall fluttered, my voice came back in racking fits, "I'll get him for you, he won't hurt you anymore, I'll make it up to you, oh Betty Jesus fuck I will."

31

THE AIRPLANE flew east, slicing through cloud banks and bright blue sky. My pockets were stuffed with cash from my all but liquidated bank account, Lieutenant Getchell had bought my line about a grievously ill high school pal in Boston and had granted me a week's accumulated sick leave. A stack of notes from the Boston PD's background check was on my lap—laboriously copied from the El Nido file. I already had an interrogation itinerary printed out, aided by the metropolitan Boston street atlas I'd purchased at the L.A. airport. When the plane landed, it would be Medford/Cambridge/Stoneham and Elizabeth Short's past—the part that didn't get smeared across page one.

I'd hit the master file yesterday afternoon, as soon as I quit shaking and was able to put how close I'd gotten to havoc out of my brain—at least the front part of it. One quick skimming told me that the L.A. end of the investigation was dead, a second and third told me it was deader, a fourth convinced me that if I stayed in town I'd go batshit over Madeleine and Kay. I had to run, and if my vow to Elizabeth Short was to mean anything, it had to be in her direction. And if it was a wild-goose chase, then at least it was a trip to clean territory—where my badge and live women wouldn't get me into trouble.

The revulsion on the hooker's face wouldn't leave me; I could still smell her cheap perfume and imagined her spitting indictments, the same words Kay had used earlier that day, only worse—because she knew what I was: a whore with a badge. Thinking about her was like scraping the bottom of my life on my knees—the only comfort in it the fact that I couldn't go any lower—that I'd chew the muzzle of my .38 first.

The plane landed at 7:35; I was the first in line to disembark, notebook and satchel in hand. There was a car rental place in the terminal; I rented a Chevy coupe and headed into the Boston metropolis, anxious to take advantage of the hour or so of daylight left.

My itinerary included the addresses of Elizabeth's mother, two of her sisters, her high school, a Harvard Square hash house where she slung plates in '42 and the movie theater where she worked as a candy girl in '39 and '40. I decided on a loop through Boston to Cambridge, then Medford—Betty's real stomping ground.

Boston, quaint and old, hit me like a blur. I followed street signs to the Charles River Bridge and crossed over into Cambridge: ritzy Georgian pads and streets packed with college kids. More signs led me to Harvard Square; there was stop one—Otto's Hofbrau, a gingerbread structure spilling the aroma of cabbage and beer.

I parked in a meter space and walked in. The Hansel and Gretel motif extended to the whole place—carved wood booths, beer steins lining the walls, waitresses in dirndl skirts. I looked around for the boss, my eyes settling on a smock-clad older man standing by the cash register.

I walked over, and something kept me from badging him. "Excuse me. I'm a reporter, and I'm writing a story on Elizabeth Short. I understand that she worked here back in '42, and I thought you could tell me a little about her then."

The man said, "Elizabeth who? She some sort of movie star?"

"She was killed in Los Angeles a few years ago. It's a famous case. Do you—"

"I bought this place in '46, and the only employee I got left from the war is Roz. Rozzie, come here! Man wants to talk to you!"

The battle-axe waitress of them all materialized—a baby elephant in a thigh-length skirt. The boss said, "This guy's a reporter. Wants to talk to you about Elizabeth Short. You remember her?"

Rozzie popped her gum at me. "I told the *Globe* and the *Sentinel* and the cops the first time around, and I ain't changing my story. Betsy Short was a dish dropper and a dreamer, and if she didn't bring in so much Harvard business, she wouldn't a lasted a day. I heard she put out for the war effort, but I didn't know none of her boyfriends. End of story. And you ain't no reporter, you're a cop."

I said, "Thank you for that perceptive comment," and left.

My atlas placed Medford twelve miles away, a straight run out Massachusetts Avenue. I got there just as night was falling, smelling it first, then seeing it.

Medford was a factory town, smoke-belching foundry stacks forming its perimeter. I rolled up my window to hold off the sulfur stink; the industrial area dwindled into blocks of narrow red-brick houses crammed together with less than a foot between them. Every block had at least two gin mills, and when I saw Swasey Boulevard—the street the movie theater was on—I opened my wind wing to see if the foundry stench was dissipating. It wasn't—and the windshield was already bearing a film of greasy soot.

I found the Majestic a few blocks down, a typical Medford red-brick building, the marquee heralding *Criss Cross* with Burt Lancaster and *Duel in the Sun*—"All Star Cast." The ticket booth was empty, so I walked straight into the theater and up to the snack stand. The man behind it said, "Anything wrong, officer?" I groaned that the locals had my number—three thousand miles from home.

"No, nothing's wrong. Are you the manager?"

"The owner. Ted Carmody. You BPD?"

I reluctantly displayed my shield. "Los Angeles Police Department. It's about Beth Short."

Ted Carmody crossed himself. "Poor Lizzie. You got some hot leads? That why you're here?"

I put a nickel on the counter, grabbed a Snickers bar and unwrapped it. "Let's just say I owe Betty one, and I've got a few questions."

"Ask on."

"First off, I've seen the Boston Police background check file, and your name wasn't listed on the interview sheet. Didn't they talk to you?"

Carmody handed me back my nickel. "On the house, and I didn't talk to the Boston cops because they talked Lizzie up like she was some sort of tramp. I don't cooperate with bad-mouthers."

"That's admirable, Mr. Carmody. But what would you have told them?"

"Nothing dirty, that's for damn sure. Lizzie was all aces to me. If the cops had been properly respectful of the dead, I'd have told 'em that."

The man was exhausting me. "I'm a respectful guy. Pretend that it's two years ago and tell me."

Carmody couldn't quite peg my style, so I chomped the candy bar to ease him into some slack. "I'd have told 'em Lizzie was a bad worker," he said finally. "And I'd have told 'em I didn't care. She brought the boys in like a magnet, and if she kept sneaking in to watch the picture, so what? For fifty cents an hour I didn't expect her to slave for me."

I said, "What about her boyfriends?"

Carmody slammed the counter; Jujubes and Milk Duds top-pled over. "Lizzie wasn't no roundheels! The only boyfriend I knew she had was this blind guy, and I knew it was just palship. Listen, you want to know what kind of kid Lizzie was? I'll tell you. I used to let the blind guy in for free, so he could listen to the picture, and Lizzie kept sneaking in to tell him what was on the screen. You know, describe it to him. That sound like tramp behavior to you?"

It felt like a punch to the heart. "No, it doesn't. Do you remember the guy's name?"

"Tommy something. He's got a room over the VFW Hall down the block, and if he's a killer I'll flap my arms and fly to Nantucket."

I stuck out my hand. "Thanks for the candy bar, Mr. Carmody."

We shook. Carmody said, "You get the guy who killed Lizzie, I'll buy you the factory that makes the goddamn things."

As I said the words, I knew it was one of the finest moments of my life:

"I will."

The VFW Hall was across the street and down from the Majestic, yet another red-brick structure streaked with soot. I walked there thinking of blind Tommy as a big washout, someone I had to talk to to soften up Betty, make her live more easily in me.

Side steps took me upstairs, past a mailbox labeled T. GILFOYLE. Ringing the bell, I heard music; looking in the one window I saw pitch darkness. Then a soft male voice came from the other side of the door. "Yes? Who is it?"

"Los Angeles Police, Mr. Gilfoyle. It's about Elizabeth Short."

Light hit the window, the music died. The door opened, and a tall pudgy man wearing dark glasses pointed me inside. He was immaculate in striped sportshirt and slacks, but the room was a pigsty, dust and grime everywhere, an army of bugs scattering from the unaccustomed blast of brightness.

Tommy Gilfoyle said, "My Braille teacher read me the L.A. papers. Why did they say such nasty things about Beth?"

I tried diplomacy. "Because they didn't know her like you did."

Tommy smiled and plopped into a ratty chair. "Is the apartment really disreputable?"

The couch was littered with phonograph records; I scooped a handful aside and sat down. "It could use a lick and a promise."

"I get slothful sometimes. Is Beth's investigation active again? Priority stuff?"

"No, I'm here on my own. Where did you pick up the cop lingo?"

"I have a policeman friend."

I brushed a fat bug off my sleeve. "Tommy, tell me about you and Beth. Give me something that didn't make the papers. Something good."

"Is this personal with you? Like a vendetta?"

"It's more than that."

"My friend said policemen who take their work personally get in trouble."

I stomped a cockroach exploring my shoe. "I just want to get the bastard."

"You don't have to yell. I'm blind, not deaf, and I wasn't blind to Beth's little faults, either."

"How so?"

Tommy fingered the cane by his chair. "Well, I won't dwell on it, but Beth was promiscuous, just like the newspapers implied. I knew the reason, but I kept still because I didn't want to disgrace her memory, and I knew that it wouldn't help the police find her killer."

The man was wheedling now, caught between wanting to kick loose and keep secrets. I said, "You let *me* judge that. I'm an experienced detective."

"At your age? I can tell by your voice that you're young. My friend said that to make detective you have to serve at least ten years on the force."

"Goddamn it, don't dick me around. I came here on my own and I didn't come to—"

I stopped when I saw that the man was frightened, one hand going for the telephone. "Look, I'm sorry. It's been a long day, and I'm a long way from home."

Tommy surprised me by smiling. "I'm sorry, too. I was just being coy to prolong the company, and that's rude. So I'll tell you about Beth, her little foibles and all.

"You probably know she was star-struck, and that's true. You probably guessed that she didn't have much talent, and that's true, too. Beth read plays to me—acting all the parts, and she was a terrible ham—just awful. I understand the spoken word, so believe me, I know.

"What Beth was good at was writing. I used to sit in on movies at the Majestic, and Beth used to describe things so I'd have something to go with the dialogue. She was brilliant, and I encouraged her to write for the movies, but she just wanted to be an actress like every other silly girl who wanted to get out of Medford."

I would have committed mass murder to get out. "Tommy, you said you know the reason Beth was promiscuous."

Tommy sighed. "When Beth was sixteen or seventeen, these two thugs assaulted her, somewhere in Boston. One actually raped her, and the other was going to, but a sailor and a marine came by and chased them away.

"Beth thought the man might have made her pregnant, so she went to a doctor for an examination. He told her she had benign ovarian cysts, that she'd never be able to have children. Beth went crazy, because she'd always wanted lots of babies. She looked up the sailor and marine who'd saved her, and she begged them to father her child. The marine turned her down, and the sailor ... he used Beth until he was shipped overseas."

I thought immediately of Frenchman Joe Dulange—his account of the Dahlia hipped on being pregnant, how he fixed her up with a "doctor buddy" and a bogus exam. That part of Dulange's story obviously wasn't as booze-addled as Russ Millard and I had originally thought—it was now a solid lead on Betty's missing days, the "doctor buddy" at least a major witness, maybe a major suspect. I said, "Tommy, do you know the names of the sailor and marine? The doctor?"

Tommy shook his head. "No. But that was when Beth became so loose with servicemen. She thought they were her saviors, that they could give her a child, a little girl to be a great actress in case she never made it. It's sad, but the only place I heard Beth was a great actress was in bed."

I stood up. "What happened with you and Beth then?"

"We lost touch. She left Medford."

"You've given me a good lead, Tommy. Thanks."

The blind man tapped his cane at the sound of my voice. "Then get who did it, but don't let Beth get hurt anymore."

"I won't."

32

THE SHORT case was hot again—if only with me.

Hours of Medford pub crawling gave me promiscuous Betty, East Coast style—a big anticlimax after Tommy Gilfoyle's revelations. I caught a midnight flight back to L.A. and called Russ Millard from the airport. He agreed: Frenchman Joe's "roach doctor" was probably legit, independent of Dulange's DTs. He proposed a call to the Fort Dix CID to try to get more details from the discharged loony, then a three-man canvassing of downtown doctors' offices, concentrating on the area around the Havana Hotel, where Dulange coupled with Betty. I suggested that the "doctor" was most likely a barfly, an abortionist or a quack; Russ concurred. He said he would talk to R&I and his snitches, and he and Harry Sears would be knocking on doors inside of an hour. We divvied up the territory: Figueroa to Hill, 6th Street to 9th Street for me; Figueroa to Hill, 5th to 1st for them. I hung up and drove straight downtown.

I stole a Yellow Pages and made a list: legitimate MD's and chiropractors, herb pushers and mystics—bloodsuckers who sold religion and patent medicine under the "doctor" aegis. The book had a few listings for obstetricians and gynecologists, but instinct told me that Joe Dulange's doctor ploy was happenstance—not the result of his consciously seeking a specialist to calm Betty down. Running on adrenaline, I worked.

I caught most of the doctors early in their day, and got the widest assortment of sincere denials I'd ever encountered as a cop. Every solid citizen croaker I talked to convinced me a little bit more that Frenchy's pal had to be at least a little bit hinky. After a wolfed sandwich lunch, I hit the quasi types.

The herb loonies were all Chinese; the mystics were half women, half squarejohn lames. I believed all of their bewildered no's; I pictured all of them too terrified by the Frenchman to consider his offer. I was about to start hitting bars for scuttlebutt on barfly docs when exhaustion hit me. I drove "home" to the El Nido and slept—for all of twenty minutes.

Too itchy to try sleep again, I tried thinking logically. It was 6:00, doctors' offices were closing for the day, the bars wouldn't be ripe for canvassing for at least three hours. Russ and Harry would call me if they got something hot. I reached for the master file and started reading.

Time flew; names, dates and locations in police jargon kept me awake. Then I saw something that I'd perused a dozen times before, only this time it seemed off.

It was two memo slips:

1/18/47: Harry - Call Buzz Meeks at Hughes and
have him call around on possible E. Short movie bus.

associations. Bleichert says the girl was star struck.
Do this independent of Loew - Russ.
  1/22/47: Russ - Meeks says goose egg. Too bad.
He was anxious to help - Harry.

With Betty's movie mania fresh in my mind, the memos
looked different. I remembered Russ telling me that he was going
to query Meeks, the Hughes security boss and the Department's
"unofficial liaison" to the Hollywood community; I recalled that
this was during the time when Ellis Loew was suppressing evidence on Betty's promiscuity in order to secure himself a better
prosecuting attorney's showcase. Also: Betty's little black book
listed a number of lower-echelon movie people—names that
were checked out during the '47 black book interrogations.
  The big question:
  If Meeks really had checked around, why didn't he come up
with at least a few of the black book names and forward them to
Russ and Harry?
  I went out to the hall, got the Hughes Security number from
the White Pages and dialed it. A singsong woman answered:
"Security. May I help you?"
  "Buzz Meeks, please."
  "Mr. Meeks is out of his office right now. Whom shall I say is
calling?"
  "Detective Bleichert, LAPD. When will he be back?"
  "When the budget meeting breaks up. May I ask what this is
in reference to?"
  "Police business. Tell him I'll be at his office in half an hour."
  I hung up and leadfooted it to Santa Monica in twenty-five
minutes. The gate guard admitted me to the plant parking lot,
pointing to the security office—a Quonset hut at the end of a
long string of aircraft hangars. I parked and knocked on the door;
the woman with the singsong voice opened it. "Mr. Meeks said
you should wait in his office. He won't be very long."
  I walked in; the woman left, looking relieved that her day's
work was over. The hut was wallpapered with paintings of
Hughes aircraft, military art on a par with the drawings on cereal boxes. Meeks' office was better decorated: photos of a burly
crewcut man with various Hollywood hotshots—actresses
I couldn't place by name along with George Raft and Mickey
Rooney.

I took a seat. The burly man showed up a few minutes later, hand out automatically, like someone whose job was ninety-five percent public relations. "Hello there. Detective Blyewell, is it?"

I stood up. We shook; I could tell that Meeks was put off by my two-day clothes and three-day beard. "It's Bleichert."

"Of course. What can I do for you?"

"I have a few questions about an old case you helped Homicide out with."

"I see. You're with the Bureau, then?"

"Newton Patrol."

Meeks sat down behind his desk. "A little out of your baili-wick, aren't you? And my secretary said you were a detective."

I closed the door and leaned against it. "This is personal with me."

"Then you'll top out your twenty rousting nigger piss bums. Or hasn't anyone told you that cops who take things personal end up from hunger?"

"They keep telling me, and I keep telling them that's my hometown. You fuck a lot of starlets, Meeks?"

"I fucked Carole Lombard. I'd give you her number, but she's dead."

"Did you fuck Elizabeth Short?"

Tilt, bingo, jackpot, lie detector perfect as Meeks flushed and fingered the papers on his blotter; a wheezing voice to back it up: "You catch a few too many in the Blanchard fight? The Short cooze is dead."

I pulled back my jacket to show Meeks the .45 I was carrying. "Don't call her that again."

"All right, tough guy. Now suppose you tell me what you want. Then we settle up and end this little charade before it gets out of hand. Comprende?"

"In '47, Harry Sears asked you to query your movie contacts on Betty Short. You reported back that it was a washout. You were lying. Why?"

Meeks picked up a letter opener. He ran a finger along the blade, saw what he was doing and put it down. "I didn't kill her and I don't know who did."

"Convince me, or I call up Hedda Hopper and give her to-morrow's column. How's this sound: 'Hollywood hanger-on sup-pressed Dahlia evidence because blank, blank, blank'? You fill in those blanks for me, or I fill them in for Hedda. Comprende?"

Meeks gave bravado another try. "Bleichert, you are fucking with the wrong man."

I pulled out the .45, made sure the silencer was on tight and slid a round into the chamber. "No, you are."

Meeks reached for a decanter on the sideboard by his desk; he poured himself a bracer and gulped it. "What I got was a dead-end lead, but you can have it if you want it so bad."

I dangled my gun by the trigger guard. "From hunger, shitbird. So give it to me."

Meeks opened up a safe built into his desk and pulled out a sheaf of papers. He studied them, then swiveled his chair and spoke to the wall. "I got a tip on Burt Lindscott, a producer at Universal. I got it from a guy who hated Lindscott's pal Scotty Bennett. Scotty was a pimp and a bookie, and he gave out Lindscott's home phone number in Malibu to all the good-looking young stuff who applied at the Universal casting office. The Short girl got one of Scotty's cards, and she called Lindscott.

"The rest, the dates and so forth, I got from Lindscott himself. On the night of January tenth, the girl called from the Biltmore downtown. Burty had her describe herself, and he liked what he heard. He told the girl he'd give her a screen test in the morning, when he got back from a poker session at his club. The girl said she didn't have any place to go until then, so Lindscott told her to come over and spend the night at his place—his houseboy would feed her and keep her company. She took a bus out to Malibu, and the houseboy—he was queer—did keep her company. Then, the next day around noon, Lindscott and three buddies of his came home drunk.

"The guys thought they'd have some fun, so they gave the girl this screen test, reading from a screenplay Burt had lying around. She was bad, and they laughed her out, then Lindscott made her an offer: service the four of them and he'd give her a bit part in his next picture. The kid was still mad at them for laughing at her screen test, and she threw a tantrum. She called them draft dodgers and traitors and said they weren't fit to be soldiers. Burt kicked her out around two-thirty that afternoon, Saturday the eleventh. The houseboy said she was broke and that she said she was gonna walk back downtown."

So Betty walked, or hitched, twenty-five miles downtown, meeting Sally Stinson and Johnny Vogel in the Biltmore lobby six hours or so later. I said, "Meeks, why didn't you report this? And look at me."

Meeks swiveled around; his features were smeared with shame. "I tried to get ahold of Russ and Harry, but they were out in the field, so I called Ellis Loew. He told me not to report what I'd found out, and he threatened to revoke my security clearance. Later on I found out that Lindscott was a Republican bigwig, and he'd promised Loew a bundle for his run at DA. Loew didn't want him implicated with the Dahlia."

I shut my eyes so I wouldn't have to look at the man; Meeks copped pleas while I ran pictures of Betty hooted at, propositioned, kicked out to die. "Bleichert, I checked out Lindscott and his houseboy and his buddies. These are legit depositions I've got—the megillah. None of them could have killed her. They were all at home and at their jobs from the twelfth straight through Friday the seventeenth. None of them could have done it, and I wouldn't have sat on it if one of the bastards snuffed her. I've got the depositions right here, and I'll show you."

I opened my eyes; Meeks was twirling the dial of a wall safe. I said, "How much did Loew pay you to keep quiet?"

Meeks blurted, "A grand," and backed off as if fearing a blow. I loathed him too much to give him the satisfaction of punishment, and left with his price tag hanging in the air.

* * *

I now had Elizabeth Short's missing days halfway filled in:

Red Manley dropped her in front of the Biltmore at dusk on Friday, January tenth; she called Burt Lindscott from there, and her Malibu adventures lasted until 2:30 the following afternoon. She was back at the Biltmore that evening, Saturday the eleventh, met Sally Stinson and Johnny Vogel in the lobby, tricked with Johnny until shortly after midnight, then took off. She met Corporal Joseph Dulange then, or later in the morning, at the Night Owl Bar on 6th and Hill—two blocks from the Biltmore. She was with Dulange, there and at the Havana Hotel, until the afternoon or evening of Sunday, January twelfth, when he took her to see his "doctor buddy."

Driving back to the El Nido, some missing piece of legwork nagged at me through my exhaustion. Passing a phone booth it came to me: if Betty called Lindscott in Malibu—a toll call— there would be a record with Pacific Coast Bell. If she made other toll calls, at that time or on the eleventh, before or after her coupling with Johnny Vogel, PCB would have the information in its records—the company saved tallies of pay phone transactions for cost and price studies.

My fatigue nosedived once more. I took side streets the rest of the way, running stop signs and red lights; arriving, I parked in front of a hydrant and ran up to the room for a notebook. I was heading for the hallway phone when it foiled me by ringing.

"Yes?"

"Bucky? Sweet, is that you?"

It was Madeleine. "Look, I can't talk to you now."

"We had a date yesterday, remember?"

"I had to leave town. It was for work."

"You could have called. If you hadn't told me about this little hideaway of yours I'd have thought you were dead."

"Madeleine, Jesus Christ—"

"Sweet, I need to see you. They're tearing those letters off the Hollywoodland sign tomorrow, *and* demolishing some bungalows Daddy owns up there. Bucky, the deeds lapsed to the city, but Daddy bought that property and built those places under his own name. He used *the* worst materials, and an investigator from the City Council has been nosing around Daddy's tax lawyers. One of them told him this old enemy of his who committed suicide left the Council a brief on Daddy's holdings and—"

It sounded like gibberish—tough guy Daddy in trouble, tough boy Bucky the second choice for consolation duty. I said, "Look, I can't talk to you now," and hung up.

Now it was real detective shitwork. I arrayed my notebook and pen on the ledge by the phone and emptied a four-day accumulation of coins from my pockets, counting close to two dollars—enough for forty calls. First I called the night supervisor at Pacific Coast Bell, requesting a list of all toll and collect calls made from Biltmore Hotel pay phones on the evenings of January 10, 11, and 12, 1947; the names and addresses of the called parties and the times of the calls.

I stood nervously holding the receiver while the woman did her work, shooting dirty looks to other El Nido residents who wanted to use the phone. Then, a half hour later, she came back on the line and started talking.

The Lindscott number and address was there among the 1/10 listings, but nothing else that night registered as hinky. I wrote all the information down anyway; then, when the woman got to the evening of 1/11—right around the time Betty met Sally Stinson and Johnny Vogel in the Biltmore lobby—I hit paydirt:

Four toll calls were made to obstetricians' offices in Beverly Hills. I took down the names and numbers, along with the numbers for the doctors' night answering services, and the immediately following toll call listings. They produced no sparks—but I copied them anyway. Then I attacked Beverly Hills with an arsenal of nickels.

It took all my change to get what I wanted.

I told the answering service operators it was a police emergency; they put me through to the doctors at home. They had their secretaries drive to the office to check their back records, then call me at the El Nido. The whole process took two hours. At the end of it I had this:

On the early evening of January 11, 1947, a "Mrs. Fickling" and a "Mrs. Gordon" called a total of four different obstetricians' offices in Beverly Hills, requesting appointments for pregnancy testing. The after-hours service operators made appointments for the mornings of January 14 and 15. Lieutenant Joseph Fickling and Major Matt Gordon were two of the war heroes Betty dated and pretended to be married to; the appointments were never kept because on the fourteenth she was getting tortured to death; on the fifteenth she was a mutilated pile of flesh at 39th and Norton.

I called Russ Millard at the Bureau; a vaguely familiar voice answered: "Homicide."

"Lieutenant Millard, please."

"He's in Tucson extraditing a prisoner."

"Harry Sears, too?"

"Yeah. How are you, Bucky? It's Dick Cavanaugh."

"I'm surprised you could place my voice."

"Harry Sears told me you'd be calling. He left a list of doctors for you, but I can't find it. That what you want?"

"Yeah, and I need to talk to Russ. When's he coming back?"

"Late tomorrow, I think. Is there someplace I can call you if I find the list?"

"I'm rolling. I'll call you."

The other phone numbers had to be tried, but the obstetrician lead was too potent to sit on. I headed back downtown to look for Dulange's doctor buddy, my exhaustion dropped like a hot rock.

I kept at it until midnight, concentrating on the bars around 6th and Hill, talking up barflies, buying them drinks, racking up booze rebop and a couple of tips on abortion mills that almost sounded legit.

Another sleepless day ended; I took to driving from bar to bar, playing the radio to keep from dozing off. The news kept droning on about the "milestone refurbishing" of the Hollywoodland sign—playing up the lopping off of L-A-N-D as the biggest thing since Jesus. Mack Sennett and his Hollywoodland tract got a lot of air time, and a theater in Hollywood was reviving a bunch of his old Keystone Kops pictures.

Toward bar-closing time, I felt like a Keystone Kop and looked like a bum—scraggly beard, soiled clothes, fevered attention that kept wandering off. When drunks eager for more booze and camaraderie began giving me the brush, I took it as a strong hint, drove to a deserted parking lot, pulled in and slept.

* * *

Leg cramps woke me up at dawn. I stumbled out of the car looking for a phone; a black-and-white cruised by, the driver giving me a long fisheye. I found a booth at the corner and dialed the padre's number.

"Homicide Bureau. Sergeant Cavanaugh."

"Dick, it's Bucky Bleichert."

"Just the man I wanted to talk to. I've got the list. You got the pencil?"

I dug out a pocket notebook. "Shoot."

"Okay. These are licensed-revoked doctors. Harry said they were practicing downtown in '47. One, Gerald Constanzo, 1841½ Breakwater, Long Beach. Two, Melvin Praeger, 9661 North Verdugo, Glendale. Three, Willis Roach. That's Roach like in the bug, in custody at Wayside Honor Rancho, convicted of selling morph in ..."

Dulange.

The DTs.

"So I take Dahlia down the street to see the *roach doctor*. I slip him a tensky, and he gives her a fake examination ..."

Breathing shallowly, I said, "Dick, did Harry write down the address where Roach was practicing?"

"Yeah. 614 South Olive."

The Havana Hotel was two blocks away. "Dick, call Wayside and tell the warden that I'll be driving up immediately to question Roach on the Elizabeth Short homicide."

"Mother dog."

"Motherfucking dog."

* * *

A shower, shave and change of clothes at the El Nido had me looking like a homicide detective; Dick Cavanaugh's call to Wayside would give me the rest of the juice I needed. I took the Angeles Crest Highway north, laying 50–50 odds that Dr. Willis Roach was Elizabeth Short's murderer.

The trip took a little over an hour; Hollywoodland sign spiel accompanied me on the radio. The deputy sheriff in the gate hut examined my badge and ID card and called the main building to clear me; whatever he was told made him snap to attention and salute. The barbed-wire fence swung open; I drove past the inmate barracks and over to a large Spanish-style structure fronted by a tile portico. As I parked, an LASD captain in uniform walked over, hand out, nervous grin on. "Detective Bleichert, I'm Warden Patchett."

I got out and gave the man a Lee Blanchard bonecrusher. "A pleasure, Warden. Has Roach been told anything?"

"No. He's in an interrogation room waiting for you. Do you think he killed the Dahlia?"

I started walking; Patchett steered me in the right direction. "I'm not sure yet. What can you tell me about him?"

"He's forty-eight years old, he's an anesthesiologist, and he was arrested in October of '47 for selling hospital morphine to an LAPD narcotics officer. He got five to ten, did a year at Quentin. He's down here because we needed help in the infirmary and the Adult Authority thought he'd be a safe risk. He's got no prior arrests, and he's been a model prisoner."

We turned into a low, tan brick building, a typical county "utility" job—long corridors, recessed steel doors embossed with numbers and no names. Passing a string of one-way glass windows, Patchett grabbed my arm. "There. That's Roach."

I stared in. A bony middle-aged man in county denims was seated at a card table, reading a magazine. He was a smart-looking bird—high forehead covered by wisps of thinning gray hair, bright eyes, the kind of large, veiny hands you associate with doctors. I said, "Care to sit in, Warden?"

Patchett opened the door. "Wouldn't miss it."

Roach looked up. Patchett said, "Doc, this is Detective Bleichert. He's with the Los Angeles Police, and he's got a few questions for you."

Roach put down his magazine—*American Anesthesiologist*. Patchett and I took seats across from him; the doctor/dope peddler said, "However I can be of service," his voice eastern and educated.

I went right for the throat. "Dr. Roach, why did you kill Elizabeth Short?"

Roach smiled slowly; gradually his grin spread ear to ear. "I expected you back in '47. After Corporal Dulange made that sad little confession of his, I expected you to break down my office door any second. Two and a half years after the fact surprises me, however."

My skin was buzzing; it felt like bugs were getting ready to eat me for breakfast. "There's no statute of limitations on murder."

Roach's grin disappeared, replaced by a serious look, the movie doctor getting ready to deliver some bad news. "Gentlemen, on Monday, January 13, 1947, I flew to San Francisco and checked in at the Saint Francis Hotel, preparatory to delivering my Tuesday night keynote speech at the annual convention of the Academy of American Anesthesiologists. I gave the speech Tuesday night, and was featured speaker at the farewell breakfast, Wednesday morning, January fifteenth. I was in the constant company of colleagues through the afternoon of the fifteenth, and I slept with my ex-wife at the Saint Francis both Monday and Tuesday nights. If you would like corroboration, call the Academy at their Los Angeles number, and my ex-wife, Alice Carstairs Roach, at San Francisco CR-1786."

I said, "Check that out for me, would you please, Warden?," my eyes on Roach.

Patchett left; the doctor said, "You look disappointed."

"Bravo, Willis. Now tell me about you and Dulange and Elizabeth Short."

"Will you inform the Parole Board that I cooperated with you?"

"No, but if you don't tell me I'll have the L.A. District Attorney file charges on you for obstruction of justice."

Roach acknowledged match point with a grin. "Bravo, Detective Bleichert. You know, of course, that the reason the dates are so well fixed in my mind is due to all the publicity Miss Short's death garnered. So please trust my memory."

I got out a pen and notepad. "Go, Willis."

Roach said, "In '47 I had a lucrative little sideline selling pharmaceuticals. I sold them primarily in cocktail lounges, primarily to servicemen who had discovered their pleasures overseas during the war. That was how I met Corporal Dulange. I approached him, but he informed me that he appreciated the pleasures of Johnnie Walker Red Label scotch whisky exclusively."

"Where was this?"

"At the Yorkshire House Bar, 6th and Olive Streets, near my office."

"Go on."

"Well, that was the Thursday or Friday before Miss Short's demise. I gave Corporal Dulange my card—injudiciously, as it turned out—and I assumed that I would never see the man again. Sadly, I was wrong.

"I was in poor shape financially at that time, owing to the ponies, and I was living in my office. On the early evening of Sunday, January twelfth, Corporal Dulange showed up at my door with a lovely young woman named Beth in tow. He was quite drunk, and he took me aside, pressed ten dollars into my hand and told me lovely Beth was hipped on being pregnant. Would I please give her a quick examination and tell her it was so?

"Well, I obliged. Corporal Dulange waited in my outer office, and I took lovely Beth's pulse and blood pressure and informed her that yes indeed, she was pregnant. Her response was quite strange: she seemed sad and relieved at the same time. My interpretation was that she needed a reason to justify her obvious promiscuity, and child bearing seemed like the ticket."

I sighed. "And when her death became news, you didn't go to the police because you didn't want them nosing around your dope racket?"

"Yes, that's correct. But there's more. Beth asked to use my phone. I acceded, and she dialed a number with a Webster prefix and asked to speak to Marcy. She said, 'It's Betty,' and listened for a while, then said, 'Really? A man with a medical background?' I didn't hear the rest of the conversation, and Beth hung up and said, 'I've got a date.' She joined Corporal Dulange in my waiting room, and they left. I looked out the window, and she was giving him the brush-off. Corporal Dulange stormed away, and

Beth walked across 6th Street and sat down at the westbound Wilshire Boulevard bus stop. That was about seven-thirty, Sunday the twelfth. There. You didn't know that last part, did you?"

I finished up my shorthand version of it. "No, I didn't."

"Will you tell the Parole Board that I gave you a valuable clue?"

Patchett opened the door. "He's clean, Bleichert."

"No shit," I said.

* * *

Another piece of Betty's missing days revealed; another trip back to the El Nido, this time to check the master file for Webster prefix phone numbers. Going through the paperwork, I kept thinking that the Spragues had a Webster number, the Wilshire bus passed within a couple of blocks of their place and Roach's "Marcy" could be a mistaken "Maddy" or "Martha." It didn't follow logically—the whole family was down at their Laguna beach house the week of Betty's disappearance, Roach was certain about the "Marcy" and I had squeezed every ounce of Dahlia knowledge out of Madeleine.

Still, the thought simmered, like some buried part of me wanted to hurt the family for the way I'd rolled in the gutter with their daughter and sucked up to their wealth. I threw out another hook to keep it going; it fell flat when confronted with logic:

When Lee Blanchard disappeared in '47, his "R," "S" and "T" files were missing; maybe the Sprague file was among them.

But there was no Sprague file, Lee did not know that the Spragues existed, I kept everything pertaining to them away from him out of a desire to keep Madeleine's lesbian bar doings under wraps.

I continued skimming the file, sweating in the hot, airless room. No Webster prefixes appeared, and I started getting nightmare flashes: Betty sitting on the westbound Wilshire bus stop, 7:30 P.M., 1/12/47, waving bye-bye Bucky, about to jump into eternity. I thought about querying the bus company, a general rousting of drivers on that route—then realized it was too cold, that any driver who remembered picking up Betty would have come forward during all the '47 publicity. I thought of calling the other numbers I'd gotten from Pacific Coast Bell—then jacked that chronologically they were off—they didn't jibe with my new knowledge of where Betty was at what time. I called Russ at the Bureau and learned that he was still in Tucson, while Harry was working crowd control up by the Hollywoodland sign. I finished my paper prowl, with a total of zero Webster prefixes. I thought of yanking Roach's PCB file, nixing the notion immediately. Downtown L.A., Madison prefix to Webster, was *not* a toll call—there would be no record, ditto on the Biltmore listings.

It came on then, big and ugly: bye-bye Bleichert at the bus stop, adios shitbird, has-been, never-was, stool pigeon niggertown harness bull. You traded a good woman for skunk pussy, you've turned everything that's been handed you to pure undiluted shit, your "I will's" amount to the eighth round at the Academy gym when you stepped into a Blanchard right hand—pratfalling into another pile of shit, clover that you turned to horse dung. Bye-bye Betty, Beth, Betsy, Liz, we were a couple of tramps, too bad we didn't meet before 39th and Norton, it just might have worked, maybe *us* would've been the one thing we wouldn't have fucked up past redemption—

I bolted downstairs, grabbed the car and rolled code three civilian, peeling rubber and grinding gears, wishing I had red lights and siren to sanction me faster. Passing Sunset and Vine, traffic got bottlenecked: shitloads of cars turning north on Gower and Beachwood. Even from miles away I could see the Hollywoodland sign dripping with scaffolding, scores of antlike people climbing up the face of Mount Lee. The lull in movement calmed me down, gave me a destination.

I told myself it wasn't over, that I'd drive to the Bureau and wait for Russ, that with two of us we'd put the rest of it together, that all *I* had to do was get downtown.

The traffic jam got worse—film trucks were shooting straight north while motorcycle bulls held back east- and westbound vehicles. Kids walked the lanes hawking plastic Hollywoodland sign souvenirs and passing out handbills. I heard, "Keystone Kops at the Admiral! Air-cooled! See the great new revival!" A piece of paper was shoved in my face, the printed "Keystone Kops," "Mack Sennett" and "Deluxe Air-Cooled Admiral Theatre" barely registering, the photo on the bottom registering hugely loud and wrong, like your own scream.

Three Keystone Kops were standing between pillars shaped like snakes swallowing each other's tails; a wall inset with Egyptian hieroglyphics was behind them. A flapper girl was lying on a tufted divan in the right-hand corner of the picture. It was unmistakably the background that appeared in the Linda Martin/ Betty Short stag film.

I made myself sit still; I told myself that just because Emmett Sprague knew Mack Sennett in the '20s and had helped him build sets in Edendale, *this* didn't mean that he had anything to do with a 1946 smut film. Linda Martin had said the movie was shot in Tijuana; the still unfound Duke Wellington admitted making it. When traffic started moving, I hung a quick left up to the Boulevard and ditched the car; when I bought my ticket at the Admiral box office the girl recoiled from me—and I saw that I was hyperventilating and rank with sweat.

Inside, the air-conditioning froze that sweat, so that my clothes felt like an ice dressing. Final credits were rolling on the screen, replaced immediately by new opening ones, superimposed on papier mâché pyramids. I balled my fists when "Emmett Sprague, Assistant Director," flashed; I held my breath for a title that said where the thing was shot. Then a printed prologue came on, and I settled into an aisle seat to watch.

The story was something about the Keystone Kops transplanted to biblical days; the action was chases and pie throwing and kicks in the ass. The stag film set recurred several times, confirmed by more details each showing. The exterior shots looked like the Hollywood Hills, but there were no outside-inside scenes to pin down whether the set was in a studio or a private dwelling. I knew what I was going to do, but I wanted another hard fact to buttress all the logical "What if's" that were stacking up inside me.

The movie dragged on interminably; I shivered from icy sweats. Then the end titles rolled, "Filmed in Hollywood, U.S.A.," and the "What if's" fell like tenpins.

I left the theater, shaking from the blast-oven heat outside. I saw that I'd left the El Nido without either my service revolver or off-duty .45, took side streets back and grabbed the handcannon. Then I heard, "Hey, fella. Are you Officer Bleichert?"

It was the next-door tenant, standing in the hallway holding the phone at the end of its cord. I made a running grab for it, blurting, "Russ?"

"It's Harry. I'm up at the end of B-B-Beachwood Drive. They're tearing down a b-bunch of b-bungalows, and t-t-this patrolman f-f-found t-this shack all b-b-b-bloodstained. T-T-There was an FI card filed up here on the twelfth and th-th-thirteenth and I-I-I—"

And Emmett Sprague owned property up there; and it was the first time I'd heard Harry stutter in the afternoon. "I'll bring my evidence kit. Twenty minutes."

I hung up, took the Betty Short print abstract from the file and ran down to the car. Traffic had slackened; in the distance I could see the Hollywoodland sign missing its last two letters. I hauled east to Beachwood Drive, then north. As I approached the park area that bordered Mount Lee, I saw that all the excitement was contained behind ropes guarded by a cordon of bluesuits; double-parking, I glimpsed Harry Sears walking over, badge pinned to his coat front.

His breath was now rife with liquor, the stutter gone. "Jesus Christ, what a piece of luck. This foot hack was assigned to clear out the vagrants before they started the demolitions. He stumbled onto the shack and came down and got me. It looks like tramps have been in and out since '47, but maybe you could still forensic it."

I grabbed my evidence kit; Harry and I walked uphill. Wrecking crews were tearing down bungalows on the street paralleling Beachwood, the workers shouting about gas leaking from pipes. Fire trucks stood by, hoses manned and pointed at huge rubble heaps. Bulldozers and earthmovers were lined up on the sidewalks, with patrolmen shepherding the locals out of potential harm's way. And up ahead of us, vaudeville reigned.

A system of pulleys was attached to the face of Mount Lee, supported by high scaffolding sunk into the ground at its base. The "A" of Hollywoodland, some fifty feet high, was sliding down a thick wire while cameras rolled, photographs snapped, rubberneckers gawked and political types drank champagne. Dust from uprooted scrub bushes was everywhere; the Hollywood High School band sat in folding chairs on a jerry-built bandstand a few feet from the pulley wire's terminus. When the letter "A" crashed to the dirt, they struck up "Hooray for Hollywood."

Harry said, "This way." We veered off on a dirt hiking trail circling the foot of the mountain. Dense foliage pressed in from both sides; Harry took the lead, walking sideways on a footpath pointing straight up the slope. I followed, scrub bushes snagging my clothes and brushing my face. After fifty uphill yards, the path leveled off into a small clearing fronted by a shallow stream of running water. And there was a tiny, pillbox-style cinderblock hut, the door standing wide open.

I walked in.

The side walls were papered with pornographic photographs of crippled and disfigured women. Mongoloid faces sucking dildoes, nudie girls with withered and brace-clad legs spread wide, limbless atrocities leering at the camera. There was a mattress on the floor; it was caked with layers and layers of blood. Bugs and flies were laced throughout the crust, stuck there as they feasted themselves to death. The back wall held tacked-on color photos that looked like they were torn from anatomy texts: close-up shots of diseased organs oozing blood and pus. There were spray and spatter marks on the floor; a small spotlight attached to a tripod was stationed beside the mattress, the light fixture aimed at the center of it. I wondered about electricity, then examined the gizmo's base and saw a battery hook-up. A blood-sprayed stack of books rested in one corner—mostly science fiction novels, with *Gray's Advanced Anatomy* and Victor Hugo's *The Man Who Laughs* standing out among them.

"Bucky?"

I turned around. "Go get ahold of Russ. Tell him what we've got. I'll do a forensic here."

"Russ won't get back from Tucson till tomorrow. And kid, you don't look too healthy to me right—"

"Goddamn it, get out of here and let me do this!"

Harry stormed out, spitting crushed pride; I thought of the proximity to Sprague property and dreamer Georgie Tilden, bum shack dweller, son of a famous Scottish anatomist. "Really? A man with a medical background?" Then I opened up my kit and raped the nightmare crib for evidence.

First I examined it top to bottom. Aside from obviously recent mud tracks—Harry's tramps probably—I found narrow strands of rope under the mattress. I scraped what looked like abraded flesh particles off them; I filled up another test tube with blood-matted dark hair taken from the mattress. I checked the blood crust for different color shadings, saw that it was a uniform maroon and took a dozen samples. I tagged and packed the rope away, along with the anatomy pages and smut pictures. I saw a man's bootprint, blood-outlined, on the floor, measured it and traced the sole treads onto a sheet of transparent paper.

Next it was fingerprints.

I dusted every touch, grab and press surface in the room; I dusted the few smooth spines and glossy pages in the books on the floor. The books yielded only streaks; the other surfaces brought up smudges, glove marks and two separate and distinct sets of latents. Finishing, I took a pen and circled the smaller digits on the door, doorjamb and wall molding by the mattress headboard. Then I got out my magnifying glass and Betty Short's print blow-up and made comparisons.

One identical print;

Two;

Three—enough for a courtroom.

Four, five, six, my hands shaking because this was unimpeachably where the Black Dahlia was butchered, shaking so hard I couldn't transfer the other set of latents to plates. I hacked a four-digit spread off the door with my knife and wrapped it in tissue—forensic amateur night. I packed up my kit, tremble-walked outside, saw the running water and knew that was where the killer drained the body. Then a strange flash of color by some rocks next to the stream caught my eye.

A baseball bat—the business end stained dark maroon.

I walked to the car thinking of Betty alive, happy, in love with some guy who'd never cheat on her. Passing through the park, I looked up at Mount Lee. The sign now read just *Hollywood*; the band was playing, "There's No Business Like Show Business."

* * *

I drove downtown. The L.A. city personnel office and the office of the Immigration and Naturalization Service were closed for the day. I called R&I and got goose egg on Scotland-born George Tildens—and I knew I'd go crazy if I waited overnight to make the print confirmation. It came down to calling in a superior officer, breaking and entering or bribery.

Remembering a janitor cleaning up outside the personnel office, I tried number three. The old man heard my phony story out, accepted my double-sawbuck, unlocked the door and led me to a bank of filing cabinets. I opened a drawer marked CITY PROPERTY CUSTODIAL—PART-TIME, got out my magnifying glass and powder-dusted piece of wood—and held my breath.

Tilden, George Redmond, born Aberdeen, Scotland, 3/4/1896. 5 foot 11, 185 pounds, brown hair, green eyes. No address, listed as "Transient—contact for work thru E. Sprague, WE-4391." California Driver's license # L.A. 68224, vehicle: 1939 Ford pickup, license 6B119A, rubbish-hauling territory Manchester to

Jefferson, La Brea to Hoover—39th and Norton right in the middle of it. Left- and right-hand fingerprints at the bottom of the page; one, two, three, four, five, six, seven, eight, nine matching comparison points—three for a conviction, six more for a one-way to the gas chamber. Hello, Elizabeth.

I closed the drawer, gave the janitor an extra ten-spot to keep him quiet, packed up the evidence kit and walked outside. I pinpointed the moment: 8:10 P.M., Wednesday, June 29, 1949, the night a flunky harness bull cracked the most famous unsolved homicide in California history. I touched the grass to see if it felt different, waved at office workers passing by, pictured myself breaking the news to the padre and Thad Green and Chief Horrall. I saw myself back at the Bureau, a lieutenant inside of a year, Mr. Ice exceeding the wildest Fire and Ice expectations. I saw my name in the headlines, Kay coming back to me. I saw the Spragues squeezed dry, disgraced by their complicity in the killing, all their money useless. And *that* was what kiboshed my reverie: there was no way for me to make the arrest without admitting I suppressed evidence on Madeleine and Linda Martin back in '47. It was either anonymous glory or public disaster.

Or back-door justice.

I drove to Hancock Park. Ramona's Cadillac and Martha's Lincoln were gone from the circular driveway; Emmett's Chrysler and Madeleine's Packard remained. I parked my lackluster Chevy crossways next to them, the rear tires sunk into the gardener's rose bush border. The front door looked impregnable, but a side window was open. I hoisted myself up and into the living room.

Balto the stuffed dog was there by the fireplace, guarding a score of packing crates lined up on the floor. I checked them out; they were filled to the top with clothes, silverware and ritzy bone china. A cardbox box at the end of the row was overflowing with cheap cocktail dresses—a weird anomaly. A sketch pad, the top sheet covered with drawings of women's faces, was wedged into one corner. I thought of commerical artist Martha, then heard voices upstairs.

I went to them, my .45 out, the silencer screwed on tight. They were coming from the master bedroom: Emmett's burr, Madeleine's pout. I pressed myself to the hallway wall, eased down to the doorway and listened.

"... besides, one of my foremen said the goddamn pipes are spewing gas. There'll be hell to pay, lassie. Health and safety code violations at the very least. It's time for me to show the three of you Scotland, and let our Jew friend Mickey C. utilize his talent for public relations. He'll put the onus on old Mack or the pinkos or some convenient stiff, trust me he will. And when things are kosher again, we'll come home."

"But I don't *want* to go to Europe, Daddy. Oh God, *Scotland*. You've never been able to talk about it without saying how dreadful and provincial it is."

"Is it your toothy chum you think you'll be missing? Ahh, I suspect it is. Well, let me put your heart to rest. Aberdeen's got strapping plowboys who'll put that piss-poor excuse for a man to shame. Less inquisitive, lads who know their place. You'll not lack for sturdy cocksmen, let me assure you. Bleichert served his purpose to us a long time ago, and it's just the danger-loving part of you that took him back in. An injudicious part, I might add."

"Oh Daddy, I don't—"

I wheeled and stepped into the bedroom. Emmett and Madeleine were lying on the big canopied bed, clothed, her head on his lap, his rough carpenter's hands massaging her shoulders. The father-lover noticed me first; Madeleine pouted when Daddy's caresses stopped. My shadow hit the bed; she screamed.

Emmett silenced her, a whip-fast hand glinting with gemstones over her mouth. He said, "This isn't a cuckold, lad. It's just affection, and we've a dispensation for it."

The man's reflexes and dinner table tone were pure style. I aped his calm: "Georgie Tilden killed Elizabeth Short. She called here on January twelfth, and one of you fixed her up with Georgie. She took the Wilshire bus out here to meet him. Now you fill the rest of it in."

Madeleine, eyes wide, trembled under her father's hand. Emmett looked at the none too steady gun aimed at him. "I don't dispute that statement and I don't dispute your somewhat belated desire to see justice done. Shall I tell you where George can be found?"

"No. First you tell me about you two, then you tell me about your dispensation."

"It's not germane, lad. I'll congratulate you on your detective work and tell you where Georgie can be found, and we'll leave it at that. Neither of us wants to see Maddy hurt, and discussing dour old family matters would affect her adversely."

As if to underline paternal concern, Emmett released his hand. Madeleine wiped smeared lipstick off her cheeks and murmured, "Daddy, make him stop."

I said, "Did Daddy tell you to fuck me? Did Daddy tell you to invite me to dinner so I wouldn't check your alibi? Did you all figure that a little hospitality and some cunt would brazen things out for you? Did you—"

"Daddy make him stop!"

Emmett's whip hand flashed again; Madeleine buried her face in it. The Scotchman made the next logical move. "Let's get down to brass tacks, lad. Put the Sprague family history out of your mind. What do you want?"

I looked around the bedroom, picking out objects—and the price tags that Madeleine had bragged to me. There was the Picasso oil on the back wall—a hundred and twenty grand. Two Ming vases resting on the dresser—seventeen big ones. The Dutch Master above the headboard cost two hundred odd thou; the ugly Pre-Columbian gargoyle on the nightstand a cool twelve and a half. Emmett, smiling now, said, "You appreciate nice things. I appreciate that, and nice things like those can be yours. Just tell me what you want."

I shot the Picasso first. The silencer went "Pffft" and the .45 hollow point blew the canvas in half. The two Mings were next, crockery fragments exploding all over the room. I missed the gargoyle with my first shot—a gold-bordered mirror the consolation prize. Daddy and darling daughter huddled on the bed; I took sight on Rembrandt or Titian or whoever the fuck it was. My bull's-eye blew a dandy hole out of it, along with a chunk of the wall. The frame toppled and hit Emmett's shoulder; the heat of the weapon singed my hand. I held on to it anyway, one round still in the chamber to get me my story.

Cordite, muzzle smoke and plaster haze making the air almost unbreathable. Four hundred grand in bits and pieces. The two Spragues a tangle of limbs on the bed, Emmett coming out of it first, stroking Madeleine, rubbing his eyes and squinting.

I placed the silencer to the back of his head. "You, Georgie, Betty. Make me believe it or I'll take your whole fucking house down."

Emmett coughed and patted Madeleine's stray curls; I said, "You and your own daughter."

My old brass girl looked up then, tears drying, dust and lipstick mottling her face. "Daddy's not my real daddy and we've never really ... so it's not wrong."

I said, "Then who is?"

Emmett turned, gently pushing my gun hand out of the way. He didn't look broken or angry. He looked like a businessman warming to the task of negotiating a tough new contract. "Dreamer Georgie is Maddy's father, Ramona is her mother. Do you want the details, or will that fact suffice?"

I sat down in a silk brocade chair a few feet from the bed. "All of it. And don't lie, because I'll know."

Emmett stood up and tidied his person, giving the room damage a weather eye. Madeleine went into the bathroom; a few seconds later I heard water running. Emmett sat on the edge of the bed, hands firm on his knees, like it was man-to-man confessional time. I knew he thought he could get away with telling me only what he wanted to; I knew I was going to make him spill it all, whatever it took.

"Back in the mid-20's Ramona wanted a child," he said. "I didn't, and I got damn sick and tired of being nagged about fatherhood. One night I got drunk and thought, 'Mother, you want a child I'll give you a lad just like me.' I did her without wearing a skin, sobered up and put it out of my mind. I didn't know it, but she took up with Georgie then, just to get that foal she craved so dearly. Madeleine was born, and I thought she was from that one mean time. I took to her—my little girl. Two years later I decided to go for a matched set, and we made Martha.

"Lad, I know you've killed two men, which is more than I can brag. So I know you know what it is to hurt. Maddy was eleven when I realized she was the stark spitting image of Georgie. I found him and played tic-tac-toe on his face with a nigger shiv. When I thought he'd die I took him to the hospital and bribed the administrators into putting 'car crash victim' on their records. When Georgie got out of the hospital he was a pitiful disfigured wreck. I begged him to forgive me, and I gave him money and I got him work tending my property and hauling rubbish for the city."

I recalled thinking that Madeleine resembled neither of her parents; I remembered Jane Chambers mentioning Georgie's car crash and descent to stumblebum. So far, I believed Emmett's story. "What about Georgie himself? Did you ever think he was crazy? Dangerous?"

Emmett tapped my knee, man-to-man empathy. "Georgie's father was Redmond Tilden, quite a celebrated doctor in Scotland. He was an anatomist. The Kirk was still strong in Aberdeen back then, and Doc Redmond could only legally dissect the corpses of executed criminals and the child molesters the villagers caught and stoned. Georgie liked to touch the organs his dad threw out. I heard a tale when we were boys, and I credit it. It seems that Doc Redmond bought a stiff from some body snatchers. He cut into the heart, and it was still beating. Georgie saw it, and it thrilled him. I credit the tale because in the Argonne Georgie used to take his bayonet to the dead Jerries. I'm not sure, but I think he's burgled graves here in America. Scalps and inside organs. Ghastly, all of it."

I saw an opening, a stab in the dark that might hit home. Jane Chambers had mentioned Georgie and Ramona filming pageants that centered on Emmett's World War I adventures, and two years ago at dinner, Ramona had said something about "Reenacting episodes out of Mr. Sprague's past he would rather forget." I swung out with my hunch: "How could you put up with someone so crazy?"

Emmett said, "You've been idolized in your time, lad. You know how it is when a weak man needs you to look after him. It's a special bond, like having a daft little brother."

I said, "I had a daft big brother once. I looked up to him."

Emmett laughed—fraudulently. "That's a side of the fence I've never been on."

"Oh yeah? Eldridge Chambers says otherwise. He left a brief with the City Council before he died. It seems that he witnessed some of Ramona and Georgie's pageants back in the thirties. Little girls with soldier kilts and toy muskets, Georgie holding off the Germans, you turning tail and running like a goddamn chickenshit coward."

Emmett flushed and tried to dredge up a smirk; his mouth twitched spastically with the effort. I shouted, "Coward!" and slapped him full force—and the hardcase Scotchman son of a bitch sobbed like a child. Madeleine came out of the bathroom, fresh makeup, clean clothes. She moved to the bed and embraced her "Daddy," holding him the way he'd held her just a few minutes before.

I said, "Tell me, Emmett."

The man wept on the shoulder of his ersatz daughter; she stroked him with ten times more tenderness than she'd ever given me. Finally he got out a shell-shocked whisper: "I couldn't let Georgie go because he saved my life. We got separated from our company, all alone in a big field of stiffs. A German patrol was reconnoitering, sticking bayonets in everything British, dead or alive. Georgie piled Germans on top of us. They were all in pieces from a mortar attack. Georgie made me crawl under all these arms and legs and guts and stay there, and when it was over he cleaned me up and talked about America to cheer me up. So you see I couldn't ..."

Emmett's whisper died out. Madeleine caressed his shoulders, ruffled his hair. I said, "I know that the stag film with Betty and Linda Martin wasn't shot in TJ. Did Georgie have anything to do with it?"

Madeleine's voice had the timbre Emmett's had earlier, when he was the one holding up the front. "No. Linda and I were talking at La Verne's Hideaway. She told me she needed a place to make a little movie. I knew what she meant, and I wanted to be with Betty again, so I let them use one of my daddy's vacant houses, one that had an old set in the living room. Betty and Linda and Duke Wellington shot the movie, and Georgie saw them doing it. He was always sneaking around Daddy's empty houses, and he got crazy over Betty. Probably because she looked like me ... his daughter."

I turned away to make it easier for her to spill the rest. "Then?"

"Then, around Thanksgiving, Georgie came to Daddy and said, 'Give me that girl.' He said he'd tell the whole world that Daddy wasn't my daddy, and he'd lie about what we did together, like it was incest. I looked around for Betty, but I couldn't find her. Later I found out she was in San Diego then. Daddy was letting Georgie stay in the garage, because he was making more and more demands. He gave him money to keep him quiet, but he was still acting nasty and awful.

"Then, that Sunday night, Betty called, out of the blue. She'd been drinking, and she called me Mary or something like that. She said she'd been calling all the friends in her little black book trying to get a loan. I put Daddy on, and he offered Betty money to date a nice man he knew. You see, we thought Georgie just wanted Betty for ... sex."

I said, "After all you knew about him, you believed that?"

Emmett shouted, "He liked to touch dead things! He was passive! I didn't think he was a goddamned killer!"

I eased them into the rest. "And you told her Georgie had a medical background?"

"Because Betty respected doctors," Madeleine said. "Because we didn't want her to feel like a whore."

I almost laughed. "Then?"

"Then I think you know the rest."

"Tell me anyway."

Madeleine delivered, hate oozing out of her. "Betty took the bus out here. She and Georgie left. We thought they'd go someplace decent to be together."

"Like the Red Arrow Motel?"

"No! Like one of Daddy's old houses that Georgie took care of! Betty forgot her purse, so we thought she'd be back for it, but she never came back and neither did Georgie, and then the papers came out and we knew what must have happened."

If Madeleine thought her confession was over, she was wrong. "Tell me what you did then. How you covered things up."

Madeleine caressed Emmett while she spoke. "I went looking for Linda Martin, and I found her at a motel in the Valley. I gave her money and told her that if the police picked her up and asked her about the movie she was to say it was filmed in Tijuana with a Mexican crew. She kept her part of the bargain when you captured her, and she only mentioned the movie because she had the print in her purse. I tried to find Duke Wellington, but I couldn't. That worried me, then he sent in his alibi to the *Herald-Express*, and it didn't mention where the movie was shot. So we were safe. Then—"

"Then I came along. And you pumped me for dope on the case, and you threw me little tidbits about Georgie to see if I bit."

Madeleine quit stroking Daddy and studied her manicure. "Yes."

"What about the alibi you gave me? Laguna Beach, check with the servants?"

"We gave them money in case you actually did check. They don't speak English too well, and of course you believed me."

Madeleine was smiling now. I said, "Who mailed Betty's pictures and little black book in? There were envelopes sent, and you said Betty left her purse here."

Madeleine laughed. "That was genius sister Martha. She knew I knew Betty, but she wasn't home that night Betty and Georgie were here. She didn't know Georgie was blackmailing Daddy or that he killed Betty. She ripped the page with our number on it out of the book, and she scratched the faces off the men in the pictures as her way of saying, 'Look for a lesbian,' namely me. She just wanted me smeared, implicated. She also called the police and gave them a tip on La Verne's. The scratched faces were très genius Martha—she always scratches like a cat when she's mad."

Something in her statement hit me as wrong, but I couldn't pin it down. "Martha told you this?"

Madeleine buffed her red claws. "When the little black book stuff made the papers, I knew it had to be Martha. I scratched a confession out of her."

I turned to Emmett. "Where's Georgie?"

The old man stirred. "He's probably staying at one of my vacant houses. I'll bring you a list."

"Bring me all four of your passports, too."

Emmett walked out of the battlefield bedroom. Madeleine said, "I really did like you, Bucky. I really did."

"Save it for Daddy. You're wearing the pants now, so save the sugar for him."

"What are you going to do?"

"First I'm going home and putting all of this on paper, attached to material witness warrants for you and Daddy. Then I'm leaving them with another officer in case Daddy goes to his friend Mickey Cohen with an offer for my head. Then I'm going after Georgie."

Emmett came back and handed me four U.S. passport holders and a sheet of paper. Madeleine said, "If you turn in those warrants, we'll ruin you in court. Everything about us will come out."

I stood up and kissed the brass girl hard on the lips. "Then we'll all go down together."

*   *   *

I didn't drive home to write it all out. I parked a few blocks from the Sprague manse and studied the list of addresses, spooked by the juice Madeleine had shown, by her sense of how deep our stalemate went.

The houses were situated in two locales: Echo Park and Silverlake, and across town in Watts—bad territory for a fifty-three-year-old white man. Silverlake-Echo was several miles due east of Mount Lee, a hilly area with lots of twisting streets, greenery and seclusion, the kind of terrain a necrophiliac might find soothing. I drove there, five addresses circled on Emmett's sheet.

The first three were plain deserted shacks: no electricity, broken windows, Mexican gang slogans painted on the walls. No '39 Ford pickup 6B119A nearby—only desolation accompanied by Santa Ana winds blowing down from the Hollywood Hills. Heading toward the fourth pad just after midnight was when I got the idea—or the idea got me.

Kill him.

No public glory, no public disgrace—private justice. Let the Spragues go or coerce a detailed confession out of Georgie before you pull the trigger. Get it on paper, then figure out a way to hurt them with it at your leisure.

Kill him.

And try to live with it.

And try to lead a normal life with Mickey Cohen's good pal running the same type of schemes on you.

I put it all out of mind when I saw that the fourth house was intact at the dead end of a cul-de-sac—chaste exterior, the lawn neatly tended. I parked two doors down, then prowled the street on foot. There were no Ford trucks—and plenty of curbside spaces for them.

I studied the house from the sidewalk. It was a '20s stucco job, small, cube-shaped, off-white with a wood-beam roof. I circled it, driveway to tiny backyard and around a flagstone path to the front. No lights—the windows were all covered with what looked like thick blackout curtains. The place was utterly silent.

Gun out, I rang the buzzer. Twenty seconds, no answer. I ran my fingers down the door-doorjamb meeting point, felt cracked wood, got out my handcuffs and wedged in the narrow part of one ratchet. The teeth held; I whittled at the wood near the lock until I felt the door play slacken. Then I gave it a gentle kick—and it opened.

Light from outside guided me to a wall switch; I flipped it on, saw a cobweb-streaked empty room, walked to the porch and shut the door. The blackout curtains held in every bit of illumination. I moved back into the house, closed the door and stuck wood slivers into the bolt fixture to jam the lock.

With front access blocked off, I walked to the rear of the house. A medicinal stench was issuing from a room adjoining the kitchen. I toed the door open and tapped the inside wall for a switch. I hit one; harsh light blinded me. Then my vision cleared and I placed the smell: formaldehyde.

The walls were lined with shelves holding jars of preserved organs; there was a mattress on the floor, half covered by an army blanket. A red-headed scalp and two notebooks lay on top of it. I took a wheezing breath and forced myself to see it *all*.

Brains, eyes, hearts and intestines floating in fluid. A woman's hand, wedding ring still attached to her finger. Ovaries, globs of shapeless viscera, a jar filled with penises. Gum sections replete with gold teeth.

I felt dry heaves coming on, and squatted by the mattress so I wouldn't have to see any more gore. I picked up one of the notebooks and leafed through it; the pages were filled with neatly typed descriptions of grave robberies—cemeteries, plot names and dates in separate columns. When I saw "East Los Angeles Lutheran," where my mother was buried, I dropped the book and reached for the blanket for something to hold; crusted semen top to bottom made me throw it at the doorway. I opened the other binder to the middle then, neat masculine printing taking me back to January 14, 1947:

> *When she woke up Tuesday morning I knew she couldn't take much more and I knew I couldn't risk staying in the hills much longer. Derelicts and lovebirds were sure to be out and about sooner or later. I could tell she was so damn proud of her little titties even while I took Chesterfields to them yesterday. I decided to cut them off slowly.*
>
> *She was still in a stupor, maybe even shock. I showed her the Joe DiMaggio Louisville Slugger which had given me so much pleasure since Sunday night. I teased her with it. That took her out of her shock. I poked it at her little hole and she almost swallowed her gag. I wished there were nails to put in it, like the iron maiden or a chastity belt she would not soon forget. I held the bat in front of her, then I opened up a cigarette burn on her left tittie with my knife. She bit on her gag and blood from where I took the Joe DiMaggio to her teeth came out due to her biting so hard. I stuck the knife down to a little bone I felt, then I twisted it. She tried to scream and the gag slipped deeper into her throat. I pulled it out for one second and she yelled for her mother. I put it back in hard and cut her again on the right tittie.*

*She's getting infected where's she's tied up now. The ropes
are cutting her ankles and they're squishy with pus ..."*

I put the notebook down, knowing I could do it, knowing if
I faltered, a few more pages would turn me around. I stood up;
the organ jars caught my attention, dead things all in a row, so
neat, so perfect. I was wondering whether Georgie had ever
killed before when I noticed a jar all by itself on the window
ledge above the head of the mattress.

A triangular piece of flesh, tattooed. A heart with the Army
Air Corps insignia inside it, the words "Betty & Major Matt"
below.

I closed my eyes and shook head to toe; I wrapped my arms
around myself and tried to tell Betty I was sorry I'd seen that
special part of her, that I didn't mean to pry so far, that I was just
trying to help. I tried to say it and say it and say it. Then something touched me softly, and I was grateful for the gentleness.

I turned around and saw a man, his face all scars, his hands
holding little hooked instruments, tools for cutting and probing.
He touched the scalpels to his cheeks; I gasped at where I'd been
and reached for my gun. Twin streaks of steel lashed at me; the .45
slipped out of my waistband and hit the floor.

I sidestepped; the blades snagged my jacket and ripped a piece
of my collarbone. I sent a kick at Tilden's groin; the grave raper
caught the blow off balance, buckled and leaped forward, crashing into me, knocking me back into the wall shelving.

Jars broke, formaldehyde sprayed, awful pieces of flesh were
loosed. Tilden was right on top of me, trying to bring his scalpels down. I held his wrists up, then shot a knee between his
legs. He grunted but didn't retreat, his face getting closer and
closer to mine. Inches away, he bared his teeth and snapped; I
felt my cheek tearing. I kneed him again, his arm pressure slackened, I caught another bite on the chin, then dropped my hands.
The scalpels hit the shelf in back of me; I flailed for a weapon
and touched a big piece of glass. I dug it into Georgie's face just
as he yanked the blades free; he screamed; steel dug into my
shoulder.

The shelving collapsed. Georgie fell on top of me, blood
pouring from an empty eye socket. I saw my .45 on the floor a
few feet away, dragged the two of us there and grabbed it. Georgie raised his head, making animal screeches. He went for my

throat, his mouth huge in front of me. I jammed the silencer into his eye hole and blew his brains out.

33

RUSS MILLARD supplied the Short case epitaph.

Adrenaline-fried, I left the death house and drove straight to City Hall. The padre had just gotten in from Tucson with his prisoner; when the man was ensconced in a holding cell, I took Russ aside and told him the entire story of my involvement with the Spragues—from Marjorie Graham's lez tip to the shooting of Georgie Tilden. Russ, dumbstruck at first, drove me to Central Receiving Hospital. The emergency room doc gave me a tetanus shot, said, "God, those bites look almost human," and sutured them up. The scalpel wounds were superficial—and required only cleansing and bandaging.

Outside, Russ said, "The case has to stay open. You'll be canned from the Department if you tell anyone else what happened. Now let's go take care of Georgie."

It was 3:00 A.M. when we got to Silverlake. The padre was shaken by what he saw, but held his composure ramrod stiff. Then the best man I ever knew astonished me.

First he said, "Go over and stand by the car"; then he fiddled with some pipes on the side of the house, paced off twenty yards and emptied his service revolver at the spot. Gas ignited; the house went up in flames. We highballed out of there without headlights. Russ shot me his line: "That obscenity did not deserve to stand."

Then it was incredible exhaustion—and sleep. Russ dropped me at the El Nido, I dived onto the bed and into twenty-odd hours of pitch-black unconsciousness. Waking up, the first thing I saw was the four Sprague passports on the dresser: the first thing I thought was: *they have to pay.*

If health and safety code violations or worse came down, I wanted the family in the country where they would suffer. I called the U.S. passport office, impersonated a detective captain and put a police hold on passport reissues for all four Spragues. It felt like an impotent gesture—a slap on the wrist. I shaved and showered then, extra careful not to wet my bandages or sutures. I thought about the end of the case so I wouldn't think about the shambles my life was in. I recalled that something Madeleine said the other day was off, wrong, out of sync. I played with the question while I dressed; going out the door to get something to eat, it hit home:

Madeleine said that Martha called the police with a tip on La Verne's Hideaway. But: I knew the Short case paperwork better then any cop alive, and there were no notations anywhere pertaining to the place. Two incidents sparked me then. Lee getting a long call during our phone-answering stint the morning after I met Madeleine; Lee going directly to La Verne's after he cracked up at the stag film showing. Only "Genius" Martha could give me answers. I drove to Ad Agency Row to brace her.

* * *

I found Emmett Sprague's real daughter alone, eating lunch on a bench in the shade of the Young & Rubicam Building. She didn't look up when I sat down across from her; I remembered that Betty Short's little black book and pictures were taken out of a mailbox a block away.

I watched the pudgy girl-woman nibble a salad and read the newspaper. In the two and a half years since I'd seen her she'd held her own against fat and bad skin—but she still looked like a tough distaff version of Emmett.

Martha put the paper down and noticed me. I expected rage to light up her eyes; she surprised me by saying, "Hello, Mr. Bleichert," with just a touch of a smile.

I walked over and sat down beside her. The *Times* was folded over to a Metro section piece: "Bizarre Fire in Silverlake Foothills—Body Found Charred Beyond Recognition."

Martha said, "I'm sorry for that picture I drew of you that night you came to dinner."

I pointed to the newspaper. "You don't seem surprised to see me."

"Poor Georgie. No, I'm not surprised to see you. Father told me you knew. I've been underestimated all my life, and I always had a feeling Maddy and Father were underestimating you."

I pushed the compliment aside. "Do you know what 'Poor Georgie' did?"

"Yes. From the beginning. I saw Georgie and the Short girl leave the house that night in Georgie's truck. Maddy and Father didn't know I knew, but I did. Only Mother never figured it out. Did you kill him?"

I didn't answer.

"Are you going to hurt my family?"

The pride in the "my" knifed me. "I don't know what I'm going to do."

"I don't blame you for wanting to hurt them. Father and Maddy are dreadful people, and I went way out on a limb to hurt them myself."

"When you sent in Betty's things?"

Now Martha's eyes fired up. "Yes. I tore out the page in the book that had our number, but I thought there might be other numbers to lead the police to Father and Maddy. I didn't have the courage to send *our* number in. I should have. I—"

I held up a hand. "Why, Martha? Do you know what would have happened if the police got the whole story about Georgie? Accessory charges, court, jail."

"I didn't care. Maddy had you and Father, Mother and I had nothing. I just wanted the whole ship to sink. Mother has lupus now, she's only got a few years left. She's going to die, and that is so unfair."

"The pictures and scratch marks. What did you mean by them?"

Martha laced her fingers together and twisted them until the knuckles were white. "I was nineteen, and all I could do was draw. I wanted Maddy smeared as a dyke, and the last picture was Father himself—his face scratched out. I thought he might have left fingerprints on the back. I was desperate to hurt him."

"Because he touches you like he touches Madeleine?"

"Because he doesn't!"

I braced myself for the spooky stuff. "Martha, did you call the police with a tip on La Verne's Hideaway?"

Martha lowered her eyes. "Yes."

"Did you talk to—"

"I told the man about my dyke sister, how she met a cop named Bucky Bleichert at La Verne's last night and had a date with him tonight. Maddy was gloating to the whole family about you, and I was jealous. But I only wanted to hurt her—not you."

Lee taking the call while I sat across a desk from him in University squadroom; Lee going directly to La Verne's when *Slave Girls From Hell* drove him around the twist. I said, "Martha, you come clean on the rest of it."

Martha looked around and clenched herself—legs together, arms to her sides, fists balled. "Lee Blanchard came to the house and told Father he'd talked to women at La Verne's—lesbians who could tie Maddy in to the Black Dahlia. He said he had to leave town, and for a price he wouldn't report his information on Maddy. Father agreed, and gave him all the money he had in his safe."

Lee, Benzie-crazed, absent from City Hall and University Station; Bobby De Witt's imminent parole his reason for blowing town. Emmett's money the cash he was flaunting in Mexico. My own voice numb: "Is there more?"

Martha's body was coiled spring-tight. "Blanchard came back the next day. He demanded more money. Father turned him down, and he beat Father up and asked him all these questions about Elizabeth Short. Maddy and I heard it from the next room. I loved it and Maddy was wicked mad. She left when she couldn't take any more of her beloved daddy-poo groveling, but I kept listening. Father was afraid that Blanchard would frame one of us for the killing, so he agreed to give him a hundred thousand dollars and told him what happened with Georgie and Elizabeth Short."

Lee's bruised knuckles; his lie: "Penance for Junior Nash." Madeleine on the phone that day: "Don't come over. Daddy's having a business soiree." Our desperate rutting at the Red Arrow an hour later. *Lee filthy rich in Mexico. Lee letting Georgie Tilden go scot fucking free.*

Martha dabbed at her eyes, saw that they were dry and put a hand on my arm. "The next day a woman came by and picked up the money. And that's all of it."

I took out my wallet snapshot of Kay and showed it to her. Martha said, "Yes. That's the woman."

I stood up, alone for the first time since the triad was formed. Martha said, "Don't hurt my family anymore. Please."

I said, "Get out, Martha. Don't let them ruin you."

*   *   *

I drove to West Hollywood Elementary School, sat in the car and kept an eyeball fix on Kay's Plymouth in the faculty parking lot. Lee's ghost buzzed in my head as I waited—bad company for close to two hours. The 3:00 bell rang right on time; Kay exited the building in a swarm of children and teachers a few minutes later. When she was alone by her car, I walked over.

She was arranging a load of books and papers in the trunk, her back to me. I said, "How much of the hundred grand did Lee let you keep?"

Kay froze, her hands on a stack of fingerpaintings. "Did Lee tell you about Madeleine Sprague and me back then? Is that why you've hated Betty Short all this time?"

Kay ran her fingers over the kiddie artwork, then turned and faced me. "You are so, so good at some things."

It was another compliment I didn't want to hear. "Answer my questions."

Kay slammed the trunk, her eyes dead on mine. "I did not accept a cent of that money, and I didn't know about you and Madeleine Sprague until those detectives I hired gave me her name. Lee was going to run away no matter what. I didn't know if I'd ever see him again, and I wanted him to be comfortable, if such a thing was possible. He didn't trust himself to deal with Emmett Sprague again, so I picked up the money. Dwight, he knew I was in love with you, and he wanted us to be together. That was one of the reasons he left."

I felt like I was sinking in a quicksand of all our old lies. "He didn't leave, he *ran* from the Boulevard-Citizens job, from the frame on De Witt, from the trouble he was in with the Depart—"

"He loved us! Don't take that away from him!"

I looked around the parking lot. Teachers were standing by their cars, eyeing the husband and wife spat. They were too far away to hear; I imagined them chalking up the fight to kids or mortgages or cheating. I said, "Kay, Lee knew who killed Elizabeth Short. Did you know that?"

Kay stared at the ground. "Yes."

"He just let it go."

"Things got crazy then. Lee went down to Mexico after Bobby, and he said he'd go after the killer when he got back. But he didn't come back, and I didn't want you going down there too."

I grabbed my wife's shoulders and squeezed them until she looked at me.

"And you didn't tell me later? You didn't tell *anyone*?"

Kay lowered her head again; I jerked it back up with both my hands. "And you didn't tell anyone?"

In her calmest schoolteacher voice, Kay Lake Bleichert said, "I almost told you. But you started whoring again, collecting her pictures. I just wanted revenge on the woman who ruined the two men I loved."

I raised a hand to hit her—but a flash of Georgie Tilden stopped me.

34

I CALLED in the last of my accumulated sick leave and spent a week killing time at the El Nido. I read and played the jazz stations, trying not to think about my future. I pored over the master file repeatedly, even though I knew the case was closed. Child versions of Martha Sprague and Lee racked my dreams; sometimes Jane Chambers' slash-mouth clown joined them, hurling taunts, speaking through gaping holes in his face.

I bought all four L.A. papers every day, and read them cover to cover. The Hollywood sign hubbub had passed, there was no mention of Emmett Sprague, Grand Jury probes into faulty buildings or the torched house and stiff. I began to get a feeling that something was wrong.

It took a while—long hours spent staring at the four walls thinking of nothing—but finally I nailed it.

"It" was a tenuous hunch that Emmett Sprague set Lee and I up to kill Georgie Tilden. With me he was blatant: "Shall I tell you where Georgie can be found?"—perfectly in character for the man—I would have been more suspicious if he had tried a round-about approach. He sent Lee after Georgie immediately after Lee beat him up. Was he hoping Lee's anger would peak when he saw the Dahlia killer? Did he know of Georgie's grave robbery treasure trove—and count on it making us killing mad? Did he count on Georgie to initiate a confrontation—one that would either eliminate him or the greedy/nosy cops who were creating such a nuisance? And why? For what motive? *To protect himself?*

The theory had one huge hole: namely, the incredible, almost suicidal audacity of Emmett, not the suicidal type.

And with Georgie Tilden—the Black Dahlia killer pure and clean—nailed—there was no logical reason to pursue it. But "It" was backstopped by a tenuous loose end:

When I first coupled with Madeleine in '47, she mentioned leaving notes for Betty Short at various bars: "Your lookalike would like to meet you." I told her the act might come back to haunt her; she said, "I'll take care of it."

The most likely one to have "taken care of it" was a policeman—and I refused to. *And*, chronologically, Madeleine spoke those words right around the time Lee Blanchard made his initial blackmail demand.

It was tenuous, circumstantial and theoretical, probably just another lie or half truth or thread of useless information. A loose end unraveled by a coming-from-hunger cop whose life was built on a foundation of lies. Which was the only good reason I could think of to pursue the ghost of a chance. Without the case, I had nothing.

* * *

I borrowed Harry Sears' civilian car and ran rolling stakeouts on the Spragues for three days and nights. Martha drove to work and back home; Ramona stayed in; Emmett and Madeleine shopped and did other daytime errands. All four stuck to the manse on evenings one and two; on the third night Madeleine prowled as the Dahlia.

I tailed her to the 8th Street bar strip, to the Zimba Room, to a cadre of sailors and flyboys and ultimately the 9th and Irolo fuck pad with a navy ensign. I felt no jealousy, no sex pull this time. I listened outside room twelve and heard KMPC; the venetian blinds were down, no visual access. The only departure from Madeleine's previous MO was when she ditched her paramour at 2:00 A.M. and drove home—the light going on in Emmett's bedroom a few moments after she walked in the door.

I gave day four a pass, and returned to my surveillance spot on Muirfield Road shortly after dark that night. I was getting out of the car to give my cramped legs a breather when I heard, "Bucky? Is that you?"

It was Jane Chambers, walking a brown and white spaniel. I felt like a kid with his hand caught in the cookie jar. "Hello, Jane."

"Hello, yourself. What are you doing? Spying? Torching for Madeleine?"

I remembered our conversation on the Spragues. "Enjoying the crisp night air. How's that sound?"

"Like a lie. Want to enjoy a crisp drink at my place?"

I looked over at the Tudor fortress; Jane said, "Boy, have you got a bee in your bonnet with that family."

I laughed—and felt little aches in my bite wounds. "Boy, have you got my number. Let's go get that drink."

We walked around the corner to June Street. Jane unhooked the dog's leash; he trotted ahead of us, down the sidewalk and up the steps to the front door of the Chambers' colonial. We caught up with him a moment later; Jane opened the door. And there was my nightmare buddy—the scar-mouth clown.

I shuddered. "That goddamn thing."

Jane smiled. "Shall I wrap it up for you?"

"Please don't."

"You know, after that first time we talked about it, I looked into its history. I've been getting rid of a lot of Eldridge's things, and I was thinking about giving it to charity. It's too valuable to give away, though. It's a Frederick Yannantuono original, and it's inspired by an old classic novel—*The Man Who Laughs* by Victor Hugo. The book is about—"

There was a copy of *The Man Who Laughs* in the shack where Betty Short was killed. I was buzzing so hard I could hardly hear what Jane was saying.

"—a group of Spaniards back in the fifteenth and sixteenth centuries. They were called the Comprachicos, and they kidnapped and tortured children, then mutilated them and sold them to the aristocracy so that they could be used as court jesters. Isn't that hideous? The clown in the painting is the book's main character, Gwynplaine. When he was a child he had his mouth slashed ear to ear. Bucky, are you all right?"

MOUTH SLASHED EAR TO EAR.

I shuddered, then forced a smile. "I'm fine. The book just reminded me of something. Old stuff, just a coincidence."

Jane scrutinized me. "You don't look fine, and you want to hear another coincidence? I thought Eldridge wasn't on speaking terms with any of the family, but I found the receipt. It was Ramona Sprague who sold him the painting."

For a split second I thought Gwynplaine was spitting blood at me. Jane grabbed my arms. "Bucky, what is it?"

I found my voice. "You told me your husband bought that picture for your birthday two years ago. Right?"

"Yes. What—"

"In '47?"

"Yes. Buck—"

"What *is* your birthday?"

"January fifteenth."

"Let me see the receipt."

Jane, spooky eyed, fumbled at some papers on the end table across the hall. I stared at Gwynplaine, transposing 39th and Norton glossies against his face. Then: "Here. Now will you tell me what's going on?"

I took the piece of paper. It was purple stationery, covered with incongruously masculine block printing: "Received from Eldridge Chambers, $3500.00 for the sale of the Frederick Yannantuono painting 'The Man Who Laughs.' This receipt constitutes Mr. Chambers' proof of ownership. Ramona Cathcart Sprague, January 15, 1947."

The printing was identical to the script in the torture diary I read just before I killed Georgie Tilden.

Ramona Sprague murdered Elizabeth Short.

I grabbed Jane in a hard bear hug, then took off while she stood there looking stunned. I went back to the car, decided it was a single-o play, watched lights go on and off in the big house and sweated through a long night of reconstructions: Ramona and Georgie torturing together, separately, bisecting, divvying up the spare parts, running a two-car caravan to Leimert Park. I played every kind of variation imaginable; I ran riffs on how the thing ignited. I thought of everything but what I was going to do when I got Ramona Sprague alone.

At 8:19 Martha walked out the front door carrying an art portfolio, and drove east in her Chrysler.

At 10:37, Madeleine, valise in hand, got into her Packard and headed north on Muirfield. Emmett waved from the doorway; I decided to give him an hour or so to leave—or take him down along with his wife. Shortly after noon, he played into my hand—tooling off, his car radio humming light opera.

My month of playing house with Madeleine had taught me the servants' routine: today, Thursday, the housekeeper and gardener were off; the cook showed up at 4:30 to prepare dinner. Madeleine's valise implied some time away; Martha wouldn't return from work until 6:00. Emmett was the only wild card.

I walked across the street and reconnoitered. The front door was locked, the side windows were bolted. It was either ring the bell or B&E.

Then I heard tapping on the other side of the glass and saw a blurry white shape moving back into the living room. A few seconds later the sound of the front door opening echoed down the driveway. I walked around to meet the woman head on.

Ramona was standing in the doorway, spectral in a shapeless silk dressing gown. Her hair was a frizzy mess, her face was blotchy red and puffed up—probably from tears and sleep. Her dark brown eyes—identical in color to mine—were scary alert. She pulled a ladylike automatic from the folds of her gown and pointed it at me. She said, "You told Martha to leave me."

I slapped the gun out of her hand; it hit a straw welcome mat emblazoned with THE SPRAGUE FAMILY. Ramona gnawed at her lips; her eyes lost their focus. I said, "Martha deserves better than a murderer."

Ramona smoothed her gown and patted at her hair. I pegged the reaction as the class of a well-bred hophead. Her voice was pure cold Sprague: "You didn't tell, did you?"

I picked up the gun and put it in my pocket, then looked at the woman. She had to be jacked on a twenty-year residue of drugstore hop, but her eyes were so dark that I couldn't tell if they were pinned or not. "Are you telling me Martha doesn't know what you did?"

Ramona stood aside and bid me to enter. She said, "Emmett told me it was safe now. He said that you'd taken care of Georgie and you had too much to lose by coming back. Martha told Emmett you wouldn't hurt us, and he said you wouldn't. I believed him. He was always so accurate about business matters."

I walked inside. Except for the packing crates on the floor, the living room looked like business as usual. "Emmett sent me after Georgie, and Martha doesn't know you killed Betty Short?"

Ramona shut the door. "Yes. Emmett counted on you to take care of Georgie. He was confident that he wouldn't implicate me—the man was quite insane. Emmett is a physical coward, you see. He didn't have the courage to do it, so he sent an underling. And my God, do you honestly think I'd let Martha know what I'm capable of?"

The torture murderess was genuinely aghast that I'd impugned her as a mother. "She'll find out sooner or later. And I know she was here that night. She saw Georgie and Betty leave together."

"Martha left to visit a chum in Palm Springs an hour or so later. She was gone for the next week. Emmett and Maddy know. Martha doesn't. And my dear God, she mustn't."

"Mrs. Sprague, do you know what you've—"

"I'm not Mrs. Sprague, I'm Ramona Upshaw Cathcart! You can't tell Martha what I did or she'll leave me! She said she wants to get her own apartment, and I haven't that much more time left!"

I turned my back on the spectacle and walked around the living room, wondering what to do. I looked at the pictures on the walls: generations of kilt-clad Spragues, Cathcarts cutting the ribbons in front of orange groves and vacant lots ripe for development. There was a fat little girl Ramona wearing a corset that must have strictured her bloody. Emmett holding a dark-haired child, beaming. Glassy-eyed Ramona poising Martha's brush hand over a toy easel. Mack Sennett and Emmett giving each other the cuckold's horns. At the back of an Edendale group shot I thought I could see a young Georgie Tilden—handsome, no scars on his face.

I felt Ramona behind me, trembling. I said, "Tell me all of it. Tell me why."

* * *

Ramona sat down on a divan and spoke for three hours, her tone sometimes angry, sometimes sad, sometimes brutally detached from what she was saying. There was a table covered with tiny ceramic figurines beside her; her hands played with them constantly. I circled the walls, looking at the family pictures, feeling them meld into her story.

She met Emmett and Georgie in 1921, when they were Scottish immigrant boys on the make in Hollywood. She hated Emmett for treating Georgie like a lackey—and she hated herself for not speaking up about it. She didn't speak up because Emmett wanted to marry her—for her father's money, she knew—and she was a homely woman with slender husband prospects.

Emmett proposed. She accepted and settled into married life with the ruthless young contractor and budding real estate tycoon. Who she gradually grew to hate. Who she passively fought by gathering information.

Georgie lived in the apartment above the garage the first years they were married. She learned that he liked to touch dead things, and that Emmett reviled him for it. She took to poisoning the stray cats who trampled her garden, leaving them on Georgie's doorstep. When Emmett spurned her desire for him to give her a child, she went to Georgie and seduced him—exulting that she had the power to excite him with something alive—the fat body that Emmett derided and only plundered at odd times.

Their affair was brief, but resulted in a child—Madeleine. She lived in terror of a resemblance to Georgie asserting itself, and took to doctor-prescribed opiates. Two years later Martha was born of Emmett. This felt like a betrayal of Georgie—and she went back to poisoning stray animals for him. Emmett caught her in the act one day; he beat her for taking part in "Georgie's perversion."

When she told Georgie of the beating, he told her of saving the coward Emmett's life in the war—putting the lie to Emmett's version of the story: that *he* saved Georgie. She started planning her pageants then—how she would get back at Emmett symbolically in ways so subtle that he would never know he was being thrashed.

Madeleine cleaved to Emmett. She was the lovely child, and he doted on her. Martha became her mother's little girl—even though she was Emmett's spitting image. Emmett and Madeleine disdained Martha as a fatso and a crybaby; Ramona protected her, teaching her to draw, putting her to bed each night with admonishings not to hate her sister and father—even though she did. Protecting Martha and instructing her in the love of art became her reason for living, her strength in the intolerable marriage.

When Maddy was eleven, Emmett noted her resemblance to Georgie, and slashed her real father's face beyond recognition. Ramona fell in love with Georgie; he was now even more physically bereft than she—and she felt a parity had been achieved between them.

Georgie rebuffed her persistent advances. She came across Hugo's *The Man Who Laughs* then, and was moved by both the Comprachicos and their disfigured victims. She bought the Yannantuono painting and kept it hidden, staring at it as a memento of Georgie in her private hours.

When Maddy hit her teens she became promiscuous, sharing the details with Emmett, cuddling on the bed with him. Martha drew obscene pictures of the sister she hated; Ramona forced her to draw pastoral landscapes to keep her anger from going haywire. To get back at Emmett she staged her long-planned pageants; they spoke obliquely of his greed and cowardice. Toy houses falling down signified Emmett's jerry-built shacks crashing in the '33 earthquake; children hiding under store mannequins dressed in ersatz German uniforms portrayed Emmett the yellow. A number of parents found the pageants disturbing, and forbade their children to play with the Sprague girls. Around that time Georgie drifted out of their lives, doing his yard work and rubbish hauling, living in Emmett's abandoned houses.

Time passed. She concentrated on looking after Martha, pressing her to finish high school early, establishing funds at Otis Art Institute so that she would get special treatment. Martha thrived and excelled at Otis; Ramona lived through her accomplishments, on and off sedatives, often thinking of Georgie—missing him, wanting him.

Then, in the fall of '46, Georgie returned. She overheard him make his blackmail demand of Emmett: "Give him" the girl in the dirty movie, or risk exposure of a good deal of the family's sordid past and present.

She became frighteningly jealous and hateful of "that girl," and when Elizabeth Short showed up at the Sprague house on January 12, 1947, her rage exploded. "That girl" looked so much like Madeleine that it felt like the cruelest of jokes was being played on her. When Elizabeth and Georgie left in his truck, she saw that Martha had gone to her room to pack for her Palm Springs trip. She left a note on her door saying good-bye, that she was sleeping now. Then she casually asked Emmett where "that girl" and Georgie were going.

He told her he heard Georgie mention one of his abandoneds up on North Beachwood. She went out the backdoor, grabbed their spare Packard, sped to Hollywoodland and waited. Georgie and the girl arrived at the base of the Mount Lee park area a few minutes later. She followed them on foot to the shack in the woods. They went inside; she saw a light go on. It cast shadows over a shiny wood object leaning against a tree trunk—a baseball bat. When she heard the girl giggle, "Did you get those scars in the war?" she went in the door, bat first.

Elizabeth Short tried to run. She knocked her unconscious and made Georgie strip her and gag her and tie her to the mattress. She promised him parts of the girl to keep forever. She took a copy of *The Man Who Laughs* from her purse and read aloud from it, casting occasional glances at the girl spread-eagled. Then she cut her and burned her and batted her and wrote in the notebook she always carried while the girl was passed out from the pain. Georgie watched, and together they shouted the chants of the Comprachicos. And after two full days of it, she slashed Elizabeth Short ear to ear like Gwynplaine, so she wouldn't hate her after she was dead. Georgie cut the body in two, washed the halves in the stream outside the shack and carried them to her car. Late at night, they drove to 39th and Norton—a lot that Georgie used to tend for the city. They left Elizabeth Short there to become the Black Dahlia, then she drove Georgie back to his truck and returned to Emmett and Madeleine, telling them that soon enough they would find out where she had been and finally respect her will. As an act of purging, she sold her Gwynplaine painting to the bargain-loving art worshipper Eldridge Chambers down the street—making a profit on the deal. Then it was days and weeks of the horror that Martha would find out and hate her—and more and more laudanum and codeine and sleep potion to make it go away.

* * *

I was looking at a row of framed magazine ads—award-winning Martha artwork—when Ramona stopped talking. The silence jarred me; her story rolled on in my head, back and forth in sequence. The room was cool—but I was sweating.

Martha's 1948 Advertising Council first prizer featured a handsome guy in a seersucker suit walking on the beach, ogling a blonde dish sunbathing. He was so oblivious to everything else around him that he was about to get creamed by a big wave. The caption at the top of the page read: "Not to worry! In his Hart, Shaffner & Marx Featherweight he'll be dried out and crisp—and ready to woo her at the club tonight!" The dish was sleek. Her features were Martha's—a soft, pretty version. The Sprague mansion was in the background, surrounded by palm trees.

Ramona broke the silence. "What are you going to do?"

I couldn't look at her. "I don't know."

"Martha mustn't know."

"You told me that already."

The guy in the ad was starting to look like an idealized Emmett—the Scotchman as a Hollywood pretty boy. I threw out the one cop question Ramona's story inspired: "In the fall of '46 someone was throwing dead cats into cemeteries in Hollywood. Was that you?"

"Yes. I was so jealous of her then, and I just wanted Georgie to know I still cared. *What are you going to do?*"

"I don't know. Go upstairs, Ramona. Leave me alone."

I heard soft footfalls moving out of the room, then sobs, then nothing. I thought about the family's united front to save Ramona, how arresting her would blow my police career: charges of withholding evidence, obstruction of justice. Sprague money would keep her out of the gas chamber, she'd get eaten alive at Atascadero or a women's prison until the lupus got her, Martha would be ravaged, and Emmett and Madeleine would still have each other—withholding/obstruction beefs against them would be too second-hand to prosecute on. If I took Ramona in I was shot to shit as a policeman; if I let her go I was finished as a man, and in either case Emmett and Madeleine would survive— together.

So the patented Bucky Bleichert advance, stymied and stale-mated, sat still in a big plush room full of ancestor icons. I looked through the packing crates on the floor—the Sprague getaway if the City Council got uppity—and saw the cheap cocktail dresses and the sketch pad covered with women's faces, no doubt Martha sketching alter egos to plaster over ads huckstering toothpaste and cosmetics and cornflakes. Maybe she could design an advertising campaign to spring Ramona from Tehachapi. Maybe without torturer Mommy she wouldn't have the guts to work anymore.

I left the manse and killed time making rounds of old haunts. I checked out the rest home—my father didn't recognize me, but looked full of malicious spunk. Lincoln Heights was rife with new houses—prefab pads waiting for tenants—"No Down Pay-ment" for GIs. The Eagle Rock Legion Hall still had a sign bally-hooing Friday night boxing, and my Central Division beat was still winos, rag suckers and Jesus shriekers. At twilight, I gave in: one last shot at the brass girl before I took her mommy down; one last chance to ask her why she was still playing Dahlia when she knew I'd never touch her again.

I drove to the 8th Street bar strip, parked at the corner of Irolo and waited with an eye on the Zimba Room entrance. I was hoping that the valise I'd seen Madeleine carrying in the morning didn't mean a trip somewhere; I was hoping her Dahlia prowl of two nights ago wasn't a one-shot deal.

I sat there eyeballing foot traffic: servicemen, civilian booze-hounds, neighborhood squares going in and out of the hash house next door. I thought of packing it in, then got frightened of the next stop—Ramona—and stuck. Just past midnight

Madeleine's Packard pulled up. She got out—carrying her valise, looking like herself, not Elizabeth Short.

Startled, I watched her walk into the restaurant. Fifteen minutes passed slowly. Then she sashayed out, Black Dahlia to the nines. She tossed her valise in the Packard's backseat and hit the Zimba Room.

I gave her a minute's slack, then went over and peered in the doorway. The bar was serving a skeleton crew of army brass; the zebra-striped booths were empty. Madeleine was drinking by herself. Two soldiers were primping at stools down from her, getting ready to make the big move. They swooped a half second apart. The dump was too deserted for me to hold surveillance in; I retreated to the car.

Madeleine and a first lieutenant in summer dress khakis walked out an hour or so later. Per her old MO, they got in the Packard and headed around the corner to the 9th and Irolo auto court. I was right behind them.

Madeleine parked and walked to the manager's hut for the key; the soldier waited by the door of room twelve. I thought of frustration: KMPC on loud, venetian blinds down to the sill. Then Madeleine left the office, called to the lieutenant and pointed across the courtyard to a different unit. He shrugged and went over; Madeleine joined him and opened the door. The light went on and off inside.

I gave them ten minutes, then moved to the bungalow, resigned to big band standards and darkness. Moans were coming from inside, unaccompanied by music. I saw that the one window was open two feet or so, dried paint on the runner holding it stuck. I found shelter beside a trellis overgrown with vines, squatted down and listened.

Heavier moans, bed springs creaking, male grunts. Her love sounds reaching fever pitch—stagy, more soprano than when she was with me. The soldier groaning hard, all noise subsiding, then Madeleine, speaking with a feigned accent:

"I wish there was a radio. Back home all the motels had them. They were bolted down and you had to put dimes in, but at least there was music."

The soldier, trying to catch his breath: "I heard Boston's a nice town."

I placed Madeleine's fake voice then: New England blue collar, the way Betty Short was supposed to speak. "Medford's not nice, not nice at all. I had one lousy job after another. Waitress, candy girl at a theater, file clerk at a factory. That was why I came to California to seek my fortune. Because Medford was so awful."

Madeleine's "A's" were getting broader and broader; she sounded like a Boston guttersnipe. The man said, "You came out here during the war?"

"Uh-huh. I got a job at the Camp Cooke PX. This soldier beat me up, and this rich man, this award-winning contractor, he saved me. He's my stepdaddy now. He lets me be with whoever I want to be with so long as I come home to him. He bought me my nice white car and all my nice black dresses, and he gives me back rubs 'cause he's not my real daddy."

"That's the kind of dad to have. My dad bought me a bicycle once, and he gave me a couple of bucks toward a soap box derby racer. But he never bought me any Packards, that's for damn sure. You've got yourself a real sugar daddy, Betty."

I knelt down lower and peered through the window crack; all I could see were dark shapes on a bed in the middle of the room. Madeleine/Betty said, "Sometimes my stepdaddy doesn't like my boyfriends. He never makes a fuss, because he's not my real daddy and I let him give me back rubs. There was this one boy, a policeman. My stepdaddy said he was wishy-washy with a mean streak. I didn't believe him, because the boy was big and strong, and he had these cute buck teeth. He tried to hurt me, but Daddy settled his hash. Daddy knows how to deal with weak men who suck around money and try to hurt nice girls. He was a big hero in the First World War and the policeman was a draft dodger."

Madeleine's accent was slipping, moving into another voice, low and guttural. I braced myself for more verbal lashing; the soldier said, "Draft dodgers should either be deported to Russia or shot. No, shooting's too merciful. Hanged by the you know what, that's more like it."

Madeleine, a vibrato rasp, a perfect Mexican accent: "An axe ees better, no? The policeman have a partner. He tie up some loose ends for me—some notes I should not 'ave lef' for a not so nice girl. The partner beat up my stepdaddy an' run away to May-hee-co. I draw pictures of a face to be and buy cheap dress. I hire a detective to find him, an' I make a pageant. I go down to Ense-nada in dees-guise, I wear cheap dress, preten' to be beggar and knock on hees door. 'Gringo, gringo, I need money.' He turn hees back, I grab axe an' chop him down. I take money he steal from stepdaddy. Seventy-one thousan' dollar I bring back home."

The soldier jabbered, "Look, is this some kind of joke?" I pulled out my .38 and cocked the hammer. Madeleine as Milt Dolphine's "rich Mex woman" slipped into Spanish, a streak of raspy obscenities. I aimed through the window crack; the light went on inside; lover boy thrashing himself into his uniform spoiled my shot at the killer. I saw Lee in a sand pit, worms crawling out of his eyes.

The soldier bolted out the door, half dressed. Madeleine, slipping into her tight black gown, was an easy target. I drew a bead; a last flash of her nakedness made me empty the gun into the air. I kicked the window in.

Madeleine watched me climb over the sill. Undaunted by gunshots and flying glass, she spoke with soft savoir faire: "She was the only thing real to me, and I had to tell people about her. I felt so contrived next to her. She was a natural and I was just an imposter. And she was ours, sweet. You brought her back to me. She was what made it so good with us. She was ours."

I mussed up Madeleine's Dahlia hairdo, so that she looked like just another raven-clad floozy; I cuffed her wrists behind her back and saw myself in the sand pit, worm bait along with my partner. Sirens blared down from all directions; flashlights shined in the broken window. Out in the Big Nowhere, Lee Blanchard reprised his line from the Zoot Suit riot:

"Cherchez la femme, Bucky. Remember that."

35

WE TOOK the fall together.

Four black-and-whites responded to my shots. I explained to the officers that it was a lights and siren roll to Wilshire Station—I was booking the woman for Murder One. At the Wilshire squadroom, Madeleine confessed to the killing of Lee Blanchard, concocting a brilliant fantasy—a lovers' triangle of Lee/Madeleine/Bucky, how she was intimately involved with both of us in the winter of 1947. I sat in on the interrogation, and Madeleine was flawless. Seasoned Homicide dicks bought her tale hook, line and sinker: Lee and I rivals for her hand, Madeleine preferring me as a potential husband. Lee going to Emmett, demanding that he "give him" his daughter, beating the man half to death when he refused. Madeleine revenge-stalking Lee in Mexico, axing him to death in Ensenada. No mention of the Black Dahlia murder case at all.

I corroborated Madeleine's story, saying that I only recently figured out that Lee had been murdered. I then confronted Madeleine with a circumstantial run-though on the snuff and coerced a partial confession out of her. Madeleine was transported to the L.A. women's jail, and I went back to the El Nido—still wondering what I was going to do about Ramona.

The next day I returned to duty. At the end of my tour a team of Metro goons was waiting for me in the Newton locker room. They grilled me for three hours; I ran with the fantasy ball Madeleine started rolling. The grit of her story and my wild departmental rep carried me through the interrogation—and nobody mentioned the Dahlia.

Over the next week the legal machinery took over.

The Mexican government refused to indict Madeleine for the murder of Lee Blanchard—without a corpse and backup evidence extradition proceedings could not be initiated. A Grand Jury was called up to decide her fate; Ellis Loew was slated to present the case for the City of Los Angeles. I told him I would testify only by deposition. Knowing my unpredictability only too well, he agreed. I filled up ten pages with lies on the "lovers' triangle," fantasy embellishments worthy of romantic Betty Short at her best. I kept wondering if she would appreciate the irony.

Emmett Sprague was indicted by a separate Grand Jury—for health and safety code violations stemming from his mob-fronted ownership of dangerously faulty property. He was given fines in excess of $50,000—but no criminal charges were filed. Counting the $71,000 that Madeleine stole from Lee, he was still close to twenty grand in the black on the deal.

The lovers' triangle hit the papers the day after Madeleine's case went to the Grand Jury. The Blanchard-Bleichert fight and the Southside shootout were resurrected, and for a week I was big-time local stuff. Then I got a call from Bevo Means of the *Herald*: "Watch out, Bucky. Emmett Sprague's about to hit back, and the shit's about to hit the fan. 'Nuff said."

It was *Confidential* magazine that nailed me.

The July 12 issue ran an article on the triangle. It featured quotes from Madeleine, leaked to the scandal rag by Emmett. The brass girl had me ditching out on duty to couple with her at the Red Arrow Motel; stealing fifths of her father's whiskey to see me through nightwatch; giving her the inside lowdown on the LAPD's traffic ticket quota system and how I "beat up niggers." Innuendos pointed to worse offenses—but everything Madeleine said was true.

I was fired from the Los Angeles Police Department on grounds of moral turpitude and conduct unbecoming an officer. It was the unanimous decision of a specially convened board of inspectors and deputy chiefs, and I did not protest it. I thought of turning over Ramona in hopes of pulling a grandstander's turn-about, but kiboshed the idea. Russ Millard might be compelled to admit what he knew and get hurt; Lee's name would get coated with more slime; Martha would *know*. The firing was about two and a half years overdue; the *Confidential* exposé my final embarrassment to the Department. No one knew that better than I did.

I turned in my service revolver, my outlaw .45 and badge 1611. I moved back to the house that Lee bought, borrowed $500 from the padre and waited for my notoriety to die down before I started looking for work. Betty Short and Kay weighed on me, and I went by Kay's school to look for her. The principal, eyeing me like a bug who just crawled out of the woodwork, said that Kay left a resignation letter the day after I hit the newsstands. It stated that she was going on a long cross-country automobile trip and would not be returning to Los Angeles.

The Grand Jury bound Madeleine over for trial on Manslaughter Three—"premeditated homicide under psychological duress and with mitigating circumstances." Her lawyer, the great Jerry Giesler, had her plead guilty and request a judge's chambers sentencing. Taking into account the recommendations of psychiatrists who found Madeleine to be a "severely delusional violent schizophrenic adept at acting out many different personalities," the judge sentenced her to Atascadero State Hospital for an "indeterminate period of treatment not to subscribe below the minimum time allotted by the state penalties code: ten years of imprisonment."

So the brass girl took the heat for her family and I took it for myself. My farewell to the Spragues was a front-page photo in the L.A. *Daily News*. Matrons were leading Madeleine out of the courtroom while Emmett wept at the defense table. Ramona, hollow-cheeked with disease, was being shepherded by Martha, all good strong business in a tailored suit. The picture was a lock on my silence forever.

36

A MONTH later I got a letter from Kay.

Sioux Falls, S.D.
8/17/49

Dear Dwight,

I didn't know if you'd moved back to the house, so I don't know if this letter will reach you. I've been checking the library for L.A. papers, and I know you're not with the Department anymore, so that's another place where I can't write to you. I'll just have to send this out and see what happens.

I'm in Sioux Falls, living at the Plainsman Hotel. It's the best one in town, and I've wanted to stay here since I was a little girl. It's not the way I imagined it, of course. I just wanted to wash the taste of L.A. out of my mouth, and Sioux Falls is as antithetical to L.A. as you can get without flying to the moon.

My grade school girlfriends are all married and have children, and two of them are widows from the war. Everyone talks about the war like it's still going on, and the high prairies outside of town are being plowed for housing developments. The ones that have been constructed so far are so ugly, such bright, jarring colors. They make me miss our old house. I know you hate it, but it was a sanctuary for nine years of my life.

Dwight, I've read all the papers and that trashy magazine piece. I must have counted a dozen lies. Lies by omission and the blatant kind. I keep wondering what happened, even though I don't really want to know. I keep wondering why Elizabeth Short was never mentioned. I would have felt self-righteous, but I spent last night in my room just counting lies. All the lies I told you and things I never told you, even when it was good with us. I'm too embarrassed to tell you how many I came up with.

I'm sorry for them. And I admire what you did with Madeleine Sprague. I never knew what she was to you, but I know what arresting her cost you. Did she really kill Lee? Is that just another lie? Why can't I believe it?

I have some money that Lee left me (a lie by omission, I know) and I'm going to head east in a day or so. I want to be far away from Los Angeles, someplace cool and pretty and old. Maybe New England, maybe the Great Lakes. All I know is that when I see the place, I'll know it.

Hoping this finds you,

Kay.

P.S. Do you still think about Elizabeth Short? I think about her constantly. I don't hate her, I just *think* about her. Strange after all this time.

K.L.B.

I kept the letter and re-read it at least a couple of hundred times. I didn't think about what it meant, or implied about my future, or Kay's, or ours together. I just re-read it and thought about Betty.

I dumped the El Nido master file in the garbage and thought about her. H.J. Caruso gave me a job selling cars, and I thought about her while I was hawking the 1950 line. I drove by 39th and Norton, saw that houses were going up on the vacant lot and thought about her. I didn't question the morality of letting Ramona walk or wonder whether Betty would approve. I just thought about her. And it took Kay, always the smarter of the two of us, to put it together for me.

Her second letter was postmarked Cambridge, Massachusetts, and was written on stationery for the Harvard Motor Lodge.

9/11/49

Dear Dwight—

I'm still such a liar, proscrastinator and chicken heart. I've known for two months, and I just got up the courage to tell you. If this letter doesn't reach you I'll actually have to call the house or Russ Millard. Better to try this way first.

Dwight, I'm pregnant. It had to have happened that one awful time about a month before you moved out. I'm due around Christmas and I want to keep it.

This is the patented Kay Lake retreat advancing. Will you please call or write? Soon? <u>Now?</u>

That's the big news. Per the P.S. on my last letter, something strange? Elegiac? Plain funny happened.

I kept thinking about Elizabeth Short. How she disrupted all our lives, and we never even knew her. When I got to Cambridge (God, how I love academic communities!) I remembered that she was raised nearby. I drove to Medford, stopped for dinner and got into a conversation with a blind man sitting at the next table. I was feeling gabby and mentioned Elizabeth Short. The man was sad at first, then he perked up. He told me about an L.A. policeman who came to Medford three months ago to find "Beth's" killer. He described your voice and verbal style to a "T." I felt very proud, but I didn't tell him that cop was my husband, because I don't know if you still are.

Wondering,

Kay

I didn't call or write. I put Lee Blanchard's house on the market and caught a flight to Boston.

37

ON THE plane I thought of all the things I'd have to explain to Kay, evidence to keep a new foundation of lies from destroying the two—or three—of us.

She would have to know that I was a detective without a badge, that for one month in the year 1949 I possessed brilliance and courage and the will to make sacrifices. She would have to know that the heat of that time would always make me vulnerable, prey to dark curiosities. She would have to believe that my strongest resolve was not to let any of it hurt her.

And she had to know that it was Elizabeth Short who was giving us our second chance.

Nearing Boston, the plane got swallowed up by clouds. I felt heavy with fear, like the reunion and fatherhood had turned me into a stone plummeting. I reached for Betty then; a wish, almost a prayer. The clouds broke up and the plane descended, a big bright city at twilight below. I asked Betty to grant me safe passage in return for my love.

THE BIG NOWHERE

To Glenda Revelle

It was written that I should
be loyal to the nightmare of my choice—

Joseph Conrad
Heart of Darkness

PART ONE
RED CROSSCURRENTS

1

THUNDERSHOWERS HIT just before midnight, drowning out the horn honks and noisemaker blare that usually signaled New Year's on the Strip, bringing 1950 to the West Hollywood Substation in a wave of hot squeals with meat wagon backup.

At 12:03, a four-vehicle fender bender at Sunset and La Cienega resulted in a half dozen injuries; the deputies who responded got eyewitness testimony: the crash was caused by the clown in the brown DeSoto and the army major in the Camp Cooke staff car racing no-hands with dogs wearing paper party hats on their laps. Two arrests; one call to the Verdugo Street Animal Shelter. At 12:14, an uninhabited vet's shack on Sweetzer collapsed in a heap of drenched prefab, killing a teenaged boy and girl necking under the foundation; two County Morgue DOA's. At 12:29, a neon lawn display featuring Santa Claus and his helpers short-circuited, shooting flames along the electrical cord to its inside terminus—a plug attached to a maze of adapters fueling a large, brightly lit Christmas tree and nativity scene—severely burning three children heaping tissue-wrapped presents on a glow-in-the-dark baby Jesus. One fire truck, one ambulance and three Sheriff's prowl cars to the scene, a minor jurisdictional foul-up when the LAPD appeared in force, a rookie dispatcher mistaking the Sierra Bonita Drive address as City—not County—territory. Then five drunk drivings; then a slew of drunk and disorderlies as the clubs on the Strip let out; then a strongarm heist in front of Dave's Blue Room, the victims two Iowa yokels in town for the Rose Bowl, the muscle two niggers who escaped in a '47 Merc with purple fender skirts. When the rain petered out shortly after 3:00, Detective Deputy Danny Upshaw, the station's acting watch commander, predicted that the 1950's were going to be a shit decade.

Except for the drunks and nonbooze misdemeanants in the holding tank, he was alone. Every black-and-white and unmarked was out working graveyard; there was no chain of command, no switchboard/clerical girl, no plainclothes deputies in the squadroom. No khaki and olive drab patrolmen strutting around, smirking over their plum duty—the Strip, glossy women, Christmas baskets from Mickey Cohen, the real grief over the city line with the LAPD. No one to give him the fisheye when he picked up his criminology textbooks: Vollmer, Thorwald, Maslick—grid-searching crime scenes, blood spatter marks explained, how to toss an 18-foot-by-24-foot room for hard evidence in an hour flat.

Danny settled in to read, his feet up on the front desk, the station-to-prowler two-way turned down low. Hans Maslick was digressing on how to roll fingerprints off severely burned flesh, the best chemical compounds to remove scabbed tissue without singeing the skin below the surface of the print pattern. Maslick had perfected his technique during the aftermath of a prison fire in Düsseldorf in 1931. He had plenty of stiffs and fingerprint abstracts to work from; there was a chemical plant nearby, with an ambitious young lab assistant eager to help him. Together, they worked rapid fire: caustic solutions burning too deep, milder compounds not penetrating scarred flesh. Danny jotted chemical symbols on a notepad as he read; he pictured himself as Maslick's assistant, working side by side with the great criminologist, who would give him a fatherly embrace every time he made a brilliant logical jump. Soon he was transposing the scorched nativity scene kids against his reading, going solo, lifting prints off tiny fingers, double-checking them against birth records, the hospital precaution they took in case newborns got switched around—

"Boss, we got a hot one."

Danny glanced up. Hosford, a uniformed deputy working the northeast border of the division, was in the doorway. "What? Why didn't you call it in?"

"I did. You mustn't of—"

Danny pushed his text and notepad out of sight. "What is it?"

"Man down. I found him—Allegro, a half mile up from the Strip. Jesus dog, you ain't ever seen noth—"

"You stay here, I'm going."

* * *

Allegro Street was a narrow residential road, half Spanish bungalow courts, half building sites fronted by signs promising DELUXE LIVING in the Tudor, French Provincial and Streamline Moderne styles. Danny drove up it in his civilian car, slowing when he saw a barrier of sawhorses with red blinkers, three black-and-whites parked behind it, their headlights beaming out into a weed-strewn vacant lot.

He left his Chevy at the curb and walked over. A knot of deputies in rain slickers were pointing flashlights at the ground; cherry lamp glow fluttered over a sign for the ALLEGRO PLANTATION ARMS—FULL TENANCY BY SPRING 1951. The prowlers' low beams crisscrossed the lot, picking out booze empties, sodden lumber and paper debris. Danny cleared his throat; one of the men wheeled and pulled his gun, spastic twitchy. Danny said, "Easy, Gibbs. It's me, Upshaw."

Gibbs reholstered his piece; the other cops separated. Danny looked down at the corpse, felt his knees buckle and made like a criminologist so he wouldn't pass out or vomit:

"Deffry, Henderson, keep your lights on the decedent. Gibbs, write down what I say verbatim.

"Dead male Caucasian, nude. Approximate age thirty to thirty-five. The cadaver is lying supine, the arms and legs spread. There are ligature marks on the neck, the eyes have been removed and the empty sockets are extruding a gelatinous substance."

Danny squatted by the corpse; Deffry and Henderson moved their flashlights in to give him some close-ups. "The genitals are bruised and swollen, there are bite marks on the glans of the penis." He reached under the dead man's back and felt wet dirt; he touched the chest near the heart, got dry skin and a residue of body heat. "There is no precipitation on the cadaver, and since it rained heavily between midnight and three A.M., we can assume the victim was placed here within the past hour."

A siren wailed toward the scene. Danny grabbed Deffry's flashlight and went in extra close, examining the worst of it. "There is a total of six oval, irregular, circumscribed wounds on the torso between the navel and rib cage. Shredded flesh outlines the perimeters, entrails coated with congealed blood extruding from them. The skin around each wound is inflamed, directly outlining the shred marks, and—"

Henderson said, "Hickeys sure as shit."

Danny felt his textbook spiel snap. "What are you talking about?"

Henderson sighed. "You know, love bites. Like when a dame starts sucking on your neck. Gibbsey, show plainclothes here what that hat check girl at the Blue Room did to you Christmas."

Gibbs chuckled and kept writing; Danny stood up, pissed at being patronized by a flunky harness bull. Not talking made the stiff sucker-punch him; his legs were rubber and his stomach was flip-flops. He flashed the five-cell at the ground surrounding the dead man, saw that it had been thoroughly trampled by LASD-issue brogans and that the prowl cars had obliterated any possible tire tracks. Gibbs said, "I ain't sure I got all them words spelled right."

Danny found his textbook voice. "It doesn't matter. Just hold on to it and give it to Captain Dietrich in the morning."

"But I'm off at eight. The skipper don't come in till ten, and I got Bowl tickets."

"Sorry, but you're staying here until day watch relieves you or the lab techs show up."

"The County lab's closed New Year's, and I've had them tickets—"

A Coroner's wagon pulled to a stop by the sawhorses, killing its siren; Danny turned to Henderson. "Crime scene ropes, no reporters or rubberneckers. Gibbs stays posted here, you and Deffry start shaking down the locals. You know the drill: witnesses to the dumping, suspicious loiterers, vehicles."

"Upshaw, it is four-twenty fucking A.M."

"Good. Start now, and you may be finished by noon. Leave a report in duplicate with Dietrich, and write down all the addresses where no one was home, so they can be checked later."

Henderson stormed over to his cruiser; Danny watched the Coroner's men place the body on a stretcher and drape it with a blanket, Gibbs talking a blue streak to them, Rose Bowl odds and a number on the Black Dahlia case, still unsolved, still a hot topic. The profusion of cherry lights, flashlights and headbeams darted over the lot, picking out details: mud puddles reflecting moonlight and shadows, the neon haze of Hollywood in the distance. Danny thought of his six months as a detective, his own two homicides open-and-shut family jobs. The morgue men loaded the body, hung a U-turn and took off sans siren. A Vollmer maxim hit home: "In murders of extreme passion, the killer will always betray his pathology. If the detective is willing to sort physical evidence objectively and then *think* subjectively from the killer's viewpoint, he will often solve crimes that are baffling in their randomness."

Eyes poked out. Sex organs mauled. Bare flesh gored down to the quick. Danny followed the morgue wagon downtown, wishing his car had a siren to get him there faster.

* * *

The L.A. City and County morgues occupied the bottom floor of a warehouse on Alameda just south of Chinatown. A wooden partition separated the two operations: examination slabs, refrigerators and dissecting tables for bodies found within City confines, a different set of facilities for stiffs from the unincorporated area patrolled by the Sheriff's Department. Before Mickey Cohen sent the LAPD and Mayor's Office topsy-turvy with his Brenda Allen revelations—the high brass taking kickbacks from L.A.'s most famous whores—there had been solid City/County co-operation, pathologists and cadaver caddies sharing plastic sheets, bone saws and pickling fluid. Now, with the County cops giving Cohen shelter on the Strip, there was nothing but inter-agency grief.

Edicts had come down from City Personnel: *no* loan-outs of City medical tools; *no* fraternizing with the County crew while on duty; *no* Bunsen burner moonshine parties, for fear of mistagged DOA's and body parts snatched as souvenirs resulting in scandals to back up the Brenda Allen job. Danny Upshaw followed the stretcher bearing John Doe # 1—1/1/50 up the County loading dock, knowing his chance of getting his favorite City pathologist to do the autopsy was close to nil.

The County side was bustling: traffic fatalities lined up on gurneys, morgue jockeys tagging big toes, uniformed deputies writing dead body reports and Coroner's men chaining cigarettes to kill the stench of blood, formaldehyde and stale chink takeout. Danny side-stepped his way over to a fire exit, then hooked around to the City loading dock, interrupting a trio of LAPD patrolmen singing "Auld Lang Syne." Inside, the scene was identical to the one on the County turf, except that the uniforms were navy blue—not olive drab and khaki.

Danny headed straight for the office of Dr. Norton Layman, Assistant Chief Medical Examiner for the City of Los Angeles, author of *Science Against Crime* and his instructor for the USC night school course "Forensic Pathology for Beginners." A note was tacked to the door: "I'm on days starting 1/1. May God bless our new epoch with less business than the first half of this rather bloody century—N.L."

Cursing to himself, Danny got out his pen and notepad and wrote:

"Doc—I should have known you'd take the busiest night of the year off. There's an interesting 187 on the County side—male, sexually mutilated. Grist for your new book, and since I caught the squeal I'm sure I'll get the case. Will you try to get the autopsy? Capt. Dietrich says the ME on the County day shift gambles and is susceptible to bribes. Enough said—D. Upshaw." He placed the sheet of paper on Layman's desk blotter, anchored it with an ornamental human skull and walked back to County territory.

Business had slacked off. Daylight was starting to creep across the loading dock; the night's catch was lined up on steel examination slabs. Danny looked around and saw that the only live one in the place was an ME's assistant propped up in a chair by the dispatch room, alternately picking his teeth and his nose.

He walked over. The old man, breathing raisinjack, said, "Who are you?"

"Deputy Upshaw, West Hollywood Squad. Who's catching?"

"Nice duty. Ain't you a little young for a gravy job like that?"

"I'm a hard worker. Who's catching?"

The old man wiped his nose-picking finger on the wall. "I can tell conversation ain't your strong suit. Doc Katz was catching, only a snootful of juice caught him. Now he's catching a few winks in that kike kayak of his. How come the hebes all drive Cadillacs? You're a detective, you got an answer for that?"

Danny felt his fists jam into his pockets and clench, his warning to ease down. "It beats me. What's your name?"

"Ralph Carty, that's—"

"Ralph, have you ever done a preautopsy prep?"

Carty laughed. "Sonny, I done them all. I did Rudy Valentino, who was hung like a cricket. I did Lupe Velez and Carole Landis, and I got pictures of both of them. Lupe shaved her snatch. You pretend they ain't dead, you can have fun. What do you say? Lupe and Carole, five-spot a throw?"

Danny got out his billfold and peeled off two tens; Carty went for his inside jacket pocket, whipping out a deck of glossies. Danny said, "Nix. The guy I want is on a tray over there."

"What?"

"I'm doing the prep. *Now.*"

"Sonny, you ain't a certified County morgue attendant." Danny added a five-spot to his bribe and handed it to Carty; the old man kissed a faded snapshot of a dead movie star. "I guess you are now."

* * *

Danny got his evidence kit from the car and went to work, Carty standing sentry in case the duty ME showed up pissed.

He stripped the sheet off the corpse and felt the limbs for postmortem lividity; he held the arms and legs aloft, dropped them and got the buckle that indicated rigor mortis coming on. He wrote, "Death around 1:00 A.M. likely," on his notepad, then smeared the dead man's fingertips with ink and rolled his prints onto a piece of stiff cardboard, pleased that he got a perfect spread the first time around.

Next he examined the neck and head, measuring the purpled ligature marks with a caliper, writing the specs down. The marks encompassed the entire neck; much too long and broad to be a single- or double-hand span. Squinting, he saw a fiber under the chin; he picked it off with a tweezer, nailed it as white terrycloth, placed it in a test tube and on impulse forced the half-locked jaws open, holding them wide with a tongue depressor. Shining his penlight into the mouth, he saw identical fibers on the roof, tongue and gums; he wrote, "Strangled and suffocated with white terrycloth towel," took a deep breath and checked out the eye sockets.

The penlight beam picked out bruised membranes streaked with the gelatinous substance he'd noticed at the building site; Danny took a Q-tip and swabbed three slide samples from each cavity. The goo had a minty medicinal odor.

Working down the cadaver, Danny spot-checked every inch; scrutinizing the inside crook of the elbows, he tingled: old needle scars—faded, but there in force on both the right and left arms. The victim was a drug addict—maybe reformed—none of the tracks were fresh. He wrote the information down, grabbed his caliper and braced himself for the torso wounds.

The six ovals measured to within three centimeters of each other. They all bore teeth mark outlines too shredded to cut casts from—and all were too large to have been made by a human mouth biting straight down. Danny scraped congealed blood off the intestinal tubes that extended from the wounds; he smeared the samples on slides and made a speculative jump that Doc Layman would have crucified him for:

The killer used an animal or animals in the postmortem abuse of his victim.

Danny looked at the dead man's penis; saw unmistakable human teeth marks on the glans, what Layman called "homicidal affection," working for laughs in a classroom packed with ambitious off-duty cops. He knew he should check the underside and scrotum, saw Ralph Carty watching him and did it, getting no additional mutilations. Carty cackled, "Hung like a cashew"; Danny said, "Shut the fuck up."

Carty shrugged and went back to his *Screenworld*. Danny turned the corpse onto its stomach and gasped.

Deep, razor-sharp cuts, dozens of them crisscrossing the back and shoulders from every angle, wood splinters matted into the narrow strips of caked blood.

Danny stared, juxtaposing the front and backside mutilations, trying to put them together. Cold sweat was soaking his shirt cuffs, making his hands twitch. Then a gruff voice. "Carty, who is this guy? What's he doing here?"

Danny turned around, putting a pacify-the-locals grin on; he saw a fat man in a soiled white smock and party hat with "1950" in green spangles. "Deputy Upshaw. You're Dr. Katz?"

The fat man started to stick out his hand, then let it drop. "What are you doing with that cadaver? And by what authority do you come in here and disrupt my workload?"

Carty was shrinking into the background, making with supplicating eyes. Danny said, "I caught the squeal and wanted to prep the body myself. I'm qualified, and I lied and told Ralphy you said it was kosher."

Dr. Katz said, "Get out of here, Deputy Upshaw."

Danny said, "Happy New Year."

Ralph Carty said, "It's the truth, Doc—if I'm lyin', I'm flyin'."

Danny packed up his evidence kit, wavering on a destination: canvassing Allegro Street or home, sleep and dreams: Kathy Hudgens, Buddy Jastrow, the blood house on a Kern County back road. Walking out to the loading dock, he looked back. Ralph Carty was splitting his bribe money with the doctor in the rhinestone party hat.

2

LIEUTENANT MAL Considine was looking at a photograph of his wife and son, trying not to think of Buchenwald.

It was just after 8:00 A.M.; Mal was in his cubicle at the DA's Criminal Investigation Bureau, coming off a fitful sleep fueled by too much Scotch. His trouser legs were covered with confetti; the roundheeled squadroom steno had smeared kisses on his door, bracketing EXECUTIVE OFFICER in Max Factor's Crimson Decadence. The City Hall sixth floor looked like a trampled parade ground; Ellis Loew had just awakened him with a phone call: meet him and "someone else" at the Pacific Dining Car in half an hour. And he'd left Celeste and Stefan at home alone to ring in 1950—because he knew his wife would turn the occasion into a war.

Mal picked up the phone and dialed the house. Celeste answered on the third ring—"Yes? Who is this that is calling?"— her bum phrasing a giveaway that she'd been speaking Czech to Stefan.

"It's me. I just wanted to let you know that I'll be a few more hours."

"The blonde is making demands, Herr Lieutenant?"

"There's no blonde, Celeste. You know there's no blonde, and you know I always sleep at the Hall after the New Year's—"

"How do you say in English—rotkopf? Redhead? Kleine rotkopf scheisser schtupper—"

"Speak English, goddamn it! Don't pull this with me!"

Celeste laughed: the stage chortles that cut through her foreign-language routine and always made him crazy. "Put my son on, goddamn it!"

Silence, then Celeste Heisteke Considine's standard punch line: "He's not your son, Malcolm. His father was Jan Heisteke, and Stefan knows it. You are my benefactor and my husband, and the boy is eleven and must know that his heritage is not amerikanisch police talk and baseball and—"

"Put my son on, goddamn you."

Celeste laughed softly. Mal knew she was acknowledging match point—him using his cop voice. The line went silent; in the background he could hear Celeste cooing Stefan out of sleep, singsong words in Czech. Then the boy was there—smack in the middle of them. "Dad—Malcolm?"

"Yeah. Happy New Year."

"We saw the fireworks. We went on the roof and held umb-umb—"

"You held umbrellas?"

"Yes. We saw the City Hall light up, then the fireworks went, then they . . . fissured?"

Mal said, "They fizzled, Stefan. F-i-z-z-l-e-d. A fissure is a kind of hole in the ground."

Stefan tried the new word. "F-i-s-u-r-e?"

"Two s's. We'll have a lesson when I get home, maybe take a drive by Westlake Park and feed the ducks."

"Did you see the fireworks? Did you look out the window to see?"

He had been parrying Penny Diskant's offer of a cloakroom quickie then, breasts and legs grinding him, wishing he could do it. "Yeah, it was pretty. Son, I have to go now. Work. You go back to sleep so you'll be sharp for our lesson."

"Yes. Do you want to speak to Mutti?"

"No. Goodbye, Stefan."

"Goodbye, D-D-Dad."

Mal put down the phone. His hands were shaking and his eyes held a film of tears.

* * *

Downtown L.A. was shut down tight, like it was sleeping off a drunk. The only citizens in view were winos lining up for dough-nuts and coffee outside the Union Rescue Mission; cars were erratically parked—snouts to smashed fenders—in front of the hot-sheet hotels on South Main. Sodden streamers hung out of windows and confetti littered the sidewalk, and the sun that was looming above the eastern basin had the feel of heat, steam and bad hangovers. Mal drove to the Pacific Dining Car wishing the first day of the new decade an early death.

The restaurant was packed with camera-toting tourists wolf-ing the "Rose Bowl Special"—hangtown fry, flapjacks, Bloody Marys and coffee. The headwaiter told Mal that Mr. Loew and another gentleman were waiting for him in the Gold Rush Room—a private nook favored by the downtown legal crowd. Mal walked back and rapped on the door; it was opened a split second later, and the "other gentleman" stood there beaming. "Knock, knock, who's there? Dudley Smith, so Reds beware.

Please come in, Lieutenant. This is an auspicious assemblage of police brain power, and we should mark the occasion with proper amenities."

Mal shook the man's hand, recognizing his name, his style, his often imitated tenor brogue. Lieutenant Dudley Smith, LAPD Homicide. Tall, beefside broad and red-faced; Dublin born, L.A. raised, Jesuit college trained. Priority case hatchet man for every L.A. chief of police dating back to Strongarm Dick Steckel. Killed seven men in the line of duty, wore custom-made club-figured ties: 7's, handcuff ratchets and LAPD shields stitched in concentric circles. Rumored to carry an Army .45 loaded with garlic-coated dumdums and a spring-loaded toad stabber.

"Lieutenant, a pleasure."

"Call me Dudley. We're of equal rank. I'm older, but you're far better looking. I can tell we're going to be grand partners. Wouldn't you say so, Ellis?"

Mal looked past Dudley Smith to Ellis Loew. The head of the DA's Criminal Division was seated in a thronelike leather chair, picking the oysters and bacon out of his hangtown fry. "I would indeed. Sit down, Mal. Are you interested in breakfast?"

Mal took a seat across from Loew; Dudley Smith sat down between them. The two were dressed in vested tweed suits—Loew's gray, Smith's brown. Both men sported regalia: Phi Beta Kappa key for the lawyer, lodge pins dotting the cop's lapels. Mal adjusted the crease in his rumpled flannels and thought that Smith and Loew looked like two mean pups out of the same litter. "No thanks, counselor."

Loew pointed to a silver coffeepot. "Java?"

"No thanks."

Smith laughed and slapped his knees. "How about an explanation for this early morning intrusion on your peaceful family life?"

Mal said, "I'll guess. Ellis wants to be DA, I want to be Chief DA's Investigator and you want to take over the Homicide Bureau when Jack Tierney retires next month. We've got venue on some hot little snuff that I haven't heard about, the two of us as investigators, Ellis as prosecuting attorney. It's a career maker. Good guess?"

Dudley let out a whooping laugh; Loew said, "I'm glad you didn't finish law school, Malcolm. I wouldn't have relished facing you in court."

"I hit it, then?"

Loew forked an oyster and dipped it in egg juice. "No. We've got our tickets to those positions you mentioned, though. Pure and simple. Dudley volunteered for his own—"

Smith interrupted: "I volunteered out of a sense of patriotism. I hate the Red filth worse than Satan."

Mal watched Ellis take one bite of bacon, one of oyster, one of egg. Dudley lit a cigarette and watched him; Mal could see brass knuckles sticking out of his waistband. "Why am I thinking grand jury job?"

Loew leaned back and stretched; Mal knew he was reaching for his courtroom persona. "Because you're smart. Have you been keeping abreast of the local news?"

"Not really."

"Well, there's a great deal of labor trouble going on, with the Hollywood movie studios in particular. The Teamsters have been picketing against the UAES—the United Alliance of Extras and Stagehands. They've got a long-term contract with RKO and the cheapie studios on Gower. They're picketing for more money and profit points, but they're not striking, and—"

Dudley Smith slammed the tabletop with two flattened palms. "Subversive, mother-hating Pinks, every one of them."

Loew did a slow burn; Mal sized up the Irishman's huge hands as neck snappers, ear gougers, confession makers. He made a quick jump, pegged Ellis as being afraid of Smith, Smith hating Loew on general principles: as a sharpster Jew lawyer son of a bitch. "Ellis, are we talking about a *political* job?"

Loew fondled his Phi Beta Kappa key and smiled. "We are talking about an extensive grand jury investigation into Communist influence in Hollywood, you and Dudley as my chief investigators. The investigation will center around the UAES. The union is rife with subversives, and they have a so-called brain trust that runs things: one woman and a half dozen men—all heavily connected to fellow travelers who went to jail for pleading the Fifth before HUAC in '47. Collectively, UAES members have worked on a number of movies that espouse the Commie line, *and* they're connected to a veritable Dun and Bradstreet of other subversives. Communism is like a spider's web. One thread leads to a nest, another thread leads to a whole colony. The threads are names, and the names become witnesses and name more names. And you and Dudley are going to get me all those names."

Silver captain's bars danced in Mal's head; he stared at Loew and ticked off objections, devil's advocate against his own cause. "Why me instead of Captain Bledsoe? He's Chief DA's Investigator, he's Mr. Toastmaster for the whole goddamn city and he's everybody's favorite uncle—which is important, since you come across like a shark. I'm a detective specializing in collecting homicide evidence. Dudley is Homicide brass flat out. Why us? And why now—at nine A.M. New Year's morning?"

Loew counted rebuttal points on his fingers, the nails coated with clear polish and buffed to a gloss. "One, I was up late last night with the District Attorney. The Bureau's final fiscal 1950 budget has to be submitted to the City Council tomorrow, and I convinced him that the odd forty-two thousand dollars we had left over should be used to fight the Red Menace. Two, Deputy DA Gifford of the Grand Jury Division and I have agreed to switch jobs. He wants criminal prosecution experience, and you know what I want. Three, Captain Bledsoe is going senile. Two nights ago he gave a speech to the Greater Los Angeles Kiwanis Club and lapsed into a string of obscenities. He created quite a stir when he announced his intention to 'pour the pork' to Rita Hayworth, to 'hose her till she bleeds.' The DA checked with Bledsoe's doctor, and learned that our dear Captain has had a series of small strokes that he's kept under wraps. He will be retiring on April fifth—his twentieth anniversary with the Bureau—and he is strictly a figurehead until then. Fourth, you and Dudley are damn good, damn smart detectives, and an intriguing contrast in styles. Fifth—"

Mal hit the tabletop à la Dudley Smith. "Fifth, we both know the DA wants an outside man for Chief Investigator. He'll go to the Feds or fish around the LAPD before he takes me."

Ellis Loew leaned forward. "Mal, he's agreed to give it to you. Chief Investigator and a captaincy. You're thirty-eight?"

"Thirty-nine."

"A mere infant. Do well at the job and within five years you'll be fending off police chief offers with a stick. And *I'll* be District Attorney and McPherson will be Lieutenant Governor. Are you in?"

Ellis Loew's right hand was resting flat on the table; Dudley Smith covered it with his and smiled, all blarney. Mal reviewed his caseload: a hooker snuff in Chinatown, two unsolved shine killings in Watts, a stickup and ADW at a coon whorehouse frequented by LAPD brass. Low priority, no priority. He put his hand on the pile and said, "I'm in."

The pile dispersed; Dudley Smith winked at Mal. "Grand partners in a grand crusade." Ellis Loew stood up beside his chair. "First, I'll tell you what we have, then I'll tell you what we need.

"We have sworn depositions from Teamster members, stating Red encroachment within the UAES. We've got Commie front membership lists cross-filed with a UAES membership list—with a lot of matching names. We've got prints of pro-Soviet films made during the war—pure Red propaganda—that UAES members worked on. We've got the heavy artillery that I'll mention in a minute and I'm working on getting a batch of Fed surveillance photos: UAES brain trusters hobnobbing with known Communist Party members and HUAC indictees at Sleepy Lagoon protest activities back in '43 and '44. Good ammo, right from the gate."

Mal said, "The Sleepy Lagoon stuff might backfire. The kids that were convicted were innocent, they never got the real killer and the cause was too popular. Republicans signed the protest petition. You might want to rethink that approach."

Dudley Smith doused his cigarette in the remains of his coffee. "They were guilty, lad. All seventeen. I know that case. They beat José Diaz half to death, dragged him out to the Lagoon and ran him down with an old jalopy. A pachuco passion job, pure and simple. Diaz was sticking it to somebody's cousin's brother's sister. You know how those taco benders intermarry and breed. Mongoloid idiots, all of them."

Mal sighed. "It was a railroad, Lieutenant. It was right before the zoot suit riots, and everyone was cuckoo about the mexes. And a Republican governor pardoned those kids, not the Commies."

Smith looked at Loew. "Our friend here takes the word of the fourth estate over the word of a brother officer. Next he'll be telling us the Department was responsible for all our pooooor Latin brethren hurt during the riot. A popular Pinko interpretation, I might add."

Mal reached for a plate of rolls—keeping his voice steady to show the big Irishman he wasn't afraid of him. "No, a popular LAPD one. I was on the Department then, and the men I worked with tagged the job as horseshit, *pure and simple.* Besides—"

Loew raised his voice—just as Mal heard his own voice start to quiver. *"Gentlemen, please."*

The interruption allowed Mal to swallow, dredge up a cold look and shoot it at Dudley Smith. The big man shot back a bland smile, said, "Enough contentiousness over a worthless dead spic," and extended his hand. Mal shook it; Smith winked.

Ellis Loew said, "That's better, because guilty or not guilty isn't germane to the issue here. The fact is that the Sleepy Lagoon case attracted a lot of subversives and *they* exploited it to their ends. That's *our* focus. Now I know you both want to go home to your families, so I'll wind this up for today.

"Essentially, you two will be bringing in what the Feds call 'friendly witnesses'—UAESers and other lefties willing to come clean on their Commie associations and name names. You've got to get admissions that the pro-Red movies UAES worked on were part of a conscious plot—propaganda to advance the Communist cause. You've got to get proof of venue—subversive activities within L.A. City proper. It also wouldn't hurt to get some big names. It's common knowledge that a lot of big Hollywood stars are fellow travelers. That would give us some ..."

Loew paused. Mal said, "Marquee value?"

"Yes. Well put, if a bit cynical. I can tell that patriotic sentiment doesn't come easy to you, Malcolm. You might try to dredge up some fervor for this assignment, though."

Mal thought of a rumor he'd heard: that Mickey Cohen bought a piece of the L.A. Teamsters off of their East Coast front man—an ex-syndicate trigger looking for money to invest in Havana casinos. "Mickey C. might be a good one to tap for a few bucks if the City funding runs low. I'll bet he wouldn't mind seeing the UAES out and his boys in. Lots of money to be made in Hollywood, you know."

Loew flushed. Dudley Smith tapped the table with a huge knuckle. "No dummy, our friend Malcolm. Yes, lad. Mickey would like the Teamsters in and the studios would like the UAES out. Which doesn't negate the fact that the UAES is crawling with Pinks. Did you know, lad, that we were almost colleagues once before?"

Mal knew: Thad Green offering him a transfer to the Hat Squad when his sergeantcy came through back in '41. He turned it down, having no balls for armed robbery stakeouts, going in doors gun first, gunboat diplomacy police work: meeting the Quentin bus at the depot, pistol-whipping hard boys into a docile parole. Dudley Smith had killed four men working the job. "I wanted to work Ad Vice."

"I don't blame you, lad. Less risk, more chance for advancement."

The old rumors: Patrolman/Sergeant/Lieutenant Mal Considine, LAPD/DA's Bureau comer, didn't like to get his hands dirty. Ran scared as a rookie working 77th Street Division—the heart of the Congo. Mal wondered if Dudley Smith knew about the gas man at Buchenwald. "That's right. I never saw any percentage there."

"The squad was wicked fun, lad. You'd have fit right in. The others didn't think so, but you'd have convinced them."

He's got the old talk nailed. Mal looked at Ellis Loew and said, "Let's wrap this up, okay? What's the heavy ammo you mentioned?"

Loew's eyes moved back and forth between Mal and Dudley. "We've got two men assisting us. The first is an ex-Fed named Edmund J. Satterlee. He's the head of a group called Red Crosscurrents. It's on retainer to various corporations and what you might want to call 'astute' people in the entertainment industry. It screens prospective employees for Communist ties and helps weed out subversive elements that may have wormed their way in already. Ed's an expert on Communism, and he's going to give you a rundown on how to most effectively collate your evidence. The second man is a psychiatrist, Dr. Saul Lesnick. He's been the 'approved' headshrinker for the L.A. Communist Party since the '40s, and he's been an FBI informer for years. We've got access to his complete file of psychiatric records—all the UAES bigwigs—their personal dirt going back to before the war. *Heavy artillery.*"

Smith slapped the table and stood up. "A howitzer, a barrage weapon, maybe even an atom bomb. We're meeting them at your house tomorrow, Ellis? Ten o'clock?"

Loew cocked a finger at him. "Ten sharp."

Dudley aped the gesture to Mal. "Until then, partner. It's not the Hats, but we'll have fun nonetheless."

Mal nodded and watched the big man exit the room. Seconds passed; Loew said, "A rough piece of work. If I didn't think the two of you would be great together, I wouldn't have let him sign on."

"He volunteered?"

"He's got a pipeline to McPherson, and he knew about the job before I got the go-ahead. Do you think you can keep him on a tight leash?"

The question was like a road map to all the old rumors. Ellis Loew had him down straight as a Nazi killer and probably believed that he was behind the botched snuff attempt on Buzz Meeks. They had to blow the Ad Vice and 77th Street stories out of the water. Dudley Smith knew better. "I don't see any problem, counselor."

"Good. How's things with Celeste and Stefan?"

"You don't want to know."

Loew smiled. "Cheer up, then. Good things are coming our way."

3

TURNER "BUZZ" Meeks watched rental cops patrol the grounds of Hughes Aircraft, laying four to one that Howard hired the ineffectual bastards because he liked their uniforms, two to one he designed the threads himself. Which meant that the Mighty Man Agency was an RKO Pictures/Hughes Aircraft/Tool Company "Stray Dog"—the big guy's tag for tax-write-off operations that he bought and meddled in out of whim. Hughes owned a brassiere factory in San Ysidro—100 percent wetback-run; he owned a plant that manufactured electroplate trophies; he owned four strategically located snack stands—essential to the maintenance of his all-cheeseburger/chili dog diet. Buzz stood in his office doorway, noticed pleated flaps on the pockets of the Mighty Man standing by the hangar across from him, made the style as identical to a blouse Howard designed to spotlight Jane Russell's tits, and called the odds off. And for the three trillionth time in his life, he wondered why he always cut bets when he was bored.

He was now very bored.

It was shortly after 10:00 New Year's morning. Buzz, in his capacity as Head of Security at Hughes Aircraft, had been up all night directing Mighty Men in what Howard Hughes called "Perimeter Patrol." The plant's regular guards were given the night off; boozehound specters had been crisscrossing the grounds since yesterday evening. The high point of their tour was Big Howard's New Year's bonus—a flatbed truck loaded with hot dogs and Cokes arriving just as 1949 became 1950—compliments of the burger write-off in Culver City. Buzz had put down his sheet of bookie calculations to watch the Mighty Men eat; he laid six to one that Howard would hit the roof if he saw their custom-embroidered uniforms dotted with mustard and sauerkraut.

Buzz checked his watch—10:14—he could go home and sleep at noon. He slumped into a chair, scanned the walls and studied the framed photos that lined them. Each one made him figure odds for and against himself, made him think of how perfect his figurehead job and what he *really* did were.

There was himself—short, broad, running to fat, standing next to Howard Hughes, tall and handsome in a chalk stripe suit—an Oklahoma shitkicker and a millionaire eccentric giving each other the cuckold's horns. Buzz saw the photo as the two sides of a scratchy hillbilly record: one side about a sheriff corrupted by women and money, the flip a lament for the boss man who bought him out. Next was a collection of police shots— Buzz trim and fit as an LAPD rookie in '34; getting fatter and better dressed as the pictures jumped forward in time: tours with Bunco, Robbery and Narcotics divisions; cashmere and camel's hair blazers, the slightly nervous look in his eyes indigenous to bagmen everywhere. Then Detective Sergeant Turner Meeks in a bed at Queen of Angels, high brass hovering around him, pointing to the wounds he survived—while *he* wondered if it was a fellow cop who'd set him up. A string of civilian pics on the wall above his desk: a fatter, grayer Buzz with Mayor Bowron, ex-DA Buron Fitts, Errol Flynn, Mickey Cohen, producers he'd pimped for, starlets he'd gotten out of litigation and into abortions, dope cure doctors grateful for his referrals. Fixer, errand boy, hatchet wielder.

Stony broke.

Buzz sat down at his desk and jotted credits and debits. He owned fourteen acres of Ventura County farmland; parched and worthless, he'd bought it for his parents to retire to—but they foiled him by kicking in a typhus epidemic in '44. The real estate man he'd been talking to said thirty bucks an acre tops—better to hold on to it—it couldn't go much lower. He owned a mint green '48 Eldo coupé—identical to Mickey C.'s, but without the bulletproof plating. He had a shitload of suits from Oviatt's and the London Shop, the trousers all too tight in the gut—if Mickey bought secondhand threads he was home free—he and the flashy little hebe were exactly the same size. But the Mick threw away shirts he'd worn twice, and the debit list was running off the page and onto his blotter.

The phone rang; Buzz grabbed it. "Security. Who's this?"

"It's Sol Gelfman, Buzz. You remember me?"

The old geez at MGM with the car thief grandson, a nice boy who clouted convertibles out of Restaurant Row parking lots, raced Mulholland with them and always left his calling card—a big pile of shit—in the back seat. He'd bought off the arresting officer, who altered his report to show two—not twenty-seven— counts of GTA, along with no mention of the turd drop MO. The judge had let the kid off with probation, citing his good family and youthful verve. "Sure. What can I do for you, Mr. Gelfman?"

"Well, Howard said I should call you. I've got a little problem, and Howard said you could help."

"Your grandson back to his old tricks?"

"No, God forbid. There's a girl in my new picture who needs help. These goniffs have got some smut pictures of her, from before I bought her contract. I gave them some money to be nice, but they're persisting."

Buzz groaned—it was shaping up as a muscle job. "What kind of pictures?"

"Nasty. Animal stuff. Lucy and this Great Dane with a schlong like King Kong. I should have such a schlong."

Buzz grabbed a pen and turned over his debit list to the blank side. "Who's the girl and what have you got on the blackmailers?"

"On the pickup men I got bubkis—I sent my production assistant over with the money to meet them. The girl is Lucy Whitehall, and listen, I got a private detective to trace the calls. The boss of the setup is this Greek she's shacking with—Tommy Sifakis. Is that chutzpah? He's blackmailing his own girlfriend, calling in his demands from their cute little love nest. He's got pals to do the pickups and Lucy don't even know she's being had. Can you feature that chutzpah?"

Buzz thought of price tags; Gelfman continued his spiel. "Buzz, this is worth half a grand to me, and I'm doing you a favor, 'cause Lucy used to strip with Audrey Anders, Mickey Cohen's squeeze. I coulda gone to Mickey, but you did me solid once, so I'm giving you the job. Howard said you'd know what to do."

Buzz saw his old billy club hanging by a thong from the bathroom doorknob and wondered if he still had the touch. "The price is a grand, Mr. Gelfman."

"What! That's highway robbery!"

"No, it's felony extortion settled out of court. You got an address for Sifakis?"

"Mickey would do it for free!"

"Mickey would go batshit and get you a homicide conspiracy beef. What's Sifakis' address?"

Gelfman breathed out slowly. "You goddamn okie lowlife. It's 1187 Vista View Court in Studio City, and for a grand I want this thing wiped up clean."

Buzz said, "Like shit in the back seat," and hung up. He grabbed his LAPD-issue equalizer and headed for the Cahuenga Pass.

* * *

The run to the Valley took him an hour; the search for Vista View Court another twenty minutes of prowling housing developments: stucco cubes arrayed in semicircles gouged out of the Hollywood Hills. 1187 was a peach-colored prefab, the paint already fading, the aluminum siding streaked with rust. Identically built pads flanked it—lemon yellow, lavender, turquoise, salmon and hot pink alternating down the hillside, ending at a sign proclaiming, VISTA VIEW GARDENS! CALIFORNIA LIVING AT ITS FINEST! NO $ DOWN FOR VETS! Buzz parked in front of the yellow dive, thinking of gumballs tossed in a ditch.

Little kids were racing tricycles across gravel front yards; no adults were taking the sun. Buzz pinned a cereal-box badge to his lapel, got out and rang the buzzer of 1187. Ten seconds passed—no answer. Looking around, he stuck a bobby pin in the keyhole and gave the knob a jiggle. The lock popped; he pushed the door open and entered the house.

Sunlight leaking through gauze curtains gave him a shot at the living room: cheapsky furniture, movie pinups on the walls, stacks of Philco table radios next to the sofa—obvious proceeds from a warehouse job. Buzz pulled the billy club from his waistband and walked through a grease-spattered kitchen-dinette to the bedroom.

More glossies on the walls—strippers in g-strings and pasties. Buzz recognized Audrey Anders, the "Va Va Voom Girl," alleged to have a master's degree from some Podunk college; next to her, a slender blonde took up space. Buzz flicked on a floor lamp for a better look; he saw tame publicity stills: "Juicy Lucy" in a spangly one-piece bathing suit, the address of a downtown talent agency rubber-stamped on the bottom. Squinting, he noticed that the girl had unfocused eyes and a slaphappy grin—probably jacked on some kind of hop.

Buzz decided on five minutes to toss the pad, checked his watch and went to work. Scuffed drawers yielded male and female undergarments tangled up indiscriminately and a stash of marijuana cigarettes; an end cabinet held 78s and dime novels. The closet showed a woman on her way up, a man running second: dresses and skirts from Beverly Hills shops, mothball-reeking navy uniforms and slacks, dandruff-flecked jackets.

With 3:20 down, Buzz turned to the bed: blue satin sheets, upholstered headboard embroidered with cupids and hearts. He ran a hand under the mattress, felt wood and metal, grabbed and pulled out a sawed-off pump shotgun, big black muzzle, probably a .10 gauge. Checking the breech, he saw that it was loaded—five rounds, double-aught buckshot. He removed the ammo and stuffed it in his pocket; played a hunch on Tommy Sifakis' brain and looked under the pillow.

A German Luger, loaded, one in the chamber.

Buzz ejected the chambered round and emptied the clip, pissed that he didn't have time to prowl for a safe, find the doggy stuff to shove in Lucy Whitehall's face later, a jolt to scare her away from Greeks with dandruff and bedroom ordnance. He walked back to the living room, stopping when he saw an address book on the coffee table.

He leafed through it, no familiar names until he hit the G's and saw Sol Gelfman, his home and MGM numbers ringed with doodles; the M's and P's got him Donny Maslow and Chick Pardell, dinks he rousted working Narco, reefer pushers who hung out at studio commissaries—not the extortionist type. Then he hit S and got his lever to squeeze the Greek dry and maybe glom himself a few solids on the side:

Johnny Stompanato, Crestview-6103. Mickey Cohen's personal bodyguard. Rumored to have financed his way out of lowball duty with the Cleveland Combination via strongarm extortion schemes; rumored to front Mexican marijuana to local dealers for a 30 percent kickback.

Handsome Johnny Stomp. *His* name ringed in dollar signs and question marks.

Buzz went back to his car to wait. He turned the ignition key to Accessory, skimmed the radio dial across a half dozen stations, found Spade Cooley and his Cowboy Rhythm Hour and listened with the volume down low. The music was syrup on top of gravy—too sweet, too much. It made him think of the Oklahoma sticks, what it might have been like if he'd stayed. Then Spade went too far—warbling a tune about a man about to go to the state prison gallows for a crime he didn't commit. That made him think of the price he paid to get out.

In 1931 Lizard Ridge, Oklahoma, was a dying hick town in the lungs of the Dustbowl. It had one source of income: a factory that manufactured stuffed souvenir armadillos, armadillo purses and Gila monster wallets, then sold them to tourists blowing through on the highway. Locals and Indians off the reservation shot and skinned the reptiles and sold them to the factory piece-work; sometimes they got carried away and shot each other. Then the '31 dust storms closed down U.S. 1 for six months straight, the armadillos and Gilas went crazy, ate themselves diseased on jimson weed, crawled off to die or stormed Lizard Ridge's main drag and got squashed by cars. Either way, their hides were too trashed and shriveled to make anyone a dime. Turner Meeks, ace Gila killer, capable of nailing the bastards with a .22 from thirty yards out—right on the spine where the factory cut its master stitches—knew it was time to leave town.

So he moved to L.A. and got work in the movies—revolving cowboy extra—Paramount one day, Columbia the next, the Gower Gulch cut-rate outfits when things got tight. Any reasonably presentable white man who could twirl a rope and ride a horse for real was skilled labor in Depression Hollywood.

But in '34 the trend turned from westerns to musicals. Work got scarce. He was about to take a test offered by the L.A. Municipal Bus Company—three openings for an expected six hundred applicants—when Hollywood saved him again.

Monogram Studio was being besieged by picketers: a combine of unions under the AFL banner. He was hired as a strikebreaker—five dollars a day, guaranteed extra work as a bonus once the strike was quelled.

He broke heads for two weeks straight, so good with a billy club that an off-duty cop nicknamed him "Buzz" and introduced him to Captain James Culhane, the head of the LAPD's Riot Squad. Culhane knew a born policeman when he saw one. Two weeks later he was walking a beat in downtown L.A.; a month later he was a rifle instructor at the Police Academy. Teaching Chief Steckel's daughter to shoot a .22 and ride a horse earned him a sergeantcy, tours in Bunco, Robbery and the big enchilada—Narcotics.

Narco duty carried with it an unwritten ethos: you roust the lowest forms of humanity, you walk your tour knee-deep in shit, you get a dispensation. If you play the duty straight, you don't rat on those who don't. *If* you don't, you lay off a percentage of what you confiscate direct to the coloreds or the syndicate boys who sell to shines only: Jack Dragna, Benny Siegel, Mickey C. And you watch the straight arrows in other divisions—the guys who want you out so they can get your job.

When he came on Narco in '44, he struck his deal with Mickey Cohen, then the dark horse in the L.A. rackets, the hungry guy coming up. Jack Dragna hated Mickey; Mickey hated Jack; Buzz shook down Jack's niggertown pushers, skimmed five grams on the ounce and sold it to Mickey, who loved him for giving Jack grief. Mickey took him to Hollywood parties, introduced him to people who needed police favors and were willing to pay; fixed him up with a roundheeled blonde whose cop husband was serving with the MPs in Europe. He met Howard Hughes and started bird-dogging for him, picking up star-struck farm girls, ensconcing them in the fuck pads the big guy had set up all over L.A. It was going aces on all fronts: the duty, the money, the affair with Laura Considine. Until June 21, 1946, when an anonymous tip on a storefront operation at 68th and Slauson led him into an alleyway ambush: two in the shoulder, one in the arm, one through the left cheek of his ass. And a speedy wound ticket out of the LAPD, full pension, into the arms of Howard Hughes, who just happened to need a man ...

And he still didn't know who the shooters were. The slugs they took out of him indicated two men; *he* had two suspects: Dragna triggers or contract boys hired by Mal Considine, Laura's husband, the Administrative Vice sergeant back from the war. He had Considine checked out within the Department, heard that he turned tail from bar brawls in Watts, that he got his jollies sending in rookies to operate whores when he ran the night watch in Ad Vice, that he brought a Czech woman and her son back from Buchenwald and was planning to divorce Laura. Nothing concrete—one way or the other.

The only thing he had down for sure was that Considine knew about the deal with his soon-to-be ex and hated him. He'd taken a retirement tour of the Detective Bureau, a chance to say goodbye and pick up his courtesy badge, a chance to get a take on the man he cuckolded. He walked by Considine's desk in the

Ad Vice squadroom, saw a tall guy who looked more like a law-yer than a cop and stuck out his hand. Considine gave him a slow eyeball, said, "Laura always did have a thing for pimps," and looked away.

Even odds: Considine or Dragna, take your pick.

Buzz saw a late-model Pontiac ragtop pull up in front of 1187. Two women in crinoline party dresses got out and rocked toward the door on high high heels; a big Greek in a too-tight suitcoat and too-short trousers followed them. The taller of the skirts caught her stiletto spike in a pavement crack and went down on one knee; Buzz recognized Audrey Anders, hair in a pageboy, twice as beautiful as her picture. The other girl—"Juicy Lucy" from the publicity stills—helped her up and into the house, the big man right behind them. Buzz laid three to one that Tommy Sifakis wouldn't respond to the subtle approach, grabbed his billy club and walked up to the Pontiac.

His first shot sheared off the Indian-head hood ornament; his second smashed the windshield. Three, four, five and six were a Spade Cooley refrain that dented the grille into the radiator, causing steam clouds to billow all around him. Seven was a blind swing at the driver's side window, the crash followed by a loud "What the fuck!" and a familiar metal-on-metal noise: a shotgun slide jacking a shell into the chamber.

Buzz turned and saw Tommy Sifakis striding down the walkway, the sawed-off held in trembling hands. Four to one the Greek was too mad to notice the weapon's light weight; two to one he didn't have time to grab his box of shells and reload. Bluff bet, straight across.

His baton at port arms, Buzz charged. When they were within heavy damage range, the Greek pulled the trigger and got a tiny little click. Buzz countered, swinging at a hairy left hand frantic-ally trying to pump in ammo that wasn't there. Tommy Sifakis screamed and dropped the shotgun; Buzz brought him down with a forehand/backhand to the rib cage. The Greek spat blood and tried to curl into a ball, cradling his wounded parts. Buzz knelt beside him and spoke softly, accentuating his okie drawl. "Son, let's let bygones be bygones. You rip up them pictures and shitcan the negatives and I won't tell Johnny Stomp you fingered him on the squeeze. Deal?"

Sifakis spat a thick wad of blood and "F-f-fuck you"; Buzz whacked him across the knees. The Greek shrieked gobbledy-gook;

Buzz said, "I was gonna give you and Lucy another chance to work things out, but now I think I'm gonna advise her to find more suitable lodging. You feel like apologizin' to her?"

"F-f-f-y-y-you."

Buzz drew out a long sigh, just like he did playing a homesteader who'd taken enough shit in an old Monogram serial. "Son, here's my last offer. You apologize to Lucy, or I tell Johnny you snitched him, Mickey C. you're extortin' his girlfriend's pal and Donny Maslow and Chick Pardell you snitched them to Narco. Deal?"

Sifakis tried to extend a smashed middle finger; Buzz stroked his baton, catching a sidelong view of Audrey Anders and Lucy Whitehall in the doorway, jaws wide. The Greek lolled his head on the pavement and rasped, "I p-pologize."

Buzz saw flashes of Lucy and her canine co-star, Sol Gelfman botching her career with grade Z turkeys, the girl crawling back to the Greek for rough sex. He said, "Good boy," popped the baton into Sifakis' gut and walked over to the women.

Lucy Whitehall was shrinking back into the living room; Audrey Anders was blocking the doorway, barefoot. She pointed to Buzz's lapel. "It's a phony."

Buzz caught the South in her voice; remembered locker room talk: the Va Va Voom Girl could twirl her pastie tassels in opposite directions at the same time. "Wheaties. You from New Orleans? Atlanta?"

Audrey looked at Tommy Sifakis, belly-crawling over to the curb. "Mobile. Did Mickey send you to do that?"

"No. I was wonderin' why you didn't seem surprised. Now I know."

"You care to tell me about it?"

"No."

"But you've done work for Mickey?"

Buzz saw Lucy Whitehall sit down on the couch and grab a stolen radio for something to hold. Her face was blotchy red and rivers of mascara were running down her cheeks. "I certainly have. Mickey disapprove of Mr. Sifakis there?"

Audrey laughed. "He knows trash when he sees it, I'll give him that. What's your name?"

"Turner Meeks."

"*Buzz* Meeks?"

"That's right. Miss Anders, have you got a place for Miss Whitehall to stay?"

"Yes. But what—"

"Mickey still hang out New Year's at Breneman's Ham 'n' Eggs?"

"Yes."

"You get Lucy to pack a grip, then. I'll run you over there."

Audrey flushed. Buzz wondered how much of her smarts Mickey put up with before he jerked the chain; if she ever did the tassel trick for him. She went over and knelt beside Lucy Whitehall, smoothing her hair, prying the radio out of her grasp. Buzz got his car and backed it up on the gravel front yard, one eye on the Greek, still moaning low. Neighbor people were peering out their windows, spread venetian blinds all around the cul-de-sac. Audrey led Lucy out of the house a few minutes later, one arm around her shoulders, one hand carrying a cardboard suitcase. On the way to the car, she stopped to give Tommy Sifakis a kick in the balls.

* * *

Buzz took Laurel Canyon back to Hollywood—more time to figure out the play if Johnny Stompanato turned up at his boss's side. Lucy Whitehall mumbled litanies on Tommy Sifakis as a nice guy with rough edges, Audrey cooing "There, there," feeding her cigarettes to shut her up.

It was coming on as a three-horse parlay: a grand from Gelfman, whatever Mickey slipped him if he got sentimental over Lucy and a shakedown or favor pried out of Johnny Stomp. Play it soft with the Mick—he hadn't seen him since he quit the Department and their percentage deal. Since then the man had survived a pipe bomb explosion, two IRS audits, his right-hand goon Hooky Rothman stubbing his face on the business end of an Ithaca .12 gauge and the shootout outside Sherry's—chalk that one up to Jack Dragna or shooters from the LAPD, revenge for the cop heads that rolled over the Brenda Allen job. Mickey had half of bookmaking, loan-sharking, the race wire and the dope action in L.A.; he owned the West Hollywood Sheriff's and the few City high brass who didn't want to see him crucified. And Johnny Stomp had stuck with him through all of it: guinea factotum to a Jew prince. Play them both *very* soft.

Laurel Canyon ended just north of the Strip; Buzz took side streets over to Hollywood and Vine, dawdling at stoplights. He could feel Audrey Anders eyeing him from the back seat, probably trying to get a take on him and the Mick. Pulling up in front of

Breneman's, he said, "You and Lucy stay here. I got to talk to Mickey in private."

Lucy dry-sobbed and fumbled with her pack of cigarettes; Audrey reached for the door handle. "I'm going, too."

"No, you're not."

Audrey flushed; Buzz turned to Lucy. "Sweetheart, this is about them pictures of you and that big old dog. Tommy was tryin' to squeeze Mr. Gelfman, and if you go inside looking distraught, Mickey just might kill him and get all of us in heaps of trouble. Tommy's got them rough edges, but the two of you just might be able to work things—"

Lucy bawled and made him stop; Audrey's look said he was lower than the dog. Buzz headed into Breneman's at a trot. The restaurant was crowded, the radio crew for "Tom Breneman's Breakfast in Hollywood" packing up equipment and hustling it toward a side exit. Mickey Cohen was sitting in a wraparound booth, Johnny Stompanato and another muscle boy sandwiching him. A third man sat alone at an adjoining table, eyes constantly circling, a newspaper folded open on the seat beside him—obviously camouflaging a monster piece.

Buzz walked over; the gunman's hand slid under his morning *Herald*. Mickey stood up, smiling; Johnny Stomp and the other guy pasted identical grins on their faces and slid over to let him into the booth. Buzz stuck out his hand; Cohen ignored it, grabbed the back of his head and kissed him on both cheeks, scraping him with razor stubble. "Big fellow, it has been too long!"

Buzz recoiled from a blast of cologne. "Much too long, big fellow. How's business?"

Cohen laughed. "The haberdashery? I got a florist's shop and an ice cream parlor now, too."

Buzz saw that Mickey was giving him a shrewd once-over; that he'd caught his frayed shirt cuffs and home manicure. "No. *Business.*"

Cohen nudged the man on his left, a bony guy with wide blue eyes and a jailhouse pallor. "Davey, business he wants. Tell him."

Davey said, "Men got to gamble and borrow money and schtup women. The shvartzes got to fly to cloud nine on white powder airlines. Business is good."

Mickey howled with laughter. Buzz chuckled, faked a coughing attack, turned to Johnny Stompanato and whispered, "Sifakis and Lucy Whitehall. *Keep your fucking mouth shut.*"

Mickey pounded his back and held up a glass of water; Buzz kept coughing, enjoying the look on Stompanato's face—a guinea Adonis turned into a busted schoolboy, his perfectly oiled pompadour about to wilt from fright. Cohen's back slaps got harder; Buzz took a gulp of water and pretended to catch his breath. "Davey, you're a funny man."

Davey half smiled. "Best in the West. I write all Mr. Cohen's routines for the smokers at the Friar's Club. Ask him, 'How's the wife?'"

Buzz saluted Davey with his glass. "Mickey, how's the wife?"

Mickey Cohen smoothed his lapels and sniffed the carnation in the buttonhole. "Some women you want to see, my wife you want to flee. These two Dragna humps were staking out my house after the Sherry's job, my wife brought them milk and cookies, told them to shoot low, she ain't had it from me since Lucky Lindy crossed the Atlantic, she don't want nobody else getting it either. My wife is so cold that the maid calls our bedroom the polar icecap. People come up to me and ask, 'Mickey, are you getting any?', and I pull a thermometer out of my jockey shorts, it says twenty-five below. People say, 'Mickey, you're popular with the ladies, you must get reamed, steamed and dry-cleaned regularly.' I say, 'You don't know my wife—hog-tied, fried and swept to the side is more like it.' Some women you *got* to see, some you *got* to flee. Oops—here she comes now!"

Mickey ended his schtick with a broad grab for his hat. Davey the gagster collapsed on the table, convulsed with laughter. Buzz tried to drum up chortles and couldn't; he was thinking that Meyer Harris Cohen had killed eleven men that he knew of and had to rake in at *least* ten million a year tax free. Shaking his head, he said, "Mickey, you're a pisser."

A group of squarejohns at the next table was giving the routine a round of applause; Mickey tipped his hat to them. "Yeah? Then why ain't you laughing? Davey, Johnny, go sit someplace."

Stompanato and the gagster slid silently out of the booth. Cohen said, "You need work or a touch, am I right?"

"Nix."

"Howard treating you right?"

"He treats me fine."

Cohen toyed with his glass, tapping it with the six-carat rock on his pinky. "I know you're in hock to some handbooks. You should be with me, boychik. Good terms, no sweat on the payback."

"I like the risk the other way. It gets my juices goin'."

"You're a crazy fuck. What do you want? Name it."

Buzz looked around the room, saw Stompanato at the bar belting a stiff one for guts and solid citizen types giving Mickey surreptitious glances, like he was a zoo gorilla who might bolt his cage. "I want you not to lean on a guy who's about to make you real mad."

"What?"

"You know Audrey's friend Lucy Whitehall?"

Mickey traced an hourglass figure in the air. "Sure. Solly Gelfman's gonna use her in his next picture. He thinks she's going places."

Buzz said, "Hell in a bucket maybe," saw Mickey going into his patented low simmer—nostrils flaring, jaw grinding, eyes trawling for something to smash—and handed him the half-full Bloody Mary Johnny Stompanato left behind. Cohen took a gulp and licked lemon pulp off his lips. "Spill it. *Now.*"

Buzz said, "Lucy's shack job's been squeezing Solly with some dirty pictures. I broke it up, strong-armed the boy a little. Lucy needs a safe place to flop, and I know for a fact that the Greek's got pals on the West Hollywood Sheriff's—your pals. I also know he used to push reefer in Dragna territory—which made old Jack D. real mad. Two damn good reasons for you to leave him alone."

Cohen was gripping his glass with sausage fingers clenched blue-white. "What . . . kind . . . of . . . pictures?"

The big wrong question—Mickey might be talking to Sol Gelfman and get the true skinny. Buzz braced himself. "Lucy and a dog."

Mickey's hand popped the glass, shards exploding all over the table, tomato juice and vodka spritzing Buzz. Mickey looked at his bloody palm and pressed it flat on the tabletop. When the white linen started to turn red, he said, "The Greek is fucking dead. He is fucking dog food."

Two waiters had approached; they stood around shuffling their feet. The squarejohns at the next table were making with shocked faces—one old lady with her jaw practically down to her soup. Buzz waved the waiters away, slid next to Cohen and put an arm around his twitching shoulders. "Mickey, you can't, and you know it. You put out the word that anybody who bucks Jack D. is your friend, and the Greek did that—in spades. Audrey saw me work him over—and *she'd* know. And the Greek didn't

know how stand-up you are—that your woman's friends are like
kin to you. Mickey, you got to let it go. You got too much to lose.
Fix Lucy up with a nice place to stay, someplace where the Greek
can't find her. Make it a mitzvah."

Cohen took his hand from the table, shook it free of glass
slivers and licked lemon goo off his fingers. "Who was in it
besides the Greek?"

Buzz showed him his eyes, the loyal henchman who'd never
lie; he came up with two gunsels he'd run out of town for crashing
Lew the Jew Wershow's handbook at Paramount. "Bruno Geyer
and Steve Katzenbach. Fairies. You gonna find Lucy a place?"

Cohen snapped his fingers; waiters materialized and stripped
the table dervish fast. Buzz sensed wheels turning behind the
Mick's blank face—in *his* direction. He moved over to cut the
man some slack; he stayed deadpan when Mickey said, "Mitzvah,
huh? You fucking goyishe shitheel. Where's Audrey and Lucy
now?"

"Out by my car."

"What's Solly pay you?"

"A grand."

Mickey dug in his pants pockets and pulled out a roll of hundreds. He peeled off ten, placed them in a row on the table and
said, "That's the only mitzvah you know from, you hump. But
you saved me grief, so I'm matching. Buy yourself some clothes."

Buzz palmed the money and stood up. "Thanks, Mick."

"Fuck you. What do you call an elephant who moonlights as
a prostitute?"

"I don't know. What?"

Mickey cracked a big grin. "A two-ton pickup that lays for
peanuts."

"That's a riot, Mick."

"Then why ain't you laughing? Send the girls in—*now*."

Buzz walked over to the bar, catching Johnny Stompanato
working on another shot. Turning, he saw Cohen being
glad-handed by Tom Breneman and the maitre d', out of eyeshot.
Johnny Stomp swiveled around; Buzz put five Mickey C-notes in
his hand. "Sifakis snitched you, but I don't want him touched.
And I didn't tell Mickey bubkis. *You owe me.*"

Johnny smiled and pocketed the cash. "Thanks, pal."

Buzz said, "I ain't your pal, you wop cocksucker," and walked
outside, stuffing the remaining hundreds in his shirt pocket,

spitting on his necktie and using it to daub the tomato juice stains on his best Oviatt's worsted. Audrey Anders was standing on the sidewalk watching him. She said, "Nice life you've got, Meeks."

4

PART OF him knew it was just a dream—that it was 1950, not 1941; that the story would run its course while part of him grasped for new details and part tried to be dead still so as not to disrupt the unraveling.

He was speeding south on 101, wheeling a hot La Salle sedan. Highway Patrol sirens were closing the gap; Kern County scrubland loomed all around him. He saw a series of dirt roads snaking off the highway and hit the one on the far left, figuring the prowl cars would pursue straight ahead or down the middle. The road wound past farmhouses and fruit pickers' shacks into a box canyon; he heard sirens to his left and right, behind him and in front of him. Knowing any roadway was capture, he downshifted and plowed across furrowed dirt, gaining distance on the wheeirr, wheeirr, wheeirr. He saw stationary lights up ahead and made them for a farmhouse; a fence materialized; he downshifted, swung around in slow second gear and got a perfect view of a brightly lit picture window:

Two men swinging axes at a young blonde woman pressed into a doorway. A half-second flash of an arm severed off. A wide-open mouth smeared with orange lipstick screaming mute.

The dream speeded up.

He made it to Bakersfield; unloaded the La Salle; got paid. Back to San Berdoo, biology classes at JC, nightmares about the mouth and the arm. Pearl Harbor, 4F from a punctured eardrum. No amount of study, cash GTAs or *anything* can push the girl away. Months pass, and he returns to find out how and why.

It takes a while, but he comes up with a triangle: a missing local girl named Kathy Hudgens, her spurned lover Marty Sidwell—dead on Saipan—questioned by the cops and let go because no body was found. The number-two man most likely Buddy Jastrow, Folsom parolee, known for his love of torturing dogs and cats. Also missing—last seen two days after he tore across the dry cabbage field. The dream dissolving into typescript—criminology texts filled with forensic gore shots. Joining the

LASD in '44 to know WHY; advancing through jail and patrol duty; other deputies hooting at him for his perpetual all-points want on Harlan "Buddy" Jastrow.

A noise went off. Danny Upshaw snapped awake, thinking it was a siren kicking over. Then he saw the stucco swirls on his bedroom ceiling and knew it was the phone.

He picked it up. "Skipper?"

"Yeah," Captain Al Dietrich said. "How'd you know?"

"You're the only one who calls me."

Dietrich snorted. "Anyone ever call you an ascetic?"

"Yeah, you."

Dietrich laughed. "I like your luck. One night as acting watch commander and you get floods, two accident deaths and a homicide. Want to fill me in on that?"

Danny thought of the corpse: bite marks, the missing eyes. "It's as bad as anything I've seen. Did you talk to Henderson and Deffry?"

"They left canvassing reports—nothing hot. Bad, huh?"

"The worst I've seen."

Dietrich sighed. "Danny, you're a rookie squadroom dick, and you've never worked a job like this. You've only seen it in your books—in black and white."

Kathy Hudgens' mouth and arm were superimposed against the ceiling—in Technicolor. Danny held on to his temper. "Right, Skipper. It was bad, though. I went down to the morgue and . . . watched the prep. It got worse. Then I went back to help Deffry and Hender—"

"They told me. They also said you got bossy. Shitcan that, or you'll get a rep as a prima donna."

Danny swallowed dry. "Right, Captain. Any ID on the body?"

"Not yet, but I think we've got the car it was transported in. It's a '47 Buick Super, green, abandoned a half block up from the building site. White upholstery with what looks like bloodstains. It was reported stolen at ten this morning, clouted outside a jazz club on South Central. The owner was still drunk when he called in—you call him for details."

"Print man dusting it?"

"Being done now."

"Is SID going over the lot?"

"No. The print man was all I could wangle downtown."

"Shit. Captain, I want this one."

"You can have it. No publicity, though. I don't want another Black Dahlia mess."

"What about another man to work with me?"

Dietrich sighed—long and slow. "If the victim warrants it. For now, it's just you. We've only got four detectives, Danny. If this John Doe was trash, I don't want to waste another man."

Danny said, "A homicide is a homicide, sir."

Dietrich said, "You're smarter than that, Deputy."

Danny said, "Yes, sir," hung up, and rolled.

* * *

The day had turned cool and cloudy. Danny played the radio on the ride to Allegro; the weatherman was predicting more rain, maybe flooding in the canyons—and there was no news of the horrific John Doe. Passing the building site, he saw kids playing touch football in the mud and rubberneckers pointing out the scene of last night's spectacle—an SID prowl of the lot would now yield zero.

The print wagon and abandoned Buick were up at the end of the block. Danny noticed that the sedan was perfectly parked, aligned with the curb six inches or so out, the tires pointed inward to prevent the vehicle from sliding downhill. A psych lead: the killer had just brutally snuffed his victim and transported the body from fuck knows where, yet he still had the calm to coolly dispose of his car—*by the dump scene*—which meant that there were probably no witnesses to the snatch.

Danny hooked his Chevy around the print car and parked, catching sight of the tech's legs dangling out the driver's side of the Buick. Walking over, he heard the voice the legs belonged to: "Glove prints on the wheel and dashboard, Deputy. Fresh caked blood on the back seat and some white sticky stuff on the side headliner."

Danny looked in, saw an old plainclothesman dusting the glove compartment and a thin patch of dried blood dotted with white terrycloth on the rear seat cushion. The seat rests immediately behind the driver were matted with crisscross strips of blood—the terrycloth imbedded deeper into the caking. The velveteen sideboard by the window was streaked with the gelatinous substance he'd tagged at the morgue. Danny sniffed the goo, got the same mint/medicinal scent, clenched and unclenched his fists as he ran a spot reconstruction:

The killer drove his victim to the building site like a chauffeur, the stiff propped up in his white terry robe, eyeless head lolling against the sideboard, oozing the salve or ointment. The crisscross strips on the seat rests were the razorlike cuts on his back soaking through; the blood patch on the cushion was the corpse flopping over sideways when the killer made a sharp right turn.

"Hey! Deputy!"

The print man was sitting up, obviously pissed that he was taking liberties. "Look, I have to dust the back now. Do you mind . . ."

Danny looked at the rear-view mirror, saw that it was set strangely and got in behind the wheel. Another reconstruction: the mirror held a perfect view of the back seat, blood strips and goo-streaked sideboard. The killer had adjusted it in order to steal glances at his victim as he drove.

"What's your name, son?"

Now the old tech was really ticked. Danny said, "It's Deputy Upshaw, and don't bother with the back seat—this guy's too smart."

"Do you feel like telling me how you know that?"

The two-way in the print wagon crackled; the old-timer got out of the Buick, shaking his head. Danny memorized the registration card laminated to the steering column: Nestor J. Albanese, 1236 S. St. Andrews, L.A., Dunkirk-4619. He thought of Albanese as the killer—a phony car theft reported—and nixed the idea as far-fetched; he thought of the rage it took to butcher the victim, the ice it took to drive him around L.A. in New Year's Eve traffic. *Why?*

The tech called out, "For you, Upshaw."

Danny walked over to the print car and grabbed the mike. "Yeah?"

A female voice, static-filtered, answered. "Karen, Danny."

Karen Hiltscher, the clerk/dispatcher at the station; *his* errand girl—occasional sweet talk for her favors. She hadn't figured out that he wasn't interested and persisted in using first names over the County air. Danny pushed the talk button. "Yeah, Karen."

"There's an ID on your 187. Martin Mitchell Goines, male Caucasian, DOB 11/9/16. Two convictions for marijuana possession, two years County for the first, three to five State for the other. Paroled from San Quentin after three and a half, August of '48. His last known address was a halfway house on 8th and

Alvarado. He was a State parole absconder, bench warrant issued. Under employment he's listed as a musician, registered with Union Local 3126 in Hollywood."

Danny thought of the Buick stolen outside a darktown jazz club. "Have you got mugs?"

"Just came in."

He put on his sugar voice. "Help me with paperwork, sweet? Some phone calls?"

Karen's voice came out whiny and catty—even over the static. "Sure, Danny. You'll pick up the mugshots?"

"Twenty minutes." Danny looked around and saw that the print tech was back at work. He added, "You're a doll," hoping the girl bought it.

* * *

Danny called Nestor J. Albanese from a pay phone on Allegro and Sunset. The man had the raspy voice and skewed speech of a hangover sufferer; he told a booze-addled version of his New Year's Eve doings, going through it three times before Danny got the chronology straight.

He was club-hopping in darktown from 9:00 or so on, the bop joints around Slauson and Central—the Zombie, Bido Lito's, Tommy Tucker's Playroom, Malloy's Nest. Leaving the Nest around 1:00 A.M., he walked over to where he thought he left his Buick. It wasn't there, so he retraced his steps, drunk, figuring he'd ditched the car on a side street. The rain was drenching him, he was woozy from mai tais and champagne, he took a cab home and woke up—still smashed—at 8:30. He took another cab back to South Central, searched for the Buick for a solid hour, didn't find it and called the police to report it stolen. He then hailed another taxi and returned home again, to be contacted by the watch sergeant at the West Hollywood substation, who told him his pride and joy was a likely transport vehicle in a homicide case, and now, at 3:45 P.M. New Year's Day, he wanted his baby back— and that was that.

Danny 99 percent eliminated Albanese as a suspect—the man came off as legit stupid, professed to have no criminal record and seemed sincere when he denied knowing Martin Mitchell Goines. He told him the Buick would be kicked loose from the County Impound inside three days, hung up and drove to the Station for mugshots and favors.

Karen Hiltscher was out on her dinner break; Danny was grateful she wasn't around to make goo-goo eyes and poke his biceps, copping feels while the watch sergeant chuckled. She'd left the mugshot strip on her desk. Alive and with eyes, Martin Mitchell Goines looked young and tough—a huge, Butch-Waxed pompadour the main feature of his front, right and left side pics. The shots were from his second reefer roust: LAPD 4/16/44 on a mugboard hanging around his neck. Six years back; three and a half of them spent in Big Q. Goines had aged badly—and had died looking older than thirty-three.

Danny left Karen Hiltscher a memo: "Sweetheart - will you do this for me? 1 - Call Yellow, Beacon and the indy cab cos. Ask about pickups of single males on Sunset between Doheny and La Cienega and side sts. between 3:00 to 4:00 a.m. last nite. Ditto pickups of a drunk man, Central and Slauson to 1200 block S. St. Andrews, 12:30 - 1:30 a.m. Get all log entries for pickups those times and locations. 2 - Stay friendly, ok? I'm sorry about that lunch date I canceled. I had to cram for a test. Thanks - D.U."

The lie made Danny angry at the girl, the LASD and himself for kowtowing to teenaged passion. He thought of calling the 77th Street Station desk to tell them he was going to be operating in City territory, then kiboshed the idea—it was too much like bowing to the LAPD and their pout over the Sheriff's harboring Mickey Cohen. He held the thought, the contempt. A killer-hoodlum who longed to be a nightclub comic and got weepy over lost dogs and crippled kids brought a big-city police department to its knees with a wire recording: Vice cops taking bribes and chauffeuring prostitutes; the Hollywood Division night-watch screwing Brenda Allen's whores on mattresses in the Hollywood Station felony tank. Mickey C. putting out his entire smear arsenal because the City high brass upped his loan shark and bookmaking kickbacks 10 percent. Ugly. Stupid. Greedy. *Wrong*.

Danny let the litany simmer on his way down to darktown—Sunset east to Figueroa, Figueroa to Slauson, Slauson east to Central—a hypothetical route for the car thief/killer. Dusk started coming on, rain clouds eclipsing late sunshine trying to light up Negro slums: ramshackle houses encircled by chicken wire, pool halls, liquor stores and storefront churches on every street—until jazzland took over. Then loony swank amidst squalor, one long block of it.

Bido Lito's was shaped like a miniature Taj Mahal, only purple; Malloy's Nest was a bamboo hut fronted by phony Hawaiian palms strung with Christmas-tree lights. Zebra stripes comprised the paint job on Tommy Tucker's Playroom—an obvious converted warehouse with plaster saxophones, trumpets and music clefs alternating across the edge of the roof. The Zamboanga, Royal Flush and Katydid Klub were bright pink, more purple and puke green, a hangarlike building subdivided, the respective doorways outlined in neon. And Club Zombie was a Moorish mosque featuring a three-story-tall sleepwalker growing out of the facade: a gigantic darky with glowing red eyes high-stepping into the night.

Jumbo parking lots linked the clubs; big Negro bouncers stood beside doorways and signs announcing "Early Bird" chicken dinners. A scant number of cars was stationed in the lots; Danny left his Chevy on a side street and started bracing the muscle.

The doormen at the Zamboanga and Katydid recalled seeing Martin Mitchell Goines "around"; a man setting up a menu board outside the Royal Flush took the ID a step further: Goines was a second-rate utility trombone, usually hired for fill-in duty. Since "Christmas or so" he'd been playing with the house band at Bido Lito's. Danny read every suspicious black face he spoke to for signs of holding back; all he got was a sense that these guys thought Marty Goines was a lily-white fool.

Danny hit Bido Lito's. A sign in front proclaimed DICKY MCCOVER AND HIS JAZZ SULTANS—SHOWS AT 7:30, 9:30 AND 11:30 NITELY—ENJOY OUR DELUXE CHICKEN BASKET. Walking in, he thought he was entering a hallucination.

The walls were pastel satin bathed by colored baby spotlights that hued the fabric garish beyond garish; the bandstand backing was a re-creation of the Pyramids, done in sparkly cardboard. The tables had fluorescent borders, the high-yellow hostesses carrying drinks and food wore low-cut tiger costumes, the whole place smelled of deep-fried meat. Danny felt his stomach growl, realized he hadn't eaten in twenty-four hours and approached the bar. Even in the hallucinatory lighting, he saw the barman make him for a cop.

He held out the mugshot strip. "Do you know this man?"

The bartender took the strip, examined it under the cash register light and handed it back. "That's Marty. Plays 'bone with the Sultans. Comes in before the first set to eat, if you wants to talk to him."

"When was the last time you saw him?"

"Las' night."

"For the band's last set?"

The barman's mouth curled into a tight smile; Danny sensed that "band" was square nomenclature. "I asked you a question."

The man wiped the bartop with a rag. "I don' think so. Midnight set I remember seein' him. Sultans played two late ones las' night, on account of New Year's."

Danny noticed a shelf of whiskey bottles without labels. "Go get the manager."

The bartender pressed a button by the register; Danny took a stool and swiveled to face the bandstand. A group of Negro men was opening instrument cases, pulling out sax, trumpet and drum cymbals. A fat mulatto in a double-breasted suit walked over to the bar, wearing a suck-up-to-authority smile. He said, "Thought I knew all the boys on the Squad."

Danny said, "I'm with the Sheriff's."

The mulatto's smile evaporated. "I usually deal with the Seven-Seven, Mr. Sheriff."

"This is County business."

"This ain't County territory."

Danny hooked a thumb in back of him, then nodded toward the baby spots. "You've got illegal booze, those lights are a fire hazard and the County runs Beverage Control and Health and Safety Code. I've got a summons book in the car. Want me to get it?"

The smile returned. "I surely don't. How can I be of service, *sir*?"

"Tell me about Marty Goines."

"What about him?"

"Try everything."

The manager took his time lighting a cigarette; Danny knew his fuse was being tested. Finally the man exhaled and said, "Not much to tell. The local sent him down when the Sultans' regular trombone fell off the wagon. I'd have preferred colored, but Marty's got a rep for getting along with non-Caucasians, so I said okay. Except for ditching out on the guys last night, Marty never did me no dirt, just did his job copacetic. Not the world's best slideman, not the worst neither."

Danny pointed to the musicians on the bandstand. "Those guys are the Sultans, right?"

"Right."

"Goines played a set with them that ended just after midnight?"

The mulatto smiled. "Dicky McCover's up-tempo 'Old Lang Syne.' Even Bird envies that—"

"When was the set finished?"

"Set broke up maybe 12:20. Fifteen-minute break I give my guys. Like I said, Marty ditched out on that and the 2:00 closer. Only time he did me dirt."

Danny went in for the Sultans' alibi. "Were the other three men on stage for the final two sets?"

The manager nodded. "Uh-huh. Played for a private party I had going after that. What'd Marty do?"

"He got murdered."

The mulatto choked on the smoke he was inhaling. He coughed the drag out, dropped his cigarette on the floor and stepped on it, rasping, "Who you think did it?"

Danny said, "Not you, not the Sultans. Let's try this one: was Goines feeding a habit?"

"Say what?"

"Don't play dumb. Junk, H, horse, a fucking heroin habit." The manager took a step backward. "I don't hire no goddamned hopheads."

"Sure you don't, just like you don't serve hijack booze. Let's try this: Marty and women."

"Never heard nothing one way or the other."

"How about enemies? Guys with a hard-on for him?"

"Nothing."

"What about friends, known associates, men coming around asking for him?"

"No, no and *no*. Marty didn't even have no family."

Danny shifted gears with a smile—an interrogation technique he practiced in front of his bedroom mirror. "Look, I'm sorry I came on so strong."

"No, you ain't."

Danny flushed, hoping the crazy lighting didn't pick it up. "Have you got a man watching the parking lot?"

"No."

"Do you remember a green Buick in the lot last night?"

"No."

"Do your kitchen workers hang out in the lot?"

"Man, my kitchen people is too busy to hang out anyplace."

"What about your hostesses? They sell it outside after you close?"

"Man, you are out of your bailiwick and way out of line."

Danny elbowed the mulatto aside and threaded his way through the dinner crowd to the bandstand. The Sultans saw him coming and exchanged looks: cop-wise, *experienced*. The drummer quit arranging his gear; the trumpeter backed off and stood by the curtains leading backstage; the saxophone man stopped adjusting his mouthpiece and stood his ground.

Danny stepped onto the platform, blinking against the hot white light shining down. He sized up the sax as the boss and decided on a soft tack—his interrogation was playing to a full house. "Sheriff's. It's about Marty Goines."

The drummer answered him. "Marty's clean. Just took the cure."

A lead—if it wasn't one ex-con running interference for another. "I didn't know he had a habit."

The sax player snorted. "Years' worth, but he kicked."

"Where?"

"Lex. Lexington State Hospital in Kentucky. This about Marty's parole?"

Danny stepped back so he could eyeball all three men in one shot. "Marty got snuffed last night. I think he was snatched from around here right after your midnight set."

Three clean reactions: the trumpeter scared, most likely afraid of cops on general principles; the drummer trembling; the sax man spooked, but coming back mad. "We all gots alibis, 'case you don't already know."

Danny thought: RIP Martin Mitchell Goines. "I know, so let's try the usual drill. Did Marty have any enemies that you know of? Woman trouble? Old dope buddies hanging around?"

The sax said, "Marty was a fuckin' cipher. All I knew about him was that he hung up his Quentin parole, that he was so hot to kick he went to Lex as a fuckin' absconder. Big balls if you asks me—that's a Fed hospital, and they mighta run warrant checks on him. Fuckin' cipher. None of us even knew where he was stayin'."

Danny kicked the skinny around and watched the trumpet player inch over from the curtains, holding his horn like it was an ikon to ward off demons. He said, "Mister, I think I got something for you."

"What?"

"Marty told me he had to meet a guy after the midnight set, and I saw him walking across the street to the Zombie parking lot."

"Did he mention a name?"

"No, just a guy."

"Did he say *anything* else about him? What they were going to do—anything like that?"

"No, and he said he'd be coming right back."

"Do you think he was going to buy dope?"

The saxophone player bored into Danny with blue eyes lighter than his own brown ones. "Man, I fuckin' told you Marty was clean, and intended to stay clean."

Boos erupted from the audience; paper debris hit Danny's legs. He blinked against the spotlight and felt sweat creeping down his rib cage. A voice yelled, "Ofay motherfuck"; applause followed it; a half-chewed chicken wing struck Danny's back. The sax man smiled up at him, licked his mouthpiece and winked. Danny resisted an urge to kick the horn down his throat and quick-walked out of the club by a side exit.

The night air cooled his sweat and made him shiver; pulsating neon assaulted his eyes. Little bursts of music melded together like one big noise and the nigger sleepwalker atop the Club Zombie looked like doomsday. Danny knew he was scared, and headed straight for the apparition.

The doorman backed off from his badge and let him in to four walls of smoke and dissonant screeching—the combo at the front of the room heading toward a crescendo. The bar was off to the left, shaped like a coffin and embossed with the club's sleep-walker emblem. Danny beelined there, grabbing a stool, hooking a finger at a white man polishing glasses.

The barkeep placed a napkin in front of him. Danny yelled, "Double bonded!" above the din. A glass appeared; Danny knocked the bourbon back; the barman refilled. Danny drank again and felt his nerves go from sandpapered to warm. The music ended with a *thud-boom-scree*; the house lights went on amid big applause. When it trailed off, Danny reached in his pocket and pulled out a five-dollar bill and the Goines mugshot strip.

The bartender said, "Two spot for the drinks."

Danny stuffed the five in his shirt pocket and held up the strip. "Look familiar?"

Squinting, the man said, "Is this guy older now? Maybe a different haircut?"

"These are six years old. Seen him?"

The barman took glasses from his pocket, put them on and held the mugshots out at arm's length. "Does he blow around here?"

Danny missed the question—and wondered if it was sex slang he didn't know. "Explain what you mean."

"I mean does he gig, jam, play music around here?"

"Trombone at Bido Lito's."

The barman snapped his fingers. "Okay, I know him then. Marty something. He juices between sets at Bido's, been doing it since around Christmas, 'cause the bar at Bido's ain't supposed to serve the help. Hungry juicer, sort of like—"

Like *you*. Danny smiled, the booze notching down his temper. "Did you see him last night?"

"Yeah, on the street. Him and another guy heading over to a car down by the corner on 67th. Looked like he had a load on. Maybe …"

Danny leaned forward. "Maybe *what*? Spell it out."

"Maybe a junk load. You work jazz clubs awhile, you get to know the ropes. This Marty guy was walking all rubbery, like he was on a junk nod. The other guy had his arm round him, helping him over to the car."

Danny said, "Slow and easy now. The time, a description of the car and the other man. Real slow."

Customers were starting to swarm the bar—Negro men in modified zoot suits, their women a half step behind, all made up and done up to look like Lena Horne. The barkeep looked at his business, then back at Danny. "Had to be 12:15 to 12:45, around in there. Marty what's his face and the other guy were cutting across the sidewalk. I know the car was a Buick, 'cause it had them portholes on the side. All I remember about the other guy was that he was tall and had gray hair. I only saw them sort of sideways, and I thought, 'I should have such a nice head of hair.' Now can I serve these people?"

Danny was about to say no; the barkeep turned to a bearded young man with an alto sax slung around his neck. "Coleman, you know that white trombone from Bido's? Marty what the fuck?"

Coleman reached over the bar, grabbed two handfuls of ice and pressed them to his face. Danny checked him out: tall, blond, late twenties and off-kilter handsome—like the boy lead in the musical Karen Hiltscher dragged him to. His voice was reedy, exhausted. "Sure. A from-hunger horn, I heard. Why?"

"Talk to this police gentleman here, he'll tell you."

Danny pointed to his glass, going two shots over his nightly limit. The barman filled it, then slid off. The alto said, "You're with the Double Seven?"

Danny killed his drink, and on impulse stuck out his hand. "My name's Upshaw. West Hollywood Sheriff's."

The men shook. "Coleman Healy, late of Cleveland, Chicago and the planet Mars. Marty in trouble?"

The bourbon made Danny *too* warm; he loosened his tie and moved closer to Healy. "He was murdered last night."

Healy's face contorted. Danny saw every handsome plane jerk, twitch and spasm; he looked away to let him quash his shock and get hepcat again. When he turned back, Healy was bracing himself into the bar. Danny's knee brushed the alto's thigh—it was taut with tension. "How well did you know him, Coleman?"

Healy's face was now gaunt, slack under his beard. "Chewed the fat with him a couple of times around Christmas, right here at this bar. Just rebop—Bird's new record, the weather. You got an idea who did it?"

"A lead on a suspect—a tall, gray-haired man. The bartender saw him with Goines last night, walking toward a car parked on Central."

Coleman Healy ran fingers down the keys of his sax. "I've seen Marty with a guy like that a couple of times. Tall, middle-aged, dignified looking." He paused, then said, "Look, Upshaw, not to besmirch the dead, but can I give you an impression I got—on the QT?"

Danny slid his stool back, just enough to get a full-face reaction—Healy wired up, eager to help. "Go ahead, impressions help sometimes."

"Well, I think Marty was fruit. The older guy looked like a nance to me, like a sugar daddy type. The two of them were playing footsie at a table, and when I noticed it, Marty pulled away from the guy—sort of like a kid with his hand caught in the cookie jar."

Danny tingled, thinking of the tags he eschewed because they were too coarse and antithetical to Vollmer and Maslick: *PANSY SLASH. QUEER BASH. FRUIT SNUFF. HOMO PASSION JOB*. "Coleman, could you ID the older man?"

Healy played with his sax. "I don't think so. The light here is strange, and the queer stuff is just an impression I got."

"Have you seen the man before or since those times with Goines?"

"No. Never solo. And I was here all night, in case you think I did it."

Danny shook his head. "Do you know if Goines was using narcotics?"

"Nix. He was too interested in booze to be a junk fiend."

"What about other people who knew him? Other musicians around here?"

"Ixnay. We just gabbed a couple of times."

Danny put out his hand; Healy turned it upside down, twisting it from a squarejohn to a jazzman shake. He said, "See you in church," and headed for the stage.

Queer slash.

Fruit snuff.

Homo passion job.

Danny watched Coleman Healy mount the bandstand and exchange back slaps with the other musicians. Fat and cadaverous, pocked, oily and consumptive looking, they seemed wrong next to the sleek alto—like a crime scene photo with blurs that fucked up the symmetry and made you notice the wrong things. The music started: piano handing a jump melody to the trumpet, drums kicking in, Healy's sax wailing, lilting, wailing, drifting off the base refrain into chord variations. The music digressed into noise; Danny spotted a bank of phone booths next to the powder room and rolled back to police work.

His first nickel got him the watch boss at the 77th Street Station. Danny explained that he was a Sheriff's detective working a homicide—a jazz musician and possible dope addict slashed and dumped off the Sunset Strip. The victim was probably not currently using drugs—but he wanted a list of local H pushers anyway—the snuff might be tied to dope intrigue. The watch boss said, "How's Mickey these days?," added, "Submit a request through official channels," and hung up.

Pissed, Danny dialed Doc Layman's personal number at the City Morgue, one eye on the bandstand. The pathologist answered on the second ring. "Yes?"

"Danny Upshaw, Doctor."

Layman laughed. "Danny Upstart is more like it—I just autopsied the John Doe you tried to usurp."

Danny drew in a breath, turning away from Coleman Healy gyrating with his sax. "Yes? And?"

"And a question first. Did you stick a tongue depressor in the corpse's mouth?"

"Yes."

"Deputy, never, *ever*, introduce foreign elements into interior cavities until after you have thoroughly spotted the exterior. The cadaver had cuts with imbedded wood slivers all over his back— pine—and you stuck a piece of pine into his mouth, leaving similar slivers. Do you see how you could have fouled up my assessment?"

"Yes, but it was obvious the victim was strangled by a towel or a sash—the terrycloth fibers were a dead giveaway."

Layman sighed—long, exasperated. "The cause of death was a massive heroin overdose. The shot was administered into a vein by the spine, by the killer himself—the victim couldn't have reached it. The towel was placed in the mouth to absorb blood when the heroin hit the victim's heart and caused arteries to pop, which means the killer had at least elementary anatomical knowledge."

Danny said, "Jesus fuck."

Layman said, "An appropriate blasphemy, but it gets worse. Here's some incidentals first:

"One, no residual heroin in the bloodstream—Mr. Doe was not now addicted, although needle marks on his arms indicate he once was. Two, death occurred around 1:00 to 2:00 A.M., and the neck and genital bruises were both postmortem. The cuts on the back were postmortem, almost certainly made by razor blades attached to something like a pine slab or a 2 by 4. So far, brutal— but not past my ken. However . . ."

Layman stopped—his old classroom orator's pause. Danny, sweating out his jolts of bonded, said, "Come on, Doc."

"All right. The substance in the eye sockets was KY Jelly. The killer inserted his penis into the sockets and ejaculated—at least twice. I found six cubic centimeters of semen seeping back toward the cranial vault. O+ secretor—the most common blood type among white people."

Danny opened the phone booth door; he heard wisps of bebop and saw Coleman Healy going down on one knee, sax raised to the rafters. "The bites on the torso?"

Layman said, "Not human is what I'm thinking. The wounds were too shredded to make casts from—there's no way I could

have lifted any kind of viable teeth marks. Also, the ME's assistant
who took over after you pulled your little number swabbed the
affected area with alcohol, so I couldn't test for saliva or gastric
juices. The victim's blood—AB+—was all I found there. You
discovered the body when?"

"Shortly after 4:00 A.M."

"Then scavenging animals down from the hills are unlikely.
The wounds are too localized for that theory, anyway."

"Doc, are you sure we're dealing with teeth marks?"

"Absolutely. The inflammation around the wounds is from a
mouth sucking. It's too wide to be human—"

"Do you think—"

"Don't interrupt. I'm thinking that—*maybe*—the killer spread
blood bait on the affected area and let some kind of well-trained
vicious dog at the victim. How many men are working this job,
Danny?"

"Just me."

"ID on the victim? Leads?"

"It's going well, Doc."

"Get him."

"I will."

Danny hung up and walked outside. Cold air edged the heat
off his booze intake and let him collate evidence. He now had
three solid leads:

The homosexual mutilations combined with Coleman Healy's
observation of Marty Goines being "fruit"; his "nance" "sugar
daddy type"—who resembled the tall, gray-haired man the bartender saw with Goines, heading toward the stolen Buick last
night—an hour or so before the estimated time of death; the
heroin OD cause of death; the bartender's description of Goines
weaving in a junk nod—that jolt of dope a probable precursor to
the shot that burst his heart; Goines' previous addiction and
recent dope cure. Putting the possible animal mutilations out of
mind, he had one *hard* lead: the tall, gray-haired man—a sugar
daddy capable of glomming heroin, hypodermic syringes and
talking a reformed junkie into geezing up on the spot and ditching his New Year's Eve gig.

And no LAPD cooperation—yet—on local horse pushers; a
junkie squeeze was the only logical play.

Danny walked across the street to Tommy Tucker's Playroom,
found an empty booth and ordered coffee to kill the liquor in his

system and keep him awake. The music/motif was ballads and zebra-striped upholstery, cheap jungle wallpaper offset by tiki torches licking flames up to the ceiling, another fire hazard, a blaze to burn the whole block to cinder city. The coffee was black and strong and made inroads on the bonded; the bop was soft— caresses for the couples in the booths: lovebirds holding hands and sipping rum drinks. The total package made him think of San Berdoo circa '39, him and Tim in a hot Olds ragger joy-riding to a hicktown prom, changing clothes at his place while the old lady hawked *Watchtowers* outside Coulter's Department Store. Down to their skivvies, horseplay, jokes about substitutes for girls; Timmy with Roxanne Beausoleil outside the gym that night— the two of them bouncing the Olds almost off its suspension. Him the prom wallflower, declining seconds on Roxy, drinking spiked punch, getting mawkish with the slow grind numbers and the hurt.

Danny killed the memories with police work—eyeball prowls for Health and Safety Code violations, liquor infractions, *wrongness*. The doorman was admitting minors; high yellows in slit gowns were oozing around soliciting business, there was only one side exit in a huge room sixteen seconds away from fireballing. Time passed; the music went from soft to loud to soft again; coffee and constant eye circuits got his nerves fine-honed. Then he hit paydirt, spotting two Negroes by the exit curtains pulling a handoff: cash for something palmable, a quick segue into the parking lot.

Danny counted to six and followed, easing the door open, peering out. The spook who took the money was striding toward the sidewalk; the other guy was two rows of cars down, opening the door of a rig topped by a long whip antenna. Danny gave him thirty seconds to geez up, light up or snort up, then pulled his .45, hunkered down and approached.

The car was a lavender Merc; marijuana smoke was drifting out the wind wings. Danny grabbed the driver's door and swung it open; the Negro shrieked, dropped his reefer and recoiled from the gun in his face. Danny said, "Sheriff's. Hands on the dashboard slow or I'll kill you."

The youth complied, in slow motion. Danny jammed the .45's muzzle under his chin and gave him a frisk: inside and outside jacket pockets, a waistband pat for weaponry. He found a lizardskin wallet, three marijuana cigarettes and no hardware;

popped the glove compartment and flicked on the dashlight. The kid said, "Look, man"; Danny dug his gun in harder, until it cut off his air supply and forced him mute.

The reefer stench was getting brutal; Danny found the butt on the seat cushion and snuffed it. With his free hand he opened the wallet, pulled out a driver's license and over a hundred in tens and twenties. He slipped the cash in his pocket and read the license: Carlton W. Jeffries, M.N., 5′ 11″, 165, DOB 6/19/29, 439 1/4 E. 98 St., L.A. A quick toss of the glove compartment got him DMV registration under the same name and a slew of unpaid traffic citations in their mailing envelopes. Danny put the license, reefers, money and registration into an envelope and dropped it on the pavement; he pulled his .45 out from under the boy's chin and used the muzzle to turn his head toward him. Up close, he saw a chocolate brown punk next to tears, lips flapping, Adam's apple bobbing up and down as he struggled for breath.

Danny said, "Information or five years State time minimum. You call it."

Carlton W. Jeffries found a voice: high, squeaky. "What you think?"

"I think you're smart. Give me what I want, and I'll put that envelope in the mail to you tomorrow."

"You could give it back now. Please. I need that money."

"I want a hard snitch. If you play both ends and I get hurt, I've got you nailed. Evidence, and the confession you just made."

"Man, I didn't make no confession to you!"

"Sure you did. You've been selling a pound a week. You're the A-number-one Southside grasshopper."

"Man!"

Danny rested his gun barrel on Carlton W. Jeffries' nose. "I want names. Heroin pushers around here. Give."

"Man—"

Danny flipped the .45 up and grabbed the muzzle, reversing his grip so the gun could be used as a bludgeon. *"Give, goddamn you."*

Jeffries took his hands off the dash and wrapped his arms around himself. "Only guy I know is a guy name of Otis Jackson. Lives above the laundromat on 103 and Beach and please don't give me no rat jacket!"

Danny holstered his piece and backed out the car door. His foot hit the DMV envelope just as he heard Carlton W. Jeffries start bawling. He picked the evidence up, tossed it on the seat and double-timed to his Chevy so he wouldn't hear the sad little fuck blubber his gratitude.

* * *

103rd and Beach was a run-down intersection in the heart of Watts: hair-straightening parlors on two corners, a liquor store on the third, the Koin King Washeteria occupying number four. Lights were burning in the apartment above the laundromat; Danny parked across the street, doused his headbeams and scoped out the only possible access: side steps leading up to a flimsy-looking door.

He walked over and up them, tiptoes, no hand on the railing for fear it would creak. At the top, he pulled his gun, put an ear to the door and listened, picking up a man's voice counting: eight, nine, ten, eleven. Tapping the door, he faked a drawl straight from Amos 'n' Andy: "Otis? You there, man? It's me, man."

Danny heard "Shit!" inside; seconds later the door opened, held to the jamb by a chain. A hand holding a switchblade stuck out; Danny brought his gun barrel down on the shiv, then threw his weight inward.

The switchblade hit the top step; a voice screeched; the door caved in, Danny riding it. Then it was a crash to the carpet and a topsy-turvy shot of Otis Jackson scooping junk bindles off the floor, stumbling to the bathroom, a toilet flushing. Danny got to his knees, sighted in and yelled, "Sheriff's!" Otis Jackson flipped him his middle finger and weaved back to the living room wearing a shiteater grin.

Danny stood up, his head pounding with jazz chords. Otis Jackson said, "The fuckin' Sheriff's ain't fuckin' shit around here."

Danny lashed the .45 across his face. Jackson hit the rug, moaned and spit out cracked bridgework. Danny squatted beside him. "You sell to a tall, gray-haired white man?"

Jackson spat bloody phlegm and a slice of his tongue. "I'm with Jack D. and the Seven-Seven, mother—"

Danny held his gun at eye level. "I'm with Mickey and the County, so what? I asked you a question."

"I deal Hollywood, man! I know lots of gray-haired suckers!"

"Name them, and name everyone else you know who unloads at the clubs on South Central."

"I'll let you kill me first, sucker!"

The jazz noise was coming back, soundtracking images: Coleman Healy fondling his sax, the reefer guy about to beg.

Danny said, "One more time. I want skinny on a tall white man. Middle-aged, silver hair."

"An' I told you—"

Danny heard footsteps coming up the stairs, grunts and the unmistakable sound of revolvers being cocked. Otis Jackson smiled; Danny glommed the gist, holstered his piece and reached for his badge holder. Two big white men popped in the doorway aiming .38's; Danny had his shield out and a peace offering ready. "Sheriff's. I'm a Sheriff's detective."

The men walked over, guns first. The taller of the two helped Otis Jackson to his feet; the other, a fat guy with curly red hair, took Danny's ID buzzer, examined it and shook his head. "Bad enough you guys get in bed with Mickey Kike, now you gotta beat up my favorite snitch. Otis, you are one lucky nigger. Deputy Upshaw, you are one stupid white man."

The tall cop helped Otis Jackson into the bathroom. Danny stood up and grabbed his badge holder. The fat redhead said, "Get the fuck back to the County and beat up your own niggers."

5

"... AND THE most pervasive aspect of Communism, its single most insidiously efficacious tool, is that it hides under a million banners, a million different flags, titles and combinations of initials, spreading its cancer under a million guises, all of them designed to pervert and corrupt in the name of compassion and goodness and social justice. UAES, SLDC, NAACP, AFL-CIO, League for Democratic Ideals and Concerned Americans Against Bigotry. All high-sounding organizations that all good Americans should be proud to belong to. All seditious, perverted, cancerous tentacles of the Communist Conspiracy."

Mal Considine had been sizing up Edmund J. Satterlee, ex-Fed, ex-Jesuit seminarian, for close to half an hour, taking occasional glances at the rest of the audience. Satterlee was a tall man, pear-shaped, in his early forties; his verbal style was a cross between Harry Truman homespun and Pershing Square crackpot—and you never knew when he was going to shout or whisper. Dudley Smith, chain-smoking, seemed to be enjoying his pitch; Ellis Loew kept looking at his watch and at Dudley—probably afraid that he was going to drop ash all over his new living room carpet. Dr. Saul Lesnick, psychiatrist/longtime Fed informant, sat as far away from the Red Chaser as possible while remaining in the same room. He was a small, frail old man with bright blue eyes and a cough that he kept feeding with harsh European cigarettes; he had the look native to stool pigeons everywhere—loathing for the presence of his captors—even though he had allegedly volunteered his services.

Satterlee was pacing now, gesticulating to them like they were four hundred, not four. Mal squirmed in his chair, reminding himself that this guy was his ticket to a captaincy and Chief DA's Investigator.

"... and in the early days of the war I worked with the Alien Squad relocating Japs. I gained my first insights into how anti-American sentiment breeds. The Japs who wanted to be good Americans offered to enlist in the armed forces, most were resentful and confused, and the subversive element—under the guise of patriotism—attempted to coerce them into treason by concerted, heavily intellectualized attacks on alleged American racial injustices. Under a banner of American concerns: liberty, justice and free enterprise, the seditious Japs portrayed this democracy as a land of lynched Negroes and limited opportunities for coloreds, even though the Nisei were emerging as middle-class merchants when the war broke out. After the war, when the Communist Conspiracy emerged as the number-one threat to America's internal security, I saw how the same kind of thinking, of manipulation, was being used by the Reds to subvert our moral fiber. The entertainment industry and business were rife with fellow travelers, and I founded Red Crosscurrents to help weed out radicals and subversives. Organizations that want to keep themselves Red-free pay us a nominal fee to screen their employees and prospective employees for Commie associations, and *we* keep an exhaustive file on the Reds we uncover. This service also allows innocent people accused of being Pink to prove their innocence and gain employment that they might have been denied. Further—"

Mal heard Dr. Saul Lesnick cough; he looked at the old man sidelong and saw that the eruption was half laughter. Satterlee paused; Ellis Loew said, "Ed, can we gloss the background and get down to business?"

Satterlee flushed, picked up his briefcase and took out a stack of papers, four individually clipped sheafs. He handed one each

to Mal, Loew and Dudley Smith; Dr. Lesnick declined his with a
shake of the head. Mal skimmed the top sheet. It was a deposition
detailing picket line scuttlebutt: members of the United Alliance
of Extras and Stagehands mouthing Pinko platitudes overheard
by counter-pickets from the Teamsters. Mal checked the signees'
names, recognizing Morris Jahelka, Davey Goldman and Fritzie
"Icepick" Kupferman—known Mickey Cohen strongarms.

Satterlee resumed his position in front of them; Mal thought
he looked like a man who would kill for a lectern—or any resting place for his long, gangly arms. "These pieces of paper are our
first wave of ammunition. I have worked with a score of municipal grand juries nationwide, and the sworn statements of patriotic
citizens always have a salutary effect on Grand Jury members.
I think we have a great chance for a successful one here in Los
Angeles now—the labor infighting between the Teamsters and
the UAES is a great impetus, a shot at the limelight that will
probably not come again. Communist influence in Hollywood is
a broad topic, and the picket line trouble and UAES's fomenting
of subversion within both contexts is a good device to get the
public interested. Let me quote from the deposition of Mr. Morris
Jahelka: 'While picketing outside Variety International Pictures
on the morning of November 29, 1949, I heard a UAES member,
a woman named "Claire," tell another UAES member: "With the
UAES in the studios we can advance the cause better than the
entire Red Guard. Movies are the new opiate of the people.
They'll believe anything we can get on the screen."' Gentlemen,
Claire is Claire Katherine De Haven, a consort of Hollywood 10
traitors and a known member of no fewer than fourteen
organizations that have been classified as Communist Fronts
by the California State Attorney General's Office. Is that not
impressive?"

Mal raised his hand. Edmund J. Satterlee said, "Yes, Lieutenant
Considine? A question?"

"No, a statement. Morris Jahelka has two convictions for felony statch rape. Your patriotic citizen screws twelve-year-old girls."

Ellis Loew said, "Goddamnit, Malcolm."

Satterlee tried a smile, faltered at it and stuck his hands in his
pockets. "I see. Anything else on Mr. Jahelka?"

"Yes. He also likes little boys, but he's never been caught at it."

Dudley Smith laughed. "Politics makes for strange bedfellows,
which doesn't negate the fact that in this case Mr. Jahelka is on

the side of the angels. Besides, lad, we'll be damn sure his jacket is sealed, and the goddamn Pinks probably won't bring in lawyers for redirect questioning."

Mal concentrated on keeping his voice calm. "Is that true, Ellis?"

Loew fanned away plumes of Doc Lesnick's cigarette smoke. "Essentially, yes. We're trying to get as many UAESers as possible to volunteer as witnesses, and hostile witnesses—subpoenaed ones—tend to try to assert their innocence by not retaining counsel. Also, the studios have a clause in their contract with UAES, stating that they can terminate the contract if certain areas of malfeasance can be proven against the contractee. Before the grand jury convenes—if our evidence is strong enough—I'm going to the studio heads to get UAES ousted on that clause— which should make the bastards hopping mad and rabid when they hit the witness stand. An angry witness is an ineffectual witness. You know that, Mal."

Cohen and his Teamsters in; UAES out. Mal wondered if Mickey C. was a contributor to Loew's six-figure slush fund— which should hit the half million mark by the time of the '52 primaries. "You're good, counselor."

"So are you, *Captain*. Down to brass tacks, Ed. I'm due in court at noon."

Satterlee handed Mal and Dudley mimeographed sheets. "My thoughts on the interrogation of subversives," he said. "Guilt by association is a strong lever on these people—they're all connected up—everyone on the far left knows everyone else to one degree or another. In with your depositions I've got lists of Commie front meetings cross-filed with donation lists, which are excellent levers to procure information and get Reds to inform on other Reds to save their own damn skin. The donations also mean bank records that can be subpoenaed as evidence. Proffering surveillance photos to potential witnesses is my personal favorite technique—being shown at a subversive meeting puts the fear of God into the most Godless Pinks, and they'll inform on their own mother to stay out of jail. I may be able to get us some extremely damaging photos from a friend who works for Red Channels—some extremely good pictures of Sleepy Lagoon Defense Committee picnics. In fact, I've been told the photos are the Rembrandts of Federal surveillance—actual CP bigwigs and Hollywood stars along with our friends in UAES. Mr. Loew?"

Loew said, "Thank you, Ed," and gave his standard one finger up, indicating everybody stand. Dudley Smith practically leaped to his feet; Mal stood and saw Doc Lesnick walking to the bathroom holding his chest. Awful wet coughs echoed from the hallway; he pictured Lesnick retching blood. Satterlee, Smith and Loew broke up their circle of handshaking; the Red Chaser went out the door with the DA kneading his shoulders.

Dudley Smith said, "Zealots are always tiresome. Ed's good at what he does, but he doesn't know when to quit performing. Five hundred dollars a lecture he gets. Capitalist exploitation of Communism, wouldn't you say so, Captain?"

"I'm not a captain yet, Lieutenant."

"Ha! And a grand wit you have, too, to go with your rank."

Mal studied the Irishman, less scared than he was yesterday morning at the restaurant. "What's in this for you? You're a case man, you don't want Jack Tierney's job."

"Maybe I just want to get next to you, lad. You're odds on for Chief of Police or County Sheriff somewhere down the line, all that grand work you did in Europe, liberating our persecuted Jewish brethren. Speaking of which, here comes the Hebrew contingent now."

Ellis Loew was leading Lesnick into the living room and settling him into an easy chair by the fireplace. The old man arranged a pack of Gauloises, a lighter and ashtray on his lap, crossing one stick leg over the other to hold them in place. Loew pulled up chairs around him in a semicircle; Smith winked and sat down. Mal saw cardboard boxes packed with folders filling up the dining alcove, four typewriters stacked in one corner to accommodate the grand jury team's paperwork. Ellis Loew was preparing for war, his ranch house as headquarters.

Mal took the leftover chair. Doc Lesnick lit a cigarette, coughed and started talking. His voice was highbrow New York Jew working with one lung; Mal made his pitch as processed, spieled to a load of other cops and DAs.

"Mr. Satterlee did you a disservice by not going back further in his rather threadbare history of subversive elements in America. He neglected to mention the Depression, starvation and desperate people, concerned people, who wanted to change terrible conditions." Lesnick paused, got breath and stubbed out his Gauloise. Mal saw a bony chest heaving, nailed the old man as gravebait and sensed that he was wavering: the pain of speech versus a chance to justify his fink duty. Finally he sucked in a huge draft of air and kept going, some kind of fervor lighting up his eyes.

"I was one of those people, twenty years ago. I signed petitions, wrote letters and went to labor meetings that accomplished nothing. The Communist Party, despite its evil connotations, was the only organization that did not seem ineffectual. Its reputation gave it a certain panache, a cachet, and the self-righteous hypocrites who condemned it in a blanket manner made me want to belong to it in order to assert my defiance of them.

"It was an injudicious decision, one that I came to regret. Being a psychiatrist, I was designated the official CP analyst here in Los Angeles. Marxism and Freudian analysis were very much in the intellectual vogue, and a number of people whom I later realized were conspirators against this country told me their . . . secrets, so to speak, emotional and political. Many were Hollywood people, writers and actors and their satellites—working-class people as deluded as I was regarding Communism, people who wanted to get close to the Hollywood people because of their movie connections. Just before the time of the Hitler-Stalin pact I became disillusioned with the Party. In '39, during the California State HUAC probe, I volunteered to serve the FBI as an undercover informant. I have served in that capacity for over ten years, while concurrently acting as CP analyst. I secretly made my private files available to the 1947 House Un-American Activities Committee probers, and I am doing the same for this grand jury probe now. The files are for UAES members essential to your probe, and should you require assistance in interpreting them, I would be happy to be of service."

The old man nearly choked on his last words. He reached for his cigarette pack; Ellis Loew, holding a glass of water, got to him first. Lesnick gulped, coughed, gulped; Dudley Smith walked into the dining alcove and tapped the filing boxes and typewriters with his spit-shined brogues—uncharacteristically idle footwork.

A horn honked outside. Mal stood up to thank Lesnick and shake his hand. The old man looked away and pushed himself to his feet, almost not making it. The horn beeped again; Loew opened the door and gestured to the cab in the driveway. Lesnick shuffled out, gulping fresh morning air.

The taxi drove away; Loew turned on a wall fan. Dudley Smith said, "How long does he have, Ellis? Will you be sending him an invitation to your victory celebration come '52?"

Loew scooped big handfuls of files off the floor and laid them out on the dining room table; he repeated the process until there were two stacks of paper halfway to the ceiling. "Long enough to suit our purposes."

Mal walked over and looked at their evidence: information extraction thumbscrews. "He won't testify before the grand jury, though?"

"No, never. He's terrified of losing his credibility as a psychiatrist. Confidentiality, you know. It's a good hiding place for lawyers, and doctors covet it too. Of course, it's not legally binding for them. Lesnick would be kaput as a psychiatrist if he testified."

Dudley said, "You would think he would like to meet his maker as a good patriotic American, though. He did volunteer, and that should be a grand satisfaction for someone whose next life looms so imminently."

Loew laughed. "Dud, have you *ever* taken a step without spotting the angles?"

"The last time *you* did, counselor. Captain Considine, yourself?"

Mal said, "Sometime back in the Roaring Twenties," thinking that mano a mano, brain to brain, he'd favor the Dublin street thug over the Harvard Phi Beta. "Ellis, when do we start approaching witnesses?"

Loew tapped the file stacks. "Soon, after you've digested these. Based on what you learn here, you'll be making your first approaches—on weak points—weak people—who'd seem most likely to cooperate. If we can build up an array of friendly witnesses fast, fine. But if we don't get a fair amount of initial cooperation, we'll have to put in a plant. Our friends on the Teamsters have heard picket line talk—that the UAES is planning strategy meetings aimed at coercing exorbitant contract demands out of the studios. If we get a string of balks right off the bat, I want to pull back and put a decoy into the UAES. I want both of you to think of smart, tough, idealistic-looking young cops we can use if it comes to that."

Chills grabbed Mal. Sending in decoys, *operating*, had made his rep at Ad Vice—it was what he was best at as a policeman. He said, "I'll think on it. There's just Dudley and me as investigators?"

Loew made a gesture that took in his whole house. "Clerks from the City pool here to handle the paperwork, Ed Satterlee for the use of his contacts, Lesnick for our psychiatric edification.

You two to interrogate. I might get us a third man to prowl for criminal stuff, rattle cages, that kind of thing."

Mal got itchy to read, think, operate. He said, "I'm going to clear up some loose ends at the Hall, go home and work."

Loew said, "I'm going to prosecute a real estate man for drunk driving on his son's motorcycle."

Dudley Smith toasted his boss with an imaginary glass. "Have mercy. Most real estate men are good patriotic Republicans, and you might need his contribution one day."

* * *

Back at City Hall, Mal made calls to satisfy his curiosity on his two new colleagues. Bob Cathcart, a savvy Criminal Division FBI man he'd worked with, gave him the scoop on Edmund J. Satterlee. Cathcart's take: the man was a religious crackpot with a wild hair up his ass about Communism, so extreme in his views that Clyde Tolson, Hoover's number-two man at the Bureau, repeatedly issued gag orders on him when he served as Agent in Charge at the Waco, Texas, field office. Satterlee was estimated to earn fifty thousand dollars a year in anti-Communist lecture fees; Red Crosscurrents was "a shakedown racket"—"They'd clear Karl Marx if the dough was right." Satterlee was rumored to have been bounced off the Alien Squad for attempting a kickback operation: cash vouchers from interned Japanese prisoners in exchange for his safeguarding their confiscated property until they were released. Agent Cathcart's summation: Ed Satterlee was a loony, albeit a rich and very efficient one—very adept at advancing conspiracy theories that stood up in court; very good at gathering evidence; very good at running outside interference for grand jury investigators.

A call to an old pal working the LAPD Metropolitan Squad and one to an ex-DA's man now with the State Attorney General's office supplied Mal with the true story on Saul Lesnick, MD, PhD. The old man was, and remained, a CP card carrier; he had been a Fed snitch since '39—when he was approached by two L.A. office agents, who made him a deal: provide confidential psychiatric dirt to various committees and police agencies, and his daughter would be sprung from her five-to-ten-year sentence for hit and run drunk driving—one year down, four more to go minimum—the girl then currently hardtiming in Tehachapi. Lesnick agreed; his daughter was released and placed on indeterminate Federal parole—which would be revoked if the good doctor ever broke his cover or otherwise refused to cooperate. Lesnick, given six months tops in his fight with lung cancer, had secured a promise from a high-ranking Justice Department official: upon his death, all the confidential files he had loaned out would be destroyed; his daughter's vehicular manslaughter conviction and parole records would be expunged and all Fed/Municipal/State grand jury notations currently on official paper vis-à-vis Lesnick and his breaches of confidentiality with subversive patients would burn. No one would know that for ten years Saul Lesnick, Communist, psychiatrist, had played both ends against the middle—and had won his holding action.

Mal segued, new colleagues to old business, thinking that the lunger got what he paid for in spades, that his dance with the Feds was good value: a daughter spared broomstick rape and pernicious anemia from Tehachapi's famous all-starch cuisine in exchange for the rest of his life—shortened by suicide via French tobacco. And *he'd* have done the same thing for Stefan—he wouldn't have thought twice.

Paperwork was arrayed neatly across his desk; Mal, stealing glances at the huge grand jury pile, got to it. He wrote memos to Ellis Loew suggesting investigators to dig for backup evidence; he typed routing slips: case files to the green young Deputy DAs who would be prosecuting now that Loew was engaged full-time in battling Communism. A Chinatown hooker killing went to a kid six months out of the worst law school in California; the perpetrator, a pimp known for his love of inflicting pain with a metal-studded dildo, would probably walk on the charge. Two shine snuffs were routed to a youth still short of his twenty-fifth birthday—smart, but naive. This perp, a Purple Cobra warlord, had fired into a crowd of kids outside Manual Arts High School on the off-chance that there might be members of the Purple Scorpions in it. There weren't; an honor student and her boyfriend went down dead. Mal gave the kid a fifty-fifty chance for a conviction—Negroes killing Negroes bored white juries and they often dropped their verdicts on whim.

The armed robbery/ADW at Minnie Roberts' Casbah went to a Loew protégé; writing evidence summaries on the three cases took four hours and gave Mal finger cramps. Finishing, he checked his watch and saw that it was 3:10—Stefan would be home from school. If he was lucky, Celeste would be visiting her crony down the street, bullshitting in Czech, gabbing about the old country before the war. Mal grabbed his stack of psychiatric dirt and drove home, resisting a kid's urge: to stop at an army-navy store and buy himself a pair of silver captain's bars.

Home was in the Wilshire District: a big white two-story that devoured his savings and most of his salary. It was the house that was too good for Laura—a kid marriage based on rutting didn't warrant the tariff. He'd bought it when he returned from Europe in '46, knowing that Laura was out and Celeste was in, sensing that he loved the boy more than he could ever love the woman—that the marriage was for Stefan's safety. There was a park with basketball hoops and a baseball diamond nearby; the neighborhood's crime rate was near zero and the local schools had the highest academic standing in the state. It was his happy ending to Stefan's nightmare.

Mal parked in the driveway and walked across the lawn—Stefan's lackluster mowing job, Stefan's softball and bat weighing down the hedge that he'd neglected to trim. Going in the door, he heard voices: the two-language fight he'd refereed a thousand times before. Celeste was running down verb conjugations in Czech, sitting on the divan in her sewing room, gesturing to Stefan, her captive in a straight-backed chair. The boy was fiddling with objects on an end table—thimbles and thread spools—arranging them by progression of color, so smart that he had to keep occupied even while on the receiving end of a lecture. Mal stood aside from the doorway and watched, loving Stefan for his defiance; glad that he was dark and pudgy like his real father was supposed to be—not lean and sandy-haired like Celeste—even though Mal was blond, and it clued people in that they weren't blood relations.

Celeste was saying, "... and it is the language of your people."

Stefan was stacking the spools, making a little house out of them—dark colors the foundation, pastels on top. "But I am to be an American now. Malcolm told me he can get me cit-cit-citizenship."

"Malcolm is a minister's son and a policeman who does not understand our old country traditions. Stefan, your heritage. Learn to make your mother happy."

Mal could tell his boy wasn't buying it; he smiled when Stefan demolished the spool house, his dark eyes fired up. "Malcolm said Czechoslovakia is a ... a ... a ..."

"A what, darling?"

"A Bohunk rubble heap! A shit pile! Scheiss! Scheiss! In German for mutti!"

Celeste raised a hand, stopped and hit her own pinched-together knees. "In English for you—little ingrate, disgrace to your real father, a cultured man, a doctor, not a consort of whores and hoodlums—"

Stefan knocked over the end table and ran out of the room, straight into Mal, blocking the doorway. The small fat boy careened off his six-foot-three stepfather, then grabbed him around the waist and buried his head in his vest. Mal held him there, one hand steadying his shoulders, the other ruffling his hair. When Celeste stood up and saw them, he said, "You'll never give it up, will you?"

Celeste mouthed words; Mal knew they were native tongue obscenities she didn't want Stefan to hear. The boy held on tighter, then let go and ran upstairs to his room. Mal heard ting-ting-ting—Stefan's toy soldiers being hurled at the door. He said, "You know what it makes him think of, and you still won't give it up."

Celeste adjusted her arms inside her overslung cardigan—the single European affectation Mal hated the most. "Nein, herr Leutnant"—pure German, pure Celeste—Buchenwald, the gas man, Major Considine, cold-blooded killer.

Mal braced himself into the doorway. "Captain soon, *Fräulein*. Chief DA's Investigator, and climbing. Juice, *Fräulein*. Just in case I think you're ruining my son and I have to take him away from you."

Celeste sat down, knees together, a finishing school move, Prague 1934. "To the mother the child belongs. Even a failed lawyer like you should know that maxim."

A line that couldn't be topped. Mal kicked up the carpeting on his way outside; he sat on the steps and watched rain clouds hover. Celeste's sewing machine started to whir; upstairs, Stefan's soldiers were still dinging his already cracked and dented bedroom door. Mal thought that soon they'd be stripped of paint, dragoons without uniforms, and that simple fact would tear down everything he'd built up since the war.

In '45 he was an army major, stationed at a temporary MP barracks near the recently liberated Buchenwald concentration camp. His assignment was to interrogate surviving inmates, specifically the ones the medical evacuation teams deemed terminally ill—the husks of human beings who would most likely never live to identify their captors in court. The question and answer sessions were horrific; Mal knew that only the stony cold presence of his interpreter was keeping him frosty, contained, a pro. News from the home front was just as bad: friends wrote him that Laura was screwing Jerry Dunleavy, a buddy from the Homicide Bureau, and Buzz Meeks, a crooked Narcotics Squad dick and bagman for Mickey Cohen. And in San Francisco, his father, the Reverend Liam Considine, was dying of congestive heart disease and sending daily telegrams begging him to embrace Jesus before he died. Mal hated the man too much to give him the satisfaction and was too busy praying for the speedy and painless deaths of every single Buchenwald survivor, for the complete cessation of their memories and his nightmares. The old man died in October; Mal's brother Desmond, the used-car king of Sacramento, sent him a telegram rich in religious invective. It ended with words of disownment. Two days later Mal met Celeste Heisteke.

She came out of Buchenwald physically healthy and defiant, and she spoke enough English to render the interpreter unnecessary. Mal conducted his interrogations of Celeste solo; they spoke on only one topic: her whoredom with an SS lieutenant colonel named Franz Kempflerr—his price for her survival.

Celeste's stories—graphically told—killed his nightmares better than the contraband phenobarbital he'd been blasting for weeks. They excited him, disgusted him, made him hate the Nazi colonel and hate himself for being a voyeur eight thousand miles away from his legendary whore sweep operations in Ad Vice. Celeste sensed his excitement and seduced him; together, they reenacted all of her adventures with Franz Kempflerr. Mal fell in love with her—because he knew she had his number better than dumb sexpot Laura ever did. Then, when she had him hooked, she told him of her dead husband and her six-year-old son, who might still be alive somewhere in Prague. Would he, a veteran detective, be willing to search for the boy?

Mal agreed, for the challenge and the chance to become more to Celeste than a voyeur-lover, more than the sewer crawler cop his family considered him to be. He made three trips to Prague, blundering around asking questions in pidgin Czech and German. Networks of Heisteke cousins resisted him; twice he was threatened with guns and knives and retreated, fear at his back

like he was walking a beat in L.A. niggertown, whispers and
catcalls from the okie cops who dominated the nightwatch there:
college boy chickenshit, nigger scared, coward. On his final trip
he located Stefan Heisteke, a pale, dark-haired child with a distended belly, sleeping outside a cigarette vendor's stall in a rolled-
up carpet lent to him by a friendly black marketeer. The man told
Mal that the boy became frightened if people spoke to him in
Czech, the language he seemed to best understand; phrases in
German and French elicited simple yes or no answers. Mal took
Stefan to his hotel, fed him and attempted to bathe him—
stopping when he started to scream.

He let Stefan wash himself; he let him sleep for seventeen
uninterrupted hours. Then, armed with German and French
phrase books, he began his most grueling interrogation. It took
a week of long silences, long pauses and halting questions and
answers with half the room between them for Mal to get the
story straight.

Stefan Heisteke had been left with trusted first cousins just
before Celeste and her husband, gentile anti-Nazis, were
captured by the Germans; they, fleeing, had shunted him to
distant in-laws, who left him with friends who gave him
to acquaintances sequestered in a deserted factory basement.
He was there for the better part of two years, accompanied by
a man and woman gone cabin-fevered. The factory processed
dog food, and cans of horsemeat were all Stefan ate during
that time. The man and woman used him sexually, then goo-
goo-talked to him in Czech, lover's endearments to a five- and
six-year-old child. Stefan could not tolerate the sound of that
language.

Mal brought Stefan back to Celeste, gave her a mercifully abbreviated account of his lost years and told her to speak French
to him—or teach him English. He did not tell her that he considered her cousins accomplices to the boy's horror, and when
Stefan himself told his mother what had happened, Celeste
capitulated to Mal. He knew she had been using him before; now
she loved him. He had a family to replace his shattered one at
home in America.

Together, they began teaching Stefan English; Mal wrote to
Laura, requested a divorce and got the paperwork ready to bring
his new family stateside. Things were going very smoothly; then
they went haywire.

Celeste's whoremaster officer had escaped before Buchenwald was liberated; just as Mal was about to take his discharge, he was captured in Kraków and held at the MP barracks there. Mal went to Kraków just to see him; the stockade duty officer showed him the Nazi's confiscated property, which included unmistakable locks of Celeste's hair. Mal walked back to Franz Kempflerr's cell and emptied his sidearm into the man's face.

A tight net was thrown over the incident; the military governor, an Army one-star, liked Mal's style. Mal took an honorable discharge, brought Celeste and Stefan to America, returned to his LAPD sergeantcy and divorced Laura. Of his two cuckolders, Buzz Meeks was wounded in a shootout and pensioned off to civilian life; Jerry Dunleavy stayed on the job—but out of his way. Rumor had it that Meeks thought Mal was behind the shooting— revenge for the affair with Laura. Mal let the talk simmer: it played a good counterpoint to the coward innuendo he'd inspired in Watts. Word leaked out here and there on the gas man; Ellis Loew, DA's comer, Jew, draft dodger, took an interest in him and offered to swing some gravy his way once he aced the lieutenant's exam. In '47 he made lieutenant and transferred to the DA's Bureau of Investigations, cop protégé to the most ambitious Deputy District Attorney the City of Los Angeles ever saw. He married Celeste and settled into family life, a ready-made child part of the deal. And the closer father and son became, the more mother resented it; and the more he pressed to formally adopt the boy the more she refused—and tried to mold Stefan in the manner of the old Czech aristocracy that was yanked out from under her by the Nazis—language lessons and European culture and customs, Celeste oblivious to the memories they'd uprooted.

"To the mother the child belongs. Even a failed lawyer like you should know that maxim."

Mal listened to Celeste's sewing machine, Stefan's toy soldiers hitting the door. He came up with his own epigraph: saving a woman's life only induces gratitude if the woman has something to live for. All Celeste had was memories and a hated existence as a cop's hausfrau. All she wanted was to take Stefan back to the time of his horror and make him part of the memories. His final epigraph: he wouldn't let her.

Mal walked back in the house to read the Commie snitch's files: his glory grand jury and all it would reap.

Juice.

6

THE TWO picket lines moved slowly down Gower, past the entrances of the Poverty Row studios. The UAES hugged the inside, displaying banners stapled to plywood strips: FAIR PAY FOR LONG HOURS, CONTRACT NEGOTIATIONS *NOW*! PROFIT SHARES FOR ALL WORKERS. The Teamsters paced beside them, a strip of sidewalk open, their signs—REDS OUT! NO CONTRACTS FOR COMMUNISTS—atop friction-taped two-by-fours. Talk between the factions was constant; every few seconds, "Fuck" or "Shit" or "Traitor" or "Scum" would be shouted, a wave of garbled obscenities following. Across the street, reporters stood around, smoking and playing rummy on the hoods of their cars.

Buzz Meeks watched from the walkway outside Variety International Pictures' executive offices—three stories up, a balcony view. He remembered busting union heads back in the '30s; he sized up the Teamsters versus the UAES and saw a bout to rival Louis and Schmeling Number Two.

Easy: the Teamsters were sharks and the UAES were minnows. The Teamster line featured Mickey Cohen goons, union muscle and hard boys hired out of the day labor joints downtown; the UAES was old leftie types, stagehands past their prime, skinny Mexicans and a woman. If push came to shove, no cameras around, the Teamsters would use their two-by-fours as battering rams and charge—brass knuckle work in close, blood, teeth and nose cartilage on the sidewalk, maybe a few ears ripped off of heads. Then vamoose before the lackluster LAPD Riot Squad made the scene. *Easy.*

Buzz checked his watch. 4:45; Howard Hughes was forty-five minutes late. It was a cool January day, light blue sky mixed with rain clouds over the Hollywood Hills. Howard got sex crazy in the winter and probably wanted to send him out on a poontang prowl: Schwab's Drugstore, the extra huts at Fox and Universal, Brownie snapshots of well-lunged girls naked from the waist up. His Majesty's yes or no, then standard gash contracts to the yeses—one-liners in RKO turkeys in exchange for room and board at Hughes Enterprises' fuck pads and frequent nighttime visits from The Man himself. Hopefully, bonus money was involved: he was still in hock to a bookie named Leotis Dineen, a six-foot-six jungle bunny who hated people of the Oklahoma persuasion worse than poison.

Buzz heard a door opening behind him; a woman's voice called out, "Mr. Hughes will see you now, Mr. Meeks."

The woman had stuck her head out of Herman Gerstein's doorway; if the Variety International boss was involved, then bonus dough was a possible. Buzz ambled over; Hughes was seated behind Gerstein's desk, scanning the pictures on the walls: semicheesecake shots of Gower Gulch starlets going nowhere. He was dressed in his usual chalk stripe business suit, sporting his usual scars—facial wounds from his latest airplane crash. The big guy cultivated them with moisturizing lotion—he thought they gave him a certain panache.

And no Herman Gerstein; and no Gerstein's secretary. Buzz dropped the formalities that Hughes required when other people were present. "Getting any, Howard?"

Hughes pointed to a chair. "You're my bird dog, you should know. Sit, Buzz. This is important."

Buzz sat down and made a gesture that took in the whole office: cheesecake, rococo wall tapestries and a knight's suit of armor hatrack. "Why here, boss? Herman got a job for me?"

Hughes ignored the question. "Buzz, how long have we been colleagues?"

"Goin' on five years, Howard."

"And you've worked for me in various capacities?"

Buzz thought: fixer, bagman, pimp. "That's right."

"And during those five years have I given you profitable referrals to other people in need of your talents?"

"You surely have."

Hughes cocked two finger pistols, his thumbs the hammers. "Remember the premiere of *Billy the Kid*? The Legion of Decency was outside Grauman's shouting 'Whoremonger' at me and little old ladies from Pasadena were throwing tomatoes at Jane Russell. Death threats, the whole megillah."

Buzz crossed his legs and picked lint off a trouser cuff. "I was there, boss."

Hughes blew imaginary smoke off his fingertips. "Buzz, that was a dicey evening, but did I ever describe it as dangerous, or *big*?"

"No, boss. You surely didn't."

"When Bob Mitchum was arrested for those marijuana cigarettes and I called you in to help with the evidence, did I describe *that* as dangerous or big?"

"No."

"And when *Confidential Magazine* was getting ready to publish that article that alleged that I like well-endowed underage girls, and you took your billy club down to the office to reason with the editor, did I describe *that* as dangerous or big?"

Buzz winced. It was late '47, the hick pads were at full capacity, Howard was a pork-pouring dervish and was filming his teen-aged conquests' endorsing his prowess—a ploy aimed at getting him a date with Ava Gardner. One of the film cans was snatched out of the RKO editing department and ended up at *Confidential*; he broke three sets of scandal mag fingers quashing the story— then blew Hughes' bonus betting stupid on the Louis-Walcott fight. "No, Howard. You didn't."

Hughes shot Buzz with his finger guns. "Pow! Pow! Pow! Turner. I am telling you that that seditious spectacle down on the street is both dangerous *and* big, and *that* is why I called you here."

Buzz looked at the pilot/inventor/mogul, exhausted by his theatrics, wanting to get to it. "Howard, is there any cash money involved in all this big danger? And if you're askin' me to break some union heads, take another think, 'cause I am too old and too fat."

Hughes laughed. "Solly Gelfman wouldn't say that."

"Solly Gelfman is too goddamned kind. Howard, what do you want?"

Hughes draped his long legs over over Herman Gerstein's desk. "What's your opinion of Communism, Buzz?"

"I think it stinks. Why?"

"The UAES down there, they're all Commies and Pinkos and fellow travelers. The City of Los Angeles is getting a grand jury together to investigate Communist influence in Hollywood, concentrating on the UAES. A bunch of studio heads—myself, Herman and some others—have formed a group called 'Friends of the American Way in Motion Pictures' to help the City out. I've contributed to the kitty, so has Herman. We thought you'd like to help out, too."

Buzz laughed. "With a contribution out of my meager salary?"

Hughes aped the laugh, putting an exaggerated okie twang on it. "I knew appealing to your sense of patriotism was a long shot."

"Howard, you're only loyal to money, pussy and airplanes, and I buy you as a good buddy of the American Way like I buy Dracula turning down a job at a blood bank. So this grand jury thing is one of the three, and my money's on money."

Hughes flushed and fingered his favorite plane crash scar, the one a girl from the Wisconsin boonies was in love with. "Brass tacks then, Turner?"

"Yes, sir."

Hughes said, "The UAES is in at Variety International, RKO, three others here on Gower and two of the majors. Their contract is ironclad and has five more years to run. That contract is costly, and escalation clauses will cost us a fortune over the next several years. Now the goddamn union is picketing for extras: bonuses, medical coverage and profit points. Totally unacceptable. *Totally.*"

Buzz locked eyes with Hughes. "So don't renew their goddamned contract or let them strike."

"Not good enough. The escalation clauses are too costly, and they won't strike—they'll pull very subtle slow dances. When we signed with UAES in '45, no one knew how big television was going to get. We're getting reamed at the box office, and we want the Teamsters in—despite the goddamned Pinko UAES and their goddamned ironclad contract."

"How you gonna get around that contract?"

Hughes winked; scars and all, the act made him look like a big kid. "There's a fine-print clause in the contract that states the UAES can be ousted if criminal malfeasance—and that includes treason—can be proved against them. And the Teamsters will work much cheaper, if certain payments are made to certain silent partners."

Buzz winked. "Like Mickey Cohen?"

"I can't shit a shitter."

Buzz put his feet on Gerstein's desk, wishing he had a cigar to light up. "So you want the UAES smeared, before the grand jury convenes or sometime during the proceedings. That way you can boot them on the malfeasance clause and put in Mickey's boys without them Commies suin' you—for fear of gettin' in more shit."

Hughes nudged Buzz's feet off the desk with his own immaculate wing tips. "'Smeared' is a misnomer. In this case we're talking about patriotism as the handmaid to good business. Because the UAES are a bunch of card-carrying Pinko subversives."

"And you'll give me a cash money bonus to—"

"And I'll give you a leave of absence from your duties at the plant and a cash bonus to help the grand jury investigating team out. They've already got two cops as political interrogators, and the Deputy DA who's running the show wants a third man to rattle for criminal skeletons and make money pickups. Buzz, there's two things you know exceedingly well: Hollywood and our fair city's criminal elements. You can be very valuable to this operation. Can I count you in?"

Dollar signs danced in Buzz's head. "Who's the DA?"

"A man named Ellis Loew. He ran for his boss's job in '48 and lost."

Jewboy Loew, he of the colossal hard-on for the State of California. "Ellis is a sweetheart. The two cops?"

"An LAPD detective named Smith and a DA's Bureau man named Considine. Buzz, are you in?"

The old odds: 50-50, either Jack Dragna or Mal Considine set up the shooting that got him two in the shoulder, one in the arm and one through the left cheek of his ass. "I don't know, boss. There's bad blood between me and that guy Considine. Cherchez la femme, if you follow my drift. I might have to need money *really* bad before I say yes."

"Then I'm not worried. You'll get yourself into a bind—you always do."

7

CAPTAIN AL Dietrich said, "I got four phone calls about your little escapades in City territory night before last. At home yesterday. *On my day off*."

Danny Upshaw stood at parade rest in front of the station commander's desk, ready to deliver an oral rundown on the Goines homicide—a memorized pitch, to end in a plea for more Sheriff's manpower and an LAPD liaison. While Dietrich fumed, he scotched the ending and concentrated on making his evidence compelling enough so that the old man would let him work the snuff exclusively for at least two more weeks.

"... and if you wanted information on heroin pushers, you should have had *our* Narco guys contact *theirs*. You don't beat up the pushers, colored or otherwise. And the manager of Bido Lito's runs another club inside the County, and he's very simpatico with the watch sergeant at Firestone. And you were seen drinking on duty, which I do myself, but under more discreet circumstances. Follow my drift?"

Danny tried to look sheepish—a little trick he'd taught himself—eyes lowered, face scrunched up. "Yes, sir."

Dietrich lit a cigarette. "Whenever you call me sir, I know you're jerking my chain. You're very lucky I like you, Deputy. You're very lucky I think your gifts exceed your arrogance. Report on your homicide. Omit Dr. Layman's findings, I read your summary and I don't like gore this early in the morning."

Danny drew himself ramrod stiff in reflex—he'd wanted to play up the horror aspects to impress Dietrich. "Captain, so far I've got two half-assed eyewitness descriptions of the killer—tall, gray-haired, middle-aged. O+ blood typed from his semen—very common among white people. I don't think either witness could ID the man from mugs—those jazz clubs are dark and have distorted lighting. The print man who dusted the transport car got no latents except those belonging to the owner and his girl-friend. He did eliminations based on Civil Defense records—both Albanese and the girlfriend had CD jobs during the war. I checked taxi logs around the time the body was dumped and the car abandoned, and nothing but couples leaving the after-hours clubs on the Strip were picked up. Albanese's story of going back to darktown to look for his car has been verified by cab records, which eliminates him as a suspect. I spent all day yesterday and most of the evening recanvassing Central Avenue, and I couldn't find any other eyewitnesses who saw Goines with the tall, gray-haired man. I looked for the two eyewitnesses I talked to before, thinking I'd try to get some kind of composite drawing out of them, but they were gone—apparently these jazz types are mostly fly-by-nights."

Dietrich stubbed out his cigarette. "What's your next move?"

"Captain, this is a fag killing. The better of my two eyewit-nesses pegged Goines as a deviant, and the mutilations back it up. Goines was killed with a heroin OD. I want to run mugshots of known homos by Otis Jackson and other local pushers. I want—"

Dietrich was already shaking his head. "No, you cannot go back to City territory and question the man you pistol-whipped, and LAPD Narco will never cooperate with a list of local pushers—thanks to your escapades." He picked a copy of the *Herald* off his desk, folded it over and pointed to a one-column piece: "Vagrant's Body Found Dumped Off Sunset Strip New Year's Eve." "Let's keep it at this—low-key, no name on the victim. We've got great duty here at this division, we thrive on tourism, and I don't want it bollixed up because some queer slashed another queer hophead trombone player. Comprende?"

Danny twisted his fingers together behind his back, then shot his CO a Vollmer maxim. "Uniform codes of investigation are the moral foundation of criminology."

Captain Al Dietrich said, "Human garbage is human garbage. Go to work, Deputy Upshaw."

* * *

Danny went back to the squadroom and brainstormed in his cubicle, partition walls bracketing him, the station's other three detectives—all at least ten years his senior—typing and jabbering into phones, the noise coming at him like gangbusters, then subsiding into a lull that was like no sound at all.

A mug blowup of Harlan "Buddy" Jastrow, Kern County axe murderer and the jolt that made him a cop, glared from the wall above his desk; some deputy who'd heard about his all-point want on the man had drawn a Hitler mustache on him, a speech balloon extending from his mouth: "Hi! I'm Deputy Upshaw's nemesis! He wants to fry my ass, but he won't tell anybody why! Watch out for Upshaw! He's a college boy prima donna and he thinks his shit don't stink!" Captain Dietrich had discovered the artwork; he suggested that Danny leave it there as a reminder to hold on to his temper and not high-hat the other men. Danny agreed; word got back to him that his fellow detectives liked the touch—it made them think he had a sense of humor that he didn't have—and it made him angry and somehow able to brainstorm better.

So far, two and a half days in, he had the basics covered. The Central Avenue jazz strip had been canvassed around the clock; every bartender, bouncer, musician and general hepcat on the block had been braced—ditto the area where the body was dumped. Karen Hiltscher had called San Quentin and Lexington State Hospital for information on Goines and his buddies, if any, there; they were waiting the results of those queries. Rousting H pushers inside City confines was out for the time being, but he could put in a memo to Sheriff's Narco for a list of dinks dealing in the County, press on that and see if he got any crossover leads back to LAPD turf. Goines' musicians' union would be reopening after the holiday this morning, and for now he had nothing but his instincts—what was true, what wasn't true, what was too far-fetched to be true and so horrible that it *had* to be true. Going eyeball to eyeball with Buddy Jastrow, Danny reconstructed the crime.

The killer meets Goines somewhere on the jazz block and talks him into geezing up—despite Marty's recent dope cure. He's got the Buick already staked out, door jimmied open or unlocked, wires unhooked and ready to be juiced together for a quick start. They drive someplace quiet, someplace equidistant from darktown and the Sunset Strip. The killer jacks enough horse into a vein near Goines' spine to pop his heart arteries, a terrycloth towel right there to shove into his mouth and keep blood from drenching him. Figure, by the Zombie barman's estimate, that the killer and Goines left Central Avenue around 12:15 to 12:45 A.M., took a half hour to drive to the destination, ten minutes to set the snuff up and accomplish it.

1:00 to 1:30 A.M.

The killer throttles his victim postmortem; fondles his genitals until they bruise, slashes his backside with the razor blade device, pulls out his eyes, screws him in the sockets at least twice, bites—or has an animal bite—through his stomach to the intestines, then cleans him up and drives him to Allegro Street, a rainy night, no moisture atop the body, the rain having stopped shortly after 3:00, the stiff discovered at 4:00 A.M.

An hour to an hour and forty-five minutes to mutilate the body, depending on the location of the killing ground.

The killer so sex-crazed that he ejaculates twice during that time.

The killer—maybe—taking a circuitous route to the Strip, rearview mirror hooked backward so he can view the corpse he is chauffeuring.

Flaw in the reconstruction so far: Doc Layman's tenuous "blood bait" theory doesn't fit. Well-trained vicious dogs did not jibe with the scenario—they would be too difficult to deal with, a nuisance, a mess, too noisy at a murder scene, too hard to contain during moments of psychotic duress. Which meant that the teeth marks on the torso had to be human, even though the mouth imprints were too large to have been made by a human being biting down.

Which meant that the killer bit and gnawed and swiveled and gnashed his teeth to get a purchase on his victim's entrails, sucking the flesh upward to leave inflamed borders as he ravaged—

Danny bolted out of his cubicle and back to the records alcove adjoining the squadroom. One battered cabinet held the division's Vice and sex offender files—West Hollywood crime reports, complaint reports, arrest reports and trouble call sheets dating back to the station's opening in '37. Some of the folders were filed alphabetically under "Arrestee"; some under "Complainant"; some numerically by "Address of Occurrence." Some held mugshots, some didn't; gaps in the "Arrestee" folders indicated that the arrested parties had bribed deputies into stealing reports that might prove embarrassing to them—and West Hollywood was only a small fraction of County territory.

Danny spent an hour scanning "Arrestee" reports, looking for tall, gray-haired, middle-aged men with violence in their MOs, knowing it was a long shot to keep him busy until Musician's Local 3126 opened at 10:30. The slipshod paperwork—rife with misspellings, smudged carbons and near illiterate recountings of sex crimes—had him to the point of screaming at LASD incompetence; turgid accounts of toilet liaisons and high school boys bribed into back seat blow jobs kept his stomach churning with a bile that tasted like fried coffee grounds and last night's six shots of bonded. The time got him four possibles—men aged forty-three to fifty-five, 6′1″ to 6′4″, with a total of twenty-one sodomy convictions among them—most of the beefs stemming from fruit tank punkings—jailhouse coitus interruptus that resulted in additional County charges being filed. At 10:20, he took the folders up to the dispatcher's office and Karen Hiltscher, sweaty, his clothes wilted before the day had hardly started.

Karen was working the switchboard, plugging in calls, a headset attached to her Veronica Lake hairdo. The girl was nineteen, bottle blonde and busty—a civilian LASD employee flagged for the next woman's opening at the Sheriff's Academy. Danny pegged her as bad cop stuff: the Department's mandatory eighteen-month jail tour would probably send her off the deep end and into the arms of the first male cop who promised to take her away from dyke matrons, Mex gang putas and white trash mothers in for child abuse. The heartthrob of the West Hollywood Substation wouldn't last two weeks as a policewoman.

Danny straightened his tie and smoothed his shirtfront, his beef-cake prelude to begging favors. "Karen? You busy, sweetheart?"

The girl noticed him and took off her headset. She looked pouty; Danny wondered if he should lube her with another dinner date. "Hi, Deputy Upshaw."

Danny placed the sex offender files up against the switchboard. "What happened to 'Hi, Danny'?"

Karen lit a cigarette à la Veronica Lake and coughed—she only smoked when she was trying to vamp the cops working day watch. "Sergeant Norris heard me call Eddie Edwards 'Eddie' and said I should call him Deputy Edwards, that I shouldn't be so familiar until I get rank."

"You tell Norris I said you can call me Danny."

Karen made a face. "Daniel Thomas Upshaw is a nice name. I told my mother, and she said it was a really nice name, too."

"What else did you tell her about me?"

"That you're really sweet and handsome, but you're playing hard to get. What's in those files?"

"Sex offender reports."

"For that homicide you're working?"

Danny nodded. "Sweet, did Lex and Quentin call back on my Marty Goines queries?"

Karen made another face—half vixen, half coquette. "I would have told you. Why did you give me those reports?"

Danny leaned over the switchboard and winked. "I was thinking of dinner at Mike Lyman's once I get some work cleared up. Feel like giving me a hand?"

Karen Hiltscher tried to return the wink, but her false eyelash stuck to the ridge below her eye, and she had to fumble her cigarette into an ashtray and pull it free. Danny looked away, disgusted; Karen pouted, "What do you want on those reports?"

Danny stared at the muster room wall so Karen couldn't read his face. "Call Records at the Hall of Justice Jail and get the blood types for all four men. If you get anything other than O+ for them, drop it. On the O+ 's, call County Parole for their last known addresses, rap sheets and parole disposition reports. Got it?"

Karen said, "Got it."

Danny turned around and looked at his cut-rate Veronica Lake, her left eyelash plastered to her plucked left eyebrow. "You're a doll. Lyman's when I clear this job."

* * *

Musician's Local 3126 was on Vine Street just north of Melrose, a tan Quonset hut sandwiched between a doughnut stand and a liquor store. Hepcat types were lounging around the front door, scarfing crullers and coffee, half pints and short dogs of muscatel.

Danny parked and walked in, a group of wine guzzlers scattering to let him through. The hut's interior was dank: folding chairs aligned in uneven rows, cigarette butts dotting a chipped linoleum floor, pictures from *Downbeat* and *Metronome* scotch-taped to the walls—half white guys, half Negroes, like the management was trying to establish jazzbo parity. The left wall held a built-in counter, file cabinets in back of it, a haggard white woman standing guard. Danny walked over, badge and Marty Goines mugshot strip out.

The woman ignored the badge and squinted at the strip. "This guy play trombone?"

"That's right. Martin Mitchell Goines. You sent him down to Bido Lito's around Christmas."

The woman squinted harder. "He's got trombone lips. What did he do you for?"

Danny lied discreetly. "Parole violation."

The slattern tapped the strip with a long red nail. "The same old same old. What can I do you for?"

Danny pointed to the filing cabinets. "His employment record, as far back as it goes."

The woman about-faced, opened and shut drawers, leafed through folders, yanked one and gave the top page a quick scrutiny. Laying it down on the counter, she said, "A nowhere horn. From Squaresville."

Danny opened the folder and read through it, picking up two gaps right away: '38 to '40—Goines' County jolt for marijuana possession: '44 to '48—his Quentin time for the same offense. Since '48 the entries had been sporadic: occasional two-week engagements at Gardena pokerino lounges and his fatal gig at Bido Lito's. Prior to Goines' first jail sentence he got only *very* occasional work—Hollywood roadhouse stints in '36 and '37. It was the early '40s when Marty Goines was a trombone-playing fool.

Under his self-proclaimed banner, "Mad Marty Goines & His Horn of Plenty," he'd gigged briefly with Stan Kenton; in 1941, he pulled a tour with Wild Willie Monroe. There were a whole stack of pages detailing pickup band duty in '42, '43 and early

'44—one-night stands with six- and eight-man combos playing dives in the San Fernando Valley. Only the bandleaders and/or club managers who did the hiring were listed on the employment sheets—there was no mention of other musicians.

Danny closed the folder; the woman said, "Bubkis, am I right?"

"You're right. Look, do you think any of these guys around here might have known—I mean know—Marty Goines?"

"I can ask."

"Do it. Would you mind?"

The woman rolled her eyes up to heaven, drew a dollar sign in the air and pointed to her cleavage. Danny felt his hands clenching the edge of the counter and smelled last night's liquor oozing out of his skin. He was about to come on strong when he remembered he was on City ground and his CO's shit list. He fished in his pockets for cash, came up with a five and slapped it down. "Do it now."

The slattern snapped up the bill and disappeared behind the filing cabinets. Danny saw her out on the sidewalk a few seconds later, talking to the bottle gang, then moving to the doughnut and coffee crowd. She zeroed in on a tall Negro guy holding a bass case, grabbed his arm and led him inside. Danny smelled stale sweat, leaves and mouthwash on the man, like the knee-length overcoat he was wearing was his permanent address. The woman said, "This is Chester Brown. He knows Marty Goines."

Danny pointed Brown to the nearest row of chairs. Miss Hepcat went back to her counter and the bass man shuffled over, plopped down and whipped out a bottle of Listerine. He said, "Breakfast of champions," gulped, gargled and swallowed; Danny sat two chairs over, close enough to hear, far away enough to defuse the stink. "Do you know Marty Goines, Chester?"

Brown burped and said, "Why should I tell you?"

Danny handed him a dollar. "Lunch of champions."

"I feed three times a day, officer. Snitching gives me an appetite."

Danny forked over another single; Chester Brown palmed it, chugalugged and patted the Listerine bottle. "Helps the memory. And since I ain't seen Marty since the war, you gonna need that memory."

Danny got out his pen and notepad. "Shoot."

The bass man took a deep breath. "I gigged pickup with Marty, back when he called himself the Horn of Plenty. Hunger huts out in the Valley when Ventura Boulevard was a fuckin' beanfield. Half the boys toked sweet lucy, half took the needle route. Marty was strung like a fuckin' dog."

So far, his seven-dollar story was running true—based on Goines' union jacket and what he knew of his criminal record. "Keep going, Chester."

"Weeell, Marty pushed reefers—not too good, since I heard he did time for it, and he was a righteous boss mothafuckin' burglar. All the pickup boys that was strung was doin' it. They'd grab purses off of barstools and tables, get the people's addresses and swipe their house keys while the bartender kept them drinkin'. One set you'd have no drummer, one set no trumpet, and so forth, 'cause they was utilizizin' their inside skinny to be burglarizizin' the local patrons. Marty did lots of that, solo stuff, steal a car during his break, burglarizize, then be back for his next set. Like I tol' you, he was a righteous boss mothafuckin' burglar."

Righteous new stuff—even to an ex-car thief cop who thought he knew most of the angles. "What years are you talking about, Chester? Think hard."

Brown consulted his Listerine. "I'd say this was goin' on from summer of '43 to maybe sometime in '44."

Goines copped his second marijuana beef in April of '44. "Did he work alone?"

"You mean on the burglarizizin'?"

"Right. And did he have running partners in general?"

Chester Brown said, "'Cept for this one kid, the Horn of Plenty was a righteous loner. He had this sidekick, though—a white blondy kid, tall and shy, loved jazz but couldn't learn to play no instrument. He'd been in a fire and his face was all covered up in bandages like he was the fuckin' mummy. Just a fuckin' kid—maybe nineteen, twenty years old. Him and Marty pulled a righteous fuckin' fuckload of burglaries together."

Danny's skin was tingling—even though the kid couldn't be the killer—a youth in '43–'44 wouldn't be gray and middle-aged in '50. "What happened to the sidekick, Chester?"

"I dunno, but you sure askin' a lot of questions for a parole violation, and you ain't asked me where I think Marty might be stayin'."

"I was getting to that. You got any ideas?"

Brown shook his head. "Marty always stayed to himself. Never socializized with the boys out of the club."

Danny dry-swallowed. "Is Goines a homosexual?"

"Say what?"

"Queer, fruit, homo! Did he fucking like boys!"

Brown killed the bottle of Listerine and wiped his lips. "You don't gots to shout, and that's a nasty thing to say about somebody never did you harm."

Danny said, "Then answer my question."

The bass man opened his instrument case. There was no fiddle inside, only bottles of Listerine Mouthwash. Chester Brown cracked the cap on one and took a long, slow drink. He said, "That's for Marty, 'cause I ain't the fool you think I am, and I know he's dead. And he wasn't no queer. He may not have been much for trim, but he sure as fuck wasn't no fuckin' fruitfly."

* * *

Danny took Chester Brown's old news and rolled with it to a pay phone. First he called City/County R&I, learned that Martin Mitchell Goines had no detainments on suspicion of B&E and that no blond youths were listed as accomplices on his two marijuana rousts; no blond youths with distinguishing burn marks were arrested for burglary or narcotics violations anywhere in the San Fernando Valley circa 1942–1945. The call was a fishing expedition that went nowhere.

A buzz to the West Hollywood Station switchboard got him a pouty conversation with Karen Hiltscher, who said that the four long shots from the sex offender files proved to be just that—a toss of their jail records revealed that none of the men had O+ blood. Administrators had called in from both San Quentin and Lexington State Hospital; they said that Marty Goines was an institutional loner, and his counselor at Lex stated that he was assigned a Fed case worker in L.A.—but hadn't reported to him yet, and left no word about where he would be staying when he got to Los Angeles. Even though the lead was probably a big nothing, Danny told Karen to check the station's burglary file for B&E men with jazz musician backgrounds and for mention of a burned-face burglar boy—a jazz aficionado. Rankling, the girl agreed; Danny hung up thinking he should raise the dreaded dinner ante from Mike Lyman's to the Coconut Grove to keep her happy.

At just after 1:00 P.M. there was nothing he could do but pound familiar pavement one more time. Danny drove to darktown and widened his canvassing area, talking Goines and the gray-haired man to locals on the side streets adjoining Central Avenue, getting four solid hours of nothing; at dusk he drove back to West Hollywood, parked on Sunset and Doheny and walked the Strip, west to east, east to west, residential streets north into the hills, south to Santa Monica Boulevard, wondering the whole time why the killer picked Allegro Street as his place to dump the body. He wondered if the killer lived nearby, desecrated Goines' corpse for that much more time and chose Allegro so he could gloat over the police and their efforts to nail him—the abandoned car a partial ruse to convince them he lived elsewhere. That theory played with led to others—subjective thinking—a Hans Maslick fundamental. Danny thought of the killer with his real car parked nearby for a quick getaway; the killer walking the Strip New Year's morning, sheltered by swarms of revelers, depleted from his awful back-to-back explosions. And that was when it got scary.

In a famous essay, Maslick described a technique he had developed while undergoing analysis with Sigmund Freud. It was called Man Camera, and involved screening details from the perpetrator's viewpoint. Actual camera angles and tricks were employed; the investigator's eyes became a lens capable of zooming in and out, freezing close-ups, selecting background motifs to interpret crime-scene evidence in an aesthetic light. Danny was crossing Sunset and Horn when the idea struck him—transpose 3:45 New Year's morning to now, himself as a sex slasher, walking home or to his car or to an all-night market to get calm again. But he didn't see the other people strolling the Strip or lining up to get in the Mocambo or sitting at the counter at Jack's Drive Inn. He went straight for Marty Goines' eyes and guts and groin, an ultra close-up in Technicolor, his preautopsy prep magnified ten million times. A car swerved in front of him then; he twitched with heebie-jeebies, saw a kaleidoscope of Coleman the alto man, his look-alike from the movie with Karen, Tim. When he pointed his Man Camera at the passersby he was supposed to be viewing, they were all gargoyles, all wrong.

It took long moments for him to calm down, to get it right. He hadn't eaten since yesterday; he'd postponed his bourbon ration in order to tread the Strip clear-headed. Hitting late-night clubs and restaurants with questions on a tall, gray-haired man New Year's would be straightforward police work to keep him chilled.

He did it.

And got more nothing.

Two hours' worth.

The same accounts at Cyrano's, Dave's Blue Room, Ciro's, the Mocambo, La Rue, Coffee Bob's, Sherry's, Bruno's Hideaway and the Movieland Diner: every single place was packed until dawn New Year's. No one remembered a solitary, tall, gray-haired man.

At midnight, Danny retrieved his car and drove to the Moon-glow Lounge for his four shots. Janice Modine, his favorite snitch, was hawking cigarettes to a thin weeknight crowd: lovebirds necking in wraparound booths, dancers necking while they slow-grinded to jukebox ballads. Danny took a booth that faced away from the bandstand; Janice showed up a minute later, hold-ing a tray with four shot glasses and an ice water backup.

Danny knocked the drinks back—bam, bam, bam, bam, eyes away from Janice so she'd take the hint and leave him alone—no gratitude for the prostie beefs he'd saved her from, no overheard skinny on Mickey C.—useless because West Hollywood Divi-sion's most auspicious criminal was greasing most of West Holly-wood's finest. The ploy didn't work; the girl squirmed in front of him, one spaghetti strap sliding off her shoulder, then the other. Danny waited for the first blast of heat, got it and saw all the col-ors in the lounge go from slightly wrong to right. He said, "Sit down and tell me what you want before your dress falls off."

Janice hunched into her straps and sat across the table from him. "It's about John, Mr. Upshaw. He was arrested again."

John Lembeck was Janice's lover/pimp, a car thief specializing in custom orders: stolen chassis for the basic vehicle, parts stolen to exact specifications. He was a San Berdoo native like Danny, knew from the grapevine that a County plainclothes comer used to clout cars all over Kern and Visalia and kept his mouth shut about it when he got rousted on suspicion of grand theft auto. Danny said, "Parts or a whole goddamn car?"

Janice pulled a Kleenex out of her neckline and fretted it. "Upholstery."

"City or County?"

"I—I think County. San Dimas Substation?"

Danny winced. San Dimas had the most rowdy detective squad in the Department; in '46 the daywatch boss, jacked on turpen hydrate, beat a wetback fruit picker to death. "That's the County. What's his bail?"

"No bail, because of John's last GTA. See, it's a parole violation, Mr. Upshaw. John's scared because he says the policemen there are really mean, and they made him sign a confession on all these cars he didn't really steal. John said I should tell you a San Berdoo homeboy who loves cars should go to bat for another San Berdoo homey who loves cars. He didn't say what it meant, but he said I should tell you."

Pull strings to save his career from its first hint of dirt: call the San Dimas bulls, tell them John Lembeck was his trusted snitch and that a nigger hot car gang had a jail bid out on him, shiv time if the stupid shit ever made it to a County lockup. If Lembeck was docile at the holding tank, they'd let him off with a beating. "Tell John I'll get on it in the morning."

Janice had pinched her Kleenex into little wispy shreds. "Thanks, Mr. Upshaw. John also said I should be nice to you."

Danny stood up, feeling warm and loose, wondering if he should muscle Lembeck for going cuntish on him. "You're always nice to me, sweetheart. That's why I have my nightcap here."

Janice vamped him with wide baby blues. "He said I should be *really* nice to you."

"I don't want it."

"I mean, like really *extra* nice."

Danny said, "It's wrong," and placed his usual dollar tip on the table.

8

MAL WAS in his office, on his twelfth full reading of Dr. Saul Lesnick's psychiatric files.

It was just after 1:00 A.M.; the DA's Bureau was a string of dark cubicles, illuminated only by Mal's wall light. The files were spread over his desk, interspersed with pages of notes splashed with coffee. Celeste would be asleep soon—he could go home and sleep in the den without her pestering him, sex offers because at this time of the morning he was her only friend, and giving him her mouth meant they could talk until one of them provoked a fight. Offers he'd accept tonight: the dirt in the files had him riled up like back in the Ad Vice days, when he put surveillance on the girls before they took down a whorehouse—the more you knew about who they were the better chance you had to get them to finger their pimps and money men. And after forty-eight hours of paper prowling, he felt like he had a pulse on the Reds in the UAES.

Deluded.

Traitorous.

Perverse.

Cliché shouters, sloganeers, fashion-conscious pseudoidealists. Locusts attacking social causes with the wrong information and bogus solutions, their one legit gripe—the Sleepy Lagoon case— almost blown through guilt by association: fellow travelers soliciting actual Party members for picketing and leaflet distribution, nearly discrediting everything the Sleepy Lagoon Defense Committee said and did. Hollywood writers and actors and hangers-on spouting cheap trauma, Pinko platitudes and guilt over raking in big money during the Depression, then penancing the bucks out to spurious leftist causes. People led to Lesnick's couch by their promiscuity and dipshit politics.

Deluded.

Stupid.

Selfish.

Mal took a belt of coffee and ran a mental overview of the files, a last paraphrase before getting down to tagging the individual brain trusters he and Dudley Smith should be interrogating and the ones who should be singled out for their as yet unfound operative: Loew's projected possibility, his favored tool already. What he got was a lot of people with too much money and too little brains pratfalling through the late '30s and '40s—betraying themselves, their lovers, their country and their own ideals, two events galvanizing their lunacy, spinning them out of their orbit of parties, meetings and sleeping around:

The Sleepy Lagoon case.

The 1947 House Un-American Activities Committee probe into Communist influence in the entertainment industry.

And the funny thing was—the two events gave the Pinkos some credibility, some vindication.

In August of 1942 a Mexican youth named José Diaz was beaten to death and run over with a car out at the Sleepy Lagoon—a grass-knolled meeting place for gang members in the Williams Ranch area of Central L.A. The incident was allegedly sparked by Diaz being ejected from a nearby party earlier that night; he had allegedly insulted several members of a rival youth gang, and seventeen of them hauled him out to the Lagoon and snuffed him. Evidence against them was scant; the LAPD investigation and trial were conducted in an atmosphere of hysteria: the '42–'43 zoot suit riots had produced a huge wave of anti-Mexican sentiment throughout Los Angeles. All seventeen boys received life sentences, and the Sleepy Lagoon Defense Committee—UAES brain trusters, Communist Party members, leftists and straight citizens—held rallies, circulated petitions and raised funds to employ a legal team—which ultimately got all seventeen pardoned. Hypocrisy within the idealism: Lesnick's male patients, hearts bleeding over the poor railroaded Mexicans, complained to him of Communist Party white women screwing "proletariat" taco benders—then assailed themselves as rabid bigots moments later.

Mal made a mental note to talk to Ellis Loew about the Sleepy Lagoon angle: Ed Satterlee wanted to procure SLDC rally pictures from the Feds—but since the kids were exonerated, it might backfire. Ditto the info the shrinkees poured out over '47 HUAC. Better for him and Dudley to keep it sub rosa, not jeopardize Lesnick's complicity and use the info only by implication: to squeeze the UAESers' suspected weak points. Going with the HUAC stuff full-bore might jeopardize their grand jury: J. Parnell Thomas, the Committee's chairman, was currently doing time on bribery charges; hotshot Hollywood stars had protested HUAC's methods and Lesnick's files were rife with nonpetty trauma deriving from the spring of '47—suicides, attempted suicides, frantic betrayals of friendship, booze and sex to kill the pain. If the '50 L.A. City grand jury team attempted to use the juice of '47 HUAC—*their first precedent*—they might engender sympathy for UAES members and subsidiary hostile witnesses. Better not to dip into old HUAC testimony for conspiracy evidence; imperative that the lefties be denied a chance to boo-hoo the grand jury's tactics to the press.

Mal felt his overview sink in as solid: good evidence, good thoughts on what to use, what to hold back. He killed his coffee and went to the individuals—the half dozen of the twenty-two most ripe for interrogation and operation.

His first was a maybe. Morton Ziffkin: UAES member, CP member, member of eleven other organizations classified as Commie fronts. Family man—a wife and two grown daughters. A highly paid screenwriter—100 thou a year until he told HUAC to fuck off—now working for peanuts as a film splicer. Underwent analysis with Doc Lesnick out of a stated desire to "explore Freudian thought" and allay his impulses to cheat on his wife with an onslaught of CP women "out for my gelt—not my body." A rabid, bad-tempered Marxist ideologue—a good man to bait on the witness stand—but he'd probably never snitch on his fellow Pinks. He sounded intelligent enough to make Ellis Loew seem like a fool, and his HUAC stint gave him an air of martyrdom. A maybe.

Mondo Lopez, Juan Duarte and Sammy Benavides, former Sleepy Lagoon Defense Committee bigshots, recruited out of the Sinarquistas—a zoot suit gang given to sporting Nazi regalia—by CP bosses. Now token ethnics in the UAES hierarchy, the three spent the '40s throwing it to condescending white lefty women—enraged over their airs, but grateful for the action; more enraged at being told by their "puto" cell leader to "explore" that rage by seeing a psychiatrist. Benavides, Duarte and Lopez were currently working at Variety International Pictures, half the time as stagehands, half the time playing Indians in cheapy cowboy pictures. They were also serving as picket bosses on Gower Gulch—the closest thing the UAES had to muscle—pitiful when compared to the Mickey Cohen goons the Teamsters were employing. Mal pegged them as pussy hounds who fell into clover, the Sleepy Lagoon job their only real political concern. The three probably had criminal records and connections stemming from their zoot suit days, a good approach for the team's troubleshooter—if Ellis Loew ever found one.

Now the brain trust got ugly.

Reynolds Loftis, movie character actor, snitched to HUAC by his former homo lover Chaz Minear, a Hollywood script hack. Loftis did not suspect that Minear ratted him, and in no way reciprocated the finking. Both men were still with the UAES, still friendly at their meetings and at other political functions they attended. Minear, guilt-crazed over his fink duty, had said to Doc Lesnick: "If you knew who he left me for, you'd understand why I did it." Mal had scanned both Loftis' and Minear's files for more mention of "he" and came up empty; there was a large gap in Lesnick's Loftis transcripts—from the years '42 to '44—and Minear's pages bore no other mention of the third edge of the triangle. Mal recalled Loftis from westerns he'd taken Stefan to: a tall, lanky, silver-haired man, handsome like your idealized U.S.

senator. And a Communist, and a subversive, and a hostile HUAC witness and self-described switch-hitter. A potential friendly witness par excellence—next to Chaz Minear, the Red with the most closeted skeletons.

And finally the Red Queen.

Claire De Haven did not possess a file, and several of the men had described her as too smart, strong and good to need a psychiatrist. She also screwed half her CP cell and all the SLDC bigwigs, including Benavides, Lopez and Duarte, who worshiped her. Chaz Minear was in her thrall, despite his homosexuality; Reynolds Loftis spoke of her as the "only woman I've ever really loved." Mal picked up on her smarts secondhand: Claire moved behind the scenes, tended not to shout slogans and retained the political and legal connections of her late father, a stolid rightwing counsel to the L.A. business establishment. Minear speculated to Doc Lesnick that her old man's political juice kept her from being subpoenaed by HUAC in '47—and not one other witness mentioned her name. Claire De Haven screwed like a rabbit, but didn't come off as a slut; she inspired the loyalty of homosexual screenwriters, switch-hitter actors, Mexican stagehands and Commies of all stripes.

Mal turned off his light, reminding himself to write Doc Lesnick a memo: all the files ended in the summer of '49—five months ago. Why? Walking out to the elevator, he wondered what Claire De Haven looked like, where he could get a picture, if he could get his decoy to operate her out of her lust—politics and sex to nail the woman as a friendly witness, the Red Queen squeezed like a Chinatown whore, captain's bars dancing his way at the end of a stag movie.

9

BAGMAN TIME.

His first stop was Variety International, where Herman Gerstein gave him a five-minute lecture on the evils of Communism and handed him a fat envelope stuffed with C-notes; stop two was a short stroll through the Teamster and UAES picket lines over to Hollywood Prestige National Pictures, where Wally Voldrich, the head of Security, kicked loose with a doughnut box full of fifties dusted with powdered sugar and chocolate sprinkles. Howard's ten thou was already in his pocket; Mickey C.'s contribution to the Friends of the American Way in Motion Pictures would be his last pickup of the morning.

Buzz took Sunset out to Santa Monica Canyon, to the bungalow hideaway where Mickey palled with his stooges, entertained poon and hid out from his wife. The money in his pocket had him feeling brash: if Mal Considine was around when he dropped the bag with Ellis Loew, he'd rattle his cage to see what the four years since Laura had done to his balls. If it felt right, he'd tell Howard he'd sign on to fight Communism—Leotis Dineen was pressing him for a grand and a half, and he was a bad jigaboo to fuck with.

Cohen's bungalow was a bamboo job surrounded by specially landscaped tropical foliage, camouflage for his triggermen when the Mick and Jack Dragna were skirmishing. Buzz parked in the driveway behind a white Packard ragtop, wondering where Mickey's bulletproofed Caddy was and who'd be around to hand him his envelope. He walked up to the door and rang the buzzer; a woman's deep-South voice drifted out a window screen. "Come in."

Buzz opened the door and saw Audrey Anders sitting at a living room table, hitting the keys of an adding machine. No make-up, dungarees and one of Mickey's monogrammed dress shirts didn't dent her beauty at all; she actually looked better than she did New Year's morning, pink party dress and high heels, kicking Tommy Sifakis in the balls. "Hello, Miss Anders."

Audrey pointed to a Chinese lacquered coffee table; a roll of bills secured by a rubber band was resting smack in the middle. "Mickey said to tell you mazel tov, which I guess means he's glad you're in with this grand jury thing."

Buzz sat down in an easy chair and put his feet up, his signal that he meant to stay and look awhile. "Mickey takin' advantage of that master's degree of yours?"

Audrey tapped out a transaction, checked the paper the machine expelled and wrote on a pad, all very slowly. She said, "You believe the program notes at the El Rancho Burlesque?"

"No, I just made you for the brains."

"The brains to keep books for a lending operation?"

"Loan shark's more the word, but I meant brains in general."

Audrey pointed to Buzz's feet. "Planning to stay awhile?"

"Not long. You really got a master's degree?"

"Jesus, we keep asking each other these questions. No, I do not have a master's degree, but I do have a certificate in accounting from a second-rate teachers college in Jackson, Mississippi. Satisfied?"

Buzz didn't know if the woman wanted him out the door pronto or if she welcomed the interruption—totalling shark vig on a fine winter day was his idea of hunger. He played his only ace, his one opening to see what she thought of him. "Lucy Whitehall okay?"

Audrey lit a cigarette and blew two perfect smoke rings. "Yes. Sol Gelfman has her tucked away at his place in Palm Springs, and Mickey had some friend of his on the Sheriff's Department issue something called a restraining order. If Tommy bothers Lucy, the police will arrest him. She told me she's grateful for what you did. I didn't tell her you did it for money."

Buzz ignored the jibe and smiled. "Tell Lucy hi for me. Tell her she's so pretty I might've done it for free."

Audrey laughed. "In a pig's eye you would. Meeks, what is between you and Mickey?"

"I'll answer that one with a question. Why you wanta know?"

Audrey blew two more rings and ground out her cigarette. "Because he talked about you for an hour straight last night. Because he said he can't figure out if you're the stupidest smart man or the smartest stupid man he ever met, and he can't figure out why you blow all your money with colored bookies when you could bet with him for no vig. He said that only stupid men love danger, but you love danger and you're not stupid. He said he can't figure out whether you're brave or crazy. Does any of this make sense to you?"

Buzz saw the words inscribed on his tombstone, all crimped together so they'd fit. He answered straight, not caring who Audrey told. "Miss Anders, I take the risks Mickey's afraid to, so I make him feel safe. He's a little guy and I'm a little guy, and maybe I'm just a tad better with my hands and that baton of mine. Mickey's got more to lose than me, so he runs scared more than me. And if I'm crazy, it means he's smart. You know what surprises me about this talk we're havin', Miss Anders?"

The question interrupted Audrey starting to smile—a big beam that showed off two slightly crooked teeth and a cold sore on her lower lip. "No, what?"

"That Mickey thinks enough of you to talk to you about stuff like that. That surely does surprise me."

Audrey's smile fizzled out. "He loves me."

"You mean he appreciates the favors you do him. Like when I was a cop, I skimmed that good old white powder and sold it to Mickey, not Jack D. We got to be as friendly as anybody and Mickey can be 'cause of that. I'm just surprised he plays it that close with a woman is all."

Audrey lit another cigarette; Buzz saw it as cover for bad thoughts, good banter flushed down the toilet. He said, "I'm sorry. I didn't mean to be so personal."

Audrey's eyes ignited. "Oh yes you did, Meeks. You *surely* did."

Buzz got up and walked around the room, checking out the strange chink furnishings, wondering who'd picked them out, Mickey's wife or this ex-stripper/bookkeeper who was making him feel jumpy, like a gun would go off if he said the wrong thing. He tried small talk. "Nice stuff. Hate to see Jack D. put bullet holes in it."

Audrey's voice was shaky. "Mickey and Jack are talking about burying the hatchet. Jack wants to go in on a deal with him. Maybe dope, maybe a casino in Vegas. Meeks, I love Mickey and he loves me."

Buzz heard the last words as bang, bang, bang, bang. He picked up the cash roll, stuffed it in his pocket and said, "Yeah, he loves takin' you to the Troc and the Mocambo, cause he knows every man there is droolin' for you and afraid of him. Then it's an hour at your place and back to the wife. It's real nice the two of you talk every once in awhile, but as far as I'm concerned you're gettin' short shrift from a Jewboy who ain't got the brains to know what he's got."

Audrey's jaw dropped; her cigarette fell into her lap. She picked it up and stubbed it out. "Are you *this* crazy or *that* stupid?"

Bang, bang, bang, bang—cannon loud. Buzz said, "Maybe I just trust you," walked over and kissed Audrey Anders full on the lips, one hand holding her head, cradling it. She didn't open her mouth and she didn't embrace him back and she didn't push him away. When Buzz snapped that it was all he was going to get, he broke the clinch and floated to the car with quicksand under his feet.

* * *

It was bang, bang, bang, bang on the drive downtown, rico-chets, old dumb moves kicked around to see how they stood up next to this doozie.

In '33 he'd charged six picket bulls outside MGM, caught nail-studded baseball bats upside his arms, took the boys out with his baton and caught tetanus—stupid, but the audaciousness helped get him his LAPD appointment.

Early in '42 he worked with the Alien Squad, rounding up Japs and relocating them to the horse paddocks at Santa Anita Race-track. He grabbed a wiseacre kid named Bob Takahashi just as he was en route to get his ashes hauled for the first time, felt sorry for him and took him on a six-day toot in Tijuana—booze, whores, the dog track and a teary farewell at the border—bad Bob hightailing it south, a slant-eyed stranger in a round-eyed land. Very stupid—but he covered his absent ass by shaking down a suspicious-looking car outside San Diego, busting four grass-hoppers transporting a pound of premium maryjane. The punks had a total of nineteen outstanding L.A. City warrants between them; he got a commendation letter and four felony notches on his gun. Another shit play turned into clover.

But the granddaddy was his brother Fud. Three days out of the Texas State Pen, Fud shows up at the door of then Detective-Sergeant Turner Meeks, informs him that he just stuck up a liquor store in Hermosa Beach, pistol-whipped the proprietor and intended to pay Buzz back the six yards he owed him with the proceeds. Just as Fud was digging through his blood-soaked paper bag, there was a knock at the door. Buzz looked through the spy hole, saw two blue uniforms, tagged blood as thicker than water and fired his own service revolver into the living room wall four times. The bluesuits started knocking down the door; Buzz hustled Fud to the cellar, locked him in, smashed the window leading to the back porch and trampled his landlady's prize petu-nias. When the patrolmen made it inside, Buzz told them he was LAPD and the perpetrator was a hophead he'd sent to Big Q—Davis Haskins—in reality a recent overdose in Billings, Montana; he'd picked up the info working an extradition job. The blues fanned out, called for backup and surrounded the neighborhood until dawn; Davis Haskins made the front page of the *Mirror* and *Daily News*; Buzz shat bricks for a week and kept Fud docile in the cellar with whiskey, baloney sandwiches and smut mags swiped from the Central Vice squadroom. And he walked on the caper, white trash chutzpah carrying him through, no one informing the police powers that be that a dead man robbed the Happy Time Liquor Store, drove a stolen La Salle up to the front door of Sergeant Turner "Buzz" Meeks, then shot out his living room wall and escaped on foot. When Fud bought it a year later at Guadalcanal, his squad leader sent Buzz a letter; baby brother's last words were something like, "Tell Turner thanks for the fur books and sandwiches."

Stupid, crazy, sentimental, lunatic dumb.

But kissing Audrey Anders was worse.

Buzz parked in the City Hall lot, transferred all the cash to his doughnut box and took it upstairs to Ellis Loew's office. Going in the door, he saw Loew, Big Dudley Smith and Mal Considine sitting around a table, all of them talking at once, garbled stuff about cop decoys. No one glanced up; Buzz eyeballed Considine four years after he gave him the cuckold's horns. The man still looked more like a lawyer than a cop; his blond hair was going gray; there was something nervous and raggedy-assed about him.

Buzz rapped on the door and tossed the box onto the chair holding it open. The three looked over; he fixed his eyes on Considine. Ellis Loew nodded, all business; Dudley Smith said, "Hello, Turner, old colleague," all blarney; Considine eyed him back, all curiosity, like he was examining a reptile specimen he'd never seen before.

They held the look. Buzz said, "Hello, Mal."

Mal Considine said, "Nice tie, Meeks. Who'd you roll for it?"

Buzz laughed. "How's the ex, Lieutenant? She still wearin' crotchless panties?"

Considine stared, his mouth twitching. Buzz stared back, his mouth dry.

Mexican standoff.

50-50, Considine or Dragna.

Maybe he'd hold off just a tad, cut the Red Menace just a bit more slack before he signed on.

10

IT WAS two nights of bad dreams and a day's worth of dead ends that had him making the run to Malibu Canyon.

Driving northbound on Pacific Coast Highway, Danny chalked it up as an elimination job: talk to the men on the list of fighting dog breeders he'd gotten from Sheriff's Central Vice, make nice with them and get educated confirmations or denials on Doc Layman's animal-aided killing/blood bait thesis. No such beast existed in the County Homicide files or with City R&I; if the breeders, men who would know if anyone did, laughed the theory off as nonsense, then maybe tonight he could sleep without the company of snapping hounds, entrails and screechy jazz.

It started this way:

After the Moonglow Lounge and Janice Modine's pass, he'd gotten an idea—build his own file on the Goines snuff, write down every shred of information, glom carbons of the autopsy and print reports, stick Dietrich with lackluster summaries and concentrate on *his* paperwork, *his* case—the 187 he'd follow up even if he didn't nail the bastard before the skipper pulled the plug. He drove to the Hollywood Ranch Market then, grabbed a stack of cardboard cartons, bought manila folders, colored side tabs, yellow legal pads, typing and carbon paper and drove home with them—allowing himself two extra shots of I.W. Harper as a reward for his dedication. The booze put him out on the couch—and it got hairy.

Goines' mutilations in wraparound Technicolor. Guts and big bruised penises, so close up that at first he couldn't tell what they were. Dogs rooting in the gore, him right there, Man Camera filming it until he joined the brood and started biting.

Two nights of it.

With a day of shit in between.

He put the first night's dream off as scare stuff caused by a frustrating case and no food in his system. In the morning he got double bacon, eggs, hash browns, toast and sweet rolls at the Wilshire Derby, drove downtown to the Sheriff's Central Bureau and scanned Homicide files. No animal-aided murders were on record; the only homosexual slashings even remotely similar to Marty Goines' were open-and-shut jobs—lovers' spats where the perpetrator was captured, still serving time or executed by the State of California.

Shitwork was next.

He called Karen Hiltscher at the Station and sweet-talked her into making phone queries of other musicians' locals that might have sent Marty Goines out on gigs, and L.A. area jazz clubs that might have hired his trombone independently. He told her to ring the other LASD station houses and solicit run-throughs of their burglary files: paper scans for jazz musician/burglars who might prove to be known associates of Goines. The girl reluctantly agreed; he blew kisses into the phone, promised to call for results later and drove back to Local 3126.

There, the counterwoman gave him another look at the Horn of Plenty's employment record, and Danny copied down club and roadhouse addresses going back to Mad Marty's first gig in '36. He spent the rest of the day driving by jazz spots that were now laundromats and hamburger joints; jazz spots that had changed hands a half dozen times; jazz spots that had retained the same owner for years. And he got the same response across the board: a shrug at Goines' mugshot strip, the words "Marty who?", a deadpan on the topics of jazzbo burglars and the longshot of a burglar kid with his face bandaged up.

At dusk, he called Karen for her results. Goose egg: more "Marty who?", the burglar files yielding eleven names—seven Negroes, two Mexicans, two white men whose jail records revealed AB+ and O— blood. Pure undiluted shit.

He remembered his promise to Janice Modine then, called the San Dimas Substation and talked to the boss of the Auto Theft Detail. John Lembeck was still in custody there, being sweated over a series of GTAs. Danny told the man his snitch story, stressing the angle that Lembeck was dead meat if he made it to the County jail. The squad boss agreed to roll him up for release; Danny could tell Jungle John was in for a severe thumping first— but not half as bad as he was going to give him.

Then it was back to his apartment, four shots of I.W. and work on the file, side tabs labeled and stuck to folders—"Interviews," "Eliminations," "Chronology," "Canvassing," "Physical Evidence," "Background." One thought burned throughout the writing of a detailed summary: where was Marty Goines living between the time of his release from Lexington State and his death? The thought led to a phone call—the night switchboard at the hospital for a list of other men released to California around the same time as Goines. The answer, after holding the line long distance for twenty minutes—*none*.

Exhaustion, writer's cramp and no sleep followed. Four bonus shots and a sheet-thrashing roll on the bed got him unconsciousness and the dogs again, the Man Camera with teeth—his—

biting at a whole morgueful of O+ stiffs lined up on gurneys. Morning and another big breakfast convinced him to make the elimination; he called Central Vice, got the list of breeders and was warned to go easy: the dog farms in Malibu Canyon were run by cracker strongarms, cousins from the Tennessee sticks. They bred their pit bulls there, which was not against the law; they only fought them in South L.A., and none of the men had been convicted of dog fighting since the war.

Danny turned off Pacific Coast Highway at the Canyon Road and climbed inland through scrub-covered hills laced with little streams and valleys. The road was a narrow two-laner, the left side featuring kiddie camps, stables and occasional nightclubs, the right a wood retaining wall and a long drop into green-brown bush forest. Signs pointing into the scrub indicated clearings and houses and people; Danny saw the roofs of villas, Tudor steeples, the chimneys of extravagant log cabins. Gradually, the quality of the real estate declined—no ocean view, no sea breeze, the scrub thicker and thicker, no dwellings at all. When he hit the top of Malibu Ridge and started rolling downhill, he knew the dog farms had to be nearby—his vista was now dotted with tar-papered shacks and the heat was zooming up as the shade-producing foliage thinned out.

The Vice officer he'd talked to had the three farms tagged as a mile in on a dirt access road marked by a sign: PIT PUPS—AUTO PARTS. Danny found the sign just as the two-lane leveled off into a long, flat stretch, the San Fernando Valley in the distance. He swung onto it and wracked his Chevy's undercarriage for three-quarters of a mile, sharecropper-like shacks on both sides of him. Then he saw them—three cinderblock huts encircled by a barbed-wire fence; three dirt yards littered with axles, drive shafts and cylinder blocks; three individually penned broods of squat, muscular dogs.

Danny pulled up to the fence, pinned his badge to his jacket front and tapped the horn—a little courtesy to the hut dwellers. The dogs barked at the noise; Danny walked over to the nearest stretch of wire and looked at them.

They weren't the dogs from his dreams—black and sleek with flashing white teeth—they were brindle and tan and speckled terriers, barrel-chested, jaw-heavy and all muscle. They didn't have the outsized genitalia of his dogs; their barks weren't death snaps; they weren't ugly—they were just animals bred for a mean utility. Danny eyed the ones penned up closest to him, wondering what they'd do if he gave them a pat on the head, then told them he was glad they didn't look like some other dogs he knew.

"Rape-o, Hacksaw and Night Train. Them dogs won sixteen altogether. Southern California record for one man's stable."

Danny turned to face the voice. A very fat man in overalls was standing in the doorway of the shack just off to his left; he was wearing thick glasses and probably couldn't see too well. Danny unpinned his badge and slipped it in his pocket, thinking the man was garrulous and ripe for an insurance agent ploy. "Can I talk to you for a second about your dogs?"

The man ambled to the fence, squinting and blinking. He said, "Booth Conklin. You in the market for a good pit hound?"

Danny looked into Booth Conklin's eyes, one a free-floating waller, the other cloudy and pocked with cataracts. "Dan Upshaw. You could start me off with some information on them."

Conklin said, "I kin do better than that," waddled to a speckled dog's pen and flipped the latch. The beast made a dash, hit the fence with his front paws and started licking the wire. Danny knelt and scratched his snout, a slick pink tongue sliding over his fingers. He said, "Good boy, good fellow," putting off Doc Layman's theories as long longshots then and there.

Booth Conklin waddled back, holding a long piece of wood. "First lesson with pits is don't talk baby talk to 'em or they won't respect you. Rape-o here's a leg pumper, just wants to get your trousers wet. My cousin Wallace named him Rape-o 'cause he'll mount anything with bad intentions. Down, Rape-o, down!"

The pit bull kept nuzzling Danny's fingers; Booth Conklin whacked him in the ass with his stick. Rape-o let out a shrill yowl, cowered away and started rubbing his backside in the dirt, all fours up and treading air. Danny felt his fists clenching; Conklin stuck the stick in Rape-o's mouth. The dog clamped down his jaws; Conklin lifted him up and held him out at arm's length. Danny gasped at the feat of strength.

Conklin spoke calmly, like holding seventy pounds of dog at the end of a stick was everyday stuff. "Pits dish it out, so they gotta be able to take it. I won't sell you no dog if you gonna coddle it."

Rape-o was hanging stock-still, groans vibrating from his throat. Every muscle was perfectly outlined; Danny thought that the animal was perfect mean beauty. He said, "I live in an apartment, so I can't have a dog."

"You just come out to look and jaw?"

Rape-o's groans were getting deeper and more pleasured; his balls constricted and he popped an erection. Danny looked away. "Questions more than anything else."

Conklin squinted, his eyes slits behind coke bottle glasses. "You ain't a policeman, are you?"

"No, I'm an insurance investigator. I'm working a death claim and I thought you could help me with some questions."

Conklin said, "I'm the helpful type, ain't I, Rape-o," moving the stick up and down, wrist flicks while the dog humped the air. Rape-o yowled, yipped and whimpered; Danny knew what was happening and fixed on the fat man's coke bottles. Rape-o let out a final yowl/yip/groan, let go and fell to the dirt. Conklin laughed. "You ain't got the sense of humor for pits, I can tell. Ask your questions, boy. I got a cousin who's an insurance man, so I'm prone to the breed."

Rape-o slinked over to the fence and tried to rub his snout up against Danny's knee; Danny took a step backward. "It's a murder claim. We know the victim was killed by a man, but the coroner thinks he may have let a dog or coyote or wolf at him after he was dead. What do you think of the idea?"

Conklin stuck a toothpick in his mouth and worked his words around it. "Mister, I know the canine family real good, and coyotes and wolves is out—'less the killer captured and starved them and left the dead guy out for them to pick clean someplace amenable. What kind of damage on your victim?"

Danny watched Rape-o curl up in the dirt and go to sleep, sated, his muscles slack. "Localized. Teeth marks on the stomach, the intestines bitten and sucked on. It had to have happened someplace inside, because the body was clean when the police found it."

Conklin snickered. "Then you rule out coyotes and wolves—they'd go crazy and eat the fucker whole, and you can't exactly keep them inside the house. You thinkin' pits? Dogs?"

"If anything, yes."

"You sure them teeth marks ain't human?"

"No, we're not sure."

Booth Conklin pointed to his pit pens. "Mister, I run these three farms for my cousins, and I know how to get what I want from dogs, and if I was crazy enough to want one of my pups to eat a man's guts, I imagine I could think up a way for him to do it. I'll tell you though, I've got a real taste for blood sport, and I couldn't imagine any human being doin' what you just told me."

Danny said, "If you wanted to, how would you do it?"

Conklin petted Rape-o's hindquarters; the dog lazily wagged its tail. "I'd starve him and pen him and let bitch dogs in heat parade around in front of his cage and make him crazy. I'd muzzle him and bind his legs and put a restrainer around his dick so he couldn't get himself off. I'd get me a rubber glove and tweak his dick till he just about got there, then I'd clamp his balls so he couldn't shoot. I'd get me some doggie menstrual blood and spray it in his eyes and nose for a week or so, till he came to think of it as food and love. Then, when I had me that dead man, I'd spread a big puddle of pussy blood right where I wanted him to bite. And, mister? I'd have a gun handy in case that tormented old dog decided to eat *me*. That answer satisfy you?"

Danny thought: No animals, it just isn't *right*. But—have Doc Layman do organ taps on Goines, his body parts near the mutilations, tests for a second, nonhuman, blood type. He threw Booth Conklin a long-shot question. "What kind of people buy dogs from you?"

"Boys who love blood sport, and I ain't talkin' 'bout your crazy shit either."

"Isn't dog fighting against the law?"

"You know who to grease, then there ain't no law. You sure you ain't a policeman?"

Danny shook his head. "Amalgamated Insurance. Look, do you remember selling a dog to a tall, gray-haired man, middle-aged, within the past six months or so?"

Conklin gave Rape-o a gentle kick; the dog stirred, got up and trotted back to his pen. "Mister, my customers are young studs in pickup trucks and niggers lookin' to have the toughest dog on the block."

"Do any of your customers stand out as different than that? Unusual?"

Booth Conklin laughed so hard he almost swallowed his toothpick. "Back durin' the war, these movie types saw my sign, came by and said they wanted to make a little home movie, two dogs dressed up with masks and costumes fightin' to the death. I sold them boys two twenty-dollar dogs for a C-note apiece."

"Did they make their movie?"

"I ain't seen it advertised at Grauman's Chinese, so how should I know? There's this sanitarium over on the beach side of the Canyon, dryout place for all the Hollywood types. I figured they were visitin' there and headin' to the Valley when they saw my sign."

"Were any of the men tall and gray-haired?"

Conklin shrugged. "I don't really remember. One guy had a funny European accent, that I do recall. Besides, my eyes ain't the best in the world. You about done with your questions, son?"

Ninety-five percent against on the blood bait theory; maybe a quash on his nightmares; useless dope on Hollywood lunacy. Danny said, "Thanks, Mr. Conklin. You were a big help."

"My pleasure, son. Come back sometime. Rape-o likes you."

* * *

Danny drove to the Station, sent out for a hamburger, fries and milk even though he wasn't hungry, ate half the meal and called Doc Layman at the City Morgue.

"Norton Layman speaking."

"It's Danny Upshaw, Doctor."

"Just the man I was going to call. Your news first or mine?"

Danny flashed: Rape-o chewing on Marty Goines' midsection. He threw the remains of his burger in the wastebasket and said, "Mine. I'm sure the teeth marks are human. I just talked to a man who breeds fighting dogs, and he said your blood bait theory is feasible, but it would take a lot of planning, and I think the killing wasn't *that* premeditated. He said dog menstrual blood would be the best bait, and I was thinking you could tap the cadaver's organs next to his wounds, see if you got any foreign blood."

Layman sighed. "Danny, the City of Los Angeles cremated Martin Mitchell Goines this morning. Autopsy completed, no claim on the body within forty-eight hours, ashes to ashes. I have some good news, though."

Danny thought, "Shit"; said, "Shoot."

"The slash wounds on the victim's back interested me, and I remembered Gordon Kienzle's wound book. Do you know it?"

"No."

"Well, Kienzle is a pathologist who started out as an emergency room MD. He was fascinated with nonfatal assaults, and he put together a book of photos and specifications on man-inflicted woundings. I consulted it, and the cuts on Martin Mitchell Goines' back are identical to the sample wounds listed under 'Zoot Stick,' a two-by-four with a razor blade or blades attached at the end. Now, the zoot stick dates back to '42 and '43. It was popular with anti-Mexican gangs and Riot Squad cops, who used it to slash the zoot suits certain Latin elements were sporting."

Check the City/County Homicide files for zoot stick killings. Danny said, "It's a good lead, Doc. Thanks."

"Don't thank me yet. I checked the files before I decided to call you. There are no zoot stick homicides on record. A friend of mine on the LAPD Riot Squad said 99 percent of your white-on-Mexican assaults weren't reported and the Mexicans never took the damn sticks to each other, it was considered dirty pool or whatever. But it *is* a lead."

Robe wad suffocating, hands or sash strangling, teeth biting, and now a zoot stick cutting. *Why the different forms of brutality?* Danny said, "See you in class, Doctor," hung up and walked back to his car just to be moving. Jungle John Lembeck was leaning against the hood, his face bruised, one eye purple and closed. He said, "They got real rough with me, Mr. Upshaw. I wouldn't have told Janice to ditz you, except they were hurting me so bad. I'm stand-up, Mr. Upshaw. So if you want payback, I'll understand."

Danny balled his right fist and got ready to swing it—but a flash of Booth Conklin and his pit hound stopped him.

11

THE CIGARS were Havanas, and their aroma made Mal wish he hadn't quit smoking; Herman Gerstein's pep talk and Dudley Smith's accompaniment—smiles, nods, little chuckles—made him wish that he was back at the LAPD Academy interviewing recruits for the role of idealistic young leftist. His one day of it had yielded no one near appropriate, and starting their interrogations without a decoy at the ready felt like a mistake. But Ellis Loew and Dudley, fired up by Lesnick's psychiatric dirt, were trigger-happy—and here they were getting ready to brace Mondo Lopez, Sammy Benavides and Juan Duarte, UAESers playing Indians on the set of *Tomahawk Massacre*. And now Gerstein's schtick was making him itchy, too.

The Variety International boss was pacing behind his desk, waving his Havana; Mal kept thinking of Buzz Meeks sliming back into his life at *the* worst possible moment.

"... and I can tell you this, gentlemen: through passive resistance and other Commie shit the UAES is gonna force the Teamsters into kicking some ass, which is gonna make the UAES look good and us look bad. Commies like to get hurt. They'll eat any amount of shit, smile like it's filet mignon and ask for seconds, turn the other cheek, then bite *you* on the ass. Like those pachucos down on Set 23. Zoot suit punks who got themselves a union card, a license to give shit and think their own shit don't stink. Am I right or is Eleanor Roosevelt a dyke?"

Dudley Smith laughed uproariously. "And a grand quiff diver she is. Dark meat, too, I've heard. And we all know about the late Franklin's bent for little black terriers. Mr. Gerstein, Lieutenant Considine and I would like to thank you for your contributions to our endeavor and your hospitality this morning."

Mal took the cue and stood up; Herman Gerstein reached into a humidor and grabbed a handful of cigars, Dudley got to his feet; Gerstein came at them like a fullback, pumping hands, stuffing Havanas in all their available pockets, showing them the door with hard back slaps. When it closed behind him, Dudley said, "No flair for language. You can take the Jew out of the gutter, but you can't take the gutter out of the Jew. Are you ready to interrogate, Captain?"

Mal looked down at the UAES picket line, caught a back view of a woman in slacks and wondered if she was Claire De Haven. "Okay, *Lieutenant*."

"Ah, Malcolm, what a grand wit you have!"

They took Herman Gerstein's private elevator down to ground level and two rows of sound stages separated by a center walkway. The buildings were tan stucco, silo tall and humpbacked at the top, with sandwich boards propped up by the front doors—the name, director and shooting schedule of the movie crayoned on white plastic. Actors riding bicycles—cowboys, Indians, baseball players, Revolutionary War soldiers—whizzed by; motorized carts hauled camera equipment; technicians hobnobbed by a snack cart where a Roman centurion dished out doughnuts and coffee. The enclosed sets extended for nearly a quarter mile, black numbers above the doors marking them. Mal walked ahead of Dudley Smith, running Benavides/Lopez/Duarte file dirt through his head, hoping an on-the-job bracing wasn't too much, too quick.

Dudley caught up outside Set 23. Mal rang the buzzer; a woman in a saloon girl outfit opened the door and popped her gum at them. Mal displayed his badge and identification. "We're with the District Attorney's Office, and we want to speak to Mondo Lopez, Juan Duarte and Sammy Benavides."

The saloon girl gave her gum a last pop and spoke with a thick Brooklyn accent. "They're on a take. They're the hotheaded young Indians who want to attack the fort, but the wise old chief don't want them to. They'll be finished in a few minutes, and you can—"

Dudley cut in. "We don't require a plot synopsis. If you'll tell them it's the police, they'll adjust their busy schedule to accommodate us. And please do it now."

The girl swallowed her gum and walked in front of them. Dudley smiled; Mal thought: he's a spellbinder—don't let him run the show.

The sound stage was cavernous: wire-strewn walls, lights and cameras on dollies, anemic-looking horses tethered to equipment poles and people standing around doing nothing. Right in the middle was an olive drab teepee, obviously fashioned from army surplus material, Indian symbols painted on the sides—candy apple red lacquer—like it was some brave's customized hot rod. Cameras and tripod lights were fixed on the teepee and the four actors squatting in front of it—an old pseudo-Indian white man and three pseudo-Indian Mexicans in their late twenties.

The saloon girl stopped them a few feet behind the cameras, whispering. "There. The Latin lover types." The old chief intoned words of peace; the three young braves delivered lines about the white eyes speaking with forked tongue, their voices pure Mex. Someone yelled, "Cut!" and the scene became a blur of moving bodies.

Mal elbowed into it, catching the three pulling cigarettes and lighters out of their buckskins. He made them make him as a cop; Dudley Smith walked over; the braves gave each other spooked looks.

Dudley flashed his shield. "Police. Am I talking to Mondo Lopez, Juan Duarte and Samuel Benavides?"

The tallest brave slipped a rubber band off his pony tail and shaped his hair into a pachuco do—duck's ass back, pompadour front. He said, "I'm Lopez."

Mal opened up his end strong. "Care to introduce your friends, Mr. Lopez? We don't have all day."

The other two squared their shoulders and stepped forward, the move half bravado, half kowtow to authority. Mal tagged the short, muscular one as Duarte, former Sinarquista squad leader, zoot suits and swastika armbands until the CP brought him around; his lanky pal as Benavides—Mr. Tight Lips to Doc Lesnick, his file a complete bore except for one session devoted to an account of how twelve-year-old Sammy molested his nine-year-old sister, a razor blade to her throat. Both men did a sullen foot dance; Muscles said, "I'm Benavides."

Mal pointed to a side door, then touched his tie clip—LAPD semaphore for *Let Me Run It*. "My name's Considine, and this is Lieutenant Smith. We're with the DA's Office, and we'd like to ask you a few questions. It's just routine, and we'll have you back at work in a few minutes."

Juan Duarte said, "We got a choice?"

Dudley chuckled; Mal put a hand on his arm. "Yes. Here or the Hall of Justice jail."

Lopez cocked his head toward the exit; Benavides and Duarte fell in next to him, lit cigarettes and walked outside. Actors and technicians gawked at the Indian-paleface migration. Mal schemed a razzle-dazzle, himself abrasive at first, then making nice, Dudley asking the hard questions, him playing savior at the end—the big push to glom them as friendly witnesses.

The three halted their march just out the door, leaning against the wall, nonchalant. Dudley stationed himself to the left of Mal, about a half step back. Mal let the men smoke in silence, then said, "Boy, have you guys got it made."

Three sets of eyes on the ground, three phony Indians in a cloud of cigarette smoke. Mal rattled the leader's cage. "Can I ask you a question, Mr. Lopez?"

Mondo Lopez looked up. "Sure, Officer."

"Mr. Lopez, you must be taking home close to a C-note a week. Is that true?"

Mondo Lopez said, "Eighty-one and change. Why?"

Mal smiled. "Well, you're making almost half as much as I am, and I'm a college graduate and a ranking police officer with six-teen years' experience. All of you quit high school, isn't that true?"

A quick look passed among the three. Lopez smirked, Bena-vides shrugged and Duarte took a long drag on his cigarette. Mal saw them sighting in on his ploy way too soon and tried for sugar. "Look, I'll tell you why I brought it up. You guys have beat the odds. You ran with the First Street Flats and the Sinarquistas, did some Juvie time and stayed clean. That's impressive, and we're not here to roust you for anything you yourselves did."

Juan Duarte ground out his cigarette. "You mean this is about our friends?"

Mal dredged the files for ammo, grabbing the fact that all three tried to join the service after Pearl Harbor. "Look, I've checked your Selective Service records. You quit the Sinarquistas and the Flats, you tried to fight the Japs, you were on the right side with Sleepy Lagoon. When you were wrong you copped to it. That's the sign of a good man in my book."

Sammy Benavides said, "Is a stool pigeon a good man in your book, Mr. Po—"

Duarte silenced him with a sharp elbow. "Who you trying to tell us is wrong now? Who you *want* to be wrong?"

Finally a good opening. "How about the Party, gentlemen? How about Uncle Joe Stalin getting under the sheets with Hitler? How about slave labor camps in Siberia and all the stuff the Party has pulled in America while they condoned the stuff going on over in Russia? Gentlemen, I've been a cop for sixteen years and I've never asked a man to snitch his friends. But I'll ask *any* man to snitch his *enemies*, especially if they also happen to be mine."

Mal caught his breath, thinking of Summations 115 at Stanford Law; Dudley Smith stood easy at his side. Mondo Lopez eyed the blacktop, then his *Tomahawk Massacre* co-stars. Then all three started clapping.

Dudley flushed; Mal could see his red face going toward purple. Lopez brought a flat palm slowly down, killing the applause. "How about you tell us what this is all about?"

Mal thrashed for file dirt and came up empty. "This is a preliminary investigation into Communist influence in Hollywood. And we're not asking you to snitch your friends, just *our* enemies."

Benavides pointed west, toward the front office and two picket lines. "And this has got nothing to do with Gerstein wanting our union out and the Teamsters in?"

"No, this is a preliminary investigation that has nothing to do with whatever current labor troubles your union is involved in. This is—"

Duarte interrupted. "Why *us*? Why me and Sammy and Mondo?"

"Because you're reformed criminals and you'd make damn good witnesses."

"Because you thought we'd be jail-wise and bleed easy?"

"No, because you've been zooters and Reds, and we figured that maybe you had the brains to know it was *all* shit."

Benavides kicked in, a leery eye on Dudley. "You know the HUAC Committee pulled this snitch routine, and good people got hurt. Now it's happening again, and you want us to fink?"

Mal thought of Benavides as a kiddie raper talking decency; he could *feel* Dudley thinking the same thing, going crazy with it. "Look, I *know* corruption. The HUAC chairman is in Danbury for bribery, HUAC itself was reckless. And I'll admit the LAPD screwed up on the Sleepy Lagoon thing. But you can't tell—"

Mondo Lopez shouted, "Screwed up! Pendejo, it was a fucking pogrom against my people by your people! You're sweet-talking the wrong people on the wrong case to get the wrong fuck—"

Dudley stepped in front of the three, his suitcoat open, .45 automatic, sap and brass knuckles in plain view. His bulk cast the Mexicans in one big shadow and his brogue went up octaves, but didn't crack. "Your seventeen filthy compatriots murdered José Diaz in cold blood and beat the gas chamber because traitors and perverts and deluded weaklings banded up to save them. And I will brook no disrespect for a brother officer in my presence. Do you understand?"

Complete silence, the UAES men still in Dudley's shadow, stagehands eyeballing the action from the walkway. Mal stepped up to speak for himself, taller than Dudley but half his breadth. Scared. Pendejo. He got ready to give signals, then Mondo Lopez hit back. "Those seventeen got fucked by the puto LAPD and the puto City court system. And that ees la fucking verdad."

Dudley moved forward so that all there was between him and Lopez was the arc of a short kidney punch. Benavides backed away, shaking; Duarte mumbled that the SLDC got anonymous letters making a white guy for José Diaz, but nobody believed it; Benavides pulled him out of harm's way. Mal grabbed Dudley's arm; the big man flung him back and lowered his brogue to baritone range. "Did you enjoy perverting justice with the SLDC, Mondo? Did you enjoy the favors of Claire De Haven—filthy rich capitalista, tight with the City Council, a real love for that undersized spic cock?"

Benavides and Duarte had their backs to the wall and were sliding away from the scene an inch at a time. Mal stood frozen; Lopez glared at Dudley; Dudley laughed. "Perhaps that was unfair of me, lad. We all know Claire spread her favors thin, but I doubt she would have stooped to your level. Your SLDC friend Chaz Minear, now that's another story. Was he there for the prime Mex butthole?"

Benavides moved toward Dudley; Mal snapped out of his freeze, grabbed him and pushed him into the wall, seeing razor blades held to a little girl's throat. Benavides shouted, "That puto bought boys at a puto escort service, he didn't do us!" Mal pressed harder, sweat-saturated suit against soaked buckskins, hard muscles straining at the body of a thin man almost forty. Benavides suddenly went slack; Mal took his hands off him and got a file flash: Sammy railing against queers to Doc Lesnick, a weak point they could have played smart.

Sammy Benavides slid down the wall and watched the Smith-Lopez eyeball duel. Mal tried to make his hands give signals, but couldn't. Juan Duarte was standing by the walkway, scoping the business long-distance. Dudley broke the standoff with a pivot and a lilting brogue aside. "I hope you learned a lesson today, Captain. You can't play sob sister with scum. You should have joined me on the Hat Squad. You would have learned then in grand fashion."

* * *

Round one blown to hell.

Mal drove home, thinking of captain's bars snatched away from him, smothered in Dudley Smith's huge fists. And he had been partly at fault, going too easy when the Mexicans came on too smart, thinking he could reason with them, wheedle and draw them into logical traps. He'd thought of submitting a memo to Ellis Loew—lay off Sleepy Lagoon, it's too sympathetic—then he tossed it into the pot for empathy, hit a nerve with the Mexes and upset Dudley's bee in the bonnet on the case. And Dudley had stood up for him before he himself did, which made it hard to fault him for losing his temper; which meant that maybe direct UAES approaches were dead and they should concentrate solely on decoy infiltration and sub-rosa interrogations.

His specialty—which didn't lessen the sting of Dudley's Hat Squad crack, and which increased the need for Buzz Meeks to join the grand jury team.

All debits, but on the plus side Dudley's ranting didn't put out information restricted to Lesnick's files, leaving that avenue of manipulation still open. What was troubling was a cop as smart as the Irishman taking a nondirect attack so personally, then hitting his "brother officer" below the belt.

Pendejo.

Scared.

And Dudley Smith knows it.

At home, Mal took advantage of the empty house, dumping his sweaty clothes, showering, changing to a sport shirt and khakis and settling into the den to write a long memo to Loew—heavily stressing that there should be no further direct questioning of UAES members until their decoy was planted—a decoy now being a necessity. He was a page in when he realized that it had to be partly a gloss job—there was no way to accurately describe what happened at Variety International without portraying himself as a weakling or a fool. So he did gloss it, and filled up another page with warnings on the Loew choice for troubleshooter— Buzz Meeks—the man who held the possible distinction of being the single most crooked cop in the history of the Los Angeles Police Department—heroin skimmer, shakedown artist, bagman and now a glorified pimp for Howard Hughes. After that page, he knew it was futile; if Meeks wanted in he *was* in— Hughes was the heaviest contributor to the grand jury bankroll and Meeks' bossman—what he said would go. After two pages he knew *why* the tack wasn't worth pursuing: Meeks was absolutely the best man for the job. And the best man for the job was afraid of him, just like he was afraid of Dudley Smith. Even though there was no reason for the fear.

Mal threw the Meeks memo in the wastebasket and started thinking decoy. The LAPD Academy was already out—straight arrow youths with no spark for impersonation. The Sheriff's Academy was unlikely—the Brenda Allen mess and the LASD sheltering Mickey Cohen made it unlikely that they would lend the City a smart young recruit. Their best bet was a rank-and-file City officer, smart, good-looking, adaptable and ambitious, mid to late twenties, a malleable young man without a hard-edged cop quality.

Where?

Hollywood Division was out—half the men had been implicated over Brenda Allen, had had their pictures in the paper, were running scared and angry and wild—there was even a rumor floating around that three men on the Hollywood Detective Squad had been behind last August's shootout at Sherry's—a botched snuff attempt on Mickey Cohen that wounded three and killed a Cohen utility trigger. *Out.*

And Central was packed with unqualified rookies who made the Department because of their war records; 77th Street, Newton and University featured outsized crackers hired on to keep the Negro citizenry in line. Hollenbeck might be a good place to look—but East L.A. was Mex, Benavides, Lopez and Duarte still had ties there, and that might blow their decoy's cover. The various detective divisions were a possible stalking ground—if they could find a man who didn't come off as irredeemably jaded.

Mal grabbed his LAPD station directory and started scanning it, one eye on the wall clock as it inched toward 3:00 and Stefan's home-from-school time. He was about to start calling CO's for preliminary screening talks when he heard footsteps in the hall; he swiveled in his chair, dropped his arms and got ready to let his son dogpile him.

It was Celeste. She looked at Mal's open arms until he dropped them; she said, "I told Stefan to stay late after school in order that I should talk to you."

"Yes?"

"The look on your face does not to make this easy."

"Spill it, goddamn you."

Celeste clutched her beaded opera purse, a favored relic of Prague, 1935. "I am going to divorce you. I have met a nice man, a man who is cultured and will make Stefan and me a better home."

Mal thought: perfect calm, she knows her effects. He said, "I won't let you. Don't hurt my boy or I'll hurt you."

"You cannot. To the mother the child belongs."

Maim her, let her know he *is* the law. "Is he rich, Celeste? If you have to fuck to survive, you should fuck rich men. Right, Fräulein? Or powerful men, like Kempflerr."

"You always return to that because it is so ugly and because it excites you so."

Match point; Mal felt his sense of gamesmanship go blooey. "I saved your wretched rich-girl ass. I killed the man who made you a whore. I gave you a home."

Celeste smiled, her standard parting of thin lips over perfect teeth. "You killed Kempflerr to prove yourself not a coward. You wanted to be like a real policeman, and you were willing to destroy yourself to do it. Only your dumb luck saved you. And you keep your secrets so badly."

Mal stood up on punch-drunk legs. "I killed someone who deserved to die."

Celeste fondled her purse, fingers over beadwork embroidery. Mal saw it as stage business, the buildup to a punch line. "No comeback for that one?"

Celeste put on her deepest iceberg smile. "Herr Kempflerr was very kind to me, and I only made up his nasty sexuality to excite you. He was a gentle lover, and when the war was almost over, he sabotaged the ovens and saved thousands of lives. You are lucky that military governor liked you, Malcolm. Kempflerr was going to help the Americans look for other Nazis. And I only married you because I felt very bad about the lies I seduced you with."

Mal tried to say "No," but couldn't form the word; Celeste broadened her smile. Mal saw it as a target and ran to her. He grabbed her neck, held her to the doorway and aimed hard right hands at her mouth, teeth splintering up through her lips, cutting his knuckles. He hit her and hit her and hit her; he would have gone on hitting her, but "Mutti!" and tiny fists pummeling his legs made him stop and run out of the house, afraid of a little boy—his own.

12

THE PHONE wouldn't quit ringing.

First it was Leotis Dineen, calling to tell him that Art Aragon knocked out Lupe Pimentel in the second round, raising his debt to twenty-one hundred even, with a vig payment due tomorrow. Next was the real estate man up in Ventura County. His glad tidings: the top offer for Buzz's dry-rotted, shadeless, rock-laden, non-irrigable, poorly located and generally misanthropic farmland was fourteen dollars an acre, the offerer, the pastor of First

Pentecostal Divine Eminence Church, who wanted to turn it into a cemetery for the sanctified pets of members of his congregation. Buzz said twenty per, minimum; ten minutes later the phone rang again. No salutation, just, "I didn't tell Mickey, because you're not worth going to the gas chamber for." He suggested a romantic drink somewhere; Audrey Anders replied, "Fuck you."

Skating on the stupidest stupid move of his life made him feel cocky, despite Dineen's implied warning: my money or your kneecaps. Buzz thought of cash shakedowns—him against fences and hotel crawlers he'd leaned on as a cop, then nixed the notion—he'd gotten older and flabbier, while they'd probably gotten meaner and better armed. There was just himself against 50-50 Mal Considine, who held a mean stare but otherwise looked pretty withered. He picked up the phone and dialed his boss's private number at the Bel-Air Hotel.

"Yes? Who is this?"

"Me. Howard, I want in on that grand jury turkey shoot. That job still open?"

13

DANNY WAS trying hard to stay under the speed limit, hauling into Hollywood—City jurisdiction—with the speedometer needle straddling forty. A few minutes ago a Lexington State administrator had called the station; a letter from Marty Goines, postmarked four days before, had just arrived at the hospital. It was addressed to a patient there and contained nothing but innocuous stuff about jazz—and the word that Goines had moved into an above-garage flop at 2307 North Tamarind. It was a scalding hot lead; if the address had been County ground, he'd have grabbed a black-and-white and rolled red lights and siren.

2307 was a half mile north of the Boulevard, in the middle of a long block of wood-framed Tudors. Danny parked curbside and saw that the cold afternoon had kept the locals indoors—no one was out taking the air. He grabbed his evidence kit, trotted up to the door of the front house and rang the bell.

Ten seconds, no answer. Danny walked back to the garage, saw a shacklike built-on atop it and took rickety steps up to the door. He tapped the pane three times—silence—got out his pocket knife and stuck it into the lock/door jamb juncture. A few seconds of prying, and snap! Danny scanned for witnesses, saw none, pushed the door open and closed it behind him.

The smell hit him first: metallic, acidic. Danny slow-motioned his evidence kit to the floor, drew his gun and fingered the wall for a light switch. His thumb flicked one on abruptly, before he'd clamped down his nerves to look. He saw a one-room dive turned slaughterhouse.

Blood on the walls. Huge, unmistakable streaks, exemplary textbook spit marks: the killer expelling big mouthfuls, spritzing the red out through his teeth, drawing little patterns on cheap floral wallpaper. Four whole walls of it—dips and curlicues and one design that looked like an elaborate letter W. Blood matting a threadbare throw rug, blood in large caked pools on the linoleum floor, blood saturating a light-colored sofa oozing stuffing, blood splashed across a stack of newspapers next to a table holding a hot plate, saucepan and single can of soup. Much too much blood to come from one ravaged human being.

Danny hyperventilated; he saw two doorless doorways off the left wall. He holstered his .45, jammed his hands in his pockets so as not to leave prints and checked the closest one out.

The bathroom.

White walls covered with vertical and horizontal blood lines, perfectly straight, intersecting at right angles, the killer getting the knack. A bathtub, the sides and bottom caked with a pinkish-brown matter that looked like blood mixed with soapsuds. A stack of men's clothing—shirts, trousers, a herringbone sports coat—folded atop the toilet seat.

Danny turned on the sink faucet with a knuckle, lowered his head, splashed and drank. Looking up, he caught his face in the mirror; for a second he didn't think it was him. He walked back to the main room, took rubber gloves from his evidence kit, slipped them on, returned to the bathroom and sifted through the clothing, dropping it on the floor.

Three pairs of pants. Three skivvy shirts. Three rolled-up pairs of socks. One sweater, one windbreaker, one sports jacket.

Three victims.

One other doorway.

Danny backed out of the bathroom and pivoted into a small kitchenette, expecting a gigantic rush of crimson. What he got was perfect tidiness: scrub brush, Ajax and a soap bar lined up on a rack above a clean sink; clean dishes in a plastic drainer; a 1949 calendar tacked to the wall, the first eleven months ripped off, no notations on the page for December. A telephone on a nightstand placed against the side wall and a battered Frigidaire next to the sink.

No blood, no horror artwork. Danny felt his stomach settle and his pulse take over, jolts like wires frazzling. Two other stiffs dumped someplace; a B&E on LAPD turf—Hollywood Division, where the Brenda Allen mess was the worst, where they hated the Sheriff's Department the most. His violation of Captain Dietrich's direct order: no strongarm, no prima donna in the City. No way to report what he found. An outside chance of the killer bringing number four here.

Danny gulped from the sink, swathed his face, let his gloved hands and jacket sleeves get sopping. He thought of tossing the pad for a bottle; his stomach heaved; he picked up the phone and dialed the station.

Karen Hiltscher answered. "West Hollywood Sheriff's. May I help you?"

Danny's voice wasn't his. "It's me, Karen."

"Danny? You sound strange."

"*Just listen.* I'm someplace where I shouldn't be and I need something, and I need you to call me back here when you've got it. And nobody can know. *Nobody.* Do you understand?"

"Yes. Danny, please don't be so rough."

"*Just listen.* I want your verbal on every dead body report filed city and countywide over the past forty-eight hours, and I want you to call me back here with it, *quick.* Ring twice, hang up and call again. Got it?"

"Yes. Sweetie, are you all—"

"Damnit, *just listen.* I'm at Hollywood-4619, it's *wrong* and I could get in big trouble for being here, so don't tell anybody. *Do you fucking understand?*"

Karen whispered, "Yes, sweetie," and let her end of the line go dead. Danny hung up, wiped sweat off his neck and thought of ice water. He saw the Frigidaire, reached over and opened the door, bolted for the sink when he caught what was inside.

Two eyeballs coated with clear jelly in an ashtray. A severed human finger on top of a package of green beans.

Danny vomited until his chest ached and his stomach retched itself empty; he turned on the faucet and doused himself until water seeped inside his rubber gloves and he snapped that a sopping wet cop couldn't forensic a crime scene that Vollmer or Maslick would have killed for. He turned the water off and shook himself half dry, hands braced against the sink ledge. The phone rang; he heard it as a gunshot, pulled his piece and aimed it at nothing.

Another ring, silence, a third ring. Danny picked up the receiver. "Yes? Karen?"

The girl had on her singsong pout. "Three DOAs. Two female Caucasians, one male Negro. The females were a pill suicide and a car wreck and the Negro was a wino who died of exposure, and you owe me the Coconut Grove for being so nasty."

Eight walls of blood spritz and a would-be lady cop who wanted to go dancing. Danny laughed and opened the icebox door for more comic relief. The finger was long, white and thin, and the eyeballs were brown and starting to shrivel. "Anywhere, sweetie, anywhere."

"Danny, are you sure you're—"

"Karen, listen real close. I'm staying here to see who shows up. Are you working a double shift tonight?"

"Until eight tomorrow."

"Then do this. I want the City and County air monitored for male Caucasian DBs. Stay at your switchboard, keep the City and County boxes on low and listen for homicide squeals with male Caucasian victims. Call me here the same way you just did if you get any. Have you got that?"

"Yes, Danny."

"And sweetie, nobody can know. Not Dietrich, not anyone on the squad, *not anyone.*"

A long sigh, Karen's version of Katharine Hepburn exhausted. "Yes, Deputy Upshaw," then a soft click.

Danny hung up and forensiced the pad.

He scraped dirt and dust samples off the floor in all three rooms, placing them in individually marked glassine envelopes; he got out his Rolleiflex evidence camera and shot wide angles and close-ups of the blood patterns. He scraped, tagged and tubed bathtub blood, couch and chair blood, wall blood, rug blood and floor blood; he took fiber samples from the three sets of clothes and wrote down the brand names on the labels.

Dusk came on. Danny kept the lights off, working with a pen flash held in his teeth. He dusted for latent prints, exhausting rolls of touch, grab and press surfaces, getting a rubber glove set—most likely the killer—and a full right- and partial left-hand unknown—which did not match the Marty Goines print abstract. Knowing Goines latents *should* appear, he kept going and was rewarded—a left spread off the kitchen sink ledge. Reconstructing the killer showering himself free of blood, he rolled every touch surface in the bathroom—bringing up one-, two-, three-finger and full hand spans, surgical rubber tips, the hands of a large man, widely spaced where he braced himself into the shower/tub wall.

Midnight.

Danny took the severed finger out of the icebox, rolled it in ink, then on paper. A matchup to the middle right digit on the unknown set. The cut point was jagged, just above the knuckle, cauterized by scorching—charred black flesh scabbing it up. Danny checked the hot plate in the living room. Paydirt: fried skin stuck to the coils; the killer wanted to preserve the finger, a shock to whoever discovered the carnage.

Or was he planning to return with another victim?

And was he keeping the pad under surveillance to know when that option was blown?

12:45.

Danny gave the place a last toss. The one closet was empty; there was nothing secreted under the rugs; a penlight wall scan gave him another notch on his reconstruction: approximately two thirds of the blood caking was texturally uniform—victims two and three were almost certainly killed at the same time. Checking out the floor on his knees got him a last piece of evidence: a glob of hardened white paste residue, neutral in smell. He tagged and bagged it, tagged and bagged Marty Goines' eyeballs, sat down on the nonblooded edge of the sofa, gun out and resting on his knee—and waited.

Exhaustion crept in. Danny closed his eyes and saw blood patterns superimposed on the lids, white on red, the colors reversed like photographic negatives. His hands were numb from hours of working in rubber gloves; he imagined the metallic smell of the room as the smell of good whiskey, started tasting it, shut down the thought and ran theories in his head so the taste would stay away.

2307 Tamarind was a thirty-minute drive to the Strip tops—the killer had his maximum time of two hours to play with Marty

Goines' corpse and decorate the pad. The killer was monstrously, *suicidally* bold to kill two other men—probably at the same time—in the same place. The killer probably had the subconscious desire to be captured that many psychopaths evinced; he was an exhibitionist and was probably distressed that the Goines snuff had received virtually no publicity. The other two bodies had probably been dumped someplace where they would be found, which meant that last night or yesterday was when murders two and three occurred. Questions: were the patterns on the wall significant in design or just blood spat in rage? What did the letter W mean? *Were the three victims randomly chosen on the basis of homosexuality or dope addiction, or were they previously known to the killer?*

More exhaustion, his brain wires frazzling from too much information, too few connecting threads. Danny took to looking at his luminous wristwatch dial to stay awake; 3:11 had just passed when he heard the outside lock being picked.

He got up and padded to the curtains beside the light switch, the door a foot away, his gun arm extended and braced with his left hand. The locking mechanism gave with a sharp ka-thack; the door opened; Danny hit the switch.

A fortyish fat man was frozen by the light. Danny took a step forward; the man pivoted into the muzzle of a .45 revolver. His hands jerked toward his pockets; Danny toed the door shut and barrel-lashed him across the face, knocking him into wallpaper zigzagged with blood. The fat man let out a yelp, saw the wall gore for real and hit his knees, hands clasped, ready to beg.

Danny squatted beside him, gun aimed at the trickle of blood on his cheek. The fat man mumbled Hail Marys; Danny fished out his cuffs, slid his .45 out of trouble, worked the ratchets and slapped them around prayer-pressed wrists. The bracelet teeth snapped; the man looked at Danny like *he* was Jesus. "Cop? You're a cop?"

Danny gave him the once-over. Convict pallor, prison shoes, secondhand clothes and grateful that a policeman caught him breaking and entering, a parole violation and a dime minimum. The man looked at the walls, brought his eyes down, saw that he was kneeling two inches from a pool of blood with a dead cockroach basted in the middle. "Goddamnit, tell me you're—"

Danny grabbed his throat and squeezed it. "Sheriff's. Keep your voice down and play straight with me and I'll let you walk out of here." With his free hand, he gave Fats a pocket and waist-band frisk, pulling out wallet, keys, a switchblade and a flat leather case, compact but heavy, with a zippered closure.

He eased off his throat hold and examined the wallet, dropping cards and papers to the floor. There was an expired California driver's license for Leo Theodore Bordoni, DOB 6/19/09; a County Parole identification card made out to the same name; a plasma bank donor slip stating that Leo Bordoni, type AB+, could sell his plasma again on January 18, 1950. The cards were racetrack stuff—voided betting stubs, receipts, matchbook covers with the names of hot horses and race numbers jotted on the back.

Danny let go of Leo Theodore Bordoni's neck, the fat man's reward for a parlay—reaction to the gore, blood type and physical description—that eliminated him as a killing suspect. Bordoni gurgled and wiped blood off his face; Danny unzipped the leather case and saw a set of bonaroos: pick gouger, baby glass cutter, chisel pry and window snap, all laid out on green velvet. He said, "B&E, possession of burglar's tools, parole violation. How many falls have you taken, Leo?"

Bordoni massaged his neck. "Three. Where's Marty?"

Danny pointed to the walls. "Where do you think?"

"Oh fucking God."

"That's right. Old Marty that nobody knows much about, except maybe you. You know about Governor Warren's habitual offender law?"

"Uh ... no."

Danny picked up his .45 and holstered it, helped Bordoni to his feet and shoved him into the one chair not soaked red/brown. "The law says any fourth fall costs you twenty to life. No plea bargains, no appeals, nada. You boost a fucking pack of cigarettes, it's a double dime. So you tell me everything there is to know about you and Marty Goines, or you hang twenty up at Quentin."

Bordoni flicked his eyes around the room. Danny walked to the curtains, looked out at dark yards and houses and thought of his killer leaving him, clued to a trap by the light burning. He flipped the wall switch; Bordoni let out a long breath. "Really bad for Marty? That the truth?"

Danny could see neon signs on Hollywood Boulevard, miles away. "The worst, so tell me."

Bordoni talked while Danny looked out at neon and dwindling headlights. "I came out of Quentin two weeks ago, seven out of seven for heists. I knew Marty when he did his turn for reef, and we were buddies. Marty knew I had a parole date, and he knew my sister's number in Frisco. He'd send me these letters every once in a while after he got out, phony name, no return address, 'cause he was an absconder and he didn't want the censors to get a handle on him.

"So Marty calls me at my sister's five days or so ago, maybe the thirtieth, maybe the thirty-first. He says he's playing horn for peanuts and hates it, he took the cure, he's gonna stay off horseback and pull jobs—burglaries. He says he just got together with an old partner and they needed a third man for a house-break gang. I told him I'd be down in a week or so, and he gave me this address and told me to let myself in. That's me and Marty."

Darkness made the room pulsate. Danny said, "What was the partner's name? Where did Goines know him from?"

"Marty didn't say."

"Did he describe him? Was he a partner of Marty's when he was pulling jobs back in '43 and '44?"

Bordoni said, "Mister, it was a two-minute conversation, and I didn't even know Marty pulled jobs back then."

"Did he mention an old running partner with a burned or scarred face? He'd be mid to late twenties by now."

"No. Marty was always close-mouthed. I was his only pal at Q, and I was surprised when he said he had an old partner. Marty wasn't really the partner type."

Danny shifted gears. "When Goines sent you letters, where were they postmarked and what did they say?"

Bordoni sighed like he was bored; Danny thought of giving him a peek at his old pal's eyeballs. "Spill, Leo."

"They were from all over the country, and they were just jive—jazz stuff, wish you were here, the horses, baseball."

"Did Marty mention other musicians he was playing with?"

Bordoni laughed. "No, and I think he was ashamed to. He was gigging all these Podunk clubs, and all he said was 'I'm the best trombone they've ever seen,' meaning Marty knew he wasn't much but these cats he was gigging with were really from hunger."

"Did he mention anybody at all, other than this old partner you were going to team up with?"

"Nix. Like I told you, it was a two-minute conversation."

The Miller High Life sign atop the Taft Building blipped off, jarring Danny. "Leo, was Marty Goines a homosexual?"

"Marty! Are you crazy! He wouldn't even pork nancy boys up at Q!"

"Anybody up there ever make advances to him?"

"Marty would have died before he let some brunser bust his cherry!"

Danny hit the light switch, hauled Bordoni up by his cuff chain and twisted his head so that it was level with a long slash of wall blood. "That's your friend. That's why you were never here and you never met me. That's heat you don't want, so you just stay frosty and think of this thing as a nightmare."

Bordoni bobbed his head; Danny let him go and unlocked the cuffs. Bordoni gathered his stuff up off the floor, taking extra care with his tool case. At the door, he said, "This is personal with you, right?"

Buddy Jastrow long gone, four shots a night not enough, his textbooks and classes not real. Danny said, "It's all I've got."

*   *   *

Alone again, Danny stared out the window, watching movie marquees blink off, turning the Boulevard into just another long, dark street. He added "possible burglary partner" to "tall, gray-haired," "middle-aged," "homosexual," and "heroin-wise"; he put off Bordoni's protestations that Marty wasn't fruit as sincere but wrong—and wondered how long he could stick inside the room without going crazy, without risking the landlord or some-one from the front house dropping by.

Looking for house lights that might be *Him* looking back was childish; eye prowling for sinister shapes was a kid's game—the kind of game he played by himself as a schoolboy. Danny yawned, sat down in the chair and tried to sleep.

He got something near sleep, an exhaustion shortcut where he wasn't quite out, couldn't quite form thoughts and saw pictures that he wasn't making himself. Street signs, trucks, a saxophone man running scales on his instrument, flower patterns, a dog at the end of a stick. The dog made him twitch; he tried to open his eyes, felt them gummed and eased back to wherever he was going. Autopsy instruments hot from an autoclave, Janice Modine, a '39 Olds rocking on its suspension, a look inside, Tim pumping Roxy Beausoleil, an ether-soaked rag up to her nose so she'd giggle and pretend it was nice.

Danny jerked out of it, eyes opening to light through a part in the curtains. He swallowed dry phlegm, caught a reprise of his last image, got up and went to the kitchen for a drink of sink water. He was on a big gulping handful when the phone rang.

A second ring, stop, a third ring. Danny picked it up. "Karen?"

The girl was almost breathless. "City radio. See the maintenance man, Griffith Park, the hiking trail up from the observatory parking lot. Two dead men, LAPD rolling. Sweetie, did you *know* this was going to happen?"

Danny said, "Just pretend it didn't happen," slammed the phone down, grabbed his evidence kit and walked out of the upholstered slaughterhouse. He forced himself not to run to his car, eyes circuiting for onlookers, seeing none. Griffith Park was a mile away. He stripped off his rubber gloves, felt his hand tingle and gunned it there.

*   *   *

Two LAPD black-and-whites beat him.

Danny parked beside them at the foot of the hiking trail, the last stretch of asphalt before the stretch of mountain that formed the park's northern perimeter. No other cars were in the lot; he could see four bluesuits up ahead where the trail cut into woods, a long-time haven for winos and lovebirds without the price of a room.

Danny marked the time—6:14 A.M.—got his badge out and walked up. The cops wheeled around, hands to holsters, shakes and queasy looks. Danny pointed to his tin. "West Hollywood Sheriff's. I'm working a dumped body case, and I heard what you got over the air at the station."

Two cops nodded; two turned away, like a County detective was lower than dirt. Danny swallowed dry; West Hollywood Substation was a half hour away, but the dummies didn't blink at the time glitch. They separated to give him a view; Danny got a mid-shot of hell.

Two dead men, nude, lying sideways on a little bed of dirt surrounded by low thornbushes. Rigor lock, coats of dust and leaf debris said they had been there at least twenty-four hours; the condition of the bodies said that they died at 2307 North Tamarind. Danny pulled a bush section back, knelt and zoomed his Man Camera in nightmare-close.

The men had been placed in a 69 position—head to groin, head to groin, genitals flopped toward each other's mouths. Their hands had been placed on each other's knees; the larger man was missing a right index finger. All four eyes were intact and wide open; the victims had been slashed like Marty Goines all over their backs—and their faces. Danny examined the pressed-together front sides; he could see blood and entrail residue.

He stood up. The patrolmen were smoking cigarettes, shuffling their feet, destroying the chance for a successful grid search. One by one they looked at him; the oldest of the four said, "Those guys like yours?"

Danny said, "Almost exactly," thinking of the real camera in his evidence kit, snapshots for his file before the City bulls closed off *their* end of *his* case. "Who found them?"

The old-timer cop answered him. "Maintenance man saw a wino running down the hill screaming, so he went up and looked. He called us, came back up and got sick. We sent him home, and when the squad gets here they'll send you home, too."

The other cops laughed. Danny let it pass and jogged down the trail to get the camera. He was almost to his Chevy when a plainclothes car and Coroner's wagon pulled into the lot and jammed up next to the black-and-whites.

A big, beef-faced man got out of the unmarked and looked right at him. Danny recognized him from newspaper pics: Detective Sergeant Gene Niles, squad whip at Hollywood Division, in up to his ears over Brenda Allen, no indictment, but a quashed lieutenancy and stalemated career—rumor having it that he took no cash, just trade goodies from Brenda's girls. The man's clothes said otherwise: smart navy blazer and razor-creased gray flannels, custom stuff no honest cop could afford.

Two Coroner's men hauled out collapsible gurneys; Danny saw Niles smell cop on him and head over, looking more and more curious and pissed: strange meat on his turf, too young to be working the Homicide Bureau downtown.

He met him halfway, a new story brewing, plausible stuff to satisfy a savvy cop. Face to face, he said, "I'm with the Sheriff's."

Niles laughed. "You a little bit confused about your jurisdiction, Deputy?"

The "Deputy" was all scorn, like a synonym for "cancer." Danny said, "I'm working a homicide just like the two you've got up the hill."

Niles bored in with his eyes. "You sleep in those clothes, Deputy?"

Danny squeezed his hands into fists. "I was on a stakeout."

"You ever hear of carrying a razor on all-nighters, *Deputy*?"

"You ever hear of professional courtesy, *Niles*?"

Sergeant Gene Niles looked at his watch. "A man who reads the papers. Let's try this. How'd you get up here twenty-two minutes after we logged the squeal at the station?"

Danny knew brass balls was the only way to cover his lie. "I was down at the doughnut joint on Western, and there was a black-and-white with the radio on. How come it took *you* so long? You stop for a manicure?"

"A year ago I'd have reamed you for that."

"A year ago you were going places. Do you want to hear about my homicide or do you want to sulk?"

Niles picked a piece of lint off his blazer. "The dispatcher said it looks like a queer job. I hate queer jobs, so if you've got another queer job, I don't want to hear about it. Roll, *Deputy*. And get yourself some decent threads. Mickey Kike's got a haberdashery, and I know he gives all his prat boys a discount."

Danny headed back to his Chevy seeing red. He drove down the park road to Los Feliz and Vermont and a pay phone, called Doc Layman and told him two Marty Goines companion stiffs were en route, grab them for autopsy no matter what. A minute later Niles' car and the Coroner's wagon went by southbound, no lights or sirens, flunkies killing a fine winter morning. Danny gave them a five-minute lead, took shortcuts downtown and parked in the shade of a warehouse across the street from the City Morgue loading dock. Fourteen minutes passed before the caravan appeared; Niles made a big show of shepherding the sheet-covered gurneys to the ramp; Norton Layman came out to help. Danny heard him berating Niles for separating the bodies.

He settled into his car to wait for Layman's findings; stretching out on the front seat, he closed his eyes and tried to sleep, knowing Doc would be four hours or more on the examinations. Sleep wouldn't come; a hot day started sizzling, warming up the car, making the upholstery sticky. Danny would begin to drop off, then start remembering his lies, what he could or couldn't tell whom. He could brazen his lie to the patrolmen, acting sheepish over being at the doughnut stand at 6:00 A.M., implying he'd been with a woman; he had to coddle Karen Hiltscher into keeping his stint at 2307 Tamarind under wraps. He couldn't let anyone see the contents of his evidence kit; he had to clue in LAPD to the letter that hipped him to Marty Goines' pad, post-dating the occurrence, making it seem like nothing big, letting them discover the gore for themselves. Leo Bordoni was a wild card, but he was probably con-wise enough to stay quiet; he had to fabricate a story to account for his whereabouts yesterday—a phony summary report to Dietrich was his best bet. And the big fear and big questions: if LAPD canvassed Tamarind, would a local report the tan 1947 Chevrolet parked outside 2307 overnight? Should he take advantage of his private lead, rape the neighborhood for witnesses himself, then report the letter, hoping that the worst they could get him for was *not* calling the dope in? If LAPD decided to ease off on their two homicides—Niles as catching officer hating "queer jobs"—would they canvass at *all*? *He* had taken the call from Lexington State Hospital himself, via Karen Hiltscher's switchboard. If it all got tricky, would she blab fast to save herself? Would LASD/LAPD rivalry reduce the mess to something that only he cared about?

Heat reflecting off the windshield and too many brain wires short-circuiting on angles lulled Danny to sleep. Cramps and glare woke him up sweaty and itchy; his foot hit the horn and black dreamlessness became sound waves bouncing off four bloody walls. He looked at his watch, saw 12:10 and at least four hours unconscious; the Doc might be done with his dead men. Danny got out of the car, stretched his cramps and walked across the street to the morgue.

Layman was standing near the ramp, eating lunch off an examination slab, a body sheet for a tablecloth. He saw Danny, swallowed a bite of sandwich and said, "You look bad."

"That bad?"

"You look scared, too."

Danny yawned; it made his gums ache. "I've seen the bodies, and I don't think LAPD cares. That's scary."

Layman wiped his mouth with a sheet corner. "Here's a few more scares for you, then. Times of death—twenty-six to thirty hours ago. Both men were anally raped—O+ secretor semen. The wounds on their backs were pure zoot stick, identical in size and fiber content to Martin Mitchell Goines. The missing-finger man died from a throat gash made by a sharp, serrated knife. No cause of death on the other man, but I'd be willing to bet barbiturate OD. On our missing-finger friend I found a vom-it-coated, punctured capsule, right up under the tongue. I tested some powder in it and got a home compound—sodium secobar-bital, one part, one part strychnine. The secobarbital would hit first, inducing unconsciousness, the strychnine would kill. I think missing finger got indigestion, puked up part of his Mickey Finn and fought to live—that that was when he lost his digit—fighting with the knife man. Once I test the blood on both men and pump their stomachs, I'll know for sure. The missing-finger man was bigger—a larger bloodstream, so the compound didn't kill him like it did our other friend."

Danny thought of 2307, vomit traces lost in the blood. "What about the stomach bites?"

Layman said, "Not human, but human. I found O+ saliva and human gastric juices on the wounds, and the bites were too fren-zied and overlapping to make casts from. But—I got three indi-vidual tooth cuts—too large to ascribe to any known human dental abstract and too shredded at the bottom to identify on any single-tooth forensic index. I also took a glob of dental mortar paste out of one of the wounds. He wears dentures, Danny. Most likely on top of his own teeth. They might be steel, they might be some other synthetic material, they might be teeth fashioned from animal carcasses. And he's rigged up a way to mutilate with them *and* swallow. They're not human, and I know this doesn't sound professional, but I don't think this son of a bitch is either."

14

ELLIS LOEW performed the ceremony in his office, Mal and Dudley Smith official witnesses. Buzz Meeks stood by the con-ference table, right hand raised; Loew recited the oath: "Do you, Turner Meeks, hereby swear to loyally and conscientiously per-form the duties of Special Investigator, Grand Jury Division of the District Attorney's Office for the City of Los Angeles, up-holding the laws of this municipality, protecting the rights and property of its citizens, so help you God?"

Buzz Meeks said, "Sure." Loew handed him an ID holder replete with license photostat and DA's Bureau shield. Mal wondered how much Howard Hughes was paying the bastard, guessing at least three grand.

Dudley joined Meeks and Loew in a back-slapping circle; Mal credited an old rumor still holding: Meeks thought he was behind the shooting that got him his pension, Jack D. blowing it, then forgetting his grudge when the okie was no longer LAPD. Let him think it—anything to keep his new colleague as far away as two cops working the same job could be.

And Dudley. And maybe Loew now, too.

Mal watched the three share a toast, Glenlivet in crystal glasses. He took his notepad down to the far end of the table, Meeks and Dudley trading one-liners, Ellis shooting him a scowl that said, "Let's work." Loew's half nod acknowledged that their bad blood was just temporary. Mal thought: he should owe me, now I owe him. He picked up his pen to doodle, his knuckles throbbed, he knew Loew was right.

* * *

After the thing with Celeste, he'd driven around directionless until his hand started swelling, the pain brutal, blunting all his frantic plans to make it up to his son. He hauled to Central Receiving, flashed his badge and got special treatment: an injection of something that sent him higher than ten kites, teeth fragments pulled out of his fingers, cleansing and suturing and bandaging. He called the house and talked to Stefan, rambling about why he did it, how Celeste had hurt him worse, how she wanted to separate the two of them forever. The boy had seemed shocked, dumbfounded, stuttering details about Celeste's bloodied face—but he'd ended the conversation calling him "Dad" and saying, "I love you."

And that little injection of hope made him think like a policeman. He called Ellis Loew, told him what happened, that lawyers and a custody battle were coming, don't let Celeste file charges and gain an advantage. Loew took the reins, driving to the house and shepherding Celeste to Hollywood Presbyterian, where her lawyer was waiting. The man took photographs of her bruised and bloody face; Loew convinced him not to let Celeste file criminal charges on a ranking DA's Bureau investigator, threatening reprisals if he did, promising not to intercede in the custody case if he agreed. The attorney did agree; Celeste's broken nose was set and two dental surgeons worked on her nearly destroyed gums and bridgework. Loew, enraged, called the pay phone where he was waiting and said, "You're on your own with the kid. Never ask me for another favor."

He drove back to the house then, finding Stefan asleep, breathing Celeste's old country sedative—schnapps and hot milk. He kissed the boy's cheek, moved a suitcase full of clothes and Lesnick's files to a motel on Olympic and Normandie, made arrangements for a woman cop he knew to check on Stefan once a day, slept off the painkiller on a strange bed and woke up thinking of Franz Kempflerr.

He couldn't stop thinking about him, and he couldn't put together any rationalizations that said Celeste was a liar. He did put together a series of phone calls that got him a lawyer: Jake Kellerman, a pragmatist who said continuances were the smart money, postpone the custody trial until Captain Considine was a grand jury hero. Kellerman advised him to stay away from Celeste and Stefan, said he'd call him for a strategy meeting soon—and left him with a Demerol hangover, aching knuckles and the certainty he should take the day off and stay away from his boss.

He still couldn't shake Kempflerr.

Going over Lesnick's files was just a distraction. He was getting a case on Claire De Haven, every notation on her tweaked him; he knew direct questioning was out for now, that finding an operative should be his main priority. Still, putting together the woman's past was enticing, and when he hit a piece of information he'd overlooked—Mondo Lopez bragging to the shrink about a dress he'd shoplifted for Claire's thirty-third birthday in May of '43, making her exactly *his* age—he took the woman and the Nazi down to the main public library for research.

He scanned microfilm for hours, banishing the German, bringing the woman into focus.

Buchenwald liberated, the Nuremberg trials, the biggest Nazis stating they just followed orders. The incredible mechanized brutality. Sleepy Lagoon a just cause championed by bad people. A hunch that Claire De Haven made the society pages as a debutante; confirmation in summer 1929: nineteen-year-old Claire at the Las Madrinas Ball—blurred black and white that only hinted at who she was.

With Kempflerr eclipsed by Göring, Ribbentrop, Dönitz and Keitel, the woman came on that much stronger. He called the DMV and got her driver's license stats, drove to Beverly Hills and kept her Spanish manse under surveillance. Two hours in, Claire left the house—her picture a prophecy of beauty fulfilled. She was trim, auburn-haired with just a few streaks of gray, and wore a face that was natural beauty and the best that money could buy—but *strong*. He followed her Cadillac down to the Villa Frascati; she met Reynolds Loftis there for lunch—the Mr. Dignity type he'd seen in a dozen movies. He had a drink at the bar and watched the two: the switch-hitter actor and the Red Queen held hands and kissed across the table every few minutes; they were undoubtedly lovers. He remembered Loftis to Lesnick: "Claire is the only woman I've ever loved"—and felt jealous.

* * *

Glasses and ashtrays hit the table; Mal glanced up from his doodling—swastikas and hangman's nooses—and saw his fellow Red chasers looking at him. Dudley slid a clean glass and the bottle down. Mal slid it back and said, "Lieutenant, you blew it for us with the Mexicans. This is for the record. I say no direct interrogations until Meeks gets us some hard criminal stuff that we can use, like indictment threats. I say we hit lefties outside UAES exclusively, turn them as friendly witnesses, get them to inform and plant a decoy as soon as we find one. I say we cover ourselves on the Mexicans by planting some lines in the political columns. Ed Satterlee's pals with Victor Reisel and Walter Winchell, they hate Commies, the UAES probably reads them. Something like this: 'L.A. City grand jury team slated to investigate Red influence in Hollywood scotched due to lack of funds and political infighting.' Every Pinko in the UAES knows what happened at Variety International the other day, and I say we put a lid on it and lull them to sleep."

All eyes were on the Irishman; Mal wondered how he'd field the gauntlet—two witnesses to irrefutable logic. Dudley said, "I can only apologize for my actions, Malcolm. You were circumspect, I was bull-headed, and I was wrong. But I think we should squeeze Claire De Haven before we pull back and go sub rosa. She's the fulcrum to snitch the whole brain trust, she's a virgin as far as grand juries go, breaking her would demoralize all those sad excuses for men in love with her. She's never been braced by the police, and I think she damn well might fold."

Mal laughed. "You're underestimating her. And I suppose you want to be the one to do the bracing?"

"No, lad, I think you should be the one. Of all of us here, you're the only one who comes off as even remotely idealistic. A kid gloves cop you are, kid gloves with a cruel streak. You'll nail her with that great right hook I've heard you've got."

Ellis Loew mouthed the words, "Not me," hard eyes on Mal's end of the table. Buzz Meeks sipped Scotch. Mal winced, wondering exactly how much Dudley knew. "It's a sucker play, Lieutenant. You screwed up once, now you're asking me to compound it. Ellis, a direct approach is bullshit. Tell him that."

Loew said, "Mal, control your language, because I agree with Dudley. Claire De Haven is a promiscuous woman, women like that are unbalanced, and I think we should risk the approach. In the meantime, Ed Satterlee is trying to co-opt a man for us, a man he knew in the seminary who's infiltrated Communist cells in Cleveland. He's a pro, but he doesn't work cheap. Even if the approach with De Haven fails and the UAES is alerted to us, he'll be able to get next to them so subtly that they'll never know it in a million years. And I'm sure we can get the money for our decoy from Mr. Hughes. Right, Buzz?"

Buzz Meeks winked at Mal. "Ellis, if this babe is a roundheels, I wouldn't be sendin' in a seminary boy to work her. Howard himself might do the trick. He likes poon, so maybe you could send him in in disguise."

Loew rolled his eyes; Dudley Smith laughed, like he'd heard a real knee-slapper at the Elks Club smoker. Meeks winked again, testing the water—were you the one who got me shot to shit back in '46? Mal thought of his custody juice riding with a cracker buffoon, hatchet cop and hard-on lawyer. It wasn't until Loew banged the table to dismiss them that he realized he would be meeting the Red Queen face to face, his own pawn to operate.

15

DANNY SPENT the next morning at his apartment, updating *his* file, all new stuff on the two new victims tied in to *his* case.

Twenty-four hours in, he had this:

No ID on victims two and three; Doc Layman, as a City pathologist, was privy to Hollywood Squad summary reports and would be calling when and if the bodies got names. He had already called to say that Sergeant Gene Niles was heading the LAPD investigation, deemed it lowball and was short-shrifting it so that he could return to a fur warehouse robbery that promised some newspaper ink to make up for the Brenda Allen smear that cost him his wife and kids. Uniformed cops were rousting winos

in Griffith Park and getting nowhere; Niles himself had rub-
ber-hosed two Sterno jockeys with child molester jackets. Layman's seventeen-page autopsy report—which *did* tag the smaller
of the two men as dying of a barbiturate OD—was ignored by
Niles and the handful of uniformed flunkies detached to work
under him. The Doc was convinced that a "Reverse Black Dahlia
Syndrome" was in effect—the three stiffs found so far had received a total of four inner section newspaper columns, city editors shying away because Marty Goines was trash and the whole
thing was queer shit that you couldn't print without the Legion
for Decency and Concerned Catholic Mothers on your ass.

Captain Dietrich had heard him out yesterday, facts, theories,
omissions, lies and his giant lie—the doughnut stand whopper to
cover him on 2307 Tamarind, still unreported. He'd nodded
along, then said he'd *try* to get the interagency ball rolling with
LAPD. Sheriff's dicks were out of the question—the three other
men on the station squad were deluged and the County Detective Bureau would deem the Goines job too Mickey Mouse and
messy now that City cops were involved. He had a pal working
Hollywood daywatch—a lieutenant named Poulson who'd
stayed tight with Mickey C. despite Brenda A. He'd talk to the
man about the two departments putting a Homicide team together, and again stated that he thought it would come down to
the quality of the victims. If two and three were hopheads,
ex-cons or queers—forget it. If they were squarejohns—maybe.
And unless the case got some juice, with an LAPD/LASD team
formed, he was off it in ten days, Martin Mitchell Goines, DOD
1/1/50 tossed into the open file.

On his evidence gathered at 2307 Tamarind:

With two exceptions, just repeat stuff, what Hans Maslick
called "double negatives to prove positives." He had gotten an
unknown set of prints that matched with the taller dead man's
missing finger; Layman had also rolled both stiffs. The white paste
residue he bagged was obviously the denture adhesive that led
Doc to his 99 percent sure denture theory. Leo Bordoni did not
touch print-sustaining surfaces while he was in the room; the
three sets of clothes had to be left behind in case the killer was
captured and specifically confessed to leaving them folded atop
the toilet. The dust and dirt trace elements were useless until he
got a suspect to run comparisons on—leaving him only two
jumps on LAPD and the killer: his photos of the blood streaks

and his chance to canvass Tamarind Street solo if the City bulls soft-pedaled their investigation. Nightmares and big jeopardy.

After leaving the morgue yesterday, he drove to a camera shop and paid quadruple the normal fee to have his rolls of film developed immediately. The man at the counter looked askance at his raggedy state but took his money; he waited while the job was done. The camera man handed the prints and negatives over an hour later, commenting, "Them walls what you call modern art?" He'd laughed and laughed and laughed himself home—his chuckles dying out when he tacked the photos to a corkboard evidence display he'd erected beside his file boxes.

Blood in glossy black and white was jarring, unnatural, the pictures things he could never let anyone see, even if he busted the combined homicides wide open. Thinking of them as his alone was comforting; he spent hours just staring, seeing designs within designs. Drip marks became strange body appendages; spray streaks were knives cutting at them. The eye circuits got so illogical that he turned to his case history text: blood spray marks exemplified. The cases elaborated were all German and Eastern European, psychopaths enacting vampire fantasies, spraying their victim's blood on convenient objects, asserting their lunacy by creating pictures of little or no significance. Nothing resembling the formation of the letter W; nothing pertaining to dentures.

Dentures.

His one hard lead to come out of victims two and three.

Not human.

They could be steel teeth, they could be plastic teeth, they could be teeth ripped out of animal carcasses. The next investigatory step was a complete paper chase: men capable of making dentures cross-probed against "tall, middle-aged," "gray-haired," "O+ blood" and time frame opportunity.

Needles in a haystack.

Yesterday, he had taken his first step, checking dental lab listings in the seventeen separate L.A. City/County Yellow Pages. There were a total of 349, plus, in consideration of a possible animal carcass angle, 93 taxidermists' shops. A phone call to a lab picked at random and a long talk with a cooperative foreman got him this information: the 349 number was low; L.A. was the big league for the denture industry. Some labs didn't advertise in the Yellow Pages; some dentists had denture makers working in their offices. If a man worked on human dentures he could apply the same skills to animal or plastic teeth. *He* didn't know of any labs that specialized in animal choppers, good luck Deputy Upshaw, you've got your work cut out for you.

It was a ride to the Station then. Karen Hiltscher was just swinging back on duty; he brought candy and flowers to chill down her curiosity over Tamarind and any poutiness for the largest deluge of shitwork he'd ever tossed her way: *all* individual station and Sheriff's Bureau files checked for men with dental lab work histories, plus eliminations against blood type and physical description; calls started to his list of dental labs for breakdowns of male workers with the same physical stats. The girl took the goodies while a group of muster room loungers guffawed; she seemed hurt and miffed, didn't mention 2307 and agreed in a Bette Davis bitch pout to make the queries in her "spare time." He didn't press; she knew she had gained the upper hand on him.

Danny finished up his file work, thinking of Tamarind Street as virgin canvassing territory, wondering if the burglary partner Leo Bordoni mentioned applied to the case, if he was or wasn't connected to the burn-faced boy from Marty Goines' past. His paperwork now totaled fifty-odd pages; he'd spent fifteen of the past twenty-four hours writing. He'd resisted the impulse to scour around Tamarind, wait, look, talk up the locals, jump the gun on LAPD. If Niles had gotten a lead on the place, Doc Layman would have called him; most likely the street was just existing, business as usual, while its residents forgot minor occurrences that might crack his case. Phone the Lexington Hospital lead to Dietrich, making like he just got the call at home, then brief Karen on the lie? Or do it after, no risk on the skipper handing the job to his LAPD pal, the interagency gig *he* asked for?

No contest. Danny drove to Hollywood, to Tamarind Street.

The block *was* business as usual, warmer than two days ago, foot traffic on the sidewalk, people sitting on front porches, mowing lawns and trimming shrubs. Danny parked and canvassed, straight zero into mid-afternoon: no strange occurrences in the neighborhood, no strange vehicles, no info on Marty Goines, nothing unusual going on at 2307 Tamarind, garage apartment rear. No loiterers, no strange noises, zero—and nobody mentioned his tan Chevy parked streetside. He was starting to feel cocky about his maneuvering when an old lady walking a miniature schnauzer responded to his lead question with a yes.

Three nights ago, around 10:00, she'd been strolling Wursti and saw a tall man with beautiful silver hair walking back toward the garage at 2307, a "weaving drunk" on either side of him. No, she had not seen any of the three men before; no, no strange noises from the garage apartment followed; no, she didn't know the woman who owned the front house; no, the men did not talk to each other, and she doubted she would be able to ID the silver-haired man if she saw him again.

Danny let the woman go, went back to his car, hunkered down to keep a fix on 2307. Instincts hit him hard:

Yes, the killer staked out the pad to see if cops showed up. Yes, he had the Griffith Park dump site already planned. Goines' name never made the papers, he was simply a vagrant, the killer knew his murder spot wasn't compromised by Goines' publicity. The only known Goines associates who knew of Mad Marty's demise were the jazzmen he had questioned, which eliminated jazzbos as suspects—with Goines ID'd by the law, no smart killer would bring future victims to the man's apartment. *Which meant that if no heat appeared in force on Tamarind Street, the killer might bring other victims here. Hold the lead safe from LAPD, stay staked out, pray the killer didn't witness his or Bordoni's break-in and today's canvassing, sit tight and he just might waltz right into your life with number four on his arm.*

Danny held, eyes on the house, rear-view adjusted to frame the driveway. Time stretched; a wrong-looking man strolled by, then two old ladies pushing shopping carts and a gaggle of boys wearing Hollywood High letter jackets. A siren whirred, getting closer; Danny thought of code three trouble down on the Boulevard.

Then everything went very fast.

An old lady opened the 2307 front house door; an unmarked prowler jammed into the driveway. Sergeant Gene Niles got out, looked across the street and saw him—a sitting duck in the car he'd had at Griffith Park yesterday morning. Niles started to head over; the old woman intercepted him, pointing toward the garage apartment. Niles stopped; the woman grabbed at his coat sleeves; Danny flailed for lies. Niles let himself be led down the driveway. Danny got bad heebie-jeebies—and drove to the Station to lay some cover.

*   *   *

Dietrich was standing by the squadroom entrance, wolfing a cigarette; Danny took his arm and steered him to the privacy of his own office. Dietrich went with it, swinging around as Danny shut the door. "Lieutenant Poulson just called me. Gene Niles just called him, because he caught a call from Martin Goines' landlady. Blood and bloody clothes all over Goines' apartment, a mile from Griffith Park. Our one and LAPD's two were obviously snuffed there, you were seen staking the place out and rabbited. Why? Make it good so I don't have to suspend you."

Danny had his answer down pat. "A man from Lexington State called me at home this morning and told me he'd gotten a letter from Marty Goines, addressed to another patient. The return address was 2307 North Tamarind. I thought about that talk we had, greasing things with Poulson, us being cooperative even though Niles was pulling a snit. But I didn't trust LAPD to canvass properly, so I did it myself. I was taking a breather in my car when Niles saw me."

Dietrich picked up an ashtray and stubbed out his smoke. "And you didn't call me? On a lead that hot?"

"I jumped the gun, sir. I'm sorry."

Dietrich said, "I'm not sure I buy your story. Why didn't you talk to the landlady before you canvassed? Poulson said Niles told him the woman was cherry—she was the one who discovered the mess."

Danny shrugged, trying to belittle the question. "I knocked early on, but the old girl probably didn't hear it."

"Poulson said she sounded like an alert old dame. Danny, were you in the neighborhood knocking off a matinee?"

The question didn't register. "What do you mean, a movie?"

"No, pussy. Your bimbo's got a place near that doughnut stand where you heard the squeal yesterday, and Tamarind is near there. Were you shacking on County time?"

Dietrich's tone had softened; Danny got his lies straight. "I canvassed, then I shacked. I was resting in my car when Niles showed up."

Dietrich smiled/grimaced; the phone on his desk rang. He picked it up, said, "Yes, Norton, he's here," listened and added, "One question. Have you got jackets on the two men?"

A long stretch of silence. Danny fidgeted by the door; Karen Hiltscher nudged it open, dropped a sheaf of papers on the Captain's desk and walked out, eyes lowered. Danny thought: don't let the skipper tell her I've got a woman; don't let her tell him she fielded the call from Lex. Dietrich said, "Hold on, Norton. I want to talk to him first," placed a hand over the receiver and spoke to Danny. "There's an ID on LAPD's two bodies. They're trash, so I'm telling you now: no interagency investigation, and you've got five more days on Goines before I yank you off. The Sun-Fax Market was held up this morning and if we don't clear it by then, I want you on that. I'm letting you slide for not reporting Goines' address, but I'm warning you: stay out of LAPD's way. Tom Poulson is a close friend, we've stayed friends despite Mickey and Brenda, and I don't want you fucking it up. Now here, Norton Layman wants to talk to you."

Danny grabbed the phone. "Yeah, Doc."

"It's your friendly City pipeline. Got a pencil?"

Danny fished pad and pen from his pockets. "Shoot."

"The taller man is George William Wiltsie, DOB 9/14/13. Two male prostitution arrests, booted out of the Navy in '43 for moral turpitude. The other man is address-verified as Wiltsie's known associate, maybe his brunser. Duane no middle name Lindenaur, DOB 12/5/16. One arrest for extortion—June, 1941. The beef did not go to court—the complainant dropped charges. There's no employment listed for Wiltsie; Lindenaur worked as a dialogue rewrite man at Variety International Pictures. Both men lived at 11768 Ventura Boulevard, the Leafy Glade Motel. LAPD is rolling there now, so stay clear. Does this make you happy?"

Danny counted lies. "I don't know, Doc."

* * *

From his cubicle, Danny called R&I and the DMV and got complete records readouts on victims two and three. George Wiltsie was arrested for soliciting indecent acts at cocktail lounges in '40 and '41; the DA dropped charges both times for lack of evidence, and the man possessed a lengthy list of traffic violations. Duane Lindenaur was DMV-clean, and had only the one dropped extortion beef Doc Layman mentioned. Danny had the R&I clerk break down the victims' arrests by location; Wiltsie's rousts were in City jurisdiction, Lindenaur's was in the southeastern part of the County patrolled by Firestone Division. A request for a check of Lindenaur's package got him the arresting officer's name—Sergeant Frank Skakel.

Danny called Sheriff's Personnel and learned that Skakel was still working Firestone swingwatch. He buzzed him there, got the switchboard and was put through to the squadroom.

"Skakel. Speak."

"Sergeant, this is Deputy Upshaw, West Hollywood."

"Yeah, Deputy."

"I'm working a homicide tied in to two City 187's, and you arrested one of the victims back in '41. Duane Lindenaur. Do you remember him?"

Skakel said, "Yeah. He was working a queer squeeze on a rich lawyer named Hartshorn. I always remember the money jobs. Lindenaur got bumped, huh?"

"Yes. Do you remember the case?"

"Pretty well. The complainant's name was Charles Hartshorn. He liked boys, but he was married and he had a daughter he doted on. Lindenaur met Hartshorn through some fruit introduction service, perved with him and threatened to snitch Hartshorn's queerness to the daughter. Hartshorn called us in, we rousted Lindenaur, then Hartshorn got cold feet about testifying in court and dropped the charges."

"Sergeant, was Hartshorn tall and gray-haired?"

Skakel laughed. "No. Short and bald as a beagle. What's with the job? You got leads?"

"Lindenaur's on the City end, and there's no real leads yet. What was your take on Hartshorn?"

"He's no killer, Upshaw. He's rich, he's got influence and he won't give you the time of day. Besides, pansy jobs ain't worth it, and Lindenaur was a punk. I say c'est la vie, let sleeping queers lie."

* * *

Back to the City, kid gloves this time, nothing to spawn more lies and trouble. Danny drove to Variety International Pictures, hoping Gene Niles would spend a decent amount of time at the Leafy Glade Motel. With the Goines end stalemated, victims two and three were the hot stuff, and Lindenaur as a studio scribe/extortionist felt hotter than Wiltsie as a male whore.

Rival union factions were picketing by the front gate; Danny parked across the street, put an "Official Police Vehicle" board on the windshield, ducked his head and weaved through a maze of bodies waving banners. The gate guard was reading a scandal

tabloid featuring a lurid column on *his* three killings—gory
details leaked by a "reliable source" at the L.A. morgue. Danny
scanned half a page while he got out his badge, the guard en-
grossed, chewing a cigar. The two cases were now connected in
print—if only by the L.A. *Tattler*—and that meant the possibility
of more ink, radio and television news, phony confessions, phony
leads and scads of bullshit.

Danny rapped on the wall; the cigar chewer put down his
paper and looked at the badge held up. "Yeah? Who you
here for?"

"I want to talk to the people who worked with Duane
Lindenaur."

The guard didn't flinch at the name; Lindenaur's monicker
hadn't yet made the tabloid. He checked a sheet on a clipboard,
said, "Set 23, the office next to the *Tomahawk Massacre* interior,"
hit a button and pointed. The gate opened; Danny threaded his
way down a long stretch of blacktop filled with costumed players.
The door to Set 23 was wide open; just inside it, three Mexican
men were wiping war paint off their faces. They gave Danny
bored looks; he saw a door marked REWRITE, went over and
knocked on it.

A voice called, "It's open"; Danny walked in. A lanky young
man in tweeds and horn rims was stuffing pages in a briefcase.
He said, "Are you the guy replacing Duane? He hasn't showed
up in three days and the director needs additional dialogue
quicksville."

Danny went in fast. "Duane's dead, his friend George Wiltsie
too. Murdered."

The young man dropped his briefcase; his hands twitched up
and adjusted his glasses. "Mm-mm-murdered?"

"That's right."

"And y-y-you're a policeman?"

"Deputy Sheriff. Did you know Lindenaur well?"

The youth picked up his briefcase and slumped into a chair.
"N-no, not well. Just here at work, just superficially."

"Did you see him outside the studio?"

"No."

"Did you know George Wiltsie?"

"No. I knew he and Duane lived together, because Duane
told me."

Danny swallowed. "Were they lovers?"

"I wouldn't dream of speculating on their relationship. All I know is that Duane was quiet, that he was a good rewrite man and that he worked cheap, which is a big plus at this slave labor camp."

A footstep scraped outside the door. Danny turned and saw a shadow retreating. Looking out, he caught a back view of a man fast-walking over to a bank of cameras and lighting fixtures. He followed; the man stood there, hands in his pockets, the classic "I've got nothing to hide" routine.

Danny braced him, disappointed that he was young and mid-sized, no burn scars on his face, at best a conduit for second-hand dope. "What were you doing listening outside that door?"

The man was closer to a boy—skinny, acned, a high voice with a trace of a lisp. "I work here. I'm a set dresser."

"So that gives you the right to eavesdrop on official police business?"

The kid primped his hair. Danny said, "I asked you a question."

"No, that doesn't give me—"

"Then why did you?"

"I heard you say Duaney and George were dead, and I knew them. Do you know—"

"No, I don't know who killed them, or I wouldn't be here. How well did *you* know them?"

The boy played with his pompadour. "I shared lunch with Duaney—Duane—and I knew George to say hi to when he picked Duane up."

"I guess the three of you had a lot in common, right?"

"Yes."

"Did you associate with Lindenaur and Wiltsie outside of here?"

"No."

"But you talked, because the three of you had so goddamn much in common. Is that right?"

The boy eyed the floor, one foot drawing lazy figure eights. "Yes, sir."

"Then you tell me about what they had going and who else they had going, because if anyone around here would know, you would. Isn't that right?"

The boy braced himself against a spotlight, his back to Danny. "They'd been together for a long time, but they liked to party with other guys. Georgie was rough trade, and he mostly lived off

Duane, but sometimes he turned tricks for this fancy escort service. I don't know anything else, so can I please go now?"

Danny thought of his call to Firestone Station—Lindenaur meeting the man he blackmailed through a "fruit introduction service." "No. What was the name of the escort service?"

"I don't know."

"Who else did Wiltsie and Lindenaur party with? Give me some names."

"I don't know and I don't have any names!"

"Don't whine. What about a tall, gray-haired man, middle-aged. Did either Lindenaur or Wiltsie mention a man like that?"

"No."

"Is there a man working here who fits that description?"

"There's a million men in L.A. who fit that description, so will you please—"

Danny clamped the boy's wrist, saw what he was doing and let go. "Don't raise your voice to me, just answer. Lindenaur, Wiltsie, a tall, gray-haired man."

The kid turned and rubbed his wrist. "I don't know of any men like that, but Duane liked older guys, and he told me he dug gray hair. Now are you satisfied?"

Danny couldn't meet his stare. "Did Duane and George like jazz?"

"I don't know, we never discussed music."

"Did they ever talk about burglary or a man in his late twenties with burn scars on his face?"

"No."

"Were either of them hipped on animals?"

"No, just other guys."

Danny said, "Get out of here," then moved himself, the kid still staring. The blacktop was deserted now, dusk coming on. He walked to the front gate; a voice from the guard hut stopped him. "Say, Officer. You got a minute?"

Danny halted. A bald man in a polo shirt and golf slacks stepped out and extended his hand. "I'm Herman Gerstein. I run this place."

City turf. Danny gave Gerstein a shake. "My name's Upshaw. I'm a Sheriff's detective."

Gerstein said, "I heard you were looking for the guys some script hack works with. That true?"

"Duane Lindenaur. He was murdered."

"That's too bad. I don't like it when my people check out without telling me. What's the matter, Upshaw? You ain't laughing."

"It wasn't funny."

Gerstein cleared his throat. "To each his own, and I don't have to beg for laughs, I've got comedians for that. Before you go, I want to inform you of something. I'm cooperating with a grand jury investigation into Commie influence in Hollywood, and I don't like the idea of extraneous cops asking questions around here. You dig? National security outranks a dead script hack."

Danny threw out a tweak on general principles. "A dead queer script hack."

Gerstein looked him over. "Now that really ain't funny, because I would never let a known homo work at my shop under any conditions. *Ever*. Is that clear?"

"Vividly."

Gerstein whipped three long cigars out of his slacks and stuck them in Danny's shirt pocket. "Develop a sense of humor and you might go places. And if you have to come on the lot again, see me first. You understand?"

Danny dropped the cigars on the ground, stepped on them and walked out the gate.

* * *

A check of the local papers and more phone work were next.

Danny drove to Hollywood and Vine, bought all four L.A. dailies, parked in a no-parking zone and read. The *Times* and *Daily News* had nothing on his case; the *Mirror* and *Herald* gave it a back page brush-off, "Mangled Bodies Found in Griffith Park," and "Dead Derelicts Discovered at Dawn" their respective tag-lines. Sanitized descriptions of the mutilations followed; Gene Niles blasted his horn about the job's random nature. There was no mention of ID on the victims and nothing pertaining to the death of Marty Goines.

A pay phone stood next to the newsstand. Danny called Karen Hiltscher and got what he expected—her dental lab queries were going very slowly, ten negatives since he gave her the job; her calls to other LASD stations and the Detective Bureau for checks on burglars with dental tech backgrounds got a total zero—no such men existed. Trial calls to two taxidermists yielded the fact that all stuffed animals wore plastic teeth; real animal teeth did not show up in dentures, only in the mouths of creatures still on the hoof. Danny urged Karen to keep plugging, said his goodbyes accompanied by kissy sounds and dialed the Moonglow Lounge.

Janice Modine was not waitressing that night, but John Lembeck was drinking at the bar. Danny made nice with the man he'd spared a beating; the car thief/pimp made nice back. Danny knew he was good for some free information and asked him for scoop on homosexual pimps and escort services. Lembeck said the only queer service he knew of was ritzy, hush-hush and run by a man named Felix Gordean, a legit talent agent with an office on the Strip and a suite at the Chateau Marmont. Gordean wasn't fruit himself, but provided boys to the Hollywood elite and old money L.A.

Danny admonished Lembeck to stay frosty and took his Gordean dope to R&I and the DMV night line. Two calls, two squeaky-clean records and three plush addresses: 9817 Sunset for his office, the Chateau Marmont down the Strip at 7941 for his apartment, a beach house in Malibu: 16822 Pacific Coast Highway.

With one dime and one nickel left in his pocket, Danny played a hunch. He called Firestone Station, got Sergeant Frank Skakel and asked him the name of the "fruit introduction service" where extortionist Duane Lindenaur met extortionee Charles Hartshorn. Skakel grumbled and said he'd ring Danny at his pay phone; ten minutes later he called back and said he'd dug up the original complaint report. Lindenaur met Hartshorn at a party thrown by a man who owned an escort service—Felix Gordean. Skakel ended with *his* admonition: while he was digging through the files, a buddy on the squad gave him some lowdown: Gordean was paying heavy operation kickbacks to Sheriff's Central Vice.

Danny drove to the Chateau Marmont, an apartment house-hotel done up like a swank Renaissance fortress. The main building was festooned with turrets and parapets, and there was an inner courtyard of similarly adorned bungalows connected by pathways—high, perfectly trimmed hedges surrounding them. Gaslights at the end of wrought-iron poles illuminated address plates; Danny followed a winding string of numbers to 7941, heard dance music wafting behind the hedge and started for the path to the door. Then a gust of wind scudded clouds across the sky and moonlight caught two men in evening clothes kissing, swaying together in the dark porch enclosure.

Danny watched; the moon was eclipsed by more cloud cover; the door opened and admitted the men—laughter, a jump crescendo and a few seconds' worth of brightness easing them inside. Danny went pins and needles, squeezed between the hedge and the front wall and scissor-walked over to a large picture window covered by velvet drapes. There was a narrow space where the two furls of purple were drawn apart, with a strip of light giving access to tuxedos swirling across parquet, wall tapestries, the sparkle of glasses hoisted. Danny pressed his face to the window and looked in.

That close, he got distortion blur, Man Camera malfunctions. He pulled back so that his eyes could capture a larger frame, saw tuxedos entwined in movement, cheek-to-cheek tangos, all male. The faces were up against each other so that they couldn't be distinguished individually; Danny zoomed out, in, out, in, until he was pressed into the window glass with the pins and needles localized between his legs, his eyes honing for mid-shots, close-ups, faces.

More blur, blips of arms, legs, a cart being pushed and a man in white carrying a punch bowl. Out, in, out, better focus, no faces, then Tim and Coleman the alto together, swaying to hard jazz. The pins and needles hurting; Tim gone, replaced by a blond ingenu. Then shadows killing his vision, his lens cleared by a step backward—and a perfectly framed view of two fat, ugly wallflowers tongue-kissing, all oily skin and razor burn and hair pomade glistening.

Danny bolted home, seeing San Berdoo '39 and Tim giving him the fisheye when he wouldn't take seconds on Roxie. He found his spare I. W. Harper, knocked down his standard four shots and saw it worse, Tim reproachful, saying, yeah it was just horseplay, but *you* really liked it. Two more shots, the Chateau Marmont in Technicolor, all pretty ones that he knew had Timmy's body.

He went straight to the bottle then, quality sourmash burning like rotgut, Man-Cameraing women, women, women. Karen Hiltscher, Janice Modine, strippers he'd questioned about a stick-up at the Club Largo, tits and cunt on display in the dressing room, inured to men looking at their stuff. Rita Hayworth, Ava Gardner, the hat check girl at Dave's Blue Room, his mother stepping out of the bathtub before she got fat and became a Jehovah's Witness. All ugly and wrong, just like the two wallflowers at the Marmont.

Danny drank standing up until his legs went. Going down, he managed to throw the bottle at the wall. It hit a pinup of the blood patterns at 2307 Tamarind.

16

MAL GOT his lies straight on the doorstep and rang the bell. Heels over hardwood echoed inside the house; he pulled his vest down to cover his slack waistband—too many meals forgotten. The door opened and the Red Queen was standing there, perfectly coiffed, elegantly dressed in silk and tweed—at 9:30 in the morning.

"Yes? Are you a salesman? There's a Beverly Hills ordinance against soliciting, you know."

Mal knew she knew otherwise. "I'm with the District Attorney's Office."

"Beverly Hills?"

"The City of Los Angeles."

Claire De Haven smiled—movie star quality. "My accumulation of jaywalking tickets?"

Cop-quality dissembling—Mal knew she had him pegged as the nice guy in the Lopez/Duarte/Benavides questioning. "The City needs your help."

The woman chuckled—elegantly—and held the door open. "Come in and tell me about it, Mr.... ?"

"Considine."

Claire repeated the name and stood aside; Mal walked into a large living room furnished in a floral motif: gardenia-patterned divans, tufted orchid chairs, little tables and bookstands inlaid with wooden daisies. The walls were solid movie posters— anti-Nazi pictures popular in the late '30s and early '40s. Mal strolled up to a garish job ballyhooing *Dawn of the Righteous*—a noble Russki facing off a drooling blackshirt brandishing a Luger. Sunshine haloed the good guy; the German was shadowed in darkness. With Claire De Haven watching him, he counterpunched. "Subtle."

Claire laughed. "Artful. Are you an attorney, Mr. Considine?"

Mal turned around. The Red Queen was holding a glass filled with clear liquid and ice. He couldn't smell gin and bet vodka—

more elegant, no booze breath. "No, I'm an investigator with the Grand Jury Division. May I sit down?"

Claire pointed to two chairs facing each other across a chess table. "I'm warming to this. Would you like coffee or a drink?"

Mal said, "No," and sat down. The chair was upholstered in leather; the orchids were embroidered silk. Claire De Haven took the opposite seat and crossed her legs. "You're crazy to think I'd ever inform. I won't, my friends won't, and we'll have the best legal talent money can buy."

Mal played off the three Mexicans. "Miss De Haven, this is a mop-up interview at best. My partner and I approached your friends at Variety International the wrong way, our boss is very angry and our funding has been cut. When we got our initial paperwork on the UAES—old HUAC stuff—we didn't find your name mentioned, and all your friends seemed ... well ... rather doctrinaire. I decided to play a hunch and present my case to you, hoping you'd keep an open mind and find aspects of what I'm going to tell you reasonable."

Claire De Haven smiled and sipped her drink. "You speak very well for a policeman."

Mal thought: and you blast vodka in the morning and fuck pachuco hoodlums. "I went to Stanford, and I was a major with the MPs in Europe. I was involved in processing evidence to convict Nazi war criminals, so you see I'm not entirely unsympathetic to those posters on your walls."

"You display empathy well, too. And now you've been employed by the studios, because it's easier to see Red than pay decent wages. You'll divide, conquer, get people to inform and bring in specialists. And you'll cause nothing but grief."

From banter to cool outrage in a half second flat. Mal tried to look hangdog, thinking he could take the woman if he gave her a tough fight, but let her win. "Miss De Haven, why doesn't the UAES strike in order to achieve its contract demands?"

Claire took a slow drink. "The Teamsters would get in and stay in on a temporary payroll stipulation."

A good opening; a last chance to play nice guy before they pulled back, planted newspaper dope and went decoy. "I'm glad you mentioned the Teamsters, because they worry me. Should this grand jury succeed—and I doubt that it will—a racketeering force against the Teamsters would be a logical next step. They are very heavily infiltrated with criminal elements, much the way the American left is infiltrated by Communists."

Claire De Haven sat still, not taking the bait. She looked at Mal, eyes lingering on the automatic strapped to his belt. "You're an intelligent man, so state your case. Thesis sentence style, like you learned in your freshman comp class at Stanford."

Mal thought of Celeste—juice for some indignation. "Miss De Haven, I saw Buchenwald, and I know what Stalin is doing is just as bad. We want to get to the bottom of *totalitarian* Communist influence in the movie industry and inside the UAES, *end it*, prevent the Teamsters from kicking the shit out of you on the picket line and establish through testimony some sort of demarcation line between *hard* Communist propaganda aggression and legitimate leftist political activity." A pause, a shrug, hands raised in mock frustration. "Miss De Haven, I'm a policeman. I collect evidence to put robbers and killers away. I don't like this job, but I think it needs to be done and I'm damn well going to do it as best I can. Can't you see my point?"

Claire took cigarettes and a lighter from the table and lit up. She smoked while Mal darted his eyes around the room, mock chagrin at blowing his calm. Finally she said, "You're either a very good actor or in way over your head with some very bad men. Which is it? I honestly don't know."

"Don't patronize me."

"I'm sorry."

"No, you're not."

"All right, I'm not."

Mal got up and paced the room, advance man for his decoy. He noticed a bookcase lined with picture frames, examined a shelf of them and saw a string of handsome young men. About half were Latin lover types—but Lopez, Duarte and Benavides were absent. He remembered Lopez' comment to Lesnick: Claire was the only gringa he'd met who'd suck him, and he felt guilty about it because only whores did that, and she was his Communista madonna. On a shelf by itself was a picture of Reynolds Loftis, his Anglo-Saxon rectitude incongruous. Mal turned and looked at Claire. "Your conquests, Miss De Haven?"

"My past and future. Wild oats lumped together and my fiancé all by himself."

Chaz Minear had gotten explicit on Loftis—what they did, the feel of his weight downstairs. Mal wondered how much the woman knew about them, if she even guessed Minear finked her future husband to HUAC. "He's a lucky man."

"Thank you."

"Isn't he an actor? I think I took my son to a movie he was in."

Claire stubbed out her cigarette, lit another one and smoothed her skirt. "Yes, Reynolds is an actor. When did you and your son see the movie?"

Mal sat down, juggling blacklist dates. "Right after the war, I think. Why?"

"A point that I'd like to make, as long as we're talking in a civil manner. I doubt that you're as sensitive as you portray yourself, but if you are I'd like to illustrate an example of the hurt men like you cause."

Mal hooked a thumb back at Loftis' picture. "With your fiancé?"

"Yes. You see, you probably saw the movie at a revival house. Reynolds was a *very* successful character actor in the '30s, but the California State Un-American Activities Committee hurt him when he refused to testify back in '40. Many studios wouldn't touch him because of his politics, and the only work he could get was on Poverty Row—toadying to an awful man named Herman Gerstein."

Mal played dumb. "It could have been worse. People were blacklisted outright by HUAC in '47. Your fiancé could have been."

Claire shouted, "He *was* blacklisted, and I bet you know it!"

Mal jerked back in his chair; he thought he'd had her convinced he wasn't wise to Loftis. Claire lowered her voice. "Maybe you knew it. Reynolds Loftis, Mr. Considine. Surely you know that he's in the UAES."

Mal shrugged, smokescreening a lie. "When you said Reynolds, I guessed that it was Loftis. I knew he was an actor, but I've never seen his photograph. Look, I'll tell you why I was surprised. An old lefty told my partner and me that Loftis was a homosexual. Now you tell me he's your fiancé."

Claire's eyes narrowed; for a half second she looked like a shrew in waiting. "Who told you that?"

Mal shrugged again. "Some guy who used to hang out and chase girls at the Sleepy Lagoon Committee picnics. I forget his name."

Shrew in waiting to nervous wreck; Claire's hands shaking, her legs twitching, grazing the table. Mal homed in on her eyes and thought he saw them pinning, like she was mixing pharmacy stuff with her vodka. Seconds dragged; Claire became calm again. "I'm sorry. Hearing Reynolds described as that upset me."

Mal thought: no it didn't—it was Sleepy Lagoon. "I'm sorry, I shouldn't have said it."

"Then why did you?"

"Because he's a lucky man."

The Red Queen smiled. "And not just because of me. Will you let me finish that point I wanted to make?"

"Sure."

Claire said, "In '47 someone informed on Reynolds to the House Committee—hearsay and innuendo—and he *was* black-listed outright. He went to Europe and found work acting in experimental art films directed by a Belgian man he'd met in L.A. during the war. The actors all wore masks, the films created quite a stir, and Reynolds eked out a living acting in them. He even won the French version of the Oscar in '48, and got mainstream work in Europe. Now the *real* Hollywood studios are offering him real work for real money, which will end if Reynolds is hauled before another committee or grand jury or kangaroo court or whatever you people call them."

Mal stood up and looked at the door. Claire said, "Reynolds will never name names, I'll never name names. Don't ruin the good life he's starting to have again. Don't ruin me."

She even begged with elegance. Mal made a gesture that took in leather upholstery, brocade curtains and a small fortune in embroidered silk. "How can you preach the Commie line and justify all this?"

The Red Queen smiled, beggar to muse. "The good work I do allows me a dispensation for nice things."

* * *

A stellar exit line.

Mal walked back to his car and found a note stuck under the wiper blades: "Captain—greetings! Herman Gerstein called Ellis with a complaint: a Sheriff's dick is making waves at Variety International (pansy homicide). Ellis spoke to his CO (Capt. Al Dietrich) about it—and we're supposed to tell the lad to desist. West Hollywood Substation when you finish with C.D.H., please—D.S."

Mal drove to the station, pissed at a stupid errand when he should be orchestrating the team's next move: radio and newspaper spots to convince UAES the grand jury was kaput. He saw Dudley Smith's Ford in the lot, left his car next to it and walked in the front door. Dudley was standing by the dispatching alcove, talking to a Sheriff's captain in uniform. A girl behind the switchboard was flagrantly eavesdropping, toying with the headset on her neck.

Dudley saw him and hooked a finger; Mal went over and offered the brass his hand. "Mal Considine, Captain."

The man gave him a bonecrusher shake. "Al Dietrich. Good to meet a couple of City boys who come off as human beings, and I was just telling Lieutenant Smith here not to judge Deputy Upshaw too harshly. He's got a lot of newfangled ideas about procedure and the like, and he's a bit of a hothead, but basically he's a damn good cop. Twenty-seven years old and already a detective must tell you something, right?"

Dudley boomed tenor laughter. "Smarts and naivete are a potent combination in young men. Malcolm, our friend is working on a County homo snuff tied to two City jobs. He seems to be obsessed as only a young idealist cop can be. Shall we give the lad a gentle lesson in police etiquette and priorities?"

Mal said, "A brief one," and turned to Dietrich. "Captain, where's Upshaw now?"

"In an interrogation room down the hall. Two of my men captured a robbery suspect this morning, and Danny's sweating him. Come on, I'll show you—but let him finish up first."

Dietrich led them through the muster room to a short corridor inset with cubicles fronted by one-way glass. Static was crackling out of a wall speaker above the last window on the left. The captain said, "Take a listen, the kid is good. And try to let him down easy, he's got a bad temper and I like him."

Mal strode ahead of Dudley to the one-way. Looking in, he saw a hood he'd roused before the war. Vincent Scoppettone, a Jack Dragna trigger, was sitting at a table bolted to the floor, his hands cuffed to a welded-down chair. Deputy Upshaw had his back to the window and was drawing water from a wall cooler. Scoppettone squirmed in his chair, his County denims sweat-soaked at the legs and armpits.

Dudley caught up. "Ah, grand. Vinnie the guinea. I heard that lad found out a quail of his was distributing her favors elsewhere and stuck a .12 gauge up her love canal. It must have been messy, albeit quick. Do you know the difference between an Italian grandmother and an elephant? Twenty pounds and a black dress. Isn't that grand?"

Mal ignored him. Scoppettone's voice came over the speaker, synched a fraction of a second behind his lips. "Eyeball witnesses don't mean shit. They got to be alive to testify. Understand?"

Deputy Upshaw turned around, holding a cup of water. Mal saw a medium-sized young man, even-featured with hard brown eyes, a dark brown crew cut and razor nicks on heavily shadowed pale skin. He looked lithe and muscular—and there was something about him reminiscent of Claire De Haven's picture-pretty boys. His voice was an even baritone. "Down the hatch, Vincent. Communion. Confession. Requiescat en pace."

Scoppettone gulped water, sputtered and licked his lips. "You a Catholic?"

Upshaw sat down in the opposite chair. "I'm nothing. My mother's a Jehovah's Witness and my father's dead, which is what you're gonna be when Jack D. finds out you're clouting markets on your own. And as far as the eyeball witnesses go, they'll testify. You'll be no bail downtown and Jack'll give you the go-by. You're in dutch with Jack or you wouldn't be pulling heists in the first place. Spill, Vincent. Feed me on your other jobs and the captain here will recommend honor farm."

Scoppettone coughed; water dribbled off his chin. "Without them witnesses, you got no case."

Upshaw leaned over the table; Mal wondered how much the speaker was distorting his voice. "You're ixnay with Jack, Vinnie. At best, he lets you go on the Sun-Fax, at worst he has you whacked when you hit the penitentiary. And that'll be Folsom. You're a known mob associate, and that's where they go. And the Sun-Fax is in Cohen territory. Mickey buys the gift baskets he greases judges with there, and he'll make damn sure one of those judges hears your case. In my opinion, you are just too stupid to live. Only a stupid shit would knock off a joint in Cohen territory. Are you looking to start a fucking war? You think Jack wants Mickey coming after him over a chump-change stickup?"

Dudley nudged Mal. "That lad is very, very good."

Mal said, "In spades." He pushed Dudley's elbow aside and concentrated on Upshaw and his verbal style—wondering if he could run Commie argot as well as he did gangsterese. Vincent

Scoppettone coughed again; static hit the speaker, then died out into words. "There ain't gonna be no war. Jack and Mickey been talkin' about a truce, maybe going in on a piece of business together."

Upshaw said, "You feel like talking about that?"

"You think I'm stupid?"

Upshaw laughed. Mal caught the phoniness, that Scoppettone didn't interest him—that it was just a job. But it was a Class A phony laugh—and the kid knew how to squeeze his own tension into it.

"Vinnie, I already told you I think you're stupid. You've got panic city written all over you, and I think you're on the outs with Jack bad. Let me guess: you did something to piss Jack off, you got scared, you thought you'd hightail. You needed a stake, you heisted the Sun-Fax. Am I right?"

Scoppettone was sweating heavy now—it was rolling off his face. Upshaw said, "You know what else I think? One heist wouldn't have done it. I think there's other jobs we can make you for. I think I'm gonna check robbery reports all over the City and County, maybe Ventura County, maybe Orange and San Diego. I'll bet if I wire your mugs around I'll come up with some other eyeball witnesses. Am I right?"

Scoppettone tried laughter—a long string of squeaky ha ha ha's. Upshaw joined in and mimicked them until his prisoner shut up. Mal snapped: he's wound tight as a steel spring on something else and shooting it to Vinnie because he's the one here— *and he probably doesn't know he's doing it.*

Squirming his arms, Scoppettone said, "Let's talk dealsky. I got something sweet."

"Tell me."

"Heroin. Heroin very large. That truce I told you about, Jack and Mickey partners. Quality Mex brown, twenty-five pounds. All for niggertown, cut-rate to lowball the independents down there. The God's truth. If I'm lyin', I'm flyin'."

Upshaw aped Vinnie's tone. "Then you've got wings stashed under your mattress, because the Mick and Dragna as partners is horseshit. Sherry's was six months ago, Cohen lost a man and doesn't forget stuff like that."

"That wasn't Jack, that was LAPD. Shooters out of Hollywood Station, a snuff kitty half the fuckin' division kicked in for 'cause of fuckin' Brenda. Mickey Kike knows Jack didn't do it."

Upshaw yawned—broadly. "I'm bored, Vinnie. Niggers geez-ing heroin and Jack and Mickey as partners is a fucking snore. By the way, you read the papers?"

Scoppettone shook his head, spraying sweat. "What?"

Upshaw pulled a rolled-up newspaper from his hip pocket. "This was in last Tuesday's *Herald*. 'Yesterday evening tragedy occurred at a convivial cocktail lounge in the Silverlake Dis-trict. A gunman entered the friendly Moonmist Lounge, carry-ing a large-caliber pistol. He forced the bartender and three patrons to lie on the floor, ransacked the cash register and stole jewelry, wallets and purses belonging to his four victims. The bartender tried to apprehend the robber, and he pistol-whipped him senseless. The bartender died of head injuries this morning at Queen of Angels Hospital. The surviving robbery victims described the assailant as "an Italian-looking white man, late thirties, five-ten, one hundred and ninety pounds."' Vinnie, that's you."

Scoppettone shrieked, "That ain't me!" Mal craned his neck and squinted at the print on Upshaw's newspaper, glomming a full page on last week's fight card at the Olympic. He thought: pull out the stops, bluff him down, hit him once, don't get carried away and you're my boy—

"That ain't fucking me!"

Upshaw leaned over the table, hard in Scoppettone's face. "I don't fucking care. You're standing in a lineup tonight, and the three squarejohns from the Moonmist Lounge are gonna look you over. Three white bread types who think all wops are Al Capone. See, I don't want you for the Sun-Fax, Vinnie, I want you for keeps."

"I didn't do it!"

"Prove it!"

"I can't prove it!"

"Then you'll take the fucking fall!"

Scoppettone was putting his whole body into his head, the only part of him not lashed down. He shook it; he twisted it; he thrust his chin back and forth like a ram trying to batter a fence. Mal got a flash: the kid had him nailed for a backup heist that night; the whole performance was orchestrated for the news-paper punch line. He elbowed Dudley and said, "Ours"; Dudley gave him the thumbs-up. Vinnie Scoppettone tried to jerk his chair off the floor; Danny Upshaw grabbed a handful of his hair and slapped his face—forehand, backhand, forehand, backhand—until he went limp and blubbered, "Deal. Deal. Deal."

Upshaw whispered in Scoppettone's ear; Vinnie drooled an answer. Mal stood on his tiptoes for a better shot at the speaker and heard only static. Dudley lit a cigarette and smiled; Upshaw hit a button under the table. Two uniformed deputies and a woman holding a steno pad double-timed down the corridor. They opened the interrogation room door and swooped on their live one; Danny Upshaw walked out and said, "Oh shit."

Mal studied the reaction. "Good work, Deputy. You were damn good."

Upshaw looked at him, then Dudley. "You're City, right?"

Mal said, "Right, DA's Bureau. My name's Considine, this is Lieutenant Smith."

"And it's about?"

Dudley said, "Lad, we were going to reprimand you for rattling Mr. Herman Gerstein's cage, but that's water under the bridge now. Now we're going to offer you a job."

"*What?*"

Mal took Upshaw's arm and steered him a few feet away. "It's a decoy plant for a grand jury investigation into Communist activity in the movie studios. A very well-placed DA is running the show, and he'll be able to square a temporary transfer with Captain Dietrich. The job is a career maker, and I think you should say yes."

"No."

"You can transfer to the Bureau clean after the investigation. You'll be a lieutenant before you're thirty."

"No. I don't want it."

"What *do* you want?"

"I want to supervise the triple homicide case I'm working—for the County *and* the City."

Mal thought of Ellis Loew balking, other City hotshots he could grease for the favor. "I think I can manage it."

Dudley came over, clapped Upshaw on the back and winked. "There's a woman you'll have to get next to, lad. You might have to fuck the pants off of her."

Deputy Danny Upshaw said, "I welcome the opportunity."

PART TWO

UPSHAW, CONSIDINE, MEEKS

17

HE WAS a cop again, bought and paid for, in with major leaguers playing for keeps. Howard's bonus had him out of hock with Leotis Dineen, and if the grand jury succeeded in booting the UAES from the studios he'd be minor-league rich. He had a set of keys to Ellis Loew's house and the use of the City clerks who'd be typing and filing there. He had a "target list" of Pinkos untouched by previous grand juries. And he had the *big* list: UAES top dogs to glom criminal dirt on, no direct approaches now that they were deep in subterfuge, with newspaper pieces planted that said their investigation was dead. An hour ago he'd had his secretary place query calls to his local Fed contact, City/County DMV/R&I and the criminal records bureaus of California, Nevada, Arizona and Oregon States, requesting arrest report information on Claire De Haven, Morton Ziffkin, Chaz Minear, Reynolds Loftis and three unholy-sounding pachucos: Mondo Lopez, Sammy Benavides and Juan Duarte, asterisks after their names denoting them "known youth gang members." The gang squad boss at Hollenbeck Station had been his only call back; he said that the three were bad apples—members of a zooter mob in the early '40s before they cleaned up and "got political." East L.A. would be his first stop—once his secretary logged in the rest of her responses to his call-outs.

Buzz looked around his office for something to kill time with, saw the morning *Mirror* on the doormat and picked it up. He flipped through to the editorial page and got bingo! under Victor Reisel's by-line, less than twenty-four hours after cuckold Mal told Loew his plan.

The title was "Reds 1—City of Los Angeles 0. 3 Outs, No Witnesses on Base." Buzz read:

> It all came down to money—the great equalizer and common denominator. A grand jury was in the works, an important grand jury that would have been as far-reaching as the 1947 House Un-American

Activities Committee hearings. Once again, Communist encroachment in the motion picture industry was to be delved into—this time within the context of labor trouble in the City of the Angels.

The United Alliance of Extras and Stagehands is currently under contract with a number of Hollywood studios. The union is rife with Communists and fellow travelers. The UAES is making exorbitant contract renegotiation demands, and a Teamster local which would like the opportunity to reach an amicable accord with the studios and step in to work UAES's job for reasonable wages and benefits is picketing against them. *Money.* The UAES implicitly advocates the end of the capitalist system and wants more of it. The nonideologically involved Teamsters want to prove their on-the-job mettle by working for wages that anticapitalists spurn. Hollywood, show biz: it's a crazy world.

Crazy Item #1: The glut of pro-Russian movies made during the early 1940's were largely scripted by members of the so-called UAES Brain trust.

Crazy Item #2: UAES Brain trust members belong to a total of 41 organizations that have been classified as Commie fronts by the State Attorney General's Office.

Crazy Item #3: The UAES wants more of that filthy capitalist lucre; the Teamsters want jobs for their people; a number of patriotic men in the L.A. District Attorney's Office had been slated to gather evidence for a prospective grand jury to delve into just *how* deep those green-loving UAESers' influence in the movie biz went. Let's face it: Hollywood is an unsurpassed tool for disseminating propaganda, and the Commies are the subtlest, most cruelly intelligent foe America has ever faced. Given access to the motion picture medium and its pervasiveness in our daily life, there is no end to the cancerous seeds of treason that well-placed movie Reds could plant—subtle satires and attacks on America, subliminally planted so that the public and right-thinking movie people would have no idea they were being brainwashed. The DA's men had made approaches to several subversives, and were attempting to get them to admit to the error of their ways and appear as witnesses when money—the great equalizer and common denominator—reared its head to give aid and comfort to the enemy.

Lieutenant Malcolm Considine, of the DA's Bureau of Investigations, said: "The City had promised us budget money, then withdrew. We're understaffed and now unfunded, with a backlog of criminal matters clogging up potential grand jury docket time. We might be able to begin gathering evidence again in fiscal '51 or '52, but how many inroads will the Communists have made into our culture by then?"

How many indeed. Lieutenant Dudley Smith of the Los Angeles Police Department, Lieutenant Considine's sadly short-lived partner in the DA Bureau's sadly short-lived investigation, said, "Yes, it all came down to money. The City has precious little, and it would be immoral and illegal to seek outside funding. The Reds do not balk at exploiting the capitalist system, while we live by its rules, accepting the few inherent frailties in an otherwise just and humane philosophy. That's the difference between them and us. They live by the law of the jungle, we are too peace-loving to stoop to it."

Reds—1, the City of Los Angeles and the movie-going public—0.

It's a crazy world.

Buzz put the paper down, thinking of crazy Dud circa '38—brass-knuckling a nigger hophead half to death for drooling on a cashmere overcoat Ben Siegel greased him with. He hit the intercom. "Sweetheart, any results on those calls yet?"

"Still waiting, Mr. Meeks."

"I'm going out to East L.A. Leave my messages on my desk, would you, please?"

"Yes, sir."

* * *

The morning was cool, with rain threatening. Buzz took Olympic straight out, Hughes Aircraft to Boyle Heights with a minimum of red lights, no pretty scenery, time to think. The .38 he'd strapped on made his rolls of flab hang funny; his ID buzzer and the *Racing Form* weighted his pockets wrong, bum ballast that had him picking at his crotch to even things out. Benavides, Lopez and Duarte were either White Fence, 1st Flats or Apaches; the Mexes in the Heights were good people, anxious to suck up right and be good Americans. He'd get good information from them—and the idea bored him.

He knew why: he hadn't been with a woman in years who wasn't a whore or a starlet looking to get next to Howard. Audrey Anders had him running on her time, brainstorming on her so hard that even this sweetheart of a deal with the DA's Office came a cropper. Betting with Leotis Dineen was plain stupid; chasing Audrey was stupid that meant something—a reason for him to quit gorging on porterhouse, au gratins and peach pie and lose a shitload of pounds so that his beaucoup wardrobe fit right—even though they'd never be able to go out in public together.

Downtown came and went; the woman stayed. Buzz tried concentrating on the job, turning north on Soto, heading into the terraced hillsides that formed Boyle Heights. The Jews had ceded the neighborhood to the Mexicans before the war; Brooklyn Avenue had gone from reeking of pastrami and chicken stock to reeking of cornmeal and deep-fried pork. The synagogue across from Hollenbeck Park was now a Catholic church; the old men with beanies who played chess under the pepper trees were replaced by pachucos in slit-bottom khakis—strutting, primping, walking the road camp walk, talking the jailhouse talk. Buzz circled the park, eyeing and tagging them: unemployed, mid-twenties, probably pushing fifty-cent reefers and collecting protection off the hebe merchants too poor to move to the new kosher canyon at Beverly and Fairfax. White Fence or 1st Flats or Apaches, with tattoos between their left thumbs and forefingers spelling it out. Dangerous when fired up on mescal, maryjane, goofballs and pussy; restless when bored.

Buzz parked and stuck his billy club down the back of his pants, throwing the fit off even worse. He approached a group of four young Mexicans; two saw him coming and took off, obviously to drop hot shit in the grass somewhere, reconnoiter and see what the fat puto cop wanted. The other two stood there watching a cockroach fight: two bugs in a shoebox placed on a bench, gladiators brawling for the right to devour a dead bug soaked in maple syrup. Buzz checked out the action while the pachucos pretended not to notice him; he saw a pile of dimes and quarters on the ground and dropped a five spot on it. "Finsky on the fucker with the spot on his back."

The Mexicans did double-takes; Buzz did a quick size-up: White Fence tattoos on two sinewy right forearms; both vatos lean and mean at the welterweight limit; one dirty T-shirt, one clean. Four brown eyes sizing *him* up. "I mean it. That fucker's got style. He's a dancemaster like Billy Conn."

Both pachucos pointed to the shoebox; Clean T-shirt said, "Billy muerto." Buzz looked down and saw the spotted bug belly up, stuck to the cardboard in a pool of amber goo. Dirty Shirt giggled, scooped up the change and five-spot; Clean Shirt took an ice cream stick, lifted the winner out of the box and put him on the bark of a pepper tree next to the bench. The bug hung there licking his feelers; Buzz said, "Double or nothin' on a trick I learned back in Oklahoma."

Clean Shirt said, "This some goddamn cop trick?"

Buzz fished out his baton and dangled it by the thong. "Sort of. I got a few questions about some boys who used to live around here, and maybe you can help me. I pull off the trick, you talk to me. No snitch stuff, just a few questions. I don't do the trick, you stroll. Comprende?"

The clean shirt vato started to walk away; Dirty Shirt stopped him and pointed to Buzz's stick. "What's that thing got to do with it?"

Buzz smiled and took three steps backward, eyes on the tree. "Son, you set that roach's ass on fire and I'll show you."

Clean Shirt whipped out a lighter, flicked it on and held the flame under the victor bug. The bug scampered up the tree; Buzz got a bead and overhanded his baton. It hit and clattered to the ground; Dirty Shirt picked it up and fingered pulp off the tip. "That's him. Holy fuck."

Clean Shirt made the sign of the cross, pachuco version, his right hand stroking his balls; Dirty Shirt crossed the standard way. Buzz tossed his stick in the air, bounced it off the inside crook of his elbow, caught it and twirled it behind his back, let it hit the pavement, then brought it to parade rest with a jerk of the thong. The Mexicans were slack-jawed now; Buzz braced them while their mouths were still open. "Mondo Lopez, Juan Duarte and Sammy Benavides. They used to gangsterize around here. Spill nice and I'll show you some more tricks."

Dirty Shirt spat a string of obscenities in Spanish; Clean Shirt translated. "Javier hates 1st Flats like a dog. Like a fucking evil dog."

Buzz was wondering if Audrey Anders would go for his stick routine. "So those boys ran with the Flats?"

Javier spat on the pavement—an eloquent lunger. "Traitors, man. Back maybe '43, '44, the Fence and Flats had a peace council. Lopez and Duarte was supposed to be in on it, but they joined the fuckin' Sinarquista Nazi putos, then the fuckin' Commie Sleepy Lagoon putos, when they shoulda been fightin' with us. The fuckin' Apaches cleaned the Flats' and Fences' fuckin' clock, man. I lost my cousin Caldo."

Buzz unclipped two more fivers. "What else have you got? Feel free to get ugly."

"Benavides was ugly, man! He raped his own fuckin' little sister!"

Buzz handed out the money. "Easy now. Give me some more on that, whatever else you got and some leads on family. *Easy.*"

Clean Shirt said, "It's just a rumor on Benavides, and Duarte's got a queer cousin, so maybe he's queer, too. Queerness runs in families, I read it in *Argosy* magazine."

Buzz tucked his billy club back in his pants. "What about families? Who's got family still around here?"

Javier answered. "Lopez' mother died, and I think maybe he got some cousins in Bakersfield. 'Cept for the maricón, mosta Duarte's people moved back to Mexico, and I know that puto Benavides got parents livin' on 4th and Evergreen."

"A house? An apartment?"

Clean Shirt piped in: "Little shack with all these statues in front." He twirled a finger and pointed to his head. "The mother is crazy. Loca grande."

Buzz sighed. "That's all I get for fifteen scoots and my show?"

Javier said, "Every vato in the Heights hates those cabróns, ask them."

Clean Shirt said, "We could make up some shit, you could pay us for that."

Buzz said, "Try to stay alive," and drove to 4th and Evergreen.

* * *

The lawn was a shrine.

Jesus statues were lined up facing the street; there was a stable made out of kids' Lincoln Logs behind them, a dog turd reposing in baby J.C.'s manger. Buzz walked up to the porch and rang the bell; he saw the Virgin Mary on an end table. The front of her flowing white gown bore an inscription: "Fuck me." Buzz made a snap deduction—Mr. and Mrs. Benavides couldn't see too well.

An old woman opened the door. "Quién?"

Buzz said, "Police, ma'am. And I don't speak Spanish."

The ginch fingered a string of beads around her neck. "I speak Inglés. Is about Sammy?"

"Yes, ma'am. How'd you know that?"

The old girl pointed to the wall above a chipped brick fireplace. A devil had been drawn there—red suit, horns and trident. Buzz walked over and scoped him out. A photo of a Mex kid was glued where his face should be, and a line of Jesus statues was looking up from the ledge, giving him the evil eye. The woman said, "My son Sammy. Communisto. Devil incarnate."

Buzz smiled. "It looks like you're well protected, ma'am. You've got Jesus on the job."

Mama Benavides grabbed a sheaf of papers off the mantel and handed them over. The top sheet was a State Justice Department publicity job—California-based Commie fronts in alphabetical order. The Sleepy Lagoon Defense Committee was check-marked, with a line in brackets next to it: "Write P.O. Box 465, Sacramento, 14, California, for membership list." The old woman snatched the pages, flipped through them and stabbed a finger at a column of names. Benavides, Samuel Tomás Ignacio, and De Haven, Claire Katherine, were starred in ink. "There. Is the truth, anti-Christ Communista y Communisto."

The ginch had tears in her eyes. Buzz said, "Well, Sammy's got his rough edges, but I wouldn't exactly call him the devil."

"Is true! Yo soy la madre del diablo! You arrest him! Communisto!"

Buzz pointed to Claire De Haven's notation. "Mrs. Benavides, what have you got on this woman here? Give me some good scoop and I'll beat that boogie man up with my stick."

"Communista! Drug addict! Sammy took her to clinica for cure, and she—"

Buzz saw a prime opening. "Where is that clinic, ma'am? Tell me slow."

"By ocean. Devil doctor! Communista whore!"

Satan's mother started bawling for real. Buzz blew East L.A. and headed for Malibu—a sea breeze, a doctor who owed him, no cockroach fights, no fuck me madonnas.

* * *

Pacific Sanitarium was in Malibu Canyon, a booze and dope dry-out farm nestled in foothills a half mile from the beach. The main building, lab and maintenance shacks were surrounded by electrified barbed wire; the price for kicking hooch, horse and drugstore hop was twelve hundred dollars a week; detoxification heroin was processed on the premises—per a gentleman's agreement between Dr. Terence Lux, the clinic's bossman, and the Los Angeles County Board of Supervisors—the agreement based on the proviso that L.A. politicos in need of the place could boil out for free. Buzz drove up to the gate thinking of all the referrals he'd given Lux: RKO juicers and hopheads spared jail jolts and bum publicity because Dr. Terry, plastic surgeon to the stars, had given them shelter and him a 10 percent kickback. One still rankled: a girl who'd OD'd when Howard booted her out of his A list fuck pad and back to selling it in hotel bars. He almost burned the three hundred Lux shot him for the business.

Buzz beeped his horn; the gate watchman's voice came over the squawk box: "Yes, sir?"

Buzz spoke to the receiver by the fence. "Turner Meeks to see Dr. Lux."

The guard said, "One moment, sir"; Buzz waited. Then: "Sir, follow the road all the way down the left fork to the end. Dr. Lux is in the hatchery."

The gate opened; Buzz cruised past the clinic and maintenance buildings and turned onto a road veering off into a scrub-covered miniature canyon. There was a shack at the end: low wire walls and a tin roof. Chickens squawked inside it; some of the birds were shrieking bloody murder.

Buzz parked, got out and peered through the wire. Two men in hipboots and khaki smocks were slaughtering chickens, hacking them with razor-bladed two-by-fours—the zoot sticks Riot Squad bulls used to pack back in the early '40s, emasculating Mex hoodlums by slashing their threads. The stick wielders were good: single neck shots, on to the next one. The few remaining birds were trying to run and fly away; their panic had them scudding into the walls, the roof and the zoot men. Buzz thought: no chicken marsala at the Derby tonight, and heard a voice behind him.

"Two birds with one stone. A bad pun, good business."

Buzz turned. Terry Lux was standing there—all rangy gray handsomeness, like a dictionary definition of "physician." "Hello, Doc."

"You know I prefer Doctor or Terry, but I've always made allowances for your homespun style. Is this business?"

"Not exactly. What's *that*? You doin' your own catering?"

Lux pointed to the slaughterhouse, silent now, the stick men tossing dead chickens in sacks. "Two birds, one stone. Years ago I read a study that asserted a heavy chicken diet is beneficial to people with low blood sugar, which most alcoholics and drug addicts have. Stone one. Stone two is my special cure for narcotics users. My technicians drain out all their existing contaminated blood and rotate in fresh, healthy blood filled with vitamins, minerals and animal hormones. So, I have a hatchery and a slaughterhouse. It's all very cost-effective and beneficial to my patients. What is it, Buzz? If it isn't business, then it's a favor. How can I help you?"

The smell of blood and feathers was making him gag. Buzz noticed a pulley system linking the maintenance huts to the clinic, a tram car stationed on a landing dock about ten yards in back of the chicken shack. "Let's go up to your office. I've got some questions about a woman who I'm pretty damn sure was a patient of yours."

Lux frowned and cleaned his nails with a scalpel. "I never divulge confidential patient information. You know that. It's a prime reason why Mr. Hughes and yourself use my services exclusively."

"Just a few questions, Terry."

"I suppose money instead is out of the question?"

"I don't need money, I need information."

"And if I don't proffer this information you'll take your business elsewhere?"

Buzz nodded toward the tram car. "No tickee, no washee. Be nice to me, Terry. I'm in with the City of Los Angeles these days, and I just might get the urge to spill about that dope you manufacture here."

Lux scratched his neck with the scalpel. "For medical purposes only, and politically approved."

"Doc, you tellin' me you don't trade the skim to Mickey C. for *his* referrals? The City hates Mickey, you know."

Lux bowed in the direction of the car; Buzz walked ahead and got in. The doctor hit a switch; sparks burst from the cables; they moved slowly up and docked on an overhang adjacent to a portico with a spectacular ocean view. Lux led Buzz down a series of antiseptic white hallways to a small room crammed with filing cabinets. Medical posters lined the walls: a picture primer for plastic surgeons, facial reconstruction in the style of Thomas Hart Benton. Buzz said, "Claire Katherine De Haven. She's some kind of Commie."

Lux opened a cabinet, leafed through folders, plucked one and read from the top page: "Claire Katherine De Haven, date of birth May 5, 1910. Chronic controlled alcoholic, sporadically addicted to phenobarbital, occasional Benzedrine use, occasional heroin skin-popper. She took my special cure I told you about three times—in '39, '43, and '47. That's it."

Buzz said, "Nix, I want more. That file of yours list any details? Any good dirt?"

Lux held up the folder. "It's mostly medical charts and financial accountings. You can read them if you like."

"No thanks. You remember her good, Terry. I can tell. So feed me."

Lux put the file back and slid the cabinet shut. "She seduced a few of her fellow patients while she was here the first time. It caused an upheaval, so in '43 I kept her isolated. She was on remorseful both times, and on her second go-round I gave her a little psychiatric counseling."

"You a headshrinker?"

Lux laughed. "No, but I enjoy getting people to tell me things. In '43 De Haven told me she wanted to reform because some Mexican boyfriend of hers got beat up in the zoot suit riots and she wanted to work more efficaciously for the People's Revolt. In '47 the Red hearings back east sent her around the twist—some pal of hers got his you-know-what in the wringer. HUAC was good for business, Buzz. Lots of remorse, ODs, suicide attempts. Commies with money are the best Commies, don't you agree?"

Buzz ran the rest of the target list through his head. "Who got his dick in the wringer, some bimbo of Claire's?"

"I don't remember."

"Morton Ziffkin?"

"No."

"One of her spics? Benavides, Lopez, Duarte?"

"No, it wasn't a Mex."

"Chaz Minear, Reynolds Loftis?"

Bingo on "Loftis"—Lux's face muscles tensing, coming together around a phony smile. "No, not them."

Buzz said, "Horseshit. You give on that. *Now.*"

Lux shrugged—phony. "I had a case on Claire, and so did Loftis. I was jealous. When you mentioned him, that brought it all back."

Buzz laughed—his patented shitkicker job. "Horse pucky. You've only got a case on money, so you fuckin' give me better than that."

The doctor got out his scalpel and tapped it against his leg. "Okay, let's try this. Loftis used to buy heroin for Claire, and I didn't like it—I wanted her beholden to me. Satisfied?"

A good morning's work: the woman as a hophead/Mex fucker, Benavides a maybe kiddie raper, Loftis copping H for a fellow Red. "Who'd he glom from?"

"I don't know. *Really.*"

"You got anything else good?"

"No. You have any fine young Howard rejects to spice up the ward?"

"See you in church, Doc."

* * *

A stack of messages was waiting back at the office, partial results from his secretary's phone queries. Buzz leafed through them.

Traffic ticket rebop predominated, along with some stale bread on the spics: unlawful assembly, nonfelony assault and battery resulting in Mickey Mouse juvie time. No sex shit on Samuel Tomás Ignacio Benavides, the "devil incarnate"; no political dirt on any of the three ex-White Fencers. Buzz turned to the last message slip—his secretary's call back from the Santa Monica PD.

> Mr. Meeks—
>
> 3/44—R. Loftis & another man—Charles (Eddington) Hartshorn, D.O.B. 9/6/1897, routinely questioned during Vice Squad raid of S.M. deviant bar (Knight in Armor - 1684 S. Lincoln, S.M.) This from F.I. card check. DMV/R&I on Hartshorn: no crim. rec., traffic rec. clean, attorney. Address - 419 S. Rimpau, L.A. - hope this helps - Lois.

419 South Rimpau was Hancock Park, pheasant under glass acres, old L.A. money; Reynolds Loftis had a case on Claire De Haven—and now it looked like he addressed the ball from both sides of the plate. Buzz ran an electric shaver over his face, squirted cologne at his armpits and brushed a chunk of pie crust off his necktie. Filthy rich always made him nervous; filthy rich and fruit was a combo he'd never worked before.

Audrey Anders stuck with him on the ride over; he pretended his Old Spice was her Chanel #5 in just the right places. 419 South Rimpau was a Spanish mansion fronted by a huge expanse of grass dotted with rose gardens; Buzz parked and rang the bell, hoping for a single-o play: no witnesses if it got ugly.

A peephole opened, then the door. A peaches-and-cream blonde about twenty-five had her hand on the knob, wholesome pulchritude in a tartan skirt and pink button-down shirt. "Hello. Are you the insurance man here to see Daddy?"

Buzz pulled his jacket over the butt of his .38. "Yes, I am. In private, please. No man likes to discuss such grave matters in the presence of his family."

The girl nodded, led Buzz through the foyer to a book-lined study and left him there with the door ajar. He noticed a liquor sideboard and thought about a quick one—a mid-afternoon bracer might give him some extra charm. Then "Phil, what's this in-private stuff?" took it out of his hands.

A short pudgy man, bald with a fringe, had pushed the door open. Buzz held out his badge; the man said, "What is this?"

"DA's Bureau, Mr. Hartshorn. I just wanted to keep your family out of it."

Charles Hartshorn closed the door and leaned against it. "Is this about Duane Lindenaur?"

Buzz drew a blank on the name, then remembered it from yesterday's late-edition *Tattler*: Lindenaur was a victim in the homo killings Dudley Smith told him about—the job the Sheriff's dick they just co-opted was set to run. "No, sir. I'm with the Grand Jury Division, and we're investigating the Santa Monica Police. We need to know if they abused you when they raided the Knight in Armor back in '44."

Veins throbbed in Hartshorn's forehead; his voice was boardroom-lawyer cold. "I don't believe you. Duane Lindenaur attempted to extort money from me nine years ago—spurious allegations that he threatened to leak to my family. I dealt with the man legally then, and a few days ago I read that he had been murdered. I've been expecting the police at my door, and now you show up. Am I a suspect in Lindenaur's death?"

Buzz said, "I don't know and I don't care. This is about the Santa Monica Police."

"No, it is not. This pertains to the spurious allegations Duane Lindenaur made against me and the non sequitur of my happening to be in a cocktail lounge frequented by certain not respectable people when a police raid occurred. I have an alibi for the newspapers' estimated time of Duane Lindenaur's and the other man's deaths, and I want you to corroborate it without involving my family. If you so much as breathe a word to my wife and daughter, I will have your badge and your head. Do you understand?"

The lawyer's tone had gotten calmer; his face was one massive contortion. Buzz tried diplomacy again. "Reynolds Loftis, Mr. Hartshorn. He was rousted with you. Tell me what you know about him, and I'll tell the Sheriff's detective who's workin' the Lindenaur case to leave you alone, that you're alibied up. That sound nice to you?"

Hartshorn folded his arms over his chest. "I don't know any Reynolds Loftis and I don't make deals with grubby little policemen who reek of cheap cologne. Leave my home now."

Hartshorn's "Reynolds" was all wrong. Buzz moved to the sideboard, filled a glass with whiskey and walked up to the lawyer with it. "For your nerves, Charlie. I don't want you kickin' off a heart attack on me."

"Get out of my home, you grubby little worm."

Buzz dropped the glass, grabbed Hartshorn's neck and slammed him against the wall. "You're humpin' the wrong boy, counselor. *The last boy around here you want to fuck with.* Now here's the drill: you and Reynolds Loftis or I go into the living room and tell your little girl that daddy sucks cock at the Westlake Park men's room and takes it up the ass on Selma and Las Palmas. And you breathe a word to anybody that I leaned on you, and I'll have you in *Confidential* magazine porkin' nigger drag queens. *Do you understand?"*

Hartshorn was beet red and spilling tears. Buzz let go of his neck, saw the imprint of a big ham hand and made that hand a fist. Hartshorn tremble-walked to the sideboard and picked up the whiskey decanter. Buzz swung at the wall, pulling the punch at the last second. "Spill on Loftis, goddamnit. Make it easy so I can get the fuck out of here."

Glass on glass chimed, followed by hard breathing and silence. Buzz stared at the wall. Hartshorn spoke, his voice dead hollow. "Reynolds and I were just a ... fling. We met at a party a Belgian man, a movie director, threw. The man was very au courant, and he threw lots of parties at clubs for our ... his kind. It never got serious with Reynolds because there was a screenwriter he had been seeing, and some third man they were disturbed over. I was the odd man ... so it never ..."

Buzz turned and saw Hartshorn slumped in a chair, warming his hands on a whiskey glass. "What else you got?"

"Nothing. I never saw Reynolds after that time at the Knight in Armor. Who are you going to—"

"Nobody, Charlie. Nobody's gonna know. I'll just say I got word that Loftis is ..."

"Oh God, is this the witchhunts again?"

Buzz exited to the sound of the sad bastard weeping.

* * *

Rain had hit while he was applying the strongarm—hard needle sheets of it, the kind of deluge that threatened to melt the foothills into the ocean and sieve out half the L.A. Basin. Buzz laid three to one that Hartshorn would keep his mouth shut; two to one that more cop work would drive him batshit; even money that dinner at the Nickodell and the evening at home writing up a report on the day's dirt was the ticket. He could smell the queer's sweat on himself, going stale with his own sweat; he felt a beaucoup case of the sucker punch blues coming on. Halfway to the office, he cracked the window for air and a rain bracer, changed directions and drove to his place.

Home was the Longview Apartments at Beverly and Mariposa, four rooms on the sixth floor, southern exposure, the pad furnished with leftovers from RKO movie sets. Buzz pulled into the garage, ditched his car and took the elevator up. And sitting by his door was Audrey Anders in a rain-spattered, sequin-spangled, gold lamé gown, a wet mink coat in her lap. She was using it as an ashtray; when she saw Buzz, she said, "Last year's model. Mickey'll get me a new one," and stubbed her cigarette out on the collar.

Buzz helped Audrey to her feet, holding her hands just a beat too long. "Did I really get this lucky?"

"Don't count your chickens. Lavonne Cohen took a trip with her mah-jongg club and Mickey thinks it's open season on me.

Tonight was supposed to be the Mocambo, the Grove and late drinks with the Gersteins. I pulled a snit and escaped."

"I thought you and Mickey were in love."

"Love has its flip side. Did you know you're the only Turner Meeks in the Central White Pages?"

Buzz unlocked the door. Audrey walked in, dropped her mink on the floor and scoped the living room. The furnishings included leather couches and easy chairs from *London Holiday* and zebra head wall mounts from *Jungle Bwana*; the swinging doors leading to the bedroom were scavenged off the saloon set of *Rage on the Rio Grande*. The carpeting was lime green and purple striped—the bedspread one the Amazon huntress lollygagged on in *Song of the Pampas*. Audrey said, "Meeks, did you *pay* for this?"

"Gifts from a rich uncle. You want a drink?"

"I don't drink."

"Why not?"

"My father, sister and two brothers are drunks, so I thought I'd give it a pass."

Buzz was thinking she looked good—but not as good as she did with no makeup and Mickey's shirt hanging to her knees. "And you became a stripper?"

Audrey sat down, kicked off her shoes and warmed her feet on the mink. "Yes, and don't ask me to do the tassel trick for you, because I won't. Meeks, what *is* the matter with you? I thought you'd be glad to see me."

He could still smell the queer. "I coldcocked a guy today. It was shitty."

Audrey wriggled her toes, making the coat jump. "So? That's what you do for a living."

"The guys I usually do it to give me more of a fight."

"So you're telling me it's all a game?"

He'd told Howard once that the only women worth having were the ones who had your number. "There's gotta be somethin' we're better at than buttin' heads and askin' each other questions."

The Va Va Voom Girl kicked the mink up in her lap. "Is the bedroom this outré?"

Buzz laughed. "*Casbah Nocturne* and *Paradise Is Pink*. That tell you anything?"

"That's another question. Ask *me* something provocative."

Buzz took off his jacket, unhooked his holster and threw it on a chair. "Okay. Does Mickey keep a tail on you?"

Audrey shook her head. "No. I made him stop it. It made me feel cheap."

"Where's your car?"

"Three blocks away."

All green lights to make his best stupid move an epic. "You got it all figured out."

Audrey said, "I didn't think you'd say no." She waved her mink coat. "And I brought a towel for the morning."

Buzz thought, RIP Turner Prescott Meeks, 1906–1950. He took a deep breath, sucked in his flab, pushed through the saloon doors and started peeling. Audrey came in and laughed at the bed—pink satin spread, pink canopy, pink embroidered gargoyles as foot posts. She got naked with a single flick of a clasp; Buzz felt his legs buckling as her breasts bobbed free. Audrey came to him and slipped off his tie, undid his shirt buttons, loosened his belt. He pried his shoes and socks off standing up; his shirt hit the floor via a bad case of the shivers. Audrey laughed and traced the goosebumps on his arms, then ran her hands over the parts of himself he couldn't stand: his melon gut, his side rolls, the knife scars running up into his chest hair. When she started licking him there he knew she was okay on it; he picked her up to show her how strong he was—his legs almost blowing it—and put her down on the bed. He got out of his trousers and boxers under his own steam and lay down beside her—and in a half second she was all arms and legs around him, face to face and mouth open, pushing up against him like he was everything she'd ever wanted.

He kissed her—soft, hard, soft; he rubbed his nose into her neck and smelled Ivory Soap—not the perfume he'd played pretend with. He took her breasts in his hands and pinched the nipples, remembering everything every cop had told him about the headliner at the Burbank Burlesque. Audrey made different noises for each part of her he touched; he kissed and tongued between her legs and got one big noise. The big noise got bigger and bigger; her legs and arms went spastic. Her going so crazy got him almost there, and he went inside her so he could be part of it. Audrey's hips pushing off the covers made him burst going in; he held on and she held him, and he gave her all his strength to smother their aftershocks. Half his weight, she was still able to push him up as she kept coming—and he grabbed her head and buried his head in her hair until he went limp and she quit fighting him.

Pink satin sheets and sweat bound them together. Buzz rolled over on his side, hooking a finger around Audrey's wrist so they'd keep on touching while he got his breath. Eight years without a cigarette and he was panting like a track dog—and she was lying there all still and calm, a vein on the back of her arm tapping his finger the only thing that said she was still racing inside. His chest heaved; he tried to think of something to say; Audrey made finger tracks on his knife scars. She said, "This could get complicated."

Buzz got his wind. "That mean you're thinkin' angles already?"

Audrey made like her nails were animals' claws and pretended to scratch him. "I just like to know where I stand."

The moment was slipping away from him—like it wasn't worth the danger. Buzz grabbed Audrey's hands. "So that means we're lookin' at a next time?"

"You didn't have to ask. I'd have told you in a minute or so."

"I like to know where I stand, too."

Audrey laughed and pulled her hands away. "You stand guilty, Meeks. You got me thinking the other day. So whatever happens, it's your fault."

Buzz said, "Sweetie, don't underestimate Mickey. He's sugar and spice with women and kids, but he kills people."

"He knows I'll leave him sooner or later."

"No, he doesn't. He figures you're an ex-stripper, a shiksa, you're thirty-somethin' and you've got no place to go. You give him a little bit of grief, maybe it gets his dick hard. But you stroll, that's somethin' else."

She couldn't meet his eyes. Buzz said, "Sweetie, where would you go?"

Audrey pulled a pillow down and hugged it, giving him both baby browns. "I've got some money saved. A bunch. I'm going to buy some grove property in the Valley and bankroll rentals on a shopping center. They're the coming thing, Meeks. Another ten thousand and I can get in on the ground floor with thirty-five acres."

Like his acreage: fourteen dollars per on the sure thing that should have made him rich. "Where'd you get the money?"

"I saved it."

"From Mickey's handouts?"

Audrey surprised him by chucking the pillow away and poking his chest. "Are you jealous, *sweetie*?"

Buzz grabbed her finger and gave it a little love bite. "Maybe just a tad."

"Well, don't be. Mickey's all wrapped up in his union business and his drug thing with Jack Dragna, and I know how to play this game. Don't you worry."

"Sweetie, you better. Because it is surely for keeps."

"Meeks, I wish you'd quit talking about Mickey. You'll have me looking under the bed in a minute."

Buzz thought of the .38 in the other room and the fruit lawyer with the bruised neck and tear-mottled cheeks. "I'm glad bein' with you is dangerous. It feels good."

18

ACTING SUPERVISOR Upshaw.

Task Force Boss.

Skipper.

Danny stood in the empty Hollywood Station muster room, waiting to address *his* three men on *his* homicide case—running the titles down in *the* single place where the Brenda Allen job caused the most grief. A cartoon tacked to the notice board spelled it out: Mickey Cohen wearing a Jew skullcap with a dollar sign affixed to the top, dangling two uniformed Sheriff's deputies on puppet strings. A balloon elaborated his thoughts: *Boy, did I give it to the LAPD! It's good I got the County cops to wipe my ass for me!* Danny saw little holes all over Mickey's face; L.A.'s number-one hoodlum had been used as a dartboard.

There was a lectern and blackboard at the front of the room; Danny found chalk and wrote "Deputy D. Upshaw, LASD," in boldface letters. He positioned himself behind the stand like Doc Layman with his forensics class and forced himself to think of his other assignment so he wouldn't get antsy when it came time to lay down the law to *his* men, three detectives older and much more experienced than he. That job was coming on like a snooze and a snore, maybe a little shot of elixir to keep bad thoughts down and business on; it was why he was standing triumphant in a spot where the County police were loathed more than baby rapers. The deal was like pinching yourself to make sure the great things that were happening weren't just a dream—and he pinched himself for the ten millionth time since Lieutenant Mal Considine made his offer.

Dudley Smith had called him at home yesterday afternoon, interrupting a long day of nursing watered-down highballs and working on his file. The Irishman told him to meet him and Considine at West Hollywood Station; the fix was in via Ellis Loew, with the temporary detachment order approved by both Chief Worton and Sheriff Biscailuz. He'd brushed his teeth, gargled and forced down a sandwich before he met them—anticipating one question and building a lie to field it. Since they'd already told him he would be planted around Variety International Pictures and they knew he'd incurred bossman Gerstein's wrath there, he had to convince them that only the gate guard, the rewrite man and Gerstein saw him in his cop capacity. It was Considine's *first* question—and a residue of bourbon calm helped him brazen it out. Smith bought it whole, Considine secondhand, when he ran his prerehearsed spiel on how he would completely alter his haircut and clothes to fit the role of Commie idealist. Smith gave him a stack of UAES paperwork to take home and study and made him scan a batch of psychiatric reports in their presence; then it was hard brass tacks.

His job was to approach UAES's suspected weak link—a promiscuous woman named Claire De Haven—gain entrance to the union's strategy meetings and find out what they were planning. Why haven't they called a strike? Do the meetings involve the actual advocacy of armed revolt? Is there planned subversion of motion picture content? Did the UAES brain trust fall for Considine's sub-rosa move—planting newspaper and radio pieces that said the grand jury investigation had gone down—and just how strongly is UAES connected to the Communist Party?

Career maker.

"You'll be a lieutenant before you're thirty."

"There's a woman you'll have to get next to, lad. You might have to fuck the pants off of her."

A bludgeon to smash his nightmares.

He felt cocky when he left the briefing, taking the nonpsychiatric reports under his arm, promising to report for a second confab this afternoon at City Hall. He went back to his apartment, called a dozen dental labs that Karen Hiltscher hadn't tapped and got zilch, read a dozen homosexual homicide histories without drinking or thinking of the Chateau Marmont. He then started feeling *very* cocky, took his 2307 Tamarind blood scrapings to the USC chemistry building and bribed a forensics classmate into typing them, hoping he could combine the wall spray pictures with the victims' names, reconstruct and get another fix on his man. The classmate didn't even blink at the bloodwork and did his tests; Danny took home data and put it together with the photographs.

Three victims, three different blood types—the risk of showing illegally obtained evidence was worth it. The Marty Goines AB+ blood matched the sloppiest of the wall sprays; he was the first victim, and the killer had not yet perfected his interior decorating technique. George Wiltsie and Duane Lindenaur, types O– and B+, had their blood spat out *separately*, Wiltsie in designs less intricate, less polished. Conclusions reinforced and conclusions gained: Marty Goines was a spur-of-the-moment victim, and the killer went at him in a total rage. Although filled with suicidal bravado—as witnessed by his bringing victims two and three to Goines' apartment—he had to have had an ace reason for choosing Mad Marty, which could be one of three:

He knew the man and wanted to kill him out of hatred—a well-defined personal motive;

He knew the man and found him a satisfactory victim based on convenience and/or blood lust;

He did not know Marty Goines previously, but was intimately acquainted with the darktown jazz strip, and trusted himself to find a victim there.

Have *his* men recanvass the area.

On Wiltsie/Lindenaur:

The killer bit and gnawed and swallowed and sprayed Wiltsie's blood first, because he was the one who most attracted him. The relative refinement of the Lindenaur blood designs denoted the killer's satisfaction and satiation; Wiltsie, a known male prostitute, was his primary sex fix.

Tonight, double-agency sanctioned, he'd brace talent agent/procurer Felix Gordean, connected circumstantially to Wiltsie's squeeze Duane Lindenaur—and try for a handle on who the men were.

Danny checked the clock: 8:53; the other officers should be arriving at 9:00. He decided to stick behind the lectern, got out his notepad and went over the assignments he'd laid out. A moment later, he heard a discreet throat-clearing and looked up.

A stocky blond man, thirty-fivish, was walking toward him. Danny remembered something Dudley Smith said: a Homicide Bureau "protégé" of his would be on the "team" to grease things and make sure the other men "fell in line." He pasted on a smile and stuck out his hand; the man gave him a hard shake. "Mike Breuning. You're Danny Upshaw?"

"Yes. Is it Sergeant?"

"I'm a sergeant, but call me Mike. Dudley sends regards and regrets—the station boss here says Gene Niles has to work the case with us. He was the catching officer, and the Bureau can't spare any other men. C'est la vie, I always say."

Danny winced, remembering his lies to Niles. "Who's the fourth man?"

"One of your guys, Jack Shortell, a squadroom sergeant from the San Dimas Substation. Look, Upshaw, I'm sorry about Niles. I know he hates the Sheriff's and he thinks the City end of the job should be shitcanned, but Dudley said to tell you, 'Remember, you're the boss.' Dudley likes you, by the way. He thinks you're a comer."

His take on Smith was that he enjoyed hurting people. "That's great. Tell the Lieutenant thanks for me."

"Call him Dudley, and thank him yourself—you guys are partners on that Commie thing now. Look, here's the others."

Danny looked. Gene Niles was walking to the front of the room, giving a tall man with wire-frame glasses a wide berth, like all Sheriff's personnel were disease carriers. He sat down in the first row of chairs and got out a notepad and pen—no amenities, no acknowledgment of rank. The tall man came up and gave Breuning and Danny quick shakes. He said, "I'm Jack Shortell."

He was at least fifty years old. Danny pointed to his name on the blackboard. "A pleasure, Sergeant."

"All mine, Deputy. Your first big job?"

"Yes."

"I've worked half a dozen, so don't be too proud to yelp if you get stuck."

"I won't be."

Breuning and Shortell sat down a string of chairs over from Niles; Danny pointed to a table in front of the blackboard—three stacks of LAPD/LASD paper on the Goines/Wiltsie/Lindenaur snuffs. Nothing speculative from his personal file; nothing on the lead of Felix Gordean; nothing on Duane Lindenaur as a former extortionist. The men got out cigarettes and matches and fired up; Danny put the lectern between him and them and grabbed his first command.

"Most of what we've got is in there, gentlemen. Autopsy reports, log sheets, my summary reports as catching officer on the first victim. LAPD didn't see fit to forensic the apartment where the victims were killed, so there's some potential leads blown. Of the officers working the two separate jobs, I've been the only one to turn up hard leads. I wrote out a separate chronology on what I got, and included carbons in with your official stuff. I'll run through the key points for you now."

Danny paused and looked straight at Gene Niles, who'd been staring hot pokers at him since he tweaked LAPD for fumbling the forensic ball. Niles would not move his eyes; Danny braced his legs into the lectern for some more frost. "On the night of January one, I canvassed South Central Avenue, the vicinity where the car that was used to transport Martin Goines' body was stolen from. Eyewitnesses placed Goines with a tall, gray-haired, middle-aged man, and we know from the autopsy reports that the killer has O+ blood—typed from his semen. Goines was killed by a heroin overjolt, Wiltsie and Lindenaur were poisoned by a seco-barbital/strychnine compound. All three men were mutilated in the same manner—cuts from an implement known as a zoot stick, bites with the dentures the killer was wearing all over their abdominal areas. The dentures could not possibly be duplicates of human teeth. He could be wearing plastic teeth or duplicates of animal teeth or steel teeth—but not human ones."

Danny took his eyes off Niles and scoped all three of his men. Breuning was smoking nervously; Shortell was taking notes; Big Gene was burning cigarette holes in the desktop. Danny looked at him exclusively and dropped his first lie. "So we've got a tall, gray-haired, middle-aged white man with O+ blood who can cop horse and barbs, knows some chemistry and can hotwire cars. When he slammed the horse into Goines, he stuffed a towel into his mouth, which means that he knew the bastard's heart arteries would pop and he'd vomit blood. So maybe he's got medical knowledge. I'm betting he knows how to make dentures, and yesterday I got a tip from a snitch of mine: Goines was putting together a burglary gang. When you read my summary reports you'll see that I questioned a vagrant named Chester Brown, a jazz musician. He knew Marty Goines back in the early '40s and stated that he was a burglar then. Brown mentioned a youth with a burned face who was Goines' KA, but I don't think he fits in the picture. So add 'burglar possible' to our scenario, and I'll tell you what we're going to do.

"Sergeant Shortell, you'll be making phone queries on the dental work lead. I've got a very long list of dental labs, and I want you to call them and get to whoever keeps employment records. You've got solid elimination stuff to go with: blood type, physical description, the dates of the killings. Also ask about dental workers who aroused *any* kind of suspicion at their workplace, and if your instincts tell you someone is suspicious but you've got no blood type, call for jail records or Selective Service records or hospital records—or call any place else you can think of where you can get the information."

Shortell had nodded along, writing it down; Danny gave him a nod and zeroed in on Niles and Breuning. "Sergeant Breuning and Sergeant Niles, you are to check every City, County and individual municipality Vice and sex crime file for biting aberrations and eliminate potential suspects against our man's blood type and description. I want the files of every registered sex offender in the L.A. area gone through. I want a more thorough background check on Wiltsie and Lindenaur, and Wiltsie's male prostitution jacket pulled for KAs with our guy's stats. I want you to cross-check the sex information against the burglary files of middle-aged white men city- and countywide, and look for arrest reports on youth burglars with burn marks going back to '43. For every possible you get, I want a set of mugshots.

"There's an approach that I've let lie because of jurisdictional problems, and that's where the mugs come in. I want every known heroin and goofball pusher to see those pictures—hard muscle shakedowns, especially in jigtown. I want you to shake down *your* snitches for information, call every Vice Squad commander in every division, City and County, and tell them to have their officers check with their snitches for fruit bar scuttlebutt. Who's tall, gray, middle-aged and has a biting fetish? And I want you to call County and State Parole for dope on violent loony bin parolees. I want Griffith Park, South Central and the area where Goines' body was dumped thoroughly recanvassed."

Breuning groaned; Niles spoke for the first time. "You want a lot, Upshaw. You know that?"

Danny leaned over the lectern. "It's an important case, and you'll share credit for the collar."

Niles snorted. "It's homo horseshit, we'll never get him, and if we did, so what? Do you care how many queers he cuts? I don't."

Danny flinched at "homo" and "queers"; holding a stare on Niles made his eyes flicker, and he realized that he hadn't used the word "homosexual" in his profile of the killer. "I'm a policeman, so I care. And the job is good for our careers."

"For *your* career, sonny. You've got some deal with some Jew DA downtown."

"Niles, shitcan it!"

Danny looked around to see who shouted, felt his throat vibrating and saw that he'd gripped the lectern with blue-white fingers. Niles evil-eyed him; Danny couldn't match the stare. He thought of the rest of his pitch and delivered it, a trace of a flutter in his voice. "Our last approach is pretty obscure. All three men were slashed by zoot sticks, which Doc Layman says Riot Squad cops used to use. There are no zoot stick homicides on record, and most zoot stick assaults were by Caucasians on Mexicans and not reported. Again, check with your informants on this and make your eliminations against blood type and description."

Jack Shortell was still scribbling; Mike Breuning was looking up at him strangely, eyes narrowed to slits. Danny turned back to Niles. "Got that, Sergeant?"

Niles had another cigarette going; he was scorching his desk with the tip. "You're really in tight with the Jews, huh, Upshaw? What's Mickey Kike paying you?"

"More than Brenda paid you."

Shortell laughed; Breuning's strange look broke into a smile. Niles threw his cigarette on the floor and stamped it out. "Why didn't you report your lead on Marty Goines' pad, hotshot? What the fuck was happening there?"

Danny's hands snapped a piece of wood off the lectern. He said, "Dismissed," with some other man's voice.

* * *

Considine and Smith were waiting for him in Ellis Loew's office; big Dudley was hanging up a phone with the words, "Thank you, lad." Danny sat down at Loew's conference table, sensing the "lad" was flunky Mike Breuning with a report on his briefing.

Considine was busy writing on a yellow legal pad; Smith came over and gave him the glad hand. "How was your first morning as Homicide brass, lad?"

Danny knew he knew—verbatim. "It went well, Lieutenant."

"Call me Dudley. You'll be outranking me in a few years, and you should get used to patronizing men much your senior."

"Okay, Dudley."

Smith laughed. "Lad, you're a heartbreaker. Isn't he a heart-breaker, Malcolm?"

Considine slid his chair next to Danny. "Let's hope Claire De Haven thinks so. How are you, Deputy?"

Danny said, "I'm fine, Lieutenant," picking up something wrong between his superiors—contempt or plain tension working two ways—Dudley Smith in the catbird seat.

"Good. The briefing went well, then?"

"Yes."

"Have you read that paperwork we gave you?"

"I've got it practically memorized."

Considine tapped his pad. "Excellent. We'll start now, then."

Dudley Smith sat at the far end of the table; Danny geared his brain to listen and *think* before speaking. Considine said, "Here's some rules for you to follow.

"One, you drive your civilian car everywhere, on your decoy job *and* your homicide job. We're building an identity for you, and we'll have a script ready by late tonight. You're going to be a lefty who's been living in New York for years, so we've got New York plates for your car, and we've got a whole personal background for you to memorize. When you go by your various station houses to check reports or whatever, park on the street at least two blocks away, and when you leave here, go downstairs to the barbershop. Al, Mayor Bowron's barber, is going to get rid of that crew cut of yours and cut your hair so that you look less like a cop. I need your trouser, shirt, jacket, sweater and shoe sizes, and I want you to meet me at midnight at West Hollywood Station. I'll have your new Commie wardrobe and script ready, and we'll finalize your approach. Got it?"

Danny nodded, pulled a sheet of paper off Considine's pad and wrote down his clothing sizes. Dudley Smith said, "You wear those clothes everywhere, lad. On your queer job, too. We don't want your new Pinko friends seeing you on the street looking like a dapper young copper. Malcolm, give our fair Daniel some De Haven lines to parry. Let's see how he fields them."

Considine spoke directly to Danny. "Deputy, I've met Claire De Haven, and I think that for a woman she's a tough piece of work. She's promiscuous, she may be an alcoholic and she may take drugs. We've got another man checking out her background and the background of some other Reds, so we'll know more on her soon. I spoke to the woman once, and I got the impression that she thrives on banter and one-upmanship. I think that it sexually excites her, and I know she's attracted to men of your general appearance. So we're going to try a little exercise now. I'll feed you lines that I think would be typical of Claire De Haven, you try to top them. Ready?"

Danny shut his eyes for better concentration. "Go."

"'But some people call us Communists. Doesn't that bother you?'"

"That old scarlet letter routine doesn't wash with me."

"Good. Let's follow up on that. 'Oh, really? Fascist politicians have ruined many politically enlightened people by slandering us as subversives.'"

Danny grabbed a line from a musical he saw with Karen Hiltscher. "I've always had a thing for redheads, baby."

Considine laughed. "Good, but don't call De Haven 'baby,' she'd consider it patronizing. Here's a good one. 'I find it hard to believe that you'd leave the Teamsters for us.'"

Easy. "Mickey Cohen's comedy routines would drive anybody out."

"Good, Deputy, but in your decoy role you'd never get close to Cohen, so you wouldn't know that about him."

Danny got a brainstorm: the dirty joke sheets and pulp novels his fellow jailers passed around when he worked the main County lockup. "Give me some sex banter, Lieutenant."

Considine flipped to the next note page. "'But I'm thirteen years older than you.'"

Danny made his tone satirical. "A grain of sand in our sea of passion."

Dudley Smith howled; Considine chuckled and said, "You just walk into my life when I'm engaged to be married. I don't know that I trust you."

"Claire, there's only one reason *to* trust me. And that's that around you I don't trust myself."

"Great delivery, Deputy. Here's a curveball: 'Are you here for me or the cause?'"

Extra easy: the hero of a paperback he'd read working night watch. "I want it all. That's all I know, that's all I want to know."

Considine slid the notebook away. "Let's improvise on that. 'How can you look at things so simplistically?'"

His mental gears were click-click-clicking now; Danny quit digging for lines and flew solo. "Claire, there's the fascists and us, and there's you and me. Why do *you* always complicate things?"

Considine, coming on like a femme fatale. "'You know I'm capable of eating you whole.'"

"I love your teeth."

"'I love your eyes.'"

"Claire, are we fighting the fascists or auditing Physiology 101?"

"'When you're forty, I'll be fifty-three. Will you still want me then?'"

Danny, aping Considine's vamp contralto. "We'll be dancing jigs together in Moscow, sweetheart."

"Not so satirical on the political stuff, I'm not sure I trust her sense of humor on that. Let's get dirty. 'It's so *good* with you.'"

"The others were just girls, Claire. You're my first woman."

"'How many times have you used that line?'"

Aw-shucks laughter—à la a pussy hound deputy he knew. "Every time I sleep with a woman over thirty-five."

"'Have there been many?'"

"Just a few thousand."

"'The cause needs men like you.'"

"If there were more women like you around, there'd be millions of us."

"'What's that supposed to mean?'"

"That I really like you, Claire."

"'Why?'"

"You drink like one of the boys, you know Marx chapter and verse, and you've got great legs."

Dudley Smith started clapping; Danny opened his eyes and felt them misting. Mal Considine smiled. "She does have great legs. Go get your haircut, Deputy. I'll see you at midnight."

* * *

Mayor Bowron's barber shaped Danny's outgrown crew cut into a modified pompadour that changed the whole set of his face. Before, he looked like what he was: a dark-haired, dark-eyed Anglo-Saxon, a policeman who wore suits or sports jacket/slacks combos everywhere. Now he looked slightly Bohemian, slightly Latin, more of a dude. The new hairstyle offset his clothes rakishly; any cop who didn't know him and spotted the gun bulge under his left armpit would shake him down on the spot, figuring him for some kind of outlaw muscle. The look and his banter improvisations made him feel cocky, like the Chateau Marmont was a fluke that nailing Claire De Haven would disprove once and for all. Danny drove back to Hollywood Station to prepare for his second pass at the Marmont and his first shot at Felix Gordean.

He went straight to the squadroom. Mickey Cohen was vilified on the walls: cartoons of him stuffing cash in Sheriff Biscailuz' pockets, cracking a whip at a team of sled dogs in LASD uniforms, poking innocent citizens in the ass with a switchblade sticking out of his prayer cap. Danny fielded an assortment of fisheyes, found the records alcove and hit the sex offender files—shaking hands with the beast—fuel for his Gordean interrogation.

There were six cabinets full of them: musty folders stuffed with occurrence reports, mugshots clipped to the first inner page. The filing was not alphabetical, and there was no logic to the penal code placements—homosexual occurrences were lumped with straight exhibitionism and child molestation; misdemeanants and felons brushed against each other. Danny scanned the first two files in the top cabinet and snapped why the system was so sloppy: the men on the squad wanted this wretched data out of sight and out of mind. Knowing he *had* to look, he dug in.

Most of the stuff was homo.

The Broadway Department Store on Hollywood and Vine had a fourth-floor men's room known as "Cocksucker's Paradise." Enterprising deviants had bored holes through the walls of the toilet stalls, enabling the occupants of adjoining shitters to get together for oral copulation. If you parked on a Griffith Park roadway with a blue handkerchief tied to your radio aerial, you were a queer. The corner of Selma and Las Palmas was where ex-cons with a penchant for anal rape and young boys congregated. The Latin inscription on the Pall Mall cigarette pack—"In Hoc Signo Vinces"—translated as "With this sign we shall conquer"—was a tentative means of homo identification—a sure thing when coupled with wearing a green shirt on a Thursday. The muscular Mex transvestite who blew sailors behind Grauman's Chinese was known as "Donkey Dan" or "Donkey Danielle" because he/she possessed a thirteen-inch dick. The E-Z Cab Company was run by homos, and they would deliver you a boy, queer smut films, extra KY Jelly, bennies, or your favorite liquor twenty-four hours a day.

Danny kept reading, weak in the knees and stomach, learning. When he saw a 1900–1910 birthdate or 6' and up on a male Caucasian's yellow sheet, he checked the mugstrip; every man he locked eyes with looked too ugly and pathetic to be *his* man—and prowling the ensuing arrest reports for blood types always proved him right. Thomas (NMI) Milnes, 6'2", 11/4/07, exposed himself to little boys and begged the arresting officers to rubber-hose him for it; Cletus Wardell Hanson, 6'1", 4/29/04, carried a power drill with him to pave the way for new blow job territory, restaurant men's rooms his speciality. In stir, he put his ass on the line: day room gang bangs, a pack of cigarettes per man. Willis (NMI) Burdette, 6'5", 12/1/1900, was a syphilitic street whore, beaten brainless by a half dozen johns he'd passed the disease to. Darryl "Lavender Blue" Wishnick, 6', 3/10/03, orchestrated orgies in the hills surrounding the Hollywood Sign and liked to pork pretty boys dressed in the attire of the United States armed forces.

Four hours in, four cabinets down. Danny felt his stomach settling around hunger pangs and the desire for a drink he usually got in the mid-afternoon. That was comforting; so was the new hairstyle he kept running his fingers through, and the new embellishments on his new identity that he'd mention to Considine tonight: nothing at his apartment should seem settled—he was just in from New York; he should leave his piece, cuffs and ID buzzer at home when he played Commie. Everything in the first four drawers was wrong for his man, not applicable to his bad moments outside Felix Gordean's window. Then he hit cabinet five.

This set of files was in some kind of order—"No Arraignments," "Charges Dropped" or "Check Agst. Future Arrests" stamped on the front of each folder. Danny read through the first handful and got straight male-on-male sex that went to arrest but not to court: coitus interruptus in parked cars; male shack jobs snitched by shocked landladies; a toilet assignation where the theater proprietor blew the whistle, then punked out for fear of bad publicity. Straight sex recounted in straight copese: abbreviations, technical terms for the acts, a few humorous asides by waggish Vice officers.

Danny felt shakes coming on. The files carried twin yellow sheets—two mugshot strips, both sex participants in black and white. He eyed the pages for birthdates and physical stats, but kept returning to the mugs, superimposing them against each other, playing with the faces—making them prettier, less con-wise. After a half dozen files, he fell into sync: a look at the photos, a scan of the arrest report, back to the mugs and the action visualized with prettified versions of the two plug-uglies clipped to the first page. Mouths on mouths; mouths to crotches; sodomy, fellatio, soixante-neuf, a Man Camera smut job, a little voice going, "It's for the investigation" when some detail hit him so large that his stomach queased to the point where he thought his bowels would go. *No* middle-aged tall guy's stats to make him stop and think; just the pictures, rapid fire, like nickelodeon flickers.

Bedspreads wet from fucking.

A naked blond man catching his breath, veins pumping in his legs.

Zoom-in shots of awful insertions.

"It's for the investigation."

Danny broke the string of images—making the pretty ones all gray, all forty-fivish, all his killer. Knowing the killer only had sex to hurt helped put the brakes on his fantasies; Danny got his legs back and saw that he'd twisted a lank of his new hairdo clean off his scalp. He slammed the cabinet shut; he recalled queer vernacular and interposed it into the questions he'd ask Felix Gordean—himself as a smart young detective who came prepared, who'd talk on the level of anyone—even if it was wrong sex to a queer pimp.

Cop to voyeur and back again.

Danny drove home, showered and checked his closet for the best suit to go with his new hair, settling on a black worsted Karen Hiltscher had bought him—too stylish, too tapered and skinny in the lapels. When he put it on, he saw that it made him look dangerous—and the narrow shoulders outlined his .45 revolver. After two shots and a mouthwash chaser, he drove to the Chateau Marmont.

The night was damp and chilly, hinting of rain; music echoed through the Marmont's inner courtyard—string swells, boogie jumps and odd ballad tremolos. Danny took the footpath to 7941, chafing from the fit of Karen's suit. 7941 was brightly lit, the velvet curtains he'd peered through open wide; the dance floor of three nights before gleamed behind a large picture window. Danny fidgeted with his jacket and rang the bell.

Chimes sounded; the door opened. A small man with a short dark beard and perfectly layered thin hair stood there. He was wearing a tuxedo with a tartan cummerbund, dangling a brandy snifter against his leg. Danny smelled the same fifty-year-old Napoleon he bought himself once a year as his reward for spending Christmas with his mother. The man said, "Yes? Are you with the Sheriff's?"

Danny saw that he'd unbuttoned his coat, leaving his gun exposed. "Yes. Are you Felix Gordean?"

"Yes, and I don't appreciate bureaucratic faux pas. Come in."

Gordean stood aside; Danny walked in and ran eye circuits of the room where he'd glimpsed men dancing and kissing. Gordean moved to a bookcase, reached behind the top shelf and returned with an envelope. Danny caught an address: 1611 South Bonnie Brae, the Sheriff's Central Vice operations front, where recalcitrant bookies got strong-armed, recalcitrant hookers got serviced, protections kickbacks got tallied. Gordean said, "I always mail it in. Tell Lieutenant Matthews I don't appreciate in-person calls with their implied threat of additional charges."

Danny let Gordean's hand hover in front of him—buffed nails, an emerald ring and probably close to a grand in cash. "I'm not a bagman, I'm a detective working a triple homicide."

Gordean smiled and held the envelope down at his side. "Then let me initiate you regarding my relationship with your Department, Mr.—"

"It's Deputy Upshaw."

"Mr. Upshaw, I cooperate fully with the Sheriff's Department, in exchange for certain courtesies, chief among them your contacting me by telephone when you require information. Do you understand?"

Danny got a strange sensation: Gordean's frost was making him frosty. "Yes, but as long as I'm here ..."

"As long as you're here, tell me how I can assist you. I've never been questioned on a triple homicide before, and frankly I'm curious."

Danny speedballed his three victims' names. "Martin Goines, George Wiltsie and Duane Lindenaur. Dead. Raped and hacked to death."

Gordean's reaction was more frost. "I've never heard of a Martin Goines. I brokered introductions for George Wiltsie throughout the years, and I think George mentioned Duane Lindenaur to me."

Danny felt like he was treading on an iceberg; he knew going in for shock value wouldn't play. "Duane Lindenaur was an extortionist, Mr. Gordean. He met and attempted to extort money from a man named Charles Hartshorn—who he allegedly met at a party you threw."

Gordean smoothed his tuxedo lapels. "I know Hartshorn, but I don't recall actually meeting Lindenaur. And I throw a lot of parties. When was this alleged one?"

"In '40 or '41."

"That's a long time ago. You're staring at me very acutely, Mr. Upshaw. Is there a reason for that?"

Danny touched his own lapels, caught what he was doing and stopped. "I usually get at least a 'my God' or a twitch when I tell someone that an acquaintance of theirs has been murdered. You didn't bat an eye."

"And you find that dismaying?"

"No."

"Curious?"

"Yes."

"Am I an actual suspect in these killings?"

"No, you don't fit my description of the killer."

"Do you require alibis for me to further assert my innocence?"

Danny snapped that he was being sized up by an expert. "All right. New Year's Eve and the night of January fourth. Where were you?"

Not a second's hesitation. "I was here, hosting well-attended parties. If you require verification, please have Lieutenant Matthews do it for you—we're old friends."

Danny saw flashes of *his* party: black-on-black tangos framed in velvet. He flinched and stuffed his hands in his pockets; Gordean's eyes flicked at the show of nerves. Danny said, "Tell me about George Wiltsie."

Gordean walked to a liquor cabinet, filled two glasses and returned with them. Danny smelled the good stuff and jammed his hands down deeper so he wouldn't grab. "Tell me about George Wilt—"

"George Wiltsie was a masculine image that a number of men found enticing. I paid him to attend my parties, dress well and act civilized. He made liaisons here, and I received fees from those men. I imagine that Duane Lindenaur was his lover. That's all I know about George Wiltsie."

Danny took the glass Gordean was offering—something to do with his hands. "Who did you fix Wiltsie up with?"

"I don't recall."

"You *what*?"

"I host parties, guests come and meet the young men I provide, money is discreetly sent to me. Many of my clients are married men with families, and keeping a blank memory is an extra service I provide them."

The glass was shaking in Danny's hand. "Do you expect me to believe that?"

Gordean sipped brandy. "No, but I expect you to accept that answer as all you are going to get."

"I want to see the books for your service, and I want to see a client list."

"No. I write nothing down. It might be considered pandering, you see."

"Then name names."

"No, and don't ask again."

Danny forced himself to barely touch his lips to the glass; barely taste the brandy. He swirled the liquid and sniffed it, two fingers circling the stem—and stopped when he saw he was imitating Gordean. "Mr. Gor—"

"Mr. Upshaw, we've reached an impasse. So let me suggest a compromise. You said that I don't fit your killer's description. Very well, describe your killer to me, and I will try to recall if George Wiltsie went with a man like that. If he did, I will forward the information to Lieutenant Matthews, and he can do with it what he likes. Will that satisfy you?"

Danny bolted his drink—thirty-dollar private stock guzzled. The brandy burned going down; the fire put a rasp on his voice. "I've got the LAPD with me on this case, and the DA's Bureau. They might not like you hiding behind a crooked Vice cop."

Gordean smiled—very slightly. "I won't tell Lieutenant Matthews you said that, nor will I tell Al Dietrich the next time I send him and Sheriff Biscailuz passes to play golf at my club. And I have *good* friends with both the LAPD and the Bureau. Another drink, Mr. Upshaw?"

Danny counted to himself—one, two, three, four—the kibosh on a hothead play. Gordean took his glass, moved to the bar, poured a refill and came back wearing a new smile—older brother looking to put younger brother at ease. "You know the game, Deputy. For God's sake quit coming on like an indignant boy scout."

Danny ignored the brandy and sighted in on Gordean's eyes for signs of fear. "White, forty-five to fifty, slender. Over six feet tall, with an impressive head of silver hair."

No fear; a thoughtful scrunching up of the forehead. Gordean said, "I recall a tall, dark-haired man from the Mexican Consulate going with George, but he was fiftyish during the war. I remember several rather rotund men finding George attractive, and I know that he went regularly with a very tall man with red hair. Does that help you?"

"No. What about men in general of that description? Are there any who frequent your parties or regularly use your service?"

Another thoughtful look. Gordean said, "It's the impressive head of hair that tears it. The only tall, middle-aged men I deal with are quite balding. I'm sorry."

Danny thought, no you're not—but you're probably telling the truth. He said, "What did Wiltsie tell you about Lindenaur?"

"Just that they were living together."

"Did you know that Lindenaur attempted to extort money from Charles Hartshorn?"

"No."

"Have you heard of either Wiltsie or Lindenaur pulling other extortion deals?"

"No, I have not."

"What about blackmail in general? Men like your clients are certainly susceptible to it."

Felix Gordean laughed. "My clients come to my parties and use my service because I insulate them from things like that."

Danny laughed. "You didn't insulate Charles Hartshorn too well."

"Charles was never lucky—in love or politics. He's also not a killer. Question him if you don't believe me, but be courteous, Charles has a low threshold for abuse and he has much legal power."

Gordean was holding out the glass of brandy; Danny took it and knocked the full measure back. "What about enemies of Wiltsie and Lindenaur, known associates, guys they ran with?"

"I don't know anything about that sort of thing."

"Why not?"

"I try to keep things separate and circumscribed."

"Why?"

"To avoid situations like this."

Danny felt the brandy coming on, kicking in with the shots he'd had at home. "Mr. Gordean, are you a homosexual?"

"No, Deputy. Are you?"

Danny flushed, raised his glass and found it empty. He resurrected a crack from his briefing with Considine. "That old scarlet letter routine doesn't wash with me."

Gordean said, "I don't quite understand the reference, Deputy."

"It means that I'm a professional, and I can't be shocked."

"Then you shouldn't blush so easily—your color betrays you as a naif."

The empty glass felt like a missile to heave; Danny hit back on "naif" instead. "We're talking about three people dead. Cut up with a fucking zoot stick, eyes poked out, intestines chewed on. We're talking about blackmail and burglary and jazz and guys with burned-up faces, and you think you can hurt me by calling *me* naif? You think you—"

Danny stopped when he saw Gordean's jaw tensing. The man stared down at the floor; Danny wondered if he'd stabbed a nerve or just hit him on simple revulsion. "What is it? Tell me."

Gordean looked up. "I'm sorry. I have a low threshold for brash young policemen and descriptions of violence, and I shouldn't have called—"

"Then help me. Show me your client list."

"No. I told you I don't keep a list."

"Then tell me what bothered you so much."

"I did tell you."

"And I don't feature you as that sensitive. So tell me."

Gordean said, "When you mentioned jazz, it made me think of a client, a horn player that I used to broker introductions to rough trade to. He impressed me as volatile then, but he's not tall or middle-aged."

"And that's *all*?"

"Cy Vandrich, Deputy. Your tactics have gotten you more than I would normally have been willing to part with, so be grateful."

"And that's *all*?"

Gordean's eyes were blank, giving nothing up. "No. Direct all your future inquiries through Lieutenant Matthews and learn to sip fine brandy—you'll enjoy it more."

Danny tossed his crystal snifter on a Louis XIV chair and walked out.

* * *

An hour and a half to kill before his meeting with Considine; more liquor out of the question. Danny drove to Coffee Bob's and forced down a hamburger and pie, wondering how much of the Gordean questioning slipped between the cracks: his own nerves, the pimp's police connections and savoir faire. The food calmed him down, but didn't answer his questions; he hit a pay phone and got dope on Cy Vandrich.

There was only one listed with DMV/R&I: Cyril "Cy" Vandrich, W.M., DOB 7/24/18, six arrests for petty theft, employment listed as "transient" and "musician." Currently on his sixth ninety-day observation jolt at the Camarillo loony bin. A follow-up call to the bin revealed that Vandrich kept pulling crazy man stunts when he got rousted for shoplifting; that the Misdemeanor Court judge kept recommending Camarillo. The desk woman told Danny that Vandrich was in custody there on the two killing nights; that he made himself useful teaching music to the nuts. Danny said that he might come up to question the man; the woman said that Vandrich might or might not be in control of his faculties—no one at the bin had ever been able to figure him out—whether he was malingering or seriously crazy. Danny hung up and drove to West Hollywood Station to meet Mal Considine.

The man was waiting for him in his cubicle, eyeing the Buddy Jastrow mug blowup. Danny cleared his throat; Considine wheeled around and gave him a close once-over. "I like the suit. It doesn't quite fit, but it looks like something a young lefty might affect. Did you buy it for your assignment?"

"No, Lieutenant."

"Call me Mal. I want you to get out of the habit of using rank. *Ted.*"

Danny sat down behind his desk and pointed Considine to the spare chair. "Ted?"

Considine took the seat and stretched his legs. "As of today, you're Ted Krugman. Dudley went by your apartment house and talked to the manager, and when you get home tonight you'll find T. Krugman on your mailbox. Your phone number is now listed under Theodore Krugman, so we're damn lucky you kept it unlisted before. There's a paper bag waiting for you with the manager—your new wardrobe, some fake ID and New York plates for your car. You like it?"

Danny thought of Dudley Smith inside his apartment, maybe discovering his private file. "Sure, Lieut—Mal."

Considine laughed. "No, you don't—it's all happening too fast. You're Homicide brass, you're a Commie decoy, you're a big-time comer. You're *made*, kid. I hope you know that."

Danny caught glee wafting off the DA's man; he decided to hide his file boxes and blood spray pics behind the rolled-up carpet in his hall closet. "I do, but I don't want to get fat on it. When do I make my approach?"

"Day after tomorrow. I think we've got the UAES lulled with our newspaper and radio plants, and Dudley and I are going to concentrate on lefties outside the union—KAs of the brain trusts—vulnerable types that we should be able to get to snitch. We're going over INS records for deportation levers on them, and Ed Satterlee is trying to get us some hot SLDC pictures from a rival clearance group. Call it a two-front war. Dudley and I on outside evidence, you inside."

Danny saw Considine as all frayed nerves; he saw that *his* suit fit him like a tent, the jacket sleeves riding up over soiled shirtcuffs and long, skinny arms. "How do I get inside?"

Considine pointed to a folder atop the cubicle's Out basket. "It's all in there. You're Ted Krugman, DOB 6/16/23, a Pinko New York stagehand. In reality you were killed in a car wreck on Long Island two months ago. The local Feds hushed it up and sold the identity to Ed Satterlee. All your past history and KAs are in there. There's surveillance pictures of the Commie KAs, and there's twenty-odd pages of Marxist claptrap, a little history lesson for you to memorize.

"So, day after tomorrow, around two, you go to the Gower Street picket line, portraying a Pinko who's lost his faith. You tell the Teamster picket boss that the day labor joint downtown sent you out, muscle for a buck an hour. The man knows who you are, and he'll set you up to picket with two other guys. After an hour or so, you'll get into political arguments with those guys—per the script I've written out for you. A third argument will result in a fistfight with a real bruiser—a PT instructor at the LAPD Academy. He'll pull his punches, but you fight for real. You're going to take a few lumps, but what the hell. Another Teamster man will shout obscenities about you to the UAES picket boss, who'll hopefully approach you and lead you to Claire De Haven, UAES's member screener. We've done a lot of homework, and we can't directly place Krugman with any UAESers. You look vaguely like him and at worst you'll be secondhand heard of. It's all in that folder, kid. Pictures of the men you'll be pulling this off with, everything."

A clean day to work the homicides; a full night to become Ted Krugman. Danny said, "Tell me about Claire De Haven."

Considine countered, "Have you got a girlfriend?"

Danny started to say no, then remembered the bogus paramour who helped him brazen out Tamarind. "Nothing serious. Why?"

"Well, I don't know how susceptible you are to women in general, but De Haven's a presence. Buzz Meeks just filed a report that makes her as a longtime hophead—H and drugstore—but she's still formidable—and she's damn good at getting what she wants out of men. So I want to make sure you seduce her, not the opposite. Does that answer your question?"

"No."

"Do you want a physical description?"

"No."

"The odds that you'll have to lay her?"

"No."

"Do you want her sexual background?"

Danny threw his question out before he could back down. "No. I want to know why a ranking policeman has a crush on a Commie socialite."

Considine blushed pink—the way Felix Gordean told him *he* blushed; Danny tried reading his face and caught: *got me*. Call-me-Mal laughed, slid off his wedding band and tossed it in the wastebasket. He said, "Man to man?"

Danny said, "No, brass to brass."

Considine made the sign of the cross on his vestfront. "Ashes to ashes, and not bad for a minister's son. Let's just say I'm susceptible to dangerous women, and my wife is divorcing me, so I can't chase around and give her ammo to use in court. I want custody of my son, and I will not give her one shred of evidence to spoil my case. And I don't usually offer my confessions to junior officers."

Danny thought: this man is so far out on a limb that you can say anything to him and he'll stick around—because at 1:00 A.M. he's got no place fucking else to go. "And *that's* why you're getting such a kick out of operating De Haven?"

Considine smiled and tapped the top desk drawer. "Why am I betting there's a bottle in here?"

Danny felt himself blush. "Because you're smart?"

The hand kept tapping. "No, because your nerves are right up there with mine, and because you always stink of Lavoris. Brass to rookie, here's a lesson: cops who smell of mouthwash are juicers. And juicer cops who can keep it on a tight leash are usually pretty good cops."

"Pretty good cops" flashed a green light. Danny nudged Considine's hand away, opened the drawer and pulled out a pint and two paper cups. He poured quadruple shots and offered; Considine accepted with a bow; they hoisted drinks. Danny said, "To both our cases"; Considine toasted, "To Stefan Heisteke Considine." Danny drank, warmed head to toe, drank; Considine sipped and hooked a thumb over his back at Harlan "Buddy" Jastrow. "Upshaw, who is this guy? And why are you so bent out of shape on your goddamn homo killings?"

Danny locked eyes with Jastrow. "Buddy's the guy I used to want to get, the guy who used to be the worst, the hardest nut to crack because he was just plain nowhere. Now there's this other thing, and it's just plain terror. It's incredibly brutal, and I think it might be random, but I don't quite go with that. I think I'm dealing with revenge. I think all the killer's methods are reenactments, all the mutilations are symbolic of him trying to get his past straight in his mind. I keep thinking it all out, and I keep coming back to revenge on old wrongs. Not everyday childhood trauma shit, but big, big stuff."

Danny paused, drank and sighted in on the mugboard around Jastrow's neck: Kern County Jail, 3/4/38. "Sometimes I think that if I know who this guy is and why he does it, then I'll know something so big that I'll be able to figure out all the everyday stuff like cake. I can get on with making rank and handling meat and potatoes stuff, because everything I ever sensed about what people are capable of came together on one job, and I nailed *why*. *Why*. Fucking *why*."

Considine's, "And why you do what you do yourself," was very soft. Danny looked away from Jastrow and killed his drink. "Yeah, and that. And why you're so hopped on Claire De Haven and me. And don't say out of patriotism."

Considine laughed. "Kid, would you buy patriotism if I told you the grand jury guarantees me a captaincy, Chief DA's Investigator and the prestige to keep my son?"

"Yeah, but there's still De Haven and—"

"Yeah, and me. Let's just put it this way. I have to know why, too, only I like going at it once removed. Satisfied?"

"No."

"I didn't think you would be."

"Do you *know* why?"

Considine sipped bourbon. "It wasn't hard to figure out."

"I used to steal cars, Lieut—Mal. I was the ace car thief of San Berdoo County right before the war. Turnabout?"

Lieutenant Mal Considine stuck out a long leg and hooked the wastebasket over to his chair. He rummaged in it, found his wedding band and slipped it on. "I've got a confab with my lawyer for the custody case tomorrow, and I'm sure he'll want me to keep wearing this fucking thing."

Danny leaned forward. "Turnabout, Captain?"

Considine stood up and stretched. "My brother used to blackmail me, threaten to rat me to the old man every time I said something snotty about religion. Since ten strokes with a switch was the old man's punishment for blasphemy, old Desmond pretty much got his way, which was usually me breaking into houses to steal stuff he wanted. So let's put it this way: I saw a lot of things that were pretty swell, and some things that were pretty spooky, and I liked it. So it was either become a burglar or a spy, and policeman seemed like a good compromise. And sending in the spies appealed to me more than doing it myself, sort of like Desmond in the catbird seat."

Danny stood up. "I'm going to nail De Haven for you. Trust me on that."

"I don't doubt it, Ted."

"In vino veritas, right?"

"Sure, and one more thing. I'll be Chief of Police or something else that large before too long, and I'm taking you with me."

19

MAL WOKE up thinking of Danny Upshaw.

Rolling out of bed, he looked at the four walls of Room 11, the Shangri-Lodge Motel. One framed magazine cover per wall—Norman Rockwell testimonials to happy family life. A stack of his soiled suits by the door—and no Stefan to run them to the dry cleaners. The memo corkboard he'd erected, one query tag standing out: locate Doc Lesnick. The fink/shrink could not be reached either at home or at his office and the 1942–1944 gaps in Reynolds Loftis' file had to be explained; he needed a general psych overview of the brain trusters now that their decoy was about to be in place, and all the files ended in the late summer of last year—why?

And the curtains were cheesecloth gauze; the rug was as threadbare as a tortilla; the bathroom door was scrawled over with names and phone numbers—"Sinful Cindy, DU-4927, 38-24-38, loves to fuck and suck"—worth a jingle—if he ever ran Vice raids again. And Dudley Smith was due in twenty minutes—good guy/bad guy as today's ticket: two Pinko screenwriters who avoided HUAC subpoenas because they always wrote under pseudonyms and blew the country when the shit hit the fan in '47. They had been located by Ed Satterlee operatives—private eyes on the Red Crosscurrents payroll—and both men knew the UAES bigshots intimately back in the late '30s, early '40s.

And getting so chummy with an underling was strange. A couple of shared drinks and they were spilling their guts to each other—bad chain of command policy—ambitious policemen should keep it zipped while they climbed the ladder.

Mal showered, shaved and dressed, running book—De Haven versus Upshaw, even money as his best bet. At 8:30 exactly a car horn honked; he walked outside and saw Dudley leaning against his Ford. "Good morning, Malcolm! Isn't it a grand day!"

* * *

They drove west on Wilshire, Mal silent, Dudley talking politics. "... I've been juxtaposing the Communist way of life against ours, and I keep coming back to family as the backbone of American life. Do you believe that, Malcolm?"

Mal knew that Loew had filled him in on Celeste—and that as far as partners went, he could have worse—like Buzz Meeks. "It has its place."

"I'd be a bit more emphatic on that, given the trouble you're taking to get your son back. Is it going well with your lawyer?"

Mal thought of his afternoon appointment with Jake Kellerman. "He's going to try to get me continuances until the grand jury is in session and making hay. I have the preliminary in a couple of days, and we'll start putting the stall in then."

Dudley lit a cigarette and steered with one pinky. "Yes, a crusading captain might convince the judge that water is thicker than blood. You know, lad, that I've a wife and five daughters. They serve well to keep the reins on certain unruly aspects of my nature. If he can keep them in perspective, a family is an essential thing for a man to have."

Mal rolled down his window. "I have no perspective where my son is concerned. But if I can keep you in perspective until the grand jury convenes, then I'll be in *grand* shape."

Dudley Smith exhaled laughter and smoke. "I'm fond of you, Malcolm—even though you don't reciprocate. And speaking of family, I've a little errand to run—my niece needs a talking-to. Would you mind a small detour to Westwood?"

"A brief detour, Lieutenant?"

"Very, Lieutenant."

Mal nodded; Dudley turned north on Glendon and headed up toward the UCLA campus, parking in a meter space on Sorority Row. Setting the brake, he said, "Mary Margaret, my sister Brigid's girl. Twenty-nine years old and on her third masters degree because she's afraid to go out and meet the world. Sad, isn't it?"

Mal sighed. "Tragic."

"The very thing I was thinking, but without your emphasis on sarcasm. And speaking of youths, what's your opinion of our young colleague Upshaw?"

"I think he's smart and going places. Why?"

"Well, lad, friends of mine say that he has no sense of his own place, and he impresses me as weak and ambitious, which I view as a dangerous combination in a policeman."

Mal's first thought of rising: He shouldn't have confided in the kid, because half his juice was front just waiting to crack. "Dudley, what do you want?"

"Communism vanquished. And why don't you enjoy the sight of comely young coeds while I speak to my niece?"

Mal followed Dudley up the steps of a Spanish manse fronted by a lawn display: Greek symbols sunk into the grass on wood stakes. The door was open; the lounge area buzzed: girls smoking, talking and gesturing at textbooks. Dudley pointed upstairs and said, "Toot sweet"; Mal saw a stack of magazines on an end table and sat down to read, fielding curious looks from the coeds. He thumbed through a *Collier's*, a *Newsweek* and two *Life*'s— stopping when he heard Dudley's brogue, enraged, echoing down the second-floor hallway.

It got louder and scarier, punctuated by pleas in a whimpering soprano. The girls looked at Mal; he grabbed another magazine and tried to read. Dudley's laughter took over—spookier than the bellows. The coeds were staring now; Mal dropped his *Weekly Sportsman* and walked upstairs to listen.

The hallway was long and lined with narrow wooden doors; Mal followed Ha! Ha! Ha! to a door with "Conroy" nameplated on the front. It was ajar a few inches; he looked in on a back wall lined with photos of Latino prizefighters. Dudley and the soprano were out of sight; Mal eavesdropped.

"... bull banks and piñatas and spic bantamweights. It's a fixation, lassie. Your mother may lack the stomach to set you straight, but I don't."

The soprano, groveling, "But Ricardo is a lovely boy, Uncle Dud. And I—"

A huge hand flashed across Mal's strip of vision, a slap turned to a caress, a head of curly red hair jerking into, then out of sight. "You're not to say you love him, lassie. Not in my presence. Your parents are weak, and they expect me to have a say regarding the men in your life. I will always exercise that say, lassie. Just remember the trouble I spared you before and you'll be grateful."

A plump girl/woman backed into view, hands on her face, sobbing. Dudley Smith's arms went around her; her hands turned to fists to keep him from completing the embrace. Dudley murmured sweet nothings; Mal walked back to the car and waited. His partner showed up five minutes later. "Knock, knock, who's there? Dudley Smith, so Reds beware! Lad, shall we go impress Mr. Nathan Eisler with the righteousness of our cause?"

* * *

Eisler's last known address was 11681 Presidio, a short run from the UCLA campus. Dudley hummed show tunes as he drove; Mal kept seeing his hand about to hit, the niece cowering from her genial uncle's touch. 11681 was a small pink prefab at the end of a long prefab block; Dudley double-parked, Mal jammed facts from Satterlee's report:

Nathan Eisler. Forty-nine years old. A German Jew who fled Hitler and company in '34; CP member '36 to '40, then member of a half dozen Commie front organizations. Co-scenarist on a string of pro-Russki turkeys, his writing partner Chaz Minear; poker buddies with Morton Ziffkin and Reynolds Loftis. Wrote under pseudonyms to guard his professional privacy; slipped through the HUAC investigators' hands; currently living under the alias Michael Kaukenen, the name of the hero of *Storm Over Leningrad*. Currently scripting RKO B westerns, under yet another monicker, the work fronted by a politically acceptable hack writer who glommed a 35 percent cut. Best pals with Lenny Rolff, fellow writer expatriate, today's second interrogee.

Former lover of Claire De Haven.

They took a toy-littered walkway up to the porch; Mal looked through a screen door into the perfect prefab living room: plastic furniture, linoleum floor, spangly pink wallpaper. Children squealed inside; Dudley winked and rang the buzzer.

A tall, unshaven man walked up to the screen, flanked by a toddler boy and girl. Dudley smiled; Mal watched the little boy pop a thumb in his mouth, and spoke first. "Mr. Kaukenen, we're with the District Attorney's Office and we'd like to talk to you. Alone, please."

The kids pressed themselves into the man's legs; Mal saw scared slant eyes—two little half-breeds spooked by two big boogeymen. Eisler/Kaukenen called out, "Michiko!"; a Japanese woman materialized and whisked the children away. Dudley opened the door uninvited; Eisler said, "You are three years late."

Mal walked in behind Dudley, amazed at how cheap the place looked—a white trash flop—the home of a man who made three grand a week during the Depression. He heard the kids bawling behind wafer-thin walls; he wondered if Eisler had to put up with the same foreign language shit he did—then popped that he probably dug it on general Commie principles. Dudley said, "This is a charming house, Mr. Kaukenen. The color motif especially."

Eisler/Kaukenen ignored the comment and pointed them to a door off the living room. Mal walked in and saw a small square space that looked warm and habitable: floor-to-ceiling books, chairs around an ornate coffee table and a large desk dominated by a class A typewriter. He took the seat furthest from the squeal of little voices; Dudley sat across from him. Eisler shut the door and said, "I am Nathan Eisler, as if you did not already know."

Mal thought: no nice guy, no "I loved your picture *Branding Iron.*" "Then you know why we're here."

Eisler locked the door and took the remaining chair. "The bitch is in heat again, despite reports that she had a miscarriage."

Dudley said, "You are to tell no one that we questioned you. There will be dire repercussions should you disobey us on that."

"Such as what, Herr—"

Mal cut in. "Mort Ziffkin, Chaz Minear, Reynolds Loftis and Claire De Haven. We're interested in their activities, not yours. If you cooperate fully with us, we might be able to let you testify by deposition. No open court, probably very little publicity. You slid on HUAC, you'll slide on this one." He stopped and thought of Stefan, gone with his crazy mother and her new paramour. "But we want hard facts. Names, dates, places and admissions. You cooperate, you slide. You don't, it's a subpoena and open court questioning by a DA I can only describe as a nightmare. Your choice."

Eisler inched his chair away from them. Eyes lowered, he said, "I have not seen those people in years."

Mal said, "We know, and it's their *past* activities that we're interested in."

"And they are the only people that you want to know about?"

Mal lied, thinking of Lenny Rolff. "Yes. Just them."

"And what are these repercussions you speak of?"

Mal drummed the table. "Open court badgering. Your picture in the—"

Dudley interrupted, "Mr. Eisler, if you do not cooperate, I will inform Howard Hughes that you are authoring RKO films currently being credited to another man. That man, your conduit to gainful employment as a writer, will be terminated. I will also inform the INS that you refused to cooperate with a sanctioned municipal body investigating treason, and urge that their Investigations Bureau delve into *your* seditious activities with an eye toward your deportation as an enemy alien and the deportation of your wife and children as potential enemy aliens. You are a German and your wife is Japanese, and since those two nations were responsible for our recent world conflict, I would think that the INS would enjoy seeing the two of you returned to your respective homelands."

Nathan Eisler had hunched himself up, elbows to knees, clasped hands to chin, head down. Tears rolled off his face. Dudley cracked his knuckles and said, "A simple yes or no answer will suffice."

Eisler nodded; Dudley said, "Grand." Mal got out his pen and notepad. "I know the answer, but tell me anyway. Are you now or have you ever been a member of the Communist Party, U.S.A.?"

Eisler bobbed his head; Mal said, "Yes or no answers, this is for the record."

A weak "Yes."

"Good. Where was your Party unit or cell located?"

"I—I went to meetings in Beverly Hills, West Los Angeles and Hollywood. We—we met at the homes of different members."

Mal wrote the information down—verbatim shorthand. "During what years were you a Party member?"

"April '36 until Stalin proved him—"

Dudley cut in. "Don't justify yourself, just answer."

Eisler pulled a Kleenex from his shirt pocket and wiped his nose. "Until early in '40."

Mal said, "Here are some names. You tell me which of these people were known to you as Communist Party members. Claire De Haven, Reynolds Loftis, Chaz Minear, Morton Ziffkin, Armando Lopez, Samuel Benavides and Juan Duarte."

Eisler said, "All of them." Mal heard the kids tramping through the living room and raised his voice. "You and Chaz Minear wrote the scripts for *Dawn of the Righteous*, *Eastern Front*, *Storm Over Leningrad* and *The Heroes of Yakustok*. All those films espoused nationalistic Russian sentiment. Were you told by Communist Party higher-ups to insert pro-Russian propaganda in them?"

Eisler said, "That is a naive question"; Dudley slapped the coffee table. "Don't comment, just answer."

Eisler moved his chair closer to Mal. "No. No, I was not told that."

Mal flashed Dudley two fingers of his necktie—*he's mine.* "Mr. Eisler, do you deny that those films contain pro-Russian propaganda?"

"No."

"Did you and Chaz Minear arrive at the decision to disseminate that propaganda yourselves?"

Eisler squirmed in his chair. "Chaz was responsible for the philosophizing, while I held that the story line spoke most eloquently for the points he wanted to make."

Mal said, "We have copies of those scripts, with the obvious propaganda passages annotated. We'll be back to have you initial the dialogue you attribute to Minear's disseminating of the Party line."

No response. Mal said, "Mr. Eisler, would you say that you have a good memory?"

"Yes, I would say that."

"And did you and Minear work together in the same room on your scripts?"

"Yes."

"And were there times when he said things along the lines of 'This is great propaganda' or 'This is for the Party'?"

Eisler kept squirming, shifting his arms and legs. "Yes, but he was just being satirical, poking fun. He did not—"

Dudley shouted, "Don't interpret, just answer!"

Eisler shouted back, "Yes! Yes! Yes! Goddamn you, yes!"

Mal gave Dudley the cut-off sign; he gave Eisler his most soothing voice. "Mr. Eisler, did you keep a journal during the time you worked with Chaz Minear?"

The man was wringing his hands, Kleenex shredding between fingers pumped blue-white. "Yes."

"Did it contain entries pertaining to your Communist Party activities and your script work with Chaz Minear?"

"Oh God, yes."

Mal thought of the report from Satterlee's PIs: Eisler coupling with Claire De Haven circa '38–'39. "And entries pertaining to your personal life?"

"Oh, Gott in himm … yes, yes!"

"And do you still have that journal?"

Silence, then, "I don't know."

Mal slapped the table. "Yes, you do, and you'll have to let us see it. Only the germane political entries will be placed in the official transcript."

Nathan Eisler sobbed quietly. Dudley said, "You will give us that journal, or we will subpoena it and uniformed officers will tear your quaint little abode apart, gravely upsetting your quaint little family, I fear."

Eisler gave a sharp little yes nod; Dudley eased back in his chair, the legs creaking under his weight. Mal saw a Kleenex box on the windowsill, grabbed it and placed it on Eisler's lap. Eisler cradled the box; Mal said, "We'll take the journal with us, and we'll put Minear aside for now. Here's a general question. Have you ever heard any of the people we're interested in advocate the armed overthrow of the United States government?"

Two negative shakes, Eisler with his head back down, his tears drying. Mal said, "Not in the way of a formal pronouncement, but that sentiment stated."

"Every one of us said it in anger, and it always meant nothing."

"The grand jury will decide what you meant. Be specific. Who said it, and when."

Eisler wiped his face. "Claire would say 'The end justifies the means' at meetings and Reynolds would say that he was not a violent man, but he would take up a shillelagh if it came to us versus the bosses. The Mexican boys said it a million different times in a million contexts, especially around the time of Sleepy Lagoon. Mort Ziffkin shouted it for the world to hear. He was a courageous man."

Mal caught up on his shorthand, thinking of UAES and the studios. "What about the UAES? How did it tie in to the Party and the front groups you and the others belonged to?"

"The UAES was founded while I was out of the country. The three Mexican boys had found work as stagehands and recruited members, as did Claire De Haven. Her father had served as counsel to vested movie interests and she said she intended to exploit and ... and ..."

Mal's head was buzzing. "And *what*? Tell me."

Eisler went back to his finger-clenching; Mal said "*Tell me*, 'Exploit' *and what*?"

"Seduce! She grew up around movie people and she knew actors and technicians who had been coveting her since she was a girl! She seduced them as founding members and got them to recruit for her! She said it was her penance for not getting subpoenaed by HUAC!"

Big time triple bingo.

Mal willed his voice as controlled as Dudley's. "Who specifically did she seduce?"

Eisler picked and plucked and tore at the tissue box. "I don't know, I don't know, I honestly do not know."

"A lot of men, a few men, how many?"

"I do not know. I suspect only a few influential actors and technicians who she knew could help her union."

"Who else helped her recruit? Minear, Loftis?"

"Reynolds was in Europe then, Chaz I don't know."

"What was discussed at the first UAES meetings? Was there some kind of charter or overview they worked on?"

The Kleenex box was now a pile of ripped cardboard; Eisler brushed it off his lap. "I have never attended their meetings."

"We know, but we need to know who besides the initial founders were there and what was discussed."

"I don't know!"

Mal threw an outside curve. "Are you still hot for Claire, Eisler? Are you protecting her? You know she's marrying Reynolds Loftis. How's that make you feel?"

Eisler threw his head back and laughed. "Our affair was brief, and I suspect that handsome Reynolds will always prefer young boys."

"Chaz Minear's no young boy."

"And he and Reynolds did not last."

"Nice people you know, comrade."

Eisler's laughter turned low, guttural—and supremely Germanic. "I prefer them to you, obersturmbahnführer."

Mal held his temper by looking at Dudley; Mr. Bad Guy returned him the cut-off sign. "We'll overlook that comment out of deference to your cooperation, and you may call this your initial interview. My colleague and I will go over your answers, check them against our records and send back a long list of other questions, detailed specifics pertaining to your Communist front activities and the activities of the UAES members we discussed. A City Marshal will monitor that transaction, and a court reporter will take your deposition. After that interview, providing you answer a few more questions now and allow us to take your journal, you will be given friendly witness status and full immunity from prosecution."

Eisler got up, walked on rubber legs to his desk and unlocked a lower drawer. He poked through it, pulled out a leather-bound diary, brought it back and laid it on the table. "Ask your few questions and leave."

Dudley moved a flat palm slowly down: *Go easy*. Mal said, "We have a second interview this afternoon, and I think you can help us with it."

Eisler stammered, "Wh-what, wh-who?"

Dudley, in a whisper. "Leonard Hyman Rolff."

Their interrogee rasped the single word, "No." Dudley looked at Mal; Mal placed his left hand over his right fist: *no hitting*. Dudley said, "*Yes*, and we will brook no argument, no discussion. I want you to think of something shameful and incriminating indigenous to your old friend Lenny, something that other people know, so that we can put the blame of informing on them. *You will inform*, so I advise you to think of something effective, something that will loosen Mr. Rolff's tongue and spare you a return visit from myself— without my colleague who serves so well to restrain me."

Nathan Eisler had gone slab white. He sat stock-still, looking way past tears or shock or indignation. Mal thought that he seemed familiar; a few seconds of staring gave him his connection: the Buchenwald Jews who'd beat the gas chamber only to sink to an early grave via viral anemia. The memory made him get up and prowl the bookshelves; the dead silence kept going. He was scanning a shelf devoted to Marxist economics when Dudley's whisper came back. "The repercussions, comrade. Refugee camps for your half-breed whelps. Mr. Rolff will receive his chance for friendly witness status, so if he's an obstreperous sort, you'll be doing him a favor by supplying us with information to convince him to inform. Think of Michiko forced to keep body and soul together back in Japan, all the tempting offers she'll receive."

Mal tried to look back, but couldn't make himself; he fixed on *Das Kapital—A Concordance, Marx's Theories of Commerce and Repression* and *The Proletariat Speak Out*. Quiet sank in behind him; heavy fingers tapped the table. Then Nathan Eisler's monotone: "Young girls. Prostitutes. Lenny is afraid his wife will find out he frequents them."

Dudley sighed. "Not good enough. Try harder."

"He keeps pornographic pictures of the ones—"

"Too bland, comrade."

"He cheats on his income tax."

Dudley ha! ha! ha!'d. "So do I, so does my friend Malcolm and so would our grand savior Jesus Christ should he return and settle in America. You know more than you are telling us, so please rectify that situation before I lose my temper and revoke your friendly witness status."

Mal heard the kids giggling outside, the little girl squealing in Japanese. He said, "Goddamn you, talk."

Eisler coughed, took an audible breath, coughed again. "Lenny will not inform as easily as I. He has not so much to lose."

Mal turned, saw a death's head and turned away; Dudley cracked his knuckles. Eisler said, "I will always try to think I did this for Lenny and I will always know I am lying." His next deep breath wheezed; he let it out fast, straight into his snitch. "I was traveling with Lenny and his wife Judith in Europe in '48. Paul Doinelle was making his masked series with Reynolds Loftis and hosted a party to seek financial backing for his next film. He wanted to solicit Lenny and brought a young prostitute for him to enjoy. Judith did not attend the party, and Lenny caught gonorrhea from the prostitute. Judith became ill and returned to America, and Lenny had an affair with her younger sister Sarah in Paris. He gave her the gonorrhea. Sarah told Judith she had the disease, but not that Lenny gave it to her. Lenny would not make love to Judith for many weeks after he returned to America and took a cure, employing various excuses. He has always been afraid Judith would logically connect the two events and realize what had occurred. Lenny confided in me and Reynolds and our friend David Yorkin, who I am sure you know from your wonderful list of front organizations. Since you are so concerned with Reynolds, perhaps you could make him the informant."

Dudley said, "God bless you, comrade."

Mal grabbed Eisler's journal, hoping for enough treason to make two silver bars and his boy worth the price. "Let's go nail Lenny."

* * *

They found him alone, typing at a card table in his back yard, clack-clack-clack leading them around the side of the house to a fat man in a Hawaiian shirt and chinos pecking on an ancient Underwood. Mal saw him look up and knew from his eyes that this guy was no pushover.

Dudley badged him. "Mr. Leonard Rolff?"

The man put on glasses and examined the shield. "Yes. You're policemen?"

Mal said, "We're with the District Attorney's Office."

"But you're policemen?"

"We're DA's Bureau Investigators."

"Yes, you are policemen as opposed to lawyers. And your names and ranks?"

Mal thought of their newspaper ink—and knew he had no recourse. "I'm Lieutenant Considine, this is Lieutenant Smith."

Rolff grinned. "Recently portrayed as regretting the demise of the would-be City grand jury, which I now take it is a going concern once again. The answer is no, gentlemen."

Mal played dumb. "No what, Mr. Rolff?"

Rolff looked at Dudley, like he knew he was the one he had to impress. "*No*, I will not inform on members of the UAES. *No*, I will not answer questions pertaining to my political past or the pasts of friends and acquaintances. If subpoenaed, I will be a hostile witness and stand on the Fifth Amendment, and I am prepared to go to prison for contempt of court. You cannot make me name names."

Dudley smiled at Rolff. "I respect men of principle, however deluded. Gentlemen, would you excuse me a moment? I left something in the car."

The smile was a chiller. Dudley walked out; Mal ran interference. "You may not believe this, but we're actually on the side of the legitimate, non-Communist American left."

Rolff pointed to the sheet of paper in his typewriter. "Should you fail as a policeman you have a second career as a comedian. Just like me. The fascists took away my career as a screenwriter; now I write historical romance novels under the nom de plume Erica St. Jane. And my publisher knows my politics and doesn't care. So does the employer of my wife, who has full tenure at Cal State. You cannot hurt either of us."

Out of the mouths of babes.

Mal watched Lenny Rolff resume work on page 399 of *Wake of the Lost Doubloons*. Typewriter clack filled the air; he looked at the writer's modest stone house and mused that at least he saved more of his money than Eisler and had the brains not to marry a Jap. More clack-clack-clack; Page 399 became pages 400 and 401— Rolff really churned it out. Then Dudley's brogue, the most theatrical he had ever heard it. "Bless me father, for I have sinned. My last confession was never, because I am Jewish. I will currently rectify that situation, Monsignors Smith and Considine my confessors."

Mal turned and saw Dudley holding a stack of photographs; Rolff finished typing a paragraph and looked up. Dudley pushed a snapshot in his face; Rolff said, "No," calmly. Mal walked around the table and scoped the picture close up.

It was fuzzy black and white, a teenage girl naked with her legs spread. Dudley read from the flip side. "To Lenny. You were the best. Love from Maggie at Minnie Robert's Casbah, January 19, 1946."

Mal held his breath; Rolff stood, gave Dudley an eye-to-eye deadpan and a steady voice. "*No*. My wife and I have forgiven each other our minor indiscretions. Do you think I would leave the pictures in my desk otherwise? *No. Thief. Fascist parasite. Irish pig.*"

Dudley tossed the photos on the grass; Mal shot him the no hitting sign; Rolff cleared his throat and spat in Dudley's face. Mal gasped; Dudley smiled, grabbed a manuscript sheet and wiped the spittle off. "*Yes*, because fair Judith does not know about fair Sarah and the clap you gave her, and I just played a hunch on where you took your cure. Terry Lux keeps meticulous records, and he has promised to cooperate with me should you decide not to."

Rolff, still voice steady. "Who told you?"

Dudley, making motions: *verbatim transcription*. "Reynolds Loftis, under much less duress than you were just subjected to."

Mal thought through the gamble: if Rolff approached Loftis, all their covert questionings were compromised; the UAES might put the kibosh on new members—terrified of infiltration, blowing Danny Upshaw's approach. He got out pen and pad, grabbed a chair and sat down; Dudley called his own bluff. "Yes or no, Mr. Rolff. Give me your answer."

Veins pulsed all over Leonard Rolff's face. He said, "Yes."

Dudley said, "Grand"; Mal wrote *L. Rolff, 1/8/50* at the top of a clean sheet. Their interrogee squared his glasses. "Open court testimony?"

Mal took the cue. "Most likely deposition. We'll start with—"

Dudley, his voice raised for the first time. "Let me have this witness, counselor. Would you mind?"

Mal shook his head and turned his chair around, steno pad braced on the top slat. Dudley said, "You know why we're here, so let's get to it. Communist influence in the motion picture business. Names, dates, places and seditious words spoken. Since I'm sure he's much on your mind, we'll start with Reynolds Loftis. Have you ever heard him advocate the armed overthrow of the United States government?"

"No, but—"

"Feel free to volunteer information, unless I state otherwise. Have you some grand tidbits on Loftis?"

Rolff's tone seethed. "He tailored his policeman roles to make the police look bad. He said he was doing his part to undermine the American system of jurisprudence." A pause, then, "If I testify in court, will he get the chance to tell about Sarah and me?"

Mal answered, half truth/half lies. "It's very unlikely he'll stand as a witness, and if he tries to volunteer that information the judge won't let him get two seconds in. You're covered."

"But outside of court—"

Dudley said, "Outside of court you're on your own, and you'll have to rely on the fact that repeating the story makes Loftis appear loathsome."

Rolff said, "If Loftis told you that, then he must have been cooperative in general. Why do you need information to use against him?"

Dudley, not missing a trick. "Loftis informed on you months ago, when we thought our investigation was going to be centered outside the UAES. Frankly, what with the recent labor troubles, the UAES presents a much nicer target. And frankly, you and the others were too ineffectual to bother with."

Mal looked over and saw that Rolff bought it: his squared shoulders had relaxed and his hands had quit clenching. His follow-up question was dead on target: "How do I know you won't do the same thing with me?"

Mal said, "This grand jury is officially on, and you'll be given immunity from prosecution, something we never offered Loftis. What Lieutenant Smith said about the labor trouble is true. It's now or never, and we're here to make hay now."

Rolff stared at him. "You acknowledge your opportunism so openly that it gives you an awful credibility."

Dudley ha' ha'd. "There is one difference between our factions—we're right, you're wrong. Now, concerning Reynolds Loftis. He deliberately portrayed American policemen as misanthropic, correct?"

Mal went back to transcribing; Rolff said, "Yes."

"Can you recall when he said that?"

"At a party somewhere, I think."

"Oh? A party for *the* Party?"

"No. No, I think it was a party back during the war, a summertime party."

"Were any of these people also present and making seditious comments: Claire De Haven, Chaz Minear, Mort Ziffkin, Sammy Benavides, Juan Duarte and Mondo Lopez?"

"I think Claire and Mort were there, but Sammy and Juan and Mondo were busy with SLDC around that time, so they weren't."

Mal said, "So this was summer of '43, around the time the Sleepy Lagoon Defense Committee was going strongest?"

"Yes. Yes, I think so."

Dudley said, "Think, comrade. Minear was Loftis' bedmate. Was he there and acting vociferous?"

Mal caught up on his note-taking, shorthanding Dudley's flair down to simple questions; Rolff ended a long pause. "What I remember about that party is that it was my last social contact with the people you mentioned until I became friendly with Reynolds again in Europe a few years ago. I recall that Chaz and Reynolds had been spatting and that Reynolds did not bring him to that party. After the party I saw Reynolds out by his car talking to a young man with a bandaged face. I also recall that my circle of political friends had become involved in the Sleepy Lagoon defense and were angry when I took a job in New York that precluded my joining them."

Dudley said, "Let's talk about Sleepy Lagoon." Mal thought of his memo to Loew: nothing on the case should hit the grand jury—it was political poison that made the Pinkos look good. Rolff said, "I thought you wanted me to talk about Reynolds."

"Digress a little. Sleepy Lagoon. Quite an event, wasn't it?"

"The boys your police department arrested were innocent. Concerned apolitical citizens joined the Southern California left and secured their release. *That* made it quite an event, yes."

"That's your interpretation, comrade. Mine differs, but that's what makes for horse races."

Rolff sighed. "What do you want to know?"

"Give me your recollections of the time."

"I was in Europe for the trial and appeals and release of the boys. I remember the actual murder from the previous summer—'42, I think. I remember the police investigation and the arrest of the boys and Claire De Haven becoming outraged and holding fund-raisers. I remember thinking that she was currying favor with her many Latin suitors, that that was one reason she was so carried away with the cause."

Mal butted in, thinking of culling facts from Dudley's bum tangent, wondering *why* the tangent. "At these fund-raisers, were there CP bigshots present?"

"Yes."

"We're going to be getting some SLDC surveillance pictures. You'll be required to help identify the people in them."

"Then there's more of this?"

Dudley lit a cigarette and motioned Mal to quit writing. "This is a preliminary interview. A City marshal and court reporter will be by in a few days with a long list of specific questions on specific people. Lieutenant Considine and I will prepare the questions, and if we're satisfied with your answers we'll mail you an official immunity waiver."

"Are you finished now, then?"

"Not quite. Let's return to Sleepy Lagoon for a moment."

"But I told you I was in New York then. I was gone for most of the protests."

"But you did know many of the SLDC principals. Duarte, Benavides and Lopez, for instance."

"Yes. And?"

"And they were the ones who most loudly contended that the poor persecuted Mex boys got the railroad, were they not?"

"Yes. Sleepy Lagoon sparked the zoot suit riots, *your* police department running amok. A number of Mexicans were practically beaten to death, and Sammy and Juan and Mondo were anxious to express their solidarity through the Committee."

Mal swiveled his chair around and watched. Dudley was on a big fishing expedition, soaking up a *big* dose of rhetoric in the process—not the man's style. Rolff said, "If that sounds doctrinaire to you, I'm sorry. It's simply the truth."

Dudley made a little pooh-pooh noise. "It always surprised me that the Commies and your so-called concerned citizens never proffered a suitable killer or killers of their own to take the fall on José Diaz. You people are masters of the scapegoat. Lopez, Duarte and Benavides were gang members who probably knew plenty of white punks to put the onus on. Was that ever discussed?"

"No. What you say is incomprehensible."

Dudley shot Mal a little wink. "My colleague and I know otherwise. Let's try this. Did the three Mexes or any other SLDC members proffer sincerely believed theories as to who killed José Diaz?"

Gritting his teeth, Rolff said, "No."

"What about the CP itself? Did it advance any potential scapegoats?"

"I *told* you no, I *told* you I was in New York for the bulk of the SLDC time."

Dudley, straightening his necktie knot with one finger pointed to the street: "Malcolm, any last questions for Mr. Rolff?"

Mal said, "No."

"Oh? Nothing on our fair Claire?"

Rolff stood up and was running a hand inside his collar like he couldn't wait to ditch his inquisitors and take a bath; Mal knocked his chair over getting to his feet. He dug for cracks to throw and came up empty. "No."

Dudley stayed seated, smiling. "Mr. Rolff, I need the names of five fellow travelers, people who are well acquainted with the UAES brain trust."

Rolff said, "No. Unequivocally *no.*"

Dudley said, "I'll settle for the names now, whatever intimate personal recollections you can supply us with in a few days, after a colleague of ours conducts background checks. The names, please."

Rolff dug his feet in the grass, balled fists at his sides. "Tell Judith about Sarah and me. She won't believe you."

Dudley took a piece of paper from his inside jacket pocket. "May 11, 1948. 'My Dearest Lenny. I miss you and want you in me despite what you carried with you. I keep thinking that of course you didn't know you had it and you met that prostitute before we became involved. The treatments hurt, but they still make me think of you, and if not for the fear of Judith finding out about us, I would be talking about you my every waking moment.' Armbuster 304's are the cheapest wall safes in the world, comrade. A man in your position should not be so frugal."

Lenny Rolff hit the grass on his knees. Dudley knelt beside him and coaxed out a barely audible string of names. The last name, sobbed, was "Nate Eisler." Mal double-timed it to the car, looking back once. Dudley was watching his friendly witness hurl typewriter and manuscript, table and chairs helter-skelter.

* * *

Dudley drove Mal back to his motel, no talk the whole time, Mal keeping the radio glued to a classical station: bombastic stuff played loud. Dudley's goodbye was, "You've more stomach for this work than I expected"; Mal went inside and spent an hour in the shower, until the hot water for the entire dump was used up and the manager came knocking on the door to complain. Mal calmed him down with his badge and a ten-spot, put on his last clean suit and drove downtown to see his lawyer.

Jake Kellerman's office was in the Oviatt Tower at Sixth and Olive. Mal arrived five minutes early, scanning the bare-bones reception room, wondering if Jake sacrificed a secretary for rental freight in one of L.A.'s ritziest buildings. Their first confab had been overview; this one had to be meat and potatoes.

Kellerman opened his inner office door at 3:00 on the dot; Mal walked in and sat down in a plain brown leather chair. Kellerman shook his hand, then stood behind a plain brown wooden desk. He said, "Preliminary day after tomorrow, Civil Court 32. Greenberg's on vacation, and we've got some goyishe stiff named Hardesty. I'm sorry about that, Mal. I wanted to get you a Jew who'd be impressed by your MP work overseas."

Mal shrugged, thinking of Eisler and Rolff; Kellerman smiled. "Care to enlighten me on a rumor?"

"Sure."

"I heard you coldcocked some Nazi bastard in Poland."

"That's true."

"You killed him?"

The bare little office was getting stuffy. "Yes."

Kellerman said, "Mazel tov," checked his court calendar and some papers on the desk. "At preliminary I'll start stalling for continuances and try to work out an angle to get you switched to Greenberg's docket. He'll fucking love you. How's the grand jury gig going?"

"It's going well."

"Then why are you looking so glum? Look, is there any chance you'll get your promotion before the grand jury convenes?"

Mal said, "No. Jake, what's your strategy past the continuances?"

Kellerman hooked two thumbs in his vest pockets. "Mal, it's a hatchet job on Celeste. She deserted the boy—"

"She didn't desert him, the fucking Nazis picked up her and her husband and threw them in fucking Buchenwald."

"Sssh. Easy, pal. You told me the boy was molested as a direct result of being deserted by his mother. She peddled it inside to stay alive. Your MP battalion has got her liberation interview pictures— she looks like Betty Grable compared to the other women who came out alive. I'll kill her in court with that—Greenberg or no Greenberg."

Mal took off his jacket and loosened his tie. "Jake, I don't want Stefan to hear that stuff. I want you to get a writ barring him from hearing testimony. An exclusion order. You can do it."

Kellerman laughed. "No wonder you dropped out of law school. Writs excluding minor children from overhearing testimony in custody cases cannot be legally sanctioned unless the counsel of both parents approve it—which Celeste's lawyer will never go for. If I break her down in court—and I will—he'll want Stefan there on the off-chance he runs to mommy, not daddy. It's out of our hands."

Mal saw Stefan Heisteke, Prague '45, coming off a three-year jag of canned dog food and rape. "You swing it, or you find stuff that happened after the war to hit Celeste with."

"Like her dutifully schooling Stefan in Czech? Mal, she doesn't drink or sleep around or hit the boy. You don't wrest custody from the natural mother because the woman lives in the past."

Mal got up, his head throbbing. "Then you make me the biggest fucking hero since Lucky Lindy. You make me look so fucking good I make motherhood look like shit."

Jake Kellerman pointed to the door. "Go get me a big load of Commies and I'll do my best."

* * *

Mal rolled to the Pacific Dining Car. The general idea was a feast to pamper himself away from Eisler, Rolff and Dudley Smith—the purging that an hour of scalding hot water didn't accomplish. But as soon as his food arrived he lost interest, grabbed Eisler's diary and flipped to 1938–1939, the writer's time with Claire De Haven.

No explicitness, just analysis.

The woman hated her father, screwed Mexicans to earn his wrath, had a crush on her father and got her white lefty consorts to dress stuffed-shirt traditional like him—so she could tear off their clothes and make a game out of humiliating paternal surrogates. She hated her father's money and political connections, raped his bank accounts to lavish gifts on men whose politics the old man despised; she went to tether's end on booze, opiates and sex, found causes to do penance with and fashioned herself into an exemplary leftist Joan of Arc: organizing, planning, recruiting, financing with her own money and donations often secured with her own body. The woman's political efficacy was so formidable that she was never dismissed as a camp follower or dilettante; at worst, only her psyche and motives were viewed as spurious. Eisler's fascination with Claire continued after their affair ended; he remained her friend throughout her liaisons with pachuco thugs, dryouts at Terry Lux's clinic, her big penance number over Sleepy Lagoon: a Mex boyfriend beat up in the zoot riots, a boil-out at Doc Terry's and then a full social season, stone cold sober, with the SLDC. Impressive. Dudley Smith's lunatic fixation aside, the seventeen kids accused of snuffing José Diaz were by all accounts innocent. And Claire Katherine De Haven—Commie rich girl slut—was a major force behind getting them sprung.

Mal leafed through the journal; the De Haven entries dwindled as he hit '44 and '45. He picked at his food and backtracked through a glut of pages that made Eisler look intelligent, analytical, a do-goodnik led down the primrose path by Pinko college professors and the spectre of Hitler looming over Germany. So far, zero hard evidence—if the diary were introduced to the grand jury it would actually make Eisler appear oddly heroic. Remembering the man as a Reynolds Loftis friend/Chaz Minear co-worker, Mal scanned pages for them.

Minear came off as weak, the nance of the two, the clinging vine. Mal read through accounts of Chaz and Eisler scripting *Eastern Front* and *Storm Over Leningrad* together circa 1942–1943, Eisler pissed at Minear's sloppy work habits, pissed at his mooning over Loftis, pissed at himself for despising his friends' homosexuality— tolerable in Reynolds because at least he wasn't a swish. You could see Minear's impotent rage building back in the Sleepy Lagoon days—his crying on Eisler's shoulder over some fling Loftis was having—"My God, Nate, he's just a boy, and he's been disfigured"—then refusing to go any further on the topic. Hindsight: in '47, Chaz Minear hit back at his faithless lover—the snitch to HUAC that got Reynolds Loftis blacklisted. Mal made a mental note: if Danny Upshaw couldn't infiltrate the UAES brain trust, then Chaz Minear, homosexual weak sister, might be ripe for overt bracing—exposure of his snitch duty the lever to get him to snitch again.

The rest of the diary was a bore: meetings, committees, gatherings and names for Buzz Meeks to check out along with the names Dudley coerced from Lenny Rolff. Mal killed it off while his steak got cold and his salad wilted in the bowl; he realized that he liked Nathan Eisler. And that with the journal checked out and dinner attempted, he had no place to go except back to the Shangri-Lodge Motel and nothing he wanted to do except talk to Stefan—a direct violation of Jake Kellerman's orders. All the motel had to offer was women's names scrawled on the bathroom door, and if he called Stefan he'd probably get Celeste, their first amenities since he reworked her face. Restless, he paid the check, drove up into the Pasadena foothills and parked in the middle of a totally dark box canyon: "Cordite Alley," the spot where his generation of LAPD rookies got fried on kickback booze, shot the shit and target practiced, tall clumps of sagebrush to simulate bad guys.

The ground held a thick layer of spent shells; dousing his headbeams, Mal saw that the other cop generations had blasted the sagebrushes to smithereens and had gone to work on the scrub pines: the trees were stripped of bark and covered with entry holes. He got out of the car, drew his service revolver and squeezed off six rounds into the darkness; the echo hurt his ears and the cordite stink smelled good. He reloaded and emptied the .38 again; over the hill in South Pasadena skid other guns went off, like a chain of dogs barking at the moon. Mal reloaded, fired, reloaded and fired until his box of Remingtons was empty; he heard cheers, howls, shrieks and then nothing.

The canyon rustled with a warm wind. Mal leaned against the car and thought about Ad Vice, operations, turning down the Hat Squad, where you went in the door gun first and cops like Dudley Smith respected you. In Ad Vice he busted a string of Chinatown whorehouses deemed inoperable—sending in fresh-scrubbed recruits for blow jobs, followed five minutes later by door-kicking harness bulls and lab techs with cameras. The girls were all straight off the boat and living at home with mama-san and papa-san, who thought they were working double shifts at the Shun-Wong Shirt Factory; he had a cordon of muscle cops accompany him to the storefront office of Uncle Ace Kwan, L.A.'s number-one boss chink pimp. He informed Uncle Ace that unless he took his whores over the line to the County, he would show the pictures to the papa-sans—many of them Tong-connected—and inform them that Kwan-san was getting fat off daughter-san's diet of Caucasian dick. Uncle Ace bowed, said, yes, complied and always sent him a candied duck and thoughtful card at Christmastime, and he always thought about passing the greeting on to his brother—while he was still on speaking terms with him.

Him.

Desmond.

Big Des.

Desmond Confrey Considine, who coerced him into dark houses and made him a cop, an operator.

Three years older. Three inches taller. An athlete, good at faking piety to impress the Reverend. The Reverend caught him boosting a pack of gum at the local Pig and Whistle and flayed his ass so bad that Big Des popped a bunch of tendons trying to get free of his bonds and was sidelined for the rest of the football season, a first-string linebacker with a third-string brain and a first-class case of kleptomania that he was now terrified to run with: no legs and no balls, courtesy of Liam Considine, first-string Calvinist.

So Desmond recruited his gangly kid brother, figuring his whippet thinness would get him inside the places he was now afraid to B&E, get him the things he wanted: Joe Stinson's tennis racquet, Jimmy Harris' crystal radio set, Dan Klein's elk's teeth on a string and all the other good stuff he couldn't stand to see other kids enjoying. Little Malcolm, who couldn't stop blaspheming even though the Reverend told him that now that he was four-teen the penalty was a whipping—not the dinner of pine tar soap and castor oil he was used to. Little Mally would become his stealer, or the Reverend would get an earful of Jesus doing it with Rex the Wonder Dog and Mary Magdalene jumping Willy, the old coon who delivered ice to their block on a swayback nag—stuff the Reverend knew Des didn't have the imagination to come up with.

So *he* stole, afraid of Desmond, afraid of the Reverend, afraid to confide in Mother for fear she'd tell her husband and he'd kill Des, then go to the gallows and leave them to the mercy of the cheap-shit Presbyterian Charity Board. Six feet and barely one-ten, he became the San Francisco Phantom, shinnying up drainpipes and popping window latches, stealing Desmond sporting junk that he was too afraid to use, books he was too stupid to read, clothes he was too big to wear. He knew that as long as Des kept the stuff he had the goods on him—but he kept playing the game.

Because Joe Stinson had a snazzy sister named Cloris, and he liked being alone in her room. Because Dan Klein had a parrot who'd eat crackers out of your mouth. Because Jimmy Harris' roundheels sister caught him raiding the pantry on his way out, took his cherry and said his thing was big. Because en route to swipe Biff Rice's *National Geographic*s he found Biff's baby brother out of his crib, chewing on an electrical cord—and he put him back, fed him condensed milk and maybe saved his life, pretending it was his kid brother and he was saving him from Des and the Reverend. Because being the San Francisco Phantom was a respite from being a stick-thin, scaredy-cat school grind with a crackpot father, doormat mother and idiot brother.

Until October 1, 1924.

Desmond had sent him on a second run to Jimmy Harris' place; he squeezed in through the woodbox opening, knowing roundheels Annie was there. She *was* there, but not alone: a cop with his blue serge trousers down to his ankles was on the living room carpet pumping her. *He* gasped, tripped and fell; the cop beat him silly, signet rings lacerating his face to shreds. He cleansed his wounds himself, tried to get up the guts to break into Biff Rice's place to see if the baby was okay, but couldn't get up the nerve; he went home, hid Desmond's burglary stash and told him the tables were turned: ripped tendons or not, the ringleader had to steal for the thief or he'd spill the beans to the Reverend. There was only one thing he wanted, and then they'd be quits—one of Annie Harris' negligees—and *he'd* tell him when to pull the job.

He staked the Harris house out, learning that Annie serviced Officer John Rokkas every Tuesday afternoon when the rest of the family worked at the Harris' produce stall in Oakland. On a cold November Tuesday, *he* picked the lock for Des; Des went in and came out twenty minutes later, beaten to a pulp. *He* stole Desmond's booty and secreted it in a safe deposit box, establishing a parity of fear between the two Considine brothers. Desmond flunked out of Union Theological Seminary and became a big shot in the used-car racket. Mal went to Stanford, graduated and lollygagged through a year of law school, dreaming of back-alley adventure, prowling for loose women and never really enjoying the capture. When law school became excruciatingly boring, he joined the Los Angeles Police Department, not knowing how long he'd last as a cop—or if he even could last. Then he went home for Christmas, twenty-three years old and a rookie running scared in L.A. niggertown. He wore his uniform to Christmas dinner: Sam Browne belt, silver-plated whistle, .38 revolver. Car king Desmond, still bearing the scars of Officer John Rokkas' beating, was terrified of his new persona. *He* knew he'd be a policeman until the day he died.

Mal segued from his brother to Danny Upshaw, the black box canyon surrounding him, spent ammunition sliding under his feet. How good was he? What would he see? Would what he saw be worth today multiplied fifty times—Ellis Loew stalking grand jury chambers wrapped in the American flag?

"You've more stomach for this work than I expected."

Dudley was right.

Mal picked up a handful of empty shells, hurled them at nothing and drove home to the Shangri-Lodge Motel.

20

MICKEY COHEN's hideaway was SRO.

The Mick and Davey Goldman were working on a new nightclub routine, a .12 gauge pump substituting for a floor mike. Johnny Stompanato was playing rummy with Morris Jahelka, going over plans for the Cohen-Dragna dope summit between hands. And Buzz was interviewing Mickey's Teamster goons, taking down picket line scuttlebutt, a last-minute precaution before Mal Considine sent in his operative.

So far, boring Commie jive:

The De Haven cooze and Mort Ziffkin traded clichés about overthrowing the "studio autocracy"; Fritzie "Icepick" Kupferman had a Teamster file clerk tagged as a UAES plant—they'd been spoon-feeding him only what they wanted him to hear for weeks now, letting him run the lunch truck across from the Variety International line. Mo Jahelka had a hinky feeling: UAES pickets weren't fighting back when shoved or verbally provoked— they seemed smug, like they were biding their time, even old lefty headbashers maintaining their frost. Moey seemed to think UAES had something up its sleeve. Buzz had padded the statements so Ellis Loew would think he was working harder than he was, feeling like a nice, tasty Christian in a lion's den, waiting for the lion to get hungry and notice him.

Johnny Stomp Lion.

Mickey Lion.

Johnny had been giving him the fisheye ever since he walked in the door, ten days since he kiboshed the squeeze on Lucy Whitehall and bought the guinea sharpster off with five Mickey C-notes. "Hi, Buzz," "Hi, Johnny," nothing else. He'd been with Audrey three times now, the one all-nighter at his place, two quick shots at Howard's fuck pad in the Hollywood Hills. If Mickey had any kind of surveillance on Audrey it was Johnny; if he got wise, it was mortgage his life to the fucker or kill him, no middle ground. If Mickey got wise, it was the Big Adios, when crossed, the little guy got vicious: he'd found the trigger who bumped Hooky Rothman, gave him two hollow points in the kneecaps, an evening of agony with a Fritzie Kupferman coup de grace: an icepick in the ear, Fritzie making like Toscanini conducting Beethoven, little dips and swirls with his baton before he speared the poor bastard's brain.

Mickey Lion, this bamboo bungalow his den.

Buzz put away his notepad, taking a last look at the four names Dudley Smith had called him with earlier: Reds to be background-checked, more shitwork, probably more padding. Mickey Lion and Johnny Lion were schmoozing by the fireplace now, a picture of Audrey Lioness in pasties and panties on the wall above them. The Mick hooked a finger at him; he walked over.

The comedian had some schtick ready. "A guy comes up and asks me, 'Mickey, how's business?' I tell him, 'Pal, it's like show business, there is no business.' I make a pass at this ginch, she says, 'I don't lay for every Tom, Dick and Harry.' I say, 'What about me? I'm Mickey!'"

Buzz laughed and pointed to the picture of Audrey, eyes hard on Johnny Stomp. "You should put her in your routine. Beauty and the Beast. You'll bring the house down."

Goose egg from Johnny; Mickey screwing up his face like he was actually considering the suggestion. Buzz tested the water again. "Get some big jig to play sidekick, make like he's giving it to Audrey. Coons are always good for a laugh."

More nothing. Mickey said, "Shvartzes I don't need, shvartzes I don't trust. What do you get when you cross a nigger and a Jew?"

Buzz played dumb. "I don't know. What?"

Mickey sprayed laughter. "A janitor who owns the building!"

Johnny chuckled and excused himself; Buzz eyed the Va Va Voom Girl at twenty and made quick book: a hundred to one he knew less than nothing about them. Mickey said, "You should laugh more. I don't trust guys who don't have no sense of humor."

"You don't trust anybody, Mick."

"Yeah? How's this for trust. February eighth at the haberdashery, my deal with Jack D. Twenty-five pounds of Mex brown, cash split, food and booze. All my men, all Jack's. Nobody heeled. *That* is trust."

Buzz said, "I don't believe it."

"The deal?"

"The nobody heeled. Are you fuckin' insane?"

Mickey put an arm around Buzz's shoulders. "Jack wants four neutral triggers. He's got two City bulls, I got this Sheriff's dick won the Golden Gloves last year, and I'm still one short. You want the job? Five hundred for the day?"

He'd spend the money on Audrey: tight cashmere sweaters, red and pink and green and white, a size too small to show off her uplift. "Sure, Mick."

Mickey's grip tightened. "I got a storefront on the Southside. County juice, a little sharking, a little book. Half a dozen runners. Audrey's keeping the ledgers for me, and she says I'm getting eaten alive."

"The runners?"

"Everything tallies, but the daily take-in's been short. I pay salary, the guys enforce their own stuff. Short of shaking down the guys, I got no way to know."

Buzz slid free of Mickey's arm, thinking of lioness larceny: Audrey with a hot pencil and a wet brain. "You want me to ask around on the QT? Get the squad boss at Firestone to shake down the locals, find out who's bettin' what?"

"Trust, Buzzchik. You nail who's doing me, I'll throw some bones your way."

Buzz grabbed his coat. Mickey said, "Hot date?"

"The hottest."

"Anybody I know?"

"Rita Hayworth."

"Yeah?"

"Yeah, trust me."

"She red downstairs?"

"Black at the roots, Mick. There's no business like show business."

* * *

His date was for 10:00 at Howard's spot near the Hollywood Bowl; Mickey and Johnny's no-take and the skim story had him running jumpy, his watch set to Audrey standard time, which made killing an hour somewhere pure horseshit. Buzz drove to the lion woman's house, parked behind her Packard ragtop and rang the bell.

Audrey answered the door, slacks, sweater and no makeup. "You said you didn't even want to know where I lived."

Buzz shuffled his feet, making like a swain on a prom date. "I checked your driver's license while you were asleep."

"Meeks, that's not something you do to somebody you're sleeping with."

"You're sleepin' with Mickey, ain't you?"

"Yes, but what does—"

Buzz slid past Audrey, into a bargain basement front room. "Savin' money on furnishings to bankroll your shopping center?"

"Yes. Since you ask, I am."

"Sweetie, you know what Mickey did to the ginzo killed Hooky Rothman?"

Audrey slammed the door and wrapped her arms around herself. "He beat the man senseless and had Fritzie what's his name drive him over the state line and warn him never to come back. Meeks, what is this? I can't *stand* you this way."

Buzz shoved her against the door, pinned her there and put his hands on her face, holding her still, his hands going gentle when he saw she wasn't going to fight him. "You're skimmin' off Mickey 'cause you think he won't find out and he wouldn't hurt you if he did and now *I'm* the one that has to fuckin' protect you because you are so fuckin' dumb about the fuckin' guys you fuck and I'm in way over my fuckin' head with you so you get fuckin' smart because if Mickey hurts you I'll fuckin' kill him and all his fuckin' kike guinea pigshit—"

He stopped when Audrey started bawling and trying to get out words. He stroked her hair, bending down to listen better, turning to jelly when he heard, "I love you, too."

* * *

They made love on the bargain basement living room floor and in the bedroom and in the shower, Buzz pulling the curtain loose, Audrey admitting she cheapskated on the bathroom fixtures, too. He told her he'd check with an ex-Dragna paper man he knew and show her how to redoctor Mickey's books—or fix an angle to lay the onus off on some nonexistent welcher; she said she'd quit skimming, straighten up, fly right, and play the stock market like a squarejohn woman who didn't screw gangsters or Red Squad bagmen. He said, "I love you" fifty times to make up for her saying it first; he got her sizes so he could blow all his kickback take on clothes for her; they went down on each other to seal a pact: nobody was supposed to mention Mickey unless absolutely necessary, nobody was to talk about their future or lack of it, two dates a week was their limit, Howard's fuck pads rotated, her place or his place as a treat once in a while, their cars stashed where the bad guys wouldn't see them. No outside dates, no trips together, no telling friends what they had going. Buzz asked Audrey to do the tassel trick for him; she did; she went on to model her stripper outfits, then all the clothes in her wardrobe. Buzz figured that if he spent his gambling output on threads he wanted to see her in, he'd never be bored staying inside with her: he could take the clothes off, make love to her, watch her dress again. He thought that if they stayed inside forever, he'd tell her everything about himself, all the shitty stuff included, but he'd lay it out slowly, so she'd get to know him, not get scared and run. He talked a blue streak; she talked a blue streak; he let slip about the Doberman pinscher he killed when he burglarized a lumber-yard in Tulsa in 1921, and she didn't care. Toward dawn, Audrey started falling asleep and he started thinking about Mickey and got scared. He thought about moving his car, but didn't want to upset the perfect way his lioness had her head tucked against his collarbone. The scare got worse, so he reached to the floor, grabbed his .38 and stuck it under the pillow.

21

THE NUT bin waiting room featured tables and plasticene couches in soothing colors: mint green, ice blue, pale yellow. Art-work by the nuts was tacked to the walls: finger paintings and draw-by-the-numbers jobs depicting Jesus Christ, Joe DiMaggio and Franklin D. Roosevelt. Danny sat waiting for Cyril "Cy" Vandrich, dressed in Ted Krugman garb: dungarees, skivvy shirt, steel-toed motorcycle boots and a bombardier's leather jacket. He'd been up most of the night studying Mal Considine's scenario; he'd spent yesterday doing his own background checks on Duane Lindenaur and George Wiltsie, prowling their Valley hangouts and getting nothing but a queasy sense of the two as homo slime. Slipping into the Ted role had been a relief, and when he drove up to the Camarillo gate the guard had double-taked his get-up and New York plates and openly challenged him as a cop, checking his ID and badge, calling West Hollywood Station to get the okay. So far, Upshaw into Krugman was a success—the acid test this afternoon at the picket line.

An orderly ushered a thirtyish man in khakis into the room—a shortish guy, skinny with broad hips, deep-set gray eyes and a hepcat haircut—one greasy brown lock perfectly covering his forehead. The orderly said, "Him," and exited; Vandrich sighed,

"This is a humbug. I've got connections on the switchboard, the girl said this is about murders, and I'm not a murderer. Jazz musicians are Joe Lunchmeat to you clowns. You've been trying to crucify Bird for years, now you want me."

Danny let it go, sizing up Vandrich sizing him up. "Wrong. This is about Felix Gordean, Duane Lindenaur and George Wiltsie. I know you're not a killer."

Vandrich slumped into a chair. "Felix is a piece of work, Duane what's his face I don't know from Adam and George Wiltsie padded his stuff so he'd look big to impress all the rich queens at Felix's parties. And why are you dressed up like rough trade? Think you'll get me to talk that way? That image is from hunger, and I outgrew it a long time ago."

Danny thought: smart, hep, probably wise to the game. The rough trade crack washed over him; he fondled his jacket sleeves, loving the feel of the leather. "You've got them all buffaloed, Cy. They don't know if you're crazy or not."

Vandrich smiled; he shifted in his chair and cocked a hip toward Danny. "You think I'm a malingerer?"

"I know you are, and I know that Misdemeanor Court judges get tired of giving the same old faces ninety days here when they could file on them for Petty Theft Habitual and get them some felony time. Quentin time. Up there they don't ask you for it, they take it."

"And I'm sure you know a lot about that, with your tough leather goods and all."

Danny laced his hands behind his head, the jacket's soft fur collar brushing him. "I need to know what you know about George Wiltsie and Felix Gordean, and maybe what Gordean does or doesn't know about some things. Cooperate, you'll always pull ninetys. Dick me around, the judge gets a letter saying you withheld evidence in a triple homicide case."

Vandrich giggled. "Felix got murdered?"

"No. Wiltsie, Lindenaur and a trombone man named Marty Goines, who used to call himself the 'Horn of Plenty.' Have you heard of him?"

"No, but I'm a trumpeter and I used to be known as the 'Lips of Ecstasy.' That's a double entendre, in case you haven't guessed."

Danny laughed off the vamp. "Five seconds or I walk and nudge the judge."

Vandrich smiled. "I'll play, Mr. Policeman. And I'll even give you a free introductory observation. But first I've got a question. Did Felix tell you about me?"

"Yes."

Vandrich did a little number, crossing his legs, making mincy hand motions. Danny saw it as the fuck going nance in order to knuckle to authority; he felt himself start to sweat, his lefty threads too hot, too much. "Look, just tell me."

Vandrich quieted down. "I knew Felix during the war, when I was putting on a crazy act to get out of the service. I played that act *everywhere*. I was living off an inheritance then, living it *up*. I went to Felix's parties and I trucked with Georgie once, and Felix thought I was non compos mentis, so if he sent you to see me he was probably playing a game. There. That's my free introductory observation."

And *his* Gordean instincts confirmed: the pimp couldn't draw breath without trying an angle—which meant that he *was* holding back. Danny said, "You're good," got out his notebook and turned to the list of questions he'd prepared.

"Burglary, Vandrich. Did you know George Wiltsie to be involved in it, or do you know of anyone connected to Felix Gordean who pulls burglaries?"

Vandrich shook his head. "No. Like I said, George Wiltsie I trucked with once, talk wasn't his forte, so we stuck to business. He never mentioned that guy Lindenaur. I'm sorry he got killed, but I just take nice things from stores, I don't associate with burglars."

Danny wrote down "No." "The same thing on dentists and dental technicians, men capable of making dentures."

Vandrich flashed perfect teeth. "No. And I haven't been to a dentist since high school."

"A young man, call him a boy—with a scarred, burned-up face in bandages. He was a burglar, and this would be back during the war."

"No. Ugh. Awful."

Two more "Nos." Danny said, "A zoot stick. That's a long wooden stick with a razor blade or razor blades attached at the end. It's a weapon from the war days, for cutting up the zoot suits that Mexicans used to wear."

Vandrich said, "Double ugh and an ugh on pachucos in zoot suits in general."

No, no, no, no—underlined. Danny put out his ace question. "Tall, gray-haired men, mid-forties now. Nice silver hair, guys who know jazz spots, hep enough to buy dope. Homosexual men who went to Gordean's parties back when you did."

Vandrich said, "No"; Danny turned to fresh paper. "This is where you shine, Cyril. Felix Gordean. Everything you know, everything you've heard, everything you've thought about him."

Vandrich said, "Felix Gordean is ... a ... piece of ... work," drawing the words out into a lisp. "He doesn't truck with man, woman or beast, and his only kick is bringing guys out, getting them to admit what they are, then . . . procuring for them. He has a legitimate talent agency, and he meets lots of young men, really sensitive creative types ... and ... well ... they're prone to being like ..."

Danny wanted to scream QUEER, FAGGOT, FRUIT, HOMO, PEDERAST, BRUNSER, PUNK, COCKSUCKER and ram slime from the Hollywood Squad reports down Vandrich's throat, making him spit it out in the open where *he* could spit on it. He kneaded his jacket sleeves and said, "He gets his thrills getting guys to admit that they're homosexuals, right?"

"Uh, yes."

"You can *say* it, Vandrich. Five minutes ago you were trying to flirt with me."

"It ... it's hard to say. It's so ugly and clinical and cold."

"So Gordean brings these *homosexuals* out. Then what?"

"Then he enjoys showing them off at his parties and fixing them up. Getting them acting jobs, then taking their money for the introductions he arranges. Sometimes he has parties at his beach house and watches through these mirrors he has. He can look in, but the fellows in the bedroom can't look out."

Danny remembered his first pass at the Marmont: peeping, his stuff pressed to the window, jazzing on it. "So Gordean's a fucking queer voyeur, he likes watching homos fuck and suck. Let's try this: *Does he keep records for his introduction service?*"

Vandrich had pushed his chair into the wall. "No. He didn't back then, at least. The word was that he had a great memory, and he was terrified of writing things down ... afraid of the police. But ..."

"But what?"

"B-but I h-heard he loves to keep it all in his head, and once I heard him say that his biggest dream was to have something on everybody he knew and a profitable way to use it."

"Like blackmail?"

"Y-yes, I thought of that."

"Do you think Gordean's capable of it?"

No lisp, stutter or hesitation. "Yes."

Danny felt his soft fur collar sticky with sweat. "Get out of here."

* * *

Gordean holding back.

His talent agency a tool to fuel his voyeurism.

Blackmail.

No suspicious Gordean reactions on Duane Lindenaur, extortionist; Charles Hartshorn—"Short and bald as a beagle"—
eliminated as a suspect on his appearance, that fact buttressed
by Sergeant Frank Skakel's assessment of his character and his
take on Hartshorn's juice—the lawyer unapproachable for now.
If Gordean himself was some sort of extortionist, it had to be
coincidental to Lindenaur—both men moved in a world rife
with blackmailees. The talent agency was the place to start.

Danny took PCH back to L.A., all the windows down so he
could keep his jacket on and buttoned full. Per Considine's orders,
he parked three blocks from Hollywood Station and walked the
rest of the way, heading into the muster room dead on time for
the noon meeting he'd called.

His men were already there, sitting in the first row of chairs,
Mike Breuning and Jack Shortell gabbing and smoking. Gene
Niles was four seats over, picking at a pile of papers on his lap.
Danny grabbed a chair and sat down facing them.

Shortell said, "You still look like a cop." Breuning nodded
agreement. "Yeah, but the Commies won't get it. If they were so
smart they wouldn't be Commies, right?"

Danny laughed; Niles said, "Let's get this over with, huh,
Upshaw? I've got lots of work to do."

Danny got out pad and pen. "So do I. Sergeant Shortell, you
first."

Shortell said, "Cut and dried. I've called ninety-one dental
labs, run the descriptions by the people in charge and got a total
of sixteen hinkers: strange-o's, guys with yellow sheets. I eliminated nine of them by blood type, four are currently in jail and the
other three I talked to myself. No sparks, plus the guys had alibis
for the times of death. I'll keep going, and I'll call you if anything
bites me."

Danny said, "Just make sure it's a denture bite," and turned to Breuning. "Mike, what have you and Sergeant Niles got?"

Breuning consulted a big spiral notebook. "What we've got is the old goose egg. On the biting MO, we checked LAPD, County and the muni files. We got a shine queer who bit his boyfriend's dick off, a fat blond guy with a kiddie raper jacket who bites little girls and two guys who match our description—both in Atascadero for aggravated assault. On the queer bar scuttlebutt, zero. Biters do not hang out at homo cocktail lounges and say, 'I bite. Want some?' The fruit detail cops I talked to laughed me out on that one. On the Vice and sex offender file eliminations, nothing. Burglary, ditto. I cross-checked them, nothing duplicated. Nothing on a kid with burn scars. There were six middle-aged gray-haired possibles—all either in custody on the nights of the killings or alibied—squarejohn witnesses. On the recanvassing—nada—it's too old now. Niggertown, Griffith Park, the area where Goines was dumped, nothing. Nobody saw anything, nobody gives a shit. On checking with snitches, forget it. This guy is a loner, I'd bet my pension he does not associate with criminal riffraff. I personally leaned on the only three possibles I got from State and County Parole—two queers and a real sweetheart—this tall, gray preacher type who cornholed three Marines back during the war, used to lube his prong with toothpaste. All three were in for curfew at the Midnight Mission—alibied by no less than Sister Mary Eckert herself."

Breuning stopped, out of breath, and lit a cigarette. He said, "Gene and I muscled every southside H man we could find, which wasn't many—it's dry all over. Rumor has it that Jack D. and/or Mickey C. are getting ready to move a load of cut-rate. Nothing. We leaned on the jazz musician angle, nothing with our man's description. Ditto on goofballs. Nothing. And we leaned *hard*."

Niles chuckled; Danny looked at his own absent doodling: a page of concentric zeros. "Mike, what about the zoot stick angle?— the assault files and snitch calls?"

Breuning's eyes narrowed. "Another goose. And that's old Mex stuff, pretty far afield. I know Doc Layman tagged the back wounds as zoot stick, but don't you think he could be wrong? As far as I'm concerned, it just doesn't play."

A Dudley Smith stooge patronizing Norton Layman, MD, PhD. Danny reached for some frost. "No. Layman's the best, and he's right."

"Then I don't think it's a real lead. I think our guy just read about the damn sticks or eyeballed one of the zoot riots and got a kick out of them. He's a fucking psycho, there's no reason to those guys."

Something about Breuning's take on the sticks was off; Danny shrugged to cover the thought. "I think you're wrong. I think the zoot sticks are essential to the way the killer thinks. My instincts tell me he's revenging old wrongs, and the specific mutilations are a big part of it. So I want you and Niles to comb the station files in Mex neighborhoods and check old occurrence reports—'42, '43, around in there, the zoot riots, Sleepy Lagoon—back when the Mexes were taking heat."

Breuning stared at Danny; Niles groaned and muttered, "My instincts." Danny said, "Sergeant, if you've got comments, address them to me."

Niles cracked a grin. "Okay. One, I don't like the Los Angeles County Sheriff's Department and their good buddy Mickey Kike, and I've got a County pal who says you're not the goody two shoes you pretend to be. Two, I've been doing a little work on my own, and I talked to a couple of Quentin parolees who said no way was Marty Goines a queer—and I believe them. And three, I think you personally fucked me by not calling in Tamarind Street, and I don't like that."

No Bordoni. No Bordoni. No fucking Bordoni. Danny, calm. "I don't care what you like or what you think. *And who were the parolees?*"

Two hard stares locked; Niles glancing down at his notebook. "Paul Arthur Koenig and Lester George Mazmanian. And four, I don't like you."

The bluff called. Danny looked at Niles, spoke to LASD Sergeant Shortell. "Jack, there's a poster on the notice board that shits on our Department. Rip it up."

Shortell's voice, admiring. "My pleasure, skipper."

*   *   *

Ted Krugman.

Ted Krugman.

Theodore Michael Krugman.

Teddy Krugman, Red Commie Pinko Subversive Stagehand.

Friends with Jukey Rosensweig of Young Actors Against Fascism and Bill Wilhite, a cell boss with the Brooklyn CP; ex-lover of Donna Patrice Cantrell, leftist firebrand at Columbia University circa '43, jumper suicide in '47—a dive off the George Washington Bridge when she got the news that her socialist father attempted suicide over his HUAC subpoena, turning himself into a permanent vegetable via ingestion of a scouring powder cocktail that scoured his brain down to sub-idiot quality. Ex-member of AFL-CIO, North Shore Long Island CP, Garment Workers' Defense Committee, Concerned Americans Against Bigotry, Friends of the Abraham Lincoln Brigade and the Fair Play for Paul Robeson League. Socialist summer camps as a kid, New York City College dropout, not drafted because of his subversive politics, liked to work as a theater grip because of all the politically enlightened people you met and pussy. Worked a long string of Broadway shows, plus a handful of B movies shot on location in Manhattan. Slogan shouter, brawler, hardcase. Loved to attend meetings and demonstrations, sign petitions and talk Commie rebop. Active in the New York leftist scene until '48—then nowhere.

Pictures.

Donna Patrice Cantrell was pretty but hard, a softer version of her dad the Ajax guzzler. Jukey Rosensweig was a big fat guy with bulging thyroid eyes and thick glasses; Bill Wilhite was white-bread handsome. His supporting cast of characters, caught in Fed surveillance snaps, were just faces attached to bodies wielding placards: names, dates and causes on the back, to shore him up with some more history.

Parked on Gower just north of Sunset, Danny ran through his script and photo kit. He had his co-stars' faces down pat: the Teamster picket boss he was supposed to introduce himself to, the goons he'd be picketing and arguing with, the LAPD Academy muscleman he'd fight—and finally—if Considine's scenario played to perfection—Norman Kostenz, UAES picket boss, the man who'd take him to Claire De Haven. Deep-breathing, he locked his gun, badge, cuffs and Daniel Thomas Upshaw ID in the glove compartment, sliding Theodore Michael Krugman license photostats into the sleeves in his wallet. Upshaw into Krugman completed; Danny walked over, ready to do it.

The scene was pandemonium divided into two snakelike strips of bodies: UAES, Teamsters, banners on sticks, shouts and catcalls, three feet of sidewalk separating the factions, a debris-filled gutter and studio walls bracketing the lines down a quarter-mile-long city block. Newsmen standing by their cars on the opposite side of Gower; lunch trucks dispensing coffee and doughnuts; a bunch of oldster cops stuffing their faces, watching newshounds shoot craps on a piece of cardboard laid across the hood of an LAPD black-and-white. Duelling bullhorns bombarding the street with squelch noise and static-layered repetitions of "REDS OUT!" and "FAIR PAY NOW!"

Danny found the Teamster picket boss, picture pure; the man winked on the sly and handed him a pine slab with UAES— UN–AMERICAN ESCAPED SUBVERSIVES printed on reinforced cardboard at the top. He went through a rigmarole of laying down the law and making him fill out a time card; Danny saw the guy working the Teamster lunch truck eyeball the transaction— obviously the UAES plant man mentioned in Considine's info package. The shouts got louder; the picket boss hustled Danny over to his marching buddies, Al and Jerry, picture perfect in their grubby work clothes. Tough-guy salutations per the script: three hard boys who brook no horseshit getting down to business. Then him—Ted Krugman—starring in his own Hollywood epic, surrounded by extras, one line of good guys, one of bad guys, all of them moving, separate lines going in opposite directions.

He marched, three abreast with Al and Jerry—pros who knew their stuff; signs came at him: FISCAL JUSTICE NOW!; END THE STUDIO AUTOCRACY!; NEGOTIATE FAIR WAGES! Teamster elbows dug into UAES rib cages; the bad guys winced, didn't elbow back, kept marching and yelling. It was Man Camera with something like Sound-O-Vision thrown in; Danny kept imagining mixmasters, meat grinders, buzz saws and cycle engines working overtime, not letting you think or sight on a fixed image. He kept talking his pre-planned diatribe, feeding Jerry, right on the button with Considine's first cue: "You're talkin' the fuckin' Moscow party line, pal. Whose fucking side are you on?"

Himself, coming back: "The side that's paying me a fucking buck an hour to picket, *pal!*"

Jerry, grabbing his arm as UAESers stood aside and watched: "That's not good enough—"

He broke free and kept walking and shouting per the scenario; per the scenario the picket boss came over and issued him a warning about team play, hauling Al and Jerry over, making them all shake hands like kids in a schoolyard, a bunch of anemic lefties scoping it out. All three of them played it sullen; the picket boss hotfooted it to the lunch truck; Danny saw him talking to the

coffee man—UAES's plant—hooking a thumb back at the little
fracas he just refereed. Al said, "Don't goldbrick, Krugman"; Jerry
muttered anti-Red epithets; Danny launched his "I'm one of the
guys" spiel, real real Krugman stuff in case the bad guys had a
close ear down, stuff Considine yanked out of an old NYPD Red
Squad report: garment worker unions bashing heads insanely,
the "bosses" on both sides fucking over the rank and file. Him
pleading with philistine Al and Jerry to see the *reason* behind what
he was saying; them shaking their heads and picketing away from
him, disgusted at working the same line as a rat fucker Commie traitor.

Danny marched, banner high, shouting, "REDS OUT!," meaning it, but savoring the curve he'd just pitched. His Man Camera
started working, everything seemed contained and controlled
like he'd just had his four shots and didn't want a fifth, like he was
born for this and the queer shit at Gordean's pad didn't really
send him. It felt like chaos in a vacuum, being shoved into a meat
grinder and laughing as you got chopped up. Time passed; Al and
Jerry brushed by him: once, twice, three times, side-mouthing
ugly stuff, bringing the LAPD goon with them on their fourth
go-round, a brick shithouse blocking his path, fingers on his chest,
the hump *improvising* on Considine's script: "This guy's a tough
guy Commie? He looks like a weak sister to me."

The wrong words, then, "Make it good you County fuck,"
whispered up close. Danny improvised, bending the shithouse's
fingers back, snapping them at the bottom digit. The man shrieked
and swung a bum left hook; Danny stepped inside with a counter
one-two to the solar plexus. The LAPD man doubled over; Danny
shot him a steel-toed right foot to the balls, crashing him into a
group of UAES pickets.

Shouts all around; whistles blowing. Danny picked up a discarded pine slab and got ready to swing it at his co-star's head.
Then blue uniforms surrounded him and billy clubs beat him to
the ground and he was pummeled, lifted, pummeled, lifted,
dumped and kicked at. He went stone cold out—then he tasted
blood and sidewalk and felt hands lifting him up until he was face
to face with Norman Kostenz, looking just like Mal Considine's
surveillance pic, a friendly guy who was saying, "Ted Krugman,
huh? I think I've heard of you."

* * *

The next hour went Speed-O-Vision fast.

Friendly Norm helped him clean himself up and took him to a bar on the Boulevard. Danny came out of his thumping quickly, thudding pains in the soft part of his back, loose teeth, side aches. The bluesuits had to have been in on Considine's plan—improvising in his favor—or they'd have cracked his head open for real. The script had called for them to break up a fistfight, separating the combatants, some minor roughhouse before cutting them loose. They'd obviously played off his improvisation, the kicks and gutter dump their aside for his walling on one of their own. Now the question was how hard "Call me Mal" would come down on him for the damage he'd done—he was an ex-LAPD man himself.

At the bar it was all questions, back to Ted Krugman, no time to think of repercussions.

Norm Kostenz took his photograph for a record of the assault and kissed his ass, a tough-guy worshiper; Danny moved into Ted, nursing a beer and double shot, making like he rarely boozed, that it was just to ease his aching, fascist-thumped bones. The liquor did help—it took the bite off his aches and got him moving his shoulders, working out the kinks that would come later. The juice downed, he started feeling good, proud of his performance; Kostenz ran a riff on how Jukey Rosensweig used to talk about him and Donna Cantrell. Danny put out a sob number on Donna, using it to segue into his missing years: Prof Cantrell a vegetable, his beloved Donna dead, the fascists responsible, but him too numbed by grief to organize, protest or generally fight back. Kostenz pressed on what he had been doing since Donna's suicide; Danny gave him an Upshaw/Krugman combo platter: real-life car thief stories under Red Ted's aegis, phony East Coast venues. Friendly Norm ate it up, vicarious kicks on a platter; he called for a second round of drinks and asked questions about the garment district wars, the Robeson League, stuff Jukey had told him about. Danny winged it, flying high: names and pictures from Considine's kit, long spiels extolling the virtues of various lefties, borrowing from the actual personalities of deputies and San Berdoo townies he'd known. Kostenz licked his plate and begged for more; Danny went sky high, all his aches lulled, kneading his jacket sleeves like they were his second skin. He spun tales out of thin air and Considine's facts: a long schtick about his loss of political faith, his rapacious womanizing with the Commie quail from Mal's surveillance pics, his long cross-country odyssey and how self-hatred and a desire to scope the scene brought him to the Teamster picket line, but now he knew he could never be fascist muscle—he wanted to work, fight, organize and help UAES end the blood-sucking tyranny of the studio bosses. Almost breathless, Norm Kostenz took it in, got up and said, "Can you meet me and our member screener tomorrow? The El Coyote on Beverly at noon?"

Danny stood up, weaving, knowing it was more from his Academy Award acting than from booze and a beating. He said, "I'll be there," and saluted like Uncle Joe Stalin in a newsreel he'd seen.

* * *

Danny drove home, checked to make sure his files and pictures were secure in their hiding place, hot-showered and daubed lina-ment on the bruises that were starting to form on his back. Naked, he performed intro lines to Claire De Haven in front of the bath-room mirror, then dressed from his lefty wardrobe: wool slacks with a skinny belt, T-shirt, his workboots and the leather jacket. Ted Krugman but a cop, he admired himself in the mirror, then drove to the Strip.

Dusk was falling, twilight darkening over low rain clouds. Danny parked on Sunset across from the Felix Gordean Agency, hunkered down in the seat with binoculars and fixed on the building.

It was a one-story gray French Provincial, louvered windows and an arched doorway, deco lettering in brass above the mailbox. An enclosed autoport was built on, the entrance illuminated by roof lights. Three cars were parked inside; Danny squinted and wrote down three Cal '49 license numbers: DB 6841, GX 1167, QS 3334.

Full darkness hit; Danny kept his eyes on the doorway. At 5:33, a twenty-fivish male Caucasian walked out, got into green Ford coupé GX 1167 and drove away. Danny wrote down a description of the car and the man, then went back to straight surveillance. At 5:47, a white prewar La Salle, Cal '49 TR 4191, pulled in; a hand-some young Latin type wearing a suitcoat and pegged pants got out, rang the buzzer and entered the agency. Danny jotted his stats down, kept looking, saw two older, dark-haired men in busi-ness suits leave, walk to the carport and get into DB 6841 and QS 3334, back out and go off in opposite directions on Sunset. The Latin type left ten minutes later; Danny filled in his descriptions of the men—none of whom matched his suspect.

Time dragged; Danny stayed glued, smelling linament, feeling his muscle aches return. At 6:14 a Rolls-Royce pulled into the carport; a man in a chauffeur's outfit got out, rang the agency buzzer, spoke into the intercom and walked across the street and out of sight. Lights went off inside—until only a single window was glowing.

Danny thought: Gordean's driver leaving his car, probably no more "clients" coming in. He spotted a phone booth on the corner, walked over, gave the box a coin and called the DMV Police Line.

"Yes? Who's requesting?"

Danny eyed the one light still on. "Deputy Upshaw, West Hollywood Squad, and make this fast."

The operator said, "We're a little bit backlogged on vehicle registrations, but—"

"This is the *police* line, not DMV Central. I'm a Homicide detective, so you kick loose for me."

The man sounded chastised. "We were helping regis—I'm sorry, Deputy. Give me your names."

Danny said, "I've got the numbers and the vehicle descriptions, *you* give *me* the names. Four California '49s: DB 6841, GX 1167, QS 3334 and TR 4191. Go fast."

The operator said, "Yessir." The line buzzed; Danny watched the Felix Gordean Agency. Seconds stretched; the DMV man came back on the line. "Got them, Deputy."

Danny braced his notepad against the wall. "Go."

"DB 6841 is Donald Willis Wachtel, 1638 Franklin Street, Santa Monica. GX 1167 is Timothy James Costigan, 11692 Saticoy Street, Van Nuys. On QS 3334, we've got Alan Brian Marks with a K-S, 209 4th Avenue, Venice, and TR 4191 is Augie Luis—that's L-U-I-S—Duarte, 1890 North Vendome, Los Angeles. That's it."

No sparks on the names—except the "Duarte" seemed vaguely familiar. Danny hung up just as the light in the window went off; he ran back to his car, got in behind the wheel and waited.

Felix Gordean walked out the door a few moments later. He checked the lock and flipped a switch that doused the carport lights, backed the Rolls out and hung a U-turn, then headed west on Sunset. Danny counted to five and pursued.

The Rolls was easy to track—Gordean drove cautiously and stuck to the middle lane. Danny let a car get in front of him and fixed on Gordean's radio aerial, a long strip of metal with an ornamental Union Jack at the top, oncoming headlight glare making it stand out like a marker.

They cruised west, out of the Strip and into Beverly Hills. At Linden the middle car hung a right turn and headed north; Danny closed the gap on Gordean, touching the Rolls' bumper with his headlights, then idling back. Beverly Hills became Holmby Hills and Westwood; traffic thinned out to almost nothing. Brentwood, Pacific Palisades, looming greenery dotted with Spanish houses and vacant lots—Sunset Boulevard winding through blackish green darkness. Danny caught the reflection of highbeams in back of him.

He let the throttle up; the beams came on that much stronger, then disappeared. He looked in the rear-view, saw low headlights three car lengths back and no one else on the road; he hit the gas and jammed forward until Gordean's Rolls was less than a short stone's throw from the snout of his Chevy. Another check of the rear-view; the back car right on his ass.

Tail.

Moving surveillance on *him*.

Three-car rolling stakeout.

Danny swallowed and glimpsed a string of vacant lots, dirt shouldered, off the right side of the street. He downshifted, swung a hard right turn, hit the shoulder and fishtailed across rock-strewn dirt, wracking the Chevy's undercarriage. He saw the tail car on Sunset, lights off and zooming; he cut hard left, went down to first gear, back off dirt onto good hard blacktop. High beams on; second and third, the gas pedal floored. A brown postwar sedan losing ground as he gained on it; him right on the car's ass, mud smeared across its rear plate, the driver probably near blinded by his lights.

Just then the sedan turned hard right and hauled up a barely lit side street. Danny downshifted, hit the brakes and skidded into a full turnaround brody, stalling the car facing the flow of traffic. Headlights were coming straight at him; he sparked the ignition, popped the clutch and gas, banged over the curb and up the street, horns blasting down on Sunset.

Bungalows lined both sides of the street; a sign designated it "La Paloma Dr, 1900 N." Danny speeded up, the blacktop getting steeper, no other moving cars in sight. Bungalow lights gave him some illumination; La Paloma Drive became a summit and leveled off—and there was his brown sedan on the roadside, the driver's door open.

Danny pulled up behind it, hit his brights, unholstered his piece. He got out and walked over, gun arm first. He looked in the front seat and saw nothing but neat velveteen upholstery; he stepped back and saw a '48 Pontiac Super Chief, abandoned on a half-developed street surrounded by totally dark hills.

His heart was booming; his throat was dry; his legs were butter and his gun hand twitched. He listened and heard nothing but himself; he scanned for escape routes and saw a dozen driveways leading into back yards and the entire rear of the Santa Monica Mountains.

Danny thought: *think procedure, go slow, you're interagency Homicide brass.* The "brass" calmed him; he tucked his .45 into his waistband, knelt and checked out the front seat.

Nothing on the seat covers; the registration strapped to the steering column—right where it should be. Danny undid the plastic strip without touching flat surfaces, held it up to the light of his highbeams and read:

Wardell John Hascomb, 9816 1/4 South Iola, Los Angeles. Registration number Cal 416893-H; license number Cal JQ 1338.

L.A. South Central, darktown, the area where the killer stole the Marty Goines transport car.

HIM.

Danny got fresh shakes, drove back to Sunset and headed west until he spotted a filling station with a pay phone. With shaky hands, he slipped a nickel in the slot and dialed DMV Police Information.

"Yeah? Who's requesting?"

"D-Deputy Upshaw, West Hollywood Squad."

"The guy from half an hour or so ago?"

"Goddamn—yes, and check the Hot Sheet for this: 1948 Pontiac Super Chief Sedan, Cal JQ 1338. If it's hot, I want the address it was stolen from."

"Gotcha," silence. Danny stood in the phone booth, warm one second, chilled the next. He took out his pad and pen, ready to write down what the operator gave him; he saw "Augie Luis Duarte" and snapped why it seemed familiar: there was a Juan Duarte in the UAES info he studied—meaning nothing—Duarte was as common a Mex name as Garcia or Hernandez.

The operator came back. "She's hot, clouted outside 9945 South Normandie this afternoon. The owner is one Wardell J. Hascomb, male Negro, 9816 South—"

"I've got that."

"You know, Deputy, your partner was a whole lot nicer."

"What?"

The operator sounded exasperated, like he was talking to a cretin. "Deputy Jones from your squad. He called in for a repeat on those four names I gave you, said you lost your notes."

Now the booth went freezing. No such deputy existed; some-one—probably HIM—had been watching him stake Gordean's office, close enough to overhear his conversation with the clerk and glom the gist—that he was requesting vehicle registrations. Danny shivered and said, "Describe his voice."

"Your partner's? Too cultured for a County plainclothes dick, I'll—"

Danny slammed the receiver down, gave the phone his last coin and dialed the direct squadroom line at Hollywood Station. A voice answered, "Hollywood Detectives"; Danny said, "Sergeant Shortell. Tell him it's urgent."

"Okay," a soft click, the old-timer cop yawning, "Yes? Who's this?"

"Upshaw. Jack, the killer was tailing me in a hot roller."

"What the—"

"Just listen. I spotted him, and he rabbited and abandoned the car. Write this down: '48 Pontiac Super, brown, La Paloma Drive off Sunset in the Palisades, where it flattens out at the hill. Print man to dust it, you to canvass. He took off on foot and it's all hills there, so I'm pretty sure he's gone, but do it anyway. And fast—I won't be there to watchdog."

"Holy fuck."

"In spades, and get me this—records checks on these four men—Donald Wachtel, 1638 Franklin, Santa Monica. Timothy Costigan, 11692 Saticoy, Van Nuys. Alan Marks, 209 4th Avenue, Venice, and Augie Duarte, 1890 Vendome, L.A. Got it?"

Shortell said, "You've got it"; Danny hung up and trawled for HIM. He cruised back to La Paloma and found the car exactly the way he left it; he hung his flashlight out the window and shone it at bungalows, alleyways, back yards and foothills. Square-john husbands and wives taking out the trash; dogs, cats and a spooked coyote transfixed by the glare in its eyes. No tall, mid-dle-aged man with lovely silver hair calmly making his getaway from a count of Grand Theft Auto. Danny drove back to Sunset and took it slowly out to the beach, scanning both sides of the street; at Pacific Coast Highway, he dug in his memory for Felix Gordean's address, came up with 16822 PCH and rolled there.

It was on the beach side of the road, a white wood Colonial built on pilings sunk into the sand, "Felix Gordean, Esq.," in deco by the mailbox. Danny parked directly in front and rang the bell; chimes like the ones at the Marmont sounded; a pretty boy in a kimono answered. Danny badged him. "Sheriff's. I'm here to see Felix Gordean."

The boy lounged in the doorway. "Felix is indisposed right now."

Danny looked him over, his stomach queasing at blond hair straight from a peroxide bottle. The living room backdropping the boy was ultramodern, with one whole wall mirrored—tinted glass like the one-ways in police interrogation stalls. Vandrich on Gordean: he perved watching men with men. Danny said, "Tell him it's Deputy Upshaw."

"It's all right, Christopher. I'll talk to this officer."

The pretty boy jumped at Gordean's voice; Danny walked in and saw the man, elegant in a silk robe, staring at the one-way. He kept staring; Danny said, "Are you going to look at me?"

Gordean pivoted slowly. "Hello, Deputy. Did you forget something the other night?"

Christopher went over and stood by Gordean, giving the mirror a look-see and a giggle. Danny said, "Four names that I need rundowns on. Donald Wachtel, Alan Marks, Augie Duarte and Timothy Costigan."

Gordean said, "Those men are clients and friends of mine, and they were all at my office this afternoon. Have you been spying on me?"

Danny stepped toward the two, angling himself away from the mirror. "Get specific. Who are they?"

Gordean shrugged and put his hands on his hips. "As I said, clients and friends."

"Like I said, get specific."

"Very well. Don Wachtel and Al Marks are radio actors, Tim Costigan used to be a crooner with the big bands and Augie Duarte is a budding actor who I've found commercial work for. In fact, maybe you've seen him on television. I found him a job playing a fruit picker in a spot for the California Citrus Growers' Association."

Pretty Boy was hugging himself, entranced by the mirror; Danny smelled fear on Gordean. "Remember how I described my suspect the other night? Tall, gray-haired and forty-fivish?"

"Yes. So?"

"So have you seen anyone like that hanging out around your office?"

A deadpan from Gordean; Christopher turning from the mirror, his mouth opening. A brief hand squeeze, pimp to Pretty Boy; the kid's deadpan. Danny smiled, "That's it. I'm sorry I bothered you."

Two men walked into the living room. They were wearing red silk briefs; one man was removing a sequined mask. Both were young and overly muscular, with shaved legs and torsos slicked down with some kind of oil. They eyed the three standing there; the taller of them threw Danny a kissy face. His partner scowled, hooked his fingers inside his briefs, pulled him back to the hallway and out of sight. They trailed giggles; Danny felt like vomiting and went for the door.

Gordean spoke to his back. "No questions about that, Deputy?"

Danny turned around. "No."

"Wouldn't you say it runs contrary to your life? I'm sure you've got a nice family. A wife or a girlfriend, a nice family who would find that shocking. Would you like to tell me about them over a glass of that nice Napoleon brandy you enjoy so much?"

For a split second Danny felt terrified; Gordean and Pretty Boy became paper silhouettes, villains to empty his gun into. He about-faced out the door, slamming it; he puked into the street, found a hose attached to the adjoining house, drank and doused his face with water. Steadied, he pulled his Chevy around to the opposite side of PCH and parked, lights off, to wait.

Pretty Boy left the house twenty minutes later, walking toward an overpass to the beach. Danny let him get to the steps, cut him five seconds' more slack, then ran over. His motorcycle boots thunked on cement; the kid looked around and stopped. Danny slowed and walked up to him. Christopher said, "Hello. Want to enjoy the view with—"

Danny hooked him to the gut, grabbed a handful of bottle blond hair and lashed slaps across his face until he felt his knuckles wet with blood. The moon lit up that face: no tears, eyes wide open and accepting. Danny let the boy kneel to the cement and looked down at him huddling into his kimono. "You did see that man hanging around Gordean's office. Why didn't you talk?"

Christopher wiped blood from his nose. He said, "Felix didn't want me to talk to you about it," no whimper, no defiance, no nothing in his voice.

"Do you do everything Felix tells you to do?"

"Yes."

"So you saw a man like that?"

Christopher got to his feet and leaned over the railing with his head bowed. "The man had really beautiful hair, like movie star hair. I do file work at the agency, and I've seen him out at the bus stop on Sunset a lot the last few days."

Danny worked the kinks out of his knuckles, rubbing them on his jacket sleeve. "Who is he?"

"I don't know."

"Have you seen him with a car?"

"No."

"Have you seen anybody talking to him?"

"No."

"But you told Felix about him?"

"Y-yes."

"And how did he react?"

Christopher shrugged. "I don't know. He didn't react much at all."

Danny leaned over the railing, fists cocked. "Yes, he fucking did, so you fucking tell me."

"Felix wouldn't like me to tell."

"No, but you tell me, or I'll hurt you."

The boy pulled away, gulped and spoke fast, a fresh-turned snitch anxious to get it over with. "At first he seemed scared, then he seemed to be thinking, and he told me I should point the man out from the window the next time I saw him."

"Did you see him again?"

"No. No, I really didn't."

Danny thought: and you never will, now that he knows I'm wise to his stakeout. He said, "Does Gordean keep records for his introduction service?"

"No. No, he's afraid of it."

Danny shot the boy an elbow. "You people like playing games, so here's a good one. I tell you something, you put it together with Gordean, who I'm sure you know *real* well. And you look at me, so I can tell if you're lying."

The kid turned, profile to full face, pretty to beaten and slack-featured. Danny tried to evil-eye him; trembly lips made him look at the ocean instead. "Does Gordean know any jazz musicians, guys who hang at the jazz clubs down in darktown?"

"I don't think so, that's not Felix's style."

"Think fast. Zoot stick. That's a stick with razor blades at the end, a weapon."

"I don't know what you're talking about."

"A man who looks like the one you saw by the bus stop, a man who uses Gordean's service."

"No. I'd never seen that man by the bus stop before, and I don't know any—"

"Dentists, dental workers, men who can make dentures."

"No. Too chintzy for Felix. Oh God, this is so strange."

"Heroin. Guys who push it, guys who like it, guys who can get it."

"No, no, *no*. Felix hates needle fiends, he thinks they're vulgar. Can we please hurry up? I never stay out on my walks this long, and Felix might get worried."

Danny got the urge to hit again; he stared harder at the water, imagining shark fins cutting the waves. "*Shut up and just answer.* Now the service. Felix gets his kicks bringing guys out, right?"

"Oh Jesus—yes."

"Were any of those four men I mentioned queers that he brought out?"

"I—I don't know."

"Queers in general?"

"Donald and Augie, yes. Tim Costigan and Al Marks are just clients."

"Did Augie or Don ever turn tricks for the service?"

"Augie did, that's all I know."

"Christopher! Did you fall in and drown!"

Danny shifted his gaze, wave churn to beach. Felix Gordean was standing on his back porch, a tiny figure lit by a string of paper lanterns. A glass door stood half open behind him; the two muscle-men, barely visible, were entwined on the floor inside. Christopher said, "Please, can I go now?"

Danny looked back at his sharks. "Don't you tell Gordean about this."

"What should I tell him about my nose?"

"Tell him a fucking shark bit you."

"Christopher! Are you coming!"

* * *

Danny drove back to La Paloma Drive. An arclight was shining down on the abandoned Pontiac; Mike Breuning was sitting on the hood of an LAPD unmarked, watching a print man dust for latents. Danny killed his engine and beeped the horn; Breuning walked over and leaned in the window. "No prints except the shine the car belongs to—we eliminated him from a gun registration set he had on file at the station. No records on those four names you gave Shortell, and he's out canvassing now. What happened? Jack said you said the killer was tailing you."

Danny got out of the car, pissed that Breuning was gold-bricking. "I was staking a place on the Strip—a talent agency run by a guy who queer-pimps on the side. I got some license numbers and called the DMV, and somebody called up impersonating a cop and got them too. I was tailed out here, and the guy rabbited when I spotted him. This car was stolen from darktown—right near where the Marty Goines transport car was grabbed. I've got an eyeball witness that places a man matching the killer's description hanging around outside the pimp's office, which means that those four men should be put under surveillance. *Now.*"

Breuning whistled; the print man called out, "Nothing but the guy from the elimination set." Danny said, "You and Jack keep shaking down the citizens. I know it's a long shot, but do it anyway. When you finish, check cab company log sheets for pickups in the Palisades and Santa Monica Canyon and shake down the bus drivers working the Sunset line. He had to blow the area somehow. He might have stolen another car, so check with the desks at West L.A. Station, Samo PD and the Malibu Sheriff's. I'm going home for a minute, then I'll head down to the Southside and check around where the Pontiac was clouted."

Breuning pulled out a notebook. "Will do, but where do you expect to get the extra men for your stakes on those names? Gene and Jack and I have got work up the wazoo already, and Dudley told me he's got you busy on that Commie thing."

Danny thought of Mal Considine. "We'll get the men, don't worry."

The arclight went off; the stretch of roadway went dark. Breuning said, "Upshaw, what's with this name Augie Luis Duarte? The killer ain't Mex and none of his victims were, so why'd you call it in?"

Danny decided to spill on Gordean. "It's part of a lead I've been following up on my own. The pimp is a man named Felix Gordean, and he runs a classy introduction service for homos. George Wiltsie worked for him, the killer was staking his office out, Duarte was one of the names I gave the DMV clerk, and he's an ex-Gordean whore. Satisfied?"

Breuning whistled again. "Maybe Dudley can get us the extra men. He's good at that."

Danny slid back in the car, catching a funny jolt—Dudley Smith's toady was stringing him along. He said, "You and Jack go to work, and if you get anything hot, call me at home." He U-turned and took La Paloma down to Sunset, thinking of a sandwich, a weak highball and jigtown canvassing. Sunset was rife with late-evening drivers; Danny turned east and joined a jetstream of lights. His mind went nicely blank; miles passed. Then, hitting the Strip, he got terrified like the half second at the beach house—this time around Man Camera short takes.

Cy Vandrich vamping him.

Breuning going strange over the zoot sticks, like one of the things was slashing at him.

Niles and his two parolees; his "I got a County pal who says you're not the goody two shoes you pretend to be."

"Make it good you County fuck" and an LAPD man bloody at his feet.

The chase, like a car thief gig reversed; it had to be him, it couldn't be him, it was too wrong to be him and too right not to be him.

Gordean making like a mind reader.

Strong-arming a pathetic homo.

The takes dissolved into a cold craving for a drink that saw him the rest of the way home. Danny opened the door and blinked at unexpected light in his living room; he saw the bottle on the coffee table and thought he was entering a hallucination. He drew his gun, snapped that it was a crazy-man stunt and put it back; he walked up to the table, saw a note propped against the jug and read:

Ted—
      You were brilliant at the picket line today. I was camped out at a surveillance spot on De Longpre and saw the whole thing. By the way, I told the Academy man to call you a "County fuck," hoping it would give you an added incentive to kick ass. Your ability exceeded my expectations, and I now owe that offi-cer a good deal more than a bottle of whiskey—you broke all his fingers and nicely enlarged his nuts.

I wangled him a commendation, and he's mollified
for now. More good news: Captain Will Bledsoe died
this morning of a massive stroke, and DA McPherson
has promoted me to Captain and appointed me Chief
DA's Investigator. Good luck with the UAESers (I saw
Kostenz approach you). Let's nail them good, and after
the grand jury I'll recommend you for an interim
LASD Sergeantcy and start pulling strings to get you
to the Bureau. I need a good exec, and the lieutenant's
bars that come with it will make you the youngest
brass hat in City/County history. Meet me tomorrow
night at midnight at the Pacific Dining Car—we'll
celebrate and you can update me on your work.

> Yours,
> Mal.

Danny began sobbing, racking sobs that wouldn't go into tears.
He kept sobbing, forgetting all about the liquor.

22

CHIEF DA'S Investigator.

Two Silver Bars, an extra 3.5 grand a year, prestige for the custody battle. The command of twenty-four detectives culled from
other police agencies on the basis of their brains and ability to
collect evidence that would stand up in court. Substantial say-so
in *the* decision process: when or when not to seek major felony
indictments. The inside track for LAPD Chief of Detectives and
Big Chief. Power: including rank over Dudley Smith and the
noblesse oblige to make an afternoon of shitwork with Buzz Meeks
tolerable.

Mal walked into the Los Angeles office of the U.S. Immigration
and Naturalization Service. Ellis Loew had called early; he and
Meeks were to meet at INS, "Try to bury whatever hatchet exists
between you," and check the service's files on UAES sympathizers
born outside the United States for deportation levers. Loew had
phrased it like an order; captain or not, he had no choice. The DA
had also requested a detailed memo on his non-UAES questionings and an update on the overall investigation—which he was late
on—eyeballing Danny Upshaw's performance had cost him an

afternoon—he'd been playing operator boss while Dudley was out shaking down the Pinkos Lenny Rolff ratted on.

Mal settled into the file room the records supervisor had arranged for them to use. He checked his watch and saw that he was early: Meeks wasn't due until 9:00; he had forty minutes to work before the fat man slimed in. Stacks of files had been arranged on a long metal table; Mal shoved them to the far corner, sat down and started writing.

Memo—1/10/50
To: Ellis Loew
From: Mal Considine
Ellis—

My first memo as Chief DA's Investigator—if it wasn't confidential you could frame it.

First off, Upshaw made a successful approach yesterday. I didn't get a chance to tell you on the phone, but he was terrific. I observed, and saw the UAES member screener approach him. I left Upshaw a note instructing him to meet me late tonight at the Dining Car for a report, and I'm betting he'll have made contact with Claire De Haven by then. I'll call you tomorrow morning with a verbal report on what he has to say.

Two days ago, Dudley and I approached Nathan Eisler and Leonard Rolff, screenwriters not subpoenaed by HUAC. Both men corroborated UAES members Minear and Loftis as planning to subvert motion picture content with Communist doctrine and both have agreed to testify as friendly witnesses. Eisler yielded a diary which further confirms Claire De Haven as promiscuous—good news for Upshaw. Eisler stated that De Haven recruited initial UAES members by sexual means—good to have for open court should she have the audacity to seek to testify. Rolff informed on a total of 4 non-UAES leftists. Dudley questioned 2 of them yesterday and phoned me last night with the results: they agreed to appear as friendly witnesses, time-, date- and place-corroborated Ziffkin, De Haven, Loftis, Minear and the 3 Mexicans

as making inflammatory statements supporting
the overthrow of the U.S.A. by the U.S. Party and
informed on a total of 19 other fellow travelers. I'm
working on a detailed questionnaire to be submitted
to all friendly witnesses, facts for you to use in your
opening presentation, and I want low-key City
Marshals to oversee the delivery and pickup of the
paperwork. The reason for this is that Dudley is too
frightening a presence—sooner or later his intimidation tactics will have to backfire. The chance for a
successful grand jury depends on the UAES being
kept in the dark. We've lulled them to sleep, so let's
keep Dudley on a tight leash. If one of our friendlies
balks and squeals on us to the brain trust, we're screwed.

Here's some random thoughts:

1. - This thing is becoming an avalanche and
soon it's going to be an avalanche of paper. Get those
clerks out to your house: I'll be submitting reports,
questionnaires, and interview abstracts constructed
from details in Eisler's diary. Dudley, Meeks and Upshaw will be filing reports. I want all this info cross-
filed for clarity's sake.

2. - You were worried on the Upshaw secrecy
angle. Don't be. We checked and rechecked. "Ted
Krugman" was not directly known to any UAES
members, he's secondhand known at best, but *known
of.* Upshaw is a *very* smart officer, he knows how to
run with the ball and I suspect he's enjoying his
role-playing.

3. - Where's Dr. Lesnick? I need to talk to him, to
run psych overview questions by him and to get his
opinion on certain parts of Eisler's diary. Also, all his
files end in Summer '49. Why? There's a gap ('42–'44)
in the Loftis file, key to the time he was rabidly
mouthing Commie sentiment and portraying cops as
evil on screen to "undermine the American system of
jurisprudence." I hope he didn't die on us—he looked
almost dead ten days ago. Have Sgt. Bowman locate
him and make sure he calls me, will you?

4. - When we've got our evidence together and
collated, we'll need to spend a goodly amount of

time deciding which of our friendlies to call to the stand. Some will be shaky and angry, thanks to Dudley and his browbeatings. As I said before, his methods have to backfire. Once we're satisfied with the number of witnesses we've turned, I want to take over the questionings and go solo on them, kid gloves—more for the sake of the investigation's security than anything else.

5. - Dudley has a bee in his bonnet over the Sleepy Lagoon case, and he keeps bringing it up in our questionings. By all accounts, the defendants were innocent, and I think we should gag testimony pertaining to the SLDC in court—unless it tangents us to viable testimony. The case made the L.A. left look good, and we can't afford to make the UAES members (many) who also belonged to SLDC out as martyrs. I outrank Dudley now, and I'm going to dress him down on this and generally have him play it softer with witnesses. In light of the above and in keeping with my new rank and promotion, I'm asking you to promote me to commanding officer of this investigation.

> Yours,
> Captain M.E. Considine,
> Chief DA's Investigator

Writing out his new title gave Mal the chills; he thought of buying a fancy pen to commemorate the occasion. He moved down to the file stacks, heard "Think fast" and saw a little blue object lobbing toward him, Buzz Meeks the lobber. He caught it on reflex—a velvet jeweler's box. Meeks said, "A peace offering, skipper. I'll be damned if I'm gonna spend the day with a guy who mighta had me shot without kissin' some ass."

Mal opened the box and saw a pair of shiny silver captain's bars. He looked at Meeks; the fat man said, "I'm not askin' for a handshake or a 'Gee, thanks, old buddy,' but I sure would like to know if it was you sent those torpedoes after me."

Something about Meeks was off: his usual slimy charm was subdued and he had to know that whatever happened in '46 had no bearing on now. Mal snapped the box shut and tossed it back. "Thanks, but no thanks."

Meeks palmed the gift. "My last shot at civility, skipper. When I moved on Laura, I didn't know she was a cop's wife."

Mal smoothed his vest front; Meeks always made him feel like he needed steam cleaning. "Take the files on the end. You know what Ellis wants."

Meeks shrugged and complied, a pro. Mal dug into his first file, read through a long INS background check report, sensed a solid citizen type with bum politics spawned by the big European inflation and put the folder aside. Files two and three were more of the same; he kept stealing glances at Meeks grinding notes, wondering what the cracker wanted. Four, five, six, seven, eight, all Hitler refugee stuff, poison that made drifts to the far left seem justified. Meeks caught his eye and winked; Mal saw that he was happy or amused about something. Nine and ten dawdled over, then a rap on the file room door. "Knock, knock, who's there? Dudley Smith, so Reds beware!"

Mal stood up; Dudley came over and gave him a barrage of hard back slaps. "Six years my junior, and a captain you are. How grand! Lad, you have my most heartfelt congratulations."

Mal saw himself trashing the Irishman, making him eat orders and kowtow. "Congratulations accepted, Lieutenant."

"And you've a wicked wit to match your new rank. Wouldn't you say so, Turner?"

Meeks rocked in his chair. "Dudley, I can't get this boy to say much of anything."

Dudley laughed. "I suspect there's old fury between you two. What it derives from I don't know, although cherchez la femme might be a good bet. Malcolm, while I'm here let me ask you something about our friend Upshaw. Is he sticking his snout into our investigation past his decoy work? The other men on the homo job resent him and seem to think he's a meddler."

"While I'm here" echoed; "cherchez la femme" thundered— Mal knew Dudley had the story on him and Meeks. "You're as subtle as a freight train, Lieutenant. And what is it about you and Upshaw?"

Dudley ha' ha'd; Meeks said, "Mike Breuning's ditzed on the kid, too. He called me last night and ran a list of names by me, four guys Upshaw wanted tails put on. He asked me if they were from the queer job or the grand jury. I told him I didn't know, that I never met the kid, all I got on him was third-hand."

Mal cleared his throat, ticked at being talked around. "What third hand, Meeks?"

The fat man smiled. "I was workin' an angle on Reynolds Loftis, and I came up with a lead from Samo PD Vice. Loftis was rousted at a queer bar back in '44, pallin' with a lawyer named Charles Hartshorn, a big wheel downtown. I braced Hartshorn, and he thought at first I was a Homicide dick, 'cause he was acquainted with one of the dead homos from Upshaw's job. I knew the guy was no killer. I leaned on him hard, then bought myself off on him rattin' me by tellin' him I'd keep the County heat away."

Mal remembered Meeks' memo to Ellis Loew: their first outside corroboration of Loftis' homosexuality. "You're sure Hartshorn wasn't essential to Upshaw's case?"

"Boss, that guy's only crime is bein' a homo with money and a family."

Dudley laughed. "Which is preferable to being a homo with no money and no family. You're a family man, Malcolm. Wouldn't you say that's true?"

Mal's chain snapped. "Dudley, what the fuck do you want? I'm running this job and Upshaw is working for me, so you just tell me why you're so interested in him."

Dudley Smith did a master vaudeville take: a rebuked youth shuffling his feet, going hangdog with hunched shoulders and a pouting lower lip. "Lad, you hurt my feelings. I just wanted to celebrate your good fortune and make it known that Upshaw has incurred the wrath of his fellow officers, men not used to taking orders from twenty-seven-year-old dilettantes."

"The wrath of a Dragna bagman with a grudge on the Sheriff's and your protégé, you mean."

"That's one interpretation, yes."

"Lad, Upshaw is *my* protégé. And I'm a captain and you're a lieutenant. Don't forget what that means. Now please leave and let us work."

Dudley saluted crisply and walked out; Mal saw that his hands were steady and his voice hadn't quivered; Meeks started applauding. Mal smiled, remembered who he was smiling at and stopped. "Meeks, what do *you* want?"

Meeks rocked his chair. "Steak lunch at the Dining Car, maybe a vacation up at Arrowhead."

"And?"

"And I'm not hog-wild about this job and I don't like the idea of you makin' voodoo eyes at me till it's over and I liked you standin' up to Dudley Smith."

Mal half smiled. "Keep going."

"You were scared of him and you dressed him anyway. I liked that."

"I've got rank on him now. A week ago I'd have let it go."

Meeks yawned, like it was all starting to bore him. "Pal, bein' afraid of Dudley Smith means two things: that you're smart and you're sane. And I outranked him once and let him slide, because that is one smart fucker that never forgets. So, accolades, Captain Considine, and I still want that steak lunch."

Mal thought of the two silver bars. "Meeks, you're not the type to offer amends."

Buzz stood up. "Like I said, I'm not hog-wild about this job, but I need the money. So let's just say it's got me thinkin' about the amenities of life."

"I'm not hog-wild about it either, but I need it."

Meeks said, "I'm sorry about Laura."

Mal tried to remember his ex-wife naked, and couldn't. "It wasn't me that had you shot. I heard it was Dragna triggers."

Meeks tossed Mal the velvet box. "Take it while I'm feelin' generous. I just bought my girl two C-notes' worth of sweaters."

Mal pocketed the insignia and stuck out his hand; Meeks gave him a bonecrusher. "Lunch, Skipper?"

"Sure, Sarge."

They took the elevator down to ground level and walked out to the street. Two patrolmen were standing in front of a black-and-white sipping coffee; Mal picked a string of words out of their conversation: "Mickey Cohen, bomb, bad."

Meeks badged the two, hard. "DA's Bureau. What'd you just say about Cohen?"

The younger cop, a peach-fuzz rookie type, said, "Sir, we just heard on the radio. Mickey Cohen's house just got bombed. It looks bad."

Meeks took off running; Mal followed him to a mint green Caddy and got in—one look at the fat man's face telling him "why?" was a useless question. Meeks hung a tire-screeching U-ey out into Westwood traffic and hauled west, through the Veterans Administration Compound, out onto San Vicente. Mal thought of Mickey Cohen's house on Moreno; Meeks kept the pedal down, zigzagging around cars and pedestrians, muttering, "Fuck, fuck, fuck, fuck." At Moreno, he turned right; Mal saw fire engines, prowl units and tall plumes of smoke up the block. Meeks skidded up to a crime scene rope and got out; Mal stood on his tiptoes and saw a nice Spanish house smoldering, L.A.'s number-one hoodlum standing on the lawn, unsinged, ranting at a cadre of uniform brass. Rubberneckers were choking the street, the sidewalk and adjoining front lawns; Mal looked for Meeks and couldn't see him anywhere. He turned and gave his backside a shot—and there was his grand jury cohort, the most corrupt cop in L.A. history, engaged in pure suicide.

Buzz was just past the edge of the commotion, smothering a showstopper blonde with kisses. Mal recognized her from gossip column pics: Audrey Anders, the Va Va Voom Girl, Mickey Cohen's on-the-side woman. Buzz and Audrey kissed; Mal gawked from a distance, then turned around and checked the lovebirds' flank, scoping for witnesses, Cohen goons who'd squeal to their master. The whole crowd was contained behind the crime scene ropes, occupied with Mickey's tirade; Mal kept scanning anyway. He felt a hard tap on his shoulder; Buzz Meeks was there wiping lipstick off his face. "Boss, I am in your power. Now we gonna go get that steak?"

23

"... AND NORM says you can fight. He's a prizefighting fan, so it must be true. Now the question is, are you willing to fight in other ways—and for us."

Danny looked across the table at Claire De Haven and Norman Kostenz. Five minutes into his audition; the woman all business so far, keeping friendly Norm businesslike with little taps that chilled his gushing about the picket line fracas. A handsome woman who had to keep touching things: her cigarettes and lighter, Kostenz when he gabbed too heavy or said something that pleased her. Five minutes in and he knew this about acting: a big part of the trick was sneaking what was really going on with you into your performance. He'd been up all night canvassing darktown straight off a weird jag of sobbing, coming up with nothing on the stolen Pontiac, but sensing HIM watching; the La Paloma Drive canvassing was a zero, ditto the bus line and cab company checks, and

Mike Breuning had called to tell him he was trying to wangle four officers to tail the men on his surveillance list. He felt tired and edgy and knew it showed; he was running with *his* case, not this Commie shit, and if De Haven pressed for background verification he was going to play pissed and bring the conversation down to brass tacks: his resurgence of political faith and what UAES had for him to prove it with. "Miss De Haven—"

"Claire."

"Claire, I want to help. I want to get moving again. I'm rusty with everything but my fists, and I have to find a job pretty soon, but I want to help."

Claire De Haven lit a cigarette and sent a hovering waitress packing with a wave of her lighter. "I think for now you should embrace a philosophy of nonviolence. I need someone to come with me when I go out courting contributors. You'd be good at helping me secure contributions from HUAC widows, I can tell."

Danny took "HUAC widows" as a cue and frowned, wounded by sudden memories of Donna Cantrell—hot love drowned in the Hudson River. Claire said, "Is something wrong, Ted?"; Norm Kostenz touched her hand as if to say, "Man stuff." Danny winced, his muscle aches kicking in for real. "No, you just reminded me of someone I used to know."

Claire smiled. "I reminded you or what I said did?"

Danny exaggerated a grimace. "Both, Claire."

"Care to elaborate?"

"Not quite yet."

Claire called the waitress over and said, "A pitcher of martinis"; the girl curtsied away, writing the order down. Danny said, "No more action on the picket line, then?"

Kostenz said, "The time isn't right, but pretty soon we'll lower the boom"; Claire shushed him—a mere flicker of her zealot's eyes. Danny horned in, Red Ted the pushy guy who'd step on anybody's toes. "What 'boom'? What are you talking about?"

Claire played with her lighter. "Norm has a precipitate streak, and for a boxing fan he's read a lot of Gandhi. Ted, he's impatient and I'm impatient. There was a grand jury investigation forming up, sort of a baby HUAC, but now it looks like it went bust. That's still scary. And I listened to the radio on the ride over. There was another attempt on Mickey Cohen's life. Sooner or later, he'll go crazy and sic his goons on the picket line at us. We'll have to have cameras there to catch it."

She hadn't really answered his question, and the passive resistance spiel sounded like subterfuge. Danny got ready to deliver a flirt line; the waitress returning stopped him. Claire said, "Just two glasses, please"; Norm Kostenz said, "I'm on the wagon," and left with a wave. Claire poured two tall ones; Danny hoisted his glass and toasted, "To the cause." Claire said, "To all things good."

Danny drank, making an ugh face, a nonboozer notching points with a juicehead woman; Claire sipped and said, "Car thief, revolutionary, ladies' man. I am suitably impressed."

Cut her slack, let *her* move, reel her in. "Don't be, because it's all phony."

"Oh? Meaning?"

"Meaning I was a punk kid revolutionary and a scared car thief."

"And the ladies' man?"

The hook baited. "Let's just say I was trying to recapture an image."

"Did you ever succeed?"

"No."

"Because she's that special?"

Danny took a long drink, booze on top of no sleep making him misty. "She was."

"Was?"

Danny knew she'd gotten the story from Kostenz, but played along. "Yeah, was. I'm a HUAC widower, Claire. The other women were just not …"

Claire said, "Not her."

"Right, not her. Not strong, not committed, not …"

"Not her."

Danny laughed. "Yeah, not her. Shit, I feel like a broken record."

Claire laughed. "I'd give you a snappy rejoinder about broken hearts, but you'd hit me."

"I only beat up fascists."

"No rough stuff with women?"

"Not my style."

"It's mine occasionally."

"I'm shocked."

"I doubt that."

Danny killed the drink. "Claire, I want to work for the union, more than just lubing old biddies for money."

"You'll get your chance. And they're not old biddies—unless you think women *my* age are old."

A prime opening. "How old are you? Thirty-one, thirty-two?"

Claire laughed the compliment out. "Diplomat. How old are you?"

Danny reached for Ted Krugman's age, coming up with it maybe a beat too slow. "I'm twenty-six."

"Well, I'm too old for boys and too young for gigolos. How's that for an answer?"

"Evasive."

Claire laughed and fondled her ashtray. "I'll be forty in May. So thanks for the subtraction."

"It was sincere."

"No, it wasn't."

Hook her now, get to the station early. "Claire, do I have political credibility with you?"

"Yes, you do."

"Then let's try this on the other. I'd like to see you outside our work for the union."

Claire's whole face softened; Danny got an urge to slap the bitch silly so she'd get mad and be a fit enemy. He said, "I mean it," Joe Clean Cut Sincere, Commie version.

Claire said, "Ted, I'm engaged"; Danny said, "I don't care." Claire reached into her purse, pulled out a scented calling card and placed it on the table. "We should at least get better acquainted. Some of us in the union are meeting at my house tonight. Why don't you come for the end of the meeting and say hello to everybody. Then, if you feel like it, we can take a drive and talk."

Danny palmed the card and stood up. "What time?"

"8:30."

He'd be there early; pure cop, pure work. "I look forward to it."

Claire De Haven had gotten herself back together, her face set and dignified. "So do I."

* * *

Krugman back to Upshaw.

Danny drove to Hollywood Station, parked three blocks away and walked over. Mike Breuning met him in the muster room doorway, grinning. "You owe me one, Deputy."

"What for?"

"Those guys on your list are now being tailed. Dudley authorized it, so you owe him one, too."

Danny smiled. "Fucking A. Who are they? Did you give them my number?"

"No. They're what you might wanta call Dudley's boys. You know, Homicide Bureau guys Dudley's brought up from rookies. They're smart guys, but they'll only report to Dud."

"Breuning, this is my investigation."

"Upshaw, I know. But you're damn lucky to have the men you've got, and Dudley's working the grand jury job too, so he wants to keep you happy. Have some goddamn gratitude. You've got no rank and you're running seven full-time men. When I was your age, I was rousting piss bums on skid row."

Danny moved past Breuning into the muster room, knowing he was right, pissed anyway. Plainclothesmen and bluesuits were milling around, chuckling over something on the notice board. He looked over their shoulders and saw a new cartoon, worse than the one Jack Shortell ripped down.

Mickey Cohen, fangs, skullcap and a giant hard-on, pouring it up the ass of a guy in an LASD uniform. The deputy's pockets were spilling greenbacks; Cohen's speech balloon said: "Smile, sweetie! Mickey C. gives it kosher!"

Danny shoved a line of blues aside and pulled the obscenity off the wall; he pivoted around, faced a full contingent of enemy cops and tore the piece of cardboard to shreds. The LAPD men gawked, simmered and plain stared; Gene Niles pushed through them and faced Danny down. He said, "I talked to a guy named Leo Bordoni. He wouldn't blab outright, but I could tell he'd been questioned before. I think you rousted him, and I think it was inside Goines' pad. When I described the place it was like he'd already fucking been there."

Except for Niles, the room was a blur. Danny said, "Not now, Sergeant," brass, the voice of authority.

"Up your ass, not now. I think you B&E'd in my jurisdiction. I know you didn't catch that squeal at the doughnut stand, and I've got a damn good lead where you did get it. If I can prove it, you're—"

"Niles not now."

"Up your ass, not now. I had a good robbery case going until you came along with your crazy homo shit. You've got a queer fix, you're cuckoo on it and maybe you are a fucking queer!"

Danny lashed out, quick lefts and rights, short speed punches that caught Niles flush, ripped his face but didn't move his body back one inch. The enemy cops dispersed; Danny launched a hook to the gut; Niles feinted and came in with a hard uppercut, slamming Danny into the wall. He hung there, a stationary target, pretending to be gone; Niles telegraphed a huge right hand at his midsection. Danny slid away just before contact; Niles' fist hit the wall; he screeched into the sound of bones crunching. Danny sidestepped, swung Niles around and rolled sets at his stomach; Niles doubled over; Danny felt the enemy cops moving in. Somebody yelled, "Stop it!"; strong arms bear-hugged and picked him up. Jack Shortell materialized, whispering, "Easy, easy," in the bear hugger's ear; the arms let go; another somebody yelled "Watch Commander walking!" Danny went limp and let the old-timer cop lead him out a side exit.

* * *

Krugman to Upshaw to Krugman.

Shortell got Danny back to his car, extracting a promise that he'd try to sleep. Danny drove home, woozy one second, all jitters the next. Finally pure exhaustion hit him and he employed Ted-Claire repartee to stay awake. The banter saw him straight to bed, a pass on Mal Considine's bottle. With the Krugman leather jacket as his blanket, he fell asleep immediately.

And was joined by odd women and HIM.

The San Berdoo High senior hop, 1939. Glenn Miller and Tommy Dorsey on the PA system, Susan Leffert leading him out of the gym and into the boys' locker room, a Mason jar of schnapps as bait. Inside, she fumbles at his shirt buttons, licking his chest, biting the hair. He tries to drum up enthusiasm by staring at his body in the dressing mirror, but keeps thinking of Tim; that feels good, but hurts, and finally having it both ways is just bad. He tells Susan he met an older woman he wants to be loyal to, she reminds him of Suicide Donna who bought him his nice bombardier jacket, a real war hero number. Susan says, "What war?"; the action fades because he knows something's off, Pearl Harbor is still two years away. Then this tall, faceless man, silver-haired, naked, is there, all around him in a circle, and squinting to see his face makes him go soft in Susan's mouth.

Then a whole corridor of mirrors, him chasing HIM, Karen Hiltscher, Roxy Beausoleil, Janice Modine and a bevy of Sunset Strip gash swooping down while he hurls excuses.

"I can't today, I have to study."

"I don't dance, it makes me self-conscious."

"Some other time, okay?"

"Sweetie, let's keep this light. We work together."

"I don't want it."

"No."

"Claire, you're the only real woman I've met since Donna."

"Claire, I want to fuck you so bad just like I used to fuck Donna and all the others. They all loved it because I loved doing it so much."

He was gaining ground on HIM, gaining focus on the gray man's brick shithouse build. The apparition twirled around; he had no face, but Tim's body and bigger stuff than Demon Don Eversall, who use to hang out in the shower, trap water in his jumbo foreskin, hold his thing out and croon, "Come drink from my cup of love." Hard kissing; bodies mashed together, the two of them inside each other, Claire walking out of the mirror, saying, "That's impossible."

Then a gunshot, then another and another.

Danny jolted awake. He heard a fourth ring, saw that he'd sweated the bed sopping, felt like he had to piss and threw off the jacket to find his trousers wet. He fumbled over to the phone and blurted, "Yes?"

"Danny, it's Jack."

"Yeah, Jack."

"Son, I cleared you with the assistant watch commander, this lieutenant named Poulson. He's pals with Al Dietrich, and he's reasonable about our Department."

Danny thought: and Dietrich's pals with Felix Gordean, who's got LAPD and DA's Bureau pals, and Niles is pals with God knows who on the Sheriff's. "What about Niles?"

"He's been yanked from our job. I told Poulson he'd been riding you, that he provoked the fight. I think you'll be okay." A pause, then, "Are you okay? Did you sleep?"

The dream was coming back; Danny stifled a shot of HIM. "Yeah, I slept. Jack, I don't want Mal Considine to hear about what happened."

"He's your boss on the grand jury?"

"Right."

"Well, I won't tell him, but somebody probably will."

Mike Breuning and Dudley Smith replaced HIM. "Jack, I have to do some work on the other job. I'll call you tomorrow."

Shortell said, "One more thing. We got minor league lucky on our hot car queries—an Olds was snatched two blocks from La Paloma. Abandoned at the Samo Pier, no prints, but I'm adding 'car thief' to our records checks. And we're a hundred and forty-one down on the dental queries. It's going slow, but I have a hunch we'll get him."

HIM.

Danny laughed, yesterday's wounds aching, new bone bruises firing up in his knuckles. "Yeah, we'll get him."

* * *

Danny segued back to Krugman with a shower and change of clothes, Red Ted the stud in Karen Hiltscher's sports jacket, pegged flannels and a silk shirt from Considine's disguise kit. He drove to Beverly Hills middle-lane slow, checking his rear-view every few seconds for cars riding his tail too close and a no-face man peering too intently, shining his headlights too bright because deep down he wanted to be caught, wanted everyone to know *WHY*. No likely suspects appeared in the mirror; twice his trawling almost got him into fender benders. He arrived at Claire De Haven's house forty-five minutes early; he saw Caddies and Lincolns in the driveway, muted lights glowing behind curtained windows and one narrow side dormer cracked for air, screened and shade covered—but open. The dormer faced a stone footpath and tall shrubs separating the De Haven property from the neighboring house; Danny walked over, squatted down and listened.

Words came at him, filtered through coughs and garbled interruptions. He picked out a man's shout: "Cohen and his farshtunkener lackeys have to go nutso first"; Claire's "It's all in knowing when to squeeze." A soft, mid-Atlantic drawl: "We have to give the studios an out to save face with, that's why knowing when is so important. It has to hit the fan just right."

Danny kept checking his blind side for witnesses; he heard a long digression on the '52 presidential election—who'd run, who wouldn't—that degenerated into a childish shouting match, Claire finally dominating with her opinion of Stevenson and Taft, fascist minions of varying stripes. There was something about a movie director named Paul Doinelle and his "Cocteau-like" classics; then an almost complete duet: the soft-voiced man chuckling over "old flames," a man with a stentorian Southern accent punch-lining, "But I got Claire." Danny recalled the psychiatric files: Reynolds

Loftis and Chaz Minear were lovers years ago; Considine told him that now Claire and Loftis were engaged to be married. He got stomach flip-flops and looked at his watch: 8:27, time to meet the enemy.

He walked around and rang the bell. Claire opened the door and said, "Right on time"; Danny saw that her makeup and slacks suit tamped down her wrinkles and showed off her curves better than the powder job and dress at the restaurant. He said, "You look lovely, Claire."

Claire whispered, "Save it for later," took his arm and led him into the living room, subtle swank offset by framed movie posters: Pinko titles from the grand jury package. Three men were standing around holding drinks: a Semitic-looking guy in tweeds, a small, trim number wearing a tennis sweater and white ducks, and a dead ringer composite for HIM—a silver-maned man pushing fifty, topping six feet by at least two inches, as lanky as Mal Considine but ten times as handsome. Danny stared at his face, thinking something about the set of his eyes was familiar, then looked away—queer or ex-queer or whatever, he was just an image—a Commie, not a killer.

Claire made the introductions. "Gentlemen, Ted Krugman. Ted, left to right we have Mort Ziffkin, Chaz Minear and Reynolds Loftis."

Danny shook their hands, getting, "Hey there, slugger," from Ziffkin, "A pleasure," from Minear and a wry smile out of Loftis, an implicit aside: I allow my fiancée to dally with younger guys. He gave the tall man his strongest grip, snapping hard into Ted K. "The pleasure's all mine, and I'm looking forward to working with you."

Minear smiled; Ziffkin said, "Attaboy"; Loftis said, "You and Claire have a good strategy talk, but get her home early, you hear?"—a Southern accent, but no syrup and another aside: he was sleeping with De Haven tonight.

Danny laughed, knowing he'd just memorized Loftis' features; Claire sighed, "Let's go, Ted. Strategy awaits."

They walked outside. Danny thought of rolling tails and steered Claire to his car. She said, "Where do you want to strategize"; *her* aside, her parody on Loftis playing cute. Danny opened the passenger door, getting an idea: prowl darktown with the protective coloration of a woman in tow. It was nearly two weeks since he'd gone strongarming down there, he probably wouldn't be recognized in his non-cop outfit and HE was near the South-side strip just yesterday. "I like jazz. Do you?"

"I love it, and I know a great spot in Hollywood."

"I know some places on South Central that really bop. What do you say?"

Claire hesitated, then said, "Sure, sounds like fun."

* * *

East on Wilshire, south on Normandie. Danny drove fast, think-ing of his midnight meeting and ways to chill Considine on the Niles ruckus; he kept checking the rear-view mock casual, gifting Claire with a smile each time so she'd think he was thinking of her. Nothing strange appeared in the mirror; Reynolds Loftis' face stayed in his mind, a non-face to make *the* face jump out and bite him. Claire chain-smoked and drummed her nails on the dashboard.

The silence played right, two idealists deep in thought. East on Slauson, south on Central, more mirror checks now that they were on HIS stomping ground. Danny pulled up in front of the Club Zombie; Claire said, "Ted, what are you afraid of?"

The question caught him checking his waistband for the sap he always packed on niggertown assignments; he stopped and grabbed the wheel, Red Ted the persecuted Negro's buddy. "The Teamsters, I guess. I'm rusty."

Claire put a hand on his cheek. "You're tired and lonely and driven. You want to please and do the right thing so badly that it just about breaks my heart."

Danny leaned into the caress, a catch in his throat like when he saw Considine's bottle. Claire took her hand away and kissed the spot she'd touched. "I am such a sucker for strays. Come on, strong silent type. We're going to listen to music and hold hands, and we're *not* going to talk about politics."

The catch stuck; the kiss was still warm. Danny walked ahead of Claire to the door; the bouncer from New Year's Day was there and eyed him like he was just another white hepcat. Claire caught up just as the cold air got him back to normal: Krugman the Commie on a hot date, Upshaw the Homicide cop on overtime. He took her arm and led her inside.

The Zombie interior was just like two weeks before, with an even louder, more dissonant combo wailing on the bandstand. This time the clientele was all Negro: a sea of black faces offset by colored lighting, a flickering canvas where a white/gray face would stand out and scream, "Me!" Danny slipped the maitre d' a five-spot and requested a wall table with a floor view; the man led them to seats near the back exit, took their order for a double bonded and a dry martini, bowed and motioned for a waitress. Danny settled Claire into the chair closest to the bandstand; he grabbed the one facing the bar and the audience.

Claire laced her fingers through Danny's and beat time on the table with their hands, a gentle beat, counterpoint to the screechy bebop that filled the room. The drinks arrived; Claire paid, a fiver to the high-yellow waitress, her free hand up to refuse the change. The girl sashayed off; Danny sipped bourbon—cheap house stuff that burned. Claire squeezed his hand; he squeezed back, grateful for loud music that made talk impossible. Looking out at the crowd, he sensed that HIM here was just as impossible—he'd know the police now had him pegged as a darktown car thief—he'd avoid South Central like the plague.

But the place felt right, safe and dark. Danny closed his eyes and listened to the music, Claire's hand on his still making a beat. The combo's rhythm was complex: drums shooting a melody to the sax, the sax winging it off on digressions, returning to simpler and simpler chords, then the main theme, then the trumpet and bass taking flight, going crazy with more and more complicated riffs. Listening for the handoffs was hypnotic; half the sounds were ugly and strange, making him wish for the simple, pretty themes to come back. Danny listened, ignoring his drink, trying to figure the music out and predict where it was going. He felt like he was getting the synchronization when a crescendo came out of nowhere, the players quit playing, applause hit like thunder and bright lights came on.

Claire dropped his hand and started clapping; a mulatto lounge lizard sidled by the table, saying, "Hello, sweet. I ain't seen you in a dog's age." Claire averted her eyes; Danny stood up; the mulatto said, "Forget old friends, see if I care," and kept sidling.

Claire lit a cigarette, her lighter shaking. Danny said, "Who was that?"

"Oh, a friend of a friend. I used to have a thing for jazz musicians."

The mulatto had made his way up to the bandstand; Danny saw him slip something into the bass player's hand, a flash of green picked up at the same time. Considine on De Haven: she was a skin-popper and devotee of pharmacy hop.

Danny sat down; Claire stubbed out her cigarette and sparked another one. The lights were dimmed; the music started—a slow, romantic ballad. Danny tried the beating time maneuver, but Claire's hand wouldn't move. Her eyes were darting around the room; he saw the exit door across from them open up, spotlighting Carlton W. Jeffries, the grasshopper he'd strong-armed for a snitch on H pushers. The doorway cast a strip of light all the way over to Claire De Haven making with rabbity eyes, a rich white girl with a snout for lowlife afraid that more embarrassment might ruin her date with an undercover cop out to get her indicted for treason. The door closed; Danny felt her fear jump on him and turn the nice, dark, safe place bad, full of crazy jungle niggers who'd eat him whole, revenging all the niggers he'd pushed around. He said, "Claire, let's leave, okay?"

Claire said, "Yes, let's."

* * *

The ride back was all Claire with the jitters, rambling on what she'd accomplished with what organizations—a litany that sounded harmless and probably contained not one shred of information that Considine and Loew would find interesting. Danny let it wash over him, thinking of his meeting, wondering what Leo Bordoni told Gene Niles, if Niles really had a County source to place him inside 2307, and if he could prove it, would anybody care? Should he grease Karen Hiltscher on general principles, her being the only *real* snitch possibility, even though her even knowing Niles was unlikely? And how should he lay off the blame for the fight? How to make Considine think his future exec beating up one of his own men was kosher, when that man might just have him by the balls?

Danny turned onto Claire's block, thinking of good exit lines; slowing down and stopping, he had two at the ready. He smiled and prepared to perform; Claire touched his cheek, softer than the first time. "I'm sorry, Teddy. It was a lousy first date. Rain check?"

Danny said, "Sure," going all warm, the catch again.

"Tomorrow night, here? Just us, strategy and whatever the spirit moves us to?"

Her hand had reversed itself, knuckles lightly tracing his jawline. "Sure ... darling."

She stopped then, eyes shut, lips parted. Danny moved into the kiss, wanting the soft hand, not the hungry mouth painted pinkish red. Just as they touched, he froze and almost pulled away. Claire's tongue slid across his teeth, probing. He thought of Reynolds Loftis, gave the woman his face and did it.

24

MAL WAS watching Buzz Meeks eat, thinking that suicide love must be good for the appetite: the fat man had devoured a plate of stuffed shrimp, two double-thick pork chops with onion rings, and was now killing a huge piece of peach pie buried in ice cream. It was their second meal together, with INS file work and his run by Jake Kellerman's office in between; at lunch Meeks had wolfed a porterhouse, home fries and three orders of rice pudding. Mal picked at a plate of chicken salad and shook his head; Meeks said, "A growin' boy's got to feed. What time's Upshaw due?"

Mal checked his watch. "I told him midnight. Why, do you have plans?"

"A late one with my sweetie. Howard's usin' his spot up by the Bowl, so we're meetin' at her place. I told her I'd be there by one at the latest, and I mean to be punctual."

"Meeks, are you taking precautions?"

Buzz said, "We use the rhythm method. Her place when Howard's rhythm moves us." He dug in his coat pockets and fished out an envelope. "I forgot to tell you. When you were at your lawyer's, Ellis came by. I gave him your memo, and he read it and wrote you one. Apparently, your boy traded blows with some LAPD dick. Ellis said to read this and abide by it."

Mal opened the envelope and pulled out a slip of paper covered with Ellis Loew's handwriting. He read:

M.C.—

I agree wholeheartedly with everything but your assessment of Dudley's methods. What you don't realize is that Dudley is so effective that his methods minimize the chance that potential witness will balk and inform on us to UAES. Also, I can't give you command of the investigation, not with the obvious dislike that exists between you and Dudley. It would ruffle the feathers of a man who up until yesterday shared your rank with many more years in grade.

You're equals in this investigation, and once we go to court you'll never have to work with him again.

Something has come up on Deputy Upshaw. A Sgt. Breuning (LAPD) called to tell me that Upshaw got into a fistfight with another City officer (Sgt. G. Niles) this afternoon, over a stupid remark Niles made about "queers." This is, in light of the interagency command we set up for Upshaw, intolerable. Breuning also stated that Upshaw demanded four officers for surveillance work, and that Dudley, wanting to keep him happy, found the men. This is also intolerable. Upshaw is a young, inexperienced officer who, however gifted, has no right to be making such demands. I want you to sternly inform him that we will tolerate no more fisticuffs or prima donna behavior.

Sgt. Bowman is now looking for Dr. Lesnick. I hope he didn't die on us, too—he's a valuable addition to our team.

E.L.

P.S.—Good luck in court tomorrow. Your promotion and current duties should help you secure a continuance.

I think Jake Kellerman's strategy is sound.

Mal wadded the paper up and hurled it blindly; it bounced off the back of the booth and landed on Meeks' butter plate. Buzz said, "Whoa, partner"; Mal looked up and saw Danny Upshaw hovering. He said, "Sit down, Deputy," ticked until he noticed the kid's hands were shaking.

Danny slid into the booth next to Meeks. Buzz said, "Turner Meeks" and gave him a shake; Danny nodded and turned to Mal. "Congratulations, Captain. And thanks for the jug."

Mal eyed his decoy, thinking that right now he looked not one iota cop. "Thank you, and my pleasure. And before we get to business, what happened with Sergeant Niles?"

Danny gripped an empty water glass. "He's got a crazy idea I B&E'd the place where the second and third victims were found. Essentially, he's miffed at taking orders from me. Jack Shortell told me the watch commander yanked him off the case, so I'm glad he's out of my hair."

The answer sounded rehearsed. Mal said, "That's all of it?"

"Yes."

"And did you B&E?"

"No, of course not."

Mal thought of the "queer" remark, but let it pass. "All right, then consider this a reprimand, from Ellis Loew *and* myself. No more of that, *period*. Don't let it happen again. Got that?"

Danny raised the glass, looking chagrined when he found it empty. "Yes, Captain."

"It's still 'Mal.' Do you want something to eat?"

"No thanks."

"A drink?"

Danny pushed the glass away. "No."

Buzz said, "Save your dukes for the Police Golden Gloves. I knew a guy made Sergeant beatin' up on guys his CO hated."

Danny laughed; Mal wished that he'd order a shot for his nerves. "Tell me about the approach. Have you met with De Haven?"

"Yeah, twice."

"And?"

"And she's making a play for me."

His operative was actually blushing. Mal said, "Tell me about it."

"There's not much to tell yet. We had a date tonight, we've got another one set for tomorrow night. I listened outside her house while a meeting was going on, and I picked up some stuff. Pretty vague, but enough to tell me that they have some kind of extortion angle going against the studios and they're planning to time it with the Teamsters going crazy on the picket line. So tell Mickey to keep his guys in check. I could tell this angle is important to their strategy, and when I see De Haven tomorrow, I'm going to press her for details."

Mal kicked the dope around, thinking that it played true to his take on the brain trusters: they were duplicitous, they talked a lot, they took their own sweet time acting and let outside events call the tune. "Who have you met besides Kostenz and De Haven?"

"Loftis, Minear and Ziffkin, but just briefly."

"How did they impress you?"

Danny made an open-handed gesture. "They didn't really impress me at all. I only spoke to them for a minute or so."

Buzz chuckled and loosened his belt. "You were lucky old Reynolds didn't jump your bones instead of De Haven. Nice-lookin' young guy like you would probably get that old prowler stiffin' up a hard yard."

Danny flushed again. Mal thought of him working two twenty-four-hour-a-day cases, jamming them into one twenty-four-hour day. He said, "Tell me how your other job's going."

Danny's eyes were darting, flicking over the neighboring booths, lingering on men at the bar before returning to Mal. He said, "Slow but well, I think. I've got my own home file, all the evidence and all my impressions, and that's a help. I've got a bunch of records checks going, and so far that's slow, but steady. Where I think I'm getting close is on the victims, putting them together. He's not a random psycho, I *know* that. If I get closer, I might need a decoy to help draw him out. Would it be possible to get another man?"

Mal said, "No"; he watched Danny's eyes follow two men walking past their booth. "No, not after your stunt with Niles. You've got those four officers Dudley Smith swung you—"

"They're Dudley's men, not mine! They won't even report to me, and Mike Breuning's jerking my chain! For all I know he's bunked out on the whole job!"

Mal slapped the table, bringing Danny's eyes back to him. "Look at me and listen. I want you to calm down and take things slow. You're doing all you can on both your assignments, and aside from Niles you're doing great. Now you've lost one man, but you've got your tailing officers, so just figure you've cut your god-damn losses, knuckle down and be a professional. *Be a policeman.*"

Danny's eyes, blurry, held on Mal. Buzz said, "Deputy, you got any hard leads on your victims, any whatcha call common denominators?"

The operative spoke to his operator. "A man named Felix Gordean. He's a homosexual procurer connected to one of the victims, and I *know* the killer's got some kind of fix on him. I haven't leaned on him too hard yet, because he's paying off County Central Vice and he says he's got influence with LAPD and the Bureau."

Mal said, "Well, I've never heard of him, and I'm top Bureau dog. Buzz, do you know this guy?"

"Sure do, boss. Large City juice, larger County. One lean and mean fruitfly, plays golf with Sheriff Eugene Biscailuz, puts a few shekels in Al Dietrich's pockets come Christmastime, too."

As he said the words, Mal knew it was one of the finest moments of his life. "Lean on him, Danny. I'll stand the heat, and if anyone gives you grief, you've got the Chief DA's Investigator for the City of Los Angeles in your corner."

Danny stood up, looking heartbreaker grateful. Mal said, "Go home and sleep, Ted. Have a nightcap on me." The decoy left, saluting his brother officers; Buzz breathed out slowly. "That boy is up on a tall old tree limb lookin' down at a tall old boy with a saw, and you've got more balls than brains."

It was just about the nicest thing anyone ever told him. Mal said, "Have another piece of pie, lad. I'm picking up the check."

25

THE HALL window scraping, three soft footsteps on the bedroom floor.

Buzz stirred, rolled away from Audrey, reached under the pillow and palmed his .38, camouflaging the movement with a sleep sigh. Two more footsteps, Audrey snoring, light through a crack in the curtains eclipsed. A shape coming around his side of the bed; the sound of a hammer being cocked; "Mickey, you're dead."

Buzz stiff-armed Audrey to the floor, away from the voice; a silencer snicked and muzzle flash lit up a big man in a dark over-coat. Audrey screamed; Buzz felt the mattress rip an inch from his legs. In one swipe, he grabbed his billy club off the nightstand and swung it at the man's knees; wood-encased steel cracked bone; the man stumbled toward the bed. Audrey shrieked, "Meeks!"; a shot ripped the far wall; another half second of muzzle light gave Buzz a sighting. He grabbed the man's coat and pulled him to the bed, smothered his head with a pillow and shot him twice in the face point-blank.

The explosions were muffled; Audrey screeching was siren loud. Buzz moved around the bed and bear-hugged her, killing her tremors with his own shakes. He whispered, "Go into the bathroom, keep the light off and your head down. This was for Mickey, and if there's a back-up man outside, he's comin'. Stay fuckin' down and stay fuckin' calm."

Audrey retreated on her knees; Buzz went into the living room, parted the front curtains and looked out. There was a sedan parked directly across the street that wasn't there when he walked in; no other cars were stationed curbside. He did a run-through on what probably happened:

He looked like Mickey from a distance; *he* drove a green '48 Eldo. Mickey's house was bombed yesterday; Mickey, wife and pet bulldog survived. *He* parked his car the standard three blocks away; half-assed surveillance convinced the gunman *he* was Mickey, a short fat okie subbing for a short fat Jew.

Buzz kept eyeballing the sedan; it stayed still, no tell-tale cigarette glow. Five minutes went by; no cops or backup men appeared. Buzz took it as a single-o play, walked back to the bedroom and flicked on the overhead light.

The room reeked of cordite; the bed was soaked in blood; the pillow was solid saturated crimson. Buzz lifted it off and propped up the dead man's head. It had no face, there were no exit wounds, all the red was leaking out his ears. He rifled his pockets—and the wicked bad willies came on.

An LAPD badge and ID buzzer: Detective Sergeant Eugene J. Niles, Hollywood Squad. An Automobile Club card, vehicle dope in the lower left corner—maroon '46 Ford Crown Victoria Sedan, Cal '49 JS 1497. A California driver's license made out to Eugene Niles, residence 3987 Melbourne Avenue, Hollywood. Car keys and other keys and pieces of paper with Audrey's address and an architectural floor plan for a house that looked like Mickey's pad in Brentwood.

Old rumors, new facts, killer shakes.

The LAPD was behind the shootout at Sherry's; Jack D. and Mickey had buried the hatchet; Niles worked Hollywood Division, the eye of the Brenda Allen storm. Buzz ran across the street on fear overdrive, saw that the sedan was '46 Vicky JS 1497, unlocked the trunk and ran back. He hauled out a big bed quilt, wrapped Niles and his gun up in it, shoulder-slung him up and over to the Vicky and locked him in the trunk, folding him double next to the spare tire. Panting, sweat-soaked and shaky, he walked back and braced Audrey.

She was sitting on the toilet, naked, smoking. A half dozen butts littered the floor; the bathroom was a tobacco cloud. She looked like the woman from Mars: tears had melted her makeup and her lipstick was still smudged from their lovemaking.

Buzz knelt in front of her. "Honey, I'll take care of it. This was for Mickey, so I think we're okay. But I should stay away from you for a while, just in case this guy had partners—we don't want them figurin' out it was you and me instead of you and Mickey."

Audrey dropped her cigarette on the floor and snuffed it with her bare feet, no pain registering. She said, "All right," a hoarse smoker's croak.

Buzz said, "You strip the bed and burn it in the incinerator. There's bullets in the mattress and the wall, you dig 'em out and toss 'em. And you don't tell *nobody*."

Audrey said, "Tell me it'll be all right." Buzz kissed the part in her hair, seeing the two of them strapped down in the gas chamber. "Honey, this will surely be all right."

* * *

Buzz drove Niles' car to the Hollywood Hills. He found gardening tools in the back seat, a level patch of hardscrabble off the access road to the Hollywood Sign and buried Mickey Cohen's would-be assassin in a plot about 4 by 4 by 4, working with an earth spade and grub hoe. He packed the dirt hard and tight so coyotes wouldn't smell flesh rot and get hungry; he put branches atop the spot and pissed on it: an epitaph for a fellow bad cop who'd put him in the biggest trouble of his trouble-prone life. He buried Niles' gun under a thornbush, drove the car out to the Valley, wiped it down, yanked the distributor and left it in an abandoned garage atop Suicide Hill—a youth gang fuck turf near the Sepulveda VA Hospital. Undrivable, the Vicky would be spare parts inside twenty-four hours.

It was 4:30 A.M.

Buzz walked down to Victory Boulevard, caught a cab to Hollywood and Vermont, walked the remaining half mile to Melbourne Avenue. He found a pay phone, glommed "Eugene Niles" from the White Pages, dialed the number and let it ring twenty times—no answer. He located 3987—the bottom left apartment of a pink stucco four-flat—and let himself in with Niles' keys, set to prowl for one thing: evidence that other men were in on the Mickey hit.

It was a typical bachelor flop: sitting/sleeping room with Murphy bed, bathroom, kitchenette. There was a desk facing a boarded-up window; Buzz went straight for it, handling everything he touched with his shirttails. Ten minutes in, he had solid circumstantial evidence:

A certificate from the U.S. Army Demolition School, Camp Polk, Louisiana, stating that Corporal Eugene Niles successfully completed explosives training in December 1931—make the fucker for the bomb under Mickey's house.

Letters from Niles' ex-wife, condemning him for trucking with Brenda Allen's hookers. She'd read the grand jury transcript and knew her husband did his share of porking in the Hollywood Station felony tank—Niles' motive to want Mickey dead.

An address book that included the names and phone numbers of four ranking Jack Dragna strongarms, listings for three other Dragna bagmen—cops he knew when he was LAPD—and a weird listing: "Karen Hiltscher, W. Hollywood Sheriff's," with "!!!!" in bright red doodles. That aside, more verification of Niles hating Mickey before the truce with Jack D. All told, it looked like a poorly planned single-o play, Niles desperate when his bomb didn't blow the Mick to shit.

Buzz killed the lights and wiped both sides of the doorknob on his way out. He walked to Sunset and Vermont, dropped Niles' house and car keys down a sewer grate and started laughing, wildly, stitches in his side. He'd just saved the life of the most dangerous, most generous man he'd ever met, and there was no way in the world he could tell him. The laughter got worse, until he doubled over and had to sit down on a bus bench. He laughed until the punch line sucker-punched him—then he froze.

Danny Upshaw beat up Gene Niles. The City cops hated the County cops. When Niles was tagged as missing, LAPD would be like flies over shit on a green kid already in shit up to his knees.

26

DANNY WAS trying to get Felix Gordean alone.

He'd begun his stakeout in the Chateau Marmont parking lot; Gordean foiled him by driving to his office with Pretty Boy Christopher in tow. Rain had been pouring down the whole three hours he'd been eyeing the agency's front door; no cars had hit the carport, the street was flooded and he was parked in a tow-away zone with his ID, badge and .45 at home because he was really Red Ted Krugman. Ted's leather jacket and Considine's sanction kept him warm and dry with the window cracked; Danny decided that if Gordean didn't leave the office by 1:00, he'd lean on him then and there.

At 12:35, the door opened. Gordean walked out, popped an umbrella and skipped across Sunset. Danny turned on his wiper blades and watched him duck into Cyrano's, the doorman fussing over him like he was the joint's most popular customer. He gave

Gordean thirty seconds to get seated, turned up his collar and ran over, ducking rain.

The doorman looked at him funny, but let him in; Danny blinked water, saw gilt and red velvet walls, a long oak bar and Felix Gordean sipping a martini at a side table. He threaded his way past a clutch of businessman types and sat down across from him; Gordean almost swallowed the toothpick he was nibbling.

Danny said, "I want to know what you know. I want you to tell me everything about the men you've brought out, and I want a report on all your customers and clients. I want it now."

Gordean toyed with the toothpick. "Have Lieutenant Matthews call me. Perhaps he and I can effect a compromise."

"Fuck Lieutenant Matthews. Are you going to tell me what I want to know? *Now?*"

"No, I am not."

Danny smiled. "You've got forty-eight hours to change your mind."

"Or?"

"Or I'm taking everything I know about you to the papers."

Gordean snapped his fingers; a waiter came over; Danny walked out of the restaurant and into the rain. He remembered his promise to call Jack Shortell, hit the phone booth across from the agency, dialed the Hollywood Station squadroom and heard, "Yes?," Shortell himself speaking, his voice strained.

"It's Upshaw, Jack. What have you got on—"

"What we've got is another one. LAPD found him last night, on an embankment up from the L.A. River. Doc Layman's doing him now, so—"

Danny left the receiver dangling and Shortell shouting, "Upshaw!"; he highballed it downtown, parked in front of the City Morgue loading dock and almost tripped over a stiff on a gurney running in. Jack Shortell was already there, sweating, his badge pinned to his coat front; he saw Danny, blocked the path to Layman's examination room and said, "Brace yourself."

Danny got his breath. "For what?"

Shortell said, "It's Augie Luis Duarte, one of the guys on your tailing list. The bluesuits who found him ID'd him from his driver's license. LAPD's had the stiff since 12:30 last night—the squad guy who caught didn't know about our team. Breuning was here and just left, and he was making noises that Duarte blew *his* tail last night. Danny, I know that's horseshit. I was calling around last night looking for you, to tell you our car thief and zoot stick queries were bust. I talked to a clerk at Wilshire Station, and she told me Breuning was there all evening with Dudley Smith. I called back later, and the clerk said they were still there. Breuning said the other three men are still under surveillance, but I don't believe him."

Danny's head boomed; morgue effluvia turned his stomach and stung his razor burns. He beelined for a door marked "Norton Layman MD," pushed it open and saw the country's premier forensic pathologist writing on a clipboard. A nude shape was slab-prone behind him; Layman stepped aside as if to say, "Feast your eyes."

Augie Duarte, the handsome Mex who'd walked out the Gordean Agency door two nights ago, was supine on a stainless steel tray. He was blood-free; bite wounds extruding intestinal tubes covered his stomach; bite marks ran up his torso in a pattern free of overlaps. His cheeks were slashed down to the gums and jawbone and his penis had been cut off, inserted into the deepest of the cuts and hooked around so that the head extended out his mouth, teeth clamped on the foreskin, rigor mortis holding the obscenity intact. Danny blurted, "Oh God fuck no"; Layman said, "The rain drained the body and kept the cuts fresh. I found a tooth chip in one of them and made a wet cast of it. It's unmistakably animal, and I had an attendant run it down to a forensic orthodontist at the Natural History Museum. It's being examined now."

Danny tore his eyes off the corpse; he walked out to the dock looking for Jack Shortell, gagging on the stench of formaldehyde, his lungs heaving for fresh air. A group of Mexicans with a bereaved-family look was standing by the loading ramp staring in; a pachuco type stared at him extra hard. Danny strained to see Shortell, then felt a hand on his shoulder.

It was Norton Layman. He said, "I just talked to the man at the Museum, and he identified my specimen. The killer wears wolverine teeth."

Danny saw a blood W on cheap wallpaper. He saw W's in black and white, W's burned into Felix Gordean's face, W's all over the rosary-clutching wetbacks huddled together grieving. He saw W's until Jack Shortell walked up the dock and grabbed his arm and he heard himself say, "Get Breuning. I don't trust myself on it."

Then he saw plain blood.

27

A STAKEOUT for his own son.

Mal sat on the steps outside Division 32, Los Angeles Civil Court. He was flanked by lawyers smoking; keeping his back to them kept light conversation away while he scanned for Stefan, Celeste and her shyster. When he saw them, it would be a quick men's room confab: don't believe the bad things you hear about me; when my man gets ugly about your mother, try not to listen.

Ten of the hour; no Stefan, Celeste and lawyer. Mal heard an animated burst of talk behind him.

"You know Charlie Hartshorn?"

"Sure. A nice guy, if a bit of a bleeding heart. He worked the Sleepy Lagoon defense for free."

"Well, he's dead. Suicide. Hung himself at his house last night. Beautiful house, right off Wilshire and Rimpau. It was on the radio. I went to a party at that house once."

"Poor Charlie. What a goddamn shame."

Mal turned around; the two men were gone. He remembered Meeks telling him Reynolds Loftis was connected to Hartshorn via a queer-bar roust, but he didn't mention the man being associated with the Sleepy Lagoon Defense Committee at all. There was no mention of Hartshorn in any of the psychiatric or other grand jury files, and Meeks had also said that the lawyer had turned up—as a non-suspect—in Danny Upshaw's homicide investigation.

The Hartshorn coincidence simmered; Mal wondered how Meeks would take his suicide—he said he'd gut-shot the man with his queerness. Looking streetside, he saw Celeste, Stefan and a young guy with a briefcase get out of a cab; his boy glanced up, lit up and took off running.

Mal met him halfway down the steps, scooped him up laughing and pinwheeled him upside down and over. Stefan squealed; Celeste and briefcase double-timed; Mal whipped his son over his shoulder, quick-marched inside and turned hard into the men's room. Out of breath, he put Stefan down and said, "Your dad's a captain," dug in his pockets and pulled out one of the insignia Buzz gave him. "You're a captain, too. Remember that. Remember that if your mother's lawyer starts talking me down."

Stefan squeezed the silver bars; Mal saw that he had that bewildered fat-kid look he got when Celeste stuffed him with starchy Czech food. "How have you been? How's your mother been treating you?"

Stefan spoke hesitantly, like he'd been force-fed old country talk since the breakup. "Mutti ... wants that we should move out. She said we ... we must move away before she decides to marry Rich-Richard."

Richard.

"I—I don't like Richard. He's nice to Mutti, but he's n-nasty to his d-d-dog."

Mal put his arms around the boy. "I won't let it happen. She's a crazy woman, and I won't let her take you away."

"Malcolm—"

"*Dad*, Stefan."

"Dad, please not to don't hit Mutti again. *Please*."

Mal held Stefan tighter, trying to squeeze the bad words out and make him say, "I love you." The boy felt wrong, flabby, like he was too skinny wrong as a kid. "Sssh. I'll never hit her again and I'll never let her take you away from me. Sssh."

The door opened behind them; Mal heard the voice of an old City bailiff who'd been working Division 32 forever. "Lieutenant Considine, court's convening and I'm supposed to bring the boy into chambers."

Mal gave Stefan a last hug. "I'm a captain now. Stefan, you go with this man and I'll see you inside."

Stefan hugged back—hard.

* * *

Court convened ten minutes later. Mal sat with Jake Kellerman at a table facing the judge's bench; Celeste, her attorney and Stefan were seated in chairs stationed diagonally across from the witness stand. The old bailiff intoned, "Hear ye, hear ye, court is now in session, the Honorable Arthur F. Hardesty presiding."

Mal stood up. Jake Kellerman whispered, "In a second the old fart'll say, 'Counsel will approach the bench.' I'll hit him for a first continuance for a month from now, citing your grand jury duties. Then, we'll get another stay until the jury convenes and you're gold. *Then* we'll get you Greenberg."

Mal gripped Kellerman's arm. "Jake, make this happen."

Kellerman whispered extra low, "It will. Just pray a rumor I heard isn't true."

Judge Arthur F. Hardesty banged his gavel. "Counsel will approach the bench."

Jake Kellerman and Celeste's lawyer approached, huddling around Hardesty; Mal strained to hear and picked up nothing but garbles—Jake sounding agitated. The huddle ended with a gavel slam; Kellerman walked back, fuming.

Hardesty said, "Mr. Considine, your counsel's request for a one-month continuance has been denied. Despite your police duties, I'm sure you can find enough time to consult with Mr. Kellerman. All parties will meet here in my chambers ten days hence, Monday, January 22. Both contestants should be ready to testify. Mr. Kellerman, Mr. Castleberry, make sure your witnesses are informed of the date and bring whatever documents you wish to be considered as evidence. This preliminary is dismissed."

The judge banged his gavel; Castleberry led Celeste and Stefan outside. The boy turned around and waved; Mal flashed him the V for victory sign, tried to smile and couldn't. His son was gone in a breath; Kellerman said, "I heard Castleberry heard about your promotion and went batshit. I heard he leaked the hospital pictures to one of Hardesty's clerks, who told the judge. Mal, I'm sorry and I'm angry. I'm going to tell Ellis what Castleberry did and make sure that punk gets reamed for it."

Mal stared at the spot where his son waved goodbye. "Ream her. Pull out all the stops. If Stefan has to hear, he has to hear. Just fucking take her down."

28

LOOKING AROUND Ellis Loew's living room, Buzz set odds: Twenty to one the grand jury handed down beaucoup UAES indictments; twenty to one the studios booted them on the treason clause prior to the official word, with the Teamsters signing to take their place inside twenty-four hours. If he convinced Mickey to make book on the proceedings, he could lay a bundle down and get well on top of Howard's bonus. Because the action in Loew's little command post said the Pinkos were buying one-way tickets for the Big Fungoo.

Except for tables and chairs set aside for clerks, all the furniture had been removed and dumped in the back yard. Filing cabinets

filled with friendly witness depositions covered the fireplace; a
corkboard was nailed to the front window, space for reports from
the team's four investigators: M. Considine, D. Smith, T. Meeks
and D. Upshaw. Captain Mal's stack of interrogation forms—
questions tailored to individual lefties, delivered and notarized by
City Marshals—was thick; Dudley's field summaries stacked out
at five times their width—he had now turned fourteen hostiles
into groveling snitch friendlies, picking up dirt on over a hundred
snitches in the process. His own reports comprised six pages:
Sammy Benavides porking his sister, Claire De Haven skin-popping
H and Reynolds Loftis as a homo bar hopper, the rest padding, all
of it snoozeville compared to Mal's and Dudley's contributions.
Danny Upshaw's stuff ran two pages—eavesdrop speculation and
necking with Pinko Claire—him and the kid were not exactly
burning down barns in their effort to destroy the Communist
Conspiracy. There were tables with "In" and "Out" baskets for the
exchange of information, tables for the photographic evidence
Crazy Ed Satterlee was accumulating, a huge cardboard box filled
with cross-referenced names, dates, political organizations and
documented admissions: Commies, pinkers and fellow travelers
embracing Mother Russia and calling for the end of the U.S.A. by
means fair and foul. And—across the broadest stretch of bare wall—
Ed Satterlee's conspiracy graph, his grand jury thumbscrew.

In one horizontal column, the UAES brain trust; in another,
the names of the Communist front organizations they belonged
to; in a vertical column atop the graph the names of friendly
witnesses and their "accusation power" rated by stars, with lines
running down to intersect with the brainers and the fronts. Each
star was Satterlee's assessment of the number of days' testimony a
friendly was worth, based on the sheer power of time, place and
hearsay: which Pinko attended where, said what, and which recanted
Red was there to listen—a brain-frying, mind-boggling, super-
stupendous and absolutely amazing glut of information impossible to disprove.

And he kept seeing Danny Upshaw smack in the middle of it,
treading shit, even though the kid was on the side of the angels.

Buzz walked out to the back porch. He'd been brainstorming
escape routes under the guise of writing reports for hours; three
phone calls had fixed Audrey's skimming spree. One was to
Mickey, handing him a convoluted epic on how a bettor skimmed
an unnamed runner who was screwing the bettor's sister and

couldn't turn him in, but finally made him cough up the six grand he'd welched—the exact amount Audrey had grifted off the Mick. The second was to Petey Skouras, a tight-lipped runner who agreed to play the lovesick fool who finally made good to his boss for a cool grand—knowing Johnny Stompanato would come snouting around for the name Buzz wouldn't give on, find him acting hinky and pound a confession out of him—the returned cash his assurance that that was his only punishment. The third was to an indy shylock: seven thousand dollars at 20 percent, $8,400 due April 10—his woman out of trouble, his gift for her grief: Gene Niles with his face blown off on her bed. Seven come eleven, thank God for the Commie gravy train. If they didn't succumb to the hots for each other, he and his lioness would probably survive.

The kid was still the wild card he didn't know how to play.

It was twelve hours since he'd prowled Niles' pad. Should he go back and make it look like Niles hightailed it? Should he have planted some incriminating shit? When the fucker was missed, would LAPD fix on him as a Dragna bad apple and let it lie? Would they make him for the bomb job and press Mickey? Would they assume a snuff and go hog-wild to find the killer?

Buzz saw Dudley Smith and Mike Breuning at the back edge of the yard, standing by Ellis Loew's couch, left out in the rain because the DA put business before comfort. A late sun was up; Dudley was laughing and pointing at it. Buzz watched dark clouds barreling in from the ocean. He thought: fix it, fix it, fix it, be a fixer. Be what Captain Mal told the kid to be.

Be a policeman.

29

DANNY UNLOCKED his door and tapped the wall light. The blood W's he'd been seeing since the morgue became his front room, spare and tidy, but with something skewed. He eyed the room in grids until he got it: the rug was puckered near the coffee table—he always toed it smooth on his way out.

He tried to remember if he did it *this* morning. He recalled dressing as Ted Krugman, nude to leather jacket in front of the bathroom mirror; he remembered walking outside thinking of Felix Gordean, Mal Considine's "Lean on him, Danny" ringing in his ears. He did not remember his methodical rug number, probably because Teddy K. wasn't the meticulous type. Nothing else in the room looked askew; there was no way in the world HE would break into a policeman's apartment ...

Danny thought of his file, ran for the hall closet and opened the door. It was there, pictures and paperwork intact, covered by wadded-up carpeting puckered just the right way. He checked the bathroom, kitchen and bedroom, saw the same old same old, sat down in a chair by the phone and skimmed the book he'd just bought.

The Weasel Family—Physiology and Habits, hot off a back shelf at Stanley Rose's Bookshop.

Chapter 6, page 59: The Wolverine.

A 40- to 50-pound member of the weasel family indigenous to Canada, the Pacific Northwest and the upper Midwest; pound for pound, the most vicious animal on earth. Utterly fearless and known for attacking animals many times its size; known to drive bears and cougars from their kills. A beast that cannot stand to watch other creatures enjoying a good feed—often blitzing them just to get at what remained of their food. Equipped with a highly efficient digestive system: wolverines ate fast, digested fast, shit fast and were always hungry; they possessed a huge appetite to match their general nastiness. All the vicious little bastards wanted to do was kill, eat and occasionally fuck other members of their misanthropic breed.

W
W
W
W
W
W
W
W

The Wolverine.

Alter ego of a biting, gouging, raping, flesh-eating killer of immense hunger: sexual and emotional. A man who possessed total identification with an obscenely rapacious animal, an identity he has assumed to right old wrongs, animal mutilations the specific means, *his specific inner reconstruction of what was done to him*.

Danny turned to the pictures at the back of the book, ripped three wolverine shots out, dug through his file for the 2307 blood pics and made a collage above the bed. He tacked the awful weasel thing in the middle; he shone his floor lamp on the collection of images, stood back, looked and thought.

A fat, shuffle-footed creature with beady eyes and a thick brown coat to ward off the cold. A slinky tail, a short, pointed snout, sharp nails and long, sharp teeth bared at the camera. An ugly child who knew he was ugly and made up for it by hurting the people he blamed for making him that way. Snap flashes as the animal and 2307 merged: the killer was somehow disfigured or thought he was; since eyewitnesses tagged him as not facially marred, the disfigurement might be somewhere on his body. The killer thought he was ugly and tied it to sex, hence Augie Duarte slashed cheek to bone with his thing sticking out his mouth. A big snap, all instinct, but feeling gut solid: HE knew the burned-face burglar boy, who was too young to be the killer himself; HE drew inspiration or sex from his disfigurement— hence the facial slashing. Zoot stick assaults were being tapped at station houses citywide; car thief MO's were being collated; he told Jack Shortell to start calling wild-animal breeders, zoo suppliers, animal trappers and fur wholesalers, cross-reference them with dental tech and go. Burglar, jazz fiend, H copper, teeth maker, car thief, animal worshiper, queer, homo, pederast, brunser and devotee of male whores. It was there waiting for them, some fact in a police file, some nonplussed dental worker saying, "Yeah, I remember that guy."

Danny wrote down his new impressions, thinking of Mike Breuning bullshitting him on the Augie Duarte tail, the other tails probably horseshit. Breuning's only possible motive was humoring him—keeping him happy on the homicide case so he'd be a good Commie operative and keep Dudley Smith happy on his anti-Red crusade. Shortell had called the other three men, warned them of possible danger and was trying to set up interviews: the only cop he could trust now, Jack would be tapping into Dudley's "boys" to see if the three Gordean "friends" had ever been under surveillance at all. He himself had stuck outside Gordean's agency trawling for more license plates, more potential victims, more information and maybe Gordean alone for a little strongarm—but the carport had stayed empty, the pimp hadn't showed and there was no traffic at his front door—rain had probably kept the "clients" and "friends" away. And he'd had to break the stakeout for his date with Claire De Haven.

A thud echoed outside the door—the sound of the paperboy chucking the *Evening Herald*. Danny walked out and picked it up, scanning a headline on Truman and trade embargoes, opening to the second page on the off-chance there was an item on his case. Another scan told him the answer was no; a short column in the bottom right corner caught his attention.

Attorney Charles Hartshorn a Suicide—Served Both the Society Elite and Society's Unfortunate

This morning Charles E. (Eddington) Hartshorn, 52, a prominent society lawyer who dabbled in social causes, was found dead in the living room of his Hancock Park home, an apparent self-asphyxiation suicide. Hartshorn's body was discovered by his daughter Betsy, 24, who had just arrived home from a trip and told Metro reporter Bevo Means: "Daddy was despondent. A man had been around talking to him—Daddy was certain it had to do with a grand jury investigation he'd heard about. People always bothered him because he did volunteer work for the Sleepy Lagoon Defense Committee, and they found it strange that a rich man wanted to help poor Mexicans."

Lieutenant Walter Reddin of the LAPD's Wilshire Station said, "It was suicide by hanging, pure and simple. There was no note, but no signs of a struggle. Harts-horn simply found a rope and a ceiling beam and did it, and it's a darn shame his daughter had to find him."

Hartshorn, a senior partner of Hartshorn, Welborn and Hayes, is survived by daughter Betsy and wife Margaret, 49. Funeral service notices are pending.

Danny put the paper down, stunned. Hartshorn was Duane Lindenaur's extortionee in 1941; Felix Gordean said that he attended his parties and was "unlucky in love and politics." He never questioned the man for three reasons: he did not fit the killer's description; the extortion was nearly nine years prior; Sergeant Frank Skakel, the investigating officer on the beef, had said that Hartshorn would refuse to talk to the police regarding the incident—and he stressed old precedents. Hartshorn was just another name in the file, a tangent name that led to Gordean. Nothing about the lawyer had seemed wrong; aside from Gordean's offhand "politics" remark, there was nothing that tagged him as having a yen for causes, and there were no notations in the grand jury file on him—despite the preponderance of Sleepy Lagoon information. *But he was questioned by a member of the grand jury team.*

Danny called Mal Considine's number at the DA's Bureau, got no answer and dialed Ellis Loew's house. Three rings, then, "Yeah? Who's this?", Buzz Meeks' okie twang.

"It's Deputy Upshaw. Is Mal around?"

"He's not here, Deputy. This is Meeks. You need somethin'?"

The man sounded subdued. Danny said, "Do you know if anybody questioned a lawyer named Charles Hartshorn?"

"Yeah, I did. Last week. Why?"

"I just read in the paper that he killed himself."

A long silence, a long breath. Meeks said, "Oh shit."

Danny said, "What do you mean?"

"Nothin', kid. This on your homicide case?"

"Yes. How did you know that?"

"Well, I braced Hartshorn, and he thought I had to be a Homicide cop, 'cause a guy who tried to shake him down on his queerness years ago just got bumped off. This was right around when you joined up with us, and I remembered somethin' about this dink Lindenaur from the papers. Kid, I was a cop for years, and this guy Hartshorn wasn't holdin' nothin' back 'cept the fact he likes boys, so I didn't tell you about him—I just figured he was no kind of suspect."

"Meeks, you should have told me anyway."

"Upshaw, you gave me some barter on the old queen. I owe you on that, 'cause I had to rough him up, and I bought out by tellin' him I'd keep the Homicide dicks away. And kid, that poor sucker couldn't of killed a fly."

"Shit! Why did you go talk to him in the first place? Because he was connected to the Sleepy Lagoon Committee?"

"No. I was trackin' corroboration dirt on the Commies and I got a note said Hartshorn was rousted with Reynolds Loftis at a fruit bar in Santa Monica in '44. I wanted to see if I could squeeze some more dirt on Loftis out of him."

Danny put the phone to his chest so Meeks wouldn't hear him hyperventilating, wouldn't hear his brain banging around the facts he'd just been handed and the way they *might just really play:*

Reynolds Loftis was tall, gray-haired, middle-aged.

He was connected to Charles Hartshorn, a suicide, the blackmail victim of Duane Lindenaur, homicide victim number three.

He was the homosexual lover of Chaz Minear circa early '40s; in the grand jury psychiatric files, Sammy Benavides had mentioned "puto" Chaz buying sex via a "queer date-a-boy gig"—a possible reference to Felix Gordean's introduction service, which employed snuff victims George Wiltsie and Augie Duarte.

Last night in darktown, Claire De Haven had been all nerves; the killer had picked up Goines on that block and a hop pusher at the Zombie had addressed her. She sloughed it off, but was known to the grand jury team as a longtime hophead. Did she procure the junk load that killed Marty Goines?

Danny's hands twitched the receiver off his chest; he heard Meeks on the other end of the line—"Kid, you there? You there, kid?"—and managed to hook the mouthpiece into his chin. "Yeah, I'm here."

"There something you ain't tellin' me?"

"Yes—no—fuck, I don't know."

The line hung silent for good long seconds; Danny stared at his wolverine pinups; Meeks said, "Deputy, are you tellin' me Loftis is a suspect for your killin's?"

Danny said, "I'm telling you *maybe.* Maybe real strong. He fits the killer's description, and he ... fits."

Buzz Meeks said, "Holy fuckin' dog."

Danny hung up, thinking he'd kissed Reynolds Loftis in his mind—and he liked it.

* * *

Krugman into Upshaw into Krugman, pure Homicide cop.

Danny drove to Beverly Hills, no rear-view trawling. He Man Camera'd Reynolds Loftis wolverine slashing; the combination of 2307 pictures, Augie Duarte's body and Loftis' handsome face rooting in gore had him riding the clutch, shifting when he didn't need to just to keep the images a little bit at bay. Pulling up, he saw the house lights on bright—cheery, like the people inside had nothing to hide; he walked up to the door and found a note under the knocker: "Ted. Back in a few minutes. Make yourself at home—C."

More nothing to hide. Danny opened the door, moved inside and saw a writing table wedged against a wall by the stairwell. A floor lamp was casting light on it; papers were strewn across the blotter, a leather-bound portfolio weighing them down, nothing to hide blinking neon. He walked over, picked it up and opened it; the top page bore clean typescript: "MINUTES AND ATTENDANCE, UAES EXECUTIVE COMMITTEE, 1950 MEETINGS."

Danny opened to the first page. More perfect typescript: the meeting/New Year's party on 12/31/49. Present—scrawled signatures—were C. De Haven, M. Ziffkin, R. Loftis, S. Benavides, M. Lopez, and one name crossed out, illegible. Topics of discussion were "Picket Assignments," "Secretary's Report," "Treasurer's Report" and whether or not to hire private detectives to look into the criminal records of Teamster picketers. The soiree commenced at 11:00 P.M. and ended at 6:00 A.M.; Danny winced at the gist: the ledger could be construed as an alibi for Reynolds Loftis—he was here during the time Marty Goines was snatched and killed—and the minutes contained nothing at all subversive.

Too much nothing to hide.

Danny flipped forward, finding a meeting on 1/4/50, the same people in attendance during the time frame of the Wiltsie/Lindenaur killings, the same strange crossout, the same boring topics discussed. And Loftis was with Claire last night when Augie Duarte probably got it—he'd have to check with Doc Layman on the estimated time of death. Perfect group alibis, no treason on the side, Loftis not HIM, unless the whole brain trust was behind the killings—which was ridiculous.

Danny stopped thinking, replaced the ledger, jammed his jumpy hands into his warm leather pockets. It was too much nothing to hide, because there was nothing to hide, because none of the brain trusters knew he was a Homicide cop, Loftis could have forged his name, a five-time corroborated alibi would stand up in court ironclad, even if the alibiers were Commie traitors, none of it meant anything, get your cases straight and identities straight and be a policeman.

The house was getting hot. Danny shucked his jacket, hung it on a coatrack, went into the living room and pretended to admire the poster for *Storm Over Leningrad*. It reminded him of the stupid turkeys Karen Hiltscher coerced him to; he was making a note to lube her on 2307 when he heard, "Ted, how the hell are you?"

HIM.

Danny turned around. Reynolds Loftis and Claire were doffing their coats in the foyer. She looked coiled; he looked handsome, like a cultured blood sport connoisseur. Danny said, "Hi. Good to see you, but I've got some bad news."

Claire said, "Oh"; Loftis rubbed his hands together and blew on them, "Hark, what bad news?"

Danny walked up to frame their reactions. "It was in the papers. A lawyer named Charles Hartshorn killed himself. It said he worked with the SLDC, and it implied he was being hounded by some fascist DA's cops."

Clean reactions: Claire giving her coat a brush, saying, "We'd heard. Charlie was a good friend to our cause"; Loftis tensing up just a tad—maybe because he and the lawyer had sex going. "That grand jury went down, but it took Charlie with them. He was a frail man and a kind one, and men like that are easy pickings for the fascists."

Danny flashed: he's talking about himself, he's weak, Claire's his strength. He moved into close-up range and hit bold. "I read a tabloid sheet that said Hartshorn was questioned about a string of killings. Some crazy queer killing people he knew."

Loftis turned his back, moving into a shamefully fake coughing attack; Claire played supporting actress, bending to him with her face averted, mumbling, "Bad for your bronchitis." Danny held his close-up and brain-screened what his eyes couldn't see: Claire giving her fiancé guts; Loftis the actor, knowing faces don't lie, keeping his hidden.

Danny walked into the kitchen and filled a glass with sink water, a break to give the players time to recover. He walked back slowly and found them acting nonchalant, Claire smoking, Loftis leaning against the staircase, sheepish, a Southern gentleman who thought coughing déclassé. "Poor Charlie. He liked Greek revelry once in a while, and I'm sure the powers that be would have loved to crucify him for that, too."

Danny handed him the water. "They'll crucify you for anything they can. It's a shame about Hartshorn, but personally, I like women."

Loftis drank, grabbed his coat and winked. He said, "So do I," kissed Claire on the cheek and went out the door.

Danny said, "We've got bad luck so far. Last night, your friend Charlie."

Claire tossed her purse on the table holding the meeting ledger—too casual. Her tad too-studied glance said she'd arranged the still life for him—Loftis' alibi—*even though they couldn't know who he was.* The threads of who was who, knew who, knew what got tangled again; Danny quashed them with a lewd wink. "Let's stay in, huh?"

Claire said, "My idea, too. Care to see a movie?"

"You've got a television set?"

"No, silly. I've got a screening room."

Danny smiled shyly, proletarian Ted wowed by Hollywood customs. Claire took his hand and led him through the kitchen to a room lined with bookcases, the front wall covered by a projection screen. A long leather couch faced the screen; a projector was mounted on a tripod a few feet behind it, a reel of film already fed in. Danny sat down; Claire hit switches, doused the lights and snuggled into him, legs curled under a swell of skirt. Light took over the screen, the movie started.

A test pattern; a black-and-white fade-in; a zoftig blonde and a Mexican with a duck's ass haircut stripping. A motel room backdrop: bed, chipped stucco walls, sombrero lamps and a bullfight poster on the closet door. Tijuana, pure and simple.

Danny felt Claire's hand hovering. The blonde rolled her eyes to heaven; she'd just seen her co-star's cock—huge, veiny, hooked at the middle like a dowsing rod. She salaamed before him, hit her knees and started sucking. The camera caught her acne scars and his needle tracks. She sucked while the hophead gyrated his hips; he pulled out of her mouth and sprayed.

Danny looked away; Claire touched his thigh. Danny flinched, tried to relax but kept flinching; Claire fingered a ridge of coiled muscle inches from his stuff. Hophead screwed Pimples from behind, the insertion close in. Danny's stomach growled—worse than when he was on a no-food jag. Claire's hand kept probing; Danny felt himself shriveling—cold shower time where you shrunk down to nothing.

The blonde and the Mexican fucked with abandon; Claire kneaded muscles that would not yield. Danny started to cramp, grabbed Claire's hand and squeezed it to his knee, like they were back at the jazz club and he was calling the shots. Claire pulled away; the movie ended with a close-up of the blonde and the Mex tongue-kissing.

Film snapped off the cylinder; Claire got up, hit the lights and exchanged reels. Danny uncramped into his best version of Ted Krugman at ease—legs loosely crossed, hands laced behind his head. Claire turned and said, "I was saving this for après bed, but I think we might need it now."

Danny winked—his whole head twitching—lady-killer Ted. Claire turned the projector on and the lights off; she came back to the couch and snuggled down again. The second half of their double feature hit the screen.

No music, no opening credits, no subtitles like in the old silents—just blackness—gray flecks the only indication that film was running. The darkness broke down at the corners of the screen, a shape took form and a dog's head came into focus: a pit bull wearing a mask. The dog snapped at the camera, the screen went black again, then slowly dissolved into white.

Danny remembered the dog breeder and his tale of Hollywood types buying pits to film; he jumped to the masked men at Felix Gordean's house; he saw that he'd shut his eyes and was holding his breath, the better to think who knew what, said what, lied what. He opened his eyes, saw two dogs ripping at each other, animated red splashed in surreal patterns across black-and-white celluloid, disappearing and coloring the real blood its real color, a spritz fogging the camera lens, gray first, cartoon red next. He thought of Walt Disney gone insane; as if in answer, an evil-looking Donald Duck flashed on the screen, feathered phallus hanging to his webbed feet. The duck hopped around, impotent angry like the real Donald; Claire laughed; Danny watched the snapping dogs circle each other and charge, the darker dog getting a purchase on the speckled dog's midsection, plunging in with his teeth. And he knew his killer, whoever he was, had gone crazy watching this movie.

A black screen; Danny going light-headed from holding his breath, sensing Claire's eyes on him. Then all color footage, naked men circling each other just like the dogs, going for each other with sucking mouths, 69 close-ups, a pullback shot and Felix Gordean in a red devil costume, capering, prancing. Danny got hard; Claire's hand went there—like she *knew.* Danny squirmed, tried to shut his eyes, *couldn't* and kept looking.

A quick cut; then Pretty Boy Christopher, naked and hard, pointing his thing at the camera, the head nearly eclipsing the screen like a giant battering ram, white background borders looking just like parted lips and teeth holding the image intact through rigor mortis—

Danny bolted, double-timed to the front of the house, found a bathroom and locked the door. He got his shakes chilled with a litany: BE A POLICEMAN BE A POLICEMAN BE A POLICEMAN; he made himself think *facts*, flung the medicine cabinet open and got one immediately: a prescription bottle of sodium secobarbital, Wiltsie's and Lindenaur's death ticket in a little vial, Reynolds Loftis' sleep pills administered by D. Waltrow, MD, 11/14/49. Fumbling through shelves of ointments, salves and more pills got him nothing else; he noticed a second door, ajar, next to the shower stall.

He pushed it open and saw a little den all done up cozy, more bookshelves, chairs arranged around a leather ottoman, another desk with another cluttered blotter. He checked the clutter—mimeographed movie scripts with hand scrawl in the margins—opened drawers and found stacks of Claire De Haven stationery, envelopes, rolls of stamps and an old leather wallet. Flipping through the sleeves, he saw expired Reynolds Loftis ID: library card, membership cards to Pinko organizations, a '36 California driver's license with a tag stuck to the back side, Emergency Medical Data—allergic to penicillin, minor recurring arthritis, O+ *blood*.

HIM?

Danny closed the drawers, unlocked the bathroom door, wiped a towel across his face and slow-walked back to the screening room. The lights were on, the screen was blank and Claire was sitting on the couch. She said, "I didn't think a tough boy like you would be so squeamish."

Danny sat beside her, their legs brushing. Claire pulled away, then leaned forward. Danny thought: *she knows, she can't know.* He said, "I'm not much of an aesthete."

Claire put a warm hand to his face; her face was cold. "Really? All my friends in the New York Party were mad for New Drama and Kabuki and the like. Didn't the movie remind you of Cocteau, only with more of a sense of humor?"

He didn't know who Cocteau was. "Cocteau never jazzed me. Neither did Salvador Dali or any of those guys. I'm just a square from Long Island."

Claire's hand kept stroking. It was warm, but the to-die-for soft-ness of last night was all gone. "I used to summer in Easthampton when I was a girl. It was lovely."

Danny laughed, glad he'd read Considine's tourist brochure. "Huntington wasn't exactly Easthampton, sweetie."

Claire cringed at the endearment, started to let her hand go, then made with more caresses. Danny said, "Who filmed that movie?"

"A brilliant man named Paul Doinelle."

"Just for friends to see?"

"Why do you say that?"

"Because it's smut. You can't release films like that. It's against the law."

"You say that so vehemently, like you care about a bourgeois law that abridges artistic freedom."

"It was ugly. I was just wondering what kind of man would enjoy something like that."

"Why do you say 'man'? I'm a woman, and I appreciate art of that nature. You're strictured in your views, Ted. It's a bad trait for people in our cause to have. And I *know* that film aroused you."

"That's not true."

Claire laughed. "Don't be so evasive. Tell me what you want. Tell me what you want to do with me."

She was going to fuck him just to get what he knew, which meant she knew, which meant—

Danny made Claire a blank frame and kissed her neck and cheeks; she sighed—phony—sounding just like a Club Largo girl pretending stripping was ecstasy. She touched his back and chest and shoulders—hands kneading—it felt like she was try-ing to restrain herself from gouging him. He tried to kiss her lips, but her mouth stayed crimped; she reached between his legs. He was frozen and shriveled there, and her hand made it worse.

Danny felt his whole body choking him. Claire took her hands away, reached behind her back and removed her sweater and bra in one movement. Her breasts were freckled—spots that looked cancerous—the left one was bigger and hung strange and the nipples were dark and flat and surrounded by crinkled skin. Danny thought of traitors and Mexicans sucking them; Claire whispered, "Here, babe," a lullaby to mother him into telling what he knew, who he knew, what he lied. She fondled her breasts toward his face; he shut his eyes and couldn't; thought of boys and Tim and HIM and couldn't—

Claire said, "Ladies' man? Oh Teddy, how were you ever able to pull that charade off?" Danny shoved her away, left the house slamming doors and drove home thinking: *SHE CANNOT KNOW WHO I AM*. Inside, he went straight for his copy of the grand jury package, prowled pages to prove it for sure, saw "Juan Duarte—UAES brain trust, extra actor/stagehand at Variety Intl Picts" on a personnel sheet, snapped to Augie Duarte choking on his cock on a morgue slab, snapped to the three Mexes on the *Tomahawk Massacre* set the day he questioned Duane Lindenaur's KAs, snapped on Norm Kostenz taking his picture after the picket line brawl. Snap, snap, snap, snap to two final snaps: the Mex at the morgue who eyed him funny was a Mex actor on the movie set, he had to be an Augie Duarte relative, Juan Duarte the spic Commie actor/stagehand. The crossout on the meeting ledger had to be his name, which meant that he saw Kostenz' picture and told Loftis and Claire that Ted Krugman was a police detective working on Augie's snuff.

Which meant that the ledger was a setup alibi.

Which meant that the movie was a device to test his reactions and find out what he knew.

Which meant that the Red Bitch was trying to do to him what Mal Considine set him up to do to her.

WHICH MEANT THAT THEY KNEW WHO HE WAS.

Danny went for the shelf over the refrigerator, the place where he stashed his Deputy D. Upshaw persona. He picked up his badge and handcuffs and held them to himself; he unholstered his .45 revolver and aimed it at the world.

30

CHIEF OF Detectives Thad Green nodded first to Mal, then to Dudley Smith. "Gentlemen, I wouldn't have called you in this early in the morning if it wasn't urgent. What I'm going to tell you has not been leaked yet, and it will remain that way."

Mal looked at his LAPD mentor. The man, rarely grave, was coming on almost funeral. "What is it, sir?"

Green lit a cigarette. "The rain caused some mudslides up in the hills. About an hour ago, a body was found on the access road going up to the Hollywood Sign. Sergeant Eugene Niles, Hollywood Squad. Buried, shot in the face. I called Nort Layman in for a quick one, and he took two .38's out of the cranial vault. They were fired from an Iver-Johnson Police Special, which you know is standard LAPD/LASD issue. Niles was last seen day before yesterday at Hollywood Station, where he got into a fistfight with your grand jury chum Deputy Daniel Upshaw. You men have been working with Upshaw, and I called you in for your conclusions. Mal, you first."

Mal made himself swallow his shock, think, then speak. "Sir, I don't think Upshaw is capable of killing a man. I reprimanded him on Niles night before last, and he took it like a good cop. He seemed relieved that Niles was off his Homicide detail, and we all know that Niles was in up to here on Brenda Allen. I've heard he ran bag for Jack Dragna, and I'd look to Jack and Mickey before I accused a brother officer."

Green nodded. "Lieutenant Smith."

Dudley said, "Sir, I disagree with Captain Considine. Sergeant Mike Breuning, who's also working that Homicide detail with Upshaw, told me that Niles was afraid of the lad and that he was convinced that Upshaw had committed a break-in in LAPD territory in order to get evidence. Niles told Sergeant Breuning that Upshaw lied about how he came to get word of the second and third victims, and that he was going to try to accrue criminal charges against him. Moreover, Niles was convinced that Upshaw had a very strange fixation on these deviant killings he's so concerned with, and Niles calling Upshaw a 'queer' was what precipitated their fight. An informant of mine told me that Upshaw was seen threatening a known queer pimp named Felix Gordean, a man who is known to heavily pay off Sheriff's Central Vice. Gordean told my man that Upshaw is crazy, obsessed with some sort of homo conspiracy, and that he made extortion demands on him—threatening to go to the newspapers unless he gave him special information—information that Gordean asserts does not even exist."

Mal took the indictment in. "Who's your informant, Dudley? And why do you and Breuning care so much about Upshaw?"

Dudley smiled—a bland shark. "I would not want that lad's unstable violent behavior to upset his work for our grand jury, and I would no more divulge the names of my snitches than you would, Captain."

"No, but you'd smear a brother officer. A man who I think is a dedicated and brilliant young policeman."

"I've always heard you had a soft spot for your operatives, Malcolm. You should be more circumspect in displaying it, though. Especially now that you're a captain. I personally consider Upshaw capable of murder. Violence is often the province of weak men."

Mal thought that with the right conditions and one drink too many, the kid could shoot in cold blood. He said, "Chief, Dudley's persuasive, but I don't make Upshaw for this at all."

Thad Green stubbed out his cigarette. "You men are too personally involved. I'll put some unbiased officers on it."

31

THE PHONE rang. Danny reached for the bedside extension, saw that he'd passed out on the floor and tripped over dead bottles and file folders getting to it. "Yeah? Jack?"

Jack Shortell said, "It's me. You listening?"

Danny blinked away wicked sunlight, grabbed paper and a pencil. "Go."

"First, Breuning's tails were all fake. I called in an old favor at LAPD Homicide, checked the work sheets for the men Dudley uses regularly and found out they were all working regular assignments full-time. I looked around for Gene Niles to see if I could sweet-talk him and get some more dope on it, but that bastard is nowhere. LAPD canvassed the area where Duarte's body was found—they caught the squeal and some rookie squadroom dick out of Central hopped on it. Nothing so far. Doc Layman's grid-searching for trace elements there—he wants complete forensics on Duarte so he can put him in his next textbook. He thinks the rain will kibosh it, but he's trying anyway, and on the autopsy it's the same story as the first three: sedated, strangled, mutilated after death. I called the other men on your tailing list, and they're going on little vacations until this blows over. Danny, did you know that guy Hartshorn you told me about killed himself?"

Danny said, "Yeah, and I don't know if it plays with our case or not."

"Well, I went by Wilshire Station and checked the report, and it looks clean—no forced entry, no struggle. Hartshorn's daughter said Pops was despondent over your grand jury."

Danny was getting nervous; the scene with De Haven was coming back: she knew, they knew, no more Red Ted. "Jack, have you got anything hot?"

Shortell said, "Maybe a scorcher. I was up all night on the wolverine thing, and I got a great lead on an old man named Thomas Cormier, that's C-O-R-M-I-E-R. He's an amateur naturalist, famous, I guess you'd call him. He lives on Bunker Hill, and he rents weasel genus things to the movies and animal shows. He has a batch of individually penned-up wolverines, the only known batch in L.A. Now listen, because this is where it gets good.

"Last night I went by the West Hollywood Substation to talk to a pal of mine who just transferred over. I heard the girl at the switchboard ragging you to the watch sergeant, and I played nice and sweet-talked her. She told me she was dragging her heels on her set of dental queries because she thought you were just using her. She gave me a list that had notes on it—negative on the killer's description, but positive on the animal teeth—Joredco Dental Lab on Beverly and Beaudry. They do animal dentures for taxidermists, and they're the only lab in L.A. that works with actual animal teeth—that lead you had that said all taxidermists use plastic teeth was wrong. And Beverly and Beaudry is seven blocks from Thomas Cormier's house—343 South Corondelet."

Red hot and biting.

Danny said, "I'm rolling," and hung up. He put muscling Felix Gordean aside, cleaned up and stashed his files, cleaned up his person and dressed as Daniel T. Upshaw, policeman, replete with badge, gun and official ID. Ted Krugman dead and buried, he drove to Bunker Hill.

* * *

343 South Corondelet was an eaved and gabled Victorian house sandwiched between vacant lots on the west edge of the Hill. Danny parked in front and heard animal yapping; he followed the sounds down the driveway and around to a terraced back yard with a picture postcard view of Angel's Flight. Lean-tos with corrugated metal roofs were arranged in L-shapes, one to each level of grass; the structures were fronted by heavy wire mesh, and the longest L had what looked like a generator device built onto its rear side. The whole yard reeked of animals, animal piss and animal shit.

"The smell getting to you, Officer?"

Danny turned around. The mind reader was a grizzled old man wearing dungarees and hipboots, walking toward him waving a fat cigar that blended in perfectly with the shit stink and made it worse. He smiled, adding bad breath to the effluvia. "Are you from Animal Regulation or Department of Health?"

Danny felt the sun and the smell go to work on his skinful of booze, sandpapering him. "I'm a Sheriff's Homicide detective. Are you Thomas Cormier?"

"I am indeed, and I've never killed anyone and I don't associate with killers. I've got some killer mustelids, but they only kill the rodents I feed them. If that's a crime, I'll take the blame. I keep my mustelidae in captivity, so if they called a bum tune, I'll pay the piper."

The man looked too intelligent to be an outright loony. Danny said, "Mr. Cormier, I heard you're an expert on wolverines."

"That is the God's truth. I have eleven in captivity right this instant, my baby refrigeration unit keeping them nice and cool, the way they like it."

Danny queased on cigar smoke and halitosis; he willed himself pro. "This is why I'm here, Mr. Cormier. Four men have been killed between New Year's and now. They were mutilated by a man wearing denture plates with wolverine teeth attached. There's a dental lab several blocks from here—the only one in L.A. that manufactures actual animal dentures. I think that's a strange coincidence, and I thought maybe you could help me out with it."

Thomas Cormier snuffed his cigar and pocketed the butt. "That is just about the strangest thing I have heard in my entire time on this planet, which dates back to 1887. What else have you got on your killer?"

Danny said, "He's tall, middle-aged, gray-haired. He knows the jazz world, he can purchase heroin, he knows his way around male prostitutes." He stopped, thinking of Reynolds Loftis, wondering if he'd get anything that wasn't circumstantial on him. "And he's a homosexual."

Cormier laughed. "Sounds like a nice fellow, and sorry I can't help you. I don't know anybody like that, and if I did, I think I'd keep my back to the wall and my trusty rifle out when he came to call. And this fellow's enamored of *Gulo luscus*?"

"If you mean wolverines, yes."

"Lord. Well, I admire his taste in mustelids, if not the way he displays his appreciation."

Danny sighed. "Mr. Cormier, do you know anything about the Joredco Dental Lab?"

"Sure, just down the street. I think they make animal choppers."

A clean take. Danny saw takes from Claire De Haven's movie, pictured HIM seeing it, getting aroused, wanting more. "I'd like to see your wolverines."

Cormier said, "Thought you'd never ask," and walked ahead of Danny to the refrigeration shed. The air went from warm to freezing; the yapping became snarling; dark shapes lashed out and banged the mesh fronts of their pens. Cormier said, "*Gulo luscus.* Carcajou—evil spirit—to the Indians. The most insatiable carnivore alive and pound for pound the meanest mammal. Like I said, I admire your killer's taste."

Danny found a good sun angle—light square on a middle pen; he squatted down and looked, his nose to the wire. Inside, a long creature paced, turning in circles, snapping at the walls. Its teeth glinted; its claws scraped the floor; it looked like a coiled muscle that would not stop coiling until it killed and slept in satiation—or died. Danny watched, feeling the beast's power, feeling HIM feeling it; Cormier talked. "*Gulo luscus* is two things: smart and intractable. I've known them to develop a taste for deer, hide in trees and toss nice edible bark down to lure them over, then jump down and rip the deer's jugular out clean to the windpipe. Once they get a whiff of blood, they will not stop persisting. I've heard of wolverines stalking cougars wounded in mating battles. They'll jab them from behind, take nips out and run away, a little meat here and there until the cougar nearly bleeds to death. When the poor fellow's almost dead, *Gulo* attacks frontally, claws the cougar's eyes out of his head and eats them like gumballs."

Danny winced, transposing the image: Marty Goines, HIM, the creature he was watching. "I need to look at your records. All the wolverines you've lent out to movies and animal shows."

Cormier said, "Officer, you can't lend *Gulos* out, much as I'd like to make the money. They're my private passion, I love them and I keep them around because they shore up my reputation as a mustelidologist. You lend *Gulos* out, they'll attack anything human or animal within biting range. I had one stolen out of its pen five or six years ago, and my only consolation was that the stealer sure as hell got himself mangled."

Danny looked up. "Tell me about that. What happened?"

Cormier took out his cigar butt and fingered it. "In the summer of '42 I worked nights at the Griffith Park Zoo, resident zoologist doing research on nocturnal mustelid habits. I had an earlier bunch of wolverines that were getting real fat. I knew somebody must have been feeding them, and I started finding extra mouse and hamster carcasses in the pens. Somebody was lifting the food latches and feeding my *Gulos*, and I figured it for a neighborhood kid who'd heard about my reputation and thought he'd see for himself. Truth be told, it didn't bother me, and it kind of gave me a cozy feeling, here's this fellow *Gulo* lover and all. Then, late in July, it stopped. I knew it stopped because there were no more extra carcasses in the cages and my *Gulos* went back to their normal weights. About a year and a half or so went by, and one night my *Gulo* Otto was stolen. I laughed like hell. I figured the feeder had to have a *Gulo* for himself and stole Otto. Otto was a pistol. If the stealer got away with keeping him, I'm sure Otto bit him real good. I called hospitals around here to see if they stitched a bite victim, but it was no go, no Otto."

Bit him real good.

Danny thought of sedation—a wolverine Mickey Finned and stolen—HIM with his own evil mascot—*the story might just play*. He looked back in the pen; the wolverine noticed something and lashed the wire, making screechy blood W noises. Cormier laughed and said, "Juno, *you're* a pistol." Danny put his face up to the mesh, tasting the animal's breath. He said, "Thanks, Mr. Cormier," pulled himself away and drove to the Joredco Dental Lab.

*   *   *

He was almost expecting a neon sign facade, an animal mouth open wide, the address numbers done up as teeth. He was wrong: the lab was just a tan stucco building, a subtly lettered sign above the door its only advertisement.

Danny parked in front and walked into a tiny receiving area: a secretary behind a desk, a switchboard and calendar art on the walls—1950 repeated a dozen times over, handsome wild animals representing January for local taxidermist's shops. The girl smiled at him and said, "Yes?"

Danny showed his badge. "Sheriff's. I'd like to speak to the man in charge."

"Regarding?"

"Regarding animal teeth."

The girl tapped an intercom switch and said, "Policeman to see you, Mr. Carmichael." Danny looked at pictures of moose, bears, wolves and buffalos; he noticed a sleek mountain cat and thought of a wolverine stalking it, killing it off with sheer ugly persistence.

A connecting door swung open; a man in a bloody white smock came in. Danny said, "Mr. Carmichael?"

"Yes, mister?"

"It's Deputy Upshaw."

"And this regards, Deputy?"

"It regards wolverine teeth."

No reaction except impatience—the man obviously anxious to get back to work. "Then I can't help you. Joredco is the only lab in Los Angeles that fashions animal dentures, and we've never done them for a wolverine."

"Why?"

"Why? Because taxidermists do not stuff wolverines—they are not an item that people want mounted in their home or lodge. I've worked here for thirteen years and I've never filled an order for wolverine teeth."

Danny thought it over. "Could someone who learned the rudiments of animal-denture making here do it himself?"

"Yes, but it would be bloody and very slapdash without the proper tools."

"Good. Because I'm looking for a man who likes blood."

Carmichael wiped his hands on his smock. "Deputy, what is this in regard to?"

"Quadruple homicide. How far back do your employment records go?"

The "quadruple homicide" got to Carmichael—he looked shaken under his brusqueness. "My God. Our records go back to '40, but Joredco employs mostly women. You don't think—"

Danny was thinking Reynolds Loftis wouldn't sully his hands in a place like this. "I think maybe. Tell me about the men you've had working here."

"There haven't been many. Frankly, women work for a lower wage. Our current staff has been here for years, and when we get rush orders, we hire bums out of day labor and kids from Lincoln and Belmont High School to do the scut work. During the war, we hired lots of temporaries that way."

The Joredco connection felt—strangely—like it was clicking in, with Loftis clicking out. "Mr. Carmichael, do you have a medical plan for your regular employees?"

"Yes."

"May I see your records?"

Carmichael turned to the receptionist. "Sally, let Deputy whatever here see the files."

Danny let the remark slide; Carmichael went back through the connecting door. Sally pointed to a filing cabinet. "Nasty prick, if you'll pardon my French. Medicals are in the bottom drawer, men in with the women. You don't think a real killer worked here, do you?"

Danny laughed. "No, but maybe a real live monster did."

* * *

It took him an hour to go through the medical charts.

Since November '39, sixteen men had been hired on as dental techs. Three were Japanese, hired immediately after the Jap internment ended in '44; four were Caucasian and now in their thirties; three were white and now middle-aged; six were Mexican. All sixteen men had, at one time or another, given blood to the annual Red Cross Drive. Five of the sixteen possessed O+ blood, the most common human blood type. Three of the men were Mexican, two were Japanese—but Joredco still felt right.

Danny went back to the shop and spent another hour chatting up the techs, talking to them while they pried teeth out of gum sections removed from the heads of elk, deer and Catalina Island boar. He asked questions about tall, gray-haired men who acted strange; jazz; heroin; guys with wolverine fixations. He breathed blood and animal tooth infection and stressed strange behavior among the temporary workers who came and went; he threw out teasers on a handsome Hollywood actor who just might have made the scene. The techs deadpanned him, no'd him and worked around him; his only lead was elimination stuff: most of the temps were Mex, wetbacks going to Belmont and Lincoln High sans green cards, veterans of the Vernon slaughterhouses, where the work was twice as gory and the money was even worse than the coolie wages Mr. Carmichael paid. Danny left thinking Reynolds Loftis would faint the second he hit the Joredco line; thinking the actor might be circumstantial linkage only. But Joredco/Cormier still felt right; the blood and decay smelled like something HE would love.

The day was warming up; heat that felt all the worse for coming after heavy rain. Danny sat in the car and sweated out last night's drunk; he thought elimination, thought that the day labor joints kept no records in order to dodge taxes, that the high school employment offices were long shots he had to try anyway. He drove to Belmont High, talked to the employment counselor, learned that her records only went back to '45 and checked the Joredco referrals—twenty-seven of them—all Mexes and Japs. Even though he knew the age range was wrong, he repeated the process at Lincoln: Mexes, Japs and a mentally deficient white boy hired because he was strong enough to haul two deer carcasses at a time. Gooser. But the rightness kept nagging him.

Danny drove to a bar in Chinatown. After two shots of house bonded, he knew this was his last day as Homicide brass: when he told Considine Ted Krugman was shot, he'd be shot back to the West Hollywood Squad, packing some large blame if Ellis Loew thought he'd jeopardized the chance for a successful grand jury. He could keep looking for HIM on his off-hours—but there was a good chance Felix Gordean would talk to his golf buddies Sheriff Biscailuz and Al Dietrich and he'd get dumped back into uniform or jail duty. He'd made an enemy of Gene Niles and pissed off Dudley Smith and Mike Breuning; Karen Hiltscher wouldn't play pratgirl for him anymore; if Niles could prove he B&E'd 2307, he'd be in real trouble.

Two more shots; warm wisps edging out the gloom. He had a friend with rank and juice—if he could make up for blowing his decoy job, he could still ride Considine's coattails. A last shot; HIM again, HIM pure and abstract, like there was never a time when he didn't exist, even though they'd been together only a few weeks. He thought of HIM free of Reynolds Loftis and last night with Claire, taking it back chronologically, stopping at Augie Duarte dead on a stainless steel slab.

The facial cuts. Jump forward to last night's file work. His instinct: the killer knew Marty Goines' pal—the youth with the bandaged face—and drew sexual inspiration from him. Jump to Thomas Cormier, whose wolverines were overfed—worshiped?—during the summer of '42, Sleepy Lagoon summer, when zoot sticks were most in use. Cormier's interpretation: a neighborhood kid. Jump to Joredco. They hired youths, maybe youths out of skid row day labor, where they didn't keep records. The burn boy was white; all the high school referrals were Mex and Jap, except for the non-play retard. Maybe the workers he talked to never met the kid because he only worked there briefly, maybe they forgot about him, maybe they just didn't notice him. Jump forward to now. The burned-face boy was a burglar—Listerine Chester Brown tagged him as burglarizing with Goines circa '43 to '44, his face bandaged. If he was the one who stole Thomas Cormier's wolverine some eighteen months after his summer of '42 worship, and he was a local kid, he might have committed other burglaries in the Bunker Hill area during that time period.

Danny drove to Rampart Station, the LAPD division that handled Bunker Hill felonies. Mal Considine's name got him the squad lieutenant's attention; a few minutes later he was in a musty storeroom checking boxes of discarded occurrence reports.

The boxes were marked according to year; Danny found two grocery cartons stenciled "1942." The reports inside were loose, the multi-page jobs stapled together with no carbons in between. There was no rhyme or reason to the order they were filed in— purse snatchings, muggings, petty thefts, burglaries, indecent exposures and loiterings were all lumped together. Danny sat down on a box of '48 reports and dug in.

He scanned upper right corners for penal code numbers— Burglary, 459.1. The two boxes for '42 yielded thirty-one; location was his next breakdown step. He carried the reports into the squadroom, sat at an empty desk facing a wall map of Rampart Division and looked for Bunker Hill street names to match. Four reports in, he got one; six reports in, three more. He memorized the ten north-south and eight east-west blocks of the Hill, tore through the rest of the pages and ended with eleven burglaries, unsolved occurrences, on Bunker Hill in the year 1942. And the eleven addresses were all within walking distance of Thomas Cormier's house and the Joredco Dental Lab.

Next was dates.

Danny flipped through the reports again quickly; the time and date of occurrence were typed at the bottom of each first page. May 16, 1942; July 1, 1942; May 27, 1942; May 9, 1942; June 16, 1942, and six more to make eleven: an unsolved burglary spree, May 9 to August 1, 1942. His head buzzing, he read "Items Stolen"—and saw why Rampart didn't put out beaucoup men to catch the burglar:

Trinkets, family portraits, costume jewelry, cash out of purses and wallets. A deco wall clock. A cedar cigar humidor. A collection of glass figurines. A stuffed ringneck pheasant, a stuffed bobcat mounted on rosewood.

More HIM, more not Loftis HIM. It had to be.

Danny tingled, like he was being dangled on electric strings. He went back to the storeroom, found the '43 and '44 boxes, looked through them and got zero Bunker Hill trinket jobs—the only burglary occurrence reports for those years denoted *real* 459.1's, real valuables taken; burglary reports resulting in arrest had already been checked City- and County wide. Danny finished and kicked at the boxes; two facts kicked him.

The killer was ID'd as middle-aged; he had to be connected to the wolverine-worshiping burglar—a youth—who was emerging from today's work. Chester Brown told him that Marty Goines and his burned-face accomplice B&E'd in the San Fernando Valley '43 to '44; station houses out there might have occurrence reports—he could roll there after he muscled a certain Commie stagehand. And summer '42 was the height of the wartime blackout, curfew was rigidly enforced and field interrogation cards were written up on people caught out after 10:00 P.M.—when the wolverine lover was most likely prowling. If the cards were saved—

Danny tore the storeroom apart, throwing empty boxes; he sweated out his booze lunch, got sprayed with cobwebs, mildew and mouse turds. He found a box marked "FI's '41–'43," thumbed back the first few cards and saw that they were—amazingly—in chronological order. He kept flipping; the late spring and summer of '42 yielded eight names: eight white men aged nineteen to forty-seven stopped for being out after curfew, questioned and released.

The cards were filled out slapdash: all had the name, race and date of birth of the interrogee; only half had home addresses listed—in most cases downtown hotels. Five of the men would now be middle-aged and possibles for HIM; the other three were youths who could be the burned-face boy pre-burns—or—if *he* was tangential to the case—Thomas Cormier's neighborhood kid wolverine lover.

Danny pocketed the cards, drove to a pay phone and called Jack Shortell at the Hollywood squadroom. The squad lieutenant put the call through; Shortell came on the line sounding harried. "Yeah? Danny?"

"It's me. What's wrong?"

"Nothing, except I'm getting the fisheye from every City bull in the place, like all of a sudden I'm *worse* than worse than poison. What have you got?"

"Names, maybe a hot one right in the middle. I talked to that Cormier guy and hit Joredco, and I couldn't put them straight together, but I'm damn sure our guy got kissing close to Cormier's wolverines. You remember that old burglary accomplice of Marty Goines I told you about?"

"Yeah."

"I think I've got a line on him, and I just about think he plays. There was a bunch of unsolved burglaries on Bunker Hill, May to August of '42. Mickey Mouse stuff clouted, right near Cormier and Joredco. LAPD was enforcing curfew then, and I picked out eight possible FI cards from the area—May through August. I've got a hunch the killings stem from then—the Sleepy Lagoon killing and the SLDC time—and I need you to do eliminations—current address, blood type, dental tech background, criminal record and the rest."

"Go, I'm writing it down."

Danny got out his cards. "Some have addresses, some don't. One, James George Whitacre, DOB 10/5/03, Havana Hotel, Ninth and Olive. Two, Ronald NMI Dennison, 6/30/20, no address. Three, Coleman Masskie, 5/9/23, 236 South Beaudry. Four, Lawrence Thomas Waznicki with a K-I, 11/29/08, 641 1/4 Bunker Hill Avenue. Five, Leland NMI Hardell, 6/4/24, American Eagle Hotel, 4th and Hill Streets. Six, Loren Harold Nadick, 3/2/02, no address. Seven, David NMI Villers, 1/15/04, no address. And Bruno Andrew Gaffney, 7/29/06, no address."

Shortell said, "All down. Son, are you getting close?"

Another electric jolt: the Bunker Hill burglaries ended on August 1, 1942; the Sleepy Lagoon murder—*the victim's clothes zoot stick slashed*—occurred on August 2. "Almost, Jack. Some right answers and luck and that fucker is mine."

* * *

Danny got to Variety International Pictures just as dusk was falling and the picket lines were breaking up for the day. He parked in plain view, put an "Official Police Vehicle" sign on his windshield and pinned his badge to his coat front; he walked to the guard hut, no familiar faces, pissed that he was ignored. The gate man buzzed him in; he walked straight back to Set 23.

The sign on the wall had *Tomahawk Massacre* still in production; the door was open. Danny heard gunfire, looked in and saw a cowboy and an Indian exchange shots across papier-mâché foothills. Lights were shining down on them; cameras were rolling; the Mexican guy he'd seen outside the morgue was sweeping up fake snow in front of another backdrop: grazing buffalos painted on cardboard.

Danny hugged the wall going over; the Mex looked up, dropped his broom and took off running, right in front of the cameras. Danny ran after him, sliding on soap flakes; the moviemaking stopped; someone yelled, "Juan, goddamn you! Cut! Cut!"

Juan ran out a side exit, slamming the door; Danny ran across the set, slowed and eased the door open. It was slammed against him, reinforced steel knocking him back; he slid on phony snow, hauled outside and saw Duarte racing down an alley toward a chain-link fence.

Danny ran full out; Juan Duarte hit the fence and started climbing. He snagged his trouser legs; he kicked, pulled and twisted to get free. Danny caught up, yanked him down by his waistband and caught a hard right hand in the face. Stunned, he let go; Duarte collapsed on top of him.

Danny kneed upward, a jerky shot; Duarte hit down, missing, smashing his fist on the pavement. Danny rolled away, came up behind him and pinned him with his weight; the Mex gasped, "Puto fascist shitfuck fascist cop fascist shitfuck." Danny fumbled out his cuffs, ratcheted Duarte's left hand and attached the spare bracelet to a fence link. The Mex flopped on his stomach and tried to tear the fence down, spitting epithets in Spanish; Danny got his breath, let Duarte shake and shout himself out, then knelt beside him. "I know you saw my picture, and you saw me at the morgue and you snitched me to Claire. I don't care and I give a fuck about UAES and the fucking Red Menace. I want to get Augie's killer and I've got a hunch it goes back to Sleepy Lagoon. Now you can talk to me, or I'll nail you for Assault on a Police Officer right here. Call it now."

Duarte shook his cuff chain; Danny said, "Two to five minimum, and I don't give a shit about the UAES." A crowd was forming in the alley; Danny waved them back; they retreated with sidelong looks and slow head shakes. Duarte said, "Take these things off me and *maybe* I'll talk to you."

Danny unlocked the cuffs. Duarte rubbed his wrist, stood up, got rubber-legged and slid down to a sitting position, his back against the fence. He said, "Why's a hired gun for the studios give a damn about my dead fag cousin?"

Danny said, "Get up, Duarte."

"I talk better on my ass. Answer me. How come you care about a maricón who wanted to be a puto movie star like every other puto in this puto town?"

"I don't know. But I want the guy who killed Augie nailed."

"And what's that got to do with you trying to get next to Claire De Haven?"

"I told you I don't care about that."

"Norm Kostenz said you sure care. When I told him you were the fucking law, he said you should get a fucking Oscar for your bonaroo portrayal of Ted Krug—"

Danny squatted by Duarte, holding the fence. "Are you going to spill or not?"

Duarte said, "I'll spill, pendejo. You said you thought Augie's snuff went back to Sleepy Lagoon, and that got my interest. Charlie Hartshorn thought that too, so—"

Danny's hand shook the fence; he braced his whole body into it to stay steady. "What did you say?"

"I said Charlie Hartshorn thought the same thing maybe, so maybe talking to a puto cop ain't all poison."

Danny slid down the fence so he could eyeball Duarte close. "Tell me all of it, slow and easy. You know Hartshorn killed himself, don't you?"

Duarte said, "Maybe he did. You tell me."

"No. You tell me, because I don't know and I've got to know."

Duarte stared at Danny, squinty-eyed, like he couldn't figure him out. "Charlie was a lawyer. He was a maricón, but he wasn't a swish or nothing. He worked Sleepy Lagoon, filing briefs and shit for free."

"I know that."

"Okay, here's what you don't know, and here's the kind of guy he was. When you saw me at the morgue it was my second time there. I got a call from a buddy who works there, maybe one in the morning, and he told me about Augie—the zoot cuts, all of it. I went to Charlie's house. He had legal juice, and I wanted to see if he'd goose the cops so they'd give Augie's snuff a good investigation. He told me he'd been goosed by some cop about the death of a guy named Duane Lindenaur, even though the cop pretended he didn't care about that. Charlie read this scandal rag that said Lindenaur and some clown named Wiltsie got cut up by a zoot stick, and my morgue buddy said Augie got chopped like that, too. I told Charlie, and he got the idea all three snuffs went back to Sleepy Lagoon. He called the cops and spoke to some guy named Sergeant Bruner or something—"

Danny cut in. "Breuning? Sergeant Mike Breuning?"

"Yeah, that's him. Charlie told Breuning what I just told you and Breuning said he'd come to see him at his crib right away to talk to him about it. I took off then. So if Charlie thought there was something to this Sleepy Lagoon theory, maybe you ain't such a cabrón."

Danny's brain stoked on overdrive:

Breuning's curiosity on the zoot stick queries, his making light of them. His strange reaction to the four surveillance names—Augie Duarte singled out—because he was Mex, a KA of a Sleepy Lagoon Committee member? Mal telling him that Dudley Smith asked to join the grand jury team, even though, as an LAPD Homicide lieutenant, there was no logical reason for him to work the job. Mal's story: *Dudley brutally interrogating Duarte/Sammy Benavides/Mondo Lopez, stressing the Sleepy Lagoon case and the guilt of the seventeen youths originally charged with the crime—even though the questioning tack was not germane to UAES.*

Hartshorn mentioning "zoot stick" on the phone to Breuning.

Jack Shortell's oral report: Dudley Smith and Breuning were seen hobnobbing at Wilshire Station the night before last—the night Hartshorn killed himself. Did they make a quick run to Hartshorn's house—a scant mile from the station—kill him and return to the Wilshire squadroom, hoping that no one saw them leave and return—a perfect cop alibi?

And why?

Juan Duarte was looking at him like he was from outer space; Danny got his brain simmered down to where he could talk. "Think fast on this. Jazz musicians, burglary, wolverines, heroin, queer escort services."

Duarte slid a few feet away. "I think they all stink. Why?"

"A kid who worships wolverines."

Duarte put a finger to his head and twirled it. "Loco mierda. A wolverine's a fucking rat, right?"

Danny saw Juno's claws lashing out. "Try this, Duarte. Sleepy Lagoon, the Defense Committee, '42 to '44 and Reynolds Loftis. Think slow, go slow."

Duarte said, "Easy. Reynolds and his kid brother."

Danny started to say, "What?", stopped and thought. He'd read the entire grand jury package twice on arrival and twice last night; he'd read the psychiatric files twice before Considine took them back. In all the paperwork there was no mention of Loftis having a brother. But there was a gap—'42 to '44—in Loftis' shrink file. "Tell me about the kid brother, Duarte. Nice and slow."

Duarte spoke rapidamente. "He was a punk, a lame-o. Reynolds started bringing him around around the time the SLDC was hot. I forget the kid's name, but he was a kid, eighteen, nineteen, in there. He had his face bandaged up. He was in a fire and he got burned bad. When he got his burns all healed up and the bandages and gauze and shit came off, all the girls in the Committee thought he was real cute. He looked just like Reynolds, but even handsomer."

The new facts coming together went tap, tap, tap, knocks on a door that was still a long way from opening. A Loftis burn-faced brother put the actor back in contention for HIM, but contradicted his instinct that the killer drew sex inspiration from the youth's disfigurement; it played into Wolverine Prowler and Burn Face as one man and tapped the possibility that he was a killing accomplice—one way to explain the new welter of age contradictions. Danny said, "Tell me about the kid. Why did you call him a punk?"

Duarte said, "He was always sucking up to the Mexican guys. He told this fish story about how a big white man killed José Diaz, like we were supposed to like him because he said the killer wasn't Mexican. Everybody knew the killer was Mexican—the cops just railroaded the wrong Mexicans. He told this crazy story about seeing the killing, but he didn't have no real details, and when guys pressed him, he clammed up. The SLDC got some anonymous letters saying a white guy did it, and you could tell the kid brother sent them—it was crazy-man stuff. The kid said he was running from the killer, and once I said, 'Pendejo, if the killer's looking for you, what the fuck you doing coming to these rallies where he could grab your crazy ass?' The kid said he had special protection, but wouldn't tell me no more. Like I said, he was a lame-o. If he wasn't Reynolds' brother, nobody woulda tolerated him at all."

Tap, tap, tap, tap, tap. Danny said, "What happened to him?"

Duarte shrugged. "I don't know. I haven't see him since the SLDC, and I don't think nobody else has either. Reynolds don't talk about him. It's strange. I don't think I've heard Chaz or Claire or Reynolds talk about him in years."

"What about Benavides and Lopez? Where are they now?"

"On location with some other puto cowboy turkey. You think this stuff about Reynolds' brother has got something to do with Augie?"

Danny brainstormed off the question. Reynolds Loftis' brother was the burned-face burglar boy, Marty Goines' burglar accomplice, very possibly the Bunker Hill prowler/wolverine lover. The Bunker Hill B&Es stopped August 1, 1942; the next night, José Diaz was killed at the Sleepy Lagoon, three miles or so southeast of the Hill. The kid brother alleged that he witnessed a "big white man" killing José Diaz.

Tap, tap, tap. Jump, jump, jump.

Dudley Smith was a big white man with a bone-deep cruel streak. He joined the grand jury team out of a desire to keep incriminating Sleepy Lagoon testimony kiboshed, thinking that with access to witnesses and case paperwork, he could get the jump on damaging evidence about to come out. Hartshorn's zoot stick call to Mike Breuning scared him; he and Breuning or one of them alone drove over from Wilshire Station to talk to the man; Hartshorn got suspicious. Either premeditatedly or on the spur of the moment, Smith and/or Breuning killed him, faking a suicide. Tap, tap, tap—thunder loud—with the door still closed on the most important question: *How did Smith killing José Diaz, his attempts to keep possible evidence quashed and his killing Charles Hartshorn connect to the Goines/Wiltsie/Lindenaur/Duarte murders? And why did Smith kill Diaz?*

Danny looked around at set doors spilling glimpses: the wild west, jungle swampland, trees in a forest. He said, "Vaya con Dios," left Duarte sitting there and drove home to hit the grand jury file, thinking he'd finally made detective in the eyes of Maslick and Vollmer. He walked in his building, light as air; he pushed the elevator button and heard footsteps behind him. Turning, he saw two big men with guns drawn. He reached for his own gun, but a big fist holding a set of big brass knucks hit him first.

* * *

He came awake handcuffed to a chair. His head was woozy, his wrists were numb and his tongue felt huge. His eyes homed in on an interrogation cubicle, three fuzzy men seated around a table, a big black revolver lying square in the middle. A voice said, ".38's are standard issue for your Department, Upshaw. Why do you carry a .45?"

Danny blinked and coughed up a bloody lunger; he blinked again and recognized the voice man: Thad Green, LAPD Chief of Detectives. The two men flanking Green fell into focus; they were the biggest plainclothes cops he'd ever seen.

"I asked you a question, Deputy."

Danny tried to remember the last time he had a drink, came up with Chinatown and knew he couldn't have gone crazy while fried on bonded. He coughed dry and said, "I sold it when I made detective."

Green lit a cigarette. "That's an interdepartmental offense. Do you consider yourself above the law?"

"No!"

"Your friend Karen Hiltscher says otherwise. She says you've manipulated her for special favors ever since you made detective. She told Sergeant Eugene Niles you broke into 2307 Tamarind and knew that two murder victims had recently been killed there. She told Sergeant Niles that your story about a girlfriend near the doughnut stand on Franklin and Western is a lie, that she phoned you the information off the City air. Niles was going to inform on you, Deputy. Did you know that?"

Danny's head woozed. He swallowed blood; he recognized the man to Green's left as the knuck wielder. "Yeah. Yes, I knew."

Green said, "Who'd you sell your .38 to?"

"A guy in a bar."

"That's a misdemeanor, Deputy. A criminal charge. You really don't care much for the law, do you?"

"Yes, yes, I care! I'm a policeman! Goddamn it, what is this!"

The knuck man said, "You were seen arguing with a known homo procurer named Felix Gordean. Are you on his payroll?"

"No!"

"Mickey Cohen's payroll?"

"No!"

Green took over. "You were given command of a Homicide team, a carrot for your grand jury work. Sergeant Niles and Sergeant Mike Breuning found it very strange that a smart young officer would be so concerned about a string of queer slashes. Would you like to tell us why?"

"No! What the fuck is this! I B&E'd Tamarind! What do you fucking want from me!"

The third cop, a huge bodybuilder type, said, "Why did you and Niles trade blows?"

"He was ditzing me with Tamarind Street, threatening to rat me."

"So that made you mad?"

"Yes."

"Fighting mad?"

"Yes!"

Green said, "We heard a different version, Deputy. We heard Niles called you a queer."

Danny froze, reached for a comeback and kept freezing. He thought of ratting Dudley and kiboshed it—they'd never believe him—*yet*. "If Niles said that, I didn't hear it."

The knuck cop laughed. "Strike a nerve, Sonny?"

"Fuck you!"

The weightlifter cop backhanded him; Danny spat in his face. Green yelled, "No!"

The knuck man put his arms around weightlifter and held him back; Green chained another cigarette, butt to tip. Danny gasped, *"Tell me what this is all about."*

Green waved the strongarms to the back of the cubicle, dragged on his smoke and stubbed it out. "Where were you night before last between 2:00 and 7:00 A.M.?"

"I was at home in bed. Asleep."

"Alone, Deputy?"

"Yes."

"Deputy, during that time Sergeant Gene Niles was shot and killed, then buried in the Hollywood Hills. Did you do it?"

"No!"

"Tell us who did."

"Jack! Mickey! Niles was fucking rogue!"

The knuck cop stepped forward; the weightlifter cop grabbed him, mumbling, "Spit on my Hathaway shirt you queer-loving hump. Gene Niles was my pal, my good buddy from the army, you queer lover."

Danny dug his feet in and pushed his chair against the wall. "Gene Niles was an incompetent bagman son of a bitch."

Weightlifter charged, straight for Danny's throat. The cubicle door opened and Mal Considine rushed in; Thad Green shouted commands impossible to hear. Danny brought his knees up, toppling the chair; the monster cop's hands closed on air. Mal crashed into him, winging rabbit punches; the knuck cop pulled him off and wrestled him out to the corridor. Shouts of "Danny!" echoed; Green stationed himself between the chair and the monster, going, "No, Harry, no," like he was reprimanding an unruly monster dog. Danny ate linoleum and cigarette butts, heard, "Get Considine to a holding tank", was lifted, chair and all, to an upright position. The knuck man went behind him and unlocked his cuffs; Thad Green reached for his .45 on the table.

Danny stood up, swaying; Green handed him his gun. "I don't know if you did it or not, but there's one way to find out. Report back here to City Hall, room 1003, tomorrow at noon. You'll be given a polygraph test and sodium pentothal, and you'll be asked extensive questions about these homicides you're working and your relationships with Felix Gordean and Gene Niles. Good night, Deputy."

Danny weaved to the elevator, rode to the ground floor and walked outside, his legs slowly coming back. He cut across the lawn toward the Temple Street cabstand, stopping for a soft voice.

"Lad."

Danny froze; Dudley Smith stepped out of a shadow. He said, "It's a grand night, is it not?"

Small talk with a murderer. Danny said, "You killed José Diaz. You and Breuning killed Charles Hartshorn. And I'm going to prove it."

Dudley Smith smiled. "I never doubted your intelligence, lad. Your courage, yes. Your intelligence, never. And I'll admit I underestimated your persistence. I'm only human, you know."

"Oh, no you're not."

"I'm skin and bone, lad. Eros and dust like all us frail mortals. Like you, lad. Crawling in sewers for answers you'd be better off without."

"You're finished."

"No, lad. You are. I've been talking to my old friend Felix Gordean, and he painted me a vivid picture of your emergence. Lad, next to myself Felix has the finest eye for weakness I've ever encountered. He knows, and when you take that lie detector test tomorrow, the whole world will know."

Danny said, "No."

Dudley Smith said, "Yes," kissed him full on the lips and walked away whistling a love song.

* * *

Machines that know.

Drugs that don't let you lie.

Danny took a cab home. He unlocked the door and went straight for his files: facts you could put together for the truth, Dudley and Breuning and HIM nailed by 11:59, a last-minute reprieve like in the movies. He hit the hall light, opened the closet door. No file boxes, the rugs that covered them neatly folded on the floor.

Danny tore up the hall carpet and looked under it, dumped the bedroom cabinet and emptied the drawers, stripped the bed and yanked the medicine chest off the bathroom wall. He upended the living room furniture, looked under the cushions and tossed the kitchen drawers until the floor was all cutlery and broken dishes. He saw a half-full bottle by the radio, opened it, found his throat muscles too constricted and hurled it, knocking down the venetian blinds. He walked to the window, looked out and saw Dudley Smith haloed by a streetlight.

And he knew he knew. And tomorrow they would all know.

Blackmail bait.

His name in sex files.

His name bandied in queer chitchat at the Chateau Marmont.

Machines that know.

Drugs that don't let you lie.

Polygraph needles fluttering off the paper every time they asked him why he cared so much about a string of queer fag homo fruit snuffs.

No reprieve.

Danny unholstered his gun and stuck the barrel in his mouth. The taste of oil made him gag and he saw how it would look, the cops who found him making jokes about why he did it that way. He put the .45 down and walked to the kitchen.

Weapons galore.

Danny picked up a serrated-edged carving knife. He tested the heft, found it substantial and said goodbye to Mal and Jack and Doc. He apologized for the cars he stole and the guys he beat up who didn't deserve it, who were just there when he wanted to hit something. He thought of his killer, thought that he murdered because someone made him what he himself was. He held the knife up and forgave him; he put the blade to his throat and slashed himself ear to ear, down to the windpipe in one clean stroke.

PART THREE

WOLVERINE

32

A WEEK later Buzz went by the grave, his fourth visit since LASD hustled the kid into the ground. The plot was a low-rent number in an East L.A. cemetery; the stone read:

Daniel Thomas Upshaw

1922–1950

No beloved whatever of.

No son of whoever.

No crucifix cut into the tablet and no RIP. Nothing juicy to catch a passerby's interest, like "Cop Killer" or "Almost DA's Bureau Brass." Nothing to spell it out true to whoever read the half-column hush job on the kid's accidental death—a slip off a chair, a nose dive onto a kitchen cutlery rack.

Fall Guy.

Buzz bent down and pulled out a clump of crabgrass; the butt of the gun he'd killed Gene Niles with dug into his side. He stood up and kicked the marker; he thought that "Free Ride" and "Gravy Train" and "Dumb Okie Luck" might look good too, followed by a soliloquy on Deputy Danny Upshaw's last days, lots of details on a tombstone skyscraper high, like the ones voodoo nigger pimps bought for themselves. Because Deputy Danny Upshaw was voodooing him, little pins stuck in a fat little Buzz Meeks voodoo doll.

Mal had called him with the word. The rain dug up Niles' body, LAPD grabbed Danny as a suspect, roughhoused him and cut him loose with orders to report for a lie detector test and sodium pentothal questioning the next day. When the kid didn't show, City bulls hit his pad in force and found him dead on the living room floor, throat slashed, the pad trashed. Nort Layman, distraught, did the autopsy, dying to call it a 187; the evidence wouldn't let him: fingerprints on the knife and the angle of the cut and fall said "self-inflicted," case closed. Doc called the death wound "amazing"—no hesitation marks, Danny Upshaw wanted out bad and now.

LASD double-timed the kid graveside; four people attended the funeral: Layman, Mal, a County cop named Jack Shortell and himself. The homo investigation was immediately disbanded and Shortell took off for a vacation in the Montana boonies; LAPD closed the book on Gene Niles, Upshaw's suicide their confession and trip to the gas chamber. City-County police relations were all-time bad—and he skated, thin-icing it, trying to fix an angle to save both their asses, no luck, too late to do the kid any good.

Free Ride.

What kept nagging at him was that he fixed Audrey's skim spree first. Petey Skouras paid Mickey back the dough the lioness bilked; Mickey was generous and let him off with a beating: Johnny Stomp and a little blackjack work on the kidneys. Petey took off for Frisco then—even though the Mick, impressed with his repentance, would have kept him on the payroll. Petey had played into his fix by skedaddling; Mickey, Mr. Effusiveness, had upped his payoff on the dope summit guard gig to a grand, telling him the charming Lieutenant Dudley Smith would also be standing trigger. More cash in his pocket—while Danny Upshaw climbed the gallows.

Dumb Okie Luck.

Mal took it hard, going on a two-day drunk, sobering up with a direct frontal attack on the Red Menace. A strongarmed lefty told Dudley Smith that Claire De Haven made "Ted Krugman" as a cop; Mal was enraged, but the consensus of the team was that they now had enough snitch testimony to take UAES down without Upshaw's covert dirt. Docket time was being set up; if all went well, the grand jury would convene in two weeks. Mal had gone off the deep end, crucifying Reds to perk his juice for *his* court battle. He'd turned Nathan Eisler's diary upside down for names, turning out snitches from four of the men Claire De Haven serviced to start her union. His flop at the Shangri-Lodge Motel now looked like Ellis Loew's living room: graphs, charts and cross-referenced hearsay, Mal's ode to Danny Upshaw, all of it proving one thing: that Commies were long on talk. And when the grand jury heard that talk, they probably wouldn't have the brains to think it out one step further: that the sad, deluded fuckers talked because they didn't have the balls to do anything else.

Buzz kicked the gravestone again; he thought that Captain Mal Considine almost had himself convinced that UAES was a hot damn threat to America's internal security—that he had to believe it so he could keep his son and still call himself a good guy. Odds on the Hollywood Commies subverting the country with their cornball propaganda turkeys, rallies and picket line highjinks: thirty trillion to one against, a longshot from Mars. The entire deal was a duck shoot, a play to save the studios money and make Ellis Loew District Attorney and Governor of California.

Bagman.

Fixer.

He'd been skating since the moment Mal called him with the news. Ellis told him to run background checks on the names in Eisler's diary; he called R&I, got their dope and let it go at that. Mal told him to conduct phone interviews with HUAC snitches back east; he gave a third of the numbers cursory calls, asked half the questions he was supposed to and edited the answers down to two pages per man, easy stuff for his secretary to type up. His big job was to locate Dr. Saul Lesnick, the grand jury's boss fink; he'd skated entirely on that gig—and kept skating in general. And always in the same direction—toward Danny Upshaw.

When he knew the hush was in, he drove up to San Bernardino for a look-see at the kid's past. He talked to his widowed mother, a faded ginch living on Social Security; she told him she didn't attend the funeral because Danny had been curt with her on his last several visits and she disapproved of his drinking. He got her talking; she painted a picture of Danny the child as smart and cold, a youngster who read, studied and kept to himself. When his father died, he expressed no grief; he liked cars and fix-it things and science books; he never chased girls and always kept his room spotless. Since he became a policeman, he visited her only on Christmas and her birthday, never more, never less. He got straight B's in high school and straight A's in junior college. He ignored the floozies who chased after him; he tinkered with hot rods. He had one close friend: a boy named Tim Bergstrom, now a phys ed teacher at San Berdoo High.

Buzz drove to the school and badged Bergstrom. The man had seen the newspaper plant on Upshaw's death, said Danny was born to die young and elaborated over beers in a nearby bar. He said that Danny liked to figure things like motors and engines and arithmetic out, that he stole cars because he loved the danger, that he was always trying to prove himself, but kept quiet about it. You could tell he was crazy inside, but you couldn't figure out how or why; you could tell he was really smart, but you didn't know what he'd end up doing with his brains. Girls liked him because he was mysterious and played hard to get; he was a terrific street fighter. Years ago, drunk, Danny told him a story about witnessing a murder; that was when he got hipped on being a cop, hipped on scientific forensic stuff. He was a cold drunk: booze just made him more inside, more mysterious and persistent, and sooner or later you knew he'd persist with the wrong guy and get himself shot— what surprised him was that Danny died accidentally. Buzz let that one go and said, "Was Danny a queer?" Bergstrom flushed, twitched, sputtered into his beer and said, "Hell, no"—and two seconds later was whipping out pictures of his wife and kids.

Buzz drove back to L.A., called a County pal, learned that Danny Upshaw's Personnel file had been yanked and that for all intents and purposes the kid was never a member of the Los Angeles County Sheriff's Department. He took a trip by the West Hollywood Substation, talked to the guys on the squad, learned that Danny never accepted bribes or trade pussy; he never moved on his snitch Janice Modine or on switchboard Karen Hiltscher— both of whom were dying to give it to him. Upshaw's fellow deputies either respected his brains or wrote him off as an idealistic fool with a mean streak; Captain Al Dietrich was rumored to like him because he was methodical, hard-working and ambitious. Buzz thought of him as a kid graduating from machines to people at the wrong time, fishing for WHY? in a river of shit, getting the worst answer two bad cases had to give and ending up dead because he couldn't lie to himself.

Daniel Thomas Upshaw, 1922–1950. Queer.

Turner Prescott Meeks, 1906–? Free ride because the kid couldn't take it.

"It" couldn't be anything else. Danny Upshaw didn't kill Gene Niles. Mal said Thad Green and two hardnoses roughed him up; they probably recounted Niles calling him a queer and went over what Dudley Smith told Mal and Green: that Danny was seen shaking down Felix Gordean. With a poly test and silly syrup pending, Green let the kid go home with his gun, hoping he'd spare LAPD the grief of a trial and Niles as a Dragna bagman coming out. Danny had obliged—but for the wrong reason and not with his gun.

Scapegoat.

Who got some kind of last laugh.

He couldn't sleep for shit; when he did put three or four hours together he dreamed of all the crappy stunts he'd pulled: farm girls coerced into Howard's bed; heroin bootjacked and sold to Mickey, cash in his pocket, the junk sidetracked on its way to some hophead's arm. Sleeping with Audrey was the only cure—she'd played her string since Niles like a trooper—and touching her and keeping her safe kept the kid away. But their four nights in a row at Howard's place was dangerous too, and every time he left her he got scared and knew he had to do something about it.

Keeping his take on Danny away from Mal was one way. The cop couldn't believe the kid killed Niles, and he was pretty shrewd in tagging Cohen gunmen for the job—he'd watched Danny question a Dragna hump named Vinnie Scoppettone, who spilled on the shooting at Sherry's: LAPD shooters. But that was as far as his reconstruction went, and he still idealized Upshaw as a smart young cop headed for rank and glory. Keeping the kid's secret was the beginning.

Buzz cocked a finger at the gravestone and made up his mind around two facts. One, when LAPD crashed Upshaw's pad, they found it thoroughly trashed; Nort Layman did a forensic, came up with Danny's prints on a shitload of tossed furniture and pegged him going crazy in the last moments of his life. LAPD's property report—the contents of the apartment inventoried—carried no mention of the grand jury paperwork *or* the personal file Danny kept on his homicides. He broke into the place and tossed it extra good; no files were secreted anywhere inside the four rooms. Mal was there when the body was discovered; he said LAPD sealed the crib tight, with only Danny and the knife leaving the premises. Two, the night before he died, Danny called him: he was amazed that his two cases had crossed at the juncture of Charles Hartshorn and Reynolds Loftis.

"Deputy, are you tellin' me Loftis is a suspect for your killin's?"

"I'm telling you maybe. Maybe real strong. He fits the killer's description ... and he fits."

No way was Danny Upshaw a murder victim. No way did the file thief wreck his apartment. Dudley Smith had a strange fix on the kid, but there was no reason for him to steal the files, and if he did he would have faked a burglary.

Person or persons unknown—a good starting point for some payback.

* * *

Buzz found Mal in Ellis Loew's back yard, sitting on a sun-bleached sofa, going over papers. He looked skinny beyond skinny, like he was starving himself to make the bantamweight limit. "Hey, boss."

Mal nodded and kept working. Buzz said, "I want to talk to you."

"About what?"

"Not some Commie plot, that's for damn sure."

Mal connected a series of names with pencil lines. "I know you don't take this seriously, but it is serious."

"It's a serious piece of gravy, I'll give you that. And I sure want my share. It's just that I've got some other boogeymen on my mind right now."

"Like who?"

"Like Upshaw."

Mal put his paper and pencil down. "He's LAPD's boogeyman, not yours."

"I'm pretty sure he didn't kill Niles, boss."

"We've been over that, Buzz. It was Mickey or Jack, and we'd never be able to prove it in a million years."

Buzz sat down on the couch—it stank of mildew and some Red chaser had burned the arms with cigarette butts. "Mal, you remember Upshaw tellin' us about his file on the queer snuffs?"

"Sure."

"It was stolen from his apartment, and so was his copy of the grand jury package."

"What?"

"I'm certain about it. You said LAPD sealed the pad and didn't take nothin', and I checked Upshaw's desk at West Hollywood Station. Lots of old paperwork, but zilch on the 187's and the grand jury. You been so absorbed chasin' pinkers you probably didn't even think about it."

Mal tapped Buzz with his pencil. "You're right, I didn't, and where are you fishing? The kid's dead and buried, he was in trouble over that B&E he pulled, he was probably finished as a cop. He could have been the best, and I miss him. But he dug his own grave."

Buzz clamped down on Mal's hand. "Boss, *we* dug his grave. You pushed him too hard on De Haven, and I ... oh fuck it."

Mal pulled his hand free. "You what?"

"The kid had a fix on Reynolds Loftis. We talked on the phone the night before he died. He'd read about Charles Hartshorn's suicide, the paper made him as a Sleepy Lagoon lawyer and Upshaw had him as a lead on his homicides—Hartshorn was blackmailed by one of the victims. I told him Loftis was rousted with Hartshorn at a queer bar back in '44, and the kid went nuts. He didn't know Hartshorn was involved with Sleepy Lagoon, and that sure did seem to set him off. I asked him if Loftis was a suspect, and he said, 'Maybe real strong.'"

Mal said, "Have you talked to that County man Shortell about this?"

"No, he's in Montana on vacation."

"Mike Breuning?"

"I don't trust that boy to answer straight. Remember how Danny told us Breuning fluffed the job and was jerkin' his chain?"

"Meeks, you sure took your time telling me this."

"I've been thinkin' it over, and it took me a while to figure out what I was gonna do."

"Which is?"

Buzz smiled. "Maybe Loftis is a hot suspect, maybe he ain't. Whatever, I'm gonna get me that queer slasher, whoever he is."

Mal smiled. "And then what?"

"Then arrest him or kill him."

Mal said, "You're out of your mind."

Buzz said, "I was sorta thinkin' about askin' you to join me. A captain out of his mind has got more juice than a loner cop with a few loose."

"I've got the grand jury, Meeks. And day after tomorrow's the divorce trial."

Buzz cracked his knuckles. "You in?"

"No. It's crazy. And I don't feature you as the dramatic gesture type, either."

"I owe him. *We* owe him."

"No, it's wrong."

"Think of the angles, skipper. Loftis as a psycho killer. You pop him for that before the grand jury convenes and UAES'll go in the toilet so large they'll hear it flush in Cleveland."

Mal laughed; Buzz laughed and said, "We'll give it a week or so. We'll put together what we can get out of the grand jury file and we'll talk to Shortell and see what he's got. We'll brace Loftis, and if it goes bust, it goes bust."

"There's the grand jury, Meeks."

"A Commie like Loftis popped for four 187's makes you so large that no judge in this state would fuck you over on your custody case. Think of that."

Mal broke his pencil in two. "I need a continuance, *now*, and I won't frame Loftis."

"That mean you're in?"

"I don't know."

Buzz went for the kill. "Well, shit there, *Captain*. I thought appealin' to your career would get you, but I guess I was wrong. Just think about Danny Upshaw and how bad he wanted it, and how you got your rocks off sendin' him after Claire De Haven. Think how maybe her and Loftis played with that cherry kid right before he cut his fuckin' throat. Then you—"

Mal slapped Buzz hard in the face.

Buzz sat on his hands so he wouldn't hit back.

Mal threw his list of names on the grass and said, "I'm in. But if this fucks up my grand jury shot, it's you and me for real. For keeps."

Buzz smiled. "Yessir, Captain."

33

CLAIRE DE Haven said, "I take it this means all pretenses are off."

A weak intro—he knew she had Upshaw made and the grand jury on track. Mal said, "This is about four murders."

"Oh?"

"Where's Reynolds Loftis? I want to talk to him."

"Reynolds is out, and I told you before that he and I will not name names."

Mal walked into the house. He saw the front page of last Wednesday's *Herald* on a chair; he knew Claire had seen the piece on Danny's death, Sheriff's Academy picture included. She closed the door—*her* no pretense—she wanted to know what *he* had. Mal said, "Four killings. No political stuff unless you tell me otherwise."

Claire said, "I'll tell you I don't know what you're talking about."

Mal pointed to the paper. "What's so interesting about last week's news?"

"A sad little obituary on a young man I knew."

Mal played in. "What kind of young man?"

"I think frightened, impotent and treacherous describes him best."

The epitaph stung; Mal wondered for the ten millionth time what Danny Upshaw and Claire De Haven did to each other. "Four men raped and cut up. No political stuff for you to get noble about. Do you want to get down off your high Commie horse and tell me what you know about it? What Reynolds Loftis knows?"

Claire walked up to him, perfume right in his face. "You sent that boy to fuck information out of me and now *you* want to preach decency?"

Mal grabbed her shoulders and squeezed them; he got his night's worth of report study straight in his head. "January 1, Marty Goines snatched from South Central, shot with heroin, mutilated and killed. January 4, George Wiltsie and Duane Lindenaur, secobarbital sedated, mutilated and killed. January 14, Augie Luis Duarte, the same thing. Wiltsie and Duarte were male whores, we know that certain men in your union frequent male whores and the killer's description is a dead ringer for Loftis. Still want to play cute?"

Claire squirmed; Mal saw her as something wrong to touch and let go. She wheeled to a desk by the stairwell, grabbed a ledger and shoved it at him. "On January first, fourth, and fourteenth, Reynolds was here in full view of myself and others. You're insane to think he could kill anybody, and this proves it."

Mal took the ledger, skimmed it and shoved it back to her. "It's a fake. I don't know what the crossouts mean, but only your signature and Loftis' are real. The others are traced over, and the minutes are like Dick and Jane join the Party. It's a fake, and you had it out and ready. Now you explain that, or I go get a material witness warrant for Loftis."

Claire held the ledger to herself. "I don't believe that threat. I think this is some kind of personal vendetta with you."

"Just answer me."

"My answer is that your young Deputy Ted kept pressing me about what Reynolds was doing on those nights, and when I discovered that he was a policeman I thought he must have convinced himself that Reynolds did something terrible. Reynolds was here then for meetings, so I left this out for the boy to see, so he wouldn't launch some awful circumstantial pogrom."

A perfect right answer. "You didn't know a graphologist would eat that ledger up in court?"

"No."

"And what did you think Danny Upshaw was trying to prove against Loftis?"

"I don't know! Some kind of treason, but not sex murders!"

Mal couldn't tell if she'd raised her voice to cover a lie. "Why didn't you show Upshaw your real ledger? You were taking a risk that he'd spot a fake one."

"I couldn't. A policeman would probably consider our real minutes treason."

"Treason" was a howler; profundity from a roundheels who'd spread for anything pretty in pants. Mal laughed, caught himself and stopped; Claire said, "Care to tell me what's so amusing?"

"Nothing."

"You sound patronizing."

"Let's change the subject. Danny Upshaw had a file on the murders, and it was stolen from his apartment. Do you know anything about that?"

"No. I'm not a thief. Or a comedienne."

Getting mad shaved ten years off the woman's age. "Then don't give yourself more credit than you're worth."

Claire raised a hand, then held it back. "If you don't consider my friends and me serious, then why are you trying to smear us and ruin our lives?"

Mal fizzled at a wisecrack; he said, "I want to talk to Loftis."

"You didn't answer my question."

"I'm doing the asking. When's Loftis coming back?"

Claire laughed. "Oh mein policeman, what your face just said. You know it's a travesty, don't you? You think we're too ineffectual to be dangerous, which is just about as wrong as thinking we're traitors."

Mal thought of Dudley Smith; he thought of the Red Queen eating Danny Upshaw alive. "What happened with you and Ted Krugman?"

"Get your names straight. You mean Deputy Upshaw, don't you?"

"Just tell me."

"I'll tell you he was naive and eager to please and all bluff where women were concerned, and I'll tell you you shouldn't have sent such a frail American patriot after us. Frail and clumsy. Did he *really* fall on a cutlery rack?"

Mal swung an open hand; Claire flinched at the blow and slapped back, no tears, just smeared lipstick and a welt forming on her cheek. Mal turned and braced himself against the banister, afraid of the way he looked; Claire said, "You could just quit. You could denounce the wrongness of it, say we're ineffectual and not worth the money and effort and still sound like a big tough cop."

Mal tasted blood on his lips. "I want it."

"For what? Glory? You're too smart for patriotism."

Mal saw Stefan waving goodbye; Claire said, "For your son?"

Mal, trembling, said, "What did you say?"

"We're not the fools you think we are, recently promoted Captain. We know how to hire private detectives and they know how to check records and verify old rumors. You know, I'm impressed with the Nazi you killed and rather surprised that you can't see the parallels between that regime and your own."

Mal kept looking away; Claire stepped closer to him. "I understand what you must feel for your son. And I think we both know the fix is in."

Mal pushed himself off the railing and looked at her. "Yeah. The fix is in, and this conversation didn't happen. And I still want to talk to Reynolds Loftis. And if he killed those men, I'm taking him down."

"Reynolds has not killed anyone."

"Where is he?"

Claire said, "He'll be back tonight, and you can talk to him then. He'll convince you, and I'll make you a deal. I know you need a continuance on your custody trial, and I have friends on the bench who can get it for you. But I don't want Reynolds smeared to the grand jury."

"You can't mean that."

"Don't make a career out of underestimating me. Reynolds was hurt badly in '47, and I don't think he'd be able to go through it again. I'll do everything I can to help you with your son, but I don't want Reynolds hurt."

"What about you?"

"I'll take my knocks."

"It's impossible."

"Reynolds has not killed anyone."

"Maybe that's true, but he's been named as a subversive too many times."

"Then destroy those depositions and don't call those witnesses."

"You don't understand. His name is all over our paperwork a thousand goddamn times."

Claire held Mal's arms. "Just tell me you'll try to keep him from being hurt too badly. Tell me yes and I'll make my calls, and you won't have to go to trial tomorrow."

Mal saw himself doctoring transcripts, shuffling names and realigning graphs to point to other Commies, going mano a mano: his editorial skill versus Dudley Smith's memory. "Do it. Have Loftis here at 8:00 and tell him it's going to be ugly."

Claire took her hands away. "It won't be any worse than your precious grand jury."

"Don't go noble on me, because I know who you are."

"Don't cheat me, because I'll use my friends to ruin you."

A deal with a real red devil: the continuance buying him time to un-nail a subversive, nail a killer and nail himself as a hero. And just maybe cross Claire De Haven. "I won't cheat you."

"I'll have to trust you. And can I ask you something? Off the record?"

"What?"

"Your opinion of this grand jury."

Mal said, "It's a goddamn waste and a goddamn shame."

34

MICKEY COHEN was pitching a tantrum; Johnny Stompanato was fueling it; Buzz was watching—scared shitless.

They were at the Mick's hideaway, surrounded by muscle. After the bomb under the house went off, Mickey sent Lavonne back east and moved into the Samo Canyon bungalow, wondering who the fuck wanted him dead. Jack D. called to say it wasn't him—Mickey believed it. Brenda Allen was still in jail, the City cops had settled into a slow burn and cop bombers played like science fiction. Mickey decided it was the Commies. Some Pinko ordnance expert got word he was fronting the Teamsters, popped his cork and planted the bomb that destroyed thirty-four of his custom suits. It was a Commie plot—it couldn't be anything else.

Buzz kept watching, waiting by the phone for a call from Mal Considine. Davey Goldman and Mo Jahelka were prowling the grounds; a bunch of goons were oiling the shotguns stashed in the fake panel between the living room and bedroom. Mickey had started squawking half an hour ago, topics ranging from Audrey not giving him any to passive resistance on the picket line and how he was going to fix the UAES's red wagon. Comedy time until Johnny Stomp showed up and started talking *his* conspiracy.

The guinea Adonis brought bad news: when Petey Skouras blew to Frisco he took a week's worth of receipts with him—Audrey told him when he picked up the Southside front's cash take. Buzz horned in on the conversation, thinking the lioness couldn't be stupid enough to try to play Petey's splitsville for a profit—Petey himself had to have done it—his bonus atop the thousand-dollar beating. Johnny's news got worse: he took a baseball bat to a guy on the welcher list, who told him Petey was no skimmer, Petey would never protect a girlfriend's brother because Petey liked boys—young darky stuff—a habit he picked up in a U.S. army stockade in Alabama. Mickey went around the twist then, spraying spit like a rabid dog, spitting obscenities in Yiddish, making his Jew strongarms squirm. Johnny had to know that his story contradicted Buzz's story; the fact that he wouldn't give him an even eyeball clinched it. When Mickey stopped ranting and started thinking, he'd snap to that, too—then he'd start asking questions and it would be another convoluted epic to explain the lie, something along the lines of Skouras protecting his *boyfriend's* brother, how he didn't want poor Greek Petey smeared as taking it Greek. Mickey would believe him—probably.

Buzz got out his notepad and wrote a memo to Mal and Ellis Loew—abbreviated skinny from three triggermen moonlighting as picket goons. Their consensus: UAES still biding its time, the Teamster rank and file on fire to whomp some ass, the only new wrinkle a suspicious-looking van parked on Gower, a man with a movie camera in the back. The man, a studious bird with Trotsky glasses, was seen talking to Norm Kostenz, the UAES picket boss. Conclusion: UAES wanted the Teamsters to rumble, so they could capture the ass-whomping on film.

His skate work done, Buzz listened to Mickey rant and checked his real notes—the grand jury and shrink files read over and put together with a few records prowls and a brief talk with Jack Shortell's partner at the San Dimas Substation. Shortell would be returning from Montana tomorrow; he could hit him for a real rundown on Upshaw's case then. The partner said that Jack said Danny seemed to think the killings derived from the time of the Sleepy Lagoon murder and the SLDC—it was the last thing the kid talked up before LAPD grabbed him. That in mind, Buzz matched the theory to his file facts.

He got:

Danny told him Reynolds Loftis fit his killing suspect's description—and in general—"he fits." Charles Hartshorn, a recent suicide, was rousted with Loftis at a local fruit bar in '44.

Two identical names and an R&I and DMV check got him Augie Duarte, snuff victim number four, and his cousin, SLDC/UAES hotshot Juan Duarte, currently working at Variety International Pictures—on a set next to the room where victim number three, Duane Lindenaur, worked as a rewrite man. SLDC Lawyer Hartshorn was blackmailed by Lindenaur years ago—a check on the crime report led him to an LASD Sergeant named Skakel, who had also talked to Danny Upshaw. Skakel told him that Lindenaur met Hartshorn at a party thrown by fag impresario Felix Gordean, the man Danny said the killer had a fix on.

The first victim, Marty Goines, died of a heroin overjolt. Loftis' fiancée Claire De Haven was a skin-popper; she took Dr. Terry Lux's cure three times. Terry said Loftis copped H for her.

From Mal's report on the Sammy Benavides/Mondo Lopez/Juan Duarte questioning:

Benavides shouted something about Chaz Minear, Loftis' fag squeeze, buying boys at a "puto escort service"—Gordean's?

Also on Minear: in his psych file, Chaz justified snitching Loftis to HUAC by pointing to a third man in a love triangle—"If you knew who he was, you'd understand why I did it."

Two strange-o deals:

The '42 to '44 pages were missing from Loftis' psych file and Doc Lesnick couldn't be found. At the three Mexes' questioning, one of the guys muttered an aside—the SLDC got letters tapping a "big white man" for the Sleepy Lagoon murder.

Strange-o stuff aside, all circumstantial—but too solid to be coincidence.

The phone rang, cutting through Mickey's tirade on Commies. Buzz picked it up; Johnny Stomp watched him talk.

"Yeah. Cap, that you?"

"It's me, Turner, my lad."

"You sound happy, boss."

"I just got a ninety-day continuance, so I am happy. Did you do your homework?"

Stompanato was still staring. Buzz said, "Sure did. Circumstantial but tight. You talk to Loftis?"

"Meet me at 463 Canon Drive in an hour. We've got him as a friendly witness."

"No shit?"

"No shit."

Buzz hung up. Johnny Stomp winked at him and turned back to Mickey.

35

HEADLIGHTS BOUNCED over the street, caught his windshield and went off. Mal heard a car door slamming and tapped his highbeams; Buzz walked over and said, "You do *your* homework?"

"Yeah. Like you said, circumstantial. But it's there."

"How'd you fix this up, Cap?"

Mal held back on the De Haven deal. "Danny wasn't too subtle hitting up Claire for Loftis' whereabouts on the killing dates, so she faked a meeting diary—Loftis alibied for the three nights. She says there were meetings, and he was there, but they were planning seditious stuff—that's why she sugar-coated the damn thing. She says Loftis is clean."

"You believe it?"

"Maybe, but my gut tells me they're connected to the whole deal. This afternoon I checked Loftis' bank records going back to '40. Three times in the spring and summer of '44 he made cash withdrawals of ten grand. Last week he made another one. Interesting?"

Buzz whistled. "From old Reynolds' missing-file time. It's gotta be blackmail, there's blackmail all over this mess. You wanna play him white hat-black hat?"

Mal got out of the car. "You be the bad guy. I'll get De Haven out of the way, and we'll work him."

They walked up to the door and rang the bell. Claire De Haven answered; Mal said, "You go somewhere for a couple of hours."

Claire looked at Buzz, lingering on his ratty sharkskin and heater. "You mustn't touch him."

Mal hooked a thumb over his back. "Go somewhere."

"No thank yous for what I did?"

Mal caught Buzz catching it. "Go somewhere, Claire."

The Red Queen brushed past them out the door; she gave Buzz a wide berth. Mal whispered, "Hand signals. Three fingers on my tie means hit him."

"You got the stomach for this?"

"Yes. You?"

"One for the kid, boss."

Mal said, "I still don't make you for the sentimental gesture type."

"I guess old dogs can learn. What just happened with you and the princess?"

"Nothing."

"Sure, boss."

Mal heard coughing in the living room; Buzz said, "I'll kickstart him." A voice called, "Gentlemen, can we get this over with?"

Buzz walked in first, whistling at the furnishings; Mal followed, taking a long look at Loftis. The man was tall and gray per Upshaw's suspect description; he was dashingly handsome at fifty or so and his whole manner was would-be slick—a costume of tweed slacks and cardigan sweater, a sprawl on the divan, one leg hooked over the other at the knee.

Mal sat next to him; Buzz thunked a chair down a hard breath away. "You and that honey Claire are gettin' married, huh?"

Loftis said, "Yes, we are."

Buzz smiled, soft and homespun. "That's sweet. She gonna let you pork boys on the side?"

Loftis sighed. "I don't have to answer that question."

"The fuck you don't. You answer it, you answer it now."

Mal came in. "Mr. Loftis is right, Sergeant. That question is not germane. Mr. Loftis, where were you on the nights of January first, fourth and the fourteenth of this year?"

"I was here, at meetings of the UAES Executive Committee."

"And what was discussed at those meetings?"

"Claire said I didn't have to discuss that with you."

Buzz snickered. "You take orders from a woman?"

"Claire is no ordinary woman."

"She sure ain't. A rich bitch Commie that shacks with a fruit-fly sure ain't everyday stuff to me."

Loftis sighed again. "Claire told me this would be ugly, and she was correct. She also told me your sole purpose was to convince yourselves that I didn't kill anyone, and that I did not have to discuss the UAES business that was transacted on those three nights."

Mal knew Meeks would figure out the Claire deal before too long; he joined his partner on the black hat side. "Loftis, I don't think you did kill anybody. But I think you're in deep on some other things, and I'm not talking politics. We want the killer, and you're going to help us get him."

Loftis licked his lips and knotted his fingers together; Mal touched his tie bar: *go in full*. Buzz said, "What's your blood type?"

Loftis said, "O positive."

"That's the killer's blood type, boss. You know that?"

"It's the most common blood type among white people, and your friend just said I'm no longer a suspect."

"My friend's a soft touch. You know a trombone man named Marty Goines?"

"No."

"Duane Lindenaur?"

"No."

"George Wiltsie?"

Tilt: Loftis crossing and recrossing his legs, licking his lips. "No."

Buzz said, "Horse fucking pucky, you don't. *Give*."

"I said I never knew him!"

"Then why'd you describe him in the past tense?"

"Oh God—"

Mal flashed two fingers, then his left hand over his right fist: *He's mine, no hitting*. "Augie Duarte, Loftis. What about him?"

"I don't know him"—a dry tongue over dry lips.

Buzz cracked his knuckles—loud. Loftis flinched; Mal said, "George Wiltsie was a male prostitute. Did you ever traffic with him? Tell the truth or my partner will get angry."

Loftis looked down at his lap. "Yes."

Mal said, "Who set it up?"

"Nobody set it up! It was just ... a date."

Buzz said, "A date you paid for, boss?"

"No."

Mal said, "Felix Gordean set you up with him, right?"

"No!"

"I don't believe you."

"No!"

Mal knew a straight admission was out; he jabbed Loftis hard on the shoulder. "Augie Duarte. Was he just a date?"

"No!"

"Tell the truth, or I'll leave you alone with the sergeant."

Loftis pinched his knees together and hunched his shoulders down. "Yes."

"Yes what?"

"Yes. We dated once."

Buzz said, "You sound like a one-night stand man. A date with Wiltsie, a date with Duarte. Where'd you meet those guys?"

"Nowhere ... at a bar."

"What bar?"

"The Oak Room at the Biltmore, the Macombo, I don't know."

"You're rattlin' my cage, boy. Duarte was Mex and those joints don't serve spics. So try again. Two goddamn queer slash murder victims you got between the sheets with. Where'd you meet them?"

Reynolds Loftis stayed crimped up and silent; Buzz said, "You paid for them, right? It ain't no sin. I've paid for pussy, so why shouldn't somebody of your persuasion pay for boys?"

"No. No. No, that's not true."

Mal, very soft. "Felix Gordean."

Loftis, trembling. "No no no no no."

Buzz twirled a finger and smoothed his necktie—the switch-eroo sign. "Charles Hartshorn. Why'd he kill himself?"

"He was tortured by people like you!"

Mal's switcheroo. "You copped horse for Claire. Who'd you get it from?"

"Who told you that?"—Loftis actually sounding indignant.

Buzz leaned over and whispered, "Felix Gordean"; Loftis jerked back and banged his head on the wall. Mal said, "Duane Lindenaur worked at Variety International, where your friends Lopez, Duarte and Benavides are working. Juan Duarte is Augie Duarte's cousin. You used to appear in Variety International movies. Duane Lindenaur was blackmailing Charles Hartshorn. Why don't you put all that together for me."

Loftis was sweating; Mal caught a twitch at *blackmail*. "Three times in '44 and once last week you withdrew ten grand from your bank account. Who's blackmailing you?"

The man was oozing sweat. Buzz flashed a fist on the QT; Mal shook his head and gave him the switch sign. Buzz said, "Tell us about the Sleepy Lagoon Defense Committee. Some strange stuff happened, right?"

Loftis wiped sweat off his brow; he said, "What strange stuff?", his voice cracking.

"Like the letters the Committee got that said a big white man snuffed José Diaz. A deputy pal of ours seemed to think these here killings went back to Sleepy Lagoon—zoot stick time. All the victims were cut with zoot sticks."

Loftis wrung his hands, popping more sweat; his eyes were glazed. Mal could tell Meeks went for a soft shot—innocuous stuff from his interrogation notes—but came up with a bludgeon. Buzz looked bewildered; Mal tamped down his black hat. "Loftis, who's blackmailing you?"

Loftis squeaked, "No"; Mal saw that he'd sweated his clothes through. "What happened with the SLDC?"

"No!"

"Is Gordean blackmailing you?"

"I refuse to answer on the grounds that my answ—"

"You're a slimy piece of Commie shit. What kind of treason are you planning at your meetings? Cop on that!"

"Claire said I didn't have to!"

"Who's that piece of tail you and Chaz Minear were fighting over during the war? Who's that piece of fluff?"

Loftis sobbed and keened and managed a squeaky singsong. "I refuse to answer on the grounds that my answers might tend to incriminate me, but I never hurt anybody and neither did my friends so please don't hurt us."

Mal made a fist, Stanford ring stone out to do maximum damage. Buzz put a hand on his own fist and squeezed it, a new semaphore: *don't hit him or I'll hit you.* Mal got scared and went for big verbal ammo: Loftis didn't know Chaz Minear ratted him to HUAC. "Are you protecting Minear? You shouldn't, because he was the one who snitched you to the Feds. He was the one who got you blacklisted."

Loftis curled into a ball; he murmured his Fifth Amendment spiel, like their interrogation was legal and defense counsel would swoop to the rescue. Buzz said, "You dumb shit, we coulda had him." Mal turned and saw Claire De Haven standing there. She was saying, "Chaz," over and over.

36

THE PICKET line action was simmering.

Buzz watched from the Variety International walkway, three stories up. Jack Shortell and Mal were supposed to call; Ellis Loew had called him at home, yanking him out of another Danny nightmare. The DA's command: convince Herman Gerstein to kick an additonal five thou into the grand jury war chest. Herman was out—probably muff-diving Betty Grable—and there was nothing for him to do but stew on Considine's foul-up and scope the prelim to slaughter down on the street.

You could see it plain:

A Teamster goon with a baseball bat was lounging near the UAES camera van; when the shit hit the fan and the film rolled, he'd be Johnny on the spot to neutralize the cinematographer and bust up his equipment. Teamster pickets were carrying double and triple banner sticks, taped grips, good shillelaghs. Four muscle boys were skulking by the Pinkos' lunch truck—just the right number to tip it over and coffee-scald the guy inside. A minute ago he saw a Cohen triggerman make an on-the-sly delivery: riot guns with rubber-bullet attachments, wrapped in swaddling cloth like Baby Jesus. Over on De Longpre, the Teamsters had *their* moviemaking crew at the ready: actor/picketers who'd wade in, provoke just the right way and make sure a few UAES pickets whomped them; three camera guys in the back of a tarp-covered pickup. When the dust cleared, Mickey's boys would survive on celluloid as the good guys.

Buzz kept posing Mal against the action. The Cap had almost shot Doc Lesnick's confidentiality on the psych files—blowing the whistle on Minear squealing Loftis—just when they were getting close on the blackmail angle and Felix Gordean. He'd hustled him out of the house quicksville, so he wouldn't keep trashing the team's cover—if they were lucky, De Haven and Loftis figured a HUAC source gave them the dope on Minear. For a smart cop, Captain Malcolm Considine kept making stupid moves: it was twenty to one he'd cut a deal with Red Claire for the custody case continuance; ten to one his attack on Loftis came close to deep sixing it. The old nance was no killer, but the '42 to '44 gap in his psych file—a time he was terrified remembering—talked volumes, and he and De Haven were looking like prime suspects on the snatch of the kid's paperwork. And Doc Lesnick being no-place was starting to look as wrong as Mal fucking up his own wet dream.

The Teamster men were passing around bottles; UAES was marching and shouting its sad old refrain: "Fair Wages Now," "End the Studio Tyranny." Buzz thought of a cat about to pounce on a mouse nibbling cheese on the edge of a cliff; he gave the matinee a pass and walked into Herman Gerstein's office.

Still no mogul; the switchboard girl at the plant knew to forward his calls to Herman's private line. Buzz sat behind Gerstein's desk, sniffed his humidor, admired his starlet pics on the wall. He was speculating on his grand jury bonus when the phone rang.

"Hello."

"Meeks?"

Not Mal, not Shortell—but a familiar voice. "It's me. Who's this?"

"Johnny."

"Stompanato?"

"How soon they forget."

"Johnny, what're you callin' me for?"

"How soon they forget their good deeds. I owe you one, remember?"

Buzz remembered the Lucy Whitehall gig—it seemed like a million years ago. "Go, Johnny."

"I'm paying you back, you cracker shitbird. Mickey knows Audrey's the skimmer. I didn't tell him, and I even kept hush on what you pulled with Petey S. It was the bank. Audrey put her skim in the Hollywood bank where Mick puts his race wire dough. The manager got suspicious and called him. Mickey's sending Fritzie over to get her. You're closer, so we're even."

Buzz saw Icepick Fritzie carving. "You knew about us?"

"I thought Audrey looked nervous lately, so I tailed her up to Hollywood, and she met you. Mickey doesn't know about you and her, so stay icy."

Buzz blew a wet kiss into the phone, hung up and called Audrey's number; he got a busy signal, hauled down to the back lot and his car. He ran red lights and yellow lights and took every shortcut he knew speeding over; he saw Audrey's Packard in the driveway, jumped the curb and skidded up on the lawn. He left the motor running, pulled his .38, ran to the door and shouldered it open.

Audrey was sitting on her bargain basement lounge chair, hair in curlers, cold cream on her face. She saw Buzz and tried to cover herself; Buzz beelined for her and started kissing, getting all gooey. He said, "Mickey knows you skimmed him," between kisses; Audrey squealed. "This isn't fair!" and "You're not supposed to see me this way!" Buzz thought of Fritzie K. gaining ground, grabbed the lioness and slung her out to her car. He gasped, "Ventura by

Pacific Coast Highway, and I'm right behind you. It ain't the Beverly Wilshire, but it's safe."

Audrey said, "Five minutes to pack?"

Buzz said, "No."

Audrey said, "Oh shit. I really liked L.A."

Buzz said, "Say goodbye to it."

Audrey popped off a handful of curlers and wiped her face. "Bye-bye, L.A."

*   *   *

The two-car caravan made it to Ventura in an hour ten. Buzz ensconced Audrey in the shack at the edge of his farmland, hid her Packard in a pine grove, left her all his money except a tensky and a single and told her to call a friend of his on the Ventura Sheriff's for a place to stay—the man owed him almost as much as he owed Johnny Stompanato. Audrey started crying when she realized it really was bye-bye L.A., bye-bye house, bank account, clothes and everything else except her bagman lover; Buzz kissed off the rest of her cold cream, told her he'd call his buddy to grease the skids and ring her at the guy's place tonight. The lioness left him with a dry-eyed sigh. "Mickey was good with a buck, but he was lousy in bed. I'll try not to miss him."

*   *   *

Buzz drove straight into Oxnard, the next town south. He found a pay phone, called Dave Kleckner at the Ventura Courthouse, made arrangements for him to pick up Audrey and dialed his own line at Hughes Aircraft. His secretary said Jack Shortell had called; she'd forwarded him to Herman Gerstein's office and Mal Considine's extension at the Bureau. Buzz changed his dollar into dimes and had the operator ring Madison-4609; Mal answered, "Yes?"

"It's me."

"Where are you? I've been trying to get you all morning."

"Ventura. A little errand."

"Well, you missed the goodies. Mickey went nuts. He gave his boys on Gower Gulch carte blanche, and they're busting heads as we speak. I just got a call from a Riot Squad lieutenant, and he said it's the worst he's ever seen. Want to place bets?"

Odds on him getting the lioness out of the country: even money. "Boss, Mickey's nuts on Audrey, that's what probably ripped his cork. He found out she was skimmin' at his shark mill."

"Jesus. Does he know about—"

"Ixnay, and I wanta keep it that way. She's stashed up here for now, but it can't last forever."

Mal said, "We'll fix something. Are you still hot on payback?"

"More than ever. You talk to Shortell?"

"Ten minutes ago. Do you have something to write on?"

"No, but I got a memory. Shoot me."

Mal said, "The last thing Danny worked was a connection between the Joredco Dental Lab on Bunker Hill—they make animal dentures—and a naturalist who raises wolverines a few blocks away. Nort Layman identified bite marks on the victims as coming from wolverine teeth—that's what this is all about."

Buzz whistled. "Christ on a crutch."

"Yeah, and it gets stranger. One, Dudley Smith never put tails on those men Danny wanted under surveillance. Shortell found out, and he doesn't know if it means anything or not. Two, Danny's fix on the Sleepy Lagoon killing and the SLDC ties in to some burglary accomplice of Marty Goines—a youth back in the early '40s—a kid with a burned face. Bunker Hill had a lot of unsolved B&Es the summer of '42, and Danny gave Shortell eight names from FI cards—curfew was being enforced then, so there were plenty of them. Shortell ran eliminations on the names and came up with one man with O+ blood—Coleman Masskie, DOB 5/9/23, 236 South Beaudry, Bunker Hill. Shortell thinks this guy may be a good bet as Goines' burglar buddy."

Buzz got the numbers down. "Boss, this Masskie guy ain't even twenty-seven years old, which sorta contradicts the middle-aged killer theory."

Mal said, "I know, that bothers me too. But Shortell thinks Danny was close to cracking the case—and *he* thought this burglary angle was a scorcher."

"Boss, we gotta take down Felix Gordean. We were gettin' close last night, when you ..."

Silence, then Mal sounding disgusted. "Yeah, I know. Look, you take the Masskie lead, I'll shake Juan Duarte. I put four Bureau men out to find Doc Lesnick, and if he's alive and findable, he's ours. Let's meet tonight in front of the Chateau Marmont, 5:30. We'll stretch Gordean."

Buzz said, "Let's do it."

Mal said, "Did you figure out De Haven and me?"

"Took about two seconds. You don't think she'll cross you?"

"No, I've got the ace high hand. You and Mickey Cohen's woman. Jesus."

"You're invited to the wedding, boss."

"Stay alive for it, lad."

* * *

Buzz took Pacific Coast Highway down to L.A., Wilshire east to Bunker Hill. Dark clouds were brewing, threatening a deluge to soak the Southland, maybe unearth a few more stiffs, send a few more hardnoses out for payback. Two thirty-six South Beaudry was a low-rent Victorian, every single shingle weather-stripped and splintered; Buzz pulled up and saw an old woman raking leaves on a front lawn as jaundiced as the pad.

He got out and approached her. Closer up, she showed a real faded beauty: pale, almost transparent skin over haute couture cheekbones, full lips and the comeliest head of gray-brown hair he'd ever seen. Only her eyes were off—they were too bright, too protruding.

Buzz said, "Ma'am?"

The old girl leaned on her rake; there was all of one leaf caught on the tines—and it was the only leaf on the whole lawn. "Yes, young man? Are you here to make a contribution to Sister Aimee's crusade?"

"Sister Aimee's been out of business awhile, ma'am."

The woman held out her hand—withered and arthritic looking—a beggar's paw. Buzz dropped some odd dimes in it. "I'm lookin' for a man named Coleman Masskie. Do you know him? He used to live here seven, eight years ago."

Now the old girl smiled. "I remember Coleman well. I'm Delores Masskie Tucker Kafesjian Luderman Jensen Tyson Jones. I'm Coleman's mother. Coleman was one of the staunchest slaves I bore to proselytize for Sister Aimee."

Buzz swallowed. "Slaves, ma'am? And you certainly do have a lot of names."

The woman laughed. "I tried to remember my maiden name the other day, and I couldn't. You see, young man, I have had many lovers in my role as child breeder to Sister Aimee. God made me beautiful and fertile so that I might provide Sister Aimee Semple McPherson with acolytes, and the County of Los Angeles has given me many a Relief dollar so that I might feed my young. Certain cynics consider me a fanatic and a welfare chiseler, but they are the devil speaking. Don't you think that spawning good white progeny for Sister Aimee is a noble vocation?"

Buzz said, "I certainly do, and I was sorta thinkin' about doin' it myself. Ma'am, where's Coleman now? I got some money for him, and I figure he'll kick some of it back to you."

Delores scratched the grass with her rake. "Coleman was always generous. I had a total of nine children—six boys, three girls. Two of the girls became Sister Aimee followers, one, I'm ashamed to say, became a prostitute. The boys ran away when they turned fourteen or fifteen—eight hours a day of prayer and Bible reading was too strenuous for them. Coleman remained the longest—until he was nineteen. I gave him a dispensation: no prayer and Bible reading because he did chores around the neighborhood and gave me half the money. How much money do you owe Coleman, young man?"

Buzz said, "Lots of it. Where is Coleman, ma'am?"

"In hell, I'm afraid. Those who rebuke Sister Aimee are doomed to boil forever in a scalding cauldron of pus and Negro semen."

"Ma'am, when did you last see Coleman?"

"I believe I last saw him in the late fall of 1942."

A half-sane answer—one that played into Upshaw's timetable. "What was old Coleman doin' then, ma'am?"

Delores pulled the leaf from her rake and crumbled it to dust. "Coleman was developing worldly ways. He listened to jazz records on a Victrola, prowled around in the evenings and quit high school prematurely, which angered me, because Sister Aimee prefers her slaves to have a high school diploma. He got a dreadful job at a dental laboratory, and quite frankly he became a thief. I used to find strange trinkets in his room, but I let him be when he confessed his transgressions against private property and pledged ten percent of his proceeds to Sister Aimee."

The dental lab, Coleman as a burglar—Upshaw's theory coming through. "Ma'am, was this '42 when Coleman was doin' his thievery?"

"Yes. The summer before he left home."

"And did Coleman have a burned face? Was he disfigured somehow?"

The old loon was aghast. "Coleman was male slave beauty personified! He was as handsome as a matinee idol!"

Buzz said, "Sorry for impugnin' the boy's looks. Ma'am, who was Masskie? He the boy's daddy?"

"I don't really recall. I was spreading myself quite thin with men back in the early nineteen twenties, and I only took the surnames of men with large endowments—the better for when I chanted my breeding incantations. Exactly how much money do you owe Coleman? He's in hell, you know. Giving me the money might win a reprieve on his soul."

Buzz forked over his last ten-spot. "Ma'am, you said Coleman hightailed in the fall of '42?"

"Yes, that's true, and Sister Aimee thanks you."

"Why did he take off? Where did he go?"

Delores looked scared—her skin sank over her cheekbones and her eyes bugged out another couple of inches. "Coleman went looking for his father, whoever he was. A nasty man with a nasty brogue came around asking for him, and Coleman became terrified and ran away. The brogue man kept returning with questions on Coleman's whereabouts, but I kept invoking the power of Sister Aimee and he desisted."

Sleepy Lagoon killing time; Dudley Smith asking to join the grand jury team; Dudley's off-the-track hard-on for the José Diaz murder and the SLDC. "Ma'am, are you talkin' about an Irish brogue? A big man, late thirties then, red-faced, brown hair and eyes?"

Delores made signs, hands to her chest and up to her face, like she was warding off vampires in an old horror movie. "Get behind me, Satan! Feel the power of Foursquare Church, Angelus Temple and Sister Aimee Semple McPherson, and I will not answer another single question until you provide adequate cash tribute. Get behind me or risk hell!"

Buzz turned out his pockets for bubkis; he knew a brick wall when he saw one. "Ma'am, you tell Sister Aimee to hold her horses—I'll be back."

* * *

Buzz drove home, ripped a photo of then-Patrolman Dudley Smith out of his LAPD Academy yearbook and rolled to the Chateau Marmont. Dusk and light rain were falling as he parked on Sunset by the front entrance; he was settling into a fret on the lioness when Mal tapped the windshield and got in the car.

Buzz said, "Gravy. You?"

"Double gravy."

"Boss, it plays like a ricochet, and it contradicts 'middle-aged' again."

Mal stretched his legs. "So does my stuff. Nort Layman called Jack Shortell, he called me. Doc's been grid-searching the L.A. River near where Augie Duarte's body was found—he wants a complete forensic for some book he's writing. Get this: he found silver-gray wig strands with O+ blood—obviously from a head scratch—at the exact spot where the killer would have had to scale a fence to get away. That's why your ricochet plays."

Buzz said, "And why Loftis doesn't. Boss, you think somebody's tryin' to frame that old pansy?"

"It occurred to me, yes."

"What'd you get off Juan Duarte?"

"Scary stuff, worse than goddamn wolverine teeth. Danny talked to Duarte, did you know that?"

"No."

"It was right before LAPD grabbed him. Duarte told Danny that around the SLDC time Reynolds Loftis had a much younger kid brother hanging around—who looked just like him. At first, the kid had his face bandaged, because he'd been burned in a fire. Nobody knew how much he resembled Loftis until the bandages came off. The kid blabbed at the SLDC rallies—about how a big white man killed José Diaz—but nobody believed him. He was supposed to be running from the killer, but when Duarte said, 'How come you're showing up here where the killer might see you,' the brother said, 'I've got special protection.' Buzz, there are no notations on a Loftis kid brother in any of the grand jury files. And it gets better."

Buzz thought: I know it does; he wondered who'd say "Dudley Smith" first. "Keep going. My stuff fits right in."

Mal said, "Duarte went to see Charles Hartshorn right before his alleged suicide, to see if he could get the cops to put some juice into investigating Augie's murder. Hartshorn said he'd been ditzed on Duane Lindenaur's killing—you, partner—and he read about the zoot stick mutilations on the other victims in a scandal sheet and thought the snuffs might be SLDC connected. Hartshorn called the LAPD then, and talked to a Sergeant Breuning, who said he'd be right over. Duarte left, and the next morning Hartshorn's body was found. Bingo."

Buzz said it first. "Dudley Smith. He was the big white man and he joined the team so he could keep the SLDC testimony watchdogged. That's why he was interested in Upshaw. Danny was hipped on the zoot stick mutilations, and Augie Duarte—Juan's cousin—was on his surveillance list. That's why Dudley blew off the tails. He went with Breuning to see Hartshorn, and somebody said the wrong thing. Necktie party, bye-bye, Charlie."

Mal hit the dashboard. "I can't fucking believe it."

"I can. Now here's a good question. You been around Dudley lots more than I have lately. Is he tied to the queer snuffs?"

Mal shook his head. "No. I've been racking my brain on it, and I can't put the two together. Dudley wanted Upshaw to join the team, and he couldn't have cared less about dead homos. It was when Danny pushed on 'zoot stick' and 'Augie Duarte' that Dudley got scared. Wasn't José Diaz a zooter?"

Buzz said, "His threads were slashed with a zoot stick, I think I remember that. You got a motive for Dudley killin' Diaz?"

"Maybe. I went with Dudley to visit his niece. Apparently she's got a bent for Mexes and Dudley can't stand it."

"Pretty slim, boss."

"Dudley's insane! What the fuck more do you want!"

Buzz squeezed his partner's arm. "Whoa, boy, and just listen to my stuff. Coleman Masskie's crazy mama and I had a little chat. She had lots of different kids by different daddies, she don't know who's whose. Coleman left home in the late fall of '42. He was a burglar, he loved jazz, he worked at that dental lab. All that fits Upshaw's scenario. Now, dig this: fall of '42, a big man with a brogue comes around askin' for Coleman. I describe Dudley, the ginch gets terrified and clams. I say Coleman's the one runnin' from the big white man, who's Dudley, who bumped José Diaz— and Coleman saw it. I say we stretch Gordean now—then go back and ply that old girl and try to tie her to Reynolds Loftis."

Mal said, "I'm taking Dudley down."

Buzz shook his head. "You take another think on that. No proof, no evidence on Hartshorn, an eight-year-old spic homicide. A cop with Dudley's juice. You're as nuts as he is if you think that plays."

Mal put on a lilting tenor brogue. "Then I'll kill him, *lad*."

"The fuck you will."

"I've killed a man before, Meeks. I can do it again."

Buzz saw that he was out to do it—enjoying the view off the cliff. "Partner, a Nazi in the war ain't the same thing."

"You knew about that?"

"Why'd you think I was always afraid it was you 'stead of Dragna set me up? A mild-mannered guy like you kills once, he *can* do it again."

Mal laughed. "You ever kill anyone?"

"I stand on the Fifth Amendment, boss. Now you wanta go roust that queer pimp?"

Mal nodded. "7941's the address—I think it's back in the bungalow part."

"You be the bad guy tonight. You're good at it."

"After you, lad."

Buzz took the lead. They walked through the lobby and out a side door to the courtyard; it was dark, and high hedges hid the individual bungalows. Buzz tracked the numbers marked on wrought-iron poles, saw 7939 and said, "It's gotta be the next one."

Gunshots.

One, two, three, four—close, the odd-numbered side of the walkway. Buzz pulled his .38; Mal pulled and cocked his. They ran to 7941, pinned themselves to the wall on opposite sides of the door and listened. Buzz heard footsteps inside, moving away from them; he looked at Mal, counted one, two, three on his fingers, wheeled and kicked the door in.

Two shots splintered the wood above his head; a muzzle flickered from a dark back room. Buzz hit the floor; Mal piled on top of him and fired twice blindly; Buzz saw a man spread-eagled on the carpet, his yellow silk robe soaked red from sash to collar. Cash wrapped in bank tabs surrounded the body.

Mal stumbled and charged. Buzz let him go, heard thumping, crashing, glass breaking and no more shots. He got up and checked the stiff—a fancy man with a neat beard, a neat manicure and not much of a torso left. The bank tabs were marked Beverly Hills Federal, and there was at least three thousand in half-grand packets within grabbing distance. Buzz resisted; Mal came back, panting. He wheezed, "Car waiting. Late model white sedan."

Buzz kicked a pack of greenbacks; they hit an embroidered "F.G." on the dead man's sleeve. "Beverly Hills Fed. That where Loftis withdrew his money?"

"That's the place."

Sirens in the distance.

Buzz waved goodbye to the cash. "Loftis, Claire, the killer, what do you think?"

"Let's hit their place now. Before the Sheriffs ask us what we're—"

Buzz said, "Separate cars," and took off running as fast as he could.

* * *

Mal got there first.

Buzz saw him standing across the street from the De Haven house, U-turned and killed his engine. Mal leaned in the window. "What took you?"

"I run slow."

"Anybody see you?"

"No. You?"

"I don't think so. Buzz, we weren't there."

"You're learnin' this game better every day, boss. What'd you get here?"

"Two cold cars. I looked in a window and saw De Haven and Loftis playing cards. They're clean. You make the killer for it?"

Buzz said, "Nix. It's wrong. He's a psycho fuckin' rat worshiper, and it's my considered opinion that psycho rat worshipers don't carry guns. I'm thinkin' Minear. He fits with Loftis, and there was a line on him from the files, said he liked to buy boys."

"You could be right. The Masskie woman next?"

"236 South Beaudry, boss."

"Let's do it."

* * *

Buzz got there first; he rang the bell and went eyeball to eyeball with Delores in a long white robe. She said, "Did you bring monetary tribute for Sister?"

Buzz said, "My bagman's comin' in a minute." He took out the picture of Dudley Smith. "Ma'am, is this the fella who was inquirin' after Coleman?"

Delores blinked at the photograph and crossed herself. "Get behind me, Satan. Yes, that's him."

Seven come eleven, one more for Danny Upshaw. "Ma'am, do you know the name Reynolds Loftis?"

"No, I don't think so."

"Anybody named Loftis?"

"No."

"Any chance you messed with a man named Loftis around the time Coleman was born?"

The old girl harumphed. "If by 'messed' you mean engaged in breeding activities for Sister Aimee, the answer is no."

Buzz said, "Ma'am, you told me Coleman went lookin' for his daddy when he took off in '42. If you didn't know who his daddy was, how'd the boy know where to look?"

Delores said, "Twenty dollars for Sister Aimee and I'll show you."

Buzz slid off his high school ring. "Yours to keep, sweetie. Just show me."

Delores examined the ring, pocketed it and walked away; Buzz stood on the porch wondering where Mal was. Minutes dragged; the woman returned with an old leather scrapbook. She said, "The genealogy of my slave breeding. I took pictures of all the men who gave me their seed, with appropriate comments on the back. When Coleman decided he had to find his father, he looked at this book for pictures of the men he most resembled. I hid the book when the brogue man came by, and I still want twenty dollars for this information."

Buzz opened the scrapbook, saw that the pages contained stapled-on photographs of dozens of men, held it up to the porch light and started looking. Four pages down, a picture caught his eye: a spellbinder youthful, spellbinder handsome Reynolds Loftis in a tweed knicker suit. He pulled the photo out and read the writing on the back.

"Randolph Lawrence (a nom de guerre?), summer stock actor, the Ramona Pageant, August 30, 1922. A real Southern gentleman. Good white stock. I hope his seed springs fertile."

1942: burglar, tooth technician, rat lover Coleman witnesses Dudley Smith killing José Diaz, sees this picture or others and locates Daddy Reynolds Loftis. 1943: Coleman, his face burned in a fire???, hangs out at SLDC rallies with his father/phony brother, talks up the big white man, nobody believes him. 1942 to 1944: Loftis' psych file missing. 1950: killer Coleman. Was the psycho trying to frame Daddy/Reynolds for the queer murders, dressed up like Loftis himself—Doc Layman's wig fragments the final kicker?

Buzz held out the picture. "That Coleman, ma'am?"

Delores smiled. "Rather close. What a nice-looking man. A shame I can't remember spawning with him."

A car door slammed; Mal got out and trotted up the steps. Buzz took him aside and showed him the photo. "Loftis, 1922. AKA Randolph Lawrence, summer stock actor. He's Coleman's father, not his brother."

Mal tapped the picture. "Now I'm wondering how the boy got burned and why the brother charade. And you were right on Minear."

"What do you mean?"

"I called the DMV. Minear owns a white '49 Chrysler New Yorker sedan. I went by his place in Chapman Park on my way here. It was in his building's garage, warm, and it looked just like the car at the Marmont."

Buzz put an arm around Mal's shoulders. "Gifts in a manger, and here's another one. That crazy woman in the doorway ID'd Dudley from a picture I got. He's the brogue man."

Mal looked over at Delores. "Do you think Dudley copped Danny's files?"

"No, I think he'd have faked a burglary. Coleman's our killer, boss. All we gotta do now is find him."

"Shit. Loftis and Claire won't talk. I know it."

Buzz took his arm away. "No, but I bet we could squeeze Chaz beauty. He was tight with Loftis back in '43, '44, and I know a good squeeze artist to help us. You give that lady a double-saw and I'll go give him a call."

Mal went for his billfold; Buzz walked into the house and found a phone by the kitchen door. He called Information, got the number he wanted and dialed it; Johnny Stompanato's slick guinea baritone oiled on the line. "Talk to me."

"It's Meeks. You wanta make some money? Number-one muscle on a strongarm job, make sure my buddy don't go crazy and hurt someone?"

Johnny Stomp said, "You're a dead man. Mickey found out about you and Audrey. The neighbors saw you hustling her away, and I'm lucky he didn't figure out I tipped you. Nice to know you, Meeks. I always thought you had style."

Move over Danny Upshaw, fat man coming through. Buzz looked at Mal paying off the rat killer's mother; he got an idea—or the idea got him. "Contract out?"

"Ten grand. Fifteen if they get you alive so Mickey can get his jollies."

"Chump change. Johnny, you wanna make twenty grand for two hours' work?"

"You slay me. Next you'll be offering me a date with Lana Turner."

"I mean it."

"Where you gonna get that dough?"

"I'll have it inside two weeks. Deal?"

"What makes you think you'll live that long?"

"Ain't you a gambler?"

"Oh shit. Deal."

Buzz said, "I'll call you back," and hung up. Mal was standing beside him, shaking his head. "Mickey knows?"

"Yeah, Mickey knows. You got a couch?"

Mal gave Buzz a soft punch in the arm. "Lad, I think people are starting to get your number."

"Say what?"

"I figured out something today."

"What?"

"You killed Gene Niles."

37

MAL'S TAKE on Johnny Stompanato: two parts olive-oil charm, two parts hepcat, six parts plug-ugly. His take on the whole situation: Buzz was doomed, and his voice talking to Audrey on the phone said he knew it. Coleman arrested for four sex murders plus grand jury indictments added up to Stefan dropped on his doorstep like a Christmas bundle. The *Herald* and *Mirror* were playing up the Gordean killing, no suspects, puff pieces on the victim as a straight-arrow talent agent, no mention of the bank money—the catching officers probably got fat. The papers made UAES the instigators of the riot the Teamsters started; Buzz was impressed with his shot in the dark on Gene Niles and believed his promise not to spill on it. The fat man was going to brace Dudley's niece while he and Stompanato braced Chaz Minear, and when they had Coleman placed, he'd call his newspaper contacts so they could be in on the capture: first interviews with Captain Malcolm E. Considine, captor of the Wolverine Monster. And then Dudley Smith.

They were sitting in Stompanato's car, 8:00 A.M., a cop-crook stakeout. Mal knew his scenario; Buzz had filled Johnny in on his and had greased the doorman of Minear's building. The man told him Chaz left for breakfast every morning at 8:10 or so, walked over Mariposa to the Wilshire Derby and returned with the newspaper around 9:30. Buzz gave him a C-note to be gone from 9:30 to 10:00; during that half hour they'd have a wide-open shot.

Mal watched the door; Stompanato gave himself a pocket-knife manicure and hummed opera. At 8:09 a small man in tennis sweater and slacks walked out the entrance of the Conquistador Apartments; the doorman gave them the high sign. Stompanato sliced a cuticle and smiled; Mal jacked his plug-ugly quotient way up.

They waited.

At 9:30, the doorman tipped his cap, got into a car and drove off; at 9:33 Chaz Minear walked into the building holding a newspaper. Stompanato put his knife away; Mal said, "Now."

They quick-marched into the lobby. Minear was checking his mail slot; Johnny Stomp strode ahead to the elevator and opened the door. Mal dawdled by a wall mirror, straightening his necktie, getting a reverse view of Minear grabbing letters, Stompanato keeping the elevator door open with his foot, smiling like a good neighbor. Little Chaz walked over and into the trap; Mal came up behind him, nudged Johnny's foot away and let the door close.

Minear pushed the button for three. Mal saw his door key already in his hand, grabbed it and rabbit-punched him. Minear dropped his newspaper and mail and doubled over; Johnny pinned him to the wall, a hand on his neck. Minear went purply blue; it looked like his eyes were about to pop out. Mal talked to him, a mimic of Dudley Smith. "We know you killed Felix Gordean. We were his partners on the Loftis job, and you're going to tell us allll about Reynolds and his son. Allll about it. *Lad*."

The door slid open; Mal saw "311" on the key and an empty hallway. He walked out, located the apartment four doorways over, unlocked the door and stood back. Stompanato forced Minear inside and released his neck; Chaz fell down rasping for breath. Mal said, "You know what to ask him. Do it while I toss for the files."

Minear coughed words; Johnny stepped on his neck. Mal took off his jacket, rolled up his sleeves and tossed.

The apartment had five rooms: living room, bedroom, kitchen, bathroom, study. Mal hit the study first—it was the furthest from Stompanato and the nance. A radio went on, the dial skimming across jazz, commercial jingles and the news, stopping at an opera, a baritone and a soprano going at each other over a thunderous orchestra. Mal thought he heard Minear scream; the music was turned up.

Mal worked.

The study—desk, filing cabinets and a chest of drawers—yielded stacks of movie scripts, carbons of Minear's political letters, correspondence to him, miscellaneous memoranda and a .32

revolver, the cylinder empty, a cordited barrel. The bedroom was pastel-appointed and filled with piles of books; there was a wardrobe closet crammed with expensive clothes and rows of shoes arrayed in trees. An antique cabinet featured drawers spilling propaganda tracts; there was nothing but more shoes under the bed.

The opera kept wailing; Mal checked his watch, saw 10:25, an hour down and two rooms clean. He gave the bathroom a cursory toss; the music stopped; Stompanato popped his head in the doorway. He said, "The pansy spilled. Tell Meeks he better stay alive to get me my money."

The hard boy looked green at the gills. Mal said, "I'll do the kitchen and talk to him."

"Forget it. Loftis and Claire what's her face got the files. Come on, you've gotta hear this."

Mal followed Johnny into the living room. Chaz Minear was sitting prim and proper in a rattan chair; there were welts on his cheeks and blood had congealed below his nostrils. His tennis whites were still spotless, his eyes were unfocused, he was wearing an exhausted, almost slaphappy grin. Mal looked at Stompanato; Johnny said, "I poured half a pint of Beefeater's into him." He tapped the sap hooked into his belt. "In vino veritas, capiche?"

Danny Upshaw had said the same thing to him—the one time they drank together. Mal took a chair facing Minear. "Why did you kill Gordean? Tell me."

Minear, an easy mid-Atlantic accent. "Pride."

He sounded proud. Mal said, "What do you mean?"

"Pride. Gordean was tormenting Reynolds."

"He started tormenting him back in '44. It took you a while to get around to revenge."

Minear focused on Mal. "The police told Reynolds and Claire that I informed on Reynolds to the House Committee. I don't know how they knew, but they did. They confronted me about it, and I could tell Reynolds' poor heart was broken. I knew Gordean was blackmailing him again, so I did penance. Claire and Reynolds and I had gotten so close again, and I imagine you could present a case for me acting in my own self-interest. It was good having friends, and it was awful when they started hating me."

The rap was falling on him—he was the one who snitched the snitch. "Why didn't you take the money?"

"Oh Lord, I couldn't. It would have destroyed the gesture. And Claire has all the money in the world. She shares so generously with Reynolds ... and with all her friends. You're not really a criminal, are you? You look more like an attorney or an accountant."

Mal laughed—a kamikaze queer romantic had his number. "I'm a policeman."

"Are you going to arrest me?"

"No. Do you want to be arrested?"

"I want everyone to know what I did for Reynolds, but ..."

"But you don't want them to know why? Why Gordean was blackmailing Loftis?"

"Yes. That's true."

Mal threw a switcheroo. "Why did Reynolds and Claire steal Upshaw's files? To protect all of you from the grand jury?"

"No."

"Because of Reynolds' kid brother? *His son?* Was it Upshaw's *homicide* file they were most interested in?"

Minear sat mute; Mal waved Stompanato toward the back of the apartment. "Chaz, you've said it once. Now you have to say it to me."

No answer.

"Chaz, I'll make you a deal. I'll make sure everyone knows you killed Gordean, but I won't let Reynolds get hurt anymore. All you'll get is what you want. Reynolds will know you had courage and you paid him back. He'll love you again. He'll forgive you."

"Love you" and "forgive you" made Minear cry, sputters of tears that he dried with his sweater sleeves. He said, "Reynolds left me for him. That's why I informed to HUAC."

Mal leaned closer. "Left you for who?"

"For *him.*"

"Who's 'him'?"

Minear said, "Reynolds' little brother was really his son. His mother was a crazy religious woman Reynolds had an affair with. She got money from him and kept the boy. When Coleman was nineteen, he ran away from the woman and found Reynolds. Reynolds took him in and became his lover. He left me to be with his own son."

Mal pushed his chair back, the confession a horror movie he wanted to run screaming from. He said, "All of it," before he bolted for real.

Minear raised his voice, like he was afraid of his confessor running; he speeded up, like he was anxious to be absolved or punished. "Felix Gordean was blackmailing Reynolds back in '44 or so. Somehow he figured out about him and Coleman, and he threatened to tell Herman Gerstein about it. Gerstein hates men like us, and he would have ruined Reynolds. When that policeman came around questioning Felix about the first three killings, Felix put things together. George Wiltsie had been with Reynolds, Marty Goines and Coleman were both jazz men. Then Augie Duarte was killed, and more details had been in the newspapers. The policeman had let some things slip and Felix knew Coleman had to be the killer. He renewed his blackmail demands, and Reynolds gave him another ten thousand.

"Claire and Reynolds confided in me, and I knew I could make up for informing. They knew after the first three killings that it had to be Coleman—they read a tabloid that had details on the mutilations, and they knew from the names of the victims. They knew about it before the policeman tried to infiltrate UAES, and they were looking for Coleman to try to stop him. Juan Duarte saw Upshaw at the morgue when Augie was there, and recognized him from a picture Norm Kostenz took. He told Claire and Reynolds who Upshaw really was, and they got scared. They had read that the police were looking for a man who resembled Reynolds, and they thought Coleman must be trying to frame his father. They left out clues to exonerate Reynolds, and I followed Upshaw home from Claire's house. The next day, Claire got Mondo Lopez to pick the lock on his apartment and look for things on the killings—things that would help them find Coleman. Mondo found his files and brought them to Claire. She and Reynolds were desperate to stop Coleman and keep the ..."

Keep the whole horror epic from ruining Reynolds Loftis worse than the grand jury ever could.

Mal thought of Claire—terrified of a harmless Sleepy Lagoon remark the first time they talked; he thought of Coleman's burn face, put it aside and went straight for the woman. "Claire and Coleman. What's between them?"

The queer redeemer glowed. "Claire nurtured Coleman back in the SLDC days. He was in love with her, and he told her he always thought about her when he was with Reynolds. She heard out all his ugly, violent fantasies. She forgave them for being together. She was always so strong and accepting. The killings started a few weeks after the papers ran the wedding announcements. When

Coleman learned that Reynolds was getting Claire forever, it
must have made him crazy. Are you going to arrest me now?"

Mal couldn't make himself say no and break the rest of Chaz
Minear. He couldn't say anything, because Johnny Stompanato
had just walked into the room with his olive-oil charm back in
place, and all he could think of was that he could never keep
Stefan safe from the horror.

38

MARY MARGARET Conroy was coming across as a major league
Mexophile.

Buzz had tailed her from her sorority house to a hand-holding
kaffeeklatch at the UCLA Student Union; she was a simpering
frail in the presence of a handsome taco bender named Ricardo.
Their conversation was all in Spanish, and all he recognized were
words like "corazon" and "felicidad," love stuff he knew from the
juke box music at Mexican restaurants. From there, Dudley
Smith's dough-faced niece went to a meeting of the Pan American Students' League, a class in Argentine history, lunch and more
fondling with Ricardo. She'd been sequestered in a classroom
with "Art of the Mayans" for over an hour now, and when she
walked out he'd pop the question—shit or get off the pot time.

He kept checking his flank, seeing bad guys everywhere, like
Mickey with the Commies. Only his were real: Mickey himself,
Cohen goons armed with icepicks and saps and garottes and
silencered heaters that could leave you dead in a crowd, a heart
attack victim, squarejohns summoning an ambulance while the
triggerman walked away. He kept checking faces and kept trying
not to cut odds, because he was too good an oddsmaker to give
himself and Audrey much of a chance.

And he had a monster hangover.

And his back ached from boozy catnaps on Mal Considine's
floor.

They'd been up most of the night, planning. He called Dave
Kleckner in Ventura—Audrey was safely tucked in at his pad.
He'd called Johnny Stomp with details on the Minear squeeze
and gave Mal the lowdown on Gene Niles. Mal said he'd tagged
him as the killer on a hunch—that payback for Danny was so
antithetical to his style that he knew the debt had to be huge.

Mal got weepy on the kid, then went loony on Dudley Smith—Dudley made for José Diaz, Charles Hartshorn, suppression of evidence and a fuckload of conspiracy raps, Dudley sucking gas up at Q. He never made the next jump: the powers that be would never let Dudley Smith stand trial for anything—his rank, juice and reputation were diplomatic immunity.

They talked escape routes next. Buzz held back on his idea—it would have sounded as crazy as Mal taking down Dudley. They talked East Coast hideouts, slow boats to China, soldier of fortune gigs in Central America, where the local strongmen paid gringos good pesos to keep the Red Menace in check. They talked the pros and cons of taking Audrey, leaving Audrey, the lioness stashed someplace safe for a couple of years. They came to one conclusion: he'd give payback another forty-eight hours tops, then go in a hole somewhere.

A classroom bell sounded; Buzz got pissed: Mary Margaret Conroy would never blab, only confirm by her actions—all he was doing was humoring Mal's hump on Dudley. "Art of the Mayans" adjourned in a swirl of students, Mary Margaret the oldest by a good ten years. Buzz followed her outside, tapped her shoulder and said, "Miss Conroy, could I talk to you for a second?"

Mary Margaret turned around, hugging her armload of books. She eyed Buzz with distaste and said, "You're not with the faculty, are you?"

Buzz forced himself not to laugh. "No, I'm not. Sweetie, wouldn't you say Uncle Dudley went a bit too far warnin' José Diaz away from you?"

Mary Margaret went sheet white and passed out on the grass.

* * *

Dudley for Diaz.

Buzz left Mary Margaret on the grass with a firm pulse and fellow students hovering. He got off the campus quick and drove to Ellis Loew's house to play a hunch: Doc Lesnick's absence while UAESer lunacy raged on all fronts was too pat. The four Bureau dicks trying to find the man were filing reports at the house, and there might be something in them to give him a spark atop the hunch and the flicker that caused it: all the psych files ended in the summer of '49, even though the brain trusters were still seeing Lesnick. That fact reeked of wrong.

Buzz parked on Loew's front lawn, already crowded with cars. He heard voices coming from the back yard, walked around and saw Ellis holding court on the patio. Champagne was cooling on an ice cart; Loew, Herman Gerstein, Ed Satterlee and Mickey Cohen were hoisting glasses. Two Cohen boys were standing sentry with their backs to him; nobody had seen him yet. He ducked behind a trellis and listened.

Gerstein was exulting: yesterday's picket brawl was blamed on the UAES; the Teamster film crew leaked their version of the riot to Movietone News, who'd be captioning it "Red Rampage Rocks Hollywood" and shoving it into theaters nationwide. Ellis came on with his good news: the grand jury members being appointed by the City Council looked mucho simpatico, his house was packed with great evidence, mucho indictments seemed imminent. Satterlee kept talking about the climate being perfect, the grand jury a sweetheart deal that was preordained by God for this time and place only, a deal that would never come again. The geek looked about two seconds away from asking them to kneel in prayer; Mickey shut him up and not too subtly started asking questions about the whereabouts of Special Investigator Turner "Buzz" Meeks.

Buzz walked to the front of the house and let himself in. Typists were typing; clerks were filing; there was enough documentation in the living room to make confetti for a thousand ticker tape parades. He moved to the report board and saw that it had been replaced by a whole wall of photographs.

Federal evidence stamps were attached to the borders; Buzz saw "SLDC" a dozen times over and looked closer. The pics were obviously the surveillance shots Ed Satterlee was trying to buy off a rival clearance group; another scope and he noticed *every* photo was marked SLDC, with '43 and '44 dates tagged at the bottom, the pictures arranged chronologically, probably waiting for some artwork: circling the faces of known Commies. Buzz thought: Coleman, and started looking for a face swathed in bandages.

Most of the photos were overhead group shots; some were enlarged sections where faces were reproduced more clearly. The quality on all of them was excellent—the Feds knew their stuff. Buzz saw some blurry, too white faces in the earlier pics, crowd shots from the spring of '43; he followed the pictures across the wall, hoping for Coleman sans gauze and dressings, an aid to ID the rat killer in person. He got bandage glimpses through the summer of '43; little looks at Claire De Haven and Reynolds Loftis along the way. Then—blam!—a Reynolds Loftis view that was way off; the handsome queer too, too short in the tooth, with too much hair.

Buzz checked the date—8/17/43—rechecked the Loftis glimpses, rechecked the clothes on the bandaged man. Reynolds had noticeably thinning hair throughout; the too young Reynolds sported a full head of thick stuff. In three of the overhead shots, bandage man was wearing a striped skivvy shirt; in the close-up, too young Reynolds was wearing the same thing. Juan Duarte had told Mal that Reynolds' "kid brother" looked just like him—but *this man* was Reynolds in every respect except the hair, every facial plane and angle exactly like his father—a mirror image of Daddy twenty years younger.

Buzz thought semantics, thought "just like" might be an uneducated greaseball's synonym for "identical twin"; Delores Masskie called the resemblance "rather close." He grabbed a magnifying glass off a typist's desk; he followed the pictures, looking for more Coleman. Three over he got a close shot of the boy with a man and a woman; he put the lens up to it and squinted for all he was worth.

No burn scars of any kind; no pocked and shiny skin; no uneven patches where flesh was grafted.

Two photos over, one row down. November 10, 1943. The boy standing sideways facing Claire De Haven, shirtless. Deep, perfectly straight scars on his right arm, a row of them, scars identical to scars he saw on the arm of an RKO actor who'd had his face reconstructed after an auto wreck, scars that actor had pointed to with pride, telling him that only Doctor Terry Lux did arm grafts, the skin there was the best, so good that it was worth upper body tissue removal. The actor said that Terry made him look *exactly* like he did before the accident—when he looked at himself even he couldn't tell the difference.

Terry Lux dried Claire De Haven out at his clinic three times.

Terry Lux had workers who slaughtered chickens with zoot sticks.

Terry Lux told him Loftis used to cop H for Claire; Marty Goines was snuffed by a heroin overjolt. Terry Lux diluted the morphine for his dope cures on the premises at his clinic.

Buzz kept the magnifying glass to the wall, kept scanning. He got a back view of Coleman shirtless, saw a patchwork of perfectly straight scars that made him think of zoot stick wounds; he found another set of group shots that looked like Coleman fawning all over Claire De Haven. Hard evidence: Coleman Masskie Loftis was plastic surgery altered to look more like his father. He resembled his father enough to ID him from Delores' pictures before; now he *was* him. His "special protection" from Dudley Smith was being disguised as Loftis.

Buzz ripped the best Coleman pic off the wall, pocketed it and found a table stacked with reports from the Bureau men. He quick-skimmed the latest update; all the officers had accomplished was a shakedown of Lesnick's parolee daughter—she said the old man was just about gone from his lung cancer and was thinking about checking into a rest home to check out. He was about to pocket a list of local sanitariums when he heard "Traitor," and saw Mickey and Herman Gerstein standing a few feet away.

Cohen with a clean shot, but a half dozen witnesses spoiling his chance. Buzz said, "I suppose this means my guard gig's kaput. Huh, Mick?"

The man looked hurt as much as he looked mad. "Goyishe shitheel traitor. Cocksucker. Communist. How much money did I give you? How much money did I set up for you that you should do me like you did?"

Buzz said, "Too much, Mick."

"That is no smart answer, you fuck. You should beg. You should beg that I don't do you slow."

"Would it help?"

"No."

"There you go, boss."

Mickey said, "Herman, leave this room"; Gerstein exited. The typers kept typing and the clerks kept clerking. Buzz gave the little hump's cage a rattle. "No hard feelin's, huh?"

Mickey said, "I will make you a deal, because when I say 'deal,' it is always to trust. Right?"

"Trust" and "deal" were the man's bond—it was why he went with him instead of Siegel or Dragna. "Sure, Mick."

"Send Audrey back to me and I will not hurt a hair on her head and I will not do you slow. Do you trust my word?"

"Yes."

"Do you trust I'll get you?"

"You're the odds-on favorite, boss."

"Then be smart and do it."

"No deal. Take care, Jewboy. I'll miss you. I really will."

* * *

Pacific Sanitarium—fast.

Buzz turned off PCH and beeped his horn at the gate; the squawk box barked, "Yes?"

"Turner Meeks to see Dr. Lux."

Static sounds for a good ten seconds, then: "Park off to your left by the door marked 'Visiting,' go through the lounge and take the elevator up to the second floor. Doctor will meet you in his office."

Buzz did it, parking, walking through the lounge. The elevator was in use; he took stairs up to the second floor, saw the connecting door open, heard, "Okie baboon" and stopped just short of the last step.

Terry Lux's voice: "... but I have to talk to him, he's a pipeline to Howard Hughes. Listen, there should be something in the papers today I'm interested in—a guy I used to do business with was murdered. I just heard about it on the radio, so go get me all the L.A. dailies while I talk to this clown."

Odds on Lux-Gordean business: six to one in favor of. Buzz retraced his steps to the car, grabbed his billy club, stuck it down the back of his pants and took his time walking inside. The elevator was empty; he pushed the button for 2 and glided up thinking how much Terry loved money, how little he cared where it came from. The door opened; the dope doc himself was there to greet him. "Buzzy, long time no see."

The administrative corridor looked nice and deserted—no nurses or orderlies around. Buzz said, "Terry, how are you?"

"Is this business, Buzz?"

"Sure is, boss. And on the extra QT. You got a place where we can talk?"

Lux led Buzz down the hall, to a little room with filing cabinets and facial reconstruction charts. He closed the door; Buzz locked it and leaned on it. Lux said, "What the hell are you doing?"

Buzz felt the billy club tickling his spine. "Spring of '43 you did a plastic job on Reynolds Loftis' son. Tell me about it."

"I don't know what you're talking about. Check my '43 files if you like."

"This ain't negotiable, Terry. This is you spill all, Gordean included."

"There's nothing to negotiate, because I don't know what you're talking about."

Buzz pulled out his baton and hit Lux behind the knees. The blow sent Lux pitching into the wall; Buzz grabbed a fistful of his hair and banged his face against the door jamb. Lux slid to the floor, trailing blood on polished mahogany, sputtering, "Don't hit me. Don't hit me."

Buzz backed up a step. "Stay there, the floor looks good on you. Why'd you cut the boy to look like his old man? Who told you to do that?"

Lux tilted his head back, gurgled and shook himself like a dog shedding water. "You scarred me. You ... you scarred me."

"Give yourself a plastic. And answer me."

"Loftis had me do it. He paid me a lot, and he paid me never to tell anybody about it. Loftis and the psycho had essentially the same bone structure, and I did it."

"Why'd Loftis want it done?"

Lux moved into a sitting position and massaged his knees. His eyes darted to an intercom phone atop a filing cabinet just out of reach; Buzz smashed the contraption with his stick. "Why? And don't tell me Loftis wanted the boy to look like him so he could be a movie star."

"He did tell me that!"

Buzz tapped the baton against his leg. "Why'd you call Coleman a psycho?"

"He did his post-op here, and I caught him raiding the hatchery! He was cutting up the chickens with one of those zoot sticks my men use! He was drinking their goddamn blood!"

Buzz said, "That's a psycho, all right"; he thought Terry *had* to be clean on snuff knowledge: the fool thought chickens were as bad as it got. "Boss, what kind of business did you do with Felix Gordean?"

"I didn't kill him!"

"I know you didn't, and I'm pretty damn sure you don't know who did. But I'll bet you hipped him to something about Reynolds Loftis back around '43, '44 or so, and Gordean started collectin' hush money on it. That sound about right?"

Lux said nothing; Buzz said, "Answer me, or I'll go to work on your kidneys."

"When I tell Howard about this, you'll be in trouble."

"I'm finished with Howard."

Lux made an overdue move. "Money, Buzz. That's what this is about, right? You've got an angle you want to buy in on and you need help. Am I right?"

Buzz tossed his stick out, holding the end of the thong. The tip hit Lux in the chest; Buzz jerked it back like a yo-yo on a string. Lux yipped at the little wonder; Buzz said, "Coleman, Loftis and Gordean. Put them together."

Lux stood up and straightened the folds of his smock. He said, "About a year after the reconstruction on Coleman I went to a party in Bel Air. Loftis and his so-called kid brother were there. I pretended not to know them, because Reynolds didn't want anyone to know about the surgery. Later on that night, I was out by the cabanas. I saw Coleman and Loftis kissing. It made me mad. I'd plasticed the kid for an incestuous pervert. I knew Felix liked to put the squeeze on queers, so I sold him the information. I figured he blackmailed Loftis. Don't look so shocked, Meeks. You would have done the same thing."

Minear's file quote: "If you knew who *he* was, you'd know why I snitched"—the one reference Doc Lesnick let slip into the grand jury team's hands—*the half-dead old stoolie had to know the whole story*. Buzz looked at Lux culling back his dignity, pushed him into the wall and held him there with his stick. "When's the last time you saw Coleman?"

Lux's voice was high and thin. "Around '45. Daddy and Sonny must have had a spat. Coleman came to me with two grand and told me he didn't want to look so much like Daddy anymore. He asked me to break his face up scientifically. I told him that since I enjoy inflicting pain, I'd only take a grand and a half. I strapped him into a dental chair, put on heavy bag gloves and broke every bone in his face. I kept him on morph while he recovered down by the chicken shed. He left with a teeny weeny little habit and some not so teeny little bruises. He started wearing a beard, and all that was left of Reynolds was the set of his eyes. Now, do you want to take that goddamn club off of me?"

Bingo—the Goines heroin angle. Buzz held off on the baton. "I know you dilute your own morph here on the grounds."

Lux took a scalpel from his pocket and started cleaning his nails. "Police sanctioned."

"You told me Loftis copped horse for Claire De Haven. Did you and him use the same suppliers?"

"A few of them. Coloreds with cop connections down in south-town. I only deal with officially sanctioned lackeys—like you."

"Did Coleman have info on them?"

"Sure. After the first surgery, I gave him a list. He had a crush on Claire, and he said he wanted to help her get the stuff, make the runs himself so she wouldn't have to truck with niggers. When he left after my second surgery, he probably used them for his own habit."

A round of applause for Coleman Loftis: he kicked morph and took up rat worship slaughter. "I want that list. Now."

Lux unlocked the filing cabinet by the demolished phone. He pulled out a slip of lined paper and reached for some blank sheets; Buzz said, "I'll keep the original," and grabbed it.

The doctor shrugged and went back to cleaning his nails. Buzz started to tuck his baton away; Lux said, "Didn't your mother tell you it's not polite to stare?"

Buzz kept quiet.

"The strong, silent type. I'm impressed."

"I'm impressed with you, Terry."

"How so?"

"Your recuperative powers. I'll bet you got yourself convinced this little humiliation didn't really happen."

Lux sighed. "I'm Hollywood, Buzz. Easy come, easy go, and it's already a dim memory. Got a sec for a question?"

"Sure."

"What's this about? There has to be money in it somewhere. You don't work for free."

Adios, Terry.

Buzz kidney-punched Lux, his hardest stick shot. The scalpel fell from the doctor's hand. Buzz caught it, kneed Lux in the balls, smothered him into the wall and placed his right palm against it Jesus style. Lux screamed; Buzz rammed the scalpel into the hand and pounded it down to the hilt with his baton. Lux screamed some more, his eyes rolling back. Buzz shoved a handful of pocket cash into his mouth. "It's about payback. This is for Coleman."

39

MAL MADE another circuit of the De Haven house, wondering if they'd ever leave and give him a crack at the files, wondering if they'd got the word on Gordean yet. If Chaz Minear had called, they would have run to him; the killing was front page and all over the radio, and friends of theirs had to know that Loftis at least knew the man. But both cars stayed put and there was nothing he could do but keep waiting, moving, waiting to swoop.

Canon Drive to Elevado, Comstock to Hillcrest to Santa Monica and around again—sitting surveillance was an invitation for the ubiquitous Beverly Hills cops to roust him, out of his jurisdiction and getting ready to pull a Class B felony. Every time around the house he imagined more horrors inside—Loftis and his own son, a knife to the part of him that lived to protect Stefan. Two hours of circling had him dizzy; he'd called Meeks' switchboard and left a message: meet me on Canon Drive—but Buzz's Caddy hadn't showed and it was getting to the point where he was close to going in the door gun first.

Santa Monica around to Canon. Mal saw a paperboy tossing newspapers on front porches and lawns, hooked an idea, pulled over three houses up from Claire's and fixed her porch in his rear-view. The boy hurled his bundle and hit the door; the door opened and an androgynous arm scooped the newspaper up. If they didn't already know, they soon would—and if their brains held over their fear they'd think *Chaz*.

A slow minute passed. Mal fidgeted and found an old sweater in the back seat—a good window punch. Another slow bunch of seconds, then Claire and Loftis hurrying out to the Lincoln in the driveway. She got behind the wheel; he sat beside her; the car backed out and headed south—the direction of Minear's place.

Mal walked over to the house—a tall, dignified man in a three-piece suit carrying a loosely folded sweater. He saw a side window by the door, punched it in, reached around and picked the lock. The door snapped open; Mal let himself in, closed the door and threw the top bolt.

There were at least fifteen rooms to toss. Mal thought: closets, dens, places with desks—and hit the writing table by the stairwell. He pulled out a half dozen drawers, rummaged in a coat closet adjacent, feeling for folders and loose paper as much as looking.

No loot.

Back to the rear of the house; two more closets. Vacuum cleaners and carpet sweepers, mink coats, a prayer to his old Presbyterian God: please don't let them keep it in a safe. A den off a rear bathroom, bookshelves, a desk there—eight drawers of potpourri—movie scripts, stationery, old Loftis personal papers and no false bottoms or secret compartments.

Mal left the den by a side door and smelled coffee. He followed the scent to a large room with a movie screen and projector set up at the rear. A drop leaf table holding a coffeepot and a scattering of papers was stationed square in the middle, two chairs tucked under it—a study scene. He walked over, started reading and saw how good Danny Upshaw could have been.

The kid block-printed cleanly, thought intelligently, wrote with clarity and would have cracked the four killings easy if LAPD had given him an extra day or so. It was right there on his first summary report, page three, his second eyewitness on the Goines snatch. Claire and Reynolds had circled the information, confirming what Minear said: they were trying to find Loftis' son.

Page three.

Eyewitness Coleman Healy, questioned by Danny Upshaw on his first full day working the case.

He was late twenties—the right age. *He* was described as tall, slender and wearing a beard, which was undoubtedly a fake, one that he took off when he impersonated his father/lover. He *front-view*-confirmed a bartender's side view description of himself, filling in the middle-aged part. *He* was the first—and only, according to Jack Shortell—witness to identify Marty Goines as a homosexual, Upshaw's first homo lead outside of the mutilations. Put makeup on Coleman, and he could look middle-aged; put it all together with Doc Layman's silver wig strands found by the L.A. River and you had Coleman Masskie/Loftis/Healy committing murders out of his own blood lust and some kind of desire for revenge on incest raper Reynolds.

But one thing didn't play: Danny had questioned Coleman and met Reynolds. Why didn't he snap to their obvious resemblance?

Mal went through the rest of the pages, feeling the kid giving him juice. Everything was perfectly logical and boldly intelligent: Danny was beginning to get the killer's psyche down cold. There was a six-page report on his Tamarind Street break-in—he *did* do it—devil take the hindmost, fuck City/County strictures; he was afraid LAPD would ruin him for it, so he didn't take the polygraph that would have cleared him on Niles and night-trained it instead. Photographs showing blood patterns were mixed in with the reports; Danny had to have taken them himself, he'd risked a forensic in enemy territory. Mal felt tears in his eyes, saw himself building Ellis Loew's prosecution with Danny's evidence, making his own name soar on it. The Wolverine Killer in the gas chamber—sent there by the two of them and the unlikeliest best friend a ranking cop ever had: Buzz Meeks.

Mal dried his eyes; he made a neat stack of the pages and photographs. He saw feminine script in the margins of a jigtown canvassing list: Southside hotels, with jazz clubs check-marked against Danny's printing. He stuffed that page in his pocket, bundled the rest of the file up and walked to the front door with it. Tripping the bolt, he heard a key go in the lock; he opened the door bold, like Danny Upshaw at Tamarind Street.

Claire and Loftis were there on the porch; they looked at the broken glass, then at Mal and his armful of paper. Claire said, "You broke our deal."

"Fuck our deal."

"I was going to kill him. I finally figured out there was no other way."

Mal saw a bag of groceries in Loftis' arms; he realized they didn't have time to see Minear. "For justice? People's justice?"

"We just talked to our lawyer. He said there's no way you can prove any kind of homicide charges against us."

Mal looked at Loftis. "It's all coming out. You and Coleman, all of it. The grand jury and Coleman's trial."

Loftis stepped behind Claire, his head bowed. Mal glanced streetside and saw Buzz getting out of his car. Claire embraced her fiancé; Mal said, "Go look after Chaz. He killed a man for you."

40

DOWN TO darktown in Mal's car, Lux's list of heroin pushers and the Danny/Claire list taped to the dashboard. Mal drove; Buzz wondered if he'd killed the Plastic Surgeon to the Stars; they both talked.

Buzz filled in first: Mary Margaret's swooning confirmation and Lux minus the crucifixion. He talked up the plastic surgery on Coleman, a ploy to keep him safe from Dudley and fulfill his father's perv; Lux shooting Gordean the incest dope for blackmail purposes, the story of the burned face a device to hide the perv from Loftis' fellow lefties, the bandages simply the surgery scars healing. Buzz saved Lux rebreaking Coleman's face for last; Mal whooped and used the point to segue to sax man Healy, questioned by Danny Upshaw on New Year's Day—that was why the kid never snapped to a perfect Loftis/Coleman resemblance—it didn't exist anymore.

From there, Mal talked Coleman. Coleman's intro lead on Marty Goines as a fruit, Coleman stressing the tall, gray man, Coleman wearing a gray wig and probably makeup when he glommed his victims, shucking the beard Upshaw saw on him. Loftis and Claire had Mondo Lopez steal Danny's files when they found out he was working the homo killings—Juan Duarte had snitched him as a cop. Mal recounted the Minear interrogation, Coleman the third point of the '42–'44 love triangle, Chaz shooting blackmailer Gordean to redeem himself in Claire and Loftis' eyes, Claire and Loftis searching for Coleman. And they both agreed: Marty Goines, a longtime Coleman pal, was probably a victim of opportunity—he was there when the rat man *had* to kill. Victims two, three and four were to tie in to Daddy Reynolds—a hellish smear tactic.

They hit the Central Avenue Strip, daytime quiet, a block of spangly facades: the Taj Mahal, palm trees hung with Christmas lights, sequined music clefs, zebra stripes and a big plaster jigaboo with shiny red eyes. None of the clubs appeared to be open: bouncer-doormen and parking lot attendants sweeping up butts and broken glass were the only citizens out on the street. Mal parked and took the west side; Buzz took the east.

He talked to bouncers; he talked to auto park flunkies; he handed out all the cash he didn't stuff down Terry Lux's throat. Three of the darkies gave him "Huh?"; two hadn't seen Coleman the alto guy in a couple of weeks; a clown in a purple admiral's tunic said he'd heard Healy was gigging at a private sepia club in Watts that let whiteys perform if they were hep and kept their lily-white meathooks off the colored trim. Buzz crossed the street and started canvassing toward his partner; three more "Huh?'s" and Mal came trotting over to him.

He said, "I talked to a guy who saw Coleman last week at Bido Lito's. He said he was talking to a sickly old Jewish man about half dead. The guy said he looked like one of the old jazz fiends from the rest home on 78th and Normandie."

Buzz said, "You think Lesnick?"

"We're on the same track, lad."

"Quit callin' me lad, it gives me the willies. Boss, I read a Bureau memo at Ellis' house. Lesnick's daughter said Pops was thinkin' about checkin' in to a rest bin to kick. There was a list of them, but I couldn't grab it."

"Let's hit that Normandie place first. You get anything?"

"Coleman might be playin' his horn at some private jig club in Watts."

Mal said, "Shit. I worked 77th Street Division years ago, and there were tons of places like that. No more details?"

"Nix."

"Come on, let's move."

They made it to the Star of David Rest Home fast, Mal running yellow lights, busting the speed limit by twenty miles an hour. The structure was a low tan stucco; it looked like a minimum security prison for people waiting to die. Mal parked and walked straight to the reception desk; Buzz found a pay phone outside and looked up "Sanitariums" in the Yellow Pages.

There were thirty-four of them on the Southside. Buzz tore the page of listings out; he saw Mal standing by the car and walked over shaking his head. "Thirty-four bins around here. A long fuckin' day."

Mal said, "Nothing inside. No Lesnick registered, nobody dying of lung cancer on the ward. No Coleman."

Buzz said, "Let's try the hotels and pushers. If that's no go, we'll get some nickels and start callin' the sanitariums. You know, I think Lesnick's a lamster. If that was him with Coleman, he's in this somehow, and he wouldn't be registered under his own name."

Mal tapped the hood of the car. "Buzz, Claire wrote that hotel list out. Minear said she and Loftis have been trying to find Coleman. If they've already tried—"

"That don't mean spit. Coleman's been seen around here inside a week. He could be movin' around, but always stayin' close to the music. Somethin's goin' on with him and music, 'cause nobody made him for playin' an instrument, now these boogies down here say he's a hot alto sax. I say we hit hotels and H men while it's still light out, then come dark we hit those jig joints."

"Let's go."

The Tevere Hotel on 84th and Beach—no Caucasians in residence. The Galleon Hotel on 91st and Bekin—the one white man staying there a three-hundred-pound rummy squeezed into a single room with his negress wife and their four kids. Walking back to the car, Buzz checked the two lists and grabbed Mal's arm. "Whoa."

Mal said, "What?"

"A matcher. Purple Eagle Hotel, 96th and Central on Claire's list. Roland Navarette, Room 402 at the Purple Eagle on Lux's."

"It took you a while."

"Ink's all smudged."

Mal handed him the keys. "You drive, I'll see what else you missed."

They drove southeast. Buzz ground gears and kept popping the clutch; Mal studied the two lists and said, "The only matchup. You know what I was thinking?"

"What?"

"Lux knows Loftis and De Haven, and Loftis used to cop Claire's stuff. They could have access to Lux's suppliers, too."

Buzz saw the Purple Eagle—a six-story cinderblock dump with a collection of chrome hood ornaments affixed above a tattered purple awning. He said, "Could be," and double-parked; Mal got out first and practically ran inside.

Buzz caught up at the desk. Mal was badging the clerk, a scrawny Negro with his shirt cuffs buttoned full in a sweltering lobby. He was muttering, "Yessir, yessir, yessir," one eye on Mal, one hand reaching under the desk.

Mal said, "Roland Navarette. Is he still in 402?"

The hophead said, "Nossir, nossir," his hand still reaching; Buzz swooped around and pinned his wrist just as he was closing in on a junk bindle. He bent the fingers back; the hophead went, "Yessir, yessir, yessir"; Buzz said, "A white man, late twenties, maybe a beard. A jazz guy. He glom horse from Navarette?"

"Nossir, nossir, nossir."

"Boy, you tell true or I break the hand you geez up with and throw you in the cracker tank at the Seven-Seven."

"Yessir, yessir, yessir."

Buzz let go and laid the bindle out on the desk. The clerk rubbed his fingers. "White man, white woman here askin' same thing twenty minutes 'go. I tol' them, I tell you, Roland straighten up, fly right, don't sell no sweet horsey nohow."

The punk's eyes strayed to a house phone; Buzz ripped it out and chucked it on the floor. Mal ran for the stairs.

Buzz huffed and puffed after him, catching up on the fourth-floor landing. Mal was in the middle of a putrid-smelling hallway, gun out, pointing to a doorway. Buzz got his breath, pulled his piece and walked over.

Mal ticked numbers; at three they kicked in the door. A Negro in soiled underwear was sitting on the floor sticking a needle in his arm, pushing the plunger down, oblivious to the noise and two white men pointing guns at him. Mal kicked his legs and pulled the spike out of his arm; Buzz saw a C-note resting under a fresh syringe on the dresser and knew Claire and Loftis had bought themselves a hot lead.

Mal was slapping the H man, trying to bring him back from cloud nine; Buzz knew that was futile. He hauled him away from Mal, dragged him to the bathroom, stuck his head in the toilet and flushed. Roland Navarette came back to earth with shakes, shivers and sputters; the first thing he saw out of the bowl was a .38 in his face. Buzz said, "Where'd you send them white people after Coleman?"

Roland Navarette said, "Man, this a humbug."

Buzz cocked the gun. "Don't make me."

Roland Navarette said, "Coleman gigging at this after-hours on 106 an' Avalon."

* * *

Watts, code three without a siren. Buzz fingered his billy club; Mal leadfooted through twilight traffic. 106 and Avalon was the heart of the heart of Watts: every tarpaper shack on the block had goats and chickens behind barbed-wire fences. Buzz thought of crazed darkies sacrificing them for voodoo rituals, maybe inviting Coleman over for some wolverine stew and a night of jazz hot. He saw a string of blue lights flickering around the doorway of a corner stucco; he said, "Pull over, I see it."

Mal swung hard right and killed his engine at the curb. Buzz pointed across the street. "That white car was in De Haven's driveway." Mal nodded, opened the glove compartment and took out a pair of handcuffs. "I was going to let the papers in on this, but I guess there's no time."

Buzz said, "He might not be here. Loftis and Claire might be waitin' him out, or there'd of been grief already. *You* ready?"

Mal nodded. Buzz saw a group of Negroes line up by the blue-lit door and start filing in. He motioned Mal out of the car; they hurried across the sidewalk and rode the last jazzbo's coattails.

The doorman was a gigantic shine in a blue bongo shirt. He started to block the way in, then stepped back and bowed—an obvious police courtesy.

Buzz went in first. Except for blue Christmas bulbs taped to the walls and a baby spot illuminating the bar, the joint was dark. People sat at card tables facing the stage and a combo back-lit by more blue lights: blinkers covered with cellophane. The music was ear-splitting shit, one step down from noise. The trumpet, bass, drums, piano and trombone were Negro guys in blue bongo shirts. The alto sax was Coleman, no beard, a cracked blue bulb blinking across the set of Daddy Reynolds' eyes.

Mal nudged Buzz and spoke loud in his ear. "Claire and Loftis at the bar. Over in the corner, tucked away."

Buzz pivoted, saw the two, half shouted to make himself heard: "Coleman can't see 'em. We'll take him when this goddamn noise shuts off."

Mal moved to the left side wall, ducking his head, moving up toward the bandstand; Buzz followed a few feet behind, doing a little shuffle: I'm not conspicuous, I'm not a cop. When they were almost to the edge of the stage, he looked back at the bar. Claire was still there; Loftis wasn't; a door on the right side of the room was just closing, showing a slice of light.

Buzz tapped Mal; Mal pointed over like he already knew. Buzz switched his gun from his holster to his right pants pocket; Mal had his piece pressed to his leg. The jigs quit playing and Coleman flew solo: squeals, rasps, honks, barks, growls, squeaks— Buzz thought of giant rats ripping flesh to the beat. There was a keening noise that seemed to go on forever, Coleman pitching his sax to the stars. The blue lights died; the keen went low note shuba-shuba-shuba in darkness and died. Real lights went on and the audience stampeded the bandstand, applauding.

Buzz pushed into the crush of bodies, Mal beside him, extra tall on his tiptoes. Everyone surrounding them was black; Buzz blinked for white and saw Coleman, sax held above his head, going through the right side door.

Mal looked at him; Buzz looked back. They pushed, punched, shoved, elbowed and kneed their way over, getting elbows, shoves and tossed drinks in their faces. Buzz came up on the door wiping bourbon sting out of his eyes; he heard a scream and a shot on the other side—and Mal went through the door gun first.

Another shot; Buzz ran after Mal's shadow. A smelly linoleum corridor. Two shapes struggling on the floor twenty feet down; Mal aiming, gun hand braced. A black guy turned a side corner and tried to block his aim; Mal shot him twice. The man careened off the walls and went down face first; Buzz got a look at the two on the floor. It was Loftis being strangled by Coleman Healy, big ugly pink dentures with fangs attached in his mouth. Coleman's chest was bloodied; Loftis was soaked dark red at the legs and groin. A revolver lay beside them.

Mal yelled, "Coleman, get back!" Buzz slid down the wall, .38 out, looking for a clean shot at the rat man. Coleman made a denture-muffled bleat and bit off his father's nose; Mal fired three times, hitting Loftis in the side and chest, pitching him away from the thing attacking him. Coleman wrapped his arms around Daddy like an animal starved for food and went for his throat. Buzz aimed at his gorging head; Mal blocked his arm and fired again, a ricochet that tore the walls with zigzags. Buzz got free and squeezed a shot; Coleman grabbed his shoulder; Mal fumbled out his handcuffs and ran over.

Buzz threw himself prone and tried to find a shot; Mal's legs and flapping suitcoat made it impossible. He stumbled up and ran himself; he saw Coleman grab the gun on the floor and aim. One, two, three shots—Mal lifted clean off his feet and spun around with his face blown away. The body collapsed in front of him; Buzz walked to Coleman; Coleman leered behind bloody fangs and raised his gun. Buzz shot first, emptying his piece at the wolverine toothwork, screaming when he finally got an empty chamber. He kept screaming, and he was still screaming when a shitload of cops stormed in and tried to take Mal Considine away from him.

PART FOUR
THE RED CHASER BLUES

41

TEN DAYS went by; Buzz hid out at a motel in San Pedro. Johnny Stompanato brought him information and bothered him for his fee on the Minear squeeze; the chink restaurant down the street delivered three greasy squares a day; the newspapers and radio supplied more info. He called Audrey in Ventura every night, spinning her tall tales about Rio and Buenos Aires, where the U.S. government couldn't extradite and Mickey was too cheap to send men. He fretted on the last and craziest money-making scheme of his L.A. career, wondering if he'd survive to spend the proceeds. He listened to hillbilly music, and Hank Williams and Spade Cooley did terrible things to him. He missed Mal Considine wicked bad.

After the shootout, an LAPD army got the citizens quelled and the bodies removed. Four dead: Coleman, Loftis, Mal and the back door bouncer he shot. Claire De Haven disappeared—she probably sent Reynolds on his lunatic mission, heard the shots, decided one redemption for the night was sufficient and calmly caught a cab home to plan more People's Revolts, Beverly Hills style. He followed Mal to the morgue and gave a statement at the Seven-Seven squadroom, tying in the Healy/Loftis deaths to the homo snuffs and insisting the late Deputy Danny Upshaw get credit for cracking the case. His statement glossed the illegalities he and Mal pulled; he didn't mention Felix Gordean, Chaz Minear, Dudley Smith or Mike Breuning at all. Let fruitfly Chaz live to enjoy his redemption; crazy Dud was too large to tap for the José Diaz kill or Charles Hartshorn's "suicide."

Reading between newspaper lines, you could follow the upshot: the Gordean killing unsolved, no suspects; the shootout explained as Mal and himself "following up a lead on an old case"; the dead boogie attributed to Coleman. No Commie or queer homicide angle on it at all—Ellis Loew had beaucoup press connections and hated complications. Reynolds and his son-lover were dismissed as "old enemies settling a grudge"—the howler to top all howlers.

Mal Considine got a hero's funeral. Mayor Bowron attended, as did the entire L.A. City Council, Board of Supervisors and selected LAPD brass. Dudley Smith gave a moving eulogy, citing Mal's "grand crusade" against Communism. The *Herald* ran a picture of Dudley chucking Mal's kid Stefan under the chin, exhorting him to "be a trouper."

Johnny Stomp was his conduit for dope on the grand jury, Ellis Loew to Mickey to him—and it looked like 24-karat stuff on all fronts:

Loew would begin his presentation of evidence next week—perfect timing—the UAES was still bearing the brunt of radio and newspaper editorials blaming them for the Gower Gulch bloodshed. Herman Gerstein, Howard Hughes and two other studio heads had told Loew they would oust UAES the day the grand jury convened—violating the union's contract on the basis of fine-print clauses pertaining to expulsion for subversive activities.

Johnny's other glad tidings: Terry Lux had suffered a stroke—the result of "prolonged oxygen deprivation" caused by a mouthful of money and a popped artery in his right hand. He was recuperating well, but ruined tendons in that hand would prevent him from performing plastic surgery again. Mickey Cohen had upped the ante on the Meeks contract to $20,000; Buzz jacked his payoff on the Minear job to $25,000 so Stompanato wouldn't put a bullet in his head. The Mick was pulling his hair out over Audrey; he'd erected a shrine out of Audrey memorabilia: her stripper publicity pics, the costumes she wore when she headlined the Burbank in '38. Mickey locked the stuff up in his bedroom at the hideaway and spent hours mooning over it. Sometimes you could hear him crying like a baby.

And Turner Meeks himself, holder of the Va Va Voom Girl's real true love, was getting fat, fat, fatter on moo shu duck, sweet and sour pork, shrimp chop suey and beef kowloon—a shitload of condemned man's last meals. And with his money shot a day away, he knew there were two things he wanted to know before he stuck his head in the noose: the whole story on Coleman and why the UAES hadn't played its extortion scheme against the studios—whatever it was—yet. And he had a hunch he knew where to get the answers.

Buzz went to the motel office, changed a five into nickels and walked to the phone booth in the parking lot. He got out the list of rest homes he'd torn from the Yellow Pages the day of the shootout and started calling, impersonating a police officer. He figured Lesnick would be hiding under an alias, but he hit the flunkies he talked to with his real name anyway, along with "old," "Jewish," "dying of lung cancer." He was $3.10 poorer when a girl said, "That sounds like Mr. Leon Trotsky." She went on to say that the oldster had checked out against medical advice and left a forwarding address: the Seaspray Motel, 10671 Hibiscus Lane, Redondo Beach.

A cheap Commie joke making it easy for him.

Buzz walked to a U-Drive and rented an old Ford sedan, thinking it looked pretty long in the tooth for a getaway car. He paid a week's fee in advance, gave the clerk a look at his driver's license and asked him for a pen and paper. The clerk complied; Buzz wrote:

> Dr. Lesnick—
> I was in with the grand jury for a while. I was there
> when Coleman and Reynolds Loftis were killed and
> I know what happened with them '42–'44. I didn't
> let any of that information out. Check the news-
> papers if you don't believe me. I have to leave Los
> Angeles because of some trouble I've gotten into and
> I would like to talk to you about Coleman. I won't
> tell what you tell me to the grand jury—I would get
> hurt if I did.
> > T. Meeks.

Buzz drove to the Seaspray Motel, hoping Mal's death kiboshed the Bureau men looking for Lesnick. It was an auto court at the tail of a dead-end street facing the beach; the office was shaped like a rocket ship pointed at the stars. Buzz walked in and punched the bell.

A youth with godawful pimples came in from the back. "You want a room?"

Buzz said, "Mr. Trotsky still alive?"

"Barely. Why?"

Buzz handed him the note and a five-spot. "Is he in?"

"He's always in. Here or the beach. Where's he gonna go? Jitterbugging?"

"Give him the paper, sonny. Keep the five. If he says he'll talk to me, Abe Lincoln's got a brother."

The pimple boy motioned Buzz outside; Buzz stood by his car and watched him walk to the middle of the court and knock on a door. The door opened, the boy went in; a minute later he came out lugging two beach chairs, a stooped old man holding his arm. The hunch played—Lesnick wanted some friendly ears on his way out.

Buzz let them come to him. The old man had a hand extended from ten yards away; his eyes were bright with sickness, his face was muddy beige and everything about him looked caved-in. His voice was strong—and the smile that went with it said he was proud of the fact. "Mr. Meeks?"

Buzz gave the hand a little tug, afraid of breaking bones. "Yessir, Doctor."

"And what is your rank?"

"I'm not a policeman."

"Oh? And what were you doing with the grand jury?"

Buzz handed the clerk a fiver and grabbed the beach chairs. The boy walked off smiling; Lesnick held Buzz's arm. "Why, then? I had thought Ellis Loew's minions were all policemen."

Lesnick's weight on his was almost nothing—a stiff breeze would blow the fucker to Catalina. Buzz said, "I did it for money. You wanta talk on the beach?"

Lesnick pointed to a spot near some rocks—it was free of glass and candy bar wrappers. Buzz shepherded him over, the chairs more of a strain than the man. He set the seats down facing each other, close, so he could hear if the Doc's voice went bum; he settled him in and watched him hunch into folds of terrycloth. Lesnick said, "Do you know how I was convinced to become an informant?"

True snitch behavior—he had to justify himself. Buzz sat down and said, "I'm not sure."

Lesnick smiled, like he was glad he could tell it. "In 1939 representatives of the Federal government offered me a chance to secure my daughter's release from Tehachapi Prison, where she was incarcerated for vehicular manslaughter. I was the official CP analyst in Los Angeles then, as I have remained. They told me that if I gave them access to my psychiatric files for evaluation by the 1940 State Attorney General's probe and other probes that might come up, they would release Andrea immediately. Since Andrea had a minimum of four more years to serve and had told me terrible stories of the abuse the matrons and her fellow inmates inflicted, I did not hesitate one second in agreeing."

Buzz let Lesnick catch some breath—and cut to Coleman. "And the reason you didn't kick loose with Loftis' file from '42 to '44 was because Coleman was smeared all over it. That right?"

Lesnick said, "Yes. It would have meant much unnecessary suffering for Reynolds and Coleman. Before I turned the files over in toto I checked for other Coleman references. Chaz Minear alluded to Coleman, but only elliptically, so his file I relinquished. I did that same sort of editing when I gave my files to the HUAC investigators, but I lied and told them the Loftis file had been lost. I didn't think Ellis Loew would believe that lie, so I just secreted Reynolds' file portion and hoped I would die before they asked me for it."

"Why didn't you just chuck the damn thing?"

Lesnick coughed and hunched deeper into his robe. "I had to keep studying it. It compelled me greatly. Why did you leave the grand jury? Was it moral qualms over Ellis Loew's methods?"

"I just didn't think UAES was worth the trouble."

"Your statement on the newspapers gives you credibility, and I find myself wondering exactly how much you know."

Buzz shouted over a sudden crash of waves. "I worked the killings *and* the grand jury! What I don't know is the history!"

The ocean noise subsided; Lesnick coughed and said, "You know all ..."

"Doc, I know the incest stuff, and the plastic surgery and all about Coleman tryin' to frame his daddy. The only other guy who knew was that DA's captain who was killed at the jazz club. And I think you wanta tell what you got, or you wouldn't of pulled that juvenile 'Trotsky' number. Make sense, headshrinker?"

Lesnick laughed, coughed, laughed. "You understand the concept of subliminal motivation, Mr. Meeks."

"I got a half-assed brain, boss. Wanta hear my theory why you held the files back from summer '49 on?"

"Please expound."

"The UAESers who knew were talkin' about Reynolds and Claire gettin' married and how Coleman would take it. That right?"

"Yes. I was afraid the investigators would seize the Coleman references and try to locate him as one of their friendly witnesses. Claire tried to keep news of the wedding out of the papers so Coleman wouldn't see it, but she did not succeed. At a terrible price, as I'm sure you know."

Buzz stared at the water, stone quiet: his favorite trick to open suspects up. After a minute or so, Lesnick said, "When the second two victims were reported in the scandal tabloids, I knew the killer had to be Coleman. He was my analysand during the SLDC time. I knew he would have to be living somewhere near the Central Avenue jazz clubs, and I located him. We were close once, and I thought I could reason with him, get him to a locked institution and stop his senseless slaughter. Augie Duarte proved me wrong, but I tried. *I tried*. Think of that before you judge me too harshly."

Buzz looked at the walking dead man. "Doc, I'm not judgin' anybody in this fuckin' thing. I'm just leavin' town in a day or so, and I sure would like you to fill in what I don't know."

"And nobody else will be told?"

Buzz threw Lesnick some crumbs. "You tried to spare your friends grief while you played the game, and I've pulled tricks like that too. I've got these two friends who'd like to know why, but they ain't ever gonna. So could you maybe just tell me?"

* * *

Saul Lesnick told. It took him two hours, with many long pauses to suck in air and keep himself fueled. Sometimes he looked at Buzz, sometimes he looked out at the ocean. He faltered at some of the worst of it, but he always kept telling.

1942.

Wartime blackouts in L.A., 10:00 P.M. curfew. Coleman was nineteen, living on Bunker Hill with his crazy mother Delores and two of his quasi-sisters. He used the surname "Masskie" because slave breeder mommy needed a paternal monicker to get Relief payments for her son and the seven letters jibed with Sister Aimee's dictates on numerology. Coleman dropped out of Belmont High when they wouldn't let him play in the school band; he was heartbroken when the band teacher told him the stupid saxophone flubbing he did was just noise that indicated no talent, only strong lungs.

Coleman tried to join the army two months after Pearl Harbor; he flunked the physical on trick knees and a spastic colon. He passed out handbills for Angelus Temple, earned enough money to buy himself a new alto sax and spent hours running chords and improvisational charts that sounded good only to him. Delores wouldn't let him practice at home, so he took his horn to the Griffith Park hills and honked at the squirrels and coyotes and stray dogs that trucked there. Sometimes he walked to the downtown library and listened to Victrola records with earphones. His favorite was "Wolverine Blues," sung by an old coon named Hudson Healy. The jig mushed words, and you could hardly hear him; Coleman invented his own words, dirty stuff about wolverines fucking, and sometimes he sang along under his breath. He listened to the record so much that he wore down the grooves to where you could hardly hear anything, and he started singing a little bit louder to make up for it. Finally, the old biddy who ran the Victrola Room got wind of his lyrics and gave him the boot. For weeks he jerked off to fantasies of Coleman the Wolverine butt raping her.

Delores kept bothering Coleman for Sister Aimee money; he took a job at the Joredco Dental Lab and gave her a percentage tithe. The work was pulling animal teeth out of decapitated trophy heads, and he loved it. He watched the more skilled workers make dentures with the teeth, fashioning plastic and mortar paste into choppers that could bite for eternity. He stole a set of bobcat plates and played with them when he honked his sax up in the hills. He pretended he was a bobcat and that Delores and his phony brothers and sisters were afraid of him.

Joredco laid Coleman off when the boss found a wetback family who'd work for an extra-low group rate. Coleman was hurt and tried to get a job at a couple of other dental labs, but found out Joredco was the only one that made dentures with *real* animal teeth. He took to prowling around after dark—*real* dark—everybody shut in behind blackout curtains so the Japs wouldn't see all the lights and do L.A. like they did Pearl Harbor.

Coleman composed music in his head while he prowled; curiosity about life behind the curtains almost drove him crazy. There was a list on the wall at a local barber shop: Bunker Hill citizens who were *good* citizens working defense jobs. The list said who was working days, swing and graveyard. Coleman took the names to the phone book and matched them to addresses; from there he made phone calls—a phony census poll—and figured out who was married and who wasn't. Unmarried and graveyard meant a Coleman foray.

He forayed a bunch of times: in through an unlocked window, busting open a woodbox door, sometimes chiseling a door jamb. He took little things and money to keep Delores off his back. His best catch was a stuffed bobcat. But Coleman liked just *being* in the empty houses best. It was fun to pretend to be an animal that could appreciate music. It was fun to be in dark places and pretend you could see in the dark.

Early in June, Coleman was on the Hill Street trolley and heard two guys talking about a strange-o named Thomas Cormier and the smelly animals he kept behind his house on Carondelet. One man recited the names: weasels, ferrets, badgers, otters and wolverines. Coleman got excited, census-called Thomas Cormier and learned he worked nights at the Griffith Park Zoo. The next night, armed with a flashlight, he visited the wolverines and fell in love with them.

They were nasty. They were vicious. They took shit from no one. They tried to chew through the front of their cages to get at him. They had a snarl that sounded like the high notes on his sax.

Coleman left; he didn't burglarize the house, because he wanted to keep coming back for more visits. He read up on the lore of the wolverine and reveled in tales of its savagery. He set rat traps in Griffith Park and brought his catch back for the wolverines to eat dead. He brought hamsters and fed them to the wolverines live. He shone his flashlight on the wolverines and watched them gorge on his goodies. He came without touching himself while he watched.

Coleman's summer was marred by Delores pestering him for more money. Late in July, he read in the paper about a local bachelor who worked swing shift at Lockheed and owned a valuable coin collection. He decided to steal it, sell it and parcel the money out to Delores so she'd leave him alone.

On the night of August 2, Coleman tried—and was captured inside the house by the owner and two friends of his. He went for the owner's eyes like a good wolverine—unsuccessfully—but managed to get away. He ran the six blocks home, found Delores and a strange man going 69 on the couch with the lights on, was repulsed and ran back outside in a panic. He tried to run for the wolverine house, but the coin collection man and his pals—trawling in a car—found him. They drove him out to Sleepy Lagoon Park and beat him; the coin collection man wanted to castrate him, but his friends held him back. They left him there beaten bloody, composing music in his head.

Coleman stumbled over to a grassy knoll and saw—*or thought he saw*—a big white man beating a Mexican youth with his fists, slashing at his clothes with a razor-bladed two-by-four. The white man railed in a thick brogue: "Spic filth! I'll teach you to traffic with clean young white girls!" He ran the boy down with a car and drove away.

Coleman examined the Mexican youth and found him dead. He made it home, lied to Delores about his injuries and spent time recuperating. Seventeen Mexican boys were indicted for the Sleepy Lagoon killing; a social ruckus over their innocence ensued; the boys were quickly put on trial and languished in jail. Coleman sent the L.A. Police Department anonymous letters during the trial—he described the monster he had come to call the Scotch Voice Man and told what really happened. Months passed; Coleman played his sax, afraid to burglarize, afraid to visit his wolverine friends. He worked skid row day labor and kicked back most of the scratch to keep Delores off his case. Then one day the Scotch Voice Man himself came walking up the steps of 236 South Beaudry.

Delores and his half sisters were gone for the day; Coleman hid out, realizing what must have happened: he left fingerprints on the letters and Scotch Voice retrieved the notes and compared the prints against the prints in his Selective Service file. Coleman hid out all that day and the next; Delores told him an "evil man" was looking for him. He knew he had to run, but had no money; he got an idea: check crazy momma's scrapbook of old flames for men that he resembled.

Coleman found four photographs of a summer-stock actor named Randolph Lawrence—the dates on the back of the pictures and a strongish facial resemblance said this was his daddy. He copped two of the snapshots, hitchhiked to Hollywood and told a fish story to a clerk at the Screen Actors Guild. She believed his abridged tale of parental abandonment, checked the Guild files and informed him that Randolph Lawrence was really Reynolds Loftis, a character actor of some note: 816 Belvedere, Santa Monica Canyon.

The child showed up at his father's door. Reynolds Loftis was touched, pooh-poohed the story of the Scotch Voice Man, admitted his parentage and gave Coleman shelter.

Loftis was living with a screenwriter named Chaz Minear; the two men were lovers. They were members of the Hollywood leftist community, they were party-hopping devotees of avant-garde cinema. Coleman spied on them in bed—he both loved and hated it. He went with them to parties thrown by a Belgian film-maker; the man screened movies featuring naked men and snapping dogs that reminded him of his wolverines—and the films obsessed him. Reynolds was generous with money and didn't mind that he spent his days in the back yard honking his alto. Coleman started hanging out at jazz clubs in the Valley and met a trombone player named Mad Marty Goines.

Mad Marty was a heroin fiend, a reefer seller, a burglar and a second-rate horn. He was a lowlife's lowlife, with a legitimate gift: teaching thievery and music. Marty taught Coleman how to hot-wire cars and really blow alto, showing him how to shape notes, read music, take his repertoire of noises and powerful lungs and use them to make sounds that meant something.

It was now the winter of '43. Coleman was shedding his baby fat, getting handsome. Reynolds became demonstrative to him, physically affectionate—lots of hugs and kisses on the cheek. He suddenly credited the story of the Scotch Voice Man. He joined the Sleepy Lagoon Defense Committee—a hot lefty item now that the seventeen boys had been convicted—to prove his faith in Coleman.

Reynolds told Coleman to be quiet about the Scotch Voice Man—nobody would believe him, and the important thing was to get the poor persecuted boys out of jail. He told him Scotch Voice would never be caught, but the evil man was probably still looking for Coleman—who needed protective coloration to remain safe from him. Reynolds took Coleman to Dr. Terence Lux and had his face physically altered to his own specifications. While recuperating at the clinic, Coleman went crazy, killing chickens in the hatchery, pretending he was a wolverine while he drank their blood. He got leaves from the clinic and pulled burglaries with Mad Marty, his face bandaged like a movie monster; he went to SLDC rallies with his attentive father—and against his wishes told the story of José Diaz and the Scotch Voice Man. Nobody believed him, everyone patronized him as Reynolds Loftis' nutty kid brother burned in a fire—lies his father told him to go along with. Then the bandages came off and Coleman *was* his father twenty years younger. And Reynolds seduced his own youthful mirror image.

Coleman went with it. He knew he was safe from Scotch Voice; while recovering from the surgery he did not know how his new face would look, but he knew now that he was beautiful.

The perversion was awful but continually exciting, like being a wolverine prowling a strange dark house twenty-four hours a day. Acting the part of a platonic kid brother was an intriguing subterfuge; Coleman knew Daddy was terrified of their secret coming out and kept mum—he knew also that Reynolds was going to rallies and donating money to causes because he felt guilty for seducing him. Maybe the surgery was not for his safety—just for the seduction. Chaz moved out—bitter over the horrific cuckolding—spurning Reynolds' offer to make it a ménage à trois. Minear went on a sex bender then, a different Felix Gordean male prostitute every night—Reynolds lived in terror of his ex-lover telling them of the incest and tricked with a bunch of prosties himself, for the sex and to keep his ear down. Coleman was jealous, but kept still about it, and his father's sudden frugality and displays of nervousness convinced him that Reynolds was being blackmailed. Then Coleman met Claire De Haven and fell in love with her.

She was Reynolds' friend and confrere in various leftist organizations, and she became Coleman's confidante. Coleman had begun to find sex with his father intolerable; he pretended the man was Claire to get through their nights together. Claire heard Coleman's horror story out and convinced him to see Dr. Lesnick, the CP's approved psychiatrist—Saul would never violate confidentiality with an analysand.

Lesnick heard Coleman out—in a series of arduously detailed two-hour sessions. He believed the Sleepy Lagoon story to be fabricated on two levels: Coleman needing to justify his search for his father and his own latent homosexuality; Coleman wanting to curry favor with SLDC Latins by saying the killer was white—not the unfound Mexican gang members the leftist community asserted the slayers to be. That aside, he believed Coleman's narratives, comforted him and urged him to break off the affair with his father.

Lesnick was also seeing Loftis as a patient; he knew Reynolds was guilt-crazed over the affair, giving more and more money to more and more causes—especially the SLDC—an adjunct of the lever of manipulation he had applied to get Coleman to consent to the plastic job. Coleman felt reality closing in and began visiting Thomas Cormier's wolverines again, feeding and loving them. One night he felt an incredible urge to pet and hold one. He opened a pen, tried to embrace the beast and was bitten all over his arms. He and the wolverine fought; Coleman won with a stranglehold. He took the carcass home, skinned it, ate its flesh raw and made dentures out of its teeth, wearing them in his private hours, pretending to be the wolverine—stalking, fucking, killing.

Time passed.

Reynolds, convinced by Claire and Lesnick, broke off the liaison with Coleman. Coleman resented his sex power being usurped and started hating Daddy outright. The boys convicted of the Sleepy Lagoon killing were exonerated and released from prison—the SLDC largely responsible for securing the piece of justice. Claire and Coleman continued to talk, but now sporadically. Coleman copped Southside heroin for her to dally with; Claire was more disturbed than pleased by the gesture, but she did give Coleman a two-thousand-dollar loan he asked for. He used the money to buy himself a second Terry Lux surgery, the doctor going at his face with weighted boxing gloves, then holing him up at the hatchery with morphine and syringes to keep himself painless. Coleman read anatomy and physiology texts there; he left the clinic, kicked the drug cold turkey and showed up at Claire's door black and blue, but not looking like his father. When he asked Claire to sleep with him, she ran away in horror.

1945.

Coleman moved out of Los Angeles, Claire's revulsion a hot wind at his back. He bummed around the country and played alto with pickup bands, taking Hudson Healy's surname. In '47, Reynolds Loftis went before HUAC, refused to inform and was blacklisted; Coleman read about it and was delighted. Coleman was living in a world of impacted rage: fantasies of hurting his father, possessing Claire, raping men who looked at him the wrong way and eating their flesh with the wolverine teeth he still carried everywhere. Composing music and playing it was the only thing holding him glued. Then, back in L.A. at the end of '49, he read that Daddy and Claire were getting married. His threadbare, jerry-built world crashed in.

Coleman's fantasies escalated to where he couldn't even think of music. He knew he had to act on the fantasies and build a purpose around them, clear and precise like what his music meant to him. He found out about Reynolds' UAES membership and learned when the union held its Executive Committee meetings. He decided to kill sex partners of his father's—ones he remembered from the time of Daddy's breakup with Chaz. Coleman recalled George Wiltsie and Latin lover Augie by face and name, but they would never be able to identify him: at the time he was protectively colored as a lowly kid brother. He remembered other Reynolds conquests strictly by face, but knew the bars they frequented. Finding victims would be easy, the rest of it more difficult.

The plan:

Kill the Reynolds lovers on UAES meeting nights, disguised as Reynolds, spreading Reynolds' identical O+ seed, dropping clues to point to Reynolds as the killer, forcing him to—at worst—be implicated in the murders, or—milder punishment—cough up his treasonous UAES meetings as alibis. Daddy could be convicted of the crimes; he could be a suspect and have to admit his homosexuality to the police; he might get smeared in the press, and if he used his precious union soirees as alibis, he might ruin his newly resurrected movie career on grounds of Pinko associations.

Coleman knew he needed money to finance his killing spree, and he was only making chump change gigging on Central Avenue. On Christmas Eve he ran into his old pal Marty Goines at Bido Lito's. Marty was surprised—and happy—it was the first time he'd seen Coleman post-bandages, years had gone by, the boy had become a man with a new face—and was not a bad alto. Coleman suggested they pull another B&E string; Mad Marty agreed. They made plans to talk after New Year's; then, early New Year's Eve, Goines saw Coleman outside Malloy's Nest and told him he'd called a Quentin buddy in Frisco, Leo Bordoni, and invited him to join their gang. Coleman, enraged at not being consulted—but not showing it—determined that Goines hadn't mentioned him or described him to Bordoni and decided that his old jazz mentor was prime wolverine bait. He told Marty to meet him at 67th and Central at 12:15, and to be quiet about it—there was a reason.

Coleman went to his room and got the Reynolds gray wig and makeup kit he'd brought. He fashioned a zoot stick from a plank he found in the garbage and a Gillette five-pack. He snapped that UAES was holding a party/meeting that night, copped four H bindles and a hypo from his old source Roland Navarette, pegged an unlocked Buick on 67th as his wheels, played his last gig at the Zombie, walked into the men's can at the Texaco Station on 68th as Coleman, walked out as Daddy.

Marty was right on time, but drunk—he didn't even blink at
Coleman's disguise. Coleman coldcocked him on the sidewalk,
slung him against his shoulder like a boozed-out buddy, got him
into the Buick and hot-wired it. He geezed Marty up with a
heavy junk load, drove him to his crib in Hollywood, shot him
with the other three bindles and stuffed the hood of a terrycloth
robe in his mouth so he wouldn't vomit blood on him when his
cardiac arteries burst. Marty's heart popped big; Coleman strangled the rest of his life out, zoot slashed his back, pulled out his
eyes like he tried to with the coin collection man back at Sleepy
Lagoon. He raped those bare sockets; he put on his wolverine
teeth and feasted, spraying blood on the walls to wild alto riffs in
his head. When he was finished he left the eyeballs in the Frigidaire, dressed Goines in the white terry robe, carried him downstairs and propped him up in the back seat of the Buick. He adjusted
the rear-view mirror so he could watch Marty with his eyeless
head lolling; he drove to Sunset Strip in the rain, thinking of
Daddy and Claire reamed to their teeth in every orifice. He depos-
ited Marty nude in a vacant lot on Allegro, prime fruit territory,
a corpse on display like the Black Dahlia. If he was lucky, victim
number one would get just as much ink.

Coleman went back to his music, his other life. The Goines
kill did not reap the publicity he hoped it would—the Dahlia was
a beautiful woman, Marty an anonymous transient. Coleman
rented U-Drive cars and patrolled 2307 Tamarind at odd times;
no cops showed up—he could use the place again. He got George
Wiltsie's address from the phone book and decided that Wiltsie
would be victim number two. He spent nights cruising queer
bars near the pad, saw Wiltsie at the dives, but always in the company of his squeeze, a guy he called "Duane." He almost decided
to let the bastard live—but thinking of the possibilities a duo kill
presented made him tingly and reminded him of Delores and the
man going 69. Then Duane mentioned to a barman that he
worked at Variety International—old Daddy turf.

Providence.

Coleman approached George and Duane, carrying a little kill
kit he'd concocted: secobarbital caps bought from Roland Navarette,
and strychnine from the drugstore. Two to one, barbiturate to
poison—pinpricks on the capsules for a quick effect. Coleman
suggested a party at "his place" in Hollywood; George and Duane
accepted. On the ride over in his U-Drive, he gave them a pint

of rye to slug from. When they were half gassed, he asked them if they'd like to try some real Spanish Fly. Both men eagerly swallowed death pills; by the time they got to Marty's dump they were so woozy Coleman had to help them upstairs. Lindenaur was DOA, Wiltsie in a deep slumber. Coleman undressed them and went to work zooting the dead guy.

Wiltsie woke up and fought to live. Coleman slashed one of the fruiter's fingers off defending himself and killed him with a knife thrust to the throat. With both men dead, he zooted, wolverined, raped the standard way and drew music pictures and a trademark W on the walls. He put Wiltsie's digit in the icebox; he showered Duane and George free of blood, wrapped them in spare blankets, carried them down and drove to Griffith Park, his old sax-honking territory. He stripped them and carried them up to the hiking trail; he 69'd them for the world to see. If *he* was seen, he was seen as his father.

Two events coincided.

Dr. Saul Lesnick, near death and wanting to somehow recoup his moral losses, read a scandal tabloid account of the Wiltsie/ Lindenaur murders. He recalled Wiltsie as a name bandied in a Reynolds Loftis psychiatric session years before; the zoot slashing reminded him of Coleman's fantasies regarding the Scotch Voice Man and the weapons at Terry Lux's hatchery. What finally convinced him that Coleman was the killer was the hunger behind the obliquely described bite marks. Coleman was hunger personified. Coleman wanted to be the most vicious, insatiable animal on earth, and now he was proving that he was.

Lesnick knew the police would kill Coleman if they caught him. Lesnick knew he had to try to get him to a locked-ward institution before he killed anyone else or took it in mind to go after Reynolds and Claire. He knew Coleman had to be close to the music, and found him playing at a club on Central Avenue. He regained Coleman's confidence as the one person who had never hurt him, secured him a cheap apartment in Compton and talked, talked, talked to him, hiding with him when a friend in the leftist community told him Reynolds and Claire were also seeking Coleman out. Coleman was experiencing moments of clarity—a classic behavior pattern in sexual psychopaths who had succumbed to murder to satisfy their lusts. He poured out the story of his first three killings; Lesnick knew that chauffeuring a dead man in the back seat and the second two victims brought to

Tamarind Street were a pure subconscious attempt to be caught. Psychological craters existed for a skilled psychologist to drive wedges into—Saul Lesnick's redemption for ten years of informing on people he loved.

Coleman was fighting his urges inchoately, with music. He was working on a long solo piece filled with eerie silences to signify lies and duplicities. The riffs would spotlight the unique high sounds he got with his sax, loud at first, then getting softer, with longer intervals of silence. The piece would end on a scale of diminishing notes, then unbroken quiet—which Coleman saw as being louder than any noise he could produce. He wanted to call his composition The Big Nowhere. Lesnick told him that if he got to a hospital, he would survive to perform it. The doctor saw Coleman faltering, clarity gaining. Then Coleman told him about Danny Upshaw.

He'd met Upshaw the night after he killed Marty Goines. The detective was on a routine canvassing assignment, and Coleman brazened him out with his "I was in plain view all night" alibi, knowing Upshaw believed it. That belief meant Goines had kept mum about meeting him, and Coleman took the opportunity to lie about Marty being fruit and drop clues on tall, gray Daddy. He put Upshaw out of his mind and went on with his plan, killing Wiltsie and Lindenaur, wavering between Augie Duarte or another Daddy squeeze he knew as victim number four. But he'd started having dreams about the young detective, steamy stuff that said he really was what Daddy tried to make him. Coleman made a decision to murder Reynolds and Claire if he couldn't smear Daddy to the rafters—he thought that potential added blood to his stew would spice him up and make him dream about the women he once loved.

The plan didn't work. Coleman had more Upshaw dreams, more Upshaw fantasies. He was Daddy-garbed and in the process of staking out Felix Gordean's office for leads on old Reynolds lovers when he spotted Upshaw holding down his own surveillance; he was nearby when Upshaw phoned the DMV Police Information Line. He caught the gist of his talk, and tailed Upshaw in the Pontiac he'd stolen—just to get close to him. Upshaw spotted the tail; a chase followed; Coleman got away, stole another car, called the DMV and pretended to be the deputy's partner. One of the names the clerk read back to him was Augie Duarte; Coleman decided it was providence again and settled on him as victim four then and there. He drove to Gordean's beach house, spotted Upshaw's car, hid and listened to Gordean and one of his musclemen talking. The pimp/queer expert said, "That policeman is coming out of the closet. I know it."

The next day, Coleman let himself into Upshaw's apartment and savored it. He saw no mementoes of women, nothing but a too-tidy, impersonal pad. Coleman *knew* then, and began to feel a complete identification with Upshaw, a symbiosis. That night, Lesnick left the apartment to get medicine at County General, thinking Coleman's Upshaw fixation would break him down on his homosexuality, stymie and stalemate him. He was wrong. Coleman picked up Augie Duarte at a downtown bar, sedated him and took him to an abandoned garage in Lincoln Heights. He strangled him and hacked him and ate him and emasculated him like Daddy and all the others had tried to do to him. He left the body in the L.A. River wash, drove back to Compton and told Lesnick he had finally put Upshaw in perspective. He was going to compete with the man, killer against detective. Saul Lesnick left the apartment and took a cab back to his rest home, knowing Coleman Healy would wreak slaughter until he was slaughtered himself. And the frail old headshrinker had been trying to get up the guts for a mercy killing ever since.

* * *

Lesnick ended his narrative with a deft storyteller's flourish, pulling a revolver from the folds of his robe. He said, "I saw Coleman one more time. He had read that Upshaw died accidentally and was very disturbed by it. He had just purchased opiates from Navarette and was going to kill another man, a man who had been an extra on one of Reynolds' films, an opium dabbler. The man had a brief fling with Reynolds and Coleman was going to kill him. He told me, like he thought I would do nothing to stop it. I bought this gun at a pawn shop in Watts. I was going to kill Coleman that night, but you and Captain Considine got to him first."

Buzz looked at the piece. It was old and rusted and would probably misfire, like the shrinker's nutso take on Sleepy Lagoon as a fantasy. Coleman would have slapped it out of his bony hand before Pops could pull the trigger. "You pleased the way it turned out, Doc?"

"No. I am sorry for Reynolds."

Buzz thought of Mal shooting straight at Daddy—wanting Coleman alive for his career and maybe something to do with his own kid. "I've got a cop question, Doc."

Lesnick said, "Please. Ask me."

"Well, I thought Terry Lux hipped Gordean to all the stuff Gordean blackmailed Loftis with. Your story makes me think Chaz Minear told Felix some details, details that he put together when he blackmailed Loftis a second time just lately. Stuff that made him think Coleman was killin' people."

Lesnick smiled. "Yes, Chaz told Felix Gordean many things about Coleman's clinic stay that could be construed as clues when put together with newspaper facts. I read that Gordean was murdered. Was it Chaz?"

"Yeah. Does that please you?"

"It's a small happy ending, yes."

"Any thoughts on Claire?"

"Yes. She'll survive your grand jury pogrom like a Tigress. She'll find another weak man to protect and other causes to champion. She'll do good for people who deserve good done for them, and I will not comment on her character."

Buzz said, "Before things got out of control, it looked like the UAES had some kind of extortion scheme brewin' against the studios. Were you playin' both ends? Holdin' back stuff you heard as a psychiatrist to help the union?"

Lesnick coughed and said, "Who wants to know?"

"Two dead men and me."

"And who else will hear?"

"Just me."

"I believe you. Why, I don't know."

"Dead men got no reason to lie. Come on, Doc. Spill."

Lesnick fondled his pawnshop piece. "I have verified information on Mr. Howard Hughes and his penchant for underaged girls, and much information on various RKO and Variety International actors and the narcotics cures they periodically undergo. I have information on the underworld associations of many studio executives, including one RKO gentleman who ran down a family of four in his car and killed them. The arrest was fixed, and it never went to trial, but that allegation by itself would be most embarrassing. So the UAES is not without weapons, you see."

Buzz said, "Boss, I pimped them girls to Howard and fixed up most of them dope cures. I got that RKO guy off the hook and ran the payoff to the judge that woulda arraigned him. Doc, the papers would never print what you got and the radio would never put it on the air. Howard Hughes and Herman Gerstein would laugh your extortion right back in your face. I'm the best fixer this town ever saw, and believe me the UAES is crucified."

Saul Lesnick got to his feet, wobbled, but stayed standing. He said, "And how will you fix that?"

Buzz walked on the question.

* * *

When he got back to his motel, there was a note from the manager on the door: "Call Johnny S." Buzz went to the pay phone and dialed Stompanato's number.

"Talk to me."

"It's Meeks. What's up?"

"Your number, but hopefully not my money. I just got a lead, through a friend of Mickey's. LAPD did a routine ballistics run-through on that jazz club shootout you were in. That hot-shot coroner Layman examined the report on the pills they took out of that rat guy you told me about. It looked familiar, so he checked back. Bullets from your gun matched the pills they took out of Gene Niles. LAPD makes you for the Niles snuff, and they're out to get you in force. Shoot to kill. And I hate to men-tion it, but you owe me a lot of money."

Buzz sighed. "Johnny, you're a rich man."

"What?"

Buzz said, "Meet me here tomorrow at noon," and hung up. He dialed an East L.A. number and got, "Quien? Quien es?"

"Speak English, Chico, it's Meeks."

"Buzz! My Padrone!"

"I'm changin' my order, Chico. No thirty-thirty, make it a sawed-off."

".12 gauge, Padrone?"

"Bigger, Chico. The biggest you got."

42

THE SHOTGUN was a .10 gauge pump with a foot-long barrel. The slugs held triple-aught buckshot. The five rounds in the breech were enough to turn Mickey Cohen's haberdashery and the dope summit personnel into dog food. Buzz was carrying the weapon in a venetian blind container covered with Christmas wrapping paper.

His U-Drive clunker was at the curb a half block south of Sunset. The haberdashery lot was packed with Jew canoes and guinea gunboats; one sentry was stationed by the front door shooing away customers; the man by the back door looked half asleep, sitting in a chair catching a full blast of late-morning sun. Two neutral triggers accounted for—Dudley and the fourth man had to be inside with the action.

Buzz waved at the guy up on the corner—his prepaid accomplice recruited from a wine bar. The guy walked into the lot looking furtive, trying Caddy and Lincoln door handles, skirting the last row of cars by the fence. Buzz eased up slowly, waiting for the sentry to take note and pounce.

It took the sunbird almost half a minute to stir, get wise and tread over, a hand inside his jacket pocket. Buzz ran full speed, fat lightning on sneakered feet.

The sentry turned around at the last second; Buzz swung the Christmas box in his face and knocked him against the hood of a '49 Continental. The man pulled his gun; Buzz kneed him in the nards, popped his nose with a flat palm and watched the .45 auto hit the blacktop. Another knee spear put him down and keening; Buzz kicked the gun away, whipped off the box and used the butt of his sawed-off to beat him quiet.

The accomplice was gone; the sentry was bleeding at the mouth and nose, deep off in dreamland—maybe for keeps. Buzz pocketed the loose cannon, walked over to the back door and let himself in.

Laughter and hail-fellow dialogue booming; a short corridor lined with dressing rooms. Buzz inched up to a curtain, pulled a corner back and looked.

The summit was in full swing. Mickey Cohen and Jack Dragna were glad-handing each other, standing by a table laid out with cold cuts, bottles of beer and liquor. Davey Goldman, Mo Jahelka and Dudley Smith were knocking back highballs; a line of Dragna humps was standing by the front window curtains. Johnny Stompanato was nowhere to be seen because Johnny Stompanato was probably halfway to Pedro by now, hoping a certain fat man survived the morning. Over by the left wall, the real business was happening: two Mex National types counting a suitcase full of money while one Mickey guy and one Jack guy taste-tested the white-brown powder stuffed into reinforced paper bags in another suitcase. Their smiles said the stuff tasted good.

Buzz pulled the curtain aside and joined the party, sliding a round into the chamber to get some attention. The noise caused heads to turn, drinks and plates of food to drop; Dudley Smith smiled; Jack Dragna eyed the barrel. Buzz saw a cop type by the Mexes. Twenty to one he and Dudley were the only ones heeled; Dud was much too smart to try something. Mickey Cohen looked hurt. He said, "As God is my witness I will do you worse than I did the guy who did Hooky Rothman."

Buzz felt his whole body floating away from him. The Mexes were starting to look scared; a rap on the window would bring the outside man. He stepped over to where he could see every face in the room and trained his muzzle for a blast spread: Jack and Mickey vaporized the second he pulled the trigger. "The money and the dope in one of your garment bags, Mick. Now and slow."

Mickey said, "Davey, he'll shoot. *Do it.*"

Buzz saw Davey Goldman cross his vision and start talking low Spanish to the Mexes. He caught a slant view of paper sacks and greenbacks being ladled into a zippered hanger bag, tan canvas with red piping and Mickey Cohen's face embossed on the front. Mickey said, "If you send Audrey back to me I will not harm a hair on her head and I will not do you slow. If I find her with you, mercy I cannot promise. Send her back to me."

A million-dollar deal blown—and all Mickey Cohen could think of was a woman. "No."

The bag was zipped up; Goldman walked it over extra slow. Buzz held his left arm out straight; Mickey was shaking like a hophead dying for a fix. Buzz wondered what he'd say next; the little big man said, "*Please.*"

The garment bag settled; Buzz felt his arm buckling. Dudley Smith winked. Buzz said, "I'll be back for you, lad. Diaz and Hartshorn."

Dudley laughed. "You won't live the day."

Buzz backed into the curtains. "Don't go out the rear door, it's booby-trapped."

Mickey Cohen said, "*Please.* You can't run with her. Not a hair on her head will I hurt."

Buzz getawayed.

*　*　*

Johnny Stompanato was waiting for him at the motel, lying on the bed listening to an opera on the radio. Buzz dropped the garment bag, unzipped it and pulled out ten ten-thousand-dollar bank stacks. Johnny's jaw dropped; his cigarette hit his chest and burned a hole in his shirt. He snuffed the butt with a pillow and said, "You did it."

Buzz threw the money on the bed. "Fifty for you, fifty for Mrs. Celeste Considine, 641 South Gramercy, L.A. You make the delivery, and tell her it's for the kid's education."

Stompanato hoarded the money into a tight little pile and gloated over it. "How do you know I won't keep it all?"

"You like my style too much to fuck me."

*   *   *

Buzz drove up to Ventura, parked in front of Deputy Dave Kleckner's house and rang the bell. Audrey answered. She was wearing an old Mickey shirt and dungarees, just like she was the first time he kissed her. She looked at the garment bag and said, "Planning to stay awhile?"

"Maybe. You look tired."

"I was up all night thinking."

Buzz put his hands to her face, smoothing a wisp of stray hair. "Dave home?"

"Dave's on duty until late, and I think he's in love with me."

"Everybody's in love with you."

"Why?"

"Because you make them afraid to be alone."

"Does that include you?"

"Me especially."

Audrey jumped into his arms. Buzz let go of the garment bag and kicked it for luck. He carried his lioness into the front bedroom and made a swipe at the light switch; Audrey grabbed his hand. "Leave it on. I want to see you."

Buzz got out of his clothes and sat on the edge of the bed; Audrey slow-grinded herself naked and leaped on him. They kissed ten times as long as they usually did and strung out everything else they'd ever done together. Buzz went into her fast, but moved extra slow; she pushed up with her hips harder than she did their first time. He couldn't hold it and didn't want to; she went crazy when he did. Like the first time, they thrashed the sheets off the bed and held each other, sweating. Buzz remembered how he'd hooked a finger around Audrey's wrist so they'd still be touching while he caught his breath. He did it again, but this time she squeezed his whole hand like she didn't know what the gesture meant.

They curled up, Audrey nuzzling. Buzz looked around the strange bedroom. Passport applications and stacks of South American tourist brochures were resting on the nightstand and boxes of women's clothing were arrayed by the door next to a brand-new suitcase. Audrey yawned, kissed his chest like it was sleep time and yawned again. Buzz said, "Sweetie, did Mickey ever hit you?"

A drowsy head shake in answer. "Talk later. *Lots* of talk later."

"Did he ever?"

"No, only men." Another yawn. "No Mickey talk, remember our deal?"

"Yeah, I remember."

Audrey gave him a squeeze and settled into sleep. Buzz picked up the brochure closest to him, a huckster job for Rio de Janeiro. He flipped pages, saw that Audrey had circled listings for guest cottages offering newlywed rates and tried to picture an on-the-lam cop-killer and a thirty-seven-year-old ex-stripper basking in the South American sun. He couldn't. He tried to picture Audrey waiting for him while he attempted to lay off twenty-five pounds of heroin to some renegade mob guy who hadn't already heard of the heist and the contract that went with it. He couldn't. He tried to picture Audrey with him when the LAPD closed in, hard-on glory cops holding their fire because the killer was with a woman. He couldn't. He thought of Icepick Fritzie finding them together, going icepick crazy on Audrey's face—and that picture was easy. Mickey saying "Please" and going mushy with forgiveness was even easier.

Buzz listened to Audrey's breath; he felt her sweaty skin cooling. He tried to picture her getting some kind of bookkeeper's job, going home to Mobile, Alabama, and meeting a nice insurance man looking for a Southern belle. He couldn't. He made a big last try at the two of them buying their way out of the country with a nationwide cop-killer APB on his head. He tried extra, extra hard on that one—and couldn't find a way to make it stick.

Audrey stirred and rolled away from him. Buzz saw Mickey tired of her in a few years, cutting her loose for some younger stuff, a nice cash money separation gift. He saw Sheriff's, City cops, Feds and Cohen goons chasing his okie ass to the moon. He saw Ellis Loew and Ed Satterlee on easy street and old Doc Lesnick hounding him with, "And how will you fix that?"

Lesnick was the kicker. Buzz got up, walked into the living room, grabbed the phone and had the operator get him Los Angeles CR-4619. A voice answered, "Yeah?"

It was Mickey. Buzz said, "She's at 1006 Montebello Drive in Ventura. You hurt her and I'll do you slower than you ever thought of doin' me."

Mickey said, "Mazel tov. My friend, you are still dead, but you are dead very fast."

Buzz let the receiver down gently, went back to the bedroom and dressed. Audrey was in the same position, her head buried in the pillow, no way to see her face. Buzz said, "You were the one," and turned off the light. He grabbed his garment bag on the way out and left the door unlocked.

* * *

Dawdling on back roads got him to the San Fernando Valley just after 7:30—full evening, black and starry. Ellis Loew's house was dark and there were no cars parked out front.

Buzz walked around to the garage, broke a clasp on the door and pushed it open. Moonlight picked out a roof bulb at the end of a string. He pulled the cord and saw what he wanted on a low shelf: two double-gallon cans of gasoline. He picked them up, found them near full, carried them to the front door and let himself in with his special-investigator's key.

A flick of the overhead light; the living room jarring white— walls, tables, cartons, shelves and odd mounds of paper—Loew and company's once-in-a-lifetime shot at the political moon. Graphs and charts and thousands of pages of coerced testimony. Boxes of photographs with linked faces to prove treason. A big fuckload of lies glued together to prove a single theory that was easy to believe because believing was easier than wading through the glut of horseshit to say, "Wrong."

Buzz doused the walls and shelves and tables and stacks of paper with gasoline. He soaked the Sleepy Lagoon Committee photos. He ripped down Ed Satterlee's graphs, emptied the cans on the floor and made a gas trail out to the porch. He lit a match, dropped it and watched the white whoosh into red and explode.

The fire spread back and upward; the house became a giant sheet of flame. Buzz got in his car and drove away, red glow lighting up the windshield. He took back streets northbound until the glow disappeared and he heard sirens whirring in the opposite direction. When the noise died, he was climbing into the foothills, Los Angeles just a neon smear in his rear-view mirror. He touched his future there on the seat: sawed-off, heroin, a hundred and fifty grand. It didn't feel right, so he turned on the radio and found a hillbilly station. The music was too soft and too sad, like a lament for a time when it all came cheap. He listened anyway. The songs made him think of himself and Mal and poor Danny Upshaw. Hardcases, rogue cops and Red chasers. Three dangerous men gone for parts unknown.

L.A. CONFIDENTIAL

To Mary Doherty Ellroy

A glory that costs everything and means nothing—

Steve Erickson

PROLOGUE

FEBRUARY 21, 1950

AN ABANDONED auto court in the San Berdoo foothills; Buzz Meeks checked in with ninety-four thousand dollars, eighteen pounds of high-grade heroin, a 10-gauge pump, a .38 special, a .45 automatic and a switchblade he'd bought off a pachuco at the border—right before he spotted the car parked across the line: Mickey Cohen goons in an LAPD unmarked, Tijuana cops standing by to bootjack a piece of his goodies, dump his body in the San Ysidro River.

He'd been running a week; he'd spent fifty-six grand staying alive: cars, hideouts at four and five thousand a night—risk rates—the innkeepers knew Mickey C. was after him for heisting his dope summit and his woman, the L.A. Police wanted him for killing one of their own. The Cohen contract kiboshed an outright dope sale—nobody could move the shit for fear of reprisals; the best he could do was lay it off with Doc Englekling's sons—Doc would freeze it, package it, sell it later and get him his percentage. Doc used to work with Mickey and had the smarts to be afraid of the prick; the brothers, charging fifteen grand, sent him to the El Serrano Motel and were setting up his escape. Tonight at dusk, two men—wetback runners—would drive him to a beanfield, shoot him to Guatemala City via white powder airlines. He'd have twenty-odd pounds of Big H working for him stateside—if *he* could trust Doc's boys and *they* could trust the runners.

Meeks ditched his car in a pine grove, hauled his suitcase out, scoped the set-up:

The motel was horseshoe-shaped, a dozen rooms, foothills against the back of them—no rear approach possible.

The courtyard was loose gravel covered with twigs, paper debris, empty wine bottles—footsteps would crunch, tires would crack wood and glass.

There was only one access—the road he drove in on—reconnoiterers would have to trek thick timber to take a potshot.

Or they could be waiting in one of the rooms.

Meeks grabbed the 10-gauge, started kicking in doors. One, two, three, four—cobwebs, rats, bathrooms with plugged-up toilets, rotted food, magazines in Spanish—the runners probably used the place to house their spics en route to the slave farms up in Kern County. Five, six, seven, bingo on that—Mex families huddled on mattresses, scared of a white man with a gun, "There, there" to keep them pacified. The last string of rooms stood empty; Meeks got his satchel, plopped it down just inside unit 12: front/courtyard view, a mattress on box springs spilling kapok, not bad for a last American flop.

A cheesecake calendar tacked to the wall; Meeks turned to April and looked for his birthday. A Thursday—the model had bad teeth, looked good anyway, made him think of Audrey: ex-stripper, ex–Mickey inamorata; the reason he killed a cop, took down the Cohen/Dragna "H" deal. He flipped through to December, cut odds on whether he'd survive the year and got scared: gut flutters, a vein on his forehead going tap, tap, tap, making him sweat.

It got worse—the heebie-jeebies. Meeks laid his arsenal on a window ledge, stuffed his pockets with ammo: shells for the .38, spare clips for the automatic. He tucked the switchblade into his belt, covered the back window with the mattress, cracked the front window for air. A breeze cooled his sweat; he looked out at spic kids chucking a baseball.

He stuck there. Wetbacks congregated outside: pointing at the sun like they were telling time by it, hot for the truck to arrive— stoop labor for three hots and a cot. Dusk came on; the beaners started jabbering; Meeks saw two white men—one fat, one skinny—walk into the courtyard. They waved glad-hander style; the spics waved back. They didn't look like cops or Cohen goons. Meeks stepped outside, his 10-gauge right behind him.

The men waved: big smiles, no harm meant. Meeks checked the road—a green sedan parked crossways, blocking something light blue, too shiny to be sky through fir trees. He caught light off a metallic paint job, snapped: Bakersfield, the meet with the guys who needed time to get the money. *The robin's-egg coupe that tried to broadside him a minute later.*

Meeks smiled: friendly guy, no harm meant. A finger on the trigger; a make on the skinny guy: Mal Lunceford, a Hollywood Station harness bull—he used to ogle the carhops at Scrivener's

Drive-in, puff out his chest to show off his pistol medals. The fat man, closer, said, "We got that airplane waiting."

Meeks swung the shotgun around, triggered a spread. Fat Man caught buckshot and flew, covering Lunceford—knocking him backward. The wetbacks tore helter-skelter; Meeks ran into the room, heard the back window breaking, yanked the mattress. Sitting ducks: two men, three triple-aught rounds close in.

The two blew up; glass and blood covered three more men inching along the wall. Meeks leaped, hit the ground, fired at three sets of legs pressed together; his free hand flailed, caught a revolver off a dead man's waistband.

Shrieks from the courtyard; running feet on gravel. Meeks dropped the shotgun, stumbled to the wall. Over to the men, tasting blood—point-blank head shots.

Thumps in the room; two rifles in grabbing range. Meeks yelled, "We got him!," heard answering whoops, saw arms and legs coming out the window. He picked up the closest piece and let fly, full automatic: trapped targets, plaster chips exploding, dry wood igniting.

Over the bodies, into the room. The front door stood open; his pistols were still on the ledge. A strange thump sounded; Meeks saw a man spread prone—aiming from behind the mattress box.

He threw himself to the floor, kicked, missed. The man got off a shot—close; Meeks grabbed his switchblade, leaped, stabbed: the neck, the face, the man screaming, shooting—wide ricochets. Meeks slit his throat, crawled over and toed the door shut, grabbed the pistols and just plain breathed.

The fire spreading: cooking up bodies, fir pines; the front door his only way out. *How many more men standing trigger?*

Shots.

From the courtyard: heavy rounds knocking out wall chunks. Meeks caught one in the leg; a shot grazed his back. He hit the floor, the shots kept coming, the door went down—he was smack in the crossfire.

No more shots.

Meeks tucked his guns under his chest, spread himself dead-man style. Seconds dragged; four men walked in holding rifles. Whispers: "Dead meat"—"Let's be reeel careful"—"Crazy Okie fuck." Through the doorway, Mal Lunceford not one of them, footsteps.

Kicks in his side, hard breathing, sneers. A foot went under him. A voice said, "Fat fucker."

Meeks jerked the foot; the foot man tripped backward. Meeks spun around shooting—close range, all hits. Four men went down; Meeks got a topsy-turvy view: the courtyard, Mal Lunceford turning tail. Then, behind him, "Hello, lad."

Dudley Smith stepped through flames, dressed in a fire department greatcoat. Meeks saw his suitcase—ninety-four grand, dope—over by the mattress. "Dud, you came prepared."

"Like the Boy Scouts, lad. And have you a valediction?"

Suicide: heisting a deal Dudley S. watchdogged. Meeks raised his guns; Smith shot first. Meeks died—thinking the El Serrano Motel looked just like the Alamo.

PART ONE

BLOODY CHRISTMAS

1

BUD WHITE in an unmarked, watching the "1951" on the City Hall Christmas tree blink. The back seat was packed with liquor for the station party; he'd scrounged merchants all day, avoiding Parker's dictate: married men had the 24th and Christmas off, all duty rosters were bachelors only, the Central detective squad was detached to round up vagrants: the chief wanted local stumble-bums chilled so they wouldn't crash Mayor Bowron's lawn party for underprivileged kids and snarf up all the cookies. Last Christmas, some crazy nigger whipped out his wang, pissed in a pitcher of lemonade earmarked for some orphanage brats and ordered Mrs. Bowron to "Strap on, bitch." William H. Parker's first yuletide as chief of the Los Angeles Police Department was spent transporting the mayor's wife to Central Receiving for sedation, and now, a year later, *he* was paying the price.

The back seat, booze-packed, had his spine jammed to Jell-O. Ed Exley, the assistant watch commander, was a straight arrow who might get uppity over a hundred cops juicing in the muster room. And Johnny Stompanato was twenty minutes late.

Bud turned on his two-way. A hum settled: shopliftings, a liquor store heist in Chinatown. The passenger door opened; Johnny Stompanato slid in.

Bud turned on the dash light. Stompanato said, "Holiday cheers. And where's Stensland? I've got stuff for both of you."

Bud sized him up. Mickey Cohen's bodyguard was a month out of work—Mickey went up on a tax beef, Fed time, three to seven at McNeil Island. Johnny Stomp was back to home manicures and pressing his own pants. "It's *Sergeant* Stensland. He's rousting vags and the payoff's the same anyway."

"Too bad. I like Dick's style. You know that, *Wendell*."

Cute Johnny: guinea handsome, curls in a tight pompadour. Bud heard he was hung like a horse and padded his basket on top of it. "Spill what you got."

"Dick's better at the amenities than you, *Officer White*."

"You got a hard-on for me, or you just want small talk?"

"I've got a hard-on for Lana Turner, you've got a hard-on for wife beaters. I also heard you're a real sweetheart with the ladies and you're not too selective as far as looks are concerned."

Bud cracked his knuckles. "And you fuck people up for a living, and all the money Mickey gives to charity won't make him no better than a dope pusher and a pimp. So my fucking complaints for hardnosing wife beaters don't make me you. *Capisce*, shitbird?"

Stompanato smiled—nervous; Bud looked out the window. A Salvation Army Santa palmed coins from his kettle, an eye on the liquor store across the street. Stomp said, "Look, you want information and I need money. Mickey and Davey Goldman are doing time, and Mo Jahelka's looking after things while they're gone. Mo's diving for scraps, and he's got no work for me. Jack Whalen wouldn't hire me on a bet and there was no goddamn envelope from Mickey."

"No envelope? Mickey went up flush. I heard he got back the junk that got clouted off his deal with Jack D."

Stompanato shook his head. "You heard wrong. Mickey got the heister, but that junk is nowhere and the guy got away with a hundred and fifty grand of Mickey's money. So, Officer White, *I* need money. And if your snitch fund's still green, I'll get you some fucking-A collars."

"Go legit, Johnny. Be a white man like me and Dick Stensland."

Stomp snickered—it came off weak. "A key thief for twenty or a shoplifter who beats his wife for thirty. Go for the quick thrill, I saw the guy boosting Ohrbach's on the way over."

Bud took out a twenty and a ten; Stompanato grabbed them. "Ralphie Kinnard. He's blond and fat, about forty. He's wearing a suede loafer jacket and gray flannels. I heard he's been beating up his wife and pimping her to cover his poker losses."

Bud wrote it down. Stompanato said, "Yuletide cheer, Wendell."

Bud grabbed necktie and yanked; Stomp banged his head on the dashboard.

"Happy New Year, greaseball."

* * *

Ohrbach's was packed—shoppers swarmed counters and garment racks. Bud elbowed up to floor 3, prime shoplifter turf: jewelry, decanter liquor.

Countertops strewn with watches; cash register lines thirty deep. Bud trawled for blond males, got sideswiped by housewives and kids. Then—a flash view—a blond guy in a suede loafer ducking into the men's room.

Bud shoved over and in. Two geezers stood at urinals; gray flannels hit the toilet stall floor. Bud squatted, looked in—bingo on hands fondling jewelry. The oldsters zipped up and walked out; Bud rapped on the stall. "Come on, it's St. Nick."

The door flew open; a fist flew out. Bud caught it flush, hit a sink, tripped. Cufflinks in his face, Kinnard speedballing. Bud got up and chased.

Through the door, shoppers blocking him; Kinnard ducking out a side exit. Bud chased—over, down the fire escape. The lot was clean: no cars hauling, no Ralphie. Bud ran to his prowler, hit the two-way. "4A31 to dispatcher, requesting."

Static, then: "Roger, 4A31."

"Last known address. White male, first name Ralph, last name Kinnard. I guess that's K-I-N-N-A-R-D. Move it, huh?"

The man rogered; Bud threw jabs: bam-bam-bam-bam-bam. The radio crackled: "4A31, roger your request."

"4A31, roger."

"Positive on Kinnard, Ralph Thomas, white male, DOB—"

"Just the goddamn address, I told you—"

The dispatcher blew a raspberry. "For your Christmas stocking, shitbird. The address is 1486 Evergreen, and I hope you—"

Bud flipped off the box, headed east to City Terrace. Up to forty, hard on the horn, Evergreen in five minutes flat. The 12, 1300 blocks whizzed by; 1400—vet's prefabs—leaped out.

He parked, followed curb plates to 1486—a stucco job with a neon Santa sled on the roof. Lights inside; a prewar Ford in the driveway. Through a plate-glass window: Ralphie Kinnard browbeating a woman in a bathrobe.

The woman was puff-faced, thirty-fivish. She backed away from Kinnard; her robe fell open. Her breasts were bruised, her ribs lacerated.

Bud walked back for his cuffs, saw the two-way light blinking and rogered. "4A31 responding."

"Roger, 4A31, on an APO. Two patrolmen assaulted outside a tavern at 1990 Riverside, six suspects at large. They've been ID'd from their license plates and other units have been alerted."

Bud got tingles. "Bad for ours?"

"That's a roger. Go to 5314 Avenue 53, Lincoln Heights. Apprehend Dinardo, D-I-N-A-R-D-O, Sanchez, age twenty-one, male Mexican."

"Roger, and you send a prowler to 1486 Evergreen. White male suspect in custody. I won't be there, but they'll see him. Tell them I'll write it up."

"Book at Hollenbeck Station?"

Bud rogered, grabbed his cuffs. Back to the house and an outside circuit box—switches tapped until the lights popped off. Santa's sled stayed lit; Bud grabbed an outlet cord and yanked. The display hit the ground: exploding reindeer.

Kinnard ran out, tripped over Rudolph. Bud cuffed his wrists, bounced his face on the pavement. Ralphie yelped and chewed gravel; Bud launched his wife beater spiel. "You'll be out in a year and a half, and I'll know when. I'll find out who your parole officer is and get cozy with him, I'll visit you and say hi. You touch her again I'm gonna know, and I'm gonna get you violated on a kiddie raper beef. You know what they do to kiddie rapers up at Quentin? Huh? The Pope a fuckin' guinea?"

Lights went on—Kinnard's wife was futzing with the fuse box. She said, "Can I go to my mother's?"

Bud emptied Ralphie's pockets—keys, a cash roll. "Take the car and get yourself fixed up."

Kinnard spat teeth. Mrs. Ralphie grabbed the keys and peeled a ten-spot. Bud said, "Merry Christmas, huh?"

Mrs. Ralphie blew a kiss and backed the car out, wheels over blinking reindeer.

*　*　*

Avenue 53—Code 2 no siren. A black-and-white just beat him; two blues and Dick Stensland got out and huddled.

Bud tapped his horn; Stensland came over. "Who's there, partner?"

Stensland pointed to a shack. "The one guy on the air, maybe more. It was maybe four spics, two white guys did our guys in. Brownell and Helenowski. Brownell's maybe got brain damage, Helenowski maybe lost an eye."

"Big maybes."

Stens reeked: Listerine, gin. "You want to quibble?"

Bud got out of the car. "No quibble. How many in custody?"

"Goose. We get the first collar."

"Then tell the blues to stay put."

Stens shook his head. "They're pals with Brownell. They want a piece."

"Nix, this is ours. We get them booked, we write it up and make the party by watch change. I got three cases: Walker Black, Jim Beam and Cutty."

"Exley's assistant watch commander. He's a nosebleed, and you can bet he don't approve of on-duty imbibing."

"Yeah, and Frieling's *the* watch boss, and he's a fucking drunk like you. So don't worry about Exley. And I got a report to write up first—so let's just do it."

Stens laughed. "Aggravated assault on a woman? What's that—six twenty-three point one in the California Penal Code? So I'm a fucking drunk and you're a fucking do-gooder."

"Yeah, and you're ranking. So now?"

Stens winked; Bud walked flank—up to the porch, gun out. The shack was curtained dark; Bud caught a radio ad: Felix the Cat Chevrolet. Dick kicked the door in.

Yells, a Mex man and woman hauling. Stens aimed head high; Bud blocked his shot. Down a hallway, Bud close in, Stens wheezing, knocking over furniture. The kitchen—the spics dead-ended at a window.

They turned, raised their hands: a pachuco punk, a pretty girl maybe six months pregnant.

The boy kissed the wall—a pro friskee. Bud searched him: Dinardo Sanchez ID, chump change. The girl boo-hooed; sirens scree'd outside. Bud turned Sanchez around, kicked him in the balls. "For ours, Pancho. And you got off easy."

Stens grabbed the girl. Bud said, "Go somewhere, sweetheart. Before my friend checks your green card."

"Green card" spooked her—*madre mia! Madre mia!* Stens shoved her to the door; Sanchez moaned. Bud saw blues swarm the driveway. "We'll let them take Pancho in."

Stens caught some breath. "We'll give him to Brownell's pals."

Two rookie types walked in—Bud saw his out. "Cuff him and book him. APO and resisting arrest."

The rookies dragged Sanchez out. Stens said, "You and women. What's next? Kids and dogs?"

Mrs. Ralphie—all bruised up for Christmas. "I'm working on it. Come on, let's move that booze. Be nice and I'll let you have your own bottle."

2

PRESTON EXLEY yanked the drop-cloth. His guests oohed and ahhed; a city councilman clapped, spilled eggnog on a society matron. Ed Exley thought: this is not a typical policeman's Christmas Eve.

He checked his watch—8:46—he had to be at the station by midnight. Preston Exley pointed to the model.

It took up half his den: an amusement park filled with papier-mâché mountains, rocket ships, Wild West towns. Cartoon creatures at the gate: Moochie Mouse, Scooter Squirrel, Danny Duck—Raymond Dieterling's brood—featured in the *Dream-a-Dream Hour* and scores of cartoons.

"Ladies and gentlemen, presenting Dream-a-Dreamland. Exley Construction will build it, in Pomona, California, and the opening date will be April 1953. It will be the most sophisticated amusement park in history, a self-contained universe where children of all ages can enjoy the message of fun and goodwill that is the hallmark of Raymond Dieterling, the father of modern animation. Dream-a-Dreamland will feature all your favorite Dieterling characters, and it will be a haven for the young and young at heart."

Ed stared at his father: fifty-seven coming off forty-five, a cop from a long line of cops holding forth in a Hancock Park mansion, politicos giving up their Christmas Eve at a snap of his fingers. The guests applauded; Preston pointed to a snowcapped mountain. "Paul's World, ladies and gentlemen. An exact-scale replica of a mountain in the Sierra Nevada. Paul's World will feature a thrilling toboggan ride and a ski lodge where Moochie, Scooter and Danny will perform skits for the whole family. And who is the Paul of Paul's World? Paul was Raymond Dieterling's son, lost tragically as a teenager in 1936, lost in an avalanche on a camping trip—lost on a mountain just like this one here. So, out of tragedy, an affirmation of innocence. And, ladies and gentlemen, every nickel out of every dollar spent at Paul's World will go to the Children's Polio Foundation."

Wild applause. Preston nodded at Timmy Valburn—the actor who played Moochie Mouse on the *Dream-a-Dream Hour*—always nibbling cheese with his big buck teeth. Valburn nudged the man beside him; the man nudged back.

Art De Spain caught Ed's eye; Valburn kicked off a Moochie routine. Ed steered De Spain to the hallway. "This is a hell of a surprise, Art."

"Dieterling's announcing it on the *Dream Hour*. Didn't your dad tell you?"

"No, and I didn't know he knew Dieterling. Did he meet him back during the Atherton case? Wasn't Wee Willie Wennerholm one of Dieterling's kid stars?"

De Spain smiled. "I was your dad's lowly adjutant then, and I don't think the two great men ever crossed paths. Preston just *knows* people. And by the way, did you spot the mouse man and his pal?"

Ed nodded. "Who is he?"

Laughter from the den; De Spain steered Ed to the study. "He's Billy Dieterling, Ray's son. He's a cameraman on *Badge of Honor*, which lauds our beloved LAPD to millions of television viewers each week. Maybe Timmy spreads some cheese on his whatsis before he blows him."

Ed laughed. "Art, you're a pisser."

De Spain sprawled in a chair. "Eddie, ex-cop to cop, you say words like 'pisser' and you sound like a college professor. And you're not really an 'Eddie,' you're an 'Edmund.'"

Ed squared his glasses. "I see avuncular advice coming. Stick in Patrol, because Parker made chief that way. Administrate my way up because I have no command presence."

"You've got no sense of humor. And can't you get rid of those specs? Squint or something. Outside of Thad Green, I can't think of one Bureau guy who wears glasses."

"God, you miss the Department. I think that if you could give up Exley Construction and fifty thousand a year for a spot as an LAPD rookie, you would."

De Spain lit a cigar. "Only if your dad came with me."

"Just like that?"

"Just like that. I was a lieutenant to Preston's inspector, and I'm still a number two man. It'd be nice to be even with him."

"If you didn't know lumber, Exley Construction wouldn't exist."

"Thanks. And get rid of those glasses."

Ed picked up a framed photo: his brother Thomas in uniform—taken the day before he died. "If you were a rookie, I'd break you for insubordination."

"You would, too. What did you place on the lieutenant's exam?"

"First out of twenty-three applicants. I was the youngest applicant by eight years, with the shortest time in grade as a sergeant and the shortest amount of time on the Department."

"And you want the Detective Bureau."

Ed put the photo down. "Yes."

"Then, first you have to figure a year minimum for an opening to come up, then you have to realize that it will probably be a Patrol opening, then you have to realize that a transfer to the Bureau will take years and lots of ass kissing. You're twenty-nine now?"

"Yes."

"Then you'll be a lieutenant at thirty or thirty-one. Brass that young create resentment. Ed, all kidding aside. You're not one of the guys. You're not a strongarm type. *You're not Bureau.* And Parker as Chief has set a precedent for Patrol officers to go all the way. Think about that."

Ed said, "Art, I want to work cases. I'm connected and I won the Distinguished Service Cross, which some people might construe as strongarm. And I will *have* a Bureau appointment."

De Spain brushed ash off his cummerbund. "Can we talk turkey, Sunny Jim?"

The endearment rankled. "Of course."

"Well … you're good, and in time you might be really good. And I don't doubt your killer instinct for a second. But your father was ruthless and likable. And you're not, so . . ."

Ed made fists. "So, Uncle Arthur? Cop who left the Department for money to cop who never would—what's your advice?"

De Spain flinched. "So be a sycophant and suck up to the right men. Kiss William H. Parker's ass and pray to be in the right place at the right time."

"Like you and my father?"

"*Touché*, Sunny Jim."

Ed looked at his uniform: custom blues on a hanger. Razor-creased, sergeant's stripes, a single hashmark. De Spain said, "Gold bars soon, Eddie. And braid on your cap. And I wouldn't jerk your chain if I didn't care."

"I know."

"And you *are* a goddamned war hero."

Ed changed the subject. "It's Christmas. You're thinking about Thomas."

"I keep thinking I could have told him something. He didn't even have his holster flap open."

"A purse snatcher with a gun? He couldn't have known."

De Spain put out his cigar. "Thomas was a natural, and I always thought he should be telling me things. That's why I tend to spell things out for you."

"He's twelve years dead and I'll bury him as a policeman."

"I'll forget you said that."

"No, remember it. Remember it when I make the Bureau. And when Father offers toasts to Thomas and Mother, don't get maudlin. It ruins him for days."

De Spain stood up, flushing; Preston Exley walked in with snifters and a bottle.

Ed said, "Merry Christmas, Father. And congratulations."

Preston poured drinks. "Thank you. Exley Construction tops the Arroyo Seco Freeway job with a kingdom for a glorified rodent, and I'll never eat another piece of cheese. A toast, gentlemen. To the eternal rest of my son Thomas and my wife Marguerite, to the three of us assembled here."

The men drank; De Spain fixed refills. Ed offered his father's favorite toast: "To the solving of crimes that require absolute justice."

Three more shots downed. Ed said, "Father, I didn't know you knew Raymond Dieterling."

Preston smiled. "I've known him in a business sense for years. Art and I have kept the contract secret at Raymond's request—he wants to announce it on that infantile television program of his."

"Did you meet him during the Atherton case?"

"No, and of course I wasn't in the construction business then. Arthur, do you have a toast to propose?"

De Spain poured short ones. "To a Bureau assignment for our soon-to-be lieutenant."

Laughter, hear-hears. Preston said, "Joan Morrow was inquiring about your love life, Edmund. I think she's smitten."

"Do you see a debutante as a cop's wife?"

"No, but I could picture her married to a ranking policeman."

"Chief of Detectives?"

"No, I was thinking more along the lines of commander of the Patrol Division."

"Father, Thomas was going to be your chief of detectives, but he's dead. Don't deny me my opportunity. Don't make me live an old dream of yours."

Preston stared at his son. "Point taken, and I commend you for speaking up. And granted, that was my original dream. But the truth is that I don't think you have the eye for human weakness that makes a good detective."

His brother: a math brain crazed for pretty girls. "And Thomas did?"

"Yes."

"Father, I would have shot that purse snatcher the second he went for his pocket."

De Spain said, "Goddammit"; Preston shushed him. "That's all right. Edmund, a few questions before I return to my guests. One, would you be willing to plant corroborative evidence on a suspect you knew was guilty in order to ensure an indictment?"

"I'd have to—"

"Answer yes or no."

"I ... no."

"Would you be willing to shoot hardened armed robbers in the back to offset the chance that they might utilize flaws in the legal system and go free?"

"I ..."

"Yes or no, Edmund."

"No."

"And would you be willing to beat confessions out of suspects you knew to be guilty?"

"No."

"Would you be willing to rig crime scene evidence to support a prosecuting attorney's working hypothesis?"

"No."

Preston sighed. "Then for God's sake, stick to assignments where you won't have to make those choices. Use the superior intelligence the good Lord gave you."

Ed looked at his uniform. "I'll use that intelligence as a detective."

Preston smiled. "Detective or not, you have qualities of persistence that Thomas lacked. You'll excel, my war hero."

The phone rang; De Spain picked it up. Ed thought of rigged Jap trenches—and couldn't meet Preston's eyes. De Spain said, "It's Lieutenant Frieling at the station. He said the jail's almost full, and two officers were assaulted earlier in the evening. Two suspects are in custody, with four more outstanding. He said you should clock in early."

Ed turned back to his father. Preston was down the hall, swapping jokes with Mayor Bowron in a Moochie Mouse hat.

3

PRESS CLIPPINGS on his corkboard: "Dope Crusader Wounded in Shootout"; "Actor Mitchum Seized in Marijuana Shack Raid." *Hush-Hush* articles, framed on his desk: "Hopheads Quake When Dope Scourge Cop Walks Tall"; "Actors Agree: *Badge of Honor* Owes Authenticity to Hard-hitting Technical Advisor." The *Badge* piece featured a photo: Sergeant Jack Vincennes with the show's star, Brett Chase. The piece did not feature dirt from the editor's private file: Brett Chase as a pedophile with three quashed sodomy beefs.

Jack Vincennes glanced around the Narco pen—deserted, dark—just the light in his cubicle. Ten minutes short of midnight; he'd promised Dudley Smith he'd type up an organized crime report for Intelligence Division; he'd promised Lieutenant Frieling a case of booze for the station party—Hush-Hush Sid Hudgens was supposed to come across with rum but hadn't called. Dudley's report: a favor shot his way because he typed a hundred words a minute; a favor returned tomorrow: a meet with Dud and Ellis Loew, Pacific Dining Car lunch—work on the line, work to earn him juice with the DA's Office. Jack lit a cigarette, read.

Some report: eleven pages long, very verbal, very Dudley. The topic: L.A. mob activity with Mickey Cohen in stir. Jack edited, typed.

Cohen was at McNeil Island Federal Prison: three to seven, income tax evasion. Davey Goldman, Mickey's money man, was there: three to seven, down on six counts of federal tax fraud. Smith predicted possible skirmishing between Cohen minion Morris Jahelka and Jack "The Enforcer" Whalen; with Mafia overlord Jack Dragna deported, they loomed as the two men most likely to control loansharking, bookmaking, prostitution and the race wire racket. Smith stated that Jahelka was too ineffectual to require police surveillance; that John Stompanato and Abe Teitlebaum, key Cohen strongarms, seemed to have gone legitimate. Lee Vachss, contract trigger employed by Cohen, was working a religious racket—selling patent medicines guaranteed to induce mystical experiences.

Jack kept typing. Dud's take hit wrong: Johnny Stomp and Kikey Teitlebaum were pure bent—they could never go pure straight. He fed in a fresh sheet.

A new topic: the February '50 Cohen/Dragna truce meeting—twenty-five pounds of heroin and a hundred and fifty grand allegedly stolen. Jack heard rumors: an ex-cop named Buzz Meeks heisted the summit, took off and was gunned down near San Bernardino—Cohen goons and rogue L.A. cops killed him, a Mickey contract: Meeks stole the Mick blind and fucked his woman. The horse was supposedly long gone unfound. Dudley's theory: Meeks buried the money and shit someplace unknown and was later killed by "person or persons unknown"—probably a Cohen gunman. Jack smiled: if LAPD was in on a Meeks hit, Dud would never implicate the Department—even in an interdepartmental report.

Next, Smith's summary: with Mickey C. gone, mob action was at a lull; the LAPD should stay alert for new faces looking to crash Cohen's old rackets; prostitution was sticking over the county line—with Sheriff's Department sanction. Jack signed the last page "Respectfully, Lieutenant D. L. Smith."

The phone rang. "Narcotics, Vincennes."

"It's me. You hungry?"

Jack kiboshed a temper fit—easy—what Hudgens just might have on him. "Sid, you're late. And the party's already on."

"I got better than booze, I got cash."

"Talk."

"Talk this: Tammy Reynolds, co-star of *Hope's Harvest*, opens tomorrow citywide. A guy I know just sold her some reefer, a guaranteed felony pinch. She's tripping the light fantastic at 2245 Maravilla, Hollywood Hills. You pinch, I do you up feature in the next issue. Because it's Christmas, I leak my notes to Morty Bendish at the *Mirror*, so you make the dailies, too. Plus fifty cash and your rum. Am I fucking Santa Claus?"

"Pictures?"

"In spades. Wear the blue blazer, it goes with your eyes."

"A hundred, Sid. I need two patrolmen at twenty apiece and a dime for the watch commander at Hollywood Station. And *you* set it up."

"Jack! It's Christmas!"

"No, it's felony possession of marijuana."

"Shit. Half an hour?"

"Twenty-five minutes."

"I'm there, you fucking extortionist."

Jack hung up, made an X mark on his calendar. Another day, no booze, no hop—four years, two months running.

* * *

His stage was waiting—Maravilla cordoned off, two bluesuits by Sid Hudgens' Packard, their black-and-white up on the sidewalk. The street was dark and still; Sid had an arclight set up. They had a view of the Boulevard—Grauman's Chinese included—great for an establishing shot. Jack parked, walked over.

Sid greeted him with cash. "She's sitting in the dark, goofing on the Christmas tree. The door looks flimsy."

Jack drew his .38. "Have the boys put the booze in my trunk. You want Grauman's in the background?"

"I like it! Jackie, you're the best in the West!"

Jack scoped him: scarecrow skinny, somewhere between thirty-five and fifty—keeper of inside dirt supreme. He either knew about 10/24/47 or he didn't; *if* he did, their arrangement was lifetime stuff. "Sid, when I bring her out the door, I do not want that goddamned baby spot in my eyes. Tell your camera guy that."

"Consider him told."

"Good, now count twenty on down."

Hudgens ticked numbers; Jack walked up and kicked the door in. The arclight snapped on, a living room caught flush: Christmas tree, two kids necking in their undies. Jack shouted "Police!"; the lovebirds froze; light on a fat bag of weed on the couch.

The girl started bawling; the boy reached for his trousers. Jack put a foot on his chest. "The hands, slow."

The boy pressed his wrists together; Jack cuffed him onehanded. The blues stormed in and gathered up evidence; Jack matched a name to the punk: Rock Rockwell, RKO ingenue. The girl ran; Jack grabbed her. Two suspects by the neck—out the door, down the steps.

Hudgens yelled, "Grauman's while we've still got the light!"

Jack framed them: half-naked pretties in their BVDs. Flashbulbs popped; Hudgens yelled, "Cut! Wrap it!"

The blues took over: Rockwell and the girl hauled bawling to their prowler. Window lights popped on; rubberneckers opened doors. Jack went back to the house.

A maryjane haze—four years later the shit still smelled good. Hudgens was opening drawers, pulling out dildoes, spiked dog collars. Jack found the phone, checked the address book for pushers—goose egg. A calling card fell out: "Fleur-de-Lis. Twenty-four Hours a Day—Whatever You Desire."

Sid started muttering. Jack put the card back. "Let's hear how it sounds."

Hudgens cleared his throat. "It's Christmas morning in the City of the Angels, and while decent citizens sleep the sleep of the righteous, hopheads prowl for marijuana, the weed with roots in Hell. Tammy Reynolds and Rock Rockwell, movie stars with one foot in Hades, toke sweet tea in Tammy's swank Hollywood digs, not knowing they are playing with fire without asbestos gloves, not knowing that a man is coming to put out that fire: the free-wheeling, big-time Big V, celebrity crimestopper Jack Vincennes, the scourge of grasshoppers and junk fiends everywhere. Acting on the tip of an unnamed informant, Sergeant Vincennes, blah, blah, blah. You like it, Jackie?"

"Yeah, it's subtle."

"No, it's circulation nine hundred thousand and climbing. I think I'll work in you're divorced twice 'cause your wives couldn't stand your crusade and you got your name from an orphanage in Vincennes, Indiana. The Biggg Veeeee."

His Narco tag: Trashcan Jack—a nod to the time he popped Charlie "Yardbird" Parker and tossed him into a garbage bin outside the Klub Zamboanga. "You should beat the drum on *Badge of Honor*. Miller Stanton's my buddy, how I taught Brett Chase to play a cop. Technical advisor kingpin, that kind of thing."

Hudgens laughed. "Brett still like them prepubescent?"

"Can niggers dance?"

"South of Jefferson Boulevard only. Thanks for the story, Jack."

"Sure."

"I mean it. It's always nice seeing you."

You fucking cockroach, you're going to wink because you know you can nail me to that moralistic shitbird William H. Parker anytime you want—cash rousts going back to '48, you've probably got documentation worked around to let you off clean and crucify me—

Hudgens winked.

Jack wondered if he had it *all* down on paper.

4

THE PARTY in full swing, the muster room SRO.

An open bar: scotch, bourbon, a case of rum Trashcan Jack Vincennes brought in. Dick Stensland's brew in the water cooler: Old Crow, eggnog mix. A phonograph spewed dirty Christmas carols: Santa and his reindeer fucking and sucking. The floor was packed: nightwatch blues, the Central squad—thirsty from chasing vagrants.

Bud watched the crowd. Fred Turentine tossed darts at Wanted posters; Mike Krugman and Walt Dukeshearer played "Name That Nigger," trying to ID Negro mugshots at a quarter a bet. Jack Vincennes was drinking club soda; Lieutenant Frieling was passed out at his desk. Ed Exley tried to quiet the men down, gave up, stuck to the lock-up: logging in prisoners, filing arrest reports.

Almost every man was drunk or working on it.

Almost every man was talking up Helenowski and Brownell, the cop beaters in custody, the two still at large.

Bud stood by the window. Garbled rumors tweaked him: Brownie Brownell had his lip split up through his nose, one of the taco benders chewed off Helenowski's left ear. Dick Stens grabbed a shotgun, went spic hunting. He credited that one: he'd seen Dick carrying an Ithaca pump out to the parking lot.

The noise was getting brutal—Bud walked out to the lot, lounged against a prowler.

A drizzle started up. A ruckus by the jail door—Dick Stens shoving two men inside. A scream; Bud cut odds on Stens finishing out his twenty: with him watchdogging, even money; without him, two to one against. From the muster room: Frank Doherty's tenor, a weepy "Silver Bells."

Bud moved away from the music—it made him think of his mother. He lit a cigarette, thought of her anyway.

He'd seen the killing: sixteen years old, helpless to stop it. The old man came home; he must have believed his son's warning: you touch Mother again and I will kill you. Asleep—cuffs on his wrists and ankles, awake—he saw the fuck beat Mother dead with a tire iron. He screamed his throat raw; he stayed cuffed in the room with the body: a week, no water, delirious—he watched his mother rot. A truant officer found him; the L.A. Sheriff's found the old man. The trial, a diminished capacity defense, a plea bargain down to Manslaughter Two. Life imprisonment, the old man paroled in twelve years. His son—Officer Wendell White, LAPD—decided to kill him.

The old man was nowhere.

He'd jumped parole; prowling his L.A. haunts turned up nothing. Bud kept looking, kept waking to the sound of women screaming. He always investigated; it was always just wisps of noise. Once he kicked in a door and found a woman who'd burned her hand. Once he crashed in on a husband and wife making love.

The old man was nowhere.

He made the Bureau, partnered up with Dick Stens. Dick showed him the ropes, heard out his story, told him to pick his shots to get even. Pops would stay nowhere, but thumping wife beaters might drive the nightmares out of his system. Bud picked a great first shot: a domestic squawk, the complainant a longtime punching bag, the arrestee a three-time loser. He detoured on the way to the station, asked the guy if he'd like to tango with a man for a change: no cuffs, a walk on the charge if he won. The guy agreed; Bud broke his nose, his jaw, ruptured his spleen with a dropkick. Dick was right: his bad dreams stopped.

His rep as *the* toughest man in the LAPD grew.

He kept it up; he followed up: intimidation calls if the fuckers got acquitted, welcome home strongarms if they did time and got parole. He forced himself not to take gratitude lays and found women elsewhere. He kept a list of court and parole dates and sent the fuckers postcards at the honor farm; he got hit with excessive-force complaints and toughed them out. Dick Stens made him a decent detective; now he played nursemaid to his teacher: keeping him half sober on duty, holding him back when he got a hard-on to shoot for kicks. He'd learned to keep himself in check; Stens was now all bad habits: scrounging at bars, letting stick-up men slide for snitch dope.

The music inside went off key—wrong, not really music. Bud caught screeches—screams from the jail.

The noise doubled, tripled. Bud saw a stampede: muster room to cellblock. A flash: Stens going crazy, booze, a jamboree—bash the cop bashers. He ran over, hit the door at a sprint.

The catwalk packed tight, cell doors open, lines forming. Exley shouting for order, pressing into the swarm, getting nowhere.

Bud found the prisoner list; checkmarks after "Sanchez, Dinardo," "Carbijal, Juan," "Garcia, Ezekiel," "Chasco, Reyes," "Rice, Dennis," "Valupeyk, Clinton"—all six cop beaters in custody.

The bums in the drunk cage egged the men on.

Stens hit the #4 cell—waving brass knucks.

Willie Tristano pinned Exley to the wall; Crum Crumley grabbed his keys.

Cops shoved cell to cell. Elmer Lentz, blood splattered, grinning. Jack Vincennes by the watch commander's office— Lieutenant Frieling snoring at his desk.

Bud stormed into it.

He caught elbows going in; the men saw who it was and cleared a path. Stens slid into 3; Bud pushed in. Dick was working a skinny pachuco—head saps—the kid on his knees, catching teeth. Bud grabbed Stensland; the Mex spat blood. "Heey, Mister White. I knowww you, *puto.* You beat up my frien' Caldo 'cause he whipped his *puto* wife. She was a fuckin' hooer, *pendejo.* Ain' you got no fuckin' brains?"

Bud let Stens go; the Mex gave him the finger. Bud kicked him prone, picked him up by the neck. Cheers, attaboys, holy fucks. Bud banged the punk's head on the ceiling; a bluesuit moved in hard. Ed Exley's rich-kid voice: "Stop it, Officer—that's an order!"

The Mex kicked him in the balls—a dangling shot. Bud keeled into the bars; the kid stumbled out of the cell, smack into Vincennes. Trashcan, aghast—blood on his cashmere blazer. He put the punk down with a left-right; Exley ran out of the cellblock.

Yells, shouts, shrieks: louder than a thousand Code 3 sirens.

Stens whipped out a pint of gin. Bud saw every man there skunked to niggertown forever. Up on his tiptoes, a prime view— Exley dumping booze in the storeroom.

Voices: attaboy, Big Bud. Faces to the voices—skewed, wrong. Exley still dumping, Mr. Teetotaler Witness. Bud ran down the catwalk, locked him in tight.

5

SHUT INTO a room eight feet square. No windows, no tele- phone, no intercom. Shelves spilling forms, mops, brooms, a clogged-up sink filled with vodka and rum. The door was steel-reinforced; the liquor stew smelled like vomit. Shouts and thudding sounds boomed through a heat vent.

Ed banged on the door—no response. He yelled into the vent—hot air hit his face. He saw himself pinioned and pickpocketed, Bureau guys who figured he'd never squeal. He wondered what his father would do.

Time dragged; the jail noise stopped, fired up, stopped, started. Ed banged on the door—no luck. The room went hot; booze stench smothered the air. Ed felt Guadalcanal: hiding from the Japs, bodies piled over him. His uniform was sopping wet; if he shot the lock the bullets could ricochet off the plating and kill him. The beatings had to go wide: an IA investigation, civil suits, the grand jury. Police brutality charges; careers flushed down the toilet. Sergeant Edmund J. Exley crucified because he could not maintain order. Ed made a decision: fight back with his brains.

He wrote on the back of official departmental forms—version one, the truth:

A rumor started it: John Helenowski lost an eye. Sergeant Richard Stensland logged in Rice, Dennis, and Valupeyk, Clinton—he spread the word. It ignited all at once; Lieutenant Frieling, the watch commander, was asleep, unconscious from drinking alcohol on duty in violation of interdepartmental regulation 4319. Now in charge, Sergeant E. J. Exley found his office keys misplaced. The bulk of the men attending the station Christmas party stormed the cellblock. The cells containing the six alleged assaulters were opened with the misplaced keys. Sergeant Exley attempted to relock those cells, but the beatings had already commenced and Sergeant Willis Tristano held Sergeant Exley while Sergeant Walter Crumley stole the spare keys attached to his belt.

Sergeant Exley did not use force to get the spare keys back.

More details:

Stensland going crazy, policemen beating helpless prisoners. Bud White: lifting a squirming man, one hand on his neck.

Sergeant Exley ordering Officer White to stop; Officer White ignoring the order; Sergeant Exley relieved when the prisoner freed himself and eliminated the need for a further confrontation.

Ed winced, kept writing—12/25/51, the Central Jail assaults in detail. Probable grand jury indictments, interdepartmental trial boards—Chief Parker's prestige ruined. Fresh paper, thoughts of inmate witnesses—mostly drunks—and the fact that virtually every officer had been drinking heavily. *They* were compromised witnesses; *he* was sober, uncompromised, and had made attempts to control the situation. *He* needed a graceful out; the Department needed to save face; the high brass would be grateful to a man who tried to circumvent bad press—who had the foresight to see it coming and plan ahead. He wrote down version two.

A digression on number one, the action shifted to limit the blame to fewer officers: Stensland, Johnny Brownell, Bud White and a handful of other men who'd already earned or were close to their pensions—Krugman, Tucker, Heineke, Huff, Disbrow, Doherty—older fish to throw the DA's Office if indictment fever ran high. A subjective viewpoint, tailored to fit what the drunk tank prisoners saw, the assaulters trying to flee the cellblock and liberate other inmates. The truth twisted a few turns—impossible for other witnesses to disprove. Ed signed it, listened through the vent for version three.

It came slowly. Voices urged "Stens" to "wake up for a piece"; White left the cellblock, muttering what a waste it all was. Krugman and Tucker yelled insults; whimpers answered them. No further sound of White or Johnny Brownell; Lentz, Huff, Doherty prowling the catwalk. Sobs, *Madre mia* over and over.

6:14 A.M.

Ed wrote out number three: no whimpers, no *madre mia*, the cop beaters inciting other inmates. He wondered how his father would rate the crimes: brother officers assaulted, the assaulters ravaged. Which required absolute justice?

The vent noise dwindled; Ed tried to sleep and couldn't; a key went in the door.

Lieutenant Frieling—pale, trembling. Ed nudged him aside, walked down the corridor.

Six cells wide open—the walls slick with blood. Juan Carbijal on his bunk, a shirt under his head soaked red. Clinton Valupeyk washing blood off his face with toilet water. Reyes Chasco one giant contusion; Dennis Rice working his fingers—swollen blue, broken. Dinardo Sanchez and Ezekiel Garcia curled up together by the drunk cage.

Ed called for ambulances. The words "Prison Ward, County General" almost made him retch.

6

DUDLEY SMITH said, "You're not eating, lad. Did a late night with your chums spoil your appetite?"

Jack looked at his plate: T-bone, baked potato, asparagus. "I always order large when the DA's Office picks up the tab. Where's Loew? I want him to see what he's buying."

Smith laughed; Jack eyed the cut of his suit: baggy, good camouflage—make me a stage Irishman, cover my .45 automatic, knuckle dusters and sap. "What's Loew have in mind?"

Dudley checked his watch. "Yes, thirty-odd minutes of amenities should be a sufficient prelude to business on our grand savior's birthday. Lad, what Ellis wants is to be district attorney of our fair city, then governor of California. He's been a deputy DA for eight years, he ran for DA in '48 and lost, there's an off-year election coming up in March of '53, and Ellis thinks he can win. He's a vigorous prosecutor of criminal scum, he's a grand friend to the Department, and despite his Hebraic genealogy I'm fond of him and think he'll make a splendid district attorney. And, lad, you can help elect him. And make yourself a very valuable friend."

The Mex he'd duked out—the whole deal might go wide. "I might need a favor pretty soon."

"One which he'll supply willingly, lad."

"He wants me to run bag?"

"'Bagman' is a colloquialism I find offensive, lad. 'Reciprocity of friendship' is a more suitable phrase, especially given the splendid connections you have. But money is at the root of Mr. Loew's request, and I'd be remiss in not stating that at the outset."

Jack pushed his plate aside. "Loew wants me to shake down the *Badge of Honor* guys. Campaign contributions."

"Yes, and to keep that damnable *Hush-Hush* scandal rag off his back. And since reciprocity is our watchword here, he has specific favors to grant in return."

"Such as?"

Smith lit a cigarette. "Max Peltz, the producer of the show, has had tax trouble for years, and Loew will see to it that he never stands another audit. Brett Chase, whom you have so brilliantly taught to portray a policeman, is a degenerate pederast, and Loew will never prosecute him. Loew will contribute DA's Bureau files to the show's story editor and you will be rewarded thusly: Sergeant Bob Gallaudet, the DA's Bureau whip, is going to law

school, doing well and will be joining the DA's Office as a prosecutor once he passes the bar. You will then be given the chance
to assume his old position—along with a lieutenantcy. Lad, does
my proposal impress you?"

Jack took a smoke from Dudley's pack. "Boss, you know I'd
never leave Narco and you know I'm gonna say yes. And I just
figured out that Loew's gonna show up, give me a thank-you and
not stay for dessert. So yes."

Dudley winked; Ellis Loew slid into the booth. "Gentlemen,
I'm sorry I'm so late."

Jack said, "I'll do it."

"Oh? Lieutenant Smith has explained the situation to you?"

Dudley said, "Some lads don't require detailed explanations."

Loew fingered his Phi Beta chain. "Thank you then, Sergeant.
And if I can help you in any way, *any way at all*, don't hesitate to
call me."

"I won't. Dessert, sir?"

"I would like to stay, but I have depositions waiting for me.
We'll break bread another time, I'm sure."

"Whatever you need, Mr. Loew."

Loew dropped a twenty on the table. "Again, thank you. Lieutenant, I'll talk to you soon. And gentlemen—Merry Christmas."

Jack nodded; Loew walked off. Dudley said, "There's more, lad."

"More work?"

"Of sorts. Are you providing security at Welton Morrow's
Christmas party this year?"

His annual gig—a C-note to mingle. "Yeah, it's tonight. Does
Loew want an invitation?"

"Not quite. You did a large favor for Mr. Morrow once, did
you not?"

October '47—too large. "Yeah, I did."

"And you're still friendly with the Morrows?"

"In a hired-hand sort of way, sure. Why?"

Dudley laughed. "Lad, Ellis Loew wants a wife. Preferably a
Gentile with a social pedigree. He's seen Joan Morrow at various
civic functions and fancies her. Will you play Cupid and ask fair
Joan what she thinks of the idea?"

"Dud, are you asking me to get the future L.A. DA a fucking date?"

"I am indeed. Do you think Miss Morrow will be amenable?"

"It's worth a try. She's a social climber and she's always wanted
to marry well. I don't know about a hebe, though."

"Yes, lad, there is that. But you'll broach the subject?"

"Sure."

"Then it's out of our hands. And along those lines—was it bad at the station last night?"

Now he gets to it. "It was very bad."

"Do you think it will blow over?"

"I don't know. What about Brownell and Helenowski? How bad did they get it?"

"Superficial contusions, lad. I'd say the payback went a bit further. Did you partake?"

"I got hit, hit back and got out. Is Loew afraid of prosecuting?"

"Only of losing friends if he does."

"He made a friend today. Tell him he's ahead of the game."

* * *

Jack drove home, fell asleep on the couch. He slept through the afternoon, woke up to the *Mirror* on his porch. On page four: "Yuletide Surprise for *Hope's Harvest* co-stars."

No pix, but Morty Bendish got in the "Big V" shtick; "One of his many informants" made it sound like Jack Vincennes had minions prowling, their pockets stuffed with *his* money—it was well known that the Big V financed his dope crusade with his own salary. Jack clipped the article, thumbed the rest of the paper for Helenowski, Brownell and the cop beaters.

Nothing.

Predictable: two cops with minor contusions was small potatoes, the punks hadn't had time to glom a shyster. Jack got out his ledger.

Pages divided into three columns: date, cashier's check number, amount of money. The amounts ranged from a C-note to two grand; the checks were made out to Donald and Marsha Scoggins of Cedar Rapids, Iowa. The bottom of the third column held a running total: $32,350. Jack got out his bankbook, checked the balance, decided his next payment would be five hundred flat. Five yards for Christmas. Big money until your Uncle Jack drops dead—and it'll never be enough.

Every Christmas he ran it through—it started with the Morrows and he saw them at Christmastime; he was an orphan, he'd made the Scoggins kids orphans, Christmas was a notoriously shitty time for orphans. He forced himself through the story.

Late September 1947.

Old Chief Worton called him in. Welton Morrow's daughter Karen was running with a high school crowd experimenting with dope—they got the shit from a sax player named Les Weiskopf. Morrow was a filthy-rich lawyer, a heavy contributor to LAPD fund drives; he wanted Weiskopf leaned on—with no publicity.

Jack knew Weiskopf: he sold Dilaudid, wore his hair in a jig conk, liked young gash. Worton told him a sergeantcy came with the job.

He found Weiskopf—in bed with a fifteen-year-old redhead. The girl skedaddled; Jack pistol-whipped Weiskopf, tossed his pad, found a trunk full of goofballs and bennies. He took it with him—he figured he'd sell the shit to Mickey Cohen. Welton Morrow offered him the security man gig; Jack accepted; Karen Morrow was hustled off to boarding school. The sergeantcy came through; Mickey C. wasn't interested in the dope—only Big H flipped his switch. Jack kept the trunk—and dipped into it for bennies to keep him juiced on all-night stakeouts. Linda, wife number two, took off with one of his snitches: a trombone player who sold maryjane on the side. Jack hit the trunk for real, mixing goofballs, bennies, scotch, taking down half the names on the *down beat* poll: THE MAN, jazzster's public enemy number one. Then it was 10/24/47—

He was cramped in his car, staking the Malibu Rendezvous parking lot: eyes on two "H" pushers in a Packard sedan. Near midnight: he'd been drinking scotch, he blew a reefer on the way over, the bennies he'd been swallowing weren't catching up with the booze. A tip on a midnight buy: the "H" men and a skinny shine, seven feet tall, a real geek.

The boogie showed at a quarter past twelve, walked to the Packard, palmed a package. Jack tripped getting out of the car; the geek started running; the "H" men got out with guns drawn. Jack stumbled up and drew his piece; the geek wheeled and fired; he saw two shapes closer in, tagged them as the nigger's backup, squeezed off a clip. The shapes went down; the "H" men shot at the spook and at him; the spook nosedived a '46 Studebaker.

Jack ate cement, prayed the rosary. A shot ripped his shoulder; a shot grazed his legs. He crawled under the car; a shitload of tires squealed; a shitload of people screamed. An ambulance showed up; a bull dyke Sheriff's deputy loaded him on a gurney. Sirens, a hospital bed, a doctor and the dyke whispering about the dope in his system—blood test validated. Lots of drugged sleep, a newspaper on his lap:"Three Dead in Malibu Shootout—Heroic Cop Survives."

The "H" guys escaped clean—the deaths pinned on them.

The spook was dead at the scene.

The shapes weren't the nigger's backup—they were Mr. and Mrs. Harold J. Scoggins, tourists from Cedar Rapids, Iowa, the proud parents of Donald, seventeen, and Marsha, sixteen.

The doctors kept looking at him funny; the dyke turned out to be Dot Rothstein, Kikey Teitlebaum's cousin, known associate of the legendary Dudley Smith.

A routine autopsy would show that the pills taken out of Mr. and Mrs. Scoggins came from Sergeant Jack Vincennes' gun.

The kids saved him.

He sweated out a week at the hospital. Thad Green and Chief Worton visited; the Narco guys came by. Dudley Smith offered his patronage; he wondered just how much he knew. Sid Hudgens, chief writer for *Hush-Hush* Magazine, stopped in with an offer: Jack to roust celebrated hopheads, *Hush-Hush* to be in on the arrests—cash to discreetly change hands. He accepted—and wondered just how much Hudgens knew.

The kids demanded no autopsy: the family was Seventh-Day Adventist, autopsies were a sacrilege. Since the county coroner knew damn well who the shooters were, he shipped Mr. and Mrs. Harold J. Scoggins back to Iowa to be cremated.

Sergeant Jack Vincennes skated—with newspaper honors.

His wounds healed.

He quit drinking.

He quit taking dope, dumped the trunk. He marked abstinent days on his calendar, worked his deal with Sid Hudgens, built his name as a local celebrity. He did favors for Dudley Smith; Mr. and Mrs. Harold J. Scoggins torched his dreams; he figured booze and hop would put out the flames but get him killed in the process. Sid got him the "technical advisor" job with *Badge of Honor*—then just a radio show. Money started rolling in; spending it on clothes and women wasn't the kick he thought it would be. Bars and dope shakedowns were awful temptations. Terrorizing hopheads helped a little—but not enough. He decided to pay the kids back.

His first check ran two hundred; he included a letter: "Anonymous Friend," a spiel on the Scoggins tragedy. He called the bank a week later: the check had been cashed. He'd been financing his free ride ever since; unless Hudgens had 10/24/47 on paper he was safe.

Jack laid out his party clothes. The blazer was London Shop—he'd bought it with Sid's payoff for the Bob Mitchum roust. The tassel loafers and gray flannels were proceeds from a *Hush-Hush* exposé linking jazz musicians to the Communist Conspiracy—he squeezed some pinko stuff out of a bass player he popped for needle marks. He dressed, spritzed on Lucky Tiger, drove to Beverly Hills.

*   *   *

A backyard bash: a full acre covered by awnings. College kids parked cars; a buffet featured prime rib, smoked ham, turkey. Waiters carried hors d'oeuvres; a giant Christmas tree stood out in the open, getting drizzled on. Guests ate off paper plates; gas torches lit the lawn. Jack arrived on time and worked the crowd.

Welton Morrow showed him to his first audience: a group of Superior Court judges. Jack spun yarns: Charlie Parker trying to buy him off with a high-yellow hooker, how he cracked the Shapiro case: a queer Mickey Cohen stooge pushing amyl nitrite—his customers transvestite strippers at a fruit bar. The Big V to the rescue: Jack Vincennes single-handedly arresting a roomful of bruisers auditioning for a Rita Hayworth lookalike contest. A round of applause; Jack bowed, saw Joan Morrow by the Christmas tree—alone, maybe bored.

He walked over. Joan said, "Happy holidays, Jack."

Pretty, built, thirty-one or -two. No job and no husband taking its toll: she came off pouty most of the time. "Hi, Joan."

"Hi, yourself. I read about you in the paper today. Those people you arrested."

"It was nothing."

Joan laughed. "Sooo modest. What's going to happen to them? Rock what's-his-name and the girl, I mean."

"Ninety days for the girl, maybe a year honor farm for Rockwell. They should hire your dad—he'd get them off."

"You don't really care, do you?"

"I hope they cop a plea and save me a court date. And I hope they do some time and learn their lesson."

"I smoked marijuana once, in college. It made me hungry and I ate a whole box of cookies and got sick. You wouldn't have arrested me, would you?"

"No, you're too nice."

"I'm *bored* enough to try it again, I'll tell you that."

His opening. "How's your love life, Joanie?"

"It isn't. Do you know a policeman named Edmund Exley? He's tall and he wears these cute glasses. He's Preston Exley's son."

Straight-arrow Eddie: war hero with a poker up his ass. "I know who he is, but I don't really know him."

"Isn't he cute? I saw him at his father's house last night."

"Rich-kid cops are from hunger, but I know a nice fellow who's interested in you."

"You do? Who?"

"A man named Ellis Loew. He's a deputy district attorney."

Joan smiled, frowned. "I heard him address the Rotary Club once. Isn't he Jewish?"

"Yeah, but look to the bright side. He's a Republican and a comer."

"Is he nice?"

"Sure, he's a sweetheart."

Joan flicked the tree; fake snow swirled. "Welll, tell him to call me. Tell him I'm booked up for a while, but he can stand in line."

"Thanks, Joanie."

"Thank *you*, Miles Standish. Look, I think I see Daddy giving me the come-hither. Bye, Jackie!"

Joan skipped off; Jack geared up for more shtick—maybe the Mitchum job, a soft version. A soft voice: "Mr. Vincennes. Hello."

Jack turned around. Karen Morrow in a green cocktail dress, her shoulders beaded with rain. The last time he'd seen her she was a too-tall, too-gawky kid forced to say thank you to a cop who'd strongarmed a hop pusher. Four years later just the too-tall stuck—the rest was a girl-to-woman changeover. "Karen, I almost didn't recognize you."

Karen smiled. Jack said, "I'd tell you you've gotten beautiful, but you've heard it before."

"Not from you."

Jack laughed. "How was college?"

"An epic, and not a story to tell you while I'm freezing. I told my parents to hold the party indoors, that England did not inure me to the cold. I have a speech prepared. Do you want to help me feed the neighbor's cats?"

"I'm on the job."

"Talking to my sister?"

"A guy I know has a crush on her."

"Poor guy. No, poor Joanie. Shit, this is not going the way I planned."

"Shit, then let's go feed those cats."

Karen smiled and led the way, wobbling, high heels on grass. Thunder, lightning, rain—Karen kicked off her shoes and ran barefoot. Jack caught up at the next-door porch—wet, close to laughing.

Karen opened the door. A foyer light was on; Jack looked at her—shivering, goose bumps. Karen shook water from her hair. "The cats are upstairs."

Jack took off his blazer. "No, I want to hear your speech."

"I'm sure you know what it is. I'm sure lots of people have thanked you."

"You haven't."

Karen shivered. "Shit. I'm sorry, but this is not going the way I planned."

Jack draped his coat around her shoulders. "You got the L.A. papers over in England?"

"Yes."

"And you read about me?"

"Yes. You—"

"Karen, they exaggerate sometimes. They build things up."

"Are you telling me those things I've read are lies?"

"Not ex—no, they're not."

Karen turned away. "Good, I knew they were true, so here's your speech, and don't look at me, because I'm flustered. One, you got me away from taking pills. Two, you convinced my father to send me abroad, where I got a damn good education and met nice people. Three, you arrested that terrible man who sold me the pills."

Jack touched her; Karen flinched away. "No, let me tell it! Four, what I wasn't going to mention, is that Les Weiskopf gave girls pills for free if they slept with him. Father was stingy with my allowance and sooner or later I would have done it. So there—you kept my goddamned virtue intact."

Jack laughed. "Am I your goddamned hero?"

"Yes, and I'm twenty-two years old and not the school-girl-crush type."

"Good, because I'd like to take you to dinner sometime."

Karen swung around. Her mascara was ruined; she'd chewed off most of her lipstick. "Yes. Mother and Father will have coronaries, but yes."

Jack said, "This is the first stupid move I've made in years."

7

A MONTH of shit.

Bud ripped January 1952 off his calendar, counted felony arrests. January 1 through January 11: zero—he'd worked crowd control at a movie location—Parker wanted a muscle guy there to shoo away autograph hounds. January 14: the cop beaters acquitted on assault charges, Helenowski and Brownell chewed up—the spics' lawyer made it look like they instigated the whole thing. Civil suits threatened; "get a lawyer?" scribbled by the date.

January 16, 19, 22: wife thumpers paroled, welcome home visits. January 23–25: stakeouts on a burglary ring, him and Stens acting on a tip from Johnny Stomp, who just seemed to know things, per a rumor: he used to run a blackmail racket. Gangland activity at a weird lull, Stomp scuffling to stay solvent, Mo Jahelka—looking after Mickey C.'s interests—probably afraid to push too much muscle. Seven arrests total, good for his quota, but the papers were working the station brouhaha, dubbing it "Bloody Christmas," and a rumor hit: the DA's Office had contacted Parker, IAD was going to question the men partying on Christmas Eve, the county grand jury was drooling for a presentation. More notes: "talk to Dick," "*lawyer*???," "*lawyer when*??"

The last week of the month—comic relief. Dick off duty, drying out at a health ranch in Twenty-nine Palms; the squad boss thought he was attending his father's funeral in Nebraska—the guys took up a collection to send flowers to a mortuary that didn't exist. Two felony notches on the 29th: parole violators he'd glommed off another Stomp snitch—but he'd had to beat the shit out of them, kidnap them, haul them from county turf to city so the Sheriff's couldn't claim the roust. The 31st: a dance with Chick Nadel, a barkeep who ran hot appliances out of the Moonglow Lounge. An impromptu raid; Chick with a stash of hot radios; a snitch on the guys who boosted the truck, holed up in San Diego, no way to make it an LAPD caper. He busted Chick instead: receiving stolen goods with a prior, ten felony arrests for the month—at least a double-digit tally.

Pure shit—straight into February.

Back to uniform, six days of directing traffic—Parker's idea, Detective Division personnel rotating to Patrol for a week a year. Alphabetically: as a "W" he stood at the rear of the pack. The late bird loses the worm—it rained all six of those days.

Floods on the job, a drought with the women.

Bud thumbed his address book. Lorene from the Silver Star, Jane from the Zimba Room, Nancy from the Orbit Lounge—late-breaking numbers. They had the look: late thirties, hungry—grateful for a younger guy who treated them nice and gave them a taste all men weren't shitheels. Lorene was heavyset—the mattress springs always banged the floor. Jane played opera records to set the mood—they sounded like cats fucking. Nancy was a lush, par for bar-prowl course. The jaded type—the type to break things off even quicker than he usually did.

"White, check this."

Bud looked up. Elmer Lentz held out the *Herald* front page.

The headline: "Police Beating Victims to File Suit."

Subheadings: "Grand Jury Ready to Hear Evidence," "Parker Vows Full LAPD Cooperation."

Lentz said, "This could be trouble."

Bud said, "No shit, Sherlock."

8

PRESTON EXLEY finished reading. "Edmund, all three versions are brilliant, but you should have gone to Parker immediately. Now, with all the publicity, your coming forth smacks of panic. Are you prepared to be an informant?"

Ed squared his glasses. "Yes."

"Are you prepared to be despised within the Department?"

"Yes, and I'm prepared for whatever displays of gratitude Parker has to offer."

Preston skimmed pages. "Interesting. Shifting most of the guilt to men with their pensions already secured is salutary, and this Officer White sounds a bit fearsome."

Ed got chills. "He is. Internal Affairs is interviewing me tomorrow, and I don't relish telling them about his stunt with the Mexican."

"Afraid of reprisals?"

"Not really."

"Don't ignore your fear, Edmund. That's weakness. White and his friend Stensland behaved with despicable disregard for departmental bylaws, and they're both obvious thugs. Are you prepared for your interview?"

"Yes."

"They'll be brutal."

"I know, Father."

"They'll stress your inability to keep order and the fact that you let those officers steal your keys."

Ed flushed. "It was getting chaotic, and fighting those men would have created more chaos."

"Don't raise your voice and don't justify yourself. Not with me, not with the IA men. It makes you appear—"

A breaking voice. "Don't say 'weak,' Father. Don't draw any sort of parallel with Thomas. And don't assume that I can't handle this situation."

Preston picked up the phone. "I know you're capable of holding your own. But are you capable of seizing Bill Parker's gratitude before he displays it?"

"Father, you told me once that Thomas was your heir as a natural and I was your heir as an opportunist. What does that tell you?"

Preston smiled, dialed a number. "Bill? Hello, it's Preston Exley ...Yes, fine, thank you ... No, I wouldn't have called your personal line for that ... No, Bill, it's about my son Edmund. He was on duty at Central Station Christmas Eve, and I think he has valuable information for you ...Yes, tonight? Certainly, he'll be there ...Yes, and my regards to Helen ...Yes, goodbye, Bill."

Ed felt his heart slamming. Preston said, "Meet Chief Parker at the Pacific Dining Car tonight at eight. He'll arrange for a private room where you can talk."

"Which one of the depositions do I show him?"

Preston handed the paperwork back. "Opportunities like this don't come very often. I had the Atherton case, you had a little taste with Guadalcanal. Read the family scrapbook and *remember those precedents*."

"Yes, but which deposition?"

"You figure it out. And have a good meal at the Dining Car. The supper invitation is a good sign, and Bill doesn't like finicky eaters."

* * *

Ed drove to his apartment, read, remembered. The scrapbook held clippings arranged in chronological order; what the newspapers didn't tell him he'd burned into his memory.

1934—the Atherton case.

Children: Mexican, Negro, Oriental—three male, two female—are found dismembered, the trunks of their bodies discovered in L.A. area storm drains. The arms and legs have been severed; the internal organs removed. The press dubs the killer "Dr. Frankenstein." Inspector Preston Exley heads the investigation.

He deems the Frankenstein tag appropriate: tennis racket strings were found at all five crime scenes, the third victim had darning-needle holes in his armpits. Exley concludes that the fiend is re-creating children with stitching and a knife; he begins hauling in deviates, cranks, loony bin parolees. He wonders what the killer will do for a face—and learns a week later.

Wee Willie Wennerholm, child star in Raymond Dieterling's stable, is kidnapped from a studio tutorial school. The following day his body is found on the Glendale railroad tracks—decapitated.

Then a break: administrators from the Glenhaven State Mental Hospital call the LAPD—Loren Atherton, a child molester with a vampire fixation, was paroled to Los Angeles two months before—and has not yet reported to his parole officer.

Exley locates Atherton on skid row: he has a job washing bottles at a blood bank. Surveillance reveals that he steals blood, mixes it with cheap wine and drinks it. Exley's men arrest Atherton at a downtown theater—masturbating during a horror movie. Exley raids his hotel room, finds a set of keys—the keys to an abandoned storage garage. He goes there—and finds Hell.

A prototype child packed in dry ice: male Negro arms, male Mexican legs, a male Chinese torso with spliced-in female genitalia and Wee Willie Wennerholm's head. Wings cut from birds stitched to the child's back. Accoutrements rest nearby: horror movie reels, gutted tennis rackets, diagrams for creating hybrid children. Photographs of children in various stages of dismemberment, a closet/darkroom filled with developing supplies.

Hell.

Atherton confesses to the killings; he is tried, convicted, hanged at San Quentin. Preston Exley keeps copies of the death photos; he shows them to his policemen sons—so that they will know the brutality of crimes that require absolute justice.

Ed flipped pages: past his mother's obit, Thomas' death. Outside of his father's triumphs, the only time the Exleys made the papers was when somebody died. He made the *Examiner*: an article on the sons of famous men fighting World War II. Like Bloody Christmas, there was more than one version.

The *Examiner* ran the version that won him his DSC: Corporal Ed Exley, sole survivor of a platoon wiped out in hand-to-hand combat, takes down three trenches filled with Jap infantry, twenty-nine dead total, if there were an officer present to witness the act he would have won the Congressional Medal of Honor. Version two: Ed Exley seizes the opportunity to make a scout run when a Jap bayonet charge is imminent, dawdles, comes back to find his platoon obliterated and a Jap patrol approaching. He hides under Sergeant Peters and Pfc Wasnicki, feels them buckle when the Japs strafe bodies; he bites into Wasnicki's arm, chews his wristwatch strap clean off. He waits for dusk, sobbing, covered by dead men, a tiny passage between bodies feeding him air. Then a terror run for battalion HQ—halted when he sees another slaughter scene.

A little Shinto shrine, tucked into a clearing covered with camouflage netting. Dead Japs on pallets, jaundice green, emaciated. Every man ripped stomach to ribcage; ornately carved swords, blood-caked, stacked neatly. Mass suicide—soldiers too proud to risk capture or die from malaria.

Three trenches cut into the ground behind the temple; weaponry nearby—rifles and pistols rusted out from heavy rain. A flamethrower wrapped in camouflage cloth—in working order.

He held it, knowing just one thing: he would not survive Guadalcanal. He'd be assigned to a new platoon; his scout run dawdlings wouldn't wash. He could not request an HQ assignment—his father would deem the act cowardice. He would have to live with contempt—fellow LAPD men wounded, awarded medals.

"Medals" led to "Bond Tours" led to crime scene reconstructions. He saw his opportunity.

He found a Jap machine gun. He hauled the hara-kiri men to the trenches, put useless weapons in their hands, arranged them facing an opening in the clearing. He dropped the machine gun there, pointed toward the opening, three rounds left in the feeder belt. He got the flamethrower, torched the Japs and the shrine past forensic recognition. He got his story straight, made it back to battalion HQ.

Recon patrols confirmed the story: fighting Ed Exley, armed with Jap ordnance, french-fried twenty-nine of the little fuckers.

The Distinguished Service Cross—the second highest medal his country could bestow. A stateside bond tour, a hero's welcome, back to the LAPD a champion.

Some kind of wary respect from Preston Exley.

"Read the family scrapbook. Remember those precedents."

Ed put the book away, still not sure how he'd play Bloody Christmas—but certain what the man meant.

Opportunities fall easy—you pay for them later.

Father, I've known it since I picked up that flamethrower.

9

"IF IT goes to the grand jury, you won't swing. And the DA and I will try to keep it from going there."

Jack counted favors on deposit. Sixteen G's to Loew's slush fund—Miller Stanton helped him lube the *Badge of Honor* gang. He tweaked Brett Chase himself, a concise little threat—a *Hush-Hush* exposé on his queerness. Max Peltz coughed up large—Loew frosted out a tax audit. A Cupid favor—tonight the man meets pouty Joan Morrow. "Ellis, I don't even want to testify. I'm talking to some IAD goons tomorrow, and it *is* going to the grand jury. So fix it."

Loew played with his Phi Beta chain. "Jack, a prisoner assaulted you, and you responded in kind. You're clean. You're also somewhat of a public figure and the preliminary depositions that we've received from the plaintiff's attorneys state that four of the beating victims recognized you. You'll testify, Jack. But you won't swing."

"I just thought I'd run it by you. But if you ask me to squeal on my brother officers, I'll plead fucking amnesia. *Comprende*, Counselor?"

Loew leaned across his desk. "We shouldn't argue—we're doing too well together. Officer Wendell White and Sergeant Richard Stensland are the ones who should be worrying, not you. Besides, the grapevine tells me you have a new lady in your life."

"You mean Joan Morrow told you."

"Yes, and frankly she and her parents disapprove. You are fifteen years older than the girl, and you've had a checkered past."

Caddy, ski instructor—an orphanage kid good at servicing rich folks. "Joanie offer details?"

"Just that the girl has a mad crush on you and believes your press clippings. I assured Joan that those clippings are true. Karen tells Joan that so far you've behaved like a gentleman, which I find hard to believe."

"That ends tonight, I hope. After our little double date, it's the *Badge of Honor* wrap party and an intimate interlude somewhere."

Loew twisted his vest chain. "Jack, has Joan been playing hard to get or does she really have that many men chasing her?"

Jack twisted the knife. "She's a popular kid, but all those movie star guys are just fluff. Stick to your guns."

"Movie stars?"

"Fluff, Ellis. Cute, but fluff."

"Jack, I want to thank you for coming along tonight. I'm sure you and Karen will be superb icebreakers."

"Then let's hit it."

* * *

Don the Beachcomber's—the women waiting in a wraparound booth. Jack made introductions. "Ellis Loew, Karen Morrow and Joan Morrow. Karen, don't they make a lovely couple?"

Karen said, "Hello," no hand squeeze—six dates and all she put out were bland good-night kisses. Loew sat next to Joan; Joanie checked him out—probably sniffing for signs of Jewishness. "Ellis and I are good phone chums already. Aren't we?"

"We are indeed"—Loew working his courtroom voice.

Joan finished her drink. "How do you two know each other? Do the police work closely with the District Attorney's Office?"

Jack kiboshed a laugh: I'm Jewboy's bagman. "We build cases together. I get the evidence, Ellis prosecutes the bad guys."

A waiter hovered. Joan ordered an Islander Punch; Jack asked for coffee. Loew said, "Beefeater martini." Karen put a hand over her glass. "Then this Bloody Christmas thing will strain relations between the police and Mr. Loew's office. Isn't that likely?"

Loew hit quick. "No, because the LAPD rank and file wish to see the wrongdoers dealt with severely. Right, Jack?"

"Sure. Things like that give all policemen a black eye."

The drinks arrived—Joan took hers down in three gulps. "You were there, weren't you, Jack? Daddy said you always go to that station party, at least since your second wife left you."

Karen: "*Joanie!*"

Jack said, "I was there."

"Did you take a few licks for justice?"

"It wasn't worth it to me."

"You mean there weren't any headlines to be had?"

"Joanie, be quiet. You're drunk."

Loew fingered his tie; Karen fingered an ashtray. Joan slurped the rest of her drink. "Teetotalers are always so judgmental. You used to attend that party after your *first* wife left you, didn't you, Sergeant?"

Karen gripped the ashtray. "You goddamn bitch."

Joan laughed. "If you want a hero policeman, I know a man named Exley who at least risked his life for his country. Granted, Jack's smooth, but can't you see what he is?"

Karen threw the ashtray—it hit the wall, then Ellis Loew's lap. Loew stuck his head in a menu; Joanie bitch glowered. Jack led Karen out of the restaurant.

* * *

Over to Variety International Pictures—Karen bad-mouthing Joanie non-stop. Jack parked by the *Badge of Honor* set; hillbilly music drifted out. Karen sighed. "My parents will get used to the idea."

Jack turned on the dash light. The girl had dark brown hair done in waves, freckles, a touch of an overbite. "What idea?"

"Well ... the idea of us seeing each other."

"Which is going pretty slow."

"That's partly my fault. One minute you're telling me these wonderful stories and the next minute you just stop. I keep wondering what you're thinking about and thinking that there's so many things you can't tell me. It makes me think you think I'm too young, so I pull away."

Jack opened the door. "Keep getting my number and you won't be too young. And tell me some of your stories, because sometimes I get tired of mine."

"Deal? My stories after the party?"

"Deal. And by the way, what do you think of your sister and Ellis Loew?"

Karen didn't blink. "She'll marry him. My parents will overlook the fact that he's Jewish because he's ambitious and a Republican. He'll tolerate Joanie's scenes in public and hit her in private. Their kids will be a mess."

Jack laughed. "Let's dance. And don't get star-struck, people will think you're a hick."

They entered arm in arm. Karen went in starry-eyed; Jack scoped his biggest wrap bash yet.

Spade Cooley and his boys on a bandstand, Spade at the mike with Burt Arthur "Deuce" Perkins, his bass player, called "Deuce" for his two-spot on a chain gang: unnatural acts against dogs. Spade smoked opium; Deuce popped "H"—a *Hush-Hush* roust just looking to happen. Max Peltz glad-handing the camera crew; Brett Chase beside him, talking to Billy Dieterling, the head cameraman. Billy's eyes on his twist, Timmy Valburn, Moochie Mouse on the *Dream-a-Dream Hour.* Tables up against the back wall—covered with liquor bottles, cold cuts. Kikey Teitlebaum there with the food—Peltz probably had his deli cater the party. Johnny Stompanato with Kikey, ex–Mickey Cohen boys huddling. Every *Badge of Honor* actor, crew member and general hanger-on eating, drinking, dancing.

Jack swept Karen onto the floor: swirls through a fast-tune medley, grinds when Spade switched to ballads. Karen kept her eyes closed; Jack kept his open—the better to dig the shmaltz. He felt a tap on the shoulder.

Miller Stanton cutting in. Karen opened her eyes and gasped: a TV star wanted to dance with her. Jack bowed. "Karen Morrow, Miller Stanton."

Karen yelled over the music. "Hi! I saw all those old Raymond Dieterling movies you made. You were great!"

Stanton hoisted her hands square-dance style. "I was a brat! Jack, go see Max—he wants to talk to you."

Jack walked to the rear of the set—quiet, the music lulled. Max Peltz handed him two envelopes. "Your season bonus and a boost for Mr. Loew. It's from Spade Cooley."

Loew's bag was fat. "What's Cooley want?"

"I'd say insurance you won't mess with his habit."

Jack lit a cigarette. "Spade doesn't interest me."

"Not a big enough name?"

"Be nice, Max."

Peltz leaned in close. "Jack, *you* try to be nicer, 'cause you're getting a bad rep in the Industry. People say you're a hard-on, you don't play the game. You shook down Brett for Mr. Loew, fine, he's a goddamn faigeleh, he's got it coming. But you can't bite the hand that feeds you, not when half the people in the Industry blow tea from time to time. Stick with the shvartzes—those jazz guys make good copy."

Jack eyeballed the set. Brett Chase in a hobnob: Billy Dieterling, Timmy Valburn—a regular fruit convention. Kikey T. and Johnny Stomp shmoozing—Deuce Perkins, Lee Vachss joining in. Peltz said, "Seriously, Jack. Play the game."

Jack pointed to the hard boys. "Max, the game is my life. You see those guys over there?"

"Sure. What's that—"

"Max, that's what the Department calls a known criminal assembly. Perkins is an ex-con wheelman who fucks dogs, and Abe Teitlebaum's on parole. The tall guy with the mustache is Lee Vachss, and he's made for at least a dozen snuffs for Mickey C. The good-looking wop is Johnny Stompanato. I doubt if he's thirty years old, and he's got a racket sheet as long as your arm. I am empowered by the Los Angeles Police Department to roust those cocksuckers on general suspicion, and I'm derelict in my duty for not doing it. Because I'm *playing the game*."

Peltz waved a cigar. "So keep playing it—but pianissimo on the tough-guy stuff. And look, Miller's bird-dogging your quail. Jesus, you like them young."

Rumors: Max and high school trim. "Not as young as you."

"Ha! Go, you fucking gonif. Your girl's looking for you."

Karen by a wall poster: Brett Chase as Lieutenant Vance Vincent. Jack walked over; Karen's eyes lit up. "God, this is so wonderful! Tell me who everyone is!"

Full-blast music—Cooley yodeling, Deuce Perkins banging his bass. Jack danced Karen across the floor—over to a corner crammed with arclights. A perfect spot—quiet, a scope on the whole gang.

Jack pointed out the players. "Brett Chase you already know about. He's not dancing because he's queer. The old guy with the cigar is Max Peltz. He's the producer, and he directs most of the episodes. You danced with Miller, so you know him. The two guys in skivvies are Augie Luger and Hank Kraft—they're grips. The girl with the clipboard is Penny Fulweider, she couldn't quit working even if she wanted to—she's the script supervisor. You know how the sets on the show are so modernistic? Well, the blond guy across from the bandstand is David Mertens, the set designer. Sometimes you'd think he was drunk, but he's not—he's got some rare kind of epilepsy, and he takes medicine for it.

I heard he was in an accident and hit his head, that that started it. He's got these scars on his neck, so maybe that's it. Next to him there's Phil Shenkel, the assistant director, and the guy next to him is Jerry Marsalas, the male nurse who looks after Mertens. Terry Riegert, the actor who plays Captain Jeffries, is dancing with that tall redhead. The guys by the water cooler are Billy Dieterling, Chuck Maxwell and Dick Harwell, the camera crew, and the rest of the people are dates."

Karen looked straight at him. "It's your milieu, and you love it. And you care about those people."

"I like them—and Miller's a good friend."

"Jack, you can't fool me."

"Karen, this is Hollywood. And ninety percent of Hollywood is moonshine."

"Spoilsport. I'm gearing myself up to be reckless, so don't put a damper on it."

Daring him.

Jack tumbled; Karen leaned into the kiss. They probed, tasted, pulled back the same instant—Jack broke off the clinch dizzy.

Karen let her hands linger. "The neighbors are still on vacation. We could go feed the cats."

"Yeah ... sure."

"Will you get me a brandy before we go?"

Jack walked to the food table. Deuce Perkins said, "Nice stuff, Vincennes. You got the same taste as me."

A skinny cracker in a black cowboy shirt with pink piping. Boots put him close to six-six; his hands were enormous. "Perkins, your stuff sniffs fire hydrants."

"Spade might not like you talkin' to me that way. Not with that envelope you got in your pocket."

Lee Vachss, Abe Teitlebaum watching them. "Not another word, Perkins."

Deuce chewed a toothpick. "Your quiff know you get your jollies shakin' down niggers?"

Jack pointed to the wall. "Roll up your sleeves, spread your legs."

Perkins spat out his toothpick. "You ain't that crazy."

Johnny Stomp, Vachss, Teitlebaum—all in earshot. Jack said, "Kiss the wall, shitbird."

Perkins leaned over the table, palms on the wall. Jack pulled up his sleeves—fresh tracks—emptied his pockets. Paydirt—a hypo syringe. A crowd forming up—Jack played to it. "Needle marks and that outfit are good for three years State. Hand up the guy who sold you the hypo and you skate."

Deuce oozed sweat. Jack said, "Squeal in front of your friends and you stroll."

Perkins licked his lips. "Barney Stinson. Orderly at Queen of Angels."

Jack kicked his legs out from under him.

Perkins landed face first in the cold cuts; the table crashed to the floor.

The room let out one big breath.

Jack walked outside, groups breaking up to let him through. Karen by the car, shivering. "Did you have to do that?"

He'd sweated his shirt clean through. "Yeah, I did."

"I wish I hadn't seen it."

"So do I."

"I guess reading about things like that are one thing and seeing them is another. Would you try to—"

Jack put his arms around her. "I'll keep that stuff separate from you."

"But you'll still tell me your stories?"

"No ... yeah, sure."

"I wish we could turn back the clock on tonight."

"So do I. Look, do you want some dinner?"

"No. Do you still want to go see the cats?"

*   *   *

There were three cats—friendly guys who tried to take over the bed while they made love. Karen called the gray one Pavement, the tabby Tiger, the skinny one Ellis Loew. Jack resigned himself to the entourage—they made Karen giggle, he figured every laugh put Deuce Perkins further behind them. They made love, talked, played with the cats; Karen tried a cigarette—and coughed her lungs out. She begged for stories; Jack borrowed from the exploits of Officer Wendell White and spun gentler versions of his own cases: minimum strongarm, lots of sugar daddy— the bighearted Big V, protecting kids from the scourge of dope. At first the lies were hard—but Karen's warmth made them easier and easier. Near dawn, the girl dozed off; he stayed wide awake, the cats driving him crazy. He kept wishing she'd wake up so he could tell her more stories; he got little jolts of worry: that he'd never remember all the phony parts, she'd catch him in whoppers, it would blow their deal sky high. Karen's body grew warmer as she slept; Jack pressed closer to her. He fell asleep getting his stories straight.

10

A CORRIDOR forty feet long, both sides lined with benches: scuffed, dusty, just hauled up from some storage hole. Packed: men in plainclothes and uniform, most of them reading—newspapers screaming *Bloody Christmas.* Bud thought of him and Stens front page smeared: nailed by the spics and their lawyers. He'd gotten his call to appear at 4:00 A.M., pure IA scare tactics. Dick across the hall—back from the dry-out farm, into the jug. Six Internal Affairs interviews apiece—neither of them had snitched. A regular Christmas reunion, the gang's all here—except Ed Exley.

Time dragged, traffic flowed: interrogation room grillings. Elmer Lentz dropped a bomb: the radio said the grand jury requested a presentation—all the officers at Central Station 12/25/51 were to stand a show-up tomorrow, prisoners would be there to ID the roughnecks. Chief Parker's door opened; Thad Green stepped outside. "Officer White, please."

Bud walked over; Green pointed him in. A small room: Parker's desk, chairs facing it. No wall mementoes, a gray-tinted mirror— maybe a two-way. The chief behind his desk, in uniform, four gold stars on his shoulders. Dudley Smith in the middle chair; Green back in the chair nearest Parker. Bud took the hot seat—a spot where all three men could see him. Parker said, "Officer, you know Deputy Chief Green, and I'm sure you know of Lieutenant Smith. The lieutenant has been serving me as an advisor during this crisis we've been having."

Green lit a cigarette. "Officer, you're being given a last chance to cooperate. You've been questioned repeatedly by Internal Affairs, and you've repeatedly refused to cooperate. Normally, you would have been suspended from duty. But you're a fine detective, and Chief Parker and I are convinced that your actions at the party were relatively blameless. You were provoked, Officer. You were not wantonly violent like most of the men accused."

Bud started to talk; Smith cut him off. "Lad, I'm sure that I speak for Chief Parker in this, so I will take the liberty of stating it without ellipses. It's a damn pity that the six scum who assaulted our brother officers weren't shot on the spot, and the violence visited upon them I deem mild. But, parenthetically, police officers who cannot control their impulses have no business being police officers, and the shenanigans perpetrated by the men outside have made the Los Angeles Police Department a laughingstock. This cannot be tolerated. Heads must roll. We must have cooperative policemen witnesses to offset the damage done to the Department's image—an image that has vastly improved under the leadership of Chief Parker. We have one major policeman witness already, and Deputy DA Ellis Loew stands firm in his desire not to prosecute LAPD officers—even if the grand jury hands down true bills. Lad, will you testify? For the Department, not the prosecution."

Bud checked the mirror—a two-way for sure—make DA's Bureau goons taking notes. "No, sir. I won't."

Parker scanned a sheet of paper. "Officer, you picked a man up by the neck and tried to bash his brains out. That looks very bad, and even though you were verbally provoked, the action stands out more than most of the abuse heaped on the prisoners. That goes against you. But you were heard muttering 'This is a goddamned disgrace' when you left the cellblock, which is in your favor. Now, do you see how appearing as a voluntary witness could offset the disadvantages caused by your ... imaginative show of force?"

A snap: Exley's their boy, *he* heard me, locked in the storeroom. "Sir, I won't testify."

Parker flushed bright red. Smith said, "Lad, let's talk turkey. I admire your refusal to betray fellow officers, and I sense that loyalty to your partner is what stands behind it. I admire that especially, and Chief Parker has authorized me to offer you a deal. If you testify as to Dick Stensland's actions and the grand jury hands down a bill against him, Stensland will serve no time in jail if convicted. We have Ellis Loew's word on that. Stensland will be dismissed from the Department without pension, but his pension will be paid to him sub rosa, through monies diverted from the Widows and Orphans Fund. Lad, will you testify?"

Bud stared at the mirror. "Sir, I won't testify."

Thad Green pointed to the door. "Be at Division 43 grand jury chambers tomorrow at 9:00. Be prepared to stand in a show-up and be called to testify. If you refuse to testify, you'll receive a subpoena and be suspended from duty pending a trial board. Get out of here, White."

Dudley Smith smiled—very slightly. Bud shot the mirror a stiff middle finger.

11

STREAKS AND smudges on the two-way—expressions came off blurred. Thad Green tough to read; Parker simple—he turned ugly colors. Dudley Smith—lexophile with a brogue—too calculated to figure. Bud White too *too* easy: the chief quoted, "This is a goddamned disgrace"; a big thought balloon popped up: "Ed Exley is the stool pigeon." The middle finger salute was just icing.

Ed tapped the speaker; static crackled. The closet was hot— but not stifling like the Central Jail storeroom. He thought of his last two weeks.

He'd played it brass balls with Parker, presenting all three depositions, agreeing to testify as the Department's key witness. Parker considered his assessment of the situation brilliant, the mark of an exemplary officer. He gave the least damaging of the three statements to Ellis Loew and his favorite DA's investigator, a young law school graduate—Bob Gallaudet. The blame was shifted, more than deservedly, to Sergeant Richard Stensland and Officer Wendell White; less deservedly to three men with their pensions already secured. The chief's reward to his exemplary witness: a transfer to a detective squadroom—a huge promotion. With the lieutenant's exam aced, within a year he would stand as Detective Lieutenant E. J. Exley.

Green left the office; Ellis Loew and Gallaudet walked in. Loew and Parker conferred; Gallaudet opened the door. "Sergeant Vincennes, please"—static out of the speaker.

Trashcan Jack: sleek in a chalk-striped suit. No amenities—he took the middle seat checking his watch. A look passed—Trash, Ellis Loew. Parker eyed the new fish, an easy read—pure contempt. Gallaudet stood by the door, smoking.

Loew said, "Sergeant, we'll get right to it. You've been very cooperative with IA, which is to your credit. But nine witnesses have identified you as hitting Juan Carbijal, and four drunk tank prisoners saw you carrying in a case of rum. You see, your notoriety preceded you. Even drunks read the scandal sheets."

Dudley Smith took over. "Lad, we need your notoriety. We have a stellar witness who will tell the grand jury that you hit back only after being hit, and since that is probably the truth, further prisoner testimony will vindicate you. But we need you to admit bringing the liquor the men got drunk on. Admit to that interdepartmental infraction and you'll get off with a trial board. Mr. Loew guarantees a quashed criminal indictment should one arise."

Trashcan kept still. Ed read in: Bud White brought most of the booze, he's afraid to inform on him. Parker said, "There will have to be a large shake-up within the Department. Testify, and you'll receive a minor trial board, no suspension, no demotion. I'll guarantee you a light slap on the wrist—a transfer to Administrative Vice for a year or so."

Vincennes to Loew. "Ellis, have I got any more truck with you on this? You know what working Narco means to me."

Loew flinched. Parker said, "None, and there's more. You'll have to stand in the show-up tomorrow, and we want you to testify against Officer Krugman, Sergeant Tucker and Officer Pratt. All three men have already earned their pensions. Our key witness will testify roundly, but you can plead ignorance to questions directed at the other men. Frankly, we must sate the public's clamor for blood by giving up some of our own."

Dudley Smith: "I doubt if you've ever drawn a stupid breath, lad. Don't do it now."

Trashcan Jack: "I'll do it."

Smiles all around. Gallaudet said, "I'll go over your testimony with you, Sergeant. Dining Car lunch on Mr. Loew." Vincennes stood up; Loew walked him to the door.

Whispers out the speaker: "... and I told Cooley you wouldn't do it again"—"Okay, boss." Parker nodded at the mirror.

Ed walked in, straight to the hot seat. Smith said, "Lad, you're very much the man of the hour."

Parker smiled. "Ed, I had you watch because your assessment of this situation has been very astute. Any last thoughts before you testify?"

"Sir, am I correct in assuming that whatever criminal bills the grand jury hands down will be stalled or quashed during Mr. Loew's post-indictment process?"

Loew grimaced. He'd hit a nerve—just like his father said he would. "Sir, am I correct in that?"

Loew, patronizing. "Have you attended law school, Sergeant?"

"No, sir. I haven't."

"Then your esteemed father has given you good counsel."

Voice steady. "No, sir. He hasn't."

Smith said, "Let's assume you're correct. Let's assume that we are bending our efforts toward what all loyal policemen want: no brother officers tried publicly. Assuming that, what do you advise?"

The pitch he'd rehearsed—verbatim. "The public will demand more than true bills, stalling tactics and dismissed indictments. Interdepartmental trial boards, suspensions and a big transfer shake-up won't be enough. You told Officer White that heads must roll. I agree, and for the sake of the chief's prestige and the prestige of the Department, I think we need criminal convictions and jail sentences."

"Lad, I am shocked at the relish with which you just said that."

Ed to Parker. "Sir, you've brought the Department back from Horrall and Worton. Your reputation is exemplary and the Department's has greatly improved. You can assure that it stays that way."

Loew said, "Spill it, Exley. Exactly what does our junior officer informant think we should do?"

Ed, eyes on Parker. "Dismiss the indictments on the men with their twenty in. Publicize the transfer shake-up and give the bulk of the men trial boards and suspensions. Indict Johnny Brownell, tell him to request a no-jury venue and have the judge let him off with a suspended sentence—his brother was one of the officers initially assaulted. And indict, try and convict Dick Stensland and Bud White. Secure them jail time. Boot them off the Department. Stensland's a drunken thug, White almost killed a man and supplied more liquor than Vincennes. Feed them to the goddamn sharks. Protect yourself, protect the Department."

Silence, stretching. Smith broke it. "Gentlemen, I think our young sergeant's advice is rash and hypocritical. Stensland has his rough edges, but Wendell White is a valuable officer."

"Sir, White is a homicidal thug."

Smith started to speak; Parker raised a hand. "I think Ed's advice is worth considering. Ace them at the grand jury tomorrow, son. Wear a smart-looking suit and ace them."

Ed said, "Yes, sir." He forced himself not to shout his joy to the rafters.

12

SPOTLIGHTS, HEIGHT strips: Jack at 5´11˝; Frank Doherty, Dick Stens, John Brownell the short guys, Wilbert Huff, Bud White topping six. Central Jail punks across the glass, couched with DA's cops taking names.

A speaker squawked, "Left profile"; six men turned. "Right profile," "Face the wall," "Face the mirror"; "At ease, gentlemen." Silence; then: "Fourteen IDs apiece on Doherty, Stensland, Vincennes, White and Brownell, four for Huff. Oh shit, the PA's on!"

Stens cracked up. Frank Doherty said, "Eat shit, cocksucker." White stayed expressionless—like he was already at the honor farm protecting Stens from niggers. The speaker: "Sergeant Vincennes to room 114, Officer White report to Chief Green's office. The rest of you men are dismissed."

114—the grand jury witness room.

Jack walked ahead, through curtains down to 114. A crowded room: Bloody Christmas plaintiffs, Ed Exley in a too-new suit, loose threads at the sleeves. The Xmas boys sneered; Jack braced Exley. "You're the key witness?"

"That's right."

"I should've known it was you. What's Parker throwing you?"

"Throwing me?"

"Yeah, Exley. *Throwing you.* The deal, the payoff. You think *I'm* testifying for free?"

Exley futzed with his glasses. "I'm just doing my duty."

Jack laughed. "You're playing an angle, college boy. You're getting something out of this, so you won't have to hobnob with the fucking rank-and-file cops who are going to hate your fucking guts for snitching. And if Parker promised you the Bureau, watch out. Some Bureau guys are gonna burn in this thing and you're gonna have to work with friends of theirs."

Exley flinched; Jack laughed. "Good payoff, I'll admit that."

"You're the payoff expert. Not me."

"You'll be outranking me pretty soon, so I should be nice. Did you know Ellis Loew's new girlfriend has the hots for you?"

A clerk called, "Edmund J. Exley to chambers."

Jack winked. "Go. And clip those threads on your coat or you'll look like a rube."

Exley walked across the hall—primping, pulling threads.

* * *

Jack killed time—thinking about Karen. Ten days since the party; life was mostly aces. He had to apologize to Spade Cooley; Welton Morrow was pissed over him and Karen—but the luke-warm Joanie/Ellis Loew deal almost made it up for him. Hotel shacks were a strain—Karen lived at home, his place was a dive, he'd been neglecting his payments to the Scoggins kids to make the freight at the Ambassador. Karen loved the illicit romance; he loved her loving it. Aces. But Sid Hudgens hadn't called and L.A. was heroin dry—no Narco jollies. A year at Ad Vice loomed like the gas chamber.

He felt like a fighter ready to dive. The Christmas geeks kept staring; the punk he'd thumped had on a nose splint—probably a phony some Jew lawyer told him to wear. The grand jury room door stood ajar; Jack walked over, looked in.

Six jurors at a table facing the witness stand; Ellis Loew hurl-ing questions—Ed Exley in the box.

He didn't play with his glasses; he didn't hem and haw. His voice went an octave lower than normal—and stayed even. Skinny, not a cop type, he still had authority—and his timing was perfect. Loew pitched perfect outside sliders; Exley knew they were coming, but acted surprised. Whoever coached him did a fucking-A bang-up job.

Jack picked out details, sensed Exley reaching, a war hero—not a weak sister in a cellblock full of rowdies. Loew glossed over that; Exley's answers hit smart: he was outnumbered, his keys were snatched, he was locked in a storeroom—and that was that. He was a man who knew who he was, knew the futility of cheap heroics.

Exley spieled: rat-offs on Brownell, Huff, Doherty. He called Dick Stensland the worst of the worst, didn't blink snitching Bud White. Jack smiled when it hit him: everything is skewed toward our side. Krugman, Pratt, Tucker, pension safe—were set up—for *his* testimony. Stensland and White—heading for indictment city. What a fucking performance.

Loew called for a summation. Exley obliged: pap about justice. Loew excused him; the jurors almost swooned. Exley left the box limping—he'd probably jammed his legs asleep.

Jack met him outside. "You were good. Parker would've loved it."

Exley stretched his legs. "You think he'll read the transcript?"

"He'll have it inside ten minutes, and Bud White'll fuck you for this if it takes the rest of his life. He was called in to Thad

Green after the show-up, and you can bet Green suspended him. You had better pray he cops a deal and stays on the Department, because that is one civilian you do not want on your case."

"Is that why you didn't tell Loew he brought most of the liquor?"

A clerk called, "John Vincennes, five minutes."

Jack got up some nerve. "I'm snitching three old-timers who'll be fishing in Oregon next week. Next to you, I'm clean. *And smart.*"

"We're both doing the right thing. Only you hate yourself for it, and that's not smart."

Jack saw Ellis Loew and Karen down the hall. Loew walked up. "I told Joan you were testifying today, and she told Karen. I'm sorry, and I told Joan in confidence. *Jack, I'm sorry.* I told Karen she couldn't watch in chambers, that she'll have to listen over the speaker in my office. *Jack, I'm sorry.*"

"Jewboy, you sure know how to guarantee a witness."

13

BUD NURSED a highball. Jukebox noise pounded him; he had the worst seat in the bar—a sofa back by the pay phones. His old football wounds throbbed—like his hard-on for Exley. No badge, no gun, indictments shooting his way—the fortyish redhead looked like the best thing he'd ever seen. He carried his drink over.

She smiled at him. The red looked fake—but she had a kind face. Bud smiled. "That an old-fashioned you're drinking?"

"Yes, and my name's Angela."

"My name's Bud."

"Nobody was born with the name 'Bud.'"

"They stick you with a name like 'Wendell,' you look for an alias."

Angela laughed. "What do you do, *Bud*?"

"I'm sorta between jobs right now."

"Oh? Well, what *did* you do?"

SUSPENDED! YOU DUMB FUCK LOOKING A GIFT HORSE IN THE MOUTH! "I wouldn't play ball with my boss. Angela, what do you say—"

"You mean like a union dispute or something? I'm in the United Federation of Teachers, and my ex-husband was a shop steward with the Teamsters. Is that what you—"

Bud felt a hand on his shoulder. "Lad, might I have a word with you?"

Dudley Smith. CALL IT IA RUNNING TAILS.

"This business, Lieutenant?"

"It is indeed. Say good night to your new friend and join me by those back tables. I've told the bartender to turn the music down so we can talk."

A jump tune went soft; Smith walked off. A sailor had his hooks into Angela. Bud eased over to the lounges.

Cozy: Smith, two chairs, a table—a newspaper covering the top, a little mound underneath. Bud sat down. "Is IA tailing me?"

"Yes, and other likely indictees. It was your chum Exley's idea. The lad has a piece of Chief Parker's ear, and he told him that you and Stensland might be driven to commit rash acts. Exley vilified you and many other fine men on the witness stand, lad. I've read the transcript. His testimony was high treason and a despicable affront to all honorable policemen."

Stens—holed up on a bender. "Don't that paper say we been indicted?"

"Don't be precipitous, lad. I've used my piece of the chief's ear to have your tail called off, so you're with a friend."

"Lieutenant, what do you want?"

Smith said, "Call me Dudley."

"*Dudley*, what do you want?"

Ho, ho, ho—a beautiful tenor. "Lad, you impress me. I admire your refusal to testify and your loyalty to your partner, however unfounded. I admire you as a policeman, particularly your adherence to violence where needed as a necessary adjunct to the job, and I am most impressed by your punishment of woman beaters. Do you hate them, lad?"

Big words—his head spun. "Yeah, I hate them."

"And for good reason, judging from what I know of your background. Do you hate anything else quite so much?"

Fists so tight his hands ached. "Exley. Fucking Exley. Trashcan Jack, he's gotta be up there, too. Dick Stens is giving himself cirrhosis 'cause those two squealed us off."

Smith shook his head. "Not Vincennes, lad. He was the stalking horse for the Department, and we needed him to give the DA's Office some bodies. He only snitched twenty-year men, and he took the blame for the liquor you brought to the party. No, lad, Jack does not deserve your hatred."

Bud leaned over the table. "Dudley, what do you want?"

"I want you to avoid an indictment and return to duty, and I have a way for you to do it."

Bud looked at the newspaper. "How?"

"Work for me."

"Doing what?"

"No, more questions first. Lad, do you recognize the need to contain crime, to keep it south of Jefferson with the dark element?"

"Sure."

"And do you think a certain organized crime element should be allowed to exist and perpetuate acceptable vices that hurt no one?"

"Sure, pork barrel. The game's gotta be played that way a little. What's this got to do—"

Smith yanked the paper—a badge and .38 special gleamed up. Bud, scalp prickles. "I knew you had juice. You squared it with Green?"

"Yes, lad, I squared it—with Parker. With the part of his ear that Exley hasn't poisoned. He said if the grand jury didn't hand down a bill against you, your refusal to testify would not be punished. Now pick up your things before the proprietor calls the police."

GLEAMING—Bud grabbed his goodies. "There's no goddamn bill on me?"

Ho, ho, ho—mocking. "Lad, the chief knew he was giving me a long shot, and I'm glad you haven't read the Four Star *Herald*."

Bud said, "*How?*"

"Not yet, lad."

"What about Dick?"

"He's through, lad. And don't protest, because it's unavoidable. He's been billed, he'll be indicted and he'll swing. He's the Department's scapegoat, on Parker's orders. And it was Exley who convinced him to hand Dick over. Criminal charges and jail time."

A broiling hot room—Bud pulled his necktie loose, closed his eyes.

"Lad, I'll get Dick a nice berth at the honor farm. I know a woman deputy there who can fix things, and when he gets out I'll guarantee him a shot at Exley."

Bud opened his eyes; Smith had the *Herald* spread full. The headline: "Policemen Indicted in Bloody Christmas Scandal."

Below, a column circled: Sergeant Richard Stensland flagged on four charges, three old-timer cops billed, Lentz, Brownell, Huff swinging on two bills apiece. Underlined: "Officer Wendell White, 33, received no true bills, although several sources within the District Attorney's Bureau had stated that first-degree assault bills seemed imminent. The grand jury's foreman stated that four police-beating victims recanted their previous testimony, which had Officer White attempting to strangle Juan Carbijal, age 19. The recanted testimony directly contradicted the testimony of LAPD Sergeant Edmund J. Exley, who had sworn under oath that White had, in fact, attempted to grievously injure Carbijal. Sergeant Exley's testimony is not considered tainted, since it resulted in probable indictments against seven other officers; however, although the grand jurors doubted the credibility of the recantings, they deemed them sufficient to deny the DA's Office true bills against Officer White. Deputy DA Ellis Loew told reporters: 'Something suspicious happened, but I don't know what it was. Four retractions have to supersede the testimony of one witness, even as splendid a witness as Sergeant Exley, a decorated war hero.'"

Newsprint swirling. Bud said, "Why? Why'd you do that for me? And how?"

Smith crumpled the paper. "Lad, I need you for a new assignment Parker has given me the go-ahead on. It's a containment measure, an adjunct to Homicide. We're going to call it the Surveillance Detail, an innocuous name for a duty that few men are fit for, but you were born for. It's a muscle job and a shooting job and a job that entails asking very few questions. Lad, do you follow my drift?"

"In Technicolor."

"You'll be transferred out of Central dicks when Parker announces his shake-up. Will you work for me?"

"I'd be crazy not to. Why, Dudley?"

"Why what, lad?"

"You shivved Ellis Loew to help me out, and everyone in the Bureau knows you and him are tight. Why?"

"Because I like your style, lad. Will that answer suffice?"

"I guess it'll have to. Now let's try 'how?'"

"How what, lad?"

"How you got the spics to retract."

Smith laid brass knucks on the table: chipped, caked with blood.

CALENDAR

1952

EXTRACT: L.A. *Mirror-News*, March 19:

POLICE BEATING SCANDAL:
COPS DISCIPLINE THEIR OWN
BEFORE WORST CULPRITS STAND TRIAL

LAPD CHIEF William H. Parker promised that he would seek justice—"wherever the search takes me"—in the tangled web of police brutality and civilian lawsuits that has come to be known as the "Bloody Christmas" scandal.

Seven officers have received criminal assault indictments stemming from their actions at the Central Division Jail on Christmas morning of last year. Those officers are:

Sergeant Ward Tucker, indicted for Second Degree Assault.

Officer Michael Krugman, Second Degree Assault and Battery.

Officer Henry Pratt, Second Degree Assault.

Sergeant Elmer Lentz, First Degree Assault with Battery.

Sergeant Wilbert Huff, First Degree Assault with Battery.

Officer John Brownell, First Degree Assault and Aggravated Assault.

Sergeant Richard Stensland, First Degree Assault, Aggravated Assault, First Degree Battery and Mayhem.

Parker did not dwell on the charges facing the indicted policemen, or on the scores of civil suits that beating victims Dinardo Sanchez, Juan Carbijal, Dennis Rice, Ezekiel Garcia, Clinton Rice and Reyes Chasco have filed against individual policemen and the Los Angeles Police Department. He announced that the following officers would receive interdepartmental trial boards, and, if not vindicated, would be severely disciplined within the Department.

Sergeant Walter Crumley, Sergeant Walter Dukeshearer, Sergeant Francis Doherty, Officer Charles Heinz, Officer Joseph Hernandez, Sergeant Willis Tristano, Officer Frederick Turentine, Lieutenant James Frieling, Officer Wendell White, Officer John Heineke and Sergeant John Vincennes.

Parker closed his press conference praising Sergeant Edmund J. Exley, the Central Division officer who came forward to testify before the grand jury. "It took great courage to do what Ed Exley did," the chief said. "The man has my greatest admiration."

EXTRACT: L.A. *Examiner*, April 11:

FIVE "BLOODY CHRISTMAS" INDICTMENTS DISMISSED; PARKER REVEALS RESULTS OF TRIAL BOARD ACTIONS

THE DISTRICT Attorney's Office announced today that five future defendants in last year's "Bloody Christmas" police brutality scandal will not stand trial. Officer Michael Krugman, Officer Henry Pratt and Sergeant Ward Tucker, all forced to resign from the Los Angeles Police Department as the result of being charged, had their indictments dismissed on the basis of abandoned testimony. Deputy DA Ellis Loew, who had been set to prosecute them, explained. "Many minor witnesses, prisoners at the Central Station Jail last Christmas, cannot be located."

In a related development, LAPD Chief William H. Parker announced the results of his "massive shake-up" of police personnel. The following indicted and non-indicted officers were found guilty of various interdepartmental infractions pertaining to their behavior last Christmas morning.

Sergeant Walter Crumley, six months suspension from duty without pay, transferred to Hollenbeck Division.

Sergeant Walter Dukeshearer, six months suspension from duty without pay, transferred to Newton Street Division.

Sergeant Francis Doherty, four months suspension from duty without pay, transferred to Wilshire Division.

Officer Charles Heinz, six months suspension from duty without pay, transferred to the Southside Vagrant Detail.

Officer Joseph Hernandez, four months suspension from duty without pay, transferred to 77th Street Division.

Sergeant Wilbert Huff, nine months suspension from duty without pay, transferred to Wilshire Division.

Sergeant Willis Tristano, three months suspension from duty without pay, transferred to Newton Street Division.

Officer Frederick Turentine, three months suspension from duty without pay, transferred to East Valley Division.

Lieutenant James Frieling, six months suspension from duty without pay, transferred to the LAPD Academy Instruction Bureau.

Officer John Heineke, four months suspension from duty without pay, transferred to Venice Division.

Sergeant Elmer Lentz, nine months suspension from duty without pay, transferred to Hollywood Division.

Officer Wendell White, no suspension, transferred to the Homicide Adjunct Surveillance Detail.

Sergeant John Vincennes, no suspension, transferred to Administrative Vice.

EXTRACT: L.A. *Times*, May 3:

POLICE SCANDAL DEFENDANT
RECEIVES SUSPENDED SENTENCE

OFFICER JOHN Brownell, 38, the first Los Angeles policeman involved in the "Bloody Christmas" scandal to face public trial, pleaded guilty at arraignment today and asked Judge Arthur J. Fitzhugh to sentence him immediately on the First Degree Assault and Aggravated Assault charges he was facing.

Brownell is the older brother of LAPD patrolman Frank D. Brownell, one of two officers injured in a bar brawl with six young men last Christmas Eve. Judge Fitzhugh, taking into account the facts that Officer Brownell was under psychological duress over the injury of his brother and that he had been discharged from the Los Angeles Police Department without pension, read the County Probation Department's report, which recommended formal probation and no jail time. He then gave Brownell a year in the County Jail, sentence suspended, and ordered him to report to the county's chief probation officer, Randall Milteer.

EXTRACT: L.A. *Examiner*, May 29:

STENSLAND CONVICTED—JAIL
FOR L.A. POLICEMAN

...THE EIGHT-MAN, four-woman jury found Stensland guilty on four counts: First Degree Assault, Aggravated Assault, First Degree

Battery and Mayhem, the charges stemming from the former police detective's alleged maltreatment of Central Jail prisoners during last year's "Bloody Christmas" scandal. In biting testimony, Sergeant E. J. Exley of the LAPD described Stensland's "rampage against unarmed men." Stensland's attorney, Jacob Kellerman, attacked Exley's credibility, stating that he was locked in a storeroom throughout most of the morning the events took place. In the end, the jurors believed Sergeant Exley, and Kellerman, citing the suspended sentence received by Bloody Christmas defendant John Brownell, asked Judge Arthur Fitzhugh to take mercy on his client. The judge did not oblige. He sentenced Stensland, already dismissed from the LAPD, to a year in the County Jail and remanded him to the custody of the Sheriff's deputies who would escort him to Wayside Honor Rancho. As he was led away, Stensland shouted obscenities regarding Sergeant Exley, who could not be reached for comment.

FEATURE: *Cavalcade Weekend*
Magazine, L.A. *Mirror*, July 3:

TWO EXLEY GENERATIONS SERVE
THE SOUTHLAND

THE FIRST thing that strikes you about Preston Exley and his son Edmund is that they don't talk like cops, even though Preston served with the Los Angeles Police Department for fourteen years and Ed has been with the LAPD since 1943, shortly before he went off to war and won himself the Distinguished Service Cross in the Pacific Theater. In fact, before the Exley clan emigrated to America, their family tree spawned generations of Scotland Yard detectives. So police work is in the clan's blood, but even more so is a thirst for advancement.

Item: Preston Exley took an engineering degree at USC, studying by night while he pounded a dangerous downtown beat by day.

Item: The late Thomas Exley, Preston's eldest son, achieved the highest scholastic average in the history of the LAPD Academy, and a plaque commemorating him is hung in the Academy's administration building. Tragically, Thomas was killed in the line of duty soon after his graduation. Further item: The second highest average was earned by Ed Exley himself, a summa cum laude UCLA graduate—at nineteen!—in 1941. Evidence going back generations: the Exleys don't talk like cops because they are not typical policemen.

Both men have been in the news lately. Preston, 58, has teamed up with world-renowned cartoonist/movie-maker/TV show host Raymond Dieterling to build Dream-a-Dreamland, the monumental amusement park that broke ground six months ago, with completion and opening scheduled for late April of next year. Exley Senior began his career in the construction business after he left the LAPD in 1936, taking his chief aide, Lieutenant Arthur De Spain, with him. At his spacious Hancock Park mansion, Preston Exley spoke with *Mirror* correspondent Dick St. Germain.

"I had an engineering degree and Art knew building materials," he said. "We had our combined life savings and borrowed from some independent investors who appreciated the wildcat mentality. We started Exley Construction and built cheap houses, then better houses, then office buildings, then the Arroyo Seco Freeway. We flourished beyond my wildest dreams. Now Dream-a-Dreamland, the gentle dreams of millions of people realized on two hundred acres. In a way, it's a hard one to top."

Exley smiled. "Ray Dieterling is a visionary," he said. "Dream-a-Dreamland will give people the chance to live the many worlds he has created through films and animation. The mountain that he's calling Paul's World is a perfect example. Paul Dieterling, Ray's son, died tragically in an avalanche back in the mid-30s. Now there will be a mountain that serves as a benevolent testimony to the boy, a mountain that brings people joy, with a percentage of the revenues earned going to children's charities. That's a hard one to top."

But will he try to top it?

Exley smiled again. "I'm addressing the Los Angeles County Board of Supervisors and the State Legislature next week," he said. "The subject will be the cost of Southern California mass rapid transit and the best way to link the Southland by freeway. Frankly, I want the job and I'm ready to offer the county an enticing bid."

And then?

Exley smiled and sighed. "And then there's all these politico fellows who've been pestering me," he said. "They think I'd be a natural for mayor, governor, senator or whatever, even though I keep telling them that Fletcher Bowron, Dick Nixon and Earl Warren are friends of mine."

But is he ruling politics out?

"I rule nothing out," Preston Exley said. "Setting limitations is against my nature."

And, as our reporters discovered, his son Edmund, now a detective sergeant with the LAPD's Hollywood Division, feels the same way. Recently in the news for testifying in a trial related to the "Bloody Christmas" police scandal, Ed Exley sees blue skies ahead—although he plans to keep police work his sole career. Speaking to our correspondent at his family's Lake Arrowhead cabin, Exley Junior said, "I want nothing other than to be a valuable, ranking detective presented with challenging cases. My father had the Loren Atherton case"—a reference to the 1934 child murderer who claimed six victims, including child star Wee Willie Wennerholm—"and I'd like to be in a position to work cases of that importance. Being in the right place at the right time is important, and I have a deep need to solve things and create order out of chaotic situations, which I believe is a good drive for a detective to have."

Exley was certainly in the right place at the right time in the fall of 1943, when, the sole survivor of a bayonet attack on his platoon, he single-handedly wiped out three trenches full of Japanese infantry. He was in the right place at the right time for justice when he courageously testified against fellow officers in a massive police brutality scandal. Exley says of the two incidents: "That's the past, and right now I'm building for my future. I'm getting solid experience working Hollywood Detectives, and my father, Art De Spain and I spend evenings performing mock questionings to help me perfect my interrogation techniques. My father wants the world, but all I want is the most this police department has to offer."

Preston Exley and Ed Exley survive Thomas, and Marguerite (nee Tibbetts) Exley, the clan's matriarch, who died of cancer six years ago. Do they feel the loss in their personal lives?

Preston said, "God, yes, every day. They are both irreplaceable."

On that subject, Edmund was more reflective. "Thomas was Thomas," he said. "I was seventeen when he died and I don't think I ever knew him. My mother was different. I knew her, she was kind and brave and strong, and there was something sad about her. I miss her, and I think the woman I marry will probably be like her, only a bit more volatile."

Two generations for this week's Profile—two men going places and serving the Southland while they do it.

BANNER: L.A. *Times*, July 9:

LOEW ANNOUNCES DA'S CANDIDACY

BANNER: Society Page,
L.A. *Herald-Express*, September 12:

GALA LOEW/MORROW WEDDING
ATTRACTS HOLLYWOOD, LEGAL CROWDS

EXTRACT: L.A. *Times*, November 7:

McPHERSON AND LOEW TOP DA'S
FIELD: WILL CLASH IN SPRING ELECTION

WILLIAM MCPHERSON, seeking his fourth term as Los Angeles District Attorney, will face upstart Deputy DA Ellis Loew in next March's general election, the two colleagues leading an eight-man field by a wide margin.

McPherson, 56, received 38 percent of the votes cast; Loew, 41, received 36 percent. Their closest rival was Donald Chapman, the former city parks commissioner, with 14 percent. The remaining five candidates, considered long shots with little chance of winning, received a total of 12 percent of the votes cast between them.

McPherson, in a scheduled press conference, predicted a down-to-the-wire campaign and stressed that he is an incumbent civil servant first and a political candidate second. Loew, at home with his wife, Joan, echoed those sentiments, predicted victory next March and thanked the voters at large and the law enforcement community in particular for their support.

1953

LAPD Annual Fitness Report,
Marked *Confidential*, dated
1/3/53, filed by Lt. Dudley
Smith, copies to Personnel and
Administration Divisions:

1/2/53
ANNUAL FITNESS REPORT

DUTY DATES: 4/4/52–12/31/52
SUBJECT: White, Wendell A., Badge 916
GRADE: Police Officer (Detective) (Civil Serv.
  Rate 4)
DIVISION: Detective Bureau
  (Homicide Adjunct Surveillance Detail)
COMMANDING OFFICER: Lt. Dudley L. Smith,
  Badge 410.

Gentlemen:

This memorandum serves both as a fitness report on Officer White and an update on the first nine months of the Surveillance Detail's existence. Of the sixteen men working the squad, I consider White my finest officer. To date he has been attentive, thorough, and has put in long hours without complaint. He has a perfect attendance record, and has often worked two-week stretches of eighteen-hour days. White transferred to Surveillance under the cloud of last year's unfortunate Christmas mess, and Deputy Chief Green, citing the four excessive-force complaints filed against him, had some misgivings about the transfer (i.e.: that White's propensity for violence and the potentially violent nature of the assignment would prove to be a disastrous combination). This has not proven to be the case, and I unhesitatingly give Officer White straight "A" markings in every fitness category. He has often evinced spectacular bravery. By way of example, I would like to cite several instances of White's performance above and beyond the call of duty.

1. 5/8/52. On a liquor store stakeout, Officer White (who is plagued by old football injuries) chased a fleeing armed suspect for a half mile. The suspect fired repeatedly back at Officer White, who did not return his fire for fear of hitting innocent civilians. The suspect took a woman hostage and held a gun to her head, which held off the backup officers who had caught up with Officer White. White then walked through a side alley while his partners attempted to calm the suspect down. The suspect refused to release the woman, and White shot and killed him at point-blank range. The woman was unharmed.

2. Numerous instances. One of the key duties of the Surveillance Detail is to meet paroled prison inmates upon their return to Los Angeles and try to convince them of the folly of committing

violent crimes in our city. This job requires great physical presence, and Officer White has, frankly, been instrumental in scaring many hardened criminals into a docile parole. He has spent much off-duty time tailing parolees with particularly violent records, and he is responsible for the arrest of John "Big Dog" Cassese, a twice-convicted rapist and armed robber. On 7/20/52, White, while surveilling Cassese inside a cocktail lounge, overheard him attempting to suborn a minor female into prostitution. Cassese attempted to resist arrest, and Officer White subdued him through physical means. Later, White and two other Surveillance officers (Sgt. Michael Breuning, Officer R. J. Carlisle) questioned Cassese extensively about his post-parole activities. Cassese confessed to the rape/murders of three women. (See Homicide arrest report 168-A, dated 7/22/52.) Cassese was tried, convicted and executed at San Quentin.

3. 10/18/52. Officer White, while surveilling parolee Percy Haskins, observed Haskins in a known criminal assembly with Robert Mackey and Karl Carter Goff. All three men possessed long armed-robbery records, and White sensed that a major felony was in the making and proceeded on that assumption. He tailed Haskins, Mackey and Goff to a market at 1683 S. Berendo. The three robbed the market, and White attempted to arrest them outside. The three refused to relinquish their weapons. White shot and killed Goff and severely wounded Mackey. Haskins surrendered. Mackey later died of his wounds and Haskins pleaded guilty to armed robbery with priors and was given a life sentence.

In summary, Officer White has taken the high ground and has been instrumental in making the Surveillance Detail's first year a resounding success. I will be returning to my regular Homicide duties effective 3/15/53 and would like Officer White to join my squad as a regular Homicide detective. In my opinion, he has the makings of a fine case man.

Respectfully,
Dudley L. Smith, Badge 410,
Lieutenant, Homicide Division

LAPD Annual Fitness Report,
marked *Confidential*, dated 1/6/53,
filed by Capt. Russell Millard,
copies to Personnel and Administration
Divisions:

1/6/53

ANNUAL FITNESS REPORT

DUTY DATES: 4/13/52–12/31/52

SUBJECT: Vincennes, John, Badge 2302

GRADE: Detective Sergeant (Civil Serv. Rate 5)

DIVISION: Detective Bureau (Administrative Vice)

COMMANDING OFFICER: Capt. Russell A. Millard, Badge 5009

Gentlemen:

An overall "D+" fitness rating for Sergeant Vincennes, along with some comments.

A. Since he doesn't drink, Vincennes is excellent at liquor violation operations.

B. Vincennes oversteps his bounds where narcotics are concerned, insisting on making possession arrests when dope is found collaterally at Ad Vice crime scenes.

C. He has not fulfilled my fears that he would neglect his Ad Vice duties to offer assistance to his Bureau mentor, Lt. Dudley Smith. This is to Vincennes' credit.

D. Vincennes is not terribly resented for his testimony in the Christmas assaults matter, because he lost his much coveted Narco assignment and because none of the officers he specifically informed on went to jail.

E. Vincennes is continually pressing me to return him to Narco. I will not sign his transfer papers until he makes a major case at Ad Vice—this is a long-standing Ad Vice transfer stipulation. Vincennes has had Deputy DA Ellis Loew exert pressure on me to transfer him, and I have refused. I will continue to refuse, even if Loew is elected DA.

F. There are rumors that Vincennes leaks interdepartmental information to the *Hush-Hush* scandal rag. I have warned him: never leak word of our work or I will have your hide.

G. In conclusion, Vincennes has proven himself a barely adequate Ad Vice officer. His attendance is good, his reports are well written (and, I suspect, padded). He is too well known to operate bookmakers and adequate at working prostitution sweeps. He has not neglected his duties to fulfill his TV show commitments, which is to his credit. Ad Vice has a probable pornography crackdown coming up within the next few months and Vincennes has a chance to prove his mettle (and earn his major case transfer requirement) on that. Again, an overall "D+" rating.

Respectfully,
Russell A. Millard, Badge 5009,
Commanding Officer,
Administrative Vice

LAPD Annual Fitness Report,
marked *Confidential*, dated 1/11/53,
filed by Lt. Arnold Reddin,
Commander, Hollywood Division Detective
Squad, copies to Personnel and
Administration Divisions:

1/11/53
ANNUAL FITNESS REPORT
DUTY DATES: 3/1/52–12/31/52
SUBJECT: Exley, Edmund J., Badge 1104
GRADE: Detective Sergeant (Civil Serv. Rate 5)
DIVISION: Detective (Hollywood Squad)
COMMANDING OFFICER: Lt. Arnold D. Reddin, Badge 556

Gentlemen:

On Sergeant Exley:

This man has obvious gifts as a detective. He is thorough, intelligent, seems to have no personal life and works very long hours. He is only thirty years old and in his nine months as a detective he has amassed a brilliant arrest record, with a 95 percent conviction rate on the cases (mostly minor felony property crimes) he has made. He is a thorough and succinct report writer.

Exley works poorly with partners and well by himself, so I have let him conduct interviews alone. He is a peerless interrogator and to my mind has gotten many miraculous confessions (without physical force). All well and good, and my overall fitness grade on Exley is a solid "A."

But he is roundly hated by his fellow officers, the result of his serving as an informant in the Christmas shake-up, and he is despised for receiving a Bureau assignment out of it. (It seems to be common knowledge that Exley made the Detective Bureau as a result of his informing.) Also, Exley does not like to employ force with suspects, and most of the men consider him a coward.

Exley has passed the lieutenant's exam with very high marks and an opening is probably coming up for him. I think he is both too young and too inexperienced to be a detective lieutenant and that such a promotion would create great resentment. I think he would be a roundly hated supervisor.

Respectfully,
Lt. Arnold D. Reddin, Badge 556

EXTRACT: L.A. *Daily News*, February 9:

IT'S OFFICIAL: CONSTRUCTION KING EXLEY TO LINK SOUTHLAND WITH SUPERHIGHWAYS

TODAY, THE Tri-County Highway Commission announced that Preston Exley, ex–San Francisco paperboy and L.A. cop, would be the man to build the freeway system that will link Hollywood to downtown L.A., downtown to San Pedro, Pomona to San Bernardino and the South Bay to the San Fernando Valley.

"Details will be forthcoming," Exley told the *News* by phone. "I'll be holding a televised press conference tomorrow, and representatives of the State Legislature and the Tri-County Commission will be there with me."

February 1953 Issue, *Hush-Hush* Magazine:

L.A. DA TAKES TIME OFF FROM CAMPAIGN—RELAXING WITH COPPER CUTIE!!!
by Sidney Hudgens

Bill McPherson, the district attorney for the City of Los Angeles, likes them long and leggy, zesty and chesty—and dark and dusky. From Harlem's Sugar Hill to L.A.'s Darktown, the 57-year-old married man with three teenaged daughters is known as a sugar daddy who likes to toss around that long slush-fund green— in dark hot spots where the drinks are tall, the jazz is cool, reefer smoke hangs humid and black-white romance bebops to the jungle throb of a wailing tenor sax.

Can you dig it, hepcat? McPherson, engaged in a reelection campaign, the fight of his political life against ace crimebuster Ellis Loew, needs time to relax. Does he go to the pool at the staid Jonathan Club? No. Does he take the family to Mike Lyman's or the Pacific Dining Car? No. Where *does* he go? To the Darktown Strutter's Ball.

It's all shakin' south of Jefferson, hepcat. It's a different world down there. Get your hair marcelled, get yourself a purple shark-skin suit and trip the dark fantastic. DA Bill McPherson does—every Thursday nite.

But let's talk facts. Marion McPherson, Darktown Bill's long-suffering hausfrau, thinks Billy Boy spends Thursday nites watching Mexican bantamweights pound each other silly at the Olympic Auditorium. She's wrongsky—Bad Billy craves amour, not mayhem, on his Thursdays.

Fact numero uno—Bill McPherson is a regular at Minnie Roberts' Casbah—the swankiest colored cat-house on L.A.'s southside. Call it sinuendo, hepcat—but we've heard he likes the thirty-five-dollar milkbath, plied by two very large Congo cuties. Fact numero twosky—McPherson was seen listening to Charlie "Bird" Parker (a notorious hophead) at Tommy Tucker's Playroom, on cloud ten from the Playroom's potent Plantation Punch. His date that night was one Lynette Brown, age eighteen, a dusky deelite with two juvenile arrests for possession of marijuana. Lynette told a secret *Hush-Hush* correspondent, "Bill like his black. He say, 'Once you had black you can't go back.' He dig jazz and he like to party slow. He really married? He really distric' 'turney?"

He sure is, sweet thing. But for how much longer? There's a bunch of Thursdays between now and Election Day, and will Bad Bebop Billy be able to control his dark desires until then?

Remember, dear reader, you heard it first here—off the record, on the Q.T. and *very Hush-Hush*.

EXTRACT: L.A. *Herald-Express*, March 1:

BLOODY CHRISTMAS POLICEMAN TO LEAVE JAIL SOON

ON APRIL 2, Richard Alex Stensland leaves Wayside Honor Rancho a free man. Convicted last year on four assault charges related to the 1951 Bloody Christmas police brutality scandal, he walks out an ex–cop with an uncertain future.

Stensland's former partner, Officer Wendell White, spoke to the *Herald*. He said, "It was the luck of the draw, that —— Christmas thing. I was there, and I could have been the guy that swung.

It was Dick, though. He made a good cop out of me. I owe him for that and I'm —— mad at what happened to him. I'm still Dick's friend and I bet he's still got lots of friends in the Department."

And among the civilian population, it appears. Stensland told a *Herald* reporter that upon his release he'll go to work for Abraham Teitlebaum, the owner of Abe's Noshery, a delicatessen in West Los Angeles. Asked whether he bears grudges against any of the people who put him in jail, Stensland said, "Only one. But I'm too law-abiding to do anything about it."

L.A. *Daily News*, March 6:

SCANDAL TURNS CLOSE DA'S RACE TO LANDSLIDE

IT WAS expected to go down to the wire: incumbent city DA William McPherson vs. Deputy DA Ellis Loew, the winner to hold the job as top elected crimefighter in the Southland for the next four years. Both men campaigned on the issues: how to deploy the city's legal budget the best way, how to most efficaciously fight crime. Both men, predictably, claimed they would fight crime the hardest. The L.A. law enforcement establishment considered McPherson soft on crime and too liberal in general and threw their support to Loew. Union organizations supported the incumbent. McPherson stood pat on his status quo record and played off his nice-guy personality, and Loew tried a young firebrand routine that didn't work: he came off as theatrical and vote-hungry. It was a gentleman's campaign until the February issue of *Hush-Hush* magazine hit the stands.

Most people take *Hush-Hush* and other scandal sheets with a grain of salt, but this was election time. An article alleged that DA McPherson, happily married for twenty-six years, cavorted with young Negro women. The DA ignored the article, which was accompanied by photographs of him and a Negro girl, taken at a nightclub in south central Los Angeles. Mrs. McPherson did not ignore the article—she filed for divorce. Ellis Loew did not mention the article in his campaign, and McPherson began to slip in the polls. Then, three days before the election, Sheriff's deputies raided the Lilac View Motel on the Sunset Strip, acting on the tip of an "unknown informant" who called in with word of an illegal assignation in room 9. The assignators proved to be DA McPherson and a young Negro prostitute, age 14. The deputies arrested McPherson on statutory rape charges and heard out the story of Marvell Wilkins, a minor with two soliciting arrests.

She told them that McPherson picked her up on South Western Avenue, offered her twenty dollars for an hour of her time and drove her to the Lilac View. McPherson pleaded amnesia: he recalled having "several martinis" at a dinner meeting with supporters at the Pacific Dining Car restaurant, then getting into his car. He remembers nothing after that. The rest is history: reporters and photographers arrived at the Lilac View Motel shortly after the deputies, McPherson became front-page news and on Tuesday Ellis Loew was elected city district attorney by a landslide.

Something seems fishy here. Scandal-rag journalism should not dictate the thrust of political campaigns, although we at the *Daily News* (admitted McPherson supporters) would never abridge their right to print whatever filth they desire. We have tried to locate Marvell Wilkins, but the girl, released from custody, seems to have disappeared off the face of the earth. Without pointing fingers, we at the *Daily News* ask District Attorney-elect Loew to initiate a grand jury investigation into this matter, if for no other reason than his desire to assume his new office with no dark clouds overhead.

PART TWO

NITE OWL MASSACRE

14

THE WHOLE squadroom to himself. A retirement party down-stairs—he wasn't invited. The weekly crime report to be read, summarized, tacked to the bulletin board—nobody else ever did it, they knew he did it best. The papers ballyhooing the Dream-a-Dreamland opening—the other cops Moochie Mouse-squeaked him ad nauseam. Space Cooley playing the party; pervert Deuce Perkins roaming the halls. Midnight and nowhere near sleepy—Ed read, typed.

4/9/53: a transvestite shoplifter hit four stores on Hollywood Boulevard, disabled two salesclerks with judo chops. 4/10/53: an usher at Grauman's Chinese stabbed to death by two male Caucasians—he told them to put out their cigarettes. Suspects still at large; Lieutenant Reddin said he was too inexperienced to handle a homicide—he didn't get the job. 4/11/53: a stack of crime sheets—several times over the past two weeks a carload of Negro youths were seen discharging shotguns into the air in the Griffith Park hills. No IDs, the kids driving a '48–'50 purple Mercury coupe. 4/11–4/13/53: five daytime burglaries, private homes north of the Boulevard, jewelry stolen. Nobody assigned yet; Ed made a note: bootjack the job, dust before the access points got pawed. Today was the fourteenth—he might have a chance.

Ed finished up. The empty squadroom made him happy: nobody who hated him, a big space filled with desks and filing cabinets. Official forms on the walls—empty spaces you filled in when you notched an arrest and made somebody confess. Confessions could be ciphers, nothing past an admission of the crime. But if you twisted your man the right way—loved him and hated him to precisely the right degree—then he would tell you things—small details—that would create a reality to buttress your case and give you that much more intelligence to bend the next suspect with. Art De Spain and his father taught how to find the spark point. They had boxloads of old steno transcripts: kiddie rapers, heisters, assorted riffraff who'd confessed to them. Art would rabbit-punch—but he used the threat more than the act. Preston Exley rarely hit—he considered it the criminal defeating the policeman and creating disorder. They read elliptical answers and made him guess the questions; they gave him a rundown of common criminal experiences—wedges to get the flow started. They showed him that men have levels of weakness that are acceptable because other men condone them and levels of weakness that produce a great shame, something to hide from all but a brilliant confessor. They honed his instinct for the jugular of weakness. It got so sharp that sometimes he couldn't look at himself in the mirror.

The sessions ran late—two widowers, a young man without a woman. Art had a bug on multiple murders—he had his father rehash the Loren Atherton case repeatedly: horror snatches, witness testimony. Preston obliged with psychological theories, grudgingly—he wanted his glory case to stay sealed off, complete, in his mind. Art's old cases were scrutinized—and *he* reaped the efforts of three fine minds: confessions straight across, 95 percent convictions. But so far his drive to crack criminal knowledge hadn't been challenged—much less sated.

Ed walked down to the parking lot, sleep coming on. "Quack, quack," behind him—hands turned him around.

A man in a kid's mask—Danny Duck. A left-right knocked off his glasses; a kidney shot put him down. Kicks to the ribs drove him into a ball.

Ed curled hard, caught kicks in the face. A flashbulb popped; two men walked away: one quacking, one laughing. Easy IDs: Dick Stensland's bray, Bud White's football limp. Ed spat blood, swore payback.

15

RUSS MILLARD addressed Ad Vice squad 4—the topic pornography.

"Picture-book smut, gentlemen. There's been a bunch of it found at collateral crime scenes lately: narcotics, bookmaking and prostitution collars. Normally this kind of stuff is made in Mexico, so it's not our jurisdiction. Normally it's an organized crime sideline, because the big mobs have the money to manufacture it and the connections to get it distributed. But Jack Dragna's been deported, Mickey Cohen's in prison and probably too puritanical anyway, and Mo Jahelka's foundering on his own. Stag pix aren't

Jack Whalen's style—he's a bookie looking to get his hands on a Vegas casino. And the stuff that's surfaced is too high quality for the L.A. area print mills: Newton Street Vice rousted them, they're clean, they just don't have the facilities to make magazines of this quality. But the backdrops in the pictures indicate L.A. venue: you can see what looks like the Hollywood Hills out some windows, and the furnishings in a lot of the places look like your typical cheap Los Angeles apartments. So our job is to track this filth to its source and arrest whoever made it, posed for it and distributed it."

Jack groaned: the Great Jerk-off Book Caper of 1953. The other guys looked hot to glom the smut, maybe fuel up their wives. Millard popped a Digitalis. "Newton Street dicks questioned everyone at the collateral rousts, and they all denied possessing the stuff. Nobody at the print mills knows where it was made. The mags have been shown around the Bureau and our station vice squads, and we've got zero IDs on the posers. So, gentlemen, look yourself."

Henderson and Kifka had their hands out; Stathis looked ready to drool. Millard passed the smut over. "Vincennes, is there someplace you'd rather be?"

"Yeah, Captain. Narcotics Division."

"Oh? Anyplace else?"

"Maybe working whores with squad two."

"Make a major case, Sergeant. I'd love to sign you out of here."

Oohs, ahhs, cackles, oo-la-las; three men shook their heads no. Jack grabbed the books.

Seven mags, high-quality glossy paper, plain black covers. Sixteen pages apiece: photos in color, black and white. Two books ripped in half; explicit pictures: men and women, men and men, girls and girls. Insertion close-ups: straight, queer, dykes with dildoes. The Hollywood sign out windows; Murphy-bed fuck shots, cheap pads: stucco-swirled walls, the hot plate on a table that came with every bachelor flop in L.A. Par for the stag-book course—but the posers weren't glassy-eyed hopheads, they were good-looking, well-built young kids—nude, costumed: Elizabethan garb, Jap kimonos. Jack put the ripped mags back together for a bingo: Bobby Inge—a male prostitute he'd popped for reefer—blowing a guy in a whalebone corset.

Millard said, "Anybody familiar, Vincennes?"

An angle. "Nothing, Cap. But where did you get these torn-up jobs?"

"They were found in a trash bin behind an apartment house in Beverly Hills. The manager, an old woman named Loretta Downey, found them and called the Beverly Hills PD. They called us."

"You got an address on the building?"

Millard checked an evidence form. "9849 Charleville. Why?"

"I just thought I'd take that part of the job. I've got good connections in Beverly Hills."

"Well, they do call you 'Trashcan.' All right, follow up in Beverly Hills. Henderson, you and Kifka try to locate the arrestees in the crime reports and try to find out *again* where they got the stuff—I'll get you carbons in a minute. Tell them there'll be no additional charges filed if they talk. Stathis, take that filth by the costume supply companies and see if you can get a matchup to their inventory, then find out who rented the costumes the … performers were wearing. Let's try it this way first—if we have to go through mugshots for IDs we'll lose a goddamn week. Dismissed, gentlemen. Roll, Vincennes. And don't get sidetracked—this is Ad Vice, not Narco."

* * *

Jack rolled: R&I, Bobby Inge's file, his angle flushed out: Beverly Hills, see the old biddy, see what he could find out and concoct a hot lead that told him what he already knew—Bobby Inge was guilty of conspiracy to distribute obscene material, a felony bounce. Bobby would snitch his co-stars and the guys who took the pix—one major class transfer requirement dicked.

The day was breezy, cool; Jack took Olympic straight west. He kept the radio going; a newscast featured Ellis Loew: budget cuts at the DA's Office. Ellis droned on; Jack flipped the dial—a kibosh on thoughts of Bill McPherson. He caught a happy Broadway tune, thought about him anyway.

Hush-Hush was his idea: McPherson liked colored poon, Sid Hudgens loved writing up jig-fuckers. Ellis Loew knew about it, approved of it, considered it another favor on deposit. McPherson's wife filed for divorce; Loew was satisfied—he took a lead in the polls. Dudley Smith wanted more—and set up the tank job.

An easy parlay:

Dot Rothstein knew a colored girl doing a stretch at Juvenile Hall: soliciting beefs, Dot and the girl kept a thing sizzling whenever she did time. Dot got the little twist sprung; Dudley and his ace goon Mike Breuning fixed up a room at the Lilac View Motel: the most notorious fuck pad on the Sunset Strip, county ground where the city DA would be just another john caught with his pants down. McPherson attended a Dining Car soiree; Dudley had Marvell Wilkins—fourteen, dark, witchy—waiting outside. Breuning alerted the West Hollywood Sheriff's and the press; the Big V dropped chloral hydrates in McPherson's last martini. Mr. DA left the restaurant woozy, swerved his Cadillac a mile or so, pulled over at Wilshire and Alvarado and passed out. Breuning cruised up behind him with the bait: Marvell in a cocktail gown. He took the wheel of McPherson's Caddy, hustled Bad Bill and the girl to their tryst spot—the rest was political history.

Ellis Loew wasn't told—he figured he just got lucky. Dot sent Marvell down to Tijuana, all expenses paid—skim off the Woman's Jail budget. McPherson lost his wife and his job; his statch rape charge was dismissed—Marvell couldn't be located. Something snapped inside the Bigggg V—

The snap: one shitty favor over the line. The reason: Dot Rothstein in the ambulance October '47—she knew, Dudley probably knew. If they knew, the game had to be played so the rest of the world wouldn't know—so Karen wouldn't.

He'd been her hero a solid year; somehow the bit got real. He stopped sending the Scoggins kids money, closing out his debt at forty grand—he needed cash to court Karen, being with her gave him some distance on the Malibu Rendezvous. Joan Morrow Loew stayed bitchy; Welton and the old lady grudgingly accepted him—and Karen loved him so hard it almost hurt. Working Ad Vice hurt—the job was a snore, he hot-dogged on dope every time he got a shot. Sid Hudgens didn't call so much—he wasn't a Narco dick now. After the McPherson gig he was glad—he didn't know if he could pull another shakedown.

Karen had her own lies going—they helped his hero bit play true. Trust fund, beach pad paid for by Daddy, grad school. Dilettante stuff: he was thirty-eight, she was twenty-three, in time she'd figure it out. She wanted to marry him; he resisted; Ellis Loew as an in-law meant bagman duty until he dropped dead. He knew why his hero role worked: Karen was the audience he'd always wanted to impress. He knew what she could take, what she couldn't; her love had shaped his performance so that all he had to do was act natural—and keep certain secrets hidden.

Traffic snagged; Jack turned north on Doheny, west on Charleville. 9849—a two-story Tudor—stood a block off Wilshire. Jack double-parked, checked mailboxes.

Six slots: Loretta Downey, five other names—three Mr. & Mrs., one man, one woman. Jack wrote them down, walked to Wilshire, found a pay phone. Calls to R&I and the DMV police information line; two waits. No criminal records on the tenants; one standout vehicle sheet: Christine Bergeron, the mailbox "Miss," four reckless-driving convictions, no license revocation. Jack got extra stats off the clerk: the woman was thirty-seven years old, her occupation was listed as actress/car hop, as of 7/52 she was working at Stan's Drive-in in Hollywood.

Instincts: carhops don't live in Beverly Hills; maybe Christine Bergeron hopped some bones to stretch the rent. Jack walked back to 9849, knocked on the door marked "Manager."

An old biddy opened up. "Yes, young man?"

Jack flashed his badge. "L.A. Police, ma'am. It's about those books you found."

The biddy squinted through Coke-bottle glasses. "My late husband would have seen to justice himself, Mr. Harold Downey had no tolerance for dirty things."

"Did you find those magazines yourself, Mrs. Downey?"

"No, young man, my cleaning lady did. *She* tore them up and threw them in the trash, where I found them. I questioned Eula about it after I called the Beverly Hills police."

"Where did Eula find the books?"

"Well ... I ... don't know if I should ..."

A switcheroo. "Tell me about Christine Bergeron."

Harumph. "That woman! And that boy of hers! I don't know who's worse!"

"Is she a difficult tenant, ma'am?"

"She entertains men at all hours! She roller-skates on the floor in those tight waitress outfits of hers! She's got a no-goodnik son who never goes to school! Seventeen years old and a truant who associates with lounge lizards!"

Jack held out a Bobby Inge mugshot; the biddy held it up to her glasses. "Yes, this is one of Daryl's no-goodnik friends, I've seen him skulking around here a dozen times. Who *is* he?"

"Ma'am, did Eula find those dirty books in the Bergeron apartment?"

"Well ..."

"Ma'am, are Christine Bergeron and the boy at home now?"

"No, I heard them leave a few hours ago. I have keen ears to make up for my poor eyesight."

"Ma'am, if you let me into their apartment and I find some more dirty books, you could earn a reward."

"Well ..."

"Have you got keys, ma'am?"

"Of course I have keys, I'm the manager. Now, I'll let you look if you promise not to touch and I don't have to pay withholding tax on my reward."

Jack took the mugshot back. "Whatever you want, ma'am."

The old woman walked upstairs, up to the second-floor units. Jack followed; granny unlocked the third door down. "Five minutes, young man. And be respectful of the furnishings—my brother-in-law owns this building."

Jack walked in. Tidy living room, scratched floor—probably roller-skate tracks. Quality furniture, worn, ill-cared-for. Bare walls, no TV, two framed photos on an end table—publicity-type shots.

Jack checked them out; old lady Downey stuck close. Matching pewter frames—two good-looking people.

A pretty woman—light hair in a pageboy, eyes putting out a cheap sparkle. A pretty boy who looked just like her—extra blond, big stupid eyes. "Is this Christine and her son?"

"Yes, and they are an attractive pair, I'll give them that. Young man, what is the amount of that reward you mentioned?"

Jack ignored her and hit the bedroom: through the drawers, in the closet, under the mattress. No smut, no dope, nothing hinky—negligees the only shit worth a sniff.

"Young man, your five minutes are up. And I want a written guarantee that I will receive that reward."

Jack turned around smiling. "I'll mail it to you. And I need another minute or so to check their address book."

"No! No! They could come home at any moment! I want you to leave this instant!"

"Just one minute, ma'am."

"No, no, no! Out with you this second!"

Jack made for the door. The old bat said, "You remind me of that policeman on that television program that's so popular."

"I taught him everything he knows."

* * *

He felt a quickie shaping up.

Bobby Inge rats off the smut peddlers, turns state's, some kind of morals rap on him and Daryl Bergeron: the kid was a minor, Bobby was a notorious fruitfly with a rap sheet full of homo-pandering beefs. Wrap it up tight: confessions, suspects located, lots of paperwork for Millard. The big-time Big V cracks the big-time filth ring and wings back to Narco a hero.

Up to Hollywood, a loop by Stan's Drive-in—Christine Bergeron slinging hash on skates. Pouty, provocative—the quasi-hooker type, maybe the type to pose with a dick in her mouth.

Jack parked, read the Bobby Inge sheet. Two outstanding bench warrants: traffic tickets, a failure-to-appear probation citation. Last known address 1424 North Hamel, West Hollywood—the heart of Lavender Gulch. Three fruit bars for "known haunts"—Leo's Hideaway, the Knight in Armor, B.J.'s Rumpus Room—all on Santa Monica Boulevard nearby. Jack drove to Hamel Drive, his cuffs out and open.

A bungalow court off the Strip: county turf, "Inge—Apt 6" on a mailbox. Jack found the pad, knocked, no answer. "Bobby, hey, sugar," a falsetto trill—still no bite. A locked door, drawn curtains—the whole place dead quiet. Jack went back to his car, drove south.

Fag bar city: Inge's haunts in a two-block stretch. Leo's Hideaway closed until 4:00; the Knight in Armor empty. The barkeep vamped him—"Bobby who?"—like he really didn't know. Jack hit B.J.'s Rumpus Room.

Tufted Naugahyde inside—the walls, ceiling, booths adjoining a small bandstand. Queers at the bar; the barman sniffed cop right off. Jack walked over, laid his mugshots out face up.

The barman picked them up. "That's Bobby something. He comes in pretty often."

"How often?"

"Oh, like several times a week."

"The afternoon or the evening?"

"Both."

"When was the last time he was here?"

"Yesterday. Actually, it was around this time yesterday. Are you—"

"I'm going to sit at one of those booths over there and wait for him. If he shows up, keep quiet about me. Do you understand?"

"Yes. But look, you've cleared the whole dance floor out already."

"Write it off your taxes."

The barkeep giggled; Jack walked over to a booth near the bandstand. A clean view: the front door, back door, bar. Darkness covered him. He watched.

Queer mating rituals:

Glances, tête-à-têtes, out the door. A mirror above the bar: the fruits could check each other out, meet eyes and swoon. Two hours, half a pack of cigarettes—no Bobby Inge.

His stomach growled; his throat felt raw; the bottles on the bar smiled at him. Itchy boredom: at 4:00 he'd hit Leo's Hideaway.

3:53—Bobby Inge walked in.

He took a stool; the barman poured him a drink. Jack walked up.

The barman, spooked: darting eyes, shaky hands. Inge swiveled around. Jack said, "Police. Hands on your head."

Inge tossed his drink. Jack tasted scotch; scotch burned his eyes. He blinked, stumbled, tripped blind to the floor. He tried to cough the taste out, got up, got blurry sight back—Bobby Inge was gone.

He ran outside. No Bobby on the sidewalk, a sedan peeling rubber. His own car two blocks away.

Liquor brutalizing him.

Jack crossed the street, over to a gas station. He hit the men's room, threw his blazer in a trashcan. He washed his face, smeared soap on his shirt, tried to vomit the booze taste out—no go. Soapy water in the sink—he swallowed it, guzzled it, retched.

Coming to: his heart quit skidding, his legs firmed up. He took off his holster, wrapped it in paper towels, went back to the car. He saw a pay phone—and made the call on instinct.

Sid Hudgens picked up. "*Hush-Hush*, off the record and on the QT."

"Sid, it's Vincennes."

"Jackie, are you back on Narco? I need copy."

"No, I've got something going with Ad Vice."

"Something good? Celebrity oriented?"

"I don't know if it's good, but if it gets good you've got it."

"You sound out of breath, Jackie. You been shtupping?"

Jack coughed—soap bubbles. "Sid, I'm chasing some smut books. Picture stuff. Fuck shots, but the people don't look like junkies and they're wearing these expensive costumes. It's well-done stuff, and I thought you might have heard something about it."

"No. No, I've heard bupkis."

Too quick, no snappy one-liner. "What about a male prostie named Bobby Inge or a woman named Christine Bergeron? She carhops, maybe peddles it on the side."

"Never heard of them, Jackie."

"Shit. Sid, what about independent smut pushers in general. What do you know?"

"Jack, I know that that is secret shit that I know nothing about. And the thing about secrets, Jack, is that everybody's got them. Including you. Jack, I'll talk to you later. Call when you get work."

The line clicked off.

EVERYBODY'S GOT SECRETS—INCLUDING YOU.

Sid wasn't quite Sid, his exit line wasn't quite a warning.

DOES HE FUCKING KNOW?

Jack drove by Stan's Drive-in, shaky, the windows down to kill the soap smell. Christine Bergeron nowhere on the premises. Back to 9849 Charleville, knock knock on the door of her apartment— no answer, slack between the lock and the doorjamb. He gave a shove; the door popped.

A trail of clothes on the living room floor. The picture frame gone.

Into the bedroom, scared, his gun in the car.

Empty cabinets and drawers. The bed stripped. Into the bathroom.

Toothpaste and Kotex spilled in the shower. Glass shelves smashed in the sink.

Getaway—fifteen-minute style.

Back to West Hollywood—fast. Bobby Inge's door caved in easy; Jack went in gun first.

Clean-out number two—a better job.

A clean living room, pristine bathroom, bedroom showing empty dresser drawers. A can of sardines in the icebox. The kitchen trashcan clean, a fresh paper bag lining it.

Jack tore the pad up: living room, bedroom, bathroom, kitchen—shelves knocked over, rugs pulled, the toilet yanked apart. He stopped on a flash: garbage cans, full, lined both sides of the street—

There or gone.

Figure an hour-twenty since his run-in with Inge: the fuck wouldn't run straight to his crib. He probably got off the street, cruised back slow, risked the move out with his car parked in the alley. He figured the roust was for his old warrants or the smut gig; he knew he was standing heat and couldn't be caught harboring pornography. He wouldn't risk carrying it in his car—the odds on a shake were too strong. The gutter or the trash, right near the top of the cans, maybe more skin IDs for Big Trashcan Jack.

Jack hit the sidewalk, rooted in trashcans—gaggles of kids laughed at him. One, two, three, four, five—two left before the corner. No lid on the last can; glossy black paper sticking out.

Jack beelined.

Three fuck mags right on top. Jack grabbed them, ran back to his car, skimmed—the kids made goo-goo eyes at the windshield. The same Hollywood backdrops, Bobby Inge with boys and girls, unknown pretties screwing. Halfway through the third book the pix went haywire.

Orgies, hole-to-hole daisy chains, a dozen people on a quilt-covered floor. Disembodied limbs: red sprays off arms, legs. Jack squinted, eye-strain, the red was colored ink, the photos doctored—limb severings faked, ink blood flowing in artful little swirls.

Jack tried for IDs; obscene perfection distracted him: ink-bleeding nudes, no faces he knew until the last page: Christine Bergeron and her son fucking, standing on skates planted on a scuffed hardwood floor.

16

A PHOTOGRAPH, dropped in his mailbox: Sergeant Ed Exley bleeding and terrified. No printing on the back, no need for it: Stensland and White had the negative, insurance that he'd never try to break them.

Ed, alone in the squadroom, 6:00 A.M. The stitches on his chin itched; loose teeth made eating impossible. Thirty-odd hours since the moment—his hands still trembled.

Payback.

He didn't tell his father; he couldn't risk the ignominy of going to Parker or Internal Affairs. Revenge on Bud White would be tricky: he was Dudley Smith's boy, Smith just got him a straight Homicide spot and was grooming him for his chief strongarm. Stensland was more vulnerable: on probation, working for Abe Teitlebaum, an ex-Mickey Cohen goon. A drunk, begging to go back inside.

Payback—already in the works.

Two Sheriff's men bought and paid for: a dip in his mother's trust fund. A two-man tail on Dick Stens, two men to swoop on his slightest probation fuckup.

Payback.

Ed did paperwork. His stomach growled: no food, loose trousers weighted down by his holster. A voice out the squawk box: loud, spooked.

"Squad call! Nite Owl Coffee Shop one-eight-two-four Cherokee! Multiple homicides! See the patrolmen! Code three!"

Ed banged his legs getting up. No other detectives on call—it was his.

* * *

Patrol cars at Hollywood and Cherokee; blues setting up crime scene blockades. No plainclothesmen in sight—he might get first crack.

Ed pulled up, doused his siren. A patrolman ran over. "Load of people down, maybe some of them women. I found them, stopped for coffee and saw this phony sign on the door, 'Closed for Illness.' Man, the Nite Owl *never* closes. It was dark inside and I knew this was a hinky deal. Exley, this ain't your squawk, this has gotta be downtown stuff, so—"

Ed pushed him aside, pushed over to the door. Open, a sign taped on: "Clossed Due to Illness." Ed stepped inside, memorized.

A long, rectangular interior. On the right: a string of tables, four chairs per. The side wall mural-papered: winking owls perched on street signs. A checkered linoleum floor; to the left a counter—a dozen stools. A service runway behind it, the kitchen in back, fronted by a cook's station: fryers, spatulas on hooks, a platform for laying down plates. At front left: a cash register.

Open, empty—coins on the floor mat beside it.

Three tables in disarray: food spilled, plates dumped; napkin containers, broken dishes on the floor. Drag marks leading back to the kitchen; one high-heeled pump by an upended chair.

Ed walked into the kitchen. Half-fried food, broken dishes, pans on the floor. A wall safe under the cook's counter—open, spilling coins. Crisscrossed drag marks connecting with the other drag marks, dark black heel smudges ending at the door of a walk-in food locker.

Ajar, the cord out of the socket—no cool air as a preservative. Ed opened it.

Bodies—a blood-soaked pile on the floor. Brains, blood and buckshot on the walls. Blood two feet deep collecting in a drainage trough. Dozens of shotgun shells floating in blood.

NEGRO YOUTHS DRIVING PURPLE '48–'50 MERC COUPE SEEN DISCHARGING SHOTGUNS INTO AIR IN GRIFFITH PARK HILLS SEVERAL TIMES OVER PAST TWO WEEKS.

Ed gagged, tried for a body count.

No discernible faces. Maybe five people dead for the cash register and safe take and what they had on them—

"Holy shit fuck."

A rookie type—pale, almost green. Ed said, "How many men outside?"

"I...I dunno. Lots."

"Don't get sick, just get everybody together to start canvassing. We need to know if a certain type of car was seen around here tonight."

"S-s-sir, there's this Detective Bureau man wants to see you."

Ed walked out. Dawn up: fresh light on a mob scene. Patrolmen held back reporters; rubberneckers swarmed. Horns blasted; motorcycles ran interference: meat wagons cut off by the crowd. Ed looked for high brass; newsmen shouting questions stampeded him.

Pushed off the sidewalk, pinned to a patrol car. Flashbulbs pop pop pop—he turned so his bruises wouldn't show. Strong hands grabbed him. "Go home, lad. I've been given the command here."

17

THE FIRST all-Bureau call-in in history—every downtown-based detective standing ready. The chief's briefing room jammed to the rafters.

Thad Green, Dudley Smith by a floor mike; the men facing them, itchy to go. Bud looked for Ed Exley—a chance to scope out his wounds. No Exley—scotch a rumor he caught the Nite Owl squeal.

Smith grabbed the mike. "Lads, you all know why we're here. 'Nite Owl Massacre' hyperbole aside, this is a heinous crime that requires a hard and swift resolution. The press and public will demand it, and since we already have solid leads, we will give it to them.

"There were six people dead in that locker—three men and three women. I have spoken to the Nite Owl's owner, and he told me that three of the dead are likely Patty Chesimard and Donna DeLuca, female Caucasians, the late-shift waitress and cash register girl, and Gilbert Escobar, male Mexican, the cook and dishwasher. The three other victims—two men, one woman—were almost certainly customers. The cash register and safe were empty and the victims' pockets and handbags were picked clean, which means that robbery was obviously the motive. SID is doing the forensic now—so far they have nothing but rubber glove prints on the cash register and food locker door. No time of death on the victims, but the scant number of customers and another lead we have indicates 3:00 A.M. as the time of the killings. A total of forty-five spent 12-gauge Remington shotgun shells were found in the locker. This indicates three men with five-shot-capacity pumps, all of them reloading twice. I do not have to tell you how gratuitous forty of those rounds were, lads. We are dealing with stark raving mad beasts here."

Bud looked around. Still no Exley, a hundred men jotting notes. Jack Vincennes in a corner, no notebook. Thad Green took over.

"No blood tracks leading outside. We were hoping for footprints to run eliminations against, but we didn't find any, and Ray Pinker from SID says the forensic will take at least forty-eight hours. The coroner says IDs on the customer victims will be extremely difficult because of the condition of the bodies. But we do have one very hot lead.

"Hollywood Division has taken a total of four crime reports on this, so listen well. Over the past two weeks a carload of Negro youths were seen discharging shotguns into the air up at Griffith Park. There were three of them, and the shotguns were pumps. The punks were not apprehended, but eyeball witnesses ID'd them as driving a 1948 to 1950 Mercury coupe, purple in color. And just an hour ago Lieutenant Smith's canvassing crew found a witness: a news vendor who saw a purple Merc coupe, '48–'50 vintage, parked across from the Nite Owl last night around 3:00 A.M."

The room went loud: a big rumbling. Green gestured for quiet. "It gets better, so listen well. There are no '48 to '50 purple Mercurys on the hot sheet, so it is very doubtful that we're dealing with a stolen car, and the state DMV has given us a registration list on '48 to '50 Mercurys statewide. Purple was an original color on the '48 to '50 coupe models, and those models were favored by Negroes. Over sixteen hundred are registered to Negroes in the State of California, and in Southern California there are only a very few registered to Caucasians. There are one hundred and fifty-six registered to Negroes in L.A. County, and there are almost a hundred of you men here. We have a list compiled: home and work addresses. The Hollywood squad is cross-checking for rap sheets. I want fifty two-man teams to shake three names apiece. There's a special phone line being set up at Hollywood Station, so if you need information on past addresses or known associates, you can call there. If you get hot suspects, bring them here to the Hall. We've got a string of interrogation rooms set up, along with a man to head the interrogations. Lieutenant Smith will give out the assignments in a second, and Chief Parker would like a word with you. Any questions first?"

A man yelled, "Sir, who's running the interrogations?"

Green said, "Sergeant Ed Exley, Hollywood squad."

Catcalls, boos. Parker walked up to the mike. "Enough on that. Gentlemen, just go out and get them. Use all necessary force."

Bud smiled. The real message: kill the niggers clean.

18

JACK'S LIST:

George NMI Yelburton, male Negro, 9781 South Beach; Leonard Timothy Bidwell, male Negro, 10062 South Duquesne; Dale William Pritchford, male Negro, 8211 South Normandie.

Jack's temporary partner: Sergeant Cal Denton, Bunco Squad, a former guard at the Texas State Pen.

Denton's car down to Darktown, the radio humming: jazz on the "Nite Owl Massacre." Denton hummed: Leonard Bidwell used to fight welterweight, he saw him go ten with Kid Gavilan—he was one tough shine. Jack brooded on his back-to-Narco ticket: Bobby Inge, Christine Bergeron gone, no smut leads from the other squad guys. The orgy pix—beautiful in a way. His own private leads, fucked up by some crazy spooks killing six people for a couple hundred bucks. He could still taste the booze, still hear Sid Hudgens: "We've all got secrets."

Snitch call-ins first: his, Denton's. Shine stands, pool halls, hair-processing parlors, storefront churches—informants palmed, leaned on, queried. The Darktown shuffle—purple car/shotgun rebop, hazy, distorted—riffraff gone on Tokay and hair tonic. Four hours down, no hard names, back to the names on the list.

9781 Beach—a tar-paper shack, a purple '48 Merc on the lawn. The car stood sans wheels, a rusted axle sunk in the grass. Denton pulled up. "Maybe that's their alibi. Maybe they fucked up the car after they did the Nite Owl so we'd think they couldn't drive it nowhere."

Jack pointed over. "There's weeds wrapped around the brake linings. Nobody drove that thing up to Hollywood last night."

"You think?"

"I think."

"You sure?"

"Yeah, I'm sure."

Denton hauled to the South Duquesne address—another tar-paper dive. A purple Mercury in the driveway—a coon coach featuring fender skirts, mud flaps, "Purple Pagans" on a hood plaque. Bolted to the porch: a heavy bag/speed bag combo. Jack said, "There's your welterweight."

Denton smiled; Jack walked up, pushed the buzzer. Dog barks inside—a real monster howling. Denton stood flank: the driveway, a bead on the door.

A Negro man opened up: wiry, a tough hump restraining a mastiff. The dog growled; the man said, "This 'cause I ain' paid my alimony? That a goddamn po-lice offense?"

"Are you Leonard Timothy Bidwell?"

"That's right."

"And that's your car in the driveway?"

"That's right. And if you a po-lice doin' repos on the side you barkin' up the wrong tree, 'cause my baby is paid for outright with my purse from my losin' effort 'gainst Johnny Saxton."

Jack pointed to the dog. "Put him back inside and close the door, walk out and put your hands on the wall."

Bidwell did it extra slow; Jack frisked him, turned him around. Denton walked over. "Boy, you like 12-gauge pumps?"

Bidwell shook his head. "Say what?"; Jack threw a change-up. "Where were you last night at 3:00 A.M.?"

"Right here at my crib."

"By yourself? If you got laid you got lucky. Tell me you got lucky, before my buddy gets pissed."

"I gots custody of my kids fo' the week. They was with me."

"Are they here?"

"They asleep."

Denton prodded him—a gun poke to the ribs. "Boy, you know what happened last night? Bad juju, and I ain't woofin'. You own a shotgun, boy?"

"Man, I don't need no fuckin' shotgun."

Denton poked harder. "Boy, don't you use curse words with me. Now, before we get your pickaninnies out here, you gonna tell me who you lent your automobile to last night?"

"Man, I don' lend my sled to nobody!"

"Then who'd you lend your 12-gauge pump shotguns to? Boy, you spill on that."

"Man, I tol' you I don't own no shotgun!"

Jack stepped in. "Tell me about the Purple Pagans. Are they a bunch of guys who like purple cars?"

"Man, that is just a name for our club. I gots a purple car, some other cats in the club gots them too. Man, what is this all about?"

Jack took out his DMV sheet—the Merc owners all typed up. "Leonard, did you read the papers this morning?"

"No. Man, what is—"

"Sssh. You listen to the radio or watch television?"

"I ain't got either of them. What's that—"

"Sssh. Leonard, we're looking for three colored guys who like to pop off shotguns and a Merc like yours, a '48, a '49, or a '50. I know you wouldn't hurt anybody, I saw you fight Gavilan and I like your style. We're looking for some *bad* guys. Guys with a car like yours, guys who might belong to your club."

Bidwell shrugged. "Why should I help you?"

"Because I'll cut my partner loose on you if you don't."

"Yeah, and you get me a fuckin' snitch jacket, too."

"No jacket, and you don't have to say anything. Just look at this list and point. Here, read it over."

Bidwell shook his head. "They's bad, so I jus' tell you. Sugar Ray Coates, drives a '49 coupe, a beautiful ride. He gots two buddies, Leroy and Tyrone. Sugar loves to party with a shotgun, I heard he gets his thrills shootin' dogs. He tried to get in my club, but we turned him down 'cause he is righteous trash."

Jack checked his list—bingo on "Coates, Raymond NMI, 9611 South Central, Room 114." Denton had his own sheet out. "Two minutes from here. We haul, we might get there first."

Hero headlines. "Let's do it."

* * *

The Tevere Hotel: an L-shaped walk-up above a washateria. Denton coasted into the lot; Jack saw stairs going up—just one floor of rooms, a wide-open doorway.

Up and in—a short corridor, flimsy-looking doors. Jack drew his piece; Denton pulled two guns: a .38, an ankle rig automatic. They counted room numbers; 114 came up. Denton reared back; Jack reared back; they kicked the same instant. The door flew off its hinges for a pure clean shot: a colored kid jumping out of bed.

The kid put up his hands. Denton smiled, aimed. Jack blocked him—two reflex pulls tore the ceiling. Jack ran in; the kid tried to run; Jack nailed him: gun-butt shots to the head. No more resistance—Denton cuffed his hands behind his back. Jack slipped on brass knucks and made fists. "Leroy, Tyrone. *Where*?"

The kid dribbled teeth—"One-two-one" came out bloody. Denton yanked him up by his hair; Jack said, "Don't you fucking kill him."

Denton spat in his face; shouts boomed down the hall. Jack ran out, around the "L," a skid to a stop in front of 121—

A closed door. Background noise huge—no way to take a listen. Jack kicked; wood splintered; the door creaked open. Two coloreds inside—one asleep on a cot, one snoring on a mattress.

Jack walked in. Sirens whirring up very close. The mattress kid stirred—Jack bludgeoned him quiet, bashed the other punk before he could move. The sirens screeched, died. Jack saw a box on the dresser.

Shotgun shells: Remington 12-gauge double-aught buck. A box of fifty, most of them gone.

19

ED SKIMMED Jack Vincennes' report. Thad Green watched, his phone ringing off the hook.

Solid, concise—Trash knew how to write a good quickie.

Three male Negroes in custody: Raymond "Sugar Ray" Coates, Leroy Fontaine, Tyrone Jones. Treated for wounds received while resisting arrest; snitched by another male Negro—who described Coates as a shotgun toter who liked to blast dogs. Coates was on the DMV sheet; the informant stated that he ran with two other men—"Tyrone and Leroy"—also living at the Tevere Hotel. The three were arrested in their underwear; Vincennes turned them over to prowl car officers responding to shots fired and searched their rooms for evidence. He found a fifty-unit box of Remington 12-gauge double-aught shotgun shells, forty-odd missing—but no shotguns, no rubber gloves, no bloodstained clothing, no large amounts of cash or coins and no other weaponry. The only clothing in the rooms: soiled T-shirts, boxer shorts, neatly pressed garments covered by dry cleaner's cellophane. Vincennes checked the incinerator in back of the hotel; it was burning—the manager told him he saw Sugar Coates dump a load of clothes in at approximately 7:00 this morning. Vincennes said Jones and Fontaine appeared to be inebriated or under the influence of narcotics—they slept through gunfire and the general ruckus of Coates resisting arrest. Vincennes told late-arriving patrolmen to search for Coates' car—it was not in the parking lot or anywhere in a three-block radius. An APB was issued; Vincennes stated that all three suspects' hands and arms reeked of perfume—a paraffin test would be inconclusive.

Ed laid the report on Green's desk. "I'm surprised he didn't kill them."

The phone rang—Green let it keep going. "More headlines this way, he's shacking with Ellis Loew's sister-in-law. And if the coons doused their paws with perfume to foil a paraffin test, we can thank Jack for that—he gave that little piece of information to *Badge of Honor*. Ed, are you up for this?"

Ed's stomach jumped. "Yes, sir. I am."

"The chief wanted Dudley Smith to work with you, but I talked him out of it. As good as he is, the man is off the deep end on coloreds."

"Sir, I know how important this is."

Green lit a cigarette. "Ed, I want confessions. Fifteen of the rounds we retrieved at the Nite Owl were nicked at the strike point, so if we get the guns we've got the case. I want the location of the guns, the location of the car and confessions before we arraign them. We've got seventy-one hours before they see the judge. I want this wrapped up by then. *Clean*."

Specifics. "Rap sheets on the kids?"

Green said, "Joyriding and B&E for all three. Peeping Tom beefs for Coates and Fontaine. And they're not kids—Coates is twenty-two, the others are twenty. This is a gas chamber bounce pure and clean."

"What about the Griffith Park angle? Shell samples to compare, witnesses to the guys letting off the shotguns."

"Shell samples might be good backup evidence, if we can find them and the coloreds don't confess. The park ranger who called in the complaints is coming down to try for an ID. Ed, Arnie Reddin says you're the best interrogator he's ever seen, but you've never worked anything this—"

Ed stood up. "I'll do it."

"Son, if you do, you'll have my job one day."

Ed smiled—his loose teeth ached. Green said, "What happened to your face?"

"I tripped chasing a shoplifter. Sir, who's talked to the suspects?"

"Just the doctor who cleaned them up. Dudley wanted Bud White to have first shot, but—"

"Sir, I don't think—"

"Don't interrupt me, I was about to agree with you. No, I want *voluntary* confessions, so White is out. You've got first shot at all three. You'll be observed through the two-ways, and if you want a partner for a Mutt and Jeff, touch your necktie. There'll be a group of us listening through an outside speaker, and a recorder will be running. The three are in separate rooms, and if you want to play them off on each other, you know the buttons to hit."

Ed said, "I'll break them."

*   *   *

His stage: a corridor off the Homicide pen. Three cubicles set up—mirror-fronted, speaker-connected—flip switches and a string of suspects could hear their partners rat each other off. The rooms: six-by-six square, welded-down tables, bolted-down chairs. In 1, 2 and 3: Sugar Ray Coates, Leroy Fontaine, Tyrone Jones. Rap sheets taped to the wall outside—Ed memorized dates, locations, known associates. A deep breath to kill stage fright—in the #1 door.

Sugar Ray Coates cuffed to a chair, dressed in baggy County denims. Tall, light-complected—close to a mulatto. One eye swollen shut; lips puffed and split. A smashed nose—both nostrils sutured. Ed said, "Looks like we both took a beating."

Coates squinted—one-eyed, spooky. Ed unlocked his cuffs, tossed cigarettes and matches on the table. Coates flexed his wrists. Ed smiled. "They call you Sugar Ray because of Ray Robinson?"

No answer.

Ed took the other chair. "They say Ray Robinson can throw a four-punch combination in one second. I don't believe it myself."

Coates lifted his arms—they flopped, dead weight. Ed opened the cigarette pack. "I know, they cut off the circulation. You're twenty-two, aren't you, Ray?"

Coates: "Say what and so what," a scratchy voice. Ed scoped his throat—bruised, finger marks. "Did one of the officers do a little throttling on you?"

No answer. Ed said, "Sergeant Vincennes? The snazzy dresser guy?"

Silence.

"Not him, huh? Was it Denton? Fat guy with a Texas drawl, sounds like Spade Cooley on TV?"

Coates' good eye twitched. Ed said, "Yeah, I commiserate—that guy Denton is one choice creep. You see *my* face? Denton and I went a couple of rounds."

No bite.

"Goddamn that Denton. Sugar Ray, you and I look like Robinson and LaMotta after that last fight they had."

Still no bite.

"So you're twenty-two, right?"

"Man, why you ask me that!"

Ed shrugged. "Just getting my facts straight. Leroy and Tyrone are twenty, so they can't burn on a capital charge. Ray, you should have pulled this caper a couple of years ago. Get life, do a little Youth Authority jolt, transfer to Folsom a big man. Get yourself a sissy, orbit on some of that good prison brew."

"Sissy" hit home: Coates' hands twitched. He picked up a cigarette, lit it, coughed. "I never truck with no sissies."

Ed smiled. "I know that, son."

"I ain't your son, you ofay fuck. You the sissy."

Ed laughed. "You know the drill, I'll give you that. You've done juvie time, you know I'm the nice guy cop trying to get you to talk. That fucking Tyrone, I almost believed him. Denton must have knocked a few of my screws loose. How could I fall for a line like that?"

"Say what, man? What line you mean?"

"Nothing, Ray. Let's change the subject. What did you do with the shotguns?"

Coates rubbed his neck—shaky hands. "What shotguns?"

Ed leaned close. "The pumps you and your friends were shooting in Griffith Park."

"Don't know 'bout no shotguns."

"You don't? Leroy and Tyrone had a box of shells in their room."

"That their bidness."

Ed shook his head. "That Tyrone, he's a pisser. You did the Casitas Youth Camp with him, didn't you?"

A shrug. "So what and say what?"

"Nothing, Ray. Just thinking out loud."

"Man, why you talkin' 'bout Tyrone? Tyrone's bidness is Tyrone's bidness."

Ed reached under the table, found the audio switch for room 3. "Sugar, Tyrone told me you went sissy up at Casitas. You couldn't do the time so you found yourself a big white boy to look after you. He said they call you 'Sugar' because you gave it out so sweet."

Coates hit the table. Ed hit the switch. "Say what, *Sugar*?"

"Say I *took* it! *Tyrone* give it! Man, I was the fuckin' boss jocker on my dorm! Tyrone the sissy! Tyrone give it for candy bars! Tyrone love it!"

Switch back up. "Ray, let's change the subject. Why do you think you and your friends are under arrest?"

Coates fingered the cigarette pack. "Some humbug beef, maybe like dischargin' firearms inside city limit, some humbug like that. Wha's Tyrone say 'bout that?"

"Ray, Tyrone said lots of things, but let's get to meat and potatoes. Where were you at 3:00 A.M. last night?"

Coates chained a smoke butt to tip. "I was at my crib. Asleep."

"Were you on hop? Tyrone and Leroy must have been, they were passed out while those officers arrested you. Some crime partners. Tyrone calls you a fairy, then him and Leroy sleep through you getting beat up by some cracker shitbird. I thought you colored guys stuck together. Were you hopped up, Ray? You couldn't take what you did, so you got yourself some dope and—"

"Take what! What you mean! Tyrone and Leroy fuck with them goofballs, not me!"

Ed hit the 2 and 3 switches. "Ray, you protected Tyrone and Leroy up at Casitas, didn't you?"

Coates coughed out a big rush of smoke. "You ain't woofin' I did. Tyrone give his boodie and Leroy so scared he almos' throw hisself off the roof and drink hisself blind on pruno. Stupid down home niggers got no more sense than a fuckin' dog."

Switches back up. "Ray, I heard you like to shoot dogs."

A shrug. "Dogs got no reason to live."

"Oh? You feel that way about people, too?"

"Man, what you sayin'?"

Switches down. "Well, you must feel that way about Leroy and Tyrone."

"Shit, Leroy and Tyrone almos' too stupid to live."

Switches up. "Ray, where's the shotguns you were shooting in Griffith Park?"

"They—I...I don't own no shotguns."

"Where's your 1949 Mercury coupe?"

"I let ... it just be safe."

"Come on, Ray. A cherry rig like that? Where is it? I'd keep a nice sled like that under lock and key."

"I said it safe!"

Ed slapped the table—two palms flat down. "Did you sell it? Ditch it? It's a felony transport car. Ray, don't you think—"

"I didn't do no felony!"

"The hell you say! Where's the car?"

"I ain't sayin'!"

"Where's the shotguns?"

"I ain't—I don't know!"

"Where's the car?"

"I ain't sayin'!"

Ed drummed the table. "Why, Ray? You got shotguns and rubber gloves in the trunk? You got wallets and purses and blood all over the seats? Listen to me, you dumb son of a bitch, I'm trying to save you a gas chamber bounce like your buddies—they're underage and you're not, and somebody has to fry for this—"

"I don't know what you talkin' 'bout!"

Ed sighed. "Ray, let's change the subject."

Coates lit another cigarette. "I don' like your subjects."

"Ray, why were you burning clothes at 7:00 this morning?"

Coates trembled. "Say what?"

"Say this. You, Leroy and Tyrone were arrested this morning. None of you had last night's clothes with you. You were seen burning a big pile of clothes at 7:00. Add that to the fact that you hid the car that you, Tyrone and Leroy were cruising around in last night. Ray, it doesn't look good, but if you give me something good to give the DA, it'll make me look good and I'll say, 'Sugar Ray wasn't a punk like his sissy partners.' Ray, just give me something."

"Such as what, since I innocent of all this rebop you shuckin' me with."

Ed flipped 2 and 3. "Well, you've said bad things about Leroy and Tyrone, you've implied that they're hopheads. Let's try this: where do they get their stuff?"

Coates stared at the floor. Ed said, "The DA hates hop pushers. And you met Jack Vincennes, the Big V."

"Crazy fuckin' fool."

Ed laughed. "Yeah, Jack is a little on the crazy side. Personally, I think anyone who wants to ruin their life with narcotics should have the right, it's a free country. But Jack's good buddies with the new DA, and they've both got hard-ons for hop pushers. Ray, give me one to give the DA. Just a little one."

Coates hooked a finger; Ed let the switches up and leaned in. Sugar Ray, a whisper. "Roland Navarette, lives on Bunker Hill. Runs a hole-up for parole 'sconders and sells red devils, and that ain't for the fuckin' DA, that's 'cause Tyrone shoot off his fat fuckin' mouth."

Switches down. "All right, Ray. You've told me that Roland Navarette sells barbiturates to Leroy and Tyrone, so now we're making some progress. And you're scared shitless, you know this is gas chamber stuff and you haven't even asked me what it's all about. Ray, you have a big guilty sign around your neck."

Coates cracked his knuckles; his good eye darted, flickered. Ed killed the audio. "Ray, let's change the subject."

"How 'bout baseball, motherfucker?"

"No, let's talk about pussy. Did you get laid last night or did you put that perfume on yourself to fuck up a paraffin test?"

Heebie-jeebie shakes.

Ed said, "Where were you at 3:00 last night?"

No answer, more shakes.

"Strike a nerve, Sugar Ray? *Perfume? Women?* Even a piece of shit like you has to have some women he cares about. You got a mother? Sisters?"

"Man, don't you talk 'bout my mother!"

"Ray, if I didn't know you I'd say you were protecting some nice girl's virtue. She was your alibi, you were shacked somewhere. But Tyrone and Leroy have got that same perfume on their mitts, and I'm betting against a gang bang, I'm betting you learned about paraffin tests up in road camp, I'm betting you've got just enough decency to feel some guilt over killing three innocent women."

"I AIN'T KILLED NOBODY!"

Ed pulled out the morning *Herald*. "Patty Chesimard, Donna DeLuca and one unidentified. Read this while I take a breather.

When I come back you'll get the chance to tell me about it and make a deal that just might save your life."

Coates, Tremor City—all twitches, soaked denims. Ed threw the paper in his face and walked out.

Thad Green in the hall; Dudley Smith, Bud White at the listening post. Green said, "We got an eyeball confirmation from that ranger—those *were* the guys in Griffith Park. And you were great."

Ed smelled his own sweat. "Sir, Coates was hinked on the women. I can feel it."

"So can I, so just keep going."

"Have we turned the guns or the car?"

"No, and the 77th Street squad is shaking down their relatives and KA's. We'll get them."

"I want to lean on Jones next. Will you do something for me?"

"Name it."

"Set up Fontaine. Unlock his cuffs and let him read the morning paper."

Green pointed to the #3 mirror. "*He'll* break soon. Sniveling bastard."

Tyrone Jones—weeping, a piss puddle on the floor by his chair. Ed looked away. "Sir, have Lieutenant Smith read the paper into his speaker, nice and slow, especially the lines about the car spotted by the Nite Owl. I want this guy primed to fold."

Green said, "You've got it." Ed checked out Tyrone Jones—dark-skinned, flabby, pockmarked. Bawling—cuffed in, welded down.

A whistle up the hall. Dudley Smith spoke into a microphone—silent lip movements. Ed fixed on Jones.

The kid twisted, heaved, buckled, like a film clip they showed at the Academy: an electric chair malfunction, a dozen jolts before the man fried. A sharp whistle up the corridor—Jones slumped, legs splayed, chin down.

Ed walked in. "Tyrone, Ray Coates ratted you off. He said the Nite Owl was your idea, he said you got the idea while you were cruising Griffith Park. Tyrone, tell me about it. I think it was Ray's idea. He made you do it. Tell me where the guns and car are and I think we can save your life."

No answer.

"Tyrone, this is a gas chamber job. If you don't talk to me you'll be dead in six months."

No answer—Jones kept his head down.

"Son, all you have to do is tell me where the guns are and tell me where Sugar left the car."

No answer.

"Son, this can be over in one minute. You tell me, and I get you transferred to a protective custody cell. Sugar won't be able to get you, Leroy won't be able to get you. The DA will let you turn state's. *You won't go to the gas chamber.*"

No response.

"Son, six people are dead and somebody has to pay. It can be you or it can be Ray."

No answer.

"Tyrone, he called you a queer. He called you a sissy and a homo. He said you took it up the—"

"I DIDN' KILL NOBODY!"

A strong voice—Ed almost jumped back. "Son, we have witnesses. We have evidence. Coates is confessing right now. He's saying you planned the whole thing. Son, save yourself. The guns, the car. *Tell me where they are.*"

"I didn' kill nobody!"

"Sssh. Tyrone, do you know what Ray Coates said about you?"

Jones lifted his head. "I know he lie."

"I think he lied, too. I don't think you're a queer. I think he's a queer, because he hates women. I think he liked killing those women. I think you feel bad about—"

"We didn' kill no women!"

"Tyrone, where were you last night at 3:00 A.M.?"

No answer.

"Tyrone, why did Sugar Ray hide his car?"

No answer.

"Tyrone, why did you guys hide the shotguns you were shooting in Griffith Park? We have a witness who ID'd you on that."

No answer. Jones lolled his head—eyes shut, spilling tears.

"Son, why did Ray burn the clothes you guys were wearing last night?"

Jones keening now—animal stuff.

"They had blood on them, didn't they? You killed six goddamn people, you got sprayed. Ray did the clean-up, he tidied the loose ends, *he's* the one who hid the shotguns, he's the boss man, he's been giving the orders since you were giving out butthole up at Casitas. Spill, goddamn you!"

"WE DIDN' KILL NOBODY! I AIN'T NO FUCKIN' QUEER!"

Ed circled the table—walking fast, talking slow. "Here's what I think. I think Sugar Ray's the boss, Leroy's just a dummy, you're the fat boy Sugar likes to tease. You all did road camp together, you and Sugar Ray got popped for Peeping Tom. Sugar liked looking at girls, you liked looking at boys. You both like looking at white folks, because that is the colored man's forbidden fruit. You had your 12-gauge pumps, you had your snazzy '49 Merc, you had some red devils you bought off Roland Navarette. You were up in Hollywood, white folks' neck of the woods. Sugar was teasing you about being fruit, you kept saying it was just because there were no girls around. Sugar says prove it, prove it, and you guys start peeping. You're getting mad, you're all flying on hop, it's late at night and there's nothing to look at, all those nice white folks have their curtains down. You drive by the Nite Owl, there's these nice white people inside—and it is just too fucking much to take. Poor fat sissy Tyrone, he takes over. He leads his boys into the Nite Owl. Six people are there—three of them women. You drag them into the locker, you hit the cash register and make the cook open the safe. You take their billfolds and purses and you spill some perfume on your hands. Sugar says, 'Touch the girlies, sissy. Prove you ain't queer.' You can't do it so you start shooting and everybody starts shooting and you love it because finally you're more than a poor queer fat little nigger and—"

"NO! NO NO NO NO NO NO!"

"Yes! Where's the guns? You fucking confess and turn over the evidence or you'll go to the fucking gas chamber!"

"No! Didn' kill nobody!"

Ed hit the table. "Why'd you ditch the car?"

Jones lashed his head, spraying sweat.

"Why'd you burn the clothes?"

No answer.

"Where did the perfume come from?"

No answer.

"Did Sugar and Leroy rape the women first?"

"No!"

"Oh? You mean all three of you did?"

"We didn' kill nobody! We wasn't even there!"

"Where were you?"

No answer.

"Tyrone, where were you last night?"

Jones sobbed; Ed gripped his shoulders. "Son, you know what's going to happen if you don't talk. So for God's sake admit what you did."

"Didn' kill nobody. None of us. Wasn't even there."

"Son, you did."

"No!"

"Son, you did, so tell me."

"We didn'!"

"Hush now. Just tell me—*nice and slowly*."

Jones started babbling. Ed knelt by his chair, listened.

He heard: "Please God, I just wanted to lose my cherry"; he heard: "Didn't mean to hurt her so's we'd have to die." He heard: "Not right punish what we didn' do ... maybe she be okay, she don't die so I don't die, 'cause I ain't no queer." He felt himself buzzing, electric chair, a sign on top: THEY DIDN'T DO IT.

Jones slipped into a reverie—Jesus, Jesus, Jesus, Father Divine. Ed hit the #2 cubicle.

Rank: sweat, cigarette smoke. Leroy Fontaine—big, dark, processed hair, his feet up on the table. Ed said, "Be smarter than your friends. Even if you killed her, it's not as bad as killing six people."

Fontaine tweaked his nose—bandaged, spread over half his face. "This newspaper shit ain't shit."

Ed closed the door, scared. "Leroy, you'd better hope she was with you at the coroner's estimated time of death."

No answer.

"Was she a hooker?"

No answer.

"Did you kill her?"

No answer.

"You wanted Tyrone to lose his cherry, but things got out of hand. Isn't that right?"

No answer.

"Leroy, if she's dead and she was colored you can cop a plea. If she was white you might have a chance. Remember, we can make you for the Nite Owl, and we can make it stick. Unless you convince me you were somewhere else doing something bad, we'll nail you for what's in that newspaper."

No answer—Fontaine cleaned his nails with a matchbook.

A big lie. "If you kidnapped her and she's still alive, that's not a Little Lindbergh violation. It's not a capital charge."

No answer.

"Leroy, where are the guns and the car?"

No answer.

"Leroy, is she still alive?"

Fontaine smiled—Ed felt ice on his spine. "If she's still alive, she's your alibi. I won't kid you, it could get bad: kidnap, rape, assault. But if you eliminate yourself on the Nite Owl now, you'll save us time and the DA will like you for it. Kick loose, Leroy. Do yourself a favor."

No answer.

"Leroy, look how it can go both ways. I think you kidnapped a girl at gunpoint. You made her bleed up the car, so you hid the car. She bled on your clothes, so you burned the clothes. You got her perfume all over yourselves. If you didn't do the Nite Owl, I don't know why you hid the shotguns, maybe you thought she could identify them. Son, if that girl is alive she is the only chance you've got."

Fontaine said, "I thinks she alive."

Ed sat down. "*You think?*"

"Yeah, I thinks."

"Who is she? *Where is she?*"

No answer.

"Is she colored?"

"She Mex."

"What's her name?"

"I don' know. College-type bitch."

"Where did you pick her up?"

"I don' know. Eastside someplace."

"Where did you assault her?"

"I don' know ... old building on Dunkirk somewheres."

"Where's the car and the shotguns?"

"I don' know. Sugar, he took care of them."

"If you didn't kill her, why did Coates hide the shotguns?"

No answer.

"Why, Leroy?"

No answer.

"Why, son? Tell me."

No answer.

Ed hit the table. "Tell me, goddammit!"

Fontaine hit the table—harder. "Sugar, he poked her with them guns! He 'fraid it be evidence!"

Ed closed his eyes. "Where is she now?"

No answer.

"Did you leave her at the building?"

No answer.

Eyes open. "Did you leave her someplace else?"

No answer.

Leaps: none of the three had cash on them, call their money evidence—stashed when Sugar burned the clothes. "Leroy, did you sell her out? Bring some buddies by that place on Dunkirk?"

"We … we drove her 'roun'."

"Where? Your friends' pads?"

"Tha's right."

"Up in Hollywood?"

"We didn' shoot them people!"

"Prove it, Leroy. Where were you guys at 3:00 A.M.?"

"Man, I cain't tell you!"

Ed slapped the table. "Then you'll burn for the Nite Owl!"

"We didn't do it!"

"Who did you sell the girl to?"

No answer.

"Where is she now?"

No answer.

"Are you afraid of reprisals? You left the girl somewhere, right? *Leroy, where did you leave her, who did you leave her with, she is your only chance to stay out of the fucking gas chamber!*"

"Man, I cain't tell you, Sugar, he like to kill me!"

"Leroy, where is she?"

No answer.

"Leroy, you turn state's you'll get out years before Sugar and Tyrone."

No response.

"Leroy, I'll get you a one-man cell where nobody can hurt you."

No response.

"Son, you have to tell me. I'm the only friend you've got."

No response.

"Leroy, are you afraid of the man you left the girl with?"

No answer.

"Son, he can't be as bad as the gas chamber. *Tell me where the girl is.*"

The door banged open. Bud White stepped in, threw Fontaine against the wall.

Ed froze.

White pulled out his .38, broke the cylinder, dropped shells on the floor. Fontaine shook head to toe; Ed kept freezing. White snapped the cylinder shut, stuck the gun in Fontaine's mouth. "One in six. Where's the girl?"

Fontaine chewed steel; White squeezed the trigger twice: clicks, empty chambers. Fontaine slid down the wall; White pulled the gun back, held him up by his hair. "*Where's the girl?*"

Ed kept freezing. White pulled the trigger—another little click. Fontaine, bug-eyed. "S-ss-sylvester F-fitch, one-o-nine and Avalon, gray corner house please don' hurt me no—"

White ran out.

Fontaine passed out.

Riot sounds in the corridor—Ed tried to stand up, couldn't get his legs.

20

A FOUR-CAR cordon: two black-and-whites, two unmarkeds. Sirens to a half mile out; a coast up to the gray corner house.

Dudley Smith drove the lead prowler; Bud rode shotgun reloading his piece. A four-car flank: black-and-whites in the alley, Mike Breuning and Dick Carlisle parked streetside—rifles on the gray house door. Bud said, "Boss, he's mine."

Dudley winked. "Grand, lad."

Bud went in the back way—through the alley, a fence vault. On the rear porch: a screen door, inside hook and eye. He slipped the catch with his penknife, walked in on tiptoes.

Darkness, dim shapes: a washing machine, a blind-covered door—strips of light through the cracks.

Bud tried the door—unlocked—eased it open. A hallway: light bouncing from two side rooms. A rug to walk on; music to give him more cover. He tiptoed up to the first room, wheeled in.

A nude woman spread-eagled on a mattress—bound with neckties, a necktie in her mouth. Bud hit the next room loud.

A fat mulatto at a table—naked, wolfing Kellogg's Rice Krispies. He put down his spoon, raised his hands. "Nossir, don't want no trouble."

Bud shot him in the face, pulled a spare piece—bang bang from the coon's line of fire. The man hit the floor dead spread—a prime entry wound oozing blood. Bud put the spare in his hand; the front door crashed in. He dumped Rice Krispies on the stiff, called an ambulance.

21

JACK WATCHED Karen sleep, putting their fight behind him.

Newspaper pix caused it: the Big V and Cal Denton rousting three colored punks—suspects in L.A.'s "Crime of the Century." Denton dragged Fontaine by his conk; Big V had neck holds on the other two. Karen said they reminded her of the Scottsboro Boys; Jack told her he saved their goddamned lives, but now that he knew they gang-raped a Mexican girl he wished he'd let Denton kill them outright. The argument deteriorated from there.

Karen slept curled away from him—covered tight like she thought he might hit her. Jack watched her while he dressed; his last two days hit him.

He was off the Nite Owl, back to Ad Vice. Ed Exley's interrogations tentatively cleared the spooks—pending questioning of the woman they'd been abusing. Bud White played some Russian roulette—the three clammed up. So far, there was no way to know if they had time to leave the woman, drive to the Nite Owl, return to Darktown and gang-rape. Maybe Coates or Fontaine left Jones in charge of the girl and pulled the snuffs with other partners. No luck finding the shotguns; Coates' purple Merc was still missing. No restaurant loot found at their hotel; the debris in the incinerator too far gone for blood-on-fabric analysis. The perfume on the jigs' hands skunked a late paraffin test. Huge pressure at the Bureau: solve the fucking case fast.

The coroner was trying to ID the patron victims, working from dental abstracts and their physical stats cross-checked against missing persons bulletins, call-ins. Made: the cook/dishwasher, waitress, cash register girl; nothing yet on the three customers, the autopsies showed no sexual abuse on the women. Maybe Coates/Jones/Fontaine weren't the triggers; Dudley Smith on the job—his men bracing armed robbers, nuthouse parolees, every known L.A. geek with a gun jacket. The news vendor who spotted the purple Merc across from the Nite Owl was requestioned; now he

said it could have been a Ford or a Chevy. Ford and Chevy registrations being checked; *now* the park ranger who ID'd the spooks
said he wasn't sure. Ed Exley told Green and Parker the purple
car might have been placed by the Nite Owl to put the onus on
the jigs; Dudley pooh-poohed the theory—he said it was probably
just a coincidence. A sure-thing case unraveling into a shitload of
possibilities.

Huge press coverage—Sid Hudgens had already called—zero
hink on the smut, nothing like "We've *all* got secrets." A heroic
version of the arrests for fifty scoots—Sid hung up quick.

The Nite Owl cost him a day on the smut. He'd checked the
squadroom postings: no leads, none of the other men tracked the
shit. He filed a phony report himself: nothing on Christine
Bergeron and Bobby Inge, nothing on the other mags he found.
Nothing on his filth dreams: his sweetheart Karen orgied up.

Jack kissed Karen's neck, hoping she'd wake up and smile.

No luck.

*   *   *

Canvassing first.

Charleville Drive, questions, no luck: none of the tenants in
Christine Bergeron's building heard the woman and her son
move out; none knew a thing about the men she entertained. The
adjoining apartment houses—ditto straight across. Jack called
Beverly Hills High, learned that Daryl Bergeron was a chronic
truant who hadn't attended classes in a week; the vice-principal
said the boy kept to himself, didn't cause trouble—he was never
in school *to* cause trouble. Jack didn't tell him Daryl was too tired
to cause trouble: fucking your mother on roller skates takes a lot
out of a kid.

His next call: Stan's Drive-in. The manager told him Chris
Bergeron splitsvilled day before yesterday, two seconds after getting a phone call. No, he didn't know who the caller was; yes, he
would buzz Sergeant Vincennes if she showed up; no, Chris did
not unduly fraternize with customers or receive visitors while
carhopping.

Out to West Hollywood.

Bobby Inge's place, talks—fellow tenants and neighbors.
Bobby paid his rent on time, kept to himself, nobody saw him
move out. The swish next door said he "played the field—he
wasn't seeing anyone in particular." Tweaks: "smut books,"

"Chris Bergeron," "this little twist Daryl"—the fruit dead-panned him cold.

Call West Hollywood dead—after B.J.'s Rumpus Room Bobby wouldn't be caught near the fag-bar strip. Jack grabbed a hamburger, checked his Inge rap sheet—no KA's listed. He studied his private filth stash, hard to concentrate, the contradictions in the pictures kept distracting him.

Attractive posers, trashy backdrops. Beautiful costumes that made you look twice at disgusting homo action. Artful orgy shots: inked-in blood, bodies connected over quilts—pix that made you squint to see female forms held in check by too much explicitness—the sex organ extravaganza made you want to see the women plain nude. The shit was pornography manufactured for money—but somewhere in the process an artist was involved.

A brainstorm.

Jack drove to a dime store, bought scissors, Scotch tape, a drawing pad. He worked in the car: faces cut from the mags, taped to the paper, men and women separated, repeats placed together to make IDs easier. Downtown to the Bureau for matchups: stag pix to Caucasian mug books. Four hours of squinting: eyestrain, zero identifications. Over to Hollywood Station, their separate Vice mugs, another zero; the West Hollywood Sheriff's Substation made zero number three. Bobby Inge aside, his smut beauties were virgins—no criminal records.

4:30 P.M.—Jack felt his options dwindling fast. Another idea caught: check Bobby Inge through the DMV; check Chris Bergeron through again—a complete paper prowl. R&I/Inge one more time—updates on his sheet.

He hit a pay phone, made the calls. Bobby Inge was DMV clean: no citations, no court appearances. Complete Bergeron paper: traffic violation dates, the names of her surety bond guarantors. R&I's only Inge update: a year-old bail report. One name crossed over—Bergeron to Inge.

Bail on an Inge prostie charge—fronted by Sharon Kostenza, 1649 North Havenhurst, West Hollywood. The same woman paid a Bergeron reckless-driving bond.

Jack called R&I back, ran Sharon Kostenza and her address through—no California criminal record. He told the clerk to check the forty-eight-state list; that took a full ten minutes. "Sorry, Sarge. Nothing at all on the name."

Back to the DMV; a shocker: no one named Sharon Kostenza possessed or had ever possessed a California driver's license. Jack drove to North Havenhurst—the address 1649 did not exist.

Brain circuits: prostie Bobby Inge, Kostenza bailed him on a prostie beef, prosties used phony names, prosties posed for stag pix. North Havenhurst a longtime call-house block—

He started knocking on doors.

A dozen quickie interviews; tags on nearby fuck joints. Two, on Havenhurst: 1611, 1564.

6:10 P.M.

1611 open for business; the boss deadpanned Sharon Kostenza, Bobby Inge, the Bergerons. Ditto the faces clipped from the fuck mags—the girls working the joint panned out likewise. The madam at 1564 cooperated—the names and faces were Greek to her and her whores.

Another burger, back to West Hollywood Substation. A run through the alias file: another flat busted dead end.

7:20—no more names to check. Jack drove to North Hamel, parked with a view: Bobby Inge's door.

He kept a fix on the courtyard. No foot traffic, street traffic slow—the Strip wouldn't jump for hours. He waited: smoking, smut pictures in his head.

At 8:46 a quiff ragtop cruised by—a slow trawl close to the curb. Twenty minutes later—one more time. Jack tried to read plate numbers—nix, too dark out. A hunch: he's looking for window lights. If he's looking for Bobby's, he's got them.

He walked into the courtyard, lucked out on witnesses—none. Handcuff ratchets popped the door: teeth cutting cheap wood. He felt for a wall light, tripped a switch.

The same cleaned-out living room; the pad in the same disarray. Jack sat by the door, waited.

Boredom time stretched—fifteen minutes, thirty, an hour. Knocks on the front windowpane.

Jack drew down: the door, eye-level. He faked a fag lilt: "It's open."

A pretty boy sashayed in. Jack said, "Shit."

Timmy Valburn, a.k.a. Moochie Mouse—Billy Dieterling's squeeze.

"Timmy, what the fuck are you doing here?"

Valburn slouched, one hip cocked, no fear. "Bobby's a friend. He doesn't use narcotics, if that's what you're here for. And isn't this a tad out of your jurisdiction?"

Jack closed the door. "Christine Bergeron, Daryl Bergeron, Sharon Kostenza. They friends of yours?"

"I don't know those names. Jack, what is this?"

"You tell me, you've been getting up the nerve to knock for hours. Let's start with where's Bobby?"

"I don't know. Would I be here if I knew where—"

"Do you trick with Bobby? You got a thing going with him?"

"He's just a friend."

"Does Billy know about you and Bobby?"

"Jack, you're being vile. *Bobby is a friend.* I don't think Billy knows we're friends, but friends is all we are."

Jack took out his notepad. "So I'm sure you have a lot of friends in common."

"No. Put that away, because I don't know any of Bobby's friends."

"All right, then where did you meet him?"

"At a bar."

"Name the bar."

"Leo's Hideaway."

"Billy know you chase stuff behind his back?"

"Jack, don't be crude. I'm not some criminal you can slap around, I'm a citizen who can report you for breaking into this apartment."

Change-up. "Smut. Picture-book stuff, regular and homo. That your bent, Timmy?"

One little eye flicker—not quite a hink. "You get your kicks that way? You and Billy take shit like that to bed with you?"

No flinch. "Don't be vile, Jack. It's not your style, but be nice. Remember what I am to Billy, remember what Billy is to the show that gives you the celebrity you grovel for. Remember who Billy knows."

Jack moved extra slow: the smut mags and face sheets to a chair, a lamp pulled over for some light. "Look at those pictures. If you recognize anybody, tell me. That's all I want."

Valburn rolled his eyes, looked. The face sheets first: quizzical, curious. On to the costume skin books—nonchalant, a queer sophisticate. Jack stuck close, eyes on his eyes.

The orgy book last. Timmy saw inked-on blood and kept looking; Jack saw a neck vein working overtime.

Valburn shrugged. "No, I'm sorry."

A tough read—a skilled actor. "You didn't recognize anybody?"

"No, I didn't."

"But you did recognize Bobby."

"Of course, because I know him."

"But nobody else?"

"Jack, really."

"Nobody familiar? Nobody you've seen at the bars your type goes to?"

"*My type?* Jack, haven't you been sucking around the Industry long enough to call a spade a spade and still be nice about it?"

Let it pass. "Timmy, you keep your thoughts hidden. Maybe you've been playing Moochie Mouse too long."

"What kind of thoughts are you looking for? I'm an actor, so give me a cue."

"Not thoughts, *reactions.* You didn't blink an eye at some of the strangest stuff I've seen in fifteen years as a cop. Arty-farty red ink shooting out of a dozen people fucking and sucking. Is that everyday stuff to you?"

An elegant shrug. "Jack, I'm *très* Hollywood. I dress up as a rodent to entertain children. Nothing in this town surprises me."

"I'm not sure I buy that."

"I'm telling you the truth. I don't know any of the people in those pictures, and I haven't seen those magazines before."

"People of your type know people who know people. You know Bobby Inge, and he was in those pictures. I want to see your little black book."

Timmy said, "No."

Jack said, "Yes, or I give *Hush-Hush* a little item on you and Billy Dieterling as soul sisters. *Badge of Honor*, the *Dream-a-Dream Hour* and queers. You like that for a three-horse parlay?"

Timmy smiled. "Max Peltz would fire you for that. He wants you to be nice. *So be nice.*"

"You carry your book with you?"

"No, I don't. Jack, remember who Billy's father is. Remember all the money you can make in the Industry after you retire."

Pissed now, almost seeing red. "Hand me your wallet. Do it or I'll lose my temper and put you up against the wall."

Valburn shrugged, pulled out a billfold. Jack glommed what he wanted: calling cards, names and numbers on paper scraps.

"I want those returned."

Jack handed the wallet back light. "Sure, Timmy."

"You are going to fuck up very auspiciously one day, Jack. Do you know that?"

"I already have, and I made money on the deal. Remember that if you decide to rat me to Max."

Valburn walked out—elegant.

*   *   *

Fruit-bar pickings: first names, phone numbers. One card looked familiar: "Fleur-de-Lis. Twenty-four Hours a Day— Whatever You Desire. HO-01239." No writing on the back— Jack racked his brain, couldn't make a connection.

New plan: call the numbers, impersonate Bobby Inge, drop lines about stag books—see who bit. Stick at the pad, see who called or showed up: long-shot stuff.

Jack called "Ted—DU-6831"—busy signal; "Geoff—CR-9640" —no bite on a lisping "Hi, it's Bobby Inge." "Bing—AX-6005"— no answer; back to "Ted"—"Bobby who? I'm sorry, but I don't think I know you." "Jim," "Nat," "Otto": no answers; he still couldn't make the odd card. Last-ditch stuff: buzz the cop line at Pacific Coast Bell.

Ring, ring. "Miss Sutherland speaking."

"This is Sergeant Vincennes, LAPD. I need a name and address on a phone number."

"Don't you have a reverse directory, Sergeant?"

"I'm in a phone booth, and the number I want checked is Hollywood 01239."

"Very well. Please hold the line."

Jack held; the woman came back on. "No such number is assigned. Bell is just beginning to assign five-digit numbers, and that one has not been assigned. Frankly, it may never be, the changeover is going so slow."

"You're sure about this?"

"Of course I'm sure."

Jack hung up. First thoughts: bootleg line. Bookies had them— bent guys at PC Bell rigged the lines, kept the numbers from being assigned. Free phone service, no way police agencies could subpoena records, no make on incoming calls.

A reflex call: The DMV police line.

"Yes? Who's requesting?"

"Sergeant Vincennes, LAPD. Address only on a Timothy V-A-L-B-U-R-N, white male, mid to late twenties. I think he lives in the Wilshire District."

"I copy. Please hold."

Jack held; the clerk returned. "Wilshire it is. 432 South Lucerne. Say, isn't Valburn that mouse guy on the Dieterling show?"

"Yeah."

"Well ... uh ... what are you after him for?"

"Possession of contraband cheese."

* * *

Chez Mouse: an old French Provincial with new money accoutrements—floodlights, topiary bushes—Moochie, the rest of the Dieterling flock. Two cars in the driveway: the ragtop prowling Hamel, Billy Dieterling's Packard Caribbean—a fixture on the *Badge of Honor* lot.

Jack staked the pad spooked: the queers were too well connected to burn, his smut job stood dead-ended—"Whatever You Desire" some kind of dead-end tangent. He could level with Timmy and Billy, shake them down, squeeze their contacts: people who knew people who knew Bobby Inge—who knew who made the shit. He kept the radio tuned in low; a string of love songs helped him pin things down.

He wanted to track the filth because part of him wondered how something could be so ugly and so beautiful and part of him plain jazzed on it.

He got itchy, anxious to move. A throaty soprano pushed him out of the car.

Up the driveway, skirting the floodlights. Windows: closed, uncurtained. He looked in.

Moochie Mouse gimcracks in force, no Timmy and Billy. Bingo through the last window: the lovebirds in a panicky spat.

An ear to the glass—all he got was mumbles. A car door slammed; door chimes ting-tinged. A look-see in—Billy walking toward the front of the house.

Jack kept watching. Timmy pranced hands-on-hips; Billy brought a big muscle guy back. Muscles forked over goodies: pill vials, a glassine bag full of weed. Jack sprinted for the street.

A Buick sedan at the curb—mud on the front and back plates. Locked doors—kick glass or go home empty.

Jack kicked out the driver's-side window. Glass on his front seat booty—a single brown paper bag.

He grabbed it, ran to his car.

Valburn's door opened.

Jack peeled rubber—east on 5th, zigzags down to Western and a big bright parking lot. He ripped the bag open.

Absinthe—190 proof on the label, viscous green liquid.

Hashish.

Black-and-white glossies: women in opera masks blowing horses.

"Whatever You Desire."

22

PARKER SAID, "Ed, you were brilliant the other day. I disapprove of Officer White's intrusion, but I can't complain with the results. I need smart men like you, and ... direct men like Bud. And I want both of you on the Nite Owl job."

"Sir, I don't think White and I can work together."

"You won't have to. Dudley Smith's heading up the investigation, and White will report directly to him. Two other men, Mike Breuning and Dick Carlisle, will work with White—however Dudley wants to play it. The Hollywood squad will be in on the job, reporting to Lieutenant Reddin, who'll report to Dudley. We've got divisional contacts assigned, and every man in the Bureau is calling in informant favors. Chief Green says Russ Millard wants to be detached from Ad Vice to run the show with Dud, so that's a possibility. That makes twenty-four full-time officers."

"What specifically do I do?"

Parker pointed to a case graph on an easel. "One, we have not found the shotguns or Coates' car, and until that girl those thugs assaulted clears them on the time element we have to assume that they are still our prime suspects. Since White's little escapade they've refused to talk, and they've been booked on kidnap and rape charges. I think—"

"Sir, I'd be glad to have another try at them."

"Let me finish. Two, we still have no IDs on the other three victims. Doc Layman's working overtime on that, and we're logging in four hundred calls a day from people worried about missing loved ones. There's an outside chance that this might be more than just a set of robbery killings, and if that proves to be the case I want you on that end of things. As of now, you're liaison to SID, the DA's Office and the divisional contacts. I want you to go over every field report every day, assess them and share your thoughts with me personally. I want daily written summaries, copies to Chief Green and myself."

Ed tried not to smile—the stitches in his chin helped. "Sir, some thoughts before we continue?"

Parker leaned his chair back. "Of course."

Ed ticked points. "One, what about searching for comparable shell samples in Griffith Park? Two, if the girl clears our suspects on the time element, what was that purple car doing across from the Nite Owl? Three, how likely are we to turn the guns and the car? Four, the suspects said they took the girl to a building on Dunkirk first. What kind of evidence did we get there?"

"Good points. But one, shell samples to compare is a long shot. With breech-load weapons the rounds might have expelled back into the car those punks were driving, the actual locations listed in the crime reports were vague, Griffith Park is all hillsides, we've had rain and mudslides over the past two weeks and that park ranger has waffled on ID'ing the three in custody. Two, the news vendor who ID'd the car by the Nite Owl says now that maybe it was a Ford or a Chevy, so our registration checks are now a nightmare. If you're thinking the car was placed there as a plant, I think that's nonsense—how would anyone know *to* plant it there? Three, the 77th Street squad is tearing up the goddamn southside for the car and the guns, muscling KA's, the megillah. And four, there was blood and semen all over a mattress in that building on Dunkirk."

Ed said, "It all comes back to the girl."

Parker picked up a report form. "Inez Soto, age twenty-one. A college student. She's at Queen of Angels, and she just came out of sedation this morning."

"Has anyone spoken to her?"

"Bud White went with her to the hospital. Nobody's talked to her in thirty-six hours, and I don't envy you the task."

"Sir, can I do this alone?"

"No. Ellis Loew wants to prosecute our boys for Little Lindbergh—kidnapping and rape. He wants them in the gas chamber for that, the Nite Owl, or both. And he wants a DA's investigator and a woman officer present. You're to meet Bob Gallaudet and a Sheriff's matron at Queen of Angels in an hour. I don't have to mention that the course of this investigation will be determined by what our Miss Soto tells you."

Ed stood up. Parker said, "Off the record, do you make the coloreds for the job?"

"Sir, I'm not sure."

"You cleared them temporarily. Did you think I'd be angry with you for that?"

"Sir, we both want absolute justice. And you like me too much."

Parker smiled. "Edmund, don't dwell on what White did the other day. You're worth a dozen of him. He's killed three men, line of duty, but that's nothing compared to what you did in the war. Remember that."

*   *   *

Gallaudet met him outside the girl's room. The hall reeked of disinfectant—familiar, his mother died one floor down. "Hello, Sergeant."

"It's Bob, and Ellis Loew sends his thanks. He was afraid the suspects would get beaten to death and he wouldn't get to prosecute."

Ed laughed. "They might be cleared on the Nite Owl."

"I don't care, and neither does Loew. Little Lindbergh with rape carries the death penalty. Loew wants those guys in the ground, so do I, so will you once you talk to the girl. So here's the sixty-four-dollar question. Did they do it?"

Ed shook his head. "Based on their reactions, I'd lean against it. But Fontaine said they drove the girl around. 'Sold her out' was the phrase he reacted to. I think it *could* have been Sugar Coates and a little pickup gang, maybe two of the guys they sold her to. None of the three had money on them when they were arrested, and either way—Nite Owl or gang rape—I think that money is stashed somewhere, covered with blood—like the bloody clothes Coates burned."

Gallaudet whistled. "So we need the girl's word on the time element *and* IDs on the other rapers."

"Right. *And* our suspects are clammed, *and* Bud White killed the one witness who could have helped us."

"That guy White's a pisser, isn't he? Don't look so spooked, being scared of him means you're sane. Now come on, let's talk to the young lady."

They walked into the room. A Sheriff's matron blocked the bed—tall, fat, short hair waxed straight back. Gallaudet said, "Ed Exley, Dot Rothstein." The woman nodded, stepped aside.

Inez Soto.

Black eyes, her face cut and bruised. Dark hair shaved to the forehead, sutures. Tubes in her arms, tubes under the sheets. Cut knuckles, split nails—she fought. Ed saw his mother: bald, sixty pounds in an iron lung.

Gallaudet said, "Miss Soto, this is Sergeant Exley."

Ed leaned on the bed rail. "I'm sorry we couldn't have given you more time to recuperate, and I'll try to make this as brief as possible."

Inez Soto stared at him—dark eyes, bloodshot. A raspy voice: "I won't look at any more pictures."

Gallaudet: "Miss Soto identified Coates, Fontaine and Jones from mugshots. I told her we might need her to look at some mugshots for IDs on the other men."

Ed shook his head. "That won't be necessary right now. Right now, Miss Soto, I need you to try to remember a chronology of the events that happened to you two nights ago. We can do this very slowly, and for now we won't need details. When you're more rested, we can go over it again. Please take your time and start when the three men kidnapped you."

Inez pushed up on her pillows. "They weren't men!"

Ed gripped the rail. "I know. And they're going to be punished for what they did to you. But before we can do that we need to eliminate or confirm them as suspects on another crime."

"I want them dead! I heard the radio! *I want them dead for that!*"

"We can't do that, because then the other ones who hurt you will go free. We have to do this correctly."

A hoarse whisper. "Correctly means six white people are more important than a Mexican girl from Boyle Heights. Those animals ripped me up and did their business in my mouth. They stuck guns in me. My family thinks I brought it on myself because I didn't marry a stupid *cholo* when I was sixteen. I will tell you nothing, *cabrón*."

Gallaudet: "Miss Soto, Sergeant Exley saved your life."

"He ruined my life! Officer White said he cleared the *negritos* on a murder charge! Officer White's the hero—he killed the *puto* who took me up my ass!"

Inez sobbed. Gallaudet gave the cut-off sign. Ed walked down to the gift shop—familiar, his deathwatch. Flowers for 875: fat cheerful bouquets every day.

23

BUD CAME on duty early, found a memo on his desk.

4/19/53

Lad—

Paperwork is not your forte, but I need you to run records checks (two) for me. (Dr. Layman has identified the three patron victims.) Use the standard procedure I've taught you and first check bulletin 11 on the squadroom board: it updates the overall status of the case and details the duties of the other investigating officers, which will prevent you from doing gratuitous and extraneous tasks.

1. Susan Nancy Lefferts, W.F., DOB 1/29/22, no criminal record. A San Bernardino native recently arrived in Los Angeles. Worked as a salesgirl at Bullock's Wilshire (background check assigned to Sgt. Exley).

2. Delbert Melvin Cathcart, a.k.a. "Duke," W.M., DOB 11/14/14. Two statutory rape convictions, served three years at San Quentin. Three procuring arrests, no convictions. (A tough ID: laundry markings and the body cross-checked against prison measurement charts got us our match.) No known place of employment, last known address 9819 Vendome, Silverlake District.

3. Malcolm Robert Lunceford, a.k.a. "Mal," W.M., DOB 6/02/12. No last known address, worked as a security guard at the Mighty Man Agency, 1680 North Cahuenga. Former LAPD officer (patrolman), assigned to Hollywood Division throughout most of his eleven-year career. Fired for incompetence 6/50. Known to be a late night habitué of the Nite Owl. I've checked Lunceford's personnel file and concluded that the man was a disgraceful police officer (straight "D" fitness reports from every C.O.). You check whatever paperwork exists on him at Hollywood Station (Breuning and Carlisle will be there to shag errands for you).

Summation: I still think the Negroes are our men, but Cathcart's criminal record and Lunceford's ex-policeman status mean that more than cursory

background checks should be conducted. I want
you as my adjutant on this job, an excellent baptism
of fire for you as a straight Homicide detective.
Meet me tonight (9:30) at the Pacific Dining Car.
We'll discuss the job and related matters.

D.S.

Bud checked the main bulletin board. Nite Owl thick: field
reports, autopsy reports, summaries. He found bulletin 11,
skimmed it.

Six R&I clerks detached to check criminal records and auto
registrations; the 77th Street squad shaking down jigtown for the
shotguns and Ray Coates' Merc. Breuning and Carlisle muscling
known gun jockeys; the area around the Nite Owl canvassed
nine times without turning a single extra eyewitness. The spooks
refused to talk to LAPD men, DA's Bureau investigators, Ellis
Loew himself. Inez Soto refused to cooperate on clearing up the
time frame; Ed Exley blew a questioning session, said they should
treat her kid-gloves.

Down the board: Malcolm Lunceford's LAPD personnel
sheets. Bad news—Lunceford as a free-meal scrounger, general
incompetent. A putrid arrest record; cited for dereliction of duty
three times. An interdepartmental information request issued; four
officers who worked with Lunceford responded. Grafter/buffoon:
Mal drank on duty, shook down hookers for blowjobs, tried to
shake down Hollywood merchants for his off-duty "protection
service"—letting him sleep on their premises while he was locked
out of his apartment for nonpayment of rent. One complaint too
many got Lunceford bounced in June 1950; all four responding
officers stated that he probably wasn't a deliberate Nite Owl victim: as a policeman he habituated all-night coffee shops—usually
to scrounge chow; he was probably at the Nite Owl at 3:00 A.M.
because he was hooked on sweet Lucy and sleeping in the weeds
and the Nite Owl looked cozy and warm.

Bud drove to Hollywood Station—Inez on his mind, Dudley,
Dick Stens along with her. Guts: she tried to claw herself off the
gurney to get at Sylvester Fitch, strapped dead to a morgue cot;
she screamed: "I'm dead, I want them dead!" He hustled her to
the ambulance, filched morphine and a hypo, shot her up while
no one was looking. The worst of it should have been over—but
the worst was still coming.

Exley would interrogate her, make her spit out details, look at sex offender pix until she cracked. Ellis Loew wanted an airtight case—that meant show-ups, courtroom testimony. Inez Soto: the first headliner witness for the most ambitious DA who ever breathed—all he could do was see her at the hospital, say "Hi," try to muffle the blows. A brave woman shoved at Ed Exley—fodder for a cowardly hard-on.

Inez to Stens.

Good revenge: Danny Duck masks, Exley whimpering. The photo good insurance; Dick still jacked up on blood—a taste that told him he was still on the muscle. His job at Kikey T.'s deli stunk—the dump was a known grifter hangout, a probation rap waiting to happen. Stens sleeping in his car, boozing, gambling—jail taught him absolutely shit.

Bud cut north on Vine; sunlight picked up his reflection in the windshield. His necktie stood out: LAPD shields, 2's. The 2's stood for the men he killed; he'd have to get some new ties made up—3's to add on Sylvester Fitch. Dudley's idea: *esprit de corps* for Surveillance. Snappy stuff: women got a kick out of them. Dudley was a kick—in the teeth, in the brains.

He owed him more than he owed Dick Stens—the man frosted Bloody Christmas, got him Surveillance, then Homicide. But when Dudley Smith brought you along you belonged to him—and he was so much smarter than everyone else that you were never sure what he wanted from you or how he was using you—shit got lost in all his fancy language. It didn't quite rankle, but you felt it; it scared you to see how Mike Breuning and Dick Carlisle gave the man their souls. Dudley could bend you, shape you, twist you, turn you, point you—and never make you feel like some dumb lump of clay. But he always let you know one thing: he knew you better than you knew yourself.

No streetside parking—every space taken. Bud parked three blocks over, walked up to the squadroom. No Exley, every desk occupied: men talking into phones, taking notes. A giant bulletin board all Nite Owl—paper six inches thick. Two women at a table, a switchboard behind them, a sign by their feet: "R&I/ DMV Requests." Bud went over, talked over phone noise. "I'm on the Cathcart check, and I want all you can get me, known associates, the works. This clown was popped twice for statch rape. I want full details on the complainants, plus current addresses. He had three pimping rousts, no convictions, and I want you to check all the local city and county vice squads to see if he's got a file. If he does, I want names on the girls he was running. If you get names, get DOBs and run them back through R&I, DMV, City/County Parole, the Woman's Jail. *Details.* You got it?"

The girls hit the switchboard; Bud hit the bulletin board: paper tagged "Victim Lunceford." One update: a Hollywood squad officer talked to Lunceford's boss at the Mighty Man Agency. Facts: Lunceford patronized the Nite Owl virtually every early A.M.—after he got off his 6:00-to-2:00 shift at the Pickwick Bookstore Building; Lunceford was a typical wino security guard not permitted to carry a sidearm; Lunceford had no known enemies, no known friends, no known lady friends, did not associate with his fellow Mighty Men, slept in a pup tent behind the Hollywood Bowl. The tent was checked out, inventoried: a sleeping bag, four Mighty Man uniforms, six bottles of Old Monterey muscatel.

Adiós, shitbird—you were in *the* wrong place at *the* wrong time. Bud checked Lunceford's arrest record: nineteen minor felony pops in eleven years as a cop, scratch revenge as a motive, kill six to get one stunk as a motive anyway. Still no Exley, no Breuning and Carlisle. Bud remembered Dudley's memo: check the station files for Lunceford listings.

A good bet: field interrogation cards filed by officer surname. Bud hit the storage room, pulled the "L" cabinet—no folder for "Lunceford, Officer Malcolm." An hour checking misfiles "A" to "Z"—zero. No FI's—strange—maybe Wino Mal never filed his field cards.

Almost noon, time for a chow run—a sandwich, talk to Dick. Carlisle and Breuning showed up—loafing, drinking coffee. Bud found a free phone, buzzed snitches.

Snake Tucker heard bupkis; ditto Fats Rice and Johnny Stomp. Jerry Katzenbach said it was the Rosenbergs—they ordered the snuffs from death row, make Jerry back on the needle. An R&I girl hovered.

She handed him a tear sheet. "There's not much. Nothing on Cathcart's KA's, not much detail besides his rap sheet. I couldn't get much on the statutory rape complainants, except that they were fourteen and blonde and worked at Lockheed during the war. My bet is they were transients. Sheriff's Central Vice had a file on Cathcart, with nine suspected prostitutes listed. I followed up. Two are dead of syphilis, three were underaged and left the state as a probation stipulation, two I couldn't get a line on. The remaining two are on that page. Does it help?"

Bud waved Breuning and Carlisle over. "Yeah, it does. Thanks."

The clerk walked off; Bud checked her sheet, two names circled: Jane (a.k.a. "Feather") Royko, Cynthia (a.k.a. "Sinful Cindy") Benavides. Last known addresses, known haunts: pads on Poinsettia and Yucca, cocktail lounges.

Dudley's strongarms hovered. Bud said, "The two names here. Shag them, will you?"

Carlisle said, "This background check shit is the bunk. I say it's the shines."

Breuning grabbed the sheet. "Dud says do it, we do it."

Bud checked their neckties—five dead men total. Fat Breuning, skinny Carlisle—somehow they looked just like twins. "So do it, huh?"

*　*　*

Abe's Noshery, no parking, around the block. Dick's Chevy out back, booze empties on the seat: probation violation number one. Bud found a space, walked up and checked the window: Stens guzzling Manischewitz, bullshitting with ex-cons—Lee Vachss, Deuce Perkins, Johnny Stomp. A cop type eating at the counter: a bite, a glance at the known criminal assembly, another bite—clockwork. Back to Hollywood Station—pissed that he was still playing nursemaid.

Waiting for him: Breuning, two hooker types—laughing up a storm in the sweatbox. Bud tapped the glass; Breuning walked out.

Bud said, "Who's who?"

"The blonde's Feather Royko. Hey, did you hear the one about the well-hung elephant?"

"What'd you tell them?"

"I told them it was a routine background check on Duke Cathcart. They read the papers, so they weren't surprised. Bud, it's the niggers. They're gonna burn for that Mex ginch, Dudley's just going through this rigamarole 'cause Parker wants a showcase and he's listening to that punk kid Exley with all his highfalut—"

Hard fingers to the chest. "Inez Soto ain't a ginch, and maybe it ain't the jigs. So you and Carlisle go do some police work."

Kowtow—Breuning shambled off smoothing his shirt. Bud walked into the box. The whores looked bad: a peroxide blonde, a henna redhead, too much makeup on too many miles.

Bud said, "So you read the papers this morning."

Feather Royko said, "Yeah. Poor Dukey."

"It don't sound like you're exactly grieving for him."

"Dukey was Dukey. He was cheap, but he never hit you. He had a thing about chiliburgers, and the Nite Owl had good ones. One chiliburg too many, RIP Dukey."

"Then you girls buy all that robbery stuff in the papers?"

Cindy Benavides nodded. Feather said, "Sure. That's what it was, wasn't it? I mean, don't you think so?"

"Probably. What about enemies? Duke have any?"

"No, Dukey was Dukey."

"How many other girls was he running?"

"Just us. We are the meager remnants of Dukey-poo's stable."

"I heard Duke ran nine girls once. What happened? Rival pimp stuff?"

"Mister, Dukey was a dreamer. He liked young stuff personally, and he liked to run young stuff. Young stuff gets bored and moves on unless their guy gets mean. Dukey could get mean with other men, but never with females. RIP Dukey."

"Then Duke must've had something else going. A two-girl string wouldn't cover him."

Feather picked at her nail polish. "Dukey was jazzed up on some new business scheme. You see, he always had some kind of scheme going. He was a dreamer. And the schemes made him happy, made him feel like the meager coin Cindy and me turned for him wasn't so bad."

"Did he give you details?"

"No."

Cindy had her lipstick out, smearing on another coat. "Cindy, he tell *you* anything?"

"No"—a little squeak.

"Nothing about enemies?"

"No."

"What about girlfriends? Duke have any young stuff going lately?"

Cindy grabbed a tissue, blotted. "N-no."

"Feather, you buy that?"

"I guess Dukey wasn't talking up nobody. Can we go now? I mean—"

"Go. There's a cabstand up the street."

The girls moved out fast; Bud gave them a lead, ran to his car. Up to Sunset across from the cabstand; a two-minute wait. Cindy and Feather walked up.

Separate cabs, different directions. Cindy shot due north on Wilcox, maybe toward home—5814 Yucca. Bud took a shortcut; the cab showed right on time. Cindy walked to a green De Soto, took off westbound. Bud counted to ten, followed.

Up to Highland, the Cahuenga Pass to the Valley, west on Ventura Boulevard. Bud stuck close; Cindy drove middle lane fast. A last-second swerve to the curb by a motel—rooms circling a murky swimming pool.

Bud braked, U-turned, watched. Cindy walked to a left-side room, knocked. A girl—fifteenish, blond—let her in. Young stuff—Duke Cathcart's statch rape type.

Eyeball Surveillance.

Cindy walked out ten minutes later—zoom—a U-turn back toward Hollywood. Bud knocked on the girl's door.

She opened it—teary-eyed. A radio blasted: "Nite Owl Massacre," "Crime of the Southland's Century." The girl focused in. "Are you the police?"

Bud nodded. "Sweetie, how old are you?"

No more focus—her eyes went blurry.

"Sweetie, what's your name?"

"Kathy Janeway. Kathy with a 'K.' "

Bud closed the door. "How old are you?"

"Fourteen. Why do men always ask you that?"

A prairie twang.

"Where are you from?"

"North Dakota. But if you send me back I'll just run away again."

"Why?"

"You want it in VistaVision? Duke said lots of guys get their jollies that way."

"Don't be such a tough cookie, huh? I'm on your side."

"That's a laugh."

Bud scoped the room. Panda bears, movie mags, schoolgirl smocks on the dresser. No whore threads, no dope paraphernalia. "Was Duke nice to you?"

"He didn't make me do it with guys, if that's what you mean."

"You mean you only did it with him?"

"No, I mean my daddy did it to me and this other guy made me do it with guys, but Duke bought me away from him."

Pimp intrigue. "What was the guy's name?"

"No! I won't tell you and you can't make me and I forgot it anyway!"

"Which one of those, sweetie?"

"I don't want to tell!"

"Sssh. So Duke was nice to you?"

"Don't shush me. Duke was a panda bear, all he wanted was to sleep in the same bed with me and play pinochle. Is that so bad?"

"Honey—"

"My daddy was worse! My Uncle Arthur was *lots* worse!"

"Hush, now, huh?"

"You can't make me!"

Bud took her hands. "What did Cindy want?"

Kathy pulled away. "She told me Duke was dead, which any dunce with a radio knows. She told me Duke said that if anything happened to him she should look after me, and she gave me ten dollars. She said the police bothered her. I said ten dollars isn't very much, and she got insulted and yelled at me. And how'd you know Cindy was here?"

"Never mind."

"The rent here's nine dollars a week and I—"

"I'll get you some more money if you'll—"

"Duke was *never* that cheap with me!"

"*Kathy, hush now and let me ask you a few questions and maybe we'll get the guys who killed Duke. All right? Huh?*"

A kid's sigh. "Okay, all right, ask me."

Bud, soft. "Cindy said Duke told her to look after you if something happened to him. Do you think he figured something was gonna happen?"

"I don't know. Maybe."

"Why maybe?"

"Maybe 'cause Duke was nervous lately."

"Why was he nervous?"

"I don't know."

"Did you ask him?"

"He said, 'Just biz.'"

Feather on Cathcart: "Jazzed on some new business scheme."

"Kathy, was Duke starting some new kind of thing up?"

"I don't know, Duke said girls don't need shoptalk. And I *know* he left me more than a crummy ten dollars."

Bud gave her a Bureau card. "That's my number at work. You call me, huh?"

Kathy plucked a panda off the bed. "Duke was so messy and such a slob, but I didn't care. He had a cute smile and this cute scar on his chest, and he never yelled at me. My daddy and Uncle Arthur always yelled at me, so Duke never did. Wasn't that a nice thing to do?"

Bud left her with a hand squeeze. Halfway out to the street he heard her sobbing.

*   *   *

Back to the car, a brainstorm on the Cathcart play so far. Call Duke's "new gig" and pimp intrigue weak maybes; call Nite Owl chiliburgers 99 percent sure the ink on his death warrant. A pimp statch raper and a grifter ex-cop for victims—strange—but par for the Hollywood Boulevard 3:00 A.M. course. Call it busywork for Dudley—maybe Cindy was hinked on more than the cash she held back. He could muscle the money out of her, glom some pimp scuttlebutt, close out the Cathcart end and ask Dud to send him down to Darktown. Simple—but Cindy was who-knows-where and Kathy had him dancing to her tune: savior with no place to go. He snapped to something missing from the bulletins: no checkout on Cathcart's apartment. A chance Duke's whore book might be there—leads on his gig and the pimp he bought Kathy from—a good time-killer.

Bud headed over Cahuenga. He saw a red sedan hovering back— he thought he'd seen it by the motel. He speeded up, made a run by Cindy's pad—no green De Soto, no red sedan. He drove to Silverlake checking his rearview. No tail car—just his imagination.

9819 Vendome looked virgin—a garage apartment behind a small stucco house. No reporters, no crime scene ropes, no locals out taking some sun. Bud popped the door with his hand.

A typical bachelor flop: living room/bedroom combo, bathroom, kitchenette. Lights on for a quick inventory—the way Dudley taught him.

A Murphy bed in the down position. Cheapie seascapes on the walls. One dresser, a walk-in closet. No doors on the bathroom and kitchenette—neat, clean. The whole pad looked spanking neat—at odds with Kathy: "Duke was so messy and such a slob."

Detail prowls—another Dudley trick. A phone on an end table, check the drawers: pencils, no address book, no whore book. A stack of Yellow Page directories, a toss—L.A. County, Riverside County, San Bernardino County, Ventura County. San Berdoo the only book used—ruffled pages, a cracked spine. Check the rufflings: "Printshop" listings thumbed through. A connection, probably nothing: victim Susan Lefferts, San Berdoo native.

Bud eyeball-prowled, click/click/click. The bathroom and kitchen immaculate; neady folded shirts in the dresser. The carpet clean, a bit grimy in the corners. A final click: the crib had been checked out, cleaned up—maybe tossed by a pro.

He went through the closet: jackets and slacks slipping off hangers. Cathcart had a nifty wardrobe—someone had been trying on his threads or this was the real Duke—Kathy's slob—and the tosser didn't bother with his clothes.

Bud checked every pocket, every garment: lint, spare change, nothing hot. A click: a test to test the tosser. He walked down to the car, got his evidence kit, dusted: the dresser a sure thing for latents. One more click: scouring powder wipe marks. Nail the pad as professionally print-wiped.

Bud packed up, got out, brainstormed some more—pimp war clicks, clickouts—Duke Cathcart had two skags in his stable, no stomach for pushing a fourteen-year-old nymphet—he was a pimp disaster area. He tried to click Duke's pad tossed to the Nite Owl—no gears meshed, odds on the coons stayed high. If the tossing played, tie it to Cathcart's "new gig"—Feather Royko talked it up—she came off as clean as Sinful Cindy came off hinky. Cindy next—and she owed Kathy money.

Dusk settling in. Bud drove to Cindy's pad, saw the green De Soto. Moans out a half-cracked window—he shoved the sill up, vaulted in.

A dark hallway, grunt-grunt-grunt one door down. Bud walked over, looked in. Cindy and a fat man wearing argyles, the bed about ready to break. Fattie's trousers on the doorknob—Bud filched a billfold, emptied it, whistled.

Cindy shrieked; Fats kept pumping. Bud: "SHITBIRD, WHAT YOU DOIN' WITH MY WOMAN!!!!"

Things speeded up.

Fattie ran out holding his dick; Cindy dove under the sheets. Bud saw a purse, dumped it, grabbed money. Cindy shrieked willy-nilly. Bud kicked the bed. "Duke's enemies. Spill and I won't roust you."

Cindy poked her head out. "I ... don't ... know ... nothin'."

"The fuck you don't. Let's try this: somebody broke into Duke's place, you give me a suspect."

"I ... don't ... know."

"Last chance. You held back at the station, Feather came clean. You went to Kathy Janeway's motel and stiffed her with a ten-spot. What else you hold back on?"

"Look—"

"Give."

"Give on what?"

"Give on Duke's new gig and his enemies. Tell me who used to pimp Kathy."

"I don't know who pimped her!"

"Then give on the other two."

Cindy wiped her face—smeared lipstick, runny makeup. "All I know's this guy was going around talking up cocktail-bar girls, acting like Duke. You know, the same one-liners, real Dukey shtick. I heard he was trying to get girls to do call jobs for him. He didn't talk to me or Feather, this is just stale-bread stuff I heard, like from two weeks ago."

Click: "This Guy" maybe the pad tosser, "This Guy" trying on Cathcart's clothes. "Keep going on that."

"That is all I heard, just the way I heard it."

"What did the guy look like?"

"I don't know."

"Who told you about him?"

"I don't even know that, they were just girls gabbing at the next table at this goddamned bar."

"All right, easy. Duke's new gig. Give on that."

"Mister, it was just another Dukey pipe dream."

"Then why didn't you tell me before?"

"You know the old adage 'Don't speak ill of the dead'?"

"Yeah. You know the bull daggers at the Woman's Jail?"

Cindy sighed. "Dukey pipe dream number six thousand—smut peddler. Is that a yuck? Dukey said he was going to push this weird smut. That's all I know, we had a two-second conversation on the topic and that's all Duke said. I didn't press it 'cause I know a pipe dream when I hear one. Now will you get out of here?"

Loose Bureau talk: Ad Vice working pornography. "What kind of smut?"

"Mister, I told you I don't know, it was just a two-second conversation."

"You gonna pay Kathy back what Duke left you?"

"Sure, Good Samaritan. Ten here, ten there. If I gave her the money all at once she'd just blow it on movie mags anyway."

"I might be back."

"I wait with bated breath."

* * *

Bud drove to a mailbox, sent the cash out special delivery: Kathy Janeway, Orchid View Motel, plenty of stamps and a friendly note. Four hundred plus—a small fortune for a kid.

7:00—time to kill before he met Dudley. The Bureau for a time-killer: Ad Vice, the squadroom board.

Squad 4 on the smut job—Kifka, Henderson, Vincennes, Stathis—four men tracking stag books, all reporting no leads. Nobody around, he could check by in the morning, it was probably nothing anyway. He walked over to Homicide, called Abe's Noshery.

Stens answered. "Abe's."

"Dick, it's me."

"Oh? Checking up on me, *Officer*?"

"Dick, come on."

"No, I mean it. You're a Dudley man now. Maybe Dud don't like the people I push my corned beef to. Maybe Dud wants skinny, thinks I'll talk to you. It ain't like you're your own man no more."

"You been drinking, partner?"

"I drink kosher now. Tell Exley that. Tell him Danny Duck wants to dance with him. Tell him I read about his old man and Dream-a-fucking-Dreamland. Tell him I might come to the opening, Danny Duck requests the presence of Sergeant Ed cocksucker Exley for one more fucking dance."

"Dick, you're way out of line."

"The fuck you say. One more dance, Danny Duck's gonna break his glasses and chew his fuckin' throat—"

"Dick, goddammit–"

"Hey, fuck you! I read the papers, I saw the personnel on that Nite Owl job. You, Dudley S., Exley, the rest of Dudley's hard-ons. You're fucking partners with the cocksucker who put me away, you're sucking the same gravy case, so if you th—"

Bud threw the phone out the window. He walked down to the lot kicking things—then the Big Picture kicked him.

He should have swung for Bloody Christmas.

Dudley saved him.

Make Exley the Nite Owl hero so far—he'd be the one to send Inez back through Hell.

Strangeness on the Cathcart end, the case might go wide, more than a psycho robbery gang. *He* could make the case, twist Exley, work an angle to help out Stens. Which meant:

Not greasing Ad Vice for smut leads.

Holding back evidence from Dudley.

BEING A DETECTIVE—NOT A HEADBASHER— ON HIS OWN.

He fed himself drunk talk for guts:

It ain't like you're your own man.

It ain't like you're your own man.

It ain't like you're your own man.

He was scared.

He owed Dudley.

He was crossing the only man on earth more dangerous than he was.

24

RAY PINKER walked Ed through the Nite Owl, reconstructing.

"Bim, bam, I'm betting it happened like this. First, the three enter and show their weaponry. One man takes the cash register girl, the kitchen boy and the waitress. This guy hits Donna DeLuca with his shotgun butt—she's standing by the cash register, and we found a piece of her scalp on the floor there. She gives him the money and the money from her purse, he shoves her and Patty Chesimard to the locker, picking up Gilbert Escobar in the kitchen en route. Gilbert resists—note the drag marks, the pots and pans on the floor. A pop to the head—bim, bam—that little pool of blood you see outlined in chalk. The safe is exposed under the cook's stand, one of the three employee victims opens it, note the spilled coins. Bim, bam, Gilbert resists some more, another gun-butt shot, note the circle marked 1-A on the floor, we found three gold teeth there, bagged them and matched them: Gilbert Luis Escobar. The drag marks start there, old Gil has quit fighting, bim, bam, suspect number one plants victims one, two and three inside the food locker."

Back to the restaurant proper—still sealed three nights post-mortem. Gawkers pressed up to the windows; Pinker kept talking. "Meanwhile, gunmen two and three are rounding up victims four through six. The drag marks going back to the locker and the spilled food and dishes speak for themselves. You might not be able to see it because the linoleum's so dark, but there's blood under the first two tables: Cathcart and Lunceford, sitting separately, two gun-butt shots. We know who was where through blood typing. Cathcart drops by table two, Lunceford by table one. Now—"

Ed cut in. "Did you dust the plates for more confirmation?"

Pinker nodded. "Smudges and smears, two viable latents on dishes under Lunceford's table. That's how we ID'd him—we got a match to the set they took when he joined the LAPD. Cathcart and Susan Lefferts had their hands blown off, no way to cross-check on that, their dishes were too smudged anyway. We tagged Cathcart on a partial dental and his prison measurement chart, Lefferts on a full dental. Now, you see the shoe on the floor?"

"Yes."

"Well, from an angle study it looks like Lefferts was flailing to get to Cathcart at the next table, even though they were sitting separately. Dumb panic, she obviously didn't know him. She started screaming, and one of the gunmen stuck a wad of napkins from that container there in her mouth. Doc Layman found a big wad of swallowed tissue in her throat at autopsy, he thinks she might have gagged and suffocated just as the shooting started. Bim, bam, Cathcart and Lefferts are dragged to the locker, Lunceford walks, the poor bastard probably thinks it's just a stickup. At the locker, purses and wallets are taken—we found a scrap of Gilbert Escobar's driver's license floating in blood just inside the door, along with six wax-saturated cotton balls. The gunmen had the brains to protect their ears."

The last bit didn't play: his coloreds were too impetuous. "It doesn't seem like enough men to do the job."

Pinker shrugged. "It worked. Are you suggesting one or more of the victims knew one or more of the killers?"

"I know, it's unlikely."

"Do you want to see the locker? It'll have to be now, we promised the owner he could have the place back."

"I saw it that night."

"I saw the pictures. Jesus, you couldn't tell they were human. You're working the Lefferts background check, right?"

Ed looked out the window; a pretty girl waved at him. Dark-haired, Latin—she looked like Inez Soto. "Right."

"And?"

"And I spent a full day in San Bernardino and got nowhere. The woman used to live with her mother, who was half-sedated and wouldn't talk to me. I talked to acquaintances, and they told me Sue Lefferts was a chronic insomniac who listened to the radio all night. She had no boyfriends in recent memory, no enemies ever. I checked her apartment in L.A., which was just about what you'd expect for a thirty-one-year-old salesgirl. One of the San Berdoo people said she was a bit of a roundheels, one said she belly-danced at a Greek restaurant a few times for laughs. Nothing suspicious."

"It keeps coming back to the Negroes."

"Yes, it does."

"Any luck on the car or the weapons?"

"No, and 77th Street's checking trashcans and sewer grates for the purses and wallets. And I know an approach we can make and save the investigation a lot of time."

Pinker smiled. "Check Griffith Park for the nicked shells?"

Ed turned to the window—the Inez type was gone. "If we place those shells, then it's either the Negroes in custody or another three."

"Sergeant, that is one large long shot."

"I know, and I'll help."

Pinker checked his watch. "It's 10:30 now. I'll find the occurrence reports on those shootings, try to pinpoint the locations and meet you with a sapper squad tomorrow at dawn. Say the Observatory parking lot?"

"I'll be there."

"Should I get clearance from Lieutenant Smith?"

"Do it on my say-so, okay? I'm reporting directly to Parker on this."

"The park at dawn then. Wear some old clothes, it'll be filthy work."

* * *

Ed ate Chinese on Alvarado. He knew why he was heading that way: Queen of Angels was close, Inez Soto might be awake. He'd called the hospital: Inez was healing up quickly, her family hadn't visited, her sister called, said Mama and Papa blamed her for the nightmare—provocative clothing, worldly ways. She'd been crying for her stuffed animals; he had the gift shop send up an assortment—gifts to ease his conscience—he wanted her as a major witness in his first big homicide case. And he just wanted her to like him, wanted her to disown four words: "Officer White's the hero."

He stalled with a last cup of tea. Stitches, dental work—his wounds were healing, made small: his mother and Inez blurred together. He'd gotten a report: Dick Stens hung out with known armed robbers, bet with bookies, took his salary in cash and frequented whorehouses. When his men had him pinned cold they'd call County Probation and fix an arrest.

Which paled beside "Officer White's the hero" and Inez Soto with the fire to hate him.

Ed paid the check, drove to Queen of Angels.

* * *

Bud White was walking out.

They crossed by the elevator. White got the first word in. "Give your career a rest and let her sleep."

"What are you doing here?"

"Not looking to pump a witness. Leave her alone, you'll get your chance."

"This is just a visit."

"She sees through you, Exley. You can't buy her off with teddy bears."

"Don't you want the case cleared? Or are you just frustrated that there's nobody else for you to kill?"

"Big talk from a brownnosing snitch."

"Did you come here to get laid?"

"Different circumstances, I'd eat you for that."

"Sooner or later, I'll take you and Stensland down."

"That goes two ways. War hero, huh? Those Japs must've rolled over for you."

Ed flinched.

White winked.

Tremors—all the way up to her room. Ed looked before he knocked.

Inez was awake—reading a magazine. Stuffed animals strewn on the floor, one creature on the bed: Scooter Squirrel as a footrest. Inez saw him, said, "No."

Faded bruises, her features coming back hard. "No what, Miss Soto?"

"No, I won't go through it with you."

"Not even a few questions?"

"No."

Ed pulled a chair up. "You don't seem surprised to see me here so late."

"I'm not, you're the subtle type." She pointed to the animals. "Did the district attorney reimburse you for those?"

"No, that was out of my own pocket. Did Ellis Loew visit you?"

"Yes, and I told him no. I told him that the three *negrito putos* drove me around, took money from other *putos* and left me with the *negrito puto* that Officer White killed. I told him that I can't remember or won't remember or don't want to remember any more details, he can take his pick and that is *absolutamente* all there is to it."

Ed said, "Miss Soto, I just came to say hello."

She laughed in his face. "You want the rest of the story? An hour later my brother Juan calls and tells me I can't go home, that I disgraced the family. Then *puto* Mr. Loew calls and says he can put me up in a hotel if I cooperate, then the gift shop girl brings me those *puto* animals and says they're gifts from the nice policeman with the glasses. I've been to college, *pendejo*. Don't you think I can follow the chain of events?"

Ed pointed to Scooter Squirrel. "You didn't throw him away."

"He's special."

"Do you like Dieterling characters?"

"So what if I do!"

"Just asking. And where do you put Bud White in your chain of events?"

Inez fluffed her pillows. "He killed a man for me."

"He killed him for himself."

"And that *puto* animal is dead just the same. Officer White just comes by to say hello. He warns me about you and Mr. Loew. He tells me I should cooperate, but he doesn't press the subject. He hates you, subtle man. I can tell."

"You're a smart girl, Inez."

"You want to say 'for a Mexican,' I know that."

"No, you're wrong. You're just plain smart. And you're lonely, or you would have asked me to leave."

Inez threw her magazine down. "So what if I am!"

Ed picked it up. Dog-eared pages: a piece on Dream-a-Dreamland. "I'm going to recommend that we give you some time to get well and recommend that when this mess goes to court you be allowed to testify by written deposition. If we get enough Nite Owl corroboration from other sources, you might not have to testify at all. And I won't come back if you don't want me to."

She stared at him. "I've still got no place to go."

"Did you read that article on the Dream-a-Dreamland opening?"

"Yes."

"Did you see the name 'Preston Exley'?"

"Yes."

"He's my father."

"So what? I know you're a rich kid, blowing your money on stuffed animals. So what? Where will I go?"

Ed held the bed rail. "I've got a cabin at Lake Arrowhead. You can stay there. I won't touch you, and I'll take you to the Dream-a-Dreamland opening."

Inez touched her head. "What about my hair?"

"I'll get you a nice bonnet."

Inez sobbed, hugged Scooter Squirrel.

* * *

Ed met the sappers at dawn, groggy from dreams: Inez, other women. Ray Pinker brought flashlights, spades, metal detectors; he'd had Communications Division issue a public appeal: witnesses to the Griffith Park shotgun blastings were asked to come forth to ID the blasters. The occurrence report locations were marked out into grids—all steep, scrub-covered hillsides. The men dug, uprooted, scanned with gizmos going tick, tick, tick—they found coins, tin cans, a .32 revolver. Hours came, went; the sun beat down. Ed worked hard—breathing dirt, risking sunstroke. His dreams returned, circles leading back to Inez.

Anne from the Marlborough School Cotillion—they did it in a '38 Dodge, his legs banged the doors. Penny from his UCLA biology class: rum punch at his frat house, a quick backyard coupling. A string of patriotic roundheels on his bond tour, a one-night stand with an older woman—a Central Division dispatcher. Their faces were hard to remember; he tried and kept seeing Inez—Inez without bruises, no hospital smock. It was dizzying, the heat was dizzying, he was filthy, exhausted—it all felt good. More hours went—he couldn't think of women or anything else. More time down, yells in the distance, a hand on his shoulder.

Ray Pinker holding out two spent shotgun shells and a photo of a shotgun shell strike surface. A perfect match: identical firing pin marks straight across.

25

TWO DAYS since the Fleur-de-Lis grab—no way to tell how far he could take it.

Two days, one suspect: Lamar Hinton, age twenty-six, arrested for strongarm assault, a conviction on an ADW, a deuce at Chino—paroled 3/51. Current employment: telephone installer at PC Bell—his parole officer suspected he moonlighted rigging bootleg bookie lines. A mugshot match: Hinton the muscle boy at Timmy Valburn's house.

Two days, no break on his stalemate: a made case would ticket him back to Narco, making *this* case meant Valburn and Billy Dieterling for material witnesses—well-connected homos who could flush his Hollywood career down the toilet.

Two days of page prowling—every roundabout approach tapped out. He checked the collateral case reports, talked to the arrestees—more denials—nobody admitted buying the smut. One day wasted; nothing at Ad Vice to goose his leads: Stathis, Henderson, Kifka reported zero, Millard was trying to co-boss the Nite Owl—pornography was not on his mind.

Two days since: midway through day two he hit hard—the bootleg number, Muscle Boy.

No Fleur-de-Lis phone listing; brain gymnastics tagged his personal connection—the first time he saw the calling card.

Tilt:

Xmas Eve '51, right before Bloody Christmas. Sid Hudgens set up a reefer roust—he popped two grasshoppers, found the card at their pad, thought nothing else of it.

Scary Sid: "We've all got secrets, Jack."

He pushed ahead anyway, that undertow driving him: he wanted to know who made the smut—and why. He hit the PC Bell employment office, cross-checked records against physical stats until he hit Lamar Hinton—tilt, tilt, tilt, tilt, tilt—

Jack looked around the squadroom—men talking Nite Owl, Nite Owl, Nite Owl, the Big V chasing hand-job books.

The orgy pix.
Vertigo.
Jack chased.

* * *

Hinton's route: Gower to La Brea, Franklin to the Hollywood Reservoir. His A.M. installations: Creston Drive, North Ivar. Jack found Creston on his car map: Hollywood Hills, a cul-de-sac way up.

He drove there, saw the phone truck: parked by a pseudo-French chateau. Lamar Hinton on a pole across the street—monster huge in broad daylight.

Jack parked, checked the truck—the loading door wide open. Tools, phone books, Spade Cooley albums—no suspicious-looking brown paper bags. Hinton stared at him; Jack went over badge first.

Hinton trundled down the pole: six-four easy, blond, muscles on muscles. "You with Parole?"

"Los Angeles Police Department."

"Then this ain't about my parole?"

"No, this is about you cooperating to avoid a parole rap."

"What do you—"

"Your parole officer don't really approve of this job you've got, Lamar. He thinks you might start doing some bootlegs."

Hinton flexed muscles: neck, arms, chest. Jack said, "Fleur-de-Lis, 'Whatever You Desire.' You desire no violation, you talk. You don't talk, then back to Chino."

One last flex. "You broke into my car."

"You're a regular Einstein. Now, you got the brains to be an informant?"

Hinton shifted; Jack put a hand on his gun. "Fleur-de-Lis. Who runs it, how does it work, what do you push? Dieterling and Valburn. Tell me and I'm out of your life in five minutes."

Muscles thought it through: his T-shirt bulged, puckered. Jack pulled out a fuck mag—an orgy pic spread full. "Conspiracy to distribute pornographic material, possession and sales of felony narcotics. I've got enough to send you back to Chino until nineteen-fucking-seventy. Now, did you move this smut for Fleur-de-Lis?"

Hinton bobbed his head. "Y-y-yeah."

"Smart boy. Now, who made it?"

"I d-don't know. Really, honest, I d-don't."

"Who posed for it?"

"I don't kn-know, I just d-d-delivered it."

"Billy Dieterling and Timmy Valburn. *Go*."

"J-just c-customers. Queers, you know, they like to fag party."

"You're doing great, so here's the big question. Who—"

"Officer, please don't—"

Jack pulled his .38, cocked it. "You want to be on the next train to Chino?"

"N-no."

"Then answer me."

Hinton turned, gripped the pole. "P-pierce Patchett. He runs the business. He-he's some kind of legit businessman."

"Description, phone number, address."

"He's maybe fifty something. I th-think he lives in B-brentwood and I don't know his n-number 'cause I get paid b-by the m-mail."

"More on Patchett. Go."

"H-he sugar-p-pimps girls made up like movie stars. H-he's rich. I-I only met him once."

"Who introduced you?"

"This guy Ch-chester I used to see at M-m-muscle Beach."

"Chester who?"

"I don't know."

Hinton: bunching, flexing—Jack figured hot seconds and he'd snap. "What else does Patchett push?"

"L-lots of b-boys and girls."

"What about through Fleur-de-Lis?"

"W-whatever you d-desire."

"Not the sales pitch, what specifically?"

Pissed more than scared. "Boys, girls, liquor, dope, picture books, bondage stuff!"

"Easy, now. Who else makes the deliveries?"

"Me and Chester. He works days. I don't like—"

"Where's Chester live?"

"I don't know!"

"*Easy, now*. Lots of nice people with lots of money use Fleur-de-Lis, right?"

"R-right."

The records in the truck. "Spade Cooley? Is he a customer?"

"N-no, I just get free albums 'cause I party with this guy Burt Perkins."

"You fucking would know him. The names of some customers. *Go*."

Hinton dug into the pole. Jack flashed: the monster turning, six .38s not enough. "Are you working tonight?"

"Y-yes."

"The address."

"No ... please."

Jack frisked: wallet, change, butch wax, a key on a fob. He held the key up; Hinton bobbed his head bam bam—blood on the pole.

"The address and I'm gone."

Bam bam—blood on the monster's forehead. "5261B Cheramoya."

Jack dropped the pocket trash. "You don't show up tonight. You call your parole officer and tell him you helped me, you tell him you want to be picked up on a violation, you have him put you up someplace. You're clean on this, and if I get to Patchett I'll make like one of the smut people snitched. *And if you clean that place out you are Chino-fucking-bound.*"

"B-but you *t-told* me."

Jack ran to his car, gunned it. Hinton tore at the pole barehanded.

* * *

Pierce Patchett, fifty-something, "some kind of legit businessman."

Jack found a pay phone, called R&I, the DMV. A make: Pierce Morehouse Patchett, DOB 6/30/02, Grosse Pointe, Michigan. No criminal record, 1184 Gretna Green, Brentwood. Three minor traffic violations since 1931.

Not much. Sid Hudgens next—fuck his smut hink. A busy signal, a buzz to Morty Bendish at the *Mirror*.

"City Room, Bendish."

"Morty, it's Jack Vincennes."

"The Big V! Jack, when are you going back to the Narco Squad? I need some good dope stories."

Morty wanted shtick. "As soon as I get squeaky-clean Russ Millard off my case and make a case for him. And *you* can help."

"Keep talking, I'm all ears."

"Pierce Patchett. Ring a bell?"

Bendish whistled. "What's this about?"

"I can't tell you yet. But if it breaks his way, you've got the exclusive."

"You'd feed me before you feed Sid?"

"Yeah. Now I'm all ears."

Another whistle. "There's not much, but what there is is choice. Patchett's a big handsome guy, maybe fifty, but he looks thirty-eight. He goes back maybe twenty-five years in L.A. He's some kind of judo or jujitsu expert, he's either a chemist by trade or he was a chemistry major in college. He's worth a boatload of greenbacks, and I know he lends money to businessman types at thirty percent interest and a cut of their biz, I know he's bankrolled a lot of movies under the table. Interesting, huh? Now try this on: he's rumored to be some kind of periodic heroin sniffer, rumored to dry out at Terry Lux's clinic. All in all, he's what you might wanta call a powerful behind-the-scenes strange-o."

Terry Lux—plastic surgeon to the stars. Sanitarium boss: booze, dope cures, abortions, detoxification heroin available—the cops looked the other way, Terry treated L.A. politicos free. "Morty, that's all you've got?"

"Ain't that enough? Look, what I don't have, Sid might. Call him, but remember I got the exclusive."

Jack hung up, called Sid Hudgens. Sid answered: "*Hush-Hush*. Off the record and on the QT."

"It's Vincennes."

"Jackie! You got some good Nite Owl scoop for the Sidster?"

"No, but I'll keep an ear down."

"Narco skinny maybe? I want to put out an all-hophead issue— shvartze jazz musicians and movie stars, maybe tie it in to the Commies, this Rosenberg thing has got the public running hot with a thermometer up their ass. You like it?"

"It's cute. Sid, have you heard of a man named Pierce Patchett?"

Silence—seconds ticking off long. Sid, too Sid-like. "Jackie, all I know on the man is that he is very wealthy and what I like to call 'Twilight.' He ain't queer, he ain't Red, he don't know any-body I can use in my quest for prime sinuendo. Where'd you hear about him?"

Bullshitting him—he could taste it. "A smut peddler told me."

Static—breath catching sharp. "Jack, smut is from hunger, strictly for sad sacks who can't get their ashes hauled. Leave it alone and write when you get work, *gabishe*?"

Hang up—bang!—a door slamming, cutting you off, some line you couldn't cross back to. Jack drove to the Bureau, MALIBU RENDEZVOUS stamped on that door.

* * *

The Ad Vice pen stood empty, just Millard and Thad Green in a huddle by the cloakroom. Jack checked the assignment board—more no-leads—walked around to the supply room on the QT. Unlocked—easy to pull off a snatch. Downwind: the high brass talking Nite Owl.

"Russ, I know you want in. But Parker wants Dudley."

"He's too volatile on Negroes, Chief. We both know it."

"You only call me 'Chief' when you want something, *Captain*."

Millard laughed. "Thad, the sappers found matching spents in Griffith Park, and I heard 77th Street turned the wallets and purses. Is that true?"

"Yes, an hour ago, in a sewer. Blood-caked, print-wiped. SID matched to the victims' blood. It's the coloreds, Russ. I know it."

"I don't think it's the ones in custody. Do you see them leaving a rape scene on the southside, then driving the girl around to let their friends abuse her, *then* driving all the way to Hollywood to pull the Nite Owl job—when two of them are high on barbiturates?"

"It's a stretch, I'll admit that. We need to nail down the outside rapists and get Inez Soto to talk. So far she's refused. But Ed Exley is working on her, and Ed Exley is very good."

"Thad, I won't let my ego get in the way. I'm a captain, Dudley's a lieutenant. We'll share the command."

"I worry about your heart."

"A heart attack five years ago doesn't make me a cripple."

Green laughed. "I'll talk to Parker. Jesus, you and Dudley. What a pair."

Jack found what he wanted: a tape recorder/phone tapper, bolt-on style, headphones. He hustled it out a side door, no witnesses.

* * *

Dusk, Cheramoya Avenue: Hollywood, a block off Franklin. 5261: a Tudor four-flat, two pads upstairs, two down. No lights—probably too late to glom "Chester" the day man. Jack rang the B buzzer—no response. An ear to the door, a listen—no sounds, period. In with the key.

Jackpot: one glance told him Hinton played it straight—no cleanout. Pervert fucking Utopia—floor-to-ceiling shelves jammed with goodies.

Maryjane: leaf, prime buds. Pills—bennies, goofballs, red devils, yellow jackets, blue heavens. Patent dope: laudanum, codeine mixtures, catchy brand names: Dreamscope, Hollywood Sunrise, Martian Moonglow. Absinthe, pure alcohol in pints, quarts, half gallons. Ether, hormone pills, envelopes of cocaine, heroin. Film cans, smutty titles: *Mr. Big Dick, Anal Love, Gang Bang, High School Rapist, Rape Club, Virgin Cocksucker, Hot Negro Love, Fuck Me Tonite, Susie's Butthole Deelite, Boys in Love, Locker Room Lust, Blow the Man Down, Jesus Porks the Pope, Cocksucker's Paradise, Cornholers Meet the Ramrod Boys, Rex the Randy Rottweiler.* Old stag books: TJ venues, women sucking cock, boys sucking cock, up-the-hole close-ups. Dusty—not a hot item; empty spaces alongside, maybe the good smut, *his smut*, was piled there: make Lamar for cleaning *that* out? Why? The rest of the shit spelled felony time to the year 2000. Snapshots—candid-type pix—real-life movie stars in the raw. Lupe Velez, Gary Cooper, Johnny Weissmuller, Carole Landis, Clark Gable, Tallulah Bankhead muff-diving, corpses going 69 on morgue slabs. A color pic: Joan Crawford and a notoriously well hung Samoan extra named "O.K. Freddy" fucking. Dildoes, dog collars, whips, chains, amyl nitrite poppers, panties, brassieres, cock rings, catheters, enema bags, black lizard pumps with six-inch heels and a female mannequin covered by a tarp—plasterboard, rubber lips, glued-on pubic hair, a snatch made from a garden hose.

Jack found the bathroom and pissed. A mirror threw his face back: old, strange. He went to work: tapper to the phone, the oldie smut skimmed.

Cheap stuff, probably Mex-made: spic hairstyles on skinny junkie posers. Vertigo: he felt swirly, like a good hop jolt. The dope on the shelves made him drool; he mixed Karen in with the pictures. He paced the room, tapped a hollow place, pulled up the rug. Bingo on a cute hidey-hole: a basement, stairs leading to an empty black space.

The phone rang.

Jack hit the tapper, picked up. "Hi. Whatever You Desire"— Lamar Hinton mimicked.

Click, a hang-up, he shouldn't have used the slogan. A half hour passed—the phone rang. "Hi, it's Lamar"—casual.

A pause, click.

A chain of smokes—his throat hurt. The phone rang.

Try a mumble. "Yeah?"

"Hi, it's Seth up in Bel Air. You feel like bringing something over?"

"Sure."

"Make it a jug of the wormwood. Make it fast and you made a nice tip."

"Uh ... gimme the address again, would ya?"

"Who could forget digs like mine? It's 941 Roscomere, and don't dawdle."

Jack hung up. Ring ring again.

"Yeah?"

"Lamar, tell Pierce I need to ... Lamar, is that you, boychik?" SID HUDGENS.

Lamar—with a tremor. "Uh, yeah. Who's this?"

Click.

Jack pushed "Replay." Hudgens talked, recognition creeped in— SID KNEW PATCHETT. SID KNEW LAMAR. SID KNEW THE FLEUR-DE-LIS RACKET.

The phone rang—Jack ignored it. Splitsville—grab the tapper, wipe the phone, wipe all the filth he'd touched. Out the door queasy—night air peaking his nerves.

He heard a car revving.

A shot took out the front window; two shots smashed the door. Jack drew, fired—the car hauling, no lights.

Clumsy: two shots hit a tree and sprayed wood. Three more pulls, no hits, the car fishtailing. Doors opening—eyewitnesses.

Jack got his car—skids, brodies, no lights until Franklin and a main traffic flow. No make on the shooter car: dark, no lights, the cars all around him looked alike: sleek, wrong. A cigarette slowed him down. He drove straight west to Bel Air.

Roscomere Road: twisty, all uphill, mansions fronted by palm trees. Jack found 941, pulled into the driveway.

Circular, looping a big pseudo-Spanish: one story, low slate roof. Cars in a row—a Jag, a Packard, two Caddies, a Rolls. Jack got out— nobody braced him. He hunkered down, took plate numbers.

Five cars: classy, no Fleur-de-Lis bags on plush front seats. The house: bright windows, silk swirls. Jack walked up and looked in.

He knew he'd never forget the women.

One almost Rita Hayworth à la *Gilda*. One almost Ava Gardner in an emerald-green gown. A near Betty Grable—sequined swimsuit, fishnet stockings. Men in tuxedos mingled—background debris. He couldn't stray his eyes from the women.

Astonishing make-believe. Hinton on Patchett: "He sugar-pimps these girls made up to look like movie stars." "Made up" didn't cut it: call these women chosen, cultivated, enhanced by an expert. Astonishing.

Veronica Lake walked through the light. Her face wasn't as close: she just oozed that cat-girl grace. Background men flocked to her.

Jack pressed up to the glass. Smut vertigo, real live women. Sid, that door slamming, that line. He drove home, bad vertigo—achy, itchy, jumpy. He saw a *Hush-Hush* card on his door, "Malibu Rendezvous" inked on the bottom.

He saw headlines:

DOPED-OUT DOPE CRUSADER SHOOTS INNO-CENT CITIZENS!

CELEBRITY COP INDICTED FOR KILLINGS!

GAS CHAMBER FOR THE BIG-TIME BIG V! RICH KID GIRLFRIEND BIDS DEATH ROW AU REVOIR!

26

AN ARM-IN-ARM entrance—Inez in her best dress and a veil to hide her bruises. Ed kept his badge out—it got them past the press. Attendants formed the guests into lines—Dream-a-Dream-land was open for business.

Inez was awestruck: quick breaths billowed her veil. Ed looked up, down, sideways—every detail made him think of his father.

A grand promenade—Main Drag, U.S.A., 1920—soda fountains, nickelodeons, dancing extras: the cop on the beat, a paperboy juggling apples, ingenues doing the Charleston. The Amazon River: motorized crocodiles, jungle excursion boats. Snow-capped mountains; vendors handing out mouse-ear beanies. The Moochie Mouse Monorail, tropical isles—acres and acres of magic.

They rode the monorail: the first car, the first run. High speed, upside down, right side up—Inez unbuckled herself giggling. The Paul's World toboggan; lunch: hot dogs, snow cones, Moochie Mouse cheese balls.

On to "Desert Idyll," "Danny's Fun House," an exhibit on outer space travel. Inez seemed to be tiring: gorged on excitement. Ed yawned—his own late night catching up.

A late squeal at the station: a shootout on Cheramoya, no perpetrators caught. He had to go to the scene: an apartment house, shots riddling a downstairs unit. Weird: .38s, .45s retrieved, the living room all shelving—empty except for some sadomasochist paraphernalia—and no telephone. The building's owner couldn't be traced; the manager said he was paid by mail, cashier's checks, he got a free flop and a C-note a month, so he was happy and didn't ask questions—he couldn't even name the dump's tenant. The condition of the apartment indicated a rapid clean-out—but no one saw a thing. Four hours of report writing—four hours snatched from the Nite Owl.

The exhibit was a bore—a sop to culture. Inez pointed to the ladies' room; Ed stepped outside.

A VIP tour on the promenade—Timmy Valburn shepherding bigwigs. The *Herald* front page hit him: Dream-a-Dreamland, the Nite Owl, like nothing else mattered.

He tried to reinterrogate Coates, Jones and Fontaine—they would not give him one word. Eyewitnesses responded to the appeal for IDs on the Griffith Park shooters and could not identify the three in custody: they said they "can't quite be sure." Vehicle checks now extended to '48–'50 Fords and Chevys—nothing hot so far. Jockeying for command of the case: Chief Parker supported Dudley Smith, Thad Green pumped up Russ Millard. No shotguns found, no trace of Sugar Ray's Merc. Wallets and purses belonging to the victims were found in a sewer a few blocks from the Tevere Hotel—combine that with the matching shells found in Griffith Park and you got what the papers didn't report: Ellis Loew bullying Parker to bully him: "It's all circumstantial so far, so have your boy Exley keep working on that Mexican girl, it looks like he's getting next to her, have him talk her into a questioning session under sodium pentothal, let's get some juicy Little Lindbergh details and fix the Nite Owl time frame once and for all."

Inez sat down beside him. They had a view: the Amazon, plaster mountains. Ed said, "Are you all right? Do you want to go back?"

"What I want is a cigarette, and I don't even smoke."

"Then don't start. Inez—"

"Yes, I'll move into your cabin."

Ed smiled. "When did you make up your mind?"

Inez tucked her veil under her hat. "I saw a newspaper in the bathroom, and Ellis Loew was gloating about me. He sounded happy, so I figured I'd put some distance between us. You know, I never thanked you for my bonnet."

"You don't have to."

"Yes I do, because I'm naturally bad-mannered around Anglos who treat me nice."

"If you're waiting for the punch line, there isn't any."

"Yes, there is. And for the record again, I won't tell you about it, I won't look at pictures, and I won't testify."

"Inez, I submitted a recommendation that we let you rest up for now."

"And 'for now's' a punch line, and the other punch line's that you go for me, which is okay, because I've looked better in my time and no Mexican man would ever want a Mexican girl who was gang-raped by a bunch of *negrito putos*, not that I've ever gone for Mexican guys anyway. You know what's scary, Exley?"

"I told you, it's Ed."

Inez rolled her eyes. "I've got a creep brother named Eduardo, so I'll call you Exley. You know what's scary? What's scary is that I feel good today because this place is like a wonderful dream, but I know that it's got to get really bad again because what happened was a hundred times more real than this. Do you understand?"

"I understand. For now, though, you should try trusting me."

"I don't trust you, Exley. Not 'for now,' maybe not ever."

"I'm the only one you can trust."

Inez flipped her veil down. "I don't trust you because you don't hate them for what they did. Maybe you think you do, but you're helping your career out at the same time. Officer White, he hates them. He killed a man who hurt me. He's not as smart as you, so maybe I can trust him."

Ed reached a hand out—Inez slid away. "I want them dead. *Absolutamente muerto. Comprende?*"

"I *comprende*. Do you *comprende* that your beloved Officer White is a goddamned thug?"

"Only if you *comprende* that you're jealous of him. Look, oh God."

Ray Dieterling, his father. Ed stood up; Inez stood up starry-eyed. Preston said, "Raymond Dieterling, my son Edmund. Edmund, will you introduce the young lady?"

Inez, straight to Dieterling. "Sir, it's a pleasure to meet you. I've been ... oh, I'm just a big fan."

Dieterling took her hand. "Thank you, dear. And your name?"

"Inez Soto. I've seen ... oh, I'm just a big fan."

Dieterling smiled, sad—the girl's story front-page news. He turned to Ed. "Sergeant, a pleasure."

A good handshake. "Sir, an honor. And congratulations."

"Thank you, and I share those congratulations with your father. Preston, your son has an eye for the ladies, doesn't he?"

Preston laughed. "Miss Soto, Edmund has rarely evinced such good taste." He handed Ed a slip of paper. "A Sheriff's officer called the house looking for you. I took the message."

Ed palmed the paper; Inez blushed through her veil. Dieterling smiled. "Miss Soto, did you enjoy Dream-a-Dreamland?"

"Yes, I did. Oh God, yes."

"I'm glad, and I want you to know that you have a good job here anytime you wish. All you have to do is say the word."

"Thank you, thank you, sir"—Inez wobbly. Ed steadied her, looked at his message: "Stensland on toot at Raincheck Room, 3871 W. Gage. Felony assembly, parole off. alerted. Waiting for you—Keefer."

The partners walked off bowing; Inez waved to them. Ed said, "I'll take you back, but I've got a little stop to make first."

* * *

They drove back to L.A., the radio going, Inez beating time on the dashboard. Ed played scenes: Stensland crushed with snappy one-liners. An hour to Raincheck Room—Ed parked behind a Sheriff's unmarked. "I'll only be a few minutes. You stay here, all right?"

Inez nodded. Pat Keefer left the bar; Ed got out, whistled.

Keefer came over; Ed steered him away from Inez. "Is he still there?"

"Yeah, skunk drunk. I'd just about given up on you, you know."

A dark alley by the bar. "Where's the Parole man?"

"He told me to take him, this is county jurisdiction. His pals took off, so there's just him."

Ed pointed to the alley. "Bring him out cuffed."

Keefer went back in; Ed waited by the alleyway door. Shouts, thuds, Dick Stens muscled out: smelly, disheveled. Keefer pulled his head back; Ed hit him: upstairs, downstairs, flails until his arms gave out. Stens hit the ground retching; Ed kicked him in the face, stumbled away. Inez on the sidewalk. Her one-liner: "Officer White's the thug?"

27

BUD FED the woman coffee—get her out, go see Stens at the lock-up.

Carolyn something, she looked okay at the Orbit Lounge, morning light put ten years on her. He picked her up on a flash: he just got the word on Dick, if he couldn't find a woman he was going to find Exley and kill him. She wasn't bad in bed—but he had to think of Inez to charge up enthusiasm, it made him feel cheap, the odds on Inez ever doing it for love were about six trillion to one. He stopped thinking about her—the rest of the night was all bad talk and brandy.

Carolyn said, "I think I should go."

"I'll call you."

The doorbell rang.

Bud walked Carolyn over. Across the screen: Dudley Smith and a West Valley dick—Joe DiCenzo.

Dudley smiled; DiCenzo nodded. Carolyn ducked out—like she knew they knew the score. Bud scoped his front room: the fold-out down, a bottle, two tumblers.

DiCenzo pointed to the bed. "There's his alibi, and I didn't think he did it anyway."

Bud shut the door. "Did *what*? Boss, what is this?"

Dudley sighed. "Lad, I'm afraid I'm the bearer of bad tidings. Last night a young lassie named Kathy Janeway was found in her motel room, raped and beaten to death. Your calling card was found in her purse. Sergeant DiCenzo took the squeal, knew you were a protégé of mine and called me. I visited the crime scene, found an envelope addressed to Miss Janeway, and recognized your rather unformed handwriting immediately. Explain with brevity, lad—Sergeant DiCenzo is heading the investigation and wants you eliminated as a suspect."

A body shot—little Kathy sobbing. Bud got his lies straight. "I was on the Cathcart background check and this hooker who worked for Cathcart told me the Janeway girl was Cathcart's last squeeze, but he didn't pimp her. I talked to the girl, but she didn't know nothing worth reporting. She told me the hooker was holding cash from Cathcart for her, but she wouldn't kick loose. I shook her down and mailed the money to the kid."

DiCenzo shook his head. "Do you routinely shake down hookers?"

Dudley sighed. "Bud has a sentimental weakness for females, and I find his account plausible within the limitations of that limitation. Lad, who was this 'hooker' you mentioned?"

"Cynthia Benavides, a.k.a. 'Sinful Cindy.'"

"Lad, you didn't include mention of her in any of the reports you've filed. Which have been rather threadbare, I might add."

Lies: hold back on smut, Cathcart's pad tossed, the pimp who sold Kathy to Duke. "I didn't think she was important stuff."

"Lad, she is a tangential Nite Owl witness. And haven't I taught you to be thorough in your reports?"

Mad now—Kathy on a morgue slab. "Yeah, you have."

"And what precisely have you accomplished since that dinner meeting of ours—which is when you *should* have reported on Miss Janeway and Miss Benavides?"

"I'm still checking out Lunceford and Cathcart KA's."

"Lad, Lunceford's known associates are extraneous to this investigation. Have you learned of anything else on Cathcart?"

"No."

Dudley to DiCenzo. "Lad, are you satisfied that Bud isn't your man?"

DiCenzo pulled out a cigar. "I'm satisfied. And I'm satisfied he ain't the smartest human being ever to breathe. White, toss me a bone. Who do you think did the girl?"

The red sedan: the motel, Cahuenga. "I don't know."

"A succinct answer. Joe, let me have a few minutes alone with my friend, would you please?"

DiCenzo walked out smoking; Dudley leaned against the door. "Lad, you cannot shake down prostitutes for money to pay off underaged mistresses. I understand your sentimental attachment to women, and I know that it is an essential component of your policeman's persona, but such overinvolvement cannot be tolerated, and as of this moment you are off the Cathcart and Lunceford checks and back on the Darktown end of the case. Now, Chief Parker and I are convinced that the three Negroes in custody are our perpetrators, or, at the very most, another jigaboo gang is responsible. We still have no murder weapons and no shake on Coates' car, and Ellis Loew wants more evidence for a grand jury presentation. Our fair Miss Soto will not talk, and I'm afraid we must urge her to take pentothal and endure a questioning session. Your job is to check files and question known Negro sex offenders. We need to find the men our unholy three let abuse Miss Soto, and I think the job is right up your alley. Will you do this for me?"

Big words—more body shots. "Sure, Dud."

"Good lad. Clock in and out at 77th Street Station, and make your reports more detailed."

"Sure, Boss."

Smith opened the door. "I tendered that reprimand with much affection, lad. Do you know that?"

"Sure."

"Grand. You are much in my thoughts, lad. Chief Parker has given me approval on a new containment measure, and I've already signed on Dick Carlisle and Mike Breuning. Once we close the Nite Owl, I'm going to ask you to join us."

"That sounds good, Boss."

"Grand. And, lad? I'm sure you know that Dick Stensland was arrested and Ed Exley had a part in it. You are not to retaliate. Do you understand?"

* * *

The red sedan—call it a maybe.

Cathcart's pad tossed and wiped, his clothes prowled—?????

Sinful Cindy: Duke's smut peddler pipe dream.

Feather Royko on Duke: "Hopped up on some new biz."

The Dukey shtick man trying to recruit B-girls. Ad Vice checked out: zero on their smut job. Trashcan Jack V., ace report padder, asked for a transfer to the Nite Owl—he said the job was from hunger. Russ Millard's last c.o.'s summary: 86 the gig—call it a wash.

He lied to Dudley and strolled on it.

If he'd ratted little Kathy to Juvie she'd be reading a movie mag somewhere.

THE PIMP WHO SOLD HER TO DUKE: "THIS GUY MADE ME DO IT WITH GUYS."

EXLEY EXLEY EXLEY EXLEY EXLEY EXLEY EXLEY—

* * *

Sinful Cindy's rap sheet—four known haunt whore bars listed. Her pad first—no Cindy. Hal's Nest, the Moonmist Lounge, the Firefly Room, the Cinnabar at the Roosevelt—no Cindy. An old Vice cop's story: whores congregating at Tiny Naylor's Drive-in—the carhops scouted tricks for them. Over to Tiny's, Cindy's De Soto outside—a food tray hooked to the door.

Bud parked beside her. Cindy saw him, dumped her tray, rolled up her window. Wham—the De Soto in reverse. Bud sprinted, popped the hood, yanked the distributor—the car stalled dead.

Cindy rolled down her window. "You stole my money! You ruined my lunch!"

Bud dropped a five on her lap. "Lunch is on me."

"Mister big shot! Mister big spender!"

"Kathy Janeway got raped and beaten to death. Give on the guy who used to pimp her, give on her tricks."

Cindy put her head on the wheel. The horn beeped; she came back up pale, no tears. "Dwight Gilette. He's some kind of colored guy passing. I don't know nothing about her old tricks."

"Gilette drive a red car?"

"I don't know."

"You got an address?"

"I heard he lives in this tract in Eagle Rock. It's white only, so he plays it that way. But I know he didn't kill her."

"How do you figure?"

"He's a swish. He's careful about his hands, and he'd never put it in a girl."

"Anything else?"

"He carried a knife. His girls call him 'Blue Blade' 'cause his name's Gilette."

"You don't seem surprised Kathy got it that way."

Cindy touched her eyes—bone dry. "She was born for it. Dukey softened her up, so she quit hating men. A few more years and she would've learned. Shit, I should have treated her better."

"Yeah, me too."

* * *

Eagle Rock, an R&I check: Dwight Gilette, a.k.a. "Blade," a.k.a. "Blue Blade," 3245 Hibiscus, Eagle's Aerie Housing Development. Six suborning arrests, no convictions, listed as a male Caucasian—if he was a shine he was passing with style. Bud found the tract, the street: cozy stucco cubes, Hibiscus a prime spot: a smoggy L.A. view.

3245: peach paint job, steel flamingos on the lawn, a blue sedan in the driveway. Bud walked up, pushed the buzzer—jingly chimes sounded.

A high-yellow guy opened up. Thirtyish, short, plump, slacks and a silk shirt with a Mr. B. collar. "I heard on the radio, so I thought you fellows might be coming by. The radio said midnight, and I have an alibi. He lives a block away and I can have him here toot-sweet. Kathy was a sweet kid and I don't know who'd do a thing like that. And don't you fellows usually come in pairs?"

"You finished?"

"No. My alibi is my lawyer, he still lives a block away and he's very well placed in the American Civil Liberties Union."

Bud shouldered him into the house, whistled.

Fruit heaven: deep pile rugs, Greek god statues. Male nudes on the wall—paint on velvet flocking. Bud said, "Cute."

Gilette pointed to the phone. "Two seconds or I call my attorney."

Quick throw. "Duke Cathcart. You sold Kathy to him, right?"

"Kathy was headstrong, Duke made me an offer. Duke's dead in that awful Nite Owl thing, so don't tell me you suspect me of that."

No hink. "I heard Duke was pushing smut. You hear that?"

"Smut is déclassé and the answer is no."

More no hink. "Give me some trade talk on Duke. What've you heard?"

Gilette stood one hip jutting. "I heard a guy was asking around about Duke, coming on like Duke, maybe thinking about crashing his stable, not that he had much of a stable left, I've heard. Now will you please leave me alone before I call my friend?"

The phone rang—Gilette walked to the kitchen, grabbed an extension. Bud walked in slow. Nice stuff: Frigidaire, coil burner stove on full blast: eggs, boiling water, stew.

Gilette made kissy sounds, hung up. "Are *you* still here?"

"Nice pad, Dwight. Business must be good."

"Business is excellent, thank you very much."

"Good. I need skinny on Kathy's old tricks, so cough up your whore book."

Gilette hit a switch above the sink. A motor growled; he shoved scrapings down a garbage hole. Bud flipped the switch up. "Your whore book."

"No, *nein, nyet* and never."

Bud hooked him to the gut. Gilette rolled with it, grabbed a knife, swung. Bud sidestepped, kicked at his balls. Gilette doubled up; Bud hit the garbage switch. The motor *scree'd*; Bud jammed the queer's knife hand down the chute.

SCREEEE—the sink shot back blood, bone. Bud yanked the hand out minus fingers—SCREEEEE fifty times louder. Stumps to the burner coils, stumps to the icebox sizzling. "GIVE ME THE FUCKING WHORE BOOK"—through a SCREEEEEEEE echo chamber.

Gilette, eyes rolling back. "Drawer ... by TV ... ambulance."

Bud dropped him, ran to the living room. Empty drawers, back to the kitchen—Gilette on the floor eating paper.

Choke hold: Gilette spat out a half-chewed page. Bud picked up the wad, stumbled outside, burned flesh making him gag. He smoothed the paper out: names, phone numbers—smeared, two legible: Lynn Bracken, Pierce Patchett.

28

JACK AT his desk, counting lies.

At work: a string of dead-end reports; legit zeros from the other squad guys totaled luck: Millard wanted to dump the smut job. Count duty no-shows as lies—he'd spent a full day chasing names—matches to the cars in Bel Air. Four names tagged; no luck at a modeling agency specializing in movie star look-alikes—none of the girls came close to his beauties. Put the names aside, chalk up the day as a wash—Sid Hudgens made pursuit a dead issue. He just wanted to see the women again—add that one to his lies to Karen.

They spent the morning at her beach place. Karen wanted to make love; he put her off with bullshit: he was distracted, he'd asked to be detached to the Nite Owl because justice was so important. Karen tried to undress him; he told her he had a sprained back; he didn't say he wasn't interested because all he wanted to do was use her, make her do it with other women, re-create fuck book scenarios. His biggest lie: he didn't tell her that he'd finally stepped in shit that didn't turn to clover, that he'd played an angle that played him back to the gas chamber door, that his home-to-Narco ticket read adiós, lovebirds—because she'd trace 10/24/47 to all his other lies and his carefully constructed nice-guy Big V would go down in flames.

He didn't tell her he was terrified. She didn't sense it—his front was still strong.

Other fronts holding—dumb luck.

Sid hadn't called, his monthly *Hush-Hush* came on schedule—no note, some "sinuendo" on Max Peltz and teenage poon—nothing scary. He checked the report on the Fleur-de-Lis shootout: bright boy Ed Exley caught the squeal. Exley baffled: no make on the drop-pad tenants, the shelves cleaned out—only some bondage shit left—make the rest of the filth down the hidey-hole. Make Lamar Hinton for the shots—a free ride—the Big V was off the case, the Big V had a new mission.

Sid Hudgens knew Pierce Patchett and Fleur-de-Lis; Sid Hudgens knew the Malibu Rendezvous. Sid had a load of private dirt files stashed. The Big V's job: find *his* file, destroy it.

Jack checked his plate list, names matched to DMV pics.

Seth David Krugliak, the owner of the Bel Air manse—fat, oily, a movie biz lawyer. Pierce Morehouse Patchett, Fleur-de-Lis Boss—Mr. Debonair. Charles Walker Champlain, investment banker—shaved head, goatee. Lynn Margaret Bracken, age twenty-nine—Veronica Lake. No criminal records.

"Hello, lad."

Jack swiveled around. "Dud, how are you? What brings you to Ad Vice?"

"A confab with Russ Millard, my colleague on the Nite Owl now. And on that topic, I heard you want in."

"You heard right. Can you swing it?"

Smith passed him a mimeo sheet. "I already have, lad. You're to join in the search for Coates' car. Every garage within the radius on this page is to be checked—with or without the owner's consent. You're to begin immediately."

A map carbon: southside L.A. in street grids. "Lad, I need a personal favor."

"Name it."

"I want you to keep a tail on Bud White. He's gotten personally involved in the unfortunate killing of a child prostitute, and I need him stable. Will you stick to him nights, great tailer that you are?"

Bad Bud—always a sucker for strays. "Sure, Dud. Where's he working out of?"

"77th Street Station. He's been assigned to roust jigaboos with sex offender records. He's on daywatch at 77th, and you'll be clocking in and out there as well."

"Dud, you're a lifesaver."

"Would you care to elaborate on that, lad?"

"No."

29

MEMO:

"From: Chief Parker. To: Dep. Chief Green, Capt. R. Millard, Lt. D. Smith, Sgt. E. Exley. Conference: Chief's Office, 4:00 P.M., 4/23/53. Topic: Questioning of witness Inez Soto." His father's note: "She's wonderful and Ray Dieterling's much taken with her. But she's a material witness and a Mexican, and I advise you not to get too attached to her. And under no circumstances should you shack up with her. Cohabitation is against departmental regs and being with a Mexican woman could seriously stall your career."

Parker kicked things off. "Ed, the Nite Owl case is narrowing down to the Negroes in custody or some other colored gang. Now, word has it that you've gotten close to the Soto girl. Lieutenant Smith and I deem it imperative that she undergo questioning in order to clear up the time element, alibi or not alibi the three in custody, and identify the other men who assaulted her. We think pentothal is the best way to get results, and pentothal works best when a subject is at ease. We want you to convince Miss Soto to cooperate. She probably trusts you, so you'll have credibility."

Inez post-Stensland: shell-shocked, hard-pressed to move to Arrowhead. "Sir, I think all our evidence so far is circumstantial. I think we should get other corroboration before I approach Miss Soto, and I want to try questioning Coates, Jones and Fontaine again."

Smith laughed. "Lad, they refused to talk to you the other day, and now they have a pinko public defender who's advising them to stay mute. Ellis Loew wants a grand jury presentation—Nite Owl and Little Lindbergh—and you can facilitate it. Kid gloves has gotten us nowhere with our fair Miss Soto, and it's time we quit coddling her."

Russ Millard: "Lieutenant, I agree with Sergeant Exley. If we keep pressing on the southside, we'll turn rape witnesses and maybe find Coates' car and the murder weapons. My instincts tell me the girl's recollections of that night might be too muddled to do us any good, and if we make her remember, it might wreck her life more than it's been wrecked already. Can you picture Ellis Loew badgering her in front of the grand jury? Not very pretty, is it?"

Smith laughed—straight at Millard. "Captain, you politicked very hard to share this command with me, and now you advance a sob sister sensibility. This is a brutal mass murder that requires a swift and hard resolution, not a sorority party. And Ellis Loew is a brilliant attorney and a compassionate man. I'm sure he would handle Miss Soto with care."

Millard swallowed a pill, chased it with water. "Ellis Loew is a headline-grubbing buffoon, not a policeman, and he should not be directing the thrust of this investigation."

"Fair Captain, I deem that comment near seditious in its—"

Parker raised a hand. "Gentlemen, enough. Thad, will you take Captain Millard and Lieutenant Smith down the hall and buy them coffee while I talk to the sergeant here?"

Green ushered the two outside. Parker said, "Ed, Dudley's right."

Ed kept quiet. Parker pointed to a stack of newspapers. "The press and the public demand justice. We'll look very bad if we don't clear this up soon."

"Sir, I know."

"Do you care about the girl?"

"Yes."

"You know that sooner or later she'll have to cooperate?"

"Sir, don't underestimate her. She's steel inside."

Parker smiled. "Then let's see how much steel you possess. Convince her to cooperate, and if we get enough corroboration to convince Ellis Loew he's got a showstopper grand jury case, I'll jump you on the promotion list. You'll be a detective lieutenant immediately."

"And a command?"

"Arnie Reddin retires next month. I'll give you the Hollywood detective squad."

Ed tingled.

"Ed, you're thirty-one. Your father didn't make lieutenant until he was thirty-three."

"I'll do it."

30

PERVERT PATROL:

Cleotis Johnson, registered sex offender, pastor of the New Bethel Methodist Episcopal Church of Zion, had an alibi for the night Inez Soto was kidnapped: he was in the 77th Street drunk tank. Davis Walter Bush, registered sex offender, alibied up by a half dozen witnesses: they were engaged in an all-night crap game in the rec room of the New Bethel Methodist Episcopal Church of Zion. Fleming Peter Hanley, registered sex offender, spent that night at Central Receiving: a drag queen bit his dick; a team of emergency room docs labored to save the organ so he could notch up a few more convictions for sodomy with mayhem.

Pervert patrol, a call to Eagle Rock Hospital: Dwight Gilette made it there. A skate: the swish didn't die on him.

Four more RSOs alibied; a run by the Hall of Justice Jail. Stens flying high on raisinjack—a jailer fixed him a toilet brew cocktail. Rants: Ed Exley, Danny Duck porking Ellis Loew.

Home, a shower, DMV checks: Pierce Patchett, Lynn Bracken. Calls—a pal working Internal Affairs, West Valley Station. Good results: no Gilette complaint, three men on the Kathy snuff.

Another shower—he could still smell the day on himself.

* * *

Bud drove to Brentwood: squeeze Pierce Morehouse Patchett, no criminal record—strange for a name in a pimp's whore book. 1184 Gretna Green, a big Spanish mansion: all pink, lots of tile.

He parked, walked up. Porch lights came on: soft focus on a man in a chair. He matched Patchett's DMV stats, looked shitloads younger than his DOB. "Are you a police officer?"

His cuffs were hooked on his belt. "Yeah. Are you Pierce Patchett?"

"I am. Are you soliciting for police charities? The last time, you people called at my office."

Pinned eyes—maybe zoned on some kind of hop. Bodybuilder muscles, a tight shirt to show them off. An easy voice—he came on like he always sat in the dark waiting for cops to call. "I'm a Homicide detective."

"Oh? Who was killed and why do you think I can help you?"

"A girl named Kathy Janeway."

"That's only half an answer, Mr.—?"

"It's Officer White."

"Mr. White, then. Again, why do you think I can help you?"

Bud pulled up a chair. "Did you know Kathy Janeway?"

"No, I did not. Did she claim to know me?"

"No. Where were you last night at midnight?"

"I was here, hosting a party. If push comes to shove, which I hope it won't, I'll supply you with a guest list. Why do you—"

Bud cut in: "Delbert 'Duke' Cathcart."

Patchett sighed. "I don't know him either. Mr. White—"

"Dwight Gilette, Lynn Bracken."

A big smile. "Yes, I know those people."

"Yeah? Then keep going."

"Now let me interrupt. Did one of them give you my name?"

"I shook down Gilette for his whore book. He tried to chew up the page that had your name and this Bracken woman's name on it. Patchett, why's a shit pimp have your phone number?"

Patchett leaned forward. "Do you care about criminal matters peripheral to the Janeway killing?"

"No."

"Then you wouldn't feel obliged to report them."

The fucker had style. "That's right."

"Then listen closely, because I'll only say it once, and if it gets repeated I'll deny it. I run call girls. Lynn Bracken is one of them. I bought Lynn from Gilette a few years ago, and if Gilette tried to chew up my name it was because he knows that I hate and fear the police, and he thought—correctly—that I would squash him like a bug if I thought he put the police on to me. Now, I treat my girls very well. I have grown daughters myself, and I lost a baby girl to crib death. I do not like the thought of women being hurt and I frankly have a great deal of money to indulge my fancies. Did this Kathy Janeway girl die badly?"

Beaten to death, semen in the mouth, rectum, vagina. "Yeah, very bad."

"Then find her killer, Mr. White. Succeed, and I'll give you a handsome reward. If that goes against your moral grain, I'll donate the money to a police charity."

"Thanks, but no thanks."

"Against your code?"

"I don't have one. Tell me about Lynn Bracken. She street?"

"No, call. Gilette was ruining her with bad clients. *I'm* very selective who my girls truck with, by the way."

"So you bought her off Gilette."

"That's correct."

"Why?"

Patchett smiled. "Lynn looks very much like the actress Veronica Lake, and I needed her to fill out my little studio."

"What 'little studio'?"

Patchett shook his head. "No. I admire your intrusive style and I sense you're on your best behavior, but that's all I'll give you. I've cooperated, and if you persist I'll meet you with my attorney.

Now, would you like Lynn Bracken's address? I doubt that she knows anything about the late Miss Janeway, but if you like I'll call her and tell her to cooperate."

Bud pointed to the house. "I got her address. You get this address running call girls?"

"I'm a financier. I have an advanced degree in chemistry, I worked as a pharmacist for several years and invested wisely. 'Entrepreneur' sums me up best, I think. And don't tweak me with criminal slang, Mr. White. Don't make me regret I leveled with you."

Bud scoped him. Two to one he *was* leveling, thought cops were bugs that leveling worked with sometimes. "Okay, then I'll wrap it up."

"Please do."

Notebook out. "You said Gilette was pimping Lynn Bracken, right?"

"I dislike the word 'pimp,' but yes."

"Okay, were any of your other girls street-pimped, call-pimped?"

"No, all my girls are either models or girls that I saved from general Hollywood heartbreak."

Switcheroo. "You don't read the papers too good, right?"

"Correct. I try to avoid bad news."

"But you heard of the Nite Owl Massacre."

"Yes, because I do not dwell in a cave."

"That guy Duke Cathcart was one of the victims. He was a pimp, and lately a guy's been asking around about him, trying to get girls to do call jobs for him. Now Gilette street-pimped Kathy Janeway, and you know him. I'm thinking maybe you might do business with some other people who might give me a line on this guy."

Patchett crossed his legs, stretched. "So you think 'this guy' might have killed Kathy Janeway?"

"No, I don't think that."

"Or you think he's behind that Nite Owl thing. I thought Negro youths were supposed to be the killers. What crime are you investigating, Mr. White?"

Bud gripped the chair—fabric ripped. Patchett put his hands up, palms out. "The answer to your questions is no. Dwight Gilette is the only person of that breed I've ever dealt with. Low-level prostitution is not my field of expertise."

"What about B&E?"

"B and E?"

"Breaking and entering. Cathcart's apartment was tossed, and the walls were wiped."

Patchett shrugged. "Mr. White, you're speaking in Sanskrit now. I simply don't know what you're talking about."

"Yeah? Then what about smut? You know Gilette, Gilette sold you Lynn Bracken, Gilette sold Kathy Janeway to Cathcart. Cathcart was supposed to be starting up a smut biz."

"Smut" buzzed him—little eye flickers. Bud said, "Ring a bell?"

Patchett picked up a glass, swirled ice cubes. "No bells, and your questions are getting further and further afield. Your approach has been novel, so I've tolerated it. But you're wearing me thin and I'm beginning to think that your motives for being here are quite muddled."

Bud stood up pissed, no handle on the man. Patchett said, "One of your tangents is personal with you, isn't it?"

"Yeah."

"If it's the Janeway girl, I meant what I said. I may suborn women into illicit activities, but they're handsomely compensated, I treat them very well and make sure the men they deal with show them every due respect. Good night, Mr. White."

*   *   *

Thoughts for the ride: how did Patchett get his number so quick, did his evidence suppression bit backfire—Dudley suspicious, wise to how far he'd go to hurt Exley. Lynn Bracken lived on Nottingham off Los Feliz; he found the address easy—a modern-style triplex. Colored lights beamed out the windows—he looked before he rang.

Red, blue, yellow—figures cut through the beams. Bud watched his very own stag show.

A Veronica Lake dead ringer, nude on her tiptoes: slender, full breasted. Blond—hair in a perfect pageboy cut. A man moving inside her, straining, crouching for the fit.

Bud watched; street sounds faded. He blotted out the man, studied the woman: every inch of her body in every shade of light. He drove home tunnel-vision—nothing but her.

Inez Soto on his doorstep.

Bud walked over. She said, "I was at Exley's place in Lake Arrowhead. He said there was no strings, then he showed up and told me I had to take this drug to make me remember. I told him no. Did you know you're the only Wendell White in the Central Directory?"

Bud straightened her hat, tucked a loose piece of veil under the crown. "How'd you get down here?"

"I took a cab. A hundred of Exley's dollars, so at least he's good for something. Officer White, I don't want to remember."

"Sweetie, you already do. Come on, I'll fix you up with a place."

"I want to stay with you."

"All I've got's a fold-out."

"Fine by me. I figure there has to be a first time again."

"Give it a rest and get yourself a college boy."

Inez stood up. "I was starting to trust him."

Bud opened the door. The first thing he saw was the bed—trashed from Carolyn or whatever her name was. Inez plopped down on it—seconds later she was sleeping. Bud tucked her in, stretched out in the hall with his suitcoat for a pillow. Sleep came slow—his long strange day kept replaying. He went out seeing Lynn Bracken; toward dawn he stirred and found Inez curled up next to him.

He let her stay.

31

HE KNEW he was dreaming, knew he couldn't stop. He kept flinching with the replay.

Inez at the cabin: "Coward," "Opportunist," "Using me to further your career." Her out-the-door salvo: "Officer White's ten times the man you are, with half the brains and no big-shot daddy." He let her go, then chased: back to L.A., the Soto family shack. Three pachuco brothers came on strong; old man Soto supplied an epitaph: "I don't have that daughter no more."

The phone rang. Ed rolled over, grabbed it. "Exley."

"It's Bob Gallaudet. Congratulate me."

Ed pushed his dream away. "Why?"

"I passed the bar exam, making me both an attorney and a DA's Bureau investigator. Aren't you impressed?"

"Congratulations, and you didn't call at 8:00 A.M. to tell me that."

"Right you are, so listen close. Last night a lawyer named Jake Kellerman called Ellis Loew. He's representing two witnesses, brothers, who say they've got a viable Duke Cathcart connection to Mickey Cohen. They say they can clear the Nite Owl. They've got some outstanding L.A. warrants for pushing Benzedrine, and Ellis is giving them immunity on that, plus possible immunity on

any conspiracy charges that might stem from their connection to the
Nite Owl. We're having a meeting at the Mirimar Hotel in an
hour—the brothers and Kellerman, you, me, Loew and Russ
Millard. Dudley S. won't be there. Thad Green's orders—he
thinks Millard's the better man for this."

Ed swung out of bed. "So who are these brothers?"

"Peter and Baxter Englekling. Heard of them?"

"No. Is this an interrogation?"

Gallaudet laughed. "Wouldn't you love that. No, it's Kellerman
reads a prepared statement, we hobnob with Loew over whether to
let them turn state's and take it from there. I'll brief you. Mirimar
parking lot in forty-five minutes?"

"I'll be there."

* * *

Forty-five on the button. Gallaudet met him in the lobby—
no handshake, straight to it. "Want to hear what we've got?"

"Go."

They talked walking. "They're waiting for us, a steno included,
and what we've got are Pete and Bax Englekling, age thirty-six,
age thirty-two, San Bernardino-based ... quasi-hoods, I guess
you'd call them. They both did Youth Authority time for pushing
maryjane back in the early '40s, and except for the bennie pushing warrants, they've stayed clean. They own a legit printshop up
in San Berdoo, they're what you'd call genius fix-it guys, and their
late father was a real piece of work. Get this: he was a college chemistry teacher and some kind of pioneering pharmaceuticalist who
developed early antipsychotic drugs. Impressive, right? Now get
this: Pops, who kicked off in the summer of '50, developed dope
compounds for the old mobs—and Mickey C. was his protector
back in his bodyguard days."

"This won't be dull. But do *you* make Cohen for the Nite Owl?
He's in prison, for one thing."

"Exley, I make those colored guys in custody. Gangsters *never*
kill innocent citizens. But frankly, Loew likes the idea of a mob
angle. Come on, they're waiting."

Into suite 309, the meeting in a small living room. One long
table—Loew and Millard across from three men: a middle-aged
lawyer, near twins in overalls—thinning hair, beady eyes, bad teeth.
A steno by the bedroom door, perched with her machine set to go.

Gallaudet carried chairs over. Ed nodded around, sat by Millard.
The lawyer checked papers; the brothers lit cigarettes. Loew said,

"For the official record, it is 8:53 A.M., April 24, 1953. Present are myself, Ellis Loew, district attorney for the City of Los Angeles, Sergeant Bob Gallaudet of the DA's Bureau, Captain Russ Millard and Sergeant Ed Exley of the Los Angeles Police Department. Jacob Kellerman represents Peter and Baxter Englekling, potential prosecution witnesses in the matter of the multiple homicides perpetrated at the Nite Owl Coffee Shop on April 14 of this year. Mr. Kellerman will read a prepared statement given to him by his clients, they will initial the stenographer's transcript. As a courtesy for this voluntary statement, the District Attorney's Office is dismissing felony warrant number 16114, dated June 8, 1951, against Peter and Baxter Englekling. Should this statement result in the arrests of the perpetrators of the aforementioned multiple homicides, Peter and Baxter Englekling will be granted immunity from prosecution in all matters pertaining to the said, including accessory, conspiracy and all collateral felonies and misdemeanors. Mr. Kellerman, do your clients understand the aforesaid?"

"Yes, Mr. Loew, they do."

"Do they understand that they may be asked to submit to questioning after their statement has been read?"

"They do."

"Read the statement, Counselor."

Kellerman put on bifocals. "I've eliminated Peter and Baxter's more colorful colloquialisms and cleaned up their language and syntax, please bear that in mind."

Loew tugged at his vest. "We're capable of discerning that. Please continue."

Kellerman read: "We, Peter and Baxter Englekling, do swear that this statement is entirely true. In late March of this year, approximately three weeks before the Nite Owl killings, we were approached at our legitimate business, the Speedy King Printshop in San Bernardino. The man who approached us was one Delbert 'Duke' Cathcart, who said that he had gotten our names from 'Mr. XY,' an acquaintance from our youth camp sentence days. Mr. XY had informed Cathcart that we ran a printshop which featured a high-speed offset press of our own design, which was true. Mr. XY had also told Cathcart that we were always interested in quote turning a quick buck unquote, which was also true."

Chuckles. Ed wrote, "Vict. Susan Lefferts from S. Berdoo—connection?" Loew said, "Continue, Mr. Kellerman. We're all capable of laughing and thinking at the same time."

Kellerman: "Cathcart showed us photographs of people engaged in explicit sexual activities, some of them homosexual in nature. Some of the photographs were quote arty-farty unquote. I.E.: people in colorful costumes and animated red ink embossed on some of the snapshots. Cathcart said that he heard we could manufacture high-quality magazine-type books very fast, and we said this was true. Cathcart also stated that a number of magazine-type books had already been manufactured, using the obscene photographs, and quoted us the cost involved. We knew we could make the books at one eighth of that cost."

Ed passed Millard a note: "Isn't Ad Vice working a pornography job?" The brothers smirked; Loew and Gallaudet whispered. Millard passed a note back: "Yes—no leads from a 4 man team. A cold trail tracking the ('strange costumed' per the statement) books—we're dropping it. Also, no field reports submitted so far link Cathcart to pornography."

Kellerman sipped water. "Cathcart then told us that he heard our late father, Franz 'Doc' Englekling, was friends with Meyer Harris 'Mickey' Cohen, Los Angeles mobster currently incarcerated at McNeil Island Penitentiary. We said this was true. Cathcart then made his basic proposal. He said that distribution of the pornographic books would have to be quote very close unquote, because the quote strange cats unquote who took the photographs and did the pasteup work seemed like they had lots to hide. He did not elaborate on this further. He said that he had access to a network of quote rich perverts unquote who would pay large sums for the books and proposed that we could also manufacture quote regular fuck-suck shit unquote, that could be distributed in large quantities. Cathcart claimed to have access to quote pervert mailing list unquote, quote junkies and whores unquote to serve as models, and access to quote classy call girls unquote, who might pose for a lark if their quote crazy sugar daddy-o unquote agreed. Again, Cathcart did not elaborate on any of his claims, nor did he mention specific names or locations."

Kellerman flipped pages. "Cathcart told us that he would be the procurer, talent scout and middleman. We would be the manufacturers of the books. We were also to visit Mickey Cohen at McNeil Island and get him to release funds to get the business started. We were also to solicit his advice on starting a distribution system. In exchange for the above Cohen would be given a quote bonaroo unquote percentage cut."

Ed passed a note: "No follow-up names—it's too convenient." Millard whispered, "And the Nite Owl is not Mickey's style." Bax Englekling chuckled; Pete poked his ears with a pencil. Kellerman read: "We visited Mickey Cohen in his cell at McNeil, approximately two weeks before the Nite Owl killings. We proposed the idea to him. He refused to help and became very angry when we told him the idea was conceived by Duke Cathcart, whom he referred to as quote a notorious statch rape-o shitbird unquote. In conclusion, we believe that gunmen employed by Mickey Cohen perpetrated the Nite Owl Massacre, a kill-six-to-get-one ruse undertaken out of his hatred for Duke Cathcart. Another possibility is that Cohen talked up Cathcart's proposed scheme on the prison yard and word got out to Cohen rival Jack 'The Enforcer' Whalen, who, always looking for new rackets to crash, assassinated Cathcart and five innocent bystanders as subterfuge. We believe that if the killings were the result of pornography intrigue, we too might become victims. We swear that this deposition is true and not rendered under physical or mental duress."

The brothers clapped. Kellerman said, "My clients welcome questions."

Loew pointed to the bedroom. "After I talk to my colleagues."

They walked in; Loew closed the door. "Conclusions. Bob, you first."

Gallaudet lit a cigarette. "Mickey Cohen, despite his many faults, does not murder people out of pique, and Jack Whalen's only interested in gambling rackets. I believe their story, but everything we've dug up on Cathcart makes him look like a pathetic chump who couldn't get something this big going. I say it's tangent stuff at best. I still make the boogies for the job."

"I agree. Captain, your opinion."

Millard said, "I like one possible scenario—with major reservations. *Maybe* Cohen talked up the job on the yard at McNeil, word got to the outside and somebody took it from there. *But*—if this deal is smut-connected, then the Englekling boys would either have been killed or approached by now. I've been running a stag book investigation out of Ad Vice for two weeks and my squad has heard nothing on this and hit one brick wall after another. I think Ed and Bob should talk to Whalen, then fly up to McNeil and talk to Mickey. I'll question those lowlifes in the next room, and I'll talk to my Ad Vice men. I've read every field report filed by every man on the Nite Owl, and there is not one mention of pornography. I think Bob's right. It's a tangent we're dealing with."

"Agreed. Bob, you and Exley talk to Cohen and Whalen. Captain, did you have capable men on your job?"

Millard smiled. "Three capable men and Trashcan Jack Vincennes. No offense, Ellis. I know he's involved with your wife's sister."

Loew flushed. "Exley, do you have anything to add?"

"Bob and the captain covered my points, but there's two things I want to mention. One, Susan Lefferts was from San Berdoo. Two, if it's not the Negroes in custody or another colored gang, then the car by the Nite Owl was a plant and we are dealing with one huge conspiracy."

"I think we have our killers. And on that note, are you making progress with Miss Soto?"

"I'm working at it."

"Work harder. Good efforts are for schoolboys, results are what counts. Go to it, gentlemen."

* * *

Ed drove to his apartment—a change of clothes for the run to McNeil. He found a note on the door.

> Exley—
>
> I still think you're everything I said you were, but I called the house and talked to my sister and she said you came by and were obviously concerned about my welfare, so I'm thawing a little bit. You've been nice to me (when you weren't covering angles or beating up people) and maybe I'm an opportunist myself and I'm just using you for shelter until I get better and can accept Mr. Dieterling's offer, so since I live in a glass house I shouldn't throw stones at you. That's as close to an apology as I'm going to give you and I will continue to refuse to cooperate. Get the picture? Is Mr. Dieterling for real about a job at Dream-a-Dreamland? I'm going shopping today with the rest of the money you gave me. Keeping busy makes me think about it less. I'll come by tonight. Leave a light burning.
>
> Inez

Ed changed and taped his spare key to the door. He left a light burning.

32

JACK IN his car, waiting to tail Bud White. Mangled hands, fruit-caked clothes—a shift breaking down garage doors, high-spirited darkies japping the search teams—rooftop hit-and-runs. No luck on Coates' Merc; Millard's bomb still exploding, lucky he heard by phone—he would have shit his pants otherwise.

"Vincennes, two witnesses have contacted Ellis Loew. They said Duke Cathcart was involved in some kind of unrealized scheme to push that smut we've been chasing. My guess is that it doesn't connect to the Nite Owl, but have you come up with anything?"

He said, "No." He asked if the other guys on the squad hit pay dirt. Millard said, "No."

He didn't tell him his reports were all bullshit. He didn't tell him he didn't care if the smut gig and the Nite Owl were doubled up from here to Mars. He didn't tell him he wouldn't rest easy until he had Sid Hudgens' file in his hand and the niggers sucked gas—guilty or not.

Eyes on the bullpen back door: blues hauling in sex geeks. Bud White inside—rubber hose work. He blew his tail last night—Dudley was pissed. Tonight he'd stick close, then hit Hudgens: get the Malibu Rendezvous wiped.

White walked out. Good light: Jack saw blood on his shirt. He hit the ignition, waited.

33

NO COLORED lights—white light behind closed curtains. Bud pushed the buzzer.

The door opened—backlight on Lynn Bracken. "Yes? Are you the policeman Pierce told me about?"

"That's right. Did Patchett tell you what it was about?"

She held the door open. "He said you weren't quite sure your-self, and he said I should be candid and cooperate with you."

"You do everything he tells you?"

"Yes, I do."

Bud walked in. Lynn said, "The paintings are real and I'm a prostitute. I've never heard of Kathy what's-her-name, and Dwight Gilette would never sexually abuse a female. If he were going to kill one, he would have used a knife. I have heard of that man Duke

Cathcart, essentially that he was a loser with a soft spot for his girls. And that's all the news that's fit to print."

"You finished?"

"No. I have no information on Dwight's other girls, and all I know about that Nite Owl thing is what I read in the papers. Satisfied?"

Bud almost laughed. "You and Patchett had *some* talk. Did he call you last night?"

"No, this morning. Why?"

"Never mind."

"It's Officer White, isn't it?"

"It's Bud."

Lynn laughed. "*Bud*, do you believe what Pierce and I have told you?"

"Yeah, pretty much."

"And you know why we're humoring you."

"You use words like that, you might make me mad."

"Yes. But you know."

"Yeah, I know. Patchett's running whores, maybe other stuff on the side. You don't want me to report you on it."

"That's right. Our motives are selfish, so we're cooperating."

"You want some advice, Miss Bracken?"

"It's Lynn."

"Miss Bracken, here's my advice. Keep cooperating and don't fucking ever try to bribe me or threaten me or I'll have you and Patchett in shit up to your ears."

Lynn smiled. Bud caught it—Veronica Lake in some turkey he saw, Alan Ladd comes home from the war to find his bitch wife snuffed. "Do you want a drink, *Bud*?"

"Yeah, plain scotch."

Lynn walked to the kitchen, came back with two short ones. "Are they making progress on the girl's killing?"

Bud knocked his back. "There's three men on it. It's a sex job, so they'll round up all the usual perverts. They'll give it a decent shot for a couple of weeks, then let it go."

"But you won't let it go."

"Maybe, maybe not."

"Why are you so concerned?"

"Old stuff."

"Old personal stuff?"

"Yeah."

Lynn sipped her drink. "Just asking. And what about the Nite Owl thing?"

"That's coming down to these nig—colored guys we arrested. It's a big fucking mess."

"You say 'fuck' a lot."

"You fuck for money."

"There's blood on your shirt. Is that an integral part of your job?"

"Yeah."

"Do you enjoy it?"

"When they deserve it."

"Meaning men who hurt women."

"Bright girl."

"Did they deserve it today?"

"No."

"But you did it anyway."

"Yeah, just like the half dozen guys you screwed today."

Lynn laughed. "Actually, it was two. Off the record, did you beat up Dwight Gilette?"

"Off the record, I stuck his hand down a garbage disposal."

No gasp, no double take. "Did you enjoy it?"

"Well … no."

Lynn coughed. "I'm being a bad hostess. Would you like to sit down?"

Bud sat on the sofa; Lynn sat an arm's length over. "Homicide detectives are different. You're the first man I've met in five years who didn't tell me I look like Veronica Lake inside of a minute."

"You look better than Veronica Lake."

Lynn lit a cigarette. "Thank you. I won't tell your lady friend you said that."

"How do you know I got a lady friend?"

"Your jacket is a mess and reeks of perfume."

"You're wrong. This is me taking a pass on a pass."

"Which you …"

"Yeah, which I seldom fucking do. Keep cooperating, Miss Bracken. Tell me about Pierce Patchett and this racket of his."

"Off the—"

"Yeah, off the record."

Lynn smoked, sipped scotch. "Well, putting what he's done for me aside, Pierce is a Renaissance man. He dabbles in chemistry, he knows judo, he takes good care of his body. He loves having beautiful women beholden to him. He had a marriage that failed, he had a daughter who died very young. He's very honest with his girls, and he only lets us date well-behaved, wealthy men. So call it a savior complex. Pierce loves beautiful women. He loves manipulating them and making money off them, but there's real affection there, too. When I first met Pierce I told him my little sister was killed by a drunken driver. He actually cried. Pierce Patchett is a hardcase businessman, and yes, he runs call girls. But he's a good man."

It played straight. "What else has Patchett got going?"

"Nothing illegal. He puts business deals and movie deals together. He advises his girls on business matters."

"Smut?"

"God, not Pierce. He likes to *do* it, not look at it."

"Or sell it?"

"Yes, or sell it."

Almost too smooth—like Patchett's smut hink needed a whitewash. "I'm starting to think you're snowing me. There's gotta be a perv deal here. Sugar-pimping's one thing, but you make this guy out to be fucking Jesus. Let's start with Patchett's 'little studio.'"

Lynn put out her cigarette. "Suppose I don't want to talk about that?"

"Suppose I give you and Patchett to Administrative Vice?"

Lynn shook her head. "Pierce thinks you have your own private vendetta going, that it's in your best interest to eliminate him as a suspect in whatever it is you're investigating and keep quiet about his dealings. He thinks you won't inform on him, that it would be stupid for you to do it."

"Stupid is my middle name. What else does Patchett think?"

"He's waiting for you to mention money."

"I don't do shakedowns."

"Then why—"

"Maybe I'm just fucking curious."

"So be it. Do you know who Dr. Terry Lux is?"

"Sure, he runs a dry-out farm in Malibu. He's dirty to the core."

"Correct on both counts, and he's also a plastic surgeon."

"He did a plastic on Patchett, right? Nobody his age looks that young."

"I don't know about that. What Terry Lux *does* do is alter girls for Pierce's little studio. There's Ava and Kate and Rita and Betty.

Read that as Gardner, Hepburn, Hayworth and Grable. Pierce finds girls with middling resemblances to movie stars, Terry performs plastic surgery for exact resemblances. Call them Pierce's concubines. They sleep with Pierce and selected clients—men who can help him put together movie and business deals. Perverse? Perhaps. But Pierce takes a cut of all his girls' earnings and invests it for them. He makes his girls quit the life at thirty—no exceptions. He doesn't let his girls use narcotics and he doesn't abuse them, and I owe him a great deal. Can your policeman's mentality grasp those contradictions?"

Bud said, "Jesus fucking Christ."

"No, Mr. White. Pierce Morehouse Patchett."

"Lux cut you to look like Veronica Lake?"

Lynn touched her hair. "No, I refused. Pierce loved me for it. I'm really a brunette, but the rest is me."

"And how old are you?"

"I'll be thirty next month, and I'll be opening up a dress shop. See how time changes things? If you'd met me a month from now, I wouldn't be a whore. I'd be a brunette who didn't look quite so much like Veronica Lake."

"Jesus Christ."

"No, Lynn Margaret Bracken."

Too quick—almost a blurt. "Look, I want to see you again."

"Are you asking me for a date?"

"Yeah, because I can't afford what Patchett charges."

"You could wait a month."

"No, I can't."

"No more shoptalk, then. I don't want to be somebody's suspect."

Bud made a check mark in the air: Patchett crossed off for Kathy and the Nite Owl. "Deal."

34

MICKEY COHEN's cell.

Gallaudet laughed: velvet-covered bed, velvet-flocked shelves, commode with a velvet-flocked seat. Heat through a wall vent—Washington State, still cold in April. Ed was tired: they talked to Jack "The Enforcer" Whalen, eliminated him, flew a thousand miles. 1:00 A.M.—two cops waiting for a psychopathic hoodlum busy with a late pinochle game. Gallaudet patted Cohen's pet bulldog: Mickey Cohen, Jr., snazzy in a velvet-flocked sweater. Ed checked his Whalen notes.

Rambling—they couldn't shut him up. Whalen laughed off the Englekling theory, digressed on L.A. organized crime.

Mob activity in a general lull since Mickey C. hit stir. The insider view: the Mick power broke, Swiss bank money tucked away— cash to rebuild with. Morris Jahelka, Cohen underboss, given a fiefdom—he promptly blew it, investing badly, no funds to pay his men. Whalen said *he* was doing well and offered his Cohen theory.

He figured Mickey was parceling out bookmaking, loansharking, dope and prostitution franchises—small, choosy who they dealt with; when paroled he'd consolidate, grab the money the franchise men invested for him, rebuild. Whalen based his theory on hink: Lee Vachss, ex-Cohen trigger, seemed to have gone legit; Johnny Stompanato and Abe Teitlebaum ditto—two wrong-o's who couldn't walk a straight line. Make all three of them still on the grift—maybe safeguarding Cohen's interests. Chief Parker— afraid the lull might lead to Mafia encroachment—just fielded a new front line against out-of-town muscle: Dudley Smith and two of his goons set up shop at a motel in Gardena: they beat gang guys half to death, stole their money for police charity contributions, put them back on the bus, train or plane to wherever they came from—all very much on the QT.

Whalen concluded:

He's allowed to operate because somebody had to provide gambling services or a bunch of crazy independents would shoot L.A. to shit. "Containment"—a Dudley S. word—said it all: the police establishment knew he only shot when shot at; he *played the game.* The idea of him or Mickey blasting six people over jack-off books was pure bullshit. Still, things were too quiet, shit had to be brewing.

Mickey Cohen, Jr., yipped; Ed looked up. Mickey Cohen walked in, holding a box of dog biscuits. He said, "I have never killed no man that did not deserve killing by the standards of our way of life. I have never distributed no obscene shit to be used for the purpose of masturbation and only took a confabulation with Pete and Bax Englekling because of my fondness for their late father, may God rest his soul even though he was a fucking kraut. I do not kill innocent bystanders because it's a mitzvah not to and because I adhere to the Ten Commandments except when it is bad for business. Warden Hopkins told me why you was here and I made you wait because you must be stupid morons to make me for this vicious and stupid caper, obviously the handiwork of stupid shvartzes. But since Mickey Junior likes you I will give you five minutes of my time. Come to Daddy, bubeleh!"

Gallaudet howled. Cohen knelt on the floor, put a biscuit in his mouth. The dog ran to him, grabbed the biscuit, kissed him. Mickey nuzzled the beast; Cohen Junior squealed, pissed. Ed saw a man on the catwalk: Davey Goldman, Mickey's chief accountant, at McNeil on his own tax beef.

Goldman sidled away. Gallaudet said, "Mickey, the Englekling brothers said you went crazy when they mentioned Duke Cathcart was behind their idea."

Cohen spat biscuit crumbs. "Are you familiar with the old saying 'blowing off steam'?"

Ed said, "Yes, but what about other names? Did the Engleklings mention any other names besides Cathcart?"

"No, and Cathcart I never met myself. I heard he had a statch rape jacket, so I judged him on that. The Bible says, 'Judge not, lest ye be judged,' so since I am willing to be judged, I say, 'Judge on, O Mickster.'"

"Did you give the brothers any advice on setting up a distribution system?"

"No! As God and my beloved Mickey Junior are my witnesses, no!"

Gallaudet: "Mick, here's the key question. Did you talk up the deal on the yard? Who else did you tell about it?"

"I told nobody! Jerk-off books are from sin and hunger! I even chased Davey away when those meshugeneh brothers came calling! Davey's my ears, that's how much I respect the cardinal virtue of confidentiality!"

Gallaudet said, "Ed, I called Russ Millard while you were talking to the warden. He said he checked with his Ad Vice guys on the pornography job, and they've got nothing. No Cathcart, no leads on the books. Russ went through all the Nite Owl field reports and got nothing. Bud White background checked Cathcart, and he reported nothing. Ed, Susie Lefferts from San Berdoo is just a coincidence. Cathcart couldn't make a smut deal happen if he tried. This whole thing was the Engleklings' buying out of some old warrants and a dog show."

Ed nodded. Mickey Cohen, Sr., cradled Mickey Cohen, Jr. "Fathers and sons are food for thought, are they not a veritable feast? My canine offspring and me, old Doc Franz and his gap-toothed white trash lowlifes. Franz was a chemical genius, great things he did for the drool case mentally disturbed. When a boatload of Big H was stole from me way back, I thought of Franz, and how if I had his brains instead of my own poetic genius I would have re-created my own white powder to sell. Go home, boychiks. Dirty books will not win you your murder case. It's the shvartzes, it's the fucking shvoogies."

35

BOTTLES: WHISKY, gin, brandy. Flashing signs: Schlitz, Pabst Blue Ribbon. Sailors downing cold beers, happy folks juicing their lights out. Hudgens' pad a block away—booze would give him the guts. He knew it before he tailed Bud White—now he had a thousand times the reason.

The barman yelled, "Last call." Jack killed his club soda, pressed the glass to his neck. His day hit him—again.

Millard says Duke Cathcart was involved in some scheme to push *his* smut.

Bud White visits Lynn Bracken, one of the lookalike whores. He stays inside two hours; the whore walks him out. He tails White home, starts thinking evidence: White knows Bracken, she knows Pierce Patchett, he knows Hudgens. Sid knows about the Malibu Rendezvous, Dudley Smith probably knows. Big Dud's reason for the tail job: White bent out of shape on a *hooker* snuff.

Pulsing beer signs: neon monsters. Brass knucks in the car, the Sidster might fold, kick loose with his file—

Jack bolted: Hudgens' place, no lights on, Sid's Packard at the curb. The door—brass knucks for a knocker.

Thirty seconds—nothing. Jack tried the door—no give— shouldered the jamb. The door popped open.

That smell.

Slow motion: handkerchief out, gun out, elbow to the wall— the switch, no prints. Switch down, lights on.

Sid Hudgens hacked up on the floor—a rug soaked black, the floor a blood slick.

Arms and legs severed, out at weird angles off his torso.

Split open crotch to neck, bones showing white through red.

Cabinets upended behind him—folders dumped on a clean patch of rug.

Jack bit his arms to kill screams.

No blood tracks, say the killer got out the back door. Hudgens naked, coated red-black. Limbs off his torso, strands of gore at the cut points, swirls like his inked-in fuck books—

Jack bolted.

Around the house, down the driveway. The back door: ajar, spilling light. Inside: a water-slick floor—no blood prints, tracks covered. He walked in, found grocery bags under the sink. Shaky steps to the living room. File cabinet dirt: folders, folders, folders—one, two, three, four, five bags—two trips to his car.

A quiet L.A. street at 2:20 A.M., calm down mumbo jumbo.

Fifty trillion people had motives. Nobody knew he'd seen the inked-in books. The mutilations would get written off—just psycho stuff.

He had to find his file.

Jack doused lights, sawed the front door with his handcuffs—let them think it's a burglar. He took off, no destination, just driving.

* * *

Just driving wore thin. He found a motel strip, a hot-sheet flop: Oscar's Sleepytime Lodge.

He paid a week's rent, hauled his bags in, took a shower and put his stale clothes back on. A cockroach palace: bugs, grease on the wall above the bed. He smelled himself: stale working on foul. He locked the door, prowled dirt.

Hush-Hush back issues, clippings, pilfered police documents. Files: Montgomery Clift as the smallest dick in Hollywood, Errol Flynn as a Nazi agent. A hot item: Flynn and some homo writer named Truman Capote. Commies, Commie sympathizers, celebrity spook fuckers ranging from Joan Crawford to former DA Bill McPherson. Hopheads galore: shit on Charlie Parker, Anita O'Day, Art Pepper, Tom Neal, Barbara Payton, Gail Russell. Intact *Hush-Hush* articles: "Mafia Ties to the Vatican!!!," "Lavender Liturgy: Is 'Rock' Hudson Really 'Rockette'?," "Grasshopper Alert: Beware of Hollywood's Tea Bag Babies." Complete files, too tame to be Hudgens' secret stash—Commies, queers, lezbos, dopesters, satyrs, nymphos, misogynists, mob-bought politicos.

Nothing on Sergeant Jack Vincennes.

Nothing on *Badge of Honor*—a big Hudgens fixation—he knew Sid had a file on Brett Chase.

Strange.

More strange: *Hush-Hush* ran a smear on Max Peltz—there was nothing on him.

Nothing on Pierce Patchett, Lynn Bracken, Lamar Hinton, Fleur-de-Lis.

Jack measured his filth pile. Big—make the killer a file thief, if he got any files it wasn't many—his pile looked like it would jam the cabinets to bursting.

ALIBI.

Jack stuffed his files in the closet. "Do Not Disturb" on the door, back to his apartment.

5:10 A.M.

Under the knocker: "Jack—remember our date Thurs." "Jack sweetie—are you hibernating? XXXX—K." He walked in, grabbed the phone, dialed 888.

"Police Emergency."

A hepcat drawl. "Man, I want to report a murder. If I'm lyin', I'm flyin'."

"Sir, is this legitimate?"

"Yeah, if I'm—"

"What is your address, sir?"

"My address is nowhere, but I was gonna burglarize this house, then I saw this body."

"Sir—"

"421 South Alexandria, got that?"

"Sir, where are—"

Jack hung up, stripped, lay down on the bed. Figure twenty minutes for the bluesuits, ten to ID Hudgens. They putz around, make it as a big case, call Homicide. The desk man thinks brass, shakes a boss case man out of bed. Thad Green, Russ Millard, Dudley S.—they'd all think Big V pronto—his phone would ring in a hot hour.

Jack lay there—sweating up a clean set of sheets. Ring ring—at 6:58.

Jack, yawning. "Yeah?"

"Vincennes, it's Russ Millard."

"Yeah, Cap. What time is it? What's—"

"Never mind. Do you know where Sid Hudgens lives?"

"Yeah, Chapman Park somewhere. Cap, what's—"

"421 South Alexandria. *Now*, Vincennes."

* * *

Shave, shower, clothes that stayed dry. Forty minutes to the scene—a fuckload of cop cars on Sid Hudgens' lawn. Morgue men hefting plastic bags: blood, body parts.

Jack parked on the lawn. An attendant wheeled out a gurney: gore wrapped in sheets. Russ Millard by the door; two comers—Don Kleckner, Duane Fisk—down the driveway. Patrolmen shooed away spectators; reporters crowded the sidewalk. Jack walked up to Millard. "Hudgens?"—not too much shock, a pro.

"Yes, your buddy. A bit chewed up, I'm afraid. A burglar called it in. He was about to tap the house, then he saw the body. Pry marks on the doorjamb, so I buy it. Don't look inside if you've eaten."

Jack looked. Dried blood, white tape outlines: arms, legs, torso—the severing points marked. Millard said, "Somebody *hated* him. You see those drawers over there? I think the killer snuffed him for his files. I had Kleckner call the *Hush-Hush* publisher. He's going to open up the office and give us copies of the recent stuff Hudgens was working on."

Old Russ wanted a comment. Jack crossed himself: his first time since the orphanage, where the fuck did it come from.

"Vincennes, you were his friend. What do you think?"

"I think he was scum! Everybody hated him! You've got all L.A. for suspects!"

"Easy, now, *easy*. I know you've leaked information to Hudgens, I know you two did business. If we don't wrap this in a few days, I'm going to want a statement."

Duane Fisk spieling Morty Bendish—make book on a *Mirror* scoop. Jack said, "I'll kick loose. What am I going to do, impede the progress of an official investigation?"

"Your sense of duty is admirable. Now, let's talk about Hudgens. Girls, boys, what did he like?"

Jack lit a cigarette. "He liked dirt. He was a goddamned degenerate. Maybe he pulled his pud while he looked at his own goddamn shitrag, I don't know."

Don Kleckner walked up, a copy of *Hush-Hush* spread open: "TV Mogul Loves to Ogle—And Then Some!!! And Teen Queens Are His Scene!!!" "Captain, I bought this at that newsstand on the corner. And the publisher told me *Badge of Honor* was a bee in Hudgens' bonnet."

"This is good. Don, you start canvassing. Vincennes, come here."

Over to the lawn. Millard said, "This keeps coming back to people you know."

"I'm a cop and I'm Hollywood. I know lots of people, and I know Max Peltz likes young trim. So what? He's sixty years old and he's no killer."

"We'll decide that this afternoon. You're block searching on the Nite Owl, right? Looking for Coates' car?"

"Yeah."

"Then go back to that now and report to the Bureau at 2:00. I'm going to ask some key people from *Badge of Honor* to come in for some friendly questioning. You can help grease things."

Billy Dieterling, Timmy Valburn—"People He Knew" closing in. "Sure, I'll be there."

Morty Bendish ran up. "Jackie, does this mean I'll get *all* your exclusives now?"

* * *

Garage door break-ins, niggers hurling fruit—*real* work back at the motel. He was heading into Darktown when it hit him.

He cut east, parked by the Royal Flush. Claude Dineen's Buick up on blocks—he was probably dealing shit in the men's room.

Jack walked in. Everything froze: the Big V meant grief. The barman poured a double Old Forester; Jack downed it—cutting off five years kosher. The juice warmed him. He kicked the men's room door in.

Claude Dineen geezing up.

Jack kicked him prone, yanked the spike from his arm. A frisk, no resistance—Claude was up on cloud ten. Bingo: tinfoil Benzedrine. He swallowed a roll dry, flushed the hypo down the toilet. He said, "I'm back."

* * *

He hit the motel juiced, primed to figure angles. File go-round number two.

Nothing new jumped out; one instinct buzzed him: Hudgens didn't keep his "secret" files at home. If the killer snuffed him for a particular file, he tried to torture the location out of him first.

The killer didn't glom a lot of files—the cabinets wouldn't hold much more than what he stole. Sid's Big V file was still at large—if the killer found it he might keep it, might throw it away.

Jump: Hudgens/Patchett connected, pornography/vice rackets the connection. Put the Cathcart/Nite Owl connection aside: Millard/Exley called it a bust—denials from Whalen and Mickey C., Cathcart never got his smut gig going. Millard's report: the Englekling brothers didn't know who took the pictures; Cathcart got ahold of some of the stag books, went crazy with a harebrained scheme. Put that aside and what he had was:

Bobby Inge, Christine and Daryl Bergeron—gone. Lamar Hinton, the probable shooter at the Fleur-de-Lis drop—undoubtedly gone. Timmy Valburn, a Fleur-de-Lis customer, rousted by him—a connection to Billy Dieterling, a *Badge of Honor* cameraman, catch him at Millard's questioning party—*stay calm on that.* Say Timmy told Billy about the roust; Billy was there when he trashed Hinton's car, *keep calm,* the queers had shitloads to lose by admitting their connection to Fleur-de-Lis—which Russ Millard did not know existed.

Brainstorming, chain-smoking.

Mutilations on Hudgens' body matched the inked-in poses in the fuck books he found outside Bobby Inge's pad. *No other cops had seen those specific books*—Millard viewed the stiff, tagged the chopped limbs as straight amputations.

Hudgens warned him away from Fleur-de-Lis. Lynn Bracken was a Patchett whore—maybe she knew Sid.

Wild card: Dudley Smith told him to tail Bud White. His reason: White running maverick on a hooker killing. Bracken was a hooker, Patchett ran hookers. But: *Dudley did not mention any tie-ins to the Nite Owl or pornography—Patchett/Bracken/smut/ Fleur-de-Lis et fucking al were probably Greek to him. The Englekling brothers/Cathcart wash aside, smut/Patchett/Bracken/Fleur-de-Lis/ Hudgens in no way made its way into the incredible glut of interdivision posted Nite Owl paperwork.*

Sky high: Benzedrine, cop logic. 11:20—time to kill before the Bureau. Two real leads—Pierce Patchett, Lynn Bracken. Bracken was closer.

* * *

Jack drove to her apartment, settled in behind her car. Give her an hour, play it by ear if she left.

Time Benzedrine-flew; Bracken's door stayed shut. 12:33—a kid chucked a newspaper at it. If Morty Bendish speedballed his story and that kid pitched the *Mirror*—

The door opened; Lynn Bracken picked the paper up, yawned back inside. The paperboy swooped by, carrier sacks in plain view: Los Angeles *Mirror-News.* Be in there, Morty.

Bang!—Bracken slammed the door, ran to her car. She gunned it, swerved west on Los Feliz. Jack cut her two seconds slack, tailed her.

Southwest: Los Feliz to Western to Sunset, Sunset straight out— ten miles over the speed limit. Odds on: a fear run to Patchett's place, she didn't want to use the phone.

Jack looped south, shortcutted, made 1184 Gretna Green burning rubber. A huge Spanish manse, a huge front lawn—Lynn Bracken hadn't showed yet.

A skidding heart: he forgot what you paid to eat bennies. He parked, checked out the house: nobody out and about. Up to the door, a duck around the side—find some windows.

All closed. A gardener working around back—no way to circuit without being seen. A car door slammed; Jack ran to a front win- dow: closed, a part in the curtains he could squint through.

The doorbell rang; Jack squinted in. Patchett walked to the door, opened it. Lynn Bracken shoved her newspaper at him— zoom into a panic duet: mute lip movements, fear very large. Jack put an ear to the glass—all he heard was his own heart thumping. No need for sound: they didn't know Sid was dead, they're scared anyway, they didn't kill him.

They walked into the next room—full curtains, no way to look or listen. Jack ran to his car.

* * *

He made the Bureau ten minutes late. The Homicide pen was jam-packed *Badge of Honor*: Brett Chase, Miller Stanton, David Mertens the set man, Jerry Marsalas his nurse—one long bench crammed tight. Standing: Billy Dieterling, the camera crew, a half dozen briefcase men: attorneys for sure. The gang looked nervous; Duane Fisk and Don Kleckner paced with clipboards. No Max Peltz, no Russ Millard.

Billy D. shot him the fisheye; the rest of the gang waved. Jack waved back; Kleckner buttonholed him. "Ellis Loew wants to see you. Booth number six."

Jack walked down. Loew was staring out a back wall mirror—a lie detector stall across the glass. Polygraph time: Millard questioning Peltz, Ray Pinker working the machine.

Loew noticed him. "I'd rather Max didn't have to go through that. Can you fix it?"

Protecting a slush-fund contributor. "Ellis, I've got no truck with Millard. If Max's lawyer advised him to do it, he'll have to do it."

"Can Dudley fix it?"

"Dud's got no truck with him either, Millard's the pious type. And before you ask me, I don't know who killed Sid, and I don't care. Has Max got an alibi?"

"Yes, but one that he would rather not use."

"How old is she?"

"Quite young. Would—"

"Yeah, Russ would file on him for it."

"My God, all this for scum like Hudgens."

Jack laughed. "Counselor, one of his little mudslings got you elected."

"Yes, politics makes for strange bedfellows, but I doubt if he'll be grieved. You know, we've got nothing. I talked to those attorneys outside, and they all assured me their clients have valid alibis. They'll give statements and be eliminated, the rest of the *Badge of Honor* people will be alibied and then we'll only have the rest of Hollywood to deal with."

An opening. "Ellis, you want some advice?"

"Yes, give me your appropriately cynical view."

"Let it play out. Push on the Nite Owl, that's the one the public wants cleared. Hudgens was shit, the investigation'll be a shit show and we'll never get the killer. Let it play out."

The door opened; Duane Fisk put two thumbs down. "No luck, Mr. Loew. Alibis straight across, and they sound like good ones. The coroner estimated Hudgens' death at midnight to 1:00 A.M., and these people were all in plain view somewhere else. We'll go for corroboration, but I think it's a wipe."

Loew nodded; Fisk walked out. Jack said, "Let it go."

Loew smiled. "What's your alibi? Were you in bed with my sister-in-law?"

"I was in bed alone."

"I'm not surprised—Karen said you've been moody and scarce lately. You look edgy, Jack. Are you afraid your arrangement with Hudgens will be publicized?"

"Millard wants a deposition, I'll give him one. You buy Sid and me as lodge brothers?"

"Of course. Along with Dudley Smith, myself and several other well-known choirboys. You're right on Hudgens, Jack. I'll broach it to Bill Parker."

A yawn—the bennies were losing their kick. "It's a dog of a case, and you don't want to prosecute it."

"Yes, since the victim did facilitate *my* election, and he might have left word that *you* leaked word to him on Mr. McPherson's quote dark desires. Jack …"

"Yeah, I'll keep my nose down, and if your name turns up on paper I'll destroy it."

"Good man. And if I …"

"Yeah, there is something. Track the reports on the investigation. Sid kept some secret dirt files, and if your name's anywhere, it's there. And if I get a lead on where, I'll be there with a match."

Loew, pale. "Done, and I'll talk to Parker this afternoon."

Ray Pinker rapped on the mirror, pressed a graph to the glass: twin needle lines—no wild fluctuations. Out the speaker: "Not guilty, but no give on his alibi. Was he *en flagrante*?"

Loew smiled. Russ Millard, speaker loud. "Go to work, Vincennes. Nite Owl block canvassing, if you recall. Your cockamamie TV show hasn't panned out so far, and I want a written statement on your dealings with Hudgens. *By 0800 tomorrow*."

Darktown beckoned.

* * *

South to 77th. Jack popped another roll and picked up his search map; the desk sergeant told him the spooks were getting feistier, some pinko agitators put a bug up their ass, more garbage attacks, the garage men were going out in threes: one detective, two patrolmen, teams on opposite sides of the street. Meet his guys at 116th and Wills—they'd been one man short since noon.

The bennies kicked in—Jack zoomed back up. He drove to 116 and Wills: a stretch of cinderblock shacks, windows stuffed with cardboard. Dirt alleys, a bicycle brigade: colored kids packing fruit. His guys up ahead: two patrolmen on the left, two blues and a plainclothes on the right. Armed: tin snips, rifles. Jack parked, made the left-side team a threesome.

Pure shitwork.

Knock on the door, get permission to search the garage. Three quarters of the locals played possum; back to the garage, open the door, cut the lock. The right-side team didn't ask—they went in snips first, dawdled, brandished their hardware at the bicycle kids. The left-side kids tried to look mean; one kid chucked a tomato over their heads. The blues fired over his head—taking out a pigeon coop, chewing up a palm tree. Dusty garage after dusty garage after dusty garage—no '49 Merc license DG114.

Twilight, a block of deserted houses—broken windows, weed jungle lawns. Jack started feeling punk: achy teeth, chest pings. He heard rebel yells across the street; the right-side team triggered shots. He looked at his partners—then they all tore ass over.

The Holy Grail in a rat-infested garage: a purple '49 Merc, jig rig to the hilt. California license DG114—registered to Raymond "Sugar Ray" Coates.

Two patrolmen whipped out bottles.

A couple of bicycle kids jabbered: the bonaroo paint job, a white cat hanging around the alley.

The left-side guys broke into a rain dance.

Jack squinted through a side window. Three pump shotguns on the floor between the seats: big bore, probably 12-gauge.

Yells—deafening; back slaps—bonecrusher hard. The kids yelled along; a patrolman let them slug from his bottle. Jack took a big gulp, emptied his gun at a streetlight, got it with his last shot. Whoops, rebel yells; Jack let the kids play quick draw with his piece. Sid Hudgens buzzed him—he took a big drink, chased him away.

36

A PRIVATE room at the Pacific Dining Car. Dudley Smith, Ellis Loew, Bud across the table. Blistered hands, three days of hose work: sex offenders blurred in his head.

Dudley said, "Lad, we found the car and the shotguns an hour ago. No prints, but one of the firing pins perfectly matches the nicked shells we found at the Nite Owl. We took the victims' purses and wallets out of a sewer grate near the Tevere Hotel, which means that we have a damn near airtight case. But Mr. Loew and I want the whole hog. We want confessions."

Bud shoved his plate away. It all came back to the spooks—scotch his shot at Exley. "So you'll put bright boy on the niggers again."

Loew shook his head. "No, Exley's too soft. I want you and Dudley to question them, inside the jail, tomorrow morning. Ray Coates has been in the infirmary with an ear infection, but they're releasing him back into general population early tomorrow. I want you and Dud there bright and early, say 7:00."

"What about Carlisle and Breuning?"

Dudley laughed. "Lad, you're a much more frightful presence. This job has the name 'Wendell White' on it, as does another assignment I've kicked off lately. One you'll be interested in."

Loew said, "Officer, it's been Ed Exley's case so far, but now you can share the glory. And I'll grant you a favor in return."

"Yeah?"

"Yes. Dick Stensland has been handed a six-count probation indictment. Do it, and I'll drop four of those charges and put him in front of a lenient judge. He'll be sentenced to no more than ninety days."

Bud stood up. "Deal, Mr. Loew. And thanks for dinner."

Dudley beamed. "Until 7:00 tomorrow, lad. And why are you leaving so abruptly, is it a hot date you have?"

"Yeah, Veronica Lake."

* * *

She opened the door, all Veronica: spangly gown, blond curl over one eye. "If you'd called first, I wouldn't look this ridiculous."

She looked edgy. Her dye job was off: uneven, dark at the roots. "Bad date?"

"An investment banker Pierce wants to curry favor with."

"Did you fake it good?"

"He was so self-absorbed that I didn't have to fake it."

Bud laughed. "You turn thirty, you do it strictly for thrills."

Lynn laughed, still edgy, she might touch him first just to have something to do with her hands. "If men don't try to be Alan Ladd, they might get the real Lynn Margaret."

"Worth the wait?"

"You know it is, and you're wondering if Pierce told me to be receptive."

He couldn't think of a comeback.

Lynn took his arm. "I'm glad you thought of that, and I like you. And if you wait in the bedroom I'll scrub off Veronica and that investment banker."

* * *

She came to him naked, a brunette, her hair still wet. Bud forced himself to go slow, take time with his kisses, like she was a lonely woman he wanted to love to death. Lynn played off his timing: her kisses back, her touches. Bud kept thinking she was faking—he rushed to taste her so he'd know.

Lynn moaned, put his hands on her breasts, set up a rhythm for his fingers. Bud followed her lead, loved it when she gasped and came over and over, hair-trigger. Real—so real he forgot about himself; he heard something like "In me, please in me." He rubbed himself hard on the bed, went in her, kept his hands on her breasts like she taught him. Hard inside her—he let himself go just as her legs pulsed and her hips pushed him up off the sheets—then his face pressing wet hair, their arms locked on each other tight.

They rested, talked. Lynn talked up her diary: a thousand pages back to high school in Bisbee, Arizona. Bud rambled on the Nite Owl, his strongarm job in the morning—sitting-duck stuff he couldn't take much more of. Lynn's look said, "Then just give it up"; he didn't have an answer, so he spieled on Dudley, the heart-breaker rape girl with a crush on him, how he'd hoped the Nite Owl would swing another way so he could use it to juke this guy he hated. Lynn talked back with little touches; Bud told her he was letting the Kathy snuff go for now, it was too easy to go crazy on—crazy like his play with Dwight Gilette. Lynn pressed on his family; he told her "I don't have one"; he ran down his outlaw job: Cathcart, his pad tossed, his smut dream, the San Berdoo Yellow Pages open to printshops clicking in to the Englekling brothers plea bargain, then clicking out, back to the colored punks they had on ice. He knew she knew the gist: he was frustrated because he wasn't that smart, he wasn't really a Homicide detective—he was the guy they brought in to scare other guys shitless. After a while, the talk petered out—Bud felt restless, pissed at himself for spilling too much too fast. Lynn seemed to sense it: she bent down and drove him crazy with her mouth. Bud stroked her hair, still a little wet, glad she didn't have to fake it with him.

37

EVIDENCE—THE VICTIMS' belongings found near the Tevere Hotel; Coates' Merc and the shotguns located: forensic verification on the piece that shot the strangely marked rounds. No grand jury on earth would refuse to hand down Murder One. The Nite Owl case was made.

Ed at his kitchen table, writing a report: Parker's last summary. Inez in the bedroom, her bedroom now, he couldn't get up the nerve to say: "Just let me sleep with you, we'll see how things go, wait on the other." She'd been moody—reading books on Raymond Dieterling, getting up nerve to ask the man for a job. The news on the guns didn't bolster her—even though it meant no testimony. Evidence—her outside wounds had healed, there was no physical pain to distract her. She kept feeling it happen.

The phone rang; Ed grabbed it. An extra click—Inez picking up in the bedroom.

"Hello?"

"Russ Millard, Ed."

"Captain, how are you?"

"It's Russ to sergeants and up, son."

"Russ, have you heard about the car and the guns? The Nite Owl's history."

"Not exactly, and that's why I called. I just talked to a Sheriff's lieutenant I know, a man on the Jail Bureau. He told me he heard a rumor. Dudley Smith's taking Bud White in to beat confessions out of our boys. Tomorrow morning, early. I had them moved to another cellblock where they can't get at them."

"Jesus Christ."

"The savior indeed. Son, I have a plan. We go in early, confront them with the new evidence and try for legitimate confessions. You play the bad guy, I'll play savior."

Ed squared his glasses. "What time?"

"Say 7:00?"

"All right."

"Son, it means making an enemy out of Dudley."

The bedroom line clicked off. "So be it. Russ, I'll see you tomorrow."

"Sleep well, son. I need you alert."

Ed hung up. Inez in the doorway, wearing his robe—huge on her. "You can't do this to me."

"You shouldn't eavesdrop."

"I was expecting a call from my sister. Exley, you can't."

"You wanted them in the gas chamber, they're going there. You didn't want to testify, now I doubt if you'll have to."

"I want them hurt. I want them to suffer."

"No. It's wrong. This is a case that demands absolute justice."

She laughed. "Absolute justice fits you like this robe fits me, *pendejo.*"

"You got what you wanted, Inez. Let it go at that and get on with your life."

"What life? Living with you? You'll never marry me, you're so deferential around me that I want to scream and every time I've got myself convinced you're a pretty decent guy you do something that makes me say, '*Madre mia*, how can I be so dumb?' And now you'd deny me this? *This little thing?*"

Ed held up his report. "Dozens of men built this case. Those animals will be dead by Christmas. *Todos*, Inez. *Absolutamente.* Isn't that enough?"

She laughed—harder. "No. Ten seconds and they go to sleep. Six hours they beat me and fucked me and stuck things in me. No, it's not enough."

Ed stood up. "So you'll let Bud White jeopardize our case. Ellis Loew probably arranged this, Inez. He's thinking airtight grand jury presentation, a two day trial with half of it him grandstanding. He'd jeopardize what he's already got for that. Be smart and recognize it."

"No, you recognize that the fix is in. The *negritos* die because that's the way it is. I'm just a witness nobody needs anymore, so maybe tomorrow Officer White takes a few licks for my justice."

Ed made fists. "White's a brutal disgrace of a policeman and a slimy, womanizing son of a bitch."

"No, he's just a guy who calls a spade a spade and doesn't look six ways before he crosses the street."

"He's shit. *Mierda.*"

"Then he's my *mierda*. Exley, I *know* you. You don't give a damn about justice, you just care about yourself. You're only doing that thing tomorrow to hurt Officer White, and you're only doing it because you know that he knows what you are. You treat me like you want to love me, then you give me nothing but money and social connections, which you've got plenty of and won't miss. You take no risks for me, and Officer White risks his *estúpido* life and doesn't weigh the consequences, and when I get better you'll want to fuck me and set me up someplace where you won't have to be seen in public with me, which is revolting to me, and if for no other reason I love *estúpido* Officer White because at least he has the sense to know what you are."

Ed walked up to her. "And what am I?"

"Just a run-of-the-mill coward."

Ed raised a fist, flinched when she flinched. Inez pulled off her robe. Ed looked, looked away—at the wall and his framed army medals. A target—he threw them across the room. Not enough. He took a bead on a window, reared back, hit soft padded curtains instead.

38

JACK WOKE up seeing smut.

Karen in orgy shots—Veronica Lake loving her. Blood: fuck pix as coroner's pix, beautiful women drenched red. The first real thing he saw was daybreak—then Bud White's car parked by Lynn Bracken's pad.

Cracked lips, bone aches head to toe. He swallowed his last bennies, brought back his last thoughts before oblivion.

Nothing in the files, Patchett and Bracken his only Hudgens leads. Patchett had servants living in. Bracken lived alone—he'd brace her when White left her bed.

Jack brainstormed a tailing report—lies to snow Dudley Smith. A door slammed—a sound like a gunshot. Bud White walked to his car.

Jack hit the seat prone. The car pulled away, seconds, another gunshot/door slam. A quick look: a brunette Lynn Bracken heading out.

Over to her car, up to Los Feliz, east. Jack followed: the right lane, dawdling back. Sparse early morning traffic: call the woman too distracted to spot him.

Due east, into Glendale. North on Brand, a swerve to the curb in front of a bank. Jack pulled around the corner to a sighting point—the corner store, a grocer's—milk cartons stacked by the door.

He squatted down, watched the sidewalk. Lynn B. was talking to a man: nervous, a shaky little guy. He opened the bank and hustled her in; a Ford and Dodge were parked further down—no way to nail plate numbers. Lamar Hinton walked outside lugging boxes.

Files, files, files—it had to be.

Bracken and the bank geek hauled boxes: a run to the Dodge and Lynn's Packard. The geek locked up the bank, hit the Ford and U-turned southbound; Hinton and Bracken formed a chain—separate cars heading north.

Seconds tick tick tick—Jack counted to ten, chased.

He caught them a mile out—weaving, creeping up, falling back—downtown Glendale, north into foothills. Traffic dwindled; Jack found a lookout spot: a clean view of the road winding upward. He parked, watched: the cars kept climbing, took a fork, disappeared.

He followed their route straight to a campsite—picnic tables, barbecue pits. Two cars behind a pine row; Bracken and Hinton carrying boxes—muscle boy dangling a gas can off one pinky.

Jack ditched his car, snuck up behind some scrub pines. Bracken and Hinton dumped: paper in a big charcoal pit. They turned their backs; Jack sprinted over, ducked down.

They came back, another load: Bracken with a lighter out, Hinton's arms full. Jack stood up, kicked, pistolwhipped—the balls, left/right/left to the face. Hinton went down dropping paper; Jack broke his arms—knees to the elbows, jerks at the wrists.

Hinton went white—shock coming on.

Bracken had hold of the gas can and a lighter.

Jack stood in front of the pit, his .38 cocked.

Standoff.

Lynn held the can, the cap loose, spilling fumes. Flick—a flame on the lighter. Jack drew down—right in her face.

Standoff.

Hinton tried to crawl. Jack's gun hand started shaking. "Sid Hudgens, Patchett and Fleur-de-Lis. It's either me or Bud White, and I can be bought."

Lynn killed the flame, lowered the gas. "What about Lamar?"

Hinton: pawing at the dirt, spitting blood. Jack lowered his gun. "He'll live. And he shot at me, so now we're quits."

"He didn't shoot at you. Pierce ... I just know he didn't."

"Then who did?"

"I don't know. Really. And Pierce and I don't know who killed Hudgens. The first we heard of it was the newspapers yesterday."

The pit—folders on charcoal. "Hudgens' private dirt, right?"

"Yes."

"Yes and keep going."

"No, let's talk about your price. Lamar told Pierce about you, and Pierce figured out that you were that policeman who always seems to wind up in the scandal sheets. So as you say, you can be bought. Now, for how much?"

"What I want's in with those files."

"And what do you—"

"I know about you and the other girls Patchett runs. I know all about Fleur-de-Lis and the shit Patchett pushes, including the smut."

No fluster—the woman put out a stone face. "Some of your stag books have pictures with animated ink. Red, like blood. I saw pictures of Hudgens' body. He was cut up to match those photos."

The stone face held. "So now you're going to ask me about Pierce and Hudgens."

"Yeah, and who doctored up the photos in the books."

Lynn shook her head. "I don't know who made those books, and neither does Pierce. He bought them bulk from a rich Mexican man."

"I don't think I believe you."

"I don't care. Do you want money besides?"

"No, and I'm betting whoever made those photographs killed Hudgens."

"Maybe somebody who got excited by the pictures killed him. Do you care either way? Why am I betting Hudgens had dirt on you, and that's what's behind all this?"

"Smart lady. And I'm betting Patchett and Hudgens didn't play golf or—"

Lynn cut him off. "Pierce and Sid were planning on working a deal together. I won't tell you any more than that."

Extortion—it had to be. "And those files were for that?"

"No comment. I haven't looked at the files, and let's keep this a stalemate and make sure nobody gets hurt."

"Then tell me what happened at the bank."

Lynn watched Hinton try to crawl. "Pierce knew that Sid kept his private files in safe-deposit boxes at that B of A. After we read that he'd been killed, Pierce figured the police would locate the files. You see, Sid had files on Pierce's dealings—dealings legitimate policemen would disapprove of. Pierce bribed the manager into letting us have the files. And here we are."

Jack smelled paper, charcoal. "You and Bud White."

Lynn made fists, pressed them to her legs. "He has nothing to do with any of this."

"Tell me anyway."

"Why?"

"Because I don't make you two as the hot item of 1953."

A smile from deep nowhere—Jack almost smiled back. Lynn said, "We're going to strike a deal, aren't we? A truce?"

"Yeah, a non-aggression pact."

"Then make this part of it. Bud approached Pierce, investigating the murder of a young girl named Kathy Janeway. He'd gotten Pierce's name and mine from a man who used to know her. Of course, we didn't kill her, and Pierce didn't want a policeman coming around. He told me to be nice to Bud ... and now I'm starting to like him. And I don't want you to tell him anything about this. *Please*."

She even begged with class. "Deal, and you can tell Patchett the DA thinks the Hudgens case is a loser. It's heading for the back burner, and if I find what I want in that pile, today didn't happen."

Lynn smiled—this time he smiled back. "Go look after Hinton."

She walked over to him. Jack dug into the folders, found name tabs, kept digging. A spate of *T*'s, a run of *V*'s, the kicker. "Vincennes, John."

Eyewitness accounts: squarejohns at the beach that night. Nice folks who saw him drill Mr. & Mrs. Harold J. Scoggins, nice folks who told Sid about it for cash, nice folks who didn't tell the "authorities" for fear of "getting involved." The results of the blood test Sid bribed the examining doctor into suppressing: the Big V with a snootful of maryjane, Benzedrine, liquor. His own doped-up statement in the ambulance: confessions to a dozen shakedowns. Conclusive proof: Jack V. snuffed two innocent citizens outside the Malibu Rendezvous.

"I got Lamar back to my car. I'll drive him to a hospital."

Jack turned around. "This is too good to be true. Patchett's got carbons, right?"

That smile again. "Yes, for his deal with Hudgens. Sid gave him carbons of every file except the files he kept on Pierce himself. Pierce wanted the carbons as his insurance policy. I'm sure he didn't trust Sid, and since we have all of Hudgens' files right here, I'm sure Pierce's files are in there."

"Yeah, and you have a carbon on mine."

"Yes, Mr. Vincennes. We do."

Jack tried to ape that smile. "Everything I know about you, Patchett, his rackets and Sid Hudgens is going into a deposition, *multiple* copies to *multiple* safe-deposit boxes. If anything happens to me or mine, they go to the LAPD, the DA's Office and the L.A. *Mirror.*"

"Stalemate, then. Do you want to light the match?"

Jack bowed. Lynn doused the files, torched them. Paper sizzled, fireballed—Jack stared until his eyes stung.

"Go home and sleep, Sergeant. You look terrible."

* * *

Not home—Karen's.

He drove there woozy, keyed up. He started to feel the close-out: bad debts settled bad, a clean slate. He got the idea just like he got the idea to shake down Claude Dineen. He didn't say the words, didn't rehearse it. He turned the radio on so he'd keep the notion fresh.

A stern-voiced announcer:

"... and the southside of Los Angeles is now the focus of the largest manhunt in California history. We repeat, an hour and a half ago, just after dawn, Raymond Coates, Tyrone Jones and Leroy Fontaine, the accused killers in the Nite Owl massacre case, escaped from the Hall of Justice Jail in downtown Los Angeles. The three had been moved to a minimum security cellblock to await requestioning and made their escape by the means of knotted-together bedsheets and a jump out a second-story window. Here, recorded immediately after the escape, are the comments of Captain Russell Millard of the Los Angeles Police Department, co-supervisor of the Nite Owl investigation.

"'I ... assume full responsibility for this incident. I was the one who ordered the three suspects sequestered in a minimum security unit. I ... every effort will be made to recapture them with all due speed. I ...'"

Jack turned the radio off. Close-out: pious Russ Millard's career. Call-out: figure the whole Bureau yanked from bed for the dragnet. He yawned the rest of the way to Karen's, rang her bell seeing double.

Karen opened up. "Sweetie, *where have you been?*"

Jack plucked curlers out of her hair. "Will you marry me?"

Karen said, "Yes."

39

ED, STAKED out at 1st and Olive. His father's shotgun for backup, a replay on his hunch.

Sugar Ray Coates: "Roland Navarette, lives on Bunker Hill. Runs a hole-up for parole absconders."

A whispered snitch: the speakers didn't catch it, doubtful Coates remembered he said it. R&I, Navarette's mugshot, address: a rooming house midway down Olive, half a mile from the Hall of Justice Jail. A dawn breakout—they couldn't make Darktown unseen. Figure all four of them armed.

Scared—like Guadalcanal '43.

Outlaw—he didn't report the lead.

Ed drove to mid-block. A clapboard Victorian: four stories, peeling paint. He jumped the steps, checked out the mail slots: R. Navarette, 408.

Inside, his suitcoat around the shotgun. A long hallway, glass-fronted elevator, stairs. Up those stairs—he couldn't feel his foot-steps. The fourth-floor landing—nobody in sight. Down to 408, drop the suitcoat. Inez screaming primed him—he kicked the door in.

Four men eating sandwiches.

Jones and Navarette at a table. Fontaine on the floor. Sugar Coates by the window, picking his teeth.

No weapons in sight. Nobody moved.

Odd sounds—"You're under arrest" strangling out. Jones put his hands up. Navarette raised his hands. Fontaine laced his hands behind his head. Sugar Ray said, "Cat got your goddamn tongue, sissy?"

Ed jerked the trigger: once, twice—buckshot took off Coates' legs. Recoil—Ed braced against the doorway, aimed. Fontaine and Navarette stood up screaming; Ed SQUEEZED the trigger, blew them up in one spread. Recoil, a bad pull: half the back wall came down.

Blood spray thick—Ed stumbled, wiped his eyes. He saw Jones make the elevator.

He ran after him: slid, tripped, caught up. Jones was pushing buttons, screaming prayers—inches from the glass, "Please Jesus." Ed aimed point-blank, squeezed twice. Glass and buckshot took his head off.

Strong legs now, fuck civilian screams all around him.

Ed ran downstairs, into a crowd: blues, plainclothesmen. Hands pounded his back; men shouted his name. A voice close by: "Millard's dead. Heart attack at the Bureau."

40

RAIN FOR the funeral. A graveside service: Dudley Smith's eulogy, a priest's last words.

Every Bureau man attended: Thad Green's orders. Parker called out the press: a little ceremony after they planted Russ Millard. Bud watched Ed Exley comfort the widow—his best profile to the cameras.

A week of cameras, headlines: Ed Exley, "L.A.'s Greatest Hero"—World War II stalwart, the man who slayed the Nite Owl slayers and their accomplice. Ellis Loew told the press the three confessed before they escaped—nobody mentioned the niggers were unarmed. Ed Exley was made.

The priest's spiel picked up steam. The widow started weeping—Exley put an arm around her shoulders. Bud walked away.

Lightning, more rain—Bud ducked into the chapel. Parker's soiree was set up: lectern, chairs, a table laid out with sandwiches. More lightning—Bud looked out the window, saw the casket hit the dirt. Ashes to fucking ashes—Stens got six months, scuttlebutt had Exley and Inez a hot item: kill four jigs, get the girl.

The mourners headed up—Ellis Loew slipped, took a pratfall. Bud hit on the good stuff: Lynn, West Valley on the Kathy snuff. Let the bad shit go for now.

Into the chapel: raincoats and umbrellas dumped, a rush for seats. Parker and Exley stood by the lectern. Bud sprawled in a chair at the back.

Reporters, notepads. Front row seats: Loew, the widow Millard, Preston Exley—hot news for Dream-a-Dreamland.

Parker spoke into the mike. "This is a sad occasion, an occasion of mourning. We mourn a kind and good man and a dedicated policeman. We mark his passing with regret. The loss of Captain Russell A. Millard is the loss of Mrs. Millard, the Millard family and all of us here. It will be a hard loss to bear, but bear it we will. There is a passage I recall from somewhere in the annals of litera-ture. That passage is 'If there was no God, how could I be a Cap-tain?' It is God who will see us through our grief and our loss.

The God who allowed Russ Millard to become a captain, His captain."

Parker pulled out a small velvet case. "And life continues through our losses. The loss of one splendid policeman coincides with the emergence of another one. Edmund J. Exley, detective sergeant, has amassed a brilliant record in his ten years with the Los Angeles Police Department, three of those years given over to service in the United States Army. Ed Exley received the Distinguished Service Cross for gallantry in the Pacific Theater, and last week he evinced spectacular bravery in the line of duty. It is my honor to present him with the highest measure of honor this police department can bestow: our Medal of Valor."

Exley stepped forward. Parker opened the case, took out a gold medallion hung from a blue satin ribbon and placed it around his neck. The men shook hands—Exley had tears in his eyes. Flashbulbs popped, reporters scribbled, no applause. Parker tapped the mike.

"The Medal of Valor is a very high expression of esteem, but not one with practical everyday applications. Spiritual ramifications aside, it does not reward the recipient with the challenge of good, hard police work. Today I am going to utilize a rarely used chief's prerogative and reward Ed Exley with *work*. I am promoting him two entire ranks, to captain, and assigning him as the Los Angeles Police Department's floating divisional commander, the assignment formerly held by our much loved colleague Russ Millard."

Preston Exley stood up. Civilians stood up; the Bureau men stood on cue—Thad Green flashed them two thumbs. Scattered applause, lackluster. Ed Exley stood ramrod straight; Bud stayed sprawled in his chair. He took out his gun, kissed it, blew pretend smoke off the barrel.

41

A GALA lawn wedding, a Presbyterian service—old man Morrow called the shots and picked up the tab. June 19, 1953: the Big V ties the knot.

Miller Stanton best man; Joanie Loew—swacked on champagne punch—matron of honor. Dudley Smith the hit of the reception—stories, Gaelic songs. Parker and Green came at Ellis Loew's request;

boy captain Ed Exley showed up. The Morrows' social circle pals rounded out the guest list—and swelled old Welton's huge backyard to bursting.

Marriage vows for his close-out. Bad debts settled good: new calendar days, his "insurance policy deposition" stashed in fourteen different bank vaults. Scary vows: he pumped himself up at the altar.

Parker buried the Hudgens killing. Bracken and Patchett stalemated. Dudley called off his tail on White, bought his phony reports: no Lynn, White prowling bars at night. He staked Lynn's place for a couple of days, it looked like she had a good thing going with Bud—who always was a sucker.

Like himself.

The minister said the words; they said the words; Jack kissed his bride. Hugs, backslaps—well wishers swept them away from each other. Parker drummed up some warmth; Ed Exley worked the crowd, no sign of his Mexican girl. Nicknames now: "Shotgun Ed," "Triggerman Eddie." "L.A.'s Greatest Hero" smiles on a bag-man cop marrying up.

Jack found a spot above the pool house—a little rise with a view. Two celebrants stuck out: Karen, Exley. Give him credit: he seized the opportunity, made the Department look bold. *He* wouldn't have had the stomach for it—or the rage.

Exley. White. Himself.

Jack counted secrets: his own, whatever lived at that edge where pornography touched a dead scandal monger and lightly brushed the Nite Owl Massacre. He thought of Bud White, Ed Exley. He sent up a wedding day prayer: the Nite Owl dead and buried, safe passage for ruthless men in love.

CALENDAR

1954

EXTRACT: L.A. *Herald-Express*, June 16:

EX-POLICEMAN ARRESTED
FOR MURDEROUS
ROBBERY SPREE

RICHARD ALEX Stensland, 40, former Los Angeles police detective and a defendant in the 1951 "Bloody Christmas" police scandal, was arrested early this morning and charged with six counts of armed robbery and two counts of first-degree murder. Arrested with him at his hideout in Pacoima were Dennis "The Weasel" Burns, 43, and Lester John Miciak, 37. The other men were charged with four armed-robbery counts and two counts of first-degree murder.

The arrest raid was led by Captain Edmund J. Exley, divisional floating commander for the Los Angeles Police Department, currently assigned to head up the LAPD's Robbery Division. Assisting Captain Exley were Sergeants Duane Fisk and Donald Kleckner. Exley, whose testimony in the Bloody Christmas scandal sent Stensland to jail in 1952, told reporters: "Eyewitnesses identified photographs of the three men. We have conclusive proof that these men are responsible for stickups at six central Los Angeles liquor stores, including the robbery of Sol's Liquors in the Silverlake District on June 9. The proprietor of that store and his son were shot and killed during that robbery and eyewitnesses place both Stensland and Burns at the scene. Intensive questioning of the suspects will begin soon, and we expect to clear up many other unsolved robberies."

Stensland, Burns and Miciak offered no resistance during their arrest. They were taken to the Hall of Justice Jail, where Stensland was restrained from attacking Captain Exley.

BANNER: L.A. *Mirror-News*, June 21:

STENSLAND CONFESSES, DESCRIBES
REIGN OF ROBBERY TERROR

BANNER: L.A. *Herald-Express*, September 23:

LIQUOR STORE KILLERS CONVICTED; DEATH PENALTY FOR EX-POLICEMAN

EXTRACT: L.A. *Times*, November 11:

STENSLAND DIES FOR LIQUOR STORE KILLINGS—GUNMAN FORMER POLICEMAN

AT 10:03 yesterday morning, Richard Stensland, 41 and a former Los Angeles police officer, died in the gas chamber at San Quentin Prison for the June 9 murders of Solomon and David Abramowitz. The killings took place during a liquor store hold-up. Stensland was convicted and sentenced on September 22 and refused to appeal his sentence.

The execution went off smoothly, although Stensland appeared inebriated. Present among the press and prison officials were two LAPD detectives: Captain Edmund J. Exley, the man responsible for Stensland's capture, and Officer Wendell White, the condemned killer's former partner. Officer White visited Stensland in his death row cell on execution eve and stayed through the night with him. Assistant Warden B. D. Terwilliger denied that Officer White supplied Stensland with intoxicating liquor and denied that White viewed the execution while drunk himself. Stensland verbally abused the prison chaplain who was present and his last words were obscenities directed at Captain Exley.

1955

Hush-Hush Magazine, May 1995 Issue:

WHO KILLED SID HUDGENS?

JUSTICE IN the City of the Fallen Angels reminds us of a line from that sin-sational sepia show *Porgy and Bess*. Like "a man," it's "a sometime thing." As in for instance: if you're a well-connected contributor to demon DA Ellis Loew's slush fund and you get murdered—killer beware!!!—L.A. Chief of Police William H. Parker will spare no expense unearthing the fiend who put you on the night train to the Big Adios. But if you're a crusading journalist writing for this magazine and you get chopped into Ken-L Ration in your own living room—killer rejoice!!!—Chief Parker and his moralistic, misanthropic, mindless mongolians will sit on their hands (well worn from palming payoffs) and whistle "justice is a sometime thing" while the killer whistles Dixie.

It has now been two years since Sid Hudgens was fatally slashed in his Chapman Park living room. Two years ago the LAPD had its (sticky, graft-ridden) hands full with the infamous Nite Owl murder case, which was resolved when one of their members took the law into his own (overweeningly ambitious, opportunistic) hands and shotgunned the shotgunners to the Big Au Revoir. Sid Hudgens' murder was assigned to two flunky detectives with a total of zero "made" homicide cases between them. They, of course, did not find the killer or killers, spent most of their days here at the *Hush-Hush* office reading back issues for clues, scarfing coffee and doughnuts and ogling the comely editorial assistants who flock to *Hush-Hush* because we know where the bodies are buried ...

We at *Hush-Hush* tap the inside pulse of the City of the Fallen Angels, and we *have* investigated the Sidster's death on our own. We have gotten nowhere, and we ask the Los Angeles Police Department the following questions:

Sid's pad was ransacked. What happened to the ultra on the QT, ultra secret and ultra *Hush-Hush* files the Sidster was supposed to be keeping—sinuendo even too scalding for us to publish?

Why didn't DA Ellis Loew, elected largely on the strength of a *Hush-Hush* article exposing the peccadillos of his incumbent

opponent, give us a backscratch in return and use his legal juice
to force the LAPD to track down the Sidster's slayer?

Celebrity cop John "Jack" Vincennes, the famous dope
scourge "Big V," was a close friend of Sid's and was responsible
for many of his crusading exposés on the menace of narcotics.
Why didn't Jack (heavily connected to Ellis Loew—*we* won't
utter the word "bagman," but feel free to *think* it) investigate
the killing on his own, out of palship for his beloved buddy the
Sidster?

Unanswerable questions for now—unless *you*, the reading
public, take up the cry. Look for updates in future issues—and
remember, dear reader, you heard it first here: off the record, on
the QT and *very Hush-Hush*.

Hush-Hush Magazine, December 1955 Issue:

JUSTICE WATCH: BEWARE THE
LOEW/VINCENNES COMBINE!!!!

WE'VE PUSSYFOOTED long enough, dear reader. In our May
issue we marked the second anniversary of the fiendish murder of
ace *Hush-Hush* scribe Sid Hudgens. We lamented the fact that his
killing remains unsolved, gently prodded the Los Angeles Police
Department, DA Ellis Loew and his brother-in-law by marriage
LAPD Sergeant Jack Vincennes to do something about it, asked a
few pertinent questions and got no response. Seven months have
passed without justice being done, so here's some more questions:

Where *are* Sid Hudgens' *ultra* sin-tillating and sin-sational
secret files—the files too hot for even scalding *Hush-Hush* to
handle?

Did DA Loew quash the Hudgens murder investigation because the crusading Sidster recently published an exposé on *Badge
of Honor* producer/director Max Peltz and his bent for teenage
girls, and Peltz was a (five figure!!!) contributor to Loew's 1953
DA's campaign fund?

Has Loew ignored our pleas for justice because he's too busy
gearing up for his spring 1957 reelection campaign? Is Jack "We
won't use the word 'Bagman'" Vincennes again shaking down
Hollywoodites for contributions for brother-in-law Ellis and thus
unable to investigate the Sidster's death?

More on the Big-time Big V:

Is Vincennes, dope-buster supreme, on the sauce and feuding with his much younger rich-girl wife, who persuaded him to leave his beloved Narco Division, but now frets over his working the hazardous LAPD Surveillance Detail????

Fuel for thought, dear reader—and a gentle prodding for belated justice. The search for justice for Sid Hudgens continues. Remember, dear reader: you heard it first here, off the record, on the QT and *very Hush-Hush*.

1956

"Crimewatch" feature,
Hush-Hush Magazine, October 1956 Issue:

GANGLAND DROUGHT AS COHEN PAROLE APPROACHES: WILL FEAST FOLLOW FAMINE WITH THE MICKSTER REDUX?

YOU, DEAR reader, probably haven't noticed, since you're a law-abiding citizen who relies on *Hush-Hush* to keep you abreast of the dark and sin-sational side of life. This publication has been accused of being sin-ical, but we're also sin-cere in our desire to inform you of the perils of crime, organized and otherwise, which is why this periodical periodically offers a "Crimewatch" feature. This month we offer a palpably percolating potpourri centering on malicious L.A. mob activity or the lack of it, our focus the currently incarcerated Meyer Harris Cohen, 43, also known as the misanthropic Mickster, the inimitable Mickey C.

The Mick has been reposing at McNeil Island Federal pen since November of 1951, and he should be paroled sometime next year, certainly by the end of 1957. You all know Mickey by reputation: he's the dapper little gent who ruled the L.A. rackets circa '45 to '51, until Uncle Sammy popped him for income tax evasion. He's a headline grabber, he's a big mocher, face it: he's a mensch. And he's up at McNeil, freezing his toches in the admittedly plush cell, his pet bulldog Mickey Cohen, Jr., keeping his tootsies warm, his money man Davey Goldman, also convicted of tax beefs, warming a cell down the hall. L.A. gangland activity has been—enjoying? enduring?—a strange lull since Mickey packed his PJs for Puget Sound, and we at *Hush-Hush*, privy to many unnamable insider sources, have a theory as to what's been shaking. Listen close, dear reader: this is off the record, on the QT and *very Hush-Hush*.

November '51: adiós Mickey, pack a toothbrush and don't forget to write. Before catching the McNeil Island Express, the Mickster informs his number two man, Morris Jahelka, that he (Mo) will remain titular boss of Kingdom Cohen, which Mickey has "long-term loan" divested to various legit, non-criminal businessmen that he trusts, to be quietly run by out-of-town muscle on a drastically scaled-down basis. Mickey may come off like a vicious buffoon, but Mrs. Cohen's little boy has a head on his simian shoulders.

Are you on our wavelength so far, dear reader? Yes? Good, now listen even more closely.

Mickey languishes in his cell, living the prison life of Riley, and time goes by. The Mick gets percentage fees from his "franchise holders," funneled straight to Swiss bank accounts, and when he's paroled he'll get "give-back fees" and have Kingdom Cohen returned to him on a platter. He'll rebuild his evil empire and happy days will be here again.

Such is the power of the ubiquitous Mickey C. that for several years no upstart gangsters try to crash his lulled-down, on-siesta rackets. Jack "The Enforcer" Whalen, however, a well-known thug/gambler, somehow knows of Mickey's plan to let sleeping dogs snooze while he's stuck in stir and the police are gratefully twiddling their thumbs with no mobster nests to swat. Whalen does not attack the diminutized Kingdom Cohen—he simply builds up a rival, strictly bookmaking kingdom with no fear of reprisals.

Meanwhile, what has happened to some of the Mickster's chief goons? Well, nebbish-like Mo Jahelka keeps triplicate sets of books for the franchise holders, whiz at figures that he is, and Davey Goldman, stuck in stir with his boss, walks Mickey Cohen, Jr., around the McNeil Island yard. Abe Teitlebaum, Cohen muscle goon, owns a delicatessen that features greasy sandwiches named after Borscht Belt comedians, and Lee Vachss, Mr. Icepick To The Ear, sells patent medicine. *Our* favorite Mickey misanthrope, Johnny Stompanato (sometimes known as "Oscar" because of his Academy Award-size appendage), nurses a long-term case of the hots for Lana Turner, and may have returned to his old pre-Cohen ways: running blackmail/extortion rackets. Assuming that Whalen and Mickey don't collide upon the Mick's release, things look hunky-dory and copacetic, don't they? Gangland amity all around?

Perhaps *no*.

Item: in August of 1954, John Fisher Diskant, an alleged Cohen franchise holder, was gunned down outside a motel in Culver City. No suspects, no arrests, current disposition: the case reposes in the open file of the Culver City PD.

Item: May 1955: two alleged Cohen prostitution bosses, franchise holders both—Nathan Janklow and George Palevsky—are

gunned down outside the Torch Song Tavern in Riverside. No
suspects, no arrests, current disposition: the Riverside County
sheriff says case closed due to lack of evidence.

Item: July 1956: Walker Ted Turow, known drug peddler who
had recently stated his desire to "push white horse very large and
become a bonaroo racketeer" is found shot to death at his pad in
San Pedro. You guessed it: no clues, no suspects, no arrests, current disposition with the LAPD's Harbor Division: open file,
we're not holding our breath.

Now, dig it, children: all four of these gang-connected or
would be gang-connected chumps were shot dead by three-man
trigger gangs. The cases were barely investigated because the respective investigating agencies considered the victims lowlifes
whose deaths did not merit justice. We wish we could say that
ballistics reports indicate that the same guns were used for all
three shootings, but they weren't—although .30-30 ripples pistols
were the killers' MO all three times. And we at *Hush-Hush* know
that no interagency effort has been launched to catch the killers.
In fact, we at *Hush-Hush* are the first even to connect the crimes
in theory. Tsk, tsk. We *do* know that Jack Whalen and his chief
factotums are alibied up tight as a crab's pincer for the times of
the killings and that Mickey C. and Davey G. have been questioned
and have no idea who the bad boys are. Intriguing, right, dear
reader? So far, no overt moves have been made to take over siesta
time Kingdom Cohen, but we have word that Mickey minion
Morris Jahelka has packed up and moved to Florida, scared wit-
less ...

And the Mickster is soon to be paroled. What will happen
then??????

Remember, dear reader, you saw it here first. Off the record,
on the QT and *very Hush-Hush*.

1957

CONFIDENTIAL LAPD REPORT: compiled
   by Internal Affairs Division, dated 2/10/57
INVESTIGATING OFFICER: Sgt. D.W. Fisk,
   Badge 6129, IAD. Submitted at the request of
   Deputy Chief Thad Green, Chief of Detectives
SUBJECT: White, Wendell A., Homicide Division

Sir:

   When you initiated this investigation you stated that Officer
White passing the sergeant's exam with high marks after two failing attempts and nine years in the Bureau startled you, especially
in the light of Lt. Dudley Smith's recent promotion to captain.
I have thoroughly investigated Officer White and have come up
with many contradictory items which should interest you. Since
you already have access to Officer White's arrest record and personnel sheet, I will concentrate solely on those items.

   1. White, who is unmarried and without immediate family,
has been intimately involved on a sporadic basis with one Lynn
Margaret Bracken, age 33, for the past several years. This woman,
the owner of Veronica's Dress Shop in Santa Monica, is rumored
(unsubstantiated by police records) to be an ex-prostitute.

   2. White, who was brought into Homicide by Lt. Smith in
1952, has, of course, not turned into the superior case man that
(now) Capt. Smith assumed he would be. His 1952–53 work under
Lt. Smith with the Surveillance Detail was, of course, legendary,
and resulted in White's killing two men in the line of duty. Since
his (April 1953) shooting of Nite Owl case collateral suspect
Sylvester Fitch, White has served under Lt./Capt. Smith with little
formal distinction. However (rather amazingly), there have been
no excessive force complaints filed against him (see White's personnel sheets 1948–51 for records of his previous dismissed complaints). It is known that during those years and up until the spring
of 1953 White visited paroled wife beaters and verbally and/or
physically abused them. Evidence points to the fact that these
illegal forays have not recurred for almost four years. White
remains volatile (as you know, he received a departmental reprimand for punching out windows in the Homicide pen when he
received word that his former partner, Sgt. R. A. Stensland, had

been sentenced to death), but it is known that he has sometimes avoided work with Lt./Capt. Smith's Mobster Squad, straining his relationship with Smith, his Bureau mentor. Citing the violent nature of the assignment, White has been quoted as saying, "I've got no more stomach left for that stuff." Interesting, when given White's reputation and past record.

3. In spring 1956, White took nine months' accumulated sick leave and vacation time when Capt. E. J. Exley rotated in as acting commander of Homicide. (A well-known hatred exists between White and Capt. Exley, deriving from the 1951 Christmas brutality affair.) During his time off from duty, White (whose Academy scores indicate only average intelligence and below average literacy) attended criminology and forensics classes at USC and took and passed (at his own expense) the FBI's "Criminal Investigation Procedures" seminar at Quantico, Virginia. White had failed the sergeant's exam twice before embarking on these studies, and on his third attempt passed with a score of 89. His sergeantcy should come in before the end of the 1957 calendar year.

4. In November 1954, R. A. Stensland was executed at San Quentin. White asked for and received permission to attend the execution. He spent the night before the execution on death row drinking with Stensland. (I was told the assistant warden overlooked this infraction of prison rules out of a regard for Stensland's ex-policeman status.) Capt. Exley also attended the execution, and it is not known if he and White had words before or after the event.

5. I saved the most interesting item for last. It is interesting in that it illustrates White's continued (and perhaps increasing) tendency to overinvolve himself in matters pertaining to abused and (now) murdered women. I.e., White has shown undue curiosity in a number of unsolved prostitute killings that he believes to be connected: murders that have taken place in California and various parts of the West over the past several years. The victims' names, DODs and locations of death are:

Jane Mildred Hamsher, 3/08/51, San Diego
Kathy NMI Janeway, 4/19/53, Los Angeles
Sharon Susan Palwick, 8/29/53, Bakersfield, Calif.
Sally NMI DeWayne, 11/02/55, Needles, Ariz.
Chrissie Virginia Renfro, 7/16/56, San Francisco

White has told other Homicide officers that he thinks evidential similarities point to one killer, and he has traveled (at his own expense) to the above-listed cities where the crimes occurred. Naturally, the detectives that White has talked to considered him a pest and were reluctant to share information with him, and it is not known whether he has made progress toward solving any of the above cases. Lt. J. S. DiCenzo, Commander of the West Valley Station squad, stated that he thinks White's hooker-killing fixation dates back to the time of the Nite Owl case, when White became personally concerned about the murder of a young prostitute (Kathy Janeway) he was acquainted with.

6. All in all, a surprising investigation. Personally, I admire White's initiative and persistence in pursuing a sergeantcy and his (albeit untoward) tenacity in the matter of the prostitute homicides. A list of my interview references will follow in a separate memo.

Respectfully,
Sgt. D. W. Fisk, 6129, IAD

CONFIDENTIAL LAPD REPORT: Compiled by Internal Affairs Division, dated 3/11/57
INVESTIGATING OFFICER: Sgt. Donald
    Kleckner, badge 688, IAD. Submitted at the
    request of William H. Parker, Chief of Police
SUBJECT: Vincennes, John, Sergeant,
    Surveillance Detail

Sir:

You stated that you wished to explore, in light of Sgt. Vincennes' deteriorating duty performance, the advisability of offering him early retirement by stress pension before the twentieth anniversary of his LAPD appointment comes up in May 1958. I deem that measure inappropriate at this time. Granted, Vincennes is an obvious alcoholic; granted also, his alcoholism cost him his job with *Badge of Honor* and thus cost the LAPD a small fortune in promotional considerations. Granted again, at 42 he is too old to be working a high-risk assignment such as the Surveillance Detail. As for his admittedly deteriorating performance, it is only deteriorating because Vincennes was, during his Narcotics Division heyday, a bold and inspired policeman. From my interviews I have

concluded that he does not drink on duty and that his deteriorating performance can best be summed up by "sluggishness" and
"bad reflexes." Moreover, should Vincennes reject an early retirement offer, my guess is that the pension board would back him up.

Sir, I know that you consider Vincennes a disgrace as a policeman. I agree with you, but advise you to consider his connection
to District Attorney Loew. The Department needs Loew to prosecute our cases, as your new chief aide, Capt. Smith, will tell you.
Vincennes continues to solicit funds and run errands for Loew,
and should Loew, as expected, be reelected next week, he would
most likely intercede if you decided to pressure Vincennes out
of the Department. My recommendation is as follows: keep
Vincennes on Surveillance until 3/58, when a new commander
is scheduled to rotate in with his own replacement officers, then
assign him to menial duties in a patrol division until his 5/15/58
retirement date arrives. At that time, Vincennes, humbled by a return
to uniformed duty, could probably be persuaded to separate from
the Department with all due speed.

Respectfully,
Donald J. Kleckner, IAD

BANNER: L.A. *Times*, March 15:

LOEW REELECTED IN LANDSLIDE;
STATEHOUSE BID NEXT?

EXTRACT: L.A. *Times*, July 8:

MICKEY COHEN WOUNDED IN
PRISON YARD ATTACK

MCNEIL ISLAND Federal Prison officials announced that yesterday mobsters Meyer Harris "Mickey" Cohen and David "Davey"
Goldman were wounded in a vicious daylight attack.

Cohen and Goldman, both slated to be paroled in September,
were watching a softball game on the prison yard when three
hooded assailants wielding pipes and handmade "shivs" descended.
Goldman was stabbed twice in the shoulder and beaten viciously
about the head, and Cohen escaped with superficial puncture

wounds. Prison doctors said that Goldman's injuries are severe and that he may have suffered irreparable brain damage. The assailants escaped, and at this moment a massive investigation is being conducted to discover who they are. McNeil administrator R. J. Wolf said, "We believe this was a so-called death contract, contracted to in-prison inmates by outside sources. Every effort will be made to get to the bottom of this incident."

Hush-Hush Magazine, October 1957 Issue:

MICKEY COHEN BACK IN L.A.!!! ARE HIS BAD OLD GOOD TIMES HERE TO STAY???

HE WAS the most colorful mobster the City of Fallen Angels had ever seen, Hepcat—and to dig his act at the Mocambo or the Troc was like watching Daddy-o Stradivarius chop a fiddle from a tree trunk. He'd crack jokes written by gagster Davey Goldman, slip fat envelopes to the bagmen from the Sheriff's Department and do a wicked Lindy hop with his squeeze Audrey Anders or the other comely quail sashaying on the premises. Eyes would dart to his table and the ladies would surreptitiously survey his chief bodyguard, Johnny Stompanato, and wonder, "Is he really *that* large?" Sycophants, stooges, glad-handers, pissanters and general rimbamboos would drop by the Mickster's side, to be rewarded with jokes, a backslap, a handout. The Mick was a soft touch for crippled kids, stray dogs, the Salvation Army and the United Jewish Appeal. The Mick also ran bookmaking, loan-sharking, gambling, prostitution and dope rackets and killed an average of a dozen people a year. Nobody's perfect, right, Hepcat? You leave your toenail trimmings on the bathroom floor, Mickey sends people on the night train to Slice City.

Dig it, Hepcat: people also tried to kill Mickey!!! A mensch like that?—No!!!! Yes, Hepcat, what goes around comes around. The trouble was, the Mick had more lives than the proverbial feline, kept dodging bombs, bullets and dynamite while those around him went down dead, survived six years at McNeil Island Pen, including a recent shiv/pipe attack—and now he's back! Sy Devore, watch out: the Mickster will be in for a few dozen shiny new sharkskin suits; Trocadero and Mocambo cigarette girls, get ready for some C-note tips. Mickey and his entourage will soon descend on the Sunset Strip, and—*very Hush-Hush*—yes, ladies, Johnny Stompanato is *that* large, but he only has eyes for Lana

Turner, and word is that he and Lana have been playing more than footsie lately ...

But back to Mickey C. Avid *Hush-Hush* readers will recall our October '56 Crimewatch feature, where we speculated on the gangland "lull" that has been going on since the Mick went to stir. Well, some *still* unsolved deaths occurred, and that pipe/shiv attack that wounded Mickey and left his stooge Davey Goldman a vegetable? Well ... they never got the hooded inmate assailants who attempted to send Mickey and his man to Slice City ...

Call this a warning, children: he's a mensch, he's local color to the nth degree, he's the marvelous, malevolent benevolent Mickster. He's tough to kill, 'cause innocent bystanders take the hot lead with his name on it. Mickey's back, and his old gang might be forming up again. Hepcat, when you club hop on the sin-tillating Sunset Strip, bring a bulletproof vest in case Meyer Harris Cohen sits nearby.

EXTRACT: L.A. *Herald-Express*, November 10:

MOBSTER COHEN SURVIVES BOMB ATTEMPT

A BOMB exploded under the home of paroled mobster Mickey Cohen early this morning. Cohen and his wife, Lavonne, were not injured, but the bomb did destroy a wardrobe room that housed three hundred of Cohen's custom-made suits. Cohen's pet bulldog, alseep nearby, was treated for a singed tail at Westside Veterinary Hospital and released. Cohen could not be reached for comment.

Confidential letter, addendum to the outside agency investigation report required on all incoming commanders of Internal Affairs Division, Los Angeles Police Department. Requested by Chief William H. Parker.

11/29/57

Dear Bill—

God, we were sergeants together! It seems like a million years ago, and you were right. I did relish the chance to slip briefly back into harness and play detective again. I felt slightly treacherous interviewing officers behind Ed and Preston's back, but again you were right: firstly in your overall policy of outside agency validation for incoming IA chiefs, and secondly in choosing an ex-policeman predisposed to like Ed Exley to query brother officers on the man. Hell, Bill, we both love Ed. Which makes me happy to state that, basic investigation aside (the DA's Bureau is conducting it, aren't they?), I have nothing but positives to report.

I spoke to a number of Detective Bureau men and a number of uniformed officers. One consensus of opinion held: Ed Exley is very well respected. Some officers considered his shooting of the Nite Owl suspects injudicious, most considered it bold and a few tagged it as intentionally grandstanding. Whatever, my opinion is that that act is what Ed Exley is most remembered for and that it has largely eclipsed the bad feelings he generated by serving as an informant in the Bloody Christmas matter. Ed's jump from sergeant to captain was greatly resented, but he is considered to have proven his mettle as divisional floater: the man has run seven divisions in under five years, established many valuable contacts and has earned the general respect of the men serving under him. Your basic concern: that his "not one of the boys" nature would provoke anger when it was learned that he would be running IA, seems so far to be unfounded. Word is out that Ed will take over IA early in '58, and it is tacitly assumed that he will vigorously pursue the assignment. My guess is that his reputation for sternness and intelligence will deter many potentially bent cops into sticking to the straight and narrow.

It is also known that Ed has passed the exam for promotion to inspector and is first on the promotion list. Here some notes of discord appear. It is generally viewed that Thad Green will retire in the next several years and that Ed might well be chosen to replace him as chief of detectives. The great majority of the men I spoke to voiced the opinion that Capt. Dudley Smith, older, much more experienced and more the leader type, should have the job.

Some personal observations to supplant your outside agency report. (1) Ed's relationship with Inez Soto is physically intimate, but I know he would never violate departmental regs by cohabitating with her. Inez is a great kid, by the way. She's become good friends with Preston, Ray Dieterling and myself, and her public relations work for Dream-a-Dreamland is near brilliant. And so what if she's a Mexican? (2) I spoke to IA Sgts. Fisk and Kleckner about Ed—the two worked Robbery under him, are junior straight-arrow Exley types and are positively ecstatic that their hero is about to become their CO. (3) As someone who has known Ed Exley since he was a child, and as an ex-police officer, I'll go on the record: he's as good as his father and I'd be willing to bet that if you made a tally you'd see that he's made more major cases than any LAPD detective ever. I'm also willing to bet that he's wise to this affectionate little ploy you've initiated: all good cops have intelligence networks.

I'll close with a favor. I'm thinking of writing a book of reminiscences about my years with the Department. Would it be possible for me to borrow the file on the Loren Atherton case? Without Preston and Ed knowing, please—I don't want them to think I've gone arty-farty in my waning years.

I hope this little addendum serves you well. Best to Helen, and thanks for the opportunity to be a cop again.

Sincerely,
Art De Spain

LAPD TRANSFER BULLETINS

1. Officer Wendell A. White, Homicide Division to the Hollywood Station Detective Squad (and to assume the rank of Sergeant), effective 1/2/58.

2. Sgt. John Vincennes, Surveillance Detail to Wilshire Division Patrol, effective when a replacement officer is assigned, but no later than 3/15/58.

3. Capt. Edmund J. Exley to permanent duty station: Commander, Internal Affairs Division, effective 1/2/58.

PART THREE
INTERNAL AFFAIRS

42

THE DINING Car had a New Year's hangover: drooping crepe paper, "1958" signs losing spangles. Ed took his favorite booth: a view of the lounge, his image in a mirror. He marked the time— 3:24 P.M., 1/2/58. Let Bob Gallaudet show up late—anything to stretch the moment.

In an hour, the ceremony: Captain E. J. Exley assumes a permanent duty station—Commander, Internal Affairs Division. Gallaudet was bringing the results of his outside agency validation—the DA's Bureau had gone over his personal life with a magnifying glass. He'd pass—his personal life was squeaky clean, putting the Nite Owl boys in the ground outgunned his Bloody Christmas snitching—he'd known it for years.

Ed sipped coffee, eyes on the mirror. His reflection: a man a month from thirty-six who looked forty-five. Blond hair gone gray; crease lines in his forehead. Inez said his eyes were getting smaller and colder; his wire rims made him look harsh. He'd told her harsh was better than soft—boy captains needed help. She'd laughed—it was a few years ago, when they were still laughing.

He placed the conversation: late '54, Inez analytical—"You're a ghoul for watching that man Stensland die." A year and a half post-Nite Owl; today made four years and nine months. A look in the mirror, a claim on those years—and what he'd had with Inez.

His killings pushed Bud White out: four deaths eclipsed one death. Those first months she was all his: he'd proven himself to her specifications. He bought her a house down the block; she loved their gentle sex; she accepted Ray Dieterling's job offer. Dieterling fell in love with Inez and her story: a beautiful rape victim abandoned by her family dovetailed with his own losses— once divorced, once widowered, his son Paul dead in an avalanche, his son Billy a homosexual. Ray and Inez became father and daughter—colleagues, deep friends. Preston Exley and Art De Spain joined Dieterling in devotion—a circle of hardcase men and a woman who made them grateful for the chance to feel gentle.

Inez took friendships from a fantasy kingdom: the builders, the second generation—Billy Dieterling, Timmy Valburn. A chatty little clique: they talked up Hollywood gossip, poked fun at male foibles. The word "men" sent them into gales of laughter. They made fun of policemen and played charades in a house bought by Captain Ed Exley.

All claims came back to Inez.

After the killings, he had nightmares: were they innocent? Impotent rage made his finger jerk the trigger; the dramatic resolution made the Department look so good that little facts like "Unarmed" and "Not Dangerous" would never surface to crush him. Inez stilled his fears with a statement: the rapists drove her to Sylvester Fitch's house in the middle of the night and left her there—giving them time to take down the Nite Owl. She never told the police about it because she did not want to recount the especially ugly things that Fitch did to her. He was relieved: *guilty* dead men shored up the justice in his rage.

Inez.

Time passed, the glow wore off—her pain and his heroism couldn't sustain them. Inez knew he'd never marry her: a high-ranking cop, a Mexican wife—career suicide. His love held by threads; Inez grew remote—a sometime lover in practice. Two people molded by extraordinary events, a powerful supporting cast hovering: the Nite Owl dead, Bud White.

White's face in the green room: pure hatred while Dick Stensland sucked gas. A look at Dicky Stens dying, a look his way, no words necessary. Leave time called in so they wouldn't have to work together when he took over Homicide. He'd surpassed his brother, grown closer to his father. His major case record was astounding; in May he'd be an inspector, in a few years he'd compete with Dudley Smith for chief of detectives. Smith had always given him a wide berth and a wary respect couched in contempt—and Dudley was the most feared man in the LAPD. Did he know that his rival feared only one thing: revenge perpetrated by a thug/cop without the brains to be imaginative?

The bar was filling up: DA's personnel, a few women. The last time with Inez was bad—she just serviced the man who paid the mortgage. Ed smiled at a tall woman—she turned away.

"Congratulations, Cap. You're Boy Scout clean."

Gallaudet sat down—strained, nervous.

"Then why do you look so grim? Come on, Bob, we're partners."

"*You're* clean, but Inez was put under loose surveillance for two weeks, just routine. Ed ... oh shit, she's sleeping with Bud White."

* * *

The ceremony—one big blur.

Parker made a speech: policemen were subject to the same temptations as civilians, but needed to keep their baser urges in check to a greater degree in order to serve as moral exemplars for a society increasingly undercut by the pervasive influence of Communism, crime, liberalism and general moral turpitude. A morally upright exemplar was needed to command the division that served as a guarantor of police morality, and Captain Edmund J. Exley, war hero and hero of the Nite Owl murder case, was that man.

He made a speech himself: more pap on morality. Duane Fisk and Don Kleckner wished him luck; he read their minds through his blur: they wanted his chief assistant spots. Dudley Smith winked, easy to read: "I will be our next chief of detectives—not you." Excuses for leaving took forever—he made it to her place with the blur clearing hard.

6:00—Inez got home around 7:00. Ed let himself in, waited with the lights out.

Time dragged; Ed watched his watch hands move. 6:50—a key in the door.

"Exley, are you skulking? I saw your car outside."

"No lights. I don't want to see your face." Noises—keys rattling, a purse dropped to the floor. "And I don't want to see all that faggot Dreamland junk you've plastered on the walls."

"You mean the walls of the house you paid for?"

"You said it, not me."

Sounds: Inez resting herself against the door. "Who told you?"

"It doesn't matter."

"Are you going to ruin him for it?"

"*Him?* No, there's no way I could do it without making myself look even more foolish than I've been. And you can say his name."

No answer.

"Did you help him with the sergeant's exam? He didn't have the brains to pass it on his own."

No answer.

"How long? How many fucks behind my back?"

No answer.

"How long, *puta*?"

Inez sighed. "Maybe four years. On and off, when we each needed a friend."

"You mean when you didn't need me?"

"I mean when I got exhausted being treated like a rape victim. When I got terrified of how far you'd go to impress me."

Ed said, "I took you out of Boyle Heights and gave you a life."

Inez said, "Exley, you started to scare me. I just wanted to be a girl seeing a guy, and Bud gave me that."

"Don't you say his name in this house."

"You mean in *your* house?"

"I gave you a decent life. You'd be pounding tortillas on a rock if it wasn't for me."

"*Querido*, you turn ugly so well."

"How many other lies, Inez? How many other lies besides him?"

"Exley, let's break this off."

"No, give me a rundown."

No answer.

"How many other men? How many other lies?"

No answer.

"Tell me."

No answer.

"You fucking whore, after what I did for you. *Tell me*."

No answer.

"I let you be friends with my father. *Preston Exley is your friend because of me.* How many other men have you fucked behind my back? How many other lies after what I did for you?"

Inez, a small voice. "You don't want to know."

"Yes I do, you fucking whore."

Inez pushed off the door. "Here's the only lie that counts, and it's all for you. Not even my sweetie pie Bud knows it, so I hope it makes you feel special."

Ed stood up. "Lies don't scare me."

Inez laughed. "*Everything* scares you."

No answer.

Inez, calm. "The *negritos* who hurt me couldn't have killed the people at the Nite Owl, because they were with me the whole night. They never left my sight. I lied because I didn't want you to feel bad that you'd killed four men for me. And you want to know what the *big* lie is? You and your precious absolute justice."

Ed pushed out the door, hands on his ears to kill the roar. Dark, cold outside—he saw Dick Stens strapped down dead.

43

BUD CHECKED out his new badge: "Sergeant" where "Police-man" used to be. He put his feet up on his desk, said goodbye to Homicide.

His cubicle was a mess—five years' worth of paper. Dudley said the Hollywood squad transfer was just temporary—his sergeantcy shocked the brass, Thad Green was juking him for his window-punching number: Dick Stens green room bound, left/right hooks into glass. A fair trade: he never became a crackerjack case man because the only cases that mattered were case closed and case/cases shitcanned. Transfer blues: leaving Bureau HQ meant no early crack at dead-body reports—a good way to keep tabs on the Kathy Janeway case and the hooker snuff string he knew tied to it.

Stuff to take with him:

His new nameplate—"Sergeant Wendell White," a picture of Lynn: brunette, goodbye Veronica Lake.

A Mobster Squad photo: him and Dud at the Victory Motel. Mobster Squad goodies—brass knuckles, a ball-bearing sap—he might leave them behind.

Lock and key stuff:

His FBI and forensics class diplomas; Dick Stensland's legacy: six grand from his robbery take. Dick's last words—a note a guard passed him.

> Partner—
>   I regret the bad things I done. I especially regret the people I hurt when I was a policeman who just got in my way when I was feeling mean and the Christmas guys and the liquor store man and his son. It's too late to change it all. So all I can do is say I'm sorry, which don't mean anything worthwhile. I'll try to take my punishment like a man. I keep think-ing it could be you instead of me who did what I did, that it was just the luck of the draw and I know maybe you've thought the same thing. I wish being

sorry counted for more with guys like you and me. I payed the piper and called the tune and all that, but Exley kept the piper tune going when he didn't have to and if I got a last request it is that you get him for his share and don't be stupid and do something dumb like I would have did. Use your brains and that money I told you where to find and give it to him good, a good one in the keester from Sergeant Dick Stens. Good luck, partner. I can't hardly believe that when you read this I'll be dead.

Dick

Double-locked in the bottom drawer:

His file on the Janeway/hooker snuffs, his private Nite Owl file—textbook pure, like he learned in school.

Two cases that proved he was a real detective; Dick's shot at Ed Exley. He pulled them out, read them over—college boy stuff all the way.

The Janeway string.

When things sizzled down with Lynn, he started looking for stuff to jazz him. Prowling for women didn't cut it—ditto his on-and-off thing with Inez. He flunked the sergeant's exam twice, paid his way through school with Dick's stash, worked the Mobster Squad part-time: meeting trains, planes, buses, taking would-be racketeers to the Victory Motel, beating the shit out of them and escorting them back to planes, trains, buses. Dud called it "containment"; he called it too much to take and still like looking at yourself in the mirror. Good cases never came his way at Homicide: Thad Green bootjacked them, assigned different men. His classes taught him interesting stuff about forensics, criminal psychology and procedure—he decided to apply what he'd learned to an old case that still simmered with him: the Kathy Janeway job.

He read Joe DiCenzo's case file: no leads, no suspects, written off as a random sex kill. He read the autopsy reconstruction: Kathy beaten to death, face blows, a man with rings on both fists. B+ secretor semen in the mouth, rectum, vagina—three separate ejaculations, the bastard took his time. He got a flash backed up by case histories: a sex fiend like that doesn't kill just once, then go back to twiddling his thumbs.

He started paper-prowling—the kind of thing he used to hate.

No similar solveds or unsolveds anywhere in the LAPD and Sheriff's Department files—the search took him eight months. He worked his way through other police agencies—Stens' money for a stake. Zero for Orange County, San Bernardino County; four months in and a match with the San Diego PD: Jane Mildred Hamsher, 19, hooker, DOD 3/8/51, the same handwork and three-way rape: no clues, no suspects, case closed.

He read LAPD and SDPD MO files and got nowhere; he remembered Dudley warning him off the Janeway case—ragging him for going crazy on woman basher jobs. He went ahead anyway; paydirt on a tri-state teletype: Sharon Susan Palwick, 20, hooker, DOD 8/29/53, Bakersfield, California. The same specs: no suspects, no leads, case closed. Dud never mentioned the teletype—if he knew it existed.

He went to Diego and Bakersfield—read files, pestered detectives who worked the cases. They were bored with the jobs—and gave him the brush. He tried reconstructing the time and place element: who was in those cities on the dates of the killings. He checked old train, bus and airplane records, got no crossover names, put out standing tri-state teletypes requesting information on the killer's MO, asking for call-ins should his killer ply that MO again. Nothing came in on the info request; three dead-body reports trickled in over the years: Sally NMI DeWayne, 17, hooker, Needles, Arizona, 11/2/55; Chrissie Virginia Renfro, 21, hooker, San Francisco, 7/14/56; Maria NMI Waldo, 20, hooker, Seattle two months ago: 11/28/57. The call-ins logged in late, the same results: goose egg. Every angle, every schoolboy approach tapped—for nothing. Kathy Janeway and five other prostitutes raped, beaten to death—open stuff only with him.

A 116-page dead-end file to take to the Hollywood squad—his own case, dead for now.

And his major case—pages and pages he kept checking over. Dick Stens' case: nails in Ed Exley's coffin. He got goose bumps just saying the words.

The Nite Owl case.

Starting in on the Janeway job brought it back: the Duke Cathcart/smut connection, evidence withheld, insider stuff to fuck Exley. Timing was against him then: he didn't have the smarts to pursue it, the niggers escaped, Exley gunned them down. The Nite Owl case was closed—the weird side bits around it forgotten. Years passed; he went back to the Janeway snuff, discovered a string. And little Kathy made him think Nite Owl, Nite Owl, Nite Owl.

Brainwork.

Back in '53, Dwight Gilette and Cindy Benavides—Kathy Janeway KA's—told him a guy who came on like Duke Cathcart was talking up muscling Cathcart's pimp business. What "pimp business"?—Duke had only two skags in his stable, but he had been talking up going into the smut biz—at first it sounded like a pipe dream coming from a major-league pipe dreamer—but it got validated when the Englekling brothers came forward and told their story of Cathcart approaching them with a deal: they'd print the smut, he'd distribute it, they'd approach Mickey Cohen for financing.

Cut to facts:

He was inside Duke's pad post–Nite Owl. It was tidied up and print-wiped; Duke's clothes had been gone through. The San Bernardino Yellow Pages were ruffled—the pages for printing shops especially. Pete and Bax Englekling owned a printshop in San Berdoo; Nite Owl victim Susan Nancy Lefferts was origin-ally from San Berdoo.

Cut to the coroner's report:

The examining pathologist based his identification of Cathcart's body on two things: dental plate *fragments* cross-checked against Cathcart's prison dental records and the "D.C." monogrammed sports jacket the stiff was wearing. The plate fragments were stand-ard California prison issue—any ex-con who'd done time in the state penal system could have plastic like that in his mouth.

Cut to his insider skinny:

Kathy Janeway mentioned a "cute" scar on Duke's chest. There was no mention of that scar anywhere in Doc Layman's autopsy report—and Cathcart's chest was not obliterated by shotgun pellets. A final kicker: the Nite Owl stiff was measured at 5'8"; Cathcart's prison measurement chart listed him at 5'9¼".

Conclusion:

A Cathcart impersonator was killed at the Nite Owl.

Cut to:

Smut.

Cindy Benavides said Duke was getting ready to push it; Ad Vice was investigating smut back then—he'd read through Squad 4's reports—all the men reported no leads, Russ Millard died, the fuck book gig fell by the wayside. The Englekling brothers told their story of Duke Cathcart's smut approach, how they visited Mickey Cohen in prison, how he refused to bankroll the deal. They thought Cohen ordered the Nite Owl snuffs out of batshit moral convictions—a ridiculous idea—but what if some kind of Nite Owl plot got started with the Mick? Exley submitted a report that said he and Bob Gallaudet talked up that theory, but the jigs escaped around then—and the Nite Owl got pinned on them.

Cut to:

His theory.

What if Cohen told some prison punk about the Cathcart/ Englekling plan—or his man Davey Goldman did? What if the punk got paroled, talked up crashing Duke's stable while he was really just shoring up juice for his Duke impersonation? What if he killed Duke, stole some of his clothes and ended up at the Nite Owl by chance—because Duke frequented the place, or more likely—*as part of some kind of criminal rendezvous that went bad, the killers leaving, coming back with shotguns, blasting the Cathcart impersonator and five innocent bystanders to make it look like a robbery?*

Flaw in his theory so far:

He'd checked McNeil parole records: only Negroes, Latins and white men too large or too small to be the Cathcart impersonator were released between the time of the Cohen–Englekling brothers meeting and the Nite Owl. But—Cohen could have talked up the Cathcart smut proposal, word could have leaked to the outside, the impersonation could have been four or five times fucking removed.

Theories on top of theories, theories that proved he had the brains to call himself a detective:

Say the Nite Owl snuffs came out of smut intrigue. That meant the niggers were innocent, the real killers planted the shotguns in Ray Coates' car—which meant that the purple Merc seen outside the Nite Owl was a coincidence—the killers couldn't have known that three spooks were recently seen discharging shotguns in Griffith Park and would rank as natural first suspects. Somehow the killers found Coates' car before the LAPD—and planted the shotguns, print-wiped. It could have happened a half dozen ways.

1. Coates, in jail, could have told his lawyer where the car was stashed; the killers or their front man could have approached him

for the information—or could have coerced him into making Coates talk.

2. The jigs could have spilled the location to one of their fellow inmates—maybe a planted inmate in with the killers.

3. His favorite, because it was simplest: the killers were smarter than the LAPD, did their own garage search, checked out garages behind deserted houses first—while the police went at it in grids.

Or the spooks told other inmates, who got released and got approached by the killers; or—unlikely—a cop finger man told them how the block search was breaking down. Impossible to check it all out: the Hall of Justice Jail destroyed its 1935–55 records to make way for more storage space.

Or the jigs really were guilty.

Or it was some other bunch of boogies riding around, blasting the air in Griffith Park, killing six people at the Nite Owl. Their 1948–50 Ford/Chevy/Merc was never located because the purple paint job was homemade, never listed on a DMV form.

Brainwork from a guy who never thought he had much of a brain—and he didn't make a shine gang for the snuffs, because—

The Englekling brothers sold their printshop mid-'54, then dropped off the face of the earth. Two years ago, he issued a "Whereabouts" bulletin: no results, no positive results on the cadaver bulletins he'd been tracking statewide: zilch on the brothers, no stiffs that might be the real Duke Cathcart. And—six months ago, following up in San Berdoo, he got a hot lead.

He found a San Berdoo townie who'd seen Susan Nancy Lefferts with a man matching Duke Cathcart's description—two weeks before the Nite Owl killings. He showed him some Cathcart mugshots; the man said, "Close, but no cigar." The Nite Owl forensic had Susan Nancy "flailing" to touch the man sitting at the next table: Duke Cathcart, really the impersonator, supposedly unknown to her. Why were they sitting at *different tables*? The kicker: he tried to interview Sue Lefferts' mother, a chance to run the boyfriend by her. She refused to talk to him.

Why?

Bud packed up: mementoes, ten pounds of paper. Stalemates for now—no new whore leads, the Nite Owl dead until he braced Mickey Cohen. Out to the elevator—adiós, Homicide.

Ed Exley walked by staring.

He knows about Inez and me.

44

STAKEOUT: HANK'S Ranch Market, 52nd and Central. A sign above the door: "Welfare Checks Cashed." January 3, relief day— check-cashers shooting craps on the sidewalk. Surveillance Squad 5 got a tip—some anonymous ginch said her boyfriend and his buddy were going to take the market off, she was pissed at the boyfriend for porking her sister. Jack in the point car, watching the door, Sergeant John Petievich parked on 52—scowling like he wanted to kill something.

Lunch: Fritos, straight vodka. Jack yawned, stretched, cut odds: Aragon vs. Pimentel, what Ellis Loew wanted—he was supposed to meet him at a political soiree tonight. The vodka burned his stomach; he had to piss wicked bad.

Horn toots—his signal. Petievich pointed to the sidewalk. Two white men entered the market.

Jack walked across the street. Petievich walked over. A frame on the doorway, a look in. The robbers at the checkstand, backs to the door—guns out, spare hands full of money.

No proprietor. No customers. A squint down the far aisle— blood and brains on the wall. SILENCER. BACK DOOR MAN. Jack shot the heisters in the back.

Petievich screamed; back door footsteps; Jack fired blind, chased. Bottles broke over his head: blind shots, silencer rounds— no noise, muffled thwaps. Down the far aisle, two dead winos, a door closing. Petievich fired, blew the door off—a man sprinted across the alley. Jack emptied his piece; the man vaulted a fence. Shouts from the sidewalk; crapshooters cheering. Jack reloaded, jumped the fence, hit a backyard. A Doberman jumped at him, snarling, snapping teeth in his face—Jack shot him point-blank. The dog belched blood; Jack heard shots, saw the fence explode.

Two bluesuits hit the yard running. Jack dropped his gun; they fired anyway—wide—blowing out fence pickets. Jack put his hands up. "Police officer! Police officer! Policeman!"

They came up slow, frisked him—peach-fuzz rookies. The taller kid found his ID. "Hey, Vincennes. You used to be some kind of hotshot, didn't you?"

Jack cold-cocked him—a knee to the nuts. The kid went down; the other kid gawked.

Jack went looking for a place to drink.

*   *   *

He found a juke joint, ordered a line of shots. Two drinks killed his shakes; two more made him a toastmaster.

To the men I just killed: sorry, I'm really better at shooting unarmed civilians. I'm being squeezed into retirement, so I thought I'd 86 a couple of real bad guys before I capped my twenty.

To my wife: you thought you married a hero, but you grew up and learned you were wrong. Now you want to go to law school and be a lawyer like Daddy and Ellis. No sweat on the money: Daddy bought the house, Daddy upgrades your marriage, Daddy will pay for tuition. When you read the paper and see that your husband drilled two evil robbers, you'll think they're the first notches on his gun. Wrong—in '47 dope crusader Jack blasted two innocent people, the big secret he almost wants to spill just to get some life kicking back into his marriage.

Jack downed three more shots. He went where he always went when with a certain amount of shit in his system—back to '53 and smut.

He felt safe on the blackmail: his depositions for insurance, the Hudgens snuff buried—*Hush-Hush* resurrected it, got nowhere. Patchett and Bracken never approached him—they had the carbon of Sid's Big V file, kept their end of the bargain. He heard Lynn and Bud White were still an item; call the brainy whore and Patchett memories—bad news from that bad bloody spring. What drove him was the smut.

He kept it in a safe-deposit box. He knew it was there, knew it excited him—knew that loving it would trash his marriage. He threw himself into the marriage, building walls to keep them safe from that spring. A string of sober days helped; the marriage helped. Nothing he did changed things—Karen just learned who he was.

She saw him muscle Deuce Perkins; he said "nigger" in front of her parents. She figured out his press exploits were lies. She saw him drunk, pissed off. He hated her friends; his one friend—Miller Stanton—dropped out of sight when he blew *Badge of Honor.* He got bored with Karen, ran to the smut, went crazy with it.

He tried to ID the posers again—still no go. He went to Tijuana, bought other fuck books—no go. He went looking for Christine Bergeron, couldn't find her, put out teletypes that got him bupkis. No way to have the real thing—he decided to fake it.

He bought hookers, shook down call girls. He fixed them up to look like the girls in his books. He had them three and four at a pop, chains of bodies on quilts. He costumed them, choreographed them. He aped the pictures, took his own pictures, recaptured; sometimes he thought of the blood pix and got scared: perfect matches to murder mutilations.

Real women never thrilled him like the pictures did; fear kept him from going to Fleur-de-Lis—straight to the source. He couldn't figure out Karen's fear—why she didn't leave him.

A last drink—bad thoughts adieu.

Jack cleaned up, walked back to his car. No hubcaps, broken wiper blades. Crime scene tape around Hank's Ranch Market; two black-and-whites in the lot. No reprimand note on his windshield—the vandals probably stole it.

* * *

He hit the bash at full swing: Ellis Loew, a suite packed with Republican bigshots. Women in cocktail gowns; men in dark suits. The Big V: chinos, a sport shirt sprayed with dog blood.

Jack flagged a waiter, grabbed a martini off his tray. Framed pictures on the wall caught his eye.

Political progress: *Harvard Law Review*, the '53 election, a howler shot: Loew telling the press the Nite Owl killers confessed before they escaped. Jack laughed, sprayed gin, almost choked on his olive. Behind him: "You used to dress a bit more nicely."

Jack turned around. "I used to be some kind of hotshot."

"Do you have an excuse for your appearance?"

"Yeah, I killed two men today."

"I see. Anything else?"

"Yeah, I shot them in the back, plugged a dog and took off before my superior officers showed up. And here's a news flash: I've been drinking. Ellis, this is getting stale, so let's get to it. Who do you want me to touch?"

"Jack, lower your voice."

"What is it, boss? The Senate or the statehouse?"

"Jack, it's not the time to discuss this."

"Sure it is. Tell true. You're gearing up for the '60 elections."

Loew, on the QT. "All right, it's the Senate. I did have some favors to ask, but your current condition precludes my asking them. We'll talk when you're in better shape."

An audience now: the whole suite. "Come on, I'm dying to run bag for you. Who do I shake down first?"

"*Sergeant, lower your voice.*"

Raise that voice. "Cocksucker, I shit where you breathe. I put Bill McPherson in the tank for you, I cold-cocked him and put him in bed with that colored girl, I fucking deserve to know who you want me to put the screws to next."

Loew, a hoarse whisper. "Vincennes, you're through."

Jack tossed gin in his face. "God, I fucking hope so."

45

". . . AND WE'RE more than the moral exemplars that Chief Parker spoke of the other day. We are the dividing line between the old police work and the new, the old system of promotion through patronage and enforcement through intimidation and a new emerging system: the elite police corps that impartially asserts its authority in the name of a stern and unbiased justice, that punishes its own with a stern moral vigor should they prove duplicitous to the higher moral standards an elite corps demands of its members. And, finally, we are the protectors of the public image of the Los Angeles Police Department. Know that when you read interdepartmental complaints filed against your brother officers and feel the urge to be forgiving. Know that when I assign you to investigate a man you once worked with and liked. Know that our business is stern, absolute justice, whatever the price."

Ed paused, looked at his men: twenty-two sergeants, two lieutenants. "Nuts and bolts now, gentlemen. Under my predecessor, Lieutenant Phillips and Lieutenant Stinson supervised field investigations autonomously. As of now, I will assume direct field command, with Lieutenant Phillips and Lieutenant Stinson serving as my execs on an alternating basis. Incoming complaints and information requests will be routed through my office first, I'll read the material and make my assignments accordingly. Sergeant Kleckner and Sergeant Fisk will serve as my personal assistants and will meet with me every morning at 0730. Lieutenant Stinson and Lieutenant Phillips, please meet me in my office in one hour to discuss my assuming command of your ongoing investigations. Gentlemen, you're dismissed."

The meeting dispersed in silence; the muster room emptied. Ed replayed his speech, hitting key phrases. "Absolute justice" hit with Inez Soto's voice.

Dump ashtrays, straighten chairs, tidy the bulletin board. Unfurl the flags by the lectern, check them for dust. Back to his speech, his father's voice: "Duplicitous to the higher moral standards an elite corps demands of its members." Two days ago, his speech would have been the truth. Inez Soto's speech made it a lie.

Flags, gold-fringed. Gold-plated opportunism: he killed those men out of a weak man's rage. As the Nite Owl killers they gave the rage meaning: absolute justice boldly taken. He twisted the meaning to support what the public was telling him: you're L.A.'s greatest hero, you're going to the top and beyond. Bud White's revenge, the man too stupid to grasp it: a simple cuckold accompanied by a woman's few words had him treading lies at the top, thrashing for a way to make his stale glory real.

Ed walked into his office: clean, neat—no order to secure. Complaint forms on his desk—he sat down, worked.

Jack Vincennes in big trouble.

1/3/58: while on a Surveillance Detail stakeout, Vincennes shot and killed two armed robbers—gunmen who had murdered three people at a southside market. Vincennes gave chase to a third gunman/robber, lost him, was approached by two patrolmen who did not know he was a police officer. The patrolmen fired at Vincennes, assuming him to be a member of the robbery gang; Vincennes dropped his gun and allowed himself to be frisked—then assaulted one of the officers and vacated the crime scene before Homicide and the coroner arrived. The third suspect remained at large; Vincennes went to a political gathering honoring DA Ellis Loew, his brother-in-law by marriage. Presumed to be drunk, he verbally abused Loew and threw a drink in his face—in full view of the guests.

Ed skimmed Vincennes' personnel file. A 5/58 pension securement date—goodbye, Trashcan Jack—you were close. Stacks of his Narcotics Squad reports: thorough, detailed to the point of being padded. Between the lines: Vincennes had a hard-on for minor dope violators—especially Hollywood celebrities and jazz musicians—substantiating an old rumor: he called *Hush-Hush* Magazine to be in on his gravy rousts. Vincennes was transferred to Administrative Vice as part of the Bloody Christmas shake-up; another stack of reports: bookmaking and liquor infraction operations, no zeal, plenty of verbal padding. Ad Vice assignment into the spring of '53: Russ Millard commanding the division, a pornography investigation running concurrent with the Nite Owl.

And a *big* anomaly: assigned to trace smut, Vincennes repeatedly reported no leads, commented that the other men on the assignment were coming up empty, twice offered the opinion that the investigation should be dropped.

Antithetical Jack V. behavior.

Smut brushed shoulders with the Nite Owl.

Ed thought back.

The Englekling brothers, Duke Cathcart, Mickey Cohen. Smut dismissed as a viable Nite Owl lead—three dead Negroes, case closed.

Ed read the file again. Years of padded reports, one assignment bereft of paper. Vincennes returned to Narco in July '53—he went back to his old ways, continued them straight through to the end of his duty with Surveillance.

Big-time anomaly.

Coinciding with the Nite Owl.

Spring '53, another connection: Sid Hudgens was murdered then—unsolved. Ed hit the intercom.

"Yes, Captain?"

"Susan, find out who besides Sergeant John Vincennes was assigned to the Fourth Squad at Administrative Vice in April of 1953. Do that, then locate them."

* * *

A half hour for results. Sergeant George Henderson, Officer Thomas Kifka retired; Sergeant Lewis Stathis working Bunco. Ed called his CO; Stathis walked in ten minutes later.

A burly man—tall, stooped. Nervous—an IA bracing out of nowhere was a spooker. Ed pointed him to a chair. Stathis said, "Sir, this is about ..."

"Sergeant, this has nothing to do with you. This has to do with an officer you worked Ad Vice with."

"Captain, my Ad Vice tour was years ago."

"I know, late '51 through the summer of '53. You transferred out just as I rotated in on my floater assignment. Sergeant, how closely did you work with Jack Vincennes?"

Stathis smiled. Ed said, "Why are you grinning?"

"Well, I read in the paper that Vincennes juked these two heist guys, and talk around the Bureau has it that he bugged out on the scene unannounced. That's a big infraction, so I was smiling 'cause it figured he'd be the Ad Vice guy you'd be interested in."

"I see. And did you work closely with him?"

Stathis shook his head. "Jack was strictly the single-o type. You know, the beat of a different drummer. Sometimes we worked the same general assignments, but that was it."

"Your squad worked a pornography investigation in the spring of '53, do you recall that?"

"Yeah, it was a colossal waste of time. Dirty skin books, a waste of time."

"You yourself reported no leads."

"Yeah, and neither did Trashcan or the other guys. Russ Millard got co-opted to that Nite Owl thing, and the skin book caper fell through."

"Do you recall Vincennes acting strangely during that time?"

"Not really. I remember he only showed up at the squadroom at odd times and that him and Russ Millard didn't like each other. Like I said, Vincennes was a loner. He didn't pal around with the guys on the squad."

"Do you recall Millard making specific queries of the squad when two printshop operators came forward with smut information?"

Stathis nodded. "Yeah, something to do with the Nite Owl that didn't pan out. We all told old Russ that those skin books could not be traced hell or high water."

One hunch going dry. "Sergeant, the Department was running a fever with the Nite Owl back then. Can you recall how Vincennes reacted to it? Any little thing out of the ordinary?"

Stathis said, "Sir, can I be blunt?"

"Of course."

"Well, then I'll tell you that I always figured Vincennes was a cheap-shot cop on the take somehow. Put that aside, I remember he was sort of nervous around the time of the skin book job. On the Nite Owl, I'd say he was bored with it. He was in on the arrest of those colored guys, he was there when our guys found the car and the shotguns, and he still seemed bored by it."

Coming on again—no facts, just instincts. "Sergeant, think. Vincennes' behavior around the time of the Nite Owl and the pornography investigation. Anything out of the ordinary with him. *Think.*"

Stathis shrugged. "Maybe one thing, but I don't think it amounts to—"

"Tell me anyway."

"Well, back then Vincennes had the cubicle next to mine, and sometimes I could hear him pretty good. I was at my desk and heard part of a conversation, him and Dudley Smith."

"And?"

"And Smith asked Vincennes to put a tail on Bud White. He said White'd gotten personally involved in a hooker homicide and he didn't want him doing nothing rash."

Skin prickles. "What else did you hear?"

"I heard Vincennes agree, and the rest of it was garbled."

"This was during the Nite Owl investigation?"

"Yes, sir. Right in the middle of it."

"Sergeant, do you remember Sid Hudgens, the scandal sheet man, being killed around that time?"

"Yeah, an unsolved."

"Do you recall Vincennes talking about it?"

"No, but the rumor was that him and Hudgens were buddies."

Ed smiled. "Sergeant, thank you. This was off the record, but I don't want you to repeat our conversation. Do you understand?"

Stathis got up. "I won't, but I feel bad about Vincennes. I heard he's topping out his twenty in a few months. Maybe he vamoosed 'cause shooting those heist guys got to him."

Ed said, "Good day, Sergeant."

* * *

Something old, wrong.

Ed sat with his door open. Gold-braided flags just outside—opportunities knocked.

Vincennes might have dirt on Bud White.

Instincts: Trash running scared in the spring of '53.

Connect the "skin-book caper" to the Nite Owl.

Inez Soto's indictment—he killed three innocent men.

If he cut Vincennes a break on his IA investigation—

Ed hit the intercom. "Susan, get me District Attorney Loew."

46

MICKEY COHEN said, "I got my own problems to worry about. The fershtunkener Nite Owl case and fershtunkener dirty books I don't know from the Bible, another book I never read. That rebop bored me five years ago, now it is an even further distance from hunger. I got my own problems, such as look at my poor baby."

Bud looked. A raggedy-assed bulldog by the Mickster's fireplace—wheezing, his tail in a splint. Cohen said, "That is Mickey Cohen, Jr., my heir who is not long for this canine world. A bomb attempt in November he survived, though a goodly number of my Sy Devore suits did not. His poor tail has remained steadily infected and his appetite is dyspeptic. Cops resurrecting old grief is not good for his health."

"Mr. Cohen—"

"I like a man who addresses me with proper decorum. What did you say your name was again?"

"Sergeant White."

"Sergeant White then, I will tell you there is no end to the grief in my life. I am like Jesus your goy savior carrying the weight of the world on his back. Back in prison these fershtunkener goons attack me and my man Davey Goldman, Davey gets his brains scrambled, gets paroled and starts walking around in public with his shlong hanging out, it's big, I don't blame him for advertising, but the Beverly Hills cops ain't so enlightened and now he's doing ninety days observation at the Camarillo nut bin. As if that is not enough grief for your yiddisher Jesus to undergo, then feature that while I was in prison some colleagues looking after my interests were bumped off by persons unknown. And now my old boys won't form back together with me. My God, Kikey T., Lee Vachss, Johnny Stompanato—"

Kill the tirade. "I know Johnny Stomp."

Cohen hit the roof. "Ferstunkener Johnny, Judas from the best-selling Bible is his middle name! Lana Turner is his Jezebel and not his Mary Magdalene, his cock leads him to grovel for her like a dowsing rod. Granted, he is even better hung than Davey G., but my blessed Jesus I took him away from being a two-bit extortionist and made him my bodyguard, and now he refuses to re-enlist, he'd rather nosh grease at Kikey's fucking deli and hobnob with Deuce Perkins, who I have it on good authority plays hide the salami with members of the canine persuasion. Did you say your name was White?"

"That's right, Mr. Cohen."

"Wendell White? *Bud* White?"

"That's me."

"Boychik, why didn't you tell me?"

Cohen Junior pissed in the fireplace. Bud said, "I didn't think you'd heard of me."

"Heard, shmeard, word gets out. Word is you're Dudley Smith's lad. Word is you and the Dudster and a couple of his other hard boys been keeping L.A. safe for democracy while this so-called crime drought's been going on. A motel in Gardena, a little blackjack work to the kidneys, va va va voom. Maybe now, maybe if I can get my old guys to quit noshing grease and associating with dog fuckers, I can get business going again. I should be nice to you so's you and the Dudster reciprocate. So what's with this Nite Owl rehash?"

His pitch—canned. "I heard how the Englekling brothers visited you up at McNeil, how they talked up Duke Cathcart's deal. I was thinking that you or Davey Goldman might have talked it up on the yard and word got out that way."

Mickey said, "Nix. Not possible, 'cause I never told Davey. True, I am well known for my cell business confabs, but not a soul on this earth did I tell. I told that guy Exley that when we shmoozed on the topic years ago. And here's a bonus insight from the Mickster. It is my considered opinion that dirty books are a high-profit item worth killing innocent bystanders over only if an established high-profit market already exists. Give the fucking Nite Owl up, those shvartzes the hero kid bumped took the ticket and probably did the job anyway."

Bud said, "I don't think Duke Cathcart was killed at the Nite Owl. I think it was a guy impersonating him. I think the guy killed Cathcart, took over his identity and wound up at the Nite Owl. I was thinking the whole thing got started up at McNeil."

Cohen rolled his eyes. "Not with me it didn't, boychik, 'cause I told nobody, and I can't feature Pete and Bax stopping to spread the word out on the yard. Where'd this clown Cathcart live?"

"Silverlake."

"Then dig up the Silverlake Hills. Maybe you'll find a nice vintage stiff."

A flash—San Berdoo, Sue Lefferts' mother at her pad—eyes darting to a built-on room. "Thanks, Mr. Cohen."

Cohen said, "Forget the fershtunkener Nite Owl."

Cohen Junior took a bead on Bud's crotch.

* * *

San Bernardino, Hilda Lefferts. Last time she shoved him out pronto; this time he'd hit on the boyfriend: Susan Nancy was seen with a guy matching Duke Cathcart's description—press, intimidate.

A two-hour run. The San Berdoo Freeway would be working soon—cut the trip in half. Exley Senior to Junior: the coward knew about him and Inez, his look the other day spelled it plain. They were both biding their time. But if things fell his way he'd hit harder—Exley would *never* tag him for the brains to hit smart.

Hilda Lefferts lived in a dump: a shingle shack with a cinder block add-on. Bud walked up, checked out the mailbox. Good intimidation stuff: Lockheed pension check, Social Security check, County Relief check. He pushed the buzzer.

The door opened a crack. Hilda Lefferts looked over the chain. "Told you before, now I'll say it again. I'm not buying what you're selling, so let my poor daughter rest in peace."

Bud fanned out the checks. "County Relief told me to hold these back until you cooperate. No tickee, no washee."

Hilda squealed; Bud popped the chain, walked in. Hilda backed away. "Please. I need that money."

Susan Nancy smiled down from four walls: vamp poses on a nightclub floor. Bud said, "Come on, be nice, huh? You remember what I tried to ask you last time? Susan had a boyfriend here in San Berdoo right before she moved to L.A. You looked scared when I told you before, you look scared now. *Come on.* Five minutes on that and I'm gone. And nobody's gonna know."

Hilda, eyeball circuits: the checks, the add-on room. "Nobody?"

Bud forked over Lockheed. "Nobody. Come on. I'll give you the other two after you tell me."

Hilda spoke straight to her daughter—the picture by the door. "Susie, you told me you met the man at a cocktail lounge and I told you I didn't approve. You said he was a nice man who'd paid his debt to society, but you wouldn't tell me his name. I saw you with him one day, and you called him Don or Dean or Dick or Dee, and he said, 'No, Duke. Get used to it.' Then I was out one day and old Mrs. Jensen next door saw you with the man here at the house and thought she heard a ruckus ..."

Match it: "debt to society" equals "ex-con." "Did you ever learn the man's name?"

"No, I didn't. I ..."

"Did Susan know two brothers named Englekling? They lived here in San Bernardino."

Hilda squinted at the picture. "Oh, Susie. No, I don't think I know that name."

"Did Susan's boyfriend ever mention the name 'Duke Cathcart' or mention a pornography business?"

"No! Cathcart was the name of one of the dead people where Susie died, and Susie was a good girl who would never associate with filth!"

Bud forked over County Relief. "Easy now. Tell me about the ruckus."

Hilda, tears coming on. "I came home the next day, and I thought I saw dried blood on the floor of the new den, I'd just had it built with the money from my husband's insurance policy. Susan and the man came back and acted nervous. The man crawled around under the house and called a Los Angeles phone number, then he and Susan Nancy left. A week later she was killed ... and ... I, well, I thought all that suspicious behavior meant the killings ... I just thought of conspiracies and reprisals, and when that nice man who became such a hero came by a few days later with his background check, I just stayed quiet."

Goose bumps: Susie Lefferts' boyfriend the Cathcart impersonator. "The ruckus": the boyfriend kills Cathcart—probably in San Berdoo to talk to the Engleklings. Susie at the Nite Owl, scoping out some kind of meeting, the boyfriend playing Cathcart—which meant the killers never saw the real Cathcart face-to-face.

THE BOYFRIEND CRAWLING AROUND UNDER THE HOUSE.

Bud got the phone, the operator, an L.A. number: PC Bell police information. A clerk came on. "Yes, who's requesting?"

"Sergeant W. White, LAPD. I'm in San Bernardino at RAnchview 04617. I need a list of all calls to Los Angeles from that number, say from March 20 to April 12, 1953. Got that?"

The clerk said, "I copy." Seconds, two minutes plus, the clerk back on. "Three calls, Sergeant. April 2 and April 8, all to the same number, HO-21118. That's a pay phone, the corner of Sunset and Las Palmas."

Bud hung up. Phone booth calls a half mile from the Nite Owl; the deal or the meet worked out—extra cautious.

Hilda fretted Kleenex. Bud saw a flashlight on an end table. He grabbed it, ran with it.

Outside to the add-on, a foundation crawlspace—one tight fit. Down, under, in.

Dirt, wood pilings, a long burlap sack up ahead. Smells: mothballs, rot. An elbow crawl to the bag—mothballs and rot getting stronger. He poked the sack, saw a rat's nest explode.

All around him: rats blinded by light.

Bud ripped burlap. In with the flashlight, rats, a skull caked with gristle. Drop the flash, rip two-handed, rats and mothballs in his face. A huge rip, a bullet hole in the skull, a skeleton hand out a sleeve—"D.C." on flannel.

He crawled out gulping air. Hilda Lefferts was right there. Her eyes said, "Please God, not that."

Clean air; clean daylight almost blinding. White light gave him the idea—his shiv at Exley.

A scandal mag leak. A guy at *Whisper* owed him—a pinko rag, they bled for Commies and jigs and hated cops.

Hilda, about to shit her drawers. "Was … there … anything under there?"

"Nothing but some rats. I want you to stay put, though. I'm gonna bring back some mugshots for you to look at."

"May I have that last check?"

The envelope—flecked with rat droppings. "Here. Compliments of Captain Ed Exley."

47

A NICE interrogation room—no bolted-down chairs, no piss smell. Jack looked at Ed Exley. "I knew I was in the shit, but I didn't think I rated the top dog."

Exley: "You're probably wondering why you haven't been suspended."

Jack stretched. His uniform chafed—he hadn't worn it since 1945. Exley looked creepy—skinny, gray-haired, rimless glasses that made his eyes come off brutal. "I was wondering. My guess is Ellis had second thoughts on the complaint he filed. Bad publicity and all that."

Exley shook his head. "Loew considers you a liability to his career and his marriage, and leaving that crime scene and assaulting that officer are enough in themselves to warrant a suspension and a dismissal."

"Yeah? Then why haven't I been suspended?"

"Because for the moment I've interceded with Loew and Chief Parker. Any other questions?"

"Yeah, where's the tape recorder and the steno?"

"I didn't want them here."

Jack pulled his chair up. "Captain, what *do* you want?"

"I'll throw that back at you. Do you want to flush your career down the toilet or would you like to skate for a few months and cash out your twenty?"

Easy: Karen's face when he told her. "Okay, I'll play. Now what do you want?"

Exley leaned close. "In the spring of '53 your friend and business associate Sid Hudgens was murdered and two detectives who worked the case under Russ Millard told me you referred to Hudgens as 'scum' and were visibly agitated on the morning his body was discovered. During this time frame Dudley Smith asked you to tail Bud White, and you agreed. During this time frame the Nite Owl case was active and you worked a pornography investigation with Ad Vice and repeatedly submitted no-lead reports, when your long-standing procedure was to jam every report you wrote full of filler. During this time two men, Peter and Baxter Englekling, came forward to offer state's evidence on an alleged pornography link to the Nite Owl. Russ Millard queried you on it, you went along with your 'no leads' routine. Throughout the smut investigation you repeatedly urged that the job be dropped. Those same two detectives, Sergeants Fisk and Kleckner, overheard you urging Ellis Loew to soft-pedal the Hudgens investigation, and one of your fellow Ad Vice officers recalls you as being atypically nervous throughout the smut job and absent from the squadroom for unusually long periods of time. Put it all together for me, would you, Jack?"

Ten counts guilty—he knew he was gawking, blinking, twitching. "How ... the ... fuck did you ..."

"It doesn't matter. Now let's hear your interpretation of what I want."

Jack caught some breath. "Okay, so I tailed Bud White. Dud was afraid he'd go apeshit over some hooker snuff, 'cause White had that tendency where young stuff was concerned. Okay, so I tailed him and didn't pick up anything worth a damn. You and White hate each other, everyone knows it. You figure someday he'll try to get you for your job on Dick Stensland and you'll cut me slack with Loew and Parker in exchange for some dirt on him. *Is that what you want?*"

"Call that twenty percent of it and give me something you learned about White."

"Such as?"

"How about him and women?"

"White likes women, but that's no news flash."

"IAD ran a personal on White after he passed the sergeant's exam. The report had him seeing a woman named Lynn Bracken. Did White know her back in '53?"

Jack shrugged. "I don't know. I never heard that name."

"Vincennes, your face says you're a liar, but put the Bracken woman aside, she doesn't interest me. Was White seeing Inez Soto during the time you were tailing him?"

He almost laughed. "No, not while I had my tail on him. Is that what you're so worked up on? You think White and your—"

Exley raised a hand. "I'm not going to ask you if you killed Hudgens, I'm not going to make you put that spring together for me, not yet and maybe never. Just give me your opinion on something. You were up to your ears on the smut job *and* you worked the Nite Owl. Do you make the three Negroes for the killings?"

Jack inched back—get away from those eyes. "There's loose ends out there, I knew it then. If it wasn't the three you got, maybe it was some other spooks, maybe they knew where Coates hid his car and planted the shotguns. Maybe it's tied to the smut. Do you care? Those niggers raped your woman, so what you did was right. What's this about, Captain?"

Exley smiled. Jack pegged it: a man sticking one foot off a cliff, hopping on one leg. "Captain, what's this—"

"No, my motives are my business, and here's my first guess. Hudgens was connected to the smut somehow, and he had a file on you. That's why you were all over that mess."

Quicksand. "Yeah, I did something really bad once. You know ... shit, sometimes I think ... sometimes I think I don't care who finds out anymore."

Exley stood up. "I've already squared the complaints against you. There'll be no trial board, no charges. Part of the agreement I made with Chief Parker is a stipulation that you voluntarily retire in May. I told him you'd agree, and I convinced him that you deserve a full pension. He didn't question my motives, and I don't want you to question them either."

Jack stood up. "And the trade?"

"If the Nite Owl ever goes wide, you and everything you know belong to me."

Jack stuck out his hand. "Jesus, you turned into a cold son of a bitch."

CALENDAR
FEBRUARY–MARCH 1958

Whisper Magazine, February 1958 Issue:

WRONG MAN KILLED IN
NITE OWL SLAUGHTER?
WEB OF MYSTERY SPREADS ...

YOU REMEMBER the Nite Owl brouhaha, don't you? On April 14, 1953, three shotgun-toting killers entered the convivial Nite Owl Coffee Shop, just off Hollywood Boulevard in sunny Los Angeles, robbed and murdered three employees and three patrons and got away with an estimated three hundred scoots, which divided by six comes to about fifty bucks a life. The Los Angeles Police Department threw itself into the case with characteristic zeal, arrested three young Negro men on suspicion of committing the murders and also charged them with kidnapping and raping a young Mexican girl. The LAPD was not quite certain that the three Negroes—Raymond "Sugar Ray" Coates, Tyrone Jones and Leroy Fontaine—committed the Nite Owl killings, but they were sure that the young men were the rapists of Inez Soto, 21, a college student. The Nite Owl investigation continued, with much attendant publicity and great pressure on the LAPD to solve L.A.'s "Crime of the Century."

The LAPD pursued fruitless leads for two weeks, then discovered the murder weapons inside Ray Coates' car, stored in an abandoned South Los Angeles garage. Shortly after that, Coates, Jones and Fontaine escaped from the Hall of Justice Jail ...

Enter a young police detective: Sergeant Edmund J. Exley of the LAPD. World War II hero, UCLA grad, informant against his fellow cops in the 1951 "Bloody Christmas" police brutality scandal and the son of construction mogul Preston Exley, the builder of Raymond Dieterling's mammoth Dream-a-Dreamland and the massive Southern California freeway system. The plot thickens ...

Item: Sergeant Ed Exley was in love with rape victim Inez Soto.

Item: Sergeant Ed Exley located, shot and killed Raymond Coates, Tyrone Jones and Leroy Fontaine, with—poetic justice—a shotgun.

Item: Sergeant Ed Exley was promoted (two whole ranks!!!) to captain a week later, a large reward for his justice-by-the-sword resolution of a case the LAPD needed to solve quicksville in order to ensure perpetuation of its (overblown?) reputation.

Item: *Captain* Ed Exley (a rich kid with a substantial private trust fund left to him by his late mother) soon became very cozy with Inez Soto and bought her a house down the block from his apartment.

Item: we at *Whisper* have it on very good authority that Raymond Coates, Leroy Fontaine, Tyrone Jones and the man who was sheltering them—Roland Navarette—were unarmed when hero Ed Exley gunned them down ... and, now, nearly five years since the Nite Owl killings, the plot thickens again ...

Now, *Whisper* is the underdog of what the squaresville press calls "Scandal Sheet Journalism." We're not the mighty *Hush-Hush*, we're based out of New York and our beat is primarily the East Coast. But we do have our L.A. sources, and among them is a crusading private eye who wishes to remain anonymous. This man has been obsessed with the Nite Owl case for years, has investigated it extensively and has come up with some startling revelations. This man, whom we shall call "Private Eye X," spoke to *Whisper* correspondents and revealed the following:

Private Eye eye-tem: during the Nite Owl investigation, two brothers, *Peter and Baxter Englekling*, printshop operators from San Bernardino, California, came forth and told authorities an account of how *Nite Owl victim Delbert "Duke" Cathcart* approached them with a plan to print pornographic material, then theorized that the Nite Owl killings were the result of intrigue within the pornography underworld. The LAPD pooh-poohed the brothers' theory in their haste to pin the crime on the Negroes, and now the Engleklings seem to have disappeared off the face of the globe ...

Private Eye eye-tem: Mrs. Hilda Lefferts, mother of San Bernardino born and bred *Nite Owl victim Susan Nancy Lefferts*, told Private Eye X that immediately before the killings her daughter had a mysterious, unnamed boyfriend who greatly resembled Duke Cathcart, and she even heard him tell Susan Nancy: "Call me 'Duke.' Get used to the idea."!!! Mrs. Lefferts could not identify the man from privately hoarded mugshots that Private Eye X showed her. X then developed what we consider an x-cellent and x-citing theory!

X theory eye-tem: we think that mystery boyfriend X killed Duke Cathcart in an attempt to take over his pornography business, impersonated Duke Cathcart and wound up at the Nite Owl Coffee Shop to do biz with the three men who perpetrated the slaughter. Susan Nancy sat nearby in order to watch her boyfriend wheel and deal. Private Eye X offers the following unimpeachable evidence as proof:

Mrs. Lefferts said boyfriend X looked just like Duke Cathcart.

The body identified as Cathcart's was too decimated to correctly ID. The coroner's final identification was based on a *partial* dental plate reconstruction crosschecked against Cathcart's prison dental records—yet other prison records listed Cathcart's height at 5′8″, while the body discovered at the Nite Owl was 5′9¼″. All in all, unmistakable proof that an impersonator, not Duke Cathcart, was killed at the Nite Owl Coffee Shop ...

X-citing x-trapolations that we believe will lead to some x-tremely interesting revelations, x-asperate the trigger-happy Los Angeles Police Department and perhaps x-onerate the three Negroes falsely accused of the Nite Owl killings. We at *Whisper* urge the Los Angeles District Attorney's Office to x-hume the bodies of the Nite Owl victims; we x-coriate Captain Ed Exley for his cold-blooded murder of four societal victims and x-pressly petition the LAPD: redeem your old wrongs in the name of justice! Reopen the Nite Owl case!!!

EXTRACT: San Francisco *Chronicle*, February 27:

GAITSVILLE SLAYINGS BAFFLE POLICE

GAITSVILLE, CALIF., Feb. 27, 1958—A bizarre double murder has the citizens of Gaitsville, a small town sixty miles north of San Francisco, scared—and the Marin County Sheriffs baffled.

Two days ago, the bodies of Peter and Baxter Englekling, 41 and 37, were discovered at their apartment next door to the printshop where they were employed as typesetters. The two brothers, in the words of Marin County Sheriff's Lieutenant Eugene Hatcher, were "shady characters with criminal connections." The lieutenant guardedly elaborated to *Chronicle* reporter George Woods.

"Both Engleklings had criminal records for narcotics offenses," Lieutenant Hatcher said. "Granted, they've been clean for a number of years, but they were still shady characters. For instance, they were working at the printing shop under assumed names. So far we have no clues, but we do think we're dealing with a torture-for-information scenario."

The Englekling brothers worked at Rapid Bob's Printing on East Verdugo Road in Gaitsville and lived in the apartment building next door. Their employer, Robert Dunkquist, 53, knew the pair as Pete and Bax Girard, and discovered their bodies on Tuesday morning. "Pete and Bax had worked for me for a year and they were as regular as clockwork. When they were late for work on Tuesday I knew something was up. Also, the shop had been ransacked and I wanted them to help me find the culprits."

The Englekling brothers, whose true identities were revealed by a fingerprint teletype check, were shot to death, and Lieutenant Hatcher is certain the killer used a .38 revolver equipped with a silencer. "Our ballistics man found iron shavings embedded in the rounds we took out of the victims. This indicates a silencer and also indicates why the neighbors never reported any shots."

Lieutenant Hatcher would not reveal the status of his investigation, but he did state that all the standard investigatory approaches are being utilized. He stated that both victims were tortured prior to being shot, but would not describe the crime scene. "We want to keep that knowledge private," he said. "Sometimes publicity-seeking lunatics confess to crimes like this, even though they didn't commit them. Keeping your facts private helps eliminate the guilty from the innocent."

Peter and Baxter Englekling have no known living relatives, and their bodies are being held at the Gaitsville city coroner's office. Lieutenant Hatcher urged all parties who might have information concerning the homicides to contact the Marin County Sheriff's Department.

EXTRACT: San Francisco *Examiner*, March 1:

MURDER VICTIMS LINKED TO CELEBRATED LOS ANGELES CRIME

PETER AND Baxter Englekling, murder victims killed in Gaitsville, California, on February 25, were material witnesses in the famous Nite Owl murder case that occurred in Los Angeles in

April 1953, Marin County Sheriff's Lieutenant Eugene Hatcher revealed today.

"We got an anonymous tip on it yesterday," Lieutenant Hatcher told the *Examiner*. "A man just called in the information, then hung up. We verified it with the DA's Bureau down in L.A., and they said it was true. I don't think it has anything to do with our case, but I called the Los Angeles Police Department anyway and ran it by them. They gave me the brush-off, so I say the heck with them."

EXTRACT: L.A. *Daily News*, March 6:

NITE OWL REDIVIVUS—SHOCKING NEW REVELATIONS POINT TO INNOCENT MEN KILLED

THIS IS an ugly story. The *Daily News*, frankly Los Angeles' only exposé-oriented newspaper and the only Southland paper proud to call itself "muckraking," does not shy away from such stories. This story punctures the hero image of a man considered by many to be a perfect exemplar of law-and-order righteousness, and when heroes possess feet of clay, we at the *Daily News* believe that it is our duty to expose their shortcomings to public scrutiny. The issues here are great, as notable as the crime that spawned them, so we are frankly sending up a muckraking hue and cry. That hue and cry: the infamous Nite Owl murder case—six people brutally robbed and shotgunned to death at a Hollywood coffee shop in April 1953—was solved incorrectly, at a great cost to justice. We want to see the case reopened and true justice achieved.

Raymond Coates, Leroy Fontaine and Tyrone Jones—do you recall those names? They were the three Negro youths, criminals and sex offenders to be sure, who were railroaded by the Los Angeles Police Department. Arrested shortly after the Nite Owl murders, they offered a hellish alibi: they could not have committed the killings because they were engaged in the kidnap and gang rape of a young woman named Inez Soto. They abused Miss Soto at a deserted building in South Los Angeles, then confessed that they drove her around and "sold her out" to their friends for more sexual abuse. They left Miss Soto with a man named Sylvester Fitch, and an LAPD officer shot and killed him while effecting the brave young woman's escape.

Miss Soto refused to cooperate with the police investigation, which at the time centered on the imperative of establishing where Coates, Jones and Fontaine were at the time of the Nite Owl killings. Were they with her and the other alleged rapists (none of whom, besides Fitch, were ever identified)? Did they have time to drive from South Los Angeles to Hollywood, commit the Nite Owl killings, then return to heap more abuse upon her? Was she conscious throughout the total sum of her degradation?

Unanswered questions—until now.

The police investigation spread into two forks: searching for evidence to corroborate Jones, Coates and Fontaine as the killers; searching for general evidence, standard police work based on the supposition that the three youths were guilty only of kidnap and rape, but not murder. Miss Soto still refused to cooperate. Both investigatory forks proved moot when Coates, Jones and Fontaine escaped from jail and were gunned down by our aforementioned hero: LAPD Sergeant Edmund Exley.

College man, World War II hero, son of the illustrious Preston Exley, Ed Exley used the Nite Owl case as a springboard for his ruthless personal ambition. He was promoted to captain at age 31 and as of this writing will soon become an inspector—at 36, the youngest in LAPD history. He is mentioned as a potential Republican office-seeker almost as often as his construction-king father. A few persistent rumors surround him: that the men killed were unarmed, that DA Ellis Loew dreamed up the Nite Owl confession that Coates, Jones and Fontaine allegedly made before they escaped. What is not generally known is that Ed Exley was in love with Inez Soto and condoned her lack of cooperation during the investigation, later bought her a house and has been intimately involved with her for close to five years.

And now, two recent developments have blown the Nite Owl case wide open.

Back in 1953, two men, brothers, came forward as material witnesses with information on the Nite Owl killings. Those men, Peter and Baxter Englekling, asserted that a pornography plot was at the base of the coffee shop massacre, per a scheme devised by one of the victims: ex-convict Delbert "Duke" Cathcart. The LAPD chose to ignore this information. Then, almost five years later, Peter and Baxter Englekling were viciously murdered in the small upstate town of Gaitsville. Those killings, which took place on February 25, are unsolved with a complete absence of clues. But a long-unanswered question was about to be answered.

At San Quentin Penitentiary, a Negro prisoner named Otis John Shortell read a San Francisco newspaper account of the Englekling brothers' killings, an account which mentioned their tenuous connection to the Nite Owl case. The article got Otis John Shortell thinking. He requested an audience with the assistant warden and made a startling confession.

Otis John Shortell, in prison on an accumulation of grand-theft auto convictions and frankly desiring a sentence reduction as a reward for his cooperation, confessed that he was one of the men Coates, Fontaine and Jones "sold" Inez Soto to. He was with Miss Soto and the three youths between the hours of 2:30 and 5:00 on the morning of the Nite Owl killings, *during the entire murder time frame*. He told the warden that he never came forward to exonerate the three for fear of rape charges being filed against him. He further stated that Coates had a large quantity of narcotics in his car and that that was the reason he never relinquished its location to the police. Shortell cited a recent conversion to Pentecostal Christianity as his reason for finally making his confession, but prison authorities were dubious. Shortell petitioned for an in-cell lie detector test to prove his veracity and was given a total of four polygraph examinations. He passed all four tests conclusively. Shortell's attorney, Morris Waxman, has sent notarized copies of the polygraph examiner's reports to the *Daily News* and the LAPD. We have advanced this article. What will the LAPD do?

We decry the injustice of shotgun justice. We decry the motives of triggerman Ed Exley. We openly challenge the Los Angeles Police Department to reopen the Nite Owl Murder Case.

EXTRACT: L.A. *Times*, March 11:

NITE OWL HUE AND CRY BUILDING

A WELTER of unrelated events and a fire fanned by a series of articles in the Los Angeles *Daily News* are pressuring the Los Angeles Police Department to reopen the 1953 Nite Owl murder case investigation.

LAPD Chief William H. Parker called the controversy "a powder keg with a wet fuse. It's all a bunch of baloney. The testimony of a degenerate criminal and an unrelated double murder do not constitute a reason to reopen a case successfully solved five years ago. I stood by Captain Ed Exley's actions in 1953 and I stand by them now."

Chief Parker's references allude to the February 25 murders of Peter and Baxter Englekling, material witnesses to the original Nite Owl investigation, and the recent testimony of San Quentin inmate Otis John Shortell, who claimed to be with the three formerly accused killers during the time frame of the Nite Owl murders. Citing Shortell's in-prison lie detector tests, his attorney Morris Waxman stated, "Polygraphs don't lie. Otis is a religious man who carries a great burden of guilt for not coming forth to exonerate innocent men five years ago, and now he wants to see justice done. He has given three dead victims a lie detector validated alibi and now he wants to see the real killers punished. I will not cease publicizing this matter until the LAPD agrees to do their duty and reopen the case."

Richard Tunstell, city editor of the Los Angeles *Daily News*, echoed that sentiment. "We've got our teeth sunk into something important. We're not going to let go."

BANNERS

L.A. *Daily News*, March 14:

J'ACCUSE—LAPD IN NITE OWL COVER-UP

L.A. *Daily News*, March 15:

OPEN LETTER TO TRIGGERMAN EXLEY

L.A. *Times*, March 16:

CONVICT'S LAWYER PETITIONS STATE ATTORNEY GENERAL FOR NITE OWL CASE REOPENING

L.A. *Herald-Express*, March 17:

PARKER TO THE PRESS: NITE OWL A DEAD ISSUE

L.A. *Daily News*, March 19:

CITIZENS DEMAND JUSTICE—PICKETS STALK THE LAPD

L.A. *Herald-Express*, March 20:

PARKER/LOEW IN HOT SEAT
GOVERNOR KNIGHT: NITE OWL A "POWDER KEG"

L.A. *Mirror-News*, March 20:

THE WAGES OF DEATH—EXCLUSIVE
PICS OF EXLEY/SOTO LOVE NEST

L.A. *Examiner*, March 20:

POLICE SWITCHBOARDS FLOODED:
CITIZENS VOICE NITE OWL OPINIONS

L.A. *Times*, March 20:

PARKER BACKS EXLEY AND HOLDS FIRM:
"NO NITE OWL REOPENING"

L.A. *Daily News*, March 20:

JUSTICE MUST PREVAIL!
DEMAND POLICE ACCOUNTABILITY!
REOPEN THE NITE OWL CASE NOW!

PART FOUR

DESTINATION: MORGUE

48

THE PHONE rang: odds on the press 20 to 1. Ed picked up anyway. "Yes?"

"Bill Parker, Ed."

"Sir, how are you? And thanks for that quote in the *Times*."

"I meant it, son. We're going to tough this thing out and let it pass. How's Inez taking it? The publicity, I mean."

"My father said she's staying at Ray Dieterling's place in Laguna. And we broke it off a few months ago. It just wasn't working."

"I'm sorry. Inez is a plucky girl, though. Compared to what she's been through, this thing should be cake."

Ed rubbed his eyes. "I'm not so sure it'll pass."

"I think it will. The Gaitsville Police won't cooperate on the Englekling homicides and that Negro at Quentin has nil value as a witness. His polygraph seems valid, but his attorney is a grandstanding shyster only interested in getting his client out of—"

"Sir, all that aside, I don't think the men I killed did the Nite Owl and—"

"Don't interrupt me and don't tell me you're so suicidally naive as to think reopening the case will do one whit of good. Now, I'm waiting for it to pass and the attorney general up in Sacramento is waiting for it to pass. Bad publicity, petitions for justice and the like *always* peak out and pass."

"And if it doesn't?"

Parker sighed. "If the AG orders a state-run special investigation, I'll file an LAPD injunction against him and preempt him with an investigation of our own. I have Ellis Loew's full support on that strategy—but it *will* pass."

Ed said, "I'm not so sure I want it to."

49

MOBSTER SQUAD duty: room 6, the Victory Motel. Bud, Mike Breuning, a Frisco boy cuffed to the hot seat—Joe Sifakis, three loanshark falls, snatched off a train at Union Station. Breuning worked the hose; Bud watched.

Fourteen hundred on the dresser—a police charity donation. A get-out-of-town pitch in high gear—dental work coming up. Bud checked his watch—4:20—Dudley was late. Sifakis screamed.

Bud walked into the bathroom. Four obscene walls: sex ditties, some dated. '53 entries—he thought Nite Owl straight off. Scary: the Nite Owl big-time news, Dud wanted to talk to him bad. He turned on the sink—cover the screams. He tested *his* Nite Owl string, found it watertight.

Nobody knew he leaked his story to *Whisper*—if the high brass knew he would have heard—and Cathcart's stiff was still under the house. Nobody knew he tipped the Gaitsville Sheriff's to the Englekling connection to the Nite Owl. Lucky breaks: the brothers dead, the spook up at Quentin—probably a legit alibi. He was clean on the evidence he suppressed in '53—if Dudley had an inkling he was holding stuff back it probably tied to his fix on the Kathy snuff. Dud was the Nite Owl supervisor, he'd want the brouhaha to pass—a reopening would make him look like a supporting player chump—second banana to hero chump Ed Exley. Parker was trying to keep a reopening kiboshed, call the odds against it 5 to 1, 5 to 1 that Exley would come out smelling—

Sifakis screamed—the door shook.

Bud doused his head in the sink. A scrawl by the mirror: Meg Greunwitz fucks good—AX-74022. Girls' names on the walls; last week the L.A. Sheriff's bagged a dead hooker, add it to his list: Lynette Ellen Kendrick, age 21, DOD 3/17/58. Beaten, ring lacerations, three-hole rape—the county cops wouldn't give him the time of—

Sifakis started babbling. The bathroom got too hot to take.

Bud walked out. Sifakis, snitch-frenzied. "... and I know things, I *hear* things. Like, dig, with the Mick out it's open season. Things was on this weird slowdown while he was inside, but these shooter teams took out these guys that was running his franchises, then these maverick guys, three triggers bang bang bang, they 86'd Mickey's men and these guys trying to crash his loanouts. Everybody used to respect Dud S. as a trucemaker, but now he don't do a damn thing. You want a prostie roust? Huh? Huh? You want a good tip on a ..."

Breuning looked bored. Bud went out to the courtyard: crab-grass, barbed-wire fenced. Fourteen empty rooms—LAPD bought the property cheap.

"Lad."

Dudley on the sidewalk. Bud lit a cigarette, walked over.

"Lad, I'm sorry I'm late."

"It don't matter, you said it was serious."

"Yes, it is all of that. How are you enjoying the Hollywood squad, lad? Is it to your liking?"

"I liked Homicide better."

"Grand, and I'll see to it that you return sometime soon. And have you been relishing the spectacle of friend Exley ridiculed by the fourth estate?"

Smoke made him cough. "Yeah, sure. Too bad the case won't get reopened and really make him squirm. Not that I'd want to see you stand heat for it, though."

Dudley laughed. "I see the conflicts inherent in your perspective. And I feel a certain ambivalence myself, especially since a little birdie in Sacramento has informed me that the attorney general will soon press to reopen the case. Ellis Loew has an injunction prepared should things get dicey, so I think it is safe to assume that the Nite Owl is regrettably our hot potato once again. Political infighting, lad. The pinko Democrats have taken the tack of jigaboos wrongly accused, intend to press the issue during the primary elections, and the Republican AG has side-stepped and counterpunched. Lad, do you possess any Nite Owl information that you haven't presented to me?"

Ready, prepared. "No."

"Ah, grand. That aside then, I have an assignment for you here at the Victory tonight. A very large and muscular man requires a bracing, and frankly Mike and Dick lack the presence to appropriately impress him. It's a small world, lad—I think this chap knew our friend Duke Cathcart back in '53. Maybe he can give you some information on your Kathy Janeway fixation. Does fair Kathy's fate still concern you, lad?"

Bud swallowed—dry.

"Lad, forget that I asked. Fixations like that are like prostitutes—they can reform, but their old ways still linger. Tonight at 10:00, lad. And be of good cheer. I have some extracurricular work for you soon, work that should rekindle your old fearsome habits."

Bud blinked.

Dudley smiled, walked to room 6.

Prostitute equals Lynn. Janeway jibe equals just how much?

Joe Sifakis screamed—through four walls, out to the edge of the courtyard.

50

GALLAUDET SLIPPED him the news: the Attorney General's Office was set to press for a reopening: state-financed, state-run. Ellis Loew was set to usurp their investigation—the LAPD, Nite Owl redux. Time to call it all in.

Ed in a coffee shop on La Brea. Jack Vincennes due, paperwork on the table: Nite Owl, notes on the Hudgens case.

Check mark: was the man at San Quentin telling the truth? Most likely yes—whatever his motives.

Check mark: did the Englekling killings tie in to the Nite Owl? No way to tell until the Marin Sheriff's shared their information.

Check mark: the purple car by the Nite Owl. A hunch: it was an innocent vehicle, the real killers followed the publicity, located Ray Coates' car before the LAPD, planted the shotguns. This meant—astoundingly—that they planted the spent shells found in Griffith Park. Hall of Justice Jail records '35 to '55 had been destroyed—if the killers gleaned the information as part of a jail connection, finding that connection would most likely prove impossible. Have Kleckner and Fisk thoroughly investigate every logical possibility pertaining to the purple car/planted shotguns.

Check mark: victim Malcolm Lunceford, ex–LAPD officer/wino security guard. Did he tie in to some kind of criminal conspiracy that resulted in the Nite Owl massacre? Answer: unlikely—he was a certified, long-term Nite Owl habitué, late nights always.

Ed sipped coffee, thought POWER. Abused: IAD was autonomous inside and outside the Department; he'd had Fisk and Kleckner working toward a possible reopening—LAPD's or his own. Vincennes admitted his tail on Bud White and lied about White knowing his sporadic girlfriend—Lynn Bracken—during the spring of '53. Lynn Bracken was placed under loose surveillance; Fisk just submitted a report.

The woman was rumored to be an ex-prostitute; she co-owned a dress shop in Santa Monica. Her partner: Pierce Morehouse

Patchett, age fifty-six. Kleckner secured a financial report: Patchett emerged as a wealthy investor known to pimp call girls to business associates. The financial kicker:

Patchett owned an apartment building in Hollywood. A weird shootout took place there—in the middle of the Nite Owl time frame. He caught the squeal himself: no suspects apprehended, sadomasochist gear in a shot-riddled downstairs unit. The manager claimed not to know the building's owner—he was paid by mail, suspected a dummy corporation issued him his paycheck. He knew the first name of the apartment's tenant—"Lamar," a "big blond guy." The manager blamed Lamar for the shootout; a Hollywood Division follow-up report stated that Lamar had not been seen since the incident. Incident closed.

Trashcan was late. Move to the Hudgens notes.

God-awful butchery, no hard suspects, Hudgens roundly hated. A lackluster investigation—heat fell briefly on Max Peltz and the *Badge of Honor* crew—*Hush-Hush* published an article "exposing" Peltz and his lust for teenage girls. Peltz passed a polygraph test; the rest of the "crew" proffered alibis. Between the lines—Parker considered the victim scum, short-shrifted the case.

Still no Trash. Ed skimmed the alibi sheet.

Max Peltz engaged in statutory rape—heavily implied, no charges filed. Script girl Penny Fulweider home with her husband; Billy Dieterling alibied—Timmy Valburn. Set designer David Mertens—a sickly man suffering from epilepsy and other ailments—alibied by Jerry Marsalas, his live-in male nurse. Star Brett Chase at a party; co-star Miller Stanton likewise. A bust—but Hudgens' death had to play central to Vincennes' spring '53.

Trashcan walked up, sat down. No prelims. "You're calling it in?"

"I'm meeting with Parker tomorrow. I'm sure he's going to announce a reopening."

Vincennes laughed. "Then don't look so grim. If you're crazy enough to want it, at least act happy."

Ed placed six shell casings on the table. "Three of these are target rounds I retrieved from your last range practice, three are rounds I took out of a Hollywood Division evidence locker. Identical lands and grooves. April '53, Jack. You remember that shootout on Cheramoya?"

Trash grabbed the table. "Keep going."

"Pierce Patchett owns that building on Cheramoya, and it's a nicely hidden ownership. S&M gear was found on the premises, and Patchett is a KA of Lynn Bracken, Bud White's girlfriend, who you denied knowing. You were working a smut job for Ad Vice then, and smut and sadomasochist paraphernalia are in the same ballpark. The last time we talked you admitted that Hudgens had a file on you, that that was why you were all over the place then. Here's my big leap, so correct me if I'm wrong. Bracken and Patchett were KA's of Hudgens."

Vincennes dug his hands in—the table shook. "So you're a smart fucker. So what?"

"So did Bud White know Hudgens?"

"No, I don't think—"

"What does White have on Patchett and Bracken?"

"I don't know. Exley, look—"

"No, *you* look. And you answer me. Did you get Hudgens' file on you?"

Trashcan, sweating. "Yeah, I did."

"Who from?"

"The Bracken woman."

"How did you get it out of her?"

"Deposition threat. I wrote out a deposition on her and Patchett, everything I put together about them. I made carbons and stashed them in safe-deposit boxes."

"And you—"

"Yeah, I've still got them. And they've still got a carbon on me."

Educated guess. "And Patchett was pushing that smut you were chasing?"

"Yeah. Exley, look—"

"No, Vincennes, *you* look. Do you still have copies of the smut books?"

"I've got the depositions and the books. You want them, I get my evidence suppression wiped. And half the Nite Owl collar."

"A third. There's no way to make the case without White."

51

ROOM 6 at Victory. Dudley, a muscle creep chained to the hot seat. Dot Rothstein ogling *Playboy*. Bud watched her scope cheesecake: a bull-dyke cop in a Hughes Aircraft jumpsuit.

Dudley skimmed a rap sheet. "Lamar Hinton, age thirty-one. One ADW conviction, a former telephone company employee strongly suspected of installing bootleg bookie lines for Jack 'The Enforcer' Whalen. A parole absconder since April 1953. Lad, I think it is safe to refer to you as an organized crime associate, thus someone in need of reeducation in the ways of polite society."

Hinton licked his lips; Dudley smiled. "You came along peacefully, which is to your credit. You did not give us a song and dance about your civil rights, which, since you don't have any, speaks well of your intelligence. Now, my job is to deter and contain organized crime in Los Angeles, and I have found that physical force often serves as the most persuasive corrective measure. Lad, I will ask questions, you will answer them. If I am satisfied with your answers, Sergeant Wendell White will remain in his chair. Now, why did you abscond your parole in April 1953?"

Hinton stuttered. Bud threw backhands—eyes on the wall so he wouldn't have to see. Left/right/left/right/left/right—Dot flashed the cut-off sign.

Cease fire. Dudley: "A little admonishing to show you what Sergeant White is capable of. Now, from here on in I will accommodate your stammer. Do you recall the question? Why did you abscond your parole in April 1953?"

Stut-stut-stutter: Hinton with his eyes squeezed shut.

"Lad, we're waiting."

Hinton: "H-h-had b-b-blow t-town."

"Ah, grand. And what precipitated your need to leave?"

"J-just w-woman t-t-trouble."

"Lad, I don't believe you."

"Th-th-the t-truth."

Dudley nodded. Bud threw backhands—pulled, fake full force. Dot said, "This boy could take a lot of grief. Come on, sugar, make it easy on yourself. April '53. Why'd you blow town?"

Bud heard Breuning and Carlisle next door. It hit him: 4/53— the Nite Owl.

"Lad, I overestimated the power of your memory, so let me help it along. Pierce Patchett. You were acquainted with him back then, weren't you?"

Bud, chills: evidence suppression, he shouldn't know Patchett existed—

Hinton jerked, thrashed.

"Ah, grand, I think we touched a nerve."

Dot sighed. "God, such muscles. I should have such muscles."

Dudley howled.

Kill the chills: he's on the reopening—maybe Hinton works in. *If he knew about my evidence dance I wouldn't be here.*

Dot sapped Hinton: the arms, the knees. Muscles took it stoic: no yelps, no whimpers.

Dudley laughed. "Lad, you have a high threshold for discomfort. Comment on the following, please: Pierce Patchett, Duke Cathcart and pornography. Be concise or Sergeant White will test that threshold."

Hinton, no stutter. "Fuck you, Irish cocksucker."

Ho, ho, ho. "Lad, you're a regular Jack Benny. Wendell, show our organized crime associate your opinion of unsolicited comedy acts."

Bud grabbed Dot's sap. "What are you looking for, boss?"

"Full and docile cooperation."

"Is this the Nite Owl? You said Duke Cathcart."

"I want full and docile cooperation on all topics. Have you objections to that?"

Dot said, "White, just do it. God, I should have such muscles."

Bud got close. "Let me play him solo. Just a couple minutes."

"A return to your old methods, lad? It's been a while since you evinced enthusiasm for this kind of work."

Bud whispered. "I'm gonna let him think he can take me, then shiv him. You and Dot wait outside, okay?"

Dudley nodded, walked Dot out. Bud turned the radio on: a commercial, used-car values at Yeakel Olds.

Hinton rattled his chains. "Fuck you, fuck that Irish guy and fuck that fucking diesel dyke."

Bud pulled up a chair. "I don't like this stuff, so you be good and give me some answers on the side and I'll tell the man to cut you loose. You got that? No parole roust."

"Fuck you."

"Hinton, I think you know Pierce Patchett, and maybe you knew Duke Cathcart. You can tell me some side stuff and I'll—"

"Fuck your mother."

Bud threw Hinton and his chair across the room. The hot seat landed sideways—slats popped off. Shelves collapsed—the radio broke, spewing static.

Bud uprighted the chair one-handed. Hinton pissed his pants. Bud heard himself talking, a weird voice like a brogue. "Give me some pimp stuff, lad. Cathcart, a coon named Dwight Gilette—they both ran this girl Kathy Janeway. She got snuffed and I don't like that. You got information on them, *lad*?"

Eyeball to eyeball—Hinton's wide wide. No stutter, don't rile the fucking animal. "Sir, I just had this driver job for Mr. Patchett, me and this guy Chester Yorkin. All we did was deliver these ... these illegal things ... and Cathcart, him I don't know from Adam. I heard Gilette was a swish, all I know's he used to get hooers for Spade Cooley's parties. You want skinny on Spade? I know he blows opium, he's a righteous degenerate dope fiend. He's playing the El Rancho now, you roust him. But I don't know no hooer killers and I don't know no girl Kathy Janeway."

Bud shook the chair—Hinton kept snitching. "Sir, Mr. Patchett, he ran call girls. Gorgeous tail, all fixed up like movie stars. His favorite was this gorgeous cunt Lynn, looked just like—"

Bud went straight for his face. The face went red, big men pressed in—arms around him—lifting him. The ceiling zooming down, cracked stucco swirls going black.

*   *   *

Questions and answers through black, shouts and whimpers through gauze—a wall that held faces back. Stag books, Cathcart, Pierce P.—the full drift couldn't get through. A strain to hear "Lynn Bracken," no yield on the name, the black going that much blacker. Mickey Cohen, '53 and why'd you run—he tore at the gauze for that name. Shrieks that made him burrow into softness—snapshots of Lynn all around him.

Lynn blond and a whore, brunette and herself. Lynn on his thing with Inez: "Be kind to her and spare me the details." Lynn filling up her diary while he punked out on reading it because he knew she had him down cold. Lynn thinking two steps ahead of him, drifting in and out of his life while he drifted in and out of hers. That black gauze throbbing—questions, answers. Black silence, cracked stucco swirls going light.

Room 7 at the Victory: cots for the Mobster Squad guys. The door to 6 wide open.

Bud rolled off his cot, stood up. His head throbbed, his jaw ached, he'd ripped up his pillow burrowing in. Into 6, a shambles: the hot seat, blood on the walls. No Hinton, no Dot, no Dudley and his boys. 1:10 A.M.—no way to figure out the questions and answers.

He drove home woozy, too trashed to think. He unlocked his door yawning—the overhead light went on. Something/some-body grabbed him.

Cuffs on his wrists. Ed Exley, Jack Vincennes—square in front
of him. A side check: Fisk and Kleckner—IA shitbirds—pinning
his arms.

Exley slapped him. Fisk grabbed his neck, popped a finger on
his carotid.

A folder in his face. Exley: "IA ran a personal on you when you
made sergeant, so we already know about Lynn Bracken. Vincennes had a tail on you back in '53, and he's got you, Bracken and
Pierce Patchett in this deposition here. You braced Patchett on the
Kathy Janeway homicide, and you were all over the Nite Owl like
a plague. I need what you know, and if you don't cooperate I'll
begin an IA investigation into your evidence suppression immediately. The Department needs a scapegoat on the old Nite Owl
job—and I'm too valuable to take the fall. If you don't cooperate,
I'll use every bit of my juice to ruin you."

The choke hold went slack—Bud tried to pull away. Kleckner
and Fisk dug in. "You fuck, I'll fucking kill you."

Exley laughed. "I don't think so, and if you play you get
your evidence suppression chilled, part of the collar and a little
plum—a liaison to those hooker snuffs you care so much
about."

Black gauze coming back. "Lynn?"

"She's our first interrogation—with pentothal. If she's clean,
she walks."

He doesn't know about *Whisper*, I've still got that stiff in San
Berdoo. "And you and me when it's over."

52

NO SLEEP—VINCENNES' deposition wouldn't let him. The
wake-up call he didn't need: a reporter at 6:00 A.M. Radio news
riding over: reopening speculation, a *mano a mano* with his father—
the freeway system near done, the Nite Owl hero now a villain.
Parking lot pickets—Commie types demanding justice.

Early—for the most important meeting of his career.

Parker's conference room was set up—notepads on the table.
Ed wrote "Patchett," "Bracken," "Patchett's 'deal' with Hudgens—extortion?"; he underlined "Pornography pictures match
Hudgens mutilations—have Vincennes bring smut books to Bureau." White's contribution: "Patchett hinked on smut in '53";

"Patchett/Englekling bros and father chem background"; "Duke Cathcart's pad tossed & San Berdoo Yellow Pages (printshops) ruffled." White was still holding back—he knew it.

Deposition underlined: "Patchett involved (through Fleur-de-Lis racket) in (contained) distribution of smut AdVice chasing in '53, smut Cathcart developed distribution scheme around, smut connected to mutilations on Hudgens' body."

Conclusion:

A dense series of criminal conspiracies at least five years old resulting in no fewer than four and perhaps as many as a dozen major crimes.

The other men filed in—Parker, Dudley Smith, Ellis Loew. Nods, quick sit-downs.

Parker said, "We're reopening. The AG's Office wants to usurp the job, but Ellis has filed a restraining order against them, which should buy us two weeks' time. We've got two weeks to clear the case and recover the respect we lost. We've got two weeks before Sacramento comes down here and makes us a laughingstock. I want this case cleared, legally inviolate and in the hands of the grand jury within twelve days. Do you understand, gentlemen?"

Nods all around. Loew said, "I'm personally in a difficult position here, since Coates, Jones and Fontaine *did* confess to me. On reflection, I must admit that they were stupid and naive boys psychologically susceptible to suggestion, so—"

Smith cut in. "Ellis, that's blood under the bridge. We simply got the wrong coloreds, not the ones who fired off those shotguns in Griffith Park. The real culprits are some smart Darktown strutters who knew where Coates stashed his car, then planted the weapons. Lads who knew niggertown well and simply beat us to the location. The purple car seen by the Nite Owl was just a coincidence that the killers capitalized on. I think the Griffith Park car was stolen or out of state, and in any event I think it's not applicable. We have to begin by shaking down the southside again."

Ed smiled—Smith's tack played into his plan. "Essentially I agree, and I've got one of my IA men checking old registrations. But aren't we ahead of ourselves? Shouldn't we set up a chain of command first?"

Loew coughed. "Ed, I think your shooting those thugs was a noble act, whatever your motives. But I think giving you the command would just make the press and the public more resentful. I think you should take a subsidiary role in this investigation."

Outrage down pat. "I'm tired of being the bad guy on the six o'clock news and I'm tired of my sex life in the papers. I'm also the best detective in the—"

Parker cut in. "You are the best detective we have, and I understand your need to cut your losses. But Ellis is right, this is too personal with you. I've given Dudley the command. He'll recruit a team from Homicide and various squadrooms and take it from there."

"And me? Do I get a piece of the case?"

Parker nodded. "I'll give you anything within reason."

The kill. "I want the chance to develop my own evidence with IA autonomy. I want the use of my two personal aides from IA and my choice of two officers to serve as field runners."

"That's fine by me. Dudley?"

"Yes, I think that's fair. Lad, who did you have in mind for runners?"

"Jack Vincennes and Bud White."

Smith almost gawked. Parker said, "Strange bedfellows, but then it's a strange case. Twelve days, gentlemen. Not one minute longer."

53

JACK WOKE up on the couch, wrote Karen a note.

> Sweetie—
>   Fairs fair & yeah I screwed up with Ellis. But this goddamn sofa for two months isn't fair & if the Department can forgive me then you should be able to too. I haven't had a drink for six weeks, which if you checked the calendar by my closet you'd know. I don't expect you to think that makes everything right with us, but give me some credit for trying. I'll try—you want to go to law school, great, but I bet you'll hate it. In May I'll retire, maybe I can get a police chief job in some hick town near a good law school. I'll try, but cut me some slack because this deep freeze number is driving me crazy & right now I can't afford to be crazy because I've been detached back to work plainclothes on something that's very

important to me. I'll probably be working late for the next week or so, but I'll call & check in.

J.

He dressed, waited for the phone to ring. Coffee in the kitchen, a note from Karen.

J.–

I've been a bitch lately. I'm sorry and I think we should try to figure some things out. You were asleep when I got home or I would have invited you into the boudoir.

XXXXX—K

P.S. A girl at work showed me this magazine that I thought you might be interested in seeing. I know you know that man Exley it mentions and it certainly is pertinent to what's been in the papers lately.

On the table: *Whisper*—"All the Dirt That's Fit to Print." Jack thumbed it smiling, caught a Nite Owl spread.

Hopped-up stuff—"Crusading Private Eye," "Duke Cathcart impersonator," smut speculation. Ed Exley raked over hot coals—Exley hatred big. A snap take: "PI" Bud White shivs Exley—a February issue on sale in January, out before the Englekling brothers got clipped and that shine up at Quentin dropped that alibi. East Coast circulation, you probably couldn't find the rag in L.A. Exley and the high brass couldn't have seen it—or *he* would have heard.

The phone rang—Jack grabbed it. "Exley?"

"Yes, and you're officially detached. White talked to Lynn Bracken. She's agreed to be pentothaled, and I want you to bring her in. She'll be waiting at that Chinese restaurant across from the Bureau in an hour. Meet her there and bring her up to IA, and if she's got a lawyer get rid of him."

"Look, I saw something I think you should see."

"Just bring me the woman."

* * *

The woman five years post-file burning—Lynn Bracken sipping tea at Al Wong's. Jack watched her through the window.

Still a showstopper. A brunette now, a thirty-fivish beauty drawing stares. She saw him. Jack got flutters: his file.

She walked out. Jack said, "I didn't want this to happen."

"You let it. And aren't you afraid of what I know about you?"

Something skewed: she was too calm five minutes from a bracing. "I've got this scary captain looking after me. If it came out, I'm betting he'd kibosh it."

"Don't make any bets you can't cover. And I'm only doing this because Bud told me he'd get hurt if I didn't."

"What else did Bud tell you?"

"Bad things about your scary captain. Can we go now? I want to get this over with."

They walked across the street, up the back Bureau stairs. Fisk met them outside IA, steered them to Exley's office. A scary set-up: scary Captain Ed. Ray Pinker, a desk covered with medical stuff—vials, syringes. A polygraph machine—backup if the truth juice failed.

Pinker filled a hypo. Exley pointed Lynn to a chair. "Please, Miss Bracken."

Lynn sat down. Pinker swabbed her left arm, fitted a tourniquet. Exley, all business. "I don't know what Bud White told you, but essentially this is an investigation involving several interrelated criminal conspiracies. If you provide us with viable information we're prepared to grant you immunity on any possible criminal charges you might accrue."

Lynn made a fist. "I can't very well lie. Can we get this over with, please?"

Pinker took her arm, injected her. Exley punched a tape machine. Lynn went dreamy-eyed—not quite pentothal gaga. Exley talked into a hand mike. "Witness Lynn Bracken, March 22, 1958. Miss Bracken, please count backward from one hundred."

Slurs right off. "Hundred, ninety-nine, ninety-eight, ninety-sev, nine-six ..."

Pinker checked her eyes, nodded. Jack grabbed a chair. Still too calm—he could taste it.

Exley coughed. "3/22/58, present with the witness are myself, Sergeant Duane Fisk, Sergeant John Vincennes and forensic chemist Ray Pinker. Duane, transcribe in shorthand."

Fisk grabbed a notepad. Exley said, "Miss Bracken, how old are you?"

A slight slur. "Thirty-four."

"And your occupation?"

"Businesswoman."

"Do you own Veronica's Dress Shop in Santa Monica?"

"Yes."

"Why did you choose the name 'Veronica's'?"

"A personal joke."

"Please elaborate."

"It's a name from my old life."

"How specifically?"

A dreamy smile. "I used to be a prostitute made up to resemble Veronica Lake."

"Who convinced you to do that?"

"Pierce Patchett."

"I see. Did Pierce Patchett kill a man named Sid Hudgens in April 1953?"

"No. I mean I don't know. Why would he?"

"Do you know who Sid Hudgens was?"

"Yes. A scandal-sheet writer."

"Did Patchett know Hudgens?"

"No. I mean if he did know him, he would have told me, a famous man like that."

A lie—she couldn't be full on the juice. She had to know he knew she was lying—she was thinking he'd cover her to protect himself.

Exley: "Miss Bracken, do you know who killed a girl named Kathy Janeway in the spring of 1953?"

"No."

"Do you know a man named Lamar Hinton?"

"Yes."

"Please elaborate."

"He worked for Pierce."

"In what capacity?"

"As a driver."

"And when was this?"

"Several years ago."

"Do you know where Hinton is now?"

"No."

"Elaborate on your answer, please."

"No, he went away, I don't know where he went."

"Did Hinton attempt to kill Sergeant Jack Vincennes in April 1953?"

"No."

She told him no back then.

"Who did try to kill him?"

"I don't know."

"Who else worked or works as a driver for Patchett?"

"Chester Yorkin."

"Please elaborate."

"Chet, Chester Yorkin, he lives in Long Beach somewhere."

"Does Pierce Patchett suborn women into prostitution?"

"Yes."

"Who killed the six people at the Nite Owl Coffee Shop in April 1953?"

"I don't know."

"Does Pierce Patchett sell a variety of illegal items through a service known as Fleur-de-Lis?"

"I don't know."

A huge lie. Hink on her face: veins pulsing.

Exley: "Does Dr. Terry Lux perform plastic surgery on Patchett's prostitutes in order to increase their resemblance to movie stars?"

Veins smoothing out. "Yes."

"Is Patchett in fact a long-term procurer of expensive call girls?"

"Yes."

"Did Patchett distribute expensive and artfully produced pornography during the spring of 1953?"

"I don't know."

White knuckles. Jack grabbed a notepad, wrote: "Patchett a chem whiz. L.B.'s lying & I think she's on dope to counter pentothal. Get blood sample."

"Miss Bracken, does—"

Jack passed the note. Exley scanned it, passed it to Pinker. Pinker fixed up a spike.

"Miss Bracken, does Patchett possess secret files stolen from Sid Hudgens?"

"I don't kn—"

Pinker grabbed Lynn's arm, fed the needle. Lynn jerked up; Exley grabbed her. Pinker pulled out the spike; Exley pinned Lynn to his desk. She thrashed and kicked—Fisk got behind her and cuffed her. Spitting now—she caught Exley in the face. Fisk wrestled her out to the hall.

Exley wiped his face—red, mottled. "I wasn't sure myself. I thought she might have been confused."

Jack handed him *Whisper*. "I knew how she should answer better than you. Captain, you should see this."

Scary: that red face, those eyes. Exley read the piece, tore the rag in half. "White did this. You go up to San Bernardino and talk to Sue Lefferts' mother. I'm going to break that whore."

* * *

San Berdoo in an uproar: Exley breaking that whore as a slide show. "Hilda Lefferts" in the phone book, directions, the house: white shingles, a cinderblock add-on.

A granny type watering the lawn. Jack parked, taped up the rip job on *Whisper*. The old girl saw him and rabbited—a run for the door.

He ran over. She squealed, "Let my Susie rest in peace!"

Jack shoved *Whisper* in her face. "An L.A. policeman talked to you, right? Big man about forty? You told him your daughter had a boyfriend who looked like Duke Cathcart right before the Nite Owl. He told her 'get used to calling me "Duke."' The policeman showed you mugshots and you couldn't make the boyfriend. Is this true? You read this and tell me."

She read, fast, squinting away sunlight. "But he said he was a policeman, not a private detective. Those were police-type pictures he showed me, and it wasn't my fault that I couldn't identify Susie's beau. And I want to go on record as stating that Susie was a virgin when she died."

"Ma'am, I'm sure she was—"

"And I want it to go on record that that policeman or whatever checked underneath the new wing on my house and found not a thing amiss. Young man, you're a policeman, aren't you?"

Jack shook his head—it felt sludgy. "Lady, what are you telling me?"

"I'm telling you that Mr. Private Eye Policeman or whatever crawled around under my house two months or so ago, because I told him Susan Nancy's beau did the same thing right after this ruckus they had with this other fellow right before that Nite Owl thing that you people keep tormenting me over, may Susie and the other victims rest in peace. All he found were rodents, not signs of foul play, so there."

So there.

Granny pointed to a crawlspace flush with the ground—so there.

It fucking could not be. Bud White did not have the brains to let a card that strong sit.

Jack took a flashlight down under—Hilda Lefferts stood watching, so there. Dust, rot, mothball stink—light on dirt, rats, rat eyes glowing. Burlap, mothballs, gristle-caked bones, a skull with a hole between the eyes.

54

ED WATCHED Lynn Bracken through the two-way.

Kleckner was questioning her, a nice guy set-up for Mr. Bad Guy—himself. She'd been repentothaled; Ray Pinker was testing her blood. Three hours in a cell hadn't broken her—she was still lying with style.

Ed turned the speaker up. Kleckner: "I'm not saying that I don't believe you, I'm just saying my policeman's experience has shown me that pimps usually hate women, so I don't buy Patchett as such a philanthropist."

"You have to look at his background, how he lost a little girl to crib death. I'm sure your policeman's mentality can grasp the cause and effect, even if you can't accept it."

"Let's talk about his background then. You've described Patchett as a financier with L.A. roots going back thirty years. You've said that he puts deals together, so be specific about the deals."

Lynn sighed—pure panache. "Movie financing deals, real estate and contracting deals. Here's one for all you movie fans in the audience: Pierce told me he'd financed a few of Raymond Dieterling's early shorts."

Cozy: Bud White's girlfriend's pimp knew Preston Exley's good buddy. Kleckner changed tape. Ed studied the whore.

Beautiful—a good part of it hung on the fact that she wasn't perfect. Her nose was too pointed; she had crease lines on her forehead. Big shoulders, big hands—beautifully formed, all the more stunning for being large. Blue eyes that probably danced when a man said the right thing; she probably thought Bud White had primitive integrity and respected him for not trying to impress her with gifts he didn't have. She kept her clothing subtle because she knew it would make more of an impression on the people she wanted to impress; she thought most men were weak and trusted her brains to slide her through anything. Suppositions leading up to a hunch: couple her brains with the counterdope in her system and you got a pentothal-immune witness dissembling with impunity—and style.

"Captain, you got a call. It's Vincennes."

Fisk had his phone, stretched to the end of the cord. Ed took it. "Vincennes?"

"Yeah, and listen close, 'cause that scandal sheet story was kosher and there's lots more."

"White?"

"Yeah, White was that phony PI, and he braced old lady Lefferts two months or so ago. She told him that story of her daughter's boyfriend who looked like Duke Cathcart and another doozie."

"*What?*"

"Just listen. A couple weeks before the Nite Owl, a neighbor saw Susie and the boyfriend alone at the house and heard them get into a ruckus with another guy. The boyfriend was seen crawling around under the house later that same day. Now, when White braced the old lady, he called PC Bell and checked their records for toll calls from the house to L.A. mid-March to mid-April '53. I did the same thing and got three tollers, all to a pay phone in Hollywood near the Nite Owl. Now, you think that's hot, you—"

"Goddammit—"

"Captain, *listen*. White crawled around under the house and told granny there was nothing there. I went under and found a stiff, wrapped in mothballs to kill the stink and a fucking bullet hole in the head. I got Doc Layman up to San Berdoo. He brought Duke Carthcart's prison dental file, the Coroner's Office copy. It was a perfect match. The first ID was bogus, off a partial plate, just like that article said. Fuck, I can't believe White put all this together and just left the stiff there. Captain, you there?"

Ed grabbed Fisk. "Where's Bud White?"

Fisk looked scared. "I heard he went up north with Dudley Smith. The Marin Sheriff's decided to kick loose on the Engleklings."

Back to Trashcan. "That article said the woman saw some mugs."

"Yeah, White brought back some shots marked 'State Records Bureau.' Now we both know the state sets run light, so my guess is White didn't want to bring her down here to check our books. Anyway, she couldn't ID the boyfriend, and if the boyfriend was one of the Nite Owl stiffs we'll have him, 'cause Nort Layman took prison dental plate fragments out of his head back in '53. Bring her down? Show her our books?"

"Do it."

Fisk took the phone. Ray Pinker walked up, holding a chem sheet. "Prestilphyozine, Captain. It's an extremely rare experimental antipsychotic drug used to tranquilize violent mental patients. Somebody professional slipped it to our lady friend, because only a pro would know this breed of phyozine would be likely to counteract pentothal. Skipper, you should sit down, you look like you're about to have a coronary."

Chemistry whiz Patchett; the Englekling brothers' father: a chemist who developed antipsychotic compounds. Bud White's whore across the glass—alone now, a tape recorder spinning.

Ed walked in. Lynn said, "You again?"

"That's right."

"Don't you have to charge me or release me?"

"Not for another sixty-eight hours."

"Aren't you violating my constitutional rights?"

"Constitutional rights have been waived for this one."

"*This one?*"

"Don't play dumb. This one is Pierce Patchett distributing pornography, including picture-book photographs that exactly match the mutilations on a murder victim, namely his late 'partner' Sid Hudgens. This one is one of the supposed Nite Owl victims tied in to a conspiracy to distribute that pornography and your friend Bud White withholding major evidence on who the real victim was. Now, White told you to cooperate and you came here under the influence of a drug to counteract pentothal. That's against you, but you can still save yourself *and White* a lot of trouble by cooperating."

"Bud can look after himself. And you look terrible. Your face is all red."

Ed sat down, turned off the tape. "You don't even feel the dosage, do you?"

"I feel like I've had four martinis, and four martinis just make me that much more lucid."

"Patchett sent you in without a lawyer to buy time, I know it. He knows you were called in as part of the Nite Owl reopening, so he knows he's a material witness at least. Personally, I don't see him as a killer. I know a great deal about Patchett's various enterprises, and you can save him a great deal of trouble by cooperating with me."

Lynn smiled. "Bud said you were quite smart."

"What else did he say?"

"That you were a weak, angry man competing with your father."

Let it pass. "Then let's concentrate on my smarts. Patchett is a chemist, and it may be reaching, but I'm betting he studied under Franz Englekling, a pharmacologist who developed drugs such as the antipsychotic compound Patchett put you under to beat the pentothal. Englekling had two sons, who were murdered in Northern California last month. Those two men came forward during the base Nite Owl investigation and mentioned a quote crazy sugar daddy-o unquote who had access to lots of quote high-class call girls unquote. Obviously Patchett, obviously tied to a would-be smut merchant named Duke Cathcart, one of the alleged Nite Owl victims. Obviously Patchett is all over this thing and in for some trouble he doesn't need and you can help circumvent."

Lynn lit a cigarette. "So you're very, very smart."

"Yes, and I'm a very good detective with a five-year backlog of withheld evidence to work from. I know about your file-burning episode, I know about Patchett's proposed extortion plan with Hudgens. I've read the deposition Vincennes bargained you with and I know all about Patchett's various enterprises, including Fleur-de-Lis."

"So you're assuming that Pierce has some very damaging information on Vincennes."

"Yes, which the district attorney and I will quash in the interest of protecting the reputation of the Los Angeles Police Department."

Fluster: Lynn dropped her cigarette, fumbled her lighter. Ed said, "You and Patchett can't win. I've got twelve days to square this thing right, and if I can't do it I'm going to start looking for subsidiary indictments. There's at least a dozen I can hang on Patchett, and believe me if I don't make this case I'll do anything I can to make myself look good."

Lynn stared at him. Ed stared back. "Patchett made you, didn't he? You were a pom-pom girl from Bisbee, Arizona, and a whore.

He taught you how to dress and talk and think, and I am very impressed with the results. But I've got twelve days to keep my life out of the toilet, and if I can't do it I'm going to take you and Patchett down."

Lynn turned on the tape player. "Pierce Patchett's whore for the record. I'm not afraid of you and I've never loved Bud White more. It makes me happy that he withheld evidence and got the better of you, and you're a fool for underestimating him. I used to be jealous of him sleeping with Inez Soto, but now I respect the poor girl's good sense in leaving a moral coward for a man."

Ed pressed "Erase," "Stop," "Start." "For the record, sixty-seven hours to go and my next interrogation won't be so cordial."

Kleckner opened the door, passed him a folder. "Captain, Vincennes brought the Lefferts woman in. They're checking out mugs, and he said you wanted these."

Ed stepped outside. A thick folder—glossy-paper smut.

The top books: pretty kids, explicit action, colorful costumes. Some of the heads had been cropped and taped back on—per the deposition—Jack tried to ID the posers from mugshots and thought cropping would facilitate the effort. Ugly/arty stuff—just like Trashcan said.

The bottom books—plain black covers—Trashcan's garbage can find. The first inked-in shots—embossed red streaming from disembodied limbs, posers linked orifice to orifice. The homicide match: a spread-eagled boy in sync to the Hudgens crime scene stills.

Past astonishing—and whoever posed the smut pics killed Hudgens.

Ed hit the last book, froze. A nude pretty boy, arms spread— ink/blood gouting off his torso. Familiar, too familiar, not from a Hudgens coroner's shot. He turned pages and caught a foldout: boys, girls, offset limbs touching, ink designs linking them.

AND HE KNEW.

He ran down the hall to Homicide, found their 1934 records, found "Atherton, Loren, 187 PC (multiple)." Three thick folders, then the photos—shot by Dr. Frankenstein himself.

Children immediately after their dismemberment.

Their arms and legs arranged just off their torsos.

White waxed paper under the bodies.

Blood fingerpainted around their limbs, red on white, intricate designs identical to the pornographic ink shots, limb spreads identical to the Hudgens severings.

Ed mangled his fingers slamming the cabinet, Code 2'd to Hancock Park.

* * *

A party at Preston Exley's mansion: valets parking cars, music in the back—probably a rose garden bash. Ed went in the front door and stopped short—his mother's library was gone.

Replacing it: a long space eclipsed by a model—lengths of highway over papier-mâché cities. Directional markers at the perimeters—the entire freeway system.

Perfection—it jerked him out of his filth-picture haze. Boats in San Pedro Harbor, the San Gabriel Mountains, tiny autos on asphalt. Preston Exley's greatest triumph on the eve of its completion.

Ed pushed a car—ocean to foothills. His father's voice: "I thought you'd be working South Central today."

Ed turned around. "What?"

Preston smiled. "I thought you'd be making up for your recent bad press."

Non sequiturs—the Atherton photos came back. "Father, excuse me, but I don't know what you're talking about."

Preston laughed. "We've seen each other so seldom lately that we've forgotten the amenities."

"Father, there's something—"

"I'm sorry, I was referring to Dudley Smith's statement to the *Herald* today. He said the reopening investigation was being centered on the southside, that you're looking for another Negro gang."

"No, that's not the way it's going."

Preston put a hand on his shoulder. "You look frightened, Edmund. You do not look like a ranking policeman and you did not come here to enjoy my completion celebration."

The hand felt warm. "Father, outside of the Department, who's seen the old Atherton photographs?"

"Now I'll say 'what?' You're referring to the photographs in the case file? The ones I showed you and Thomas years ago?"

"Yes."

"Son, what are you talking about? Those photographs are sealed LAPD evidence, never released to the press or the public. Now tell me—"

"Father, the Nite Owl is collateral to several other major crimes, and Negro gangs have nothing to do with it. One of them is—"

"Then explain the evidence the way I taught you. I've had cases like—"

"Nobody has ever had a case like this, I'm a better detective than you *ever* were and *I've* never had a case like this."

Preston clamped both hands down—Ed felt his shoulders go numb. "I'm sorry for that, but it's true and I've got a five-year-old mutilation homicide connected to the Nite Owl case that says so. The victim was cut *identically* to Loren Atherton's victims and *identical* to some ink-embossed pornographic photographs tangential to the Nite Owl. Which means that either somebody saw the Atherton pictures and took it from there or you got the wrong suspect in '34."

The man didn't even blink. "Loren Atherton was incontrovertibly guilty, with a confession and eyewitness vertification. You and Thomas saw his photographs, and I doubt seriously that those photographs have ever left the Homicide pen downtown. Unless you hypothesize a policeman killer, which I find absurd, then the only explanation is that Atherton showed the photographs to some person or persons prior to his arrest. *You* got the wrong men in your glory case—I did not make that error. *Think* before you raise your voice to your father."

Ed stepped back—his legs brushed the model, broke off a piece of freeway. "I apologize, and I should be asking your advice, not competing with you. Father, is there anything about the Atherton case you haven't told me?"

"Apology accepted, and no, there isn't. You, Art and I went over the case constantly during our seminar period, and I expect that you know it as well as I do."

"Did Atherton have *any* known associates?"

Preston shook his head. "Emphatically no. He was the very model of a psychotic loner."

A deep breath. "I want to interview Ray Dieterling."

"Why? Because one of his child stars was killed by Atherton?"

"No, because a witness identified Dieterling as a KA of a criminal tangential to the Nite Owl."

"How long ago?"

"Thirty years or so."

"This person's name?"

"Pierce Patchett."

Preston shrugged. "I've never heard of him and I don't want you bothering Raymond. Emphatically no, a thirty-year-old acquaintanceship does not warrant bothering a man of Ray Dieterling's stature. *I'll* ask Ray about him and report back to you. Will that suffice?"

Ed looked at the model. Hypnotic: L.A. grown huge, Exley Construction containing it. His father's hands, gentle now. "Son, you've come very far and you've earned my respect absolutely. You've taken a beating for Inez and those men you killed, and I think you're bearing up strongly. For now, though, I want you to consider this. The Nite Owl case got you where you are today and a quick resolution on the reopening will keep you there. Collateral homicide investigations, however compelling, might seriously distract you from your main objective and thus destroy your career. Please remember that."

Ed squeezed his father's hands. "Absolute justice. Remember that?"

55

BOTH CRIME scenes sealed—the printshop, the pad next door. One Marin sheriff—a fat guy named Hatcher. A lab man talking nonstop.

Crime Scene 1: the back room at Rapid Bob's Printing. Bud scoped Dudley nonstop, flashing back to *his* pitch: "We thought you were going to kill him, so we stopped you. I'm sorry if we were untoward, but you were a handful. Hinton is associated with some very bad people, and I'll elaborate in all due time."

He didn't press it—Dud might have stuff on him.

Lynn in custody.

Exley's slap in the face.

The lab man pointed to a rack of dumped shelves. "... okay, so the front of the shop looked hunky-dory, so our perpetrator didn't bother with it. We found cigarette butts in an ashtray here, two brands, so let's assume the Engleklings were working late. Let's assume the perpetrator picked the front door lock, tiptoed up and got the drop on them. Glove prints on the jamb of the connecting door, so that backs it up. He comes in, he makes our boys open those cabinets I showed you, he doesn't find what he wants. He gets pissed and yanks those shelves to the floor, glove prints on the fourth shelf up indicate a right-handed man of average height. The brothers open the boxes that spilled off—we got a whole load of smudged latents that indicate Pete and Bax were a bit panicked by this time. So, the perpetrator obviously didn't find what he wanted and marched our boys across the driveway to their apartment. Gentlemen, follow me."

Out the door, across an alley. The lab guy carried a flashlight; Bud stuck to the back.

Lynn cocky—convinced she could beat truth juice with her brains.

Dud probably had his own insider leads—but he still kept talking up niggers.

The lab man said, "Note the dirt on the driveway. On the morning the bodies were found our tech crew discovered and photographed three sets of footmarks too shallowly placed to make exemplars from. Two sets walking ahead of a single set, which indicates a march at gunpoint."

Over to a bungalow court. Dudley stone quiet—on the plane he hardly talked.

Would *Whisper* hit?

Play the stiff under the house against Exley—*HOW?*

Tape on the door—Hatcher peeled it off. The lab man opened up with a pass key. Lights inside—Bud squeezed in first.

A shambles—all forensicked up.

Blood spills on a wall-to-wall carpet—tape-marked. Glass tubes on the floor—circled, held in see-through evidence bags. Scattered around: photo negatives—dozens—cracked, scalded surfaces. Overturned chairs, a dumped dresser, a sofa with the stuffing ripped out. Tucked in the largest rip: a glassine bag tagged "Heroin."

The lab guy spieled. "Those tubes contain chemicals that we've ID'd as antipsychotic drugs. The negatives were mostly too blurred to identify, but we were able to figure out that most of them were pornographic photographs. The images were mostly burned off with chemicals taken from the refrigerator in the kitchen: our boys owned a whole cornucopia of corrosive solutions. I'll hypothesize here: Peter and Baxter Englekling were tortured before they were shot to death—that we know. I think the killer showed them each negative individually, asked them questions, then burned them—and the pictures. What was he looking for? I don't know, maybe he wanted the picture participants identified. We found a magnifying glass under the couch, so I'm leaning toward that theory now. Also, note the plastic bag marked 'Heroin' extruding from the couch, the contents of which, of course, we locked up. Four bags total in a safe little hidey-hole. The killer left a small fortune in salable dope behind."

Into the kitchen, more chaos, the icebox open—spilling tubes, bottles marked with chemical symbols. Stacked by the sink: something like printing press plates.

The tech man pointed to the mess. "Another hypothesis, gentlemen. In my crime scene report you'll note that I've listed no less than twenty-six separate chemical substances found on the premises. The killer tortured Pete and Bax Englekling with chemicals, and he knew which chemicals would scald flesh. I'd call his torture method a means of opportunity, so I'm betting the man had an engineering, a medical or a chemistry background. Now the bedroom."

Bud thought: PATCHETT.

Back to the bedroom, blood drops in the hall along the way. A small room, a twelve-by-twelve slaughterhouse.

Two body outlines—one on the bed, one on the floor, dried blood tape-to-tape both places. Clothesline sash wrapped around the bedposts; more sash on the floor; taped circles on the bedsheets, the floor, a nightstand by the bed. A bullet hole circled on one wall; a forensic display on a corkboard: more scalded negatives.

Lab man: "Just glove prints and Englekling prints on the negatives, we dusted every one of them, then placed most of them back in their original locations. The ones on the board were found here in the bedroom, which as you can tell was where the torture and the killings took place. Now, those small circles on the bed and elsewhere indicate sections of torso, arm and leg tissue scalded off the Englekling brothers, and if you look closely at the floor you'll be able to see patches of singed carpet caused by chemical spills. Both men were shot twice with a silencer-fitted .38 revolver. Baffling threads we took off the shells indicate the silencer and indicate why no shots were heard. The bullet hole in the wall is our one real lead, and it's easy to reconstruct what happened. Bax Englekling got free of his bonds, got ahold of the gun and fired a wounding shot before the killer got the gun back and shot him. The shell we took out of the wall had shredded Caucasian flesh and gray arm hair stuck to it, along with O-plus blood. Both Englekling boys were AB-minus, so we know the perpetrator was hit. The blood drops leading out to the living room and the negatives that he took out to look at indicate that it wasn't a major wound. Lieutenant Hatcher's crew found a blood-soaked O-plus towel in a sewer down the street, so that was his tourniquet. My last hypothesis is that this bastard really had a hard-on for those negatives."

Hatcher spoke up. "And we've got nothing. We've canvassed two dozen times, we've got no eyewitnesses and those goddamned brothers did not have a single KA that we've been able to turn. We hit doctors' offices, emergency rooms, train stations, airports and bus stations looking for sightings of a wounded man and got nothing. If the brothers had an address book, it was taken. Nobody saw anything or heard anything. Like my science buddy says, our guy really had a boner for those negatives, which might— and I emphasize 'might'—have something to do with our victims coming forth on that Nite Owl case of yours years ago. They had a dirty-picture theory then, right?"

Dudley said, "They did indeed, quite unsubstantiated."

"And the L.A. papers said you just reopened the case."

"Yes, that's correct."

"Captain, I regret that we didn't decide to cooperate with you earlier, but put that aside. Have you got anything to give me on the new end of your case that I can use?"

Dudley smiled. "Chief Parker has authorized me to secure a copy of your case file to read. He said that if I find evidential links to our homicides, he'll release a transcription of the Englekling brothers' 1953 testimony."

"Which you say pertains to pornography, which our case sure as hell does."

Dudley lit a cigarette. "Yes, if it doesn't pertain to heroin just as much."

Hatcher snorted. "Captain, if our boy got his chops licked over white horse, he'd have stolen that stuff stashed in the couch."

"Yes, or the killer was simply a frothing-at-the-mouth psychopath who evinced a psychopathic reaction to the negatives for unfathomable reasons of his own. Frankly, the heroin angle interests me. Have you any evidence that the brothers were either selling or manufacturing it?"

Hatcher shook his head. "None, and as far as *our* case goes, I don't think it plays. Have you got a pornography angle on the reopening?"

"No, not as yet. Again, after I've read your case file I'll be in touch."

Hatcher—ready to bust. "Captain, you came all the way up here for our evidence, and you got nothing to give in return?"

"I came up here at the urging of Chief Parker, who pledges his full cooperation should your case warrant reciprocity."

"Big words, sahib, that I don't like the sound of."

Getting ugly—Dudley dug in with a big blarney smile. Bud walked out to the curb, dug in by their rental.

Scared, standing on GO.

Dudley walked out; Hatcher and the lab man locked the printshop. Bud said, "I don't follow you at all these days, boss."

"Starting when, lad?"

"Let's try last night with Hinton."

Dudley laughed. "You were your old cruel self last night. It warmed my heart and convinced me that the extracurricular work I have planned for you remains within your grasp."

"What work?"

"In due time."

"What happened to Hinton?"

"We released him well-chastised and terrified of Sergeant Wendell White."

"Yeah, but what were you pressing him on?"

"Lad, you have your extracurricular secrets, I have mine. We'll hold a clarification session soon."

GO. "No. I just want to know where we both stand on the Nite Owl. *Now.*"

"Edmund Exley, lad. We both stand there."

"What?"—scared to his own ears.

"*Edmund Jennings Exley.* He's been your raison d'être since Bloody Christmas, and he's why you don't tell me certain things. I love you, so I respect your omissions. Now reciprocate my love and respect my lack of clarification for the next twelve days and you'll see him destroyed."

"What are you—" a little kid's voice.

"You've never accorded him credit, so I'll tell you now. As a man he's less than negligible, but as a detective he far exceeds even myself. There. God and yourself witness plaudits for a man I despise. Now will you respect my omissions—as I respect yours?"

Past GO. "No. Just fucking tell me what you want me to do. Just explain it."

Dudley laughed, smiled. "Do nothing for now but listen. I've found out that Thad Green will be retiring to take over the

U.S. Border Patrol later this spring. Our new chief of detectives will be either Edmund Exley or myself. His upcoming inspectorship gives Exley the inside track, and Parker favors him personally. I plan on using certain aspects of our mutually withheld evidence to clear the Nite Owl posthaste, establish myself as the new frontrunner and ruin Exley in the process. Lad, bear with me for a few more days and I'll guarantee you your own personal revenge."

The deal was Exley/Dudley vs. Exley.

No contest.

Past GO: the crumbs he spilled to Exley, Exley's promise—liaison, the hooker snuffs. "Boss, is there a carrot in this for me?"

"Besides our friend's downfall?"

"Yeah."

"And in exchange for a full disclosure? Beyond what you gave Exley as part of your field runner agreement?"

Jesus, what the man knew. "Right."

Ho Ho Ho. "Lad, you drive a hard bargain, but will a Chief of Detectives' Special Inquiry suffice? Say 187 PC multiple, various jurisdictions?"

Bud stuck out his hand. "Deal."

Dudley said, "Stay away from Exley and treat yourself to a grand clean room at the Victory. I'll be by to see you in a day or so."

"You take the car, I got business in Frisco first."

* * *

He blew forty bucks on a cab, cruised the Golden Gate high on adrenaline. Double cross: a bad deal to survive, then a good deal to win—up from the minors to the majors. Exley had insider tips and sad Trashcan Jack; Dudley had insider juice that almost went psychic. Turnaround: he lied to Dudley to burn down Exley; five years later the man calls it in: lies forgiven, two cops, one torch. San Francisco bright in the distance, Dudley Smith's voice: "Edmund Jennings Exley." Chills just saying the name.

Over the bridge, a stop at a pay phone. Long-distance: Lynn's number, ten rings, no answer. 9:10 P.M., a spooker—she should have been home from the Bureau by dark.

Across town for the drop-off: San Francisco Police Department, Detective Division HQ. Bud pinned on his badge, walked in.

Homicide on floor three—arrows painted on the wall pointed him up. Creaky stairs, a huge squad bay. Nightwatch lull: two men up by the coffee.

They walked over. The younger guy pointed to his shield. "L.A., huh? Help you with something?"

Bud held his ID out. "You've got an old 187, like one a pal of mine on the L.A. Sheriff's caught. He asked me to check out your case file."

"Well, the captain's not here now. Maybe you should try in the morning."

The older man checked his ID. "You're the guy that's bugs on prostie jobs. The captain said you keep calling up and you're a royal pain in the keester. What's the matter, you got another one?"

"Yeah, Lynette Ellen Kendrick, L.A. County last week. Come on, ten minutes with the file and I'm out of your hair."

The young guy: "Hey, catch the drift? The captain wanted you to see the file, he woulda sent you an invitation."

The old guy: "The captain's a jack-off. What's our victim's name and DOD?"

"Chrissie Virginia Renfro, July 16, '56."

"Well then, I'll tell you what you do. You hit the records room around the corner, find your 1956 unsolved cabinet and go to the R's. You don't take anything out and you skedaddle before junior here has a migraine. Got it?"

"Got it."

* * *

Autopsy pictures: orifice rips, facial close-ups—pulp, no real face, ring fragments embedded in cheekbones. Wide-angle shots: the body, found at Chrissie's pad—a dive across from the St. Francis Hotel.

Pervert shakedown reports—local deviates brought in, questioned, released for lack of evidence. Foot fuckers, sadist pimps, Chrissie's pimp himself—in the Frisco City Jail when Chrissie was snuffed. Panty sniffers, rape-o's, Chrissie's regular johns—all alibied up, no names that crossed to the other case files he'd read.

Canvassing reports: local yokels, guests at the St. Francis. Six loser sheets, a grabber.

7/16/56: a St. Francis bellhop told detectives he caught Spade Cooley's late show at the hotel's Lariat Room, then saw Chrissie Virginia Renfro, weaving—"maybe on hop"—walk into her building.

Grabber—Bud sat still, worked it up.

Grab Lynette Ellen Kendrick, DOD L.A. County last week. Grab an unrelated snitch—Lamar Hinton stooling everything in sight. Grabs: Dwight Gilette—Kathy Janeway's ex-pimp—supplied whores for Spade Cooley's parties. Spade was an opium smoker, a "degenerate dope fiend." Spade was in L.A., playing the El Rancho Klub on the Strip—a mile from Lynette Kendrick's pad.

First glitch: Spade couldn't have a jacket, no way to check his blood type—he rode in Sheriff Biscailuz' volunteer posse—PR stuff—nobody with a yellow sheet allowed.

Keep grabbing, check the ME's report, "Bloodstream Contents." Page 2, a scorcher—"undigested foodstuffs, semen, a heavily narcotizing amount of food-dispersed opium further verified by tar residue in teeth."

Bud threw his arms up—like he could reach through the roof and haul down the moon. He banged the ceiling, came back to earth thinking—this was not a solo job, he was hiding out from Exley, Dudley just didn't care. He saw a phone, hit the ceiling, came down with a partner:

Ellis Loew—sex murders made him drool.

He grabbed the phone.

56

HILDA LEFFERTS tapped a mugshot. "There, that's Susan Nancy's beau. Will you take me home now?"

Bingo—a pudgy hardcase type, a real Duke Cathcart lookalike. Dean NMI Van Gelder, W.M., DOB 3/4/21. 5'8¾", 178 lbs., blue eyes, brown hair. One armed-robbery bounce—6/42—ten to twenty, released from Folsom 6/52, full minimum sentence topped—no parole. No further arrests—chalk it up to Bud White's theory—Van Gelder got it at the Nite Owl.

Hilda said, "That's it—*Dean*. Susan Nancy called him 'Dean,' but he said, 'No, get used to calling me "Duke."'"

Jack said, "You sure?"

"Yes, I'm sure. Six hours of looking at these awful pictures and you ask me if I'm sure? If I wanted to lie I would have pointed somebody out hours ago. *Please*, Officer. First you find a body under my house, next you subject me to these pictures. Now will you please take me home?"

Jack shook his head no. Work it: Who? to Van Gelder to Cathcart to the Nite Owl. One parlay made sense—the Englekling brothers to Cathcart to a brush with Mickey Cohen—in stir back in '53. He picked up the phone, dialed O.

"Operator."

"Operator, this is a police emergency. I need to be put through to somebody in administration at McNeil Federal Penitentiary, Puget Sound, Washington."

"I see. And your name?"

"Sergeant Vincennes, Los Angeles Police Department. Tell them I'm on a homicide investigation."

"I see. Circuits to Wasington State have been—"

"Shit. I'm at MAdison 60042. Will you—"

"I'll try your call now, sir."

Jack hung up. Forty seconds by the wall clock—*bbring brinng.*

"Vincennes."

"Deputy Warden Cahill at McNeil. This pertains to a homicide?"

Hilda Lefferts was pouting—Jack turned away from her. "Yeah, and all I need's one answer. Got a pencil?"

"Of course."

"Okay. I need to know if a white male named Dean Van Gelder, that's two separate words on the last name, visited an inmate at McNeil say from February through April 1953. All I need's a yes or no and the names of any inmates he visited."

A sigh. "All right, please hold. This may take a while."

Jack held counting minutes—Cahill came back on at twelve plus. "That's a positive. Dean Van Gelder, DOB 3/4/21, visited inmate David Goldman on three occasions: 3/27/53, 4/1/53 and 4/3/53. Goldman was at McNeil on tax charges. Perhaps you've heard—"

Work in Davey G.—Mickey Cohen's man. Work in Van Gelder's last visit—two weeks before the Nite Owl, the same time the Englekling brothers lubed Mickey—the meet where they spilled the smut plan. The prison man kept babbling—Jack hung up on him. The Nite Owl case started to shake.

57

ED DROVE Lynn Bracken home, a last shot before having her arrested. She protested, then went along: her day of truth dope, counterdope and browbeating showed—she looked frazzled, exhausted. Call her smart, strong and chemically fortified; she gave up nothing but Pierce Patchett crumbs—however she managed it. Patchett knew a whitewash wouldn't wash; Lynn funneled out her call girl tale—and Patchett had to have lawyers waiting in case that crumb went to indictments. Reopening day one was pure insane: Dudley Smith up in Gaitsville while his hot dogs shook down Darktown; Vincennes' body under the house and his ID on Dean Van Gelder—Davey Goldman's McNeil visitor pre-Nite Owl. Bud White for a runner, then his *Whisper* leak breaking—he was a fool to trust him for a second. All of that he could take: he was a professional detective used to dealing with chaos.

But the Atherton case and his father circuiting in was something else. Now he felt suspended, one simple instinct running him: the Nite Owl had a life past any detective's volition—and the will to make its horror known whether he was there to probe evidence or not, whether he was capable of forming plans or just hanging on for the ride.

He had a plan to work Bracken and Patchett.

Lynn blew smoke rings out the window. "Down two blocks and turn left. You can stop there, I'm right near the corner."

Ed braked short. "One last question. At the Bureau you implied that you knew Patchett and Sid Hudgens were planning to work an extortion racket."

"I don't recall endorsing that statement."

"You didn't dispute it."

"I was tired and bored."

"You endorsed it, implicitly. And it's in Jack Vincennes' deposition."

"Then perhaps Vincennes lied about that part. He used to be quite a celebrity. Wouldn't you also call him quite a self-dramatist?"

An opening. "Yes."

"And do you think you can trust him?"

Fake chagrin oozing. "I don't know. He's my weak point."

"So there you are. Mr. Exley, are you going to arrest me?"

"I'm beginning to think it wouldn't do any good. What did White say when he told you to come in for questioning?"

"Just to come clean. Did you show him Vincennes' deposition?"

The truth—make her grateful. "No."

"I'm glad, because I'm sure it's full of lies. Why didn't you show it to him?"

"Because he's a limited detective, and the less he knows the better. He's also a protégé of a rival officer on the case, and I didn't want him passing information to him."

"Are you speaking of Dudley Smith?"

"Yes. Do you know him?"

"No, but Bud speaks of him often. I think he's afraid of him, which means that Smith must be quite a man."

"Dudley's brilliant and vicious to the core, but I'm better. And look, it's late."

"Can I give you a drink?"

"Why? You spat in my face today."

"Well, given the circumstances."

Her smile made his smile easy. "Given the circumstances, one drink."

Lynn got out of the car. Ed watched her move: high heels, a shit day—but her feet hardly touched the ground. She led him to her building, unlocked the bottom door and hit a light.

Ed walked in. Exquisite—the fabrics, the art. Lynn kicked off her shoes and poured brandies; Ed sat on a sofa—pure velvet.

Lynn joined him. Ed took his drink, sipped. Lynn warmed the glass with her hands. "Do you know why I invited you in?"

"You're too intelligent to try to wrangle a deal, so I'll guess you're just curious about me."

"Bud hates you more than he loves me or anyone else. I'm beginning to see why."

"I don't really want your opinion."

"I was leading up to a compliment."

"Some other time, all right?"

"I'll change the subject then. How's Inez Soto handling the publicity? She's been all over the papers."

"She's taking it poorly, and I don't want to talk about her."

"It galls you that I know so much about you. You don't have information to compete."

Move the wedge. "I have Vincennes' deposition."

"Which I suspect you doubt the truth of."

Throw the change-up. "You mentioned that Patchett financed some early Raymond Dieterling films. Can you elaborate on that?"

"Why? Because your father is associated with Dieterling? You see the disadvantages of being the son of a famous man?"

No hink, a deft touch with the knife. "Just a policeman's question."

Lynn shrugged. "Pierce mentioned it to me in passing several years ago."

The phone rang—Lynn ignored it. "I can tell you don't want to talk about Jack Vincennes."

"I can tell you do."

"I haven't seen much in the news about him lately."

"That's because he flushed everything he had down the toilet. *Badge of Honor*, his friendship with Miller Stanton, all of it. Sid Hudgens getting murdered didn't help, since *Hush-Hush* owed half its filth to Vincennes' shakedowns."

Lynn sipped brandy. "You don't like Jack."

"No, but there's part of his deposition that I believe absolutely. Patchett has carbons of Sid Hudgens' private dirt files, including a carbon of a file on Vincennes himself. You can do yourself some good by acknowledging it."

If she bit she'd start now.

"I can't acknowledge it, and the next time we speak I'll have a lawyer. But I can tell you that I think I know what such a file would contain."

First wedge in place. "And?"

"Well, I think the year was 1947. Vincennes got involved in a gunfight at the beach. He was under the influence of narcotics and shot and killed two innocent people, a husband and wife. My source has verification, including the testimony of an ambulance deputy and a notarized statement from the doctor who treated Jack for his wounds. My source has blood test results that show the drugs in his system and testimony from eyewitnesses who didn't come forth. Is that information you'd suppress to protect a brother officer, Captain?"

The Malibu Rendezvous: Trashcan's glory job. The phone rang—Lynn let it go. Ed said, "Jesus Christ," no need to fake.

"Yes. You know, when I read about Vincennes I always thought he had some very dark reasons for persecuting dope users, so I wasn't surprised when I found that out. And, Captain? If Pierce did have file carbons, I'm sure he would have destroyed them."

Her last bit rang fake—Ed played a lie off it. "I know Jack loves dope, it's been a rumor around the Bureau for years. And I know you're lying about the files and I know Vincennes would do anything to get his file back. You and Patchett shouldn't underestimate him."

"The way you've underestimated Bud White?"

Her smile came on like a target—he thought for a second that he'd hit her. She laughed before he could; he leaned in and kissed her instead. Lynn pulled back, then kissed back; they rolled to the floor shedding clothes. The phone rang—Ed kicked it off the hook. Lynn pulled him inside her; they rolled, moved together, trashed furniture. It ended as fast as it started—he could feel Lynn reaching to peak. Seconds apart for that, good enough, rest. His story laid out between sighs, like it was a burden too heavy to carry.

Rogue cop Jack Vincennes, on dope and too hot to handle. He'd do anything to get his file back, he had to get that file. Captain E. J. Exley had to use him for what he knew—but Vincennes was doped up, boozed up, going psycho on him—

58

BUD HIT L.A. at dawn, off the midnight bus down from Frisco. His city looked strange, new—like everything else in his life.

He got a taxi and dozed; he kept snapping awake to Ellis Loew: "It sounds like a great case, but multiple homicides are tricky and Spade Cooley is a well-known figure. I'll put a DA's Bureau team on it and *you stay out of it for now.*" Cut to Lynn: calls, the phone off the hook, smothered. Strange, but like her—when she wanted to sleep she wanted to sleep.

He couldn't believe his life, it was just too goddamn amazing.

The cab dropped him off. He found a note on his door— "Sergeant Duane W. Fisk" on the letterhead.

> Sgt. White—
>   Captain Exley wants to see you immediately (something pertaining to *Whisper* magazine and a body under a house). Report to IA immediately upon your return to Los Angeles.

Bud laughed, packed a bag: clothes, his paper stash—the hooker killings, the Nite Owl—Dudley's for the asking. He threw the note in the toilet, pissed on it.

* * *

He drove to Gardena, checked into the Victory: a room with clean sheets, a hot plate, no bloodstains on the walls. Fuck sleep— he fixed coffee, worked.

Everything he knew on Spade Cooley—half a longhand page.

Cooley was an Okie fiddler/singer, a skinny guy, maybe late forties. He had a couple of hit records, his TV show was big for a while. His bass player, Burt Arthur Perkins, a.k.a. "Deuce," did

time on a chain gang for sodomy on dogs and was rumored to
have a shitload of mob KA's.

On the investigation:

Lamar Hinton said Spade smoked opium; Spade played the
Lariat Room in Frisco—across from Chrissie Renfro's place of
death. Chrissie died with "O" in her system; Spade was currently
playing the El Rancho Klub in L.A., close by Lynette Ellen Kendrick's apartment. Lamar Hinton said Dwight Gilette—Kathy
Janeway's old pimp—supplied whores for Cooley's parties.

Circumstantial—but tight.

A phone wired to the wall—Bud grabbed it, called the County
Coroner's Office.

"Medical Examinations, Jensen."

"Sergeant White for Dr. Harris. I know he's busy, but tell him
it's just one thing."

"Hold, please," click, click, click. "Sergeant, what is it this time?"

"One thing off your autopsy report."

"You're not even a county officer."

"Stomach and bloodstream contents on Lynette Kendrick.
Come on, huh?"

"That's easy, because Kendrick won our best stomach award
last week. Are you ready? Frankfurters with sauerkraut, french
fries, Coca-Cola, opium, sperm. Jesus, what a last supper."

Bud hung up. Ellis Loew said stay out of it. Kathy Janeway said GO.

*　*　*

He drove to the Strip, put the MO together.

First the El Rancho Klub, closed, "Spade Cooley and His Cowboy Rhythm Band Appearing Nitely." A publicity still by the door:
Spade, Deuce Perkins, three other cracker types. No heavily ringed
fingers; a lead rubber-stamped at the bottom: "Represented by Nat
Penzler Associates, 653 North La Cienega, Los Angeles."

Across the street: the Hot Dog Hut, kraut dogs and fries on
the menu. Down the Strip by Crescent Heights: a well-known
prostie stroll. A mile south at Melrose and Sweetzer: Lynette Ellen
Kendrick's apartment.

Easy:

Spade picked her up late, no witnesses. He had the food and
the dope, suggested a cozy all-nighter, took Lynette home. They
got high, chowed down—Spade beat her to death, raped her
three times postmortem.

Bud hooked south to La Cienega. 653: a redwood A-frame, "Nat Penzler Assoc." by the mailbox. The door propped open; a girl inside making coffee.

Bud walked in. The girl said, "Yes, can I help you?"

"The boss around?"

"Mr. Penzler's on the telephone. Can *I* help you?"

One connecting door—"N.P." brass-stamped. Bud pushed it open; an old man yelled, "Hey! I'm on a call! What are you, a bill collector? Hey, Gail! Give this clown a magazine!"

Bud flashed his badge. The man hung up the phone, pushed back from his desk. Bud said, "You're Nat Penzler?"

"Call me Natsky. Are you looking for representation? I could get you work playing thugs. You have that Neanderthal look currently in vogue."

Let it go. "You're Spade Cooley's agent, right?"

"Right. You want to join Spade's band? Spade's a moneymaker, but my shvartze cleaning lady sings better than him, so maybe I can get you a spot, a bouncer gig at the El Rancho at least. Lots of trim there, boychik. A moose like you could get reamed, steamed and dry-cleaned."

"You through, pops?"

Penzler flushed. "Mr. Natsky to you, caveman."

Bud shut the door. "I need to see Cooley's booking records going back to '51. You want to do this nice or not?"

Penzler got up, blocked his filing cabinets. "Showtime's over, Godzilla. I never divulge client information, even under threat of a subpoena. So amscray and come back for lunch sometime, say on the twelfth of never."

Bud tore the phone cord from the wall; Penzler slid the top drawer open. "No rough stuff, please, caveman! I do my best work with my face!"

Bud thumbed folders, hit "Cooley, Donnell Clyde," dumped it on the desk. A picture hit the blotter: Spade, four rings on ten fingers. Pink sheets, white sheets, then blue sheets—booking records clipped by year.

Penzler stood by muttering. Bud matched dates.

Jane Mildred Hamsher, 3/8/51, San Diego—Spade there at the El Cortez Sky Room. April '53, Kathy Janeway, the Cowboy Rhythm Band at Bido Lito's—South L.A. Sharon, Sally, Chrissie Virginia, Maria up to Lynette: Bakersfield, Needles, Arizona, Frisco, Seattle, back to L.A., shifting personnel listed on pay cards: Deuce

Perkins playing bass most of the time, drum and sax guys coming and going, Spade Cooley *always* headlining, in those cities on those DODs.

Blue sheets dripping wet—his own sweat. "Where's the band staying?"

Penzler: "The Biltmore, and you didn't get it from Natsky."

"That's good, 'cause this is Murder One and I wasn't here."

"I am like the Sphinx, I swear to you. My God, Spade and his lowlife crew. My God, do you know what he grossed last year?"

* * *

He called the lead in to Ellis Loew; Loew hit the roof: "I told you to stay out! I've got three *civilized* men on it, and I'll tell them what you've got, but you stay out and get back to the Nite Owl, *do you understand me?*"

He understood: Kathy Janeway kept saying GO.

The Biltmore.

He forced himself to drive there slow, park by the back entrance, politely ask the clerk where to find Mr. Cooley's party. The clerk said, "The El Presidente Suite, floor nine"; he said "Thank you" so calm that everything went into slow motion and he thought for a second he was swimming.

The stairs were like swimming upstream—Little Kathy kept saying KILL HIM. The suite: double doors, gold-filigreed—eagles, American flags. He jiggled the knob, the doors opened.

High swank gone white trash—three crackers passed out on the floor. Booze empties, dumped ashtrays, no Spade.

Connecting doors—the one on the right featured noise. Bud kicked it in.

Deuce Perkins in bed watching cartoons. Bud pulled his gun. "Where's Cooley?"

Perkins popped in a toothpick. "On a drunk, which is where I'm goin'. You want to see him, come to the El Rancho tonight. Chances are he'll show up."

"The fuck, he's the headliner."

"Most times. But Spade's been erratic lately, so I been fillin' in. I sing good as him and I'm better lookin', so nobody seems to mind. Now, you want to get out of here and leave me alone with my entertainment?"

"Where's he drinking?"

"Put that gun away, junior. The worse you got him for's non-payment of child support, and Spade always pays sooner or later."

"Nix, this is Murder One, and I heard he likes opium."

Perkins coughed out his toothpick. "What'd you say?"

"Hookers. Spade like young girls?"

"He don't like to kill them, just play hide the tubesteak like you and me."

"*Where is he?*"

"Man, I'm not no snitch."

Backhanded pistolwhips—Perkins yelped, spat teeth. The TV went loud: kids squealing for Kellogg's Cornflakes. Bud shot the screen out.

Deuce snitched: "Check the 'O' joints in Chinatown and please fuckin' leave me alone!"

Kathy said KILL HIM. Bud thought of his mother for the first time in years.

59

THE DOCTOR said, "I told this to your Captain Exley, and I told him an interview with Mr. Goldman would most likely prove fruitless—the man is simply not lucid most of the time. However, since he insisted on sending you up here, I'll run through it again."

Jack looked around. Camarillo was creepy: lots of geeks, geek artwork on the walls. "Would you? The captain wants a statement from him."

"Well, he'll be lucky to get one. Last July, Mr. Goldman and his confrere Mickey Cohen were attacked with knives and pipes at McNeil Island Prison. Unidentified assailants apparently, and Cohen was relatively unharmed while Mr. Goldman suffered serious brain damage. Both men were paroled late last year, and Mr. Goldman began to behave quite erratically. Late in December he was arrested for urinating in public in Beverly Hills, and the judge ordered him here for ninety days' observation. We've had him since Christmas and we've just recycled him in for another ninety. Frankly, we can't do a thing with him, and the only thing mysterious is that Mr. Cohen visited and offered to transfer Mr. Goldman to a private treatment facility at his own expense, but Mr. Goldman refused and acted terrified of him. Isn't that odd?"

"Maybe not. Where is he?"

"On the other side of that door. Be gentle with him, please. The man was a gangster, but he's just a sad human being now."

Jack opened the door. A small padded room; Davey Goldman on a long padded bench. He needed a shave; he reeked of Lysol. Slack-jawed Davey scoping a *National Geographic*.

Jack sat beside him—Goldman moved away. Jack said, "This place is the shits. You should've let Mickey spring you."

Goldman picked his nose, ate it.

"Davey, you on the outs with Mickey?"

Goldman held out his magazine—naked Negroes waving spears.

"Cute, and when they start showing white stuff I'll subscribe. Davey, you remember me? Jack Vincennes? I used to work LAPD Narco and we used to run into each other on the Strip."

Goldman scratched his balls. He smiled, low voltage, nobody home.

"Is this an act? Come on, Davey. You and the Mick go way back. You know he'd take care of you."

Goldman squashed an invisible bug. "Not anymore."

A gone man's voice—nobody could fake it that good. "Say, Davey, whatever happened to Dean Van Gelder? You remember him, he used to visit you at McNeil."

Goldman picked his nose, wiped it on his feet. Jack said, "Dean Van Gelder. He visited you at McNeil in '53, right around the time these two guys Pete and Bax Englekling visited Mickey. Now you're afraid of Mickey, and Van Gelder clipped a guy named Duke Cathcart and got clipped himself during the world famous Nite Owl fucking Massacre. You got any brains left to talk about that?"

No lights blinked on.

"Come on, Davey. You tell me, you won't feel so sad. Talk to your Uncle Jack."

"Dutchman! Dutch fuck! Mickey should know to hurt me but he don't. Hub rachmones, Meyer, hub rachmones, Meyer Harris Cohen te absolvo my sins."

His mouth did the talking—the rest of the man came off dead. Jack parlayed: Van Gelder the Dutchman, Yiddish to Latin, something like betrayal. "Come on, keep going. Confess to Father Jack and I'll make it allll better."

Goldman picked his nose; Jack shoved him. "Come on!"

"Dutchman blew it!"

?????—maybe—a jail bid on Duke Cathcart. "Blew what, come on!"

Goldman, a gone monotone. "Franchise boys got theirs three triggers blip blip blip. Fucking slowdown ain't no hoedown, Mickey thinks he'll get the fish but the Irish Cheshire got the fishy and Mickey gets the bones no gravy he is dead meat for the meow monster. Hub rachmones Meyer, I could trust you, not them, it's all on ice but not for us te absolvo ..."

??????????? "Who are these guys you're talking about?"

Goldman hummed a tune, off key, familiar. Jack caught the melody: "Take the 'A' Train." "Davey, *talk* to me."

Davey sang. "Bumpa—bump bump bump bump bump bump bump bump the cute train bump bump bump bump the cute train."

??????????????????????—worse, like his brain had padded walls. "Davey, just talk."

Geek talk: "Bzz, bzz bzz talking bug to hear. Betty, Benny bug to listen, Barney bug. Hub rachmones Meyer my dear friend."

????????? into just maybe something:

The Engleklings saw Cohen *in his cell*, pitched him on Duke Cathcart's smut scheme. Mickey swore he did not tell a soul. Goldman found out about it, decided to crash the racket, dispatched Dean Van Gelder to snuff Cathcart—or maybe buy in on the deal. ????????—How—??????—DID HE HAVE A BUG PLANTED IN COHEN'S CELL?

"Davey, *tell me about the bug.*"

Goldman started humming "In the Mood."

The doctor opened the door. "That's it, Officer. You've bothered this man long enough."

* * *

Exley okayed it on the phone: a run to McNeil to check for evidence of bugging apparatus in Mickey Cohen's former cell. The Ventura County Airport was a few miles away—he was to fly to Puget Sound, take a cab to the pen. Bob Gallaudet would have a Prison's Bureau man there to run liaison—the McNeil administrators pampered Cohen, probably took bribes for the service, might not cooperate without a push. Exley called the bug theory a long shot; he ranted that Bud White was missing—Fisk and Kleckner were out looking for him, the bastard was probably running from his *Whisper* piece and the body in San Berdoo—Fisk left him a note, mentioned the discovery. Parker said Dudley Smith was studying the Englekling case file and would report on it soon; Lynn Bracken was still holding back. Jack said, "What do we do about that?" Exley said, "The Dining Car at midnight. We'll discuss it."

Scary Captain Ed closing ominous.

Jack drove to Ventura, caught his flight—Exley called ahead, vouchered his ticket. A stewardess handed out newspapers; he grabbed a *Times* and *Daily News* and read Nite Owl.

Dudley's boys were ripping up Darktown, hauling in known Negro offenders, looking for the *real* punks popping shotguns in Griffith Park. Pure bullshit: whoever planted the weapons in Ray Coates' car planted the matching shells in the park, feeding off location leads in the press—only pros would have the brains and the balls to do it. Mike Breuning and Dick Carlisle were running a command post at 77th Street Station—the entire squad and twenty extra men from Homicide detached to work the case. No way were crazed darkies guilty—it was starting to look like 1953 all over again. The *Daily News* showed photos: Central Avenue swarmed by placard-waving boogies, the house Exley bought Inez Soto. A dandy shot in the *Times*—Inez outside Ray Dieterling's place in Laguna, shielding her eyes from flashbulbs.

Jack kept reading.

The State Attorney General's Office issued a statement: Ellis Loew outfoxed them by planting a restraining order, but they were still interested in the case and would intercede when the order lapsed—unless the LAPD solved the Nite Owl mess to the satisfaction of the Los Angeles County Grand Jury within a suitable period of time. LAPD issued a press release—a detail-packed doozie on Inez Soto's 1953 gang rape accompanied by a heartwarming rendition of how Captain Ed Exley helped her rebuild her life. Exley's old man got a treatment: the *Daily News* played up the completion of the Southern California freeway system and reported a late-breaking rumor—Big Preston was soon to announce his candidacy in the governor's race, a scant two and a half months before the Republican primary, the eleventh-hour announcement strategy a ploy to capitalize on upcoming freeway brouhaha. How would his son's bad press affect his chances?

Jack measured his own chances. He was back on with Karen because she saw he was trying; the best way to keep it going was to cash in his twenty, grab his pension, get out of L.A. The next two months would be a sprint dodging bullets: the reopening, what Patchett and Bracken had on him. Odds you couldn't figure—for a sprinter he was scared and tired—and starting to feel old. Exley had sprint moves in mind—late dinner meets weren't his style. Bracken and Patchett might deal his dirt in; Parker might quash it to protect the Department. But Karen would know, and what was left of the marriage would go down—because she could just barely take that she'd married a drunk and a bagman. "Murderer" was one bullet they both couldn't dodge.

Three hours in the air; three hours pent up thinking. The plane touched down at Puget Sound; Jack caught a cab to McNeil.

Ugly: a gray monolith on a gray rock island. Gray walls, gray fog, barbed wire at the edge of gray water. Jack got out at the guard hut; the gatekeeper checked his ID, nodded. Steel gates slid back into stone.

Jack walked in. A wiry little man met him in the sallyport. "Sergeant Vincennes? I'm Agent Goddard, Prison's Bureau."

A good handshake. "Did Exley tell you what it's about?"

"Bob Gallaudet did. You're on the Nite Owl and related conspiracy cases and you think Cohen's cell might have been bugged. We're looking for evidence to support that theory, which I don't think is so farfetched."

"Why?"

They walked bucking wind—Goddard talked above it. "Cohen got the royal treatment here, Goldman too. Privileges up the wazoo, unlimited visitors and not too much scrutiny on the stuff brought into their tier, so a bug could have been planted. Are you thinking Goldman crossed Mickey?"

"Something like that."

"Well, could be. They had cells two doors apart, on a tier Mickey requested, because half the cells had ruined plumbing and you couldn't house inmates in them. You'll see, I've got the whole row vacated and closed off."

Checkpoints, the blocks—six-story tiers linked by catwalks. Upstairs to a corridor—eight empty cells. Goddard said, "The penthouse. Quiet, underpopulated and a nice day room for the boys to play cards in. We have an informant who says Cohen got approval on the inmates placed up here. Can you feature the cheek of that?"

Jack said, "Jesus, you're good. And fast."

"Well, Exley and Gallaudet carry weight, and the powers that be here didn't have time to prepare. Now check the goodies I brought."

On the day room table: crowbars, chisels, mallets, a long thin pole with a hook at the end. On a blanket: a tape recorder, a tangle of wires. Goddard said, "First we tear this tier up. I admit it's a long shot, but I brought a recorder along in case we find tape."

"I'd call that a maybe. Goldman and Cohen got paroled last fall, but they got bushwhacked in July and Davey got his brains scrambled. I'm thinking if he was the one monitoring the tape then maybe he was too wet-brained to pull the machine."

"Enough gabbing. Let's dig."

*   *   *

They dug.

Goddard plumbed a line from the heat duct in Cohen's cell to the heat duct in Goldman's, marked a line on the ceilings of the two cells in between, started probing with a mallet and chisel. Jack pried a protection plate off the duct on Mickey's wall, banged around inside the chute with the hook device. Nothing but hollow tin walls, no wires just inside. Frustrating: it was the logical place to plant a microphone. Heat boomed out the duct; Jack changed his mind, Washington was cold, the heat would be on too much of the time, drowning out conversation. He checked the walls and ceiling for other conduits—nothing—then the area around the vent. Irregularly applied spackling dotted with pinholes right by the protector plate; he smashed his mallet until half the wall came down and a small Spackle-covered microphone dangling off a wire came loose. The wire jerked from his hand, straight back into the wall. Five seconds later Goddard stood there holding it—attached to a tape recorder covered with plastic. "Halfway between the cells, a little hidey-hole right off the vent. Let's listen, huh?"

*   *   *

They fired it up in the day room. Goddard hooked up his machine, changed spools, pushed buttons—tape-recorded tape.

Static, a dog yipping, "There, there, bubeleh"—Mickey Cohen's voice. Goddard said, "They let him keep a dog in his cell. Only in America, huh?"

Cohen: "Quit licking your schnitzel, little precious." More yips, a long silence, a click-off sound. Goddard said, "I was timing it. Voice-activated mike. Five minutes and it goes off automatically."

Jack brushed plaster off his hands. "How'd Goldman get in to change the tape?"

"He must have had some kind of hook thing, like that pole I gave you. The grate on his heat vent was loose, so we know somebody was poking around in there. Jesus, this thing has been in there how long? And Goldman had to have help, this is no one-man operation. Listen, hear that click?"

Another click, a strange voice: "For how much? I'll have that guard place the bet." Cohen: "A thousand on Basilio, that little guinea is mean. And take a run by the infirmary and see Davey, my God a goddamn turnip those goons turned him into, I swear I will live to see them in a vegetable puree." Overlapping voices, mumbles, Mickey cooing, his dog yipping.

Nail the time: Goldman and Cohen had been attacked; Mickey laid down an early bet on the Robinson-Basilio fight last September, he was probably out by then—he got down before the odds dropped.

Click off, click on, forty-six minutes of Mickey and at least two other men playing cards, mumbling, flushing the toilet. The used tape almost gone; click off, click on, the fucking dog yowling.

Mickey: "Six years and ten months here and to lose Davey's redoubtable brain right before I leave. Such tsurus to go home on. Mickey Junior, quit licking your putz, you faigeleh."

A strange voice: "Get him a bitch, and he won't have to."

Cohen: "My God to be so nimble and so hung, like Heifetz on the fiddle with his shlong that dog is, and hung like Johnny Stompanato to boot. And on the topic of boots, I read Hedda Hopper's column and see Johnny's putting the boots to Lana Turner, such a crush he's had for so long, she must have a cunt like chinchilla."

The strange-voice man cracked up. Cohen: "Enough already, you brownnoser, save some for Jack Benny. Johnny I need now, Johnny I can't locate 'cause he's playing bury the brisket with movie stars. My franchise guys keep getting clipped and I need Johnny to put an ear down for who, but that big dick dago cunt-bandit is nowhere! I want those cocksuckers clipped! I want those shitbirds who hurt Davey to cease residence on this earth!"

Mickey cough, cough, coughed. Strange Voice: "How about Lee Vachss and Abe Teitlebaum? You could put them on it."

Cohen:"Such a shmendrik you are for a confidant, but you do play cribbage good. No, Abe has grown too soft to work muscle, too much grease noshed at his deli, such grease clogs the arteries that inspire mayhem, and Lee Vachss loves death too much to be discerning. Lana, what a snatch she must have, like cashmere."

The tape ran out. Goddard said, "Mickey sure does have a verbal style, but what did all that have to do with the Nite Owl case?"

"How's 'nothing' sound?"

60

ONE WALL of his den was now a graph: Nite Owl related case players connected by horizontal lines, vertical lines linking them to a large sheet of cardboard blocked off into information sections—events culled from Vincennes' deposition. Ed wrote margin notes; his father's call still hammered him: "Edmund, I'm running for governor. Your recent notoriety may have hurt me, but put that aside. I don't want the Atherton case resurrected in print and tied to your various cases, and I don't want Ray Dieterling bothered. I want you to direct all your queries along those lines to me, and between the two of us we'll work things out."

He agreed. It rankled. It made him feel like a child—like sleeping with Lynn Bracken made him feel whorish. And too many Dieterling names were popping up on the graph.

Ed crossed lines.

Sid Hudgens lined to the ink smut Vincennes found in '53; the smut lined to Pierce Patchett. Line to: Christine Bergeron, her son Daryl and Bobby Inge, smut posers who disappeared almost concurrent with the Nite Owl. Have Fisk and Kleckner initiate a new search for them; attempt to identify the other posers—one more time. Put the smut/Hudgens line to the Atherton case aside, former Inspector Preston Exley would make discreet inquiries when asked.

A theoretical line—Pierce Patchett to Duke Cathcart. Lynn Bracken denied it, a lie, Vincennes' deposition had Patchett pushing the smut Cathcart planned to distribute—*but who made it?* Hudgens to Patchett and Bracken: the dirtmonger was terrified that Vincennes was nosing around Fleur-de-Lis; Lynn told Jack that Patchett and Hudgens were going in on a gig together, she now denied it, another lie. He needed another graph just to chart lies—he didn't have a room big enough to hold it.

More lines:

Davey Goldman to Dean Van Gelder to Duke Cathcart and
Susan Nancy Lefferts—incomprehensible until Vincennes reported
back from McNeil Island, and Bud White, obviously hiding out,
was questioned on what he might be suppressing. Vocational lines—
Patchett, the Englekling brothers and their father possessed chemistry backgrounds; Patchett, a reputed heroin sniffer, had plastic
surgery connections to Dr. Terry Lux, the owner of a booze/
dope sanitarium. Dudley Smith's report to Parker stated that Pete
and Bax Englekling were tortured to death with corrosive chemicals, no other details added. Conclusion: the link to decipher
every interconnected line had to be Patchett—his whores, his
smut posers, Patchett the conduit to the man who made the
blood smut, killed Hudgens and formed the final line stretching
back to 1934 and his own father's glory case.

Too many lines to ignore.

Patchett bankrolled early Dieterling films. Dieterling's son Billy
and boyfriend Timmy Valburn used Fleur-de-Lis; Valburn was a
Bobby Inge KA. Billy worked on *Badge of Honor*, the first focus of
the Hudgens homicide investigation. *Badge of Honor* co-star Miller
Stanton was a Dieterling kid star around the same time that Wee
Willie Wennerholm was murdered—by Loren Atherton? Slash
lines—Atherton to the smut to Hudgens; lines of coincidence too
convenient not to cut at family loyalty—seventeen years post-
Atherton, Preston Exley builds Dream-a-Dreamland.

Governor Exley. Chief of Detectives Exley.

Ed thought of Lynn, tasted her, shuddered. A quick jump to
Inez—a new line to utilize.

He drove to Laguna Beach.

* * *

The press, swarming: perched by their cars, playing cards on
Ray Dieterling's lawn. Ed pulled around the block, walked up,
sprinted.

They saw him, chased him. He made the door, slammed the
knocker. The door opened—straight into Inez.

She slammed it, bolted it. Ed walked into the living room—
Dream-a-Dreamland smiled all around him.

Gimcracks, porcelain statues: Moochie, Danny, Scooter. Wall
photos: Dieterling and crippled children. Canceled checks encased
in plastic—six figures to fight kids' diseases.

"See, I've got company."

Ed turned to face her. "Thanks for letting me in."

"They've been treating you worse than me, so I figured I owed you."

She looked pale. "Thanks. And you know it'll pass, just like last time."

"Maybe. You look lousy, Exley."

"People keep telling me that."

"Then maybe it's true. Look, if you want to stay and talk awhile, fine, but please don't talk about Bud or all this *mierda* that's going on."

"I wasn't planning on it, but small talk was never our forte."

She walked up. Ed embraced her; she grabbed his arms and pushed herself away. Ed tried a smile. "I saw some gray hairs. When you're my age you'll probably be as gray as I am. How's that for small talk?"

"Small, and I can do better. Preston's running for governor, unless his notorious son ruins his chances. I'm going to be his campaign coordinator."

"Governor Dad. Did he say I'd ruin his chances?"

"No, because he'd never say bad things about you. Just try to do what you can not to hurt him."

Reporters outside—Ed heard them laughing. "I don't want Father to be hurt either. And you can help me prevent it."

"How?"

"A favor. A favor between you and me, nobody else to know."

"What? Explain it."

"It's very complicated, and it involves Ray Dieterling. Do you know the name 'Pierce Patchett'?"

Inez shook her head. "No, who is he?"

"He's an investor of sorts, that's all I can tell you. I need you to use your access at Dream-a-Dreamland to check his financial connections to Dieterling. Check back to the late '20s, very quietly. Will you do that for me?"

"Exley, this sounds like police business. And what does it have to do with your father?"

Recoiling: doubting the man who formed him. "Father might be in some tax trouble. I need you to check Dieterling's financial records for mention of him."

"Bad trouble?"

"Yes."

"Check back to '50 or so? When they began planning for Dream-a-Dreamland?"

"No, go back to 1932. I know you've seen the books at Dieterling Productions, and I know you can do it."

"With explanations to follow?"

More recoil. "On Election Day. Come on, Inez. You love him almost as much as I do."

"All right. For your father."

"No other reason?"

"All right, for what you've done for me and the friends you gave me. And if that sounds cruel, I'm sorry."

A Moochie Mouse clock struck ten. Ed said, "I should go, I've got a meeting in L.A."

"Go out the back way. I think I still hear the vultures."

* * *

The recoil got squared driving back.

Call it standard elimination procedure:

If his father really did know Ray Dieterling during the time of the Atherton case, he had a valid reason for not revealing it, he was probably embarrassed at plumbing business deals with a man he once rubbed shoulders with in the process of a hellish murder investigation. Preston Exley believed that policemen striking friendships with influential civilians was inimical to the concept of impartial absolute justice, and if he fell short of his own standards it was understandable that he would not want the fact known.

Squared with love and respect.

Ed made the Dining Car early; the maître d' said his guest was waiting. He walked back to his favorite booth—a private nook behind the bar. Vincennes was there, holding a tape spool.

Ed sat down. "That's tape off a bug?"

Vincennes slid the spool over. "Yeah, filled with Mickey C. running off at the mouth on stuff that has nothing to do with the Nite Owl. Too bad, but I think we can put Davey down as a traitor to Mickey, and I think he must have heard the Engleklings offer Mick the Cathcart deal. He liked the sound of it and sent Van Gelder after Duke. And that's as far as I can take it."

The man looked shot. "Good work, Jack. Really, I mean it."

"Thanks, and that first name bit just went over large."

Ed picked up a menu, emptied his pockets underneath it. "It's midnight and I'm all out of subtlety."

"You're working up to something. What'd you get out of Bracken?"

"Nothing but lies. And you're right, Sergeant. The McNeil end is dead for now."

"So?"

"So tomorrow I'm hitting Patchett. I'm sealing IA off from Dudley and his men and bringing in Terry Lux, Chester Yorkin and every Patchett flunky that Fisk and Kleckner can find."

"Yeah, but what about Bracken and Patchett?"

Ed saw Lynn naked. "Bracken tried to buy out of your deposition. She snitched you on that escapade in Malibu, and I played her back on it."

Trash slammed his head down on two clenched fists. Ed said, "I told her you'd do anything to get the file back. I told her you still love dope and you're in hock to some bookies. You're up for a trial board and you want to crash Patchett's rackets."

Vincennes raised his head—pale, knuckle-gouged. "So tell me you'll square what's in the file."

Ed picked up his menu. Underneath: heroin, Benzedrine, a switchblade, a 9mm automatic. "You're going to shake Patchett down. He snorts heroin, so you offer him some. If you want some stuff to get your own juice up, you've got it. You're going after him to get your file back and to find out who made the blood smut and killed Hudgens. I'm working on a script, and you'll have it by tomorrow night. You're going to scare the shit out of Patchett and you're going to do whatever it takes to get what we both want. I know you can do it, so don't make me threaten you."

Vincennes smiled. He almost hit the chord—the old big-time Big V. "Suppose it goes bad?"

"Then kill him."

61

OPIUM FUMES banged his head; chink backtalk banged it worse: "Spade not here, my place have police sanction, I pay I pay!" Uncle Ace Kwan sent him to Fat Dewey Shin, who sent him to a string of dens on Alameda—Spade was there, but Spade was gone, "I pay! I pay!," try Uncle Minh, Uncle Chin, Uncle Chan. The Chinatown runaround, it took him hours to figure it out, a shuffle from enemy to enemy. Uncle Danny Tao pulled a shotgun; he took it away from him, blackjacked him, still couldn't force a snitch. Spade was there, Spade was gone—and if he took one more whiff of "O" he knew he'd curl up and die or start shooting. The punch line: he was shaking Chinatown for a man named Cooley.

Chinatown dead for now.

Bud called the DA's Bureau, gave the squad whip his Perkins/Cooley leads; the man yawned along, signed off bored. Out to the Strip; the Cowboy Rhythm Band on stage, no Spade, nobody had seen him in a couple of days. Hillbilly clubs, local bars, night spots—no sightings of Donnell Clyde Cooley. 1:00 fucking A.M., no place to go but Lynn's—"Where *were* you?" and a bed.

Rain came on—a downpour. Bud counted taillights to stay awake: red dots, hypnotizing. He made Nottingham Drive near gone—dizzy, numb in the limbs.

Lynn on her porch, watching the rain. Bud ran up; she held her arms out. He slipped, steadied himself with her body.

She stepped back. Bud said, "I was worried. I kept calling you last night before things got crazy."

"Crazy how?"

"The morning, it's too long a story for now. How did it—"

Lynn touched his lips. "I told them things about Pierce that you already know, and I've been getting misty with the rain and thinking about telling them more."

"More what?"

"I'm thinking that it's over with Pierce. In the morning, sweetie. Both our stories for breakfast."

Bud leaned on the porch rail. Lightning lit up the street—and dry tears on Lynn's face. "Honey, what is it? Is it Exley? Did he hardnose you?"

"It's Exley, but not what you're thinking. And I know why you hate him so much."

"What do you mean?"

"That he's just the opposite of all the good things you are. He's more like I am."

"I don't get it."

"Well, it's a credibility he has for being so calculating. I started out hating him because you do, then he made me realize some things about Pierce just by being who he is. He told me some things he didn't have to, and my own reactions surprised me."

More lightning—Lynn looked god-awful sad. Bud said, "For instance?"

"For instance Jack Vincennes is going crazy and has some kind of vendetta against Pierce. And I don't care half as much as I should."

"How did you get so friendly with Exley?"

Lynn laughed. "*In vino veritas.* You know, sweetie, you're thirty-nine years old and I keep waiting for you to get exhausted being who you are."

"I'm exhausted tonight."

"That's not what I meant."

Bud turned on the porch light. "You gonna tell me what happened with you and Exley?"

"We just talked."

Her makeup was tear streaked—it was the first time he'd seen her not beautiful. "So tell me about it."

"In the morning."

"No, now."

"Honey, I'm as tired as you are."

Her little half smile did it. "You slept with him."

Lynn looked away. Bud hit her—once, twice, three times. Lynn faced straight into the blows. Bud stopped when he saw he couldn't break her.

62

IAD—PACKED.

Chester Yorkin, the Fleur-de-Lis delivery man, stashed in booth #1; in 2 and 3: Paula Brown and Lorraine Malvasi, Patchett whores—Ava Gardner, Rita Hayworth. Lamar Hinton, Bobby Inge, Christine Bergeron and son could not be located; ditto the smut posers—Fisk and Kleckner failed to make them from extensive mugbook prowls. In booth 4: Sharon Kostenza, real name Mary Alice Mertz, a plum off Vincennes' deposition—the woman who once bailed Bobby Inge out of jail and paid a surety bond for Chris Bergeron. In booth 5: Dr. Terry Lux, his attorney—the great Jerry Geisler.

Ray Pinker standing by with counterdope—so far none of the new fish looked drugged.

Two officers guarding the squadroom—private interrogations—strict IA autonomy.

Kleckner and Fisk grilling Mertz and pseudo Ava—armed with deposition copies, smut photos, a case summary. Yorkin, Lux and phony Rita cooling their heels.

Ed worked in his office: draft three of Vincennes' script. A thought nagged him: if Lynn Bracken reported to Patchett in full, he would have yanked his people before the police could bring them in—the way Inge, Bergeron and son disappeared immediately pre-Nite Owl. Two possibles on that—she was playing an angle or their rutting had her confused and she was stalling to figure the upshot. Most likely the former—the woman cut her last confused breath at birth.

He could still taste her.

Ed drew lines on paper. Inez to check Dieterling connections to Patchett and his father—that thought still made him wince. Two IA men out looking for White—apprehend the bastard and break him. Billy Dieterling and Timmy Valburn to be questioned—kid gloves, they had prestige, juice. A line to the Hudgens kill and the Hudgens/Patchett "gig"—Vincennes' deposition stated that Hudgens' *Badge of Honor* files were missing at the time of his death, anomalous, the show was a Hudgens fixation. The *Badge of Honor* people were alibied for the murder—but another reading of the case file was in order.

Half his maze of cases read extortion.

Line to an outside issue—Dudley Smith, going crazy for a quick Darktown collar. Line to a rumor: Thad Green was going to take over the U.S. Border Patrol come May. A theoretical line: Parker would choose his new chief of detectives solely on the basis of the Nite Owl case—him or Smith. Dudley might send White back to break his autonomy; criss cross all lines to keep *his* case sealed.

Kleckner walked in. "Sir, the Mertz woman won't cooperate. All she'll say is that she lives under that Sharon Kostenza alias and that she makes bail for Patchett's people when they get arrested for outside charges. Nobody's *ever* been arrested working for him, we know that. She says she can't ID the people in the photos and she's mum on that extortion angle you told me to play up. She deadpanned the Nite Owl—and I believe her."

"Release her, I want her to go to Patchett and panic him. What did Duane get off Ava Gardner?"

Kleckner passed him a sheet of paper. "Lots. Here's the high points, and he's got the actual interview on tape."

"Good. You go soften up Yorkin for me. Bring him a beer and baby sit him."

Kleckner walked out smiling. Ed read Fisk's memo.

Witness Paula Brown 3/25/58

   1. Witness revealed names of numerous P.P. call girl/male prostitute customers (specifics to follow in separate memo & on tape)

   2. Could not ID people in photos (seems truthful on this)

   3. Extortion hook got her talking

   a. P.P. gave his girls/male prostitutes bonuses to get their customers to reveal intimate details of their lives

   b. P.P. makes his prosts quit at 30 (apparent bee in his bonnet)

   c. On in-home prostitution assignments, P.P. had prosts leave doors/windows open so men with cameras could take compromising photos. Prosts also made wax impressions of locks on certain rich custs doors

   d. P.P. had famous (T. Lux obviously) plastic surgeon cut male/female prosts to look like movie stars and thus make more $

   e. Male prosts extorted $ from married homosexual custs & split take with P.P.

   f. Bored by Nite Owl quests (obviously has no guilty knowledge)

Astounding audacious perversion.

Ed hit sweatbox row, checked the mirrors. Fisk and phony Ava talking; Kleckner and Yorkin drinking beer. Terry Lux reading a magazine, Jerry Geisler fuming. Lorraine Malvasi alone in a cloud of smoke. Astounding audacious perversion—the woman had Rita Hayworth's face down to the bone, up to the hairdo from *Gilda*.

He opened the door. Rita/Lorraine stood up, sat down, lit a cigarette. Ed handed her Fisk's memo. "Please read this, Miss Malvasi."

She read, chewing lipstick. "So?"

"So do you confirm that or not?"

"So I'm entitled to a lawyer."

"Not for seventy-two hours."

"You can't hold me here that long."

"Caaant"—a bad New York accent. "Not here, but we can hold you at the Woman's Jail."

Lorraine bit at a nail, drew blood. "You caan't."

"Sure I can. Sharon Kostenza's in custody, so she can't make bail for you. Pierce Patchett is under surveillance and your friend Ava just spilled what you read there. She talked first, and all I want you to do is fill in some blanks."

A little sob. "I caan't."

"Why not?"

"Pierce has been too nice to—"

Cut her off. "Pierce is finished. Lynn Bracken turned state's on him. She's in protective custody, and I can go to her for the answers or save myself the trouble and ask you."

"I caaan't."

"You can and you will."

"No, I caaan't."

"You'd better, because you're an accessory to eleven felonies in Paula Brown's statement alone. Are you afraid of the dykes at the jail?"

No answer.

"You should be, but the matrons are worse. Big husky bull daggers with nightsticks. You know what they do with those—"

"All right all right all right! All right I'll tell you!"

Ed took out a notepad, wrote "Chrono." Lorraine: "It's not Pierce's fault. This guy made him do it."

"What guy?"

"I don't know. Really, for real, I don't know."

"Chrono" underlined. "When did you start working for Patchett?"

"When I was twenty-one."

"Give me the year."

"1951."

"And he had Terry Lux perform surgery on you?"

"Yes! To make me more beautiful!"

"Easy now, please. Now a second ago you said that a guy—"

"I don't know who the guy is! I caan't tell you what I don't know!"

"Sssh, please. Now, you confirmed Paula Brown's statement and you said that a 'guy,' *whose identity you don't know*, coerced Patchett into the extortion plans detailed in that statement. Is that correct?"

Lorraine put out her cigarette, lit another one. "Yes. Extortion is like blackmail, right, so yes."

"When, Lorraine? Do you know *when* 'this guy' approached Patchett?"

She counted on her fingers. "Five years ago, May."

"Chrono" hard underlined. "That's May of 1953?"

"Yeah, 'cause my father died that month. Pierce called us kids in and said we had to do it, he didn't want to, but this guy had him by the you-know-whats. He didn't say the guy's name and I don't think none of the other kids know it either."

"Chrono" one month post–Nite Owl. "Think fast, Lorraine. The Nite Owl massacre. Remember that?"

"What? Some people got shot, right?"

"Never mind. What else did Patchett tell you when he called you in?"

"Nothing."

"*Nothing* else on Patchett and extortion? Remember, I'm not asking you if you did any of this. I'm not asking you to incriminate yourself."

"Well, maybe three months or so before that I heard Veronica—I mean Lynn—and Pierce talking. He said him and that scandal mag man who got killed later were gonna run this squeeze thing where Pierce would tell him about our clients' secret little ... you know, fetishes, and the man would threaten the clients with being in *Hush-Hush*. You know, pay money or be in the scandal mag."

Extortion theory validated. An instinct: on some level Lynn was playing straight, she hadn't told Patchett to prepare—he never would have let these people come in. "Lorraine, did Sergeant Kleckner show you some pornographic pictures?"

A nod. "I told him and I'll tell you. I don't know any of the people and those pictures gave me the creeps."

Ed walked out. Duane Fisk in the hallway. "Good work, sir. When you got her on that 'this guy' bit, I went back and ran it by Ava. She confirmed it and confirmed that no ID."

Ed nodded. "Tell her that Rita and Yorkin have been booked, then release her. I want her to go back to Patchett. How's Kleckner doing with Yorkin?"

Fisk shook his head. "That boy's a hardcase. He's practically daring Don to make him talk. Hey, where's Bud White now that we need him?"

"Amusing, but don't keep it up. And right now I want you to take Lux and Geisler to lunch. Lux is here voluntarily, so be nice. Tell Geisler that this is a multiple homicide major conspiracy case, and tell him Lux gets full collateral immunity for his cooperation and a signed promise of no courtroom testimony.

Tell him it's already in writing, and if he wants verification to call Ellis Loew."

Fisk nodded, walked down to booth 5. Ed checked the #1 look-in.

Chester Yorkin wising off at the mirror: making faces, flipping the bird. Skinny, a pompadour flopped over his eyes oozing grease. Welts on his arms—maybe old needle marks.

Ed opened the door. Yorkin said, "Hey, I know you. I read about you."

Tracks confirmed—scar tissue on the welts. "I've been in the news."

Giggle, giggle. "This is an old one, *kemo sabe.* Something like you saying, 'I never hit suspects 'cause that's the cop lowered to the level of the criminal.' You wanta hear my answer? I never snitch, 'cause cops are all cocksuckers who get their cookies off making guys talk."

"You through?"—Bud White's stock line.

"No. Your father takes it up the ass from Moochie Mouse."

Scared, but he did it—an elbow to the windpipe. Yorkin gasped; Ed got behind him, cuffed him, shoved him to the floor.

Scared, but steady hands: look, Dad, no fear.

Yorkin backed into a corner.

Scared, another Bad Bud move: a chair, a roundhouse swing, the chair smashed to the wall just above the suspect's head. Yorkin tried to squirm away; Ed kicked him back to his corner. Slow now: don't let your voice break, don't let your eyes go soft behind your glasses. "*Everything.* I want to know about the smut and the other shit you push through Fleur-de-Lis. *Everything.* You start with those tracks on your arms and why a smart man like Patchett trusts a junkie like you. And you know one thing right now— Patchett is finished and I'm the only one who can cut you a deal. *Do you understand me?*"

Yorkin bobbed his head yes yes yes. "Test pilot! I flew for him! Test pilot!"

Ed unlocked his cuffs. "Say that again."

Yorkin rubbed his neck. "Guinea pig."

"What?"

"I let him test horse on me. Here and there, a little at a time."

"Start over. Slowly."

Yorkin coughed. "Pierce got this heroin stolen off this Cohen– Jack Dragna deal years ago. This guy Buzz Meeks left some with these guys Pete and Bax Englekling, just a sample, and they gave it to their father, who was some kind of chemistry hotshot. He taught Pierce in college, and he laid the shit off to him and died, a heart attack or something. This other guy, I don't know his name so don't ask me, he killed Meeks or something like that. He got the rest of the shit, like eighteen pounds' worth. Pierce has been developing compounds with the stuff for years. He wants to make the cheapest and the safest and the best. I just ... I just take some test pops."

Astounding lines crossing. "You were making deliveries for Fleur-de-Lis five years ago, right?"

"Right, yeah, sure."

"You and Lamar Hinton."

"I ain't seen Lamar in years, you can't pin Lamar's shit on me!"

Ed grabbed the spare chair, brandished it. "I don't want to. Give me an answer on this, and if I like it I'll owe you a solid. It's a test and you're a test pilot, so you should do well. Who shot at Jack Vincennes outside the Hollywood drop back in '53?"

Yorkin cringed. "Me. Pierce told me to clip him. I shouldn't of done it by the drop. I fucked up and Pierce got pissed."

Patchett nailed: attempted murder on a police officer. "What did he do to you for that?"

"He tested me bad. He gave me all these bad compounds he said he had to eliminate. He made me take these bad fucking flights."

"So you hate him for it."

"Man, Pierce ain't like regular people. I hate him, but I dig him too."

Ed pushed the chair away. "Do you remember the Nite Owl shootings?"

"Sure, years ago. What's that got to do—"

"Never mind, and here's the important thing. If you fill this in for me, I'll give you a written immunity statement and put you up in protective custody until Patchett's down. Smut, Chester. You remember those orgy books Fleur-de-Lis was running five years ago?"

Yorkin bobbed his head yes.

"The ink blood on the pictures, do you remember that?"

Yorkin smiled—snitching eager now. "I know that story good. Pierce is going down for real?"

Ten hours from the script. "Maybe tonight."

"Then fuck him for all those bad flights."

"Chester, just tell me slowly."

Yorkin stood up, worked the kinks from his legs. "You know what's a bitch about Pierce? He'd say all these things around me when I was on a flight, like I was harmless 'cause I couldn't remember nothing he said."

Ed got out his notebook. "Try to tell it in order."

Yorkin rubbed his throat, coughed. "Okay, Pierce had this old string of girls that he let go, this was around when we were moving them picture books. Some guy, I don't know his name, he talked some of the girls and their johns into posing for them pictures. He made books out of them and went to Pierce to get money to move the books wide, you know, he promised Pierce a cut. Pierce, he liked the idea, but he didn't want to expose his girls or their johns. He bought a bunch of the books off the guy to move through Fleur-de-Lis, you know, just a close distribution he called it, like a test market, he figured he could keep track of the stuff that way."

Old lines crossing: the close distribution wasn't that close, Ad Vice retrieved throwaway copies—Vincennes to the case. "Keep going, Chester."

"Well, the guy who made the stuff, somehow he weaseled some info on the Englekling brothers out of Pierce, how they had this printing press place and was always bent for money. He found himself a front man, and the front man, he approached the brothers. You know, a plan to make the shit bulk and move it."

The front man: Duke Cathcart. Zigzag lines from Cohen to the brothers, the brothers to Patchett, back on a sideswipe: Mickey at McNeil Island—then Goldman and Van Gelder. *Line the heroin to the pornography.* "Chester, how do you know all this?"

Yorkin laughed. "I'd be on a mainline flight and Pierce, he'd be on safe old white horse up the nose. He'd just jaw at me like I some kind of dog you talk to."

"So Patchett and the smut are dead, right? All he's interested in is pushing the heroin."

"Nix. That guy who brought Pierce the eighteen pounds years ago? Well, he's got a hard-on for the smut. He's got lists of all these rich perverts and all these contacts in South America. Him and Pierce, they sat on the original pictures for years, then they had some new books made up who-knows-where. They got the shit in a warehouse someplace, I don't know where, just waiting to go. I think Pierce was waiting for some kind of heat to die down."

No new lines crossed. A phrase sunk in: *profit motive.* Pornography by itself was chancy; twenty pounds of heroin *developed* meant millions. Yorkin said, "One more 'case you get antsy on my deal. Pierce has got him a booby-trapped safe by his house. He's got money, dope, all kinds of stuff stashed there."

Ed kept thinking MONEY.

Yorkin: "Hey, talk to me! You want the new drop address? 8819 Linden, Long Beach. Exley, talk to me!"

"Steak in your cell, Chester. You've earned it."

* * *

Fresh lines—Ed pulled Fisk's and Kleckner's summaries, added the Yorkin/Malvasi revelations.

Heroin and pornography lined. "The Guy" who made the smut books as Sid Hudgens' killer, his front man Duke Cathcart—killed by Dean Van Gelder, ordered killed or merely approached by Davey Goldman—who learned of the smut proposal via the bug in Mickey Cohen's cell. Cohen omnipresent—his stolen heroin ended up with both the Engleklings and "The Man" who brought Patchett the eighteen pounds of "H" for development, "The Man" who also loved pornography and convinced Patchett to manufacture new books from the 1953 prototypes. An instinct: Cohen was Mr. Patsy going back eight years, in and out of jail, a focal point who never dealt his own hand into the welter of cases. A line to a conclusion: the Nite Owl killings were semiprofessional at least, an attempt to take over the heroin and pornography rackets of Pierce Patchett. Cathcart, attempting to push the smut on his own, was the focus of the killings. Did he misrepresent his importance to the wrong people, or did the shooters deliberately take out Van Gelder, knowing or not knowing he was a Cathcart impersonator? Lines to organized crime intrigue, semipro at least, with all mob lines dead or incapacitated: Franz Englekling and sons—dead, Davey Goldman a vegetable, Mickey Cohen befuddled by the action going on around him. A question line: who clipped Pete and Bax Englekling? The terror line: Loren Atherton, 1934. How could it be?

Fisk rapped on the door. "Sir, I brought Lux and Geisler back."

"And?"

"Geisler gave me a prepared statement."

"Read it."

Fisk pulled out a sheet. "'Pertaining to my relationship with Pierce Morehouse Patchett, I, Terence Lux, MD, do offer the following notarized statement. To wit: my relationship with Pierce Patchett is professional: i.e., I have performed extensive plastic surgery on a number of male and female acquaintances of his, perfecting already existing resemblances to exact resemblances of several notable actors and actresses. Unsubstantiated rumors hold that Patchett employs these young people for purposes of prostitution, but I have no conclusive evidence that this is true. Duly sworn,' et cetera."

Ed said, "Not good enough. Duane, you take Yorkin and Rita Hayworth across the street and book them. Aiding and Abetting, and leave the arrest dates blank. Allow them one phone call each, then go down to Long Beach and seize 8819 Linden. That's a Fleur-de-Lis drop, and I'm sure Patchett's cleaned it out, but do it anyway. If you find the place virgin, bust it up and leave the door open."

Fisk swallowed. "Uh, sir? Bust it up? And no booking date on our suspects?"

"*Bust it up. Make a statement. And don't question my orders.*"

Fisk said, "Uh, yes, sir." Ed closed the door, buzzed Kleckner. "Don, send Dr. Lux and Mr. Geisler in."

"Yes, sir," loud on the intercom. Whispered: "They're pissed, Captain. Thought you should know."

Ed opened the door. Geisler and Lux walked up—brusque.

No handshakes. Geisler said, "Frankly, that lunch didn't begin to cover the hourly rate I'm going to have to charge Dr. Lux. I think it's reprehensible that he came here voluntarily and was kept waiting so long."

Ed smiled. "I apologize. I accept the formal statement you offered and I have no real questions for Dr. Lux. I have just one favor to ask and a large one to grant in return. And send me your bill, Mr. Geisler. You know I can afford it."

"I know your father can. Continue, please. You're holding my interest so far."

Ed to Lux. "Doctor, I know who you know and you know who I know. And I know you deal in legal morphine cures. Help me with something and I'll pledge my friendship."

Lux cleaned his nails with a scalpel. "The *Daily News* says you're obsolescent."

"They're mistaken. Pierce Patchett and heroin, Doctor. I'll settle for rumors and I won't ask for your sources."

Geisler and Lux went into a huddle—a step out the door, whispers. Lux broke it off. "I've heard Pierce is connected to some very bad men who want to control the heroin trade in Los Angeles. He's quite the chemist, you know, and he's been developing a special blend for years. Hormones, antipsychotic strains, quite a brew. I've heard it puts regular heroin to shame, and I heard it's ready to be manufactured and sold. One in my column, Captain. Jerry, take the man at his word and send him my bill."

*　*　*

Semipro, pro—his new lines all spelled HEROIN. Ed called Bob Gallaudet, left a message with his secretary: Nite Owl maybe breaking—call me. A picture on his desk hooked him: Inez and his father at Arrowhead. He called Lynn Bracken.

"Hello?"

"Lynn, it's Exley."

"God, hello."

"You didn't go to Patchett, did you?"

"Did you think I would? Were you setting me up to?"

Ed laid the picture face down. "I want you to get out of L.A. for a week or so. I have a place at Lake Arrowhead, you can stay there. Leave this afternoon."

"Is Pierce …"

"I'll tell you later."

"Will you come up?"

Ed checked the Vincennes script. "As soon as I set something up. Have you seen White?"

"He came and went, and I don't know where he is. Is he all right?"

"Yes. No, shit, I don't know. Meet me at Fernando's on the lake. It's right by my place. Say six?"

"I'll be there."

"I figured you'd take some convincing."

"I've already convinced myself of lots of things. Leaving town just makes it easier."

"*Why*, Lynn?"

"The party was over, I guess. Do you think keeping your mouth shut's a heroic act?"

63

BUD WOKE up at the Victory. Dusk out the window—he'd slept through half a night and a day. He rubbed his eyes; Spade Cooley locked right back on him. He smelled cigarette smoke, saw Dudley sitting by the door.

"Bad dreams, lad? You were thrashing a bit."

Nightmare: Inez trashed by the press, his fault—what he did to nail Exley.

"Lad, in repose you reminded me of my daughters. And you know I care for you no less."

He'd sweated the sheets through. "What's with the job? What's next?"

"Next you listen. I've long been involved in containing hard crime so that myself and a few colleagues might someday enjoy a profit dispensation, and that day will soon be arriving. As a colleague, you will share handsomely. Grand means will be in our hands, lad. Imagine the means to keep the nigger filth sedated and extrapolate from there. One obstreperous Italian you've dealt with in the past is involved, and I think you can be particularly useful in keeping him in line."

Bud stretched, cracked his knuckles. "I meant the reopening. Talk straight, okay?"

"Edmund Jennings Exley is as straight as I can be. He's trying to prove bad things against Lynn, lad. Salt on all the old wounds he's given you."

Live wires buzzing. "You knew about us. I should've known."

"There is precious little I don't know, and nothing I would not do for you. Coward Exley has touched the only two women you've loved, lad. Think of grand ways to hurt him."

64

THEY MADE love straight off—Ed knew they'd have to talk if they didn't, Lynn seemed to sense the same thing. The cabin was musty, the bed unmade—stale from last time with Inez. Ed kept the lights on: the more he saw, the less he'd think. It helped him through the act; counting Lynn's freckles kept him from peaking. Slow on the act, both of them, making up for their tumble off the couch. Lynn had bruises; Ed knew they came from Bud White.

For a tightrope act they were gentle; their long embrace after felt like payback for their lies. When they started talking they'd never stop. Ed wondered who'd say "Bud White" first.

Lynn said it. Bud was the fulcrum that convinced her to lie to Patchett: the police investigation was a joke, they were grasping at straws. White knew of Patchett's milder doings, she was afraid he'd get in trouble if Pierce fought back. Pierce might try to buy his friendship, he thought everyone had a price tag, he didn't know her Wendell couldn't be bought. Bud got her thinking; the more she thought the more she hurt; a certain police captain kissing a certain ex-whore at the only moment she would have let him just added to the party's over, Pierce made me but he's bad deep down, if I let him go then maybe I'll get back some of the good things he's killed in me. Ed winced through the words, knew he couldn't return her candor—now Jack Vincennes was going in barefoot, he'd counted on Lynn to push Patchett to panic, past Fisk taking a fire axe to the drop, past his people grilled and arrested. Lynn met his silence with words—excerpts from her diary, a show-and-tell for fugitive lovers her pronouncement. Funny, sad—old tricks derided, a monologue on carhop hookers that almost had him laughing. Lynn on Inez and Bud White—he loved her here and there and mostly at a distance because her rage was worse than his, drained him, a night here and there was all he could take. No jealousy—so his own jealousy jumped up, almost forced him to shout questions: heroin and extortion, astounding audacious perversion, just how much do you know? The gift she gave him wouldn't let him; soft hands on his chest made him throw out a parity in candor before he started interrogating or lying just to have something to say.

He went straight to his family, spiraled past to present. Mama's boy Eddie, golden boy Thomas, the jig he danced when his brother stopped six bullets. Being a policeman/patrician from a long line of Scotland Yard detectives. Inez, four men killed out of weakness; Dudley Smith going crazy to find a suitable scapegoat that Ellis Loew and Chief Parker just might accept as a panacea. A headlong rush to the great Preston Exley in all his intractable glory and how ink-embossed pornography lined to a dead scandalmonger, vivisected children and his father and Raymond Dieterling twenty-four years ago. A rush until there was nothing left to say and Lynn kissed his lips shut and he fell asleep touching her bruises.

65

ROGUE COP Big V—give Exley credit for good casting. He synced his approach call to the drop raid—Patchett said, "Yes, I'll talk to you. Eleven tonight, and come alone."

He wore a tape wire hooked across a bulletproof vest.

He carried a bag of heroin, a switchblade, a 9mm automatic. Exley's Benzedrine down the toilet, grief he didn't need.

He walked up, rang the bell—stage fright all the way.

Patchett opened the door. Pinned-back eyes like Exley predicted—a nose junkie.

Jack, per the script: "Hello, Pierce"—all contempt.

Patchett shut the door. Jack threw the dope in his face. It hit him, fell to the floor.

Ad lib time. "Just a peace offering. Not up to that shit you tested on Yorkin anyway. Did you know my brother-in-law's the City DA? He's a bonus you get if you make a deal with me."

Patchett: "Where did you get that?" Calm, the stuff up his nose wouldn't let him show fear.

Jack pulled out the knife, scratched his neck with the blade. He felt blood, licked it off a finger—Academy Award psycho. "I shook down some niggers. You know all about that, right? *Hush-Hush* Magazine used to write me up. You and Sid Hudgens go way back, so you should know."

No fear. "You made trouble for me five years ago. I still have that file carbon on you, and I think it's fair to say that you broke your part of our bargain. I'm assuming you've shown your superiors your deposition."

Knife bit: the tip of the blade in one palm, a little push to retract it. More blood, a key Exley line. "I'm way past you in the information department. I know about the heroin you got from the Cohen-Dragna deal and what you've been doing with it. I know about the smut you were pushing in '53, and I know all about those extortion shakedowns with your whores. And all I want is my file and some information. You give me that and I'll put the fritz to everything Captain Exley has."

"What information?"

The script, verbatim. "I made a deal with Hudgens. The deal was my file destroyed and ten grand in cash in exchange for some juicy dirt I had on the LAPD high brass. I knew Sid was going to work a shakedown scheme with you, and I'd already backed down on Fleur-de-Lis—you know that's true. Sid got killed before I could pick up the money and the file, and I think the killer got both of them. I need that money, 'cause I'm getting shit canned off the Department before I can collect my pension, and I want the fucker who robbed me dead. You didn't *make* that smut back in '53, but whoever did killed Sid and robbed me. Give me the name and I'm yours."

Patchett smiled. Jack smiled—one last push before the pistol whipping. "Pierce, the Nite Owl was smut and heroin—yours. Do you want to swing for that?"

Patchett pulled out a piece, shot him three times. Silencer thwaps—the slugs shattered the tape gizmo, bounced off his vest.

Three more shots—two in the vest, one wide.

Jack crashed into a table, came up aiming. A jammed slide, Patchett on him, two misfire clicks right up close. Patchett in his face, the knife out, a blind stab, a scream—the blade catching.

Patchett's left hand nailed to the table. Another scream, his right hand arcing—a hypo in it. The needle mainline close, stab, zooooom somewhere nice. Shots rifle loud, "No, Abe, no, Lee, no!" Flames, smoke, rolling away from the grief, so he could live to love the needle again, maybe see the funny man with his hand shivved to the table.

<h1 style="text-align:center">66</h1>

THE CLOCK in his head was way off, his watch had quit working—he wasn't sure if it was Wednesday or Thursday. His Nite Owl "disclosure" ate up a whole evening—Dudley was so far ahead of him he never even took notes. The man left him at midnight, pumped up with bold language, no date for the strongarm cop's bail. Dud's date was Exley: clear the Nite Owl and ruin his career, seconds for Bad Bud White: "Think of grand ways to hurt him." Murder was all he could think of—a fair trade for Lynn; killing an LAPD captain was the springs in his clock all snapping—one more span of skewed time and he'd do it. Some point early A.M. Kathy Janeway hit him up—Kathy the way she looked then. She found him a date for the wee small hours—the man who killed her.

And Spade Cooley stood him up.

He went by the Biltmore, talked to the Cowboy Rhythm Band—Spade was still gone, Deuce Perkins was off on his own toot. The DA's Bureau night clerk gave him the brush—were they even on the case? Another tear through Chinatown, a run by his apartment—a couple of IA hard-ons parked out front. A wolfed meal at a burger stand, dawn creeping up, a pile of *Herald*s that told him it was Friday. A Nite Owl headline: jigs crying police brutality, Chief Parker promising justice.

He felt tired one second, keyed up the next. He tried to set his watch to the radio; the hands stuck; he threw a hundred-dollar Gruen out the window. Tired, he saw Kathy; keyed up, he saw Exley and Lynn. He drove to Nottingham Drive to check cars.

No white Packard—and Lynn always parked the same place.

Bud walked around the building—no sign of Exley's blue Plymouth. A neighbor woman bringing in milk. She said, "Good morning. You're Miss Bracken's friend, aren't you?"

The old snoop—Lynn said she peeped bedrooms. "That's right."

"Well, as you can see, she's not here."

"Yeah, and you don't know where she is."

"Well …"

"Well what? You seen her with a man? Tall, glasses?"

"No, I haven't. And mind your tone, young man. Well what, indeed."

Bud badged her. "*Well what*, lady? You were gonna tell me something."

"Until you got cheeky, I was going to tell you where Miss Bracken went. I heard her talking to the manager last night. She was asking for directions."

"*Where to?*"

"Lake Arrowhead, and I would have told you before you got cheeky."

* * *

Exley's place, Inez told him about it, a cabin flying flags: American, state, LAPD. Bud drove to Arrowhead, cruised by the lake, found it: banners cutting wind, no blue Plymouth. Lynn's Packard in the driveway.

A brodie to the porch; a leap up the steps. Bud punched in a window, unlatched the door. No response to the noise—just a musty front room done up hunting lodge provincial.

He walked into the bedroom. Sweat stink, lipstick blots on the bed. He kicked the feathers out of the pillows, dumped the mattress, saw a leather binder underneath. Lynn's "Scarlet Letters" for sure—she'd been talking up her diary for years.

Bud grabbed it, got ready to rip—down the spine like his old phone book trick. The smell made him stop—if he didn't look, he was a coward.

Flip to the last page. Lynn's handwriting, bold black ink, the gold pen he'd bought her.

March 26, 1958

More on E.E. He just drove off and I could tell he was chagrined by all the things he told me last night. He looked vulnerable in the A.M. light, stumbling to the bathroom without his glasses. I pity Pierce his misfortune in encountering such an essentially fright-ened and unyielding man. E.E. makes love like my Wendell, like he never wants it to end, because when it ends he will have to return to what he is. He is per-haps the only man I have ever met who is as com-promised as I am, who is so smart, circumspect and cautious that you can always see his wheels turning and thus wish you could always talk in the dark so that face value would be less complex. He is so smart and pragmatic that he makes W.W. appear childish and thus less heroic than he really is. And considering his dilemma, my betrayal of Pierce's friendship and patronage seem frankly callow. This man has been so obsessively beholden to his father for so long that the crux of it must influence every step he takes, yet he is still taking steps, which amazes me. E.E. didn't delve too far into specifics, but the basic thrust is that some of the more artful pornographic books that Pierce was selling five years ago have diagrams that match the mutilations on Sid Hudgens' body and the wounds on the victims of a murderer named Loren Atherton, who was apprehended by Preston Exley in the 1930s. P.E. is soon to announce his candidacy for governor and E.E. now considers that his father solved the Atherton case incorrectly and inferred that he suspects P.E. of establishing business relations with Raymond Dieterling at the time of that case (one of Atherton's victims was a Dieterling child star).

Another strange crux: E.E., my *très* smart pragmatist, considers his father such a moral exemplar and paragon of efficacy that he is terrified of accepting normal incompetence and rational business self-interest as within the bounds of acceptable human behavior. He is afraid that solving his "Nite Owl related" cases will reveal P.E.'s fallibility to the world and destroy his gubernatorial chances, and he is obviously even more afraid of having to accept his father as a mortal, especially difficult since he has never accepted himself as one. But he will go ahead with his cases, deep down he seems quite determined. As much as I love him, in the same situation my Wendell would just shoot everyone involved, then look for somebody a bit more intelligent to sort out the bodies, like that urbane Irishman Dudley Smith he always mentions. More on this and related matters after a walk, breakfast and three strong cups of coffee.

Now he ripped—down the spine, across the grain, leather and paper shredded to bits.

The phone, IAD direct. Buzz, buzz, "Internal Affairs, Kleckner."

"It's White. Put Exley on."

"White, you're in troub—" a new voice on the line. "This is Exley. White, where are you?"

"Arrowhead. I just read Lynn's diary and got the whole story on your old man, Atherton and Dieterling. *The whole fucking story.* I'm running a suspect down, and when I find him it's your daddy on the six o'clock news."

"I'll make a deal with you. Just listen."

"Never."

* * *

Back to L.A., the old Spade routine: Chinatown, the Strip, the Biltmore, his third circuit since time went haywire. The chinks were starting to look like the Cowboy Rhythm Band, the El Rancho guys were growing slant eyes. Every known haunt triple-checked, three times everything—except for a single hit on his agent.

Bud drove to Nat Penzler Associates. The connecting door was open—Mr. Natsky was eating a sandwich. He took a bite, said, "Oh shit."

"Spade's been ditching out on his gig. He must be costing you money."

Penzler eased a hand behind his desk. "Caveman, if you knew the grief my clients cause me."

"You don't sound so concerned."

"Bad pennies always turn up."

"Do you know where he is?"

Penzler brought his hand up. "My guess is on the planet Pluto, hanging out with his pal Jack Daniels."

"What were you doing with your hand?"

"Scratching my balls. You want the job? It pays five yards a week, but you have to kick back ten percent to your agent."

"Where is he?"

"He is somewhere in the vicinity of nowhere I know. Check with me next week and write when you get brains."

"Like that, huh?"

"Caveman, if I knew would I withhold from a bruiser like you?"

Bud kicked him out of his chair. Penzler hit the floor; the chair spun, tipped. Bud reached under the desk, pulled out a bundle wrapped with string. A foot on top, a jerk on the knot—clean black cowboy shirts.

Penzler stood up. "Lincoln Heights. The basement at Sammy Ling's, and you didn't get it from Natsky."

* * *

Ling's Chow Mein: a dive on Broadway up from Chinatown. Parking spaces in back; a rear entrance to the kitchen. No outside basement access, steam shooting from an underground vent. Bud circled the place, heard voices out the vent. Make the trapdoor in the kitchen.

He found a two-by-four in the lot, went in the back way. Two slants frying meat, an old geek skinning a duck. A fix on the trapdoor, easy: lift the pallet by the oven.

They spotted him. The young chinks jabbered; Papa-san waved them quiet. Bud held his shield out.

The old man rubbed fingers. "I pay! I pay I pay! You go!"

"Spade Cooley, Papa. You go downstairs and tell him Natsky brought the laundry. Chop-chop."

"Spade pay! You leave alone! I pay! I pay!"

The kids circled. Papa-san waved his cleaver.

"You go now! Go now! I pay!"

Bud fixed a line on the floor. Papa stepped over it.

Bud swung his stick—pops caught it waist-high. He crashed into the stove, his face hit a burner, his hair caught fire. The kids charged; Bud got their legs in one shot. They hit the floor tangled up—Bud smashed in their ribs. Pops doused his head in the sink, charged with his face scorched black.

A roundhouse to the knees—Papa went down glued to that cleaver. Bud stepped on his hand, cracked the fingers—Papa let go screaming. Bud dragged him to the oven, kicked the pallet loose. Yank the trapdoor, drag the old man downstairs.

Fumes: opium, steam. Bud kicked Papa-san quiet. Through the fumes: dope suckers on mattresses.

Bud kicked through them. All chinks—they grumbled, swatted, sucked back to dreamland. Smoke: in his face, up his nose, breathing hard so he took it down his lungs. Steam like a beacon: a sweat room at the back.

He kicked over to the door. Through a mist: naked Spade Cooley, three naked girls. Giggles, arms and legs cockeyed—an orgy on a slippery tile bench. Spade so tangled up in women that you couldn't shoot him clean.

Bud flipped a wall switch. The steam died, the mist fizzled. Spade looked over. Bud took his gun out.

KILL HIM.

Cooley moved first: a shield, two girls pressed tight. Bud moved in—yanking arms, legs, nails raking his face. The girls slipped, stumbled, tumbled out the door. Spade said, "Jesus, Mary and Joseph."

Smoke inside him, brewing up his very own dreamland. Last rites, stretch the moment. "Kathy Janeway, Jane Mildred Hamsher, Lynette Ellen Kendrick, Sharon—"

Cooley yelled, "GODDAMN YOU IT'S PERKINS!"

The moment snapped—Bud saw his gun half-triggered. Colors swirled around him; Cooley talked rapid fire. "I saw Deuce with that last girlie, that Kendrick. I know'd he liked to hurt hooers, and when that last girlie turned up dead on the TV I asked him 'bout it. Deuce, he like to scared me to death, so's I took off on this here toot. Mister, you gotta believe me."

Color flashes: Deuce Perkins, plain vicious. One color blinking— turquoise, Spade's hands. "Those rings, where'd you get them?"

Cooley pulled a towel over his lap. "Deuce, he makes them.
He brings a hobby kit with him on the road. He's been crackin'
all these vague-type jokes for years, how they protects his
hands for his intimate-type work, and now I know what he
means."

"Opium. Can he get it?"

"That cracker shitbird steals my shit! Mister, you gotta
believe me!"

Starting to. "My killing dates put you in the right place to do
the jobs. Just *you*. Your booking records show different goddamn
guys traveling with you, so how do you—"

"Deuce, he's been my road manager since '49, he *always* travels
with me. Mister, you gotta believe me!"

"*Where is he?*"

"I don't know!"

"Girlfriends, buddies, other perverts. *Give.*"

"That miserable sumbitch got no friends I know of 'cept that
wop shitbird Johnny Stompanato. Mister, you gotta believe—"

"I believe you. You believe I'll kill you if you scare him away
from me?"

"Praise Jesus, I believe."

Bud walked into the smoke. The chinks were still on the nod,
Papa was just barely breathing.

*   *   *

R&I on Perkins:

No California beefs, clean on his Alabama parole—he'd spent
'44–'46 on a chain gang for animal sodomy. Transient musician,
no known address listed. KA confirmation on Johnny Stompanato—ditto Lee Vachss and Abe Teitlebaum—mob punks all. Bud
hung up, remembered a talk with Jack Vincennes—he'd rousted
Deuce at a *Badge of Honor* party—Johnny, Teitlebaum and Vachss
were there with him.

Kid gloves: Johnny used to be his snitch, Johnny hated him,
feared him.

Bud called the DMV, got Stomp's phone number—ten rings,
no answer. Two more no-answers: the Cowboy Rhythm Band at
the Biltmore, the El Rancho. Kikey Teitlebaum's deli next—Kikey
and Johnny were tight.

A run out Pico, shaking off fumes. A keen edge settling in: get
Perkins alone, kill him. Then Exley.

Bud parked, looked in the window. A slow afternoon, pay dirt—Johnny Stomp, Kikey T. at a table.

He walked in. They spotted him, whispered. Years since he'd seen them—Abe was fatter, Stomp still guinea slick.

Kikey waved. Bud grabbed a chair, carried it over. Stomp said, "Wendell White. How's tricks, *paesano*?"

"Tricky. How's tricks with Lana Turner?"

"Trickier. Who told you?"

"Mickey C."

Teitlebaum laughed. "Must have a hole like the Third Street Tunnel. Johnny's leaving for Acapulco with her tonight, and me, I shack with Sadie five-fingers. White, what brings you here? I ain't seen you since Dick Stens used to work for me."

"I'm looking for Deuce Perkins."

Johnny tap-tapped the table. "So talk to Spade Cooley."

"Spade don't know where he is."

"So why ask me? Mickey tell you Deuce and me are close?"

No ritual question: what do you want him for? And fat-mouth Kikey too quiet. "Spade said you and him were acquaintances."

"Acquaintances is right. We go back, *paesano*, so I'll tell you I haven't seen Deuce in years."

Change-up pitch. "You ain't my *paesano*, you wop cocksucker."

Johnny smiled, maybe relieved, their old cop-snitch game one more time. A look at Kikey—the fat man working on spooked. "Abe, you're tight with Perkins, right?"

"Nix. Deuce is too meshugeneh for me. He's just a guy to say hi to once in a blue fucking moon."

A lie—Perkins' rap sheet said different. "So maybe I'm confused. I know you guys are tight with Lee Vachss, and I heard him and Deuce are tight."

Kikey laughed—too stagy. "What a yuck. Johnny, I think Wendell here is really confused."

Stomp said, "Oil and water, those two. Tight? What a howl."

Standing up for Vachss for no reason. "You guys are the howl. I figured you'd ask me what the grief was right off."

Kikey pushed his plate aside. "It occur to you we just don't care?"

"Yeah, but you guys love to shmooz and milk the grapevine."

"So shmooz."

A rumor: Kikey beat a guy to death for calling him a yid. "I'll shmooz, it's a nice day and I got nothing better to do than hobnob with a greasy wop and a fat yid."

Abe ho-ho-ho'd, cuffed his arm oh-you-kid. "You're a pisser. So what do you want Deuce for?"

Bud cuffed him back hard—"None of your fucking business, Jewboy"—throw a change-up to Johnny. "What are you doing now that Mickey's out?"

Tap, tap, tap—a pinky ring on a bottle of Schlitz. "Nothing you'd be interested in. I got things contained, so don't you worry. What are *you* doing?"

"I'm on the Nite Owl reopening."

Johnny tap-tapped too hard—his bottle almost tipped. Kikey, working on pale. "You don't think Deuce Perkins ..."

Stompanato: "Come on, Abe. Deuce for the Nite Owl, what a howl."

Bud said, "I gotta piss," walked to the bathroom. He closed the door, counted to ten, opened it a crack. The shitbirds spieling full blast—Abe wiping his face with a napkin. Let the pieces fit in.

Hink: Deuce for the Nite Owl.

Jack V. spotted Vachss, Stomp, Kikey and Perkins at a party—maybe a year pre-Nite Owl.

A Mobster Squad roust, a snitch off Joe Sifakis: *three-man* trigger gangs clipping Cohen franchise hoods, maverick hoods. The Victory Motel buzzing hard.

Bud grabbed the piece, dropped it, grabbed it.

"Contain."

Dudley's favorite big word—"containment."

His motel pitch: "containing," "profit dispensation," "obstreperous Italian you've dealt with in the past"—Johnny Stomp an old snitch who hated him. Dud hot for his "full disclosure"; the Lamar Hinton roust—a shakedown for Nite Owl information, Dot Rothstein there, Kikey Teitlebaum's cousin—

Bud washed his face, walked back calm. Stomp said, "Have a good one?"

"Yeah, and you're right. I want Deuce for some old warrants, but I got a hunch on the Nite Owl."

Calm Johnny: "Oh, yeah?"

Calm Kikey: "Some new shvoogies, right? All I know's what I read in the papers."

Bud: "Maybe, but if it wasn't some new niggers, then that purple car by the Nite Owl was a plant. Take care, guys. If you see Deuce, tell him to call me at the Bureau."

Calm Johnny tap-tap-tapped.

Calm Kikey coughed, popped sweat.

Calm Bud, not so calm: out to the car, around the corner to a pay phone. The PC Bell police number, one long fucking wait.

"Uh, yes, who's requesting?"

"Sergeant White, LAPD. It's a trace job."

"For when, Sergeant?"

"*For now.* It's a homicide priority, private lines and pay phones at a restaurant. *It's now.*"

"One second, please."

Transfer click-click-clicks—a new woman. "Sergeant, what exactly do you need?"

No Calm Bud. "Abe's Noshery at Pico and Veteran. All calls out on all phones for the next fifteen goddamn minutes. Lady, don't hump me on this."

"We can't initiate actual traces, Officer."

"Just who the calls are to, goddamn it."

"Well, if it *is* a homicide priority. What is your number now?"

Bud read off the phone. "GRanite 48112."

Harumph. "Fifteen minutes then. And next time allow us more operating leeway."

Bud hung up—Dudley Dudley Dudley Dudley Dudley—hard time cut off by *brrrinnngg*. He grabbed the phone, fumbled it, cradled it. "Yeah?"

"Two calls. One to DUnkirk 32758—a Miss Dot Rothstein holds that number. The second to AXminster 46811, the residence of a Mr. Dudley L. Smith."

Bud dropped the receiver. The clerk babbled from someplace safe and calm that he'd never see again—no Lynn, no safety in a badge.

Captain Dudley Liam Smith for the Nite Owl.

67

JACK VINCENNES confessed.

He confessed to knocking up a girl at the St. Anatole's Orphan Home, to killing Mr. and Mrs. Harold J. Scoggins. He confessed to tank-jobbing Bill McPherson with a hot little nigger girl, to planting dope on Charlie Parker, to shaking down hopheads for *Hush-Hush* Magazine. He tried to jerk out of bed and raise his hands to form the Stations of the Cross. He babbled something like hub rachmones, Mickey, and bump bump bump bump the cute train. He confessed to beating up junkies, to running bag for Ellis Loew. He begged his wife to forgive him for fucking whores who looked like women in dirty picture books. He confessed that he loved dope and was unfit to love Jesus.

Karen Vincennes stood by weeping: she couldn't listen, she had to listen. Ed tried to shoo her out—she wouldn't let him. He called the Bureau from outside Arrowhead; Fisk gave him the word: Pierce Patchett shot and killed last night, his mansion torched, burned to the ground. Firemen had discovered Vincennes in the backyard—smoke inhalation, rips in his bulletproof vest. They got him to Central Receiving, a doctor took a blood sample. The results: Trashcan on a test flight, a heroin/antipsychotic drug compound. He'd live, he'd be fine—when the OD in his system flushed out.

A nurse swabbed Vincennes' face; Karen fretted Kleenex. Ed checked Fisk's memo: "Inez Soto called. No info on R.D. $ dealings. R.D. suspicious of queries???—she was cryptic—D.W."

Ed crumpled it, tossed it. Vincennes went in barefoot—while he was shacked with Lynn. Somebody killed Patchett, left them both to burn.

Burned like Exley father and son—Bud White holding the torch.

He couldn't look at Karen.

"Captain, I've got something."

Fisk in the hallway. Ed walked over, led him away from the door. "What is it?"

"Nort Layman completed the autopsy. Patchett's cause of death was five .30-30 slugs fired from two different rifles. Ray Pinker ran ballistics tests and came up with a match to an old Riverside County bulletin. May of '55, unsolved with no leads, I checked. Two men gunned down outside a tavern. It looked like a gangland job."

All coming down to the heroin. "That's all you've got?"

"No. Bud White tore up a dope den in Chinatown and beat three Chinamen half to death. He came in asking questions, badged them and went crazy. One of them ID'd his personnel photo. Thad Green called IA on it, and I caught the squeal. Pickup order, sir? I know you want him and Chief Green said it's your call."

Ed almost laughed. "No, no pickup order."

"Sir?"

"I said no, so cut it off there. And you and Kleckner do this for me. Contact Miller Stanton, Max Peltz, Timmy Valburn and Billy Dieterling. Have them come to my office tonight at 8:00 for questioning. Tell them *I'm* the investigating officer, and if they want no publicity, then bring no lawyers. And get me Homicide's file on the old Loren Atherton case. Seal it, Sergeant. I don't want you to look at it."

"Sir ..."

Ed turned away. Karen in the doorway, dry-eyed. "Do you think Jack did those things?"

"Yes."

"He mustn't know that I know. Will you promise not to tell him?"

Ed nodded, looked in the room. The Big V begged for communion.

68

A FILE room at the main DMV— boxes stacked shoulder-high. A confirmation search—a riff on Johnny and Kikey's last hink. Riff in, out, back, around—he was so high he could think it through and prowl registration records at the same time.

Make Stomp, Teitlebaum and Lee Vachss for the Nite Owl triggers; make them the shooter gang bumping upstart mobsters and Cohen franchise holders. Deuce Perkins was part of the gang—the others didn't know he beat hookers to death— they'd consider it amateur shit, wouldn't tolerate it. Dudley was the leader—he couldn't be anything else. All his job offer stuff was a try at recruiting him; the Lamar Hinton roust was Dud frosting out loose ends on the Patchett side of things—make Patchett and Smith some kind of KA's, make Hinton dead, Breuning and Carlisle part of the gang. "Contain," "Contained," "Containment," "Profit Dispensation." Call it Dudley trying to control the L.A. rackets—and pin the Nite Owl on a new bunch of jigs.

Bud tore through boxes: auto registrations, early April '53. Schoolboy thinking: he figured the car by the Nite Owl was a plant; the shotguns in Coates' car, the shells in Griffith Park, both plants—the killers followed the case, got lucky on the Merc, found some boogies to take the heat. Wrong—LAPD conspirators were in on the job. They read crime reports, got hipped to some joyriding spooks firing shotguns—lay the onus on them—they figured the arresting officers would kill them, case closed.

So they got themselves a car that matched the crime report description. They made sure it was spotted near the Nite Owl. They wouldn't steal a car—cops wouldn't risk a late night roust. They didn't buy a purple car—they bought a different colored one and painted it.

Bud kept working. No logic to the file mess: Mercs, Chevies, Caddies, L.A., Sacramento, Frisco, whoever registered the car would've used a phony name. One luck-out: the registers' race, DOB and physical stats listed on cards attached to the initial purchase carbons. Facts to eliminate against, like he learned in school: '48–'50 Mercs, Southern California purchasers, stats that matched to Dudley, Stomp, Vachss, Teitlebaum, Perkins, Carlisle and Breuning. Hours of digging, a pile inches thick—then a strange one that felt warm.

1948 primer-gray Merc coupe, purchased April 10, 1953. Register: Margaret Louise March, W.F., DOB 7/23/18, brown and brown, 5'9", 215 lbs. Register's address: 1804 East Oxford, Los Angeles. Phone number: NOrmandie 32758.

Warm to scalding—Fat Dot Rothstein's specs. Oxford ran north-south—not east-west. The call to Dot from the Noshery—DU-32758—the dumb dyke tacked her own number onto a different exchange.

And bought herself some purple paint.

Bud whooped, punched the air, kicked boxes. Two cases made in one day—if anyone believed him. All dressed up and no one to kill. Circumstantial Dudley evidence—no hard proof. Dudley too well placed to fall, nobody who cared like he did.

Except Exley.

69

A STAKEOUT on the house he grew up in. He couldn't go in and question his father; he couldn't ask for his help. He couldn't tell the man he confided secrets to a woman—and gave a brutal enemy the means to patricide. He brought the Atherton file with him—there was nothing in it he didn't already know, the man who made the smut and killed Sid Hudgens was intrinsic to the Atherton murders, maybe the killer himself—truths Preston Exley would dispute out of pride. He couldn't go in; he couldn't stop thinking. He counted memories instead.

His father bought the house for his mother; it was really just a sop to his pride—the Exleys flee the middle class grandly. They never had Christmas lights on the lawn—Preston Exley said it was lowlife. Thomas fell off balconies—and had the style not to cry. His father threw him a "back from the war" party—only the mayor, the City Council and LAPD men who could further his career were invited.

Art De Spain walked to his car, looking frail, one arm bandaged. Ed watched him drive off, his father's man, his Dutch uncle. Memory: Art said he wasn't cut out to be a detective.

The house loomed big and cold. Ed drove back to the hospital.

* * *

Trash was up, giving Fisk a statement. Ed watched from the doorway.

"... and I was playing off Exley's script. I don't remember exactly what I said, but Patchett pulled out a gun and shot me. That shit piece Exley gave me jammed, and Patchett slammed me with a hypo. Then I heard shots and 'No, Abe, no, Lee, no.' And now you know as much as I do."

From the hall, loud: "Abe Teitlebaum, Johnny Stompanato and Lee Vachss. They did the Nite Owl. Throw in Deuce Perkins as part of the gang and get ready to shit when I tell you who else I got."

Ed smelled his sweat, his breath. White pushed him inside—firm, not too rough. "Put our stuff aside for a minute. Did you hear what I said?"

The names registered: gang muscle, a not-bad line to HEROIN. White looked insane—disheveled, a zealot. Fisk said, "Sir, do you want me to ..."

Ed moved his shoulders—White dropped his hands right on cue. "Two minutes, *Captain*."

Scared—*be a captain*. "Duane, go get yourself some coffee. White, get my interest before I ream you for the Chinamen."

Fisk walked out. Ed said, "Jack, you stay. White, you keep my interest."

White closed the door. Disheveled: soiled clothes, ink-smudged hands. "Good I heard the radio on you, Trashcan. I didn't know you were here, I mighta tried to do it all myself."

Vincennes, on the bed looking queasy. "Do *what*? Abe, Lee. You make Teitlebaum and Vachss for Patchett, spell it out."

Ed: "You took Crim 101, White. Make like you're writing an occurrence chronology."

White smiled—pure kamikaze. "I been tracking a string of hooker killings for years. It started with this girl Kathy Janeway. She got snuffed back in '53, right around the Nite Owl. She was Duke Cathcart's girlfriend."

Ed nodded. "I know that story. IA ran a personal on you when you passed the sergeant's exam."

"Oh, yeah? What you don't know is that a few years ago my case broke. I thought my killer was Spade Cooley—his band was in all the hooker snuff cities on the DODs. I was wrong. Cooley ratted off the real killer—Burt Arthur Perkins."

Vincennes spoke up. "I buy Deuce as a woman killer. He's wrong to the core."

White said, "You should know, 'cause Cooley said he was pals with Johnny Stompanato, and back around '52 you told me you rousted him hanging out with Johnny Stomp, Kikey T. and Lee Vachss. Cooley told me Johnny and Deuce were tight, so I went looking for Johnny."

Ed said, "All right, so you went to Stompanato."

White lit a cigarette. "Nix. Now I tell you that Dudley Smith has been using me for strongarm jobs on the Mobster Squad going back years. You know how he talks? 'Containment,' that's one of his favorite words. Contain crime, contain this, contain that. He's been beating around the bush about offering me outside work, and the other night he said I could be useful keeping the 'obstreperous Italian' that's afraid of me in line. Johnny Stomp's afraid of me—he used to snitch for me and I used to muscle him good. You know how Dud's this so-called gangland peacemaker? Well, the other night him, Carlisle and Breuning worked over this guy Lamar Hinton at the Victory, supposedly a Mobster Squad job. Bullshit—all Dudley asked him about was Nite Owl stuff—smut, Pierce Patchett."

Ed, bug-eyed: this can't be coming. "So you went to Stompanato looking for Perkins."

"Right. I go to Kikey's deli, and Johnny's there with Kikey. I ask Johnny about Deuce, and Johnny's all hinked. Kikey's hinked worse and they both lie and say Deuce is just some bumfuck acquaintance. They deny that Deuce is tight with Lee Vachss, when I know goddamn otherwise. Johnny uses the word 'containment,' which is not a Johnny-type word. Hink all over these guys, and I drop that I'm on the Nite Owl reopening and they almost shit, Deuce for the Nite Owl, ho, ho. I leave, go to a pay phone and have PC Bell put a fifteen-minute trace on all calls out of the deli. Two calls—one to Dot Rothstein, Dudley's good pal and Kikey's cousin, one to Dudley's house."

Vincennes said, "Holy fucking shit." Ed jerked a hand to his gun—wrong—White was a cop. "Give me corroboration."

White flicked his smoke out the window. "Crim 101. The niggers didn't do it, so Dud and his gang planted a car by the Nite Owl. I went to the DMV and checked April '53 registrations, Caucasians this time. Dot Rothstein bought a '48 Merc, primer gray, on April 10. A phony name, a phony address, but the stupid bitch used the real digits on her own phone number."

Vincennes looked shell-shocked. Ed reeled in a line so he wouldn't scream DUDLEY. "Right before the Nite Owl I was working late at Hollywood Station. Spade Cooley was playing a retirement party downstairs, and I saw Burt Perkins roaming the halls. Try this theory: Mal Lunceford, ex-LAPD patrolman. Call him the forgotten Nite Owl victim, and remember he worked Hollywood Division for most of his time on the Department. Now, did one of the shooters have a grudge against Lunceford? Was Perkins removing records of it that night at the station? Did the conspirators know that Lunceford was a Nite Owl regular and plan their Cathcart or Cathcart-impersonator hit so that they could clip him too?"

White answered. "Dudley put me on the Lunceford background check, probably because he thought I'd fuck it up. I checked for old Lunceford FI's and couldn't find a goddamn one. I buy that theory."

DUDLEY past screaming—Ed held it down. Vincennes: "Fisk told me about Patchett, how he got the Cohen-Dragna summit heroin, how him and this unnamed bad guy who's obviously Dudley were getting ready to push it. Now, I know for a fact that Dud bodyguarded that deal, and there was this rumor floating around years ago—that Dud led this posse that killed this guy Buzz Meeks who heisted the summit. Fisk said that Patchett got most of the white horse that got clouted, some from the Englekling brothers and their father, some from this bad guy who's obviously Dudley. Okay, so what I'm thinking is—could Lunceford have been in on the posse? Was *that* when Dudley got the dope?"

White shook his head—new stuff for him. "You fill me in on that, because I got a lead that ties in. Dud was talking up his containment shit, and he said something about keeping the niggers sedated, which sounds like heroin to me."

Ed said, "Call that done for now. Jack, run with the Goldman-Van Gelder angle. Put it together with our new leads."

Trash stood up, steadied himself on the bed rail. "Okay, let's say Davey G. was in with Dudley, Stompanato, Kikey, Vachss and Dot. How any of them could trust a psycho like Deuce I don't know, but fuck it. Anyway, they're all conspiring against Mickey C. White, you don't know this, but Goldman had a bug in Mickey's cell at McNeil. I'm betting Dudley and his friends were in with Davey from the beginning, but fuck it, however it happened, Davey heard the Englekling brothers approach Mickey with Duke Cathcart's smut deal."

Ed raised a hand. "Chester Yorkin said that the man who brought Patchett the bulk of the heroin—let's assume it's Dudley—had a hard-on for smut and quote 'contacts in South America and pervert mailing lists.' I always wondered about the profit on pornography, and now Dudley's connection makes it seem more feasible."

Vincennes said, "Let me keep going. Dud worked with the OSS in Paraguay after the war and he ran Ad Vice back in '39 or so, so I know he's got those contacts, but sit on that. Right now we've got Goldman going to Smith and Stompanato with the word on the smut plan. Everybody, especially Dud, likes the idea, and they decide to crash the racket. On his own, a double cross, I don't know, Davey sends Dean Van Gelder, his prison visitor, to talk to Cathcart. Van Gelder decides to crash Duke's prostie racket and the smut gig on his own. He'd been seen by Davey face-to-face, but the outside prison men had never seen him. He figured he looked like Cathcart, so he could impersonate Cathcart and cut his own deal. By the time the impersonation was found out he'd be too far in good with the outside men for Davey to care what he'd done. So Van Gelder moved to San Berdoo to be close to the Englekling brothers. He fell in with Sue Lefferts and snuffed Duke. He knew the names of at least one of the outside men, called them at a pay phone from the Lefferts' house and asked for a meet. He went in tough and suggested a public place, he figured

Sue could sit nearby and he'd be safe. One of the outside guys put Lunceford together with the Nite Owl and said let's meet there. Dud or one of his guys approached Patchett right *before* the Nite Owl and told him to get his loose ends tidied. Patchett didn't know exactly what was gonna happen, but he had Chris Bergeron and her kid and Bobby Inge blow town just as I was starting in on the smut gig for Ad Vice."

An air-cooled room—Ed felt every word boost the temperature. "Let me throw out a chronology, starting right after Van Gelder as Cathcart contacts the outside men. Now, we know Dudley loves pornography, we know he's been sitting on eighteen pounds of 'H' since the Cohen-Dragna deal. Try this theory: he breaks into Cathcart's apartment and finds something that leads him to Patchett, something that includes mention of his chemistry background and his connection to old Dr. Englekling. He goes to Patchett, they strike a deal—develop the heroin, push the smut. He's astounded that Patchett's thinking along the same lines, that he's already got some of the horse from Doc Englekling. Now Dudley wants Cathcart killed, Mal Lunceford silenced for whatever reason—and he wants Patchett terrified. He's a policeman, and he's read about those Negroes discharging shotguns in Griffith Park. He sets up the meet at the Nite Owl, knowing Lunceford will be there, and Jack's right—he was ambiguous, but he told Patchett to get rid of his loose ends. Moving ahead, the investigation goes wider than Dudley thinks it will—because the Negroes don't get killed during their arrest, and they don't confess. He puts White on the Cathcart background check, and he probably *didn't* know that Perkins killed the Janeway girl, but he wanted White steered away from getting involved on general principles—he wanted him to steer clear of possible Cathcart–Nite Owl connections."

All eyes on Bud White. The zealot: "Okay, Dudley put me on the Cathcart check because he thought I'd screw up. But I checked out Duke's pad and saw that it was print-wiped, and I figured that somebody had tried on his clothes. The Dudley guys wiped the place, but they didn't touch the phone books, and I could tell that the San Berdoo printshop listings had been looked over. Now, I got a theory. When I was on the Cathcart check, I met Kathy Janeway at this motel out in the Valley. Two days later she's raped and killed. When I left the motel I thought I was being tailed, but then I forgot about it. I think the tail was

Deuce Perkins. I think Dud put a tail on Cathcart's KA's, just to keep tabs on the investigation, which explains how he's always known so much about all this stuff that I've always kept secret. So Deuce, who's a rape-o shitbird psycho, sees Kathy and goes for her. Maybe Dudley knew he killed her, maybe he didn't. Either way he fucking pays."

Vincennes lit a cigarette, coughed. "We've got no evidence, but I've got some more stuff to tie in. One, Doc Layman took five .30-30 slugs out of Patchett, and he said they match this gang unsolved in Riverside County. When Davey Goldman was babbling away up in Camarillo, he said something about three triggers. He babbled some other stuff that keeps running through my head, but it doesn't make any sense. Exley, did you listen to that tape I found at McNeil?"

Ed nodded. "You're right. Nothing salient at all, just a passing mention of some gang hits."

White: "There's been a bunch of mob unsolveds. I know, 'cause a suspect spilled some tangent stuff on them on a Mobster Squad roust. Always three triggers, Cohen franchise holders and upstart hoods clipped. Easy money: Stompanato, Vachss and Teitlebaum keeping things copacetic for Mickey C.'s parole. They wanted to keep things chilled for their containment gig and they figured when Mickey got out they'd test the wind and either clip him or use him. My bet's on clip. They had Cohen and Goldman bushwhacked in prison—a pure cross on Davey. Mickey's house got bombed and Mickey lived to tell. They'll clip him before too long and they'll contain real good, 'cause Dud's Mr. Mobster Squad and he's got Parker's fucking—what's the word? mandate?—to keep out-of-town muscle out. Do you fucking believe it?"

Trash laughed. "Grand, lad, grand. And all the hits were paving the way for Dud to push Patchett's heroin. He got the command on the reopening so he could find some new patsies, and he's set to push the horse. He's got the smut stashed, and he didn't warn Patchett about the investigation because he was already planning to kill him. He didn't touch Lynn Bracken, because he figured Patchett kept her in the dark on all his worst stuff. He let her come in for questioning because he figured she'd stall Exley's part of the investigation."

Lynn Bracken.

Ed winced, moved toward the door. "And we still don't know who made the smut and killed Hudgens. Or the Engle-kling brothers, which doesn't look like a pro job. White, you went up to Gaitsville with Dudley, and he submitted a soft-pedal report on—"

"It was another psycho job. Heroin lying around, and the killer just left it. He tortured the brothers with chemicals and burned up a bunch of smut negatives with acid solutions. The lab tech said he thought the killer was trying to ID the people in the pictures. The chemistry stuff made me think Patchett, but then I thought he must've already known who the picture people were. I don't really think their heroin ties to our heroin, the brothers were dope peddlers on and off for years. Chemists and dope peddlers, and if Patchett wanted their dope, he would've stolen it. I think the brothers got killed by somebody, I don't know, outside the center of this mess."

Trash sighed. "*There's no evidence.* Patchett and the whole Englekling family are dead, and Dud probably killed Lamar Hinton. You got nothing at the Fleur-de-Lis drop and White's little grandstand with Stompanato and Teitlebaum means that now Dudley's been alerted and he's taking care of *his* loose ends. I don't think we've got much of a case."

Ed thought it through. "Chester Yorkin told me Patchett had a booby-trapped safe outside his house. The house is being guarded now, the West L.A. squad has a team on it. In a day or so, I'll go lift the guards. There might be something in that safe that nails Dudley."

White said, "So right now, what? No evidence, and Stompanato's leaving for Acapulco today with Lana Turner. What now?"

Ed opened the door—Fisk was outside drinking coffee. "Duane, get back in touch with Valburn, Stanton, Billy Dieterling and Peltz. Change the meeting to the downtown Statler at 8:00. Call the hotel and set up three suites and call Bob Gallaudet and tell him to call me here—tell him it's urgent."

Fisk went for a phone. Vincennes said, "You're hitting the Hudgens end."

Ed turned away from White. "*Think.* Dudley's a policeman. We need evidence, and we may get it tonight."

"I'll take Stanton. We used to be friends."

Line it—a Dieterling kid star, Preston Exley. "No ... I mean are you up to it?"

"It's my case too, Captain. I've come this far, and I went up against Patchett for you and damn near got killed."

Weigh the risk. "All right, you take Stanton."

Trash rubbed his face—pale, stubbled. "Did I ... I mean when Karen was here and I was unconscious ... did I ..."

"She doesn't know anything you don't want her to. Now go home, I want to talk to White."

Vincennes walked out—ten years older in a day. White said, "The Hudgens end is bullshit. It's all Dudley now."

"No. First we buy some time."

"Protecting Daddy? Jesus, and I thought I was dumb on women."

"*Just think.* Think what Dudley is and what taking him down means. Think, and I'll make you a deal."

"I told you *never.*"

"You'll like this one. You keep quiet about my father and the Atherton case and I'll let you have Dudley and Perkins."

White laughed. "The collars? I got them anyway."

"No. I'll let you kill them."

70

EXLEY'S RULE rankled: no hitting, Billy and Timmy were too upscale to take muscle. Hotel good guy/bad guy rankled—they should be muscling Dudley at the Victory. Bob Gallaudet took Max Peltz; Trashcan was grilling Miller Stanton. Gallaudet got briefed by Exley—everything but the Atherton angle. He thought he could prosecute Dudley Smith, Exley didn't tell him Dud and Deuce Perkins were paid for. Fucking Exley wouldn't let him out of his sight—he took him through every piece of the case step by step, like they were partners who could trust each other. The case all put together was amazing, Exley had an amazing fucking brain—but he was stupid if he didn't know one thing: after Dudley and Deuce, Preston E. was next. Easy: Dick Stens wouldn't have it otherwise.

Bud watched—a crack in the bathroom doorway.

The queers sat side by side; Mr. Good Guy pussyfooted. Yes, they bought Fleur-de-Lis dope; yes, they knew Pierce Patchett "socially." Yes, Pierce snorted "H," we heard rumors he sold pornographic books—but *we* never indulged in such things. Kid gloves: the fruits thought the Patchett snuff was why they got the royal hotel treatment. Captain Exley would never be nasty—Preston Exley was running for governor, Ray Dieterling throwing hot financial backup.

Exley, loud. "Gentlemen, there's an old homicide that might tie in to the Patchett killing."

Bud walked in. Exley said, "This is Sergeant White. He has a few questions for you, then I think we can wrap it up."

Timmy Valburn sighed. "Well, I'm not surprised. Miller Stanton and Max Peltz are down the hall, and the last time the police questioned all of us was when that awful man Sid Hudgens was killed. So *I'm* not surprised."

Bud pulled a chair up. "Why'd you say 'awful'? You kill him?"

"Oh, Sergeant *really*. Do I look like the killer type to you?"

"Yeah, you do. Guy who makes his living playing a mouse has gotta be capable of anything."

"Sergeant, *really*."

"Besides, *you* weren't called in on the Hudgens job. Billy tell you about it? A little pillow talk, maybe?"

Billy Dieterling to Exley. "Captain, I don't like this man's tone."

Exley said, "Sergeant, keep it clean."

Bud laughed. "That's the pot calling the kettle black, but screw it. You guys alibied each other for Hudgens, now it's five years later and you alibi each other up for Patchett. Hinky to me. My take on fruits is that they can't stick to the same bed for five minutes, let alone five years."

Valburn: "You're an animal."

Bud pulled out a file sheet. "Alibis on the Hudgens case. You and Billy in bed together, Max Peltz porking some teenage quiff. Miller Stanton at a party where your queer buddy Brett Chase also happens to be. So far, we got a real all-American crew on *Badge of Honor*. David Mertens the set man, he's at home with his male nurse, so maybe he's fruit, too. What I want—"

Exley, on cue: "Sergeant, watch your language and get to the point."

Valburn seethed; Billy D. faked boredom. But something in the last spiel nudged him—his eyes went from good guy to bad guy. "The point is that Sid Hudgens had a boner for *Badge of Honor* at the time he was killed. Patchett gets killed five years later, and him and Hudgens were partners. These homos here, they're both tied to *Badge of Honor* and they kicked loose with intimate details on Patchett's rackets. Captain, if it walks, talks and quacks like a duck, then it's a duck—not a mouse."

Valburn said, "Quack, quack, idiot. Captain, will you tell this man who he's dealing with?"

Exley, stern. "Sergeant, these gentlemen aren't suspects. They're voluntary interviewees."

"Well, shit, sir, I don't see no difference."

Exley, exasperated. "Gentlemen, to end this once and for all, please tell the sergeant. Did either of you even *know* Sid Hudgens personally?"

Two "No" head shakes. Bud flew—Exley poetry. "If it squeaks like a mouse and swishes, it's a queer mouse. Captain, *think*. These guys bought dope off Fleur-de-Lis, and they admitted they knew Patchett sniffed horse and pushed pornography. They've got the lowdown on Patchett's rackets, but they claim they didn't know Patchett and Hudgens were partners. I say we take them through Patchett's little enterprises and see what they do know."

Exley raised his hands—fake helpless. "A few more specific questions then, gentlemen. Again, anything illegal that you admit to will be overlooked—and will not go outside this room. Do you understand, Sergeant?"

Fucking brilliant: build them up to who made the blood smut. Trash said Timmy was spooked by the stuff—he showed it to him in '53. Credit Exley with balls—the closer they got to the smut the closer they got to his old man and Atherton. "Okay, sir."

Timmy and Billy shared a look: nice people strafed by low class. Exley flashed it over. "And, Sergeant—I'll ask the questions."

"Yes, sir. You guys tell the truth. I'll know if you're lying."

Exley sighed. "Just a few questions. First, did you know that Patchett procured call girls for business associates?"

Two "Yes" nods. Bud said, "He ran boys, too. You guys ever buy any outside stuff?"

Exley: "Not another word, Sergeant."

Timmy slid closer to Billy. "I won't dignify that last question with an answer."

Bud winked. "You're cute. I ever wind up in stir, I hope you're in my cell."

Billy mimed spitting on the floor. Exley rolled his eyes—God save us from this heathen. "Moving along. Were you aware that Patchett employed a plastic surgeon to surgically alter his prostitutes to resemble movie stars?"

Timmy said, "Yes," Billy said, "Yes." Exley smiled like that was everyday stuff. "Were you also aware that those prostitutes, both male and female, engaged in other criminal pursuits at Patchett's direction?"

Build them up to "extortion," the Patchett/Hudgens partnership. Exley told him the story: Lorraine/Rita said "This Guy" made Patchett squeeze his "clients," right when Pierce was set to go partners with Hudgens—*right after the Nite Owl killings.* A brainstorm coming—maybe a connector back to Dudley. "Answer the captain, shitbirds."

Billy said, "Ed, make him stop. Really, this has gone far enough."

Bud laughed. "*Ed?* Oops, I forgot, boss. Your daddy's pals with his daddy."

Exley riled for real—flushed, trembling. "White, shut your mouth."

The fruits loved it—smiles, titters. Exley said, "Gentlemen, please answer the question."

Timmy shrugged. "Be specific. What other 'criminal pursuits'?"

"Specifically blackmail."

Two legs brushing twitched apart—Bud caught it plain. Exley touched his necktie—GO FULL.

Brainstorm: Johnny Stomp as "This Guy." Johnny Stomp an old shake artist, no visible means of support. Crim 101—Lorraine Malvasi said the squeezes went down May '53—Dudley's gang had already teamed up with Patchett. "Yeah, *blackmail.* Married johns and pervs and queers are prone to it. It's like an occupational hazard. Ever get squeezed by one of your playmates?"

Now Billy rolled his eyes. "We don't frequent prostitutes. Male or female."

Bud pulled his chair closer. "Well, your sweetie pie here was a known associate of a known fruit hustler named Bobby Inge. If it quacks like a duck, it's a duck. So quack, quack, and kick loose with who put the arm on you."

Exley, stern. "Gentlemen, do you know the names of any specific Patchett prostitutes?"

Billy came on butch. "He's a storm trooper, and we don't have to answer his questions."

"The fuck. You crawl around in sewers, you gotta meet some rats. Ever hear of a cute little twist named Daryl Bergeron? Ever get a yen for a woman and go for his mother? Daryl did—Trashcan Jack Vincennes has got a smut book with pictures of them fucking on roller skates. You're floating in a sewer on a Popsicle stick you fucking queer bastards, so—"

Valburn: "Ed, make him stop!"

Exley: "Sergeant, enough!"

Bud, dizzy, like a man inside his head was feeding him lines. "The hell you say. These geeks are all over Patchett's schemes. One of them's a TV star, one of them's got a famous daddy. Two faggots with plenty of money just fucking ripe to be squeezed. That don't play smart to you?"

Exley—KEEP STILL—a finger to his collar. "Sergeant White has a point, although I apologize for his way of expressing it. Gentlemen, just for the record. Have either of you any knowledge of extortion schemes involving Pierce Patchett and/or his prostitutes?"

Timmy Valburn said, "No."

Billy Dieterling said, "No."

Bud got ready to whisper.

Exley leaned forward. "Have either of you ever been threatened with blackmail?"

Two more nos—two queers sweating up a nice cool room. Bud whispered, "Johnny Stompanato."

The fags froze. Bud said, "*Badge of Honor* dirt. Is that what he wanted?"

Valburn started to speak—Billy shushed him. Exley: SLOW.

The dizzy head man said NO. "Did he have dirt on your father? The great fucking Raymond Dieterling?"

Exley shot the cut-off sign. The dizzy man showed his face: Dick Stens sucking gas. "*Dirt*. Wee Willie Wennerholm, Loren Atherton and the kiddie murders. *Your father.*"

Billy trembled, pointed to Exley. "*His* father!"

Four-way stares—cut off by Valburn sobbing. Billy helped him up, embraced him. Exley said, "Get out. Now. You're free to go."

He looked sad more than mad or scared.

Billy walked Timmy out. Bud walked to the window. Exley walked over, talked to a hand mike. "Duane, Valburn and Dieterling are on their way. You and Don tail them."

Bud scoped him—a little taller, half his bulk. Something made him say, "I shouldn't have done that."

Exley looked out the window. "It'll be over soon. All of it."

Bud looked down. Fisk and Kleckner stood by the door; the queers hit the sidewalk running. The IA men chased—a bus held them back. The bus zoomed by—no Billy and Timmy. Fisk and Kleckner stood in the street looking stupid.

Exley started laughing.

Something made Bud laugh.

71

THEY REHASHED old times; Stanton drank room service bubbly. Jack laid out his pitch: Patchett/Hudgens, smut, heroin, the Nite Owl. He could tell Miller knew something; he could tell he wanted to spill it.

Old touches: how he taught Miller to play a cop; how he took Miller down to Central Avenue to get laid and wound up rousting Art Pepper. Gallaudet poked his head in, said Max Peltz was clean—Max stories ate up another hour. Miller got misty—'58 would be the show's last season. Too bad they lost touch with each other, but the Big V was acting too crazy, a pariah in the Industry. White and Exley arguing next door—Jack cut to it.

"Miller, is there something you're dying to tell me?"

"I don't know, Jack. It's old rebop."

"This mess *goes* back. You know Patchett, don't you?"

"How'd you know that?"

"Educated guess. And the captain's file said Patchett bankrolled some old Dieterling films."

Stanton checked his glass—empty. "Okay, I know Patchett from way back. It's some story, but I don't see how it applies to what you're interested in."

Jack heard the side door scrape carpet. "All I know is that you've been dying to tell me ever since I said the word 'Patchett.'"

"Damn, I don't feel like a cop around you. I feel like a fat actor about to lose his series."

Jack looked away—cut the man slack. Stanton said, "You know I was the chubby kid in Dieterling's serials way back when. Willie Wennerholm, Wee Willie, he was the big star. I used to see Patchett at the studio school, and I knew he was some kind of Dieterling business partner, because our tutor had a crush on him and told all the kids who he was."

"And?"

"And Wee Willie was kidnapped from the school and chopped up by Dr. Frankenstein. You know the case, it was famous. The police picked up this guy Loren Atherton. They said he killed Willie and all these other children. Jack, this is the hard part."

"So tell it fast."

Very fast. "Mr. Dieterling and Patchett came to me. They gave me tranquilizers and told me I had to come along with this older boy and visit a police station. I was fourteen, the older boy was maybe seventeen. Patchett and Mr. Dieterling coached me, and we went to the station. We talked to Preston Exley, he was a detective back then. We told him just what Patchett and Mr. Dieterling told us to—that we'd seen Atherton prowling around the studio school. We identified Atherton and Exley believed us."

An actor's pause. Jack said, "Goddammit, *and*?"

Slower. "I never saw the older boy again, and I can't even remember his name. Atherton was convicted and executed, and I wasn't asked to testify at his trial. It got to be '39, right in there. I was still in the Dieterling stable, but I was a boy ingenue. Mr. Dieterling had this little studio contingent go out to the opening of the Arroyo Seco Freeway, just a publicity appearance. Preston Exley, he was a big-shot contractor now, and he cut the ribbon. I heard Mr. Dieterling, Patchett and Terry Lux, you know him, talking."

Pins and needles. "Miller, come on."

"I'll never forget what they said, Jack. Patchett told Lux, 'I've got the chemicals to keep him from hurting anybody and you plasticked him.' Lux said, 'And I'll get him a keeper.' Mr. Dieterling, I'll never forget the way his voice sounded. He said, 'And I gave Preston Exley a scapegoat he believes in beyond Loren Atherton. And I think the man owes me too much now to hurt me.'"

Jack touched himself—he thought he'd stopped breathing. Breathing behind him—strained. Eyes on Exley and White in the doorway—up close to each other frozen.

72

NOW ALL his lines crossed in ink.

Red ink mutilations. An inkwell spilling blood. Cartoon characters on a marquee with Raymond Dieterling, Preston Exley, an all-star criminal cast. Ink colors: red, green for bribe money. Black for mourning—the dead supporting players. White and Vincennes knew, they'd probably tell Gallaudet—he kicked them out of the hotel knowing it. He could warn his father or not warn his father and the end would be the same. He could keep going or sit in this room and watch his life explode on television.

Long hours down—he couldn't reach for the phone. He turned on the TV, saw his father at a freeway ceremony, stuck his gun in his mouth while the man mouthed platitudes. The trigger half back—fade to a commercial. He emptied four rounds, spun the cylinder, put the barrel to his head. He squeezed the trigger twice, empty chambers, he couldn't believe what he'd done. He threw his piece out the window—a wino grabbed it off the sidewalk, shot up the sky. He laughed, sobbed, punched himself out on the furniture.

More hours down doing nothing.

The phone rang—Ed flailed for it blind. "Uh … yes?"

"Captain, you there? It's Vincennes."

"I'm here. What is it?"

"I'm at the Bureau with White. We just caught a squeal and grabbed it. 2206 North New Hampshire, Billy Dieterling's house. Billy and an unknown male dead. Fisk rolled on it already. Cap, *are you there?*"

No no no—yes. "I'm going … I'll be there."

"Will do. And by the way, White and I didn't tell Gallaudet what Stanton said. Thought you should know that."

"Thank you, Sergeant."

"Thank White. He's the one you had to worry about."

* * *

Fisk met him there—a mock Tudor lit by headlights—black-and-whites, crime lab cars on the lawn.

Ed ran up; Fisk spoke shorthand. "Neighbor woman heard screams, waited half an hour and called. She saw a man run out, get into Billy Dieterling's car and take off. He hit a tree down the block, got out and ran. I took a statement. White, male, early forties, average build. Sir, brace yourself."

Flashbulb pops inside. Ed said, "*Seal it here.* No Homicide, no station cops. No press, and I don't want Dieterling's father to find out. Have Kleckner seal the car and go get me Timmy Valburn. *Find him. Now.*"

"Sir, they blew our tail. I feel bad about this, like it's our fault."

"It doesn't matter, just do what I told you."

Fisk ran to his car; Ed walked in, looked.

Billy Dieterling on a white couch soaked red. A knife in his throat; two knives in his stomach. His scalp on the floor, stuck to the carpet with an icepick. A few feet away: a fortyish white man—disemboweled, eviscerated, knives in his cheeks, two kitchen forks in his eyes. Drug capsules soaking in floor blood.

No artful desecrations—his man was past it now.

Ed walked into the kitchen. Patchett to Lux '39: "I've got the chemicals to keep him from hurting anybody, and you plasticked him." Cupboards dumped; forks and spoons on the floor. Ray Dieterling '39: "A scapegoat he believes in." Bloody footprints in and out—his man made trips for more adornment. Lux: "I'll get him a keeper." A scalp section in the sink. "Preston Exley. He was a big-shot contractor now." A bloody handprint on the wall, a psycho passion job for Crim 101's all-time list.

Ed squinted at the print—ridges and whirls showed plainly. Psycho oblivion: his man pressed his hand there to leave an imprimatur.

Back to the living room. Trashcan Jack in the middle of a half dozen lab techs. Bad flashbulb glare, no Bud White.

Trash said, "The other man's Jerry Marsalas. He's a male nurse, and he's sort of the keeper of this guy on the *Badge of Honor* crew. David Mertens, the set designer. Very quiet, he's got epilepsy or something like that."

"Plastic surgery scars?"

"Graft scars all over his neck and back. I saw him with his shirt off once."

Techs swarming now—Ed led Vincennes out to the porch. Cool air, bright bright headlights. Trash said, "Mertens is the right age to be that older kid Stanton was talking about. Lux cut him, so Miller wouldn't have recognized him on the set. All the grafts on his back, he could have been cut lots of times. Jesus, the look on your face. You're taking it all the way?"

"I don't know. I want one more day to see what we can get on Dudley."

"And see if White tries to shank you. He could have told Gallaudet the whole story, but he didn't."

"White's as crazy as anybody in this thing."

Trash laughed. "Yeah, like you. Boss, if you and Gallaudet want this mess to go to due process, you'd better lock that boy up. He's out to kill Dudley and Deuce, and believe me he'll do it."

Ed laughed. "I told him he could."

"You'd *let him* do—"

Cut him off. "Jack, do this. Stake Mertens' place and see if you can find White, then—"

"He's chasing down Perkins, how do I—"

"Just try to find him. And with or without him, meet me at Mickey Cohen's house tomorrow at nine. We're going to brace him on Dudley."

Vincennes looked around. "I don't see anybody from Homicide here."

"You and Fisk caught it, so Homicide doesn't know. I can keep it IA-sealed for twenty-four hours or so. It's ours until the press gets it."

"No APB on Mertens?"

"I'll call out half of IA. He's a drooling psychotic. We'll get him."

"Suppose I find him. You don't want him talking old times, not with your father part of it."

"Take him alive. I want to talk to him."

Vincennes said, "For crazy, White's got nothing on you."

* * *

Ed sealed it.

He called Chief Parker, told him he had an IA-related double homicide and was keeping the victims' identities secret. He woke up five IA men, filled them in on David Mertens, sent them out to search for him. He made the neighbor lady who called in the squeal take a sedative, go to bed, promise she wouldn't spill the name "Billy Dieterling" to the press. The press arrived—he mollified them with John Doe IDs, sent them packing. He walked to the end of the block and examined the car—Kleckner watchdogging it—a Packard Caribbean with the front wheels up on the curb, the fender nosed into a tree. The driver's seat, dash and shift lever—bloody; perfect bloody handprints on the outside of the windshield. Kleckner stripped the license plates; Ed told him to drive the car home, stash it, team up with the searchers. Courtesy calls from a pay phone: the watch commander at Rampart Station, the duty ME at the City Morgue. A lie: Parker wanted a twenty-four-hour blanket on the killings—no statements to the press, no autopsy reports circulated. 3:40 A.M., no Homicide brass at the scene—Parker carte-blanched him.

Sealed.

Ed walked back to the house. Quiet—no newsmen, no rubberneckers. Tape outlines—no bodies. Techs dusting, bagging evidence. Fisk in the kitchen doorway—looking nervous. "Sir, I've got Valburn. Inez Soto's with him. I went down to Laguna on a hunch. You told me Miss Soto knew him."

"What did Valburn tell you?"

"Nothing. He said he'd only talk to you. I broke it to him, and he cried himself out on the ride up. He said he's ready to make a statement."

Inez walked out. Grief all over her, her nails chewed bloody. "I blame you for this. I blame you for pushing Billy to it."

"I don't know what you mean, but I'm sorry."

"You had me spy on Raymond. Now you did this."

Ed stepped toward her. She slapped him, hit him. "Leave us all alone!"

Fisk grabbed her, eased her outside. Gentle—soft hands, a low voice. Ed walked down the hall looking in rooms.

Valburn in the den, taking pictures off the wall. Bright eyes glazed over, a too-bright voice. "If I keep doing things I'll be fine."

A group shot came down. "I need a full statement."

"Oh, you'll get one."

"Mertens killed Hudgens, Billy and Marsalas, plus Wee Willie and those other children. I need the why. Timmy, look at me."

Timmy plucked a framed photo. "We were together since 1949. We had our little indiscretions, but we always stayed together and loved each other. Don't give me a speech about getting his killer, Ed. I just couldn't bear it. I'll tell you what you want to know, but try not to be déclassé."

"Timmy—"

Valburn threw the frame at the wall. "David Mertens, god-damn you!"

Glass shattered. The picture landed face up: Raymond Diet-erling holding an inkwell. "Start with the pornography. Jack Vincennes talked to you about it five years ago, and he thought you were holding back."

"Is this another third degree?"

"Don't make it one."

Timmy squared a stack of frames. "Jerry Marsalas made David create that strange ... filth. Jerry was a very bad man. He'd been David's companion for years, and he regulated the drugs that kept him ... relatively normal. Sometimes he'd escalate and de-escalate his dosages and get David to do commercial art piecework, just so he could keep the money. Raymond paid Jerry to look after David. He got David the job at *Badge of Honor* so that Billy could look after him, too—Billy ran the camera crew since the show first went on."

Ed said, "Don't get ahead of yourself. Where did Marsalas and Mertens find the posers?"

Timmy hugged his pictures. "Fleur-de-Lis. Marsalas had used the service for years. He'd buy call girls when he was flush, and he knew lots of Pierce's old string of girls and lots of ... sexually adventurous people that the girls told him about. He found out that a lot of Fleur-de-Lis customers had a bent for specialty smut, and he talked some of Pierce's old girls into letting him voyeur their sex parties. Jerry took pictures, David took pictures, and Jerry escalated David's drug intake and made him do pasteup work. The ink blood was all David's idea. Jerry hired some studio art director to make finished books out of the pictures and took them to Pierce. Do you follow? I don't know what *you* know."

Ed got out his notebook. "Miller Stanton told us some background things. Patchett and Dieterling were partners at the time of the Atherton killings, and you know I make Mertens for them. Just keep going. If I need something clarified, I'll tell you."

Timmy said, "All right then. If you don't know it, the ink pictures were similar to the woundings on the Atherton victims. Pierce didn't know it when he saw the books, I guess only policemen saw the evidence photos. He also didn't know that David Mertens was the Wennerholm killer's new identity, so when Marsalas hatched this plan to sell the books and went to Pierce for financing, he just thought it was dirty books that compromised his prostitutes and their customers. He turned Marsalas down on his offer, but he did buy some of the books to sell through Fleur-de-Lis. Then Marsalas went to this man Duke Cathcart, and he went to these people the Englekling brothers. Ed, your Mr. Fisk hinted that all this has to do with the Nite Owl case, but I don't—"

"I'll tell you later. You're talking about early '53, and I'm following you so far. Just keep telling it in order."

Timmy laid his pictures down. "Then Patchett went to Sid Hudgens. He and Hudgens were going to be partners in some extortion thing that I don't know anything about, and Pierce told Hudgens about Marsalas and his smut. He'd had Marsalas checked out, and he knew he was a regular on the *Badge of Honor* set, which interested Hudgens, because he had always wanted to do an exposé on the show for *Hush-Hush*. Pierce gave Hudgens a few of the books he'd held back from Fleur-de-Lis, and Hudgens approached Marsalas. He demanded information on the show's stars and threatened Jerry with exposure of his smut dealings if he didn't cooperate. Jerry gave him some tame stuff on Max Peltz, and a little while later it appeared in print. Then Hudgens was murdered, and of course it was Jerry who put David up to it. He lowered his drug dosage and drove him insane. David reverted to his old ... to the way he killed the children. Marsalas did it because he was afraid Hudgens would keep trying to extort him. He went with David, and he stole Hudgens' *Badge of Honor* files from his house, including an incomplete file Hudgens had on him and David. I don't think he knew that Pierce already had carbons of the files he and Hudgens were going to use for their blackmail thing, or that Pierce knew the bank where Hudgens kept his original files stashed."

Three key questions coming up; more corroboration first. "Timmy, when Vincennes questioned you five years ago, you acted suspiciously. Did you know back then that Mertens made the smut?"

"Yes, but I didn't know who David *was.* All I knew was that Billy kept an eye on him, so I kept quiet to Jack."

Question number one. "How do you know all this? Everything you've told me."

Timmy's eyes glazed fresh. "I found out tonight. After the hotel, Billy wanted that awful policeman's hints about Johnny Stompanato explained. Billy's known most of the story for years, but he wanted to know the rest. We went to Raymond's house in Laguna. Raymond knew about the more recent things from Pierce, and he told Billy the whole story. I just listened."

"And Inez was there."

"Yes, she heard it all. She blames you, sweetie. Pandora's box and all that."

She knew, his father probably knew. Full disclosure as good as public. "So Patchett supplied the dope that's kept Mertens docile all these years."

"Yes, he's quite physiologically ill. He gets brain inflammations periodically, and that's when he's most dangerous."

"And Dieterling got him the job with *Badge of Honor* so Billy could look after him."

"Yes. After the Hudgens killing Raymond read about the mutilations and thought they sounded like the ones from the old child murders. He contacted Patchett, who he knew was friendly with Hudgens. Raymond revealed David's identity to Pierce, and Pierce became terrified. Raymond was afraid to take David away from Jerry, and he's been paying Jerry extraordinary money to keep David drugged up."

Key question two. "You've been waiting for this one, Timmy. Why has Ray Dieterling gone to all this trouble for David?"

Timmy turned a picture around—Billy, a lump-faced man. "David is Raymond's illegitimate son. He's Billy's half brother, and look at him. Terry Lux has cut him so often that he's so ugly next to my sweet Billy that you almost can't look."

Moving on grief—Ed cut in before he snapped. "What happened tonight?"

"Tonight Raymond filled Billy in on everything going back to Sid Hudgens—he didn't know any of it. Billy made me stay with Inez at Laguna. He told me he was going to snatch David from Jerry's house and wean him off the drugs. He must have tried it, and Marsalas must have retaliated. I saw those pills on the floor ... and oh God David must have just gone insane. He couldn't understand who was good and who was bad and just ..."

Three. "At the hotel you reacted to Johnny Stompanato. Why?"

"Stompanato's been blackmailing Pierce's customers for years. He caught me with another man and got part of the Mertens story out of me. Not much, just that Raymond paid for David's upkeep. It ... it was before I knew very much. Stompanato's been preparing a dossier to bleed Raymond dry. He's been threatening Billy with notes, but I don't think he knows who David is. Billy was trying to convince his father to have him killed."

Sun broke through a window—it caught Timmy when his tears broke through. He held Billy's picture, a hand over David's face.

73

AN IA goon relieved him at 7:00—pissed that he was sleeping, slumped in the doorway with his gun out. The house stayed virgin—no blood-crazed David Mertens showed up. The IA guy said Mertens was still at large; Captain Exley's orders: meet him and Bud White at Mickey Cohen's place at 9:00. Jack rolled to a pay phone, played a hunch.

A call to the Bureau—Dudley Smith on "emergency family leave." Breuning and Carlisle working "out of state"—the squad lieutenant at 77th the temporary Nite Owl boss. A buzz to the Main Woman's Jail: Deputy Dot Rothstein on "emergency family leave." The hunch: they had nothing but theories, Dudley's loose ends were getting snipped.

Jack drove home, shaking off a dream: Davey Goldman's wet-brain ramblings. Make the "Dutchman" Dean Van Gelder, the "Irish Cheshire" Dudley. "Franchise boys got theirs three triggers blip blip blip"—call that the shooters—Stompanato, Vachss, Teitlebaum—taking out hoods. "Bump bump bump bump bump bump bump cute train"—??????? Crazy—maybe Patchett's dope was still working some voodoo.

Karen's car was gone. Jack walked in, saw a layout on the coffee table: airplane tickets, a note.

> J.—
>
> Hawaii, and note the date. May 15, the day you become an official pensioner. Ten days and nights to get reacquainted. Dinner tonight. I made reservations at Perino's, and if you're still working call me so I can cancel.
>
> xxxxx K.
>
> P.S. I know you're wondering, so I'll tell you. When you were at the hospital you talked in your sleep. Jack, I know the worst I can possibly know and I don't care. We never have to discuss it. Capt. Exley heard you and I don't think he cares either. (He's not as bad as you said he was.)
>
> Many X's
K.

Jack tried to cry—no go. He shaved, showered, put on slacks and his best sports jacket—over a Hawaiian shirt. He drove to Brentwood thinking everything around him looked new.

* * *

Exley on the sidewalk, holding a tape recorder. Bud White on the porch—IA must have found him. Jack made it a threesome.

White walked over. Exley said, "I just spoke to Gallaudet. He said without hard evidence we can't go to Loew. Mertens and Perkins are still out there, and Stompanato's in Mexico with Lana Turner. If Mickey doesn't give us anything good, then I'm going directly to Parker. Full disclosure on Dudley."

From the doorway: "Are you coming in or aren't you? You want to give me grief, give me indoor grief."

Mickey Cohen in a robe and Jew beanie. "Last call to give grief! Are you coming?"

They walked up. Cohen closed the door, pointed to a small gold coffin. "My late canine heir, Mickey Cohen, Jr. Distract me from my real grief, you goyisher cop fucks. The service is today at Mount Sinai. I bribed the rabbi to give my beloved a human sendoff. The shmendriks at the mortuary think they're burying a midget. Talk to me."

Exley talked. "We came to tell you who's been killing your franchise people."

"What 'franchise people'? Continue in this vein and I shall have to stand on the Fifth Amendment. And what is that tape doohickey you're holding?"

"Johnny Stompanato, Lee Vachss and Abe Teitlebaum. They're part of a gang, and they got the heroin you lost at your meeting with Jack Dragna back in '50. They've been killing your franchise people, and they tried to have you and Davey Goldman killed at McNeil. They bombed your house and didn't get you, but sooner or later they will."

Cohen laughed outright. "Granted, those old pals have been vacant from my life and are not amenable to rejoining me. But they do not have the intelligence to fuck with the Mickster and succeed."

White: "Davey Goldman was working with them. They crossed him when they tried to clip you two at McNeil."

Mickey Cohen, livid. "No! Never in six thousand millenniums would Davey do that to me! Never! Sedition in the same league as Communism you are talking!"

Jack said, "We got proof. Davey had your cell bugged. That's how word on the Englekling brothers and who knows what else got out."

"Lies! Combine Davey with the others and you still do not have the voltage to fuck with me!"

Exley futzed with the recorder—tape spun. Whirr, whirr, "My God to be so nimble and so hung, like Heifetz on the fiddle with his shlong that dog is, and hung like—"

Cohen hit the roof. "No! No! No man on earth is capable of shtupping me like that!"

Exley pushed buttons. Start—"Lana, what a snatch she must have"—stop, start—a card game, a toilet flushing. Mickey kicked the coffin. "All right! I believe you!"

Jack: "Now you know why Davey wouldn't let you put him in a rest home."

Cohen wiped his face with his beanie. "Not even Hitler is capable of such things. Who could be so brainy and so ruthless?"

White said, "Dudley Smith."

"Oh, Jesus Christ. Him I could believe. No ... tell me in full view of my late beloved you are joking."

"An LAPD captain? This is for real, Mick."

"No, this I don't believe. Give me proof, give me evidence."

Exley said, "Mickey, you give *us* some."

Cohen sat down on the coffin. "I think I know who tried to clip me and Davey in the pen. Coleman Stein, George Magdaleno and Sal Bonventre. They're en route to San Quentin, a pickup chain from other jails. When they land, you could talk to them, ask them who put out the bid on me and Davey. I was going to clip them, but I couldn't get a good rate, such gonifs these jailhouse killers are."

Exley packed up his tape kit. "Thanks. When the bus gets in, we'll be there."

Cohen moaned. White said, "Kleckner left me a memo. Kikey and Lee Vachss are supposed to be meeting at the deli this morning. I say we brace them."

Exley said, "Let's do it."

74

ABE'S NOSHERY: the tables full, Kikey T. at the cash register. White pressed up to the window. "Lee Vachss at a table on the right." Ed put a hand on his holster—empty—his suicide play. Trashcan opened the door.

Chimes. Kikey glanced over, reached under the register. Ed saw Vachss make heat, make like he was smoothing his trousers. Metal flashing waist-high.

People ate, talked. Waitresses circulated. Trash walked toward the register; White eyeballed Vachss. Metal flashed: under the table coming up.

Ed pulled White to the floor.

Kikey and Vincennes drew down.

Crossfire—six shots—the window went out, Kikey hit a stack of canned goods. Screams, panic runs, blind shots—Vachss firing wild toward the door. An old man went down coughing blood; White stood up shooting, a moving target—Vachss weaving back toward the kitchen. A spare on White's waistband—Ed stumbled up, grabbed it.

Two triggers on Vachss. Ed fired—Vachss spun around grabbing his shoulder. White fired wide; Vachss tripped, crawled, stood up—his gun to a waitress' head.

White walked toward him. Vincennes circled left; Ed circled right. Vachss blew the woman's brains out point-blank.

White fired. Vincennes fired. Ed fired. No hits—the woman's body took their shots. Vachss inched backward. White ran up; Vachss wiped brains off his face. White emptied his gun—all head shots.

Screams, a stampede to the door, a man bucking glass shards out the window. Ed ran to the counter, bolted it.

Kikey on the floor, blood gouting from chest wounds. Ed got right up in his face. "Give me Dudley. Give me Dudley for the Nite Owl."

Sirens loud. Ed cupped an ear, bent down.

"Grand. Begorra, lad."

Down closer. "Who took out the Nite Owl?"

Blood gurgles. "Me. Lee. Johnny Stomp. Deuce drove."

"*Abe, give me Dudley.*"

"Grand, lad."

Sirens brutal loud. Shouts, footsteps. "The Nite Owl. *Why?*"

Kikey coughed blood. "Dope. Picture books. Cathcart had go. Lunceford on posse what got dope and hung out Nite Owl. FI's on Stomp so Deucey stole. Man said scare Patchett. Two birds one stone Duke and Mal. Mal wanted money 'cause he knew man on posse."

"Give me Dudley. Say Dudley Smith was your partner."

Vincennes squatted down. The restaurant boomed: millions of voices. Blood on the counter—Ed thought of David Mertens. A flash—the Dieterling studio school—a mile from Billy D.'s house. "Abe, he can't hurt you now."

Kikey started choking.

"Abe—"

"Can too hurt can too."

Fading—Trash slammed his chest. "You fuck, give us something!"

Kikey mumbled, pulled a gold star off his neck. "Mitzvah. Johnny wants jail guys out. Q train. Dot got guns."

Vincennes, looking crazed. "It's a train, not a bus. It's a crash-out. Davey G. knew about it, he was rambling. Exley, the cute train, the *Q train*. Cohen said the guys from the jail bid are on it."

Ed grabbed at it, caught it. "YOU CALL."

Trash ran out. Ed stood up, breathed chaos: cops, shattered glass, an ambulance backed through the window loading bodies. Bud White shouting orders, a little girl in a blood-spattered dress eating a doughnut.

Trash came back—more crazed. "The train left L.A. ten minutes ago. Thirty-two inmates in one car, and the phone on board's out. I called Kleckner and told him to find Dot Rothstein. This was a set-up, Captain. Kleckner never left White that memo—this had to be Dudley."

Ed shut his eyes.

"Exley—"

"All right, you and White go to the train. I'll call the Sheriff's and Highway Patrol and have them set up a diversion."

White walked over, winked at Ed. He said, "Thanks for the push," stepped on Kikey T.'s face until he quit breathing.

75

A MOTORCYCLE escort met them, shot them out the Pomona Freeway. Half the stretch elevated: you could see the California Central tracks, a single train running north—a freight carrier, inmate cargo in the third car—barred windows, steel-reinforced doors. Surface streets outside Fontana—up to hills abutting the tracks—and a small standing army.

Nine prowl cars, sixteen men with gas masks and riot pumps. Sharpshooters in the hills, two machinegunners, three guys with smoke grenades. At the edge of the curve: a big buck deer on the tracks.

A deputy handed them shotguns, gas masks. "Your pal Kleckner called the command post, said that Rothstein woman was DOA at her apartment. She either hanged herself or somebody hanged her. Either way, we gotta assume she got the guns on. There's four guards and six crewmen on board that train. We stand ready with smoke and call for the password—every prison chain's got one. We hear the okay, we call a warning and wait. No okay, we go in."

A train whistle blew. Somebody yelled, "Now!"

The sharpshooters ducked down. The gas men hugged the ground. The fire team ran behind a pine row—Bud found a tree up close. Jack took a spot beside him.

The train made the curve—brakes caught, sparks on the tracks. The engine car stopped—nose up to the obstruction.

Megaphone: "Sheriff's! Identify yourself with the password!"

Silence—ten seconds' worth. Bud eyeballed the engine car window—blue denim flashed.

"Sheriff's! Identify yourself with the password!"

Silence—then a fake bird call.

The gas men hit the windows—grenades broke glass, slipped between the bars. Tommygunners charged car 3—full clips took down the door.

Smoke, screams.

Somebody yelled, "Now!"

Smoke out the door—men in khaki running through it. A sharpshooter picked one off; somebody yelled, "No, they're ours!"

Cops swarmed the car—masks on, shotguns up. Jack grabbed Bud. "They're not in that one!"

Bud ran, hit the car 4 platform. Open the door—a dead guard just inside, inmates running helter-skelter.

Bud fired, pumped, fired—three went down, one aimed a handgun. Bud pumped, fired, missed—a crate beside the man exploded. Jack jumped on the platform—the inmate squeezed a shot. Jack caught it in the face, spun, hit the tracks.

The shooter ran. Bud pumped, hit empty. He dropped his shotgun, pulled his .38—one, two, three, four, five, six shots—hits in the back, he was killing a dead man. Noise outside the car— convicts on the tracks by Trashcan's body. Deputies behind them firing close—buckshot and blood, black/red air.

A smoke bomb exploded—Bud ran into #5 gagging. Gunfire: white guys in denim shooting colored guys in denim, guards in khaki shooting both of them. He jumped the train, ran for the trees.

Bodies on the tracks.

Convicts picked off sitting duck-style.

Bud hit the pines, hit his car, gunned it over the tracks dragging the axles. Into a gully, fishtailing down, tires sliding on gravel. A tall man standing by a car. Bud saw who he was, aimed straight for him.

The man ran. Bud sideswiped the car, skidded to a stop. He got out—groggy, bloody from a crack on the dash. Deuce Perkins walked up shooting.

Bud caught one in the leg, one in the side. Two misses, a hit in the shoulder. Another miss—Perkins dropped the gun, pulled a knife. Bud saw rings on his fingers.

Deuce stabbed. Bud felt his chest rip, tried to make fists, couldn't. Deuce lowered his face, smirked—Bud kneed him in the balls and bit his nose off. Perkins shrieked; Bud bit into his arm, threw his weight down.

They tumbled. Perkins made animal noises. Bud thrashed his head, felt the arm rip out of its socket.

Deuce dropped the knife. Bud picked it up—blinded by rings that killed women. He dropped the knife, beat Perkins to death with his own two wounded hands.

76

THE PATCHETT estate in ruins—two acres of soot, debris. Shingles on the lawn, a scorched palm tree in the pool. The house itself rubble—collapsed stucco, soaked ashes. Find a booby-trapped safe inside a six-trillion-square-inch perimeter.

Ed kicked through the rubble. David Mertens hovered—he had to be *there*, it was just too right.

The floor collapsed into the foundation blocks—timber to be cleared away. Wood heaps, mounds of sodden fabric—no telltale metal glints. A ten-man/one-week job, a tech for the booby trap. Around to the yard.

A cement back porch—a slab with fried furniture. Solid cement—no cracks, no grooves, no obvious access to a safe hole. The pool house another rubble heap.

Wood three feet high—too much work if Mertens was *there*. Circuit the pool—burned chairs, a diving platform. A hand-grenade pin floating in the water.

Ed kicked the floating palm tree. Porcelain chips in the fronds; a piece of shrapnel embedded in the trunk. Down prone, squinting: capsules in the water, black squares that looked like detonator caps. The shallow end steps exploded plaster—metal grids showing, more pills. Check the lawn—extra-scorched grass running from the pool to the house.

Access to the safe. Grenade and dynamite safeguards. Flames shooting to the terminus, defusing the booby trap—just maybe.

Ed jumped in the water, tore at the plaster—pills and bubbles broke to the surface. Two-handed rips—plaster, water, bubbles, a swinging metal door. Pill eruptions, folders under plastic, plastic over cash and white powder. Loads and loads and loads—then nothing but a deep black hole. Sopping-wet runs to his car—the sun beat down—he was almost dry when he got the stash loaded. One last trip in case HE was THERE: pills scooped from the deep end.

* * *

The car heater warmed him up. He drove to the Dieterling school, bolted the fence.

Quiet—Saturday—no classes. A typical playground—basketball hoops, softball diamonds. Moochie Mouse on everything—backboards to base markers.

Ed walked to the south fence perimeter—the closest route from Billy Dieterling's house. Gristled skin on chain links—handholds up and over. Dark dots on faded asphalt—blood, an easy trail.

Across the playground, down steps to a boiler room door. Blood on the knob, a light on inside. He took out Bud White's spare, walked in.

David Mertens shivering in a corner. A hot room—the man sweating up bloody clothes. He showed his teeth, twisted his mouth into a screech. Ed threw the pills at him.

He grabbed them, gagged them down. Ed aimed at his mouth, couldn't pull the trigger. Mertens stared at him. Something strange happened with time—it left them alone. Mertens fell asleep, his lips curled over his gums. Ed looked at his face, tried for some outrage. He still couldn't kill him.

Time came back: the wrong way. Trials, sanity hearings, Preston Exley reviled for letting this monster go free. Time hard on the trigger—he still couldn't do it.

Ed picked the man up, carried him out to his car.

* * *

Pacific Sanitarium—Malibu Canyon. Ed told the gate guard to send down Dr. Lux—Captain Exley wanted to pay back his favor.

The guard pointed him to a space. Ed parked, ripped off Mertens' shirt. Brutal—the man was one huge scar.

Lux headed over. Ed pulled out two bags of powder, two stacks of thousand-dollar bills. He placed them on the hood, rolled down the rear windows.

Lux walked up, checked the back seat. "I know that work. That's Douglas Dieterling."

"Just like that?"

Lux tapped the powder. "The late Pierce Patchett's? Let's not be outraged, Captain. The last I heard you were no Cub Scout. And what is it that you wish?"

"That man taken care of on a locked ward for the rest of his life."

"I find that acceptable. Is this compassion or the desire to spare our future governor's reputation?"

"I don't know."

"Not a typical Exley answer. Enjoy the grounds, Captain. I'll have my orderlies clean up here."

Ed walked to a terrace, looked at the ocean. Sun, waves— maybe some sharks out feeding. A radio snapped on behind him. "... so for more on that thwarted prison train break. A Highway Patrol spokesman told reporters that the death toll now stands at twenty-eight inmates, seven guards and crew members. Four deputy sheriffs were injured and Sergeant John Vincennes, celebrated Los Angeles policeman and the former technical advisor to the *Badge of Honor* TV show, was shot and killed. Sergeant Vincennes' partner, LAPD Sergeant Wendell White, is in critical condition at Fontana General Hospital. White pursued and killed the crashout's pickup man, identified as Burt Arthur 'Deuce' Perkins, a nightclub entertainer with underworld connections. A team of doctors are now striving to save the valiant officer's life, although he is not expected to live. Captain George Rachlis of the California Highway Patrol calls this tragedy—"

The ocean blurred through his tears. White winked and said, "Thanks for the push." Ed turned around. The monster, the dope, the money—gone.

77

THE POOL stash: twenty-one pounds of heroin, $871,400, carbons of Sid Hudgens' dirt files. Included: blackmail photos, records of Pierce Patchett's criminal enterprises. The name "Dudley Smith" did not appear—nor did the names of John Stompanato, Burt

Arthur Perkins, Abe Teitlebaum, Lee Vachss, Dot Rothstein, Sergeant Mike Breuning, Officer Dick Carlisle. Coleman Stein, Sal Bonventre, George Magdaleno—killed in the crash-out. Davey Goldman reinterviewed at Camarillo State Hospital—he could not give a coherent statement. The Los Angeles County Coroner's Office ruled Dot Rothstein's death a suicide. David Mertens stayed in locked-ward custody at Pacific Sanitarium. Relatives of the three innocent citizens killed at Abe's Noshery brought suit against the LAPD for reckless endangerment. The crash-out received national news coverage, was labeled the "Blue Denim Massacre." Surviving inmates told Sheriff's detectives that squabbling among the armed prisoners resulted in guns changing hands—soon every inmate on the train was free. Racial tensions flared up, aborting the crash-out before the authorities arrived.

Jack Vincennes was posthumously awarded the LAPD's Medal of Valor. No LAPD men were invited to the funeral—the widow refused an audience with Captain Ed Exley.

Bud White refused to die. He remained in intensive care at Fontana General Hospital. He survived massive shock, neurological trauma, the loss of over half the blood in his body. Lynn Bracken stayed with him. He could not speak, but responded to questions with nods. Chief Parker presented him with his Medal of Valor. White freed an arm from a traction sling, threw the medal in his face.

Ten days passed.

A warehouse in San Pedro burned to the ground—remnants of pornographic books were discovered. Detectives labeled the fire "professional arson," reported no leads. The building was owned by Pierce Patchett. Chester Yorkin and Lorraine Malvasi were reinterrogated. They offered no salient information, were released from custody.

Ed Exley burned the heroin, kept the files and the money. His final Nite Owl report omitted mention of Dudley Smith and the fact that David Mertens, now the object of an all-points bulletin for his murders of Sid Hudgens, Billy Dieterling and Jerry Marsalas, was also the 1934 slayer of Wee Willie Wennerholm and five other children. Preston Exley's name was not spoken in any context.

Chief Parker held a press conference. He announced that the Nite Owl case had been solved—correctly this time. The gunmen were Burt Arthur "Deuce" Perkins, Lee Vachss, Abraham "Kikey" Teitlebaum—their motive to kill Dean Van Gelder, an ex-convict masquerading as the incorrectly identified Delbert "Duke" Cathcart. The shootings were conceived as a terror tactic, an attempt to take over the vice kingdom of Pierce Morehouse Patchett, a recent murder victim himself. The State Attorney General's Office reviewed Captain Ed Exley's 114-page case summary and announced that it was satisfied. Ed Exley again received credit for breaking the Nite Owl murder case. He was promoted to inspector in a televised ceremony.

The next day Preston Exley announced that he would seek the Republican Party's gubernatorial nomination. He shot to the front of a hastily conducted poll.

Johnny Stompanato returned from Acapulco, moved into Lana Turner's house in Beverly Hills. He remained there, never venturing outside, the object of a constant surveillance supervised by Sergeants Duane Fisk and Don Kleckner. Chief Parker and Ed Exley referred to him as their Nite Owl "Addendum"—the living perpetrator to feed the public now that they were temporarily mollified with dead killers. When Stompanato left Beverly Hills for Los Angeles City proper, he would be arrested. Parker wanted a clean front-page arrest just over the city line—he was willing to wait for it.

The Nite Owl case and the murders of Billy Dieterling and Jerry Marsalas remained news. They were never speculatively connected. Timmy Valburn refused to comment. Raymond Dieterling issued a press release expressing grief over the loss of his son. He closed down Dream-a-Dreamland for a one-month period of mourning. He remained in seclusion at his house in Laguna Beach, attended to by his friend and aide Inez Soto.

Sergeant Mike Breuning and Officer Dick Carlisle remained on emergency leave.

Captain Dudley Smith remained front stage center throughout the post-reopening round of press conferences and LAPD/DA's Office meetings. He served as toastmaster at Thad Green's surprise party honoring Inspector Ed Exley. He did not appear in any way flustered knowing that Johnny Stompanato remained at large, was under twenty-four-hour surveillance and thus immune to assassination. He did not seem to care that Stompanato would be arrested in the near future.

Preston Exley, Raymond Dieterling and Inez Soto did not contact Ed Exley to congratulate him on his promotion and reversal of bad press.

Ed knew they knew. He assumed Dudley knew. Vincennes dead, White fighting to live. Only he and Bob Gallaudet knew—and Gallaudet knew nothing pertaining to his father and the Atherton case.

Ed wanted to kill Dudley outright.

Gallaudet said, kill yourself instead, that's what you'd be doing.

They decided to wait it out, do it right.

Bud White made the wait unbearable.

He had tubes in his arms, splints on his fingers. His chest held three hundred stitches. Bullets had shattered bones, ripped arteries. He had a plate in his head. Lynn Bracken tended to him—she could not meet Ed's eyes. White could not talk—being able to talk in the future was doubtful. His eyes were eloquent: Dudley. Your father. What are you going to do about it? He kept trying to make the V-for-victory sign. Three visits, Ed finally got it: the Victory Motel, Mobster Squad HQ.

He went there. He found detailed notes on White's prostitute-killing investigation. The notes were a limited man reaching for the stars, pulling most of them down. Limits exceeded through a brilliantly persistent rage. Absolute justice—anonymous, no rank and glory. A single line on the Englekling brothers that told him their killer still walked free. Room 11 at the Victory Motel—Wendell "Bud" White seen for the first time.

Ed knew why he sent him there—and followed up.

A phone company check, one interview—all it took. Confirmation, an epigraph to build on it: Absolute Justice. The TV news said Ray Dieterling walked through Dream-a-Dreamland every day—easing his grief in a deserted fantasy kingdom. He'd give Bud White a full day of his justice.

* * *

Good Friday, 1958. The A.M. news showed Preston Exley entering St. James Episcopal Church. Ed drove to City Hall, walked up to Ellis Loew's office.

Still early—no receptionist. Loew at his desk, reading. Ed rapped on the door.

Loew glanced up. "Inspector Ed. Have a chair."

"I'll stand."

"Oh? Is this business?"

"Of sorts. Last month Bud White called you from San Francisco and told you Spade Cooley was a sex killer. You said you'd put a DA's Bureau team on it, and you didn't. Cooley has donated in excess of fifteen thousand dollars to your slush fund. You called the Biltmore Hotel from your place in Newport and talked to a member of Cooley's band. You told him to warn Spade and the rest of the guys that a crazy cop was going to come around and cause trouble. White braced Deuce Perkins, the real killer. Perkins sent him after Spade, he probably thought he'd kill him and save him from the rap. Perkins was warned by you and went into hiding. He stayed out long enough to turn White into a vegetable."

Loew, calm. "You can't prove any of that. And since when are you so concerned about White?"

Ed laid a folder on his desk. "Sid Hudgens had a file on you. Contribution shakedowns, felony indictments you dismissed for money. He's got the McPherson tank job documented, and Pierce Patchett had a photograph of you sucking a male prostitute's dick. Resign from office or it all goes public."

Loew—sheet white. "I'll take you with me."

"Do it. I'd enjoy the ride."

* * *

He saw it from the freeway: Rocketland and Paul's World juxtaposed—a spaceship growing out of a mountain, a big empty parking lot. He took surface streets to the gate, showed the guard his shield. The man nodded, swung the fence open.

Two figures strolled the Grand Promenade. Ed parked, walked up to them. Dream-a-Dreamland stood hear-a-pin-drop silent.

Inez saw him—a pivot, a hand on Dieterling's arm. They whispered; Inez walked off.

Dieterling turned. "Inspector."

"Mr. Dieterling."

"It's Ray. And I'm tempted to say what took you so long."

"You knew I'd be coming?"

"Yes. Your father disagreed and went on with his plans, but I knew better. And I'm grateful for the chance to tell it here."

Paul's World across from them—fake snow near blinding. Dieterling said, "Your father, Pierce and I were dreamers. Pierce's dreams were twisted, mine were kind and good. Your father's dreams were ruthless—as I suspect yours are. You should know that before you judge me."

Ed leaned against a rail, settled in. Dieterling spoke to his mountain.

* * *

1920.

His first wife, Margaret, died in an automobile accident—she bore his son Paul. 1924—his second wife, Janice, gave birth to son Billy. While married to Margaret, he had an affair with a disturbed woman named Faye Borchard. She gave him son Douglas in 1917. He gave her money to keep the boy's existence secret—he was a rising young filmmaker, wished a life free of complications, was willing to pay for it. Only he and Faye knew the facts of Douglas' parentage. Douglas knew Ray Dieterling as a kindly friend.

Douglas grew up with his mother; Dieterling visited frequently, a two-family life: wife Margaret dead, sons Paul and Billy ensconced with himself and wife Janice—a sad woman who went on to divorce him.

Faye Borchard drank laudanum. She made Douglas watch pornographic cartoons that Raymond made for money, part of a Pierce Patchett scheme—cash to finance their legitimate dealings. The films were erotic, horrific—they featured flying monsters that raped and killed. The concept was Patchett's—he put his narcotic fantasies on paper, handed Ray Dieterling an inkwell. Douglas became obsessed with flight and its sexual possibilities.

Dieterling loved his son Douglas—despite his rages and fits of strange behavior. He despised his son Paul—who was petty, tyrannical, stupid. Douglas and Paul greatly resembled each other.

Ray Dieterling grew famous; Douglas Borchard grew wild. He lived with Faye, watched his father's cartoon nightmares—birds plucking children out of schoolyards—Patchett fantasies painted on film. He grew into his teens stealing, torturing animals, hiding out in skid row strip shows. He met Loren Atherton on the row—that evil man found an accomplice.

Atherton's obsession was dismemberment; Douglas' obsession was flight. They shared an interest in photography, were sexually aroused by children. They spawned the idea of creating children to their own specifications.

They began killing and building hybrid children, photographing their works in progress. Douglas killed birds to provide wings for their creations. They needed a beautiful face; Douglas suggested Wee Willie Wennerholm's—it would be a kindly nod to kindly

"Uncle Ray"—whose early work he found so exciting. They snatched Wee Willie, butchered him.

The newspapers called the child killer "Dr. Frankenstein"—it was assumed there was only one assailant. Inspector Preston Exley commanded the police investigation. He learned of Loren Atherton, a paroled child molester. He arrested Atherton, discovered his storage garage abattoir, his collection of photographs. Atherton confessed to the crimes, said that they were his work solely, did not implicate Douglas and stated his desire to die as the King of Death. The press lauded Inspector Exley, echoed his appeal: citizens with information on Atherton were asked to come forth as witnesses.

Ray Dieterling visited Douglas. Alone in his room, he discovered a trunk full of slaughtered birds, a child's fingers packed in dry ice. He *knew* immediately.

And felt responsible—his quick-buck obscenities had created a monster. He confronted Douglas, learned that he might have been seen at the school near the time Wee Willie was kidnapped.

Protective measures:

A psychiatrist bribed to silence diagnosed Douglas: a psychotic personality, his disorder compounded by chemical brain imbalances. Remedy: the proper drugs applied for life to keep him docile. Ray Dieterling was friends with Pierce Patchett—a chemist who dabbled in such drugs. Pierce for inner protection—Pierce's friend Terry Lux for the outer.

Lux cut Douglas a whole new face. Atherton's lawyer stalled the trial. Preston Exley kept looking for witnesses—a well-publicized search. Ray Dieterling treaded panic—then formed a bold plan.

He fed drugs to Douglas and young Miller Stanton. He coached them to say they saw Loren Atherton, *alone*, kidnap Wee Willie Wennerholm—they were afraid to come forth until now—afraid Dr. Frankenstein would get them. The boys told Preston Exley their story; he believed them; they identified the monster. Atherton did not recognize his surgically altered friend.

Two years passed. Loren Atherton was tried, convicted, executed. Terry Lux cut Douglas again—destroying his resemblance to the witness boy. Douglas lived in Pierce Patchett sedation, a room at a private hospital—guarded by male nurses. Ray Dieterling became even more successful. Then Preston Exley knocked on his door.

His news: a young girl, older now, had come forth. She had seen Dieterling's son Paul with Loren Atherton—at the school the day Wee Willie was kidnapped.

Dieterling knew it was really Douglas—his resemblance to Paul was that strong. He offered Exley a large amount of money to desist. Exley took the money—then attempted to return it. He said, "Justice. I want to arrest the boy."

Dieterling saw his empire ruined. He saw the petty and mindless Paul exonerated. He saw Douglas somehow captured—destroyed for the grief his art had spawned. He insisted that Exley keep the money—Exley did not protest. He asked him if there was no other way.

Exley asked him if Paul was guilty.

Raymond Dieterling said, "Yes."

Preston Exley said, "Execution."

Raymond Dieterling agreed.

He took Paul camping in the Sierra Nevada. Preston Exley was waiting. They dosed the boy's food; Exley shot him in his sleep and buried him. The world thought Paul was lost in an avalanche—the world believed the lie. Dieterling thought he would hate the man. The price of justice on his face told him he was just another victim. They shared a bond now. Preston Exley gave up police work to build buildings with Dieterling seed money. When Thomas Exley was killed, Ray Dieterling was the first one he called. Together they built from the weight of their dead.

* * *

Dieterling ended it. "And all of this is my rather pathetic happy ending."

Mountains, rockets, rivers—they all seemed to smile. "My father never knew about Douglas? He really thought Paul was guilty?"

"Yes. Will you forgive me? In your father's name."

Ed took out a clasp. Gold oak-leafs—Preston Exley's inspector's insignia. A hand-me-down—Thomas got it first. "No. I'm going to submit a report to the county grand jury requesting that you be indicted for the murder of your son."

"A week to get my affairs in order? Where could I run to, someone as famous as I am."

Ed said, "Yes," walked to his car.

* * *

The freeway model gone—replaced by campaign posters. Art De Spain unpacking leaflets, no arm bandage—a textbook bullet scar. "Hello, Eddie."

"Where's Father?"

"He'll be back soon. And congratulations on inspector. I should have called you, but things have been hectic around here."

"Father hasn't called me either. You're all pretending everything's fine."

"Eddie ..."

A bulge on Art's left hip—he still carried a piece. "I just spoke to Ray Dieterling."

"We didn't think you would."

"Give me your gun, Art."

De Spain handed it over butt first. Silencer threads, S&W .38s. "Why?"

"Eddie ..."

Ed dumped the shells. "Dieterling told me everything. And you were Father's exec back then."

The man looked proud. "You know my MO, Sunny Jim. It was for Preston. I've always been his loyal adjutant."

"And you knew about Paul Dieterling."

De Spain took his gun back. "Yes, and I've known for years that he wasn't the real killer. I got a tip back in '48 or so. It placed the kid somewhere else at the time of the Wennerholm snatch. I didn't know if Ray gave Paul over legitimately or not, and I couldn't break Preston's heart by telling him he killed an innocent boy. I couldn't upset his friendship with Ray—it just would have hurt him too much. You know how the Atherton case has always driven me. I've always had to know who killed those kids."

"And you never found out."

De Spain shook his head. "No."

Ed said, "Get to the Englekling brothers."

Art picked up a poster: Preston backdropped by building grids. "I was visiting the Bureau. I know it was '53, right in there. I saw these pictures on the Ad Vice board. Nice-looking kids, like a stag-shot daisy chain. The design reminded me of the pictures Loren Atherton took, and I knew that just Preston and I and a few other officers had seen them. I tried to track down the pictures and didn't get anywhere. A while later I heard how the Englekling brothers gave that smut testimony for the Nite Owl investigation, but you didn't follow up on it. I figured they were a lead, but

I couldn't find them. Late last year I got a tip that they were working at this printshop up near Frisco. I went up to talk to them. All I wanted was to find out who made that smut."

White's notes: God-awful torture. "Just to talk to them? I *know* what happened there."

Awful pride glaring. "They took it for a shakedown. It went bad. They had some old smut negatives, and I tried to get them to ID the people. They had some heroin and some antipsychotic drugs. They said they knew a sugar daddy who was going to push some horse blend that would set the world on fire, but they could do better. They laughed at me, called me 'pops.' I got this notion that they had to know who made that smut. I don't know ... I know I went crazy. I think I thought they killed all those children. I think I thought they'd hurt Preston somehow. Eddie, they *laughed* at me. I figured they were dope pushers, I figured next to Preston they were nothing. And this old man took them both out."

He'd fretted the poster to shreds. "You killed two men for nothing."

"Not for nothing. For Preston. And I beg you not to tell him."

"Just another victim"—maybe the victim that justice lets slide.

"Eddie, he can't know. And he can't know that Paul Dieterling was innocent. Eddie, please."

Ed pushed him aside, walked through the house. His mother's tapestries made him think of Lynn. His old room made him think of Bud and Jack. The house felt filthy—bad money bought and paid for. He walked downstairs, saw his father in the doorway.

"Edmund?"

"I'm arresting you for the murder of Paul Dieterling. I'll be by in a few days to take you in."

The man did not budge an inch. "Paul Dieterling was a psychopathic killer who richly deserved the punishment I gave him."

"He was innocent. And it's Murder One either way."

Not one flicker of remorse. Unbudging, unyielding, unflinching, intractable rectitude. "Edmund, you're quite disturbed at this moment."

Ed walked past him. His goodbye: "Goddamn you for the bad things you made me."

* * *

Downtown to the Dining Car: a bright place full of nice people. Gallaudet at the bar, sipping a martini. "Bad news on Dudley. You don't want to hear this."

"It can't be any worse than some other things I've heard today."

"Yeah? Well, Dudley's scot-free. Lana Turner's daughter just knifed Johnny Stompanato. DO fucking A. Fisk was staked out across the street and saw the meat wagon and the Beverly Hills PD take Johnny away. No Dudley witness, no Dudley evidence. Grand, lad."

Ed grabbed the martini, killed it. "Fuck Dudley sideways. I've got a shitload of Patchett's money for a bankroll, and I'll burn down that Irish cocksucker if it's the last fucking thing I ever do. *Lad*."

Gallaudet laughed. "May I make an observation, Inspector?"

"Sure."

"You sound more like Bud White every day."

CALENDAR

APRIL 1958

EXTRACT: L.A. *Times*, April 12:

GRAND JURY REVIEWS NITE OWL
EVIDENCE; DECLARES CASE CLOSED

ALMOST FIVE years to the day after the crime, the City and County of Los Angeles bid official farewell to the Southland's "Crime of the Century," the infamous Nite Owl murder case.

On April 16, 1953, three gunmen entered the Nite Owl Coffee Shop on Hollywood Boulevard and shotgunned three employees and three patrons to death. Robbery was the assumed motive, and suspicion soon fell on three Negro youths, who were arrested on suspicion of the crime. The three: Raymond Coates, Tyrone Jones and Leroy Fontaine, escaped from jail and were killed resisting arrest. The three allegedly confessed to District Attorney Ellis Loew prior to their escape, and the case was assumed to have been solved.

Four years and ten months later, a San Quentin inmate, Otis John Shortell, came forward with information that led many to believe that the three youths were innocent of the Nite Owl killings. Shortell said that he was in the presence of Coates, Jones and Fontaine while they were engaged in the gang rape of a young woman, at the exact time of the coffee shop slaughter. Shortell's testimony, verified by lie detector tests, created a public clamor to reopen the case.

The clamor was fanned by the February 25 murders of Peter and Baxter Englekling. The brothers, convicted narcotics traffickers, were material witnesses to the 1953 Nite Owl investigation and asserted at that time that the killings originated from a web of intrigue involving pornography. The Englekling killings remain unsolved. In the words of Marin County Sheriff's Lieutenant Eugene Hatcher, "No leads at all. But we're still trying."

The Nite Owl case was reopened, and an involved pornography link was revealed. On March 27, wealthy investor Pierce Morehouse Patchett was shot and killed at his Brentwood home, and two days later police shot and killed Abraham Teitlebaum, 49, and Lee Peter Vachss, 44, his assumed slayers. Later that day the infamous "Blue Denim Massacre" occurred. Among the criminal dead: Burt Arthur "Deuce" Perkins, a nightclub singer with underworld ties. Teitlebaum, Vachss and Perkins were assumed to be the Nite Owl killers. LAPD Captain Dudley Smith elaborated.

"The Nite Owl killings derived from a grandly realized scheme to distribute heinous and soul-destroying pornographic filth. Teitlebaum, Vachss and Perkins were attempting to kill Nite Owl patron Delbert 'Duke' Cathcart, an independent smut merchant, and take over Pierce Patchett's smut racket in the process. Alas, it was really one Dean Van Gelder, a criminal impersonating Cathcart, who was there in Cathcart's place. The Nite Owl murder case will go down as a testimony to the cruel caprices of fate, and I am glad that it has finally been resolved."

Then Captain, now Inspector Edmund Exley, credited with solving the Nite Owl reopening case, said that it has finally been resolved, despite rumors that a fourth conspirator died abruptly, just as he was about to be arrested. "That's nonsense," Exley said. "I gave the county grand jury a detailed brief on the case and testified extensively myself. They accepted my findings. It's over."

At some great cost. LAPD Chief of Detectives Thad Green, soon to retire and assume command of the U.S. Border Patrol, said, "For sheer expense and the number of accumulated investigatory man-hours, the Nite Owl case has no equal. It was a once-in-a-lifetime case and the price for clearing it was very, very high."

EXTRACT: L.A. *Mirror-News*, April 15:

LOEW RESIGNATION A SHOCKER; LEGAL CROWD BUZZES

SPECULATION IN Southland legal circles rages: why did Los Angeles District Attorney Ellis Loew resign from office yesterday and scotch a brilliant political career? Loew, 49, announced his resignation at his regular weekly press conference, citing nervous exhaustion and a desire to return to private practice. Aides close to the man described the abrupt retirement as stupefyingly atypical. The DA's Office is stunned: Ellis Loew appeared happy, fit and in perfect health.

Chief Criminal Prosecutor Robert Gallaudet told this reporter: "Look, I'm stunned, and I don't stun easily. What's Ellis' underlying motive? I don't know, ask him. And when the City Council appoints an interim DA, I hope it's me."

After the shock waves subsided, plaudits rolled in. LAPD Chief William H. Parker described Loew as a "vigorous and fair-minded foe of criminals," and Parker's aide, Captain Dudley Smith, said, "We'll miss Ellis. He was a grand friend of justice." Governor Knight and Mayor Norris Poulson sent Loew telegrams asking him to reconsider his decision. Loew himself could not be reached for comment.

EXTRACT: L.A. *Herald-Express*, April 19:

DREAM-A-DREAMLAND SUICIDES: GRIEF, BEWILDERMENT CONTINUE

THEY WERE found together at Dream-a-Dreamland, temporarily closed to mourn the death of a great man's son. Preston Exley, 64, former Los Angeles policeman, master builder and neophyte politician; Inez Soto, 28, publicity director at the world's most celebrated amusement complex and a key witness in the awful Nite Owl murder case. And Raymond Dieterling, 66, the father of modern animation, the genius who virtually created the cartoon art form, the man who built Dream-a-Dreamland as a tribute to a child tragically lost. The world at large and Los Angeles in particular have expressed great grief and bewilderment.

They were found last week, together, on Dream-a-Dreamland's Grand Promenade. There were no notes, but County Coroner Frederic Newbarr quickly ruled out foul play and established the deaths as suicides. The means: all three had ingested fatal quantities of a rare antipsychotic drug. Expressions of grief greeted the news—President Eisenhower, Governor Knight and Senator William Knowland were among those who offered condolences to the loved ones of the three. Exley and Dieterling left fortunes: the building magnate willed his construction kingdom to his longtime aide Arthur De Spain and his $17-million financial estate to his son Edmund, a Los Angeles police officer. Dieterling left his more than vast holdings to a legal trust, with instructions to disperse the funds and future Dream-a-Dreamland profits among various children's charities. With the legalities taken care of and public shock and bereavement hardly abating, speculation into the motives for the suicides began to rage.

Miss Soto was romantically linked to Preston Exley's son Edmund and had been despondent over recent publicity pertaining to her involvement in the Nite Owl case. Raymond Dieterling was distraught over the recent murder of his son William. Preston Exley, however, had recently celebrated his greatest triumph, the completion of the Southern California mass freeway system, and had just announced his candidacy in the governor's race. A poll conducted shortly before his death showed him gaining and favored to win the Republican nomination. There seems to be no logical motive for the man to take his own life. Those closest to Preston Exley—Arthur De Spain and son Edmund—have refused comment.

Letters of sympathy and floral tributes flood Dream-a-Dreamland and Preston Exley's Hancock Park home. Flags fly at half mast throughout the State of California. Hollywood grieves the loss of a moviemaking colossus. The single word "Why?" rests on millions of lips.

Preston Exley and Ray Dieterling were giants. Inez Soto was a spunky hard-luck girl who became their trusted aide and close friend. Before their deaths, all three added codicils to their wills, stating that they wished to be buried at sea together. Yesterday they were, summarily, with no religious service and no guests in attendance. The Dream-a-Dreamland security chief handled the arrangements and would not disclose the location where the bodies were laid to rest. The word "Why?" still rests on millions of lips.

Mayor Norris Poulson doesn't know why. But he does offer a fitting eulogy. "Very simply, these two men symbolized the fulfillment of a vision—Los Angeles as a place of enchantment and high-quality everyday life. More than anyone else, Raymond Dieterling and Preston Exley personified the grand and good dreams that have built this city."

PART FIVE

AFTER YOU'VE GONE

78

ED IN his dress blue uniform.

Parker smiled, pinned gold stars to his shoulders. "Deputy Chief Edmund Exley. Chief of Detectives, Los Angeles Police Department."

Applause, flashbulbs. Ed shook Parker's hand, checked the crowd. Politicos, Thad Green, Dudley Smith. Lynn at the back of the room.

More applause, a handshake line. Mayor Poulson, Gallaudet, Dudley.

"Lad, you have performed so grandly. I look forward to serving under you."

"Thank you, Captain. I'm sure we'll have a grand time together." Dudley winked.

The City Council filed by; Parker led the crowd to refreshments. Lynn stayed in the doorway.

Ed walked over. Lynn said, "I can't believe it. I'm giving up a hotshot with seventeen million dollars for a cripple with a pension. Arizona, love. The air's good for pensioners and I know where everything is."

She'd aged the past month—beautiful to handsome. "When?"

"Right now, before I back down."

"Open your purse."

"What?"

"Just do it."

Lynn opened her purse—Ed dropped in a plastic bundle. "Spend it fast, it's bad money."

"How much?"

"Enough to buy Arizona. Where's White?"

"At the car."

"I'll walk you."

They skirted the party, took side stairs down. Lynn's Packard in the watch commander's space, a summons stuck to the windshield. Ed tore it up, checked the back seat.

Bud White. Braces on his legs, his head shaved and sutured. No splints on his hands—they looked strong. A wired-up mouth that made him look goofy.

Lynn stood a few feet away. White tried to smile, grimaced. Ed said, "I swear to you I'll get Dudley. I swear to you I'll do it."

White grabbed his hands, squeezed until they both winced. Ed said, "Thanks for the push."

A smile, a laugh—Bud forced them through wires. Ed touched his face. "You were my redemption."

Party noise upstairs—Dudley Smith laughing. Lynn said, "We should go now."

"Was I ever in the running?"

"Some men get the world, some men get ex-hookers and a trip to Arizona. You're in with the former, but my God I don't envy you the blood on your conscience."

Ed kissed her cheek. Lynn got in the car, rolled up the windows. Bud pressed his hands to the glass.

Ed touched his side, palms half the man's size. The car moved—Ed ran with it, hands against hands. A turn into traffic, a goodbye toot on the horn.

Gold stars. Alone with his dead.

WHITE JAZZ

To Helen Knode

In the end I possess my birthplace and am possessed by its language.

—Ross MacDonald

All I have is the will to remember. Time revoked/fever dreams—I wake up reaching, afraid I'll forget. Pictures keep the woman young.

L.A., fall 1958.

Newsprint: link the dots. Names, events—so brutal they beg to be connected. Years down—the story stays dispersed. The names are dead or too guilty to tell.

I'm old, afraid I'll forget:

I killed innocent men.

I betrayed sacred oaths.

I reaped profit from horror.

Fever—that time burning. I want to go with the music—spin, fall with it.

L.A. *Herald-Express*, 10/17/58:

BOXING PROBE IN PROGRESS;
FEDERAL GRAND JURY TO HEAR WITNESSES

YESTERDAY, A spokesman for the U.S. Attorney's Office in Los Angeles announced that Federal agents are probing the "gangland infiltrated" Southland prize fight scene, with an eye toward securing grand jury indictments.

U.S. Attorney Welles Noonan, former counsel to the McClellan Rackets Committee, said that Justice Department investigators, acting on information supplied by unnamed informants, are soon to question colorful Los Angeles "mob fringe character" Mickey Cohen. Cohen, now thirteen months out of prison, is rumored to have attempted contract infringement on a number of local prizefighters. Currently being questioned under hotel guard are Reuben Ruiz, bantamweight contender and regular attraction at the Olympic Auditorium, and Sanderline Johnson, former ranked flyweight working as a croupier at a Gardena poker establishment. A Justice Department press release stated that Ruiz and Johnson are "friendly witnesses." In a personal aside to *Herald* reporter John Eisler, U.S. Attorney Noonan said: "This investigation is now in its infancy, but we have every hope that it will prove successful. The boxing racket is just that: a racket. Its cancerous tentacles link with other branches of organized crime, and should Federal grand jury indictments result from this probe, then perhaps a general probe of Southern California mob activity will prove to be in order. Witness Johnson has assured my investigators that boxing malfeasance is not the only incriminating information he has been privy to, so perhaps we might start there. For now, though, boxing is our sole focus."

POLITICAL STEPPINGSTONES HINTED

SOME SKEPTICISM greeted news of the prize fight probe. "I'll believe it when the grand jury hands down true bills," said William F. Degnan, a former FBI agent now retired in Santa Monica. "Two witnesses do not make a successful investigation. And I'm wary of anything announced in the press: it smacks of publicity seeking."

Mr. Degnan's sentiments were echoed by a source within the Los Angeles District Attorney's Office. Queried on the probe, a prosecuting attorney who wishes to remain anonymous stated: "It's politics pure and simple. Noonan's friends with [Massachusetts Senator and presidential hopeful] John Kennedy, and I've heard he's going to run for California Attorney General himself in '60. This probe has to be fuel for that run, because Bob Gallaudet [interim Los Angeles District Attorney expected to be elected to a full term as DA ten days hence] might well be the Republican nominee. You see, what a *Federal* probe implicitly states is that *local* police and prosecutors can't control crime within their own bailiwick. I call Noonan's grand jury business a political steppingstone."

U.S. Attorney Noonan, 40, declined comment on the above speculation, but a surprise ally defended him with some vigor. Morton Diskant, civil liberties lawyer and Democratic candidate for Fifth District City Councilman, told this writer: "I distrust the Los Angeles Police Department's ability to maintain order without infringing on the civil rights of Los Angeles citizens. I distrust the Los Angeles District Attorney's Office for the same reason. I especially distrust Robert Gallaudet, most specifically for his support of [Fifth District Republican Councilman] Thomas Bethune, my incumbent opponent. Gallaudet's stand on the Chavez Ravine issue is unconscionable. He wants to evict impoverished Latin Americans from their homes to procure space for an L.A. Dodgers ballpark, a frivolity I deem criminal. Welles Noonan, on the other hand, has proven himself to be both a determined crimefighter and a friend of civil rights. Boxing is a dirty business that renders human beings walking vegetables. I applaud Mr. Noonan for taking the high ground in combatting it."

WITNESSES UNDER GUARD

U.S. ATTORNEY Noonan responded to Mr. Diskant's statement. "I appreciate his support, but I do not want partisan political comments to cloud the issue. That issue is boxing and the best way to sever its links to organized crime. The U.S. Attorney's Office does not seek to supersede the authority of the LAPD or to in any way ridicule or undermine it."

Meanwhile, the boxing probe continues. Witnesses Ruiz and Johnson are in protective custody at a downtown hotel, guarded by Federal agents and officers on loan from the Los Angeles Police Department: Lieutenant David Klein and Sergeant George Stemmons, Jr.

"Hollywood Cavalcade" Feature, *Hush-Hush* Magazine, 10/28/58:

MISANTHROPIC MICKEY SLIPS, SLIDES, AND NOSEDIVES SINCE PAROLE

DIG IT, hepcats: Meyer Harris Cohen, the marvelous, benevolent, malevolent Mickster, has been out of Federal custody since September, '57. He did 3 to 5 for income tax evasion; his ragtag band dispersed, and the former mob kingpin's life since then has been one long series of skidmarks across the City of the Fallen Angels, the town he used to rule with bullets, bribes and bullspit bonhomie. Dig, children, and smell the burning rubber of those skids: off the record, on the QT and *very Hush-Hush*.

April, '58: former Cohen henchman Johnny Stompanato is shanked by Lana Turner's daughter, a slinky 14 year old who should have been trying on prom gowns instead of skulking outside Mommy's bedroom with a knife in her hand. Too bad, Mickster: Johnny was your chief strongarm circa '49–'51, maybe *he* could have helped curtail your post prison tailspin. And tsk, tsk: you *really shouldn't* have sold Lana's sin-sational love letters to Johnny—we heard you raided the "Stomp Man's" Benedict Canyon love shack while Johnny was still in the meat wagon on his way to Slab City.

More sin-tillating scoop on the Mickster:

Under the watchful eye of his parole officer, Mickey has since made attempts to straighten up and skid right. He bought an ice cream parlor that soon became a criminal haven and went bust when parents kept their children away in droves; he financed his own niteclub act, somnambulistic shtick at the Club Largo. Snore City: bum bits on Ike's golf game, gags about Lana T. and Johnny S., the emphasis on "Oscar," the Stomp Man's Academy Award size appendage. And—Desperation City—the Mickster salaamed for Jesus during Billy Graham's Crusade at the L.A. Coliseum!!!! The chutzpah of Mickey renouncing his Jewish heritage as a

PR ploy!!!! For shame, Mickster, for shame!!!!! And now the scenario darkens.

Item:

Federal agents are soon to scold Mickey for infringing on the contracts of local prizefight palookas.

Item:

Four of Mickey's goons—Carmine Ramandelli, Nathan Palevsky, Morris Jahelka and Antoine "The Fish" Guerif—have mysteriously disappeared, presumably snuffed by person or persons unknown, and (very strangely, hepcats) Mickey is keeping his (usually on overdrive) yap shut about it.

Rumors are climbing the underworld grapevine: two surviving Cohen gunmen (ChickVecchio and his brother Salvatore "Touch" Vecchio, a failed actor rumored to be *très* lavender) are planning nefarious activities outside of Mickey's aegis. Get in on the ground floor, Mickster—we've heard that your sole source of income is Southside vending and slot machines: cigarettes, rubbers, french ticklers and one-armed bandits stuffed into smoky back rooms in Darktown jazz clubs. For shame again, Mickey! Shvartze exploitation! Penny ante and beneath you, you the man who once ruled the L.A. rackets with a paralyzingly pugnacious panache!

Get the picture, kats and kittens? Mickey Cohen is Skidsville, U.S.A., and he needs moolah, gelt, the old cashola. Which explains our most riotous rumor revelation, raffishly revealed for the frenetically foremost first time!

Digsville:

Meyer Harris Cohen is now in the movie biz!!

Move over C. B. DeMille: the fabulous, benevolent, malevolent Mickster is now sub-rosa financing a horror cheapie currently shooting in Griffith Park! He's saved his negro exploited nickels and is now partners with Variety International Pictures in the making of *Attack of the Atomic Vampire*. It's sensational, it's non-union, it's a turkey of epic proportions!

Further Digsville:

Ever anxious to parsimoniously pinch pennies, Mickey has cast lavender loverboy Touch Vecchio in a key role—and the Touchster is hot, hot, hotsville with the star of the movie: limp-wristed lothario Rock Rockwell. Off-camera homo hijinx! You heard it first here!

Final Digsville:

Enter Howard Hughes: Mr. Airplane/Tool Magnate, lascivious luster after Hollywood lovelies. He used to own RKO Studios; now he's an independent producer known for keeping wildly well-endowed wenches welded to "personal service contracts"— read as bit roles in exchange for frequent nighttime visits. Dig: we've heard that Mickey's leading lady left the mammary-mauling mogul spinning his own propeller—she actually amscrayed on a Hughes contract and car hopped until Mickey materialized at Scrivner's Drive-In dying for a chocolate malt.

Are you smitten, Mickster?

Are you heartbroken, Howard?

Hollywood Cavalcade shifts gears with an open letter to the Los Angeles Police Department.

Dear LAPD:

Recently, three wino bums were found strangled and mutilated in abandoned houses in the Hollywood area. *Very Hush-Hush*: we've heard the still-at-large killer snapped their windpipes post-mortem, utilizing great strength. The press has paid these heinously horrific killings scant attention; only the sin-sation slanted L.A. *Mirror* seems to care that three Los Angeles citizens have met such nau-seatingly nasty nadirs. The LAPD's Homicide Division has not been called in to investigate; so far only two Hollywood Division detectives are working the case. Hepcats, it's the pedigree of the victims that determine the juice of investigation—and if three squarejohn citizens got choked by a neck-snapping psychopath, then LAPD Chief of Detectives Edmund J. Exley would waste no time mounting a full scale investigation. Often it takes a catchy tag name to bring dirty criminal business into the public's conscious-ness and thus create a clamor for justice. *Hush-Hush* hereby names this anonymous killer fiend the "Wino Will-o-the-Wisp" and petitions the LAPD to find him and set him up with a hot date in San Quentin's green room. They cook with gas there, and this killer deserves a four-burner cookout.

Watch for future updates on the Wino Will-o-the-Wisp, and remember you heard it first here: off the record, on the QT and *very Hush-Hush*.

PART ONE

STRAIGHT LIFE

1

THE JOB: take down a bookie mill, let the press in—get some ink to compete with the fight probe.

Some fruit sweating a sodomy beef snitched: fourteen phones, a race wire. Exley's memo said show some force, squeeze the witnesses at the hotel later—find out what the Feds had planned.

In person: "If things get untoward, don't let the reporters take pictures. You're an attorney, Lieutenant. Remember how clean Bob Gallaudet likes his cases."

I hate Exley.

Exley thinks I bought law school with bribe money.

I said four men, shotguns, Junior Stemmons as co-boss. Exley: "Jackets and ties; this will end up on TV. And no stray bullets— you're working for me, not Mickey Cohen."

Someday I'll shove a bribe list down his throat.

Junior set it up. Perfect: a Niggertown street cordoned off; bluesuits guarding the alley. Reporters, prowl cars, four jackets and ties packing twelve-gauge pumps.

Sergeant George Stemmons, Jr., snapping quick draws.

Hubbub: porch-loafing jigs, voodoo eyes. My eyes on the target—closed curtains, a packed driveway—make a full shift inside working bets. A cinderblock shack—figure a steel plate door.

I whistled; Junior walked over twirling his piece.

"Keep it out, you might need it."

"No, I've got a riot gun in the car. We go in the door, we—"

"We *don't* go in the door, it's plated. We start banging on the door, they burn their paper. You still hunt birds?"

"Sure. Dave, what—"

"You got ammo in your car? Single-aught birdshot?"

Junior smiled. "That big window. I shoot it out, the curtain takes the pellets, we go in."

"Right, so you tell the others. And tell those clowns with the cameras to roll it, Chief Exley's compliments."

Junior ran back, dumped shells, reloaded. Cameras ready; whistles, applause: wine-guzzling loafers.

Hands up, count it down—

Eight: Junior spreads the word.

Six: the men flanked.

Three: Junior window-aiming.

One: "Now!"

Glass exploded *ka*-BOOM, loud loud loud; recoil knocked Junior flat. Cops too shocked to yell "TRIPLE AUGHT!"

Window curtains in rags.

Screams.

Run up, jump the sill. Chaos: blood spray, bet slip/cash confetti. Phone tables dumped, a stampede: out the back door bookie fistfights.

A nigger coughing glass.

A pachuco minus some fingers.

"Wrong Load" Stemmons: "Police! Stop or we'll shoot!"

Grab him, shout: "This was shots fired inside, a fucking criminal altercation. We went in the window because we figured the door wouldn't go down. You talk nice to the news guys and tell them I owe them one. You get the men together and make fucking-A sure they know the drill. *Do you understand me?*"

Junior shook free. Foot thumps—window-storming plainclothesmen. Cover noise: I pulled my spare piece. Two ceiling shots, a wipe—evidence.

Toss the gun. More chaos: suspects kicked prone, cuffed.

Moans, shouts, shotgun wadding/blood stink.

I "discovered" the gun. Reporters ran in; Junior spieled them. Out to the porch, fresh air.

"You owe me eleven hundred, Counselor."

Make the voice: Jack Woods. Mixed bag—bookie/strongarm/contract trigger.

I walked over. "Did you catch the show?"

"I was just driving up—and you should put that kid Stemmons on a leash."

"His daddy's an inspector. I'm the kid's mentor, so I've got a captain's job as a lieutenant. Did you have a bet down?"

"That's right."

"Slumming?"

"I'm in the business myself, so I spread my own bets around for good will. Dave, you owe me eleven hundred."

"How do you know you won?"

"The race was fixed."

Jabber—newsmen, the locals. "I'll get it out of the evidence vault."

"C'est la guerre. And by the way, how's your sister?"

"Meg's fine."

"Say hi for me."

Sirens; black-and-whites pulling up.

"Jack, get out of here."

"Good seeing you, Dave."

Book the fuckers—Newton Street Station.

Rap sheet checks: nine outstanding warrants total. Missing Fingers came up a sweetheart: rape, ADW, flimflam. Shock pale, maybe dying—a medic fed him coffee and aspirin.

I booked the plant gun, bet slips and money—minus Jack Woods' eleven hundred. Junior, press relations: the lieutenant owes you a story.

Two hours of pure shitwork.

4:30—back to the Bureau. Messages waiting: Meg said drop by; Welles Noonan said the guard gig, six sharp. Exley: "Report in detail."

Details—type them out, more shitwork:

4701 Naomi Avenue, 1400 hours. Set to raid a bookmaker's drop, Sgt. George Stemmons, Jr., and I heard shots fired inside the premises. We did not inform the other officers for fear of creating a panic. I ordered a shotgun round directed at the front window; Sgt. Stemmons misled the other men with a "birdshot assault" cover story. A .38 revolver was found; we arrested six bookmakers. The suspects were booked at Newton Station; the wounded received adequate first aid and hospital treatment. R&I revealed numerous extant warrants on the six, who will be remanded to the Hall of Justice Jail and arraigned on felony charges 614.5 and 859.3 of the California Penal Code. All six men will be subsequently interrogated on the shots fired and their bookmaking associations. I will conduct the interrogations myself—as Division Commander I must personally guarantee the veracity of all preferred statements. Press coverage of this occurrence will be minimal: reporters at the scene were unprepared for the rapid transpiring of events.

Sign it: Lieutenant David D. Klein, Badge 1091, Commander, Administrative Vice.

Carbons to: Junior, Chief Exley.

The phone—

"Ad Vice, Klein."

"Davey? Got a minute for an old gonif buddy?"

"Mickey, Jesus Christ."

"I know, I'm supposed to call you at home. Uh … Davey … a favor for Sam G.?"

G. for Giancana. "I guess. What?"

"You know that croupier guy you're watchdogging?"

"Yeah."

"Well … the radiator's loose in his bedroom."

2

ROCKABYE REUBEN Ruiz: "This is the tits. I could get used to this."

The Embassy Hotel: parlor, bedrooms, TV. Nine floors up, suite service: food and booze.

Ruiz belting Scotch, half-assed restless. Sanderline Johnson watching cartoons, slack-jawed.

Junior practicing quick draws.

Try some talk. "Hey, Reuben."

Popping mock jabs: "Hey, Lieutenant."

"Hey, Reuben. Did Mickey C. try to infringe on your contract?"

"He what you call strongly suggested my manager let him buy in. He sent the Vecchio brothers out to talk to him, then he punked out when Luis told them, 'Hey, kill me, 'cause I ain't signin' no release form.' You want my opinion? Mickey ain't got the stones for strongarm no more."

"But you've got the *cojones* to snitch."

Jabs, hooks. "I got a brother deserted the army, maybe lookin' at Federal time. I got three bouts coming up at the Olympic, which Welles Noonan can fuck up with subpoenas. My family's what you call from a long line of thieves, what you call trouble prone, so I sorta like making friends in what you might call the law-enforcement community."

"Do you think Noonan has good stuff on Mickey?"

"No, Lieutenant, I don't."

"Call me Dave."

"I'll call you Lieutenant, 'cause I got enough friends in the law-enforcement community."

"Such as?"

"Such as Noonan and his FBI buddy Shipstad. Hey, you know Schoolboy Johnny Duhamel?"

"Sure. He fought in the Gloves, turned pro, then quit."

"You lose your first pro fight, you better quit. I told him that, 'cause Johnny and me are old friends, and Johnny is now *Officer* Schoolboy Johnny Duhamel, on the fuckin' LAPD, on the righteous Mobster Squad, no less. He's tight with the—what you call him?—legendary?—Captain Dudley Smith. So I got enough fuck—"

"Ruiz, watch your language."

Junior—pissed. Johnson goosed the TV—Mickey Mouse ran from Donald Duck.

Junior killed the volume. "I knew Johnny Duhamel when I taught at the Academy. He was in my evidence class, and he was a damn good student. I don't like it when criminals get familiar with policemen. *Comprende, pendejo?*"

"*Pendejo,* huh? So I'm the *stupido,* and you're this punk cowboy, playin' with your gun like that sissy mouse on fuckin' television."

Necktie pull, signal Junior: FREEZE IT.

He froze—fumbling his gun.

Ruiz: "I can always use another friend, *Dave.* There something you want to know?"

I boosted the TV. Johnson stared, rapt—Daisy Duck vamping Donald. Ruiz: "Hey, *Dave.* You wangle this job to pump me?"

Huddle close, semi-private. "You want to make another friend, then give. What's Noonan have?"

"He's got what you call aspirations."

"I know that. *Give.*"

"Well ... I heard Shipstad and this other FBI guy talking. They said Noonan's maybe afraid the fight probe's too limited. Anyway, he's thinking over this backup plan."

"And?"

"And it's like a general L.A. rackets thing, mostly Southside stuff. Dope, slots, you know, illegal vending machines and that kind of shit. I heard Shipstad say something about the LAPD don't investigate colored on colored homicides, and like all this ties to Noonan making the new DA—what's his name?"

"Bob Gallaudet."

"Right, Bob Gallaudet. Anyway, it all ties to making him look bad so Noonan can run against him for attorney general."

Darktown, the coin biz—Mickey C.'s last going stuff. "What about Johnson?"

Snickers. "Look at that mulatto wetbrain. Can you believe he used to be forty-three, zero and two?"

"Reuben, *give*."

"Okay, give he's close to a fuckin' idiot, but he's got this great memory. He can memorize card decks, so some made guys gave him a job at the Lucky Nugget down in Gardena. He's good at memorizing conversations, and some guys weren't so what you call discreet talking around him. I heard Noonan's gonna make him do these memory tricks on the stand, which—"

"I get the picture."

"Good. I quit my own trouble-prone ways, but I sure got a trouble-prone family. I shouldn't of told you what I did, so since you're my friend I'm sure this ain't getting back to the Federal guys, right, *Dave*?"

"Right. Now eat your dinner and get some rest, okay?"

Midnight—lights out. I took Johnson; Junior took Ruiz—my suggestion.

Johnson, bedtime reading: "God's Secret Power Can Be Yours." I pulled a chair up and watched his lips: glom the inside track to Jesus, fight the Jew-Communist conspiracy to mongrelize Christian America. Send your contribution to Post Office Box blah, blah, blah.

"Sanderline, let me ask you something."

"Uh, yessir."

"Do you believe that pamphlet you're reading?"

"Uh, yessir. Right here it says this woman who came back to life said Jesus guarantees all gold-star contributors a new car every year in heaven."

JESUS FUCK.

"Sanderline, did you catch a few in your last couple of fights?"

"Uh, no. I stopped Bobby Calderon on cuts and lost a split decision to Ramon Sanchez. Sir, do you think Mr. Noonan will get us a hot lunch at the grand jury?"

Handcuffs out. "Put these on while I take a piss."

Johnson stood up—yawning, stretching. Check the heater—thick pipes—nix ballast.

Open window—nine-floor drop—this geek half-breed smiling.

"Sir, what do you think Jesus drives himself?"

I banged his head against the wall, threw him out the window screaming.

3

LAPD HOMICIDE said suicide, case closed.

The DA: suicide probable.

Confirmation—Junior, Ruiz—Sanderline Johnson, crazy man. Listen:

I watched him read, dozed off, woke up—Johnson announced he could fly. He went out the window before I could voice my disbelief.

Questioning: Feds, LAPD, DA's men. Basics: Johnson crash-landed on a parked De Soto, DOA, no witnesses. Bob Gallaudet seemed pleased: a rival's political progress scotched. Ed Exley: report to my office, 10:00 A.M.

Welles Noonan: incompetent disgrace of a policeman; piti-ful excuse for an attorney. Suspicious—my old nickname—"the Enforcer."

No mention: 187 PC—felonious homicide.

No mention: outside-agency investigations.

No mention: interdepartmental charges.

I drove home, showered, changed—no reporters hovering yet. Downtown, a dress for Meg—I do it every time I kill a man.

10:00 A.M.

Waiting: Exley, Gallaudet, Walt Van Meter—the boss, Intelligence Division. Coffee, pastry—fuck me.

I sat down. Exley: "Lieutenant, you know Mr. Gallaudet and Captain Van Meter."

Gallaudet, all smiles: "It's been 'Bob' and 'Dave' since law school, and I won't fake any outrage over last night. Did you see the *Mirror*, Dave?"

"No."

" 'Federal Witness Plummets to Death,' with a sidebar: 'Suicide Pronouncement: "Hallelujah, I Can Fly!"' You like it?"

"It's a pisser."

Exley, cold: "The lieutenant and I will discuss that later. In a sense it ties in to what we have here, so let's get to it."

Bob sipped coffee. "Political intrigue. Walt, you tell him."

Van Meter coughed. "Well ... Intelligence has done some pol-itical operations before, and we've got our eye on a target now—a pinko lawyer who has habitually bad-mouthed the Department and Mr. Gallaudet."

Exley: "Keep going."

"Well, Mr. Gallaudet should be elected to a regular term next week. He's an ex-policeman himself, and he speaks our language. He's got the support of the Department and some of the City Council, but—"

Bob cut in. "Morton Diskant. He's neck and neck with Tom Bethune for Fifth District city councilman, and he's been ragging me for weeks. You know, how I've only been a prosecutor for five years and how I cashed in when Ellis Loew resigned as DA. I've heard he's gotten cozy with Welles Noonan, who just might be on my dance card in '60, and Bethune is our kind of guy. It's a very close race. Diskant's been talking Bethune and I up as right-wing shitheads, and the district's twenty-five percent Negro, lots of them registered voters. You take it from there."

Play a hunch. "Diskant's been riling the spooks up with Chavez Ravine, something like 'Vote for me so your Mexican brothers won't get evicted from their shantytown shacks to make room for a ruling-class ballpark.' It's five–four in favor on the Council, and they take a final vote sometime in November after the election. Bethune's an interim incumbent, like Bob, and if he loses he has to leave office before the vote goes down. Diskant gets in, it's a deadlock. We're all civilized white men who know the Dodgers are good for business, so let's get to it."

Exley, smiling: "I met Bob in '53, when he was a DA's Bureau sergeant. He passed the bar and registered as a Republican the same day. Now the pundits tell us we'll only have him as DA for two years. Attorney General in '60, then what? Will you stop at Governor?"

Laughs all around. Van Meter: "I met Bob when he was a patrolman and I was a sergeant. Now it's 'Walt' and 'Mr. Gallaudet.' "

"I'm still 'Bob.' And you used to call me 'son.' "

"I will again, Robert. If you disown your support of district gambling."

Stupid crack—the bill wouldn't pass the State Legislature. Cards, slots and bookmaking—confined to certain areas—taxable big. Cops hated it—say Gallaudet embraced it for votes. "He'll change his mind, he's a politician."

No laughs—Bob coughed, embarrassed. "It looks like the fight probe is down. With Johnson dead, they've got no confirming witnesses, and I got the impression Noonan was just using Reuben Ruiz for his marquee value. Dave, do you agree?"

"Yeah, he's a likable local celebrity. Apparently Mickey C. made some kind of half-baked attempt to muscle his contract, so Noonan probably wanted to use Mickey for *his* marquee value."

Exley, shiv shot: "And we know you're an expert on Mickey Cohen."

"We go back, Chief."

"In what capacity?"

"I've offered him some free legal advice."

"Such as?"

"Such as 'Don't fuck with the LAPD.' Such as 'Watch out for Chief of Detectives Exley, because he never tells you exactly what he wants.' "

Gallaudet, calm: "Come on, enough. Mayor Poulson asked me to call this meeting, so we're on his time. And I have an idea, which is to keep Ruiz on our side. We use him as a front man to placate the Mexicans in Chavez Ravine, so if the evictions go down ugly, we have him as our PR guy. Doesn't he have some kind of burglary jacket?"

I nodded. "Juvie time for B&E. I heard he used to belong to a burglary gang, and I know his brothers pull jobs. You're right—we should use him, promise to keep his family out of trouble if he goes along."

Van Meter: "I like it."

Gallaudet: "What about Diskant?"

I hit hard. "He's a pinko, so he has to have some Commie associates. I'll find them and strongarm them. We'll put them on TV, and they'll snitch him."

Bob, head shakes: "No. It's too vague and there's not enough time."

"Girls, boys, liquor—give me a weakness. Look, I screwed up last night. Let me do penance."

Silence: long, *loud*. Van Meter, off a sigh: "I heard he loves young women. He supposedly cheats on his wife very discreetly. He likes college girls. Young, idealistic."

Bob, a smirk fading: "Dudley Smith can set it up. He's done this kind of thing before."

Exley, weird emphatic: "No, not Dudley. Klein, do you know the right people?"

"I know an editor at *Hush-Hush*. I can get Pete Bondurant for the pix, Fred Turentine for bugging. Ad Vice popped a call house last week, and we've got just the right girl sweating bail."

Stares all around. Exley, half smiling: "So do your penance, Lieutenant."

Bob G.—diplomat. "He let me study his crib sheets in law school. Be nice, Ed."

Exit line—he waltzed, Van Meter walked hangdog.

Say it: "Will the Feds ask for an investigation?"

"I doubt it. Johnson did ninety days observation at Camarillo last year, and the doctors there told Noonan he was unstable. Six FBI men canvassed for witnesses and got nowhere. They'd be stupid to pursue an investigation. You're clean, but I don't like the way it looks."

"You mean criminal negligence?"

"I mean your longstanding and somewhat well-known criminal associations. I'll be kind and say you're 'acquainted' with Mickey Cohen, a focus of the investigation your negligence destroyed. Imaginative people might make a slight jump to 'criminal conspiracy,' and Los Angeles is filled with such people. You see how—"

"Chief, listen to—"

"No, you listen. I gave you and Stemmons that assignment because I trusted your competence and I wanted an attorney's assessment of what the Feds had planned in our jurisdiction. What I got was 'Hallelujah, I Can Fly' and 'Detective Snoozes While Witness Jumps Out Window.'"

Quash a laugh. "So what's the upshot?"

"You tell me. Assess what the Feds have planned past the fight probe."

"I'd say with Johnson dead, not much. Ruiz told me Noonan had some vague plans to mount an investigation into the Southside rackets—dope, the Darktown slot and vending machines. If that probe flies, the Department could be made to look bad. But *if* it goes, Noonan will announce it first—he's headline happy. We'll get a chance to prepare."

Exley smiled. "Mickey Cohen runs the Southside coin business. Will you warn him to get his stuff out?"

"I wouldn't dream of it. Off the topic, did you read my report on the bookie house?"

"Yes. Except for the shots fired, it was salutary. What is it? You're looking at me like you want something."

I poured coffee. "Throw me a bone for the Diskant job."

"You're in no position to ask favors."

"After Diskant I will be."

"Then ask."

Bad coffee. "AdVice is boring me. I was passing through Robbery and saw a case that looked good on the board."

"The appliance store heist?"

"No, the Hurwitz fur warehouse job. A million in furs clouted, no leads, and Junior Stemmons popped Sol Hurwitz at a dice game just last year. He's a degenerate gambler, so I'd bet money on insurance fraud."

"No. It's Dudley Smith's case, and he's ruled insurance out. And you're a commanding officer, not a case man."

"So stretch the rules. I tank the Commie, you throw me one."

"No, it's Dudley's job. The case is three days old and he's already been assigned. Beyond that, I wouldn't want to tempt you with saleable items like furs."

Shivved—deflect it. "There's no love lost between you and Dud. He *wanted* chief of detectives, and you got it."

"COs always get bored and want cases. Is there any particular reason why you want this one?"

"Robbery's clean. You wouldn't be suspicious of my friends if I worked heist jobs."

Exley stood up. "A question before you go."

"Sir?"

"Did a friend tell you to push Sanderline Johnson out the window?"

"No, sir. But aren't you glad he jumped?"

I slept the night off, a room at the Biltmore—figure reporters had my pad staked out. No dreams, room service: 6:00 A.M. breakfast, the papers. New banners: "U.S. Attorney Blasts 'Negligent' Cop"; "Detective Voices Regret at Witness Suicide." Pure Exley—*his* press gig, *his* regret. Page three, more Exley: no Hurwitz-job leads—a gang with toolmaking/electronics expertise boosted a million plus in cold fur. Pix: a bandaged-up security guard; Dudley Smith ogling a mink.

Robbery, sweet duty: jack up heist guys and boost their shit.

Work the Commie: phone calls.

Fred Turentine, bug man—yes for five hundred. Pete Bondurant—yes for a grand—and he'd pay the photo guy. Pete, *Hush-Hush* cozy—more heat on the smear.

The Women's Jail watch boss owed me; a La Verne Benson update cashed her out. La Verne—prostitution beef number three—no bail, no trial date. La Verne to the phone—suppose we lose your rap sheet—yes! yes! yes!

Antsy—my standard postmurder shakes. Antsy to itchy—drive.

A run by my pad—reporters—no haven there. Up to Mulholland, green lights/no traffic—60, 70, 80. Fishtails, curve shimmy—slow down, think.

Think Exley.

Brilliant, cold. In '53 he gunned down four niggers—it closed out the Nite Owl case. Spring '58—evidence proved he killed the wrong men. The case was reopened; Exley and Dudley Smith ran it: *the* biggest job in L.A. history. Multiple homicides/smut intrigue/interlocked conspiracies—Exley cleared it for real. His construction-king father killed himself non sequitur; now Inspector Ed got his money. Thad Green resigned as Chief of Detectives; Chief Parker jumped Dudley to replace him: Edmund Jennings Exley, thirty-six years old.

No love lost—Exley and Dudley—two good haters.

No Detective Division reforms—just Exley going iceberg cold.

Green lights up to Meg's house—just her car out front. Meg in the kitchen window.

I watched her.

Dish duty—a lilt to her hands—maybe background music. Smiling—a face almost mine, but gentle. I hit the horn—

Yes—a primp—her glasses, her hair. A smile—anxious.

I jogged up the steps; Meg had the door open. "I had a feeling you'd bring me a gift."

"Why?"

"The last time you got in the papers you bought me a dress."

"You're the smart Klein. Go on, open it."

"Was it terrible? They had this clip on TV."

"He was a dumb bunny. Come on, open it up."

"David, we have to discuss some business."

I nudged her inside. "*Come on.*"

Rip, tear—wrapping paper in shreds. A whoop, a mirror dash—green silk, a perfect fit.

"Does it work?"

A swirl—her glasses almost flew. "Zip me?"

Shape her in, tug the zipper. Perfect—Meg kissed me, checked the mirror.

"Jesus, you and Junior. He can't stop admiring himself either."

A swirl, a flash: prom date '35. The old man said take Sissy—the guys hounding her weren't appropriate.

Meg sighed. "It's beautiful. Just like everything you give me. And how is Junior Stemmons these days?"

"Thank you, you're welcome, and Junior Stemmons is half smart. He's not really suited for the Detective Bureau, and if his father didn't swing me the command at Ad Vice I'd kick his ass back to a teaching job."

"Not a forceful enough presence?"

"Right, with a hot-dog sensibility that makes it stand out worse, and itchy nerves like he's raiding the dope vault at Narco. Where's your husband?"

"Going over some blueprints for a building he's designing. And while we're on the subject ..."

"Shit. Our buildings, right? Deadbeats? Skipouts?"

"We're slumlords, so don't act surprised. It's the Compton place. Three units in arrears."

"So advise me. You're the real estate broker."

"Two units are one month due, the other is two months behind. It takes ninety days to file an eviction notice, and that entails a court date. And *you're* the attorney."

"Fuck, I hate litigation. And will you sit down?"

She sprawled—a green chair, the green dress. Green against her hair—black—a shade darker than mine. "You're a good litigator, but I know you'll just send some goons down with fake papers."

"It's easier that way. I'll send Jack Woods or one of Mickey's guys."

"Armed?"

"Yeah, and fucking dangerous. Now tell me you love the dress again. Tell me so I can go home and get some sleep."

Counting points—our old routine. "One, I love the dress. Two, I love my big brother, even though he got all the looks and more of the brains. Three, by way of amenities, I quit smoking again, I'm bored with my job and my husband and I'm considering sleeping around before I turn forty and lose the rest of my looks. Four, if you knew any men who weren't cops or thugs I'd ask you to fix me up."

Points back: "I got the Hollywood looks, you got the real ones. Don't sleep with Jack Woods, because people have this tendency to shoot at him, and the first time you and Jack tried shacking it didn't last too long. I do know a few DAs, but they'd bore you."

"Who do I have left? I flopped as a gangster consort."

The room swayed—frazzled time. "I don't know. Come on, walk me out."

Green silk—Meg stroked it. "I was thinking of that logic class we took undergrad. You know, cause and effect."

"Yeah?"

"I ... well, a hoodlum dies in the papers, and I get a gift."

Swaying bad. "Let it go."

"Trombino and Brancato, then Jack Dragna. Honey, I can live with what we did."

"You don't love me the way I love you."

4

REPORTERS AT my door, wolfing take-out.

I parked out back, jimmied a bedroom window. Noise—newsmen gabbing *my* story. Lights off, crack that window: talk to defuse Meg's bomb.

Straight: I'm a kraut, not a Jew—the old man's handle got clipped at Ellis Island. '38—the LAPD; '42—the Marines. Pacific duty, back to the Department '45. Chief Horrall resigns; William Worton replaces him—a squeaky-clean Marine Corps major general. Semper Fi: he forms an ex-Marine goon squad. Esprit de Corps: we break strikes, beat uppity parolees back to prison.

Law school, freelance work—the GI Bill won't cover USC. Repo man, Jack Woods' collector—"the Enforcer." Work for Mickey C.: union disputes settled strongarm. Hollywood beckons—I'm tall, handsome.

Nix, but it leads to *real* work. I break up a squeeze on Liberace—two well-hung shines, blackmail pix. I'm in with Hollywood and Mickey C. I make the Bureau, make sergeant. I pass the bar, make lieutenant.

All true.

I topped my twenty last month—true. My Enforcer take bought slum pads—true. I shacked with Anita Ekberg and the redhead on "The Spade Cooley Show"—false.

Bullshit took over; talk moved to Chavez Ravine. I shut the window and tried to sleep.

No go.

Lift that window—no newsmen. TV: strictly test patterns. Turn it off, run the string out—MEG.

It was always there scary wrong—and we touched each other too long to say it. I kept the old man's fists off her; she kept me from killing him. College together, the war, letters. Other men and other women fizzled.

Rowdy postwar years—"the Enforcer." Meg—pal, repo sidekick. A fling with Jack Woods—I let it go. Study ate up my time—Meg ran wild solo. She met two hoods: Tony Trombino, Tony Brancato.

June '51—our parents dead in a car wreck.

The guts, the will—

A motel room—Franz and Hilda Klein fresh buried. Naked just to see. On each other—every taste half recoil.

Meg broke it off—no finish. Fumbles: our clothes, words, the lights off.

I still wanted it.

She didn't.

She ran crazy with Trombino and Brancato.

The fucks messed with Jack Dragna—the Outfit's number-one man in L.A. Jack showed me a picture: Meg—bruises, hickeys—Trombino/Brancato verified.

Verified—they popped a mob dice game.

Jack said five grand, you clip them—I said yes.

I set it up—a shakedown run—"We'll rob this bookie holding big." August 6, 1648 North Ogden—the Two Tonys in a '49 Dodge. I slid in the backseat and blew their brains out.

"Mob Warfare" headlines—Dragna's boss torpedo picked up quick. His alibi: Jack D.'s parish priest. Gangland unsolved—let the fucking wops kill each other.

I was paid—plus a tape bonus: a man raging at the scum who hurt his sister. Dragna's voice—squelched out. My voice: "I will fucking kill them. I will fucking kill them for free."

Mickey Cohen called. Jack said I owed the Outfit—the debt kosher for a few favors. Jack would call, I'd be paid—strictly business.

Hooked.

Called:

June 2, '53: I clipped a dope chemist in Vegas.

March 26, '55: I killed two jigs who raped a mob guy's wife.

September '57, a rumor: Jack D.—heart disease bad.

I called him.

Jack said, "Come see me."

We met at a beachfront motel—his fixing-to-die-fuck spot. Guinea heaven: booze, smut, whores next door.

I begged him: cancel my debt.

Jack said, "The whores do lez stuff."

I choked him dead with a pillow.

Coroner's verdict/mob consensus: heart attack.

Sam Giancana—my new caller. Mickey C. his front man: cop favors, clip jobs.

Meg sensed something. Lie away her part, take all the guilt. Sleep—restless, sweaty.

The phone—grab it—"Yes?"

"Dave? Dan Wilhite."

Narco—the boss. "What is it, Captain?"

"It's ... shit, do you know J. C. Kafesjian?"

"I know who he is. I know what he is to the Department."

Wilhite, low: "I'm at a crime scene. I can't really talk and I've got nobody to send over, so I called you."

Hit the lights. "Fill me in, I'll go."

"It's, shit, it's a burglary at J.C.'s house."

"Address?"

"1684 South Tremaine. That's just off—"

"I know where it is. Somebody called Wilshire dicks before they called you, right?"

"Right, J.C.'s wife. The whole family was out for the evening, but Madge, the wife, came home first. She found the house burgled and called Wilshire Station. J.C., Tommy and Lucille—that's the other kid—came home and found the house full of detectives who didn't know about our ... uh ... arrangement with the family. Apparently, it's some goddamn nutso B&E and the Wilshire guys are making pests of themselves. J.C. called my wife, she called around and found me. Dave ..."

"I'll go."

"Good. Take someone with you, and count it one in your column."

I hung up and called for backup—Riegle, Jensen—no answer. Shit luck—Junior Stemmons—"Hello?"

"It's me. I need you for an errand."

"Is it a call-out?"

"No, it's an errand for Dan Wilhite. It's smooth J.C. Kafesjian's feathers."

Junior whistled. "I heard his kid's a real psycho."

"1684 South Tremaine. Wait for me outside, I'll brief you."

"I'll be there. Hey, did you see the late news? Bob Gallaudet called us 'exemplary officers,' but Welles Noonan said we were 'incompetent freeloaders.' He said that ordering room-service booze for our witnesses contributed to Johnson's suicide. He said—"

"Just be there."

Code 3, do Wilhite solid—aid the LAPD's sanctioned pusher. Narco/J.C. Kafesjian—twenty years connected—old Chief Davis brought him in. Weed, pills, H—Darktown trash as clientele. Snitch duty got J.C. the dope franchise. Wilhite played watchdog; J.C. ratted rival pushers, per our policy: keep narcotics isolated south of Slauson. His legit work: a dry-cleaning chain; his son's work: muscle goon supreme.

Crosstown to the pad: a Moorish job lit up bright. Cars out front: Junior's Ford, a prowl unit.

Flashlight beams and voices down the driveway. "Holy shit, holy shit"—Junior Stemmons.

I parked, walked over.

Light in my eyes. Junior: "That's the lieutenant." A stink: maybe blood rot.

Junior, two plainclothesmen. "Dave, this is Officer Nash and Sergeant Miller."

"Gentlemen, Narco's taking this over. You go back to the station. Sergeant Stemmons and I will file reports if it comes to that."

Miller: " 'Comes to that'? Do you *smell* that?"

Heavy, acidic. "Is this a homicide?"

Nash: "Not exactly. Sir, you wouldn't believe the way that punk Tommy What's-His-Name talked to us. *Comes to*—"

"Go back and tell the watch commander Dan Wilhite sent me over. Tell him it's J.C. Kafesjian's place, so it's not your standard 459. If that doesn't convince him, have him wake up Chief Exley."

"Lieutenant—"

Grab a flashlight, chase the smell—back to a snipped chain-link fence. Fuck—two Dobermans—no eyes, throats slit, teeth gnashing chemical-soaked washrags. Gutted—entrails, blood— blood dripping toward a jimmied back door.

Shouts inside—two men, two women. Junior: "I shooed the squadroom guys off. Some 459, huh?"

"Lay it out for me, I don't want to question the family."

"Well, they were all at a party. The wife had a headache, so she took a cab home first. She went out to let the dogs in and found them. She called Wilshire, and Nash and Miller caught the squeal. J.C., Tommy and the daughter—the two kids live here, too—came home and raised a ruckus when they found cops in the living room."

"Did you talk to them?"

"Madge—that's the wife—showed me the damage, then J.C. shut her up. Some heirloom-type silverware was stolen, and the damage was some strange stuff. Do you feature this? I have never worked a B&E job like this one."

Yells, horn bleats.

"It's not a job. And what do you mean 'strange stuff'?"

"Nash and Miller tagged it. You'll see."

I flashed the yard—foamy meat scraps—call the dogs poisoned. Junior: "He fed them that meat, then mutilated them. He got blood on himself, then trailed it into the house."

Follow it:

Back-door pry marks. A laundry porch—bloody towels discarded—the burglar cleaned up.

The kitchen door intact—he slipped the latch. No more blood, the sink evidence tagged: "Broken Whiskey Bottles." Cabinet-drawers theft tagged: "Antique Silverware."

Them:

"You whore, to let strange policemen into our home!"

"Daddy, please don't!"

"We always call Dan when we need help!"

A dining room table, photo scraps piled on top: "Family Pictures." Sax bleats upstairs.

Walk the pad.

Too-thick carpets, velvet sofas, flocked wallpaper. Window air coolers—Jesus statues perched beside them. A rug tagged: "Broken Records/Album Covers"—*The Legendary Champ Dineen: Sooo Slow Moods*; *Straight Life*: The Art Pepper Quartet; *The Champ Plays the Duke.*

LPs by a hi-fi—stacked neat.

Junior walked in. "Like I told you, huh? Some damage."

"Who's making that noise?"

"The horn? That's Tommy Kafesjian."

"Go up and make nice. Apologize for the intrusion, offer to call Animal Control for the dogs. Ask him if he wants an investigation. Be nice, do you understand?"

"Dave, he's a criminal."

"Don't worry, I'll be brown-nosing his old man even worse."

"DADDY, DON'T!"—booming through closed doors.

"J.C., LEAVE THE GIRL ALONE!"

Spooky—Junior *ran* upstairs.

"THAT'S RIGHT, GET OUT"—a side door slamming—"Daddy" in my face.

J.C. close up: a greasy fat man getting old. Burly, pockmarked, bloody facial scratches.

"I'm Dave Klein. Dan Wilhite sent me over to square things."

Squinting: "What's so important he couldn't come himself?"

"We can do this any way you want, Mr. Kafesjian. If you want an investigation, you've got it. You want us to dust for prints, maybe get you a name, you've got it. If you want payback, Dan will support you in anything within reason, if you follow—"

"I follow what you mean and I clean my own house. I deal with Captain Dan strictly, not strangers in my parlor."

Two women snuck by. Soft brunettes—nongrease types. The daughter waved—silver nails, blood drops.

"You see my girls, now forget them. They are not for you to know."

"Any idea who did it?"

"Not for you to talk about. Not for you to mention business rivals who might want to hurt me and mine."

"Rivals in the dry-cleaning biz?"

"Not for you to make jokes! Look! Look!"

A door tag: "Mutilated Clothing." "Look! Look! Look!"—J.C. yanked the knob—"Look! Look! Look!"

Look: a small closet. Spread-legged, crotch-ripped pedal pushers tacked across the walls.

Stained—smell it—semen.

"Now it is not to laugh. I buy Lucille and Madge so many nice clothes that they must keep some down in the parlor. Perverted degenerate wants to hurt Lucille's pretty things. *You look.*"

Tijuana whore stuff: "Pretty."

"Not so funny now, Dan Wilhite's errand boy. Now you don't laugh."

"Call Dan. Tell him what you want done."

"I clean my own house!"

"Nice threads. Your daughter working her way through college?"

Fists clenching/veins popping/face-rips trickling—this fat greasy fuck pressing close.

Shouts upstairs.

I ran up. A room off the hall—scope the damage:

Tommy K. up against the wall. Reefers on the floor, tough guy Junior frisking him. Jazz posters, Nazi flags, a sax on the bed.

I laughed.

Tommy smiled nice—this skinny nongreaser.

Junior: "He *flaunted* that mary jane. He *ridiculed* the Department."

"Sergeant, apologize to Mr. Kafesjian."

Half pout, half shriek: "Dave ... God ... *I'm sorry*."

Tommy lit up a stick and blew smoke in Junior's face.

J.C., downstairs: "Go home now! I clean my own house!"

5

BAD SLEEP, no sleep.

Meg's call woke me up: get our late rent settled, no silk-dress talk. I said, "Sure, sure"—hung up and pitched Jack Woods: twenty percent on every rent dollar collected. He jewed me up to twenty-five—I agreed.

Work calls: Van Meter, Pete Bondurant, Fred Turentine. Three green lights: LaVerne's pad was bugged; a photo man was stashed in the bedroom. Diskant—tailed and overheard: drinks at Ollie Hammond's Steakhouse, 6:00 P.M.

The bait stood ready: *our* Commie consort. Pete said *Hush-Hush* loved it: pinko politico trips on his dick.

I called Narco—Dan Wilhite was out—I left a message. Bad sleep, no sleep—the nightmare Kafesjians. Junior last night, comic relief: "I know you don't think I rate the Bureau, but I'll show you, I'll really show you."

5:00 P.M.—fuck sleep.

I cleaned up, checked the *Herald*—Chavez Ravine bumped my dead man off page one. Bob Gallaudet: "The Latin Americans who lose their dwellings will be handsomely compensated, and in the end a home for the L.A. Dodgers will serve as a point of pride for Angelenos of all races, creeds and colors."

Knee-slapper stuff—it doused my Kafesjian hangover.

Ollie Hammond's—stake the bar entrance, wait.

Morton Diskant in the door, six sharp.

LaVerne Benson in at 6:03—tweed skirt, knee sox, cardigan.

6:14—Big Pete B., sliding the seat back.

"Diskant's with his friends, LaVerne's two booths down. Two seconds in and she's giving him these hot looks."

"You think he'll tumble?"

"I would, but then I'm a pig for it."

"Like your boss?"

"You can say his name—Howard Hughes. He's a busy guy—like you."

"He was a dumb fuck. If he didn't jump, I probably would have pushed him."

Pete tapped the dashboard—huge hands—they beat a drunk-tank brawler dead. The L.A. Sheriff's canned him; Howard Hughes found a soulmate.

"*You* been busy?"

"Sort of. I collect dope for *Hush-Hush*, I keep Mr. Hughes out of *Hush-Hush*. People try to sue *Hush-Hush*, I convince them otherwise. I scout pussy for Mr. Hughes, I listen to Mr. Hughes talk this crazy shit about airplanes. Right now Mr. Hughes has got me tailing this actress who jilted him. Dig this: this cooze blows out of Mr. Hughes' number-one fuck pad, with a three-yard-a-week contract to boot, all to act in some horror cheapie. Mr. Hughes has got her signed to a seven-year slave contract, and he wants to get it violated on a morality clause. Can you feature this pussy pig preaching morality?"

"Yeah, and you love it because you're—"

"Because I'm a pig for the life, like you."

I laughed, yawned. "This could go on all night."

Pete lit a cigarette. "No, La Verne's impetuous. She'll get bored and honk the Commie's shvantz. Nice kid. She actually helped Turentine set up his microphones."

"How's Freddy doing?"

"He's busy. Tonight he compromises this Commie, next week he wires some fag bathhouse for *Hush-Hush*. The trouble with Freddy T. is he's a booze pig. He's got all these drunk-driving beefs, so the last time the judge stuck him with this service job teaching electronics to the inmates up at Chino. Klein, look."

La Verne at the bar door—two thumbs up. Pete signaled back. "That means Diskant's meeting her after he ditches his friends. See that blue Chevy, that's hers."

I pulled out—La Verne in front—right turns on Wilshire. Straight west—Sweetzer, north, the Strip. Curvy side streets, up into the hills—La Verne stopped by a stucco four-flat.

Ugly: floodlights, *pink* stucco.

I parked a space back—room for the Red.

La Verne wiggled up to her door. Pete sent out love taps on my siren.

Foyer lights on and off. Window lights on—the downstairs-left apartment. Party noise: the pad across from La Verne's.

Pete stretched. "You think Diskant's got the smarts to make this for an unmarked?"

La Verne opened her curtains, stripped to peignoir and garters. "No, he's only got one thing on his mind."

"You're right, 'cause he's a pig for it. I say one hour or less."

"Twenty says fifteen minutes."

"You're on."

We settled in, eyes on that window. Lull time, party noise: show tunes, voices. Bingo—a tan Ford. Pete said, "Forty-one minutes."

I slid him twenty. Diskant walked up, hit the door, buzzed. La Verne, window framed: bumps and grinds.

Pete howled.

Diskant walked in.

Ten minutes ticking by slow ... lights off at La Verne's love shack. Hold for the photo man's signal: flashbulb pops out that front window.

Fifteen minutes ... twenty ... twenty-five—a Sheriff's unit double-parking.

Pete nudged me. "Fuck. That party. 116.84 California Penal Code, Unlawfully Loud Assembly. *Fuck.*"

Two deputies walking. Nightstick raps on the party-pad window. No response.

"Klein, this is not fucking good."

Rap rap rap—La Verne's front window. Flashbulb pops—*the bedroom window*—big-time-bad-news improvisation.

Screams—our Commie hooker.

The deputies kicked the foyer door down—I chased the fuckers, badge out—

Across the lawn, up the steps. Topsy-turvy glimpses: the photo man dropping out a window sans camera. Through the lobby—party kids mingling—La Verne's door snapped clean. I pushed through, punks tossing drinks in the face.

"Police! Police officer!"

I jumped the doorway dripping Scotch—a deputy caught me. My badge in his face: "Intelligence Division! LAPD!"

The dipshit just gawked me. Bedroom shrieks—

I ran in—

Diskant and La Verne floor-tumbling—naked, flailing, gouging. A camera on the bed; a dumbfuck shouting: "Hey! You two stop that! We're the Sheriff's!"

Pete ran in—Dumbfuck grinned familiar—old-deputy-acquaintance recognition. Fast Pete: he hustled the clown out quicksville. La Verne vs. the pinko: kicks, sissy punches.

The camera on the bed: grab it, pop the film out, seal it. Hit the button—flashbulb light in Diskant's eyes.

One blind Commie—La Verne tore free. I kicked him and punched him—he yelped, blinked and focused—ON THE FILM.

Shakedown:

"This was supposed to be some kind of setup, but those policemen broke it up. You were heading for the scandal sheets, something like 'Red Politician Blah Blah Blah.' You come across and that won't happen, because I sure would hate for your wife to see this film. Now, are you sure you want to be a city councilman?"

Sobs.

Brass knucks on. "Are you sure?"

More sobs.

Kidney shots—my knucks tore flab.

"Are you sure?"

Beet-red bawling: "Please don't hurt me!"

Two more shots—Diskant belched foam.

"You drop out tomorrow. Now say yes, because I don't like this."

"Y-yes p-p-p—"

Fucked-up shitty stuff—I hit the living room quashing shakes. No cops, La Verne draped in a sheet.

Pete, dangling bug mikes: "I took care of the deputies, and Van Meter called on your two-way. You're supposed to meet Exley at the Bureau right now."

Downtown. Exley at his desk.

I pulled a chair up, slid him the film. "He's pulling out, so we won't have to go to *Hush-Hush*."

"Did you enjoy the work?"

"Did you enjoy shooting those niggers?"

"The public has no idea what justice costs the men who perform it."

"Which means?"

"Which means thank you."

"Which means I have a favor coming."

"You've been given one already, but ask anyway."

"The fur robbery. Maybe it's insurance fraud, maybe it's not. Either way, I want to work cases."

"No, I told you it's Dudley Smith's assignment."

"Yeah, you and Dud are such good buddies. And what's with this 'already' favor?"

"Besides no reprimand or interdepartmental charges on Sanderline Johnson?"

"Chief, come on."

"I destroyed the autopsy report on Johnson. The coroner noted a non sequitur bruise with imbedded paint fragments on his forehead, as if he banged his head against a windowsill before he jumped. I'm not saying that you're culpable; but other people, notably Welles Noonan, might. I had the file destroyed. And I have a case for you. I'm detaching you from Ad Vice immediately to start working on it."

Weak knees: "What case?"

"The Kafesjian burglary. I read the Wilshire Squad occurrence report, and I've decided I want a major investigation. I'm fully aware of the family's LAPD history, and I don't care what Captain Wilhite wants. You and Sergeant Stemmons are detached as of now. Shake the family, shake their known associates. J.C. employs a runner named Abe Voldrich, so lean on him while you're at it. I want a full forensic and the files checked for similar B&Es. Start tomorrow—with a show of force."

I stood up. "This is fucking insane. Lean on *our* sanctioned Southside dope kingpin when the U.S. Attorney just might be planning a rackets probe down there. Some pervo kills two dogs and jacks off on some—"

Exley, standing/crowding: "Do it. Detach canvassing officers from Wilshire Patrol and bring in the Crime Lab. Stemmons lacks field experience, but use him anyway. *Show of force*. And don't make me regret the favors I've done you."

6

SHOW OF FORCE.

8:00 A.M., 1684 South Tremaine. Personnel: lab crew, print team, four bluesuits.

The blues deployed: house-to-house witness checks, trashcan checks. Traffic cops standing by to shoo the press off.

Show of force—Exley's wild hair up the ass.

Show of force—short-shrift it.

A compromise with Dan Wilhite—one edgy phone call. I said Exley pure had me; he called the job crazy—J.C. and the Department: twenty years of two-way profit. I owed Dan; he owed me—favors backlogged. Wilhite, scared: "I retire in three months. My dealings with the family won't stand up to outside-agency scrutiny. Dave … can you … play it easy?"

I said, "My ass first, yours second."

He said, "I'll call J.C. and jerk his leash."

8:04—showtime.

Black-and-whites, a lab van. Patrolmen, tech men. Gawkers galore, little kids.

The driveway—I walked the lab guys back. Ray Pinker: "I called Animal Control. They told me they got no dead dog reports from this address. You think the people planted them in some pet cemetery?"

Garbage day—trashcans lined up in the alley. "Maybe, but check those cans behind the back fence. I don't think Old Man Kafesjian's so sentimental."

"I heard he was a real sweetheart. We find the dogs, then what?"

"Take tissue samples for a make on what they were poisoned with. If they're still chewing on washcloths, get me a make on the chemical—it smelled like chloroform. I need ten minutes to talk up J.C., then I want you to come inside and bag fibers in the kitchen, living room and dining room. Send the print guys in then, and tell them just the downstairs—I don't think our burglar went upstairs. He jerked off on some pedal pushers, so if Pops didn't throw them out you can test the semen for blood type."

"Jesus."

"Yeah, Jesus. Listen, if he did dump them, they're probably in those garbage cans. Pastel-colored pedal pushers ripped at the crotch, not everyday stuff. And Ray? I want a nice fat summary report on all this."

"Don't shit a shitter. You want me to pad it, say it."

"Pad it. I don't know what Exley wants, so let's give him something to chew on."

Madge at the back door, looking out. Heavy makeup—Pan-Cake over bruises.

Ray nudged me. "She doesn't look Armenian."

"She's not, and their kids don't look it either. Ray—"

"Yeah, I'll pad it."

Back to the street—rubberneckers swarming. Junior and Tommy K. locking eyes.

Tommy, porch loafer: bongo shirt, pegger pants, sax.

Junior sporting his new look: whipped dog with a mean streak.

I braced him—avuncular. "Come on, don't let that guy bother you."

"It's those looks of his. Like he knows something I don't."

"Forget about it."

"You didn't have to kowtow to him."

"I didn't disobey my CO."

"Dave …"

"Dave nothing. Your father's an inspector, he got you the Bureau, and my Ad Vice command was part of the deal. It's a game. You owe your father, I owe your father, I owe Dan Wilhite. We both owe the Department, so we have to play things like Exley's off the deep end on this deal. Do you understand?"

"I understand. But it's your game, so just don't tell me it's right."

Slap his fucking face—no—don't. "You pull that idealistic shit on me and I'll hand your father a fitness report that will bounce you back to a teaching job in record goddamn time. *My game got you where you are.* You play along or you see 'ineffectual command presence,' 'overly volatile' and 'poor composure in stress situations' on Daddy's desk tonight. You call it, Sergeant."

Punk bravado: "*I'm playing.* I called the Pawnshop Detail and gave them a description of the silverware, and I got a list of Kafesjian's dry-cleaning shops. Three for you, three for me, the usual questions?"

"Good, but let's see what the patrolmen turn first. Then, after you hit your three, go downtown and check the Central burglary files and Sheriff's files for 459's with similar MOs. You turn some, great. If not, check homicide unsolveds—maybe this clown's a goddamn killer."

A stink, fly swarms—lab men hauled the dogs out, dripping garbage.

"I guess you wouldn't tell me these things if you didn't care."

"That's right."

"You'll see, Dave. I'll prove myself on this one."

Tommy K. honked his sax—spectators clapped. Tommy bowed and pumped his crotch.

"Hey, Lieutenant! You come and talk to me!"

J.C. on the porch, holding a tray out. "Hey! We have an eye opener!"

I walked up. Bottled beer—Tommy grabbed one and guzzled. Check his arms: skin-pop tracks, swastika tattoos.

J.C. smiled. "Don't tell me too early for you."

Tommy belched. "Schlitz, Breakfast of Champions."

"Five minutes, Mr. Kafesjian. Just a few questions."

"I say all right, Captain Dan said you okay, this thing is not your idea. You follow me. Tommy, you go offer the other men Breakfast of Champions."

Tommy dipped the tray à la carhop. J.C. bowed, follow-me style.

I followed him into the den: pine walls, gun racks. Check the parlor—print men, carhop Tommy hawking beer.

J.C. shut the door. "Dan told me you just going to go through the motions."

"Not quite. This is Ed Exley's case, and his rules are different than ours."

"We do business, your people and mine. He knows that."

"Yeah, and he's stretching the rules this time. He's the Chief of Detectives, and Chief Parker lets him do what he wants. I'll try to go easy, but you'll have to play along."

J.C.: greasy and ugly. Face scratches—his own daughter clawed him. "Why? Exley, he's crazy?"

"I don't know why, which is a damn good question. Exley wants the major-case treatment on this one, and he's a better god-damn detective than I am. I can only bullshit him so far."

J.C. shrugged. "Hey, you smart, you got more juice. You a lawyer, you tight with Mickey Cohen."

"No. I fix things, Exley *runs* things. You want smart? Exley's the best detective the LAPD's ever seen. Come on, help me. You don't want regular cops nosing around, I understand that. But some piece-of-shit burglar breaks in here and rips up—"

"I clean my own house! Tommy and me, we find this guy!"

Easy now: "No. *We* find him, then maybe Dan Wilhite gives you a shot. No trouble, nice and legal."

Head jerks no-no. "Dan says you got questions. You ask, I answer. I play ball."

"No you'll cooperate, no you won't?"

"I cooperate."

Notebook out. "Who did it? Any ideas?"

"No"—deadpan—no read.

"Enemies. Give me some names."

"We got no enemies."

"Come on, you sell narcotics."

"Don't say that word in my home!"

EASY NOW: "Let's call it business. Business rivals who don't like you."

Fist shakes no-no. "*You* make the rules, we play right. We do business fair and square so we don't make no enemies."

"Then let's try this. You're what we call a suborned informant. People like that make enemies. Think about it and give me some names."

"Fancy words for snitch and fink and stool pigeon."

"Names, Mr. Kafesjian."

"Men in prison can't break into nice family houses. I got no names for you."

"Then let's talk about Tommy and Lucille's enemies."

"No enemies, my kids."

"Think. This guy breaks in, breaks phonograph records and mutilates your daughter's clothing. Did those records belong to Tommy?"

"Yes, Tommy's long-play record albums."

"Right. And Tommy's a musician, so maybe the burglar had a grudge against him. He wanted to destroy his property and Lucille's, but for some reason he didn't get upstairs to their bedrooms. So, *their* enemies. Old musician buddies, Lucille's old boyfriends. *Think.*"

"No, no enemies"—soft—say his brain just clicked on.

Change-up: "I need to fingerprint you and your family. We need to compare your prints against any prints the burglar might have left."

He pulled a money clip out. "No. It's not right. I clean my own—"

I squeezed his hand shut. "Play it your way. Just remember it's Exley's show, and I owe him more than I owe Wilhite."

He tore his hand free and fanned out C-notes.

I said, "Fuck you. Fuck your whole greasy family."

Rip, tear—he trashed two grand easy.

I waltzed before it got worse.

7

SHITWORK TIME.

Pinker labbed the dogs. The print guys got smudges, partials. The crowd dwindled; blues canvassed. Junior logged reports: nothing hot that night, archetypal Kafesjian rebop.

Dig: epic family brawls, all-night sax noise. J.C. watered the lawn in a jock strap. Tommy pissed out his bedroom window. Madge and Lucille: wicked tantrum shouters. Bruises, black eyes—standard issue.

Slow time—let it drag.

Lucille and Madge took off—adiós in a pink Ford Vicky. Tommy practiced scales—the lab men popped in earplugs. Beer cans out the windows—Lunch of Champions.

Junior fetched the *Herald*. A Morton Diskant announcement: press conference, 6:00 tonight.

Time to kill—I hit the lab van, watched the techs work.

Tissue slicing, extraction—our boy jammed the dogs' eyes down their throats. Back to my car, a doze—bum sleep two nights running stretched me thin.

"Dave, rise and shine"—Ray Pinker, too goddamn soon.

Up yawning. "Results?"

"Yes, and interesting. I'm not a doctor and what I did wasn't an autopsy, but I think I can reconstruct some things conclusively."

"Go. Tell me now, then route me a summary report."

"Well, the dogs were poisoned with hamburger laced with sodium tryctozine, commonly known as ant poison. I found leather glove fragments on their teeth and gums, which leads me to believe that the burglar tossed them the meat, but didn't wait for them to die before he mutilated them. You told me you smelled chloroform, remember?"

"Yeah. I figured it was the washrags in their mouths."

"You're close so far. But it wasn't chloroform, it was stelfactiznide chloride, a dry-cleaning chemical. Now, J.C. Kafesjian owns a string of dry-cleaning shops. Interesting?"

The man broke in, stole and destroyed. A psycho, but precise—no disarray. Bold: and time-consuming. Psycho-crazy shit: *and* neat, precise.

"You're saying he might know the family, might work in one of the shops."

"Right."

"Did you find the girl's pants?"

"No. We found charred fabric mounds in that garbage can with the dogs, so there's no way to test the semen for blood type."

"Shit. Fried pedal pushers sounds just like J.C."

"Dave, listen. This verges on theory, but I like it."

"Go ahead."

"Well, the dogs were chemically scalded right around their eyes, and the bones in their snouts were broken. I think the burglar debilitated them with the poison, clamped down on their snouts, then tried to blind them while they were still alive. Stelfactiznide causes blindness when locally applied, but they flailed too much and bit him. They died from the poison, then he gutted them postmortem. He had some strange fix on their eyes, so he carefully pulled them out, stuffed them down their throats and stuffed the washrags soaked in chemical in their mouths. All four eyeballs were saturated with that chloride, so I rest my case."

Junior and a bluesuit hovering. "Dave—"

Cut him off: "Ray, have you *ever* heard of watchdog torture on a 459?"

"Never. And I'll go out on a limb for motive."

"Revenge?"

"Revenge."

"Dave ..."

"What?"

"This is Officer Bethel. Officer, tell the lieutenant."

Nervous—a rookie. "Uh, sir, I got two confirmations on a prowler on this block the night of the burglary. Sergeant Stemmons, he's had me checking on the houses where nobody was home earlier. This old lady told me she called the Wilshire desk, and this man, he said he saw him too."

"Description?"

"J-just a young male Caucasian. No other details, but I called the desk anyway. They did send a car out. No luck, and no white prowlers got arrested or FI carded anywhere in the division that night."

A lead—shove it at Junior. "Call Wilshire and get four more men to hit the not-at-home addresses, say from six o'clock on. Have them go for descriptions on possible prowlers. Check those files I told you to and go by the first three Kafesjian shops on your list. Ray?"

"Yeah, Dave."

"Ray, tell Stemmons here your chemical angle. Junior, hit that angle with the employees at the shops. If you get a rabbit, don't do something stupid like kill him."

"Why not? Live by the sword, die by the sword."

"You dumb shit, I want to hear this guy's take on the Kafesjians."

Three E-Z Kleen shops—1248 South Normandie closest. I drove over—the pink Ford stood out front.

I double-parked; a guy ran out looking anxious. Make him; Abe Voldrich, Kafesjian high-up.

"Please, Officer. They don't know anything about this god-damn break-in. Call Dan Wilhite, talk to him about the ... uh ..."

"Ramifications?"

"Yeah, that's a good word. Officer—"

"Lieutenant."

"Lieutenant, let it rest. Yes, the family has enemies. No, they won't tell you who they are. You could ask Captain Dan, but I doubt if he'd tell you."

Smart little hump. "So we won't discuss enemies."

"Now we're cooking with gas!"

"What about stelfactiznide chloride?"

"What? Now you're talking Greek to me."

"It's a dry-cleaning chemical."

"That end of the business I don't know from."

Walking in: "I want an employee list—all your shops."

"No. We hire strictly colored people for the cleaning and pressing work, and most of them are on parole and probation. They wouldn't appreciate you asking questions."

Jig crime—no—it played wrong. "Do you have colored salespeople?"

"No, J.C. doesn't trust them around money."

"Let me check your storeroom."

"For that what you call it chemical? Why?"

"The watchdogs were burned with it."

Sighing: "Go, just don't roust the workers."

I skirted the counter. A small factory in back: pressers, vats, darkies folding shirts. Wall shelves: jars, bottles.

Check labels—two run-throughs, a catch: stelfactiznide chloride, skull and crossbones.

I sniffed a jug—foul/familiar—my eyes burned. Put it back, dawdle—the women might show. No luck—just darting slave eyes. I walked back up front popping sweat.

Lucille at the counter, hanging shirts. Bump bump—ass grinds to a radio beat. Bump, flash: a vamp smile.

I smiled back. Lucille zipped her mouth, threw away a pretend key. Outside: Voldrich and Madge. Mama K.: wet makeup, tears.

I walked out to the car. Whispers—I couldn't hear shit.

I hit a pay phone—fuck the E-Z Kleen shops.

I called Ad Vice and left a message for Junior: buzz Dan Wilhite, bag a Kafesjian snitch list. Probably futile—he'd refuse, hot to placate J.C. A message *from* Junior: he'd checked around, learned stel-what-the-fuck was a standard dry-cleaning chemical used worldwide.

Back to South Tremaine—one black-and-white in front. Bethel waved me over. "Sir, we got two more confirmations on that prowler night before last."

"More details on his description?"

"No, but it looks like he's a peeper too. We got that same 'young, white' make, and both people said he was peeping in windows."

Think: burglary/mutilation tools. "Did they say he was carrying anything?"

"No, sir, but I think he could have secreted the B&E stuff on his person."

"But the people didn't call in complaints."

"No, sir, but I got a lead that might tie in."

Coax him: "So tell me, Officer."

"Well, the woman in the house directly across the street told me that sometimes Lucille Kafesjian dances naked in her bedroom window. You know, with the lights on behind her at night. She said she does it when her parents and her brother are out for the evening."

Guesswork:

Exhibitionist Lucille, peeper/prowler/B&E man hooked on the family.

"Bethel, you're going places."

"Uh, yessir. Where?"

"In general. Right now, though, you stick here. You keep going back to the addresses where no one was home earlier. You try to flesh out the description of the peeper. Got it?"

"Yessir!"

Rolling shitwork:

Wilshire Station, paper checks: arrest rosters, MO files, FI cards. Results: window-peeping young white men—zero. Dog-slashing burglars—zero.

University Station, arrest/MO—bupkis. FI cards, three recent: a "youngish," "average build" white man was reported peeping whore motels. *My* eyeball man?—maybe—but:

No motel addresses—just "South Western Avenue" listed. No complainant names or badge ID numbers listed.

No place to go right now.

I called 77th Street Station. The squad boss, bored:

No dog snuffs. A young white peeper spotted roof-prowling: fuck-pad motels, jazz clubs. No arrests, no suspects, no FI cards—the squad had a new card system pending. He'd route me the club/motel locations—if and when he found them.

Tommy K.'s *jazz* records smashed?

More calls: Central Jail, LAPD/Sheriff's R&I. Results: no dog-snuff arrests this year; zero on young white peeper/prowlers. 459 pops post-Kafesjian: no Caucasian perps.

Calls—a pay phone hogged three hours—every LAPD/Sheriff's squadroom tapped. Shit: no young white peepers in custody; two wetback dog slashers deported to Mexico.

Waiting: the Bureau pervert file.

I rolled downtown. An office check—no messages, a report on my desk:

CONFIDENTIAL

10/30/58

TO: LIEUTENANT DAVID D. KLEIN
FROM: SERGEANT GEORGE STEMMONS, JR.
TOPIC: KAFESJIAN/459 P. C.
947.1 (HEALTH & SAFETY CODE—ANIMAL MAYHEM)

SIR:

As ordered, I checked the Central Bureau and Sheriff's Central Burglary files for 459's similar to ours. None were listed. I also cross-checked 947.1 offenders (very few were listed) against the 459 files and found no crossover names. (The youngest 947.1 offender is currently 39 years old, which contradicts the prowler lead that Officer Bethel gave us.) I also checked local/statewide homicide files back to 1950. No 187's/187's collateral to burglaries similar to our perpetrator's MO were listed.

Re: Captain Wilhite. I "diplomatically" asked him to supply us with a list of pushers/addicts informed on by the Kafesjians, and he said that their snitches were never tallied, that no records were kept to protect the family. Captain Wilhite offered one name, a man recently informed on by Tommy Kafesjian: marijuana seller Wardell Henry Knox, male negro, employed as a bartender at various jazz clubs. Captain Wilhite's officers could not locate Knox. Knox was recently murdered (unsolved). It was a negro on negro homicide that presumably received only a cursory investigation.

Re the E-Z Kleen shops: at all three locations the staff flatly refused to talk to me.

Returning to Captain Wilhite. Frankly, I think he lied about the Kafesjian's snitches never being tallied. He expressed displeasure over your argument with J.C. Kafesjian and told me he has heard rumors that the Federal rackets probe will be launched, centering on narcotics dealings in South-Central Los Angeles. He expressed concern that the LAPD's suborning of the Kafesjian family will be made public and thus discredit both the Department and the individual Narcotics Division officers involved with the family.

I await further orders.

> Respectfully,
> Sgt. George Stemmons, Jr.
> Badge 2104
> Administrative Vice Division

Junior—half-ass smart when he tried. I left him a note: the peeper, stripper Lucille updates. Orders: go back to the house, run the canvassers, avoid the family.

Keyed up—glom the pervert file. Dog stuff/B&E/Peeping Tom, see what jumped:

A German shepherd-fucking Marine. Doctor "Dog": popped for shooting his daughter up with beagle pus. Dog killers—none fit my man's specs. Dog fuckers, dog suckers, dog beaters, dog worshipers, a geek who chopped his wife while dressed up as Pluto. Panty sniffers, sink shitters, masturbators—lingerie jackoffs only. Faggot burglars, transvestite break-ins, "Rita Hayworth"—Gilda gown, dyed bush hair, caught blowing a chloroformed toddler. The right age—but a jocker cut his dick off, he killed himself, a full-drag

San Quentin burial. Peepers: windows, skylights, roofs—the roof clowns a chink brother act. No watchdog choppers, the geeks read passive, caught holding their puds with a whimper. Darryl Wishnick, a cute MO: peep, break, enter, rape, watchdogs subdued by goofball-laced meat—too bad he kicked from syph in '56. One flash: peepers played passive, my guy killed badass canines.

No jumps.

5:45—keyed up, hungry. Rick's Reef the ticket—maybe Diskant on TV.

I drove over, wolfed bar pretzels. TV news: Chavez Ravine, traffic deaths, the Red.

Boost the volume:

"... and so I'm withdrawing for personal reasons. Thomas Bethune will be re-elected by default, which I fervently hope will not guarantee the facilitation of the Chavez Ravine land grab. I will continue to protest this travesty as a private citizen. I ..."

No more appetite—I took off.

Nowhere to go—just a cruise. South—some magnet pulled me.

Figueroa, Slauson, Central. A gray cop Plymouth behind me—say IAD, Exley ordered. I gunned it—adiós, maybe tail car.

Peeper turf—nightclubs, fuck flops. Bido Lito's, Klub Zamboanga, Club Zombie—low roofs, good for climbing. Lucky Time Motel, Tick Tock Motel. Easy peeping: roof access, weeds shoulder high. A brain click: catch Lester Lake at the Tiger Room.

U-turn, check the rearview, shit—a gray Plymouth cut off.

IAD or Narco? Goons keeping tabs?

Side streets—dawdling evasive—Lester's set closed at 8:00 sharp. Lester Lake: tenant, informant. Snitch duty cheap—he owed me.

Fall '52:

A call from Harry Cohn, movie kingpin. My "Enforcer" tag intrigued him; he figured "Klein" made me a Jewboy. A shvartze crooner was banging his girlfriend—clip him for ten grand.

I said no.

Mickey Cohen said no.

Cohn called Jack Dragna.

I knew I'd get the job—no refusal rights. Mickey: a taste for light poon don't rate death—but Jack insists.

I called Jack: this is petty shit, don't set a standard. Muscle Lester Lake—don't kill him.

Jack said *you* muscle him.

Jack said take the Vecchio brothers.

Jack said take the nigger someplace, cut his vocal cords—

Gulp—one split second—

"Or I'll nail you for Trombino and Brancato. I'll drag your whore sister's name through the mud."

I grabbed Lester Lake at his crib: get cut or get killed—you call it. Lester said, cut, fast, please. The Vecchios showed—Touch packed a scalpel. A few drinks to loosen things up—knockout drops for Lester.

Anesthesia—Lester moaned for Mama. I hustled a disbarred doctor over—surgery in exchange for no abortion charge. Lester healed up; Harry Cohn found a new girlfriend: Kim Novak.

Lester's voice went baritone to tenor—he chased jig poon strictly now. Touch brought boyfriends to hear him.

Lester said he owed me. Our deal: a flop at my shine-only dive—reduced rent for good information. Success: he talked spook to the spooks and snitched bookies.

The club—a tiger-striped facade, a tiger-tux doorman. Inside: tiger-fur walls, tiger-garb drink girls. Lester Lake on stage, belting "Blue Moon."

I grabbed a booth, grabbed a tigress—"Dave Klein to see Lester." She zipped backstage—slot machines clanged out the doorway. Lester: mock-humble bows, bum applause.

House lights on, dig it: jungle bunnies sprawled in tiger-fur booths. Lester right there, holding a plate.

Chicken and waffles—popping grease. "Hello, Mr. Klein. I was gonna call you."

"You're short on the rent."

He sat down. "Yeah, and you slumlords cut a man no slack. Could be worse, though. You could be a Jew slumlord."

Eyes our way. "I always meet you in public. What do people figure we're doing?"

"Nobody never asks, but I figure they figure you still collect bets for Jack Woods. I'm a betting man, so I'd say that's it. And speaking of Jack, he was collecting your rents this afternoon, which made me want to call you before he leaned on me like he leaned on that poor sucker down the hall."

"Help me out and I'll let you slide."

"You mean you asks, I answers."

"No. First you get rid of that slop, then I ask and you answer."

A tiger girl passed—Lester dumped his plate and swiped a shot glass. A gulp, a belch: "So ask."

"Let's start with burglars."

"Okay, Leroy Coates, out on parole and spending money. Wayne Layne, boss pad creeper, pimping his wife to make the nut on his habit. Alfonzo Tyrell—"

"My guy's white."

"Yeah, but I keep to the dark side of town. Last time *I* heard of a white burglar was never."

"Fair enough, but I'd call this guy a psycho. He cut up two Dobermans, stole nothing but silverware, then trashed some family-type belongings. Run with it."

"Run with it nowheres. I know nothing 'bout a crazy man like that, 'cept you don't have to be Einstein to figure he's bent on that family. Wayne Layne shits in washing machines, and he's as crazy a B&E man as I care to be acquainted with."

"Okay, peepers then."

"Say what?"

"Peeping Toms. Guys who get their kicks looking in windows. I've got peeper reports nailed at my burglary location *and* all over the Southside—hot-sheet motels and jazz clubs."

"I'll ask around, but you sure ain't getting much for your month's rent."

"Let's try Wardell Henry Knox. He sold mary jane and worked as a bartender at jazz joints, presumably down here."

"Presumably, 'cause white clubs wouldn't hire him. And *was* is correct, 'cause he got hisself snuffed a few months ago. Person or persons unknown, just in case you wants to know who did it."

Jukebox blare close—jerk the cord—instant silence. "I know he was murdered."

Indignant niggers mumbling—fuck them. Lester: "Mr. Klein, your questions are getting pretty far afield. I'll guess a motive on Wardell, though."

"I'm listening."

"Pussy. Ol' Wardell had hound blood. He was the righteous fuckin' pussy hound supreme. If it moved, he'd poke it. He'd ream it, steam it, banana cream it. He must've had a million enemies. He'd fuck a woodpile on the off chance there was a snake inside. He liked to taste it and baste it, but he'd never waste it. He—"

"Enough, Jesus Christ."

Lester winked. "Ask me something I might know something about."

In close. "The Kafesjian family. You've got to know more than I do."

Lester talked low. "I know they're tight with your people. I know they only sell to Negroes and what you'd call anybody but square white folks, 'cause that's the way Chief Parker likes things. Pills, weed, horse, they are *the* number-one suppliers in Southside L.A. I know they lend money and take the vig out in snitch information, you know, independent pushers they can rat to the LAPD, 'cause that is part of their bargain with your people. Now, I *know* J.C. and Tommy hire these inconspicuous-type Negro guys to move their stuff, with Tommy riding herd on them. And you want crazy?—try Tommy the K. He hangs out with the suedes at Bido Lito's and gets up and plays this godawful tenor sax whenever they let him, which is frequently, 'cause who wants to refuse a crazy man, even a little skinny twerp like Tommy? Tommy is craaazy. He is bad fuckin' juju. He is the Kafesjian muscle guy, and I heard he is righteous good with a knife. I also heard he will do anything to ingratiate hisself with Narco. I heard he clipped this drunk driver who hit-and-ran this Narco guy's daughter."

Craaazy. "That's all?"

"Ain't it enough?"

"What about Tommy's sister, Lucille? She's a geek, she parades around naked at her pad."

"I say say what and so what. Too bad Wardell's dead, he'd probably want to poke her. Maybe she likes it dark, like her brother. I'd poke her myself, 'cept last time I tried white stuff I got my neck sliced. You should know, you was there."

Jukebox trills—Lester himself—somebody put the plug back in. "They let you put your own songs in there?"

"Chick and Touch Vecchio do. They're more sentimental 'bout that old neck-slicin' time than slumlord Dave Klein. Long as they run the Southside slots and vending shit for Mr. Cohen, Lester Lake's rendition of 'Harbor Lights' will be on that jukebox. Which gives me pause, 'cause the past two weeks or so these new out-of-town-lookin' guys been working the hardware, which might bode bad for ol' Lester."

"Those haaarbor lights"—pure schmaltz. "Mickey should watch it, the Feds might be checking out the machinery down here. And did anyone ever tell you you sound like a homo? Like Johnnie Ray out of work?"

Howling: "Yeah, my ladyfriends. I make them think I gots queer tendencies, then they works that much harder to set me straight. Touch V. comes in with his sissy boys, and I studies his mannerisms. He brings in this bottle-blond sissy, it was like getting a righteous college degree in fruitness."

I yawned—tiger stripes spun crazy.

"Get some sleep, Mr. Klein. You look all bushed."

Fuck sleep—that magnet was still pulling me.

I zigzagged east and south—no gray Plymouths on my ass. Western Avenue—peeper turf—whore motels, no addresses to work off. Western and Adams—whore heaven—girls jungled up by Cooper's Donuts. Colored, Mex, a few white—slit-leg gowns, pedal pushers. Jump start: Lucille's hip huggers, slashed and jizzed on.

Brain jump:

Western and Adams—University Division. University Vice, hooker ID stashes there: alias files, john lists, arrest-detention reports. Lucille smiling whorish, Daddy's blood on her claws—jump to her selling it for kicks.

Big jump—odds against it.

I rolled anyway—

Uny Station, brace the squad whip—that whore stuff, a mishmash:

Loose mug shots, report carbons. Names: whores, whore monikers, men detained/booked with whores. Three cabinets' worth of paper in no discernible order.

Skimming through:

No "Kafesjian," no Armenian names—an hour wasted—no surprise—most hookers got bailed out behind monikers. Punch line: if Lucille whored, *if* she got popped—she'd probably call Dan Wilhite to chill things. 114 detention reports, 18 white girls—no physical stats matched Lucille. A half-ass system—most cops let whore reports slide, the girls always repeated. John lists: no Luce, Lucille, Lucy white girl listed—no Armenian surnames.

More mugs—some with neckboard numbers and printing: real names, john names, dates. Shine girls, Mexicans, whites—99.9 percent skank. Goosebumps: Lucille—profile, full face—no neckboard, no printing.

Go, do it: recheck all paper. Three go-rounds—zero, zilch, bupkis. No clicks back to Lucille.

Just one mug strip.

Call it lost paperwork.

Say Dan Wilhite yanked the paper—the mugs got overlooked.

Guess burglar = peeper = Lucille K. john.

I wrote it up, a note to Junior:

Check all stationhouse john/prostie lists—try for information on Lucille's tricks.

Goosebumps: that godawful family.

I hit the Bureau, dropped the note on Junior's desk. Midnight: Ad Vice empty.

"Klein?"

Dan Wilhite across the hall. I called him over—*my* squadroom.

"So?"

"So, I'm sorry for the run-in with Kafesjian."

"I'm not looking for apologies. I'll say it again: so?"

"So it's a tight situation, and I'm trying to be reasonable. I didn't ask for this job, and I don't want it."

"I know, and your Sergeant Stemmons already apologized for your behavior. He also asked for a tally of perpetrators J.C. and his people have informed on, which I refused to give him. Don't ask again, because all notations pertaining to the Kafesjians have been destroyed. *So?*"

"So it's like that. And the question should be 'So what does Exley want?' "

Wilhite crowded up, hands on hips. "Tell me what you think this 459 is. I think it's a dope mob warning. I think Narco is best suited to handle it, and I think you should tell Chief Exley that."

"I don't think so. I think the burglar's hinked on the family, maybe Lucille specifically. It might be a window peeper who's been working Darktown lately."

"Or maybe it's a crazy-man act. A rival mob using terror tactics."

"Maybe, but I don't think so. I'm not really a case man, but—"

"No, you're a thug with a law degree—"

FROST/EASY/DON'T MOVE.

"—and I regret calling you into this mess. Now I've heard that that Fed probe *is* going to happen. I've heard Welles Noonan has auditors checking tax returns—my own and some of my men. That probably means that he knows about Narco and the Kafesjians. We've all taken gratuities, we've all got expensive items we can't explain, so—"

Sweating on me, hot tobacco breath.

"—you do your duty to the Department. You've got your twenty in, I don't and my men don't. You can practice law and suck up to Mickey Cohen, and we can't. *You* owe us, because *you* let Sanderline Johnson jump. Welles Noonan has got this Southside hard-on because *you* compromised his prizefight job. The heat on my men is because of *you*, so *you* square things. Now, J.C. and Tommy are crazy. They've never dealt with hostile police agencies, and if the Feds start pressing them they'll go out of control. I want them quieted down. Stall this bullshit investigation of yours, feed Exley whatever you have to. Just get out of that family's way as quick as you can."

Crowded, elbowed in. "I'll try."

"Do it. Make like it's a paying job. Make like I think you pushed Johnson out the window."

"Do you?"

"You're greedy enough, but you're not that stupid."

Crowd him back, walk—my legs fluttered. A clerk's slip on my desk: "P. Bondurant called. Said to call H. Hughes at Bel-Air Hotel."

8

"... AND MY man Pete told me about your splendid perform-ance vis-à-vis the Morton Diskant matter. Did you know that Diskant is a member of four organizations that have been clas-sified as Communist fronts by the California State Attorney General's Office?"

Howard Hughes: tall, lanky. A hotel suite, two flunkies: Bradley Milteer, lawyer; Harold John Miciak, goon.

7:00 A.M.—distracted, a plan brewing: frame some geek for the Kafesjian job.

"No, Mr. Hughes. I didn't know that."

"Well, you should. Pete told me your methods were rough, and you should know that Diskant's record justified those methods. Among other things, I'm seeking to establish myself as an inde-pendent motion picture producer. I'm planning on producing a series of films depicting aerial warfare against the Communists, and a major theme of those films will be the end justifies the means."

Milteer: "Lieutenant Klein is also an attorney. If he accepts your offer, you'll receive an additional interpretation of the con-tractual aspects."

"I haven't practiced much law, Mr. Hughes. And I'm pretty busy right now."

Miciak coughed. Tattooed hands—zoot gang stuff. "This ain—*isn't* a lawyer job. Pete Bondurant's got his plate full, so—"

Hughes, interrupting: "'Surveillance' sums this assignment up best, Lieutenant. Bradley, will you elaborate?"

Milteer, prissy: "Mr. Hughes has a young actress named Glenda Bledsoe signed to a full-service contract. She was living in one of his guest homes and was being groomed to play lead roles in his Air Force films. She infringed on her contract by moving out of the guest home and by leaving script sessions without asking permission. She's currently playing the female lead in a non-union horror film shooting in Griffith Park. It's called *Attack of the Atomic Vampire*, so you can imagine the quality of the production."

Hughes, prissy: "Miss Bledsoe's contract allows her to make one non-Hughes film per year, so I cannot violate the contract for that. There is, however, a morality clause that we can utilize. If we can prove Miss Bledsoe to be an alcoholic, criminal, narcotics addict, Communist, lesbian, or nymphomaniac, we can violate her contract and get her blackballed from the film industry on that basis. Our one other avenue is to secure proof that she knowingly took part in publicizing non-Hughes performers outside of her work for this ridiculous monster film. Lieutenant, your job would be to surveil Glenda Bledsoe with an eye toward securing contract-violating information. Your fee would be three thousand dollars."

"Have you explained the situation to her, Mr. Milteer?"

"Yes."

"How did she react?"

"Her reply was 'Fuck you.' Your reply, Lieutenant?"

Close to "No"—freeze it—think:

Hush-Hush said Mickey C. bankrolled that movie.

"Guest home" meant "fuck pad" meant Howard Hughes left to choke his own chicken.

Think:

Glom some Bureau guys for tail work. Glom a slush fund: Kafesjian frame cash.

JEW HIM UP.

"Five thousand, Mr. Hughes. I can recommend cheaper help, but I can't neglect my regular duties for any less than that."

Hughes nodded; Milteer whipped out a cash roll. "All right, Lieutenant. This is a two-thousand-dollar retainer, and I'll expect reports at least every other day. You can call me here at the Bel-Air. Now, is there anything else you need to know about Miss Bledsoe?"

"No, I'll find an in on the movie crew."

Hughes stood up. I laid on the glad hand: "I'll nail her, sir."

A limp shake—Hughes wiped his hand on the sly.

New money—spend it smart. Think smart:

Nail Glenda Bledsoe fast. Let Junior carry some Kafesjian weight—hope his fuck-up string ended. Figure out that Dark-town tail, stay tailless.

Instinct: Exley wouldn't rat me on Johnson. Logic: he destroyed the coroner's file; I could rat him for a piece of Diskant. Instinct: call his Kafesjian fix PERSONAL. Instinct—call me bait—a bad cop sent out to draw heat.

Conclusions:

Number one: Call Wilhite and Narco more dangerous; call me a bent cop juking their meal ticket. Maybe the Fed grand jury blues upcoming: true bills, indictments. Rogue cops out of work then, one scapegoat: a lawyer-landlord with a sure police pension. Out-of-work killers, one target: me.

Number two: Find a burglar/pervert confessor—some geek to take my 459 fall. Palm squadroom bulls for leads; keep Junior on the case legit. No legit B&E man?—Joe Pervert buys the dive.

I drove over to Hollywood Station. No file-room clerk—I boosted "459 Cleared," "False Confessions," '49–'57. A 187 sheet on the board—the "Wino Will-o-the-Wisp." Perv stuff, nice—I grabbed a carbon.

Conclusion number three:

Call me still short of scared.

Griffith Park, the west road up—streams, small mountains. Steep turns, scrub-hill canyons—Movieland.

I pulled into a makeshift lot—vehicles parked tight. Shouts, picket signs bobbing way back. I hopped a flatbed, scoped the ruckus.

Union placard shakers—Chick Vecchio facing them off—the stiff-arm fungoo up close. A clearing, trailers, the set: cameras, a rocket ship half Chevy.

"Scab!" "Scab scum!"

Over, buck the line—"Police officer!" Punk pickets—they let me through, no grief. Chick greeted me—smiles, back slaps.

"Scab scum!" "Police collusion!"

We walked over to the trailers. Catcalls, no rocks—sob sisters. Chick: "You looking for Mickey? I'll bet he's got a nice envelope for you."

"He told you?"

"No, it's what my brother would call an 'inescapable conclusion to the cognoscenti.' Come on, a witness flies out the window with Dave Klein standing by. What's a card-carrying cogno supposed to think?"

"I think you almost did some union thumping."

"Hey, we should have called the old Enforcer. Seriously, you got ideas? Mickey's got a bad case of the shorts. You know any boys who won't cost us an arm and a leg?"

"Fuck it, let them picket."

"Uh-uh. They yell when we're shooting, which means scenes have to be redubbed, which costs money."

Someone, somewhere: "Cameras! Action!"

"Serious, Dave."

"Okay, call Fats Medina at the Main Street Gym. Tell him I said five sparring partners and a roadblock. Tell him you'll go fifty a man."

"For real?"

"Do it tonight, and you won't have union trouble tomorrow. Come on, I want to check out this movie."

Up to the set. Chick held a finger to his lips—scene in progress.

Two "actors" gesticulating. The spaceship close up: Chevy fins, Studebaker grille, Kotex-box launching pad.

Touch Vecchio: "Russian rocket ships have dropped atomic waste on Los Angeles—a plot to turn Angelenos into automatons susceptible to Communism! They have created a vampire virus! People have turned into monsters who devour their own families!"

His co-star—blond, padded crotch: "Family is the sacred concept that binds all Americans. We must stop this soul-usurping invasion whatever the cost!"

Chick, cupping a whisper: "The hoot is my brother's killed eight men, and he takes this noise serious. And feature—him and that bottle-blond fruitcake are porking in trailers every chance they get, *and* chasing chicken down at the Fern Dell toilets. You see that guy with the megaphone? That's Sid Frizell, the so-called director. Mickey hired him on the cheap, and to me he reads ex-con who couldn't direct a Mongolian cluster fuck. He's always talking to that guy Wylie Bullock, the cameraman, who at least has got a place to live, unlike most of the bums Mickey's hired. Feature: he hired the crew out of the slave markets down on skid row. They sleep on the set, like this is some kind of fucking hobo jungle. And the dialogue? Frizell—Mickey shoots him an extra sawbuck a day to be scriptwriter."

No Mickey, no women. Touch: "I would slay the highest echelon of the Soviet Secretariat to protect the sanctity of my family!"

Blondie: "I of course empathize. But first we must isolate the atomic waste before it seeps into the Hollywood Reservoir. Look at these wretched victims of the vampire virus!"

Cut to werewolf-mask extras hip-hopping. Hip, hop—T-Bird popped out of back pockets.

Sid Frizell: "Cut! I told you people to leave your wine back with your blankets and sleeping bags! And remember Mr. Cohen's order—no wine before your lunch break!"

A geek lurched into the spaceship. Touch squeezed Blondie's ass on the QT.

Frizell: "Five-minute break and no drinking!" Background noise: "Scab scum! Police puppets!"

No Glenda Bledsoe.

Touch oozed by the camera slow. "Hi, Dave. Looking for Mickey?"

"People keep asking me that."

"Well, it's an inescapable conclusion of the cognoscenti."

Chick winked. "He'll show up. He goes by this bakery to get week-old bread to make sandwiches with. Feature the cuisine we get: stale bread, stale doughnuts and this lunch meat sold out the back door at this slaughterhouse out in Vernon. I quit eating on the set when I caught fur on my baloney and cheese."

I laughed. Script talk: Blondie and an old geek dressed like Dracula.

Touch sighed. "Rock Rockwell is going to be such a big star. Listen, he's actually telling Elston Majeska how to interpret his lines. What does that imply to the cognoscenti?"

"Who's Elston Majeska?"

Chick: "He was some kind of silent-movie star over in Europe, and now Mickey gets him passes from this rest home. He's a junkie, so Mickey pays him off in this diluted H he gets cheap. Old Elston says his lines, shoots up and goes on a sugar jag. You ought to see him snarf those stale doughnuts."

Pops peeled a Mars Bar, weaving—Blondie grabbed his cape.

Touch, swooning: "One man sandwich with the works!"

Frizell: "Glenda to the set in five minutes!"

"When I met Mickey, he was clearing ten million a year. From that to this, Jesus Christ."

Chick: "Things come and go."

Touch: "The torch passes."

"Bullshit. Mickey got out of McNeil Island a year ago—and *nobody* has grabbed his old action. Is he scared? Four of his guys have gotten clipped, all unsolveds—and I mean *nobody* knows who did it. You guys are all the muscle he's got left, and I can't feature why you stick around. What's he got left, the Niggertown coin business? How much can he be turning on that?"

Chick shrugged. "So feature we been with Mickey a long time. Feature we don't like change. He's a scrapper, and scrappers get results sooner or later."

"Nice results. And Lester Lake told me some out-of-town guys are working the Southside coin."

Chick shrugged. Wino cheers and wolf whistles—Glenda Bledsoe in a pom-pom-girl outfit.

Feature:

Tall, lanky, honey blond. All legs, all chest—a grin said she never bought in. A little knock-kneed, big eyes, dark freckles. Pure something—maybe style, maybe juice.

Touch shot me details: "Glamorous Glenda. Rock and me are the only males on the set immune to her charms. Mickey discovered her working at Scrivner's Drive-In. He's smitten, Chick's smitten. Glenda and Rock play brother and sister. She's been infected with the vampire virus, and she puts the make on her own brother. She turns into a monster and sends Rock running off into the hills."

Frizell: "Actors on their marks! Camera! Action!"

Rock: "Susie, I'm your big brother. The vampire virus has stunted your moral growth, and you've still got two years to go at Hollywood High."

Glenda: "Todd, in times of historic struggle, the rules of the bourgeoisie don't apply."

A clinch, a kiss. Frizell: "Cut! It's a take! Print it!"

Rock broke the clinch. Whistles, cheers. A wino booed; Glenda flipped him the finger. Mickey C. ducked in a trailer, lugging groceries.

I eased around the set and tapped the door.

"Wine money not disbursed until six o'clock! The tsuris you stumblebums inflict! This is a motion picture location, not the Jesus Saves Rescue Mission!"

I opened the door, caught a flying bagel. Stale—I tossed it back.

"David Douglas Klein, the 'Douglas' a dead giveaway you are not of my kindred blood, you farshtinkener Dutch fuck. Refuse my food, but I doubt you will refuse the money Sam Giancana has transmitted to me for you."

Mickey tucked a wad under my holster. "Sammy says thank you. Sammy says damn good job on such short notice."

"It was too close to home, Mick. It caused me lots of trouble."

Mickey plopped into a chair. "Sammy doesn't care from your troubles. You of all people should know the ethos of that farshtinkener crazy cocksucker."

"He's supposed to care about *your* trouble."

"Which in his brutish spaghetti-bender fashion he does."

Glenda cheesecake—four walls' worth. "Let's say he miscalculated this time."

"As the song goes, 'I should care?'"

"You should care. Noonan's prizefight probe went out the window too, so now he's hot to get something going in Niggertown. If the Feds hit the Southside, they'll raid your coin locations. If I get a line on it I'll tell you, but I might not know. Sam put your last going business in real trouble."

Chick V. by the doorway; Mickey, cheesecake eyes. "David, such tsuris you predict, such tsuris I am nonplussed by. My desires are strictly to see district gambling get in, then retire to Galapagos and watch turtles fuck in the sun."

Laugh it out. "District gambling will never pass the State Legislature, and if it did, you'd never get a franchise. Bob Gallaudet is the only reputable politician who supports it, and he'll change his mind if he makes attorney general."

Chick coughed; Mickey shrugged. A permit on the door: "Parks-Recreation, Approval to Film." I squinted—"Robert Gallaudet," small print.

Laugh *that* out. "Bob let you film here for a campaign contribution. He's about to make DA, so you think a grand or two gets you the inside track on district gambling. Jesus, you must be shooting dope like old Dracula."

Pinups galore—Mickey blew them kisses. "The prom date I never had in 1931. I could guarantee her a corsage and many fine hours of Bury the Brisket."

"She reciprocate?"

"Tomorrow, maybe yes, but today she breaks my heart. Dinner tonight was already finalized, then Herman Gerstein called. His company is set to distribute my movie, and he needs Glenda to accompany his faygeleh heartthrob Rock Rockwell on a publicity date. Such tsuris—Herman is grooming that rump ranger for stardom apart from me, he's terrified the scandal rags will discover he takes his pleasure Greek. Such duplicity to lose her company, my comely brisketeer."

"Publicity date"—contract breaker. "Mickey, watch your coin biz. Remember what I told you."

"Go, David. Take a bagel for the road."

I walked out; Chick walked in. I checked my envelope—five G's.

A pay phone, two dimes: the DMV cop line, Junior.

Stats: Glenda Louise Bledsoe, 5´8˝, 125, blond/blue, DOB 8/3/29, Provo, Utah. California license since 8/46, five moving violations. '56 Chevrolet Corvette, red/white, Cal. DX 413. Address: 2489½ N. Mount Airy, Hollywood.

Junior at the Bureau—no luck—the Ad Vice clerk said he didn't check in. I left a message: buzz me at Stan's Drive-in.

I dawdled over, grabbed a space by the phone booth. Coffee, a burger—scan those file carbons.

Burglars, confessors—physical stats/MO/priors—I took notes. The Wino Will-o-the-Wisp—shit, still at large. Names, names, names—candidates for a psycho framee. Scribbling notes—distracted—flirty carhops, new money. Nagging me: a frame meant no payoff—no way to match Lucille and the burglar to WHY?

The phone—I ran, grabbed it. "Junior?"

"Yeah, the clerk said to call you."

Wary—not his style. "You got that note I left you, right?"

"Right."

"Right, and did you check the stationhouse whore files for paper on Lucille Kafesjian?"

"I'm working on it. Dave, I can't talk now. I'll—look, I'll call you later."

"The fuck later, you *jump* on that work—" CLICK—dead air.

Home, paperwork. Pissed at Junior—an erratic punk getting worse. Paperwork: Exley's Kafesjian report padded up fat. Lists next: potential Glenda tailers, potential pervert framees. Calls in: Meg—Jack Woods glommed our back rent. Pete B.: do Mr. Hughes solid, I convinced him you're not a Hebe. Calls out: Ad Vice, Junior's pad, no luck—find him, ream his insubordinate heart. My tailer list, bum luck holding—no men to start tonight. *My* job by default—a publicity date meant contract breaker.

Back to Hollywood: side streets, the freeway. No tails on me: dead sure. Up Gower, Mount Airy, left turn.

2489: courtyard bungalows—peach stucco. A carport—with a red and white Corvette snuggled in.

5:10—just dark. I parked close—courtyard/carport view.

Time dragged—the stakeout blues—piss in a cup, toss it, doze. Auto/foot traffic—light. 7:04—three cars at the curb.

Doors open, flashbulbs popping: Rock Rockwell—tuxedo, bouquet. A jog to the courtyard, back with Glenda—nice—a tight sweater dress. Bulb glare caught her patented Look—it's a joke and I know it. Zoom: all three cars U-turned southbound.

Rolling stakeout—four cars long—Gower, Sunset west. The Strip, Club Largo, three-car pile-out.

Valets swooped in, servile. More photos—Rockwell looked bored. I parked in the red and fixed my windshield: "Official Police Vehicle." The entourage hit the club.

I badged in, badged a Shriner off a bar stool. Turk Butler on stage—bistro belter supreme. Ringside: Rock, Glenda, scribes. Photo men by the exit—zoom lenses zoomed in.

Break that contract.

Dinner: club soda, pretzels. Easy eyeball work: Glenda talked, Rock sulked. The reporters ignored him—snore city.

Turk Butler off stage, chorus girls on. Glenda smoked and laughed. Big lungs on the dancers—Glenda pulled her sweater up for chuckles. Rock hit the sauce—whiskey sours.

A club hop at ten sharp—across Sunset on foot to the Crescendo. Another bar stool, eyeball surveillance: pure Glenda. Showstopper Glenda—odd wisps of Meg, and her own SOMETHING.

Midnight—a dash for the cars—I tailed the convoy brazen close. Back to Glenda's pad, sidewalk arc lights: a dud goodnight kiss caught on film.

The newsman took off; Glenda waved. Quiet out—voices carried.

Rock: "Hell, now I've got no wheels."

Glenda: "Take mine, and bring Touch back with you. Say two hours?"

Rock grabbed her keys and ran—gleeful. The Vette peeled out burning rubber—Glenda winced. "Bring Touch back with you" hit funny—tail him.

Gower south, Franklin east. Sparse traffic—still no tails on *me*. North on Western, say a movie set run—Mickey's permit kept the park road open.

Los Feliz, left turn, Fern Dell—streams and glades before the Griffith Park hills. Brake lights blinked—fuck—Fern Dell—Vice cops called it Cocksuckers' Paradise.

He parked—rush hour—cigarette tips red in the dark. I swung right and stopped—my beams on Rock and a cute young quiff.

I killed my lights, cracked the window. Close—I caught the proposition:

"Hi."

"Hi."

"I …I think fall is the best time in L.A., don't you?"

"Yeah, sure. Listen, I just borrowed a *really* nice car. We could maybe make last call at the Orchid Room, then go someplace. I've got some time to kill before I pick my boy—I mean somebody up."

"You don't mince words."

"I don't mince period. Come on, say yes."

"Nix, sweetie. You're big and brusque, which I like, but the last big brusque guy I said yes to turned out to be a deputy sheriff."

"Oh, come on."

"Nix, nyet, nein and no. Besides, I heard Administrative Vice has been operating Fern Dell."

Wrong—Ad Vice never popped fruits. Outside chance— gung-ho Junior, Vice cowboy.

Rock—"Thanks for the memories"—match flare, his cigarette lit. Prowling now—easy to track—I watched the tip glow queer to queer.

Time wheezed, a bum soundtrack: sex moans out in the woods. An hour, an hour ten—Rock walked back zipping his fly.

Zoom—the Vette peeled. I followed slow—no traffic—call the set his destination. A roadblock out of nowhere—baseball-bat men waved him through.

Truck headlights approaching—I backed up and watched.

Brake squeals—a big flatbed—picket clowns in back. A spotlight flashed—bright white blindness on the target.

Goons hit the truck swinging—nail-studded Louisville Sluggers. The windshield exploded—a man stumbled out belching glass. The driver ran—a nail shot took his nose off.

The bed gate crashed—goons went in close—ribcage work. Fats Medina dragged a guy by the hair—his scalp came off.

No screams—wrong—why no sound—

Back to Fern Dell, down to Glenda's. No screams—weird—then my pulse quit banging my ears so I could hear.

Wait the boys out: "Rock," "Touch"—the nance type, this eight-notch killer. Suspicious: 2:00 A.M., a B-movie siren set for hostess.

One courtyard light on—hers. I tapped the two-way, flipped bands to kill boredom. Dispatch calls—the Bureau frequency—voices.

Hurwitz fur-job talk—Robbery men. Make the voices: Dick Carlisle, Mike Breuning—Dudley Smith strongarms. No trace on the furs; Dud wanted fences braced *hard*. Crackle: station-to-station interference. Breuning: Dud pulled Johnny Duhamel off the Mobster Squad—a scary kick-ass ex-fighter. More static—I flipped dials—a liquor-store heist on La Brea.

The Vette hit the carport; the boys hit Glenda's pad nuzzled up.

One ring—the door open and shut.

Figure access.

The courtyard proper—too risky. Nix the roof—no way to get up. Behind the bungalows—maybe a window to peep.

Risk it—worth it—juicy hearsay.

I walked over, counted back doors down—one, two, three—hers locked tight. One window—curtains cracked—eyes to the glass:

A dark bedroom, a connecting door ajar.

Press the glass, slide it up. Open—no shimmy, no squeak. Vault the sill: up and in.

Smells: cotton, stale perfume. Dark going gray—I saw a bed and bookshelves. Voices—hug the door—listen:

Glenda: "Well, there is a precedent."

Touch: "Not a successful one, sweetie."

Rockwell: "Marie 'the Body' McDonald. A from-nowhere career, then this kidnapping out of nowhere. The papers smelled publicity stunt quicksville. I think—"

Glenda: "It wasn't realistic, that's why. Her hair wasn't even mussed. Remember, Mickey Cohen is bankrolling our movie. He's hot for me, so the press will think gangland intrigue right off. Howard Hughes used to keep me, so we've got him for a supporting play—"

Touch: " 'Keep,' what a euphemism."

Rock: "What's a euphemism?"

Touch: "Lucky you're gorgeous, 'cause you'd never make it on brains."

Glenda: "Cut it out, and listen. I'm wondering what the police will think. It's not a kidnapping for ransom, because frankly nobody would pay good money to get Rock and I out of trouble. What I'm think—"

Touch: "The police will think revenge on Mickey or something, and Mickey won't know a thing. The police love to bother Mickey. Bothering Mickey is a favorite activity of the Los Angeles Police Department. And you two will be *good*. Georgie Ainge will slap you around just a little bit more than a smidgin, for realism's sake. The police will buy it, so just don't worry. You'll both be kidnap victims, and you'll both get lots of publicity."

Rock: "Method acting."

Glenda: "It compromises Howard, the creep. He'd never violate the contract of a beautiful kidnap victim."

Touch: "Tell true, sweetie. Was he hung?"

Glenda: "Hung like a cashew."

They all howled. The real howler: fake kidnaps *always* bombed.

A doorway crack—I pressed up, squinted. Glenda—robe, wet hair: "He talked about airplanes to get himself excited. He called my breasts my propellers."

More laughs—Glenda edged out of my light. Needle scratches, Sinatra—wait the tune out for one more look.

No luck—just "Ebb Tide" done very slow. Through the bedroom, out the window, thinking crazy: *Don't snitch her.*

9

MONSTERS:

Charles Issler, confessor—front-page-hot female snuffs. "Hit me! Hit me!"—known to bite Homicide bulls who wouldn't oblige.

Michael Joseph Krugman, confessor—the Jesus Christ 187. His motive—revenge—Jesus fucked his wife.

Swirling:

Beaucoup confessors—find a patsy in LAPD file print. Some INSTINCT working through—

Donald Fitzhugh—queer snuff confessor; Thomas Mark Janeway—kiddie molestations strictly. That INSTINCT THING worked me over—almost a taunt. The Wino Will-o-the-Wisp: strangler/mutilator/stumblebum slayer. No hard candidates—

I woke up. THAT INSTINCT big:

The Kafesjians *knew* who trashed their pad—if I framed some geek they'd fuck things up.

Sweaty sheets/sweaty files/that rap sheet I glommed late:

George Sidney Ainge, aka "Georgie." White male, DOB 11/28/22. Pimp convictions '48, '53—fourteen months County time total. Gun sale rousts '56, '7, '8—no convictions. Last known address 1219 S. Dunsmuir, L.A. Vehicle: '51 Caddy Eldo, QUR 288.

Touch to Glenda: "Georgie Ainge will slap you around just a little bit more than a smidgin."

I shaved, showered, dressed. Glenda smiled, saying stall things for now.

The Bureau, an Exley memo waiting: "Kafesjian/459—report in full." 8:00, no daywatch men in yet—no potential Georgie Ainge skinny.

Coffee—overdue. Some DA called—that botched bookie raid—I shitted him lawyer to lawyer. Junior walking: up the side stairs, furtive. I whistled—long and shrill.

He walked over. I shut the door, shut my voice in: "Never hang up on me or get cute like that again. One more time and I'm submitting a transfer request that will ruin you in the Bureau so fast—"

"Dave—"

"Dave shit. Stemmons, you fucking toe the line. You obey my orders, you do what I tell you to do. *Now*, did you check the stationhouse files for paper on Lucille Kafesjian?"

"N-no listings, I ch-checked all around"—nervous, hinky.

Change-up: "Have you been hotdogging queers in Fern Dell Park?"

"W-what?"

"Some quiff said Ad Vice was operating the park, which we both know is bullshit. I repeat, were you—"

Hands up—placating me. "Okay, okay, guilty. I owed a favor to this old student of mine at the Academy. He's working Holly-wood Vice and he's swamped, the squad boss has him detached to that wino-killing job. I just made a few collars and let him do the booking. Look, I'm sorry if I didn't go by the rules."

"Learn the fucking rules."

"Sure, Dave, sorry."

Shaky, sweaty—I gave him a handkerchief. "Have you heard of a pimp named Georgie Ainge? He sells guns on the side."

Head bobs, eager to please. "I heard he's a rape-o. Some squad-room guy told me he likes gigs where he gets to hurt women."

"Wipe your goddamn face, you're sweating up my floor."

Junior quick-drawed—the gun bobbed at *me*. Quick—slap him—my law school ring drew blood.

White knuckles on his piece. Brains—he pointed it down.

"Stay angry, tough guy. We've got an outside job, and I want you pissed."

Separate cars, let him stew with half the picture: good guy/bad guy, no arrest. Stay pissed: I've got a moonlight gig going, a fake kidnap might deep-six it. Junior—"Sure, Dave, sure"—eager beaver.

I got there first—a mock chateau—four floors, maybe ten units per. A '51 Eldo at the curb—a match to the Ainge rap sheet.

I checked the mail slots: G. Ainge, 104. Junior's Ford hit the curb—two wheels on the sidewalk. I beelined down the hall.

Junior caught up. I winked; he winked—half twitch. I pushed the buzzer.

The door opened a crack. Ear tug—cue the bad guy.

Junior: "LAPD, open up!"—wrong—I signaled kick it in.

The door swung wide. Right there: a fat lowlife, arms raised. Old tracks—hold for the "I'm Clean" pitch.

"I'm clean, Officers. I got me a nice little job, and I got me Nalline test results that prove I don't geez no more. I'm still on County probation, and my PO knows I switched from horse to Silver Satin."

I smiled. "We're sure you're clean, Mr. Ainge. May we come in?"

Ainge stood aside; Junior closed the door. The flop: Murphy bed, wine bottles tossed helter-skelter. TV, magazines: *Hush-Hush*, girlie stuff.

Junior: "Kiss the wall, shitbird."

Ainge spread out. I scoped a *Hush-Hush* cover: Marie "the Body" McDonald, fake kidnap supreme.

Georgie ate wallpaper; Junior frisked him slow. Page two: some boyfriend drove Marie to Palm Springs and stashed her in an old mining shack. A ransom demand—her agent called the FBI. Satire: stage your own publicity kidnap, five easy steps.

Junior dropped Ainge—a kidney shot—not bad.

Georgie sucked wind. I skimmed the mags—bondage smut— women gagged and harnessed.

Junior kicked Ainge prone. A blonde looked sort of like Glenda.

Out loud: "'Lesson number one: call Hedda Hopper in advance. Lesson number two: don't hire kidnappers from Central Casting. Lesson number three: don't pay your publicist with marked ransom money.' Whose idea, Georgie? You or Touch Vecchio?"

No answer.

I flashed two fingers: GO FULL. Junior slammed kidney shots; Georgie Ainge drooled bile.

Kneel down close. "Tell us about it. It's not going to happen, but tell us anyway. Tell us nice and we won't tell your PO. Stay snotty and we'll pop you for possession of heroin."

Gurgles, "Fuck you."

Two fingers/GO FULL.

Rabbit shots—strong—Ainge curled up fetal-style. A punch hit the floor—Junior yelped and grabbed his piece.

I snatched it, worked the chamber, popped the clip.

Junior—"Dave, Jesus!"—farewell, tough guy.

Ainge groaned—Junior kicked him—ribs cracked.

"OKAY! OKAY!"

I hauled him into a chair; Junior grabbed his gun back. Silver Satin on the bed—toss it over.

Chugalug—Ainge coughed, burped blood. Junior crawled for his clip—hands and knees.

"Whose idea?"

Ainge—"How'd you tumble?"—wincing.

"Never mind. I asked you, 'Whose idea?'"

"Touch, Touch V., his idea. The deal was to goose his bun boy's career, with that blond cooze along for some cheesecake. Touch said three hundred and no rough stuff. Listen, I just took the job to get a taste."

Junior: "A taste of horse? I thought you were clean, shitbird."

"'Shitbird' went out with vaudeville. Hey, you get your badge in a cereal box?"

I held Junior back. "A taste of what?"

Giggles. "I don't sell guns no more, I don't procure females for purposes of prostitution. I switched from H to jungle juice, so my tastes are none of—"

"*A taste of what?*"

"Shit, I just wanted to bust up that Glenda cooze."

I froze—Ainge kept talking—rank wine breath.

"... you know, I just wanted to put the hurt on something Howard Hughes put the boots to. I got fired at Hughes Aircraft during the war, so you could maybe call that Glenda cunt my payback. Va-va-voom, that is some fine piece of—"

I kicked his chair over, threw the TV at his head. He ducked—tubes popped, exploded. I grabbed Junior's gun—aimed, fired—clicks, no fucking clip, fuck me.

Ainge snaked under the bed. Soft, talking nice:

"Look, you think that Glenda woman's My Fair Lady? Look, I *know* her, she used to whore for this pimp Dwight Gilette. I can hand her up to you on a *guaranteed gas-chamber bounce.*"

"Gilette"—vague—a 187 unsolved. I unloaded my own piece—safety valve.

Ainge, soft: "Look, I sold guns then. Glenda knew that. Gilette was slapping her around, so she bought a .32 to protect herself. I don't know, something happened, so Glenda shot Gilette. She shot him, and she ended up taking his knife away from him. She fucking cut him too, and then she sold me the gun back. I've got it stashed, you know, I figured maybe some day, some reason, maybe it's got prints on it, I was gonna threaten her with it on the kidnap thing. Touch, he don't know about it, *but you can make this a fucking gas-chamber job."*

Make the case:

'55, '56—Dwight Gilette, mulatto pimp, dead at his pad. Highland Park dicks handled it: fatal shots, no gun found—the stiff stabbed postmortem. Knife man Gilette—aka "Blue Blade." Forensics: two blood types made; female hair and bone chips found. Hypothesis: knife fight with a whore, some hooker shot/ shanked a skilled blade freak.

Bugs up my spine.

Ainge kept talking—gibberish—I didn't hear it. Junior scribbled up his notebook fast.

Fast—don't think why—find the gun.

One room—an easy toss—closet, dresser, cupboards. Ainge blabbing non-stop—Junior coaxing him out from under the bed. Tossing hard, tossing zero: skin mags, probation forms, rubbers. Topsy-turvy glimpses: evidence-prof Junior stacking pages.

No gun.

"Dave."

Ainge cozied up—a fresh bottle half guzzled. Junior: "Dave, we've got ourselves a homicide."

"No. It's too old, and there's just this geek's word."

"Dave, come on."

"No. Ainge, where's the gun?"

No answer.

"Tell me where the gun is, goddamn it."

No answer.

"Ainge, give up the fucking gun."

Junior, quick hand signals: LET ME WORK HIM.

Work shit—grab his notebook. Skim it—Georgie's pitch town—details, approximate dates. No locate on the gun—call odds on latent prints thirty to one.

Junior, flexing his mean streak: "Dave, give me my notebook back."

I shoved it at him. "Wait outside."

This X-ray stare—not bad for a punk.

"Stemmons, wait outside."

Junior eeeased out, tough-guy slow. I locked the door and fixed on Ainge.

"Give up the gun."

"Not on your life. I was talking scared then, but now I figure different. You want my interpretation?"

Brass knucks, get ready.

"My interpretation is the kid thinks a murder beef for the Glenda cooze is a good idea, but for some reason you don't. I also know that if I give up that gun it's a probation violation vis-à-fucking-vis harboring contraband items. You know what a 'hole card' is? You know—"

On him—knucks downstairs/upstairs—flab rippers/broken face bones/fear-of-God time:

"No kidnapping. Not a word to Touch or Rockwell. You don't talk about Glenda Bledsoe, you don't go near her. You don't give that gun up to my partner or anyone else."

Coughs/moans/sputters trying to yes me. Bloody phlegm on my hands; shock waves up my knuck arm. I kicked through TV rubble getting out.

Junior on the sidewalk, smoking. No preamble: "We pop the Bledsoe woman for Gilette. Bob Gallaudet will grant Ainge immunity on the gun charge. Dave, she's Howard Hughes' ex-girlfriend. This is a big major case."

Head throbs. "It's shit. Ainge told me the gun story was a lie. What we've got is a three-year-old homicide with one convicted-felon hearsay witness. *It's shit.*"

"No, Ainge lied *to you.* I think there is a gun extant."

"Gallaudet would never file. I'm an attorney, you're not. Believe me."

"Dave, just listen."

"No, forget it. You were damn good in there, but it's over. We came to break up an impending felony, and—"

"And protect this moonlight job of yours."

"Right, which I'll kick back to you on."

"Which is unreported income in violation of departmental regs."

Seeing red: "There's no case. We're on the Kafesjian job, which is a major case, because Exley's got a hard-on for it. If you want juice, play tight with me on that. Maybe we soft-pedal it, maybe we don't. We have to work angles on that case to protect the Department, and I don't want you going off halfcocked on some stale-bread pimp snuff."

"A homicide is a homicide. And you know what I think?"

Smug little shitbird. "What?"

"That you want to protect that woman."

Seeing red, seeing black.

"And I think that for a cop on the take, you take pretty small. If you want to steal, steal big. If I ever broke the regs, I wouldn't start at the bottom."

PURE BLACK—knucks out.

Pure rabbit—Junior tripped into his car. Pulling out, window down: "You owe me for the way you patronize me! You owe me! And I might collect damn soon!"

RED BLACK RED.

Junior fishtailed straight through a red light.

I drove to the set just to see her; I figured one look would say yes or no.

Big blue eyes looked right through me—I couldn't even guess. She acted; she laughed; she talked—her voice gave nothing away. I stuck to the trailers and framed her in longshots—Miss Vampire/ maybe pimp slasher. A change of costume, demure stuff to low-cut gown—

Shoulder-blade scars. ID them: slash marks, one puncture wound/bone notch. Call it à la *Hush-Hush*:

HOOKER/ACTRESS MURDERS HALF-BREED PIMP! AIRPLANE MOGUL SMITTEN! ROGUE COP STEPS FROM CLOVER TO SHIT!

I watched her act, watched her subtle-goof the whole silly business. Dark came on, I just watched, no one bugged the skulking stage-door Johnny.

Rain shut things down—I would have watched all night otherwise.

A pay-phone stint, zero luck: no Exley at the Bureau, no Junior to wheedle or threaten. Wilhite, my feelers out—not at Narco, not at home. Down to the Vine Street Hody's: paperwork, dinner.

I wrote out two Exley reports: full disclosure and whore Lucille omitted—insurance if I swung Wilhite's way. That frame brainstorm—nix it—Exley wouldn't bite, the Kafesjians made one big monkey wrench. Hard to concentrate—Junior hovered—taunting me with murderess Glenda.

Ex-whore Glenda; whore Lucille.

Rain blurred people outside. Hard to see faces, easy to im-agine them—easy to make women Glenda. A brunette looked in

the window—Lucille K. one split second. I banged the table getting up; she waved to a waitress, just some plain Jane.

Darktown—nowhere else to go.

Systematic:

No exact peeper locations—two divisions botched paperwork—no whore motel/jazz club addresses to work from. South
on Western, driving one-handed, one hand free to jot motel
names. Systematic: no tails on *me*, forty-one hot-sheet flops Adams
to Florence.

Jazz clubs, more confined: Central Avenue, southbound. Nineteen clubs, count bars in, boost the tally up to sixty-odd. Rain kept
foot traffic thin; neon signs hit hypnotic—half-second blips in my
windshield.

Rain fizzling—try the coffee-and-donuts routine.

A Cooper's stand on Central—whore heaven—I fed the girls
coffee and showed the Lucille pix. Big nos, one yes—a Western-
and-Adams girl stepping east. Her story: Lucille worked
"occasional"—tight pedal pushers—no street name, no truck
with other whores.

Pedal pushers—slashed/jacked off on—*my* burglar.

Midnight—half the clubs shut down. Neon blipped off; I
caught boss men locking their doors. Peeper/prowler questions—"Say what?"s straight across. The Lucille mugs—straight
deadpans.

1:00 A.M., 2:00 A.M.—shit police work. B-girls at bus stops
and cab stands—I talked Lucille with my brain revving Glenda.
More nos, more rain—I ducked into a diner.

A counter, booths. Packed—all spooks. Whispers, nudges—
niggers smelling Law. Two B-girl types in a front booth—hands
under the table furtive quick.

I joined them. One bolted—I jerked her back by the wrist.
Sitting beside me: a skanky high yellow. Bad juju percolating—I
could feel it.

"Dump your purses on the table."

Slow and cool: two pseudo-snakeskin bags turned out. Felony
tilt: tinfoil Benzedrine.

Change-up: "Okay, you're clean."

Darky: "Sheeeit!"

High Yellow: "Man, what you—?"

I flashed the Lucille pix. "Seen her?"

Purse debris zoomed back; High Yellow chased Bennies with coffee.

"*I said*, have you seen her?"

High Yellow: "No, but this other po-lice been—"

The dark girl shushed her—I felt the nudge.

"What 'other police'? And don't you lie to me."

High Yellow: " 'Nuther officer was aroun' asking questions 'bout that girl. He didn' have no photographs, but he had this, this ... po-lice sketch, he called it. Very same girl, good picture if you asks me."

"Was he a young man? Sandy-haired, late twenties?"

"That's right. He had this big pom-po-dour that he kept playin' with."

Junior—maybe working off a Bureau likeness sheet. "What kind of questions did he ask you?"

"He ask did that mousy little white girl ho' roun' here. I say, 'I don't know.' He ask did I work the bars down here, and I say yes. He ask 'bout some Peepin' Tom, I say I don't know 'bout no jive Peepin' Tom."

Brace the dark girl: "He asked you the same questions, right?"

"Tha's right, an' I told him the same answers, which is the righteous whole truth."

"Yeah, but *you* nudged your friend here, which means *you* told her something else about that policeman, because *you* are the one acting hinky. Now spill before I find something else in your purse."

Cop-hater rumbles—the whole room. "Tell me, goddamn it."

High Yellow: "Lynette tol' me she see that po-liceman shake down a man in Bido Lito's parking lot. Colored man, an' Lynette say the pom-po-dour cop take money from him. Lynette say she see that same po-lice at Bido's talkin' to that pretty-boy blond po-liceman who works for that mean Mr. Dudley Smith, who jist loves to have his strongarm men roust colored people. Ain' all that whooole truth, Lynette?"

"Sho' is, sugar. The whoooole truth, if I'm lyin', I'm flyin'."

Flying:

Junior—shakedown artist?—"If you want to steal, steal big."

"Pretty-boy blond cop"—??????

"Who was the colored man at Bido Lito's?"

Lynette: "I don't know, an' I ain't seen him before or since."

"What did you mean by 'shakedown'?"

"I mean he put the arm on that poor man for money, and he be usin' rude language besides."

"Give me a name for that blond cop."

"Ain' got a name, but I seen him with Mr. Smith, and he so cute I *give* it free to him."

Lynette laughed; High Yellow howled. The whole room laughed—at me.

Bido Lito's, 68th and Central—closed. Mark it: a lead on crazy man Junior.

I staked the parking lot—no suspicious shit—music out a door down the block. Squint, catch the marquee: "Club Alabam—Art Pepper Quartet Nitely." Art Pepper—*Straight Life*—a Tommy K. smashed record.

Strange music: pulsing, discordant. Distance distorted sounds—I synced a beat to people talking on the sidewalk. Hard to see faces, easy to imagine them: I made all the women Glenda. A crescendo, applause—I hit my brights to get a real look. Too bright—jigs passing a reefer—gone before I could blink.

I pulled up and walked in. Dark—no doorman/cover charge—four white guys on stage, backlit. Sax, bass, piano, drums—four beats—not music, not noise. I bumped a table, bumped a left-behind jug.

My eyes adjusted—bourbon and a shot glass right there. I grabbed a chair, watched, *listened*.

Sax solo—honks/blats/wails—I poured a shot, downed it.

Hot—I thought of Meg—juicehead parents scared us both away from liquor. Match flare: Tommy Kafesjian at ringside. Three shots quick—my breath timed itself to the music. Crescendos, no break, a ballad.

Pure beautiful: sax, piano, bass. Whispers: "Champ Dineen," "The Champ, that's his." Tommy's broken record: *Sooo Slow Moods*.

One more shot—bass notes—skipped heartbeats. Glenda, Meg, Lucille—some booze reflex warmed their faces.

Exit-door light—Tommy K. walking out. Validate this slumming, pure cop instincts:

Peeper/prowler/B&E man—all one man. Jazz fiend/voyeur—the noise fed the watching.

Noise/music—go, follow it—

Hot-sheet row—motels pressed tight—one long block. Stucco dives—bright colors—an alley behind them.

Ladder roof access: I parked, climbed, looked.

Vertigo—noise/music and liquor still had me. Slippery, careful, a perch—pure balls made me choose a high signpost. A breeze, a view: windows.

A few showing light: fuck flop rooms—bare walls—nothing else. I shivered out the booze—the music hit harder.

Lights on and off. Bare walls—no way to see faces, easy to imagine:

Glenda killing that pimp.

Glenda naked—Meg's body.

Chills—I got the car, cranked the heater, drove—

Meg's—dawn—no lights on. Hollywood—Glenda's place dark. Back to my place—a letter from Sam G. in the mailbox.

USC season tickets. A P.S.: "Thanks for proving jungle bunnies can fly."

Noise/music—I smashed the mailbox two-handed.

L.A. *Times*, 11/4/58:

COUNCILMANIC RACE ANTICLIMACTIC; CHAVEZ RAVINE SWING VOTE GAINED BY DEFAULT

A DOWN to the wire run was expected in the race for Fifth District City Councilman; today's election vote should have been nip and tuck. But while state, municipal, and judicial candidates nervously awaited poll news, incumbent Republican Councilman Thomas Bethune relaxed with his family at his Hancock Park home.

Up until last week, Bethune was hotly challenged by Morton Diskant, his liberal Democratic opponent. Diskant, stressing his credentials as a civil liberties lawyer, sought to portray Bethune as a pawn of the Los Angeles political establishment, his chief focus the Chavez Ravine issue. The Fifth Councilmanic District, which has a 25% Negro population, became a litmus test: how would voters respond when an entire campaign revolved around whether or not to relocate impoverished Latin Americans in an attempt to create space for a Los Angeles Dodgers ballpark?

Diskant pressed that issue, along with what he called "collateral matters": the allegedly overzealous enforcement measures of the Los Angeles Police Department and the "Gas Chamber Happy" Los Angeles District Attorney's Office. More than a litmus test, the Fifth District race was crucial to the passage of the Chavez Ravine bond issue: a Council straw vote showed that body currently standing 5 to 4 in favor, with all other Republican and Democratic candidates vying for Council seats also voicing their approval of the measure. Thus, only Diskant's election could force a City Council deadlock and legally postpone the wedding of Chavez Ravine and the Dodgers for some time.

But it was not to be. Last week, Diskant dropped out of the race, just as straw polls began to show him pulling ahead of his incumbent opponent. The Chavez Ravine Council vote will remain 5 to 4 in favor, and the bond issue is expected to be voted into law in mid-November. Diskant cited "personal reasons" as his motive for withdrawing; he did not elaborate further. Speculation in political circles has raged, and U.S. Attorney Welles Noonan, Chief Federal Prosecutor for the greater Southern California District, voiced this opinion to *Times* reporter Jerry Abrams: "I won't name names, and frankly I can't name names. But Diskant's withdrawal smacks of some sort of coercion. And I'll go on the record as a Democrat and a determined crimefighter with credentials including work for the McClellan Senate Rackets Committee: you can be both a moderate liberal and a foe of crime, as my good friend Senator John Kennedy proved by his work for the Committee."

Noonan declined to answer questions on his own political ambitions, and Morton Diskant could not be reached to voice his response. Councilman Bethune told the *Times*: "I hated to win this way, because I relish a good fight. Get those hot dogs and peanuts ready, [Dodger organization president] Walter O'Malley, because I'm putting in for season tickets. Play ball!"

L.A. *Mirror*, 11/5/58:

GALLAUDET ELECTED DA; YOUNGEST IN CITY'S HISTORY

IT WAS no surprise: Robert "Call Me Bob" Gallaudet, 38, a former LAPD and DA's Bureau officer who went to USC Law School nights, was elected Los Angeles District Attorney yesterday, topping a six man field with 59% of the total votes cast.

His election marks a fast rising career streaked with good luck, chiefly the resignation of former DA Ellis Loew last April. Gallaudet, then Loew's favored prosecutor, was appointed interim DA by the City Council, largely, it was believed, because of his friendship with LAPD Chief of Detectives Edmund Exley. A Republican, Gallaudet is expected to run for State Attorney General in 1960. He is a staunch law and order advocate, and a frequent target of death penalty repeal groups, who consider him overzealous in his recommendations of capital punishment.

A recent barb was thrown at the new District Attorney from another angle. Welles Noonan, U.S. Attorney for the Southern California Federal District and often spoken of as Gallaudet's likely opponent in the Attorney General's race, told the *Mirror*: "DA Gallaudet's support of the District Gambling Bill currently stalled in the California State Legislature stands out as a startling contradiction to this man's supposedly bedrock anti-crime philosophy. That bill [i.e.—proposed legitimate gambling zones confined to certain areas surveilled by local police agencies, where cards, slot machines, off track betting and other games of chance will be legal, but heavily surtaxed for State revenue purposes] is a moral outrage that condones compulsive gambling under the guise of political good.

It will become a magnet for organized crime, and I exhort DA Gallaudet to retract his support of the measure."

At a press conference to announce his upcoming victory gala at the Ambassador Hotel's Cocoanut Grove two nights from now, Gallaudet pooh-poohed his critics, chiefly U.S. Attorney Noonan. "Look, he's running against me for AG already, and I just got elected to *this* job. On my political future: no comment. My comment on my election as Los Angeles District Attorney: watch out, criminals. And take heart, Angelenos: I'm here to make this city a peaceful, safe haven for all its law-abiding citizens."

Hush-Hush Magazine, 11/6/58:

HELLO DODGERS!!! ADIÓS HUDDLED MASSES!!!

DIG IT, kats and kittens, chicks and charlies: we love the national pastime as much as you do, but enough is enough. Doesn't that great lady the Statue of Liberty have some kind of rebop inscribed by her tootsies? Something like: "Give us your poor, huddled, wretched masses yearning to be free?" Look, east coast geography isn't our strong suit, and we can tell you're tired of this patriotic shtick already. Look, *everybody* wants a bonaroo home for the Dodgers, us included. *But*—iconoclasm dictates that we take a different tack, if only for the sake of our circuitously circling circulation. Social protest from *Hush-Hush*! They said it couldn't happen! Remember, dear reader, you heard it first here!

Dig: The L.A. City Council is set to boot an egregiously entrenched enclave of impecunious, impoverished, impetuously machismo mangled Mexican-Americans from their sharecropper shingle shacks in that shady, smog-shrouded Shangri-La Chavez Ravine!!! Those pennant flopper, fly ball dropper L.A. Dodgers are moving in as soon as the dust clears and a stadium is built—and they'll have a new home from which to rule the National League cellar!!! Dig it!! You're happy, we're happy!! Go, Dodgers!!! But what will happen to those dourly dispossessed, Dodger doomed delinquents: the maladroitly mismanaged Mexicans?

Digsville: The California State Bureau of Land and Way is granting shack dwellers $10,500 per family relocation expenses, roughly ½ the cost of a slipshod, slapdash slum pad in such colorful locales as Watts, Willowbrook and Boyle Heights. The Bureau is also

enterprisingly examining dervishly developed dump dives proffered by rapaciously rapid real estate developers: would-be Taco
Terraces and Enchilada Estates where Burrito Bandits bounced
from shamefully sheltered Chavez Ravine could live in jerry-rigged
slum splendor, frolicking to fleabag firetrap fandangos!

Dig, we've heard that among the sites being considered are
converted horse paddock–jail cells once used to house Japanese
internees during World War II, and a converted bungalow motel
in Lynwood, replete with heart shaped beds and cheesy
gilt-edged mirrors. Say! Those places sound like the office here
at *Hush-Hush*!!!

Hey! The rent here on the sin-tillating, salivatingly sensational
Sunset Strip has steadily steepened—and we've heard that several
dismayingly disgusted dispossessees have put in for their money
and moved back to Mexico ahead of the general eviction date,
leaving behind abandoned shacks! Hey—*Hush-Hush* could move
its operations into them! As a result, we could charge a lower
price for this rag! If you believe that, we'll sell you a Pendejo
Penthouse and a brand-new Chorizo Chevrolet!

But, to close on a more serious note, it appears that the L.A.
powers-that-be have a front man chatting up the many remaining
Chavez Ravine dwellers, passing out trinkets and doing his best
to convince them to move out before the established eviction
date without seeking legal injunctions. That man: popular bantamweight battler Reuben Ruiz, currently ranked 8th by *Ring*
Magazine, a man whom *Hush-Hush* hastens to charge with a
checkably checkered past.

Item:

Reuben Ruiz served time at the Preston Reformatory for juvenile burglary.

Item:

Reuben Ruiz has three brothers: Ramon, Reyes and Reynal-
do—! God!—alliteration to make *Hush-Hush* proud!—and all
three men have burglary and/or grand theft auto convictions on
their records.

Item:

Reuben Ruiz was a guarded witness during Federal bright
boy Welles Noonan's recently short lived boxing probe. (You recall that probe, hepcats: another witness jumped out the window
while the LAPD detective guarding him resided in Snooze City.)

Item:

Reuben Ruiz was spotted a few days ago, lunching at the Pacific Dining Car with DA Bob Gallaudet and City Council-man Thomas Bethune. A late breaking extra, on the QT and *very Hush-Hush*:

Reuben Ruiz' brother Ramon was arrested for grand theft auto several days before, but now the charges have been mysteri-ously dropped....

A captivatingly corrosive coercion conclusion to consider:

Is Reuben Ruiz a bagman–PR man for the DA's Office and City Council? Does Ruiz' hellacious hermano rowdy Ramon owe his freedom to Reuben's politically prudent pandering? Will Reuben's extra-curricular efforts extricate his lethal left hook when he fights tough Stevie Moore at the Olympic next week?

Remember, dear reader, you heard it first here: off the record, on the QT and *very Hush-Hush*.

"Crimewatch" Feature, *Hush-Hush* Magazine, 11/6/58:

FUR FLIES FURTIVELY OUT OF FUR KING'S FREEZERS—FUR WHERE?

YOU ALL know Sol "The Fur King" Hurwitz, hepcats: he does his own commercials on TV's Spade Cooley Show. His running gag is an animated snowstorm descending on Grauman's Chinese Theatre while unprepared Angelenos shiver in Bermuda shorts. He cuts these commercials on a sound stage made up like an igloo, with his marionette mascot Maurizio Mink supplying a hard sell Greek chorus: scientists are predicting a new ice age several centuries down the line, buy your Hurwitz Fur now at rock bottom low prices, easy monthly payments, store your fur during the "off season" at our San Fernando Valley fur warehouse free of charge. Follow the drift, kats and kittens? Sol Hurwitz knows that fur is a preposterous Southern California item, and he's poking fun at himself while neglecting to mention the basic fact of his business: people buy furs for two reasons: to look good and to show off how much money they have.

Dig that especially L.A. ethos? Good, you're on our wavelength. Dig further that Hurwitz' free storage come-on is good for lots of biz. Shiver, shiver, brrrr. Your beloved Charlie Chinchilla, Mindy Mink and Rachel Raccoon are safe with Sol, right? Well, up until October 25th you weren't whistling Dixie....

On that fateful night, three or four daring desperadoes presumed to have toolmaking and electronics expertise *fur*tively
*fur*thered their criminal careers by overpowering a security
guard and absconding with an estimated one million dollars in
"Off-Season" storaged furs. Did you read the small print on
your "free" storage contracts, kool kats? If not, dig: in case of
theft, Hurwitz Furs' insurance carrier reimburses you at the rate
of 25% of the estimated value of your lost stole or coat, and
*fur*thermore, the police have no clues as to who these *fur*shtink-
ener *fur*tive *fur* heisters are!

Captain Dudley Smith, head of the LAPD's Robbery Division,
told reporters at Van Nuys Station: "We know that a large flatbed
truck was the means of entry and escape, and the regrettably injured
guard told us that three or four men wearing stocking masks disabled him. A complex freezer locking system was dismantled,
giving the robbers access to the furs. Technical expertise is an
obvious strong point of this gang of thieves, and I will not rest
until they are apprehended."

Assisting Captain Smith are Sergeant Michael Breuning and
Sergeant Richard Carlisle. A surprise addition to the celebrated
crimebuster's team: Officer John Duhamel, known to So Cal
fight fans as "Schoolboy" Johnny Duhamel, former middleweight
Golden Gloves champ. Captain Smith, Sergeant Breuning and
Sergeant Carlisle refused to talk to *Hush-Hush*, but ace *Hush-Hush*
scribe Duane Tucker cornered Officer "Schoolboy" Duhamel at
last week's Hollywood Legion Stadium fistfest. Off the record,
on the QT and *very Hush-Hush*, Officer "Schoolboy" spoke out
of school.

He called the robbery a baffler, and ruled out insurance fraud,
even though Sol Hurwitz is rapaciously rumored to be a dice
game degenerate. "Schoolboy" then bit his tongue and offered no
*fur*ther comments.

In a *fur*ther development, a score of *fur*ious *fur*meisters picketed
Sol Hurwitz' Pacoima scene-of-the-crime storage facility. With a
scant 25% assessed value refund coming to them, these perplexed
parents impatiently importuned Mindy Mink, Rachel Raccoon
and Charlie Chinchilla:

Come home! It's 80 degrees and we're freezing without you!

Look for *fur*ther developments in upcoming Crimewatch
features. Remember, you heard it *fur*st here: off the record, on the
QT and *very Hush-Hush*!

L.A. *Herald-Express*, 11/7/58:

U.S. ATTORNEY ANNOUNCES SOUTHSIDE RACKETS PROBE

THIS MORNING, in a brief, tersely worded prepared statement, U.S. Attorney Welles Noonan announced that Justice Department investigators assigned to the Southern California District Office would soon begin a "minutely detailed, complex and far reaching" probe into racketeering in South-Central Los Angeles. He called his investigation a "gathering of evidence aimed at establishing criminal conspiracies"; he said that his goal was to present "convincing evidence" to a specially convened Federal Grand Jury, with an eye toward securing major indictments.

Noonan, 40, former counsel to the U.S. Senate's McClellan Rackets Committee, said that his investigation would encompass crimes including narcotics trafficking, jukebox, vending machine and slot machine illegalities, and that he would "thoroughly explore" rumors that the Los Angeles Police Department allows vice to rage in Southside Los Angeles and rarely investigates homicides involving both Negro victims and perpetrators.

The U.S. Attorney declined to answer reporters' questions, but stated that his task force would include four prosecuting attorneys and at least a dozen specially selected Justice Department agents. He closed his press conference stating that he fully expects the Los Angeles Police Department to refuse to cooperate with the probe.

LAPD Chief William H. Parker and Chief of Detectives Edmund Exley were informed of U.S. Attorney Noonan's announcement. They declined to comment.

PART TWO

VAMPIRA

10

SCOPE THE party:

The Cocoanut Grove, a society band. Chief Parker, Exley—smiles for our boy: Gas Chamber Bob Gallaudet. Drink waiters, dancing—Meg brought Jack Woods so she could mambo. Dudley Smith, Mayor Poulson, Tom Bethune—no thank-you to me for the tank job.

Newsmen, Dodger execs. Gallaudet grinning, bombed by flashbulbs.

Mingle, look:

George Stemmons, Sr., two Smith goons: Mike Breuning, Dick Carlisle. Read their lips: FED PROBE, FED PROBE. Parker and Exley holding cocktails—talking FED PROBE—bet money. Meg danced Jack by—hoodlums still jazzed her—my fault.

Show-up time: I owed Bob congratulations. Better to wait, get him alone—*my* bad PR lingered. I watched the crowd, matched thoughts to faces.

Exley—tall, easy to spot. He'd read my 459 report: the Lucille/peeper leads, a bogus addendum—shitcan the job, it's dead-ended. He said keep going; some part of me rejoiced—I wanted to drag that family through the gutter. Both ends against the middle: I'd told Dan Wilhite I'd go easy.

Inspector George Stemmons, Sr., by the punchbowl—Junior twenty-odd years older. Junior missing since the Georgie Ainge roust—stalemate time—he knew Glenda Bledsoe killed Dwight Gilette. *His* Kafesjian report: fluff. No john/whore file checks, my Darktown scoop made him too busy: that shakedown outside Bido Lito's; that confab with a "pretty-boy blond cop." Pretty boy's ID: Johnny Duhamel, Dud Smith's new Mobster Squad lad.

Junior: no way to trust him; no way to dump him off the case just yet.

Solo now:

I checked the stationhouse lists—luck at University—john names, no hooker names connected. I ran them through the DMV and R&I—all phonies—most Vice cops didn't press for real

IDs—no heart to ream pussy prowlers. Luck crapped out—I saved the names to check against—most johns kept the same alias.

Darktown strutter:

I questioned Western Avenue whores, three nights' worth—no Lucille pic IDs. I checked with the 77th Squad—still no locate on the peeper complaints. I peeped myself: the Kafesjian pad, car-radio jazz to kill boredom. Two nights—family brawls; one night, Lucille alone—a window striptease—the radio pulsed to her movements. Three nights total, no other watchers—make *me* the only voyeur. That Big Instinct confirmed: prowler/peeper/ B&E man—all one man.

Homework, two nights' worth: Art Pepper, Champ Dineen— listening to what the burglar smashed. My phonograph, the volume torqued: that Instinct solid. One session pushed me back to the house—I tailed Tommy K. down to Bido Lito's. Tommy: *in with his own key*, weed bags stashed by slot machines. I called Lester Lake: glom me skinny on Tommy's known associates.

Happy chatter—the party crowd swelling. Meg and Jack Woods talking—they'd probably start up again. Jack muscled our rent; we cut a percentage deal: his dice game, our Westside vacant. Holding hands: my sister, my hood friend. Exhausted—I shifted to Glenda Overdrive—

Hooked bad—I couldn't subcontract the Hughes job. Moonlight work: I tailed her, watched for tails on me, ditched some maybes. Movie set skulks, rolling stakeouts:

Glenda raids Hughes' fuck pads; Glenda donates stolen food to "Dracula's" rest home. Frequent Glenda guests: Touch V. and Rock Rockwell—Georgie Ainge nowhere in sight. Last night, Good Deed Glenda: foie gras for the oldsters at the Sleepy Glade dump.

R&I—Bledsoe, Glenda Louise:

No wants, no warrants, no prostitution arrests. 12/46: ten days, juvie shoplifting. A Juvenile Hall file note: Glenda beat up an amorous bull dyke.

LAPD Homicide—Dwight William Gilette, DOD 4/19/55 (unsolved)—ZERO ON GLENDA LOUISE BLEDSOE.

Fake reports to Bradley Milteer: Glenda's thefts deleted, her publicity date lied off—a "friendly outing." Glenda Overdrive driving me: good scary/scary good.

I edged up to the crowd. Gallaudet had a new haircut: that Jack Kennedy/Welles Noonan style. A nod my way, but no shake—bad-press cops rated low. Walter O'Malley sidled by—Bob almost genuflected. Chavez Ravine, ballpark, ballpark—loud, happy.

"Hello, lad."

That brogue—Dudley Smith.

"Hello, Dud."

"A fine evening, is it not? Mark my words, we are celebrating the beginning of a splendid political career."

An envelope passed: Dodger man to DA's man. "Bob was always ambitious."

"Like yourself, lad. And does the prospect of a stadium for our home team thrill you?"

"Not particularly."

Dud laughed. "Nor I. Chavez Ravine was a splendid place to purchase spic trinkets, but now I fear it will be replaced by traffic jams and more smog. Do you follow baseball, lad?"

"No."

"Not interested in athletics? Is extracurricular money your only passion?"

"It's this Jew name I got stuck with."

Howls—his suitcoat gapped. Check the ordnance: magnum, sap, switchblade. "Lad, you have the power to amuse this old man."

"I only get funny when I'm bored—and baseball bores me. Boxing's more my sport."

"Ah, I should have known. Ruthless men always admire fisti-cuffs. And I phrase 'ruthless' as a compliment, lad."

"No offense taken. And speaking of boxing, Johnny Duhamel's working for you, right?"

"Correct, and a splendidly fear-inducing addition to the Mob-ster Squad he is. I've given him work on my fur-robbery job as well, and he is proving himself to be a splendid all-around young policeman. Why do you ask, lad?"

"His name came up. One of my men used to teach at the Academy. Duhamel was a student of his."

"Ahh, yes. George Stemmons, Jr., am I correct? What a memory for students past that lad must have."

"That's him."

Exley nailed me—a curt nod. Dud caught it: "Go, lad, Chief Exley beckons from across the room. Ah, the gaze of a shark he has."

"Good seeing you, Dud."

"My pleasure entirely, lad."

I walked over. Exley, straight off: "There's a briefing day after tomorrow. Nine o'clock, all Bureau COs. Be there—we're going to discuss the Fed probe. Also, I want you to get ahold of the Kafesjian family's tax records. You're an attorney—find a loophole."

"Income tax records require a Federal writ. Why don't you ask Welles Noonan? It's his district."

White knuckles—his wineglass shook. "I read your report, and the john names interest me. I want a trick sweep on Western and Adams tomorrow night. Set it up with University Vice, and detach as many men as you need. I want detailed information on Lucille Kafesjian's customers."

"Are you sure you want to risk riling that family with the Feds around the goddamn corner?"

"Do it, Lieutenant. Don't question my motives or ask why."

Pissed—I hit the lobby steaming. A phone, a dime—buzz the Bureau.

"Administrative Vice, Officer Riegle."

"Sid, it's me."

"Hi, Skipper. You telepathic? Hollenbeck just left you a message."

"Hold on, I need you to set something up first."

"All ears."

"Call University and set up a trick sweep. Say eight men and two whore wagons. Make it eleven P.M. tomorrow night, Western and Adams, Chief Exley's authorization."

Sid whistled. "Care to explain?"

BRAINSTORM:

"And tell the squad lieutenant I need a row of interrogation rooms, and tell Junior Stemmons to meet me at the station, I want him in on this."

Scribble sounds. "It's on paper. You want that message now?"

"Shoot."

"The Pawnshop Detail turned the Kafesjian silverware. Some Mexican tried to pawn it in Boyle Heights, and the shop owner saw our bulletin and stalled him. He's in custody at Hollenbeck Station."

I whooped—heads turned. "Call Hollenbeck, Sid. Tell them to put the Mex in a sweat room. I'll be right over."

"On it, Skipper."

Back to the party—Gas Chamber Bob swamped—no way to check out graceful. A blonde swirled by—Glenda—a blink—just some woman.

11

JESUS CHASCO—fat, Mex—not my peeper. No rap sheet, a '58 green card running out. Scared—the sweat room sweats.

"Habla inglés, Jesus?"

"I speak English good as you do."

Skim the crime sheet. "This says you attempted to sell stolen silverware to the Happytime Pawnshop. You told the officers that you didn't steal the silverware, but you wouldn't tell them where you got it. Okay, that's one felony—receiving stolen goods. You gave your car as your address, so that's a misdemeanor charge—vagrancy. How old are you, Jesus?"

T-shirt and khakis—sweated up. "Forty-three. Why you ask me that?"

"I'm figuring five years in San Quentin, then the boot back to Mexico. By the time you get back here, you might win a prize as the world's oldest wetback."

Chasco waved his arms; sweat flew. "I sleep in my car to save money!"

"Yeah, to bring your family up here. Now sit still or I'll cuff you to your chair."

He spit on the floor; I dangled my handcuffs eye-level. "Tell me where you got the silverware. If you prove it, I'll cut you loose."

"You mean you—"

"I mean you walk. No charges, no nada."

"Suppose I don't tell you?"

Wait him out, let him show some balls. Ten seconds—a classic pachuco shrug. "I do custodian work at this motel. It's on 53rd and Western, called the Red Arrow Inn. It's ... you know, for *putas* and their guys."

Tingles. "Keep going."

"Well ... I was fixing the sink in room 19. I found all this nice-looking silver stuck into the bed ... you know, the sheets and the mattress all ripped up. I ... I figured ... I figured the guy who rented the room went crazy ... and ... and he wouldn't press no charges if I swiped his stuff."

Grab the lead: "*What does 'the guy' look like?*"

"I don't know—a guy. I never seen him. Ask the night clerk, she'll tell you."

"She'll tell both of us."

"Hey, you said—"

"Put your hands behind your back."

Balls—two seconds' worth—another shrug. I cuffed him up loose—keep him friendly.

"Hey, I'm hungry."

"I'll get you a candy bar."

"You said you'd cut me loose!"

"I'm going to."

"But my car's back here!"

'Take a bus."

"*Pinche cabrón! Puto! Gabacho maricón!*"

A half-hour run. Praise Jesus: no backseat noise, no cuff thrashing. The Red Arrow Inn: connected cabins, two rows, a center driveway. A neon sign: "Vacancy."

I pulled up to cabin 19: dark, no car out front. Chasco: "I got my master key."

I unlocked his cuffs. High beams on—he opened 19, backlit nice.

"Come look! Just like I tol' you, man!"

I walked over. Evidence: doorjamb jimmy marks—*recent*—fresh splinters. The room itself: small, linoleum floor, no furniture. The bed: slashed sheets, ripped mattress spilling kapok.

"Go get the clerk. Don't run away, you'll piss me off."

Chasco hauled. I scoped the bed close up: fork holes in the mattress, stabs down to the springs. Semen stains—my peeper screamed CATCH ME NOW. I ripped off a sheet swatch—the jizz could be tested for blood type.

"No-good ofay trash!"

I turned around—"Ofay trash dee-stroy my nice bed!"—this jig granny flapping a rent card.

Grab it—"John Smith"—predictable—ten days paid up front, checkout time tomorrow. Granny popped spit; Chasco pointed outside.

I followed him. Jesus, eager: "Carlotta don't know who rented the room. She said she thinks it's a young white guy. She said this wino rented the room for him, and the tenant guy said he had to have room 19. She ain't seen the tenant guy herself. I ain't either, but listen, I know that wino. You give me five dollars and a ride back to my car and I find him for you."

Fork it over: two fives, the Lucille pix. "One for you, one for Carlotta. Tell her I don't want any trouble and ask her if she knows this girl. *Then* you go find me that wino."

Chasco ran back, passed the five, flashed the mugs—Moms nodded yes yes yes. Jesus, back to me: "Carlotta said that girl's like a once-in-a-while—she rent short-timer and don't fill out no rent card. She said she's a prostie, and she always ask for number 18, right next to where I found that nice silver. She said the girl likes 18 'cause she got a street view case the police show up."

Think:

Room 19, room 18: the peeper peeping Lucille's trick fucks. Room 19 jimmy marks—make some third party involved?

Granny jiggled a tin can. "For Jehovah. Jehovah get ten per-cent of all rent money spent on this sinful premises tithed back to him. I gots the slot-machine gambleitis myself, and I kicks back ten percent of my winnings to Jehovah. You a handsome young po-lice, so for one more dollar for Jehovah I give you more skinny on that slummin', thrill-seekin' white ho' Hay-soos showed me them pictures of."

Fuck it, fork it—Moms fed the can. "I seen that girl at Bido Lito's, where I was indulgin' my one-arm-bandit gambleitis to tithe Jehovah. This other po-lice, he was askin' people at the bar 'bout her. I tol' him what I tol' you: she jist a thrill-seekin', slummin' white ho'. Later on, after hours, I seen that girl in the pictures do this striptease with this bee-you-tiful mink coat. That other po-lice, he saw it too, but he actin' cool, like he *not* a po-lice, an' he didn' even stop her from makin' that disgraceful display, *or* act like he was too hot and bothered."

Think—don't jump yet. "Jesus, go get me that wino. Carlotta, what did that policeman look like?"

Chasco breezed. Moms: "He had light brown hair done up with pomade, an' he maybe thirty years old. Nice-lookin', but not as high-steppin' as you, Mister Po-lice."

Jump: Darktown Junior lead number two. Reverse jump: Rock Rockwell at Fern Dell—some quiff said Ad Vice was working the Park. Junior copped to it—"a favor"—he owed a pal working Hollywood Vice.

Rattle rattle—I shoved Moms some change. "Listen, have you ever seen the man staying in this room?"

"Praise Jehovah, I seen him from the back."

"Have you ever seen him *with* anyone else?"

"Praise Jehovah, no I hasn't."

"When was the last time you saw the girl in my photographs?"

"Praise Jehovah, when she did that striptease at Bido's maybe four, five days ago."

"When was the last time she brought a trick to this front room here?"

"Praise Jehovah, maybe a week ago."

"Where does she solicit her tricks?"

"Praise Jehovah, I don't know."

"Has she brought the same man more than once? Does she have regular tricks?"

"Praise Jehovah, I has taught myself not to look at the faces of these sinners."

Chasco walked a piss bum up. "I don't know, but I think maybe this guy's not so sharp with questions."

"This guy": Mex, Filipino—grime-caked—a tough call. "What's your name, sahib?"

Mumbles, hiccups—Jesus shushed him. "The cops call him Flame-O, 'cause sometimes he sets himself on fire when he's drunk."

Flame-O flashed some scars—Moms took off going "Uggh." Jesus: "Look, I asked him 'bout that guy he rented the room for, an' I don't think he remembers so good. You still gonna drive me—"

Back to room 19—my blinders on. Throw the lock, eyeball it—zoom—a connecting door.

Room 19 to room 18—Lucille's preferred fuck spot. Jamb-ledge jimmy marks—different than the front door marks.

Think:

Peeper hits or tries to hit Lucille's room.

Peeper trashes his own room, leaves the silver, moves out panicked. Or: *different* pry marks on peeper's front door. Say somebody else broke in. Make some third party involved?

I rattled the connecting door—no answer. A shoulder push—slack, give, snap—I rode loose hinges into room 18.

Just like 19—but no closet door. Something else: ripples on the wall above the bed.

Up close: buckled wallpaper, paste spackling. A square indentation—perforated dry wall underneath. Peeled wallpaper—one thin strip, follow the line:

The wall to the connecting door—a drop to the crack under the door.

Odds on:

A bug—planted and removed, the mike above the bed—the peeper voyeurs Lucille, basic electronics skill—

I tore up the room—empty, zero, nothing. Number 19—dump it twice, closet swag: Jockey shorts tangling up a tape spool.

Panic move-out validated.

Moms and Jesus outside pitching tantrums.

I shoved through them double time. Granny chucked her tin can at me.

The Bureau—Code 3—a lab stop, orders: test the sheet-swatch jizz for blood type. My office, my old chem kit—dust the spool.

Smudges—no latent prints. Edgy now, I glommed a tape rig from the storeroom.

Nightwatch lull—the squadroom stood quiet. I shut my door, pressed Play, killed the lights.

Listen:

Static, traffic boom, window shimmy. Outside noises: business at the Red Arrow Inn.

Spook whores talking—ten minutes of pimp/trick rebop. I could *SEE IT*: hookers outside HER window. Silence, tape hiss, a door slamming. "In advance, sweet"—pause—"Yes, that means now"—Lucille.

"Okay, okay"—a man. A pause, shoes dropped, mattress squeaks—three minutes' worth. The tape almost out, groans—his climax. Silence, garbled words, Lucille: "Let's play a little game. Now I'll be the daughter and you'll be the daddy, and if you're *reeeeal* sweet we can go again no extra."

Traffic noise, driveway noise, breath. Easy to imagine:

That wall between them.

Surveillance not enough.

My peeper breathing hard—scared to bust down that wall.

12

STATIC GARBLED dreams: Lucille talking sex jive to *me*. The lab, my wake-up call—the jizz tested out O+. Chills off a late phone stint: Hollywood Vice called Junior's queer roust story bullshit.

"Horse pucky—whoever told you that lied through his teeth. We're too busy with the Will-o-the-Wisp to work fruits, and none of our guys have popped Fern Dell Park chicken in over a year."

Coffee—half a cup—my nerves jangled.

The buzzer—loud.

I opened up—fuck—Bradley Milteer and Harold John Miciak.

Stern looks—their cop colleague in a towel. Miciak scoped my Jap sword scar.

"Come in, gentlemen."

They shut the door behind them. Milteer: "We came for a progress report."

I smiled—servile. "I have sources on the movie set accruing information on Miss Bledsoe."

"You've been in Mr. Hughes' employ for a week, Lieutenant. Frankly, so far you haven't 'accrued' the results he hoped for."

"I'm working on it."

"Then please produce results. Are your normal police duties interfering with your work for Mr. Hughes?"

"My police duties aren't quite normal."

"Well, be that as it may, you are being paid to secure information on Miss Glenda Bledsoe. Now, Mr. Hughes seems to think that Miss Bledsoe has been pilfering foodstuffs from his actress domiciles. A criminal theft charge will violate her contract, so will you surveil her even more diligently?"

Miciak flexed his hands—no gang tattoos.

"I'll begin that surveillance immediately, Mr. Milteer."

"Good. I expect results, Mr. Hughes expects results."

Miciak—jailhouse eyes, cop-hater fuck.

"First Flats or White Fence, Harold?"

"Uh, what?"

"Those tattoos Mr. Hughes made you burn off."

"Listen, I'm clean."

"Sure, Mr. Hughes had your record wiped."

Milteer: "Lieutenant, *really*."

The geek: "Where'd you get that scar, hotshot?"

"A Jap sword."

"What happened to the Jap?"

"I stuck the sword up his ass."

Milteer, rolled eyes oh-you-heathens: "Results, Mr. Klein. Harold, come."

Harold walked. Fist signals back at me—pure White Fence.

Movie-set bustle:

Wine call—Mickey C. doling out T-Bird to his "crew." "Director" Sid Frizell, "cameraman" Wylie Bullock—poke the head monster's eyes out with a stick or a knife? Glenda feeding extras sturgeon, read *her* eyes: "Who's *that* guy, I've seen him before."

Rock Rockwell's trailer—tap the door.

"It's open!"

I walked in. Cozy: a mattress, one chair. Rockwell cranking push-ups on the floor. THE LOOK: cop, oh fuck.

"It's not a roust, I'm friends with Touch."

"Did I hear my name?"

Touch stepped out of the bathroom. No fixtures—just TV sets stacked high. "David, you didn't see those."

"See what?"

Rockwell slid up on the mattress; Touch tossed him a towel. "Meg's my first customer. She told me she wants to put TV's in all your furnished vacancies so she can raise the rent. Oh, excuse me. Rock Rockwell, David Klein."

No hello—Rock toweled off. Touch: "Dave, what's this about?"

Eyes on Rockwell—Touch caught the drift. "He can keep police-type confidences."

"I had some questions about activities in Fern Dell Park."

Rockwell scratched the mattress—Touch sprawled beside him. "Vice-type activities?"

I pulled the chair up. "Sort of, and it gets tricky because I think one of my men might be pulling shakedowns in Fern Dell."

Touch tensed up.

"What? What is it?"

"David, what does this man of yours look like?"

"Five-ten, one-sixty, long sandy hair. Sort of cute—you might like him."

No laugh—Touch coiled toward Rockwell.

"Come on, tell me. We go back—you know nothing you say leaves this room."

"Well ... since it sort of involves Mickey, and you're his friend ..."

Coax him: "Come on—like the magazine says: 'off the record.'"

Touch stood up, threw a robe on, paced—"Last week, that guy, that ... policeman you just described to a T, he rousted me in Fern Dell. I told him who I was, *who I knew*, including Mickey Cohen, which *he* was oblivious to. Look, I was cruising—you know what I am, David—Rock and I, we have this arrangement—"

Rockwell—BAM!—out the door pulling on pants.

"It's the way our kind of people have to be to get along, and this ... oh shit, this *policeman* said he'd seen me installing slots and coin hardware on the Southside a while back, and he said that Fed probe would happen and he'd snitch me to it if I didn't cooperate with him, so all right, *we* both know how to do business, David, but *this policeman* was acting so hopped-up and crazy that I *knew he didn't*, so I listened. He said, 'You must know Darktown pretty well,' I said yes, I got the impression he was messed up on Bennies or goofballs *or both*, and *then* he started rambling about—and I quote you, David—this 'gorgeous'—he actually used the word 'gorgeous'—other policeman working the Mobster Squad—"

"Gorgeous" Johnny Duhamel. My head throbbed—queer lilt synchronized—

"This policeman, he just kept rambling. He wouldn't tell me *details*, he just … kept rambling. He told me this crazy story about a whore in a mink coat stripping and how the gorgeous Mobster Squad cop got panicky and made her stop. David, here's where it gets strange and funny and sort of … well … *incestuous*, because the crazy policeman saw that the fur-coat spiel made me just a tad suspicious. He came on strong, and he found a gun on me and threatened me with a concealment charge, and I said the fur thing spooked me because Johnny Duhamel, that sort-of-famous ex-boxer, he tried to sell Mickey a bulk load of hot furs, which Mickey refused. The crazy cop, he laughed and laughed and started muttering 'Gorgeous Johnny,' and then he just sort of warned me off and walked away, and David, that policeman, he is one of us, if you catch my drift, dear heart, and I only told you all this because our mutual friend Mickey played just a tad of a supporting role."

Touch—hands in his robe, out with a piece—bet he almost shoved it up Junior's ass.

Think:

Junior shakes down a guy at Bido Lito's.

Hobnobs with Johnny Duhamel—Bido Lito's.

Scopes out Lucille's fur strip—Bido Lito's.

More:

Junior—Kafesjian work fluffed off.

Fern Dell Park shakedowns—faggot Junior—Touch knew the turf—call it a maybe.

Touch: "I don't want you to tell Mickey what I told you. Duhamel just approached Mickey because he's Mickey. Mickey doesn't know anything about that extortionist policeman of yours, I just know it. Dave, are you listening to me?"

"I heard you."

"You won't tell Mickey?"

"No, I won't tell him."

"You look like you've seen a ghost."

"Lots of them."

Ghost chaser—

The Observatory lot—phone work.

Dime one: Jack Woods—set to bird-dog Junior post-trick sweep. Two: Ad Vice/Sid Riegle/confirmation: everything set, Junior told to stick at University Station. Orders: walk over to Robbery, skim the fur-heist file. Riegle: sure, I'll call you back.

Tick tick tick—my pulse outran my watch. Eleven minutes, Sid with stale news:

No suspects, fences leaned on—no furs surfacing. Three to five men, a truck, solid knowhow: electronics and toolworking. Dud Smith ruled out fraud—no profit motive—Sol Hurwitz packed low payoff-rate insurance. Sid—"Why the interest?"—cut him off, work dime three—a Personnel clerk who owed me.

My offer: your debt wiped for a file check: Officer John Duhamel. He agreed; I asked one question: did Duhamel possess technical expertise?

I held the line—twenty long minutes. Results: Duhamel, cum laude grad—engineering—USC, '56. Straight-A average—rah, rah, fellow Trojan.

Duhamel—possible fur thief. Possible partners: Reuben Ruiz and his brothers—Reuben and Johnny fought amateur together. Nix it on instinct: Ruiz boosted pads, ditto his brothers—the family topped out at auto theft. More likely:

Dudley co-opts Johnny to the fur heist; Johnny gloms some solo leads and gloms some furs. Smart into dumb—he offers Mickey Cohen the goods—the kid doesn't know Mickey's scuffling.

My scuffle—rat him to Dud?—think it through. *Tick tick tick*—not yet—too circumstantial. My priority: sort Junior and Johnny out, ease Junior off Glenda.

Ghost chaser.

Glenda.

Results.

Time before the trick sweep—tail her.

The park road—wait her out.

Her routine: drive home at 2:00, pilfer later. Time to kill, time to think—

Easy: my "crush" stretched me too thin—catch her stealing and snitch her—TODAY. Kicks: get her a Commie lawyer enraged at big money—Morton Diskant, just the ticket. Arraignment, trial— Glenda pays cunthound Morty off in trade. "Guilty," State time, Dave Klein there with flowers when they boot her.

Play the radio, drift.

Bop—maybe queer cops prowling Darktown—too jangly, too frantic. Skim the dial, ballads—"Tennessee Waltz"—Meg. '51, that song, the Two Tonys—Jack Woods probably knew the whole story. Him and Meg back on; I dumped a witness and she got suspicious—and Jack wouldn't shit her. She'd know, she'd be scared, she'd forgive me. Her and Jack—I wasn't jealous—call him dangerous and safe—safer than me.

Back to bop—jangly good now—think:

Lucille on tape: "I'll be the daughter and you'll be the daddy." Lucille, nude: fleshy like this boot camp whore I had. Big-band tunes, the war, schoolgirl Glenda—*close her out*—

Noon, 1:00, 1:30—I snoozed and woke up cramped. Stomach growls, a piss in the weeds. Early: her Vette zooming by with the top down.

I rolled—a brown Chevy cut between us—weird familiar. Squint, make the driver: Harold John Miciak.

Three-car tail string—absurd.

Up to the Observatory; down to street level. Glenda carefree, her scarf billowing. Pissed: hit the siren, ream that shitbird.

Miciak gunned it—bumper-to-bumper close. Glenda looked around; he looked around—sixty miles an hour, kill the siren, hit the mike: "Police! Pull over now!"

He swerved, banged the curb, stalled out. Glenda slowed down and stopped.

I got out.

Miciak got out.

Glenda watched—see it her way:

This big goon walks up shouting; this shoulder-holster shirt-sleeves guy shouts back: "This is mine! You'll get your results! Tell your fucking boss that!"

The goon stutters, kicks the ground, U-turns off.

The cop goes back to his car—his B-movie goddess is gone.

Time to kill, time to figure her route. I tried due east: Hughes' Glendale fuck pad.

I drove there. Paydirt: a Tudor mansion flanked by airplane-shaped hedges. A circular driveway—her Vette by the door.

I pulled up. Drizzling—I got out and touched the rain. Glenda walked out carrying groceries.

She saw me.

I just stood there.

She tossed me a tin of caviar.

13

WESTERN AND Adams—the whores briefed nice—quasi-deputies for the night.

Bluesuits out in force: popping tricks, impounding trick cars.

Prostie vans behind Cooper's Donuts; Vice bulls bagging IDs. Men stationed southbound and northbound—hot to foil sex prowlers hot to rabbit.

My perch: Copper's roof. Ordnance: binoculars, a bullhorn.

Dig the panic:

Johns soliciting whores—cops grabbing them. Vehicles impounded, van detainment—fourteen fish bagged so far, prelim Q&A:

"You married?"

"You on parole or probation?"

"You like it white or colored? Sign this waiver, we might cut you loose at the station."

No Lucille K.

Some clown tried to run—a rookie plugged his back tires.

Epidemic boo-hoo—"DON'T TELL MY WIFE!" Leg-shackle clangs—the prostie vans shook.

Luck—whores mixed fifty-fifty: white girls, coons. Fourteen tricks arrested—all Caucasian.

Panic down below: Shriners bagged en masse. Five men, fez hats flying—a whore grabbed one and pranced.

I hit the bullhorn: "We've got nineteen! Let's close it down!"

The station—dawdle over—let Sid Riegle work setup. Luck: Junior's Ford by the squadroom door. Headlight signals goosed me walking in: Jack Woods, contingency tail man.

Squadroom, muster room, jail. I badged the jailer—*click/ whoosh*—the door opened. Down the catwalk, turn the corner:

the swish tank facing the drunk tank. Drunks and tricks hooting at the floorshow: drag queens masturbating.

Riegle outside the bars, marking nametags. He shook his head—too much noise to talk.

I scanned the fish—shit—nothing peeper-aged. Fuck it—I hit the show-up room.

Chairs, a height strip stage: one-way glass lit up harsh. Rap sheets and IDs laid out for me—I checked them against my john alias list.

No crossovers—expected—I'd run the fake names through the DMV. No real-name spinoffs; driver's license ages thirty-eight and up—my peeper ten years older minimum. Six tricks misdemeanor rap-sheeted—no Peeping Toms, burglars, sex fiends. A cover note: sixteen out of nineteen men were married.

Riegle walked in. I said, "Where's Stemmons?"

"He's waiting in one of the interrogation rooms. Dave, is the scoop on this real? J.C. Kafesjian's daughter is some kind of prostie?"

"It's true, and don't ask me what Exley wants, and don't tell me how the Department doesn't need this shit with the Feds nosing around."

"I was gonna mention it, but I think I'll stay on your good side. One thing, though."

"What's that?"

"I saw Dan Wilhite in the watch commander's office. Given what he is to the Kafesjians, I'd say he's more than a little pissed."

"Shit, that's more shit I don't need."

Sid smiled. "Yeah, but it's a duck shoot—they *all* signed the false-arrest waivers."

I smiled back. "Move them in."

Riegle walked back out; I grabbed the intercom mike. Shackle clang, shackle shuffle—whore chasers lit up on stage.

"Good evening, gentlemen, and listen closely"—the speaker kicked on loud.

"You have all been arrested for soliciting for purposes of prostitution, a California Penal Code violation punishable by up to a year in the Los Angeles County Jail. Gentlemen, I can make this easy or I can make this one of the worst experiences of your life, and the way I play it depends entirely on you."

Blinks, shuffles, dry sobs—sad sacks all in a row. I read my john list and scoped reactions:

"John David Smith, George William Smith—come on, be original. John Jones, Thomas Hardesty—that's more like it. D. D.

Eisenhower—come on, that's beneath you. Mark Wilshire, Bruce Pico, Robert Normandie—street names, come on. Timothy Crenshaw, Joseph Arden, Lewis Burdette—he's a baseball player, right? Miles Swindell, Daniel Doherty, Charles Johnson, Arthur Johnson, Michael Montgomery, Craig Donaldson, Roger Hancock, Chuck Sepulveda, David San Vicente—Jesus, more street names."

Fuck—I couldn't scan faces that quick.

"Gentlemen, here's where it gets either easy or very difficult. The Los Angeles Police Department wishes to spare you grief, and frankly your *illegal* extramarital pursuits do not concern us that greatly. Essentially, you have been detained to aid us in a burglary investigation. A young woman known to occasionally sell her services on South Western Avenue is involved, and I need to isolate men who have purchased those services."

Riegle up on stage, mug shots out.

"Gentlemen, we can legally hold you for seventy-two hours prior to arraigning you in Misdemeanor Court. You are entitled to one phone call apiece, and should you decide to call your wives, you might tell them that you are being held at University Station on one-eighteen-dash-six-zero charges: soliciting for purposes of prostitution. I understand that you might be reluctant to do that, so listen closely, I'll only say it once."

Rumbles—breath fogged the glass.

"Officer Riegle will show you photographs of that young woman. If you have purchased her services, take two steps forward. If you have seen her streetwalking, but haven't purchased her services, raise your right hand."

Pause a beat.

"Gentlemen, *legitimate confirmations* will get all of you released within several hours, *with no charges filed*. If none of you admit to purchasing this woman's services, then I will conclude that either you are lying or simply that none of you have ever seen her or dallied with her, which means in either case that all nineteen of you will be subjected to intensive questioning, and all nineteen of you will be booked, held for seventy-two hours and arraigned on soliciting charges. You will be held during that time in the facility that we reserve here for homosexual prisoners, i.e. the queer tank, where those nigger queens were shaking their dicks at you. Gentlemen, if any of you do admit to dallying with the young lady, and your statements convince us that you are telling the truth, you will in no way be criminally charged and your disclosures will be kept in the strictest confidence. Once we are convinced, you will all be released and allowed to claim your confiscated property and impounded cars. Your cars are being held at a County lot nearby, and as a reward for your cooperation you will not be charged the standard impound fee. Again: we want the truth. You cannot lie your way out of here by claiming that you fucked her when you didn't—your lies won't wash. Sid, pass the mugs."

Handoff: Riegle to a scrawny granddad type.

Dizzy, lawyer high—David Klein, Juris Doctor.

I looked down, held a breath, looked up: one Shriner and one lounge lizard stood forward. I checked driver's license pix and matched up names:

Shriner: Willis Arnold Kaltenborn, Pasadena. Lizard: Vincent Michael Lo Bruto, East L.A. A rap sheet check, paydirt on the wop: child-support skips.

Sid walked in. "We did it."

"Yeah, we did. Stemmons is waiting, right?"

"Right, and the tape recorder's in with him. The fourth booth down, he's there."

"Put Kaltenborn in number 5, and the greaseball in with Junior. Take the rest of them back to the drunk tank."

"Feed them?"

"Candy bars. And no phone calls—a smart attorney could wangle writs. Where's Wilhite?"

"I don't know."

"Keep him away from the sweat rooms, Sid."

"Dave, he's a captain."

"Then … shit, just do it."

Riegle strolled out—pissed. I strolled, itchy—over to sweat box row.

Standard six-by-eights, peekaboo glass. Booth 5: fez man Kaltenborn. Number 4: Lo Bruto, Junior, a tape rig on the table.

Lo Bruto rocked his chair; Junior squirmed. Touch V.'s take: Junior doped up at Fern Dell. The Ainge roust, a late make: dope eyes. Worse now—pin slits.

Open the door, slam it. Junior nodded—half lurch.

I sat down. "What do they call you—Vince? Vinnie?"

Lo Bruto picked his nose. "The ladies call me Mr. Big Dick."

"That's what they call my partner here."

"Yeah? The nervous, silent type. He must get a lot."

"He does, but we're not here to discuss his sex life."

"Too bad, 'cause I got time. The old lady and the kids are in Tacoma, so I coulda done the whole seventy-two hours, but I figured, why spoil it for the other guys? Look, I fucked her, so why beat around the bush, no pun intended."

I slid him cigarettes. "I like you, Vinnie."

"Yeah, then call me Vincent. And save your money, 'cause I quit on March 4, 1952."

Junior stripped the pack. Shot nerves: three swipes at a match.

I leaned back. "How many times did you go with that girl?"

"Once."

"Why just once?"

"Once qualifies as strange. More than once you might as well pop your old lady for all the surprises you get with whoo-ers."

"You're a smart guy, Vincent."

"Yeah, then why am I a security guard for a buck twenty an hour?"

Junior smoking—huge drags. I said, "You tell me."

"I don't know—I get to choke my mule on the Mighty Man Agency's time. It's a living."

Hot—I took off my jacket. "So you solicited that girl just once, right?"

"Right."

"Had you seen her around before?"

"No."

"Have you seen her since?"

"There hasn't been no since. Jesus Christ, I get paid, I go cruising for some strange and some punk kid cop strongarms me. Jesus fucking—"

"Vincent, what attracted you to that girl?"

"She was white. I got no taste for nigger stuff. I'm not prejudiced, I just don't dig it. Some of my best friends are nig—I mean Negroes, but I don't go for dark cooze."

Junior smoking—hot—he kept his coat on.

Lo Bruto: "Your partner don't talk much."

"He's tired. He's been working undercover up in Hollywood."

"Yeah? Wow, now I know why he's such a pussy bandit. Man-oh-Manischewitz, they say the snatch grows fine up there."

I laughed. "It does, but he's been working fruits. Say, partner, remember how you popped those queers in Fern Dell? Remember—you helped out that Academy pal of yours?"

"Sure"—dry-mouthed, scratchy.

"Jesus, partner, it must have made you sick. Did you stop for some poon on the way home, just to get rid of the TASTE?"

Sweaty knuckle pops—his sleeves dropped. WRIST TRACKS— he tugged his cuff links to hide them.

Lo Bruto: "Hey, I thought this was my show."

"It is. Sergeant Stemmons, any questions for Vincent?"

"No"—dry, fretting those cuff links.

I smiled. "Let's get back to the girl."

Lo Bruto: "Yeah, let's do that."

"Was she good?"

"Strange is strange. She was better than the wife, but not as good as the amateur stuff handsome here probably gets."

"He likes them *blond* and *gorgeous*."

"We all do, but I'm lucky to get it plain old Caucasian."

Junior stroked his gun, spastic-handed.

"So how was she better than your wife?"

"She moved around more, and she liked to talk dirty."

"What did she call herself?"

"She didn't tell me no name."

Lucille's window striptease—use it. "Describe the girl naked."

Fast: "Chubby, low-slung tits. Big brown nipples, like she maybe had some *paisan* blood."

Tilt—he knew. "What was she wearing when you picked her up?"

"Hip huggers—you know, pedal pushers."

"Where did you screw her?"

"In the snatch, where else?"

"The location, Vincent."

"Oh. I ... uh ... I think it was a dive called the Red Arrow Inn."

I tapped the tape rig. "Listen close, Vincent. There's a man on this, but I don't think it's you. Just tell me if the girl talked up any similar stuff."

Lo Bruto nodded; I punched Play. Static hiss, "Now I'll be the daughter and you'll be the daddy, and if you're *reeeeal* sweet we can go again no extra."

I hit Stop. Junior—no reaction. Lo Bruto: "Boy, that sick kitten is just full of surprises."

"Meaning?"

"Meaning she didn't make me wear a safe."

"Maybe she uses a diaphragm."

"Nyet. Trust Mr. Big Dick, these girls *always* go the rubber route."

"And she didn't?"

"What can I tell you, she let this jockey ride bareback. And let me tell you, *paisan*, my big sausage *works*. Witness the goddamn offspring that got me slaving to feed them."

A guess: scrape jobs made Lucille sterile. "What about that tape?"

"What about it?"

"Did the girl talk up any of that daddy-daughter stuff with you?"

"No."

"But you said she talked dirty."

Tee-hee. "She said I was the biggest. I said they don't call me Mr. Big Dick for nothing. She said she's liked them big since way back when, and I said, 'Way back when to a kid like you means last week.' She said something like 'You'd be surprised.'"

Junior tugged his cuff links. Tweak him: "This Lucille sounds like a Fern Dell Park faggot, partner. Big dicks, that's a queer fix-ation. *You've* worked fruits more than me, wouldn't you say so?"

Hot seat—Junior squirmed.

"Wouldn't you say so, Sergeant?"

"Y-yeah, s-sure"—hoarse.

Back to Big Dick. "So the girl wore pedal pushers, right?"

"Right."

"Did she mention a guy perved on her, maybe peeping her trick assignations?"

"No."

"And she wore pedal pushers?"

"Yeah, I told you that already."

"What else did she wear?"

"I don't know. A blouse, I think."

"What about a *fur coat*?"

Hophead nerves—Junior twitched a cuff link clean off.

"No, no fur coat. I mean, Christ, she's a Western Avenue whoo-er."

Change-up: "So you said the girl talked dirty to you."

"Yeah. She said Mr. Big Dick sure deserved his nickname."

"Forget about your dick. Did she talk dirty besides that?"

"She said she was screwing some guy named Tommy."

Tingles/goosebumps. "Tommy who?"

"I don't know, she didn't say no last name."

"Did she say he was her brother?"

"Come on, that's crazy."

"'Come on'? You remember that tape that I just played you?"

"So that was a game. Daddy and daughter don't mean brother, and white people don't do that kind of stuff. It's a sin, it's an *infamia*, it's—"

Hit the table. *"Did she say he was her brother?"*

"No."

"Did she say his last name?"

"No"—soft—scared now.

"Did she say he was perved on her?"

"No."

"Did she say he was a musician?"

"No."

"Did she say he sold narcotics?"

"No."

"Did she say he paid her for it?"

"No."

"Did she say he was a burglar?"

"No."

"A peeper, a voyeur?"

"No."

"Did she say what he did?"

"No."

"Did she talk about her family?"

"No."

"Did she describe this guy?"

"No."

"Did she say he chased colored girls?"

"No. Officer, look—"

I slapped the table—Big Dick crossed himself.

"Did she mention a man named Tommy Kafesjian?"

"No."

"Fur coats?"

"No."

"Fur-coat robberies?"

Junior squirming, scratching his hands.

"Officer, she just said she was banging this guy Tommy. She said he wasn't that good, but he turned her out, and you always pack a torch for the guy who took your cherry."

I froze.

Junior jumped bolt upright—that cuff link rolled under the door.

Itchy scratchy nerves—he jerked the door open. Standing outside: Dan Wilhite. Hall speaker blinks—he'd heard.

"Klein, come here."

I stepped forward. Wilhite jabbed my chest—I bent his hand back. *This is my case. You don't like it, take it up with Exley.*

Narco goons right there—I let him go. Junior tried to waltz—I pulled him back.

Wilhite—pale, popping spit bubbles.

His boys flushed—wicked pissed, spoiling to trash me.

Lo Bruto: "Jesus, I'm hungry."

I shut the door.

"Hey, I'm starved. Can I have a sandwich or something?"

I hit the intercom. "Sid, bring the other man in."

Lo Bruto out, Kaltenborn in: this fat geek wearing a fez. Junior sulked and hid his eyes.

The geek—"Please, I don't want any trouble"—his voice half-ass familiar.

I hit Play.

Lucille: "In advance, sweet." Pause. "Yes, that means *now.*"

Kaltenborn winced—hot potato.

Pause, "Okay, okay"—*more* familiar. Mattress squeaks, grunts—Fats sobbed along.

Lucille: "Let's play a little game. Now I'll be the daughter and you'll be the daddy, and if you're *reeeeal* sweet we can go again no extra."

Big sobs.

I pushed Stop. "Was that you, Mr. Kaltenborn?"

Sobs, nods. Junior squirmed—junkie shitbird.

"Quit crying, Mr. Kaltenborn. The sooner you answer my questions, the sooner we'll let you go."

His fez slid down cockeyed. "Lydia?"

"What?"

"My wife, she won't ..."

"This is strictly confidential. *Is* that you on the tape, Mr. Kaltenborn?"

"Yes, yes it is. Did ... did the police record that ..."

"That *illegal* extramarital assignation? No, we didn't. Do you know who did?"

"No, of course not."

"*Did* you play the daddy?"

Muffled, sob-choked: "Yes."

"Then tell me about it."

Fretting the fez—twisting it, stroking it. "I wanted to go again, so the girl put on her clothes and begged me to rip them off. She said, 'Rip my clothes off, Daddy.' I did it, and we went again, and that's all. I don't know her name—I never saw her before and I haven't seen her since. This is all just a terrible coincidence. That girl was the only prostitute I ever trafficked with, and I was at a meeting with my Shrine brothers to discuss our charity fish fry when one of them asked me if I knew where prostitutes could be procured, so I—"

"Did the girl talk about a man named Tommy?"

"No."

"A *brother* named Tommy?"

"No."

"A man who might be following her, or tape-recording her or eavesdropping on her?"

"No, but I—"

"But what?"

"But I heard a man in the room next to us crying. Maybe it was my imagination, but it was as if he was listening to us. It was as if what he heard disturbed him."

Peeper bingo.

"Did you *see* the man?"

"No."

"Did you hear him say or mutter specific words?"

"No."

"Did the girl mention other members of her family?"

"No, she just said what I told you and what you played me on that tape. Officer … where did you get that? I … I don't want my wife to hear—"

"Are you *sure* she didn't mention a man named Tommy?"

"Please, Officer, you're shouting!"

Change-up: "I'm sorry, Mr. Kaltenborn. Sergeant, do you have any questions?"

Sergeant—this gun-fondling hophead—"N-no"—watch his hands.

"Mr. Kaltenborn, did the girl wear a FUR COAT?"

"No, she wore tight toreador pants and some sort of inexpensive wrap."

"Did she say she dug STRIPTEASE?"

"No."

"Did she say she frequented a Negro club named BIDO LITO'S?"

"No."

"Did she say that peeling off a HOT FUR COAT was ecstasy?"

"No. What are you—?"

Junior dropped his hands—watch for a quick draw.

"Mr. Kaltenborn, did she say she knew a GORGEOUS BLOND POLICEMAN who used to be a boxer?"

"No, she didn't. I ... I don't understand the thrust of these questions, Officer."

"Did she say she knew a shakedown-artist cop with a THRUST for young blond guys?"

RABBIT—

Out the door, down the hall—Junior, his piece unholstered. Outside, chase him, sprint—

He made his car—heaving breathless. I grabbed him, pinned his gun hand, bent his head back.

"I'll let you slide on all of it. I'll pull you off the Kafesjian job before you fuck things up worse. We can trade off right now."

Greasy pomade hair—he thrashed his head free. Stray headlights hit this dope face oozing spittle: "That cunt killed Dwight Gilette, and you're suppressing it. Ainge left town, and maybe I got the gun she fired. You're queer for that cunt and I think you pushed that witness out the window. *No trade*, and you just *watch* me take you and that cunt down."

I grabbed his neck and dug in to kill him. Obscene—his breath, his lips curled to bite. I edged back—slack—a knee slammed me. Down, sucking wind, kicked prone—tires spinning gravel.

Headlights: Jack Woods in tail pursuit.

West L.A., 3:00 A.M. Junior's building—four street-level units—no lights on. No Junior Ford parked nearby—pick the lock, hit the lights.

Aches groin to ribcage—hurt him, kill him. I left the lights on—*let him* show.

Bolt the door, walk the pad.

Living room, dinette, kitchen. Matched wood—fastidious. Neatness, grime: squared-off furniture, dust.

The sink: moldy food, bugs.

The icebox: amyl nitrite poppers.

Butt-filled ashtrays—Junior's brand—lipstick-smudged.

Bathroom, bedroom: grime, makeup kit—the lipstick color matched the butts. A waste basket: red-lip-blotted tissue overflowing. An unmade bed, popped poppers on the sheets. I flipped the pillow: a silencer-fitted Luger and shit-caked dildo underneath.

Paperbacks on the nightstand: *Follow the Boys*, *The Greek Way*, *Forbidden Desire*.

A padlocked trunk.

A wall photo: Lieutenant Dave Klein in LAPD dress blues. Track queer thinking, zoooom:

I'm not married.

No woman heat pre-Glenda.

Meg—he *couldn't* know.

The Luger smiling—"Go ahead, shoot something."

I fired, point-blank silent: shattered glass/ripped plaster/ripped ME. I shot the trunk—splinters/cordite haze—the lock flew.

I tore in. Neat paper stacks—fastidious Junior. Slow, inventory them pro—

Carbons:

Johnny Duhamel's Personnel file. Dudley Smith fitness reports—all Class A. Co-opt requests—Johnny to the fur job—fur-heist references checkmarked. Strange: Johnny *never* worked Patrol—he moved straight to the Bureau post-Academy.

More Duhamel—boxing programs—beefcake deluxe. Academy papers, Evidence 104—Junior told Reuben Ruiz he taught Johnny. Straight A's, blind fag love—Duhamel's prose style stunk. More fur-job paper: Robbery reports, figure Junior scooped Dudley—*he* made Johnny as the thief and Dud never tumbled.

A formal statement: Georgie Ainge rats Glenda on the Dwight Gilette 187. Lieutenant D. D. Klein suppresses the evidence; Junior tags the motive: lust. Grab those pages, safe-deposit-box info underneath: figure Junior had backup statements stashed at some bank. No mention of the gun or Glenda's prints on a gun—maybe Junior stashed the piece as a hole card.

Plaster dust settling—my shots grazed some pipes. Miscellaneous folders, file cards:

Folder number one—Chief Ed Exley clippings—the Nite Owl job. Number two—odd Exley cases '53–'58. Concise—the *Times*, *Herald*—fastidious.

WHY?

The cards—LAPD FIs—four-by-six field questioning forms. "Name," "Location," "Comments"—filled in shorthand. I read through them and interpreted:

All locations "F.D.P."—make that Fern Dell Park. Initials, no names. Numbers—California Penal Code designations—lewd and lascivious behavior.

Comments: homo coitus interruptus, Junior levies on-the-spot fines—cash, jewelry, reefers.

Sweaty, close to breathless. Three cards clipped together—initials "T.V." Comments: the Touch Vecchio roust—credit Junior with extortion skill:

Touch calls Mickey C. power-broke and desperate. He's hot to do something "on his own"; he's got his own shakedown gig brewing. Feature: Chick Vecchio to pork famous women; Touch to pork celebrated fruits. Pete Bondurant to take pix and apply the strongarm: cough up or *Hush-Hush* gets the negatives.

Chills—bad juju. The phone—once, stop, once—Jack's signal.

I grabbed the bedside extension. "Yeah?"

"Dave, listen. I tailed Stemmons to Bido Lito's. He met J.C. and Tommy Kafesjian in this back room they've got there. I saw them shake him for a wire, and I caught a few words before they shut the window."

"What?"

"What I heard was Stemmons talking. He offered to protect the Kafesjian family—he actually said 'family'—from you and somebody else, I couldn't catch the name."

Maybe Exley—that clip file. "What else?"

"Nothing else. Stemmons walked out the front door counting money, like Tommy and J.C. just palmed him. I tailed him down the street, and I saw him badge this colored guy. I think the guy was selling mary jane, and I think he palmed Stemmons."

"Where is he now?"

"Heading your way. Dave, you owe me—"

I hung up, dialed 111, got Georgie Ainge's listing. Dial it, two rings, a message: "The number you have reached has been disconnected." Junior's story held: Ainge blew town.

Options:

Stall him, threaten to rat him as a homo. Maim him, trade him: depositions and print gun for no exposé.

Shit logic—psychos don't barter.

I doused the lights, packed the Luger. Kill him/don't kill him. Pendulum: if he walks in on the wrong swing he's dead.

Think—queer pinup fever—psycho Junior hates heartthrob Glenda.

Time went nutso.

My ribs ached.

The morning paper hit the door—I shot a chair. Bullet logic: this grief for a woman I never even touched.

I walked outside. Dawn—milkman witnesses nixed murder.

I dropped the Luger in a trashcan.

I primped—don't think, just do it.

14

I KNOCKED; she answered. My move—she moved first. "Thanks for yesterday."

Set ready: gown and raincoat. My move—she moved first. "It's David Klein, right?"

"Who told you?"

She held the door open. "I saw you on the set, and I saw you following me a few times. I know what unmarked police cars look like, so I asked Mickey and Chick Vecchio about you."

"And?"

"And I'm wondering what you want."

I walked in. Nice stuff—maybe fuck-pad furnished. TVs by the couch—Vecchio stash.

"Be careful with those televisions, Miss Bledsoe."

"Tell your sister that. Touch told me he sold her a dozen of them."

I sat on the couch—hot Philcos close by. "What else did he tell you?"

"That you're a lawyer who dabbles in slum property. He said you turned down a contract at MGM because strikebreaking appealed to you more than acting."

"Do you know why I was following you?"

She pulled a chair up—not too close. "You're obviously working for Howard Hughes. When I left him, he threatened to violate my contract. You obviously know Harold Miciak, and you obviously don't like him. Mr. Klein, did you … ?"

"Scare off Georgie Ainge?"

"Yes."

I nodded. "He's a pervert, and fake kidnaps never work."

"How did you know about it?"

"Never mind. Do Touch and his boyfriend know I scared him away?"

"No, I don't think so."

"Good, then don't tell them."

She lit a cigarette—the match shook. "Did Ainge talk about me?"

"He said you used to be a prostitute."

"I was also a carhop and Miss Alhambra, and yes, I used to work for a call service in Beverly Hills. A very expensive one, Doug Ancelet's."

Shake her: "You worked for Dwight Gilette."

Stylish—that cigarette prop helped. "Yes, and I was arrested for shoplifting in 1946. Did Ainge mention anything—"

"Don't tell me things you might regret."

A smile—cheap—not *that* smile. "So you're my guardian angel."

I kicked a TV over. "Don't patronize me."

Not a blink: "Then what do you want me to do?"

"Quit stealing from Hughes, apologize to him and fulfill the stipulations of your contract."

Her raincoat slid off—bare shoulders, knife scars. "Never."

I leaned closer. "You've gone as far as you can on looks and charm, so use your brains and do the smart thing."

Smiling: "Don't *you* patronize me."

That smile—I smiled back. "Why?"

"*Why?* Because I was *dismissable* to him. Because last year I was carhopping and one of his 'talent scouts' saw me win a dance contest. He got me an 'audition,' which consisted of me taking off my brassiere and posing for pictures, which Mr. Hughes liked. Do you know what it's like to get screwed by a man who keeps naked pictures of you and six thousand other girls in his Rolodex?"

"Nice, but I'm not buying."

"Oh?"

"Yeah, I think you got bored and moved on. You're an actress, and the style angle of jilting Howard Hughes appealed to you. You figured you could get yourself out of trouble, because you've been in shitloads of trouble before."

"*Why*, Mr. Klein?"

"Why what?"

"Why are you putting yourself to such trouble to keep me out of trouble?"

"I can appreciate style."

"No, I don't believe you. And what else did Georgie Ainge say about me?"

"Nothing. What else did the Vecchio brothers say about me?"

Laughing: "Touch said he used to have a crush on you. Chick said you're dangerous. Mickey said he's never seen you with a woman, so maybe that rules out the standard reason for your being interested in me. I'm only thinking that there must be a payoff involved somewhere."

Scope the room—books, art—taste she got somewhere. "Mickey's on the skids. If you thought you traded Hughes up for a big-time gangster, you're wrong."

She chained cigarettes. "You're right, I miscalculated."

"Then square things with Hughes."

"Never."

"Do it. Get us both out of trouble."

"No. Like you said, I've been in trouble before."

Zero fear—daring me to say I KNOW.

"You should see yourself on camera, Miss Bledsoe. You're laughing at the whole thing, and it's real stylish. Too bad the movie's headed for drive-ins in Dogdick, Arkansas. Too bad no men who can help your career will see it."

A flush—one split second. "I'm not as beholden to men as you think I am."

"I didn't say you liked it, I just meant you know it's the game."

"Like being a bagman and a strikebreaker?"

"Yeah, wholesome stuff. Like you and Mickey Cohen."

Smoke rings—nice. "I'm not sleeping with him."

"Good, because guys have been trying to kill him for years, and it's the people around him who get hurt."

"He was something once, wasn't he?"

"He had style."

"Which we both know you appreciate."

This portrait on a shelf—a ghoul woman. "Who's that?"

"That's Vampira. She's the hostess of an awful horror TV show. I used to carhop her, and she gave me pointers on how to act in your own movie when you're in someone else's movie."

Shaky hands—I wanted to touch her.

"Are you fond of Mickey, Mr. Klein?"

"Sure. He had it once, so it's rough to see him diving for scraps."

"Do you think he's desperate?"

"Attack of the Atomic Vampire?"

Glenda laughed and coughed smoke. "It's worse than you think. Sid Frizell is putting in all this gore and incest, so Mickey's afraid they'll have to book it straight into drive-ins to make a profit."

I fixed the TV pile. "Be smart and go back to Hughes."

"No. Frizell's directing some stag films on the side, though. He has a place in Lynwood fixed up with mirrored bedrooms, so maybe I could get work there."

"Not your style. Does Mickey know about it?"

"He's pretending he doesn't, but Sid and Wylie Bullock have been talking it up. Mr. Klein, what are you going to do about this?"

Shelves packed tight—college texts. I opened one—comp stuff, doodling: a heart circling "G.B. & M.H."

"Yes, I stole those. What are you going—"

"What happened to M.H.?"

That smile. "He got another girl pregnant and died in Korea. David—"

"I don't know. Maybe I'll just pull out and set you up with an attorney. But the best you can hope for is a violated contract and no criminal charges."

"And the worst?"

"Howard Hughes is Howard Hughes. One word to the DA gets you indicted for grand theft."

"Mickey said you're friends with the new DA."

"Yeah, he used to study my crib sheets in law school, and Hughes put two hundred grand in his slush fund."

"David—"

"It's Dave."

"I like David better."

"No, my sister calls me that."

"So?"

"Let it rest."

The phone rang—Glenda picked up. "Hello? ...Yes, Mickey, I know I'm late.... No, I've got a cold....Yes, but Sid and Wylie can shoot around my scenes.... No, I'll try to come in this afternoon....Yes, I won't forget our dinner.... No—goodbye, Mickey."

She hung up. I said, "M.H. took off, but Mickey won't."

"Well, he's lonely. Four of his men have disappeared, and I think he knows they're dead. Business was business, but I think he misses them more than anything else."

"He's still got Chick and Touch."

A breeze—Glenda shivered. "I don't know why they stay. Mickey has this scheme to have them seduce famous people. It's so un-Mickey it's pathetic."

"Pathetic"—Junior's notes confirmed. Glenda—shivers, goosebumps.

I grabbed her raincoat and held it out—she stood up smiling. Touching her.

She slid the coat on; I pulled it back and touched her scars. Glenda: this slow turn around to kiss me.

Day/night/morning—the phone off the hook, the radio low. Talk, music—soft ballads lulled Glenda sleepy. Losing her brought it ALL back.

She slept hard, stirred hungry. Yawns, smiles—open eyes caught me scared. Kisses kept her from asking; the whole no-payoff feel kept me breathless.

Pressed hard together—no thoughts. *Her* breath peaking—no thoughts. Inside her when her eyes said don't hold back—no queers, no peepers, no dope-peddler-daughter whores taunting me.

15

"... AND THEY are out there, within our jurisdiction, supersed-ing our jurisdiction. So far as we know, there are seventeen Fed-eral agents and three Deputy U.S. Attorneys backstopping Welles Noonan. Noonan has not requested an LAPD liaison, so we must fully assume that this is a hostile investigation aimed at discredit-ing us."

Chief William H. Parker speaking. Standing by: Bob Gallaudet, Ed Exley. Seated: all stationhouse commanders and Detective Division COs. Missing: Dan Wilhite, Dudley Smith—Mike Breun-ing and Dick Carlisle pinch-hitting.

Eerie—*no* Narco men. Odd—no Dudley.

Exley at the mike: "The chief and I view this 'investigation' as conceived for political gain. Federal agents are not city policemen and certainly not conversant with the realities of maintaining order in Negro-inhabited sectors. Welles Noonan wishes to discredit both the Department and our colleague Mr. Gallaudet, and Chief Parker and I have agreed on measures to limit his success. I will be briefing each of you division heads individually, but before I commence I'll hit some key points you should all be aware of."

I yawned—bed-bruised, exhausted. Exley: "Division commanders should tell their men, both plainclothes and uniform: muscle and/or palm your informants and tell them not to cooperate with any Federal agents they might encounter. Along those lines, I want Southside club and bar owners visited. 'Visited' is a euphemism, gentlemen. 'Visited' means that the station COs at Newton, University and 77th Street should send intimidating plainclothesmen around to tell the owners that since we overlook certain infractions of theirs, they should overlook speaking candidly to the Feds. The Central Vagrant Squad will follow a parallel line: they will round up local derelicts to insure their silence vis-à-vis enforcement measures that quasi-liberals like Noonan might consider overzealous. The 77th Squad is to politely muscle white swells out of the area—we want no well-connected people federally entrapped. Robbery and Homicide Division detectives are currently sifting through recent Negro-on-Negro unsolved homicides, with an eye toward presenting indictment-ready evidence to Mr. Gallaudet—we want to counter Noonan's charge that we let colored 187s lie doggo. And finally, I think it's safe to say that the Feds might raid the slot and vending-machine locations controlled by Mickey Cohen. We will let them do this, and we will let Cohen take the fall. Central Vice has destroyed all the coin-hardware complaints that we've ignored, and we can always say that we didn't know those machines existed."

Implied: Mickey didn't yank his Southside coin. Warn him—again—tell Jack Woods to pull his Niggertown book.

Parker walked out; Exley coughed—crypto-embarrassed. "The chief has never liked white women fraternizing with Negroes, and he's hard-nosed the club owners down there who encourage it. Sergeant Breuning, Sergeant Carlisle—you men make sure that those club owners don't talk to the Feds."

Smirks—Dudley's boys loved strongarm. Exley: "That's all for now. Gentlemen, please wait outside my office, I'll be down to brief you individually. Lieutenant Klein, please remain seated."

Gavel bangs—meeting adjourned. A big exit; Gallaudet slipped me a note.

Exley walked over. Brusque: "I want you to stay on the Kafes-jian burglary. I'm thinking of stepping it up, and I want a detailed report on the trick sweep."

"Why wasn't Narco represented at this meeting?"

"Don't question my measures."

"One last time: the Kafesjians are prime Fed meat. They're twenty years dirty with the Department. Rattling their cage is suicidal."

"One last time: don't question my motives. One last time: you and Sergeant Stemmons stay on the case full priority."

"Was there any specific reason why you wanted Stemmons on this job?"

"No, he just seemed like the logical choice."

"Meaning?"

"Meaning he works closely with you at Ad Vice, and he had excellent ratings as an evidence teacher."

Deadpan—a tough read. "I can't believe this personal-involvement routine. Not from you."

"Make it personal yourself."

Tight reins—don't laugh. "It's getting there."

"Good. Now what about the family's known associates?"

"I've got my best snitch looking into it. I spoke to a man named Abe Voldrich, but I don't think he knows anything about the burglary."

"He's a longtime Kafesjian KA. Maybe he has some family background information."

"Yeah, but what do you want—a burglary suspect or family dirt?"

No retort—he walked. I checked Gallaudet's note:

Dave—

I understand your need to protect certain friends of yours who have Southside business dealings, and I think Chief Ex-ley's fix on the Kafesjians is a bit untoward. Please do what you can to protect the LAPD's Southside interests, especially in light of this damn Fed probe. And please, without telling Chief Exley, periodically update me on the Kafesjian investigation.

Four days—chase evidence, get chased back. Sprint, get chased harder—pictures I couldn't outrun.

I told Mickey to pull his machines—he shrugged the whole Fed business off. Shit-for-brains Mickey—Jack Woods yanked his biz in record time. Chase Exley with paper: Kafesjian 459 PC, record detail. Covered: the peeper tape and Q&A—those two Lucille tricks.

Exley said keep going. Small talk: how's Stemmons handling the job?

I said just fine. Mental pictures: beefcake Johnny Duhamel, lipstick on cigarette butts.

Exley said keep going; I fed Bob Gallaudet information on the sly. Politics: he didn't want Welles Noonan reaping juice off the Kafesjians.

Chase, watch for chasers. No tails—near-crack-ups making sure. Exley/Hughes/Narco/the Feds: potential chasers, big resources.

Chasing evidence:

I staked the Red Arrow Inn—no Lucille, no peeper suspects. I checked 77th: no peeper FI cards found. Tri-State MO checks: zero. Lester Lake said scoop soon— "maybe." Chasing secrets, chasing pictures—

Solo trick rousts—no new Lucille fuckers confirmed. Western and Adams, points south—pressing for stories—I stayed high-octane juiced on that family.

Like Exley.

Call it lawyer style:

Disturbing the Kafesjians with a Federal narcotics probe in progress is certifiably insane. Edmund Exley is a certifiably brilliant detective with nationally recognized leadership skills. Narco was not present at Exley's Fed probe briefing. Narco is the most autonomous LAPD division. Narco and the Kafesjian family go back autonomously twenty-odd years. Exley knows that the Fed probe will succeed. Exley wants the probe diverted from the rank-and-file LAPD. Exley knows that heads must roll. Exley has convinced Chief Parker that the least damaging, most judicious move is to sacrifice Narco to the Feds—they can be portrayed as rogue cops autonomously run amok without severely damaging the overall prestige of the Department.

I didn't quite buy it—his hard-on for that family played too ugly.

Like mine, like Junior's.

George Stemmons II—my worst pictures.

I chased him four days—call him plain gone. Ad Vice: straight no-shows. The pad I trashed: locked tight. Darktown: no. His father's house: no. Fern Dell: no. Fag bars: no, he didn't have the guts to go that blatant. Long shot—Johnny Duhamel—his known haunts.

Personnel shot me his address. I checked it three days/nights running—no Johnny, no Junior. No way to catch Duhamel on duty—I couldn't tip

Dudley Smith. An instinct said Junior's crush ran unrequited—Blond and Gorgeous didn't play fruit. Possible approach: Reuben Ruiz, Johnny's pal. Gallaudet turned him: front man set to oil the spics out of Chavez Ravine.

I fed Bob a snow job: Ruiz knew a guy I needed to lean on. Gallaudet: he's in training somewhere, check the Ravine in a few days—he'll be there working the crowd.

Tapped out.

Clay pigeon:

Junior nails Glenda dead—for Murder One. A nigger pimp victim— Gallaudet might not seek an indictment. But: Howard Hughes snaps his fingers; Gas Chamber Bob jumps. Snap—pick the judge, stack the jury— Glenda green-room bound. Accessory charges pending: on me.

The upshot:

Neutralize Junior. Hush up his Kafesjian dealings—if Exley tumbles, he'll rat Glenda to buy out. My buyout—Duhamel—feed him to Dudley, the peak moment, work for Exley—Junior/Glenda insurance.

I paid Jack Woods two grand: find me Junior Stemmens. My skip trace—HER—a movie-set trailer late nights.

Miciak kept quiet—we both made his tail strictly freelance. I wrote Milteer fake reports—Glenda fed me fake details. The set—Mickey's wino crew passed out. We talked low, made love and danced around IT.

I never said I knew; she never pressed me. Biographies, gaps: I hid Meg, she bypassed whoring.

I never said I kill people. I never said Lucille K. made me a voyeur.

She said I used people up.

She said I only bet on rigged games.

She said ranking cop/lawyer put some distance on white trash.

She said I never got burned.

I said three out of four—not bad.

PART THREE

DARKTOWN RED

16

DIRT ROADS, shacks. Hills trapping smog—Chavez Ravine.

Swamped—I parked long-distance and scanned it:

Geeks waving placards. Newsmen, bluesuits. Commie types chanting: "Justice, sí! Dodgers, no!"

Friendly throngs—eyes on Reuben Ruiz, gladhander. Sheriff's bulls, Agent Will Shipstad.

Ruiz—Fed witness?

I jogged into it—"Hey, hey! No, no! Don't drive us back to Mexico!" Badge out—blues eased me through.

Heckler hubbub:

Ruiz, fighting tonight—be there to cheer his opponent. The fascist Bureau of Land and Way: plans to relocate the spics to Lynwood slum pads. "Hey, hey! No, no! Justice, sí! Dodgers, no!"

Ruiz blasting bullhorn Spanish:

Move out early! Your relocation dough means Easy Street! New homes soon available! Enjoy the new Dodger Stadium YOU helped create!

Noise war—Reuben's bullhorn won. Deputies tossed tickets—spics genuflected, grabbed. I snatched one: Ruiz vs. Stevie Moore, Olympic Auditorium.

Chants, jabber—Ruiz saw me and bucked fans.

I shoved close. Reuben cupped a shout: "We should yak! Say my dressing room after my bout?"

I nodded yes—"Scum! Dodger pawn!"—no way to talk.

A quick run—the Bureau, my office.

A message from Lester Lake—meet me 8:00 tonight—Moonglow Lounge. Exley skirted Ad Vice—I gestured him over.

"I had a few questions."

"Ask them, as long as they're not 'What do you want?'"

"Let's try 'Why just two men on a case you're so hot to clear?'"

"No. Next question, and don't ask 'Why me?'"

"Let's try 'What's in it for me?'"

Exley smiled. "If you clear the case I'll exercise a rarely used chief of detective's prerogative and jump you to captain without a civil-service listing. I'll rotate Dudley Smith into Ad Vice and give you the Robbery Division command."

Jig heaven—don't swoon.

"Is something wrong, Lieutenant? I would have expected you to express your gratitude."

"Thanks, Ed. That's a dandy carrot you just dangled."

"Given what you are, I'd say it is. Now I'm busy, so ask your next question."

"Lucille Kafesjian's the key to this thing. I've got a hunch that the family knows damn well who the burglar is, and I want to bring her in for questioning."

"No, not yet."

Change-up: "Give me the Hurwitz fur job. Take it away from Dudley."

"No, and no emphatically, and don't ask me again. Now, let's wrap this up."

"Okay, then let me lean on Tommy Kafesjian."

"Explain 'lean on,' Lieutenant."

"*Lean on. Muscle.* I fuck Tommy up, he tells us what we want to know. You know, outré police methods, like the time you shot those unarmed niggers."

"No direct approach on the family. Other than that, you have carte blanche."

Carte blanche shitwork, overdue: big fucking distractions.

Simple:

Lucille pix/tape rig/motel list—haul them southbound and ask questions:

Have you rented to her?

Has a man requested a room adjoining hers?

Have wino/bums rented rooms here by proxy?

Bad odds—call the Red Arrow her sole trick pad.

Southbound—Central Avenue all the way. Police intrigue, big-time:

IA cars trailing Fed cars—discreet. Bum rousts—Vag cops spread thick. Prostie wagons prowling for whores.

Feds:

License-plate checks outside bars and nightclubs.

Kibitzing a sidewalk crap game.

Staking out a swanky coon whorehouse.

Crew-cut gray suit Feds Darktown rife.

I stopped at 77th Street Station and borrowed a tape rig. Sweat box row was packed: jig-on-jig 187 "clearance." Feds outside with cameras—snapping cop IDs.

Shitwork now:

Tick Tock Motel, Lucky Time Motel—no to all my questions. Darnell's Motel, De Luxe Motel—straight nos. Handsome Dan's Motel, Cyril's Lodge—No City. Hibiscus Inn, Purple Roof Lodge—NO.

Nat's Nest—81st and Normandie. "Kleen Rooms Always"— brace the clerk.

"Yessir, I know this girl. She's a short-timer rental, an' she always ask for the same room."

I gripped the counter. "Is she registered now?"

"Nosir, an' not for maybe six, seven days."

"Do you know what she uses the room for?"

"Nosir. My motto is 'See no evil, hear no evil,' an' I adheres to that policy 'cept when they be makin' too much noise doin' whatever it is they be doin'."

"Does the girl ask for a front room with a street view?"

Shocked: "Yessir. How you know that?"

"Have you rented the room next to hers to a young white man? Did a bum request that particular room and register for him?"

Shut-my-mouth shocked—he dipped behind the counter and pulled out a rent card. "See, 'John Smith,' which in my opinion be an alias. See, he gots two days left on his rent. He ain' in right now, I seen him leave this morn—"

"Show me those rooms."

He beelined outside, fumbling keys. Two doors opened quick— good and cop scared.

Separate bungalows—no connecting door.

I caught up. Easy now—frost him with a ten spot. "Watch the street. If that white guy shows up, stall him. Tell him you've got a plumber in his room, then come and get me."

"Yessir, yessir"—genuflecting streetside—

Two doors—no mutual access. Side windows—the peeper could WATCH her. Hedges below, a loose-stone walk path.

Look:

A wire out HIS window.

Into HIS hedge, out, under the stones.

I grabbed it and pulled—

Stones flew—the wire jerked taut. Into HER room—under the carpet, yank—a spackle-covered mike snapped off the wall.

Walk the cord back:

HIS window—jam the ledge up—step in. Pull—*thunk*—a tape machine under the bed.

Empty reels.

Back outside, check the doors—no pry marks. Figure HE went in HER window.

I shut both doors and tossed HIS room.

The closet:

Soiled clothes, empty suitcase, record player.

The dresser: skivvies, jazz albums—Champ Dineen, Art Pepper. Title matchers—Tommy K.'s smashed wax duplicated.

The bathroom:

Razor, shaving cream, shampoo.

Pull the rug:

Girlie mags—*Transom*—three issues. Cheesecake, text: movie-star "confessions."

No tape.

Dump the mattress, punch the pillow—a hard spot—tear, rip—

One tape spool—rig it up for a listen fast—

Nerves—I fumbled the goods, smeared potential prints. Spastic-handed—loop the tape/push Start.

Rustles, coughs. I shut my eyes and imagined it: lovers in bed.

Lucille: "You don't get tired of these games?"

Unknown Man: "Hand me a cigarette"—pause—"No, I don't tire of them. You certainly know how to—"

Sobs—distant—motel room walls shutting *my* man out.

Trick Man: "... and you know that father-daughter games have staying power. Really, given our age variance, it's quite a natural bed game to play."

A cultured voice—Tommy/J.C. antithetical.

Sobs, louder.

Lucille: "These places are filled with losers and lonesome creeps."

No hink/no recognition/no surveillance fear.

Click—figure a radio—"... chanson d'amour, ratta-tat-tatta, play encore." Blurred voices, *click*, Trick Man: "... of course, there was always that little dose you gave me."

"Dose": clap/syph?

I checked the reels—tape running out.

Sleepy voices jumbled—*more than a trick stand*. I shut my eyes—please, one more game.

Silent tape hiss—sleepy lovers. Hinge creak/"God!"—too close, too real—NOW. Eyes open—a white man standing by the door.

Fucked up blurry vision—I drew down, aimed, fired. Two shots—the doorjamb splintered; one more—wood scraps exploding.

The man ran.

I ran out aiming.

Screams, shouts.

Zigzags—my man bucking traffic. I fired running—two shots went wide. Aiming straight—a clear shot—this jolt: if you kill him, you won't know WHY?

Bolting traffic, sighting in on this white head bobbing. Horns, brakes—black faces on the sidewalk, my white speck disappearing.

I tripped, stumbled, ran. Losing him—black all around me.

Shouts.

Black faces scared.

My reflection in a window: this terrified geek.

I slowed down. Another window—black faces—follow their eyes:

A curbside roust—Feds and niggers. Welles Noonan, Will Shipstad, FBI muscle.

Grabbed, shoved—pinned to a doorway. Rabbit-punched—I dropped my piece.

Pinned—gray suit Fed gorillas. Welles Noonan sucker-punched me: spit in my face. His punch line: "That's for Sanderline Johnson."

17

THE MOONGLOW—early for Lester. Jukebox tunes killed time.

Noonan, backed by music—replays still smelling his spittle:

Those Feds—cut-rate revenge. Back to Nat's Nest—prowl cars responding to shots. I chased them off and bagged evidence: records, skin mags, tape rig, tape.

Calls next:

Orders to Ray Pinker: dust both rooms, bring a sketch man—make the clerk face-detail the peeper. Mugshot checks later—pray for good eyes.

Jack Woods, glad tidings: he spotted Junior, tailed him for two hours and lost him. Busy Junior—three indy pusher shakedowns—Jack glommed descriptions and plate numbers.

Jack, verbatim: "He looked fried to the gills and fucking insane. I checked his car out while he stopped for cigarettes. You know what I saw in the backseat? A hypodermic kit, six empty tuna-fish cans and three sawed-off shotguns. I don't know what he's got on you, but in my opinion you should clip him."

The jukebox, unmistakable—Lester Lake's "Harbor Lights"— and not on my dime.

Bingo—Lester himself, oozing fear. "Hello, Mr. Klein."

"Sit down. Tell me about it."

"Tell you about what?"

"The look on your face and why you played that goddamn song."

Sitting down: "Just reassurance. Good to know Uncle Mickey keeps my tune in his Wurlitzers."

"Mickey should pull his boxes before the Feds pull him. What is it? I haven't seen you this spooked since the Harry Cohn thing."

"Mr. Klein, you know a couple of Mr. Smith's boys named Sergeant Breuning an' Sergeant Carlisle?"

"What about them?"

"Well, they workin' overtime at the Seven-Seven."

"Come on, get to it."

Breathless: "They goin' aroun' tryin' to solve colored-on-colored killin's, word is to forestall all this potential good Federal investigation publicity. You remember you ask me 'bout a mary jane pusher named Wardell Knox? You remember I tol' you he got hisself killed by person or persons unknown?"

Tommy K. snitched Knox to Narco—Dan Wilhite told Junior. "I remember."

"Then you should remember I tol' you ol' Wardell was a cunthound with a million fuckin' enemies. He was fuckin' a million different ladies, includin' this high-yellow cooze Tilly Hopewell that I was also climbin'. Mr. Klein, I heard them Mr. Smith boys been lookin' for me on account of some bogus rumor that I snuffed fuckin' Wardell, and it looks to me like they be measurin' me for a quick statistic. Now you want skinny on the fuckin' Kafesjians and their fuckin' known associates, so I got a real knee-slapper for you, which is that I just recently heard that crazy Tommy Kafesjian popped ol' Wardell roun' September, some kind of fuckin' dope or sex grievance, 'cause he was also climbin' that fine Tilly Hopewell on occasion."

Breathless/heaving.

"Look, I'll talk to Breuning and Carlisle. They'll lay off you."

"Yeah, maybe thas' true, 'cause ol' slumlord Dave Klein knows the right people. But Mr. Smith, he hates the colored man. An' I don' see you people pinnin' the Wardell Knox job on Tommy the K., your righteous motherfuckin' informant."

"So do you want to change the world or waltz on this thing?"

"I wants you to give me an extra month's free rent for all the fine skinny I gots on the fuckin' Kafesjian family."

"Harbor Lights" snapped on again. Lester: "And on that note, I heard the daughter's a righteous semipro hooker. I heard Tommy and J.C. beat up Mama Kafesjian and her like batting practice. I heard Madge—that's Mama—used to have a thing goin' with Abe Voldrich, he's this head guy in their dope operation, an' he runs one of their dry-cleaning joints on the side. I heard Voldrich dries up big bushels of mary jane in them big dryers they got at their plants. I heard the way they keep things copacetic with rival pushers is kickbacks from little Mickey Mouse independents that they tolerates, but no righteous organizations would ever try to infringe on the Southside, 'cause they knows the LAPD would come down hard just to keep them Armenian fucks happy. I heard the only humps they snitch to you people is the indies who won't kick back no operatin' tribute. I heard the family is fuckin' skin tight, even though they don't treat each other with so much fuckin' respect. I heard that outside of Voldrich an' this colored trim Tommy the K. goes for, the family only gots employees and customers, not no fuckin' friends. I heard Tommy used to be pals with some white kid named Richie, I don't know no last name, but I heard they blew these punk square horns together, like they pretended they had talent. That crazy-ass burglary you told me about—them chopped-up watchdogs an' stolen silverware an' shit—I heard jackshit 'bout that. I also heard you thinkin' 'bout raisin' the rent in my buildin', so I—"

Cut him off: "What about Tommy fucking Lucille?"

"Say what? I didn' hear nothin' like that. I said 'skin tight,' not fuckin' skin deep."

"What about this Richie guy?"

"Shit, I tol' you what I heard, no more, no less. You want me—"

"Keep asking around about him. He might connect to this peeper guy I've been chasing."

"Yeah, you mentioned that Peepin' Tom motherfucker, an' I knows how to improvise off what a man tells me. So I been askin' aroun' 'bout that, an' I ain't heard nothin'. Now, 'bout that rent increase—"

"Ask around if the Kafesjians have been looking for a peeper themselves. I have a hunch that they know who the burglar is."

"An' I got a hunch slumlord Dave Klein gonna raise my rent."

"No, and I'll carry you to January. If Jack Woods comes around to collect, call me."

"What about Mr. Smith's boys in hot pursuit of ol' Lester?"

"I'll take care of it. Do you know Tilly Hopewell's address?"

"Can my people dance? Have I strapped on at that love shack more than a few times myself?"

"Lester—"

"8491 South Trinity, apartment 406. Say, where you goin'?"

"The fights."

"Moore and Ruiz?"

"That's right."

"Bet on the Mex. I used to climb Stevie Moore's sister, an' she tol' me Stevie couldn't take it to the breadbasket."

I badged in ringside—late.

The sixth-round break—card girls strutting. Spectator chants: "Dodgers, no! Ruiz must go!" Boos, shouts: pachucos vs. Commies.

The bell—

Rockabye Reuben circling; Moore popping right-hand leads. Mid-ring clinch—Ruiz loose, the spook winded.

"Break! Break!"—the ref in and out.

Moore stalking slow—elbows up, open downstairs. Headhunter Reuben—near-miss hooks moving back.

Lazy Reuben, bored Reuben.

A snap guess: tank job.

Moore—no steam, no juice. Ruiz—lazy hooks, lazy right-hand leads.

Moore swarming and sucking in air; Reuben eating blockable shots—the coon wide open.

Ruiz—a lazy left hook.

Moore catching wind, his guard low.

Bullseye—the wrong man went down.

Pachuco cheers.

Pinko boos.

Reuben—this oh-fuck look—stalling the count. Dawdle time—he oozed over to a neutral corner slow.

Six, seven, eight—Moore up, wobbly.

Ruiz dawdling center ring. Moore backing up—shot to shit. Bomb range, Reuben bombs—wild misses. Ten, twelve, fourteen—real air whizzers.

Ruiz fake-gasping; fake-weary arms flopping dead.

Moore threw a bolo shot.

Rockabye Reuben staggered.

Moore—left/right bolos.

Reuben hit the canvas—eyes rolling, fake out. Seven, eight, nine, ten—Moore kissed Sammy Davis, Jr., at ringside.

Bleacher attack—get the Reds—spics tossing piss-filled beer cups. Placard shields—no help—the pachucos moved in swinging bike chains.

I hit an exit—coffee down the block, let things chill. Twenty minutes, back over—shitloads of prowl cars and Commies shackled up.

Back in—follow the liniment stench. Dressing rooms, Ruiz alone—wolfing a taco plate.

"Bravo, Reuben. The best tank job I've ever seen."

"Hey, and the riot wasn't so bad neither. Hey, Lieutenant, what did those back-pedal hooks tell you?"

I shut the door—noise down the hall—newsmen and Moore. "That you know how to entertain the chosen few."

Chugging beer: "I hope Hogan Kid Bassey saw the fight, 'cause the deal was Moore gets the bantam elimination shot and I move up to the feathers and fight him. I'll kick his ass, too. Hey, Lieutenant, we ain't talked since that night Sanderline jumped."

"Call me Dave."

"Hey, Lieutenant, a nigger and a Mexican jump out a six-story window the same time. Who hits the ground first?"

"I've heard it, but tell me anyway."

"The nigger, 'cause the Mexican's got to stop on the way down and spray *'Ramón y Kiki por vida'* on the wall."

Ha, ha—polite.

"So, Lieutenant, I know you saw Will Shipstad watchdogging me at the ravine. Let me reassure you and Mr. Gallaudet that I'm grateful for this what you call public-relations gig you got me, 'specially since it got my goddamn brother off another GTA bounce. So, yeah, I'm a Fed witness again, but Noonan just wants me to testify on some stale-bread bookie stuff, and I'd never snitch Mickey C. or your buddy Jack Woods."

"I always figured you knew how to play."

"You mean play to the chosen few?"

"Yeah. Business is business, so you fuck your own people to get next to the DA."

Smiling nice: "I got a trouble-prone family, so I gotta figure they're more important than Mexicans in general. Hey, I kiss a little ass, so that what you call them—slumlords?—like you and your sister can stay fat. You know, *Dave*, the fuckin' Bureau of Land and Way's been checking out these dumps in Lynwood. There's supposed to be some what you call converted whorehouse that these hard boys want to dump my poor evicted *hermanos* into, so maybe you and your goddamn slumlord sister can buy in on the ground floor."

Brains—fuck his bravado. "You know a lot about me."

"Hey, Dave 'the Enforcer' Klein, people talk about you."

Change-up: "Is Johnny Duhamel queer?"

"Are you nuts? He is the snatch hound to end all snatch hounds."

"Seen him lately?"

"We keep in touch. Why?"

"Just checking up. He's on the Hurwitz fur case, and it's a big assignment for an inexperienced officer. Has he talked to you about it?"

Head shakes—half-ass wary. "No. Mostly he talks about this Mobster Squad job he's got."

"Anything specific?"

"No, he said he's not supposed to talk about it. Hey, why you pumping me?"

"Why did you look so sad all of a sudden?"

Hooks, jabs—air whizzed. "I saw Johnny maybe a week ago. He said he'd been doing this bad stuff. He didn't, how you say, elaborate, but he said he needed a penance beating. We put on gloves, and he let me punch him around. I remember he had these what you call blisters on his hands."

Rubber-hose work—Johnny probably hates it. "Remember Sergeant Stemmons, Reuben?"

"Sure, your partner at the hotel. Nice haircut, but a punk if you ask me."

"Have you seen him?"

"No."

"Has Johnny mentioned him to you?"

"No. Hey, what's this Johnny routine?"

I smiled. "Just routine."

"Sure, subtle guy. Hey, what do you get when you cross a Mexican and a nigger?"

"I don't know."

"A thief who's too lazy to steal!"

"That's a riot."

Fondling a Schlitz: "You ain't laughing so hard, and I can tell you're thinking: at the ravine Rockabye Reuben said we should talk."

"So talk."

Pure pachuco—he bit off the bottle cap and guzzled. "I heard Noonan talking to Will Shipstad about you. He hates you like a goddamn dog. He thinks you pushed Johnson out the window and fucked up some guy named Morton Diskant. He tried to get me to say I heard you toss Johnson, and he said he's gonna take you down."

18

FORENSICS—AT my living room desk.

Dust the magazines, tape rig, spools—smudges and four identical latents. I rolled my own prints to compare—it confirmed my own fumble-hand fuck-up.

The phone rang—

"Yes?"

"Ray Pinker, Dave."

"You're finished?"

"Finished is right. First, no viable suspect latents, and we dusted every touch surface in both rooms. We took elimination sets off the clerk, who's also the owner, the janitor and the chambermaid, all Negroes. We got *their* prints in the rooms and nothing else."

"Fuck."

"Succinctly put. We also bagged the male clothing and tested some semen-stained shorts. It's O positive again, with the same cell breakdown—your burglar or whatever is quite a motel hopper."

"Shit."

"Succinct, but we had better luck on the sketch reconstruction. The clerk and the artist worked up a portrait, and it's waiting for you at the Bureau. Now—"

"What about mug shots? Did you tell the clerk we'll need him for a viewing?"

Ray sighed—half pissed. "Dave, the man took off for Fresno. He implied that your behavior disturbed him. I offered him an LAPD reimbursement for the door you shot out, but he said it wouldn't cover the aggravation. He also said don't go looking for him, because he is gone, no forwarding. I didn't press for him to stay, because he said he'd complain about that door you destroyed."

"Shit. Ray, did you check—"

"Dave, I'm way ahead of you. I asked the other employees if *they* had seen the tenant of that room. They both said no, and I believed them."

Shit. Fuck.

Half pouty: "Lots of trouble for a one-shot 459, Dave."

"Yeah, just don't ask me why."

Click—my ear stung.

Go, keep dusting:

Smudges off the album covers—grooved records themselves wouldn't take prints. Champ Dineen on my hi-fi: *Sooo Slow Moods, The Champ Plays the Duke.*

Background music—I skimmed *Transom.*

Piano/sax/bass—soft. Cheesecake pix, innuendo: blond siren M.M. craves she-man R.H.—she'll do anything to turn him around. Nympho J.M.—gigantically endowed—seeks double-digit males at Easton's Gym. Ten inches and up, please—J.M. packs a ruler to make sure. Recent conquests: B-movie hulk F.T.; gangster M.B.; laconic cowboy star G.C.

Breathy sax, heartbeat bass.

Stories—traveling-salesman gems. Pix: big-tit slatterns drooping out of lingerie. Piano trills—gorgeous.

One issue down, Dineen percolating. *Transom,* June '58:

M.M. and baseball M.M. hot—her J.D.M. torch pushed her toward hitters. The swank Plaza Hotel—ten-day/ten-night homestand.

Alto sax riffs—Glenda/Lucille/Meg, swirling.

Ads: dick enlargers, home law school. "Mood Indigo" à la Dineen—low brass.

A daddy/daughter story—a straight-dialogue intro. Photos: this skank brunette, bikini-clad.

"Well … you look like my daddy."

"Look? Well, yeah, I'm old enough. I guess a game is a game, right? I can be the daddy because I fit the part."

"Well, like the song says, 'My heart belongs to Daddy.'"

Skim the text:

Orphan Loretta lusts for a daddy. The evil Terry deflowered her—she crawls for him, she hates it. She sells herself to older men—a preacher kills her. Accompanying pix: the skank sash-cord-strangled.

Champ Dineen roaring—think it through:

Loretta equals Lucille; Terry equals Tommy. "Orphan" Loretta—non sequitur. Lucille lusts for Daddy J.C.—hard to buy her hot for that greasy shitbird.

Call the dialogue voyeured.

Call the peeper "author."

Transom, July '58—strictly movie-star raunch. Check the masthead—a Valley address—hit it tomorrow.

The phone rang—cut the volume—catch it.

"Glen—"

"Yes. Are you psychic or just hoping?"

"I don't know, maybe both. Look, I'll come up to the set."

"No. Sid Frizell's shooting some night scenes."

"We'll go to a hotel. We can't use your place or my place—it's too risky."

That laugh. "I read it in the *Times* today. Howard Hughes and his entourage left for Chicago for some Defense Department meeting. David, the Hollywood Hills 'actress domicile' is available, and I have a key."

Past midnight—call it safe. "Half an hour?"

"Yes. Miss you."

I put the phone down and cranked the volume. Ellington/Dineen—"Cottontail." Memory lane—'42—the Marine Corps. Meg—that tune—dancing at the El Cortez Sky Room.

Raw now—sixteen years gone bad. The phone right there—do it.

"Hello?"

"I'm glad I got you, but I figured you'd be out after Stemmons."

"I had to get some sleep. Look, slavedriver—"

"Kill him, Jack."

"Okay by me. Ten?"

"Ten. Clip him and buy me some time."

19

THE HILLS—a big Spanish off Mulholland.

Lights on, Glenda's car out front. Twenty-odd rooms—fuck pad supreme.

I parked, beams on a '55 Chevy. Bad familiar: Harold John Miciak's.

Be sure, tweak the high beams—Hughes Aircraft decals on the back fender.

Late-night quiet—big dark houses, just one lit.

I got out and listened. Voices—his, hers—muffled low.

Up, try the front door—locked. Voices—his edgy, hers calm. Circuit the house, listen:

Miciak: "... you could do worse. Look, you come across for me, you pretend it's Klein. I seen him come see you in Griffith Park, and as far as that goes, you can still give it to him—I'm not possessive and I got no partners. Mr. Hughes, he's never gonna know, just you come across for me and get that money I want from Klein. I know he's got it, 'cause he's connected with some mob guys. Mr. Hughes, he told me so hisself."

Glenda: "How do I know there's just you?"

Miciak: " 'Cause Harold John's the only daddy-o in L.A. man enough to mess with Mr. Hughes and this cop who thinks he's so tough."

Around to the dining room window. Curtain gaps—look:

Glenda edging backward; Miciak pressing up, grinding his hips.

Slow walking—both of them—a knife rack behind Glenda.

I tried the window—no give.

Glenda: "How do I know there's just you?"

Glenda: one hand reaching back, one hand out come hither.

Glenda: "I think we'd be good together."

Around the back, a side door—I shoulder-popped it and ran in.

The hallway, the kitchen, there—

A clinch: his hands groping, hers grabbing knives.

Slow-motion numb—I *couldn't* move. Shock-still frozen, look:

Knives down—in his back, in his neck—twisted in hilt-deep. Bone cracks—Glenda dug in—two hands blood-wet. Miciak thrashing AT HER—

Two more knives snagged—Glenda stabbing blind.

Miciak clawing the rack, up with a cleaver.

I stumbled in close—numb legs—smell the blood—

He stabbed, missed, lurched into the knife rack. She stabbed—his back, his face—blade jabs ripped his cheeks out.

Gurgles/screeches/whines—Miciak dying loud. Knife handles sticking out at odd angles—I threw him down, twisted them, killed him.

Glenda—no screams, this look: SLOW, I've been here before.

SLOW:

We killed the lights and waited ten minutes—no outside response. Plans then—soft whispers holding each other bloody.

No dining room carpet—luck. We showered and swapped clothes—Hughes kept a male/female stash. We bagged our own stuff, washed the floor, the rack, the knives.

Blankets in a closet—we wrapped Miciak up and locked him in his car trunk. 1:50 A.M.—out, back—no witnesses. Out and back again—our cars tucked below Mulholland.

A plan, a fall guy: the Wino Will-o-the-Wisp, L.A.'s favorite at-large killer.

Out to Topanga Canyon solo—I drove Miciak's car. Hillhaven Kiddieland Kamp—defunct, wino turf. I flashlight-checked all six cabins—no bums residing.

I stashed the car out of sight.

I wiped it.

Kougar Kub Kabin—dump the body.

I throttled the corpse per the Wisp MO.

I rolled it through sawdust to stuff up the stab wounds. Forensic logic: impacted wounds made knife casting impossible.

Hope logic:

Howard Hughes, publicity shy—he might not push to find his man's killer.

I walked back to Pacific Coast Highway. SLOW fear speeding up—

Sporadic tails dogging me.

A tail tonight meant grief forever.

Glenda picked me up at PCH. Back to Mulholland, two cars to my place, bed just to talk.

Small talk—her will held. CinemaScope/Technicolor knife work—I pushed to know she didn't like it.

I hit the pillow by her face.

I shined the bed light in her eyes.

I told her:

My father shot a dog/I torched his toolshed/he hit my sister/I shot him, the gun jammed/these Two Tony fucks hurt my sister/I killed them/I killed five other men/I took money—what gives you the right to play it so stylish—

Hit the pillow, make her talk—no style, no tears:

She was floating, carhopping, this pretend actress. She was sleeping around for rent money—a guy told Dwight Gilette. He propositioned her: turn tricks for a fifty-fifty split. She agreed, she did it—sad sacks mostly. Georgie Ainge once—no rough stuff from him—but regular beatings from Gilette.

She got mad. She got this pretend-actress idea: buy a gun off Georgie and scare Dwight. Pretend actress with a prop now: a real pistol.

Dwight made her drive his "nieces" to his "brother's" place in Oxnard. It was fun—cute colored toddlers—their pictures on TV a week later.

Two four-year-olds starved, tortured and raped—found dead in an Oxnard sewer.

Pretend actress, errand girl. This real-actress idea:

Kill Gilette—before he sends any more kids out to be snuffed.

She did it.

She didn't like it.

You don't skate from things like that—you crawl stylish. I held her. I talked a Kafesjian blue streak.

Champ Dineen lulled us to sleep.

I woke up early. I heard Glenda in the bathroom, sobbing.

20

HARRIS DULANGE—fifty, bad teeth: "Since me and the magazine are as clean as a cat's snatch, I will tell you how *Transom* works. First, we hire hookers or aspiring actresses down on their luck for the photos. The written stuff is by yours truly, the editor-in-chief, or it's scribed by college kids who write out their fantasies in exchange for free issues. It's what *Hush-Hush* calls 'Sinuendo.' We tack those movie-star initials onto our stories so that our admittedly feeble-minded readers will think, 'Wow, is that really Marilyn Monroe?'"

Tired—I made an early Bureau run for Pinker's sketch. Exley said no all-points distribution—last night left me too fried to fight him.

"Lieutenant, are you daydreaming? I know this isn't the nicest office in the world, but ..."

I pulled the June '58 issue out. "Who wrote this father-daughter story?"

"I don't even have to look. If it's plump brunettes hot for some daddy surrogate, it's Champ Dineen."

"*What?* Do you know who Champ Dineen *is*?"

"*Was*, because he died some time back. I *knew* the guy was using a pseudonym."

I flashed Pinker's sketch. Dulange deadpanned it: "Who's this?"

"Odds are it's the man who wrote those stories. Haven't you *seen* him?"

"No. We only talked on the phone. Nice-looking picture, though. Surprising. I figured the guy would be a troll."

"Did he say his real name was Richie? That might be a lead on his ID."

"No. We only talked on the phone once. He said his name was Champ Dineen, and I thought, 'Copacetic, and only in L.A.' Lieutenant, let me ask you. Does the Champster have a voyeur fetish?"

"Yes."

Dulange—nodding, stretching: "Say eleven months ago, around Christmas, this pseudo-Champ guy calls me up out of the blue. He says he's got access to some good *Transom*-type stuff, something like a whorehouse peek. I said, 'Swell, send me a few samples, maybe we can do business.' So ... he sent me two stories. There was a PO-box return address, and I thought, 'What? He's on the lam or he lives in a post office box?' "

"Go on."

"So the stuff was good. *Cash good*—and I rarely pay for text, just pictures. Anyway, it was two girlie-daddy stories, and the dialogue introductions were realistic, like he eavesdropped on this sick game stuff. The accompanying stories weren't so hot, but I sent him a C-note off the books and a note: 'Keep the fires stoked, I like your stuff.' "

"Did he send the stories in handwritten?"

"Yes."

"Did you keep them?"

"No, I typed them over, then tossed them."

"You did that every time he sent stories in?"

"That's right. Four issues featuring the Champ, four times I typed the stuff up and tossed it. That was June '58 you showed me, plus the Champ also made it in February '58, May '58 and September '58. You want copies? I can have the warehouse send them to you, maybe take a week."

"No sooner?"

"The wetbacks they got working there? For them a week's Speedy Gonzales."

I laid a card down. "Send them to my office."

"Okay, but you'll be disappointed."

"Why?"

"The Champ's a one-trick jockey. It's all quasi-incest stuff featuring plump brunettes. I think I'll start editing him and change things around. Rita Hayworth looking to bang father surrogates is spicier, don't you think?"

"Sure. Now, what about a contributors' file?"

He tapped his head. "Right here. We're cramped for space in the plush offices of *Transom* magazine."

Itchy—thinking Glenda. "Do you pay the man by check?"

"No, always cash. When we talked on the phone he said cash only. Lieutenant, you're getting antsy, so I'll tell you. Check PO box 5841 at the main downtown post office. That's where I send the gelt. It's always cash, and if you're thinking of finking me to the IRS, don't—because the Champ man is covered under various petty-cash clauses."

Hot—the A.M. sweats. "How did he sound that one time you talked to him?"

"Like a square punk who always wanted to be a hepcat jazz musician. Say, did you know that my kid brother was a suspect in the Black Dahlia case?"

PO box stakeout?—too time-consuming. Glom a writ to bag the contents?—ditto. Bust the box open?—yes—call Jack Woods.

Phone dimes:

Jack—no answer. Meg—tap our property account for ten grand cash. Okay, no "Why?", news: She and Jack were an item again. I resisted a cheap laugh: give *him* the ten—he's killing Junior for me.

Shot/shivved/bludgeoned—picture it—Junior dead.

Pincushion Miciak—seeing it/*feeling* it: knife blades snagged on his spine.

More calls:

Mike Breuning and Dick Carlisle—77th, the Bureau—no luck. Picture Lester Lake scared shitless—cops out to frame him.

Picture Glenda: "Shit, David, you caught me crying."

I drove down to Darktown—a name-tossing run. Bars and early-open jazz clubs—go.

Names:

Tommy Kafesjian, Richie—an old Tommy friend? Tilly Hopewell—consort—Tommy and the late Wardell Knox. My wild card: Johnny Duhamel—ex-fighter cop.

Names tossed to:

B-girls, hopheads, loafers, juice friends, bartenders. My toss-backs: Richie—straight deadpans. White Peeping Toms—ditto. Tilly Hopewell—junkie talk—she was an ex-hype off a recent hospital cure. Wardell Knox—"He dead and I don't know who did it." Schoolboy Johnny—boxing IDs only.

My peeper sketch: zero IDs.

Dusk—more clubs open. More name tosses—zero results—I checked slot-machine traffic on reflex. A coin crew at the Rick Rack—white/spic—Feds across the street, camera ready. Mickey slot men on film—Suicide Mickey.

Cop-issue Plymouths out thick—Feds, LAPD. Intermittent heebie-jeebies—tails on me LAST NIGHT?

I stopped at a pay phone. Out of dimes—I used slugs.

Glenda—my place, her place—no answer. Jack Woods—no answer. Over to Bido Lito's—toss names, toss shit—I got nothing but sneers back.

Two-drink minimum—I grabbed a stool and ordered two scotches. Voodoo eyes: wall-to-wall niggers.

I downed the juice fast—two drinks, no more. Scotch warm, this idea: wait for Tommy K. and shove him outside. Do you fuck your sister/does your father fuck your sister—brass knucks until he coughed up family dirt.

The barman had drink three ready—I said no. A combo setting up—I waved the sax man over. He agreed: twenty dollars for a Champ Dineen medley.

Lights down. Vibes/drums/sax/trumpet—go.

Themes—loud/fast, soft/slow. Soft—the barman talked mythic Champ Dineen.

Dig:

He came out of nowhere. He looked white—but rumor made his bloodlines mongrel. He played piano and bass sax, wrote jazz and cut a few sides. Handsome, jumbo hung: he fucked in whorehouse peek shows and never had his picture taken. Champ in love: three rich-girl sisters, their mother. Four mistresses—four children born—a rich cuckold daddy shot the Champ Man dead.

A drink on the bar—I bolted it. *My* mythic peeper—dig *his* story, just maybe:

Whorehouse peek equals *Transom*; family intrigue equals KAFESJIAN.

I ran outside—across the street to a phone bank. Jack Woods' number, three rings—"Hello?"

"It's me."

"Dave, don't ask. I'm still looking for him."

"Keep going, it's not that."

"What is it?"

"It's another two grand if you want it. You know the all-night post office downtown?"

"Sure."

"Box 5841. You break in and bring me the contents. Wait until three o'clock or so, you'll get away clean."

Jack whistled. "You've got Fed trouble, right? Some kind of seizure writ won't do it, so—"

"Yes or no?"

"Yes. I like you in trouble, you're generous. Call me tomorrow, all right?"

I hung up. My memory jolted—*plate numbers*. Jack's work—those Junior shakedownees he spotted. I dug my notebook out and buzzed the DMV.

Slow—read the numbers off, wait. Cold air juked my booze rush and cleared my head—*pusher* shakedown victims—potential Junior/Tommy snitchers.

My readout:

Patrick Dennis Orchard, male caucasian—1704½ S. Hi Point; Leroy George Carpenter, male negro—819 W. 71st Street, #114; Stephen NMI Wenzel, male caucasian, 1811 S. St. Andrews, #B.

Two white men—surprising. Think: Lester Lake shot me Tilly Hopewell's address. There, grab it: 8491 South Trinity, 406.

Close by—I got there quick. A four-story walk-up—I parked curbside.

No lift—I walked up for real. 406—push the buzzer.

Spyhole clicks. "Who is it?"

"Police."

Chain noise, the door open. Tilly: a thirtyish high yellow, maybe half white.

"Miss Hopewell?"

"Yes"—no coon drawl.

"It's just a few questions."

She walked backward—dead cowed. The front room: shabby, clean. "Are you from the Probation?"

I closed the door. "LAPD."

Goosebumps: "Narco?"

"Administrative Vice."

She whipped papers off the TV. "I'm clean. I had my Nalline test today. See?"

"I don't care."

"Then ..."

"Let's start with Tommy Kafesjian."

Tilly backed up, brushed a chair, plunked down. "Say what, Mr. Po-lice?"

"Say what shit, you're not that kind of colored. *Tommy Kafesjian.*"

"I know Tommy."

"And you've been intimate with him."

"Yes."

"And you've been intimate with Wardell Knox and Lester Lake."

"That's true, and I'm not the kind of colored who thinks it's all a big sin, either."

"Wardell's dead."

"I know that."

"Tommy killed him."

"Tommy's evil, but I'm not saying he killed Wardell. And if he did, he's LAPD protected, so I'm not giving away anything you don't already know."

"You're a smart girl, Tilly."

"You mean for colored I'm smart."

"Smart's smart. Now give me a motive for Tommy killing Wardell. Was it bad blood over you?"

Sitting prim—this junkie schoolmarm. "Tommy and Wardell could never get that fired up over a woman. I'm not saying Tommy killed him, but *if* he killed him, it's because Wardell was behind on some kind of dope payment. Which doesn't mean anything to you, considering the Christmas baskets Mr. J.C. Kafesjian sends downtown."

Change-up: "Do you like Lester Lake?"

"Of course I do."

"You don't want to see him get popped for a murder he didn't commit, do you?"

"No, but who says that's going to happen? Any plain fool can tell Lester's not the kind of man who could kill anybody."

"Come on, you know things don't work that way."

Getting antsy—raw off that dope cure. "Why do you care so much about Lester?"

"We help each other out."

"You mean you're the slum man Lester snitches for? You want to help him out, fix his bathtub."

Change-up: "Johnny Duhamel."

"Now I'll say 'say what' for real. Johnny who?"

Name toss: "Leroy Carpenter ... Stephen Wenzel ... Patrick Orchard.... Let's try a policeman named George Stemmons, Jr."

Cigarettes on a tray close by—Tilly reached trembly.

Kick it over, set her off—

"That Junior is trash! Steve Wenzel's my friend, and that Junior trash stole his bankroll and his speedballs and called him a white nigger! That Junior talked this crazy talk to him! I saw that crazy Junior man popping goofballs right out in the open by this club!"

Flash it—*my* bankroll. "*What crazy talk?* Come on, you're just off the cure, you know you can use a fix. *Come on, what crazy talk?*"

"I don't know! Steve just said crazy nonsense!"

"What else did he tell you about Junior?"

"Nothing else! He just said what I told you!"

"Patrick Orchard, Leroy Carpenter. *Do you know them?*"

"No! I just know Steve! And I don't want a snitch jacket!"

Twenty, forty, sixty—I dropped cash on her lap. "Tommy and his sister Lucille. Anything ugly. Tommy will never know you told me."

Dope eyes now—fuck fear. "Tommy said that sometimes Lucille whores. He said that a man in Stan Kenton's band recommended her to this Beverly Hills call-girl man. Doug something ... Doug Ancelet? Tommy said that Lucille worked for that man for a while like several years ago, but he fired her because she gave these tricks of hers the gonorrhea."

Recoil: Glenda, ex–Ancelet girl. My peeper tape—the trick to Lucille—"that little dose you gave me."

Tilly: dope eyes, new money.

Carpenter/Wenzel/Orchard—I swung an address circuit south/ northwest. Nobody home—circuit south, crack the wind wings— cold air cleared my head.

Make Junior dead or dead soon—faggot-smear him post-mortem. Leak queer dirt to *Hush-Hush*—taint his Glenda dirt. Retoss his pad, dump evidence—pump his shakedown victims. Work Kafesjian 459—and tie in Junior dirty. Question mark: his Exley file.

Brain circuits:

Exley proffers my Kafesjian payoff: Robbery Division CO. It's a shiv to Dudley Smith, the fur-job boss—the perp his "protégé" Johnny Duhamel.

Johnny and Junior—heist partners?

My instinct: unlikely.

Reflex instinct: hand Johnny up to Dud—deflect Exley's shiv, curry Dud's favor.

South, hit the gas: talk had Smith working 77th. Over— newsmen outside—a captain grandstanding:

Ignore Negro-victim 187s—never!

Watch for zealous justice soon!

Door guards kept reporters out: civilians verboten, zealotry wrapped.

I badged in. Sweat box row was packed: nigger suspects, two cop teams twirling saps.

"Lad."

Smith in the bullpen doorway. I walked over; he shot me a bonecrusher shake. "Lad, was it me you came to see?"

Sidestep: "I was looking for Breuning and Carlisle."

"Ahh, grand. Those bad pennies should turn up, but in the meantime share a colloquy with old Dudley."

Chairs right there—I grabbed two.

"Lad, in my thirty years and four months as a policeman I have never seen anything quite like this Federal business. You've been on the Department how long?"

"Twenty years and a month."

"Ah, grand, with your wartime service included, of course. Tell me, lad, is there a difference between killing Orientals and white men?"

"I've never killed a white man."

Dud winked—oh, you kid. "Nor have I. Jungle bunnies account for the seven men I have killed in the line of duty, stretching a point to allow for them as human. Lad, this Federal business is damningly provocative, isn't it?"

"Yes."

"Concisely put. And in that concise attorney's manner of yours, what would you say is behind it?"

"Politics. Bob Gallaudet for the Republicans, Welles Noonan for the Democrats."

"Yes, strange bedfellows. And ironic that the Federal Government should be represented by a man with fellow-traveler tendencies. I understand that that man spat in your face, lad."

"You've got good eyes out there, Dud."

"Twenty-twenty vision, all my boys. Lad, do you hate Noonan? It's safe to say that he"—wink—"considers you negligent in the matter of Sanderline Johnson's unscheduled flight."

I winked back. "He thinks I bought him the ticket."

Ho, ho, ho. "Lad, you dearly amuse this old man. By any chance were you raised Catholic?"

"Lutheran."

"Aah, a Prod. Christianity's second string, God bless them. Do you still believe, lad?"

"Not since my pastor joined the German-American Bund."

"Aah, Hitler, God bless him. A bit unruly, but frankly I preferred him to the Reds. Lad, did your second-string faith feature an equivalent to confession?"

"No."

"A pity, because at this moment our interrogation rooms are filled with confessees and confessors, that grand custom being utilized to offset any untoward publicity this Federal business might foist upon the Department. Brass tacks, lad. Dan Wilhite has told me of Chief Exley's potentially provocative fixation on the Kafesjian family, with you as his agent provocateur. Lad, will you confess your opinion of what the man wants?"

Sidestep: "I don't like him any more than you do. He got chief of detectives over you, and I wish to hell you'd gotten the job."

"Grand sentiments, lad, which of course I share. But what do you think the man is doing?"

Feed him—my Johnny snitch prelim. "I think—maybe—he's sacrificing Narco to the Feds. It's a largely autonomous division, and *maybe* he's certain that the Fed probe will prove successful enough to require a scapegoat that will protect the rest of the Department *and* Bob Gallaudet. Exley is two things: intelligent and ambitious. I've always thought that he'll get tired of police work and try politics himself, and we know how tight he is with Bob. I think—*maybe*—he's convinced Parker to let Narco go, with his eye on his own goddamn future."

"A brilliant interpretation, lad. And as for the Kafesjian burglary itself, and your role as Exley's chosen investigating officer?"

I ticked points: "You're right, I'm an agent provocateur. Chronologically: Sanderline Johnson jumps, and now Noonan hates me. The Southside Fed probe is already rumored, and the Kafesjian burglary occurs coincident to it. Coincident to *that*, I operate a pinko politician who's enamored of Noonan. Now, the Kafesjian burglary is nothing—it's a pervert job. But the Kafesjians are scum personified and tight with the LAPD's most autonomous and vulnerable division. At first I thought Exley was operating Dan Wilhite, but now I think he put me out there to draw heat. I'm out there, essentially getting nowhere on a worthless pervert 459. It's a one—I mean *two*-man job, and if Exley *really* wanted the case cleared he would have put out a half-dozen men. I think he's running me. He's playing off my reputation and running me."

Dudley, beaming: "Salutary, lad—your intelligence, your lawyer-sharp articulation. Now, what does Sergeant George Stemmons, Jr., think of the job? My sources say he's been behaving rather erratically lately."

Spasms—don't flinch. "You mean your source Johnny Duhamel. Junior taught him at the Academy."

"Johnny's a good lad, and your colleague Stemmons should trim his disgraceful sideburns to regulation length. Did you know that I co-opted Johnny to the Hurwitz investigation?"

"Yeah, I'd heard. Isn't he a little green for a case like that?"

"He's a grand young copper, and I heard that you yourself sought to command the job."

"Robbery's clean, Dud. I'm looking out for too many friends working Ad Vice."

Ho-ho, wink-wink. "Lad, your powers of perception have just won you the undying friendship of a certain Irishman named Dudley Liam Smith, and I am frankly amazed that two bright lads such as ourselves have remained merely acquaintances all these many years."

SNITCH DUHAMEL.

DO IT NOW.

"On the topic of friendship, lad, I understand that you and Bob Gallaudet are quite close."

Hallway noise—grunts/thuds/"Dave Klein my friend!"

Lester—sweat box row.

I sprinted over—door number 3 was just closing. Check the window—Lester handcuffed, dribbling teeth—Breuning and Carlisle swinging saps overtime.

Shoulder wedge—I snapped the door clean.

Breuning—distracted—huh?

Carlisle—blood-fogged glasses.

Out of breath, pitch the lie: "He was with me when Wardell Knox was killed."

Carlisle: "Was that a.m. or p.m.?"

Breuning: "Hey, Sambo, try to sing 'Harbor Lights' now."

Lester spat blood and teeth in Breuning's face.

Carlisle balled his fists—I kicked his legs out. Breuning yelped, blood-blind—I sapped his knees.

That brogue:

"Lads, you'll have to release Mr. Lake. Lieutenant, bless you for expediting justice with your splendid alibi."

21

Dear Mr. Hughes, Mr. Milteer:

On the dates of 11/11, 11/12 and 11/13/58, Glenda Bledsoe participated in actively publicizing performers currently under contract to Variety International Pictures, a clear legal breach of her contract with Hughes Aircraft, Tool Company, Productions et al. Specifically, Miss Bledsoe allowed herself to be photographed and interviewed with actors Rock Rockwell and Salvatore "Touch" Vecchio, on matters pertaining to their acting careers outside the production/publicity confines of *Attack of the Atomic Vampire*, the motion picture all three are currently involved with. Specifics will follow in a subsequent note, but you should now be advised that Miss

Bledsoe's Hughes contract is legally voided: she can be sued in civil court, dunned for financial damages and blackballed from future studio film appearances under various clauses of her Hughes contract. My continued surveillance of Miss Bledsoe has revealed no instances of actress domicile theft; if items are missing from those premises, most likely they have been stolen by local youths employing loose window access: such youths would know that the domiciles were intermittently occupied and take their thievery from there. Please inform me if you wish me to continue surveilling Miss Bledsoe; be advised that you now have enough information to proceed with all legal dispatch.

Respectfully,
David D. Klein

Dawn—the trailer. Glenda sleeping; Lester curled up outside by the spaceship.

I stepped out; Lester stirred and gargled T-Bird. Confab: the camera boss and director.

"Come on, Sid, this time the head vampire *plucks* the guy's eyes out."

"But Mickey's afraid I'm making things too gruesome. I ... I don't know."

"Jesus Christ, you take the extra and pour some fake blood in his eyes."

"Wylie, *you* come on. Let me have coffee before I start thinking gore at six-forty-nine in the morning."

Lester weaved over—cut, bruised. "I always wanted to be a movie star. Maybe I stick aroun' an extra day or so, play the Negro vampire."

"No, Breuning and Carlisle will be looking for you. They didn't pin Wardell Knox on you, but they'll find something."

"I don't feel so much like runnin'."

"*You do it.* I told you last night: call Meg and tell her I said she should stake you. You want to end up dead for resisting arrest some goddamn night when you think they've forgotten about it?"

"No, I don't think I do. Say, Mr. Klein, I never thought I'd see the day Mr. Smith gave me a break."

I winked à la Dudley. "He likes my style, lad."

Lester strolled back to his bottle. The director fisheyed me—I strolled to the trailer, nonchalant.

Glenda was reading my note. "David, this could kill—I mean *ruin* me in the film business."

"We have to give them something. If they believe it, they won't press theft charges. And it diverts attention from the actress pads."

"There's been nothing on TV or in the papers."

"The more time goes by, the better. Hughes might report him missing, and the body will be found sooner or later. Either way, we might or might not be questioned. I had words with him, so I'm more likely to be a pro forma suspect. I can handle it, and I know you can handle it. We're ... oh shit."

"We're *professionals*?"

"Don't be so cruel, it's too early."

She took my hands. "When can *we* go public?"

"We may have already. I shouldn't have stayed so late, and we should probably cool things for a while."

"Until when?"

"Until we're cleared on Miciak."

"That's the first time we've said his name."

"We haven't really talked about it at all."

"No, we've been too busy sharing secrets. What about alibis?"

"For up to two weeks you were home alone. After two weeks you don't remember—nobody remembers that long."

"There's something else bothering you. I could tell last night."

Neck prickles—I blurted it. "It's the Kafesjian job. I was questioning a girl who knows Tommy K., and she said Lucille did call jobs for Doug Ancelet."

"I don't think I knew her. The girls never used their real names, and if I knew someone similar to the way you described her, I would have told you. Are you going to question him?"

"Yeah, today."

"When did she work for Doug?"

"Doug?"

Glenda laughed. "*I* worked for Doug briefly, after the Gilette thing, and you're disturbed that I used to do what I did."

"No—I just don't want you connected to any of this."

Lacing our fingers—"I'm not, except that I'm connected to you"—squeezing tighter—"So *go*. It's Premier Escorts, 481 South Rodeo, next to the Beverly Wilshire Hotel."

I kissed her. "You make things worse, then you make them better."

"No, it's just that you like your trouble in smaller doses."

"You've got me."

"I'm not so sure. And be careful with Doug. He used to pay off the Beverly Hills Police."

I walked—lightheaded. Lester serenaded winos by the spaceship—"Harbor Lights"—the gap-toothed version.

Phone news:

Woods spotted Junior in Darktown—then lost him running a red light. Jack—irked, going back out: "It looks like he's living in his car. He had his badge pinned to his coat, like he's a fucking Wild West sheriff, and I saw him buying gas with two big automatics shoved down his pants."

Bad, but:

He hit box 5841—check under his doormat, grab the key, check his mail slot. "Four envelopes, Dave. Jesus, I thought you were sending me after jewels or something. And you owe me—"

I hung up and drove over. There: the key, the slot, four letters. Back to my car—Champ Dineen mail.

Two letters sealed, two slit. I opened the sealed ones—both from *Transom* to Champ—recent postmarks. Inside: fifty-dollar bills, notes: "Champ—Thanx mucho, Harris"; "Champ—Thanx, man!"

Two slit—left for safekeeping?—no return address, Christmas '57 postmarks. Eleven months PO box stashed—why?

December 17, 1957

My Dear Son,

I am so sad to be apart from you this holiday season. Circumstances have not been kind in the keeping us together department for several years now. The others of course do not miss you the way I do, which makes me miss you more and makes me miss the pretend happy family that we once had years ago.

The strange life that you have chosen to live is a strange comfort to me, though. I don't miss the housekeeping money I send you and it's like a secret joke when your father reads my itemized household expense lists with large "miscellaneous" amounts that I refuse to explain. He, of course, considers you just someone in hiding from the real responsibilities of life. I know that the circumstances of our family life and theirs too has done something to you. You cannot live the way other people do and I love you for not pretending to. Your musical interests must give you comfort and I always buy the records you tell me to buy even though the music is not normally the type of music I enjoy. Your father and sisters ignore the records and suspect that I buy them only to be in touch with you in this difficult absence of yours, but they don't know that they are direct recommendations! I only listen to them when the others are out and with all the lights off in the house. Every day I intercept the mailman before he gets to our house so the others will not know that you are contacting me. This is our secret. We are new to living this way, you and me, but even if we have to live this way always like long lost pen pals living in the same city I will do it because I understand the terrible things this long history of insanity both our families has endured has done to you. I understand and I don't judge you. That is my Christmas gift to you.

Love,
Mother

Neat handwriting, ridged paper—non–print–sustaining. No Richie confirmation; "Long history of insanity/both our families." My peeper: mother/father/sisters. "Circumstances of our family life and theirs too has done something to you."

December 24, 1957

Dear Son,

Merry Christmas even though I don't feel the Christmas spirit and even though the jazz Christmas albums you told me to buy didn't cheer me up, because the melodies were so out of kilter to my more traditional ear. I just feel tired. Maybe I have iron poor blood like on the Geritol TV commercials, but I think it is more like an accumulation that has left me physically exhausted on top of the other. I feel like I want it to be over. I feel more than anything else like I just don't want to know any more. Three months ago I said I was close to doing

it and it spurred you to do a rash thing. I don't want to do that
again. Sometimes when I play some of the prettier songs on
the records you suggest to me I think that heaven will be like
that and I get close. Your sisters are no comfort. Since your
father gave me what that prostitute gave him I can only use
him for his money, and if I had my druthers I would give you
all the money anyway. Write to me. The mail gets bollixed
up at Xmastime, but I'll be watching for the postman at all
different times.

Love,
Mother

Sisters/music/well-heeled father.
Mother suicidal—close three months before—"it spurred you
to do a rash thing."
"Your father gave me what that prostitute gave him."
The peeper tape, Trick Man to Lucille: "that little dose you
gave me."
Doug Ancelet fires Lucille—"She gave these tricks of hers the
gonorrhea."
Snap call:
The peeper taped Lucille and *his own father*.
"Insanity."
"Both our families."
"Our family life and *theirs* too has done something to you."
I drove home, changed, grabbed the tape rig, extra sketches
and my john list. A pay-phone stop, a call to Exley—I pitched
him hard, no explanation:
Leroy   Carpenter/Steve   Wenzel/Patrick   Orchard—I
want them. Send squadroom men out—*I want those pushers
detained.*
Exley agreed—grudgingly. Agreed too: Wilshire Station deten-
tion. Suspicious: Why not 77th?
Unsaid:
I'm having a cop killed/I don't want Dudley Smith around—
he's too close to this fur-thief cop—
"I'll implement it, Lieutenant. But I want a full report on your
interrogations."
"Yes, sir!"
10:30 A.M.—Premier Escorts should be open.

Out to Beverly Hills—Rodeo off the Beverly Wilshire. Open: a ground-floor suite, a receptionist.

"Doug Ancelet, please."

"Are you a client?"

"A potential one."

"May I ask who recommended you?"

"Peter Bondurant"—pure bluff—a big-time whorehound.

Behind us: "Karen, if he knows Pete, send him in."

I walked back. A nice office—dark wood, golf prints. An old man dressed for golf, PR smile on.

"I'm Doug Ancelet."

"Dave Klein."

"How is Pete, Mr. Klein? I haven't seen him in a dog's age."

"He's busy. Between his work for Howard Hughes and *Hush-Hush* he's always on the run."

Pseudo-warm: "God, the stories that man has. You know, Pete has been both a client for several years *and* a talent scout for companions for Mr. Hughes. In fact, we've introduced Mr. Hughes to several young ladies who've gone on to become contract actresses for him."

"Pete gets around."

"He does indeed. My God, he's the man who verifies the veracity of those scurrilous stories in that scurrilous scandal rag. Has he explained how Premier Escorts works?"

"Not in detail."

Practiced: "It's by word of mouth exclusively. People know people, and they recommend us. We operate on a principle of relative anonymity, and all our clients use pseudonyms and call us when they wish to have an introduction made. That way we don't have their real names or phone numbers on file. We have picture files on the young ladies we send out on dates, and they use appropriately seductive pseudonyms themselves. With the exception of a few clients like Pete, I doubt that I know a half-dozen of my clients and girls by their real names. Those picture files on the girls also list the pseudonyms of the men they've dated, to aid us in making recommendations. *Anonymity*. We accept only cash as payment, and I assure you, Mr. Klein—I've forgotten your real name already."

Tweak him: "Lucille Kafesjian."

"I beg your pardon?"

"Another client mentioned her to me. A sexy brunette, a little on the plump side. Frankly, he said she was great. Unfortunately, he also said that you dismissed her for giving your clients venereal disease."

"Unfortunately, I've dismissed a few girls for that offense, and one of them did use an Armenian surname. Who was the client who mentioned her?"

"A man in Stan Kenton's band."

Eyeing me—cop-wise now. "Mr. Klein, what do you do for a living?"

"I'm an attorney."

"And that's a tape recorder you're carrying?"

"Yes."

"And why are you carrying a revolver in a shoulder holster?"

"Because I command the Administrative Vice Division, Los Angeles Police Department."

Turning florid: "Did Pete Bondurant give you my name?"

Flash the peeper sketch, dig his reaction: "*He* gave you my name? I've never seen him before, and that likeness reads much younger than the vast majority of my clients. Mr.—"

"Lieutenant."

"Mr. Lieutenant Whatever Out-of-Your-Jurisdiction Police-man, leave this office immediately!"

I shut the door. Ancelet flushed heart-attack red—baby him. "Are you in with Mort Riddick on the BHPD? Talk to him, he'll verify me. I bluffed in with Pete B., so call Pete and ask about me."

Turning beet-red/purple. A decanter set on his desk—I poured him a shot.

He guzzled it and made refill nods. I poured him a short one—he chased it with pills.

"You son of a bitch, using a trusted client of mine as subter-fuge, you son of a bitch."

Refill number two—*he* poured this time.

"A few minutes of your time, Mr. Ancelet. You'll make a valuable contact on the LAPD."

"No good son of a bitch"—winding down.

I flashed the john list. "These are trick names I got out of a police file."

"*I will not identify any of my client names or pseudonyms.*"

"Former clients, then, that's all I'm asking."

Squinting, finger-scanning: "There, 'Joseph Arden.' He used to be a client several years back. I remember because my daughter lives near the Arden Dairy in Culver City. This man trucks with common street girls?"

"That's right. And johns always keep the same alias. Now, did this man trick with that Armenian-named girl you told me about?"

"I don't recall. And remember what I told you: I don't keep client files, and my picture file on that clap-passing slut is strictly ancient history."

Lying fuck—file cabinets stacked wall-to-wall. "Listen to a tape. It'll take two minutes."

He tapped his watch. "*One minute.* I'm due on the tee at Hillcrest."

Fast: rig the spools, press Play. Squelch, Stop, Start, there:

Lucille: "These places are filled with losers and lonesome creeps."

Stop, Start, "Chanson d'Amour," the trick: "... of course, there was always that little dose you gave me."

I pressed Stop. Ancelet, impressed: "That's Joseph Arden. The girl sounds somewhat familiar, too. Satisfied?"

"How can you be sure? You only listened for ten seconds."

More watch taps. "*Listen*, I do most of my business on the phone, and I recognize voices. Now, follow this train of thought: I have asthma. That man had a slight wheeze. I remembered that he called me out of the blue several years ago. He wheezed, and we discussed asthma. He said he heard two men in an elevator discussing my service and got the Premier Escorts number out of the Beverly Hills Yellow Pages, where frankly I advertise my more legitimate escort business. I set the man up with a few dates and *that was that.* Satisfied?"

"And you don't recall which girls he selected."

"Correct."

"And he never came in to look at your picture file."

"Correct."

"And of course you don't keep a pseudonym file on your clients."

Tap tap. "Correct, and Jesus Christ, they'll tee off without me. Now, Mr. Policeman Friend of Pete's Who I Have Humored Past the Point of Courtesy, please—"

In his face: "*Sit down. Don't move. Don't pick up the phone.*"

He kowtowed—twitching and fuming dark red. File cabinets—nine drawers—go—

Unlocked, manilla folders, side tabs. Male names—lying old whoremaster fuck. Alphabetical: "Amour, Phil," "Anon, Dick," "Arden, Joseph"—

Pull it:

No real name/no address/no phone number.

Ancelet: "This is a rank invasion of privacy!"

Assignations:

7/14/56, 8/1/56, 8/3/56—Lacey Kartoonian—call her Lucille. 9/4/56, 9/11/56—Susan Ann Glynn, a footnote: "Make this girl use a pseudonym: I think she wants clients to be able to locate her thru normal channels to avoid paying commission."

"They are on the second hole already!"

I yanked drawers—one, two, three, four—male names only. Five, six, seven—initialed folders/nude whore pix.

"Get out now, you fucking hard-on voyeur, before I call Mort Riddick!"

Yanking folders—no L.K., no Lucille pictures—

"Karen, call Mort Riddick at the station!"

I yanked *his* phone out by the cord—watch his face throb. My own throbs: fuck L.K., find G.B.—

"Mr. Ancelet, Mort's on his way!"

No L.K., files dwindling. There, G.B. paydirt—"Gloria Benson" in brackets. Glenda's movie name—she said she chose it.

I grabbed the file, grabbed the tape rig and hauled. Outside, my car—I peeled rubber—down to my jurisdiction.

Look:

Two nude snapshots dated 3/56—Glenda looked embarrassed. Four "dates" listed, a note: "A headstrong girl who went back to carhopping."

I ripped it all up.

I hit my siren out of pure fucking joy.

22

ONE SUSAN Ann Glynn DMV-listed—Ocean View Drive, Redondo Beach.

Twenty minutes south. A clapboard shack, no view—a pregnant woman on the porch.

I parked and walked up. Blond, mid-twenties—DMV stat bullseye.

"Are you Susan Ann Glynn?"

She patted a sit-down place. Expectant: cigarettes, magazines.

"You're the policeman Doug called about?"

I sat down. "He *warned* you?"

"Uh-huh. He said you looked through an old trick file that had my name on it. He said you might come to see me and make trouble like you did with him. I said I sure hope he makes it before three-thirty, when my husband gets home."

Noon now. "Your husband doesn't know what you used to do?"

A kid yelping inside—she lit a cigarette on reflex. "Uh-uh. And I bet if I cooperate with you, you won't tell him."

"That's right."

She coughed, smiled. "The baby kicked. Now, uh, Doug said the trick was Joseph Arden, so I put on my thinking cap. This isn't for murder or anything like that, is it? Because that man behaved like a gentleman."

"I'm investigating a burglary."

Cough, wince. "You know, I remember that I liked that man. I remember him good because Doug said be nice 'cause this other service girl gave him the clap, and he had to get it treated."

"Did he tell you his real name?"

"No. I used *my* real name at the service for a while, but Doug accused me of trying to recruit customers for myself, so I stopped."

"What did Joseph Arden look like?"

"Nice looking. Cultured looking. Maybe in his late forties. He looked like he had money."

"Tall, short, heavy, slender?"

"Maybe six feet. I guess you'd say he had a medium build. Blue eyes, I think. What I guess you'd call medium-brown hair."

I showed the sketch. "Does this look like him?"

"This man looks too young. The chin sort of reminds me of him, though."

Noise inside—Susan winced. Check her magazines: *Photoplay*, *Bride's*. "Do you know what mug shots are?"

"Uh-huh, from the TV. Pictures of criminals."

Soft: "Would you—?"

"No" shakes—emphatic. "Mister, this man was no criminal. I could look at your pictures until this new baby of mine has her sweet sixteen and never see his face."

"Did he mention a son named Richie?"

"We didn't talk much, but on like our second date he said his wife just tried to kill herself. At first I didn't believe it, 'cause lots of men tell you sad things about their wives so you'll feel sorry for them and pretend you like it more."

"You said at first you didn't believe him. What convinced you?"

"He told me he and his wife had this fight a few weeks back, and she just started screaming and picked up a can of Drano and started drinking it. He said he stopped her and fetched this doctor neighbor of his so he wouldn't have to take her to the hospital. Believe me, that story was so awful that I knew he didn't make it up."

"Did he say that she went to a hospital for follow-up treatment?"

"No. He said the neighbor doctor took care of all of it. He said he was glad, 'cause that way nobody knew how crazy his wife was."

One dead lead. "Did he tell you his wife's name?"

"No."

"Did he mention the names of any other family members?"

"No, he sure didn't."

"Did he mention any other girls who worked for Doug Ancelet?"

Nods—eager. "Some girl with one of those foreign-type I-A-N names. It seemed to me he had—"

"Lacey Kartoonian?"

"Riiight."

"What did he say about her?"

"That she loved it. That's a big thing with call-service customers. They think they're the only ones who can make you love it."

"Be more specific."

"He said, 'Do it like Lacey does.' I said, 'How's that?' He said, 'Love it.' That's all he said about her, I'm sure."

"He didn't mention her as the one who gave him a dose?"

"Uh-uh, that's all he said. And I never met that girl myself, and nobody else ever brought her up to me. And if she didn't have such a funny call name I wouldn't have remembered her at all."

Chrono links:

Christmas '57: peeper's mother with the suicide blues *again*. Susan Glynn/Joseph Arden—trick dates 9/56. Mrs. Arden, Drano drinker—private treatment. Police agencies sealed suicide files. Arden, wealthy—*if* his wife killed herself, he'd buy *extra* legal closure.

Linkage:

Letters, peeper tapes, Ancelet.

Quotes:

Joseph Arden to Lucille: "that dose you gave me."

Mom to Champ/peeper: "Your father gave me what that prostitute gave him."

Conclusive:

The peeper peeped his own father fucking Lucille.

Susan: "Penny for your thoughts."

"You don't want to know."

"Ask me one."

Try her: "When you worked for the service, did you know a girl named Gloria Benson? Her real name's Glenda Bledsoe."

Smiling, pleased: "I remember her. She quit Doug's to become a movie star. When I read she was under contract to Howard Hughes it made me so happy."

23

WILSHIRE STATION—wait, work.

I dusted the Mom-peeper envelopes—two prints surfaced. I checked Jack Woods' Vice sheet—match-up—Jack pawed the goods.

No post-Christmas letters box-stashed—why?

I buzzed Sid Riegle: check white female attempted suicides/suicides Christmas '57 up. Assume Coroner's file closure; inquire station squad to squad—City/County. Look for: middle-aged/affluent/husband/son/daughters. Sid said I'll help you part time—*you* never show up—*I'm* running Ad Vice by default.

I called the Arden Dairy—a shot at a Joseph Arden make. Strikeout: no Arden-surname owners/employees; the founder dead, heirless.

I called University Station—4:00—nightwatch roll call in progress. Via intercom hookup:

Did any of you men trick-card Joseph Arden—white male alias?

One taker—"I *think* I carded that alias"—no real name, vehicle or description recalled.

Joseph Arden—dead for now.

A teletype check: no Topanga Canyon 187's—Pincushion Miciak decomposing.

Dinner: candy bars from a vending machine. Grab a sweat room, wait.

I tilted a chair back—sleep waves hit me. Half dreaming: Mr. Third Party says hi!

The Red Arrow Inn—peeper jimmies Lucille's door. Jimmy marks *on the peeper's door*—nonmatching. Kafesjian 459: watchdogs chopped and blinded—eyes shoved down their throats.

The peeper sobbing, listening to:

Lucille with odd tricks—and his own father.

Read the peeper passive.

Read the burglar brutal.

Silverware stolen, found: the peeper's bed stabbed and ripped. Assumed: the peeper himself. My new instinct: third party/door chopper = burglar/bed slasher =

One separate fiend.

Half dreaming—sex-fiend gargoyles chasing me. Half waking—"Double-header, Lieutenant"—Joe Plainclothes shoving two punks in.

One white, one colored. The plainclothesman cuffed them to chairs, their hands racked to the slats.

"Blondie's Patrick Orchard, and the Negro guy's Leroy Carpenter. My partner and me checked Stephen Wenzel's place, and it looked like he cleaned it out in a hurry."

Orchard—skinny, pimples. Carpenter—purple suit, this coon fashion plate.

"Thanks, Officer."

"Glad to oblige"—smile—"Glad to earn a few points with Chief Exley."

"Did you run them for warrants?"

"Sure did. Leroy's a child-support skip, and Pat's a Kern County probation absconder."

"If they cooperate, I'll cut them loose."

He winked. "Sure you will."

I winked. "Check the jail roster tomorrow if you don't believe me."

Orchard smiled. Leroy said, "Say what?" Plainclothes—huh?— back out shrugging.

Showtime.

I reached under the table—bingo—a sap taped on. "I meant what I said, and this has got *nothing* to do with you. This is about a policeman named George Stemmons, Jr. He was observed rousting you two and a guy named Stephen Wenzel, and all I want is for you to tell me about it."

Orchard—wet lips—snitch-eager.

Leroy—"Fuck you, ofay motherfuck, I know my rights."

I sapped him—arms, legs—and dumped his chair. He hit the floor sideways—no bleats, no yelps—good stones.

Orchard, snitch frenzied: "Hey, I know that Junior cat!"

"And?"

"And he shook me down for my roll!"

"And?"

"And he stole my ... my ..."

"And he stole your felony narcotics. *And?*"

"And he was stoned out of his fucking gourd!"

"And?"

"And he was talking this 'I'm a criminal mastermind' rebop!"

"And?"

"And he boosted my shit! He popped these goofballs right out in the open by the Club Alabam!"

Tilly Hopewell confirmed. *"And?"*

"An-an-an—"

I sapped his chair. "AND?"

"An-an-an' I know Steve Wenzel. St-St-Steve s-said J-Junior t-t-talked this crazy shit to him!"

Tilly confirmation ditto. I checked Leroy—too quiet—watch his fingers—

Waistband pokes, surreptitious.

I hauled his chair up and jerked his belt—H bindles popped out of his pants.

Improvise:

"Pat, I didn't find these on Mr. Carpenter, I found them on you. Now, do you have anything else to say about Junior Stemmons, Steve Wenzel and yourself?"

Leroy—"Crazy, daddy-o!"—dig the ofay.

"AND, Mr. Orchard?"

"An-an-and St-Steve s-said he c-cut a d-deal w-w-with c-crazy Junior. J-Junior p-promised Steve this b-big money to buy this b-bulk horse. C-couple days ago, Steve, he told me this. He s-s-said J-Junior n-needed twenty-four hours to get the money."

Leroy: "Sissy fink stool pigeon motherfucker."

Craaazy Junior—KILL HIM, JACK.

Twirling my sap: "Possession of heroin with intent to sell. Conspiracy to distribute narcotics. Assault on a police officer, because you just took a swing at me. *AND*, Mr. Orch—"

"Okay! Okay! Okay!"

I sapped the table. "AND?"

"A-and c-crazy Junior, he made me go with him to the club Alabam. Y-y-you know that b-boxer cop?"

"Johnny Duhamel?"

"R-right, who w-won the G-Golden Gloves. J-J-Junior, he started bothering the-the-the—"

Tongue tied bad—uncuff him, cut him slack.

Leroy: "You afraid to let *my* hands free, Mr. Po-lice?"

Orchard: "Fuck, that's better."

"AND?"

"And J-Junior, he was bugging the G-Golden Gloves guy."

"What was Duhamel doing at the Club Alabam?"

"It looked like he was eyeballing these guys back by this curtained-off room they got there."

"What guys? What were they doing?"

"It looked like they were filing numbers off these slot machines."

"And?"

"Man, you keeping saying that!"

I sapped the table hard—it jumped off the floor. "AND why did Junior Stemmons take you to the Club Alabam?"

Orchard, hands up, begging: "Okay okay okay. Junior what's-his-name was stoned out of his gourd. He buttonholed the Golden Gloves man and told him this crazy fantasy rebop that I had this big money to buy mink coats with. The boxer cop, he almost went nuts shushing Junior. They almost threw blows, and I saw these two *other* cops that I sorta knew by sight watching the whole thing sort of real interested."

"Describe the two other cops."

"Shit, mean looking. A heavyset blond guy, and this thin guy with glasses."

Breuning and Carlisle—go from there:

Duhamel scoping slot work—Mobster Squad duty? Goons scoping *him*—suspected fur thief?

Orchard: "Man, I got no more 'ands' for you. Whatever you threaten me with, I'll be feeding you bullshit from here on in."

Work the spook: "*Give*, Leroy."

"Give shit, I ain't no stool pigeon."

"No, you're a small-time independent narcotics pusher."

"Say what?"

"Say this heroin is a month's pay for you."

"An' say I got a bail bondsman ready to stand my bail an' a righteous Jew lawyer set to defend me. Say you book me, say I get my phone call. Say what, shit."

I uncuffed him. "Did Tommy Kafesjian ever muscle you, Leroy?"

"Tommy K. don't scare me."

"Sure he does."

"Horse pucky."

"You're either paying him protection, snitching for him or running from him."

"Horse pucky."

"Well, I don't think snitching's your style, but I think you're looking over your shoulder a lot waiting for some Kafesjian guy to notice you."

"Maybe that's true. But maybe the Kafesjians ain't gonna control the Southside traffic that much longer."

"Did Junior Stemmons tell you that?"

"Maybe he did. But maybe it's just loose talk pertainin' to this big Southside Federal thing. And either way I ain't no snitch."

Tough monkey.

"Leroy, why don't you tell me how Junior Stemmons muscled you."

"Fuck you."

"Why don't you tell me what you two talked about."

"Fuck your mother."

"You know, if you cooperate with me, it might help bring the Kafesjians down."

"Fuck you. I ain't no snitch."

"Leroy, were you acquainted with a mary jane pusher named Wardell Knox?"

"Fuck you, so what if I was."

"He was murdered."

"No shit, Sherlock."

"You know, there's quite a push to clear up these Negro homicides."

"No shit, Dick Tracy."

Tough and stupid.

I walked Orchard next door and cuffed him in tight. Back to Leroy—

"Give on you and Junior Stemmons, or I drive you down to 77th Street and tell Dudley Smith you killed Wardell Knox and molested a bunch of little white kids."

Coup de grace—I laid the H on the table. "Go ahead, I never saw it."

Leroy snatched his shit back. Zoooom—instant cooperation:

"All that Junior punk and me *did* was talk. Mostly he talked and I listened, 'cause he shook me down for my roll and some shit, and I knew that wasn't no crackerjack badge he showed me."

"Did he mention Tommy Kafesjian?"

"Not Tommy specific."

"Tommy's sister Lucille?"

"Uh-uh."

"A peeper spying on Lucille?"

"Uh-uh, he just said the Kafesjian family itself was going down, gonna get fucked up by the Federal business. He said LAPD Narco was gonna get neutralized by the Feds, and he was gonna be the new Southside dope kingpin—"

KILL HIM.

—"this snotnose little twerpy cop flying on a snootful of shit. He said he had the goods on the Kafesjians, and access to his boss's burglary investigation, which was full of dirty stuff to black-mail J.C. Kafesjian with—"

KILL HIM.

—"and he said he was gonna drive the Kafesjians out and steal their turf, and right about this time I'm biting my tongue to keep from laughing. Next he says he's got stuff on these brothers work-ing for Mickey Cohen. He said they're gonna pull these sex shakedowns on movie stars—"

Junior's FI cards—Vecchio stud service—

—"and the capper is little Junior says he's gonna take over Mickey Cohen's kingdom, which as I understand it ain't such a hot kingdom no more."

"And?"

"And I was just thinking the money and dope I lost was worth it to catch this crazy motherfucker's act."

Woods' surveillance—Junior, Tommy and J.C. at Bido Lito's. Overheard: he'd protect THEM from ME. Double-agent Junior— mercy-kill him.

"Give me the dope back."

"Man, you said I could have it!"

"Give it to me."

"Fuck you, lying motherfucker!"

I sapped him down, broke his wrists, pried it free.

24

"CRAZY MOTHERFUCKER'S act."

Junior's door—six padlocks—crazy new precautions. The dumbfuck used LAPD hardware—my master keys got me in.

Hit the lights—

Rice Krispies on the floor.

Piano wire strung ankle-high.

Closet doors nailed shut; mousetraps on the furniture.

CRAAAAZY.

Toss it slow now—the trunk distracted me last time—

I pried the closets open—nothing but food scraps inside.

Cornflakes and tacks on the kitchen floor.

Sink sludge—motor oil, glass shards; friction tape sealing the icebox. Peel it off—

Amyl nitrite poppers in an ice tray.

Reefer buds in a casserole dish.

Chocolate ice cream—plastic shoved down an open pint container. Dump it, yank—

One Minox spy camera—no film loaded in.

The hall—neck-high wires—duck. The bathroom—mousetraps, a medicine chest glued shut. Smash it open—K-Y jelly and two C-notes on a shelf.

A hamper—nailed tight—pry, pull—

Bloody hypos—spikes up—a booby trap. Dump them—a small steel strongbox underneath.

Locked—I banged it open on the wall.

Booty:

One B of A Hollywood branch passbook—balance $9,183.40.

Two safe-deposit-box keys, one instruction card. Fuck: "Box access requires password and/or visual okay."

Call it:

Evidence holes—Junior caution pre-complete CRAAAZY.

Logic:

Glenda/Klein dispositions stashed THERE—ditto the gun Georgie Ainge sold Glenda.

Find the password.

I tossed the bedroom—carpet glass spread thick—the trunk gone. The drawers—pure shit—paper scraps gibberish-scrawled.

I dumped the mattress, the couch, the chairs—no rips, no stash holes. I pulled the TV apart—mousetraps snapped. That wall section I shot out—stuffed with Kotex.

No password. No FI cards. No depositions. No Exley/no Duhamel files.

Snap, crackle, pop—Rice Krispies underfoot.

Phone *bbrinng*—

The hall extension—grab it.

"Uh, yeah?"

"It's me, Wenzel. Uh, Stemmons ... look, man ... I don't want any part of dealing with you."

I faked Junior's voice: "Meet me."

"No ... I'll get your money back to you."

"Come on, let's talk about—"

"No, you're nuts!"—*click*, say it: Junior bought Wenzel's dope; Wenzel wised up later.

Bank books, box keys—mine now. I clipped the padlocks fumble-handed—kill him, Jack.

I drove to Tilly's place. Four flights up—knock—no answer.

Peep the spyhole, listen—light, TV laughs. A shoulder wedge snapped the door.

Tilly flipping channels—sprawled on the floor, hophead-dreamy.

Bindles on a chair—say a pound's worth.

Flip—Perry Como, boxing, Patti Page. Slack-face Tilly on cloud nine.

I crammed the door shut and bolted it. Tilly flipped stations, goofy-eyed: Lawrence Welk, Spade Cooley. I grabbed her, dragged her—

Clenching up, kicking—good. The bathroom, the shower, full-blast water—

Cold—soak her clothes, freeze her sober. Wet myself—fuck it.

Freezing her: big shivers, jumbo goosebumps. Teeth clicks trying to beg me—sweat her.

Hot water—fighting now—I let her hit, kick, squirm. Back to ice-cold—"All right! All right!"—no dope slur.

I pulled her out, sat her down on the toilet.

"I think Steve Wenzel left you that dope for safekeeping. He was going to give it to that policeman Junior Stemmons we talked about the other night, and Junior already paid him for it. Now he wants to give Junior his money back because Junior's crazy and he's scared. *Now you tell me what you know about that.*"

Tilly trembled—spastic shivers. I tossed her towels and tapped the heater.

She bundled up. "Are you going to tell the Probation?"

"Not if you cooperate with me."

"And what about that ..."

"That shit in your front room that will get you a dime in some dyke farm if I decide to get ugly?"

Popping cold sweat now. "Yes."

"I won't touch it. And I know you want to geez, so the sooner you talk to me, the sooner you can."

Red coils, heat. Tilly: "Steve heard that Tommy Kafesjian's out to kill him. This seller man Pat Orchard, he knows Steve, and he was in jail this afternoon. This policeman strongarmed him—"

"That was me."

"I'm not surprised, but just let me tell you. Anyway, according to Steve, that policeman which I guess was you asked this Pat Orchard all these questions about this Junior policeman. You released him, and he went to Tommy Kafesjian and snitched that Junior man and Steve. He said that Steve sold Junior this big stash, and that the Junior policeman was talking up all this dope-kingpin jive. Steve said he moved out of his place, and he's going to try to give Junior his money back, 'cause he heard Tommy's out to get him."

"And Wenzel left his shit with you for safekeeping."

Antsy—squirming up her towels. "That's right."

"I cut Orchard loose no more than three hours ago. How did you learn all this so quickly?"

"Tommy came by here before Steve did. He told me, 'cause he knows I know Steve, and he thought I might know where he's hiding. I didn't tell him I talked to you the other night, and I said I don't know where Steve is, which is the truth. He left, then Steve came by and dropped his stash off. I told him, 'You run from that crazy Tommy and that crazy Junior.'"

Steve calls Junior—and gets me. "What else did you and Tommy talk about?"

Stifling coil heat—Tilly dripped sweat. "He wanted to do it to me, but I said no 'cause you told me he killed Wardell Knox."

"What else? The sooner I go, the sooner you can—"

"Tommy said he's looking for this guy spying on his sister, Lucille. He said he's going crazy looking for that spyer."

"What else did he tell you about him?"

"Nothing."

"Did he say his name was Richie?"

"No."

"Did he say he was a musician?"

"No."

"Did he say he had leads on where the guy was?"

"No. He said the spyer was like a f-ing phantom, and he didn't know where he was."

"Did he mention a different man, someone spying on the spyer?"

"No."

"Did he mention *any* name on the spyer?"

"No."

"Champ Dineen?"

"Do you think I'm stupid? Champ Dineen was this music writer who died years ago."

"What else did Tommy say about Lucille?"

"Nothing."

"Did he mention the name Joseph Arden?"

"No. Please, I need to—"

"Did Tommy say *he* was screwing Lucille?"

"Mister, you got an evil curiosity about that girl."

Fast: out to the front room, back with the dope.

"Mister, that belongs to Steve."

I cracked the window, looked down—a crap game in the alley dead below.

"Mister ..."

I tossed a bindle out—dice-blanket bullseye. "What else did Tommy say about Lucille?"

"*Nothing*. Mister, please!"

Shouts downstairs—dope from heaven.

Two more bindles out—"Mister, I need that!"—four, five—alleyway roars.

"TOMMY AND LUCILLE"—six, seven, eight.

Nine, ten—"It's wrong to be thinking what you're thinking. Would you be doing that with your own sister?!"

Crap-game reveries—praise Jesus.

Eleven, twelve—I threw them at Tilly.

Downtown—R&I—a run for Steve Wenzel's rap sheet and mug-shots. Wenzel—two dope falls, butt-ugly: lantern-jaw white trash. No KAs/known haunts listed—I shifted to THEM.

A run by their house—lights on, cars out front. I parked, window reconned.

Down the driveway—dark—I watched for new dogs. Hop the fence, peep around—Madge cooking, no Lucille. Dark rooms, the den—J.C., Tommy and Abe Voldrich.

I squatted down. Closed windows—no sound. Eyeball it:

J.C. waving papers; Tommy giggling. Voldrich—read his hands—be calm.

Muffled shouts—the window glass hummed.

I squinted; J.C. kept waving those papers. He moved closer—fuck—Ad Vice forms.

No way to read the fine print.

Probably Klein-to-Exley stuff—peeper leads. Stolen, leaked—maybe Junior, maybe Wilhite.

"Tommy going crazy chasing that spyer."

I circuited back to my car. Peep surveillance—*my* eyes on *her* window. Forty minutes down—there—Lucille nonchalant naked. Her lights went out too fucking soon—I scoped the front door still hungry to watch.

Ten minutes, fifteen.

Slam—the three men ran out—over to separate cars. Tommy's Merc crunched off the sidewalk dragging sparks.

J.C. and Voldrich headed northbound.

Tommy—dead south.

Follow *him*—

La Brea south, Slauson east—this purple coon coach. *Way* east, Central Avenue south.

Peeper turf.

Light traffic—lay back, tail that jig rig. Way south—Watts—east.

Tommy, brake lights on—Avalon and 103—after-hours-party-club row.

Nigger Heaven:

Two tenements wood-plank-linked—three stories up, open windows, fire-escape access.

Tommy parked. I cruised by, backed up, watched him:

He walked over to the right-side building.

He climbed up the fire escape and stepped on the plank.

Tommy creeping—wobbly wood, rope holds.

Tommy crouching.

Tommy peeping the left-side window.

Big-time-hinky wrong: Tommy just plain looking.

I bolted my car, bolted the left-side steps. No lobby lookout—sprint.

Three floors up—bouncers at the door. Looks: who's this cop know? Instant bouncer-doormen—I walked in.

Mock-zebra walls, party geeks—white, colored. Music, party noise.

I scanned the room—no peeper-sketch look-alikes, no Tommy.

Check the window—no Tommy on the plank.

Geeks packed tight—white hepcats/snazzy niggers—hard to move.

Reefer smoke close by—lantern-jaw Steve Wenzel passing a stick.

Geeks between us.

Tommy behind him, hands in his coat.

Hands out—a sawed-off pump getting loose.

I yelled—

Some nigger hit a switch—the room went black.

Shotgun roar—full auto—one long blast. Spatter spray/random pistol shots/screams—muzzle flash lit up Steve Wenzel, faceless.

Screams.

I ripped through them out the window.

I crawled the plank, glass and brains in my hair.

25

HARBOR FREEWAY northbound, two-way squawk:

"Code 3 all units vicinity 103rd and Avalon multiple homicides 10342 South Avalon third floor ambulances responding repeat all units multiple 187's 10342 South Avalon see the building superintendent—"

Breathing blood—my raincoat cleaned me up—clean, but still smelling it.

"Repeat all units four dead 10342 South Avalon Code 3 ambulances responding."

Shell shock worse than Saipan—the road blurred.

"Traffic units vicinity 103 and Avalon Code 3 see Sergeant Disbrow Code 3 urgent."

6th Street off-ramp, down to Mike Lyman's—Exley's late dinner spot. I palmed a waiter: get the Chief *now*.

Happy people all around me—gargoyles.

"Lieutenant, this way please!"

I followed the waiter. A booth at the back—Exley standing, Bob Gallaudet sprawled—what's this?

Exley: "Klein, what is it?"

Bar seats close—I gestured him over. Bob—feelers perking, out of earshot.

"Klein, what *is* it?"

"You remember that pickup order you issued this morning?"

"Yes. Three men to be detained at Wilshire Station. You owe me an explanation on it, so start—"

"One of the men was an indie pusher named Steve Wenzel, and half an hour ago Tommy Kafesjian shotgunned him at one of those sanctioned after-hours pads in Watts. I was there, I saw it, it's all over the City air. Four dead so far."

"Explain this to me."

"It all pertains to Junior Stemmons."

"Explain it."

"Fuck ... he's dirty past your wildest ... fuck, he's shooting dope, he's shaking down pushers. He's a faggot, he's extorting queers in Fern Dell Park, I think he's leaking my 459 reports to you to the Kafesjians, he's driving around Niggertown like a crazy man, talking up how he's the new—"

Restraining me: "And you've been trying to take care of it yourself."

I pulled loose. "That's right. Junior bought Wenzel's stash, to quote unquote 'set himself up as the new Southside dope kingpin.' One of the other men on that pickup order, *who I questioned extensively about Stemmons and Wenzel,* snitched both of them to Tommy K. I tailed Tommy down to Watts, and I was there when he took out Wenzel."

Pure patrician frost: "I'll send an IAD team down to seal those homicides. It was Wenzel and innocent bystanders?"

"Right."

"Then I'll make sure *his* ID is kept away from the press, which will prevent that pickup order from coming back to haunt us."

"You don't want the Feds getting ahold of this, so you'd better drop a blanket on the press right now."

"Klein, you know that you can't approach—"

"I won't go near Tommy Kafesjian—*yet*—even though I saw him kill a man, even though you won't tell me why you're using me to operate that family."

No rebuke, no comeback.

"Where's Stemmons now?"

"I don't know"—KILL HIM, JACK.

"Do you think they'll ..."

"I don't *think* they'll clip him. They might put Dan Wilhite on it, but I don't think they'd clip an LAPD man."

"I want a detailed confidential report on this within twenty-four hours."

I crowded him—Bob G. watching. "*Nothing on paper*, are you fucking insane? And while I've got you, you should know that Junior's queer for Johnny Duhamel. Next time you see Dudley, tell him he's got a fruit heartthrob working for him."

Exley blinked—simple loose talk shivved him. "There must be a reason why you didn't tell me these things about Stemmons before."

"You don't inspire friendly talks."

"No, but you're much too smart to bypass authority when it can get you what you want."

"Then help me get a bank writ. Junior has some dope stashed in safe-deposit boxes. Help me get it out before it embarrasses the Department."

"Altruistic of you to be so concerned, but *you're* the lawyer, bank writs are Fed business and Welles Noonan is the U.S. Attorney here."

"You could petition a Federal judge."

"No."

"No, *and*?"

"*No*, and right now I want you to go by that man Wenzel's place and toss it for evidence on his dealings with Junior Stemmons. If you find any, destroy it. *That* would be a service to the Department."

"Chief, let *me* take care of Stemmons."

"No. I'm going to call out every man in IAD. I'm going to wrap that Watts shootout up, find Stemmons and sequester him where the Feds can't find him."

Junior ratting Glenda—wide screen/VistaVision/3-D—

"Will you quash *anything* incriminating that comes out on me and mine?"

"Yes. But don't cloak your self-serving motives in respect for the Department. Given what you are, it's pitifully transparent."

Change-up: "Has IAD been tailing me sporadically since the Johnson thing?"

"No. If you've been under surveillance, it's the Feds. I forgave you for *that* murder, remember?"

X-ray eyes—the fuck made me blink.

"Clean yourself up, Lieutenant. You smell like blood."

I cruised by Wenzel's pad—J.C.'s car was parked outside. Call it: potential Tommy links snipped quick.

Shell-shock images:

The Feds bag Junior live. He plea bargains: queer exposure quashed in exchange for Dave Klein nailed. Junior, evidence-prof savant—all my killings, all my payoffs itemized.

Go—toss that insane hovel one more time—

I drove over, unlocked six padlocks to get in. Lights on, new horror:

Shotgun shells in the oven.

Cherry bombs crammed down a toaster.

Razor blades choking a heat duct.

Do it:

Bag the spy camera.

Bag the gibberish notes.

Dump the furniture again—four chairs in—loose stitching. Rip, reach—

Cash tucked away—$56.

Gilette 187 carbons—Homicide-pilfered.

A new Glenda/Klein report—more detail:

PRIOR TO HER FATAL SHOOTING AND STAB-BING OF GILETTE, MISS BLEDSOE FIRED TWO NON-WOUNDING SHOTS WITH THE AFOREMEN-TIONED .32 REVOLVER THAT SHE HAD PUR-CHASED FROM GEORGE AINGE. (SEE BALLISTICS REPORT # 114-55 ATTACHED TO THE HIGHLAND PARK SQUAD CASE FILE FOR DETAILS ON THE EXPENDED ROUNDS TAKEN FROM GILETTE'S

BODY AND FOUND EMBEDDED IN HIS LIVING
ROOM WALLS.) THAT REVOLVER IS NOW SAFE IN
MY POSSESSION, LEFT WITH ME BY AINGE PRIOR
TO HIS DEPARTURE FROM LOS ANGELES. I HAVE
TEST FIRED SIX ROUNDS FROM IT, AND BALLIS-
TICS ANALYSIS OF THE ROUNDS INDICATES
THAT THEY ARE *IDENTICAL* TO THE ROUNDS
TAKEN FROM BOTH GILETTE'S BODY AND THE
GILETTE PREMISES. IT IS PLASTIC WRAPPED AND
THE SMOOTH PEARL GRIPS SUSTAINED RIGHT
AND LEFT THUMB PRINTS WHICH MATCH TO
ELEVEN COMPARISON POINTS THE PRINTS ON
FILE FROM GLENDA BLEDSOE'S 1946 JUVENILE
SHOPLIFTING ARREST.

I ripped it up, flushed it.

"Safe"/"wrapped"/powdered = safety-box-stashed.

I tapped the walls—no hollow spots.

I unzipped cushions—mousetraps set with Cheez Whiz
snapped at me.

I yanked a loose floorboard—an electric dashboard Jesus
glowed up iridescent.

I laughed—

99% CRAAAZY Junior—1% sane. Sane evidence—methodical,
logical, concise, succinct, plausible—assume death provisions
rigged—willing the concise, logical, plausible, succinct evidence
to its most logical, potentially vindictive heir: Howard Fucking
Hughes.

Laughing—hard to breathe—Rice Krispies popping on the
floor. Voices next door—why's that nice Mr. Stemmons laughing
so CRAAAZY?

I grabbed the phone, fumbled it, dialed.

"Hello? Dav—"

"Yeah, it's me."

"Where are you? What happened with Doug?"

Ancelet—skewed time—ancient stuff. "I'll tell you when I see
you."

"Then come over now."

"I can't."

"Why?"

"I'm waiting someplace. There's an off chance the guy who lives here might show up."

"Then leave him a note and have him call you at my place."

Don't laugh. "I can't."

"You sound very strange."

"I'll tell you about it when I see you."

Silence—line crackle—Miciak hovered.

"David, do you …"

"Don't say his name, and if it hasn't been in the papers or on TV, figure no."

"And when it's yes, I know what to do."

"You always know what to do."

"And you'll always push me for where I learned it."

"I'm a detective."

"No, you're this man who implements things. And everything about *me* can't be explained."

"But I'll—"

"But you'll always try—so come over and try now."

"I can't. Glenda, tell me things. Distract me."

Hear it—match flare, exhale. "Well, Herman Gerstein came by the set today and raised hell with Mickey. It seems that he's seen rushes, and he's afraid Sid Frizell's making the movie too gory. Also, quote, 'This vampire incest routine might get that goddamn goy-ishe Legion of Decency on our ass,' unquote. To top that off, Touch told me that Rock gave him the crabs, and Sid's been screening outtakes from this stag film he's shooting down in Lynwood. Not the most attractive performers, but the crew seemed to enjoy it."

I checked a window—dawn coming. "I should keep this line open."

"Tonight then?"

"I'll call you."

"Be careful."

"Always."

I hung up, grabbed a chair and drifted someplace. Vampires there: Tommy, Pops chasing Meg with his fly down. Blank sleep, hands on me—"Yeah, he's the boss at Ad Vice."

"Lieutenant, wake up."

Up thrashing.

Two prototype IA men, guns out.

"Sir, Junior Stemmons is dead."

26

CODE 3 to Bido Lito's—two cars—no explanation. Spooked: Jack said he'd lose the corpse.

Side streets, there:

Reporters, prowl cars, Plymouths—Feds snapping zoom-lens pix. Civilians milling around—no crowd ropes yet.

I parked and followed a morgue team. Feds talking—duck by, listen:

"... and their pictures weren't in our Intelligence files. These were unknown, most likely out-of-town hoods seen servicing the coin machines here and at a dozen other Southside locations."

"Frank—"

"Please, just listen. Yesterday, Noonan got an anonymous tip on a garage down here. We hit it, and we found slot machines up the wazoo. *But*—it was just a separate garage on a dirty little street, and we can't trace the ownership to save our lives."

Slot intrigue—fuck it—

I ran inside. Heavy brass: Exley, Dudley Smith, Inspector George Stemmons, Sr. Lab men swarming, Dick Carlisle, Mike Breuning.

Voodoo eyes strafed me—Lester Lake's savior. They flipped stiff fingers surreptitious—Breuning kissed his.

Flashbulb pops. Stemmons shouting, close to tears.

Morgue jockeys pushed a gurney in. I chased them—past the bandstand, back hallways—a slot room.

FUCK—

Junior dead—fetal-curled on the floor.

Junkie-tied—an arm tourniquet—rigor-locked teeth on a sash cord.

A spike bent off a mainline; bulging eyes. Short sleeves—needle tracks and vein scars exposed.

A bluesuit, gawking: "I checked his pockets. He had a key to the front door on him."

A lab man: "The janitor got here early and found him. Jesus, this kind of grief right in the middle of the Fed thing."

The coroner, mind reader: "It's either a legitimate OD or a very skillful hotshot. Those marks are proof of the man's addiction. My God, a Los Angeles police officer."

Jack Woods—never.

Ray Pinker nudged me. "Dave, Chief Exley wants to see you out back."

I double-timed it out to the lot. Exley was standing by Junior's car. "Interpret this."

"Interpret shit. It's real or it's the Kafesjians."

"IA said they found you asleep at Stemmons' apartment."

"That's right."

"What were you doing there?"

"I drove over to Steve Wenzel's place and saw J.C.'s car in front. Junior's apartment was close, and I thought he might show up. What happened with Watts?"

"Five dead, and no eyewitnesses. It was dark when Tommy Kafesjian fired, is that correct?"

"Yeah, he had some nigger kill the lights. Did you—"

"Wenzel was the only white victim, and the state of his body precluded an early ID. Apparently, the shotgun rounds provoked a reaction from a number of independently armed men inside the club. Bob Gallaudet and I went down there and mollified the press. We told them all the victims were Negroes and promised them passes to the Chavez Ravine evictions if they soft-pedaled the story. Of course they agreed."

"Yeah, but you can bet the Feds were monitoring our radio calls."

"They were there taking pictures, but so far as they know it was just some sort of glorified Negro altercation."

"And since they're charging us with giving shine killings the go-by, you sent a dozen Homicide dicks over for appearances."

"Correct, and Bob and I spoke to an influential Negro minister. He has political aspirations, and he promised to talk to the victims' loved ones. While he's at it, he's going to urge them not to talk to the Feds."

Junior's car—grime-streaked windows, filthy. "What did you find here?"

"Narcotics, canned food and homosexual literature. IA's impounding it."

Noise inside the club. Check the window: Stemmons, Sr., kicking chairs. "What about Junior?"

"We'll tell the press it was accidental death. IA will investigate, very discreetly."

"And steer clear of the Kafesjians."

"They'll be dealt with in time. Do you think Narco could have done this?"

Stemmons sobbing.

"Klein—"

"No. Sure, they could rig a hotshot, but I don't think it's them. I'm leaning toward a legit OD."

"Why?"

"A patrolman said Junior had a front-door key in his pocket. He was a doped-up crazy fuck, and this place is a known Tommy K. dope drop and hangout. If they were going to kill him, they wouldn't have left the body here."

"What kind of condition did you find his apartment in?"

"You wouldn't believe me if I told you, and you should let me forensic it. I aced forensics undergrad, and I trashed the place and probably left prints up the ying-yang."

"Do it, then wipe it. And call Pacific Bell and get his phone records sealed. Now, last night you said Stemmons had dope stored in safe-deposit boxes."

"Yes."

"Do you know which banks?"

"I've got his bank books and the box keys."

"Good, and you're an attorney, so I'll go along with your 'dope stash' fantasy and tell you to study your law books and figure out a strategy to bypass Welles Noonan and secure a bank writ."

"*Fantasy?*"

Sighing: "Stemmons has dirt on you. It's most likely stored in those boxes. He was extorting you on some level, or you would have dealt with him in your inimitable strongarm fashion before this lunacy of his extended so far out of control."

NOW, SPILL IT:

"He had a clipping file on *you*. It was hidden with some Personnel forms on Johnny Duhamel. Last night I made a bullshit comment on Duhamel that jacked your blood pressure up about twenty points, so don't you fucking patronize me."

"Describe the file"—no reaction, pure frost.

"All your Bureau cases. Thorough—Junior was as good a paperwork evidence man as I've ever seen. I broke into his apartment last week and found it. *Last night* it was gone."

"Interpret."

I winked Dudley-style. "Let's just say it's nice to know that my good buddy Ed has got a personal stake in this too. And don't worry on Kafesjian 459 PC—I'm in way too deep to stop."

Window view—Papa Stemmons grieving. "You should calm
him down, Eddie. We don't want him screwing up this personal
thing of ours."

"Call me after your forensic"—about-face, watch him go.
Window view:

Exley waltzing up to Stemmons—no handshake, no embrace.
Crack the window, listen:

"Your son ... forbid you to interfere or talk to the press ...
spare you the pain of his pervert tendencies made public."

Stemmons weaving, grief-crazy.

27

CAR RADIO downtown:

KMPC: Policeman Found Dead at Southside Jazz Club—LAPD
Says Heart Attack.

KGFJ: After-Hours Shootout! Five Negroes Dead!

Press blanket—Exley working fast.

Nothing on Harold John Miciak.

Police-band check—dipshit cops ID'ing Junior by name.

The Bureau, my office—a run for clean clothes. A locker-room
shave and shower—keyed up, exhausted.

Down the hall to Personnel—I requisitioned Junior's print
abstract. Furtive: I grabbed Johnny Duhamel's.

The lab—I bagged an evidence kit and a camera. A call to PC
Bell—Exley's name dropped.

Do this:

Compile all Gladstone 4-0629 calls going back twenty days.

List the names and addresses of all people called.

Hold all George Stemmons, Jr., records—awaiting Chief Exley's
court order.

Call *me* at that number—with full results—inside four hours.

Car radio back out:

Watts killings—Negro preacher blames liquor—"the enslaver
of our people."

Exley press-leak fantasia:

During a hot pursuit through a closed-down Southside nightclub, Sergeant George Stemmons, Jr., suffers a fatal heart attack.
The robber escapes; there will be no autopsy—it violates the dead
officer's religion.

No Miciak.

No Fed stuff.

Blues guarding Junior's door—I locked them out and worked. I took photos:

Booby traps/cornflake piles/sloth.

I bagged fibers, listed property.

Print dusting next—tedious, slow. I got Junior himself—multiple sets—ten point matched to the abstract. The living room/hallway/kitchen—odd latents, featuring scar ridges. An easy make—me—Pops caught me stealing and burned my fingers.

Three rooms down—I wiped them clean. The inside doorway—a new set, a match: Duhamel, eight comparison points. Extrapolate it: Johnny scared to enter.

I wiped them. The phone rang—PC Bell, responding.

I copied:

10/28/58—BR 6-8499—Mr. & Mrs. George Stemmons, 4129 Dresden, Pasadena.

10/30/58—BR 6-8499—ditto.

11/2/58—MA 6-1147—Administrative Vice Division, LAPD.

11/2/58—Mom/Dad.

11/3/58, 11/3/58, 11/4/58, 11/4/58—Ad Vice.

11/5/58, 11/5/58, 11/6/58—GR 1-4790—John Duhamel, 10477 Oleander, Eagle Rock.

11/6/58, 11/6/58, 11/7/58, 11/9/58, 11/9/58—AX 4-1192—Victory Motel, Gardena.

11/9/58—MU 8-5888—pay phone, 81st/Central—Los Angeles.

11/9/58—MU 7-4160—pay phone, 79th/Central—Los Angeles.

11/9/58—MU 6-1171—pay phone, 67th/Central—Los Angeles.

11/9/58—Victory Motel.

11/9/58—ditto.

11/9/58—Duhamel's pad.

11/10/58—WE 5-1243—pay phone, Olympic/La Brea—Los Angeles.

11/10/58—Victory Motel.

11/10/58, 11/10/58, 11/11/58, 11/12/58—KL 6-1885—pay phone, Aviation/Hibiscus—Lynwood.

11/16/58—HO 4-6833—Glenda Bledsoe, 248½ N. Mount Airy, Hollywood.

Writer's cramp—interpret the data:

Mom-Dad/work early on—straight biz. Duhamel calls next—Junior going crazy. The Victory Motel—Mobster Squad HQ—Smith's strongarm spot/Johnny on duty.

Pay phones then—Darktown locations—say dope biz, maybe talks with Steve Wenzel. A non-sequitur phone booth—Olympic and La Brea—the Kafesjian pad six blocks south. Crazy Junior—THEY said don't call the house.

11/12 to 11/16—no calls, Junior INSANE. 11/16—*my* late Glenda call.

Logical, but:

Lynwood pay-phone calls = ????

Exhaustion-fried—I dusted the bed rail.

Fuck—

Interlocked hand spreads—laced fingers gripping. Sweat smears, viable latents: and *no* Johnny points. Obvious Junior prints linked with unknown prints: some ham-handed faggot.

Wipe them—*bbring bbring*—grab the phone, shut the bed out.

"Exley?"

"It's John Duhamel."

"What the—how did you know I was here?"

"I heard a radio call about Stemmons. I drove by his place, and the patrolmen told me you were inside. I—look, I need to talk to you."

ADRENALINE—my head buzzed.

"Where are you?"

"No ... meet me tonight."

"Come on, *now*."

"No, we'll make it eight o'clock. 4980 Spindrift. It's in Lynwood."

"Why there?"

"Evidence."

"Johnny, tell me—"

Click—dial tone—tap the button—Exley, fast.

NO.

Don't—he's hinked on Johnny—just maybe.

Option call—I dialed MA 4-8630.

"Office of the District Attorney."

"Dave Klein for Bob Gallaudet."

"I'm sorry, sir. Mr. Gallaudet is in a staff meeting."

"Tell him it's urgent."

Transfer clicks, "Dave, what can I do for you?"

"A favor."

"Name it—you've shot me a few recently."

"I need a look at an IAD personal file."

"Is this an Ed innovation? IA's very much his cadre."

"Yeah, it's an Exley thing. When a man makes the Detective Bureau, IAD does a very thorough background check. I'm meeting a man tonight, and I need more of a handle on him. It's about the Darktown trouble, and you could get a look at the file with no questions."

"You're doing this behind Ed's back."

"Yeah, like those Kafesjian reports I gave you."

A pause—seconds ticking. "Touché, so call me back in a few hours. It can't leave the Bureau, but I'll oblige you with a synopsis. What's the man's name?"

"John Duhamel."

"Schoolboy Johnny? I lost a bundle on his pro debut. Care to enlighten me?"

"When it's over, Bob. Thanks."

"Well, quid pro quo for now. And next time I see you, let me tell you about the meeting Ed and I had with this colored minister. Strange bedfellows, huh?"

That bed—laced hands. "The fucking strangest."

28

SURPLUS ADRENALINE—it jacked me up to peep the Kafesjians.

I staked their house from three doors down—no bedroom-window strip show. Nobody peeper-chasing—three cars on the lawn.

Stakeout time killer—my car radio:

Junior eulogized—LAPD chaplain Dudley Smith: "He was a grand lad. He was a dedicated crimefighter, and it is a cruel caprice of fate that so young a man should suffer cardiac arrest while chasing a common robber."

Welles Noonan on KNX: "... and I'm not saying that the surprising death of an allegedly healthy young policeman is connected to the other five deaths that have occurred within the past twenty-four hours in South Central Los Angeles, but it seems curious to me that the Los Angeles Police Department should be so eager to explain it all away and be done with it."

Smart Noonan—shit draws flies.

4:00—Tommy sax-honks—my cue to leave. My own music juicing me—I was closing in on SOMETHING.

Early dusk—clouds, rain. A phone booth stop—Bob out, Riegle in. Bum station check news—no suicides clicked in PEEPER'S MOTHER.

Up to the set—hard rain—no shooting in progress. Luck: her trailer light on. A sprint—in the door dodging puddles.

Glenda was smoking, distracted. Sprawled on the bed—no rush to touch me.

Easy guess: "Miciak?"

She nodded. "Bradley Milteer came by. Apparently he and Herman Gerstein know each other independent of his work for Hughes. He told Herman that Miciak's body and car were found, and that all of Hughes' contract players were going to be discreetly questioned. Mickey overheard him tell Herman that detectives from the Malibu Sheriff's Station would be by to talk to me."

"That's all you heard?"

"No. Mickey said the Sheriff's are keeping their investigation under wraps to avoid embarrassing Howard."

"Did he mention the Hollywood Division LAPD? A killer named the Wino Will-o-the-Wisp?"

Glenda blew smoke rings. "No. I thought—I mean *we* thought Hughes would just push this under the table."

"No, we *wished* it. And there's no evidence that Miciak was killed at …"

"At the *fuck pad* where Howard Hughes used to *fuck* me and the man I killed wanted to *fuck* me?"

Stop her/make her think. "You bought it, and now you're paying for it. Now you act your way out."

"Direct me. Tell me something to make it easy."

Touch me, tell me things.

"You say you were home alone that night. You don't flirt with the officers or try to charm them. You subtly drop that Hughes is a lech and you can spill the goods on it. You reach for whatever it is that you won't tell me about that gave you the stones to … oh shit, Glenda."

"Okay"—just like that—"Okay."

I kissed her—dripping wet. "Is there a phone I can use?"

"Outside Mickey's trailer. You know, if I could cry on cue, I would."

"Don't, please."

"You're leaving?"

"I have to meet a man."

"Later, then?"

"Yeah, I'll come by your place."

"I won't expect much. You look like you haven't slept in a week."

Raining buckets—I ducked under Mickey's trailer awning. The phone worked—I dialed Gallaudet's private line.

He picked up himself. "Hello?"

"It's me, Bob."

"Dave, hi, and quid pro quo fulfilled. Are you listening?"

"Shoot."

"John Gerald Duhamel, age twenty-five. As far as IA personal files go, not much—I checked a few others for a comparison."

"And?"

"And aside from the interesting combination of a cum laude engineering degree and an amateur boxing career, not much of note."

"Family?"

"An only child. His parents were supposedly rich, but died in a plane crash and left the kid broke while he was still in college, and under known associates we've got the somewhat dicey Reuben Ruiz and his sticky-fingered brothers, but of course Reuben's on our side now. The kid apparently has an undiscriminating appetite for poontang, which I did myself when I was twenty-five. There were unsubstantiated rumors that he tanked his one and only pro fight, and that's all the news that's fit to print."

No bells rang. "Thanks, Bob."

"I'll never high-hat you, son—I remember those crib sheets too well."

"Thanks."

"Take care, son."

I hung up, took a breath, ran—

"Dave! Over here!"

Lightning glow lit up the voice—Chick Vecchio under a tarp hang. Bums behind him, sucking T-Bird.

I dashed over—time to kill.

Chick: "Mickey's at home today."

Glenda—fifty-fifty he knew. "I should have known. Fuck, this rain."

"The *Herald* said two inches. The *Herald* also said that kid partner of yours had a heart attack. Why don't I believe the *Herald*?"

"Because your kid brother told you my kid partner shook him down in Fern Dell Park."

"Yeah, and I don't feature twenty-nine-year-old extortionist cops having heart attacks."

"Chick, *come on.*"

"All right, all right. Touch told me he told you about him and Stemmons in Fern Dell, but there's something he didn't tell you."

Preempt him: "You, Touch and Pete Bondurant are planning your own shakedown gig. It's sex, and it's cough up or *Hush-Hush* gets the pictures. Stemmons got it out of Touch, so now you're afraid that *we* know."

"Hey, *you* know."

I lied: "Stemmons told me. The regular Bureau doesn't have a clue, and if they knew they'd bury it to protect the kid's reputation. Your gig's covered."

"Copacetic, but I still don't feature no heart attack."

"Off the record?"

"Uh-huh, and on the QT, like *Hush-Hush.*"

I cupped a whisper. "The kid was fucking around with J.C. and Tommy Kafesjian. He was popping H, and he OD'd or took a hotshot. It's a toilet job, and it's headed for a whitewash."

Chick cupped a whisper. "Feature the K. boys are not to screw around with."

"Feature I'm starting to think that Ed Exley's going to take those humps down two seconds after the Fed heat peters out."

"Which may be a while, the way things are looking."

Wind, rain. "Chick, what's with Mickey? I saw some new guys moving slots out of the Rick Rack, with Feds right across the street taking pictures."

Chick shrugged. "Mickey's Mickey. He's this hebe hardhead you can't talk sense to half the time."

"The whole thing played funny. A couple of the slot guys were Mex, and Mickey never hires spics. I tipped him on the Feds early on, but he still won't pull his metal."

"Touch and me are staying out of all this Southside business. It sounds to me like Mickey's hiring freelance."

Winos pissing on the spaceship. "Yeah, and maybe cut-rate, like your crew here. Does he need money that bad? I know he's buffered, but sooner or later the Feds will pin those machines on him."

"Off the record?"

"Sure."

"Then feature Mickey's paying off a syndicate loan with his slot percentages, so he's got to let the machines linger a bit. I guess he knows it's risky, but he's scuffling."

"Yeah—'He's a scrapper, and scrappers always get results.' "

"I said it and I meant it."

"And he thinks he'll get a district gambling franchise."

"Feature that bill could pass."

"Feature the AG's office under Gas Chamber Bob Gallaudet? Feature him granting *Mickey Cohen* a franchise?"

Smirking: "Feature I don't think you came here to see Mickey."

Wet ground—the spaceship capsized—bums cheered. "I hope this movie makes money."

"So does Mickey. Hey, where you going?"

"Lynwood."

"Hot date?"

"Yeah, with a pretty-boy strongarm cop."

"I'll tell Touch—he'll be jealous."

Adrenaline—rain peaked it.

29

LYNWOOD—WIND, rain—streets running crisscross and diagonal. Dark—hard to see; Aviation and Hibiscus—that pay phone on the corner.

Tombstone laughs—Jack's call reprised:

"He kicked natural or got snuffed by somebody else? Come on, let me redeem myself. Say Welles Noonan for that same ten?"

Stucco pads—quasi slums; empty bungalow courts. Spindrift—the 4900 block—I skimmed numbers.

24, 38, 74. 4980: a two-deck stucco dive, abandoned.

One light on—downstairs left, the door open.

I walked up.

An empty living room—cobwebs, dusty floor—Schoolboy Johnny standing there calm.

No jacket, empty holster—trust me.

Trust shit—watch his hands.

"Are you grieving for Junior, Johnny?"

"What do you know about Stemmons and me?"

"I know he made you for the fur heist. I know that other stuff doesn't count."

"Other stuff" made him blink. Ten feet apart—watch his hands.

"He had evidence on you, too. He felt terrible things for certain people, and he collected evidence on them to even things out."

"We can work out a deal. I don't care about the fur job."

"You don't know the half"—eye flickers craaaazy.

Footsteps behind me.

My hands pinned/my mouth cupped—smothered/my sleeves rolled up/stabbed.

Walking air—tunnel vision—peripheral grass. Tingles/flutters up my groin/toasty warm.

Side doorways, shoes, trouser legs flapping.

Elbow dipped, shoes on concrete, right turn—

A door opened—warm air, light. Mirrored walls, herringbone patterns up close. Somebody stretched me prone.

Light overhead—snowflake blurry.

Whir, click/click—cylinder noise, like a camera. Sliding on my knees—white wax paper under me.

Propped up.

Tape strips on my eyes—slapped sticky blind.

Somebody hit me.

Somebody poked me.

Somebody burned me—hot/cold sizzles on my neck.

Not so tingly/toasty warm—no flutters up my groin.

Somebody pulled the tape off—sticky red blood in my eyes.

Cylinder click-clicks.

Propped up on white wax paper. Something in my right hand, heavy and shiny: MY souvenir Jap sword.

Shoved, focused in:

Johnny Duhamel naked, holding MY gun.

Burned: hot/cold—my neck, my hands.

Burned raw—Johnny kneeling, glassy eyes, taunting me.

Burned—steam in my face—Johnny taunting me—blue slant eyes.

Get him, cut him—wild swings, misses.

Johnny weaving—grip down, swing two-handed.

Miss, hit, miss—pale skin ripped, tattoos gouting blood. Hit, rip, rip—an arm gone, socket spray. Johnny jabbering Jap singsong, blue slant eyes—

Miss, miss—Jap Johnny prone, twitching crazy. Sight in—this chest tattoo—split it, split him—

Miss, miss—wax paper shredding.

Hit, jerk down—spine snaps/blade drag/pull—red EVERY-WHERE.

Gasping—hard to breathe—blood in my mouth.

Somebody stabbed me—I went tingly/toasty warm/flutters up my groin.

Fading out: flamethrower burns toasty nice, Jap surrender.

Floating toasty black. *Tick tick* somewhere—a clock—I counted seconds. Six thousand—drifting off—ten thou four hundred.

Jap zeros gliding, voices:

Meg: Pops never touched me—David, don't hurt him. The peeper: Daddy, Daddy. Lucille: He's *my* Daddy.

Jap zeros strafing Darktown. *Tick tick*—fourteen thousand odd.

Toasty black.

Blurry: gray herringbones, shoes.

Wall mirrors topsy-turvy; Jap zeros. I tried to wave—stupid—taped-down arms wouldn't let me.

A chair—taped in snug.

Projector clicks.

White light, a white screen.

Movie time—Pops and Meg?—don't let him grope her.

I thrashed—futile—sticky tape, no give.

A white screen.

Cut to:

Johnny Duhamel naked.

Cut to:

Dave Klein swinging a sword.

Zooming in—the sword grip: SSGT D.D. Klein USMC Saipan 7/24/43.

Cut to:

Johnny begging—"Please"—mute sound.

Cut to:

Dave Klein thrashing—stabbing, missing.

Cut to:

A severed arm twitching on wax paper.
Cut to:
Dave Klein, gutting motions—Johnny D. coughing entrails.
Cut to:
Lens glass dripping red; a finger flicking spine chips off the surface.
I screamed—
A needle stab cut me off mute.

Fading in—moving—night—windshield blur.
Niggertown—South Central.
Chest pains, neck pains. Beard stubble, no holster.
Swerving.
Sirens *whoop whoop*.
Bum aches.
Disinfectant stink—somebody washed me.
Where/what/who—Johnny Duhamel begging.
No.
Not for real.
THEY made me do it.
Please—I didn't like it.
Sirens, flames up ahead.

30

Fire trucks, prowl cars. Beard stubble—say a day's worth. Smoke, fire—Bido Lito's flaming skyward.

A roadblock—swing right—I jumped the curb. Gray suit camera men right there—monsters.

Bumper crunch, this sign: "Self-Determination Is Yours With the Prophet Muhammed."

Resting now—a nice soft dashboard. Fading out: "That's Klein. Grab him."

"I think he's got a concussion."
"He looks drugged to me."
"I don't think this is legal."
"It's dicey, but it's legal. We found him blacked out near an arson homicide scene, and he's a major suspect in our overall investigation. Mr. Noonan has a source in the Coroner's Office.

He told him that Klein's partner died of a heroin overdose, and just look at this man's condition."

"Jim, for the written record in case this reaches litigation."

"Shoot."

"All right. It's 3:40 A.M., November 19, 1958, and I am Special Agent Willis Shipstad. With me are Special Agents James Henstell and William Milner. We are at the downtown Federal Building with Lieutenant David Klein of the Los Angeles Police Department. Lieutenant Klein was picked up in a stuporous condition one hour ago at 67th Street and Central Avenue in South Los Angeles. He was unconscious and in a disheveled state. We brought him here to assure that he receives proper medical attention."

"That's a riot."

"Jim, strike Bill's comment. Resuming, Lieutenant Klein, whom our Intelligence records indicate to be forty-two years old, has sustained possible head injuries. His hands and neck have been burned, the scarring forensically consistent with burns caused by dry ice. There are bloodstains on his shirt and there is friction tape stuck to his jacket. He is unarmed. We properly parked his 1957 Plymouth police vehicle at the intersection where we found him. Prior to interrogation, Lieutenant Klein will be offered medical attention."

Propped up in a straight-backed chair.

Feds.

"Jim, have this typed and see that Mr. Noonan gets a carbon."

A sweat hole. Will Shipstad, two G-men. A table, chairs, a steno rig.

Shipstad: "He's coming to. Jim, get Mr. Noonan."

One Fed walked. I stretched—kinks and aches head to toe.

Shipstad: "You know me, Lieutenant. We met at the Embassy Hotel."

"I remember."

"This is my partner, Special Agent Milner. Do you know where you are?"

My Jap sword—wide screen/color.

"Do you want to see a doctor?"

"No."

Milner—fat, cheap cologne. "Are you sure? You're looking a little raggedy-ass."

"No."

Shipstad: "Witness that Mr. Klein refused medical attention. What about an attorney? Being one yourself, you know that we have the right to hold you for questioning."

"I waive."

"You're sure?"

Johnny—Jesus God.

"I'm sure."

"Bill, witness that Mr. Klein was offered and refused legal counsel."

"Why am I here?"

Milner: "Look at yourself. The question should be where have you been?"

Shipstad: "We picked you up at 67th and Central. A short time prior to that, the Bido Lito's club was arsoned. We had agents in the vicinity on general surveillance, and one of them heard a witness talking to LAPD detectives. The witness said he was walking by Bido Lito's shortly after the club closed for the night and saw a broken front window. Seconds later the place caught fire. That certainly sounds like a firebombing to me."

Milner: "Three people died in that fire. So far, we're assuming it was the club's two owners and the cleanup man. Lieutenant, do you know how to concoct a Molotov cocktail?"

Shipstad: "We're not suggesting that *you* torched Bido Lito's. Frankly, the condition we picked you up in suggests that you were incapable of lighting a cigarette. Lieutenant, look how this appears. Two nights ago, five people were killed at an after-hours club in Watts, and a somewhat reliable source told us that Ed Exley and Bob Gallaudet exerted a great deal of pressure to keep the details under wraps. *Now*, the following morning your colleague Sergeant George Stemmons, Jr., is found dead at Bido Lito's. Chief Exley feeds the press a song and dance about a heart attack, when we've heard that it was most likely a self-inflicted heroin overdose. *Now*, forty-odd hours after *that*, Bido Lito's is torched, and *you* drive by not long after in a state that indicates narcotic-induced intoxication. Lieutenant, do you see how all this appears?"

Kafesjian setup. Johnny D. gouting blood—

Milner: "Klein, are you with us?"

"Yes."

"Do you routinely use narcotics?"

"No."

"Oh, just occasionally?"

"Never."

"How about submitting to a blood test?"

"How about releasing me on a prima facie evidence writ?"

Milner: "Hey, he went to law school."

Shipstad: "Where were you coming from when we picked you up?"

"I refuse to answer."

Milner: "Sure, on the grounds that it might incriminate you."

"No, on the grounds of nonincriminating information disclosure as detailed in *Indiana* v. *Harkness, Bodine, et al.*, 1943."

"Hey, he went to law school. You got anything to add to that, hotshot?"

"Yeah, you're a fat piece of shit and your wife fucks Rin-Tin-Tin."

Cardiac red—fat shitbird. Shipstad: "*Enough*. Lieutenant, where were you?"

"Refuse to answer."

"What happened to your service revolver?"

"Refuse to answer."

"Can you explain the unkempt condition we found you in?"

"Refuse to answer."

"Can you explain the blood on your shirt?"

Johnny begging—

"Refuse to answer."

Milner: "Something getting to you, hotshot?"

Shipstad: "Where were you?"

"Refuse to answer."

"Did *you* torch Bido Lito's?"

"No."

"Do you know who did?"

"No."

"Did the LAPD do it as revenge for Stemmons' death?"

"No, you're crazy."

"Did Inspector George Stemmons, Sr., order the torch?"

"I don't—no, you're crazy."

"Did *you* torch Bido Lito's to avenge your partner's death?"

"No"—getting light-headed.

Milner: "We don't smell liquor on your breath."

Shipstad: "Were you under the influence of narcotics when we found you?"

"No."

"Do you use narcotics?"

"No"—speaker lights on the wall—listeners somewhere.

"Were you forcibly administered narcotics?"

"No"—a good guess—JOHNNY CO-STAR. The door opened—Welles Noonan stepped in.

Milner walked out. Noonan: "Good morning, Mr. Klein."

Jack Kennedy hair—reeking of hairspray. "I said, 'Good morning.' "

JOHNNY BEGGING.

"Klein, are you listening to me?"

"I heard you."

"Good. I had a few questions before we release you."

"Ask them."

"I will. And I look forward to sparring with you. I remember that precedent you upbraided Special Agent Milner with, so I think we'd be evenly matched."

"How do you get your hair to do that?"

"I'm not here to share my hairdressing secrets with you. Now, I'm going—"

"Cocksucker, you spit in my face."

"Yes. And you were at the very least criminally negligent in the matter of Sanderline Johnson's death. So far, these are—"

"Ten minutes or I call Jerry Geisler for habeas."

"He'll never find a judge."

"Ten minutes or I engage Kanarek, Brown and Mattingly to file nuisance claims that entail immediate court appearances."

"Mr. Klein, did you—"

"Call me 'Lieutenant.' "

"Lieutenant, how well do you know the history of the Los Angeles Police Department?"

"Get to it, don't lead me."

"Very well. Who initiated what I'll euphemistically describe as the 'arrangement' between the LAPD and Mr. J.C. Kafesjian?"

"What 'arrangement'?"

"Come, *Lieutenant*. You know you despise them as much as we do."

Lead him, cut him slack. "I think it was Chief Davis, the chief before Horrall. Why?"

"And this was circa 1936, '37?"

"Around then, I think. I joined the Department in '38."

"Yes, and I hope that the fact that your pension is secure hasn't given you a false sense of invulnerability. Lieutenant, Captain

Daniel Wilhite is the liaison between the Kafesjian family and Narcotics Division, is he not?"

"Refuse to answer."

"I understand, brother-officer loyalty. Has Wilhite operated the Kafesjians since the beginning of your arrangement?"

"The way I understand it, Chief Davis brought the Kafesjians in and operated them until Horrall took over as chief late in '39. Dan Wilhite didn't join the Department until mid-'39, so he couldn't have been their original operator, if he has fucking indeed *ever* been their operator."

Fey aristocrat: "Oh, come, Lieutenant. You know Wilhite and the Kafesjians are near-ancient allies."

"Refuse to comment. But keep asking me about the Kafesjians."

"Yes, we've heard they've piqued your interest."

JOHNNY BEGGING.

Shipstad: "You're looking queasy. Do you want a drink of—"

Noonan: "Did you tell Mickey Cohen to remove his slot and vending machines? He was lax, you know. We've got pictures of his men servicing them."

"Refuse to answer."

"We've recently turned a major witness, you know."

Don't bite.

"A *major* witness."

"Your clock's ticking."

"Yes, it is. Will, do you think Mr. Klein torched Bido Lito's?"

"No, sir, I don't."

"He can't or won't account for his whereabouts."

"Sir, I'm not so sure he knows himself."

I stood up—my legs almost went. "I'll take a cab back to my car."

"Nonsense, Special Agent Shipstad will drive you. Will, I'm curious as to where the lieutenant has spent the past day or so."

"Sir, my guess is either a hell of a woman or a run-in with a grizzly bear."

"Aptly put, and the blood on his shirt suggests the latter. Do you know how I suggest we find out?"

"No, sir."

"We monitor Southside homicide calls and see which ones Edmund Exley tries to obfuscate."

"I like it, sir."

"I thought you would. It's empirically valid, since we both know that Dave here murdered Sanderline Johnson. I think it's a family enterprise. Dave does the scut work, sister Meg invests the money. How's this for an adage? 'The family that slays together stays—'"

I jumped him—my legs caved—Shipstad pried me off. Thumbs on my carotid, hauled across the hallway blacking out—

Locked in, snapping back fast—wide awake quick. A four-by-six space—quilt walls—no chairs, no table. A wall speaker outlet and mirrored spyhole—adjoining-room access.

A padded cell/watching post—scope it out:

Scarred glass—some distortion. Audio squelch—I slapped the speaker—better. Check the mirror: Milner and Abe Voldrich next door.

Milner: "... what I'm saying is that either J.C. and Tommy will be indicted, or the publicity they get when we make the grand jury minutes available to the press will ruin them. Narco is going to be cut off at the knees, and I think Ed Exley knows it himself, because he has taken no measures to protect them or to sequester evidence. Abe, without Narco the Kafesjians are just a bunch of stupes running a marginally profitable dry-cleaning business."

Voldrich: "I ... am ... not ... an informant."

Milner: "No, you're a fifty-one-year-old Lithuanian refugee with a green card we can revoke at any time. Abe, do you want to live behind the Iron Curtain? Do you know what the Commies would do to you?"

"I am not a snitch."

"No, but you'd like to be. You're letting hints drop. You told me you dried marijuana bales in one of the E-Z Kleen dryers."

"Yes, and I told you J.C., Tommy and Madge didn't know about it."

Cigarette smoke—blurred faces.

Milner: "You know that J.C. and Tommy are scum. You always go to lengths to differentiate Madge from them. She's a nice woman, and you're an essentially decent man who fell in with bad people."

Voldrich: "Madge is a very fine woman who for many reasons ... well, she just needs Tommy and J.C."

Milner: "Did Tommy clip a drunk driver who killed a Narco cop's daughter?"

"I stand on that Fifth Amendment thing."

"You and the whole goddamn world—they never should have broadcast the Kefauver hearings. Abe—"

"Agent Milner, please charge me or release me."

"You got your phone call, and you elected to call your sister. If you'd called J.C., he would have found a smart lawyer to get you released on a writ. I think you want to do the right thing. Mr. Noonan explained the immunity agreement to you, and he's promised you a Federal service reward. I think you want it. Mr. Noonan wants to take three major witnesses to the grand jury, one of them you. And the nice thing is that if all three of you testify, everyone who could conceivably hurt you will be indicted and convicted."

"I am not an informant."

"Abe, did Tommy and J.C. kill Sergeant George Stemmons, Jr.?"

"No"—hoarse.

"He died from a heroin overdose. Tommy and J.C. could have faked something like that."

"No—I mean I don't know."

"Which one?"

"I mean no, I don't think so."

"Abe, you're not exactly a poker face. Now, along those lines, we know that Tommy plays his horn at Bido Lito's. Is he tight there?"

"Fifth Amendment."

"That's TV for you. Kids break a window, they plead the Fifth. Abe, how well did the Kafesjians know Junior Stemmons?"

"Fifth Amendment."

"Stemmons and a Lieutenant David Klein were bothering them about a burglary that occurred at their house two weeks ago. What do you know about that?"

"Fifth Amendment."

"Did they try to shake down the Kafesjians for money?"

"No—I mean Fifth Amendment."

"Abe, you're an open book. Come on, Stemmons was a junkie, and Klein's as dirty as cops get."

Voldrich coughed—the speaker caught static. *"No. Fifth Amendment."*

Milner: "Let's change the subject."

"How about politics?"

"How about Mickey Cohen? Do you know him?"

"I have never met the man."

"Maybe not, but you're an old Southside hand. What do you know about Mickey's coin racket down there?"

"I know bupkis. I know that slot machines play to a nickel-and-dime mentality, which explains their allure to stupid shvartzes."

Milner: "Let's change the subject."

"How about the Dodgers? If I was a Mexican, I'd be happy to leave Chavez Ravine."

"How about Dan Wilhite?"

"Fifth Amendment."

"We've looked at his tax records, Abe. J.C. gave him twenty percent of the E-Z Kleen shop on Alvarado."

"Fifth Amendment."

"Abe, every man working Narco owns unaffordable items that we think J.C. gave them. We've audited their tax returns, and when we call them in to explain those items and say 'Tell us where you got them and you'll skate,' J.C. will be sunk on twenty-four counts of bribery and suborning federal tax fraud."

"Fifth Amendment."

"Abe, I'll give you some advice: *always plead the Fifth across the board*. Conversational answers interspersed with the Fifth simply serve to single out the responses that indicate guilty knowledge."

Silence.

"Abe, you're looking a little green at the gills."

No answer.

"Abe, we heard Tommy's been looking for a guy named Richie. We've got no last name, but we've heard that he and Tommy used to play jazz together and pull B&E's."

I pressed up to the glass—smoke, distortion—"Fifth Amendment."

"Abe, you never won a dime at poker."

Pressing up—squinting, ears cocked.

"You really do want to help us out, Abe. Once you admit it you'll feel a lot better."

Door clangs—I eased off the wall.

Two Feds flanking Welles Noonan. I hit first: "You want to turn me as a witness."

Noonan patted his hair. "Yes, and my wife's pulling for you. She saw your picture in the papers, and she's quite smitten."

"Quid pro quo?"

"You're not desperate enough, but try me."

"Richie Something. Tell me what you've got on him."

"No, and I'll have to upbraid Agent Milner for leaving that speaker on."

"Noonan, we can deal on this."

"No, you're not ready to beg yet. Gentlemen, escort Mr. Klein to a taxi."

31

BIDO LITO'S—daybreak.

Scorched rubble, the bandstand dead center. Ash heaps, shattered glass.

Sidewalk phones intact. One dime in my pockets—be there, please.

Six rings—"Hello?" sleepy-voiced.

"It's me."

"Where are you?"

"I'm all right."

"I didn't ask you—David, where *were* you?"

Tingles—just hearing her.

"I can't—look, were you questioned?"

"Yes, two Sheriff's men. They said it was routine, that all the Hughes contract actresses were being questioned. They didn't seem to know that Howard had me under surveillance, and I didn't have to give an alibi for a specific time, because they couldn't establish the time Miciak died. They—"

"Don't say names."

"Why? Where are you calling from?"

"A pay phone."

"David, you sound frightened. Where *were* you?"

"I'll tell you if—I mean when it's over."

"Is this the Kafesjian thing?"

"How did you know that?"

"I just did. There's things you don't tell me, so—"

"There's things you don't tell me."

Silence.

"Glenda?"

"Yes, and there's things that I won't."

'Talk to me, then."

"Come over."

"I can't, I have to sleep."

"What kind of things should I tell you?"

"I don't know, good things."

Soft, sleepy-voiced: "Well, when I was seeing H.H. I pumped him for some stock tips and bought low. Those stocks are rising now, so I think I'll make a nice profit. When you stood me up night before last, I had dinner with Mickey. He's still enamored of me, and he had me critique his acting style, something to do with his making an important speech soon. My car has a loose clutch, and I—"

"Look, it's going to be all right."

"Is it *all* going to be all right?"

"Sure."

"You don't sound convinced."

"I'll call you when I can."

Vandals got my hubcaps. Movie time encore:

"PLEASE DON'T KILL ME."

"PLEASE DON'T KILL ME LIKE YOU KILLED ALL THE OTHERS."

Happytime Liquor two doors down.

I walked in, bought a pint of Scotch. Back to the car—three shots quick.

Shudders—no toasty-warm tingles.

I tossed the rest—booze was for perverts and cowards.

Meg taught me.

32

MY PLACE: neat and clean. I holstered up replacement goods: my Marine .45.

A scream then:

My Jap sword on a bookshelf—blood-flecked.

Five grand beside it.

Sleep—JOHNNY BEGGING.

Noon—I woke up reaching for the phone. A quick reflex call: Lynwood City Hall.

Inquire:

4980 Spindrift—vacant four-flat—who's it belong to? A clerk shuffle, the word:

Lynwood City foreclosed—the owner died circa '46. Abandoned for twelve years, rebuilding bids out: potential Chavez Ravine evictee housing. A title search?—impossible—storage-basement floods destroyed those records.

Lynwood—why meet there?

Duhamel: "Evidence."

Out for the papers, back for coffee. Four L.A. dailies full of Darktown:

The after-hours shootout—five dead, no clues, no suspects. Four shines ID'd—"Negro" Steve Wenzel deleted. Exley: "Experienced Homicide detectives are working this case full-time. It is a top LAPD priority."

A flash:

Movie time—mirrored walls—familiar *somehow*—

The Herald:

"Three Dead in Jazz Club Fire: Arson Cops Tag Blaze 'Accidental.'" Exley: "We believe that the fire at Bido Lito's is in no way connected to the tragic heart attack death of Sergeant George Stemmons, Jr., two days before on those same premises."

Instinct: Junior hotshot—by THEM.

Instinct: potential evidence torched.

The *Mirror-News*—skank-slanted:

Dead cop/niteclub inferno—what's shaking? Stemmons, Sr., quoted: "Negro hoodlums killed my son!" Exley's rebuttal: "Pure nonsense. Sergeant Stemmons died of cardiac arrest pure and simple. The Coroner's Office will release findings along those lines within twenty-four hours. And the notion that the Los Angeles Police Department set fire to Bido Lito's as revenge for Sergeant Stemmons' death is simply preposterous."

Junior RIP—a Catholic service upcoming. Officiating: Dudley Smith, lay chaplain.

Snide:

"With a Federal rackets probe in full swing down in South Central Los Angeles (and one generally believed to be aimed at discrediting the Los Angeles Police Department), Chief of Detectives Edmund J. Exley certainly is doing his best to pooh-pooh the current Southside crime wave to members of the press. Local sources say that there are as many Federal agents on the streets as there are LAPD men, which one would think bodes for diminished crime statistics. Something is fishy here, and it certainly isn't the catfish gumbo which used to be served at the recently scorched Bido Lito's Club."

Exley, L.A. *Times*: "I feel sorry for the Federal authorities currently seeking to manufacture a successful rackets investigation in Los Angeles. They will fail, because the enforcement measures employed by the Los Angeles Police Department have proven successful for many years. Apparently, Welles Noonan has targeted the LAPD's Narcotics Division for indictments, and I was recently asked why I have not sequestered the men working that division. My answer? Simply that those men have nothing to hide."

BIG instinct—Narco, Fed bait.

The *Times/Herald/Mirror*—no male DB's found. The *Examiner*: "Sewer Worker Makes Grisly Discovery."

Skim it:

A storm drain on the Compton/Lynwood border—Sheriff's turf. Found: a white male DB—tall, pale, 160—headless, no fingers, no feet. Dead for twenty-four to thirty-six hours—EVISCERATED, SPINE SEVERED.

"No identifying marks were found on the body. Sheriff's detectives believe that the killer or killers decapitated the victim and cut off his hands and feet to render a forensic identification impossible."

"If you have information regarding this man, John Doe #26-1958, County Homicide Bulletin 141-26-1958, call Sgt. B.W. Schenkner, Firestone Sheriff's Station, TU 3-0985."

I could call that number. I could plead:

No location or exact time-frame knowledge—I was drugged and coerced.

My assumed coercers: the Kafesjians. Two-man coercion minimum—logistics dictated it.

THEM:

Dope access.

A motive—rogue cop orbits—Duhamel linked to Junior linked to me.

I could plead details:

Johnny and Junior—fur-job filthy—maybe more. Junior—would-be "Dope Kingpin"—extorting THEM. Me—this crazed peeper chaser—THEY wanted HIM.

I could plead evidence:

My Jap sword and five grand on a bookshelf.

My hit fee—common insider knowledge.

My sword—common knowledge—I killed a shitload of Japs with it and won the Navy Cross.

I could plead linkage:

I knew Junior/Junior knew Johnny/I fucked with the Kafesjians/Junior fucked with them/Johnny fucked with them directly or indirectly—directly or indirectly due to crazy faggot Junior Stemmons/Johnny called me to plead out or buy out like I'm pleading out now/the Kafesjians made me kill him—they made me a movie star.

Home movie time.

Splicing and developing time—who did the work?

Dave Klein left alive—movie killer. Time ticking, two ways it could go:

Straight coercion: desist on the peeper.

Fed/LAPD screenings: countless angles.

I could plead theories:

Say Johnny called me legit.

Say *he* kept the meet quiet.

I told Bob Gallaudet about it; I told Chick Vecchio—obliquely.

Chick knew my clip fee.

Chick knew my sword.

Chick knew THEM—or people who did.

Chick knew Junior was fucking with the Kafesjians.

Chick tips THEM off.

99% sure—I was coerced into killing Johnny Duhamel.

1% doubt—I'm a murderer.

My closing plea:

I don't like it.

I shaved and showered. Haggard, new gray hair—forty-two going on dead. Burn tickles toweling off—dry ice coaxed my performance. My sword, five grand—fear tactics.

Invest that money—

I called Hughes Aircraft—Pete picked up.

"Bondurant."

"Dave Klein, Pete."

Caught short: "You *never* call me here. This is work, right?"

"Five grand's worth."

"Split?"

"Your share."

"Then this isn't a police gig like last time."

"No, this is a muscle job on a hard boy."

"You're good at that by yourself."

"It's Chick Vecchio, and I know about that shakedown deal you're working with him and Touch. I want to play an angle on it."

"And you're not gonna tell me how you found out about it."

"Right."

"And if I say no, you're not gonna spoil it for us."

"Right."

"And you figured you by yourself, Chick might not fold, but both of us he would."

"Right."

Knuckle pops on his end—Pete thinking angles.

"Go to seven and answer a few questions."

"Seven."

Pop, pop—ugly. "So what's the beef?"

"Chick put me in shit with the Kafesjians."

"So clip him. That's more your style."

"I need a snitch."

"Chick's a tough boy."

"Seven. Yes or no."

Pop, pop—phone static—killer hands. "Yes with a condition, because I always thought Chick was essentially a greasy wop fuck, and because Mickey changed his mind and told him and Touch not to do this sex gig. I figure Mickey was always nice to me, so I'm doing him a solid he can pay back if he ever quits this movie-mogul shit and starts behaving like a white man again. Now, what's the angle?"

"Straight strongarm, with dirt on Chick himself—in case he runs to Sam Giancana. Chick's Outfit, and the Outfit doesn't like this kind of extortion."

"So you want to catch him at it. I bring my camera, we go from there."

"Right. *If* we don't have to wait too long."

Knuckle pops—

"Pete, come on."

"I need two days."

"Fuck."

"Fuck nothing, Chick's set to bed down Joan fucking Crawford. Now *that* is worth waiting for."

Movie stars/movie time—Johnny begging.

"All right. Two days."

"There's that condition, Klein."

"What?"

"If it looks like Chick's thinking revenge, then we clip him."

"Agreed."

Walking air—tunnel vision—peripheral grass.

Side doorways.

Mirrored walls.

Gray herringbones—a coat?

I drove down to Lynwood—crowding the speed limit.

Aviation and Hibiscus first—that pay phone. Feed the slot, use it: PC Bell said *outgoing* booth calls weren't tallied.

Sid Riegle said his suicide queries yielded zero.

4980 Spindrift—still abandoned. The downstairs-left unit—unlocked.

Four empty rooms—like Johnny never showed up there.

Rainy that night, sunny now. I made street circuits—nothing clicked. Vacant bungalow courts—whole blocks of them.

Treading air that night—like I was carried. Grass, side doorways, a right turn.

Maybe: a courtyard right-side room—movie time.

Wet that night, sunny now—maybe dried footprints on grass.

GO—

Six blocks—thirty-odd courts. Epidemic crabgrass—weedy dry, no footprints. Right-side doors—boarded/nailed/locked—dusty, no fresh entry marks.

Johnny laughed: "Why Lynwood, Dave?"

More street circuits—empty courtyards forever.

Fuck.

Downtown to Central Records. Their burglary file vault—crime sheets back to '50.

Agent Milner:

"We heard Tommy's been looking for a guy named Richie. We've got no last name, but we heard that he and Tommy used to play jazz together and pull B&E's."

Tommy's rap sheet—undoubtedly expunged. Richie Something—maybe not.

GO—

Male adults—four cabinets' worth—no "Richard"-derivation Caucasians. Juvie—seven Richards—five Negro, two white—porkers topping out 250.

"Unsolved"—adult/juvie—hodgepodge stuff. '50 and up, bad typing—I got eyestrain. Tilt—11/6/51:

Music Man Murray's, 983 N. Weyburn, Westwood Village. Trumpets stolen and recovered: traced to unnamed juvies. No arrests, two kid suspects—"Tommy," "Richie"—no surnames. The detective assigned: Sgt. M.D. Breuning, West L.A. Squad.

Three more cabinets—no Tommy/Richie extant.

Easy to extrapolate:

Strongarm Breuning works a chump 459. He blows the job and gets nudged: Tommy's J.C. Kafesjian's son.

Do it—eat dirt.

I called Robbery first—"Breuning's out." 77th ditto—try the Victory Motel.

"Mobster Squad, Carlisle."

"Sergeant, it's Dave Klein."

Breath flutters—"Yeah, what is it?"

"Look, I'm sorry about that trouble with Lester Lake."

"Sure. You side with a nigger over two … Shit, all right, he was your snitch. Look, you want Dudley? He's out."

"Is Breuning in?"

"He's with Dud. What is it?"

"It's an old juvie 459 Breuning worked. November '51. Have Mike call me, all right?"

"Mike? Sure, *Dave*"—slam/dial tone.

Tapping out.

My best move now—tail THEM.

My worst move—they'd spot me.

My best nightmare: THEY approach ME. Movie time explained: threats, offers—at least I'd know WHY.

Darktown by default—go, let things happen.

Familiar now—synced to music in my head. Familiar faces staring back: black, sullen. Slow cruising, two-way-radio sputter:

County calls—no Johnny John Doe talk. No Miciak, no Bido's—half-ass comforting.

I tapped the glove box—no candy—just dope stashed and forgotten. Hiss, crackle—a gang fight at Jordan High.

North—a run by THEIR house—Fed surveillance thick. Sax noise—Will Shipstad wearing earplugs.

Radio hum—my soundtrack for Johnny begging. North on instinct overdrive: Chavez Ravine.

Feds thick—I stuck to the car. Check the view:

Eviction papers tacked door to door. A face-off: Commie geeks and pachucos. Earthmovers, dump trucks—LAPD guards standing by.

More:

The main drag cordoned off: Reuben Ruiz dancing a samba. Fans pressing close, wet-eyed women. Fed bodyguards—disgusted.

Two-way boom:

"Code 3 all units vicinity 249 South ARDEN repeat 249 South ARDEN multiple homicides 249 South ARDEN Detective units Roger your locations 249 South ARDEN on-call Homicide units that vicinity Roger your locations!"

33

ROLLING CODE 3.

South Arden/Joseph Arden/street name/trick name. A Hancock Park address—affluent—a strong maybe.

"Request animal disposal unit 249 South Arden. Be advised all units now standing."

I hit the mike: "4-ADAM-31 to Bureau base urgent. Over."

"Roger, 4-A-31."

"Urgent. Repeat urgent. Lieutenant D.D. Klein seeking Chief Exley. Over."

"Roger, 4-A-31."

Makeshift code: "Urgent. Advise Chief Exley homicides at 249 South Arden likely *major case* connected. Request permission to seal under IA autonomy. Urgent that you find Chief Exley. Over."

"Roger, 4-A-31. State your location."

"3rd and Mariposa westbound. Over."

Dead air, speeding—

"4-A-31, please Roger."

"Roger, this is 4-A-31."

"4-A-31, assume command 249 South Arden IA autonomy. Over."

"4-A-31, Roger, over."

3rd westbound—siren earaches. Arden Boulevard—right turn, right there:

A big Tudor house swamped—prowl cars, morgue cars.

Civilian cliques on the sidewalk—nervous.

Ice cream trucks, kids.

I jammed in curbside. Two brass hats on the porch, looking queasy.

I ran up. One lieutenant, one captain—green. A hedge behind them dripping vomit.

"Ed Exley wants this sealed: no press, no downtown Homicide. I'm in charge, and IA's bagging the evidence."

Nods—queasy—nobody said, "Who are you?"

"Who found them?"

The captain: "Their mailman called it in. He had a special-delivery package, and he wanted to leave it at the side door. The dogs didn't bark like they usually do, and he saw blood on a window."

"He ID'd them?"

"Right. It's a father and two daughters. Phillip Herrick, Laura and Christine. The mother's dead—the mailman said she killed herself earlier this year. Hold your nose when you—"

In—smell it—blood. Flashbulbs, gray suits—I pushed through.

The entrance foyer floor: two dead shepherds belly-up, dripping mouth foam. Tools nearby—spade/shears/pitchfork—bloody.

Meat scraps/drool/puke trails.

Stabbed and cut and forked—entrail piles soaking a throw rug.

I squatted down and pried their jaws loose—tech men gasped.

Washrags in their mouths—stelfactiznide-chloride-soaked.

Match it up—Kafesjian 459.

Walk/look/think—plainclothesmen gave me room:

The front hallway—broken records/tossed covers. Christmas jazz wax—confirm the Mom-peeper letters.

The dining room:

Booze bottles and portraits smashed—another K.-job match. *Family pictures*: a dad and two daughters.

Mom to peeper: "Your sisters."

Suicide talk/suicide confirmation.

A tech stampede—follow it—the den.

Three dead on the floor: one male, two female.

Details:

Their eyes shot out—powder-black cheeks, exit spatter.

Ripped cushions on a chair—bullet mufflers.

Shears, chainsaw, axe—bloody, propped in a corner.

The rug—soaked bubbling.

His pants down.

Castrated—his penis in an ashtray.

The women:

Cut/sawed/snipped—limbs dangling by skin shreds.

Bloody walls, windows sprayed—kids looking in.

Artery gout red: the floor, the ceiling, the walls. Plainclothesmen oozing shell shock.

A framed photo spritzed: handsome daddy, grown daughters.

Peeper kin.

"Fuuuck"/"My God"/Hail Marys. I skirted the blood and checked access.

Rear hall, back door, steps—jimmy marks, meat scraps, drool.

One high-heel pump just inside.

Work it:

He pries in quiet, throws the meat, waits outside.

The dogs smell it, eat it, quease.

He walks in.

Shoots Herrick.

Finds the tools, kills the dogs.

The girls come home, see the door, run in. One shoe lost—scattered tools—he hears them.

CRAAAZY shooting/mutilation—leaded windows kill the noise.

Homicide/symbolic destruction—he probably didn't steal.

Snap guess: the girls showed up unexpected.

I looked outside—trees, shrubs—hiding spots. No blood drip—say he stole clean clothes.

Blues and a mailman smoking—brace them. "Did the Herricks have a son?"

The mailman nodded. "Richard. He escaped from Chino something like September of last year. He went up on dope charges."

Mom—"pen pals/same city"—lamster Richie explained it. "Spurred you/rash thing"—he waltzed minimum-security Chino.

Nervous blues jabbering: Richie caught/convicted/gassed—their instant suspect.

Killer Richie?—NO—think it through:

The Red Arrow Inn—Richie's peep spot B&E'd. His bed ripped—with Kafesjian 459 silver. Dead cert—this killer/that burglar—one man—broken bottle/smashed record/snuffed dog confirmation. Richie—passive watcher—someone watching and pressing him. Tommy K. chasing him outright, flirt with the notion: Tommy stone psycho, Tommy trashes his own house, now THIS.

Back inside:

Blood drops—dark, fading—the main hallway off the den. I followed them upstairs—red into pink, a bathroom—stop.

Floor water—the toilet bowl full—a knife floating in piss water. Pink water in the shower, bloody hair clots.

Reconstruct it:

Bloody clothes ripped and flushed—the toilet floods. A shower then?—check the towel rack—one towel sodden.

Recent—broad-daylight killings.

I checked the hallway—wet footprint indentations on the carpet. Easy tracks—straight to a bedroom.

Drawers open, clothes scattered. A wallet on the floor—turned out, no cash.

A driver's license: Phillip Clark Herrick, DOB 5/14/06. The ID pic: "Fuck me Daddy" bland handsome.

Wallet sleeves—a photo—Lucille naked. A fake license: Joseph Arden—Herrick stats, a fake address.

I checked the window: South Arden was roped off. Bluesuit cordons held reporters back.

Other bedrooms—

One hallway, three doors. Two open—girlish bedrooms—undisturbed. One door locked—I shoulder-popped it.

A snap make: Richie's room preserved.

Neat, mothball-reeking.

Jazz posters.

Books: music bios, sax theory.

Kid-type paintings: Lucille softened, demure.

A graduation pic: Richie, peeper sketch perfect.

Doors slamming—check the window—IA swarming in.

Lucille—idealized, a madonna.

Books: all jazz.

Funny—no tech stuff—and Richie *knew* bugging.

Running footsteps—Exley in my face, catching breath. "You should be downstairs. Ray Pinker briefed me, but I wanted your interpretation first."

"There's nothing to interpret. It's Richie Herrick, or it's the guy who broke into his motel room. Check my early reports, I mentioned him then."

"I remember. And you've been avoiding me. I told you to call me after you forensic'd Stemmons' apartment."

"There was nothing to report."

"Where have you been?"

"People keep asking me that."

"That's not an answer."

Bloody wing tips—he got close.

"So what now? That's a question."

"I'm issuing an APB on Richard Herrick."

"Think it over first. I don't *think* this is him."

"You obviously want me to prompt you. *So*, Lieutenant?"

"So I think we should haul in Tommy K. I've got a strong tip that he's been looking for Richie Herrick. Richie's a damn good hider, but Tommy *knows* him. He's got a better chance of finding him than we do."

"No direct approach on the Kafesjians. And I am issuing that APB, because the Kafesjians are under blanket Fed surveillance, which somewhat impedes their ability to search for Herrick. Moreover, these deaths are front-page news. Herrick will read about them and act even more furtively. We can only control the press so far."

"Yeah, which must really gall you."

"Frankly, it does. Now surprise me or anticipate me. Tell me something I don't know."

I jabbed his vest—hard. "Johnny Duhamel's dead. He's a Sheriff's John Doe down near Compton, and I think you two are dirty together. You're running me on the Kafesjians, and it ties in to Duhamel. I'm not thinking so straight these days, and I'm getting to the point where I'm going to fuck you for it."

Exley stepped back. "You're detached to Homicide and in charge of this investigation. You can do anything you want except approach the Kafesjians."

Chimes streetside—ice cream trucks.

34

3RD STREET, Bureau bound. A stoplight at Normandie— Plymouths cut me off and boxed me in.

Four cars—Feds piled out aiming shotguns. Radio mike loud: "You are under arrest. Get out with your hands up."

I killed the engine, set the brake, complied. Slooow: grip the roof, arms spread.

Swamped/frisked/cuffed—crew-cut shitbirds loving it.

Milner poked me. "Reuben Ruiz said he saw you dump Johnson."

Three men tossed my car. A skinny hump checked the glove compartment.

"Milner, look. Looks like white horse to me!"

Lying snitch fuck Ruiz.

Heroin jammed in my face.

Downtown—the Fed Building—manhandled upstairs. Shoved into an office—

Four walls paper-draped—graph lines visible underneath.

Noonan and Shipstad waiting.

Milner sat me down; Shipstad took my cuffs off. My dope passed Fed to Fed—whistles all around.

Noonan: "Too bad Junior Stemmons is dead. He could have been your alibi on Johnson."

"You mean you *know* Ruiz is lying? You *know* he was sleeping when Johnson jumped?"

Shipstad: "There's no evidence sticker on this bag of white powder, Lieutenant."

Milner: "I think he's got a habit."

His partner: "Stemmons sure as hell did."

Noonan tugged his necktie—his underlings walked out.

Shipstad: "Do you wish to examine the arrest warrant, Mr. Klein?"

Noonan: "We'll have to amend it to include violation of Federal narcotics statutes."

I threw a guess out: "You rigged the warrant with a friendly judge. You told Ruiz to lie, then recant when you turned me. You told the judge what you were doing. It's a Federal warrant on some trumped-up civil-rights violation, not a California Manslaughter One paper, because no Superior Court judge would sign it."

Noonan: "Well, it got your attention. And of course we have binding evidence."

"Release me."

Noonan: "I said '*binding*.'"

Shipstad: "Shortly after we released you early this morning, Abe Voldrich was released to take care of some personal business. He was found murdered this afternoon. He left a suicide note, which a graphologist examined and said was written under physical duress. Voldrich had agreed to testify as a Federal witness, on all matters pertaining to the Kafesjian family and this perhaps tangential burglary investigation that you and the late Sergeant Stemmons were involved in. An agent went by his house to pick Voldrich up for more questioning and found him."

Noonan: "Agent Milner canvassed the area. A 1956 powder-blue Pontiac coupe was seen parked by his house around the approximate time of his death."

Shipstad: "Did you kill him?"

Noonan: "You own a blue automobile, don't you?"

"You know I didn't kill him. You know it's Tommy and J.C. You know that I own a dark blue '55 Dodge."

Shipstad: "The Kafesjians have an excellent alibi for the time of Voldrich's death."

Noonan: "They were at home, under twenty-four-hour Federal surveillance."

"So they called out a contract."

Shipstad: "No, their phone was tapped."

Noonan: "And *had* been tapped, going back prior to the time we picked up Voldrich."

"What else did they discuss on the phone?"

Shipstad: "Unrelated matters. Nothing pertaining to that Richie you seemed to be so interested in last night."

Scooped—no Herrick update—clueless on the South Arden slaughter.

"Get to it. Get to 'binding evidence.'"

Noonan: "Your appraisal of the situation first, Mr. Klein."

"You want to take three witnesses to the grand jury. I'm one, one just died, one's this so-called major surprise witness. You're short a man, so you're doubling up on me. That's my appraisal, *so let's hear your offer.*"

Noonan: "Immunity on the Johnson killing. Immunity on *all* potential criminal charges that you might accrue. A written guar-antee that no Federal tax liens will be filed against you should it be revealed that you have unreported income earned as a direct result of criminal conspiracies that you've engaged in. For this, you agree to enter Federal custody and testify in open court as to your knowledge of the Kafesjian family, their LAPD history and most importantly your own history of dealings with organized crime, *excluding* Mickey Cohen."

Light bulb—Major Witness Mickey.

Reflex jolt—never.

"You bluffed, I call."

Shipstad ripped the draping off the walls. Shredded paper in piles—column graphs underneath.

I stood up. Boldface print—easy to read.

Column one: names and dates—my mob hits.

Column two: my property transactions detailed. Corresponding dates—Real Estate Board kickbacks—five thousand dollars each—my clip fee funneled.

Column three: kickback receivers listed. Detailed: slum dives offered to me lowball cheap. Corresponding dates: escrow and closing.

Column four—Meg's tax returns '51–'57. Her *unreported* cash listed and traced: to appraisers and permit signers bribed.

Column five—witness numbers—sixty-odd bribe takers listed. Names and numbers—pulsing.

Noonan: "Much of the data regarding you is circumstantial and subject to interpretation. We've listed only the men that the underworld grapevine credits you with killing, and those five-thousand-dollar windfalls that followed are circumstantially seductive and not much more. The important thing is that you and your sister are indictable on seven counts of Federal tax fraud."

Shipstad: "I convinced Mr. Noonan to extend the immunity agreement to cover your sister. If you agree, Margaret Klein Agee will remain exempt from all Federal charges."

Noonan: "What's your answer?"

Shipstad: "Klein?"

Clock ticks, heartbeats—something short-circuiting inside me.

"I want four days' grace before I enter custody, and I want a Federal bank writ to allow me access to Junior Stemmons' safe-deposit boxes."

Shipstad, bait grabber: "Did he owe you money?"

"That's right."

Noonan: "I agree, provided a Federal agent goes with you to the bank."

A contract in my face—fine print pulsing.

I signed it.

"You sound resigned."

"It's all got a life of its own."

"Meaning?"

"Meaning you should tell me things."

"You don't mention certain things. You call me from phone booths so you won't have to."

"I want to put it all together first."

"You said it's sorting itself out."

"It is, but I'm running out of time."

"You or we?"

"Just me."

"Don't start lying to me. Please."

"I'm just trying to put things straight."

"But you still won't tell me what you're doing."

"It's this trouble I got you in. Let it go at that."

"I bought that trouble myself—you told me that."

"Now you sound resigned."

"Those Sheriff's men came by again."

"And?"

"And a cameraman told them we were sleeping together in my trailer."

"Do they know I was hired to tail you?"

"Yes."

"What did you tell them?"

"That I'm free, white and twenty-nine, and I'll sleep with whoever I want to."

"And?"

"And Bradley Milteer told them that you and Miciak had words. I said I met Miciak through Howard, and he was easy to dislike."

"Good, that was smart."

"Does this mean we're suspects?"

"It means they know my reputation."

"What reputation?"

"You know what I mean."

"That?"

"That."

"... Oh shit, David."

"Yeah, 'oh shit.'"

"Now you sound tired."

"I am tired. Tell me—"

"I knew that was coming."

"And?"

"And my clutch is still on the fritz, and Mickey asked me to marry him. He said he'd 'cut me loose' in five years and make me a star, and he's been behaving as oblique as David Douglas Klein at his most guarded. He's got some kind of strange acting bug, and he keeps talking about his 'cue' and his 'curtain call.'"

"And?"

"How do you know there's more?"

"I can tell."

"Smart man."

"And?"

"And Chick Vecchio's been coming on to me. It's almost like…"

"His whole attitude changed overnight."

"Smart man."

"Don't worry, I'll take care of it."

"But you won't tell me what it's about?"

"Just hold on for a few more days."

"Because it's all sorting itself out?"

"Because there's still a chance I can force things our way."

"Suppose you can't?"

"Then at least I'll know."

"You sound resigned again."

"It's dues time. I can feel it."

L.A. *Herald-Express*, 11/21/58:

HANCOCK PARK SLAYINGS SHOCK CITY

THE MURDERS of wealthy chemical engineer Phillip Herrick, 52, and his daughters Laura, 24, and Christine, 21, continue to shock the Southland and confound the Los Angeles Police Department with their brazen brutality.

In the mid afternoon hours of November 19th, police surmise that a man invaded the comfortable Tudor style home where widower Phillip Herrick lived with his two daughters. Forensic experts have reconstructed that he gained access through a flimsily locked back door, fatally poisoned the family's two dogs, then shot Phillip Herrick and employed gardening tools found on the premises to hideously mutilate both Mr. Herrick and the animals. Evidence indicates that Laura and Christine returned home at this point and surprised the killer, who similarly butchered them, showered himself free of their blood and donned clothes belonging to Mr. Herrick. He then either walked or drove away, accomplishing the bestial murders in something like near silence. Postal employee Roger Denton, attempting to deliver a special delivery package, saw blood on the inside den windows and immediately called police from a neighboring house.

"I was shocked," Denton told *Herald* reporters. "Because the Herricks are nice people who had already had their fill of tragedy."

FAMILY NO STRANGER TO TRAGEDY

AS POLICE began a house-to-house canvassing for possible witnesses and lab technicians sealed the premises off to search for clues, neighbors congregating outside in a state of horrified confusion told reporter Todd Walbrect of tragic recent turns in the family's affairs.

For many years the Herricks seemed to enjoy a happy life in affluent Hancock Park. Phillip Herrick, a chemist by trade and the owner of a chemical manufacturing business that supplied industrial solvents to Southland machine shops and dry-cleaning establishments, was active in the Lions Club and Rotary; Joan (Renfrew) Herrick did charitable work and headed drives to feed indigent skid row habitués festive Thanksgiving dinners. Laura and Christine matriculated at nearby Marlborough Girls' School and UCLA, and son Richard, now 26, attended public schools and played in their marching bands. But dark clouds were hovering: in August of 1955, "Richie" Herrick, 23, was arrested in Bakersfield: he sold marijuana and heroin-cocaine "goofballs" to an undercover police officer. Convicted of the offense, he was sentenced to four years in Chino Prison, a harsh sentence for a first offender, meted out by a judge anxious to establish a reputation for sternness.

Neighbors state that Richie's imprisonment broke Joan Herrick's heart. She began drinking and neglecting her charity work, and spent many hours alone listening to jazz records that Richie recommended to her in long letters from prison. In 1956 she attempted suicide; in September of 1957 Richie Herrick escaped from minimum-security Chino and remained at large, police believe, without ever contacting his mother. Joan Herrick went into what several acquaintances described as a "fugue state," and on February 14th of this year committed suicide with an overdose of sleeping pills.

Postman Roger Denton: "What a godawful shame that so much awfulness was visited on one nice family. I remember when Mr. Herrick put those heavy leaded windows in. He hated noise, and now the police say those windows helped stifle the noise of that killer fiend doing his work. I'll miss the Herricks and pray for them."

EXPRESSIONS OF SHOCK AS POLICE INVESTIGATION SPREADS OUT

SHOCK WAVES have spread through Hancock Park and indeed the entire Southland, and a memorial service for Christine and Laura Herrick drew hundreds at Occidental College, where they were both enrolled in graduate programs. Locksmiths citywide have reported a tremendous business upswing; guard dog sales have doubled locally. Private security patrols for Hancock Park are being considered, and meanwhile police are jealously guarding investigatory information.

The Herrick investigation is being headed by Lieutenant David D. Klein, the commander of the Los Angeles Police Department's Administrative Vice Division, recently in the news when a Federal witness he was guarding committed suicide in his presence. Lieutenant Klein has detached a half dozen men from the Department's Internal Affairs Detail to work under him, along with his aide, Officer Sidney Riegle.

Chief of Detectives Edmund Exley defended his choice of Lieutenant Klein, 42, a 20 year officer with no Homicide Division experience. "Dave Klein is an attorney and a very savvy detective," he said. "He has worked on a burglary case that may be tangentially connected, and he is very good at keeping evidence under wraps. I want this case cleared, and so I have selected the best possible men to achieve that end."

Lieutenant Klein addressed reporters at the LAPD Detective Bureau. "This investigation is proceeding rapidly," he said, "and progress has been made. Many known associates of the Herrick family have been questioned and eliminated as suspects, and extensive canvassing of the area surrounding the murder scene yielded no eyewitnesses to the killer entering or leaving the Herrick home. We have eliminated robbery and revenge against the family as motives, and most importantly eliminated the Herricks' Chino escapee son Richard as a suspect. He had been our initial major suspect, and we had issued an all-points-bulletin to aid in his capture, but we have now lifted that bulletin, although Richard Herrick is an escaped felon and we would very much like to talk to him. We are now centering our search on a sexual psychopath rumored to be seen near Hancock Park shortly before the killings. Although the three victims were not specifically sexually assaulted, the crime has the earmarks of being perpetrated by a sexual deviate. I, personally, am convinced that this man, whose name I cannot reveal, is the killer. We are making every effort to apprehend him."

And, meanwhile, fear besieges the Southland. Police patrols in Hancock Park have been doubled and the current boom in home security measures continues.

A funeral service for Phillip, Laura and Christine Herrick will be held today at St. Basil's Episcopal Church in Brentwood.

L.A. *Times*, 11/21/58:

SOUTHSIDE CRIME WAVE AROUSES SUSPICION

CITING CRIME statistics and current rumors, U.S. Attorney Welles Noonan stated today that Southside Los Angeles is "boiling over with violent intrigue" that may well be "connected on some as yet undetermined level."

Noonan, heading up a much-publicized Federal rackets probe centered in South Central Los Angeles, spoke to reporters at his office.

"During the past four days eight violent deaths have occurred within a three-mile South Los Angeles radius," he said. "This is *double* the average of any one-month period of any given year going back to 1920. Add on the curious heart attack of a supposedly healthy young policeman at a nightclub later burned down, and count as perhaps curious the mutilated body of an unidentified man found two miles further south on the Compton–Lynwood border. Collectively, you have fodder for much interesting speculation."

Noonan elaborated. "Three nights ago an unexplained shootout at an illegal after hours club in Watts occurred," he said. "Two Negro men and three Negro women were killed, although rumors persist that one of the victims was white. The following morning a young LAPD officer named George Stemmons, Jr., was found dead, allegedly of a heart attack, in a back room at the Bido Lito's jazz club. A scant day and a half later Bido Lito's burned to the ground. Federal agents overheard an eyewitness tell LAPD detectives that he heard a Molotov-cocktail-like explosion moments before Bido Lito's caught fire, but the LAPD Arson Squad has now attributed the blaze, which took three lives, to a carelessly tossed cigarette."

Reporters interrupted the impromptu press conference with questions. Repeatedly stressed: the Federal rackets probe is specifically targeted to discredit the Los Angeles Police Department's Southside enforcement measures; isn't the U.S. Attorney taking an adversarial position predicated on incomplete information?

Noonan responded. "Granted," he said, "that unidentified body found in the L.A. County Sheriff's jurisdiction may be a non sequitur, but I ask you to consider the following.

"One, remember what I told you about that eyewitness to the Bido Lito's fire. Two, consider that the father of the young policeman who expired of alleged heart failure at Bido Lito's earlier, himself a high-ranking Los Angeles police officer, stated that he thought his son was murdered. That man has been suspended from duty for his open criticism of Chief Ed Exley's handling of the situation, and is rumored to be resting at home under doctor-ordered sedation."

Reporters pressed: isn't the Federal–LAPD quagmire coming down to a battle waged by two highly respected, nationally known crimefighters: himself and LAPD Chief of Detectives Edmund Exley?

Noonan said, "No. I will not let personalities or political ambitions dictate the thrust of my investigation. What I do know is: after hours clubs are allowed to flourish in Watts under unofficial LAPD sanction. Five Negro citizens died as a result, and despite assigning a dozen officers to the case, Ed Exley has not been able to come up with a single arrest. He has shoved the suspicious death of a Los Angeles policeman under the carpet and has deliberately misrepresented the facts in a triple-homicide arson case."

In related developments, Noonan refused to comment on the persistent rumor that LAPD Narcotics Division officers are soon to be called in for questioning, or whether Abraham Voldrich, a rumored Federal witness recently deceased, was murdered or committed suicide.

"No comments on those questions," he said. "But on the topic of witnesses, let me state that when it comes time to present evidence to the Federal Grand Jury, I will offer a major surprise witness with extraordinary cachet and another witness prepared to give astonishing testimony."

Edmund Exley responded to the U.S. Attorney's accusations: "Welles Noonan is an unscrupulous hack politician with spurious liberal credentials. He has no grasp of the situation in Southside Los Angeles and his smear campaign against the LAPD is based on lies, fatuous rumors and innuendo. The Federal rackets probe is a politically motivated front aimed at establishing Noonan as a viable candidate for State office. It will fail because he has grievously underestimated the moral rectitude of the Los Angeles Police Department."

Dues time/time running out—RUN.

Herrick 187 PC—six IA men and Sid Riegle co-opted. Forty-eight hours in:

No eyewitnesses, no vehicle pegged. No prints, no Richie-to-Mom letters found. Confirmed: the dogs sucked stelfactiznide chloride.

Background check:

Laura and Christine Herrick—nice girls. Good students, square boyfriends—almost Hancock Park wives.

Joan Renfrew Herrick—secret boozer. Suicide attempts, suicide. A neighbor doctor told me:

Joanie burned herself, and begged morphine. Demerol prescribed; self-inflicted burns kept it coming. Zombie matron—all-day jazz on cloud nine.

"She drank *Drano*, Lieutenant. Her ultimate suicide was inevitable, and a merciful relief for the people who cared about her."

Richie Herrick—shy boy, chump musician. One friend—"This hood Tommy," "Oil and water, him and Tommy—I think Richie had a crush on Tommy's sister." Neighborhood shock expressed: shy Richie the dope peddler. The Bakersfield PD queried: Richie was bagged dead to rights, open-and-shut. No co-defendants, no Tommy involved—three-to-four Chino.

Richie's prison file—missing. Misplaced? Misfiled? Stolen?—possible suspect Dan Wilhite—just a hunch.

Warden's aides searching for it: I wanted to nail Richie's Chino KAs.

Escape reports 9/57—adiós, Richie—no details, no leads.

Mike Breuning—no call from him yet—my B&E lead was tapped out.

Phillip Herrick:

No record, no Vice Squad sheets City/County.

Chemist.

Chemical manufacturer.

PH Solvents, Inc.—dry-cleaning supplies.

Stelfactiznide chloride—made in-house.

Distributed statewide—to dry-cleaning shops and industrial plants.

NOT a customer: E-Z Kleen/J.C. Kafesjian.

PH employees alibi-checked—clean straight across.

Cross-family background check:

Phillip Herrick—DOB 5/14/06—Scranton, Pennsylvania.

John Charles Kafesjian—DOB 1/15/03—Scranton, Pennsylvania.

No Pennsylvania criminal records/State Police employment check:

1930–32—Balustrol Chemicals; Scranton. Phillip Herrick: solvent analyst; J.C. Kafesjian: laborer/mixer.

California DMV check:

6/32—both men glom driver's permits.

Birth record check:

1932–37: Tommy/Lucille, Richie/Laura/Christine born.

Time ticking—RUN—custody looming.

Running separate—Exley and Noonan—chasing bank writs.

Noonan moving east—furtive—petitioning Fed jurists. Exley sticking west—slower, no connections.

Name it ALL: the Kafesjian/Herrick case.

Breaking now—CRAAAZY volition.

Crazy fake press leaks—my idea.

We announced a fake APB, then fake withdrew it. One fake suspect fed to the press: an unnamed psycho. Bait: to calm Richie down and lure Tommy to him.

A help: Richie's mug shot on page one—a bum likeness, peeper sketch imperfect.

A hindrance: Feds dogging THEM.

Exley, page-one tweaks:

"Dave Klein is a very savvy detective."

"He has worked on a burglary case that may be tangentially connected."

Bait: push THEM toward Richie/push THEM toward me.

One glitch: Fed lockstep surveillance on the Kafesjians.

RUN—

Junior's funeral—mandatory Bureau attendance. Exley there for PR, Dudley Smith somber. Stemmons, Sr., still distraught, sedative bombed.

Father-son farewell: Sad-ass Bible readings. Thirty years since First Dutch Lutheran, catch the gist: mercy for the sick and insane.

RUN—Sheriff's Homicide chasers—"routine" questions, two sessions' worth:

Were you hired to tail Glenda Bledsoe?

Did you become intimate with her?

Did she steal from Howard Hughes' guest homes?

Yes, yes, no—one cop smirking.

Did you argue with Harold John Miciak?

Yes—this cop-hater shitbird. Instant empathy, a smirky punch line: don't you think Mr. Hughes might try to fuck you for taking his money and his girlfriend?

Running with me—Sid Riegle/six IA men: background checks/interviews/shitwork. Meg working on a title search—4980 Spindrift/"Why meet there?" My own sister: searching records, tracing money—Phillip Herrick's fortune, find me filth—

Kafesjian/Herrick—Mom to Richie: "Long history of insanity, both our families."

Killer Richie—no.

Killer Tommy—doubtful.

Leaning toward: Mr. Third Party insane.

Narco men running scared—persistent Bureau rumors. Mass cop divestment: Kafesjian gratuities dumped. Rumors had Dan Wilhite begging Exley: say something, do something.

Exley noncommittal; Fed rumors: nineteen subpoenas headed Narco's way.

My subpoenas on hold—via Fed custody extortion. Key witness Dave Klein, compromisable: if that movie showed up on Noonan's desk. Call "if" wishful thinking—I kept waiting the delivery out—time ticking slow.

Running, thinking:

THEY made the film—Chick Vecchio their point man. Make him snitch: THEY coerced my starring role.

Conspiracy indictments potentially pending—"maybe" one tainted witness skates.

Maybe wishful thinking.

Running, watching:

THEIR house—night surveillance, parked three doors down. SRO: Feds in front, Feds out back. Family tantrums inside—my nostalgia soundtrack—

The Two Tonys—pomade spatter off point-blank head shots. "No, my children"—a clip victim weeping. Rape-o doubleheader—buckshot tore this nigger faceless.

Silk dresses for Meg—penance gifts. Meg with Jack Woods now—her own killer. Meg holding ten grand—Jack stiffed, Junior otherwise dead. A stray thought: Abe Voldrich snuffed, a car spotted. Jack's car: that make, that model.

Music to watch by: car-radio bop night one. Night two—straight Champ Dineen.

Soft: Richie and Lucille, maybe lovers. Soft: Glenda turning my way off a skid, all this courage.

Champ Dineen—my car radio on low. Echoed out Lucille's window—the same station.

Lucille in her window—no makeup, new hair—Richie's bedroom pictures life-size.

A nightgown on—almost prim.

Feds on the street—family close.

Johnny begging—constant refrains—unshakable.

Two days down, two days left before custody. Two late nights with Glenda.

She said, "We might not walk."

I said, "You will."

She said, "You're tired."

She said, "You want to confess."

PART FOUR
MONEY JUNGLE

35

"WELL, THIS writ *does* appear to be in order. But what's this stamp on the bottom?"

Agent Henstell: "It's a routing stamp. The U.S. attorney here sent the paperwork to a judge back east."

"Was there a reason for that?"

To bypass Exley-friendly jurists—open the vault, you officious little shit.

"No, Mr. Noonan simply knew that the Federal judge for this district was too busy to read writ requests."

"I see. Well, I suppose—"

I goosed him: "The writ's valid, so let's move this along."

"There's no need to be brusque. This way, *gentlemen*."

Teller cages, guard station, walk-in vault. Unlocked—a Pinkerton at parade rest. Henstell: "Before we go in, I want to recap Mr. Noonan's instructions."

"I'm listening."

"One, you're allowed to keep any money you might find. Two, you're allowed to go through any personal papers you might find, alone, in an examination cubicle here on bank property. After you go through them, they are to be turned over to me, for booking as Federal evidence. Three, any contraband items such as narcotics, or firearms, will be seized as evidence immediately."

"Firearms"—icy tingles. "Agreed."

"All right, then. Mr. Welborn, after you."

Quick march—Welborn leading. Gray metal aisles—safe-deposit boxes recessed floor to ceiling. Left turn, right turn, stop.

Welborn, dangling keys: "5290 and 5291. There's an examination room around the corner."

"And you're to leave Agent Henstell and me alone."

"As you wish."

Two boxes knee-high; four key slots. Tingles—I stuck my keys in.

Welborn—master keys in—clicks simultaneous.

Handkerchiefs up my sleeves.

Welborn, prissy: "Good day, Officers."

Quick now—Henstell picking a cuticle, bored—

I cracked the drawers—paper piles bulged the boxes wide.
RIGHT THERE on top:

A revolver—evidence bagged. Powder-dusted prints on the
grips and barrel housing—protective glazed.

Henstell picking his nose.

Quick:

Unwrap the gun—bury it—paper-pile cover.

Henstell: "What have we got?"

"Folders and paperwork so far."

"Noonan wants it all, and I wouldn't mind being out of here
by lunchtime."

I dropped my hands; the handkerchiefs fell out. Block his view—
wipe the piece—

Three times—Glenda—make sure.

I handed it over. "Henstell, look at this."

He twirled the gun and snapped quick draws—bad déjà vu.

"Pearl grips—this Stemmons guy must have had a cowboy
fetish. And look, no numbers on the barrel plate."

I pulled the drawers out. "Do you want to look through these
for narcotics?"

"No, but Noonan wants it all when you're finished. He said
I should pat-search you afterwards, but that's not my style."

"Thanks."

"You're going to love Federal custody. Noonan pops for steak
lunch every day."

Fake grunts: "You want to give me a hand with this?"

"Come on, they can't be *that* heavy."

Good fake out—I moved on it—over to a catty-corner cubicle.
One table, one chair, no inside lock—I jammed the chair under
the doorknob.

Dump the drawers, check the contents:

Folders, photos, odd papers—I stacked them on the table.

Four keys on a fob—"Brownell's Locksmiths, 4024 Wabash
Ave, East Los Angeles."

Loose newspaper clippings—I smoothed out the crumples.

Go—skim it all:

Typed depositions—Glenda Bledsoe/Dwight Gilette—Murder
One. My evidence suppression—detailed in longhand.

Georgie Ainge's statement: a typed original and five carbons.

Photo blow-ups: Glenda's juvie print strip and the gun prints. A fingerprint analysis report; photo glossies with comparison points checked.

Witness Disposition Report:

"Mr. Ainge is currently living under an assumed name at an undisclosed location in the San Francisco area. I have telephone access to him and have given him money so that he might hide out and escape potential reprisals from Lieutenant David D. Klein. He remains available to me should he be called as a witness in the matter of the County of Los Angeles vs. Glenda Louise Bledsoe."

My bullshit detector clicked in—Ainge bugged out on his own—I'd bet money.

Handwritten pages—doodles, scrawls—half-legible hiero-glyphics:

(Unreadable)/"I've got a trail worked out on paper"/(unread-able)/"He's spent a fortune so far"/(unreadable)/ink smears. "So he's spent a fortune operating Officer John Duhamel"—smears— "But of course he's a rich kid policeman whose father died (April 1958) and left him millions."

Scribbles/penis drawings—doped-up homo Junior. "Rich kid" Exley—easy make—working Johnny D.—no huge surprise. Doodles/gun drawings/indecipherable gobbledygook. "Operat-ing this guy whose story you won't believe." Coffee stains/ smears/cock drawings/"See file marked Evidence #1."

Check the stack—there—a folder:

Newspaper clippings: mid-April '58. Human-interest schmaltz:

Johnny Duhamel turns pro—his "wealthy" parents died pen-niless and USC dunned their estate. Johnny: attending grad school, three jobs—no pro fight career plans. USC cracks down: repay your college debt or drop out.

That piece—the L.A. *Times*, 4/18/58. Three recaps—the *Herald/ Examiner/Mirror*—4/24, 5/2, 5/3.

Weird:

Four L.A. dailies/four stories—no new facts exposited, no new angles probed. Gallaudet's file check confirmed: Duhamel's parents died broke.

More "Evidence #1": numbered document photos. I flashed back to Junior's pad—that Minox camera.

Photos 1, 2, 3: Security First National Bank forms. Checking and savings accounts opened: Walton White, 2750 N. Edgemont,

Los Angeles. Two thirty-grand deposits coming off hinky: Edgemont stopped at 2400.

Notations on the back:

#1—"Manager described 'Walton White' as 'familiar some-how,' 6′2″, 170, blond-gray hair, glasses, late thirties."

#2—"Manager shown magazine photograph of Edmund Exley. Confirms that E.E. opened the 'Walton White' accounts."

#3—"Manager stated that 'Walton White' (E.E.) requested blank bank checks immediately so that he could begin fulfilling transactions."

Hot now—I started sweating.

Photos 4, 5, 6—cancelled "Walton White" checks. Four grand, four grand, five grand—4/23, 4/27, 4/30/58.

Made out to:

Fritzie Huntz, Paul Smitson, Frank Brigantino.

Bingo: the bylines on those copycat articles.

Photo #7—a cancelled check. Eleven grand and change paid out to: the USC Alumni Debt Fund.

"So he's spent a fortune operating Officer John Duhamel."

"Operating this guy whose story you won't believe."

Reporters bribed.

Johnny bought.

Junior glomming bank records—intimidation prowess and charm pre-CRAAAZY.

Sweating—dripping on my file swag:

Duhamel fight clippings.

A deposition—Chuck "the Greek" Chamales—matchmaker, Olympic Auditorium.

"Revealed under the threat to expose his liaison with Lurleen Ruth Cressmeyer, age 14":

Johnny D. tanked his one pro fight.

Ed Exley paid him to do it.

Duhamel told Chamales this—"one night when he was drunk." The Greek to Junior, verbatim: "He didn't get specific. He just told me on the QT that that Exley guy had special work for him."

Odd pages left—gibberish/doodling. One sheet block-printed:

ADDENDUM:

As former Academy evidence instructor I was invited to the October 16th retirement party for Sgt. Dennis Payne. Talked about my recent sergeantcy and transfer to Ad Vice with Capt. Didion, who told me my father had old Dep. Chief Green move Dave Klein up to the Ad Vice command as only a Lieutenant partially to grease things for my ultimately taking a spot there. Capt. Didion told Dave "The Enforcer" stories for half an hour, and I only listened because I wanted to tap the grapevine for information on Johnny. Capt. Didion told me that Exley personally requested that Johnny graduate early (the 7/10/58 cycle) in order to fill a potential Wilshire Patrol vacancy, which made no sense to him. Also, Dennis Payne confirmed what I suspected when Johnny was yanked early from my evidence class: that Exley urged those undercover assignments on him personally, asking Capt. Didion that he be assigned to them while still technically a cadet.

Exley and Duhamel—operating partners—operating WHO?
Suspects:
The Kafesjians.
Narco.
"This guy whose story you won't believe."
"This guy"—*singular*. A semantic fuck-up—maybe, maybe not.
Single-o suspects:
Tommy K.
J.C.
Dan Wilhite.
Skewed—I couldn't link them directly to Johnny.
Crack the door—Henstell on the walkway, pacing. Shove the chair back, jam the knob shut, go—
I lit a match and torched a file page: faggot artwork sizzled. More matches, more pages—a contained blaze right there on the table.
Smoke out the floor crack—
Henstell banged on the door. "Klein, Goddamn it, what the hell are you doing!"
Flames, charred paper, smoke. I kicked the table over, stomped the blaze out.
"Klein, Goddamn it!"
Jerk the door open, shove him back, coughing smoke—
"Tell Noonan it was personal. Tell him I'm still his witness, and now I owe *him* one."

Out to East L.A., light-headed—light smoke inhalation. Custody forty-seven hours off—two days to GET it:

"LONG HISTORY OF INSANITY BOTH OUR FAMILIES."

Olympic east—rain clouds dousing smog. Chasing/chased/partnered up/partner fucked:

Richie's Chino file was still missing—warden's aides were tossing storage bins for it. Sid Riegle was out chasing Richie—Darktown/Hancock Park—no leads.

Six IA men tapped out: no new Herrick/Kafesjian links. Links extant: Pennsylvania/chemical work/L.A. arrivals '31–'32. Late-'31 marriages: Joan Renfrew, Madge Clarkson—no criminal records—their hometowns queried.

Meg chasing real estate: a Spindrift pad title search. Zero so far, Meg persisting.

The Kafesjians at home, cabin-fevered—Feds out front, Feds out back. Partnered-up-family-tight—no way to tell them:

You and the Herricks—filthy together. Liquor bottles smashed/dogs blinded/music trashed—murder/suicide/castration—I can TASTE it. You'll tell me, you'll tell somebody—I'm partnered up strong on my ride down.

Strong and dirty: Exley. Strong/cautious/grasping: Noonan.

Use them both: fight/squirm/lie/beg/manipulate them.

Exley: Johnny D. as my wedge. The Feds—no lever yet—that fire fried my momentum. Henstell: "You know, Mr. Noonan *was* starting to think you'd be a pretty good witness."

Was/is/could be/would be: DUES TIME. Junior nullified now—Glenda safe—punch my new grief ticket: FEDERAL.

No pre-court testimony taken yet—custody meant interrogation. Noonan—cautious/grasping—shooting me wake-up phone calls:

"You're commanding a homicide case—how odd."

"Would Richard Herrick be the Richie you seem to be so interested in? The man Tommy Kafesjian seems to be rather concerned with? Chief Exley told the *Herald* that you worked on a burglary case that may be tangentially connected to the killings. We *must* discuss this after you enter custody."

"I understand the dilemma you're in, David. You may think that you can dissemble to us and be less than forthcoming vis-à-vis your organized-crime connections, thus sparing yourself a Syndicate death sentence. You will of course be given Federal protection after your grand jury testimony, but you should know now that lies and lies by omission will not be tolerated."

Smart fucker.

Holding back information—bet on it. My big fear: those Fed tails post-Johnson. Long-shot stuff, hard to shake: Abe Voldrich snuffed, a blue Pontiac spotted. Jack Woods—nine contract hits minimum—*my* preferred killer. Jack Woods, proud owner: a powder-blue '56 Pontiac.

Downtown, the 3rd Street Bridge, Boyle Heights. East to Wabash—Brownell's Locksmiths—

A parking-lot drive-up hut.

Four keys—three numbered—maybe traceable.

I pulled up, honked. A man right there, customer smile on. "Help you?"

I flashed my badge and the key fob. "158-32, 159-32, 160-32, and one unstamped. Who did you make them for?"

"I don't even have to check my files, 'cause that 32 coding's from this rent-a-locker storage place I do all the locker keys for."

"So you don't know who rented these individual lockers?"

"Right you are. The unstamped key's for the front door, the number keys are for lockers. And I don't cut no duplicates 'less the manager at the place gives the okay."

"What 'place'?"

"The Lock-Your-Self at 1750 North Echo Park Boulevard, which is open twenty-four hours, case you didn't know."

"You're pretty snappy with your answers."

"Well ..."

"Come on, tell me."

"Well ..."

"Well nothing, I'm a police officer."

Whiny, wheedling: "Well, I hate to be a stool pigeon, 'cause I sorta liked the guy."

"What guy?"

"I don't know his name, but he's that little Mex bantam fights at the Olympic all the time."

"Reuben Ruiz?"

"Right you are. He came in yesterday and told me he wanted dupes of the keys with them numbers, like he *saw* the keys but couldn't get his mitts on the two original sets I cut. I told him, 'Ixnay, not even if you was Rocky Marciano himself.'"

"You cut *two* original sets for the Lock-Your-Self place?"

"One customer original, one management original. The manager sent a guy by for a second customer set, 'cause the people who rented those lockers wanted dupes."

Set number one—Junior. Set number two—maybe Johnny D. —Reuben's pal.

"Officer, them locks and keys are being changed continually to thwart theft. So if you talk to Bob, the manager, will you tell him I'm doing my part toward keeping things—"

I hit the gas—the lock man ate exhaust fumes.

Echo Park off Sunset—a big warehouse. A parking lot, no door guard—*my* door key got me in.

Huge: crisscross hallways, locker-lined. A directory/map up front, number-coded.

The 32 codings were tagged "Jumbo." Follow the map—two corridors down, left, stop:

Three floor-to-ceiling lockers six feet wide.

Scratched up—lock-pick marks.

Keys in, crack the doors:

158-32: mink coats hung eight feet deep, six feet wide.

Seven empty hangers.

159-32: stoles and pelts—dumped shoulder-high.

160-32: fox/mink/raccoon coats—fuckloads hung/dumped/piled/folded/tossed.

Johnny/Junior/Reuben.

Dudley Smith, fur-heist boss—scooped/hoodwinked/stiffed.

Exley and Duhamel—operating WHO?

Mink—touch it, smell it. Empty hangers—Lucille's fur strip? Johnny trying to sell Mickey Cohen bulk fur??

Reuben Ruiz: ex-B&E man/burglar brothers.

His direct key approach—no go.

Break-in scratches/no door guard/Lock-Your-Self: open twenty-four hours.

Key clicks/lock clicks/brain clicks—I got my notebook and pen out. Three lockers—I dropped three identical notes inside:

I want to deal on Johnny Duhamel, Junior Stemmons
and whatever or whoever else connects to this. This
is for money, independent of Ed Exley.

                              D. Klein

Lock the doors—lock clicks/brain clicks—get to a phone.

I found a booth across Sunset. Ad Vice, two rings, "Riegle."

"Sid, it's me."

"You mean it's you and you want something."

"You're right."

"So tell me, but I'll tell *you* right now this Homicide work is wearing me thin."

"Meaning?"

"Meaning Richie Herrick is nowhere. First Exley issues an APB, then he rescinds it, and we *still* can't locate one single white man known to frequent Negro areas."

"I know, and our best bet is to let Tommy Kafesjian find him for us."

"Which doesn't seem too likely with those Armenian humps holed up with Fed surveillance outside their house. Jesus ..."

"Sid, write this down."

"Okay, I'm listening."

"The storage locker place at 1750 North Echo Park."

"All right, I wrote it down. Now what?"

"Now you get your civilian car and stake out the entrance and parking lot. You write down the plate numbers on everyone who walks in. Every five or six hours you call in the stats to the DMV, and you go through until tomorrow morning and call me."

Stage groans. "You'll explain then?"

"That's right."

"It's the Herrick job?"

"It's fucking everything."

36

REUBEN RUIZ—talk, strongarm—whatever it took.

R&I shot me his address: 229 South Loma. Not that far—a quick run over—brother Ramon on the porch.

"Reuben's at the ravine, bein' a *puto* for the City of Los Angeles."

Another quick run—Chavez Ravine.

Swarming now—evictions pending. "Police Parking"—a dirt lot going in. Cop cars jammed up tail to snout: Sheriff's, LAPD, Feds.

Hills fronting the main drag; Mex kids chucking rocks. Black-and-whites scratched and dented.

An access road up—narrow, dusty. I walked it, hit the top, caught the view:

Hecklers bucking bluesuit containment—the main road cordoned off. Shack-lined roads/hills/gulleys—eviction notices rife. Camera crews shooting door to door: Feds and a bobbing sombrero.

Dig it: shack dwellers swarming that hat.

I walked down into it; blues juked me through the cordon. Catch the view: Shipstad, Milner, Ruiz in bullfighter garb.

Reuben:

Passing out money, spics swamping him.

"Dinero!"

"El jefe Ruiz!"

Big-time Mex jabber—incomprehensible.

Milner gaga-eyed: what *is* this?

I shoved, waved—Shipstad saw me. Trembly and flushed—Henstell probably blabbed.

He shoved toward me. We collided: hands on suitcoats instinctive.

"Gracias el jefe Reuben!"—Ruiz tossing cash away.

A dirt yard off the road—Shipstad pointed over. I followed him—tree shade, a sign: "Notice to Vacate."

"Justify that firebug routine before Noonan revokes your immunity and has you arrested."

Eyeball magnet: Reuben dishing out greenbacks.

"Look at me, Klein."

At him, lawyer bullshit: "It was nontangential incriminating evidence. It in no way pertained to the Kafesjian family or to any focus of your investigation or my potential grand jury testimony. Noonan has enough on me as it is, and I didn't want to feed him more potential indictable information."

"Attorney to attorney, how can you live the way you do?"

Tongue tied—

"We're trying to help you get out of this alive. I'm developing a plan to relocate you after you testify, and frankly Noonan doesn't think I should be working so hard at it."

"Which means?"

"Which means I dislike him slightly more than I dislike you. Which means he's two seconds away from arresting you and putting you on display as a hostile witness, then releasing you and letting Sam Giancana or whoever have you killed."

Meg jailed/ brutalized/clipped—Technicolor. "Will you relocate my sister?"

"That's impossible. This last escapade has cost you credibility with Noonan, relocation for your sister was not covered in your contract and there is no established precedent for mobsters harming the loved ones of fugitive witnesses."

GET MONEY.

Ruiz throwing it away.

"We're your only hope. I'll square things with Noonan, but you be at the Federal Building by eight A.M. day after tomorrow, or we'll find you, arrest your sister and begin tax-charge proceedings."

Crowd noise, dust. Reuben watching us.

I waved the keys. Sunlight on metal—he nodded.

Shipstad: "Klein ..."

"I'll be there."

"Eight A.M."

"I heard you."

"It's your only—"

"What's Ruiz doing?"

He looked over. "Expiation of guilt or some such concept. Can you blame him? All this for a baseball stadium?"

Reuben walked up.

"Did you come to see *him*? And what's with those keys?"

"Give me some time with him."

"Is it personal?"

"Yeah, it's personal."

Shipstad walked; Ruiz passed him and winked. Rockabye Reuben: bullfight threads, grin.

"Hey, Lieutenant."

I twirled the keys. "You go first."

"No. First you tell me this is just two witness buddies gabbing, then you tell me popping Mexican bantamweights for robbery don't push your buzzer."

Bulldozers down the road—a shack crashed.

"*Keys*, Reuben. You saw the originals, memorized the numbers and tried to get that locksmith to cut dupes, and there's tool marks on the lockers at that storage place."

"I didn't hear you say anything like 'This is just two guys who'd like each other to stay out of trouble talking.' "

Gear whine/wood snap/dust—the noise made me flinch. "I'm way past arresting people."

"I sort of thought so, given what the Feds been saying."

"Reuben, *spill*. I've got this half-assed notion you want to."

"Do penance, maybe. Spill, I don't know."

"Did you boost some furs out of those lockers?"

"As many as me and my righteous B&E buddies could carry. And they're gone, in case you want a mink for your slumlord sister."

Flowers sprouting next to weeds; smog wafting in.

"So you bagged some furs, sold them and gave the money to your poor exploited brethren."

"No, I gave a silver fox pelt to Mrs. Mendoza next door, 'cause I popped her daughter's cherry and never married her, *then* I sold the furs, *then* I got drunk and gave the money away."

"Just like that?"

"Yeah, and those stupidos down there'll probably spend it on Dodger tickets."

"Reuben—"

"Fuck it, all right—me, Johnny Duhamel and my brothers took down the Hurwitz fur warehouse. You were maybe pushing that way when I saw you in my dressing room, so now you tell me what *you* got before I sober up and get bored with this penance routine."

"Let's try Ed Exley operating Johnny."

Smog—Reuben coughed. "You picked a good fucking topic."

"I figured if Johnny talked to anybody, it was you."

"You figured pretty good."

"He told you about it?"

"Most of it, I guess. Look, this is, you know, off the record?"

I nodded—easy now—cut him rope.

Tick tick tick tick.

Jerk the rope: "Reuben—"

"Yeah, okay, I guess it was like this spring, like April or something. Exley, he read this newspaper story about Johnny. You know, a what you call human-interest story, like here's this guy in graduate school working all these jobs, he used to be a comer in the Golden Gloves, but now he's gotta turn pro even though he don't want to, 'cause his parents croaked and stiffed him and his school, and how he's broke. You follow me so far?"

"Keep going."

"Okay, so Exley, he approached Johnny and what you call manipulated him. He gave Johnny money and paid off his college loan, and he paid off these debts Johnny's parents left. Exley, he's like some kind of rich-kid cop with this big inheritance, and he gave Johnny this bonaroo fucking amount of money and paid these reporter guys to write these other, you know, similar-type newspaper stories about him, playing on this angle that he had to turn pro out of, you know, financial necessity."

"And Exley made Johnny tank that one pro fight he had."

"Right."

"And the newspaper pieces and the tank job were to set Johnny up as some sort of hard-luck kid, so it would look realistic when he applied to the LAPD."

"Right."

"And Exley got Johnny eased into the Academy?"

"Right."

"And all this was to set Johnny up to work undercover."

"Right, to get next to some people or something that Exley had this hard-on for, but don't ask me who, 'cause I don't know."

THEM/Dan Wilhite/Narco—mix them, match them—

"Keep going."

Bobs, feints—Reuben oozed sweat. "So Exley, he got Johnny this outside work while he was in the Academy, this gig where he what you call infiltrated these Marine Corps guys who were beating up and robbing all these rich queers. That punk Stemmons, you know, that ex-partner of yours, he was Johnny's teacher at the Academy, and he read this report that Johnny wrote on the fruit-roller gig."

"And?"

"And Stemmons, he was both, you know, attracted to and, what you call it, repelled by homos. He had the hots for Johnny, which embarrassed the shit out of Johnny, 'cause he's a cunt man from the gate. Anyway, Johnny busted up the fruit-roller ring, and the Marine Corps police, they got, you know, convictions against the guys. Johnny graduated from the Academy and got assigned to the Detective Bureau right off, 'cause the queer gig made him look righteous good, and 'cause being a Golden Gloves champ gave him some righteous prestige. Anyway, that Irish guy, you know, Dudley Smith, he took a shine to Johnny and got him assigned to the Mobster Squad, 'cause he wanted an ex-fighter for this strongarm work they do."

Linkage clicking in—no surprises yet.

"And?"

"*And* somehow Stemmons found out that Exley was what you call operating Johnny, *and* he pulled this wild queer number on him, *and* it disgusted Johnny, but he didn't beat that *puto* faggot silly, 'cause Stemmons was this hotshot evidence teacher cop who could screw Johnny on this gig he was fuckin' embroiled in with Exley."

Popping punches, popping sweat—little moves synced to his story.

"And?"

"*And* you cops always pull that 'and' bit to keep people talking."

"Then let's try 'so.'"

"*So* I guess it was about this time that Johnny got tangled up in the fur job. He said he had inside help, and he just hired on me and my brothers to do the hauling work. He was doing these other so-called bad things, and I figured it was strongarm shit on the Mobster Squad, but Johnny said it was lots worse, like so bad he was afraid to tell his good buddy Exley about it. Fucking Stemmons, he was talking all this criminal-mastermind noise up to Johnny, and I don't know, but somehow he found out about Johnny and the fur heist."

Ruiz shit-eater-grinning—punched out, winded.

"When did Johnny tell you all this?"

"After the fur heist, when we put on gloves and he told me to give him this penance beating."

"And around that time Stemmons tried to horn in on Johnny's part of the fur job."

"Right."

"Come on, Reuben. Right, *and*?"

"And Johnny told me the fur job was an Exley setup from the gate. It was part of his what you call cover, and Exley was in with that guy Sol Hurwitz. Hurwitz was some kind of gone-bust gambler, and fuckin' rich-kid Exley, he bought all the furs and told Johnny how to stage the heist."

AUDACIOUS.

Links missing.

Exley's heist/Dudley Smith's investigation—why did Exley assign someone that good?

Linkage chronology—pure guesswork:

Johnny offers Mickey Cohen hot fur.

Dud gloms the Cohen lead and scares Mickey shitless.

Exley intercedes.

Exley operates Mickey—*toward what end?*

Mickey, skewed behavior—movie mogul, Darktown bungler—he *still* won't pull his Southside slots.

Chick Vecchio—Mickey linked.

Chick—finger man—Kafesjian movie time.

Mickey and Chick—linked to:

THEM/Narco/Dan Wilhite.

Links:

Missing/hidden/obscured/twisted CRAAAZY—

Reuben—punched out, grinning: "*So*, I guess all this is just between us witness buddies."

"That's right."

"Is Johnny dead?"

"Yes."

"Too bad he never got married. Mea fucking culpa, I could of dropped a nice mink coat on his widow."

Crash noise—another shack went down.

37

STONE'S THROW: Chavez Ravine to Silverlake. Over to Jack Woods' place—his car outside.

Powder blue gleaming: Jack's baby.

The front door stood ajar—I knocked first.

"I'm in the shower! It's open!"

I walked in—brazen Jack—phones and bet slips in plain view. A wall photo: Jack, Meg and me—the Mocambo, '49.

"You remember that night? Meg got plowed on Brandy Alexanders."

Meg sat between us—hard to tell whose girl.

"You're cruising down memory lane pretty steep, partner."

I turned around. "You clipped a guy for Mickey a couple of days before. You were flush, so you picked up the tab."

Jack cinched his robe. "Is this the pot calling the kettle black?"

"Did you pop Abe Voldrich?"

"Yeah, I did. Do you care?"

"Not exactly."

"Then you just came by to rehash old times."

"It's about Meg, but I wouldn't mind an explanation."

Jack lit a cigarette. "Chick Vecchio bought the hit for Mickey. He said Narco and Dan Wilhite wanted it. Voldrich was the Kafesjian family's bagman to the LAPD. Chick said it was Mickey's idea, that the Feds had turned Voldrich as a witness, and Mickey wanted his connections to the Kafesjians snipped. Ten grand, partner. My consolation prize for that hump Stemmons dying on me."

"I'm not so sure I buy it."

"So what? Business is business, and Mickey and those Armenians have got lots of stuff going down in Niggertown."

"Something's missing. Mickey doesn't clip people anymore, and he hasn't got ten grand liquid to save his life."

"So it was the Kafesjians direct, or Dan Wilhite through Chick. Look, what do you care who—"

"Wilhite doesn't know Chick personally, I'd bet on it."

My sister's lover—bored. "Look, Chick played on you and me as friends. He said Voldrich could spill to the Feds on you, so did I want to make ten G's and help a buddy out. *Now*, you want to tell me how you made me for the job?"

Links: obscured/hidden/fucked with—

"Dave—"

"The Feds saw a car like yours near Voldrich's place. They didn't get any plate numbers, or you'd have heard from them by now."

"So it was just an educated guess."

"You're the only clip guy I know with a powder-blue car."

"So what about Meg?"

"First you tell me how it stands with you two."

"It stands that she's thinking about leaving her husband and getting a place with me."

"A phone drop? Some crap-game pad?"

"We ruined her for squarejohn guys years ago, so don't act like she doesn't know the score."

That photo—a woman, two killers.

"The Feds have got me by the shorts. I'm going into custody day after tomorrow, and if they try to screw me on my immunity deal Meg might get hurt. I want you to tell her to pull our money out of the bank, and I want you to stash her some place safe until I call you."

"Okay."

"Just 'okay'?"

"Okay, send postcards from wherever the Feds hide you, and I've had a hunch that you were screwed for a couple of weeks now."

That picture—

Jack smiled. "Meg said she's doing this title search for you, and every time you talk on the phone you sound less like a strong-arm guy."

"And more like a lawyer?"

"No, more like a guy trying to buy his way out."

"Look after her."

"Write when you can, Counselor."

A pay-phone call to Homicide. Shit news—no trace on Richie Herrick's Chino file. A message—meet Pete Bondurant—8:00, the Smokehouse, Burbank.

The Vecchio job—looming ugly.

Time to kill. Stone's throw: Silverlake to Griffith Park. I drove up the east road to the Observatory.

Smog clearing, a view: Hollywood, points south. Coin telescopes mounted by the entrance: 180-degree swivels.

Time to kill, pocket change—I aimed one at the set.

Glass blur, asphalt, hills. Parked cars, up, over: the spaceship.

Crank the lens, squint—people.

Sid Frizell and Wylie Bullock talking: maybe their standard gore shtick. Blur, twist the lens: winos sleeping in the weeds.

Look:

A trailer door embrace: Touch and Rock Rockwell. Over right: Mickey C. spieling extras. Metal glare—Glenda's trailer, Glenda.

Sitting on the steps, her legs jammed up. Her vampire gown getting ratty—faded, threadbare.

Glass blur, sun streaks. People walking by—dark obstructions. Hard to see, easy to imagine:

Her breath catching low guiding me in.

Sweat matting her hair a shade darker.

Touching her scars—her eyes implicit: horror gave me the will—and I won't tell you how.

Sun spots, eyestrain. Twist the scope—a wino fistfight—pratfalls, gouging.

The lens clicked off—my time was up. My eyes hurt—I closed them and just stood there. Images hit me rapid-fire:

Dave Klein, strikebreaker—teeth on my truncheon.

Dave Klein, bet enforcer—baseball bat work.

Dave Klein, killer—hung over from cordite and blood stench.

Meg Klein, sobbing: "I don't want you to love me that way."

Joan Herrick: "Long history of insanity both our families."

Somebody, please: give me one last chance to know.

38

"... SO MR. HUGHES is pissed. Some psycho chopped Harold Miciak, and he was hoping it'd be open and shut, but now the Malibu Sheriff's are thinking it's not that Wino Will-o-the-Wisp guy. They're thinking somebody chopped Miciak and strangled him to make it look like the Wisp, and Miciak's ex-wife is bothering Mr. Hughes to put private eyes on the job like he's supposed to spend *money* on this thing. *Then*, on top of all *that*, Bradley Milteer finds out that *you're* porking Glenda Bledsoe and that she's been stealing from Mr. Hughes' fuck pads, but *you* never reported it."

Southbound—Pete's car. Bonus armed: knucks and sap.

"I got you the Glenda gig. Mr. Hughes didn't trust me on it, 'cause he knows I'm susceptible to snatch. I figured, give the job to the old Enforcer, 'cause he's pretty stoical in the woman department."

I stretched—neck kinks, jangly nerves. "I'm paying you seven grand for this."

"Yeah, and you bought me a barbeque beef plate and a beer, which frankly Mr. Hughes never did. What I'm saying is that Mr. Hughes is pissed at you, which is grief you don't need."

Normandie south—Pete smoking—crack the window. Replay: my call to Noonan.

"You burned up potential Federal evidence. You're lucky I haven't revoked your immunity outright, and now you want this rather outsized favor."

"PLEASE."

"I like the tremor in your voice."

"*PLEASE*. Lift the surveillance on the Kafesjians tomorrow. It's my last full day before custody, and I want to see if I can learn a few things before I go in."

"My guess is that this pertains to the Kafesjians looking for that Richie character, who may be Richard Herrick of that rather outré triple-homicide case you're working."

"You're right."

"Good. I appreciate candor, and I'll do it if you formally depose your Richie information during your pre-grand-jury interviews."

"I agree."

"It's settled, then. Go with God, Brother Klein."

"Brother" Klein—Lutheran choirboy—fists/sap/knucks—

Pete nudged me. "Chick's meeting Joan Crawford at the Lucky Nugget. She'll be camouflaged up, and they're gonna play pokerino or something, then head for the fuck spot from there. I'm gonna snap some pictures on the QT, then Chick's gonna give me the high sign. We'll tail them to the spot, let them get cozy and take it from there."

Cold air, bouncing headlights. A billboard: "Dodger Stadium Is *Your* Dream! Support the Chavez Ravine Bill!"

Pete: "Seven grand for your thoughts."

"I'm thinking Chick must have a money stash someplace."

"If you're thinking take it, it means we have to clip him."

"It's just a thought."

"And as thoughts go, not bad. Jesus, you and some ex-carhop actress. Is she—"

"Yeah, she's worth the trouble."

"I wasn't gonna ask you that."

"I know."

"Like that, huh?"

"Like that."

Straight south—Gardena—Pete talking grapevine:

Fred Turentine, *Hush-Hush* bug man: scandal duty for off-the-books cash. Boozer Freddy, AWOL: from dry-out farms and his jail teaching gig. Fed heat, restless niggers—you couldn't score good ribs or dark poon for shit.

Gardena—poker-palace row pulsing neon. The Lucky Nugget—Chick's Caddy in the lot, top down.

We pulled up behind it—tail ready. Front-seat action—Joan Crawford and Chick necking hot.

Pete said, "Duck down, they'll see you."

I ducked and listened—car doors slammed. Back up—lovebirds on the stroll.

Pete got out. "Take a snooze or something. Don't play the radio, you'll run the battery down."

Tracks inside: movie star, thug, shakedown man. I skimmed the radio dial: news, religious shit, bop.

Memory jog: rolling Gardena drunks back in high school. Bop to ballads, memory lane—zipping Meg's prom gown too slow.

Fuck it—spare the battery—I turned the music off and dozed. Pete at the door: "Wake up, they're leaving."

The Caddy rolled, ragtop up. Pete pulled out—not too close. East, north—cool air woke me up. Easy tailwork—collusion—Pete drove nonchalant. One arm out her window, oblivious: Joan fucking Crawford.

Due north—Compton, LYNWOOD—spooky turf.

Chick out front: left turn, right turn—Spindrift Drive.

48, 4900—curb plates pulsing weird/nuts/strange. 4980—Johnny D.—"Why meet there?"

Hard to breathe—I rolled the window down.

Left turn, right turn.

Empty courtyards.

Dry-ice chills: hot and cold.

Pete: "Jesus, I never made you for such a fresh-air fiend."

Chick stopped—brake-light taps, signallike.

Memory lane:

Needle stabbed.

Toasty-warm tingly doped up.

Chick and Joanie, walking love-draped:

Into a vacant courtyard, up the RIGHT side walkway.

Then:

Carried, treading air.

RIGHT turn—a skanky room—MOVIE TIME.

Now:

Sucking air—hard to breathe—Johnny replays zinging me.

Pete pulled up curbside. "Chick passed me a note. He knows some guys making smut films here, so he thought Joanie'd like that angle. Movie stars never fail to fucking amaze me."

Memory clicks—brutal late:

Glenda said Sid Frizell was shooting stag films.

"At some abandoned dive."

"Down in LYNWOOD."

"Hey, Klein, are you okay?"

Weapon check: .45, sap, knucks. "Let's go."

Pete loaded his camera. "It's all set. We go in on 'Baby, it's so good.'"

Ready: knuck teeth scraped my law-school ring.

Pete: "Now."

We ran in: stucco cubes, walkways, grass.

Place it then and now: Movie time, Johnny begging: "PLEASE DON'T KILL ME."

Sex grunts—a right-side shack midway down. Tiptoes up, listen: Smut moans, Chick: "Baby, it's so gooood."

Pete camera ready.

Looks, nods, kicks—we snapped the door clean.

Pitch black half a second.

Flashbulb pops: Joan Crawford gobbling Chick V. tonsil-deep. Speedo:

Bulb blips—Joanie running out the door bare-ass, shrieking.

Chick pawing at a wall switch—the lights on.

A magnum on the nightstand—I grabbed it and scoped the room: Mirrored walls.

Linoleum floor—maroon dots—dried blood.

Chick on the bed, zipping his fly.

Knucks/gun butt—quick—

I bashed his face, racked his nuts, cracked his arms. Bone jar up my hands—Chick balled himself tight.

A shadow on the bed—Pete restraining me. *"Ease off.* I gave Crawford some clothes and some money. *We've got time to do this right."*

Chick doubled up, quaking, good cause: two giant fists flexing straight at him.

Canned shtick—Pete gleeful:

"The left one's the hospital, the right one's death. The right one steals your life while the left steals your breath. These hands are bad juju and the bad boogaloo, they're the teeth of the demon as he slides down the flue."

Chick stood up—bloody, trembly. "I am Outfit. I am a made guy. Feature you are both dead for this."

Pete: "Dave, ask the man a question."

I said, "You set me up. I told you I was meeting a 'pretty-boy strongarm cop' in Lynwood. Now, for starters you tell me *who* you told and how they got that home-movie idea."

"Feature I will tell you nothing."

Pete grabbed him by the neck. Flick: two hundred pounds airborne. Chick hit the far wall—mirror glass shattered.

Rag doll Chick—this "huh?" look.

Pete right there—stomp, stomp—fingers cracking under his heels. Chick showed balls: no audible grief.

I knelt down. "You set me up with the Kafesjians."

"Go fuck yourself."

"Chick, we go back. This doesn't have to be ugly."

"Feature you *are* ugly."

"You fingered me to the Kafesjians. Cop to it and go from there."

"I didn't clue nobody you were meeting that cop you told me about. So you got set up, what the fuck, they set you up. Feature I knew they set you up, but feature it was after the goddamn fact."

"You said 'they.' You mean the Kafesjians?"

"I mean it's a figure of goddamn speech. You got set up 'cause you were born for it, all the shit you pulled and walked on. You got set up, but feature I didn't do it."

Pete: "I didn't know you knew the Kafesjians. I thought you were strictly a Mickey guy."

"Fuck you. You're a chump change pimp for Howard Hughes. I fucked your mother. My dog fucked your mother."

Pete laughed.

Chick—broken fingers, shock pale: "Feature I been rough-housed before. Feature I gave you a free introductory answer, but from here on in you get shit."

Blood flecks on the floor—Johnny begging.

"You said 'they.' You mean the Kafesjians? Give me some details I can use."

"You mean feed to the Feds? I know you rolled over for Welles Noonan."

This greaseball thug—sweating off Joan Crawford's perfume.

"Hand the fuckers up. Give me details."

"Detail this"—one smashed middle finger twirling. "Suck on this, you kraut cocksuck—"

I grabbed his hand—a wall socket close—jam that fuck-you finger in—

Sparks/smoke—Chick convulsing—live-wire jolts shaking me. Pete shook me: "STOP IT, YOU'LL KILL HIM!"

Chick shook free: juiced-up hip-hops on his knees, going green. Fast:

Pete tossed him on the bed. Pillows, sheets, blankets—one mummified geek inside seconds.

Hip-hops sputtering out, his green tinge fading.

Johnny Duhamel begging—IN THIS ROOM.

I grabbed the magnum and popped the cylinder. Six rounds—I dumped five.

Pete nodded: I *think* he's okay.

Show the gun, show the cylinder—spin it, lock it.

Chick—read his eyes—"You wouldn't."

I aimed point blank—my gun, his head. "You said 'they.' Did you mean the Kafesjian family?"

No response.

I pulled the trigger—*click*—empty chamber.

"How'd you get in with the Kafesjians? I didn't know you knew them."

No response.

I pulled the trigger—*click*—empty chamber.

"I know you gave Jack Woods the contract on Abe Voldrich, and Jack said Mickey ordered it. I don't believe that, so you tell me who really did."

Chick, raspy: "Fuck you."

I pulled the trigger—twice—empty chambers.

Pete whooped: "Mother dog!"

Rainbow Chick turning gray/green/blue.

Cock the hammer, eeeaase the trigger sooo slooow ...

"Okay, okay PLEASE!"

I pulled the gun back. Chick coughed, spat phlegm and talked:

"I got this order to recruit a hit on Abe Voldrich. Feature they figured I was too well known on the Southside to do it myself, so I thought, 'Dave Klein, he could get burned by this Federal biz,' and 'Jack Woods, he does a job for a price, he's Dave's buddy, he'd want to spare Dave grief,' so I talked him into it that way, not that he didn't jew me up on the ticket."

Raspy working on hoarse: "So, feature—I *talked* to Voldrich. The Feds cut him loose to take care of some stuff for a day or so, and I wanted to know what he knew before I had Jack clip him. Now, now, now"—snitch fever—"you just listen."

Pete popping his knuckles—loud, like hammer clicks.

Chick, thrashing his blankets: "Voldrich said the Feds were hot to turn you as a witness. He said he overheard Welles Noonan and this FBI man Shipstad talking. They said they bugged your pad, and they've got a tape with you talking this amorphous stuff about your mob hits, and Glenda Bledsoe saying she snuffed some nigger pimp named Dwight Gilette. Feature, Davey: Noonan told Shipstad he was going to offer you immunity, get a shitload of information, then violate the agreement unless you testify against Glenda on the murder charge. Shipstad tried to talk Noonan out of crossing you, but Noonan hates you so bad he said he'd never agree."

Feature:

The bed spinning.

The room spinning.

The gun spinning—

"Who are 'they'?"

"Davey, please. I just did you this all-time solid."

"Something's off here. You're not the one the Kafesjians would send to pump Abe Voldrich. Now, who set me up to kill Johnny Duhamel?"

"Davey, *please*."

Everything spinning—

"Please, Davey ..."

I hit him—gun-butt shots—his blankets caught the brunt. I pulled them down—ribcage work—the bed spun.

"Who set me up?"

No snitch.

"What's with Mickey? Why are those out-of-town guys working his slots with the Feds right there?"

No snitch.

"You're in with the Kafesjians? You're tight with them? *You fucking tell me what you know about Tommy chasing a guy named Richie Herrick.*"

No snitch—ribcage work—my pistol grips shattered. Pete flashed me a signal: EASY.

I spun the cylinder again. "Is Sid Frizell shooting smut films here?"

No answer.

I pulled the trigger—*click*—empty chamber.

Chick balled up, quaking—

Pull the trigger—*click*—empty chamber.

Quaking/snitch-begging eyes: "They said they needed a strongarm place, so I said take this place, Sid and his crew were editing their stag stuff, so this place was empty."

"Did they tell you they were making their own movie?"

"No! They said 'strongarm spot'! That's all they said!"

"Who developed their film? Did someone on Mickey's movie crew help them out?"

"No! Frizell and his guys are fucking clowns! They don't know anybody except me!"

"Who's been running you?"

"No, Davey, please!"

I put the gun to the mattress—next to his head. "Who are
THEY?"

"NO! I CAN'T! I WON'T!"

I pulled the trigger—*click/click/roar*—muzzle flash set his hair
on fire.

This scream.

This huge hand snuffing flames out—stretching huge to quash
that scream.

A whisper:

"We'll stash him at one of your buildings. You do what you
have to do, and I'll watchdog him. We'll work an angle on his
money, and sooner or later he'll spill."

Smoke. Mattress debris settling.

Chick torched half-bald.

EVERYTHING SPINNING.

39

BACK TO L.A.—Pete's car solo—pay-phone stops en route.

I broke it to Glenda: you're nailed for Dwight Gilette. She
said, "Oh, shit" and hatched a plan: she'd bus it to Fresno, hide out
with an old carhop pal. Phone-tap panic hit me—I spieled her
through the checkout procedure. Glenda pulled wires and
checked diodes—no tap on her line.

Her goodbye: "We're too good-looking to lose."

Jack Woods—three no-answers—Meg ditto. A booth outside
the Bureau, luck—Jack just walked in. I told him the Feds fucked
me: grab Meg, grab our money, GO.

"Okay, Dave"—no goodbye.

I ran up to Ad Vice. A clerk's slip on my desk: "Call Meg.
Important."

My In box, my Out box—no new Herrick field reports.
I checked my desk—the Kafesjian/Herrick case file was gone.

The phone rang—

"Yeah?"

"Boss, it's Riegle."

"Yeah?"

"Come on, you assigned me to a stakeout, remember? The
storage locker place, you told me—"

"Yeah, I remember. Is this routine, or something good?"

Miffed:"I got you twelve hours of DMV-certified squarejohns and one interesting bit."

"So tell me."

"*So*, a guy went in, then ran back to his car looking spooked. *So*, I got his plate number and checked him out, and I thought he looked sort of familiar. *So*, Richard Carlisle, you know him? He's LAPD, and I think he works for Dudley Smith."

Soft clicks.

"Boss, are you—"

I cradled the phone down, soft clicks building:

Dick Carlisle—fur-job detective.

Dick Carlisle—Mike Breuning's partner.

11/51—Breuning dead-ends a juvie B&E. Obvious perps: Tommy K., Richie Herrick.

My Kafesjian/Herrick case file—missing.

I walked down the hall to Personnel. File request slips on the clerk's desk—for Division COs only.

I braced the clerk:

Michael Breuning, Richard Carlisle—get me their folders. "Yes, sir," ten minutes, folders out—"not to leave the room."

Carlisle—Previous Employment—no clicks.

Breuning—movie click—Wilshire Film Processing, developing technician—'37–'39—pre-LAPD.

Click—soft, circumstantial.

1:00 A.M.—back to Ad Vice. Stray thoughts: Pete guarding Chick at my El Segundo vacant.

Chick:

"THEY."

Afraid to say "Kafesjian."

Afraid to snitch they/THEM/who?

That message slip: "Call Meg. Important."

Circumstantial—prickles up my short hairs.

Meg at Jack's—worth a try. Three rings—Jack, edgy: "Yes?"

"It's me."

Background noise: high heels tapping. Jack said, "She's here. She's taking it pretty well, maybe just a little bit nervous."

"You're leaving tomorrow?"

"Right. We'll hit the banks early, withdraw the cash and get bank drafts. Then we're going to drive down to Del Mar, open some new accounts and find a place. You want to talk to her?"

Tap tap—Meg pacing—high heels made her stocking seams bunch. "No. Tell her it's just goodbye for now, and ask her what the message was."

Tap, tap, low voices. Footsteps, Jack: "Meg said she's got a partial trace on that building in Lynwood."

"And?"

"She found some property evaluation reports in that storage basement at the City Hall. What she's got is a 1937 report listing Phillip Herrick and a Dudley L. Smith as bidders on 4980 Spindrift. Hey, you think that's *the* Dudley Smith?"

Sweaty hands—I dropped the phone.

Say it:

Ed Exley vs. Dudley Smith.

40

EMERGENCY COMMAND #'s—my desk card. Chief of Detectives (Home)—dial it.

Exley, 1:00 A.M. alert: "Yes? Who is this?"

"It's Klein. I just figured out you're working Dudley Smith."

"Come over now. My address is 432 South McCadden."

A trellised Tudor—lights on, the door ajar. I walked in uninvited.

A showroom living room, catalog perfect. Exley in a suit and knotted tie—2:00 fucking A.M.

"How did you find out?"

"I beat you to a bank writ and hit Junior Stemmons' vault boxes. He had notes on you operating Duhamel, and Reuben Ruiz filled in some blank spots on the fur heist. I found out that Dudley and Phillip Herrick went in on some property together back in '37. Herrick and J.C. Kafesjian came to L.A. a few years before, and I'm betting Dudley was the one who set J.C. up with the LAPD."

Standing there, arms crossed. "Continue."

"It fits. My Kafesjian and Herrick files were stolen, and Richie's prison records are missing. Dudley could have snatched them both easily. He loves developing protégés, so you shoved Johnny Duhamel in his face."

"Continue."

Shock him: "I killed Johnny. Dudley doped me up, provoked me and filmed it. A fucking *movie* exists. I think he's waiting to use me for something."

Exley "shock"—one neck vein pulsing. "When you said Duhamel was dead, I knew it had to be Dudley, but this film business surprises me."

"Surprise *me*. Give me your end of it."

He pulled chairs up. "Give me your take on Dudley Smith."

"He's brilliant and obsessed with order. He's cruel. It's occurred to me a few times that he's capable of anything."

"Beyond your wildest imaginings."

Scalp prickles. "And?"

"And he's been trying to set himself up to control the L.A. rackets for years."

"And?"

"And, in 1950 he acquired some heroin stolen from a Mickey Cohen–Jack Dragna truce meeting. He enlisted a chemist, who spent years developing compounds with it, in order to produce the drug more cheaply. His design was to accrue profit through selling it, to utilize it to keep Negro criminal elements sedated and then branch out into other rackets. His ultimate goal was something along the lines of 'contained' organized crime. He wanted to perpetuate illegal enterprises within specific vice zones, most notably South Los Angeles."

"Get to specifics."

Slow—tantalizing me: "In '53 Dudley became involved in an attempt to take over a pornography racket. A meet was set up at the Nite Owl Coffee Shop. Dudley sent three men in with shotguns. A robbery was faked, and six people were killed. Dudley was instrumental in attempting to frame three Negro thugs for the murders. They escaped from jail and hid out, and as you know, I shot and killed them, along with the man who was hiding them."

The room swirled—

"The case was assumed closed. As you also know, a man came forth later and gave the men I killed a valid Nite Owl alibi, which prompted a reopening. I know you know most of the story, but let two facts suffice: the actual gunmen were killed during the reopened investigation, and they left not one shred of evidence pointing to Dudley Liam Smith."

Swirling—grab for threads:

Dudley—smut fiend?—MOVIE TIME. Sid Frizell shooting stag films in that courtyard—no connection to Smith.

"Dud's got new takeover plans going—strictly Niggertown."

"Bravo, Lieutenant."

"He's running Mickey Cohen?"

"Continue."

"Mickey's been scuffling since he got out of prison. Four of his men disappeared earlier this year—Dudley killed them. All Mickey's got going is that stupid horror movie he's bankrolling, which I don't think ties to any of this."

"Continue."

"Mickey's been acting strange since the Fed business started. He won't dump his Southside coin machines, and I warned him half a dozen times. He's got some out-of-town guys servicing slots in plain sight, with the Feds right there taking pictures. I mentioned it to Chick Vecchio, who handed me a line of shit about Mickey paying off a syndicate loan with his coin percentages. Chick's in with Dudley. Dudley clipped those four Mickey guys and approached Chick. Chick's the liaison between Dud and Mickey. That slot work with the Feds watching is some kind of setup."

Exley fucking *smiled*. "You've put it together exactly as I have."

"Get to Johnny. Tell me how you operated him."

"No, tell me about your Stemmons evidence first."

I ticked points: "I know about those bank accounts you set up. I know how you paid those reporters to write stories about Johnny. I know you paid off his debts, got him to tank that fight and got him into the Academy. You set up the fur heist yourself, so I'm thinking you arranged leads to have Dudley actually *make* Johnny for the heist. You *knew* how Dudley loved developing 'protégés,' so you put a fucking humdinger right in front of his nose."

"Keep going."

"Breuning and Carlisle—they're in with Dudley."

"Correct."

"You got Johnny that Academy undercover job."

"Elaborate on that."

Leading me/pushing me/praising me—this string-pulling weak sister.

"You coached him to overreact. Dudley likes tough boys, so you made damn sure Johnny established some strongarm credentials."

"Bravo, Lieutenant"—toss the dog a bone.

"You like running people as much as Dudley does. It must gall you to know he's better at it."

"You're sure of that?"

"No, you cocksucker, I'm not. But I *know* it must get you to look in the mirror and see Dudley."

Exley "anger"—a tight little grimace.

"Continue."

"No, you give me a chronology. Dudley bit, and got Johnny assigned to the Mobster Squad. He's the Robbery Division CO, so he got the Hurwitz heist pro forma. You planted leads to put Dudley on to Johnny, then what?"

"Then Johnny became an official Mobster Squad goon. It's brutal work, Lieutenant. I always thought you'd be well suited for it."

Tight fists—my knuckles ached. "Reuben Ruiz said Johnny was doing some 'very bad things.' Dudley started working *him* then, right? He made Johnny for the robbery, and he *liked* it. It impressed him, so he let Johnny in on his plans."

"You're on track. Continue."

"Continue shit—what 'very bad things'?"

"Dudley had Johnny terrorizing out-of-town hoodlums he had plans for. Johnny told me he was having difficulty doing it."

"You should have pulled him then."

"No. I needed more."

"Do you think those out-of-town guys were the guys working Mickey's slots? Do you think it ties into Dud running Mickey?"

"Yes. I'm not entirely sure, but I think it's possible."

His chair—Scotch tape dangling off a slat.

"Wrap it up."

Exley buffed his glasses—his eyes looked soft without them. "Johnny began to lose Dudley's respect. He was too lax with the out-of-town men, and he told me that Carlisle and Breuning were surveilling him sporadically, apparently because Dudley became instinctively suspicious of him. Junior Stemmons came back into Johnny's life then, quite accidentally. Both he and Johnny were working South-Central, and somehow Stemmons got Johnny to admit his participation in the fur robbery. Johnny didn't, apparently, implicate me, but Stemmons sensed that he was being operated. Dudley became aware of how dangerously unstable Stemmons was, and I *think* he suspected him of trying to extort Johnny. I *know* for a fact that Dudley tried to get a bank writ to seize potential Stemmons evidence, and I'm assuming that he tortured Johnny for information on the extent of Junior's knowledge before he had you kill him. I had already gone to a

Federal law clerk that I know, and he stalled Dudley's writ while I tried to get one. You got to the vault boxes first, and I'm thinking that Welles Noonan must have assisted you."

That dangling tape—just maybe.

"He did."

"Are you going to be a Federal witness?"

"I'm supposed to be."

"But you're considering not testifying?"

Glenda—potential FED indictments pending.

"Mostly I'm thinking of running."

"What's stopping you?"

"The Kafesjian-Herrick job."

"You're expecting some kind of payoff?"

"No, I just want to know why."

"Is that all you want?"

"No. I want you to get me a cup of coffee, and I want to know why you assigned me to the Kafesjian burglary."

Exley stood up. "Do you think Dudley killed Junior Stemmons?"

"No, he would have ditched the body to buy more time to get at the vault boxes."

"Are you thinking it was a legitimate overdose?"

"No, I'd bet on Tommy K. My guess is that Junior came on strong and Tommy got pissed. It happened *at* Bido Lito's, so Tommy left the body there. The Kafesjians torched the place to destroy evidence."

"You could be right. Wait, I'll get you your coffee."

He walked out. Kitchen sounds—I grabbed the tape.

Safe-combination bingo: 34L–16R–31L. Squarejohn thinking: every rich stupe pulled that chair-reminder bit. I pressed the tape back and scoped the room: cold, expensive.

Exley brought coffee in on a tray. I poured a cup for show.

"You put me on the Kafesjian burglary to bait Dudley."

"Yes. Has he approached you?"

"Indirectly, and I told him flat out that you were using me as some sort of agent provocateur. He let it go at that."

"And he has you compromised with that movie you told me about."

"PLEASE DON'T KILL ME."

"Get to it. Dudley and the Kafesjians."

He sat down. "The burglary itself was just a coincidence, and I simply capitalized on the fact that Dan Wilhite sent you over to smooth things out with J.C. I suspect that the burglary and the Herrick killings, which *are* connected, are connected to Dudley at best tangentially. Essentially, after the Nite Owl reopening, I began querying retired officers about Dudley. I learned that he, not Chief Horrall, suborned the Kafesjians into the LAPD fold twenty-odd years ago. *He* was the one who initiated the notion of contained narcotics peddling in exchange for a certain amount of Southside order and snitch information, and of course many years later he went crazy with the notion of containment in general."

"What about Phillip Herrick?"

"Your property-ownership lead is my first indication of a Smith-Herrick connection. You see, I just wanted Dudley diverted. I knew he had things brewing in South-Central, and I knew he was taking a discreet percentage from J.C. Kafesjian. I wanted the Kafesjians rattled, and I had hoped that your reputation would move Dudley to approach you."

"Then you'd operate me."

"Yes."

Dawn breaking—my last free day. "I burned up Junior's evidence. He had notes, your canceled checks to those reporters, everything."

"All my dealings with Duhamel were verbal. You've just assured me that there is no evidence on my operation extant."

"It's comforting to know that you'll skate."

"You can, too."

"Don't jerk my chain. Don't offer me protection, and don't mention sparing the Department."

"You consider your situation beyond those things?"

Dawn light—my eyes stung. "I'm fucked, plain and simple."

"Ask a favor then. I'll grant it."

"I got Noonan to lift his surveillance on the Kafesjians. They'll be tail-free today only, and I think they'll go after Richie Herrick. I want a dozen mobile tail men with civilian radio cars, and a special frequency set up to monitor their calls. It's a shot at Dudley, which should please you no fucking end."

"You're assuming Richie can fill in some blanks on Dudley and the Kafesjians?"

"I'm assuming he knows all of it."

Exley stuck a hand out—Dave, my buddy. "I'll set up a radio spot at Newton Station. Be there at ten-thirty, I'll have your men briefed and ready."

That hand, persistent—I ignored it.

"You're letting Narco go. The Department needs a scapegoat, and they're it."

That hand disappeared. "I have extensive dossiers on every Narco officer. At the proper time, I'm going to present them to Welles Noonan, as a way of affecting a rapprochement. And, parenthetically, Dan Wilhite committed suicide last night. He left a note that included a brief mention of the bribes he's taken, and I'm going to send Noonan a memorandum on it before too long. He was obviously afraid of having his more outré secrets exposed, which is something you should consider should you decide to testify against the Department."

Bad morning light—glaring.

"I'm past all that."

"You're not past needing me. I can help satisfy your curiosity regarding those families, so don't forget that your interests are identical to mine."

Bad morning light—one day left.

41

10:30—NEWTON STREET Station. A briefing room—chairs facing me.

No sleep—phone work kept me up. Recap: early-A.M. check-in—the Wagon Wheel Motel.

Those fur-storage notes: Dudley knew I knew/Dudley knew where I lived.

Calls:

Glenda said she was safe in Fresno.

Pete said he had Chick V. stashed, with Fred Turentine guarding him. Safe: *my* slum building, dummy signers, untraceable. "When he heals up a little, I'm gonna lean on him. He's got money tucked away someplace, I can tell."

Implied: rob him, kill him.

Welles Noonan had Kafesjian news:

Per our bargain: all Fed tails were lifted today only. TV misinformation was planted: "Probe surveillance quashed by court injunction."

"I'm hoping our friends will think that an LAPD fix is in, and resume their outside life. Godspeed in this mission of yours,

Brother Klein—and tune in Channel 4 or KMPC at two-forty-five this afternoon. Really, you'll be in for quite a treat."

Lying treacherous hump.

Tail men walked in and sat down. Mixed bag: suits and ties, loafer types. Twelve men—eyes on me.

"Gentlemen, I'm Dave Klein. I'm commanding the Herrick homicide job, and per Chief Exley's order, you are to keep a twenty-four rolling surveillance on J.C., Tommy, Lucille and Madge Kafesjian. We are hoping that one of them will lead us to Richard Herrick, who Chief Exley and I want to question as a material witness in the Herrick 187's."

Little nods—Exley pre-briefed them.

"Gentlemen, those folders on your desks contain Intelligence Division photos of the four Kafesjians, along with State Records Bureau mugs of Richard Herrick, and a more recent artist's sketch of him. Know those faces. Memorize them. You'll be stringing three-man tails on each family member, both mobile and on foot, and I don't want you losing them."

Folders open, pix out—pros.

"You're all skilled tail men, or Chief Exley wouldn't have chosen you. You've got radio-equipped civilian cars, and Communications Division has got you hooked up on band 7, which is absolutely Fed-listening-proof. You're hooked up car to car, so you can talk among yourselves or contact me here at the base. You all know how to leapfrog suspects, and there are boom mikes outside the Kafesjian house. There's a man in a point car listening, and once you assume your perimeter posts, he'll tell you when to roll. Questions so far?"

No hands up.

"Gentlemen, if you see Richard Herrick, apprehend him alive. He's a peeper at worst, and both Chief Exley and I believe that a man peeping on him is in fact the Herrick family killer. If approached, I doubt that he'll react violently or resist arrest. He might try to flee, in which case you should pursue him and take him *alive* by any means necessary. *Should you spot one of the Kafesjians, specifically Tommy or J.C., trying to kill or in any way harm Richard Herrick, kill them.* If Tommy himself spots your tail and attempts to flee, chase him. If he makes *any* aggressive moves toward you, *kill him.*"

Whistles, smiles.

"Go—you're dismissed."

Bugs in my walls, bugs on my phone. Bugs snooping on Glenda, snooping on Meg. Fred Turentine—the "Bug King"—guarding Chick.

Bugs in my buildings—three hundred units plus. Tenants overheard: fix the roof, kill the rats. Bugs blasting bop—niggers tearing up my slum pads.

"Sir? Lieutenant Klein?"

I woke up aiming—trigger happy.

A bluesuit—scared. "S-s-sir, the point man broadcast in. He said the two Kafesjian guys are mobile, and he said he heard them talking up Richie Herrick."

42

TAIL REPORTS—band 7, continuous squawk:

11:14: Madge and Lucille at home. J.C. and Tommy driving eastbound—separate cars.

11:43: J.C. at the downtown Public Library. Tail men in foot pursuit—walkie-talkie talkback:

The music room—J.C. rousting winos. "Hey! You know Richie Herrick, he used to read books here! Hey, you seen Richie, you tell me!"

No Richie confirmations.

12:06: J.C. mobile, eastbound.

12:11: Madge and Lucille at home.

Earaches—my headset fit tight.

12:24: J.C. at a skid-row movie house.

"He's shining a flashlight at all these bums sleeping. He's getting nowhere, and he's getting mad."

12:34: J.C. walking—Q&A at the Jesus Saves Mission.

12:49: Tommy walking—skid row.

12:56: Tommy at a skin-book arcade.

12:58: Tommy talking to a clerk.

Linkage?:

Transom magazine—Richie Herrick, author.

1:01: Tommy muscling the clerk. Unit 3-B67, walkie-talkie: "The guy's pleading with Tommy. If Tommy pulls a weapon, I'll go in."

1:01: J.C. at a hot-dog stand.

1:03–1:04: Tommy driving northbound.

1:06: Unit 3-B67, walkie-talkie:

"I talked to the clown Tommy leaned on, and he said that Richie bought dirty magazines there. He said Richie said something about a pad in Lincoln Heights, and he told Tommy about it to get him off his back."

1:11: Tommy—Pasadena Freeway north.

1:14: Tommy—Lincoln Heights off-ramp.

1:19: J.C. eating lunch: five kraut dogs, Bromo Seltzer.

1:21: Lucille heading out in her Ford Vicky.

1:23: Tommy cruising North Broadway, Lincoln Heights.

1:26: Madge at home.

1:34: J.C. scarfing dessert: jelly doughnuts and beer.

1:49: Tommy cruising side streets, Lincoln Heights.

1:53: Lucille—Pasadena Freeway northbound.

1:56: Lucille—Lincoln Heights off-ramp.

1:59: 3-B67/3-B71—crosstalk:

Lucille cruising Lincoln Heights.

Tommy cruising Lincoln Heights.

North/south/east/west zigzags—missing each other.

Educated guess:

Two Richie chasers chasing Richie—cross-purposes.

Maybe Lucille got a phone tip—maybe the skin-mag clerk.

2:00–2:04: All J.C./Tommy/Lucille units:

No Richie Herrick sightings.

Transmitter static. I flipped dials—squelch, odd words: "multiple," "maybe mob stuff," "Watts."

A clerk tapped me. "Sorry, Lieutenant, a Code 3 screwed up the lines."

"What is it?"

"Homicides at the Haverford Wash. Maybe shotguns, maybe gangster stuff."

My hackles jumped. "You monitor band 7, I'm going."

Watts—Code 3, join the crowd: black-and-whites, lab vans, Fed cars. *Deep* Watts—rural—fields, scattered shacks.

A bluff—cop vehicles at the edge. I skidded up and fishtailed in close.

Men looking down—Feds and LAPD combined. Push through, scope it:

A concrete run-off ditch—twenty feet deep.

Sewage water ankle-high—tech men kicking through it.

Blood streaks down the right-side embankment.

Four garbage-soaked bodies just below.

Steep cement leading down—I skidded all the way. Tech guys snapping pix—bulb light bouncing off bloody water.

I looked up:

Trees lining the embankment—good cover.

I looked down:

Shotgun shells bobbing in the muck.

Call it:

Tree-cover ambush—buckshot blew them down.

I sloshed over—techs swarming—more sirens up top. Four bottom-sucking dead men—their backsides ripped tailbone to ribcage.

Jumbled voices on the bluff: Noonan, Shipstad, Exley. Lab men flipping bodies, getting gore-splashed.

Four stiffs face-up now—two white, two Mex. I made three: goons working Mickey C. coin.

Snap conclusion:

Dudley ambush—NO FACE SHOTS—Darktown slot geek victims.

Snap theory:

Staged killings for the Feds—some onus dropped on out-of-town gangs. A Dudley Smith charade—SOMEHOW.

Look:

Exley kicking up water—his cuffs soaked.

Noonan closer—trousers rolled, fucking garters.

Tech talk, scrambled:

Handguns on the stiffs.

Spent rounds up top—threads attached—the killers wore bulletproof vests.

Lab men swamping Exley, holding him back. Noonan on me, splashing me.

Waving photos—matching dead men—dead panicked.

"Oh God, oh no. We identified these—"

I steered him clear of Exley. Noonan kicked at the water—shotgun shells jumped.

"We identified these men. Mickey Cohen divested his Southside coin machines to them. They're part of a midwestern syndicate.... Mickey said they're the ones who killed those men of his who just disappeared a while ago. Mickey's got no stomach for the rackets anymore.... He sold them his coin business to get out of it."

Bullshit—actor Mickey—Glenda critiqued his "style."

Noonan: "We turned Mickey as a witness. We granted him immunity and promised him a Federal Service Medal. He thinks it will help him secure a district gambling franchise, which is absurd, since that bill will never pass the State Legislature."

Mr. U.S. Attorney—plaid garters.

"Klein, do *you* know anything about this?"

"Major Witness" Mickey—confirmed. A flash: Bob Gallaudet supported district gambling.

Exley watching us.

"Klein—"

"No, I don't."

"This may hurt us. Mickey was going to testify against those men."

"Us"/"we"—Glenda juked Fed royal.

"I want an extra day before I enter custody."

"Under no circumstances. Don't ask me again, and don't even consider begging additional favors. This is your last day to resolve your curiosity vis-à-vis the Kafesjians, and as of tomorrow those curiosities will become a matter of Federal testimony."

Mr. U.S. Attorney—used rubbers stuck to his ankles.

"Who do you think killed these guys?"

"I would say East Coast mafiosi. I would say the word got out that Mickey divested his coin machines, and some East Coast men are attempting to crash the racket."

Clueless dumbfuck.

"Trust ME, lad"—Dudley Smith in my head.

Shouts up top:

"Mr. Noonan! Mr. Noonan, he's on the radio!"

Noonan splashed up the hill; Exley hooked a finger my way.

Duck him—up to the bluff fighting shivers. Fed cars, Feds: Shipstad, Noonan, Milner et fucking al.

Mickey Cohen on KMPC:

"...This is a public announcement undertaken in true sincerity, so I will say it now: I am severing my rackets connections. It is a mitzvah and a good deed of atonement, and I am coming forth to aid the Federal rackets probe currently doing business in Nigger—I mean Southside Los Angeles. I do this with great personal tsuris, which is the same as agony to you many Angeleno viewers and listeners who do not understand Yiddish. I am doing this severing because vicious midwestern hoodlums killed four of my men some months ago, and they are now threatening to kill my ex-wife, and let me now state that those rumors of her leaving me for some shvartze calypso singer are false. I am doing this severing because it is the moral thing to do as taught in the Bible, that wonderful perennial bestseller with many wonderful lessons for gentiles and Jews alike. I sold my Nig—I mean Southside vending-machine business to the midwestern hoodlums to save lives. I am now prepared to aid my dear friend U.S. Attorney Welles Noonan and his courageous ..."

Mickey rambling.

Shipstad grinning.

Noonan trembling—wet feet, rage.

"... and the Federal rackets probe is undertaken out of principles espoused in the Bible, one of those goyishe chapters that serve as the basis of inspirational movies like *Samson and Delilah* or maybe the scintillating *The Ten Commandments*."

Noonan:"Mickey's testimony is a bit anticlimactic now. I would like to blame these deaths on the Kafesjians, but vending machines have never been their raison d'être. Eight A.M. tomorrow, Brother Klein. Bring Kafesjian information, and don't even think of asking for an extension."

"Trust ME, lad"—Dudley Smith sweet as Jesus.

43

4:09: J.C. and Madge at home.

4:16: Lucille walking—Lincoln Heights—bars, newsstands.

4:23:Tommy walking—Lincoln Heights. Unit 3-B67:"I think he's checking out shooting galleries. He's hit four places the past two hours, and they look like hype pads to me."

4:36: Lucille walking.

4:41:Tommy walking.

3-B67: "I called the Highland Park Squad about those places Tommy hit. They said hype pads affirmative. Him and Lucille haven't run into each other yet, which goddamn amazes me."

4:53–4:59, all units: No Richie Herrick sightings.

5:02: Base to all J.C./Madge units: proceed to Lincoln Heights and saturate for Richie Herrick.

5:09: Lucille at Kwan's Chow Mein Pagoda. 3-B71: "She walked straight to the kitchen, and I *know* this place. Uncle Ace Kwan sells white horse, so I'll bet Lucy didn't stop in for chop suey."

5:16: Lucille exiting the restaurant. 3-B71: "She looks nervous, and she's carrying a brown paper bag."

Weird—hype Lucille?—unlikely.

Junkie Richie—ditto.

Tommy cruising dope pads—????

5:21: Tommy pissing in the street in full view of children. 3-B67: "Jesus, what a whanger! This clown has gotta hold the white man's world record!"

A clerk nudged me; I pulled off my headset. "What is it?"

"High brass to see you. The parking lot, ASAP."

Exley.

Go—past the squadroom—civilian radio blaring: Gangland Slayings! Mickey Cohen Reforms! Outside—Dudley.

Lounging on a prowl car.

Breuning and Carlisle by the fence—out of earshot. Breuning wearing a herringbone coat—MOVIE TIME patterns.

"Hello, lad."

Don't flinch, don't move too sudden, don't tremble.

"I got your notes, lad."

I stepped closer. Smell him: bay rum cologne.

"I hope you availed yourself of a splendid mink stole for that lovely sister of yours. Is she still consorting with Jack Woods?"

"I've got Chick Vecchio stashed. He snitched you on the movie, the furs, you running Mickey and those slot guys you clipped in Watts."

"I would say you're dissembling. I would say Exley hearsay is your sole source of information. You're assuming I told Chick things that indeed I didn't, and frankly I doubt that he would speak indiscreetly, even under the most severe duress."

"Try to find him."

"Is he dead or just temporarily indisposed?"

"He's alive, and he'll talk to stay that way."

Breuning and Carlisle watching us bug-eyed.

"They can't hear us, lad."

Don't blink. Don't tremble—

"Lad, your notes stated that you wished to act independent of Edmund Exley. I found that encouraging, and your mention of money even more so."

"Breuning put that sword in my hand. I'll trade you Vecchio for him, the movie and fifty thousand."

"Mike was hardly the director of your cinema debut."

"Let's just say he pays."

"Lad, you surprise me. I had thought your homicidal tendencies to be strictly profit-motivated."

"I'm afraid you'll just have to accept this new aspect of my personality."

Dudley roared. "Lad, your sense of humor is beyond salutary, and I agree to your offer."

"Tonight then. A public place."

"Yes, my thoughts exactly. Shall we make it eight o'clock, the Hollywood Ranch Market parking lot?"

"Agreed."

"I'll have Mike bring the fifty. He'll think it's a payoff run, and he'll be told to accompany you to fetch Vecchio. Take him with you, and when things are settled, call me at AXminster 6-4031 to tell me where Chick can be found. And, lad? Mike will be wearing a vest—you should know that and aim accordingly."

"I'm surprised—you and Breuning go back."

"Yes, lad, but you and I go forward. And on that topic, how do you assess the extent of Edmund Exley's information?"

Seal it—touch him. That cologne—don't gag.

"Lad ..."

I draped an arm around his shoulders. "He knows everything that I do and whatever else Johnny Duhamel told him. There's nothing on paper, and his Duhamel evidence is hearsay impossible to corroborate. He ran me against you on the Kafesjian burglary, and my only regret is that he's too big to kill."

"Are you saying our transgressions might go unpunished as a result of his lack of evidence?"

"I'm saying you'll skate—*if* you curtail your plans with Mickey."

"And yourself, lad? Dare I proffer the word 'loyalty'?"

"It's the Feds, Exley or you. You're the only one with cash money."

Embracing me—Dudley Liam Smith. "You've made a wise choice, lad. We'll discuss Exley later, and I won't insult your intelligence with the word 'trust.'"

44

6:16: J.C. and Madge at home.

  6:21: Tommy prowling dope pads—Lincoln Heights.

  6:27: Lucille prowling bars—Lincoln Heights.

  6:34, all units: no Richie Herrick sightings.

6:41: Tommy eating dinner: Kwan's Chow Mein Pagoda.

3–B67, walkie-talkie: "I'm no lip reader, but I can tell Uncle Ace is telling Tommy how Lucille copped some white horse from him. Tommy's goddamn fuming. Oops, he's walking. 3–B67 to base, over and out."

6:50: Tommy cruising Lincoln Heights—random zigzags.

6:54: Lucille walking—Lincoln Park—chatting up bums.

6:55, 6:56, 6:57, 6:58—Mike Breuning pictured dead a hundred ways.

NO—

45

"...so I'LL cross Dudley. I won't hand over Vecchio—and Dudley thinks I'm going to kill Breuning. *We* nail Breuning for the Duhamel killing, and *I'll* eyewitness Tommy K. popping Steve Wenzel, which gives us a wedge on the Kafesjians. Breuning will fucking shit his pants when I ARREST him, then we'll—"

"Klein, will you calm down—"

"Calm down shit, I'm a lawyer, you listen to me."

"Klein—"

"No, you listen. Breuning snitches Dudley, then Gallaudet convenes a special County grand jury to hear evidence. We upstage the Feds on Narco and the Kafesjians tangential to Dudley, and I testify on the Duhamel killing and all conspiracies extant with the Kafesjians, Dan Wilhite, Narco, Smith, Mickey Cohen, my mob hits, all of it. I'm a cop, I'm an attorney, I'll be the goat, I'll testify when the trials start, the Feds'll be fucked, you'll look so good Welles Noonan'll wither up and die and Gas Chamber Bob'll ride the trials straight to the governorship and—"

"Klein—"

"Exley, PLEASE, let me do this. Dudley knows I'm a killer, and he thinks he's operating *me* on Breuning. Now, if I bring Breuning in, he'll punk out—without Dudley he's got no guts. Exley, PLEASE."

Tick tick tick tick tick—seconds/a minute—

"Do it."

Phone-booth sweats—drenched—I cracked the door for a breeze.

"And no backup men at the Ranch Market—Breuning might spot them."

"Agreed. Do it."

Pay phone to pay phone—bug-fear precautions. Long distance—twenty dimes—Newton Station to Mel's Drive Inn, Fresno.

Glenda talked a blue streak:

Touch told Mickey she drove to T.J. for a scrape. Dig her new stand-in—Rock Rockwell, full drag. Dig Fed witness Mickey on TV— blatant Vampire plugs.

Reckless Glenda—tell me everything.

She was carhopping now: roller skates, cowgirl outfits. A Fed fugitive— fuck it—she spilled a malt on the Fresno DA—and he loved it. Good tips, getting gooood on skates—really gooood tray dips. Stylish Glenda, strong Glenda—tell me ANYTHING.

Her blue streak dwindled; her tough-girl shtick tapped out hoarse. Scared Glenda—chain-smoking to tamp down her nerves.

I told her:

You scared me.

You cut me loose from this woman I had no business loving.

46

HOLLYWOOD RANCH Market—Fountain and Vine.

Open-air entrance, parking lot. Cars, shoppers, box boys pushing carts.

8:02 P.M.—standing curbside. Sweaty, chafing—my bulletproof vest fit tight.

Breuning walking toward me—across-the-lot diagonal.

Packing a suitcase.

Fatter than fat—*his* vest bunched up at the hips.

Parking-lot lights: humdrum shoppers lit up. No backup types dawdling.

I cut over. Breuning clenched up—fat neck toady fuck.

"Show me the money."

"Dud said you should hand up Vecchio first."

"Just show me."

He opened the bag—just a crack. Cash stacks—fifty grand easy. "Satisfied?"

A box boy circled by, hands in his apron. A toupee, familiar—
Breuning eyeballed him—Say what?

Black-and-white-glossy familiar—slot surveillance pix—

Breuning fumbled his piece up—

His suitcase hit the ground.

I snagged my .45 on my vest.

The box boy shot through his apron two-handed—Breuning caught two clean head shots.

Screams.

A breeze—money flying.

I got my piece free; the box boy swung my way—two hands out.

Point blank: three shots slammed my vest and pitched me backward. Muzzle smoke in his eyes—I shot through it.

Point blank—no way to miss—a bloody toupee sheared clean, Jesus fuck—

Screams.

Shoppers grabbing money.

Breuning and the box boy tangled up dead.

Another "box boy"—braced against a car hood, aiming at me.

People running/milling/huddling/eating pavement.

I threw myself prone. Shots—rifle loud.

Roof snipers.

That box boy blending in—human shields bobbing every which way.

Snipers—Exley backup.

Firing at the box boy—missing wide.

Bullhorn amplified: "Cease fire! Hostage!"

I stood up. "Hostage": box boy dragging an old lady backward.

Elbows flailing, clawing at him—resisting mean.

Blade flash—he slit her throat down to the windpipe.

Bullhorn roar: "Get him!"

Rifle shots strafed the old lady—box boy hit the sidewalk hauling dead weight.

Run—

Straight across diagonal—his blind side.

"DON'T SHOOT, HE'S OURS!"—somebody/somewhere.

On him, his shield up—this mouth-gaping, neck-severed thing.
I shot through her face and ripped them separate; I matched his face as one more Fed-photo dead man.

47

"THE CRIME wave that has local authorities baffled continues. A scant hour ago four people were shot and killed at the picturesque Hollywood Ranch Market, two of them identified as Midwest-based criminals posing as market employees. An LAPD officer was also gunned down, as was an innocent woman taken hostage by one of the criminals. Thousands of dollars dropped from a suitcase were scattered in the ensuing pandemonium, and when calculating in the gangland slayings in Watts earlier today that also left four dead, the City of the Angels begins to seem like the City of the Devils."

My motel room, TV news. Call it for *real*:

Exley backup, Smith targets: Breuning and me. A Dudley charade: rogue cops slain, bag cash found. Movie time pending then: my rep even more trashable postmortem.

"... LAPD Chief of Detectives Edmund J. Exley spoke to reporters at the scene."

Recap—my Newton check-in call:

"Tommy and Lucille are still cruising Lincoln Heights, and they *still* haven't seen each other. And ... uh ... sir? Your pal Officer Riegle called in ... and ... uh ... sir, he said to tell you he heard that Chief Exley issued an APB order on you 'cause you left that shooting scene without telling anybody."

Exley on camera: "At this time we are withholding the identities of the victims for legal reasons. I will neither confirm nor refute a rival television station's speculation on the identity of the officer who was killed, and at this time I can only state that he was killed in the line of duty, while attempting to entrap a criminal with marked LAPD money."

Flashback: that slot man eating that old lady's brains.

I called El Segundo. Ring, ring—"Yeah, who's this?"—Pete Bondurant.

"It's me."

"Hey, were you at the Ranch Market? Some news guy said Mike Breuning got it and one cop bugged out."

"Does Chick know about Breuning?"

"Yeah, and it's spooking him no end. Hey, *were you there*?"

"I'll be over in an hour and tell you about it. Is Turentine there?"

"He's here."

"Have him set up a tape recorder and ask him if he's got the equipment to monitor police calls. Tell him I want to tap into band 7 at Newton Street Station."

"Suppose he doesn't have the stuff?"

"Then tell him to get it."

48

THE STASH pad—*my* low-rent unit.

Pete, Freddy T.; Chick Vecchio cuffed to a heat pipe. A tape rig and shortwave set—with band 7 pickup.

Mobile units calling in to Newton. Broadcasting base to cars: Exley himself.

Incoming:

Tommy and Lucille cruising separate—Lincoln Heights, Chinatown, moving south.

The point man at the K. house:

"I heard it out the boom mike. It sounded to me like J.C. just slapped the piss out of Madge. To top it off, there's Fed cars driving by on the QT every hour or so."

Unit 3-B71: "Lucille's walking around Chinatown asking questions. She's looking sorta distraught, and that last joint she went into—the Kowloon—it looked like a dope front to me."

Pete—wolfing spareribs.

Fred—nursing a highball.

Chick—purple bruises, half his scalp scorched.

Fred poured himself a refill. "The Kafesjians and you. I don't get it."

"It's a long story."

"Sure, and I wouldn't mind listening to something other than these goddamn radio calls."

Pete said, "Don't tell him shit, it'll end up in *Hush-Hush*."

"I'm just thinking twelve mobile tail cars and Ed Exley monitoring calls himself means it's some kind of big deal, which maybe Dave should elaborate on. Like for instance, who are these Tommy and Lucille chumps looking for?"

Light bulb:

Richie "Peeper" Herrick—Chino inmate/bugging know-how. Fred Turentine, drunk driver—Chino teaching gigs.

"Freddy, when were you teaching that electronics class up at Chino?"

"Early '57 up till I got bored and hung up my probation maybe six months ago. Why? What's that got to do with—"

"Did a kid named Richie Herrick take the class?"

Light bulb—dim—juicer Freddy. "Riiiight, Richie Herrick. He escaped, and some psycho chopped his family."

"So, did he take your class?"

"Sure did. I remember him, because he was a shy kid and he played these jazz records while the class worked on their projects."

"And?"

"And that's it. There was this other white guy that he palled with, and he took the class with Herrick. He stuck close to him, but I don't think it was a queer thing."

"Do you remember his name?"

"Nooo, I can't place it."

"Description?"

"Shit, I don't know. Just your average white-trash inmate with a duck's-ass haircut. I don't even remember what he was in for."

Something?/nothing?—tough call. Chino files missing—

"Dave, what's this all ab—"

Pete: "Leave Klein alone, you're getting paid for this."

Band 7:

Tommy mobile—Chinatown.

Lucille mobile—Chinatown near Chavez Ravine.

I doused the volume and grabbed a chair. Chick edged his chair back.

In his face: "DUDLEY SMITH."

"Davey, please"—raspy dry.

"He's behind all the trouble in Niggertown, and he just sent Mike Breuning out to die. Spill on him, and I'll cut you loose and give you some money."

"Suppose I don't?"

"Then I'll kill you."

"Davey ..."

Pete signaled me: feed him liquor.

"Davey ... Davey ... please."

I handed him Freddy's glass.

"You guys don't know Dudley. You don't know the kind of stuff he'd do to me."

Bonded sour mash—three fingers. "Drink it, you'll feel better."

"Davey ..."

Drink.

Chick guzzled it down. Grab the glass, refill it, watch him swill.

Instant booze panache: "So what kind of money are you talking about? I've got expensive tastes, you know."

"Twenty grand"—pure bullshit.

"That plays lowball to me."

Pete said, "Talk to Klein or *I'll* fucking kill you."

"Okay, okay, okay"—refill gestures.

I filled the glass. "Chick, *give*."

"Okay okay okay"—sipping slow.

I propped the tape rig up by his chair and hit Record.

"*Dudley*, Chick. The furs, Duhamel, the Kafesjians, the whole takeover story."

"I guess I know most of it. Feature Dudley likes to talk, 'cause he figures everybody's too scared of him to tattle."

"*Get to it.*"

Booze-brave: "I say Domenico 'Chick' Vecchio knows when to talk and when to shut up. I say fuck 'em all except six, and save them for the pallbearers."

Pete said, "Will you *please* fucking give?"

"Okay okay, feature Dudley, he was the boss at Robbery Division. Exley, he had this hard-on for him, because he made Dud for lots of stuff over the years—"

"Like the Nite Owl job?"

"Yeah, like the Nite Owl. Anyway, Dudley always took the most interesting robbery cases for himself, 'cause that's just the way he is. So Exley shot the Hurwitz Fur case to Robbery, and Dud grabbed it, and he got some leads that he later on figured out were planted by Exley, and those fucking leads led him to his very own so-called protégé, Johnny Duhamel."

Freddy and Pete noshing spareribs—rapt.

"Keep going."

"Okay, now Dudley, he'd recruited Schoolboy Johnny for the Mobster Squad. You know how he drools for tough boys, and when Johnny was in the LAPD Academy he showed some meanness that Dud really liked. So he stayed mean on the Mobster Squad, and now Dudley sees that he's a fucking badass heist guy, which, being Dudley, pleases him no fucking end. So, Dud called Johnny on the heist, and Johnny admitted it, but he refused to snitch his partners, which also impressed Dud. So, feature, Dudley gave Johnny a skate on the fur job and confided some of his own crime gigs to him, which meant that so far Exley's trap was working."

Tape hiss. Chick, snitching nice and loose now: "So feature that Dudley bagged Johnny's furs and stored them at a storage locker joint. A couple got out, 'cause Dudley told Johnny to get next to Lucille Kafesjian when Exley assigned you and that punk Stemmons to that burglary job. Johnny, he got a little lightweight boner for Lucille and gave her one."

"Dudley told Johnny to become intimate with Lucille?"

"Yeah, sort of like a safeguard if you started leaning on the Kafesjians too hard."

"Then what?"

"Then that goddamn Stemmons blundered in. He was Johnny's teacher at the Academy, and Johnny made him for a closet fruit back then. So Junior, he saw this striptease that Lucille did with this mink Johnny gave her, I think he was working Bido Lito's on the burglary job. Johnny was there, and him and Junior talked, which resparked this fucking faggot torch Stemmons had for Johnny."

"So at first Junior came on like a pal."

"Right, and feature that all that Mobster Squad strongarm stuff wasn't really Johnny's style, it was just this role Exley had him playing. Anyway, Johnny, he was stretched pretty thin and feeling pretty bad about it, and he told Stemmons about how brutal the work was, and Junior started figuring out that some-body was running him undercover. Johnny never flat-out snitched Dudley to him, but he told him about these 'auditions' Dudley was doing without naming no names."

"What 'auditions'?"

"Dud was bringing these out-of-town guys in. He needed them to work the Southside coin, and he *wanted* the Feds to see them. Dud said later that Johnny figured out the guys were going to get clipped when Mickey went public with his Fed witness bit."

Haverford Wash—four dead. "But Johnny didn't confide *that* to Junior."

"Right."

"And the coin men were just pigeons set up to get clipped later?"

"Right."

"What about the 'auditions' themselves?"

"Dudley told the out-of-town guys they had to earn the right to work for him. He said that meant enduring pain. He paid them money to let Johnny hurt them while he watched and talked this philosophical shit to them. Dick Carlisle said Dud broke their spirits and made them goddamn slaves."

Pete said, "Holy shit."

Freddy said, "I don't believe this."

"Who clipped the slot guys?"

"Carlisle and Breuning. You want to hear a nice Dudley touch? He had them soak their buckshot in rat poison, then repack the shells."

"Get back to Johnny."

Chick stretched—his cuff chain rattled. "Dud had Johnny monitoring the slot guys—you know, watching them service the machines. He was doing that one night or something, and Dick Carlisle saw Junior come up to him and start talking this nutso rebop. Carlisle got this feeling that Johnny might be a plant, so he told Dudley, and Dud had Carlisle and Breuning keep this loose tail on him. Now, I don't know who killed Stemmons—probably Tommy or J.C. Kafesjian—but around the time Carlisle got hinky, J.C. told Dudley that Stemmons was acting crazy, shaking down pushers, shaking down him and Tommy and telling them he could monkey-wrench *your* burglary investigation. So, this nutty faggot Junior, he's talking up his own Niggertown takeover stuff, and in my opinion Dud would have clipped him himself, if he hadn't of OD'd or got snuffed by the Kafesjians."

"Then what?"

"Then Dud got a tip that Johnny called *you* to set up a meet— *and I didn't tell him.* So now he *knew* Johnny was a fucking traitor or decoy or something."

The meet: Chick knew. Bob Gallaudet knew.

"Then what?"

"So Johnny told you to meet him at that pad in Lynwood. Dud used to own it years ago, so I guess Johnny just wanted to meet you someplace close to the bungalow where ... you know."

Change-up: "Phillip Herrick."

"Who's that?"

"He was murdered in Hancock Park last week. Dudley co-owned 4980 Spindrift with him."

"So?"

Easy call: no Herrick knowledge.

"So Johnny told me to meet him there, and your little movie set was close by. What do you figure he wanted to show me?"

"Maybe the smut-movie setup."

"Maybe, but you told me Sid Frizell wasn't connected to any of Dudley's plans."

"He's not, but Dud *loves* stag stuff, and when he got tight with Mickey, Mickey told him about this batshit horror movie he was bankrolling and how Sid Frizell wanted to shoot smut films, but he couldn't find a spot. Dud told Mickey to tell Frizell to use one of the rooms in that court, so down the line Sid did, but feature I know for a fact that he doesn't even know Dudley."

SOMETHING—some CONNECTION—knifing me.

"Does Dudley own those bungalows?"

"Feature yes he does, through dummy partners. Feature he owns about twenty other abandoned dives, just bought dirt fucking cheap off the Lynwood City Council."

"And?"

Leering at me ugly drunk: "And feature Dudley Liam Smith does not get his rocks off on girls, boys or Airedale terriers. Feature he likes to watch. Feature the mirror walls in that flop where you rousted me and feature he's got a shitload of other flops just like it. Feature he's got this idea to film these on-the-sly smut movies where the fuckers and fuckees don't even know they're being watched. Feature he's got bids in with the Bureau of Land and Way to house the spics evicted from Chavez Ravine in those pads and that dump on Spindrift. Feature Dudley's going to film all these taco benders fucking and sell the movies to geeks like himself who dig all that voyeuristic horseshit."

Rumors:

Sid Frizell shooting LYNWOOD stag films.

LYNWOOD spic relocation maybe looming.

That SOMETHING—click:

Atomic Vampire.

Movie gore: incest/eye poking/blinding.

Kafesjian 459—dogs blinded.

Herrick 187—three victims eye socket blasted.

Sid Frizell—ex-con type.

Non-Dudley-connected—Chick convinced me.

Non-click: SOMETHING missing.

I said, "Dudley and Mickey."

"You mean what's the skinny on Dudley's rackets thing?"

Shortwave sputter: "Chinatown, Chinatown, Chavez Ravine."

"Right."

"Well, feature the word 'containment.' That's Dud's big word, and what he wants to do is build up this empire on the Southside, maybe stretching into Lynwood, where he's got all this property. He'll only sell dope to niggers, and he'll run whores and smut on the QT, and he'll run all the coin hardware that Mickey so-called divested. His big deal is supposed to be district gambling, with Mickey as his front man. Feature he killed all of Mickey's guys except me and Touch, and feature he fucking manipulated Mickey into cozying up to the Feds. The Mick's a hero now, he's a lovable shmuck, and Dud thinks he can buy up more Lynwood property and start so-called 'containing' the economy down there, then set Mickey up to front his district gambling franchise, all nice and legal."

"District gambling won't pass the State Legislature."

"Well, feature Dudley thinks otherwise. Feature he's got a political guy with very large juice in his pocket to make sure it does get passed."

Gas Chamber Bob Gallaudet: district gambling supporter.

Tipped off to the Duhamel meet.

Goosebumps: my dry-ice burns started tickling.

"So Dud found out you were meeting Johnny. Breuning and Carlisle slugged you and doped you up, and Dud tortured Johnny before you sliced him. They got him to admit that Exley was running him as a decoy and that he had these fake bank accounts and this operations cash stashed in a safe at his house. Johnny said he kept trying to pull out of the deal because he knew the slot guys would probably get clipped and lots of other shit would hit the fan, but Exley kept sending him back to find out more."

Radio hum: Tommy mobile, Lucille mobile.

Pete and Freddy dumbstruck—holy shit/mother dog!

"Why did Dudley make that movie? Why didn't he just kill Johnny and me?"

"He said he wanted to compromise you and use you. He said he was going to offer you this job as liaison and bagman to the LAPD. He said he could use you to take Ed Exley down. He said you were probably a pretty good lawyer, and he said you could teach him things about property maintenance."

Chick oozing brainwaves: kowtow to Dudley or die.

Pete oozing brainwaves: kill the wop and grab his money.

Freddy oozing brainwaves: *Hush-Hush* would love THIS.

Atomic Vampire—INCEST/GORE.

"Chick, what do you know about Sid Frizell?"

"Feature I know close to nothing."

"Has he done time?"

"County time for child-support skips. He's no hard-case penitentiary guy, if that's what you're thinking."

To Freddy: "*Sid Frizell*. He's a tall, skinny guy about thirty-five. He's got sort of an Okie drawl."

"No bells. Am I supposed to know him?'

"I thought he might have taken your class at Chino."

"No, I don't think so. I mean, I'm a bug man, so I listen to how people talk. Sorry, but there were no Okie drawls in my class."

SOMETHING MISSING.

I grabbed the phone and got an operator—Chino on the line. A warden's aide answered. Go, tell him:

Compile a roster for me—cons at Chino Richie Herrick concurrent. Messenger it down?—No, I'll call you back for a verbal.

2:00 A.M.—custody looming. Radio sputter, *pop/pop*—Pete cracking his knuckles. Chick loopy drunk, scorched hair—my damage.

Smells—stale food, smoke. A view out the window: overflowing trashcans. *My* building—nine G's a year net profit.

Think: snitches, deal-outs.

Last-ditch tries.

Welles Noonan—a Gallaudet rival.

Think trades: Glenda for Bob G. and Dudley.

The bedroom phone—shaky hands on the dial. MA 4-0218—Noonan.

"U.S. Attorney's Office, Special Agent Shipstad."

"It's Klein."

"Klein, this call didn't happen."—low, furtive.

"What?"

"Noonan got a film can special-delivery. It's you chopping up some guy, and *I* know it's a setup, but *he* doesn't care. A note said copies go to the press if you testify for us, and Noonan said your immunity agreement is cancelled. He's issued a Federal arrest warrant on you, and *this call did not happen.*"

CLICK—

Chairs/shelves/tables—I threw them and kicked them and dumped them. I punched myself arm-dead on the curtains; exhaustion had me swaying light-headed.

Radio squawk:

"Madge left the house alone. The point car's on her."

"Lucille's entering Chavez Ravine. She's driving erratic, she's sideswiping trees—"

49

CRISSCROSS HEADLIGHTS, dirt roads—Chavez Ravine.

Dark—no streetlights—cop lights only. Roof lights, headlights, flashlights—tail men mobile and on foot.

Bumper crunched upside a tree: Lucille's Ford, abandoned.

APBs out on me—

I ditched my car and sprinted up the access road. Zigzag flashlights down below: a shack-to-shack search.

"Lad."

Dark, just his voice. I aimed at it, half pull triggered.

"Lad, hear me out before you act precipitously."

"You sent that movie to Noonan."

"No, Bob Gallaudet did. I told him you had Chick Vecchio hidden, and Bob assumed that Chick would behave in a cowardly fashion and inform on us. Lad, Bob handed you up to Noonan. He threatened to make public a second copy of the film if you testified as a Federal witness, assuming that your testimony would damn both himself and this aging Irishman who bears quite a grudging fondness for you. Noonan was furious, of course, and Bob quite wisely retreated to a more judicious footing: he said that the film threat stood, but he would not enter the attorney general's race if Noonan promised no open-court mention of him. Noonan, bright lad that he is, agreed."

"Gallaudet ratted *you* to Noonan?"

"No, Allah be praised, he just evinced panic and spoke nebulously of complex criminal conspiracies. I'm sure Noonan considers me just an aging policeman with a gift for language and a stern reputation."

Shouts down below. Stray headlights blipped Dudley smiling benign.

"Who gave Bob that movie copy?"

"Mike Breuning. He was afraid our enterprises were in jeopardy, so he gave Robert a copy to cut a deal for himself. Alas, Mike confessed what he had done before I sent him out to meet you, which is why I set him up so harshly."

"Gallaudet?"

"Ensconced with Allah, lad. Neatly dismembered and unreachable. Kill Vecchio, if you haven't already, and there's just Exley sans hard evidence."

"Chick told me Duhamel snitched Exley."

"Yes, that's true."

"He said Exley kept money in a safe?"

"Yes, Chick is correct."

"Inside his house?"

"Yes, lad, that would be logical."

"Big money?"

"Yes, that's correct. Lad, get to the point, you're tantalizing me."

"I can tap that safe. I'll kill Vecchio and steal Exley's money. We'll split it."

"You're very generous, and I'm surprised that you haven't expressed rancor over my machinations at the Ranch Market."

"I want you to like me. If I run, I don't want you coming after the people I leave here."

"You're perceptive to assume my survival."

"The money?"

"I'll accept half graciously."

Commotion down the hill: cops kicking in shack doors.

"Chick told you the thrust of my plans, did he, lad?"

"Yes."

"Did you infer that I enjoy watching?"

"Yes."

"I view it as a dispensation for the grand work of containment I'll be doing. I view it as a means to touch compelling filth without succumbing to it."

FLASH: Lucille nude.

"You're a watcher, lad. You've touched your own dark capacities, and now you enjoy the surcease of simple watching."

FLASH: whore-pad windows.

"I empathize with your curiosities, lad."

FLASH—peeper tapes—pictures synced to sounds.

"It pleases me that the Kafesjians and Herricks seem to have piqued those curiosities. Lad, I could tell you many grand stories about those two families."

FLASH—bright open windows—TELL ME THINGS.

"Lad, do you feel the basis of an understanding starting to form? Are you beginning to see the two of us as kindred souls, brothers in curious—"

Shouts, flashlights converging—

I ran down—tripping and stumbling. Shacks pressed up tight together—lights fixed in one doorway.

Tail men huddled outside—push through, look:

Lucille and Richie Herrick—DOA.

Tourniquet tied/veins pumped/mouths frozen gasping.

Entwined on a mink coat bed.

H bindles, spikes and Drano on a fox pelt.

50

8:01 A.M.—FEDERAL fugitive.

Fugitive pad, fugitive car—a '51 Chevy bought off a junker lot. Fugitive calls:

Glenda safe—style vs. fear—style winning.

Sid Riegle, panicked—Exley men rousted my men.

Bureau talk: Lucille and Richie died from heroin-Drano cocktails. Sid: "Ray Pinker said she hotshot him, then killed herself. Doc Newbarr said no way was it murder, then suicide—everything was too nice and neat."

More talk:

Tommy and J.C.—Fed-rousted and released at 4:00 A.M. Madge K. gone for parts unknown—the point man lost her.

A call to Pete—find me that woman, she can TELL ME things.

Fugitive wheels: the Cahuenga Pass south. Rearview panic checks—everything looked strange and wrong.

Radio news: Hot L.A. Crime Wave! Mickey Cohen Federal Witness! DA Gallaudet Misses Breakfast Talk—Assembled Scribes Baffled!

Last night—Dudley's farewell:

"I'll require verification on Chick. His right hand should suffice—it bears quite a recognizable tattoo."

Brain teaser:

Vampire gore/the Kafesjian-Herrick case—who?/why?

South: Hollywood, Hancock Park. Left turn—432 South McCadden.

Virgin—no cars curb or driveway.

I walked up and knocked. Nobody watching—knife the keyhole, work the lock.

In.

Close the door, bolt it—lights on, go.

I checked the living room walls: no pictures, no fake panels.

I checked the den—framed photos—Dudley Smith, Bureau toastmaster. Pull them, look behind—

No safe.

Upstairs—three bedrooms—more walls, more pictures:

Dudley Smith as Santa Claus—a polio ward, '53.

Dudley Smith, guest speaker—Christian Anti-Communist Crusade.

Dudley Smith at a crime scene: ogling a dead jigaboo.

Three bedrooms—twenty Dudley Smith pictures—Exley hate fuel.

No safe.

Back downstairs—check the kitchen—nothing.

Check the carpets—every one tacked flat. Upstairs—hallway throw rugs—pull them—

A hinged panel under a red Persian.

Inset with a tumbler dial and handle.

Trembly—34L–16R–31L—two run-throughs, snap/thunk— yank the handle.

Drawstring bank bags. Five. Nothing else.

Hundreds, fifties, twenties. Old bills.

I shut the lid, spun the dial and fixed the rugs. Downstairs, the kitchen—

Cutlery right there. I grabbed a cleaver—heebie-jeebies—Chick.

51

"DAVEY ... PLEASE."

Psychic: begging me two seconds in the door. A tattoo on his right hand: "Sally 4-Ever."

"Davey, please."

683 grand and that cleaver. Pete out chasing Madge, Fred asleep in the bedroom.

Chick, cuffed down—panic spritzing:

We go back, we had laughs, I'm sorry I got fresh with Glenda, but how can you blame me? We had laughs, we made money, Pete wants to kill me, he's a fucking neon sign. ...

"Davey, please."

Pillow bullet mufflers. Curtains for a makeshift shroud.

"Davey ... Jesus Christ ... Davey."

Tired—no stones for it—yet.

Dead man talking:

I'll disappear ... you can trust me.... Glenda's great ... Sid Frizell says she's star stuff. Frizell ... what a chump ... no ideas ... that camera guy Wylie Bullock's got twice the smarts, and he couldn't direct traffic on Mars. You and Glenda ... I wish you the best.... Davey, I know what you got planned, I can see it in your eyes....

Tired.

No stones for it—yet.

The phone rang—I cradled it up. "Yeah?"

"It's Pete."

"And?"

"And I found Madge Kafesjian."

"Where?"

"The Skyliner Motel, Lankershim and Croft in Van Nuys. She's in room 104, and the desk man says she's on a hankie binge."

"You're staking her?"

"I'm on your payroll, and I'm watching that room till you say otherwise."

"Just stay there. I'll be out soon, so—"

"Look, I talked to Mr. Hughes. He said the Sheriff's found a witness who saw Glenda by the Hollywood Hills fuck pad like the approximate night that Miciak bought it. They think she's hinky, and they're looking for her as a suspect. It looks like she blew town, but—"

"Just stick at the motel."

"Your payroll, boss. How's Chick—"

I hung up and dialed Chino direct.

"Deputy Warden Clavell's office."

"Is he in? It's Lieutenant Klein, LAPD."

"Oh, *yes,* sir. Mr. Clavell left me a list of names to read you."

"Read off the released inmates first."

"Current addresses too?"

"The names first, I want to see if something grabs me."

"Yes, sir"—slow, precise:

"Altair, Craig V. ... Allegretto, Vincent W. ... Anderson, Samuel NMI. ... Bassett, William A. ... Beltrem, Ronald D. ... Bochner, Kurt NMI. ... Bonestell, Chester W. ... Bordenson, Walter S. ... Bosnitch, Vance B. ... Bullock, Wylie D.—"

Tilt/click/snap—SOMETHING missing/SOMETHING there:

Wylie Bullock.

Vampire cameraman.

Idea man—pressing gore on Sid Frizell.

"Burdsall, John C. ... Cantrell, Martin NMI—"

"Go back to Wylie Bullock. Give me his parole date and his last known address."

"Um ... he was paroled on November 9, 1957, and his parole disposition address is the Larkview Trailer Court, Arroyo and Brand in Glendale."

Freddy in the hallway—yawning.

"Sir, do you want the rest of these names?"

I put the phone down. "Was there a guy named Wylie Bullock in your class at Chino?"

"Yeah ... riiight ... he was that guy following Richie Herrick around."

Adrenaline—*zoooom.*

Chick: "Hail Mary full of grace the Lord is with thee."

Stay of execution: dumb guinea luck.

52

R & I / D M V:

Bullock, Wylie Davis—DOB 7/16/25. Brown/brown, 5′10″, 165. Popped 3/56—pornography beefs—3 to 5, Chino.

Occupation: photographer-cameraman. Vehicle: '54 Packard Clipper, white & salmon, Cal. GHX 617.

Freeways out to Glendale—my rat's-ass car belched smoke. Wylie/Madge/Dudley—TELL ME THINGS.

Arroyo off-ramp, south to Brand—the Larkview Trailer Court.

Parking slots: and no two-tone Packard tucked in. A map out front: "W. Bullock"—three rows over, six trailers down.

Rock gardens, jacked-up trailers, white trash wives out sunning. My SOMETHING MISSING:

Frizell-Bullock confabs—Wylie assertive: Incest! Poke the vampire's eyes out!

Three over, six down—a chromium Airstream. My .45 out surreptitious—knock.

No answer—no surprise—no Packard. I tried the door—locked—too many squarejohns around for a break-in.

The set—go.

Freeways back—my clunker wheezed. Griffith Park, the set—no Bullock vehicle in sight.

Mickey by the spaceship—wearing a Jew beanie.

"The Feds and LAPD were here chasing your tush. The Malibu Sheriff's were looking for my erstwhile star Glenda Bledsoe, who I understand you are playing Bury the Brisket with. You break my heart, you handsome snatch bandit."

No "crew"—just Mickey. "Where is everybody?"

"Shmuckface, *Attack of the Atomic Vampire* is in show-biz parlance a 'wrap.' Glenda may look a bit muscular in her concluding moments, given that Rock Rockwell portrayed her in long shots, but that aside I consider my movie a cinema landmark."

"Where's Wylie Bullock?"

"I should know? I should care?"

"Sid Frizell?"

"Paid off and on the night boat to Nowheresville for all I care."

Beanie, flag lapel pin—hero Mickey. "You look happy."

"I have a movie in the can, and I have made friends of the Federal persuasion. And do not judge me as a snitch fuck, because a certain U.S. attorney told me you have those tendencies yourself."

Dudley's lovable shmuck. "I'll miss you, Mickey."

"Run, David. The tsuris you have caused seeks retribution. Run to Galapagos and watch turtles fuck in the sun."

The Cahuenga Pass—back over coughing fumes. Lankershim and Croft—the Skyliner Motel.

Horseshoe-shaped—cut-rate pool-view cabanas. Pete staked out curbside—snoozing with the seat back.

I parked behind him. Tell-me money in the trunk—I stuffed my pockets.

Skirt the pool over—room 104. I knocked—Madge opened up quick.

Haggard—heavy makeup made it worse. "You're that policeman. Our house was broken into ... you came over...."

"Hankie binge"—wet eyes, tear tracks.

"I'm sorry about your daughter."

"It was a merciful death for both of them. Did you come to arrest me?"

"No. Why should I—"

"If you don't know, I won't tell you."

"I just wanted to talk to you."

"So you filled your pockets with money."

C-notes spilling out. "I figured it couldn't hurt."

"Did Dan Wilhite send you?"

"He's dead. He killed himself."

"Poor Dan"—one short sigh.

"Mrs. Kafesjian ..."

"Come in. I'll answer your questions if you promise not to slander the children."

"Whose children?"

"Ours. Whoever's. Just exactly what did you ... ?"

I sat her down. "Your family and the Herricks."

"What do you want to know?"

"Tell me everything."

1932—Scranton, Pennsylvania.

J.C. Kafesjian and Phillip Herrick work at Balustrol Chemicals. J.C. is a laborer, Phillip a solvent analyst. J.C. is crude, Phil is cultured—they are friends—nobody knows why.

1932: the friends move to Los Angeles together. They court women and marry them: J.C. and Madge Clarkson, Phil and Joan Renfrew.

Five years pass: the men toil at boring chemical jobs. Five children are born: Tommy and Lucille Kafesjian; Richard, Laura and Christine Herrick.

J.C. and Phil are bored, angry and poor. Their chemistry knowledge inspires a scheme: brew homemade liquor.

They do it—and thrive.

The Depression continues; poor people *need* cut-rate spirits. J.C. and Phil sell it cheap—work-camp workers their chief clientele. They accrue profits and hoard their shares.

J.C. and Phil—friends and partners.

J.C. and Phil—cuckolding each other.

Neither man knows:

Two affairs predate their weddings. Lovers: J.C. and Joan, Phillip and Madge. The adultery continues—five children are born— their patrimony inconclusive.

J.C. opens a dry-cleaning shop; Phil invests in a chemical plant. They continue their home liquor business.

J.C. pushes Phil to cut costs: lower-quality alcohol solvents mean greater profits.

Phil agrees.

They sell a batch to some CCC workers—a dozen men go permanently blind.

June 22, 1937:

A blind man carries a pump shotgun into a tavern.

He fires the weapon at random—three people are killed.

He sticks the barrel in his mouth and blows his own head off.

Sergeant Dudley Smith investigates. He learns the source of the shotgun man's blinding; he tracks the liquor to Phil and J.C. He makes them an offer: his silence for a percentage of their holdings.

They agree.

Dudley recognizes J.C.'s mean streak—and cultivates it. He believes that Negroes could be kept dope-sedated; he urges J.C. to sell them drugs. He urges Chief Davis to let J.C. "serve" them: as a sanctioned dope peddler and informant to the fledgling Narcotics Squad.

Dudley hides his role—few know that he is J.C.'s recruiter. Chief Davis retires in '39; Chief Horrall takes over. He assumes credit for the Kafesjian recruitment—and taps Officer Dan Wilhite to serve as J.C.'s contact.

Years pass; Dudley continues to extract his business percentage. J.C.'s dry-cleaning shops flourish; he builds up a Southside dope kingdom. Phil Herrick earns legitimate wealth: PH Solvents is hugely successful.

The adultery goes on: J.C. and Joan, Phillip and Madge.

Both women have assured their lovers that birth control precautions have been taken. Both have lied—they loathe their husbands, but will not leave them. Madge knows J.C. would kill her; Joan needs Phillip's money and newly developed social connections.

Five children.

Inconclusive patrimony.

No dangerous resemblances emerging.

Joan *wanted* J.C.'s baby: he treated her atypically tender. Madge wanted Phillip's: she despised her vicious husband. Guesswork fathers softens things—both women believe it.

Post–World War II:

Major Dudley Smith, OSS, sells black-market penicillin to escaped Nazis. Phil Herrick, naval officer, serves in the Pacific; J.C. Kafesjian runs his dry-cleaning shops and dope racket. Dudley returns to L.A. late in '45; Herrick, fourteen months at sea, comes home unexpectedly.

He finds Joan nine months pregnant. He beats her—and learns that J.C. has been her lover throughout their marriage. She had planned to put the child up for adoption; Phil's surprise return prevented her. She hid her pregnancy with long indoor sojourns; Laura, Christine and Richie—away at boarding school—do not know what happened.

Joan runs to J.C.

Madge hears them talking and confronts them.

J.C. brutally beats both women.

Madge admits her long affair with Phil Herrick.

Cuckold husbands, cuckold wives. Enraged men—two women beaten and raped. Terrible chaos. Abe Voldrich calls in Dudley Smith.

He has the five children blood-tested—the results are ambiguous. Joan Herrick delivers her baby; Dudley strangles it three days old.

Laura and Christine never learn the facts of their lineage.

Tommy, Lucille and Richie do—several years later.

The boys grow up friends—maybe brothers—whose father is whose? They burglarize houses and play jazz; Richie falls in love with Lucille. He comforts her with Champ Dineen—he didn't know his bloodlines either.

Tommy emulates his "name" father J.C.—selling dope while still in high school. He's always lusted after Lucille—now there's a chance she *isn't* his sister. He rapes her—and makes her his personal whore.

Richie finds out—and swears to kill Tommy.

Tommy relishes the vow—he considers Richie a weakling.

Richie drives to Bakersfield and buys a gun. He gets caught selling dope; Dudley Smith intercedes, but cannot convince the DA to drop charges. Richie Herrick, sentenced to Chino: 1955.

Tommy swears he'll kill him when he's released—he knows his personal whore Lucille deeply loves him. Richie swears to kill Tommy—he has debased the maybe sister he loves chastely.

Lucille runs wild—prostitute, window dancer, taunter of men. Phil Herrick seeks her out—his maybe daughter. Their first coupling is a street assignation. Lucille agrees just to taunt him.

His gentleness surprised her—this maybe daddy more like Richie than Tommy. They continued to meet: always talking, always playing games. Phil Herrick and Lucille: maybe daddy-daughter lovers, maybe just a whore and a john.

And Madge and Joan became friends. They hid from the madness together—fugitive time spent simply talking. Confidantes: years of partial shelter.

Richie escaped from Chino—fit only to voyeur-watch Lucille. Joan and Richie exchanged letters; Richie said a friend soon to be paroled would avenge him painlessly. This man seemed to have a hold on Richie: Richie never even said his name.

Joan killed herself nine months ago; the insanity peaked all at once. Lucille did not know Richie was watching her; Tommy read Junior Stemmons' reports and assumed that Richie was the voyeur. He vowed to kill him—afraid that Exley-linked men would find him first. Lucille found him—their ticket to shelter in a needle.

Tissues on the floor—Madge fretted a whole box to shreds.

"Would you call that 'everything,' Lieutenant?"

"I don't know."

"Then you're a very curious man."

"Do you know the name Wylie Bullock?"

"No."

"Who killed Junior Stemmons?"

"I did. He was browbeating Abe Voldrich at one of our cleaning shops. I was afraid he'd find out the truth about Richie and Lucille, and I wanted to protect them. I attacked him rather foolishly, and Abe subdued him. We knew Dudley would protect us if we killed him, and Abe knew he was an addict."

"So Abe shot him up and dumped him at Bido Lito's."

"Yes."

"And you told Tommy, and he burned the place down. He hung out there, and he was afraid we'd find evidence on him."

"Yes. And I don't feel bad about that young man Stemmons. I think he was in as much pain as Richie and Lucille were."

I emptied my pockets—big wads of cash.

"You're naive, Lieutenant. Money won't make J.C. and Tommy go away."

53

"EVERYTHING" = "MORE" = "BULLOCK."

Back to the trailer dump—a two-tone Packard in the lot. I jammed up behind it, spewing smoke.

Voices, feet kicking gravel.

Thick fumes—I got out coughing. Exley and two IA men—packing shotguns.

"Everything" means "more" means—

Fumes, gravel dust. Shotgun flankers, Exley sweating up a custom-made suit.

"Bullock killed the Herricks and trashed the Kafesjian place. How did you know—"

"I called Chino to get my own roster. That woman in the warden's office told me you went crazy over Bullock."

"Let's take him. And get those guys out of here—I *know* he's got stuff on Dudley."

"You men wait here. Fenner, give the lieutenant your shotgun."

Fenner tossed it—I pumped a shell home.

Exley said, "All right then."

Now:

We ran three rows over, six trailers down—civilians watched us slack-jawed. That Airstream—radio hum, the door open—

I stepped in aiming; Exley squeezed in behind me. Two feet away: Wylie Bullock in a lawn chair.

This bland geek:

Smiling.

Raising his hands cop-wise slow.

Spreading ten fingers wide—no harm meant.

I jammed the shotgun barrel under his chin.

Exley cuffed his hands behind his back.

Radio hum: Starfire 88's at Yeakel Olds.

"Mr. Bullock, you're under arrest for the murders of Phillip, Laura and Christine Herrick. I'm the LAPD chief of detectives, and I'd like to question you here first."

Monster's den: *Playboy* pinups, mattress. Bullock: Dodger T-shirt, calm brown eyes.

I goosed him: "I know about you and Richie Herrick. I know you told him you'd get him revenge on the Kafesjians, and I'll bet you know the name Dudley Smith."

"I want a cell by myself and pancakes for breakfast. If you say that's okay, I'll talk to you here."

I said, "Make like you're telling us a story."

"Why? Cops like to ask questions."

"This is different."

"Pancakes and *sausage*?"

"Sure, every day."

Chairs circled up, the door shut. No Q&A/no notebooks—Maniac speaks:

June, 1937—Wylie Bullock, almost twelve—"I was just a kid, you dig me?"

An only child, nice parents—but poor. "Our flop was as small as this trailer, and we ate at this gin mill every night, because you got free seconds on the cold cuts."

June 22:

A crazy blind man enters the tavern. Random shotgun blasts: his parents get vaporized.

"I got hospitalized, 'cause I was in some kind of shock."

Foster homes then—"some nice, some not so hot"—revenge dreams minus a bad guy—the shotgun man killed himself. Trade schools—a knack for cameras—"Old Wylie's a born shutterbug." Camera jobs, curiosity: 6/22/37—why?

Amateur detective Wylie—he kept pestering the cops. The brush-off: "They kept saying the case file was lost." Newspaper study: Sergeant Dudley Smith, investigating officer. Calls to now-Lieutenant Smith—none returned.

He haunted that tavern. Rumors haunted the place itself: bad bootleg trashed the shotgun man's eyes. He chased rumors: who sold bootleg whiskey back in '37?

Bad leads—years' worth—"like impossible to verify, you know?" Two rumors persistent: "dry-cleaning-cut hooch," "this Armenian guy—J.C."

He made a logical jump: the E–Z Kleen shops/J.C. Kafesjian. "I didn't have any proof—it just felt right. I kept a scrapbook on the blind man case, and I had this picture of Sergeant Smith from '37."

"It was becoming like an obsession."

Supporting that obsession: camera work. Illegal: "I took snatch pictures and sold them to sailors and Marines up from Diego."

Obsession focus: the Kafesjians.

"I sort of circled around them. I found out J.C. and Tommy pushed dope and had these police connections. Lucille was a floozy, and Tommy was vicious. It was sort of like they were my pretend family. Tommy had this buddy Richie, and the two of them played this jazz music really lousy. I used to follow them, and I watched them get into some kind of big falling-out over Lucille. Richie got popped selling dope up in Bakersfield. He got sentenced to Chino, and I was in an E-Z Kleen shop one day, and I heard Tommy tell Abe Voldrich that when he got out Richie was dead meat."

Early '56—two bombshells hit him simultaneous:

One—he's outside a Southside E-Z Kleen. Huddled up: J.C. Kafesjian and Dudley Smith—nineteen years older than that news pic.

Two—he gets popped selling snatch photos.

"I figured Dudley Smith and the Kafesjians were dirty together. I couldn't *prove* anything, but I thought maybe Smith gave J.C. a skate on that poison liquor he sold. After a while I just believed it."

He started hatching revenge plots—this Eyeball Man inside him fed him plans. He pleaded guilty to selling pornography—his lawyer said beg for mercy.

"At the County Jail this guy told me about the X-ray lab at Chino—what a good job it was. I figured I could get a job there if I got sentenced to State time, 'cause I knew so much about photography. See, I had a real plan now, and I wanted to do a Chino hitch so I could get next to Richie."

The judge hit him with three-to-five State. They bought his X-ray experience snow job: Wylie Davis Bullock, go to Chino.

"So I went to Chino and got next to Richie. He was a lonely kid, so I befriended him, and he told me this AMAZING goddamn story."

Amazing:

The Kafesjians, the Herricks—who fathered whose children? Phil Herrick and J.C.—bootleg dealers back in the '30s. The blind man killings—Richie said yes, maybe—it might be Dudley Smith's wedge. Incest: maybe/quasi/brother/father perv stuff.

"I guarantee you you have never heard *nothing* to compare to the stuff Richie told me."

Richie, sissy/voyeur:

"He told me he was in love with Lucille, but he wouldn't touch her because she might be his half-sister. He said he loved spying on her."

Richie, compulsive talker:

"He put things together for me. I figured out enough about Dudley Smith to know that he met up with Herrick and Kafesjian some time right after the killings. I figured Smith got cozy with them and took bribes not to snitch that they brewed that liquor. I knew now. I knew these two crazy families killed my family."

Richie, talking vengeance on Tommy:

"I knew he didn't have the balls for it. I said just wait—I'll get you your revenge if you promise not to bother the Kafesjians."

Richie promised.

"Then his mother wrote him and went through this sob-sister suicide routine. Richie walked Chino—fucking minimum security, he just *walked*."

Richie stayed loose.

He got paroled two months later.

"I tried to find Richie. I staked out the Kafesjian and Herrick houses, but I never saw him."

"That Lucille, though—wow. I used to watch her do the shimmy-shimmy naked."

Months ticked by. "One day right before she killed herself I saw Old Lady Herrick leave a letter in her box for the postman. I snuck up and grabbed it, and it was addressed to Champ Dineen, this jazz clown that Richie worshipped. There was a PO box address, so I figured Moms and Richie were working a mail-drop thing. I sent Richie a note at his box:'Dig Lucille do the shimmy shimmy in her window. Now you be patient and I'll get you your revenge.'"

The note worked—months ticked by—he peeped Richie peeping Lucille. AMAZING: peeper Richie, amateur bug man— that electronics class did him solid. He walked the straight and narrow himself—movie jobs, parole confabs—nobody knew the Eyeball Man kept his dick hard—

"I started getting these wild ideas.

"The Eyeball Man said I should follow the Kafesjian guys and Dudley Smith around just for kicks.

"I was dogging Smith one day. He had lunch with Mickey Cohen, and I grabbed a booth next to them. Cohen said he was fronting this horror movie shooting in Griffith Park, and this Sid Frizell guy who was directing it shot stag films on the side. Smith said he loved naughty movies, and that Cohen should tell Frizell he had a nice sound stage he could use. Cohen said Frizell was skanky enough to take him up on it."

He hit the *Vampire* set—"Man, was this flick from hunger." He offered his camera services cut-rate; Cohen hired him; he gamed dumbfuck Sid Frizell—strapped for ideas. "I fed him these incestuous-type bits and all this blinding stuff, 'cause I figured one day I'd show Richie the finished-up movie. I told Frizell I had smut experience, and he pestered this Cohen guy Chick Vecchio into talking to Smith. Smith gave the okay, so Frizell got to shoot his stuff at this dive down in Lynwood.

"So I got cozy close to things, but I still didn't have *the* fucking plan worked out. Then the Eyeball Man came through."

He said tweak the Kafesjians with a voodoo B&E. Put the onus on Richie—keep him scared—keep him hiding.

"So I did it. I guess it's like symbolism, 'cause the Eyeball Man told me exactly how to do things. I tried to blind the dogs with this dry-cleaning chemical, but that didn't work, so I pulled their eyes out. I broke liquor bottles to goose them on their bootleg gig, and I broke Tommy's records up 'cause the Eyeball Man said that would symbolize how Richie hated Tommy. Richie always hated Lucille whoring, so I cut her pedal pushers up and shot a load on them."

Wicked fun.

"The Eyeball Man said make Richie squirm, so I scoped him out at these motels, getting all weepy over Lucille, and I cut up his bed with this silverware I stole to spook him. There was lots of heat around the Kafesjians because of the B&E and the Fed thing, so the Eyeball Man told me to kill Phil Herrick early. The daughters came home unexpected, and the Eyeball Man said snuff them too. I figured Richie was a fucking escapee, so the cops would think he did it and snuff him on the spot."

Then?

"The Eyeball Man said kill Tommy and J.C. slow. He said rip Dudley Smith's eyes out and eat them."

Now?

"Pancakes and sausage, daddy-o. A nice safe cell for me and the Eyeball Man."

Licking his chops.

Flapjack batter on a shelf.

EVERYTHING.

Chest pings/headache/dry mouth—Dudley Smith meets the Eyeball Man.

Exley pointing at the door.

I followed him outside. Spooky sunlight—trailer-park geeks watching us.

"What's your assessment?"

Juke him/fuck him—LIE:

"I want to take Bullock in to Welles Noonan. I'm dodging custody, and he can help me smooth things out. He's a key witness on Dudley and the Kafesjians, and if we cooperate with the Feds we can cut their probe off at the knees, especially with you giving them Narco."

"He's insane. He's not a valid witness."

"Yeah, but all he is to *us* is a psycho. He's not even fit to stand trial."

"Gallaudet will get indictments. He'll prosecute him himself."

"Bob's dead. He was in with Dudley on some district gambling scheme. Dudley killed him."

Weak knees—I steadied him—Edmund Jennings Exley popping cold sweat.

"I've got Chick Vecchio stashed. He begged me for Federal custody, and Madge Kafesjian filled in some of Bullock's story and told me how Dudley hooked J.C. up with the Department. Exley, it's all *contained*. Vecchio, Bullock, Madge—*they* rat Dudley and only Narco gets hurt. It's *your* basic plan, and all you have to do is cut me some slack before I take Bullock in."

"Specifically?"

"Call Noonan. Tell him you're handing your Narco dossiers over. Tell him to retract his warrant on me until I bring our witnesses in."

Do it—grab the bait—I'll run with *your* money—

"Exley ..."

"Yes. Move Bullock some place safe after dark, then call me."

"You'll call Noonan?"

"Yes, I'll call him now."

"I'm surprised you're trusting me."

"I've betrayed your trust before, and I'm running out of strategies. Just keep the shotgun and try not to kill him."

*

I settled in.

Bullock talked pancakes and the Eyeball Man.

EVERYTHING spun me crazy—backward, forward—back to Meg, up to Glenda.

Escape plans. Buyouts. Schemes—nothing jelled.

Dusk came on—I kept the lights off. Music somewhere—EVERYTHING spun me fresh.

Nothing jelled.

Bullock fell asleep cuffed to his chair.

Nothing jelled.

Bullock muttered gibberish in his sleep.

Shakes, shudders—something like a whimper ripping through me.

I braced myself against the wall—

Killings, beatings, bribes, payoffs, kickbacks, shakedowns. Rent coercion, muscle jobs, strikebreaker work. Lies, intimidation, vows trashed, oaths broken, duties scorned. Thievery, duplicity, greed, lies, killings, beatings, bribes, payoffs, Meg—

That whimper got loose—Bullock cocked his head to hear it better. Sobs then—choking back tears, sobs racking through me so hard the trailer shook.

EVERYTHING.

Spinning, falling, confessing.

I don't know how long it lasted.

I came out of it thinking:

NOT ENOUGH.

I made the call.

54

THE SEARS & Roebuck parking lot: wide open, empty. A block off: *my* Eastside building.

Early. Arclights on asphalt—he'd see us.

683 grand stuffed in four attaché cases.

My .45 taped to my ankle.

Wylie Bullock in the front seat—cuffed with his hands in his lap.

Exley's cleaver beside him.

Headlights coming.

I laid the money bags on the hood. No suitcoat, no holster—frisk me.

Headlights up, brakes, lights off. Dudley Smith stepped out, smiling.

Coatless, empty holster—frisk *me*.

"Lad, you're early."

"I'm cautious."

"Given your circumstances, I would be, too. And that man I glimpse in your car?"

"He's a pilot. He's flying me south."

He looked in—the passenger window half down. Bullock stayed calm, my suitcoat draped over his cuffs.

"What grand briefcases! Have you tallied the amount?"

"Almost seven hundred thousand."

"Is this my share?"

"It's yours."

"In exchange for?"

"The safety of the people I leave here."

"You used the plural, lad. Have you loved ones beyond your sister?"

"Not really."

"Aah, grand. And Vecchio?"

"He's dead."

"Have you brought the verification I requested?"

"It's in with the money."

"Well, then given that Edmund Exley is unapproachable and somewhat compromised, I would say this is goodbye."

I stepped closer—blocking his view—cover for Bullock. "I've still got those curiosities."

"Such as?"

Louder—*barely*—don't rile him yet:

"Madge Kafesjian told me about the blind man killings. I wondered how you cut your deal with J.C. and Phil Herrick."

Dudley roared—huge stage laughs.

I reached back and freed the door.

"I was brazen then, lad. I understood the metaphors of greed and blind rage, and the absurdity of a sightless man wielding a ten-gauge did not escape me."

"I wish I could have seen you cut the deal."

"It was fairly prosaic, lad. I simply told Mr. Kafesjian and Mr. Herrick that their thriftily brewed liquor caused four deaths and assorted untold suffering. I informed them that in exchange for a percentage of their business holdings that suffering would remain strictly a point of contention between them and God."

"Just like that?"

Bullock mumbling.

"I also offered visual persuasion. A coroner's photograph of a young couple rendered headless expressed a certain shock value."

Mumbling louder—I coughed to cover the noise.

"Lad, is your pilot confrere talking to himself?"

Getting hinky—watch his hands.

"Lad, will you open the briefcase that contains my verification?"

I stepped closer.

Dudley flexed his hands one single beat too quick.

I pivoted to slam a knee shot; he sidestepped me.

Shivs dropping out his shirt cuffs—grab a briefcase, swing it—

Two stilettos palmed deft.

Stabbing at me—ripping leather—two blades stuck.

I dropped the briefcase.

Dudley stood wide open.

Bullock piled out, hands on the cleaver.

"EYEBALL MAN! EYEBALL MAN!"

I slammed a knee shot.

Dudley went down.

Bullock went at him cleaver-first.

Wild swings—the handcuffs fucked his grip up—the blade ripped Dudley's mouth ear to ear. Roundhouse coup de grace—the cleaver hit asphalt.

"EYEBALL MAN!"—Bullock on Dudley:

Biting.

Clawing.

Ripping at his eyes.

Look:

One gushing red socket.

"NO!"—*my* scream/my gun out/aiming at them tangled up together.

I fired twice—two misses—ricochets off the pavement.

Two more shots braced against the hood—Bullock's face exploded.

Bone spray in my eyes.

Firing blind—ricochet zings, a jammed slide.

Dudley on Bullock—prying at his hands.

Dudley weaving, screaming exultant—his eye cupped back to his face.

I grabbed the money and ran. Echoes boomed behind me: "EYEBALL MAN! EYEBALL MAN!"

A week—backtrack it:

I ran that one block to my building. Old bookie stash holes in the basement—I tucked the money away.

Calls from the janitor's phone:

Glenda, long distance: come down, grab the cash, hide. Pete in El Segundo: cut Chick loose—Glenda's got twenty grand for you.

Pandemonium at Sears—prowl cars responding to shots. Bullock dead, Dudley rushed to Queen of Angels. My explanation: ask Chief Exley.

I was arrested—bagged on Exley's APB. I was allowed one phone call—I buzzed Noonan.

A custody battle ensued—LAPD vs. Feds—Noonan victorious.

Material witness protection—no charges filed on me yet.

A Statler Hilton suite, friendly guards: Jim Henstell and Will Shipstad.

A TV in my room—dig the news:

Mickey Cohen—solid-citizen Fed helper.

Gas Chamber Bob G.—nine days missing, where's the DA?

Frequent visits from Welles Noonan.

My tack: total silence.

His tack: threats, lawyer logic.

Exley called him the day we glommed Bullock; dig the deal he offered:

A joint LAPD/Fed effort—Narco swings and Dave Klein brings in four witnesses. Cooperation assured; Exley quoted verbatim: "Let's bury the hatchet and work together. One of the witnesses will be a high-ranking LAPD man, more like a hostile interrogatee. He has intimate knowledge on the Kafesjian family, and I would call him federally indictable on at least a half-dozen charges. I think he will more than make up for the loss of Dan Wilhite, who regrettably committed suicide last week. Mr. Noonan, this officer is very dirty. All I ask is that he be portrayed as a contained, totally autonomous entity within the LAPD, just as you've agreed to portray the Narcotics Division."

Coming up: an LAPD/Fed press conference.

My "witnesses":

Wylie Bullock—dead.

Chick V.—probably hiding.

Madge—grieving somewhere.

Dudley Smith—on the critical list.

"Critical" PR—Exley press manipulation—no word on the Bullock thing issued. No City charges filed on me; Bullock cremated.

No "witnesses"—and Noonan was furious.

Threats:

"I'll prosecute your sister on tax charges."

"I'll give the DA's Office my bugging tapes—Glenda Bledsoe god-damn admitted she killed Dwight Gilette."

"I have you on tape telling a man named Jack to 'kill him.' If you refuse to talk to me, I'll have Federal agents comb a list of your known associates for that man."

My tack: total silence.

My ace: sole-witness status—I knew EVERYTHING.

Days dragged. No more L.A. "crime wave" news—Noonan and Exley put the fix in. Tommy and J.C.—under Fed surveillance, untouchable.

A visit from Ed Exley.

"I think you stole money from me. Cooperate with Noonan and I'll let you keep it. You'll need money—and I won't miss it."

"Without your testimony Dudley can't be touched."

"If this agreement with the Feds falls through, the Department will look disgracefully ineffectual."

My tack: total silence.

A visit from Pete B. Whispers: Glenda's got the money—and she paid me my cut. Word's out you're a Fed snitch—Sam Giancana just issued a contract.

A visit from two Sheriff's dicks: "We like Glenda Bledsoe for the Miciak job."

My tack—confession—I killed him solo. I dropped knife wound details—they bought it—they said they'd file Murder One on me.

Noonan right there: "I will use the full power of the Federal Government to keep this man in my sole custody."

A phone call—Jack Woods checking in:

"Meg's okay. Sam G. put the word out—you're dead."

Stale news.

Long days—playing cards with Will Shipstad killed time. Instincts: he hates Fed work, he hates Noonan. I threw out a bribe flyer: erase the Glenda tape for thirty grand.

He agreed.

Noonan confirmed it the next day: "Incompetent technicians!"—a huge tantrum.

Long nights—bad dreams—killings, beatings, bribes, shakedowns, lies.

Bad sleep, no sleep.

Afraid to sleep, nightmares on call: Johnny begging, one-eyed Dudley.

Glenda—hard to conjure—easy to hear:

"You want to confess."

Two nights, six legal pads—Dave "the Enforcer" Klein confesses—

Killings, beatings, bribes, payoffs, shakedowns—my police career up to Wylie Bullock. Lies, intimidation, vows trashed, oaths broken. Exley and Smith—my accessories—tell the world.

Ninety-four pages—Shipstad leaked it to Pete B.

Conduit Pete, copies to: Hush-Hush, the L.A. Times, the State AG.

Time ticking, Noonan crazed: the press conference is pending, I need you to talk.

Threats, offers, threats—

I talked:

"Give me two days of freedom under Federal guard. When I return to custody we'll prepare my testimony."

Noonan—reluctant, half crazy: "Yes."

L.A. *Herald-Express*, 12/6/58:

LAPD-FEDERAL PRESS CONFERENCE CANCELLED

THE ANNOUNCEMENT last week surprised everybody: the Los Angeles Police Department and the U.S. Attorney's Office, Southern California District, were holding a joint press conference. Adversaries during U.S. Attorney Welles Noonan's still ongoing Southside rackets probe, the two law enforcement agencies had recently come across as anything but friendly. Federal officers charged the LAPD with allowing vice to rage in South-Central Los Angeles, while LAPD Chief of Detectives Edmund Exley accused Mr. Noonan of mounting a politically motivated smear campaign against his Department. That dissension ended last week when both men issued identical statements to reporters. Now, tomorrow's press conference has been precipitously called off, leaving many members of the Southern California law enforcement community baffled.

Last week's press release was carefully worded; it hinted only that a cooperative Federal-LAPD effort had been mounted, one perhaps aimed at securing indictments against members of the LAPD's Narcotics Division. Much more was to have been revealed tomorrow, and an anonymous source within the U.S. Attorney's Office stated that he thought the joint effort was scotched due to breach of official promises. Queried as to exactly what "promises," the source stated: "A Los Angeles police officer skipped Federal custody. He was to have testified against members of the LAPD Narcotics Squad and a criminal family they have long been allied with, and he was also to have induced a total of four other potential witnesses into testifying. He did not deliver those witnesses, and when allowed two days out of custody to take care of personal matters, he attacked his guard and escaped. Frankly, without him the Federal Government has only Mickey Cohen, a former gangster, to offer testimony."

CRIME WAVE SPECULATION

THIS SITUATION occurs in the middle of a statistically staggering Los Angeles crime wave, much of it Southside based. The City homicide rate for the past month soared 1600%, and although neither the LAPD nor U.S. Attorney's Office will confirm it, speculation has linked last week's gangland killings in Watts to the

Hollywood Ranch Market shootout that also left four dead. Add on the mysterious disappearance of Los Angeles District Attorney Robert Gallaudet and the November 19 Herrick family slayings, still unsolved, and you have what Governor Goodwin J. Knight has called "a powder keg situation. I have every confidence in the ability of Chief Parker and Deputy Chief Exley to maintain order, but you still have to wonder what could cause such a drastic upsweep in crime."

Asked to comment on the press conference cancellation, Chief Exley refused. Queried on the recent crime wave, he stated: "It was simply coincidental and non-tangential, and now it's over."

L.A. *Mirror*, 12/8/58:

LAPD PRE-EMPTS FEDS IN DARING MOVE

THE LOS Angeles Police Department's famously stern Chief of Detectives Edmund J. Exley called an impromptu press conference this morning. He was expected to digress on the recent Federal Southside crime investigation and offer comments on why the LAPD and local U.S. Attorney's Office have apparently abandoned their short-lived "cooperative venture" into probing both Southside malfeasance and the Los Angeles Police Department's own Narcotics Division.

He did neither. Instead, in a terse prepared statement, he blasted the Narcotics Division himself and said that he would personally deliver incriminating evidence to a specially convened County grand jury, then offer tax fraud information unilaterally to the U.S. Attorney's Office.

Describing "Narco" as a "police unit autonomously run amok," Exley stated that he was certain its "long-standing tradition of graft" did not extend to other LAPD divisions, but Internal Affairs Division, under his supervision, was going to "comb this police department like a bloodhound sniffing out graft to make sure."

Stunned reporters asked questions; Exley refused to answer them. He did state that the commanding officer of Narcotics Division, Captain Daniel Wilhite, 44, recently committed suicide, and that Internal Affairs detectives were currently interviewing various "Narco" officers with an eye toward securing voluntary grand jury testimony.

Asked just how "dirty" "Narco" was, Chief Exley said, "Very. I am personally stating that it has been in collusion with a vicious dope-pushing family for over twenty years. It is my desire to reform the Narcotics Division from the ground up and take that family down. I will be passing pertinent Federal venue information on to U.S. Attorney Welles Noonan, but he should know that I am taking the primary responsibility for cleaning my own house."

Hush-Hush Magazine, 12/11/58:

FREEDOM OF SPEECH GAGGED!!!!! J'ACCUSE! J'ACCUSE!

JOURNALISTIC NITROGLYCERINE—that's the only way to describe it. 94 pages that arrived at *Hush-Hush* ten days ago, atom bomb accusations that were also sent to a Los Angeles newspaper and the State Attorney General's Office.

They chose to ignore it; we chose to print it. The confidential source that transmitted this literary A-bomb verified its authenticity—and we believed him. 94 pages: scorching, scalding, burning hot revelations, the confessions of a crooked Los Angeles policeman on the run from the mob, the cops and his own violent past. You *would have seen it here* on December 18th—but something happened.

Kats and kittens, we're on dicey legal ground here. We can describe the "legal" machinations that have censored us; our lawyers tell us that the vague description of the material covered in the preceding paragraph does not violate the "legal" injunction filed against us by the Los Angeles Police Department.

And we'll go just a tad further in our description: those 94 pages would have brought the LAPD to its knees. Our (regrettably) anonymous author, unflinching in his portrayal of his own corruption, also charged celebrated Los Angeles policemen with felony malfeasance on a spectacular scale and claimed that LAPD officials covered up a complex web of circumstances surrounding the recent L.A. crime wave. Scalding, scorching hot revelations—verifiably true—and we can't print them.

That's as much as our attorneys will permit us to tell you about those 94 pages. Is your appetite whetted? Good, now let us stoke your rage.

An employee of ours, a man charged with gathering electronic information, has a drinking problem. He saw those 94 pages, recognized them as dynamite and called an LAPD acquaintance. Our employee, a probation absconder ducking drunk driving warrants, leaked those pages to his acquaintance. Word spread to the LAPD hierarchy; a restraining order was secured. Our employee was rewarded: his warrants were rendered null and void. Those scalding 94 pages were seized; we cannot print any portion of them under threat of "legal" injunction.

The newspaper? The State Attorney General's Office?

They discarded their 94 pages. They ridiculed them as hogwash. The monstrous facts were too ugly to believe.

The author? He's out there among the night blooming fiends in the City of the Fallen Angels.

The upshot? You decide. Decry this fascistic censorship. Write to us. Write to the LAPD. Express your rage. Send one up for a rogue cop whose mea culpa read too explosive to print.

BANNERS:

L.A. *Times*, 12/14/58:

GRAND JURY CONVENED; "NARCO" COPS TESTIFY

L.A. *Mirror*, 12/15/58:

HUSH-HUSH "CENSORSHIP" BLAST MEETS DEAF EARS

L.A. *Herald–Express*, 12/16/58:

LAPD DERIDES HUSH-HUSH INVECTIVE

L.A. *Times*, 12/19/58:

NARCOTICS OFFICERS INDICTED

L.A. *Mirror*, 12/21/58:

EXLEY: HUSH-HUSH ACCUSATIONS "NONSENSE"

L.A. *Mirror*, 12/22/58:

REPUTED DOPE KINGPINS FACE GRAND JURY

L.A. *Herald-Express*, 12/23/58:

GRAND JURY SHOCKER: NO
KAFESJIAN INDICTMENTS—ACTING
DA SAYS NARCO TESTIMONY COMPROMISED

L.A. *Examiner*, 12/26/58:

GALLAUDET STILL MISSING; SEARCH CONTINUES

L.A. *Mirror*, 12/27/58:

MAYOR POULSON: HUSH-HUSH
ACCUSATIONS LAUGHABLE

L.A. *Mirror*, 12/28/58:

FEDERAL RACKETS PROBE DISBANDS

L.A. *Herald-Express*, 1/3/59:

TOASTMASTER POLICEMAN VOTED SPECIAL PENSION

THE SCENE was sad, touching, antithetical to recent police headlines: Narcotics officers indicted on graft charges. That scene: a
grossly injured Los Angeles policeman fighting for his life in a
hospital bed.

Dudley L. Smith, Captain, LAPD. Dublin born, Los Angeles
raised, a World War II OSS spymaster. 53 years old, thirty years a

policeman. A wife, five daughters. Numerous commendations for bravery, LAPD toastmaster, lay chaplain. Dudley L. Smith: stabbed in an altercation with a robber five weeks ago—now fighting for his life.

He's winning that fight so far: he lost an eye, he's paralyzed, he's sustained brain damage, he'll probably never walk again. When he's lucid he charms nurses with his brogue and jokes that he'll do advertisements like the eye patch man who hucksters Hathaway Shirts. He's not lucid most of the time, and that's a heartbreaker.

The LAPD will not release details on the altercation that earned Dudley Smith his wounds; they know he would prefer to spare the family of the robber he killed the ignominy of public recognition. That's a heartbreaker, as is the fact that Dudley Smith will require intensive sanitarium care for the rest of his life.

His police pension and savings won't cover it. He's too proud to accept police charity contributions. He's a legendary policeman, much beloved, a cop who has killed eight men in the line of duty. Knowing these things, LAPD Chief of Detectives Edmund Exley asked the Los Angeles City Council to exercise a rarely used option and vote him a special pension: an amount to sustain his care in a comprehensively equipped sanitarium indefinitely.

The City Council agreed and voted in Dudley Smith's pension unanimously. Chief Exley told reporters: "It's important that Captain Smith remains contained and receives the care he deserves. He'll be safe and secure, and he'll be able to live out his days free of the taxing problems of police work."

Dudley L. Smith, hero. May those days stretch long and peacefully.

PART FIVE
HUSHABYE

55

TAKE-OUT CARTONS, newspaper stacks—Pete's hole-up a month in.

A tract house outside San Diego. Safe—his ex-wife was touring Europe for six weeks. Rent pirate Pete: two grand a week.

Newspapers—the story dispersed:

My confession quashed by legal injunction.

Dudley half-dead.

The Fed probe blitzed.

Narco destroyed—Exley triumphant.

Time to think.

Phone time—outside conduit Pete reporting in:

Warrants out on me—State and Fed—nine indictments total. "They've got you on Miciak, tax charges, two State and three Federal conspiracy statutes. There's national APBs out on you, plus Fed bulletins up the wazoo. You can keep the house until January 27th, but that's it."

Pete—January 13:

"Glenda's still in Fresno. The Feds have got her under surveillance, but I think I can sneak her down for a visit before you take off."

January 14:

"I called Jack Woods. He said Meg's okay, and I checked with a Fed guy I know. He said Noonan's not going to file tax charges on her—he's too busy cooking up some new probe gig to give a shit."

January 15.

January 16.

January 17.

Tired, sludgy—chink take-out five weeks straight.

January 18:

"Dave, I can't get you a passport. I've got no legit contacts, and I heard the mob fronts aren't selling them, 'cause they figure *you're* buying."

January 19—blind run fever.

Nightmares—EVERYTHING swirling.

January 20:

"Glenda thinks they lifted the surveillance on her. She's going to bring your money down in a couple of days."

January 21—Pete, fucking scared:

"Mr. Hughes found out I've been hiding you. He's pissed that Glenda skated on Miciak and … shit, you know, you and her. He wants some personal payback, and he said he won't turn you in if you cooperate. Dave, I'll try to go easy."

56

ON MY knees—woozy. Shock waves up my spine—one punch in.

The backyard—Howard Hughes watching.

I stood up groggy—loose teeth, split lips. Left-right/left-right/left-right—my nose somewhere down my throat. Propped up—eyebrow flaps shredded loose, shading my eyes.

Howard Hughes in a business suit and wing tips.

Kicked prone—"No, use your fists."

Jerked upright—left hook/left hook—spitting gums, no nose, hard to breathe. Left hook/left hook—bones cracking.

No legs, no face—signet ring rips jaw to hairline.

"A few more."

"He can't take any more."

"Don't contradict me."

No legs, no face. Eyes to the sun—burning red—please don't blind me. Left-right/left-right—"Leave him for the doctor."

Fading somewhere—don't take my eyes.

Spinning, falling.

Music.

Darkness/light/pain—arm jabs, crazy bliss. Light = sight—don't take my eyes.

Spinning, falling—EVERYTHING synced to bop. Champ Dineen riffs—Lucille and Richie waved down from heaven.

Sweating—cold swipes at my face. Somebody's face—an old man.

Needle jabs eating up pain.

Arm pops = craaaazy bliss.

EVERYTHING—spinning, falling.

Cheek rubs half blissed—thick beard stubble.

Time—light into dark, light into dark, light into dark.

A man wearing glasses—maybe a dream. Voices—dreamy, half real.

Music.

57

FOUR DAYS sedated.

The doctor, walking out: "I left you some morphine Syrettes. You're healing up nicely, but you'll need to get some bones set within a month or so. Oh, and a friend of yours left you a package."

Numb throbs chin to forehead. Fresh newspapers—check the dates—January 22 to 25.

Mirror check:

My nose—smashed flat.

My jaw—bent sideways.

No eyebrows—scar tissue instead.

A raised hairline—scalp cuts ripped me balding.

Two new ears.

One eye squinty, one eye normal.

Dark brown hair gone pure gray inside a week.

Call it:

A new face.

Healing—bruises fading, sutures out.

I checked the package:

One blank passport.

One .38 revolver, silencer fitted.

A note, unsigned:

Klein—

IA found you, and I've decided to let you go. You served me very well and you deserve the chance I'm giving you.

Keep the money you took. I'm not optimistic, but I hope the passport helps. I won't apologize for the way I used you, since I believe the Smith situation justified it. He's neutralized now, but if you consider the justice you meted out less than absolute, you have my permission to follow it up more thoroughly. Frankly, I'm through with him. He's cost me enough as it is.

Indirect order: kill him.
Not HIM—THEM.

58

"WE USED to be a great-looking pair."

"That part's all on you now"—loose teeth, painful.

"You're different, David."

"Sure, look at me."

"No, it's that we've been together for five minutes and you haven't asked me to tell you things."

Glenda: carhop suntan, close to gaunt. "I just want to look at you."

"I've looked better."

"No, you haven't."

She touched my face. "Was I worth it?"

"Whatever it cost, whatever it took."

"Just like that?"

"Yeah, just like that."

"You should have grabbed that movie contract way back when."

Money bags by the door—time closing in.

Glenda said, "Tell *me* things."

Back to then, up to always—I told her EVERYTHING.

I faltered sometimes—pure horror jolted me silent. That silence, implicit: *you*—tell *me*.

Light kisses said no.

I told her all of it. Glenda listened, short of spellbound—like she knew.

The story hung between us. Kissing her hurt—her hands said let me.

She undressed me.

She slid out of her clothes just past my reach.

I roused slow—just let me look. Persistent Glenda, soft hands—inside her half-crazy just from looking.

She moved above me—propped up off my bruises. Just watching her felt wrong—I pulled her down.

Her weight on me hurt—I kissed her hard to rip through the pain. She started peaking—my hurt ebbed—I came blending into her spasms.

I opened my eyes. Glenda framed my face with her hands—just looking.

Sleep—day into night. Up startled—a clock by the bed—1:14.

January 26.

A camera on the dresser—Pete's ex-wife's. I checked the film—six exposures remaining.

Glenda stirred.

I walked into the bathroom. Morphine Syrettes in a dish—I popped one and mixed it with water.

I got dressed.

I stuffed two hundred grand in Glenda's purse.

The bedroom—

Glenda yawning, hands out, thirsty—I gave her the glass.

She gulped the water down. Stretches, little tucks—back to sleep.

Look:

A half-smile brushing her pillow. One shoulder outside the covers, old scars going tan.

I snapped pictures:

Her face—eyes closed—dreams she'd never tell me. Lamp light, flashbulb light: blond hair on white linen.

I sealed the film.

I picked up the money bags—heavy, obscene.

I walked out the door bracing back sobs.

59

EASY:

I took a bus to L.A. and got a hotel room. I had a typewriter sent up—one blank passport rendered valid.

My new name: Edmund L. Smith.

Picture valid: photo-booth snapshots, glue.

My ticket out: Pan Am, L.A. to Rio.

My wounds were healing up.

My new face was holding: no handsome Dave Klein showing through.

Morphine pops kept me calm and crazy exultant. This crazy notion: you walked.

Not yet.

60

I BOUGHT a new clunker—two hundred dollars cash. I took a detour airport-bound: 1684 South Tremaine.

8:00 A.M.—quiet, peaceful.

Voices inside—bellicose male.

I walked back, tried the rear door—unlocked. Laundry room, kitchen door—yank it.

J.C. and Tommy at the table, guzzling beer.

Say what?

What the—

J.C. first—silencer THWAP—brains out his ears. Tommy, beer bottle raised—THWAP—glass in his eyes.

He screamed: "DADDY!"

EYEBALL MAN! EYEBALL MAN!—I shot them both faceless blind.

61

AIRPORT HEAT: Feds, Sheriff's men, mob lookouts. Right through them—no blinks—up to the counter.

Friendly service, a glance at my passport. I checked my money bags through—"Have a pleasant flight, Mr. Smith."

Gone—just like that.

The will to remember.

Fever dreams—that time burning.

Old now—a gringo exile rich off real estate. My confession complete—but still not enough.

Postscripts:

Will Shipstad—private practice from '59 up.

Reuben Ruiz—Bantam champ, '61–'62.

Chick Vecchio—shot and killed robbing a liquor store.

Touch V.—managing drag-queen acts in Vegas.

Fred Turentine—dead—cirrhosis. Lester Lake—dead—cancer.

The place lost/the time burning/close to them somehow.

Madge Kafesjian—alone—that house, those ghosts.

Welles Noonan—convicted of jury tampering—1974. Sentenced to three to five Fed—a Seconal OD suicide en route to Leavenworth.

Meg—old, a widow—my conduit there to here. Wealthy—our slum pads traded up for condos.

Spinning, falling—afraid I'll forget:

Mickey Cohen—perpetual scuffler—two prison jolts. Dead—heart attack, '76.

Jack Woods, Pete B.—old, in failing health.

Dick Carlisle:

Retired from the LAPD—never charged as a Dudley Smith accomplice. "Dick the Fur King"—the Hurwitz stash expanded legit. Dry-cleaning mogul—the E-Z Kleen chain purchased from Madge.

Dudley Smith—still half-lucid, still a charmer: Gaelic songs for the girls who wet-nurse him.

Edmund Exley:

Chief of Detectives, Chief of Police. Congressman, Lieutenant Governor, current gubernatorial candidate.

Acknowledged Dudley Smith admirer—politically expedient, smart.

Dudley—rakish in his eye patch. Pundit when sane: snappy quotes on "containment," always good for a news retrospective. A reminder: men were men then.

Glenda:

Movie star, TV star. Sixtyish—the matriarch on a long-running series.

Glenda:

Thirty-odd years famous. Always with me—those pictures held close. Ageless—every movie, every printed photo shunned.

In my dreams—spinning, falling.

Like Exley and Dudley and Carlisle.

Exiled from me, things to tell me—prosaic horrors that define their long survival. Words to update this confession to free me.

Dreams: spinning, falling—

I'm going back. I'm going to make Exley confess every monstrous deal he ever cut with the same candor I have. I'm going to kill Carlisle, and make Dudley fill in every moment of his life—to eclipse my guilt with the sheer weight of his evil. I'm going to kill him in the name of our victims, find Glenda and say:

Tell me anything.

Tell me everything.

Revoke our time apart.

Love me fierce in danger.

CHINUA ACHEBE
The African Trilogy
Things Fall Apart

ISABEL ALLENDE
The House of the Spirits

MARTIN AMIS
London Fields

ISAAC ASIMOV
Foundation
Foundation and Empire
Second Foundation
(in 1 vol.)

MARGARET ATWOOD
The Handmaid's Tale

JAMES BALDWIN
Giovanni's Room
Go Tell It on the Mountain

JOHN BANVILLE
The Book of Evidence
The Sea
(in 1 vol.)

JULIAN BARNES
Flaubert's Parrot
A History of the World in
10½ Chapters (in 1 vol.)

GIORGIO BASSANI
The Garden of the Finzi-Continis

SIMONE DE BEAUVOIR
The Second Sex

SAMUEL BECKETT
Molloy, Malone Dies,
The Unnamable

SAUL BELLOW
The Adventures of Augie March

JORGE LUIS BORGES
Ficciones

RAY BRADBURY
The Stories of Ray Bradbury

MIKHAIL BULGAKOV
The Master and Margarita

A. S. BYATT
Possession

JAMES M. CAIN
The Postman Always Rings Twice
Double Indemnity
Mildred Pierce
Selected Stories
(1 vol. US only)

ITALO CALVINO
If on a winter's night a traveler

ALBERT CAMUS
The Outsider (UK)
The Stranger (US)
The Plague, The Fall,
Exile and the Kingdom,
and Selected Essays
(in 1 vol.)

ANGELA CARTER
The Bloody Chamber,
Wise Children,
Fireworks
(in 1 vol.)

WILLA CATHER
Death Comes for the Archbishop
(US only)
My Ántonia
O Pioneers!

RAYMOND CHANDLER
The novels (2 vols)
Collected Stories

G. K. CHESTERTON
The Everyman Chesterton

KATE CHOPIN
The Awakening

JOSEPH CONRAD
Heart of Darkness
Lord Jim
Nostromo
The Secret Agent
Typhoon and Other Stories
Under Western Eyes
Victory

JULIO CORTÁZAR
Hopscotch
Blow-Up and Other Stories
We Love Glenda So Much and
Other Tales
(in 1 vol.)

ROALD DAHL
Collected Stories

JOAN DIDION
We Tell Ourselves Stories in
Order to Live (US only)

DAPHNE DU MAURIER
Rebecca (US only)

MARGUERITE DURAS
The Lover,
Wartime Notebooks,
Practicalities
(in 1 vol.)

UMBERTO ECO
The Name of the Rose

JAMES ELLROY
The L.A. Quartet
The Underworld U.S.A. Trilogy

J. G. FARRELL
The Siege of Krishnapur
and Troubles

WILLIAM FAULKNER
The Sound and the Fury
(UK only)

F. SCOTT FITZGERALD
The Great Gatsby
This Side of Paradise
(UK only)

PENELOPE FITZGERALD
The Bookshop
The Gate of Angels
The Blue Flower
(in 1 vol.)
Offshore
Human Voices
The Beginning of Spring
(in 1 vol.)

FORD MADOX FORD
The Good Soldier
Parade's End

RICHARD FORD
The Bascombe Novels

E. M. FORSTER
A Room with a View,
Where Angels Fear to Tread
(in 1 vol., US only)
Howards End
A Passage to India

ANNE FRANK
The Diary of a Young Girl
(US only)

GEORGE MACDONALD
FRASER
Flashman
Flash for Freedom!
Flashman in the Great Game

MAVIS GALLANT
The Collected Stories

KAHLIL GIBRAN
The Collected Works

GÜNTER GRASS
The Tin Drum

ROBERT GRAVES
Goodbye to All That

GRAHAM GREENE
Brighton Rock
The Human Factor

DASHIELL HAMMETT
The Maltese Falcon
The Thin Man
Red Harvest
(in 1 vol.)
The Dain Curse
The Glass Key
and Selected Stories
(in 1 vol.)

JAROSLAV HAŠEK
The Good Soldier Švejk

JOSEPH HELLER
Catch-22

ERNEST HEMINGWAY
A Farewell to Arms
The Collected Stories
(UK only)

MICHAEL HERR
Dispatches (US only)

PATRICIA HIGHSMITH
The Talented Mr. Ripley
Ripley Under Ground
Ripley's Game
(in 1 vol.)

ALDOUS HUXLEY
Brave New World

KAZUO ISHIGURO
The Remains of the Day

JAMES JOYCE
Dubliners
A Portrait of the Artist as
a Young Man
Ulysses

FRANZ KAFKA
Collected Stories
The Castle
The Trial

MAXINE HONG KINGSTON
The Woman Warrior and
China Men
(US only)

RUDYARD KIPLING
Collected Stories
Kim

GIUSEPPE TOMASI DI
LAMPEDUSA
The Leopard

D. H. LAWRENCE
Collected Stories
The Rainbow
Sons and Lovers
Women in Love

DORIS LESSING
Stories

PRIMO LEVI
If This is a Man and The Truce
(UK only)
The Periodic Table

NAGUIB MAHFOUZ
The Cairo Trilogy
Three Novels of Ancient Egypt

THOMAS MANN
Buddenbrooks
Collected Stories (UK only)
Death in Venice and Other Stories
(US only)
Doctor Faustus
Joseph and His Brothers
The Magic Mountain

KATHERINE MANSFIELD
The Garden Party and Other
Stories

GABRIEL GARCÍA MÁRQUEZ
The General in His Labyrinth
Love in the Time of Cholera
One Hundred Years of Solitude

W. SOMERSET MAUGHAM
Collected Stories
Of Human Bondage

CORMAC McCARTHY
The Border Trilogy

IAN McEWAN
Atonement

YUKIO MISHIMA
The Temple of the
Golden Pavilion

TONI MORRISON
Beloved
Song of Solomon

ALICE MUNRO
Carried Away: A Selection
of Stories

IRIS MURDOCH
The Sea, The Sea
A Severed Head
(in 1 vol.)

VLADIMIR NABOKOV
Lolita
Pale Fire
Pnin
Speak, Memory

V. S. NAIPAUL
Collected Short Fiction (US only)
A House for Mr Biswas

R. K. NARAYAN
Swami and Friends, The Bachelor
of Arts, The Dark Room,
The English Teacher
(in 1 vol.)
Mr Sampath – The Printer of
Malgudi, The Financial Expert,
Waiting for the Mahatma
(in 1 vol.)

IRÈNE NÉMIROVSKY
David Golder
The Ball
Snow in Autumn
The Courilof Affair
(in 1 vol.)

FLANN O'BRIEN
The Complete Novels

FRANK O'CONNOR
The Best of Frank O'Connor

MICHAEL ONDAATJE
The English Patient

GEORGE ORWELL
Animal Farm
Nineteen Eighty-Four
Essays
Burmese Days, Keep the Aspidistra
Flying, Coming Up for Air
(in 1 vol.)

ORHAN PAMUK
My Name is Red
Snow

BORIS PASTERNAK
Doctor Zhivago

SYLVIA PLATH
The Bell Jar (US only)

HENRIK PONTOPPIDAN
Lucky Per

MARCEL PROUST
In Search of Lost Time
(4 vols, UK only)

PHILIP PULLMAN
His Dark Materials

ERICH MARIA REMARQUE
All Quiet on the Western Front

JOSEPH ROTH
The Radetzky March

SALMAN RUSHDIE
Midnight's Children

PAUL SCOTT
The Raj Quartet (2 vols)

JANE SMILEY
A Thousand Acres

ALEXANDER SOLZHENITSYN
One Day in the Life of
Ivan Denisovich

MURIEL SPARK
The Prime of Miss Jean Brodie
The Girls of Slender Means
The Driver's Seat
The Only Problem
(in 1 vol.)

CHRISTINA STEAD
The Man Who Loved Children

JOHN STEINBECK
The Grapes of Wrath

ITALO SVEVO
Zeno's Conscience

GRAHAM SWIFT
Waterland

JUNICHIRŌ TANIZAKI
The Makioka Sisters

JOHN UPDIKE
The Complete Henry Bech
Rabbit Angstrom

EVELYN WAUGH
(US only)
Black Mischief, Scoop, The Loved
One, The Ordeal of Gilbert
Pinfold (in 1 vol.)
Brideshead Revisited
The Complete Short Stories
Decline and Fall
A Handful of Dust
The Sword of Honour Trilogy
Waugh Abroad: Collected Travel
Writing

H. G. WELLS
The Time Machine,
The Invisible Man,
The War of the Worlds
(in 1 vol.)

EDITH WHARTON
The Age of Innocence
The Custom of the Country
Ethan Frome, Summer,
Bunner Sisters
(in 1 vol.)
The House of Mirth
The Reef

PATRICK WHITE
Voss

OSCAR WILDE
Plays, Prose Writings and Poems

P. G. WODEHOUSE
The Best of Wodehouse

VIRGINIA WOOLF
To the Lighthouse
Mrs Dalloway

RICHARD YATES
Revolutionary Road
The Easter Parade
Eleven Kinds of Loneliness
(in 1 vol.)

W. B. YEATS
The Poems (UK only)

This book is set in BEMBO which was cut
by the punch-cutter Francesco Griffo
for the Venetian printer-publisher
Aldus Manutius in early 1495
and first used in a pamphlet
by a young scholar
named Pietro
Bembo.